CLASSIC TALES OF HORROR

CLASSIC TALES OF HORROR

Introduction by Ernest Hilbert

Canterbury Classics
San Diego

Canterbury Classics
An imprint of Printers Row Publishing Group
9717 Pacific Heights Blvd, San Diego, CA 92121
www.canterburyclassicsbooks.com • mail@canterburyclassicsbooks.com

Correspondence regarding the content of this book should be sent to Canterbury Classics, Editorial Department, at the above address.

Publisher: Peter Norton
Associate Publisher: Ana Parker
Publishing/Editorial Team: April Graham, Kelly Larsen, Kathryn C. Dalby
Editorial Team: JoAnn Padgett, Melinda Allman, Dan Mansfield, Traci Douglas
Production Team: Jonathan Lopes, Rusty von Dyl
Cover and endpaper design by Ray Caramanna

Library of Congress Cataloging-in-Publication Data

Classic tales of horror / edited by editors of Canterbury Classics.
pages cm. -- (Leather-bound classics)
Summary: "This chilling collection of scary stories will keep you awake for hours! Psychological horrors, disturbing dramas, and gruesome ghosts compose this compendium of confessions made in the dead of night. From vampires and a monkey paw to an unstoppable heart and haunting apparitions, anecdotes of supernatural terror will have you turning pages long past the witching hour. Allow famous authors such as Edgar Allan Poe, H. P. Lovecraft, Henry James, Washington Irving, and more to prey upon your emotions and peace of mind at slumber parties and camping trips, or anytime you want to end the night with a delightful fright!"-- Provided by publisher.
Summary: "A collection of more than 50 classic horror stories, from well-known writers such as Edgar Allan Poe, Bram Stoker, Nathaniel Hawthorne, Franz Kafka, and Charles Dickens"-- Provided by publisher.
ISBN 9781626864658
1. Horror tales. I. Canterbury Classics.

PN6071.H727C57 2015
808.83'8738--dc23

2015002106

Printed in China
28 27 26 25 24 10 11 12 13 14

MIX
Paper | Supporting responsible forestry
FSC www.fsc.org FSC® C144853

Editor's Note: The pieces in this book have been published in their original form to preserve the authors' intent and style.

CONTENTS

INTRODUCTION

We've all felt the rush of fear in the dead of night when we wake with a fright, chilled to the bone, feeling we are not alone. Our fear of the unknown—of those things that go bump in the night—is as old as time itself. Such primordial terrors take hold in the small hours, when the world sleeps, but they are captured, like genies in bottles, by the authors you will encounter in *Classic Tales of Horror*—authors who, above all, remind us that all is not always well, that we are not always safe, nor do we fully understand the universe as much as we believe we do. In his pivotal essay "Supernatural Horror in Literature," H. P. Lovecraft, one of the undisputed masters of the genre, began by affirming quite simply that "the oldest and strongest emotion of mankind is fear, and the oldest and strongest kind of fear is fear of the unknown." It is hard to improve on this. A menace known, seen, and understood can never be as frightening as one that remains hidden, lurking in the shadows. This is the timeless element of these stories, and it contributes to their enduring appeal. They are as engaging today as they were when they first appeared.

Stephen King, one of the most successful horror writers of all time, knows this and suggests that in horror fiction "we often experience that low sense of anxiety which we call 'the creeps.' " He touches on an important point, which is that the fear of the unknown comes not only from outside phenomena but also, much more unsettlingly, sometimes from within. A recurring theme in these stories is the skeptic's struggle to retain his faith in reason—to reassure himself that he is sane and that weird phenomena can be explained away—in the face of mounting evidence to the contrary. Even if he comes to accept the evidence as real, he may find himself unwilling or unable to talk about it with others. As Charles Dickens wrote in "The Trial for Murder": "I have always noticed a prevalent want of courage, even among persons of superior intelligence and culture, as to imparting their own psychological experiences when those have been of a strange sort." The terror arises, in part, from a character's inability to be certain that what he experiences with his five senses is, in fact, real, that some presentiment or "feeling" is actually attached to a supernatural event. The horror story, from its genesis, has always relied on a strong psychological element: Ancient, primitive forces somehow persist into the present day; subterranean energies force their way to the surface; tragedies unfolded long ago are reenacted. Characters wrestle with their own psyches in a vain effort to cling to remnants of sanity.

Origins of the Genre

In 1773 John Aikin and his sister Anna Laetitia Aikin wrote an essay called "On the Pleasure Derived from Objects of Terror," in which they posed that "the apparent delight with which we dwell upon objects of pure terror, where our moral feelings are not in the least concerned, and no passion seems to be excited but the depressing one of fear, is a paradox of the heart." Indeed, it is very hard to understand the attraction. Why would we want to be frightened? Perhaps that is the most frightening aspect of the stories. They describe occurrences outside the natural run of events, beyond what seems possible to a scientific mind, and as such, they can be dismissed as absurd, yet we return to the old places, push open the creaky doors, and enter because we are searching for something we have lost, or been denied, by our calculating, rational modern society. We can agree that most horror stories share certain features, but they also tend to separate themselves into recognizable categories (even if these sometimes combine to make hybrid forms, as we will see). The most common category in this collection is the ghost story, the old standby, which can be further subdivided into a variety of haunted-house tales and other records of hauntings. The closest contender to the ghost story is the vampire story, which also assumes diverse forms, beginning with John William Polidori's groundbreaking story "The Vampyre." These are followed in frequency by the straightforward monster tale, along with stories concerning demonic activity, deals with the devil, and terrible animals large and small. Perhaps rarest of all is the work of pure psychological terror, as one finds with Charlotte Perkins Gilman's "The Yellow Wallpaper" and Franz Kafka's profoundly unsettling and highly suggestive stories, whose inhospitable visions of alienation and oppression mark him as one of the most important authors of the twentieth century.

So, we must ask, what do we call these stories? There is no easy answer, as they go by many names and arrive in many guises: horror stories, Gothic novels, dark fantasies, weird tales, works of mystery and imagination, reports of the grotesque, and chronicles of the uncanny, bizarre, and supernatural. Some prefer the dignifying designation of "spectral literature." Even fairy tales, such as those recorded by the Brothers Grimm, are at times calculated to worry us. There is no way to know the deepest origins of these stories, though they have haunted us for centuries in old wives' tales and warnings to children, and even deeper in legends and ancient myths. There is much to terrify the attentive reader of Homer's *Odyssey* (800 BC), with its cannibals, witches, and monsters (on land and in the sea), as well as its hero's descent into the underworld to spill ritual blood and commune with the restless dead. Even earlier, the Babylonian *Epic of Gilgamesh* (circa 2000 BC) depicts a battle between its hero and the monstrous giant Humbaba. In fact, Lovecraft insists that because the horror tale deals directly with primal emotion, it "is as old as human thought and speech themselves." We would do well to call them tales of horror—because that is, in fact, what the best of them actually do: place us in a state of horror.

Efforts have been made to explain the enduring appeal of the horror story in its many forms. Edith Birkhead, in her 1921 study *The Tale of Terror*, investigated medieval stories handed down by oral tradition set "in an atmosphere of supernatural wonder and enchantment." She points to the presence of horror in Thomas Malory's *Le Morte d'Arthur* (1485), Edmund Spenser's *The Faerie Queene* (1590), Christopher Marlowe's *The Tragical History of the Life and Death of Doctor Faustus* (1604), and John Bunyan's *The Pilgrim's Progress* (1678). The first great outpouring of these stories in a purer form occurred in the era of Gothic literature, which spans roughly from 1764, with Horace Walpole's novel *The Castle of Otranto*, through 1820, which saw the publication of Charles Maturin's novel *Melmoth the Wanderer*, though, as we will see, the influence of Gothic storytelling continues to linger to the present day.

Though bloodcurdling stories have been told around fires—in prehistoric caves and Victorian drawing rooms—from time immemorial, the modern horror story really begins with Walpole's *The Castle of Otranto*, set in a labyrinthine Italian castle. It was followed by many imitators, including Ann Radcliffe's 1794 novel *The Mysteries of Udolpho*, which some believe to be the archetypal Gothic novel. Walpole's wildly popular novel (originally published under a pseudonym, though he took credit in subsequent printings) initiated the vogue for stories set on the Italian peninsula, in old ruins or abandoned villas, as we observe with Lovecraft's fable "The Tree" (set in the classical period), Ambrose Bierce's graveyard story "An Inhabitant of Carcosa," Nathaniel Hawthorne's "Rappaccini's Daughter," and Edgar Allan Poe's "The Masque of the Red Death" and "The Cask of Amontillado." Walpole's book also introduced the technique of framing a story through documentation, offering it as if it had been lately found as an historical account, a collection of diary entries, or courtroom records, often alleged to be translated from a foreign language. This was the eighteenth-century equivalent of the "found footage" horror film popularized by *The Blair Witch Project* and used with great effect in the *Paranormal Activity* movies. It lends an air of credibility and antiquity—sometimes immediacy—to the stories while also making them appear more exotic.

Further, Walpole established not only the atmosphere but the location. In his 1927 book *The Haunted Castle*, Eino Railo explained that the castle so common to these stories had an essential "collection of family portraits" along with subterranean vaults and passages, hidden triggers for "a secret trap door." Indeed, one will encounter many castles, ancestral homes, manors, mansions, villas, and more modest haunted houses in these pages. Haunted houses and other evil places never seem to lose their allure. Fully half of the stories, if not more, occur in such gloomy quarters. The houses in this book laid the foundation stones for later infamous addresses, such as those in Shirley Jackson's *The Haunting of Hill House* (1959), Richard Matheson's *Hell House* (1971), Stephen King's *The Shining* (1977), and Mark Z. Danielewski's *House of Leaves* (2000).

Spooky Places

Ghosts and hauntings abound in these stories, usually associated with a particular place—a tomb, a graveyard, or, as we have seen, a haunted building. The Gothic novel, with its trappings of desolate castles and stormy nights, eventually gave way to what we call the ghost story, a child of the Victorian era. Dorothy Scarborough noted in her 1917 study *The Supernatural in Modern English Fiction* that "the ghost is the most enduring figure in supernatural fiction. He is absolutely indestructible . . . he appears as unapologetically at home in twentieth century fiction as in classical mythology, Christian hagiology, medieval legend, or Gothic romance," adding that "he changes with the styles in fiction but he never goes out of fashion." Ghosts linger, sometimes for generations, reliving their misfortunes, seeking revenge, or desperately trying to warn unwary visitors.

Algernon Blackwood begins "The Empty House" by asserting quite bluntly that "certain houses, like certain persons, manage somehow to proclaim at once their character for evil. In the case of the latter, no particular feature need betray them; they may boast an open countenance and an ingenuous smile; and yet a little of their company leaves the unalterable conviction that there is something radically amiss with their being: that they are evil." One can't help but notice how many stories include the word "house" in their titles: "The Shunned House," "The Empty House," "The Judge's House." We must begin, however, with the most famous of houses, Edgar Allan Poe's "The Fall of the House of Usher," a story of a crumbling edifice haunted by its still-living inhabitants, a frantically nervous man and his sickly sister, the two remaining heirs of a declining and degenerate family line. Horror stories of real significance begin with Poe, who is the true father of the American horror story, though his achievements are by no means limited to horror stories. He is credited with creating the detective story in 1841 with "The Murders in the Rue Morgue." He also dabbled in science fiction ("Ms. Found in a Bottle," 1833), published significant works of literary criticism, and was celebrated as a poet.

It is worth considering the opening passage of "The Fall of the House of Usher," as it is perhaps the finest description of its kind. As our narrator approaches the eponymous house, having been mysteriously summoned for a visit by a childhood friend, Poe combines several elements to achieve his effect, incorporating bleak weather, keenly felt emotion, and observation of desolate surroundings and physical decay to conjure "an utter depression of soul." This promises to be one truly ominous visit.

> During the whole of a dull, dark, and soundless day in the autumn of the year, when the clouds hung oppressively low in the heavens, I had been passing alone, on horseback, through a singularly dreary tract of country; and at length found myself, as the shades of the evening drew on, within view of the melancholy House of Usher. I know not how it was—but, with the first glimpse of the building, a sense of insufferable gloom pervaded my spirit. I say insufferable; for the feeling was unrelieved by any of that half-pleasurable, because poetic, sentiment, with which the mind usually receives even the sternest natural images of the desolate or terrible. I looked upon the scene before me—upon the mere house, and the simple landscape features of the domain—upon the bleak walls—upon the vacant eye-like windows—upon a few rank sedges—and upon a few white trunks of decayed trees—with an utter depression of soul which I can compare to no earthly sensation more properly than to the after-dream of the reveller upon opium—the bitter lapse into everyday life—the hideous dropping off of the veil. There was an iciness, a sinking, a sickening of the heart—an unredeemed dreariness of thought which no goading of the imagination could torture into aught of the sublime.

At times such landscapes seem like nothing so much as the outward manifestation of what would have been called a state of melancholy, that "utter depression of soul," what today—in an age more clinical and more cynical—might be termed major depression.

Though Poe's House of Usher may be the best of its kind, Bram Stoker, author of *Dracula*, invents a similarly terrible locale in "The Judge's House," where a young student seeks seclusion so that he may study undisturbed. He waves away the vague warnings of the locals, insisting that his studies in mathematics will give him "too much to think of to be disturbed by any of these mysterious 'somethings' . . . his work is of too exact and prosaic a kind to allow of his having any corner in his mind for mysteries of any kind." Likewise, his hired help, the sturdy Mrs. Dempster, sniffs "in a superior manner" and explains "bogies is all kinds and sorts of things—except bogies!

Rats and mice, and beetles; and creaky doors, and loose slates, and broken panes, and stiff drawer handles, that stay out when you pull them and then fall down in the middle of the night." The rats in question—and a very large, tenacious one in particular—begin to make him think that he might have placed himself into a worrying situation well out of reach of help.

Henry James—one of the indisputably major authors in this book—indulged his darker side with the novella *The Turn of the Screw*, which stands out as one of the great American ghost stories, lending itself to adaptation not only to film but also as a highly regarded opera by Benjamin Britten with a libretto by Myfanwy Piper. The story of a callow governess, sent to keep watch over two troubled, orphaned children in an isolated mansion, unfolds with immense subtlety. James carefully captures that "hush in which something gathers or crouches." His heroine, who may or may not be mad herself, who may or may not be hallucinating the figures she sees in the windows at night and on dark staircases, is altogether unsure herself, exclaiming, "No, no—there are depths, depths! The more I go over it the more I see in it, and the more I see in it the more I fear. I don't know what I *don't* see, what I *don't* fear!" James is the most indirect and refined of the authors in this collection, and his prose is exquisite. He works through suggestion and misdirection, hints and queries. "Sir Edmund Orme" is no less unsettling, though much of it is set out in broad daylight and in public. Imagine if you could see an apparition that no one else—save a single other person—could see. You would be thought mad if you so much as mentioned it. This is the terror that confronts the narrator of James's story, in the form of a personal testament found in papers of the author and presented by the executor: "I had heard all my days of apparitions, but it was a different thing to have seen one and to know that I should in all probability see it familiarly, as it were, again."

Edith Wharton, also a major American novelist, known for *The House of Mirth* and *The Age of Innocence*, composed many ghost stories. "Kerfol"—the name of an abandoned French estate, "the most romantic house in Brittany"—reminds us that not all ghosts appear in human form. A brutal mauling death is attributed to another kind of ghost, of the four-legged variety, proving that man's best friend is sometimes his greatest nemesis. In "Afterward," a wealthy American couple inquires hopefully about ghosts in an old English house called Lyng, which they intend to rent in Dorsetshire. As one often sees in these stories, they are told they "can get it for a song" (the observant reader will notice that Kerfol was also going for "a song"). They are tantalizingly informed by a friend who arranges the rental: "Oh, there *is* one, of course, but you'll never know it." They move into the shadowy old manor in hopes of luring out its resident ghost. Disappointed, they settle into a comfortable routine—she gardens, he works on his book—only to discover that they may have brought their own ghost with them from far away.

A Ghost of a Different Color

While the ghosts of James and Wharton are elusive and thin as air, F. Marion Crawford's ghosts are relentless and direct. "The Screaming Skull" begins with its narrator explaining, apologetically and somewhat defensively, "I have often heard it scream. No, I am not nervous, I am not imaginative, and I never believed in ghosts, unless that thing is one. Whatever it is, it hates me almost as much as it hated Luke Pratt, and it screams at me." We listen patiently as he continues in this vein, attempting to justify and rationalize his decision to live alone with the apparition. Despite his best efforts, he grows increasingly terrified and uncertain of himself as his tale progresses. He repeatedly offers us another glass of whiskey—"You may as well finish that glass while I'm getting it, for I don't mean to let you off with less than three before you go to bed." A stiff drink helps, but it's not enough, especially when he moves to retrieve the skull from its box to find it has gone off wandering on its own. Crawford's 1911 contribution to the vampire genre, "For the Blood Is the Life," is also, largely, a ghost story. It treats traditional themes of unrequited love, unpunished crimes, and young death with a very modern sensibility. His vampire is an innocent young woman, trying to remember what it meant to be alive by slowly feeding upon the man she once loved from a distance, draining her lover of the very life she hopes to regain.

Charles Dickens was an aficionado and a virtuoso of the ghost story. We should not forget that one of his most beloved stories, *A Christmas Carol*, is, in fact, a ghost story. Perhaps, because it is also a story of redemption, rather than ruin, it remains more popular than his other ghost stories, such as "The Trial for Murder," in which Dickens gets right at the heart of the revenge story. During the trial, the accused is seen pointing at someone he sees sitting with the jurors, who begin to wonder how many are in the box with them after all.

> "Why," says he, suddenly, "we are thirt—; but no, it's not possible. No. We are twelve."
>
> According to my counting that day, we were always right in detail, but in the gross we were always one too many.
>
> There was no appearance—no figure—to account for it; but I had now an inward foreshadowing of the figure that was surely coming.

In Dickens's most frightening ghost story, "The Signal-Man," the narrator meets a lonely signal-man, posted to a cold, remote railway embankment, who tells him, "I am troubled, sir, I am troubled." The narrator, concerned, presses him for details and learns that the signal-man nightly experiences terrible forebodings of an accident. He understands that he is being warned by spectral figures who wave and shout, but he cannot see their faces or figure out what it is he is being warned about—until it is too late.

Haunted houses have many rooms. E. F. Benson's "The Room in the Tower" ingeniously combines a story of foreboding dreams, a haunted room at the top of an old tower, and life-drinking vampires in a single chilling tale. Benson learned from the best. He was close friends with the distinguished writer M. R. James. Benson was present at a meeting of the Chitchat Society at Cambridge University when James read his first two ghost stories, "Canon Alberic's Scrap-book" and "Lost Hearts," in October 1893 (both are included in this volume). The literary influence was immediate and profound. Benson went on to write more than fifty classic ghost stories, and his 1912 story "The Room in the Tower" remains his signature work.

H. P. Lovecraft is second only to Poe among American horror writers. Like Poe, he died prematurely (Poe at forty, Lovecraft at forty-six), but he left behind a vast assortment of stories and novellas mapping out his own invented pantheon of ancient terrible gods and other beings, known collectively as the Cthulhu Mythos, after his most famous deity. In his story "The Shunned House," Lovecraft, always innovative, deepens the horror of the traditional haunted house. Locals recoil from the house in question, and the owners find themselves unable to rent it for long.

> The general fact is, that the house was never regarded by the solid part of the community as in any real sense "haunted." There were no widespread tales of rattling chains, cold currents of air, extinguished lights, or faces at the window. Extremists sometimes said the house was "unlucky," but that is as far as even they went. What was really beyond dispute is that a frightful proportion of persons died there; or more accurately, *had* died there, since after some peculiar happenings over sixty years ago the building had become deserted through the sheer impossibility of renting it.

The narrator sets out with his scientifically minded uncle to move into the basement of the house and learn its secrets. They begin digging into the basement floor and discover an evil far stranger than they had ever imagined.

Prolific French novelist Honoré de Balzac is celebrated for his massive collection of interlinked stories about French life in the first half of the nineteenth century. It is known collectively as *La Comédie Humaine*, and it contains its share of ghost stories. In "La Grande Bretèche," the narrator finds himself captivated by a derelict mansion that seems to have been suddenly abandoned. He returns nightly to gaze up at the dilapidated facade in wonder. After meeting the estate's executor in a local café, he hears a perverse tale of betrayal and revenge, in which the lord of the house walls up a man alive. In Guy de Maupassant's "A Ghost," we find a single haunted room in an old manor and its occupant, a ghost with a rather curious request, which sets the visitor careering from the house in terror. In "The Open Window" by Saki (Hector Hugh Munro), we are taught that some ghost stories do not even require ghosts to truly frighten the unwary visitor out of his wits.

Terror also lurks outside the walls of these mansions and castles. Writing about Shirley Jackson's *The Haunting of Hill House*, Stephen King alighted on the notion of "the bad place," which he uses successfully in novels like *Pet Sematary* and *The Shining*. We find many such bad places in these pages. In Algernon Blackwood's masterful story "The Willows," two friends, who stop to camp for the night on a small island while canoeing down the Danube, begin to suspect that they are not alone. The willows themselves seem to moan and move of their own accord. While the friends sleep, one of their oars disappears, and a hole is scored in the bottom of the canoe. Other things begin to go wrong. They realize that the barrier between their world and another one has become porous and that something is trying to reach them, something older than the world's religions. They begin to experience the presence "of a deliberate and malefic purpose, resentful of our audacious intrusion into their breeding-place; whereas my friend threw it into the unoriginal form at first of a trespass on some ancient shrine, some place where the old gods still held sway, where the emotional forces of former worshippers still clung, and the ancestral portion of him yielded to the old pagan spell."

One tells the other that it might be "a question wholly of the mind, and the less we think about them the better our chance of escape. Above all, don't think, for what you think happens!" Here we see yet again how menacing surroundings are reflected as the inner horrors felt by the visitors to these places. The greatest horror is always psychological.

Keeping Company with the Dead

No survey of "bad places" would be complete without a visit to desolate tombs and graveyards. There is no better place to start than with H. P. Lovecraft's unnerving story "The Tomb," about a sensitive and aloof young man who feels uncannily drawn to an old tomb he discovers near his house. In time, he finds he feels at home there. Lovecraft's description of his character's first visit rivals the opening of Poe's "The Fall of the House of Usher."

> When, upon forcing my way between two savage clumps of briers, I suddenly encountered the entrance of the vault, I had no knowledge of what I had discovered. The dark blocks of granite, the door so curiously ajar, and the funereal carvings above the arch, aroused in me no associations of mournful or terrible character. Of graves and tombs I knew and imagined much, but had on account of my peculiar temperament been kept from all personal contact with churchyards and cemeteries. The strange stone house on the woodland slope was to me only a source of interest and speculation; and its cold, damp interior, into which I vainly peered through the aperture so tantalisingly left, contained for me no hint of death or decay. But in that instant of curiosity was born the madly unreasoning desire which has brought me to this hell of confinement.

In "An Inhabitant of Carcosa," Ambrose Bierce delivers a ghost story told from a strange perspective, set in a desolate necropolis and allegedly told through "the facts imparted to the medium Bayrolles by the spirit Hoseib Alar Robardin." The narrator cannot fathom why no one responds to his calls or seems to see him. Then he begins to wonder who the real ghost might be, prefiguring Bruce Willis's role as Dr. Malcolm Crowe in M. Night Shyamalan's 1999 film *The Sixth Sense.* "An Inhabitant of Carcosa" dovetails with Lovecraft's "The Outsider," whose narrator believes he has escaped from his ancestral home, where he lived in "dismal chambers with brown hangings and maddening rows of antique books . . . twilight groves of grotesque, gigantic, and vine-encumbered trees that silently wave twisted branches far aloft. Such a lot the gods gave to me—to me, the dazed, the disappointed; the barren, the broken." When he enters a crowded ballroom, its inhabitants flee in terror.

> Flight was universal, and in the clamour and panic several fell in a swoon and were dragged away by their madly fleeing companions. Many covered their eyes with their hands, and plunged blindly and awkwardly in their race to escape; overturning furniture and stumbling against the walls before they managed to reach one of the many doors.

He then believes he too can see the source of their terror and decides to approach it. Lovecraft's surprise ending is unforgettable.

Such graveyards are home not only to ghosts but to grave robbers as well, or "resurrection men" as they were sometimes known. In nineteenth-century Britain, surgical colleges were filled with eager young students hoping to hone their skills on cadavers. According to government edict, however, only the bodies of executed criminals were to be used for this purpose. The result was a brisk demand and only a trickling supply. It was inevitable that someone would step in to meet the need. In Bierce's "One Summer Night," young medical students are greeted with a gruesome surprise in the graveyard, only to be shocked even further when they return to their dissection room the next day. Famous for his novels *Treasure Island* and *Kidnapped*, as well as his tale of split personality, *The Strange Case of Dr. Jekyll and Mr. Hyde*, Robert Louis Stevenson also dabbled in gore and ghosts. In "The Body-Snatcher," a dissolute medical student is tasked with rising before dawn to pay for recently unearthed cadavers delivered by repellent, mud-stained men. He expects the cadavers to be disinterred from local cemeteries, but he begins to wonder why they seem to be so fresh. When he recognizes in one of the cadavers a friend whom he had seen alive only the day before, he realizes that something is terribly wrong.

A Fiend for All Seasons

Considering how popular vampires are today, one might be tempted to think they had always prowled the pages of literature. The vampire first seized the public's imagination when Lord Byron published his poem "The Giaour" in 1813. Six years later, and fully seventy-eight years before Bram Stoker unleashed his swarthy Carpathian count onto an unsuspecting world, Byron's personal physician, John William Polidori, published "The Vampyre," which Christopher Frayling describes as "the first story successfully to fuse the disparate elements of vampirism into a coherent literary genre." His story, inspired by both Byron and his poem, lavishes much attention on a suave British nobleman-vampire named Lord Ruthven. (Polidori's story was also encouraged, in part, by the unfinished Byron story "The Burial: A Fragment.") Polidori gives us the first neck-biter: "Upon her neck and breast was blood, and upon her throat were the marks of teeth having opened the vein." "The Vampyre" was begun on the same rainy evening that Mary Shelley first imagined Dr. Frankenstein and his creature (the two authors, along with Lord Byron and Mary's husband Percy Bysshe Shelley, whiled away the hours at the Villa Diodati near Lake Geneva during the torrential summer rains by telling each other ghost stories). "The Vampyre" embodies eternal anxieties about infection, foreign interlopers, and repressed sexual desire, thereby setting the standard for the modern vampire story.

Beginning in 1845, James Malcolm Rymer published a sensational and very long Gothic novel in parts (issued one chapter at a time in pamphlet form) called *Varney the Vampire; or, the Feast of Blood*, but the most famous vampire story appeared in the shape of Bram Stoker's rambling 1897 novel *Dracula.* Stoker's chronicle of an ancient and immortal Transylvanian count enjoyed fantastic success. Like many popular novels at the time, it was adapted for the stages of London's West End and later New York's Broadway, where a young immigrant actor named Bela Lugosi was discovered on opening night by a Universal Pictures scout and hired on the spot to play the count in the pioneering 1931 motion picture. Universal's *Dracula* revived the paraphernalia of the Gothic tradition for the silver screen. Dracula's castle, with its crumbling curved stairways, candelabras, vast spiderwebs, long shadows, and misty crypt, would be used again in innumerable horror movies, comics, novels, and Halloween haunted houses.

Two years after his death in 1912, Stoker's widow published a collection of his stories, called *Dracula's Guest and Other Weird Stories*, claiming that the title story was a "hitherto unpublished episode from *Dracula* . . . originally excised owing to the length of the book." It is as terrifying as anything in *Dracula.* However, "Dracula's Guest" differs from the novel on several counts. It is a straightforward, first-person narrative, while the novel relies on correspondence, newspaper articles, and private diaries to tell the story of Jonathan and Mina Harker, Lucy Westenra, Dr. Abraham Van Helsing, and the great vampire. The central character of "Dracula's Guest," an Englishman, is not named, though he is most certainly Jonathan Harker. Against the advice of the German hotelier, he decides to go out into the countryside on "Walpurgis nacht . . . when, according to the belief of millions of people, the devil was abroad." He is even so bold as to leave his carriage and driver behind in order to explore the landscape on his own. Before he does, though, he and the driver, whose grasp of the English language is decidedly meager, indulge in a brief exchange on the merits of his decision to go wandering.

> "Tell me," I said, "about this place where the road leads," and I pointed down.
>
> Again he crossed himself and mumbled a prayer, before he answered, "It is unholy."
>
> "What is unholy?" I enquired.
>
> "The village."
>
> "Then there is a village?"
>
> "No, no. No one lives there hundreds of years."
>
> My curiosity was piqued. "But you said there was a village."
>
> "There was."
>
> "Where is it now?"
>
> Whereupon he burst out into a long story in German and English, so mixed up that I could not quite understand exactly what he said, but roughly I gathered that long ago, hundreds of years, men had died there

> and been buried in their graves; and sounds were heard under the clay, and when the graves were opened, men and women were found rosy with life, and their mouths red with blood.

After hearing this, our intrepid (some might say foolish) Englishman proceeds to make his way down into the dark valley during a snowstorm.

Lovecraft regarded Guy de Maupassant's "The Horla" as a masterpiece, as it astonishingly combines science fiction, vampire fiction, and ghost stories in a single, unnerving tale. Through a sequence of diary entries, our narrator tells how he comes to suspect an invisible presence in his midst. Milk and water mysteriously disappear from sealed bottles. The narrator begins to believe that the invisible presence is starting to take control of his mind. He reads in the *Revue du Monde Scientifique* that

> Information of a curious nature comes to us from Rio de Janeiro. An epidemic of madness, comparable to those contagious crazes which attacked the European peoples during the Middle Ages, is, it seems, at present, raging in the province of San Paulo. The inhabitants are leaving their houses in dismay, deserting their villages, and abandoning their crops, maintaining that they are being pursued, taken possession of, governed like a human herd of cattle, by certain invisible but tangible beings, resembling vampires, who suck upon their life-blood during their sleep, and who, besides that, take water and milk, but no other nourishment.

Maupassant leaves us to wonder what these "new" life-forms are, or if they exist at all. Are they vampires, ghosts, or merely mass hallucinations?

The fears of invasion and infection Maupassant explores in "The Horla" reach their purest form in Poe's "The Masque of the Red Death." When the Red Death, a virus even more horrific and contagious than the Black Plague, spreads into his kingdom, a wealthy prince invites his friends to retreat with him to a well-stocked villa where they can wait out the disease while enjoying endless parties. The revelries go on night and day with no expense spared and not a worry expended, until the prince is angered by the presence of someone he does not remember inviting, who arrives at the masque costumed as a victim of the dreaded Red Death.

Biological Perils

Fear of infection is linked with that of poisoning, as we find in Nathaniel Hawthorne's "Rappaccini's Daughter." A naive student falls in love with a young woman he observes tending the "gorgeously magnificent" yet "strange" flowers in the garden below his window. Oddly, her father, Rappaccini, a scientist, is seen handling the same flowers with thick gloves and a mask to cover his face. When the student inquires about Rappaccini, a fellow scientist explains that Rappaccini "cares infinitely more for science than for mankind. His patients are interesting to him only as subjects for some new experiment. He would sacrifice human life, his own among the rest, or whatever else was dearest to him, for the sake of adding so much as a grain of mustard-seed to the great heap of his accumulated knowledge." In this, he resembles Mary Shelley's Dr. Frankenstein. In fact, "Rappaccini's Daughter" also qualifies as a mad scientist story when it becomes apparent that Rappaccini's most sinister experiment is his own beautiful daughter.

While one's body can be easily poisoned, one's mind may also be contaminated. Nathaniel Hawthorne's "Young Goodman Brown" stumbles upon what he believes to be a Black Mass during his evening stroll deep in the woods outside of Salem, but he is not sure he can trust his eyes.

> Either the sudden gleams of light flashing over the obscure field bedazzled Goodman Brown, or he recognized a score of the church members of Salem village famous for their especial sanctity. Good old Deacon Gookin had arrived, and waited at the skirts of that venerable saint, his revered pastor. But, irreverently consorting with these grave, reputable, and pious people, these elders of the church, these chaste dames and dewy virgins, there were men of dissolute lives and women of spotted fame, wretches given over to all mean and filthy vice, and suspected even of horrid crimes. It was strange to see that the good shrank not from the wicked, nor were the sinners abashed by the saints.

Are his fellow citizens, including his chaste wife, really secret worshippers of the devil? Hawthorne's great-great-grandfather was a judge at the infamous Salem witch trials. One can't help but notice how this played upon the author's conscience. Part of the story's terror stems from its ambiguity—a complexity that inspired Herman Melville to declare that the story is "as deep as Dante"—though ultimately the experience, actual or imagined, results in a very real, and heartrending, loss of faith for Goodman Brown, condemning him to a life of dejection and withdrawal.

In "The Devil and Tom Walker," Washington Irving adopts a different approach to dealings with the devil, reminding the reader that when you strike a deal with the cloven-hoofed one, payment will come due eventually. A local merchant—a despicably greedy man—and his equally vile wife wonder if they are equal to doing business with the devil, hoping to profit where others have failed. When events turn against them, no one is surprised or saddened, and the "good people of Boston shook their heads and shrugged their shoulders, but had been so much accustomed to witches and goblins, and tricks of the devil, in all kinds of shapes, from the first settlement of the colony, that they were not so much horror-struck as might have been expected." This is quite amusing. Supernatural events have become so common to New Englanders of the period that they greet such news with a complete absence of wonder.

Where there are devils, one will find demons of other orders. Balzac's "The Succubus" appeared in *Les Contes Drolatiques* (*Droll Stories*), published serially from 1832 to 1837. These were tales of nymphomania and scatological pranks set in the Middle Ages and Renaissance, the author's attempt to revive a tradition of robust, comic literature. Vampires may be cold, but Balzac's succubus is sultry and irresistible. Among the vast host of hell, she is the sexy vixen. As he takes pains to explain, "Succubi or demons, having the faces of women, who, not wishing to return to hell, and having with them an insatiable fire, attempt to refresh and sustain themselves by sucking in souls." Though concerning the demonic, the story borders on the comic, as the young woman accused of being a succubus proves to be as persuasive as she is seductive, leaving her accusers and interlocutors enamored and baffled, moving Christian knights to joust for her honor. Outrage and indignation are transformed into enchantment in her presence, though she comes to a gruesome end after confronting a sexless, ice-cold priest who is unmoved by her feminine wiles.

M. R. James may be the most accomplished author of Victorian English ghost stories, and, as we will see, the two stories in this collection also delve into the demonic. Like many horror authors, James prefers to relate stories second- or thirdhand, "as told to," or discovered among old letters or diaries. Rather than muffling the horror, this technique actually makes it much more acute, as details become more vague and suggestive. In "Canon Alberic's Scrap-book," the narrator tells of an English scholar on vacation in the French village of St. Bertrand de Comminges who stumbles onto an opportunity to purchase a valuable volume of medieval manuscripts, though the seller seems downright eager to be rid of it at any price. As he leafs through its pages, he notices something disquieting in one of the miniature illustrations.

> At first you saw only a mass of coarse, matted black hair; presently it was seen that this covered a body of fearful thinness, almost a skeleton, but with the muscles standing out like wires. The hands were of a dusky pallor, covered, like the body, with long, coarse hairs, and hideously taloned. The eyes, touched in with a burning yellow, had intensely black pupils, and were fixed upon the throned King with a look of beast-like hate. Imagine one of the awful bird-catching spiders of South America translated into human form, and endowed with intelligence just less than human, and you will have some faint conception of the terror inspired by the appalling

> effigy. One remark is universally made by those to whom I have shown the picture: "It was drawn from the life."

He believes he is alone with his prized book but soon learns otherwise. In "Count Magnus," another scholar (James served as provost of King's College, Cambridge, and of Eton College) arrives to stay in an "ancient manor-house in Vestergothland" in Sweden, where he studies a venerable family's history and finds himself fascinated by a distant ancestor who, it was whispered, had made something called a "Black Pilgrimage." He finds himself asking, "What did the Count bring back with him?" He makes visits to the count's sarcophagus in the family tomb. On his final visit, the lid begins to rise, causing him to hurriedly flee Sweden and his research. He begins to worry that he is trailed back to England by "two figures . . . in dark cloaks; the taller one wore a hat, the shorter a hood. He had no time to see their faces." James placed his finger squarely on a particular type of horror. His characters find themselves unaccountably attracted to arcane or mysterious knowledge, only to find themselves visited by a long-buried menace. His scholars are killed by curiosity.

As we leave the world of devils, succubi, and demons behind, we enter a world of monstrous animals, some more loquacious than others. Poe's classic "The Raven" is the sole poem in this anthology, highly memorable and memorizable, written in trochaic octameter, a very forceful, incantatory meter, with a short refrain at the end of each stanza. As with all of Poe's verse, rhythms and rhymes entrance the reader. Poe's raven appears to rise from the abyss, a messenger from another world. Like all ravens, he is capable of mimicking sounds from his environment, including human speech.

> Then this ebony bird beguiling my sad fancy into smiling,
> By the grave and stern decorum of the countenance it wore,
> "Though thy crest be shorn and shaven, thou," I said, "art sure no craven,
> Ghastly grim and ancient raven wandering from the Nightly shore—
> Tell me what thy lordly name is on the Night's Plutonian shore!"
> Quoth the raven "Nevermore."

In "The Damned Thing," Ambrose Bierce imagines an unseen creature altogether unknown to science.

> There are sounds that we cannot hear. At either end of the scale are notes that stir no chord of that imperfect instrument, the human ear. They are too high or too grave . . . As with sounds, so with colours. At each end of the solar spectrum the chemist can detect the presence of what are known as "actinic" rays. They represent colours—integral colours in the composition of light—which we are unable to discern. The human eye is an imperfect instrument; its range is but a few octaves of the real

> "chromatic scale." I am not mad; there are colours that we cannot see. And, God help me! the Damned Thing is of such a colour!

Monster animals come in all sizes. Arthur Conan Doyle, most famous for his character Sherlock Holmes, imagined massive, prehistoric creatures lurking beneath our world, rising up when the time is right.

> All this country is hollow. Could you strike it with some gigantic hammer it would boom like a drum, or possibly cave in altogether and expose some huge subterranean sea. A great sea there must surely be, for on all sides the streams run into the mountain itself, never to reappear. There are gaps everywhere amid the rocks, and when you pass through them you find yourself in great caverns, which wind down into the bowels of the earth.

When a visitor to the limestone hills of North-West Derbyshire, in England, is told that sheep tend to go missing on pitch-black, overcast nights, he is overcome by curiosity and takes a bicycle lamp to explore an ancient Roman quarry and learn what might dwell in its depths.

Psychology and Terror

Most tales of horror depend in some way on the threat of madness and the surreal contours of psychological terror, but some raise these to such a fever pitch that they become a brand of story all their own. Stephen King has remarked that "the melodies of the horror tale are simple and repetitive, and they are melodies of disestablishment and disintegration." We are fascinated by things going wrong, faulty memories, uncertain visions, those who steadily lose their grip on reality and begin to experience sublime moments of terror. Poe's "The Pit and the Pendulum" conveys suspense to almost unbearable levels as the narrator, condemned to the fetid dungeons of Torquemada's Spanish Inquisition, struggles to survive in the lightless, damp, rat-infested pit, only to face an almost unthinkable type of murderous technology.

Poe excelled at psychological tension. In fact, Lovecraft felt that Poe "clearly and realistically understood the natural basis of the horror-appeal and the correct mechanics of its achievement." Poe's "The Cask of Amontillado," a tale of revenge and murder, is oddly comic, which makes it all the more disquieting (we cannot ignore the terrible irony of the victim's name, Fortunato). Fortunato sings and laughs in a drunken reverie while he is slowly walled into his own tomb. It is worth noting that no fewer than four of the Poe stories included in this volume feature characters entombed or otherwise trapped in subterranean crypts, dungeons, walls, or under floorboards. Perhaps Poe's most famous story is "The Tell-Tale Heart," an account of heartless murder that results in hallucination, obsession, and lunacy. It seizes our attention at the very start.

> True!—nervous—very, very dreadfully nervous I had been and am; but why will you say that I am mad? The disease had sharpened my senses—not destroyed—not dulled them. Above all was the sense of hearing acute. I heard all things in the heaven and in the earth. I heard many things in hell. How, then, am I mad? Hearken! and observe how healthily—how calmly I can tell you the whole story.

Poe places the story in the hands—and in the mind—of a truly deranged psyche. Even if we begin to believe the narrator's claims, we are quickly disabused, disconcerted, and ultimately scared stiff. Poet and critic Daniel Hoffman wrote that "Poe was born to suffer, to thrill to the exquisite torment of those sufferings, to transmute them by his symbolistic imagination into paradigms of man's divided nature." Lovecraft himself—and he knew of whence he spoke—proclaimed that to Poe "we owe the modern horror-story in its final and perfected state." All of this, and more, is on full display in "The Tell-Tale Heart." Poe's unreliable storyteller is so completely insane that he believes he can prove his sanity to us by explaining with what awful thoroughness and precision he carried out his terrible deed. He finally admits that he was called to confess by something he alone could hear.

All this talk of madness brings us to "The Yellow Wallpaper" by Charlotte Perkins Gilman, which novelist and critic Lynne Sharon Schwartz described as a story about "a trapped woman's mental disintegration." After arriving in "a colonial mansion, a hereditary estate, I would say a haunted house," where she has moved with her husband for three months in order to recuperate from "nervous depression," the narrator becomes fixated on the hideous peeling wallpaper on the walls of the former attic nursery they choose for their bedroom.

> One of those sprawling flamboyant patterns committing every artistic sin. It is dull enough to confuse the eye in following, pronounced enough to constantly irritate and provoke study, and when you follow the lame uncertain curves for a little distance they suddenly commit suicide—plunge off at outrageous angles, destroy themselves in unheard of contradictions. The color is repellent, almost revolting; a smouldering unclean yellow, strangely faded by the slow-turning sunlight.

She becomes convinced she can spot shifting patterns, like fungus, in the wallpaper, finally believing she sees a woman creeping behind the pattern, trying to get out.

While he is not typically grouped among horror writers, there is little question that Franz Kafka remains among the most terrifying of authors. In his story "In the Penal Colony," a visitor to a distant land witnesses a meticulous demonstration of a monstrous machine—a "peculiar apparatus"—that slowly kills a condemned man by writing his very death sentence onto his skin with needles until he can finally *feel* the words before being allowed to die. Kafka's stories contain such symbolic significance that they become allegories of the modern horrors experienced at the hands of totalitarian regimes of the twentieth century. "The Metamorphosis," his most harrowing tale, contains one of the best opening passages in literature.

> One morning, when Gregor Samsa woke from troubled dreams, he found himself transformed in his bed into a horrible vermin. He lay on his armour-like back, and if he lifted his head a little he could see his brown belly, slightly domed and divided by arches into stiff sections. The bedding was hardly able to cover it and seemed ready to slide off any moment. His many legs, pitifully thin compared with the size of the rest of him, waved about helplessly as he looked.

In the spirit of a true nightmare, Gregor is at first much more anxious about being late for work and disappointing his employer than in the fact that he's been transformed into a giant insect. To make his morning even more nightmarish, a representative from his firm arrives to the apartment demanding to know why Gregor has not appeared for work, causing his mother, father, and sister to bang on the door pleading with him to come out. Once he finally manages to open the door, they are utterly repulsed by him. The story, strange as it may be, is actually heartbreaking, as poor Gregor can understand his family when they speak but he is unable to communicate in any way with them. Try as he may, he cannot explain that he is not a monster. It is deservedly ranked among the greatest stories of any kind and is the crown jewel of this collection.

Like science fiction, fantasy, and mystery, horror is a living art form, and it has never fallen entirely out of favor. It continues to occasion annual anthologies, conventions, comics, and, of course, the lasting attention of Hollywood. The stories in this anthology—spanning over a century, from Polidori's "The Vampyre" in 1819 to Lovecraft's "The Outsider" in 1926—paved the way for much that followed, including television shows like *The Twilight Zone*, *Alfred Hitchcock Presents*, *The X-Files*, and *American Horror Story*, not to mention the seemingly unstoppable waves of vampire books and films.

This collection, voluminous as it may be, is but the merest peek through a crack in the doorway. Many other worthy authors could have been included in these pages, including Joseph Sheridan LeFanu, Elizabeth Gaskell, Edward Bulwer-Lytton, Mary Elizabeth Braddon, Amelia Edwards, Margaret Oliphant, Sutherland Menzies, Lafcadio Hearn, Mary Austin, Mary Wilkins Freeman, and Robert Aickman. Likewise, many chilling novels fall outside the purview of this anthology due to their sheer size, such as Mary Shelley's *Frankenstein*, Emily Brontë's *Wuthering Heights*, H. Rider Haggard's *She*, Arthur Machen's *The Great God Pan*, and even Jane Austen's *Northanger Abbey*, which satirizes the faddishness of Gothic novels. All of these are worth seeking out, and one would be commended for continuing to explore these authors and helping to restore old stories that have unjustly fallen out of taste.

Why are we drawn back to these dark corners again and again? Some part of us likes to be scared. After reading these stories, we find ourselves starting at unexpected sounds, staring out into the dark, checking over our shoulders to see if we are being followed. They take away the illusion of comfort we allow ourselves in happier moments. Clive Barker, whose six short story collections, collectively titled *The Books of Blood*, reinvigorated the horror genre in the 1980s, insists that horror fiction "shows us that the control we believe we have is purely illusory, and that every moment we teeter on chaos and oblivion." We would rightly banish horror stories from our lives if we did not believe he is correct. E. F. Benson wrote in the author's preface to his story collection *The Room in the Tower* that he "fervently wishes his readers a few uncomfortable moments." Indeed, as he points out, this is "the avowed object of ghost-stories and such tales as deal with the dim unseen forces which occasionally and perturbingly make themselves manifest." So, by all means, settle in and make yourself uncomfortable. Curl up with this collection of disturbing tales—and take care to keep the lights burning and your friends close by.

Ernest Hilbert
Philadelphia, Pennsylvania
March 13, 2015

Ernest Hilbert studied at Oxford University, where he completed a doctorate in English Literature in 2000. He is a widely published poet, critic, and opera librettist with an enduring affinity for supernatural literature and ghost stories. As an antiquarian book dealer, Hilbert has handled first editions of books by many of the authors in this volume, from Polidori to Poe and beyond.

THE TELL-TALE HEART

Edgar Allan Poe

True!—nervous—very, very dreadfully nervous I had been and am; but why will you say that I am mad? The disease had sharpened my senses—not destroyed—not dulled them. Above all was the sense of hearing acute. I heard all things in the heaven and in the earth. I heard many things in hell. How, then, am I mad? Hearken! and observe how healthily—how calmly I can tell you the whole story.

It is impossible to say how first the idea entered my brain; but once conceived, it haunted me day and night. Object there was none. Passion there was none. I loved the old man. He had never wronged me. He had never given me insult. For his gold I had no desire. I think it was his eye! yes, it was this! He had the eye of a vulture—a pale blue eye, with a film over it. Whenever it fell upon me, my blood ran cold; and so by degrees—very gradually—I made up my mind to take the life of the old man, and thus rid myself of the eye forever.

Now this is the point. You fancy me mad. Madmen know nothing. But you should have seen me. You should have seen how wisely I proceeded—with what caution—with what foresight—with what dissimulation I went to work! I was never kinder to the old man than during the whole week before I killed him. And every night, about midnight, I turned the latch of his door and opened it—oh so gently! And then, when I had made an opening sufficient for my head, I put in a dark lantern, all closed, closed, that no light shone out, and then I thrust in my head. Oh, you would have laughed to see how cunningly I thrust it in! I moved it slowly—very, very slowly, so that I might not disturb the old man's sleep. It took me an hour to place my whole head within the opening so far that I could see him as he lay upon his bed. Ha! would a madman have been so wise as this? And then, when my head was well in the room, I undid the lantern cautiously—oh, so cautiously—cautiously (for the hinges creaked)—I undid it just so much that a single thin ray fell upon the vulture eye. And this I did for seven long nights—every night just at midnight—but I found the eye always closed; and so it was impossible to do the work; for it was not the old man who vexed me, but his Evil Eye. And every morning, when the day broke, I went boldly into the chamber, and spoke courageously to him, calling him by name in a hearty tone, and inquiring how he has passed the night. So you see he would have been a very profound old man, indeed, to suspect that every night, just at twelve, I looked in upon him while he slept.

Upon the eighth night I was more than usually cautious in opening the door. A watch's minute hand moves more quickly than did mine. Never before that night had I felt the extent of my own powers—of my sagacity. I could scarcely contain my feelings of triumph. To think that there I was, opening the door, little by little, and he not even to dream of my secret deeds or thoughts. I fairly chuckled at the idea; and perhaps he heard me; for he moved on the bed suddenly, as if startled. Now you may think that I drew back—but no. His room was as black as pitch with the thick darkness, (for the shutters were close fastened, through fear of robbers,) and so I knew that he could not see the opening of the door, and I kept pushing it on steadily, steadily.

I had my head in, and was about to open the lantern, when my thumb slipped upon the tin fastening, and the old man sprang up in bed, crying out—"Who's there?"

I kept quite still and said nothing. For a whole hour I did not move a muscle, and in the meantime I did not hear him lie down. He was still sitting up in the bed listening;—just as I have done, night after night, hearkening to the death watches in the wall.

Presently I heard a slight groan, and I knew it was the groan of mortal terror. It was not a groan of pain or of grief—oh, no!—it was the low stifled sound that arises from the bottom of the soul when overcharged with awe. I knew the sound well. Many a night, just at midnight, when all the world slept, it has welled up from my own bosom, deepening, with its dreadful echo, the terrors that distracted me. I say I knew it well. I knew what the old man felt, and pitied him, although I chuckled at heart. I knew that he had been lying awake ever since the first slight noise, when he had turned in the bed. His fears had been ever since growing upon him. He had been trying to fancy them causeless, but could not. He had been saying to himself—"It is nothing but the wind in the chimney—it is only a mouse crossing the floor," or "It is merely a cricket which has made a single chirp." Yes, he had been trying to comfort himself with these suppositions: but he had found all in vain. *All in vain;* because Death, in approaching him had stalked with his black shadow before him, and enveloped the victim. And it was the mournful influence of the unperceived shadow that caused him to feel—although he neither saw nor heard—to feel the presence of my head within the room.

When I had waited a long time, very patiently, without hearing him lie down, I resolved to open a little—a very, very little crevice in the lantern. So I opened it—you cannot imagine how stealthily, stealthily—until, at length a simple dim ray, like the thread of the spider, shot from out the crevice and fell full upon the vulture eye.

It was open—wide, wide open—and I grew furious as I gazed upon it. I saw it with perfect distinctness—all a dull blue, with a hideous veil over it that chilled the very marrow in my bones; but I could see nothing else of the old man's face or person: for I had directed the ray as if by instinct, precisely upon the damned spot.

And have I not told you that what you mistake for madness is but over-acuteness of the sense?—now, I say, there came to my ears a low, dull, quick sound, such as a watch makes when enveloped in cotton. I knew *that* sound well, too. It was the beating of the old man's heart. It increased my fury, as the beating of a drum stimulates the soldier into courage.

But even yet I refrained and kept still. I scarcely breathed. I held the lantern motionless. I tried how steadily I could maintain the ray upon the eye. Meantime the hellish tattoo of the heart increased. It grew quicker and quicker, and louder and louder every instant. The old man's terror *must* have been extreme! It grew louder, I say, louder every moment!—do you mark me well I have told you that I am nervous: so I am. And now at the dead hour of the night, amid the dreadful silence of that old house, so strange a noise as this excited me to uncontrollable terror. Yet, for some minutes longer I refrained and stood still. But the beating grew louder, louder! I thought the heart must burst. And now a new anxiety seized me—the sound would be heard by a neighbour! The old man's hour had come! With a loud yell, I threw open the lantern and leaped into the room. He shrieked once—once only. In an instant I dragged him to the floor, and pulled the heavy bed over him. I then smiled gaily, to find the deed so far done. But, for many minutes, the heart beat on with a muffled sound. This, however, did not vex me; it would not be heard through the wall. At length it ceased. The old man was dead. I removed the bed and examined the corpse. Yes, he was stone, stone dead. I placed my hand upon the heart and held it there many minutes. There was no pulsation. He was stone dead. His eye would trouble me no more.

If still you think me mad, you will think so no longer when I describe the wise precautions I took for the concealment of the body. The night waned, and I worked hastily, but in silence. First of all I dismembered the corpse. I cut off the head and the arms and the legs.

I then took up three planks from the flooring of the chamber, and deposited all between the scantlings. I then replaced the boards so cleverly, so cunningly, that no human eye—not even *his*—could have detected any thing wrong. There was nothing to wash out—no stain of any kind—no blood-spot whatever. I had been too wary for that. A tub had caught all—ha! ha!

When I had made an end of these labors, it was four o'clock—still dark as midnight. As the bell sounded the hour, there came a knocking at the street door. I went down to open it with a light heart,—for what had I now to fear?

There entered three men, who introduced themselves, with perfect suavity, as officers of the police. A shriek had been heard by a neighbour during the night; suspicion of foul play had been aroused; information had been lodged at the police office, and they (the officers) had been deputed to search the premises.

I smiled—for *what* had I to fear? I bade the gentlemen welcome. The shriek, I said, was my own in a dream. The old man, I mentioned, was absent in the country. I took my visitors all over the house. I bade them search—search well. I led them, at length, to *his* chamber. I showed them his treasures, secure, undisturbed. In the enthusiasm of my confidence, I brought chairs into the room, and desired them here to rest from their fatigues, while I myself, in the wild audacity of my perfect triumph, placed my own seat upon the very spot beneath which reposed the corpse of the victim.

The officers were satisfied. My manner had convinced them. I was singularly at ease. They sat, and while I answered cheerily, they chatted of familiar things. But, ere long, I felt myself getting pale and wished them gone. My head ached, and I fancied a ringing in my ears: but still they sat and still chatted. The ringing became more distinct:—It continued and became more distinct: I talked more freely to get rid of the feeling: but it continued and gained definiteness—until, at length, I found that the noise was not within my ears.

No doubt I now grew *very* pale;—but I talked more fluently, and with a heightened voice. Yet the sound increased—and what could I do? It was a low, *dull, quick sound—much such a sound as a watch makes when enveloped in cotton.* I gasped for breath—and yet the officers heard it not. I talked more quickly—more vehemently; but the noise steadily increased. I arose and argued about trifles, in a high key and with violent gesticulations; but the noise steadily increased. Why *would* they not be gone? I paced the floor to and fro with heavy strides, as if excited to fury by the observations of the men—but the noise steadily increased. Oh God! What *could* I do? I foamed—I raved—I swore! I swung the chair upon which I had been sitting, and grated it upon the boards, but the noise arose over all and continually increased. It grew louder—louder—*louder!* And still the men chatted pleasantly, and smiled. Was it possible they heard not? Almighty God!—no, no! They heard!—they suspected!—they *knew!*—they were making a mockery of my horror!—this I thought, and this I think. But anything was better than this agony! Anything was more tolerable than this derision! I could bear those hypocritical smiles no longer! I felt that I must scream or die! and now—again!—hark! louder! louder! louder! *louder!*

"Villains!" I shrieked, "dissemble no more! I admit the deed!—tear up the planks! here, here!—It is the beating of his hideous heart!"

DRACULA'S GUEST

Bram Stoker

When we started for our drive the sun was shining brightly on Munich, and the air was full of the joyousness of early summer. Just as we were about to depart, Herr Delbrück (the maître d'hôtel of the Quatre Saisons, where I was staying) came down, bareheaded, to the carriage and, after wishing me a pleasant drive, said to the coachman, still holding his hand on the handle of the carriage door:

"Remember you are back by nightfall. The sky looks bright but there is a shiver in the north wind that says there may be a sudden storm. But I am sure you will not be late." Here he smiled, and added, "for you know what night it is."

Johann answered with an emphatic, "Ja, mein Herr," and, touching his hat, drove off quickly. When we had cleared the town, I said, after signalling to him to stop:

"Tell me, Johann, what is tonight?"

He crossed himself, as he answered laconically: "Walpurgis nacht." Then he took out his watch, a great, old-fashioned German silver thing as big as a turnip, and looked at it, with his eyebrows gathered together and a little impatient shrug of his shoulders. I realised that this was his way of respectfully protesting against the unnecessary delay, and sank back in the carriage, merely motioning him to proceed. He started off rapidly, as if to make up for lost time. Every now and then the horses seemed to throw up their heads and sniffed the air suspiciously. On such occasions I often looked round in alarm. The road was pretty bleak, for we were traversing a sort of high, wind-swept plateau. As we drove, I saw a road that looked but little used, and which seemed to dip through a little, winding valley. It looked so inviting that, even at the risk of offending him, I called Johann to stop—and when he had pulled up, I told him I would like to drive down that road. He made all sorts of excuses, and frequently crossed himself as he spoke. This somewhat piqued my curiosity, so I asked him various questions. He answered fencingly, and repeatedly looked at his watch in protest. Finally I said:

"Well, Johann, I want to go down this road. I shall not ask you to come unless you like; but tell me why you do not like to go, that is all I ask." For answer he seemed to throw himself off the box, so quickly did he reach the ground. Then he stretched out his hands appealingly to me, and implored me not to go. There was just enough of English mixed with the German for me to understand the drift of his talk. He seemed always just about to tell me something—the very idea of which evidently frightened him; but each time he pulled himself up, saying, as he crossed himself: "Walpurgis-Nacht!"

I tried to argue with him, but it was difficult to argue with a man when I did not know his language. The advantage certainly rested with him, for although he began to speak in English, of a very crude and broken kind, he always got excited and broke into his native tongue—and every time he did so, he looked at his watch. Then the horses became restless and sniffed the air. At this he grew very pale, and, looking around in a frightened way, he suddenly jumped forward, took them by the bridles and led them on some twenty feet. I followed, and asked why he had done this. For answer he crossed himself, pointed to the spot we had left and drew his carriage in the direction of the other road, indicating a cross, and said, first in German, then in English: "Buried him—him what killed themselves."

I remembered the old custom of burying suicides at cross-roads: "Ah! I see, a suicide. How interesting!" But for the life of me I could not make out why the horses were frightened.

Whilst we were talking, we heard a sort of sound between a yelp and a bark. It was far away; but the horses got very restless, and it took Johann all his time to quiet them. He was pale, and said, "It sounds like a wolf—but yet there are no wolves here now."

"No?" I said, questioning him; "isn't it long since the wolves were so near the city?"

"Long, long," he answered, "in the spring and summer; but with the snow the wolves have been here not so long."

Whilst he was petting the horses and trying to quiet them, dark clouds drifted rapidly across the sky. The sunshine passed away, and a breath of cold wind seemed to drift past us. It was only a breath, however, and more in the nature of a warning than a fact, for the sun came out brightly again. Johann looked under his lifted hand at the horizon and said:

"The storm of snow, he comes before long time." Then he looked at his watch again, and, straightway holding his reins firmly—for the horses were still pawing the ground restlessly and shaking their heads—he climbed to his box as though the time had come for proceeding on our journey.

I felt a little obstinate and did not at once get into the carriage.

"Tell me," I said, "about this place where the road leads," and I pointed down.

Again he crossed himself and mumbled a prayer, before he answered, "It is unholy."

"What is unholy?" I enquired.

"The village."

"Then there is a village?"

"No, no. No one lives there hundreds of years."

My curiosity was piqued, "But you said there was a village."

"There was."

"Where is it now?"

Whereupon he burst out into a long story in German and English, so mixed up that I could not quite understand exactly what he said, but roughly I gathered that long ago, hundreds of years, men had died there and been buried in their graves; and sounds were heard under the clay, and when the graves were opened, men and women were found rosy with life, and their mouths red with blood. And so, in haste to save their lives (aye, and their souls!—and here he crossed himself) those who were left fled away to other places, where the living lived, and the dead were dead and not—not something. He was evidently afraid to speak the last words. As he proceeded with his narration, he grew more and more excited. It seemed as if his imagination had got hold of him, and he ended in a perfect paroxysm of fear—white-faced, perspiring, trembling and looking round him, as if expecting that some dreadful presence would manifest itself there in the bright sunshine on the open plain. Finally, in an agony of desperation, he cried:

"Walpurgis nacht!" and pointed to the carriage for me to get in. All my English blood rose at this, and, standing back, I said:

"You are afraid, Johann—you are afraid. Go home; I shall return alone; the walk will do me good." The carriage door was open. I took from the seat my oak walking-stick—which I always carry on my holiday excursions—and closed the door, pointing back to Munich, and said, "Go home, Johann—Walpurgis-nacht doesn't concern Englishmen."

The horses were now more restive than ever, and Johann was trying to hold them in, while excitedly imploring me not to do anything so foolish. I pitied the poor fellow, he was deeply in earnest; but all the same I could not help laughing. His English was quite gone now. In his anxiety he had forgotten that his only means of making me understand was to talk my language, so he jabbered away in his native German. It began to be a little tedious. After giving the direction, "Home!" I turned to go down the cross-road into the valley.

With a despairing gesture, Johann turned his horses towards Munich. I leaned on my stick and looked after him. He went slowly along the road for a while: then there came over the crest of the hill a man tall and thin. I could see so much in the distance. When he drew near the horses, they began to jump and kick about, then to scream with terror. Johann could not hold them in; they bolted down the road, running away madly. I watched them out of sight, then looked for the stranger, but I found that he, too, was gone.

With a light heart I turned down the side road through the deepening valley to which Johann had objected. There was not the slightest reason, that I could see, for his objection; and I daresay I tramped for a couple of hours without thinking of time or distance, and certainly without seeing a person or a house. So far as the place was concerned, it was desolation itself. But I did not notice this particularly till, on turning a bend in the road, I came upon a scattered fringe of wood; then I recognised that I had been impressed unconsciously by the desolation of the region through which I had passed.

I sat down to rest myself, and began to look around. It struck me that it was considerably colder than it had been at the commencement of my walk—a sort of sighing sound seemed to be around me, with, now and then, high overhead, a sort of muffled roar. Looking upwards I noticed that great thick clouds were drifting rapidly across the sky from North to South at a great height. There were signs of coming storm in some lofty stratum of the air. I was a little chilly, and, thinking that it was the sitting still after the exercise of walking, I resumed my journey.

The ground I passed over was now much more picturesque. There were no striking objects that the eye might single out; but in all there was a charm of beauty. I took little heed of time and it was only when the deepening twilight forced itself upon me that I began to think of how I should find my way home. The brightness of the day had gone. The air was cold, and the drifting of clouds high overhead was more marked. They were accompanied by a sort of far-away rushing sound, through which seemed to come at intervals that mysterious cry which the driver had said came from a wolf. For a while I hesitated. I had said I would see the deserted village, so on I went, and presently came on a wide stretch of open country, shut in by hills all around. Their sides were covered with trees which spread down to the plain, dotting, in clumps, the gentler slopes and hollows which showed here and there. I followed with my eye the winding of the road, and saw that it curved close to one of the densest of these clumps and was lost behind it.

As I looked there came a cold shiver in the air, and the snow began to fall. I thought of the miles and miles of bleak country I had passed, and then hurried on to seek the shelter of the wood in front. Darker and darker grew the sky, and faster and heavier fell the snow, till the earth before and around me was a glistening white carpet the further edge of which was lost in misty vagueness. The road was here but crude, and when on the level its boundaries were not so marked, as when it passed through the cuttings; and in a little while I found that I must have strayed from it, for I missed underfoot the hard surface, and my feet sank deeper in the grass and moss. Then the wind grew stronger and blew with ever increasing force, till I was fain to run before it. The air became icy-cold, and in spite of my exercise I began to suffer. The snow was now falling so thickly and whirling around me in such rapid eddies that I could hardly keep my eyes open. Every now and then the heavens were torn asunder by vivid lightning, and in the flashes I could see ahead of me a great mass of trees, chiefly yew and cypress all heavily coated with snow.

I was soon amongst the shelter of the trees, and there, in comparative silence, I could hear the rush of the wind high overhead. Presently the blackness of the storm had become merged in the darkness of the night. By-and-by the storm seemed to be passing away: it now only came in fierce puffs or blasts. At such moments the weird sound of the wolf appeared to be echoed by many similar sounds around me.

Now and again, through the black mass of drifting cloud, came a straggling ray of moonlight, which lit up the expanse, and showed me that I was at the edge of a dense mass of cypress and yew trees. As the snow had ceased to fall, I walked out from the shelter and began to investigate more closely. It appeared to me that, amongst so many old foundations as I had passed, there might be still standing a house in which, though in ruins, I could find some sort of shelter for a while. As I skirted the edge of the copse, I found that a low wall encircled it, and following this I presently found an opening. Here the cypresses formed an alley leading up to a square mass of some kind of building. Just as I caught sight of this, however, the drifting clouds obscured the moon, and I passed up the path in darkness. The wind must have grown colder, for I felt myself shiver as I walked; but there was hope of shelter, and I groped my way blindly on.

I stopped, for there was a sudden stillness. The storm had passed; and, perhaps in sympathy with nature's silence, my heart seemed to cease to beat. But this was only momentarily; for suddenly the moonlight broke through the clouds, showing me that I was in a graveyard, and that the square object before me was a great massive tomb of marble, as white as the snow that lay on and all around it. With the moonlight there came a fierce sigh of the storm, which appeared to resume its course with a long, low howl, as of many dogs or wolves. I was awed and shocked, and felt the cold perceptibly grow upon me till it seemed to grip me by the heart. Then while the flood of moonlight still fell on the marble tomb, the storm gave further evidence of renewing, as though it was returning on its track. Impelled by some sort of fascination, I approached the sepulchre to see what it was, and why such a thing stood alone in such a place. I walked around it, and read, over the Doric door, in German:

COUNTESS DOLINGEN OF GRATZ
IN STYRIA
SOUGHT AND FOUND DEATH
1801

On the top of the tomb, seemingly driven through the solid marble—for the structure was composed of a few vast blocks of stone—was a great iron spike or stake. On going to the back I saw, graven in great Russian letters:

> "The dead travel fast."

There was something so weird and uncanny about the whole thing that it gave me a turn and made me feel quite faint. I began to wish, for the first time, that I had taken Johann's advice. Here a thought struck me, which came under almost mysterious circumstances and with a terrible shock. This was Walpurgis Night!

Walpurgis Night, when, according to the belief of millions of people, the devil was abroad—when the graves were opened and the dead came forth and walked. When all evil things of earth and air and water held revel. This very place the driver had specially shunned. This was the depopulated village of centuries ago. This was where the suicide lay; and this was the place where I was alone—unmanned, shivering with cold in a shroud of snow with a wild storm gathering again upon me! It took all my philosophy, all the religion I had been taught, all my courage, not to collapse in a paroxysm of fright.

And now a perfect tornado burst upon me. The ground shook as though thousands of horses thundered across it; and this time the storm bore on its icy wings, not snow, but great hailstones which drove with such violence that they might have come from the thongs of Balearic slingers—hailstones that beat down leaf and branch and made the shelter of the cypresses of no more avail than though their stems were standing-corn. At the first I had rushed to the nearest tree; but I was soon fain to leave it and seek the only spot that seemed to afford refuge, the deep Doric doorway of the marble tomb. There, crouching against the massive bronze door, I gained a certain amount of protection from the beating of the hailstones, for now they only drove against me as they ricocheted from the ground and the side of the marble.

As I leaned against the door, it moved slightly and opened inwards. The shelter of even a tomb was welcome in that pitiless tempest, and I was about to enter it when there came a flash of forked-lightning that lit up the whole expanse of the heavens. In the instant, as I am a living man, I saw, as my eyes were turned into the darkness of the tomb, a beautiful woman, with rounded cheeks and red lips, seemingly sleeping on a bier. As the thunder broke overhead, I was grasped as by the hand of a giant and hurled out into the storm. The whole thing was so sudden that, before I could realise the shock, moral as well as physical, I found the hailstones beating me down. At the same time I had a strange, dominating feeling that I was not alone. I looked towards the tomb. Just then there came another blinding flash, which seemed to strike the iron stake that surmounted the tomb and to pour through to the earth, blasting and crumbling the marble, as in a burst of flame. The dead woman rose for a moment of agony, while she was lapped in the flame, and her bitter scream of pain was drowned in the thundercrash. The last thing I heard was this mingling of dreadful sound, as again I was seized in the giant-grasp and dragged away, while the hailstones beat on me, and the air around seemed reverberant with the howling of wolves. The last sight that I remembered was a vague, white, moving mass, as if all the graves around me had sent out the phantoms of their sheeted-dead, and that they were closing in on me through the white cloudiness of the driving hail.

* * * * *

Gradually there came a sort of vague beginning of consciousness; then a sense of weariness that was dreadful. For a time I remembered nothing; but slowly my senses returned. My feet seemed positively racked with pain, yet I could not move them. They seemed to be numbed. There was an icy feeling at the back of my neck and all down my spine, and my ears, like my feet, were dead, yet in torment; but there was in my breast a sense of warmth which was, by comparison, delicious. It was as a nightmare—a physical nightmare, if one may use such an expression; for some heavy weight on my chest made it difficult for me to breathe.

This period of semi-lethargy seemed to remain a long time, and as it faded away I must have slept or swooned. Then came a sort of loathing, like the first stage of sea-sickness, and a wild desire to be free from something—I knew not what. A vast stillness enveloped me, as though all the world were asleep or dead—only broken by the low panting as of some animal close to me. I felt a warm rasping at my throat, then came a consciousness of the awful truth, which chilled me to the heart and sent the blood surging up through my brain. Some great animal was lying on me and now licking my throat. I feared to stir, for some instinct of prudence bade me lie still; but the brute seemed to realise that there was now some change in me, for it raised its head. Through my eyelashes I saw above me the two great flaming eyes of a gigantic wolf. Its sharp white teeth gleamed in the gaping red mouth, and I could feel its hot breath fierce and acrid upon me.

For another spell of time I remembered no more. Then I became conscious of a low growl, followed by a yelp, renewed again and again. Then, seemingly very far away, I heard a "Holloa! holloa!" as of many voices calling in unison. Cautiously I raised my head and looked in the direction whence the sound came; but the cemetery blocked my view. The wolf still continued to yelp in a strange way, and a red glare began to move round the grove of cypresses, as though following the sound. As the voices drew closer, the wolf yelped faster and louder. I feared to make either sound or motion. Nearer came the red glow, over the white pall which stretched into the darkness around me. Then all at once from beyond the trees there came at a trot a troop of horsemen bearing torches. The wolf rose from my breast and made for the cemetery. I saw one of the horsemen (soldiers by their caps and their long military cloaks) raise his carbine and take aim. A companion knocked up his arm, and I heard the ball whizz over my head. He had evidently taken my body for that of the wolf. Another sighted the animal as it slunk away, and a shot followed. Then, at a gallop, the troop rode forward—some towards me, others following the wolf as it disappeared amongst the snow-clad cypresses.

As they drew nearer I tried to move, but was powerless, although I could see and hear all that went on around me. Two or three of the soldiers jumped from their horses and knelt beside me. One of them raised my head, and placed his hand over my heart.

"Good news, comrades!" he cried. "His heart still beats!"

Then some brandy was poured down my throat; it put vigour into me, and I was able to open my eyes fully and look around. Lights and shadows were moving among the trees, and I heard men call to one another. They drew together, uttering frightened exclamations; and the lights flashed as the others came pouring out of the cemetery pell-mell, like men possessed. When the further ones came close to us, those who were around me asked them eagerly:

"Well, have you found him?"

The reply rang out hurriedly:

"No! no! Come away quick—quick! This is no place to stay, and on this of all nights!"

"What was it?" was the question, asked in all manner of keys. The answer came variously and all indefinitely as though the men were moved by some common impulse to speak, yet were restrained by some common fear from giving their thoughts.

"It—it—indeed!" gibbered one, whose wits had plainly given out for the moment.

"A wolf—and yet not a wolf!" another put in shudderingly.

"No use trying for him without the sacred bullet," a third remarked in a more ordinary manner.

"Serve us right for coming out on this night! Truly we have earned our thousand marks!" were the ejaculations of a fourth.

"There was blood on the broken marble," another said after a pause—"the lightning never brought that there. And for him—is he safe? Look at his throat! See, comrades, the wolf has been lying on him and keeping his blood warm."

The officer looked at my throat and replied:

"He is all right; the skin is not pierced. What does it all mean? We should never have found him but for the yelping of the wolf."

"What became of it?" asked the man who was holding up my head, and who seemed the least panic-stricken of the party, for his hands were steady and without tremor. On his sleeve was the chevron of a petty officer.

"It went to its home," answered the man, whose long face was pallid, and who actually shook with terror as he glanced around him fearfully. "There are graves enough there in which it may lie. Come, comrades—come quickly! Let us leave this cursed spot."

The officer raised me to a sitting posture, as he uttered a word of command; then several men placed me upon a horse. He sprang to the saddle behind me, took me in his arms, gave the word to advance; and, turning our faces away from the cypresses, we rode away in swift, military order.

As yet my tongue refused its office, and I was perforce silent. I must have fallen asleep; for the next thing I remembered was finding myself standing up, supported by a soldier on each side of me. It was almost broad daylight, and to the north a red streak of sunlight was reflected, like a path of blood, over the waste of snow. The officer was telling the men to say nothing of what they had seen, except that they found an English stranger, guarded by a large dog.

"Dog! that was no dog," cut in the man who had exhibited such fear. "I think I know a wolf when I see one."

The young officer answered calmly: "I said a dog."

"Dog!" reiterated the other ironically. It was evident that his courage was rising with the sun; and, pointing to me, he said, "Look at his throat. Is that the work of a dog, master?"

Instinctively I raised my hand to my throat, and as I touched it I cried out in pain. The men crowded round to look, some stooping down from their saddles; and again there came the calm voice of the young officer:

"A dog, as I said. If aught else were said we should only be laughed at."

I was then mounted behind a trooper, and we rode on into the suburbs of Munich. Here we came across a stray carriage, into which I was lifted, and it was driven off to the Quatre Saisons—the young officer accompanying me, whilst a trooper followed with his horse, and the others rode off to their barracks.

When we arrived, Herr Delbrück rushed so quickly down the steps to meet me, that it was apparent he had been watching within. Taking me by both hands he solicitously led me in. The officer saluted me and was turning to withdraw, when I recognised his purpose, and insisted that he should come to my rooms. Over a glass of wine I warmly thanked him and his brave comrades for saving me. He replied simply that he was more than glad, and that Herr Delbrück had at the first taken steps to make all the searching party pleased; at which ambiguous utterance the maître d'hôtel smiled, while the officer pleaded duty and withdrew.

"But Herr Delbrück," I enquired, "how and why was it that the soldiers searched for me?"

He shrugged his shoulders, as if in depreciation of his own deed, as he replied:

"I was so fortunate as to obtain leave from the commander of the regiment in which I served, to ask for volunteers."

"But how did you know I was lost?" I asked.

"The driver came hither with the remains of his carriage, which had been upset when the horses ran away."

"But surely you would not send a search-party of soldiers merely on this account?"

"Oh, no!" he answered; "but even before the coachman arrived, I had this telegram from the Boyar whose guest you are," and he took from his pocket a telegram which he handed to me, and I read:

> *Bistritz.*
> Be careful of my guest—his safety is most precious to me. Should aught happen to him, or if he be missed, spare nothing to find him and ensure his safety. He is English and therefore adventurous. There are often dangers from snow and wolves and night. Lose not a moment if you suspect harm to him. I answer your zeal with my fortune.
>
> —Dracula.

As I held the telegram in my hand, the room seemed to whirl around me; and, if the attentive maître d'hôtel had not caught me, I think I should have fallen. There was something so strange in all this, something so weird and impossible to imagine, that there grew on me a sense of my being in some way the sport of opposite forces—the mere vague idea of which seemed in a way to paralyse me. I was certainly under some form of mysterious protection. From a distant country had come, in the very nick of time, a message that took me out of the danger of the snow-sleep and the jaws of the wolf.

THE DEVIL AND TOM WALKER

Washington Irving

A few miles from Boston, in Massachusetts, there is a deep inlet winding several miles into the interior of the country from Charles Bay, and terminating in a thickly wooded swamp or morass. On one side of this inlet is a beautiful dark grove; on the opposite side the land rises abruptly from the water's edge into a high ridge, on which grow a few scattered oaks of great age and immense size. Under one of these gigantic trees, according to old stories, there was a great amount of treasure buried by Kidd the pirate. The inlet allowed a facility to bring the money in a boat secretly, and at night, to the very foot of the hill; the elevation of the place permitted a good lookout to be kept that no one was at hand; while the remarkable trees formed good landmarks by which the place might easily be found again. The old stories add, moreover, that the devil presided at the hiding of the money, and took it under his guardianship; but this, it is well known, he always does with buried treasure, particularly when it has been ill-gotten. Be that as it may, Kidd never returned to recover his wealth; being shortly after seized at Boston, sent out to England, and there hanged for a pirate.

About the year 1727, just at the time that earthquakes were prevalent in New England, and shook many tall sinners down upon their knees, there lived near this place a meagre, miserly fellow, of the name of Tom Walker. He had a wife as miserly as himself; they were so miserly that they even conspired to cheat each other. Whatever the woman could lay hands on she hid away; a hen could not cackle but she was on the alert to secure the new-laid egg. Her husband was continually prying about to detect her secret hoards, and many and fierce were the conflicts that took place about what ought to have been common property. They lived in a forlorn-looking house that stood alone and had an air of starvation. A few straggling savin-trees, emblems of sterility, grew near it; no smoke ever curled from its chimney; no traveller stopped at its door. A miserable horse, whose ribs were as articulate as the bars of a gridiron, stalked about a field, where a thin carpet of moss, scarcely covering the ragged beds of pudding-stone, tantalized and balked his hunger; and sometimes he would lean his head over the fence, look piteously at the passer-by, and seem to petition deliverance from this land of famine.

The house and its inmates had altogether a bad name. Tom's wife was a tall termagant, fierce of temper, loud of tongue, and strong of arm. Her voice was often heard in wordy warfare with her husband; and his face sometimes showed signs that their conflicts were not confined to words. No one ventured, however, to interfere between them. The lonely wayfarer shrank within himself at the horrid clamor and clapper-clawing; eyed the den of discord askance; and hurried on his way, rejoicing, if a bachelor, in his celibacy.

One day that Tom Walker had been to a distant part of the neighborhood, he took what he considered a short-cut homeward, through the swamp. Like most short-cuts, it was an ill-chosen route. The swamp was thickly grown with great, gloomy pines and hemlocks, some of them ninety feet high, which made it dark at noonday and a retreat for all the owls of the neighborhood. It was full of pits and quagmires, partly covered with weeds and mosses, where the green surface often betrayed the traveller into a gulf of black, smothering mud; there were also dark and stagnant pools, the abodes of the tadpole, the bull-frog, and the water-snake, where the trunks of pines and hemlocks lay half-drowned, half-rotting, looking like alligators sleeping in the mire.

Tom had long been picking his way cautiously through this treacherous forest, stepping from tuft to tuft of rushes and roots, which afforded precarious footholds among deep sloughs, or pacing carefully, like a cat, along the prostrate trunks of trees, startled now and then by the sudden screaming of the bittern, or the quacking of a wild duck, rising on the wing from some solitary pool. At length he arrived at a firm piece of ground, which ran like a peninsula into the deep bosom of the swamp. It had been one of the strongholds of the Indians during their wars with the first colonists. Here they had thrown up a kind of fort, which they had looked upon as almost impregnable, and had used as a place of refuge for their squaws and children. Nothing remained of the old Indian fort but a few embankments, gradually sinking to the level of the surrounding earth, and already overgrown in part by oaks and other forest trees, the foliage of which formed a contrast to the dark pines and hemlocks of the swamps.

It was late in the dusk of evening when Tom Walker reached the old fort, and he paused there awhile to rest himself. Any one but he would have felt unwilling to linger in this lonely, melancholy place, for the common people had a bad opinion of it, from the stories handed down from the times of the Indian wars, when it was asserted that the savages held incantations here and made sacrifices to the Evil Spirit.

Tom Walker, however, was not a man to be troubled with any fears of the kind. He reposed himself for some time on the trunk of a fallen hemlock, listening to the boding cry of the tree-toad, and delving with his walking-staff into a mound of black mould at his feet. As he turned up the soil unconsciously, his staff struck against something hard. He raked it out of the vegetable mould, and lo! a cloven skull, with an Indian tomahawk buried deep in it, lay before him. The rust on the weapon showed the time that had elapsed since this death-blow had been given. It was a dreary memento of the fierce struggle that had taken place in this last foothold of the Indian warriors.

"Humph!" said Tom Walker, as he gave it a kick to shake the dirt from it.

"Let that skull alone!" said a gruff voice. Tom lifted up his eyes and beheld a great black man seated directly opposite him, on the stump of a tree. He was exceedingly surprised, having neither heard nor seen any one approach; and he was still more perplexed on observing, as well as the gathering gloom would permit, that the stranger was neither negro nor Indian. It is true he was dressed in a rude Indian garb, and had a red belt or sash swathed round his body; but his face was neither black nor copper-color, but swarthy and dingy, and begrimed with soot, as if he had been accustomed to toil among fires and forges. He had a shock of coarse black hair, that stood out from his head in all directions, and bore an axe on his shoulder.

He scowled for a moment at Tom with a pair of great red eyes.

"What are you doing on my grounds?" said the black man, with a hoarse, growling voice.

"Your grounds!" said Tom, with a sneer; "no more your grounds than mine; they belong to Deacon Peabody."

"Deacon Peabody be damned," said the stranger, "as I flatter myself he will be, if he does not look more to his own sins and less to those of his neighbors. Look yonder, and see how Deacon Peabody is faring."

Tom looked in the direction that the stranger pointed, and beheld one of the great trees, fair and flourishing without, but rotten at the core, and saw that it had been nearly hewn through, so that the first high wind was likely to blow it down. On the bark of the tree was scored the name of Deacon Peabody, an eminent man who had waxed wealthy by driving shrewd bargains with the Indians. He now looked around, and found most of the tall trees marked with the name of some great man of the colony, and all more or less scored by the axe. The one on which he had been seated, and which had evidently just been hewn down, bore the name of Crowninshield; and he recollected a mighty rich man of that name, who made a vulgar display of wealth, which it was whispered he had acquired by buccaneering.

"He's just ready for burning!" said the black man, with a growl of triumph. "You see I am likely to have a good stock of firewood for winter."

"But what right have you," said Tom, "to cut down Deacon Peabody's timber?"

"The right of a prior claim," said the other. "This woodland belonged to me long before one of your white-faced race put foot upon the soil."

"And, pray, who are you, if I may be so bold?" said Tom.

"Oh, I go by various names. I am the wild huntsman in some countries; the black miner in others. In this neighborhood I am known by the name of the black woodsman. I am he to whom the red men consecrated this spot, and in honor of whom they now and then roasted a white man, by way of sweet-smelling sacrifice. Since the red men have been exterminated by you white savages, I amuse myself by presiding at the persecutions of Quakers and Anabaptists; I am the great patron and prompter of slave-dealers and the grand-master of the Salem witches."

"The upshot of all which is, that, if I mistake not," said Tom, sturdily, "you are he commonly called Old Scratch."

"The same, at your service!" replied the black man, with a half-civil nod.

Such was the opening of this interview, according to the old story; though it has almost too familiar an air to be credited. One would think that to meet with such a singular personage in this wild, lonely place would have shaken any man's nerves; but Tom was a hard-minded fellow, not easily daunted, and he had lived so long with a termagant wife that he did not even fear the devil.

It is said that after this commencement they had a long and earnest conversation together, as Tom returned homeward. The black man told him of great sums of money buried by Kidd the pirate under the oak-trees on the high ridge, not far from the morass. All these were under his command, and protected by his power, so that none could find them but such as propitiated his favor. These he offered to place within Tom Walker's reach, having conceived an especial kindness for him; but they were to be had only on certain conditions. What these conditions were may be easily surmised, though Tom never disclosed them publicly. They must have been very hard, for he required time to think of them, and he was not a man to stick at trifles when money was in view. When they had reached the edge of the swamp, the stranger paused. "What proof have I that all you have been telling me is true?" said Tom. "There's my signature," said the black man, pressing his finger on Tom's forehead. So saying, he turned off among the thickets of the swamp, and seemed, as Tom said, to go down, down, down, into the earth, until nothing but his head and shoulders could be seen, and so on, until he totally disappeared.

When Tom reached home he found the black print of a finger burned, as it were, into his forehead, which nothing could obliterate.

The first news his wife had to tell him was the sudden death of Absalom Crowninshield, the rich buccaneer. It was announced in the papers, with the usual flourish, that "A great man had fallen in Israel."

Tom recollected the tree which his black friend had just hewn down, and which was ready for burning. "Let the freebooter roast," said Tom; "who cares!" He now felt convinced that all he had heard and seen was no illusion.

He was not prone to let his wife into his confidence; but as this was an uneasy secret, he willingly shared it with her. All her avarice was awakened at the mention of hidden gold, and she urged her husband to comply with the black man's terms, and secure what would make them wealthy for life. However Tom might have felt disposed to sell himself to the devil, he was determined not to do so to oblige his wife; so he flatly refused, out of the mere spirit of contradiction. Many and bitter were the quarrels they had on the subject; but the more she talked, the more resolute was Tom not to be damned to please her.

At length she determined to drive the bargain on her own account, and, if she succeeded, to keep all the gain to herself. Being of the same fearless temper as her husband, she set off for the old Indian fort toward the close of a summer's day. She was many hours absent. When she came back, she was reserved and sullen in her replies. She spoke something of a black man, whom she had met about twilight hewing at the root of a tall tree. He was sulky, however, and would not come to terms; she was to go again with a propitiatory offering, but what it was she forbore to say.

The next evening she set off again for the swamp, with her apron heavily laden. Tom waited and waited for her, but in vain; midnight came, but she did not make her appearance; morning, noon, night returned, but still she did not come. Tom now grew uneasy for her safety, especially as he found she had carried off in her apron the silver tea-pot and spoons, and every portable article of value. Another night elapsed, another morning came; but no wife. In a word, she was never heard of more.

What was her real fate nobody knows, in consequence of so many pretending to know. It is one of those facts which have become confounded by a variety of historians. Some asserted that she lost her way among the tangled mazes of the swamp, and sank into some pit or slough; others, more uncharitable, hinted that she had eloped with the household booty, and made off to some other province; while others surmised that the tempter had decoyed her into a dismal quagmire, on the top of which her hat was found lying. In confirmation of this, it was said a great black man, with an axe on his shoulder, was seen late that very evening coming out of the swamp, carrying a bundle tied in a check apron, with an air of surly triumph.

The most current and probable story, however, observes that Tom Walker grew so anxious about the fate of his wife and his property that he set out at length to seek them both at the Indian fort. During a long summer's afternoon he searched about the gloomy place, but no wife was to be seen. He called her name repeatedly, but she was nowhere to be heard. The bittern alone responded to his voice, as he flew screaming by; or the bull-frog croaked dolefully from a neighboring pool. At length, it is said, just in the brown hour of twilight, when the owls began to hoot and the bats to flit about, his attention was attracted by the clamor of carrion crows hovering about a cypress-tree. He looked up and beheld a bundle tied in a check apron and hanging in the branches of the tree, with a great vulture perched hard by, as if keeping watch upon it. He leaped with joy, for he recognized his wife's apron, and supposed it to contain the household valuables.

"Let us get hold of the property," said he, consolingly, to himself, "and we will endeavor to do without the woman."

As he scrambled up the tree, the vulture spread its wide wings and sailed off, screaming, into the deep shadows of the forest. Tom seized the checked apron, but, woful sight! found nothing but a heart and liver tied up in it!

Such, according to this most authentic old story, was all that was to be found of Tom's wife. She had probably attempted to deal with the black man as she had been accustomed to deal with her husband; but though a female scold is generally considered a match for the devil, yet in this instance she appears to have had the worst of it. She must have died game, however; for it is said Tom noticed many prints of cloven feet deeply stamped about the tree, and found handfuls of hair, that looked as if they had been plucked from the coarse black shock of the woodsman. Tom knew his wife's prowess by experience. He shrugged his shoulders as he looked at the signs of fierce clapper-clawing. "Egad," said he to himself, "Old Scratch must have had a tough time of it!"

Tom consoled himself for the loss of his property, with the loss of his wife, for he was a man of fortitude. He even felt something like gratitude toward the black woodsman, who, he considered, had done him a kindness. He sought, therefore, to cultivate a further acquaintance with him, but for some time without success; the old black-legs played shy, for, whatever people may think, he is not always to be had for the calling; he knows how to play his cards when pretty sure of his game.

At length, it is said, when delay had whetted Tom's eagerness to the quick and prepared him to agree to anything rather than not gain the promised treasure, he met the black man one evening in his usual woodsman's dress, with his axe on his shoulder, sauntering along the swamp and humming a tune. He affected to receive Tom's advances with great indifference, made brief replies, and went on humming his tune.

By degrees, however, Tom brought him to business, and they began to haggle about the terms on which the former was to have the pirate's treasure. There was one condition which need not be mentioned, being generally understood in all cases where the devil grants favors; but there were others about which, though of less importance, he was inflexibly obstinate. He insisted that the money found through his means should be employed in his service. He proposed, therefore, that Tom should employ it in the black traffic; that is to say, that he should fit out a slave-ship. This, however, Tom resolutely refused; he was bad enough in all conscience, but the devil himself could not tempt him to turn slave-trader.

Finding Tom so squeamish on this point, he did not insist upon it, but proposed, instead, that he should turn usurer; the devil being extremely anxious for the increase of usurers, looking upon them as his peculiar people.

To this no objections were made, for it was just to Tom's taste.

"You shall open a broker's shop in Boston next month," said the black man.

"I'll do it to-morrow, if you wish," said Tom Walker.

"You shall lend money at two per cent a month."

"Egad, I'll charge four!" replied Tom Walker.

"You shall extort bonds, foreclose mortgages, drive the merchants to bankruptcy—"

"I'll drive them to the devil," cried Tom Walker.

"*You* are the usurer for my money!" said black-legs with delight. "When will you want the rhino?"

"This very night."

"Done!" said the devil.

"Done!" said Tom Walker. So they shook hands and struck a bargain.

A few days' time saw Tom Walker seated behind his desk in a counting-house in Boston.

His reputation for a ready-moneyed man, who would lend money out for a good consideration, soon spread abroad. Everybody remembers the time of Governor Belcher, when money was particularly scarce. It was a time of paper credit. The country had been deluged with government bills; the famous Land Bank had been established; there had been a rage for speculating; the people had run mad with schemes for new settlements, for building cities in the wilderness; land-jobbers went about with maps of grants and townships and Eldorados, lying nobody knew where, but which everybody was ready to purchase. In a word, the great speculating fever which breaks out every now and then in the country had raged to an alarming degree, and everybody was dreaming of making sudden fortunes from nothing. As usual, the fever had subsided, the dream had gone off, and the imaginary fortunes with it; the patients were left in doleful plight, and the whole country resounded with the consequent cry of "hard times."

At this propitious time of public distress did Tom Walker set up as usurer in Boston. His door was soon thronged by customers. The needy and adventurous, the gambling speculator, the dreaming land-jobber, the thriftless tradesman, the merchant with cracked credit—in short, everyone driven to raise money by desperate means and desperate sacrifices hurried to Tom Walker.

Thus Tom was the universal friend to the needy, and acted like "a friend in need"; that is to say, he always exacted good pay and security. In proportion to the distress of the applicant was the hardness of his terms. He accumulated bonds and mortgages, gradually squeezed his customers closer and closer, and sent them at length, dry as a sponge, from his door.

In this way he made money hand over hand, became a rich and mighty man, and exalted his cocked hat upon "Change." He built himself, as usual, a vast house, out of ostentation, but left the greater part of it unfinished and unfurnished, out of parsimony. He even set up a carriage in the fulness of his vain-glory, though he nearly starved the horses which drew it; and, as the ungreased wheels groaned and screeched on the axle-trees, you would have thought you heard the souls of the poor debtors he was squeezing.

As Tom waxed old, however, he grew thoughtful. Having secured the good things of this world, he began to feel anxious about those of the next. He thought with regret of the bargain he had made with his black friend, and set his wits to work to cheat him out of the conditions. He became, therefore, all of a sudden, a violent church-goer. He prayed loudly and strenuously, as if heaven were to be taken by force of lungs. Indeed, one might always tell when he had sinned most during the week by the clamor of his Sunday devotion. The quiet Christians who had been modestly and steadfastly travelling Zionward were struck with self-reproach at seeing themselves so suddenly outstripped in their career by this new-made convert. Tom was as rigid in religious as in money matters; he was a stern supervisor and censurer of his neighbors, and seemed to think every sin entered up to their account became a credit on his own side of the page. He even talked of the expediency of reviving the persecution of Quakers and Anabaptists. In a word, Tom's zeal became as notorious as his riches.

Still, in spite of all this strenuous attention to forms, Tom had a lurking dread that the devil, after all, would have his due. That he might not be taken unawares, therefore, it is said he always carried a small Bible in his coat-pocket. He had also a great folio Bible on his counting-house desk, and would frequently be found reading it when people called on business; on such occasions he would lay his green spectacles in the book, to mark the place, while he turned round to drive some usurious bargain.

Some say that Tom grew a little crack-brained in his old days, and that, fancying his end approaching, he had his horse new shod, saddled, and bridled, and buried with his feet uppermost; because he supposed that at the last day the world would be turned upside-down; in which case he should find his horse standing ready for mounting, and he was determined at the worst to give his old friend a run for it. This, however, is probably a mere old wives' fable. If he really did take such a precaution, it was totally superfluous; at least so says the authentic old legend, which closes his story in the following manner:

One hot summer afternoon in the dog-days, just as a terrible black thunder-gust was coming up, Tom sat in his counting-house, in his white linen cap and India silk morning-gown. He was on the point of foreclosing a mortgage, by which he would complete the ruin of an unlucky land-speculator for whom he had professed the greatest friendship. The poor land-jobber begged him to grant a few months' indulgence. Tom had grown testy and irritated, and refused another delay.

"My family will be ruined, and brought upon the parish," said the land-jobber.

"Charity begins at home," replied Tom; "I must take care of myself in these hard times."

"You have made so much money out of me," said the speculator.

Tom lost his patience and his piety. "The devil take me," said he, "if I have made a farthing!"

Just then there were three loud knocks at the street door. He stepped out to see who was there. A black man was holding a black horse, which neighed and stamped with impatience.

"Tom, you're come for," said the black fellow, gruffly. Tom shrank back, but too late. He had left his little Bible at the bottom of his coat-pocket and his big Bible on the desk buried under the mortgage he was about to foreclose: never was sinner taken more unawares. The black man whisked him like a child into the saddle, gave the horse the lash, and away he galloped, with Tom on his back, in the midst of the thunder-storm. The clerks stuck their pens behind their ears, and stared after him from the windows. Away went Tom Walker, dashing down the streets, his white cap bobbing up and down, his morning-gown fluttering in the wind, and his steed striking fire out of the pavement at every bound. When the clerks turned to look for the black man, he had disappeared.

Tom Walker never returned to foreclose the mortgage. A countryman, who lived on the border of the swamp, reported that in the height of the thunder-gust he had heard a great clattering of hoofs and a howling along the road, and running to the window caught sight of a figure, such as I have described, on a horse that galloped like mad across the fields, over the hills, and down into the black hemlock swamp toward the old Indian fort, and that shortly after a thunder-bolt falling in that direction seemed to set the whole forest in a blaze.

The good people of Boston shook their heads and shrugged their shoulders, but had been so much accustomed to witches and goblins, and tricks of the devil, in all kinds of shapes, from the first settlement of the colony, that they were not so much horror-struck as might have been expected. Trustees were appointed to take charge of Tom's effects. There was nothing, however, to administer upon. On searching his coffers, all his bonds and mortgages were reduced to cinders. In place of gold and silver, his iron chest was filled with chips and shavings; two skeletons lay in his stable instead of his half-starved horses, and the very next day his great house took fire and was burned to the ground.

Such was the end of Tom Walker and his ill-gotten wealth. Let all gripping money-brokers lay this story to heart. The truth of it is not to be doubted. The very hole under the oak-trees, whence he dug Kidd's money, is to be seen to this day; and the neighboring swamp and old Indian fort are often haunted in stormy nights by a figure on horseback, in morning-gown and white cap, which is doubtless the troubled spirit of the usurer. In fact, the story has resolved itself into a proverb, and is the origin of that popular saying, so prevalent throughout New England, of "The devil and Tom Walker."

AN OCCURRENCE AT OWL CREEK BRIDGE

Ambrose Bierce

I

A man stood upon a railroad bridge in northern Alabama, looking down into the swift water twenty feet below. The man's hands were behind his back, the wrists bound with a cord. A rope closely encircled his neck. It was attached to a stout cross-timber above his head and the slack fell to the level of his knees. Some loose boards laid upon the ties supporting the rails of the railway supplied a footing for him and his executioners—two private soldiers of the Federal army, directed by a sergeant who in civil life may have been a deputy sheriff. At a short remove upon the same temporary platform was an officer in the uniform of his rank, armed. He was a captain. A sentinel at each end of the bridge stood with his rifle in the position known as "support," that is to say, vertical in front of the left shoulder, the hammer resting on the forearm thrown straight across the chest—a formal and unnatural position, enforcing an erect carriage of the body. It did not appear to be the duty of these two men to know what was occurring at the center of the bridge; they merely blockaded the two ends of the foot planking that traversed it.

Beyond one of the sentinels nobody was in sight; the railroad ran straight away into a forest for a hundred yards, then, curving, was lost to view. Doubtless there was an outpost farther along. The other bank of the stream was open ground—a gentle slope topped with a stockade of vertical tree trunks, loopholed for rifles, with a single embrasure through which protruded the muzzle of a brass cannon commanding the bridge. Midway up the slope between the bridge and fort were the spectators—a single company of infantry in line, at "parade rest," the butts of their rifles on the ground, the barrels inclining slightly backward against the right shoulder, the hands crossed upon the stock. A lieutenant stood at the right of the line, the point of his sword upon the ground, his left hand resting upon his right. Excepting the group of four at the center of the bridge, not a man moved. The company faced the bridge, staring stonily, motionless. The sentinels, facing the banks of the stream, might have been statues to adorn the bridge. The captain stood with folded arms, silent, observing the work of his subordinates, but making no sign. Death is a dignitary who when he comes announced is to be received with formal manifestations of respect, even by those most familiar with him. In the code of military etiquette silence and fixity are forms of deference.

The man who was engaged in being hanged was apparently about thirty-five years of age. He was a civilian, if one might judge from his habit, which was that of a planter. His features were good—a straight nose, firm mouth, broad forehead, from which his long, dark hair was combed straight back, falling behind his ears to the collar of his well fitting frock coat. He wore a moustache and pointed beard, but no whiskers; his eyes were large and dark gray, and had a kindly expression which one would hardly have expected in one whose neck was in the hemp. Evidently this was no vulgar assassin. The liberal military code makes provision for hanging many kinds of persons, and gentlemen are not excluded.

The preparations being complete, the two private soldiers stepped aside and each drew away the plank upon which he had been standing. The sergeant turned to the captain, saluted and placed himself immediately behind that officer, who in turn moved apart one pace. These movements left the condemned man and the sergeant standing on the two ends of the same plank, which spanned three of the cross-ties of the bridge. The end upon which the civilian stood almost, but not quite, reached a fourth. This plank had been held in place by the weight of the captain; it was now held by that of the sergeant. At a signal from the former the latter would step aside, the plank would tilt and the condemned man go down between two ties. The arrangement commended itself to his judgement as simple and effective. His face had not been covered nor his eyes bandaged. He looked a moment at his "unsteadfast footing," then let his gaze wander to the swirling water of the stream racing madly beneath his feet. A piece of dancing driftwood caught his attention and his eyes followed it down the current. How slowly it appeared to move! What a sluggish stream!

He closed his eyes in order to fix his last thoughts upon his wife and children. The water, touched to gold by the early sun, the brooding mists under the banks at some distance down the stream, the fort, the soldiers, the piece of drift—all had distracted him. And now he became conscious of a new disturbance. Striking through the thought of his dear ones was sound which he could neither ignore nor understand, a sharp, distinct, metallic percussion like the stroke of a blacksmith's hammer upon the anvil; it had the same ringing quality. He wondered what it was, and whether immeasurably distant or near by—it seemed both. Its recurrence was regular, but as slow as the tolling of a death knell. He awaited each new stroke with impatience and—he knew not why—apprehension. The intervals of silence grew progressively longer; the delays became maddening. With their greater infrequency the sounds increased in strength and sharpness. They hurt his ear like the trust of a knife; he feared he would shriek. What he heard was the ticking of his watch.

He unclosed his eyes and saw again the water below him. "If I could free my hands," he thought, "I might throw off the noose and spring into the stream. By diving I could evade the bullets and, swimming vigorously, reach the bank, take to the woods and get away home. My home, thank God, is as yet outside their lines; my wife and little ones are still beyond the invader's farthest advance."

As these thoughts, which have here to be set down in words, were flashed into the doomed man's brain rather than evolved from it the captain nodded to the sergeant. The sergeant stepped aside.

II

Peyton Farquhar was a well to do planter, of an old and highly respected Alabama family. Being a slave owner and like other slave owners a politician, he was naturally an original secessionist and ardently devoted to the Southern cause. Circumstances of an imperious nature, which it is unnecessary to relate here, had prevented him from taking service with that gallant army which had fought the disastrous campaigns ending with the fall of Corinth, and he chafed under the inglorious restraint, longing for the release of his energies, the larger life of the soldier, the opportunity for distinction. That opportunity, he felt, would come, as it comes to all in wartime. Meanwhile he did what he could. No service was too humble for him to perform in the aid of the South, no adventure too perilous for him to undertake if consistent with the character of a civilian who was at heart a soldier, and who in good faith and without too much qualification assented to at least a part of the frankly villainous dictum that all is fair in love and war.

One evening while Farquhar and his wife were sitting on a rustic bench near the entrance to his grounds, a gray-clad soldier rode up to the gate and asked for a drink of water. Mrs. Farquhar was only too happy to serve him with her own white hands. While she was fetching the water her husband approached the dusty horseman and inquired eagerly for news from the front.

"The Yanks are repairing the railroads," said the man, "and are getting ready for another advance. They have reached the Owl Creek bridge, put it in order and built a stockade on the north bank. The commandant has issued an order, which is posted everywhere, declaring that any civilian caught interfering with the railroad, its bridges, tunnels, or trains will be summarily hanged. I saw the order."

"How far is it to the Owl Creek bridge?" Farquhar asked.

"About thirty miles."

"Is there no force on this side of the creek?"

"Only a picket post half a mile out, on the railroad, and a single sentinel at this end of the bridge."

"Suppose a man—a civilian and student of hanging—should elude the picket post and perhaps get the better of the sentinel," said Farquhar, smiling, "what could he accomplish?"

The soldier reflected. "I was there a month ago," he replied. "I observed that the flood of last winter had lodged a great quantity of driftwood against the wooden pier at this end of the bridge. It is now dry and would burn like tinder."

The lady had now brought the water, which the soldier drank. He thanked her ceremoniously, bowed to her husband and rode away. An hour later, after nightfall, he repassed the plantation, going northward in the direction from which he had come. He was a Federal scout.

III

As Peyton Farquhar fell straight downward through the bridge he lost consciousness and was as one already dead. From this state he was awakened—ages later, it seemed to him—by the pain of a sharp pressure upon his throat, followed by a sense of suffocation. Keen, poignant agonies seemed to shoot from his neck downward through every fiber of his body and limbs. These pains appeared to flash along well defined lines of ramification and to beat with an inconceivably rapid periodicity. They seemed like streams of pulsating fire heating him to an intolerable temperature. As to his head, he was conscious of nothing but a feeling of fullness—of congestion. These sensations were unaccompanied by thought. The intellectual part of his nature was already effaced; he had power only to feel, and feeling was torment. He was conscious of motion. Encompassed in a luminous cloud, of which he was now merely the fiery heart, without material substance, he swung through unthinkable arcs of oscillation, like a vast pendulum. Then all at once, with terrible suddenness, the light about him shot upward with the noise of a loud splash; a frightful roaring was in his ears, and all was cold and dark. The power of thought was restored; he knew that the rope had broken and he had fallen into the stream. There was no additional strangulation; the noose about his neck was already suffocating him and kept the water from his lungs. To die of hanging at the bottom of a river!—the idea seemed to him ludicrous. He opened his eyes in the darkness and saw above him a gleam of light, but how distant, how inaccessible! He was still sinking, for the light became fainter and fainter until it was a mere glimmer. Then it began to grow and brighten, and he knew that he was rising toward the surface—knew it with reluctance, for he was now very comfortable. "To be hanged and drowned," he thought, "that is not so bad; but I do not wish to be shot. No; I will not be shot; that is not fair."

He was not conscious of an effort, but a sharp pain in his wrist apprised him that he was trying to free his hands. He gave the struggle his attention, as an idler might observe the feat of a juggler, without interest in the outcome. What splendid effort!—what magnificent, what superhuman strength! Ah, that was a fine endeavor! Bravo! The cord fell away; his arms parted and floated upward, the hands dimly seen on each side in the growing light. He watched them with a new interest as first one and then the other pounced upon the noose at his neck. They tore it away and thrust it fiercely aside, its undulations resembling those of a water snake. "Put it back, put it back!" He thought he shouted these words to his hands, for the undoing of the noose had been succeeded by the direst pang that he had yet experienced. His neck ached horribly; his brain was on fire, his heart, which had been fluttering faintly, gave a great leap, trying to force itself out at his mouth. His whole body was racked and wrenched with an insupportable anguish! But his disobedient hands gave no heed to the command. They beat the water vigorously with quick, downward strokes, forcing him to the surface. He felt his head emerge; his eyes were blinded by the sunlight; his chest expanded convulsively, and with a supreme and crowning agony his lungs engulfed a great draught of air, which instantly he expelled in a shriek!

He was now in full possession of his physical senses. They were, indeed, preternaturally keen and alert. Something in the awful disturbance of his organic system had so exalted and refined them that they made record of things never before perceived. He felt the ripples upon his face and heard their separate sounds as they struck. He looked at the forest on the bank of the stream, saw the individual trees, the leaves and the veining of each leaf—he saw the very insects upon them: the locusts, the brilliant bodied flies, the gray spiders stretching their webs from twig to twig. He noted the prismatic colors in all the dewdrops upon a million blades of grass. The humming of the gnats that danced above the eddies of the stream, the beating of the dragon flies' wings, the strokes of the water spiders' legs, like oars which had lifted their boat—all these made audible music. A fish slid along beneath his eyes and he heard the rush of its body parting the water.

He had come to the surface facing down the stream; in a moment the visible world seemed to wheel slowly round, himself the pivotal point, and he saw the bridge, the fort, the soldiers upon the bridge, the captain, the sergeant, the two privates, his executioners. They were in silhouette against the blue sky. They shouted and gesticulated, pointing at him. The captain had drawn his pistol, but did not fire; the others were unarmed. Their movements were grotesque and horrible, their forms gigantic.

Suddenly he heard a sharp report and something struck the water smartly within a few inches of his head, spattering his face with spray. He heard a second report, and saw one of the sentinels with his rifle at his shoulder, a light cloud of blue smoke rising from the muzzle. The man in the water saw the eye of the man on the bridge gazing into his own through the sights of the rifle. He observed that it was a gray eye and remembered having read that gray eyes were keenest, and that all famous marksmen had them. Nevertheless, this one had missed.

A counter-swirl had caught Farquhar and turned him half round; he was again looking at the forest on the bank opposite the fort. The sound of a clear, high voice in a monotonous singsong now rang out behind him and came across the water with a distinctness that pierced and subdued all other sounds, even the beating of the ripples in his ears. Although no soldier, he had frequented camps enough to know the dread significance of that deliberate, drawling, aspirated chant; the lieutenant on shore was taking a part in the morning's work. How coldly and pitilessly—with what an even, calm intonation, presaging, and enforcing tranquility in the men—with what accurately measured interval fell those cruel words:

"Company! . . . Attention! . . . Shoulder arms! . . . Ready! . . . Aim! . . . Fire!"

Farquhar dived—dived as deeply as he could. The water roared in his ears like the voice of Niagara, yet he heard the dull thunder of the volley and, rising again toward the surface, met shining bits of metal, singularly flattened, oscillating slowly downward. Some of them touched him on the face and hands, then fell away, continuing their descent. One lodged between his collar and neck; it was uncomfortably warm and he snatched it out.

As he rose to the surface, gasping for breath, he saw that he had been a long time under water; he was perceptibly farther downstream—nearer to safety. The soldiers had almost finished reloading; the metal ramrods flashed all at once in the sunshine as they were drawn from the barrels, turned in the air, and thrust into their sockets. The two sentinels fired again, independently and ineffectually.

The hunted man saw all this over his shoulder; he was now swimming vigorously with the current. His brain was as energetic as his arms and legs; he thought with the rapidity of lightning:

"The officer," he reasoned, "will not make that martinet's error a second time. It is as easy to dodge a volley as a single shot. He has probably already given the command to fire at will. God help me, I cannot dodge them all!"

An appalling splash within two yards of him was followed by a loud, rushing sound, diminuendo, which seemed to travel back through the air to the fort and died in an explosion which stirred the very river to its deeps! A rising sheet of water curved over him, fell down upon him, blinded him, strangled him! The cannon had taken an hand in the game. As he shook his head free from the commotion of the smitten water he heard the deflected shot humming through the air ahead, and in an instant it was cracking and smashing the branches in the forest beyond.

"They will not do that again," he thought; "the next time they will use a charge of grape. I must keep my eye upon the gun; the smoke will apprise me—the report arrives too late; it lags behind the missile. That is a good gun."

Suddenly he felt himself whirled round and round—spinning like a top. The water, the banks, the forests, the now distant bridge, fort and men, all were commingled and blurred. Objects were represented by their colors only; circular horizontal streaks of color—that was all he saw. He had been caught in a vortex and was being whirled on with a velocity of advance and gyration that made him giddy and sick. In few moments he was flung upon the gravel at the foot of the left bank of the stream—the southern bank—and behind a projecting point which concealed him from his enemies. The sudden arrest of his motion, the abrasion of one of his hands on the gravel, restored him, and he wept with delight. He dug his fingers into the sand, threw it over himself in handfuls and audibly blessed it. It looked like diamonds, rubies, emeralds; he could think of nothing beautiful which it did not resemble. The trees upon the bank were giant garden plants; he noted a definite order in their arrangement, inhaled the fragrance of their blooms. A strange roseate light shone through the spaces among their trunks and the wind made in their branches the music of Aeolian harps. He had not wish to perfect his escape—he was content to remain in that enchanting spot until retaken.

A whiz and a rattle of grapeshot among the branches high above his head roused him from his dream. The baffled cannoneer had fired him a random farewell. He sprang to his feet, rushed up the sloping bank, and plunged into the forest.

All that day he traveled, laying his course by the rounding sun. The forest seemed interminable; nowhere did he discover a break in it, not even a woodman's road. He had not known that he lived in so wild a region. There was something uncanny in the revelation.

By nightfall he was fatigued, footsore, famished. The thought of his wife and children urged him on. At last he found a road which led him in what he knew to be the right direction. It was as wide and straight as a city street, yet it seemed untraveled. No fields bordered it, no dwelling anywhere. Not so much as the barking of a dog suggested human habitation. The black bodies of the trees formed a straight wall on both sides, terminating on the horizon in a point, like a diagram in a lesson in perspective. Overhead, as he looked up through this rift in the wood, shone great golden stars looking unfamiliar and grouped in strange constellations. He was sure they were arranged in some order which had a secret and malign significance. The wood on either side was full of singular noises, among which—once, twice, and again—he distinctly heard whispers in an unknown tongue.

His neck was in pain and lifting his hand to it found it horribly swollen. He knew that it had a circle of black where the rope had bruised it. His eyes felt congested; he could no longer close them. His tongue was swollen with thirst; he relieved its fever by thrusting it forward from between his teeth into the cold air. How softly the turf had carpeted the untraveled avenue—he could no longer feel the roadway beneath his feet!

Doubtless, despite his suffering, he had fallen asleep while walking, for now he sees another scene—perhaps he has merely recovered from a delirium. He stands at the gate of his own home. All is as he left it, and all bright and beautiful in the morning sunshine. He must have traveled the entire night. As he pushes open the gate and passes up the wide white walk, he sees a flutter of female garments; his wife, looking fresh and cool and sweet, steps down from the veranda to meet him. At the bottom of the steps she stands waiting, with a smile of ineffable joy, an attitude of matchless grace and dignity. Ah, how beautiful she is! He springs forwards with extended arms. As he is about to clasp her he feels a stunning blow upon the back of the neck; a blinding white light blazes all about him with a sound like the shock of a cannon—then all is darkness and silence!

Peyton Farquhar was dead; his body, with a broken neck, swung gently from side to side beneath the timbers of the Owl Creek bridge.

KERFOL

Edith Wharton

I

"You ought to buy it," said my host; "its just the place for a solitary-minded devil like you. And it would be rather worth while to own the most romantic house in Brittany. The present people are dead broke, and it's going for a song—you ought to buy it."

It was not with the least idea of living up to the character my friend Lanrivain ascribed to me (as a matter of fact, under my unsociable exterior I have always had secret yearnings for domesticity) that I took his hint one autumn afternoon and went to Kerfol. My friend was motoring over to Quimper on business: he dropped me on the way, at a cross-road on a heath, and said: "First turn to the right and second to the left. Then straight ahead till you see an avenue. If you meet any peasants, don't ask your way. They don't understand French, and they would pretend they did and mix you up. I'll be back for you here by sunset—and don't forget the tombs in the chapel."

I followed Lanrivain's directions with the hesitation occasioned by the usual difficulty of remembering whether he had said the first turn to the right and second to the left, or the contrary. If I had met a peasant I should certainly have asked, and probably been sent astray; but I had the desert landscape to myself, and so stumbled on the right turn and walked across the heath till I came to an avenue. It was so unlike any other avenue I have ever seen that I instantly knew it must be *the* avenue. The grey-trunked trees sprang up straight to a great height and then interwove their pale-grey branches in a long tunnel through which the autumn light fell faintly. I know most trees by name, but I haven't to this day been able to decide what those trees were. They had the tall curve of elms, the tenuity of poplars, the ashen colour of olives under a rainy sky; and they stretched ahead of me for half a mile or more without a break in their arch. If ever I saw an avenue that unmistakably led to something, it was the avenue at Kerfol. My heart beat a little as I began to walk down it.

Presently the trees ended and I came to a fortified gate in a long wall. Between me and the wall was an open space of grass, with other grey avenues radiating from it. Behind the wall were tall slate roofs mossed with silver, a chapel belfry, the top of a keep. A moat filled with wild shrubs and brambles surrounded the place; the drawbridge had been replaced by a stone arch, and the portcullis by an iron gate. I stood for a long time on the hither side of the moat, gazing about me, and letting the influence of the place sink in. I said to myself: "If I wait long enough, the guardian will turn up and show me the tombs—" and I rather hoped he wouldn't turn up too soon.

I sat down on a stone and lit a cigarette. As soon as I had done it, it struck me as a puerile and portentous thing to do, with that great blind house looking down at me, and all the empty avenues converging on me. It may have been the depth of the silence that made me so conscious of my gesture. The squeak of my match sounded as loud as the scraping of a brake, and I almost fancied I heard it fall when I tossed it onto the grass. But there was more than that: a sense of irrelevance, of littleness, of futile bravado, in sitting there puffing my cigarette-smoke into the face of such a past.

I knew nothing of the history of Kerfol—I was new to Brittany, and Lanrivain had never mentioned the name to me till the day before—but one couldn't as much as glance at that pile without feeling in it a long accumulation of history. What kind of history I was not prepared to guess: perhaps only that sheer weight of many associated lives and deaths which gives a majesty to all old houses. But the aspect of Kerfol suggested something more—a perspective of stern and cruel memories stretching away, like its own grey avenues, into a blur of darkness.

Certainly no house had ever more completely and finally broken with the present. As it stood there, lifting its proud roofs and gables to the sky, it might have been its own funeral monument. "Tombs in the chapel? The whole place is a tomb!" I reflected. I hoped more and more that the guardian would not come. The details of the place, however striking, would seem trivial compared with its collective impressiveness; and I wanted only to sit there and be penetrated by the weight of its silence.

"It's the very place for you!" Lanrivain had said; and I was overcome by the almost blasphemous frivolity of suggesting to any living being that Kerfol was the place for him. "Is it possible that any one could *not* see—?" I wondered. I did not finish the thought: what I meant was undefinable. I stood up and wandered toward the gate. I was beginning to want to know more; not to *see* more—I was by now so sure it was not a question of seeing—but to feel more: feel all the place had to communicate. "But to get in one will have to rout out the keeper," I thought reluctantly, and hesitated. Finally I crossed the bridge and tried the iron gate. It yielded, and I walked through the tunnel formed by the thickness of the *chemin de ronde*. At the farther end, a wooden barricade had been laid across the entrance, and beyond it was a court enclosed in noble architecture. The main building faced me; and I now saw that one half was a mere ruined front, with gaping windows through which the wild growths of the moat and the trees of the park were visible.

The rest of the house was still in its robust beauty. One end abutted on the round tower, the other on the small traceried chapel, and in an angle of the building stood a graceful well-head crowned with mossy urns. A few roses grew against the walls, and on an upper window-sill I remember noticing a pot of fuchsias.

My sense of the pressure of the invisible began to yield to my architectural interest. The building was so fine that I felt a desire to explore it for its own sake. I looked about the court, wondering in which corner the guardian lodged. Then I pushed open the barrier and went in. As I did so, a dog barred my way. He was such a remarkably beautiful little dog that for a moment he made me forget the splendid place he was defending. I was not sure of his breed at the time, but have since learned that it was Chinese, and that he was of a rare variety called the "Sleeve-dog." He was very small and golden brown, with large brown eyes and a ruffled throat: he looked like a large tawny chrysanthemum. I said to myself: "These little beasts always snap and scream, and somebody will be out in a minute."

The little animal stood before me, forbidding, almost menacing: there was anger in his large brown eyes. But he made no sound, he came no nearer. Instead, as I advanced, he gradually fell back, and I noticed that another dog, a vague rough brindled thing, had limped up on a lame leg. "There'll be a hubbub now," I thought; for at the same moment a third dog, a long-haired white mongrel, slipped out of a doorway and joined the others. All three stood looking at me with grave eyes; but not a sound came from them. As I advanced they continued to fall back on muffled paws, still watching me. "At a given point, they'll all charge at my ankles: it's one of the jokes that dogs who live together put up on one," I thought. I was not alarmed, for they were neither large nor formidable. But they let me wander about the court as I pleased, following me at a little distance—always the same distance—and always keeping their eyes on me. Presently I looked across at the ruined facade, and saw that in one of its empty window-frames another dog stood: a white pointer with one brown ear. He was an old grave dog, much more experienced than the others; and he seemed to be observing me with a deeper intentness. "I'll hear from him," I said to myself; but he stood in the window-frame, against the trees of the park, and continued to watch me without moving. I stared back at him for a time, to see if the sense that he was being watched would not rouse him. Half the width of the court lay between us, and we gazed at each other silently across it. But he did not stir, and at last I turned away. Behind me I found the rest of the pack, with a newcomer added: a small black greyhound with pale agate-coloured eyes. He was shivering a little, and his expression was more timid than that of the others. I noticed that he kept a little behind them. And still there was not a sound.

I stood there for fully five minutes, the circle about me—waiting, as they seemed to be waiting. At last I went up to the little golden-brown dog and stooped to pat him. As I did so, I heard myself give a nervous laugh. The little dog did not start, or growl, or take his eyes from me—he simply slipped back about a yard, and then paused and continued to look at me. "Oh, hang it!" I exclaimed, and walked across the court toward the well.

As I advanced, the dogs separated and slid away into different corners of the court. I examined the urns on the well, tried a locked door or two, and looked up and down the dumb façade; then I faced about toward the chapel. When I turned I perceived that all the dogs had disappeared except the old pointer, who still watched me from the window. It was rather a relief to be rid of that cloud of witnesses; and I began to look about me for a way to the back of the house. "Perhaps there'll be somebody in the garden," I thought. I found a way across the moat, scrambled over a wall smothered in brambles, and got into the garden. A few lean hydrangeas and geraniums pined in the flower-beds, and the ancient house looked down on them indifferently. Its garden side was plainer and severer than the other: the long granite front, with its few windows and steep roof, looked like a fortress-prison. I walked around the farther wing, went up some disjointed steps, and entered the deep twilight of a narrow and incredibly old box-walk. The walk was just wide enough for one person to slip through, and its branches met overhead. It was like the ghost of a box-walk, its lustrous green all turning to the shadowy greyness of the avenues. I walked on and on, the branches hitting me in the face and springing back with a dry rattle; and at length I came out on the grassy top of the *chemin de ronde*. I walked along it to the gate-tower, looking down into the court, which was just below me. Not a human being was in sight; and neither were the dogs. I found a flight of steps in the thickness of the wall and went down them; and when I emerged again into the court, there stood the circle of dogs, the golden-brown one a little ahead of the others, the black greyhound shivering in the rear.

"Oh, hang it—you uncomfortable beasts, you!" I exclaimed, my voice startling me with a sudden echo. The dogs stood motionless, watching me. I knew by this time that they would not try to prevent my approaching the house, and the knowledge left me free to examine them. I had a feeling that they must be horribly cowed to be so silent and inert. Yet they did not look hungry or ill-treated. Their coats were smooth and they were not thin, except the shivering greyhound. It was more as if they had lived a long time with people who never spoke to them or looked at them: as though the silence of the place had gradually benumbed their busy inquisitive natures. And this strange passivity, this almost human lassitude, seemed to me sadder than the misery of starved and beaten animals. I should have liked to rouse them for a minute, to coax them into a game or a scamper; but the longer I looked into their fixed and weary eyes the more preposterous the idea became. With the windows of that house looking down on us, how could I have imagined such a thing? The dogs knew better: they knew what the house would tolerate and what it would not. I even fancied that they knew what was passing through my mind, and pitied me for my frivolity. But even that feeling probably reached them through a thick fog of listlessness. I had an idea that their distance from me was as nothing to my remoteness from them. The impression they produced was that of having in common one memory so deep and dark that nothing that had happened since was worth either a growl or a wag.

"I say," I broke out abruptly, addressing myself to the dumb circle, "do you know what you look like, the whole lot of you? You look as if you'd seen a ghost—that's how you look! I wonder if there is a ghost here, and nobody but you left for it to appear to?" The dogs continued to gaze at me without moving . . .

* * * * *

It was dark when I saw Lanrivain's motor lamps at the cross-roads—and I wasn't exactly sorry to see them. I had the sense of having escaped from the loneliest place in the whole world, and of not liking loneliness—to that degree—as much as I had imagined I should. My friend had brought his solicitor back from Quimper for the night, and seated beside a fat and affable stranger I felt no inclination to talk of Kerfol . . .

But that evening, when Lanrivain and the solicitor were closeted in the study, Madame de Lanrivain began to question me in the drawing-room.

"Well—are you going to buy Kerfol?" she asked, tilting up her gay chin from her embroidery.

"I haven't decided yet. The fact is, I couldn't get into the house," I said, as if I had simply postponed my decision, and meant to go back for another look.

"You couldn't get in? Why, what happened? The family are mad to sell the place, and the old guardian has orders—"

"Very likely. But the old guardian wasn't there."

"What a pity! He must have gone to market. But his daughter—?"

"There was nobody about. At least I saw no one."

"How extraordinary! Literally nobody?"

"Nobody but a lot of dogs—a whole pack of them—who seemed to have the place to themselves."

Madame de Lanrivain let the embroidery slip to her knee and folded her hands on it. For several minutes she looked at me thoughtfully.

"A pack of dogs—you saw them?"

"Saw them? I saw nothing else!"

"How many?" She dropped her voice a little. "I've always wondered—"

I looked at her with surprise: I had supposed the place to be familiar to her. "Have you never been to Kerfol?" I asked.

"Oh, yes: often. But never on that day."

"What day?"

"I'd quite forgotten—and so had Hervé, I'm sure. If we'd remembered, we never should have sent you to-day—but then, after all, one doesn't half believe that sort of thing, does one?"

"What sort of thing?" I asked, involuntarily sinking my voice to the level of hers. Inwardly I was thinking: "I knew there was something . . ."

Madame de Lanrivain cleared her throat and produced a reassuring smile. "Didn't Hervé tell you the story of Kerfol? An ancestor of his was mixed up in it. You know every Breton house has its ghost-story; and some of them are rather unpleasant."

"Yes—but those dogs?"

"Well, those dogs are the ghosts of Kerfol. At least, the peasants say there's one day in the year when a lot of dogs appear there; and that day the keeper and his daughter go off to Morlaix and get drunk. The women in Brittany drink dreadfully." She stooped to match a silk; then she lifted her charming inquisitive Parisian face. "Did you really see a lot of dogs? There isn't one at Kerfol," she said.

II

Lanrivain, the next day, hunted out a shabby calf volume from the back of an upper shelf of his library.

"Yes—here it is. What does it call itself? *A History of the Assizes of the Duchy of Brittany. Quimper, 1702.* The book was written about a hundred years later than the Kerfol affair; but I believe the account is transcribed pretty literally from the judicial records. Anyhow, it's queer reading. And there's a Hervé de Lanrivain mixed up in it—not exactly *my* style, as you'll see. But then he's only a collateral. Here, take the book up to bed with you. I don't exactly remember the details; but after you've read it I'll bet anything you'll leave your light burning all night!"

I left my light burning all night, as he had predicted; but it was chiefly because, till near dawn, I was absorbed in my reading. The account of the trial of Anne de Cornault, wife of the lord of Kerfol, was long and closely printed. It was, as my friend had said, probably an almost literal transcription of what took place in the court-room; and the trial lasted nearly a month. Besides, the type of the book was very bad . . .

At first I thought of translating the old record. But it is full of wearisome repetitions, and the main lines of the story are forever straying off into side issues. So I have tried to disentangle it, and give it here in a simpler form. At times, however, I have reverted to the text because no other words could have conveyed so exactly the sense of what I felt at Kerfol; and nowhere have I added anything of my own.

III

It was in the year 16— that Yves de Cornault, lord of the domain of Kerfol, went to the pardon of Locronan to perform his religious duties. He was a rich and powerful noble, then in his sixty-second year, but hale and sturdy, a great horseman and hunter and a pious man. So all his neighbours attested. In appearance he was short and broad, with a swarthy face, legs slightly bowed from the saddle, a hanging nose and broad hands with black hairs on them. He had married young and lost his wife and son soon after, and since then had lived alone at Kerfol. Twice a year he went to Morlaix, where he had a handsome house by the river, and spent a week or ten days there; and occasionally he rode to Rennes on business. Witnesses were found to declare that during these absences he led a life different from the one he was known to lead at Kerfol, where he busied himself with his estate, attended mass daily, and found his only amusement in hunting the wild boar and water-fowl. But these rumours are not particularly relevant, and it is certain that among people of his own class in the neighbourhood he passed for a stern and even austere man, observant of his religious obligations, and keeping strictly to himself. There was no talk of any familiarity with the women on his estate, though at that time the nobility were very free with their peasants. Some people said he had never looked at a woman since his wife's death; but such things are hard to prove, and the evidence on this point was not worth much.

Well, in his sixty-second year, Yves de Cornault went to the pardon at Locronan, and saw there a young lady of Douarnenez, who had ridden over pillion behind her father to do her duty to the saint. Her name was Anne de Barrigan, and she came of good old Breton stock, but much less great and powerful than that of Yves de Cornault; and her father had squandered his fortune at cards, and lived almost like a peasant in his little granite manor on the moors . . . I have said I would add nothing of my own to this bald statement of a strange case; but I must interrupt myself here to describe the young lady who rode up to the lych-gate of Locronan at the very moment when the Baron de Cornault was also dismounting there. I take my description from a faded drawing in red crayon, sober and truthful enough to be by a late pupil of the Clouets, which hangs in Lanrivain's study, and is said to be a portrait of Anne de Barrigan. It is unsigned and has no mark of identity but the initials A. B., and the date 16—, the year after her marriage. It represents a young woman with a small oval face, almost pointed, yet wide enough for a full mouth with a tender depression at the corners. The nose is small, and the eyebrows are set rather high, far apart, and as lightly pencilled as the eyebrows in a Chinese painting. The forehead is high and serious, and the hair, which one feels to be fine and thick and fair, is drawn off it and lies close like a cap. The eyes are neither large nor small, hazel probably, with a look at once shy and steady. A pair of beautiful long hands are crossed below the lady's breast . . .

The chaplain of Kerfol, and other witnesses, averred that when the Baron came back from Locronan he jumped from his horse, ordered another to be instantly saddled, called to a young page to come with him, and rode away that same evening to the south. His steward followed the next morning with coffers laden on a pair of pack mules. The following week Yves de Cornault rode back to Kerfol, sent for his vassals and tenants, and told them he was to be married at All Saints to Anne de Barrigan of Douarnenez. And on All Saints' Day the marriage took place.

As to the next few years, the evidence on both sides seems to show that they passed happily for the couple. No one was found to say that Yves de Cornault had been unkind to his wife, and it was plain to all that he was content with his bargain. Indeed, it was admitted by the chaplain and other witnesses for the prosecution that the young lady had a softening influence on her husband, and that he became less exacting with his tenants, less harsh to peasants and dependents, and less subject to the fits of gloomy silence which had darkened his widowhood. As to his wife, the only grievance her champions could call up in her behalf was that Kerfol was a lonely place, and that when her husband was away on business at Bennes or Morlaix—whither she was never taken—she was not allowed so much as to walk in the park unaccompanied. But no one asserted that she was unhappy, though one servant-woman said she had surprised her crying, and had heard her say that she was a woman accursed to have no child, and nothing in life to call her own. But that was a natural enough feeling in a wife attached to her husband; and certainly it must have been a great grief to Yves de Cornault that she bore no son. Yet he never made her feel her childlessness as a reproach—she admits this in her evidence—but seemed to try to make her forget it by showering gifts and favours on her. Rich though he was, he had never been openhanded; but nothing was too fine for his wife, in the way of silks or gems or linen, or whatever else she fancied. Every wandering merchant was welcome at Kerfol, and when the master was called away he never came back without bringing his wife a handsome present—something curious and particular—from Morlaix or Rennes or Quimper. One of the waiting-women gave, in cross-examination, an interesting list of one year's gifts, which I copy. From Morlaix, a carved ivory junk, with Chinamen at the oars, that a strange sailor had brought back as a votive offering for Notre Dame de la Clarté, above Ploumanac'h; from Quimper, an embroidered gown, worked by the nuns of the Assumption; from Rennes, a silver rose that opened and showed an amber Virgin with a crown of garnets; from Morlaix, again, a length of Damascus velvet shot with gold, bought of a Jew from Syria; and for Michaelmas that same year, from Rennes, a necklet or bracelet of round stones—emeralds and pearls and rubies—strung like beads on a fine gold chain. This was the present that pleased the lady best, the woman said. Later on, as it happened, it was produced at the trial, and appears to have struck the Judges and the public as a curious and valuable jewel.

The very same winter, the Baron absented himself again, this time as far as Bordeaux, and on his return he brought his wife something even odder and prettier than the bracelet. It was a winter evening when he rode up to Kerfol and, walking into the hall, found her sitting by the hearth, her chin on her hand, looking into the fire. He carried a velvet box in his hand and, setting it down, lifted the lid and let out a little golden-brown dog.

Anne de Cornault exclaimed with pleasure as the little creature bounded toward her. "Oh, it looks like a bird or a butterfly!" she cried as she picked it up; and the dog put its paws on her shoulders and looked at her with eyes "like a Christian's." After that she would never have it out of her sight, and petted and talked to it as if it had been a child—as indeed it was the nearest thing to a child she was to know. Yves de Cornault was much pleased with his purchase. The dog had been brought to him by a sailor from an East India merchantman, and the sailor had bought it of a pilgrim in a bazaar at Jaffa, who had stolen it from a nobleman's wife in China: a perfectly permissible thing to do, since the pilgrim was a Christian and the nobleman a heathen doomed to hell-fire.

Yves de Cornault had paid a long price for the dog, for they were beginning to be in demand at the French court, and the sailor knew he had got hold of a good thing; but Anne's pleasure was so great that, to see her laugh and play with the little animal, her husband would doubtless have given twice the sum.

* * * * *

So far, all the evidence is at one, and the narrative plain sailing; but now the steering becomes difficult. I will try to keep as nearly as possible to Anne's own statements; though toward the end, poor thing . . .

Well, to go back. The very year after the little brown dog was brought to

Kerfol, Yves de Cornault, one winter night, was found dead at the head of a narrow flight of stairs leading down from his wife's rooms to a door opening on the court. It was his wife who found him and gave the alarm, so distracted, poor wretch, with fear and horror—for his blood was all over her—that at first the roused household could not make out what she was saying, and thought she had suddenly gone mad. But there, sure enough, at the top of the stairs lay her husband, stone dead, and head foremost, the blood from his wounds dripping down to the steps below him. He had been dreadfully scratched and gashed about the face and throat, as if with curious pointed weapons; and one of his legs had a deep tear in it which had cut an artery, and probably caused his death. But how did he come there, and who had murdered him?

His wife declared that she had been asleep in her bed, and hearing his cry had rushed out to find him lying on the stairs; but this was immediately questioned. In the first place, it was proved that from her room she could not have heard the struggle on the stairs, owing to the thickness of the walls and the length of the intervening passage; then it was evident that she had not been in bed and asleep, since she was dressed when she roused the house, and her bed had not been slept in. Moreover, the door at the bottom of the stairs was ajar, and it was noticed by the chaplain (an observant man) that the dress she wore was stained with blood about the knees, and that there were traces of small blood-stained hands low down on the staircase walls, so that it was conjectured that she had really been at the postern-door when her husband fell and, feeling her way up to him in the darkness on her hands and knees, had been stained by his blood dripping down on her. Of course it was argued on the other side that the blood-marks on her dress might have been caused by her kneeling down by her husband when she rushed out of her room; but there was the open door below, and the fact that the finger-marks in the staircase all pointed upward.

The accused held to her statement for the first two days, in spite of its improbability; but on the third day word was brought to her that Hervé de Lanrivain, a young nobleman of the neighbourhood, had been arrested for complicity in the crime. Two or three witnesses thereupon came forward to say that it was known throughout the country that Lanrivain had formerly been on good terms with the lady of Cornault; but that he had been absent from Brittany for over a year, and people had ceased to associate their names. The witnesses who made this statement were not of a very reputable sort. One was an old herb-gatherer suspected of witchcraft, another a drunken clerk from a neighbouring parish, the third a half-witted shepherd who could be made to say anything; and it was clear that the prosecution was not satisfied with its case, and would have liked to find more definite proof of Lanrivain's complicity than the statement of the herb-gatherer, who swore to having seen him climbing the wall of the park on the night of the murder. One way of patching out incomplete proofs in those days was to put some sort of pressure, moral or physical, on the accused person. It is not clear what pressure was put on Anne de Cornault; but on the third day, when she was brought in court, she "appeared weak and wandering," and after being encouraged to collect herself and speak the truth, on her honour and the wounds of her Blessed Redeemer, she confessed that she had in fact gone down the stairs to speak with Hervé de Lanrivain (who denied everything), and had been surprised there by the sound of her husband's fall. That was better; and the prosecution rubbed its hands with satisfaction. The satisfaction increased when various dependents living at Kerfol were induced to say—with apparent sincerity—that during the year or two preceding his death their master had once more grown uncertain and irascible, and subject to the fits of brooding silence which his household had learned to dread before his second marriage. This seemed to show that things had not been going well at Kerfol; though no one could be found to say that there had been any signs of open disagreement between husband and wife.

Anne de Cornault, when questioned as to her reason for going down at night to open the door to Hervé de Lanrivain, made an answer which must have sent a smile around the court. She said it was because she was lonely and wanted to talk with the young man. Was this the only reason? she was asked; and replied: "Yes, by the Cross over your Lordships' heads." "But why at midnight?" the court asked. "Because I could see him in no other way." I can see the exchange of glances across the ermine collars under the Crucifix.

Anne de Cornault, further questioned, said that her married life had been extremely lonely: "desolate" was the word she used. It was true that her husband seldom spoke harshly to her; but there were days when he did not speak at all. It was true that he had never struck or threatened her; but he kept her like a prisoner at Kerfol, and when he rode away to Morlaix or Quimper or Rennes he set so close a watch on her that she could not pick a flower in the garden without having a waiting-woman at her heels. "I am no Queen, to need such honours," she once said to him; and he had answered that a man who has a treasure does not leave the key in the lock when he goes out. "Then take me with you," she urged; but to this he said that towns were pernicious places, and young wives better off at their own firesides.

"But what did you want to say to Hervé de Lanrivain?" the court asked; and she answered: "To ask him to take me away."

"Ah—you confess that you went down to him with adulterous thoughts?"

"No."

"Then why did you want him to take you away?"

"Because I was afraid for my life."

"Of whom were you afraid?"

"Of my husband."

"Why were you afraid of your husband?"

"Because he had strangled my little dog."

Another smile must have passed around the courtroom: in days when any nobleman had a right to hang his peasants—and most of them exercised it—pinching a pet animal's wind-pipe was nothing to make a fuss about.

At this point one of the Judges, who appears to have had a certain sympathy for the accused, suggested that she should be allowed to explain herself in her own way; and she thereupon made the following statement.

The first years of her marriage had been lonely; but her husband had not been unkind to her. If she had had a child she would not have been unhappy; but the days were long, and it rained too much.

It was true that her husband, whenever he went away and left her, brought her a handsome present on his return; but this did not make up for the loneliness. At least nothing had, till he brought her the little brown dog from the East: after that she was much less unhappy. Her husband seemed pleased that she was so fond of the dog; he gave her leave to put her jewelled bracelet around its neck, and to keep it always with her.

One day she had fallen asleep in her room, with the dog at her feet, as his habit was. Her feet were bare and resting on his back. Suddenly she was waked by her husband: he stood beside her, smiling not unkindly.

"You look like my great-grandmother, Juliane de Cornault, lying in the chapel with her feet on a little dog," he said.

The analogy sent a chill through her, but she laughed and answered: "Well, when I am dead you must put me beside her, carved in marble, with my dog at my feet."

"Oho—we'll wait and see," he said, laughing also, but with his black brows close together. "The dog is the emblem of fidelity."

"And do you doubt my right to lie with mine at my feet?"

"When I'm in doubt I find out," he answered. "I am an old man," he added, "and people say I make you lead a lonely life. But I swear you shall have your monument if you earn it."

"And I swear to be faithful," she returned, "if only for the sake of having my little dog at my feet."

Not long afterward he went on business to the Quimper Assizes; and while he was away his aunt, the widow of a great nobleman of the duchy, came to spend a night at Kerfol on her way to the *pardon* of Ste. Barbe. She was a woman of piety and consequence, and much respected by Yves de Cornault, and when she proposed to Anne to go with her to Ste. Barbe no one could object, and even the chaplain declared himself in favour of the pilgrimage. So Anne set out for Ste. Barbe, and there for the first time she talked with Hervé de Lanrivain. He had come once or twice to Kerfol with his father, but she had never before exchanged a dozen words with him. They did not talk for more than five minutes now: it was under the chestnuts, as the procession was coming out of the chapel. He said: "I pity you," and she was surprised, for she had not supposed that any one thought her an object of pity. He added: "Call for me when you need me," and she smiled a little, but was glad afterward, and thought often of the meeting.

She confessed to having seen him three times afterward: not more. How or where she would not say—one had the impression that she feared to implicate some one. Their meetings had been rare and brief; and at the last he had told her that he was starting the next day for a foreign country, on a mission which was not without peril and might keep him for many months absent. He asked her for a remembrance, and she had none to give him but the collar about the little dog's neck. She was sorry afterward that she had given it, but he was so unhappy at going that she had not had the courage to refuse.

Her husband was away at the time. When he returned a few days later he picked up the animal to pet it, and noticed that its collar was missing. His wife told him that the dog had lost it in the undergrowth of the park, and that she and her maids had hunted a whole day for it. It was true, she explained to the court, that she had made the maids search for the necklet—they all believed the dog had lost it in the park . . .

Her husband made no comment, and that evening at supper he was in his usual mood, between good and bad: you could never tell which. He talked a good deal, describing what he had seen and done at Rennes; but now and then he stopped and looked hard at her, and when she went to bed she found her little dog strangled on her pillow. The little thing was dead, but still warm; she stooped to lift it, and her distress turned to horror when she discovered that it had been strangled by twisting twice round its throat the necklet she had given to Lanrivain.

The next morning at dawn she buried the dog in the garden, and hid the necklet in her breast. She said nothing to her husband, then or later, and he said nothing to her; but that day he had a peasant hanged for stealing a faggot in the park, and the next day he nearly beat to death a young horse he was breaking.

Winter set in, and the short days passed, and the long nights, one by one; and she heard nothing of Hervé de Lanrivain. It might be that her husband had killed him; or merely that he had been robbed of the necklet. Day after day by the hearth among the spinning maids, night after night alone on her bed, she wondered and trembled. Sometimes at table her husband looked across at her and smiled; and then she felt sure that Lanrivain was dead. She dared not try to get news of him, for she was sure her husband would find out if she did: she had an idea that he could find out anything. Even when a witchwoman who was a noted seer, and could show you the whole world in her crystal, came to the castle for a night's shelter, and the maids flocked to her, Anne held back.

The winter was long and black and rainy. One day, in Yves de Cornault's absence, some gypsies came to Kerfol with a troop of performing dogs. Anne bought the smallest and cleverest, a white dog with a feathery coat and one blue and one brown eye. It seemed to have been ill-treated by the gypsies, and clung to her plaintively when she took it from them. That evening her husband came back, and when she went to bed she found the dog strangled on her pillow.

After that she said to herself that she would never have another dog; but one bitter cold evening a poor lean greyhound was found whining at the castle-gate, and she took him in and forbade the maids to speak of him to her husband. She hid him in a room that no one went to, smuggled food to him from her own plate, made him a warm bed to lie on and petted him like a child.

Yves de Cornault came home, and the next day she found the greyhound strangled on her pillow. She wept in secret, but said nothing, and resolved that even if she met a dog dying of hunger she would never bring him into the castle; but one day she found a young sheepdog, a brindled puppy with good blue eyes, lying with a broken leg in the snow of the park. Yves de Cornault was at Bennes, and she brought the dog in, warmed and fed it, tied up its leg and hid it in the castle till her husband's return. The day before, she gave it to a peasant woman who lived a long way off, and paid her handsomely to care for it and say nothing; but that night she heard a whining and scratching at her door, and when she opened it the lame puppy, drenched and shivering, jumped up on her with little sobbing barks. She hid him in her bed, and the next morning was about to have him taken back to the peasant woman when she heard her husband ride into the court. She shut the dog in a chest, and went down to receive him. An hour or two later, when she returned to her room, the puppy lay strangled on her pillow . . .

After that she dared not make a pet of any other dog; and her loneliness became almost unendurable. Sometimes, when she crossed the court of the castle, and thought no one was looking, she stopped to pat the old pointer at the gate. But one day as she was caressing him her husband came out of the chapel; and the next day the old dog was gone . . .

This curious narrative was not told in one sitting of the court, or received without impatience and incredulous comment. It was plain that the Judges were surprised by its puerility, and that it did not help the accused in the eyes of the public. It was an odd tale, certainly; but what did it prove? That Yves de Cornault disliked dogs, and that his wife, to gratify her own fancy, persistently ignored this dislike. As for pleading this trivial disagreement as an excuse for her relations—whatever their nature—with her supposed accomplice, the argument was so absurd that her own lawyer manifestly regretted having let her make use of it, and tried several times to cut short her story. But she went on to the end, with a kind of hypnotized insistence, as though the scenes she evoked were so real to her that she had forgotten where she was and imagined herself to be re-living them.

At length the Judge who had previously shown a certain kindness to her said (leaning forward a little, one may suppose, from his row of dozing colleagues): "Then you would have us believe that you murdered your husband because he would not let you keep a pet dog?"

"I did not murder my husband."

"Who did, then? Hervé de Lanrivain?"

"No."

"Who then? Can you tell us?"

"Yes, I can tell you. The dogs—" At that point she was carried out of the court in a swoon.

* * * * *

It was evident that her lawyer tried to get her to abandon this line of defense. Possibly her explanation, whatever it was, had seemed convincing when she poured it out to him in the heat of their first private colloquy; but now that it was exposed to the cold daylight of judicial scrutiny, and the banter of the town, he was thoroughly ashamed of it, and would have sacrificed her without a scruple to save his professional reputation. But the obstinate Judge—who perhaps, after all, was more inquisitive than kindly—evidently wanted to hear the story out, and she was ordered, the next day, to continue her deposition.

She said that after the disappearance of the old watchdog nothing particular happened for a month or two. Her husband was much as usual: she did not remember any special incident. But one evening a pedlar woman came to the castle and was selling trinkets to the maids. She had no heart for trinkets, but she stood looking on while the women made their choice. And then, she did not know how, but the pedlar coaxed her into buying for herself a pear-shaped pomander with a strong scent in it—she had once seen something of the kind on a gypsy woman. She had no desire for the pomander, and did not know why she had bought it. The pedlar said that whoever wore it had the power to read the future; but she did not really believe that, or care much either. However, she bought the thing and took it up to her room, where she sat turning it about in her hand. Then the strange scent attracted her and she began to wonder what kind of spice was in the box. She opened it and found a grey bean rolled in a strip of paper; and on the paper she saw a sign she knew, and a message from Hervé de Lanrivain, saying that he was at home again and would be at the door in the court that night after the moon had set . . .

She burned the paper and sat down to think. It was nightfall, and her husband was at home . . . She had no way of warning Lanrivain, and there was nothing to do but to wait . . .

At this point I fancy the drowsy court-room beginning to wake up. Even to the oldest hand on the bench there must have been a certain relish in picturing the feelings of a woman on receiving such a message at nightfall from a man living twenty miles away, to whom she had no means of sending a warning . . .

She was not a clever woman, I imagine; and as the first result of her cogitation she appears to have made the mistake of being, that evening, too kind to her husband. She could not ply him with wine, according to the traditional expedient, for though he drank heavily at times he had a strong head; and when he drank beyond its strength it was because he chose to, and not because a woman coaxed him. Not his wife, at any rate—she was an old story by now. As I read the case, I fancy there was no feeling for her left in him but the hatred occasioned by his supposed dishonour.

At any rate, she tried to call up her old graces; but early in the evening he complained of pains and fever, and left the hall to go up to the closet where he sometimes slept. His servant carried him a cup of hot wine, and brought back word that he was sleeping and not to be disturbed; and an hour later, when Anne lifted the tapestry and listened at his door, she heard his loud regular breathing. She thought it might be a feint, and stayed a long time barefooted in the passage, her ear to the crack; but the breathing went on too steadily and naturally to be other than that of a man in a sound sleep. She crept back to her room reassured, and stood in the window watching the moon set through the trees of the park. The sky was misty and starless, and after the moon went down the night was black as pitch. She knew the time had come, and stole along the passage, past her husband's door—where she stopped again to listen to his breathing—to the top of the stairs. There she paused a moment, and assured herself that no one was following her; then she began to go down the stairs in the darkness. They were so steep and winding that she had to go very slowly, for fear of stumbling. Her one thought was to get the door unbolted, tell Lanrivain to make his escape, and hasten back to her room. She had tried the bolt earlier in the evening, and managed to put a little grease on it; but nevertheless, when she drew it, it gave a squeak . . . not loud, but it made her heart stop; and the next minute, overhead, she heard a noise . . .

"What noise?" the prosecution interposed.

"My husband's voice calling out my name and cursing me."

"What did you hear after that?"

"A terrible scream and a fall."

"Where was Hervé de Lanrivain at this time?"

"He was standing outside in the court. I just made him out in the darkness. I told him for God's sake to go, and then I pushed the door shut."

"What did you do next?"

"I stood at the foot of the stairs and listened."

"What did you hear?"

"I heard dogs snarling and panting." (Visible discouragement of the bench, boredom of the public, and exasperation of the lawyer for the defense. Dogs again—! But the inquisitive Judge insisted.)

"What dogs?"

She bent her head and spoke so low that she had to be told to repeat her answer: "I don't know."

"How do you mean—you don't know?"

"I don't know what dogs . . ."

The Judge again intervened: "Try to tell us exactly what happened. How long did you remain at the foot of the stairs?"

"Only a few minutes."

"And what was going on meanwhile overhead?"

"The dogs kept on snarling and panting. Once or twice he cried out. I think he moaned once. Then he was quiet."

"Then what happened?"

"Then I heard a sound like the noise of a pack when the wolf is thrown to them—gulping and lapping."

(There was a groan of disgust and repulsion through the court, and another attempted intervention by the distracted lawyer. But the inquisitive Judge was still inquisitive.)

"And all the while you did not go up?"

"Yes—I went up then—to drive them off."

"The dogs?"

"Yes."

"Well—?"

"When I got there it was quite dark. I found my husband's flint and steel and struck a spark. I saw him lying there. He was dead."

"And the dogs?"

"The dogs were gone."

"Gone—whereto?"

"I don't know. There was no way out—and there were no dogs at Kerfol."

She straightened herself to her full height, threw her arms above her head, and fell down on the stone floor with a long scream. There was a moment of confusion in the court-room. Some one on the bench was heard to say: "This is clearly a case for the ecclesiastical authorities"—and the prisoner's lawyer doubtless jumped at the suggestion.

After this, the trial loses itself in a maze of cross-questioning and squabbling. Every witness who was called corroborated Anne de Cornault's statement that there were no dogs at Kerfol: had been none for several months. The master of the house had taken a dislike to dogs, there was no denying it. But, on the other hand, at the inquest, there had been long and bitter discussions as to the nature of the dead man's wounds. One of the surgeons called in had spoken of marks that looked like bites. The suggestion of witchcraft was revived, and the opposing lawyers hurled tomes of necromancy at each other.

At last Anne de Cornault was brought back into court—at the instance of the same Judge—and asked if she knew where the dogs she spoke of could have come from. On the body of her Redeemer she swore that she did not. Then the Judge put his final question: "If the dogs you think you heard had been known to you, do you think you would have recognized them by their barking?"

"Yes."

"Did you recognize them?"

"Yes."

"What dogs do you take them to have been?"

"My dead dogs," she said in a whisper . . . She was taken out of court, not to reappear there again. There was some kind of ecclesiastical investigation, and the end of the business was that the Judges disagreed with each other, and with the ecclesiastical committee, and that Anne de Cornault was finally handed over to the keeping of her husband's family, who shut her up in the keep of Kerfol, where she is said to have died many years later, a harmless mad-woman.

So ends her story. As for that of Hervé de Lanrivain, I had only to apply to his collateral descendant for its subsequent details. The evidence against the young man being insufficient, and his family influence in the duchy considerable, he was set free, and left soon afterward for Paris. He was probably in no mood for a worldly life, and he appears to have come almost immediately under the influence of the famous M. Arnauld d'Andilly and the gentlemen of Port Royal. A year or two later he was received into their Order, and without achieving any particular distinction he followed its good and evil fortunes till his death some twenty years later. Lanrivain showed me a portrait of him by a pupil of Philippe de Champaigne: sad eyes, an impulsive mouth and a narrow brow. Poor Hervé de Lanrivain: it was a grey ending. Yet as I looked at his stiff and sallow effigy, in the dark dress of the Janséniste, I almost found myself envying his fate. After all, in the course of his life two great things had happened to him: he had loved romantically, and he must have talked with Pascal . . .

THE ELIXIR OF LIFE

Honoré de Balzac

Translated by Clara Bell and James Waring

One winter evening, in a princely palace at Ferrara, Don Juan Belvidero was giving a banquet to a prince of the house of Este. A banquet in those times was a marvelous spectacle which only royal wealth or the power of a mightly [sic] lord could furnish forth. Seated about a table lit up with perfumed tapers, seven laughter-loving women were interchanging sweet talk. The white marble of the noble works of art about them stood out against the red stucco walls, and made strong contrasts with the rich Turkey carpets. Clad in satin, glittering with gold, and covered with gems less brilliant than their eyes, each told a tale of energetic passions as diverse as their styles of beauty. They differed neither in their ideas nor in their language; but the expression of their eyes, their glances, occasional gestures, or the tones of their voices supplied a commentary, dissolute, wanton, melancholy, or satirical, to their words.

One seemed to be saying—"The frozen heart of age might kindle at my beauty."

Another—"I love to lounge upon cushions, and think with rapture of my adorers."

A third, a neophyte at these banquets, was inclined to blush. "I feel remorse in the depths of my heart! I am a Catholic, and afraid of hell. But I love you, I love you so that I can sacrifice my hereafter to you."

The fourth drained a cup of Chian wine. "Give me a joyous life!" she cried; "I begin life afresh each day with the dawn. Forgetful of the past, with the intoxication of yesterday's rapture still upon me, I drink deep of life—a whole lifetime of pleasure and of love!"

The woman who sat next to Juan Belvidero looked at him with a feverish glitter in her eyes. She was silent. Then—"I should need no hired bravo to kill my lover if he forsook me!" she cried at last, and laughed, but the marvelously wrought gold comfit box in her fingers was crushed by her convulsive clutch.

"When are you to be Grand Duke?" asked the sixth. There was the frenzy of a Bacchante in her eyes, and her teeth gleamed between the lips parted with a smile of cruel glee.

"Yes, when is that father of yours going to die?" asked the seventh, throwing her bouquet at Don Juan with bewitching playfulness. It was a childish girl who spoke, and the speaker was wont to make sport of sacred things.

"Oh! don't talk about it," cried Don Juan, the young and handsome giver of the banquet. "There is but one eternal father, and, as ill luck will have it, he is mine."

The seven Ferrarese, Don Juan's friends, the Prince himself, gave a cry of horror. Two hundred years later, in the days of Louis XV, people of taste would have laughed at this witticism. Or was it, perhaps, that at the outset of an orgy there is a certain unwonted lucidity of mind? Despite the taper light, the clamor of the senses, the gleam of gold and silver, the fumes of wine, and the exquisite beauty of the women, there may perhaps have been in the depths of the revelers' hearts some struggling glimmer of reverence for things divine and human, until it was drowned in glowing floods of wine! Yet even then the flowers had been crushed, eyes were growing dull, and drunkenness, in Rabelais' phrase, had "taken possession of them down to their sandals."

During that brief pause a door opened; and as once the Divine presence was revealed at Belshazzar's feast, so now it seemed to be manifest in the apparition of an old white-haired servant, who tottered in, and looked sadly from under knitted brows at the revelers. He gave a withering glance at the garlands, the golden cups, the pyramids of fruit, the dazzling lights of the banquet, the flushed scared faces, the hues of the cushions pressed by the white arms of the women.

"My lord, your father is dying!" he said; and at those solemn words, uttered in hollow tones, a veil of crape seemed to be drawn over the wild mirth.

Don Juan rose to his feet with a gesture to his guests that might be rendered by, "Excuse me; this kind of thing does not happen every day."

Does it so seldom happen that a father's death surprises youth in the full-blown splendor of life, in the midst of the mad riot of an orgy? Death is as unexpected in his caprice as a courtesan in her disdain; but death is truer—Death has never forsaken any man.

Don Juan closed the door of the banqueting-hall; and as he went down the long gallery, through the cold and darkness, he strove to assume an expression in keeping with the part he had to play; he had thrown off his mirthful mood, as he had thrown down his table napkin, at the first thought of this role. The night was dark. The mute servitor, his guide to the chamber where the dying man lay, lighted the way so dimly that Death, aided by cold, silence, and darkness, and it may be by a reaction of drunkenness, could send some sober thoughts through the spendthrift's soul. He examined his life, and became thoughtful, like a man involved in a lawsuit on his way to the Court.

Bartolommeo Belvidero, Don Juan's father, was an old man of ninety, who had devoted the greatest part of his life to business pursuits. He had acquired vast wealth in many a journey to magical Eastern lands, and knowledge, so it was said, more valuable than the gold and diamonds, which had almost ceased to have any value for him.

"I would give more to have a tooth in my head than for a ruby," he would say at times with a smile. The indulgent father loved to hear Don Juan's story of this and that wild freak of youth. "So long as these follies amuse you, dear boy—" he would say laughingly, as he lavished money on his son. Age never took such pleasure in the sight of youth; the fond father did not remember his own decaying powers while he looked on that brilliant young life.

Bartolommeo Belvidero, at the age of sixty, had fallen in love with an angel of peace and beauty. Don Juan had been the sole fruit of this late and short-lived love. For fifteen years the widower had mourned the loss of his beloved Juana; and to this sorrow of age, his son and his numerous household had attributed the strange habits that he had contracted. He had shut himself up in the least comfortable wing of his palace, and very seldom left his apartments; even Don Juan himself must first ask permission before seeing his father. If this hermit, unbound by vows, came or went in his palace or in the streets of Ferrara, he walked as if he were in a dream, wholly engrossed, like a man at strife with a memory, or a wrestler with some thought.

The young Don Juan might give princely banquets, the palace might echo with clamorous mirth, horses pawed the ground in the courtyards, pages quarreled and flung dice upon the stairs, but Bartolommeo ate his seven ounces of bread daily and drank water. A fowl was occasionally dressed for him, simply that the black poodle, his faithful companion, might have the bones. Bartolommeo never complained of the noise. If the huntsmen's horns and baying dogs disturbed his sleep during his illness, he only said, "Ah! Don Juan has come back again." Never on earth has there been a father so little exacting and so indulgent; and, in consequence, young Belvidero, accustomed to treat his father unceremoniously, had all the faults of a spoiled child. He treated old Bartolommeo as a wilful courtesan treats an elderly adorer; buying indemnity for insolence with a smile, selling good-humor, submitting to be loved.

Don Juan, beholding scene after scene of his younger years, saw that it would be a difficult task to find his father's indulgence at fault. Some new-born remorse stirred the depths of his heart; he felt almost ready to forgive this father now about to die for having lived so long. He had an accession of filial piety, like a thief's return in thought to honesty at the prospect of a million adroitly stolen.

Before long Don Juan had crossed the lofty, chilly suite of rooms in which his father lived; the penetrating influences of the damp close air, the mustiness diffused by old tapestries and presses thickly covered with dust had passed into him, and now he stood in the old man's antiquated room, in the repulsive presence of the deathbed, beside a dying fire. A flickering lamp on a Gothic table sent broad uncertain shafts of light, fainter or brighter, across the bed, so that the dying man's face seemed to wear a different look at every moment. The bitter wind whistled through the crannies of the ill-fitting casements; there was a smothered sound of snow lashing the windows. The harsh contrast of these sights and sounds with the scenes which Don Juan had just quitted was so sudden that he could not help shuddering. He turned cold as he came towards the bed; the lamp flared in a sudden vehement gust of wind and lighted up his father's face; the features were wasted and distorted; the skin that cleaved to their bony outlines had taken wan livid hues, all the more ghastly by force of contrast with the white pillows on which he lay. The muscles about the toothless mouth had contracted with pain and drawn apart the lips; the moans that issued between them with appalling energy found an accompaniment in the howling of the storm without.

In spite of every sign of coming dissolution, the most striking thing about the dying face was its incredible power. It was no ordinary spirit that wrestled there with Death. The eyes glared with strange fixity of gaze from the cavernous sockets hollowed by disease. It seemed as if Bartolommeo sought to kill some enemy sitting at the foot of his bed by the intent gaze of dying eyes. That steady remorseless look was the more appalling because the head that lay upon the pillow was passive and motionless as a skull upon a doctor's table. The outlines of the body, revealed by the coverlet, were no less rigid and stiff; he lay there as one dead, save for those eyes. There was something automatic about the moaning sounds that came from the mouth. Don Juan felt something like shame that he must be brought thus to his father's bedside, wearing a courtesan's bouquet, redolent of the fragrance of the banqueting-chamber and the fumes of wine.

"You were enjoying yourself!" the old man cried as he saw his son.

Even as he spoke the pure high notes of a woman's voice, sustained by the sound of the viol on which she accompanied her song, rose above the rattle of the storm against the casements, and floated up to the chamber of death. Don Juan stopped his ears against the barbarous answer to his father's speech.

"I bear you no grudge, my child," Bartolommeo went on.

The words were full of kindness, but they hurt Don Juan; he could not pardon this heart-searching goodness on his father's part.

"What a remorseful memory for me!" he cried, hypocritically.

"Poor Juanino," the dying man went on, in a smothered voice, "I have always been so kind to you, that you could not surely desire my death?"

"Oh, if it were only possible to keep you here by giving up a part of my own life!" cried Don Juan.

("We can always say this sort of thing," the spendthrift thought; "it is as if I laid the whole world at my mistress' feet.")

The thought had scarcely crossed his mind when the old poodle barked. Don Juan shivered; the response was so intelligent that he fancied the dog must have understood him.

"I was sure that I could count upon you, my son!" cried the dying man. "I shall live. So be it; you shall be satisfied. I shall live, but without depriving you of a single day of your life."

"He is raving," thought Don Juan. Aloud he added, "Yes, dearest father, yes; you shall live, of course, as long as I live, for your image will be for ever in my heart."

"It is not that kind of life that I mean," said the old noble, summoning all his strength to sit up in bed; for a thrill of doubt ran through him, one of those suspicions that come into being under a dying man's pillow. "Listen, my son," he went on, in a voice grown weak with that last effort, "I have no more wish to give up life than you to give up wine and mistresses, horses and hounds, and hawks and gold—"

"I can well believe it," thought the son; and he knelt down by the bed and kissed Bartolommeo's cold hands. "But, father, my dear father," he added aloud, "we must submit to the will of God."

"I am God!" muttered the dying man.

"Do not blaspheme!" cried the other, as he saw the menacing expression on his father's face. "Beware what you say; you have received extreme unction, and I should be inconsolable if you were to die before my eyes in mortal sin."

"Will you listen to me?" cried Bartolommeo, and his mouth twitched.

Don Juan held his peace; an ugly silence prevailed. Yet above the muffled sound of the beating of the snow against the windows rose the sounds of the beautiful voice and the viol in unison, far off and faint as the dawn. The dying man smiled.

"Thank you," he said, "for bringing those singing voices and the music, a banquet, young and lovely women with fair faces and dark tresses, all the pleasure of life! Bid them wait for me; for I am about to begin life anew."

"The delirium is at its height," said Don Juan to himself.

"I have found out a way of coming to life again," the speaker went on. "There, just look in that table drawer, press the spring hidden by the griffin, and it will fly open."

"I have found it, father."

"Well, then, now take out a little phial of rock crystal."

"I have it."

"I have spent twenty years in—" but even as he spoke the old man felt how very near the end had come, and summoned all his dying strength to say, "As soon as the breath is out of me, rub me all over with that liquid, and I shall come to life again."

"There is very little of it," his son remarked.

Though Bartolommeo could no longer speak, he could still hear and see. When those words dropped from Don Juan, his head turned with appalling quickness, his neck was twisted like the throat of some marble statue which the sculptor had condemned to remain stretched out for ever, the wide eyes had come to have a ghastly fixity.

He was dead, and in death he lost his last and sole illusion.

He had sought a shelter in his son's heart, and it had proved to be a sepulchre, a pit deeper than men dig for their dead. The hair on his head had risen and stiffened with horror, his agonized glance still spoke. He was a father rising in just anger from his tomb, to demand vengeance at the throne of God.

"There! it is all over with the old man!" cried Don Juan.

He had been so interested in holding the mysterious phial to the lamp, as a drinker holds up the wine-bottle at the end of a meal, that he had not seen his father's eyes fade. The cowering poodle looked from his master to the elixir, just as Don Juan himself glanced again and again from his father to the flask. The lamplight flickered. There was a deep silence; the viol was mute. Juan Belvidero thought that he saw his father stir, and trembled. The changeless gaze of those accusing eyes frightened him; he closed them hastily, as he would have closed a loose shutter swayed by the wind of an autumn night. He stood there motionless, lost in a world of thought.

Suddenly the silence was broken by a shrill sound like the creaking of a rusty spring. It startled Don Juan; he all but dropped the phial. A sweat, colder than the blade of a dagger, issued through every pore. It was only a piece of clockwork, a wooden cock that sprang out and crowed three times, an ingenious contrivance by which the learned of that epoch were wont to be awakened at the appointed hour to begin the labors of the day. Through the windows there came already a flush of dawn. The thing, composed of wood, and cords, and wheels, and pulleys, was more faithful in its service than he in his duty to Bartolommeo—he, a man with that peculiar piece of human mechanism within him that we call a heart.

Don Juan the sceptic shut the flask again in the secret drawer in the Gothic table—he meant to run no more risks of losing the mysterious liquid.

Even at that solemn moment he heard the murmur of a crowd in the gallery, a confused sound of voices, of stifled laughter and light footfalls, and the rustling of silks—the sounds of a band of revelers struggling for gravity. The door opened, and in came the Prince and Don Juan's friends, the seven courtesans, and the singers, disheveled and wild like dancers surprised by the dawn, when the tapers that have burned through the night struggle with the sunlight.

They had come to offer the customary condolence to the young heir.

"Oho! is poor Don Juan really taking this seriously?" said the Prince in Brambilla's ear.

"Well, his father was very good," she returned.

But Don Juan's night-thoughts had left such unmistakable traces on his features, that the crew was awed into silence. The men stood motionless. The women, with wine-parched lips and cheeks marbled with kisses, knelt down and began a prayer. Don Juan could scarce help trembling when he saw splendor and mirth and laughter and song and youth and beauty and power bowed in reverence before Death. But in those times, in that adorable Italy of the sixteenth century, religion and revelry went hand in hand; and religious excess became a sort of debauch, and a debauch a religious rite!

The Prince grasped Don Juan's hand affectionately, then when all faces had simultaneously put on the same grimace—half-gloomy, half-indifferent—the whole masque disappeared, and left the chamber of death empty. It was like an allegory of life.

As they went down the staircase, the Prince spoke to Rivabarella: "Now, who would have taken Don Juan's impiety for a boast? He loves his father."

"Did you see that black dog?" asked La Brambilla.

"He is enormously rich now," sighed Bianca Cavatolino.

"What is that to me?" cried the proud Veronese (she who had crushed the comfit-box).

"What does it matter to you, forsooth?" cried the Duke. "With his money he is as much a prince as I am."

At first Don Juan was swayed hither and thither by countless thoughts, and wavered between two decisions. He took counsel with the gold heaped up by his father, and returned in the evening to the chamber of death, his whole soul brimming over with hideous selfishness. He found all his household busy there. "His lordship" was to lie in state to-morrow; all Ferrara would flock to behold the wonderful spectacle; and the servants were busy decking the room and the couch on which the dead man lay. At a sign from Don Juan all his people stopped, dumfounded and trembling.

"Leave me alone here," he said, and his voice was changed, "and do not return until I leave the room."

When the footsteps of the old servitor, who was the last to go, echoed but faintly along the paved gallery, Don Juan hastily locked the door, and sure that he was quite alone, "Let us try," he said to himself.

Bartolommeo's body was stretched on a long table. The embalmers had laid a sheet over it, to hide from all eyes the dreadful spectacle of a corpse so wasted and shrunken that it seemed like a skeleton, and only the face was uncovered. This mummy-like figure lay in the middle of the room. The limp clinging linen lent itself to the outlines it shrouded—so sharp, bony, and thin. Large violet patches had already begun to spread over the face; the embalmers' work had not been finished too soon.

Don Juan, strong as he was in his scepticism, felt a tremor as he opened the magic crystal flask. When he stood over that face, he was trembling so violently, that he was actually obliged to wait for a moment. But Don Juan had acquired an early familiarity with evil; his morals had been corrupted by a licentious court, a reflection worthy of the Duke of Urbino crossed his mind, and it was a keen sense of curiosity that goaded him into boldness. The devil himself might have whispered the words that were echoing through his brain, *Moisten one of the eyes with the liquid!* He took up a linen cloth, moistened it sparingly with the precious fluid, and passed it lightly over the right eyelid of the corpse. The eye unclosed . . .

"Aha!" said Don Juan. He gripped the flask tightly, as we clutch in dreams the branch from which we hang suspended over a precipice.

For the eye was full of life. It was a young child's eye set in a death's head; the light quivered in the depths of its youthful liquid brightness. Shaded by the long dark lashes, it sparkled like the strange lights that travelers see in lonely places in winter nights. The eye seemed as if it would fain dart fire at Don Juan; he saw it thinking, upbraiding, condemning, uttering accusations, threatening doom; it cried aloud, and gnashed upon him. All anguish that shakes human souls was gathered there; supplications the most tender, the wrath of kings, the love in a girl's heart pleading with the headsman; then, and after all these, the deeply searching glance a man turns on his fellows as he mounts the last step of the scaffold. Life so dilated in this fragment of life that Don Juan shrank back; he walked up and down the room, he dared not meet that gaze, but he saw nothing else. The ceiling and the hangings, the whole room was sown with living points of fire and intelligence. Everywhere those gleaming eyes haunted him.

"He might very likely have lived another hundred years!" he cried involuntarily. Some diabolical influence had drawn him to his father, and again he gazed at that luminous spark. The eyelid closed and opened again abruptly; it was like a woman's sign of assent. It was an intelligent movement. If a voice had cried "Yes!" Don Juan could not have been more startled.

"What is to be done?" he thought.

He nerved himself to try to close the white eyelid. In vain.

"Kill it? That would perhaps be parricide," he debated with himself.

"Yes," the eye said, with a strange sardonic quiver of the lid.

"Aha!" said Don Juan to himself, "here is witchcraft at work!" And he went closer to crush the thing. A great tear trickled over the hollow cheeks, and fell on Don Juan's hand.

"It is scalding!" he cried. He sat down. The struggle exhausted him; it was as if, like Jacob of old, he was wrestling with an angel.

At last he rose. "So long as there is no blood—" he muttered.

Then, summoning all the courage needed for a coward's crime, he extinguished the eye, pressing it with the linen cloth, turning his head away. A terrible groan startled him. It was the poor poodle, who died with a long-drawn howl.

"Could the brute have been in the secret?" thought Don Juan, looking down at the faithful creature.

Don Juan Belvidero was looked upon as a dutiful son. He reared a white marble monument on his father's tomb, and employed the greatest sculptors of the time upon it. He did not recover perfect ease of mind till the day when his father knelt in marble before Religion, and the heavy weight of the stone had sealed the mouth of the grave in which he had laid the one feeling of remorse that sometimes flitted through his soul in moments of physical weariness.

He had drawn up a list of the wealth heaped up by the old merchant in the East, and he became a miser: had he not to provide for a second lifetime? His views of life were the more profound and penetrating; he grasped its significance, as a whole, the better, because he saw it across a grave. All men, all things, he analyzed once and for all; he summed up the Past, represented by its records; the Present in the law, its crystallized form; the Future, revealed by religion. He took spirit and matter, and flung them into his crucible, and found—Nothing. Thenceforward he became *Don Juan.*

At the outset of his life, in the prime of youth and the beauty of youth, he knew the illusions of life for what they were; he despised the world, and made the utmost of the world. His felicity could not have been of the bourgeois kind, rejoicing in periodically recurrent *bouilli*, in the comforts of a warming-pan, a lamp of a night, and a new pair of slippers once a quarter. Nay, rather he seized upon existence as a monkey snatches a nut, and after no long toying with it, proceeds deftly to strip off the mere husks to reach the savory kernel within.

Poetry and the sublime transports of passion scarcely reached ankle-depth with him now. He in nowise fell into the error of strong natures who flatter themselves now and again that little souls will believe in a great soul, and are willing to barter their own lofty thoughts of the future for the small change of our life-annuity ideas. He, even as they, had he chosen, might well have walked with his feet on the earth and his head in the skies; but he liked better to sit on earth, to wither the soft, fresh, fragrant lips of a woman with kisses, for like Death, he devoured everything without scruple as he passed; he would have full fruition; he was an Oriental lover, seeking prolonged pleasures easily obtained. He sought nothing but a woman in women, and cultivated cynicism, until it became with him a habit of mind. When his mistress, from the couch on which she lay, soared and was lost in regions of ecstatic bliss, Don Juan followed suit, earnest, expansive, serious as any German student. But he said I, while she, in the transports of intoxication, said We. He understood to admiration the art of abandoning himself to the influence of a woman; he was always clever enough to make her believe that he trembled like some boy fresh from college before his first partner at a dance, when he asks her, "Do you like dancing?" But, no less, he could be terrible at need, could unsheathe a formidable sword and make short work of Commandants. Banter lurked beneath his simplicity, mocking laughter behind his tears—for he had tears at need, like any woman nowadays who says to her husband, "Give me a carriage, or I shall go into a consumption."

For the merchant the world is a bale of goods or a mass of circulating bills; for most young men it is a woman, and for a woman here and there it is a man; for a certain order of mind it is a salon, a coterie, a quarter of the town, or some single city; but Don Juan found his world in himself.

This model of grace and dignity, this captivating wit, moored his bark by every shore; but wherever he was led he was never carried away, and was only steered in a course of his own choosing. The more he saw, the more he doubted. He watched men narrowly, and saw how, beneath the surface, courage was often rashness; and prudence, cowardice; generosity, a clever piece of calculation; justice, a wrong; delicacy, pusillanimity; honesty, a *modus vivendi;* and by some strange dispensation of fate, he must see that those who at heart were really honest, scrupulous, just, generous, prudent, or brave were held cheaply by their fellow-men.

"What a cold-blooded jest!" said he to himself. "It was not devised by a God."

From that time forth he renounced a better world, and never uncovered himself when a Name was pronounced, and for him the carven saints in the churches became works of art. He understood the mechanism of society too well to clash wantonly with its prejudices; for, after all, he was not as powerful as the executioner, but he evaded social laws with the wit and grace so well rendered in the scene with M. Dimanche. He was, in fact, Moliere's Don Juan, Goethe's Faust, Byron's Manfred, Mathurin's Melmoth—great allegorical figures drawn by the greatest men of genius in Europe, to which Mozart's harmonies, perhaps, do no more justice than Rossini's lyre. Terrible allegorical figures that shall endure as long as the principle of evil existing in the heart of man shall produce a few copies from century to century. Sometimes the type becomes half-human when incarnate as a Mirabeau, sometimes it is an inarticulate force in a Bonaparte, sometimes it overwhelms the universe with irony as a Rabelais; or, yet again, it appears when a Marechal de Richelieu elects to laugh at human beings instead of scoffing at things, or when one of the most famous of our ambassadors goes a step further and scoffs at both men and things. But the profound genius of Juan Belvidero anticipated and resumed all these. All things were a jest to him. His was the life of a mocking spirit. All men, all institutions, all realities, all ideas were within its scope. As for eternity, after half an hour of familiar conversation with Pope Julius II he said, laughing:

"If it is absolutely necessary to make a choice, I would rather believe in God than in the Devil; power combined with goodness always offers more resources than the spirit of Evil can boast."

"Yes; still God requires repentance in this present world—"

"So you always think of your indulgences," returned Don Juan Belvidero. "Well, well, I have another life in reserve in which to repent of the sins of my previous existence."

"Oh, if you regard old age in that light," cried the Pope, "you are in danger on canonization—"

"After your elevation to the Papacy nothing is incredible." And they went to watch the workmen who were building the huge basilica dedicated to Saint Peter.

"Saint Peter, as the man of genius who laid the foundation of our double power," the Pope said to Don Juan, "deserves this monument. Sometimes, though, at night, I think that a deluge will wipe all this out as with a sponge, and it will be all to begin over again."

Don Juan and the Pope began to laugh; they understood each other. A fool would have gone on the morrow to amuse himself with Julius II in Raphael's studio or at the delicious Villa Madama; not so Belvidero. He went to see the Pope as pontiff, to be convinced of any doubts that he (Don Juan) entertained. Over his cups the Rovere would have been capable of denying his own infallibility and of commenting on the Apocalypse.

Nevertheless, this legend has not been undertaken to furnish materials for future biographies of Don Juan; it is intended to prove to honest folk that Belvidero did not die in a duel with stone, as some lithographers would have us believe.

When Don Juan Belvidero reached the age of sixty he settled in Spain, and there in his old age he married a young and charming Andalusian wife. But of set purpose he was neither a good husband nor a good father. He had observed that we are never so tenderly loved as by women to whom we scarcely give a thought. Dona Elvira had been devoutly brought up by an old aunt in a castle a few leagues from San-Lucar in a remote part of Andalusia. She was a model of devotion and grace. Don Juan foresaw that this would be a woman who would struggle long against a passion before yielding, and therefore hoped to keep her virtuous until his death. It was a jest undertaken in earnest, a game of chess which he meant to reserve till his old age. Don Juan had learned wisdom from the mistakes made by his father Bartolommeo; he determined that the least details of his life in old age should be subordinated to one object—the success of the drama which was to be played out upon his death-bed.

For the same reason the largest part of his wealth was buried in the cellars of his palace at Ferrara, whither he seldom went. As for the rest of his fortune, it was invested in a life annuity, with a view to give his wife and children an interest in keeping him alive; but this Machiavellian piece of foresight was scarcely necessary. His son, young Felipe Belvidero, grew up as a Spaniard as religiously conscientious as his father was irreligious, in virtue, perhaps, of the old rule, "A miser has a spendthrift son." The Abbot of San-Lucar was chosen by Don Juan to be the director of the consciences of the Duchess of Belvidero and her son Felipe. The ecclesiastic was a holy man, well shaped, and admirably well proportioned. He had fine dark eyes, a head like that of Tiberius, worn with fasting, bleached by an ascetic life, and, like all dwellers in the wilderness, was daily tempted. The noble lord had hopes, it may be, of despatching yet another monk before his term of life was out.

But whether because the Abbot was every whit as clever as Don Juan himself, or Dona Elvira possessed more discretion or more virtue than Spanish wives are usually credited with, Don Juan was compelled to spend his declining years beneath his own roof, with no more scandal under it than if he had been an ancient country parson. Occasionally he would take wife and son to task for negligence in the duties of religion, peremptorily insisting that they should carry out to the letter the obligations imposed upon the flock by the Court of Rome. Indeed, he was never so well pleased as when he had set the courtly Abbot discussing some case of conscience with Dona Elvira and Felipe.

At length, however, despite the prodigious care that the great magnifico, Don Juan Belvidero, took of himself, the days of decrepitude came upon him, and with those days the constant importunity of physical feebleness, an importunity all the more distressing by contrast with the wealth of memories of his impetuous youth and the sensual pleasures of middle age. The unbeliever who in the height of his cynical humor had been wont to persuade others to believe in laws and principles at which he scoffed, must repose nightly upon a *perhaps*. The great Duke, the pattern of good breeding, the champion of many a carouse, the proud ornament of Courts, the man of genius, the graceful winner of hearts that he had wrung as carelessly as a peasant twists an osier withe, was now the victim of a cough, of a ruthless sciatica, of an unmannerly gout. His teeth gradually deserted him, as at the end of an evening the fairest and best-dressed women take their leave one by one till the room is left empty and desolate. The active hands became palsy-stricken, the shapely legs tottered as he walked. At last, one night, a stroke of apoplexy caught him by the throat in its icy clutch. After that fatal day he grew morose and stern.

He would reproach his wife and son with their devotion, casting it in their teeth that the affecting and thoughtful care that they lavished so tenderly upon him was bestowed because they knew that his money was invested in a life annuity. Then Elvira and Felipe would shed bitter tears and redouble their caresses, and the wicked old man's insinuating voice would take an affectionate tone—"Ah, you will forgive me, will you not, dear friends, dear wife? I am rather a nuisance. Alas, Lord in heaven, how canst Thou use me as the instrument by which Thou provest these two angelic creatures? I who should be the joy of their lives am become their scourge . . ."

In this manner he kept them tethered to his pillow, blotting out the memory of whole months of fretfulness and unkindness in one short hour when he chose to display for them the ever-new treasures of his pinchbeck tenderness and charm of manner—a system of paternity that yielded him an infinitely better return than his own father's indulgence had formerly gained. At length his bodily infirmities reached a point when the task of laying him in bed became as difficult as the navigation of a felucca in the perils of an intricate channel. Then came the day of his death; and this brilliant sceptic, whose mental faculties alone had survived the most dreadful of all destructions, found himself between his two special antipathies—the doctor and the confessor. But he was jovial with them. Did he not see a light gleaming in the future beyond the veil? The pall that is like lead for other men was thin and translucent for him; the light-footed, irresistible delights of youth danced beyond it like shadows.

It was on a beautiful summer evening that Don Juan felt the near approach of death. The sky of Spain was serene and cloudless; the air was full of the scent of orange-blossom; the stars shed clear, pure gleams of light; nature without seemed to give the dying man assurance of resurrection; a dutiful and obedient son sat there watching him with loving and respectful eyes. Towards eleven o'clock he desired to be left alone with this single-hearted being.

"Felipe," said the father, in tones so soft and affectionate that the young man trembled, and tears of gladness came to his eyes; never had that stern father spoken his name in such a tone. "Listen, my son," the dying man went on. "I am a great sinner. All my life long, however, I have thought of my death. I was once the friend of the great Pope Julius II; and that illustrious Pontiff, fearing lest the excessive excitability of my senses should entangle me in mortal sin between the moment of my death and the time of my anointing with the holy oil, gave me a flask that contains a little of the holy water that once issued from the rock in the wilderness. I have kept the secret of this squandering of a treasure belonging to Holy Church, but I am permitted to reveal the mystery *in articulo mortis* to my son. You will find the flask in a drawer in that Gothic table that always stands by the head of the bed . . . The precious little crystal flask may be of use yet again for you, dearest Felipe. Will you swear to me, by your salvation, to carry out my instructions faithfully?"

Felipe looked at his father, and Don Juan was too deeply learned in the lore of the human countenance not to die in peace with that look as his warrant, as his own father had died in despair at meeting the expression in his son's eyes.

"You deserved to have a better father," Don Juan went on. "I dare to confess, my child, that while the reverend Abbot of San-Lucar was administering the Viaticum I was thinking of the incompatibility of the co-existence of two powers so infinite as God and the Devil—"

"Oh, father!"

"And I said to myself, when Satan makes his peace he ought surely to stipulate for the pardon of his followers, or he will be the veriest scoundrel. The thought haunted me; so I shall go to hell, my son, unless you carry out my wishes."

"Oh, quick; tell me quickly, father."

"As soon as I have closed my eyes," Don Juan went on, "and that may be in a few minutes, you must take my body before it grows cold and lay it on a table in this room. Then put out the lamp; the light of the stars should be sufficient. Take off my clothes, reciting Aves and Paters the while, raising your soul to God in prayer, and carefully anoint my lips and eyes with this holy water; begin with the face, and proceed successively to my limbs and the rest of my body; my dear son, the power of God is so great that you must be astonished at nothing."

Don Juan felt death so near, that he added in a terrible voice, "Be careful not to drop the flask."

Then he breathed his last gently in the arms of his son, and his son's tears fell fast over his sardonic, haggard features.

It was almost midnight when Don Felipe Belvidero laid his father's body upon the table. He kissed the sinister brow and the gray hair; then he put out the lamp.

By the soft moonlight that lit strange gleams across the country without, Felipe could dimly see his father's body, a vague white thing among the shadows. The dutiful son moistened a linen cloth with the liquid, and, absorbed in prayer, he anointed the revered face. A deep silence reigned. Felipe heard faint, indescribable rustlings; it was the breeze in the tree-tops, he thought. But when he had moistened the right arm, he felt himself caught by the throat, a young strong hand held him in a tight grip—it was his father's hand! He shrieked aloud; the flask dropped from his hand and broke in pieces. The liquid evaporated; the whole household hurried into the room, holding torches aloft. That shriek had startled them, and filled them with as much terror as if the Trumpet of the Angel sounding on the Last Day had rung through earth and sky. The room was full of people, and a horror-stricken crowd beheld the fainting Felipe upheld by the strong arm of his father, who clutched him by the throat. They saw another thing, an unearthly spectacle—Don Juan's face grown young and beautiful as Antinous, with its dark hair and brilliant eyes and red lips, a head that made horrible efforts, but could not move the dead, wasted body.

An old servitor cried, "A miracle! a miracle!" and all the Spaniards echoed, "A miracle! a miracle!"

Dona Elvira, too pious to attribute this to magic, sent for the Abbot of San-Lucar; and the Prior beholding the miracle with his own eyes, being a clever man, and withal an Abbot desirous of augmenting his revenues, determined to turn the occasion to profit. He immediately gave out that Don Juan would certainly be canonized; he appointed a day for the celebration of the apotheosis in his convent, which thenceforward, he said, should be called the convent of San Juan of Lucar. At these words a sufficiently facetious grimace passed over the features of the late Duke.

The taste of the Spanish people for ecclesiastical solemnities is so well known, that it should not be difficult to imagine the religious pantomime by which the Convent of San-Lucar celebrated the translation of the *blessed Don Juan Belvidero* to the abbey-church. The tale of the partial resurrection had spread so quickly from village to village, that a day or two after the death of the illustrious nobleman the report had reached every place within fifty miles of San-Lucar, and it was as good as a play to see the roads covered already with crowds flocking in on all sides, their curiosity whetted still further by the prospect of a *Te Deum* sung by torchlight. The old abbey church of San-Lucar, a marvelous building erected by the Moors, a mosque of Allah, which for three centuries had heard the name of Christ, could not hold the throng that poured in to see the ceremony. Hidalgos in their velvet mantles, with their good swords at their sides, swarmed like ants, and were so tightly packed in among the pillars that they had not room to bend the knees, which never bent save to God. Charming peasant girls, in the basquina that defines the luxuriant outlines of their figures, lent an arm to white-haired old men. Young men, with eyes of fire, walked beside aged crones in holiday array. Then came couples tremulous with joy, young lovers led thither by curiosity, newly-wedded folk; children timidly clasping each other by the hand. This throng, so rich in coloring, in vivid contrasts, laden with flowers, enameled like a meadow, sent up a soft murmur through the quiet night. Then the great doors of the church opened.

Late comers who remained without saw afar, through the three great open doorways, a scene of which the theatrical illusions of modern opera can give but a faint idea. The vast church was lighted up by thousands of candles, offered by saints and sinners alike eager to win the favor of this new candidate for canonization, and these self-commending illuminations turned the great building into an enchanted fairyland. The black archways, the shafts and capitals, the recessed chapels with gold and silver gleaming in their depths, the galleries, the Arab traceries, all the most delicate outlines of that delicate sculpture, burned in the excess of light like the fantastic figures in the red heart of a brazier. At the further end of the church, above that blazing sea, rose the high altar like a splendid dawn. All the glories of the golden lamps and silver candlesticks, of banners and tassels, of the shrines of the saints and votive offerings, paled before the gorgeous brightness of the reliquary in which Don Juan lay. The blasphemer's body sparkled with gems, and flowers, and crystal, with diamonds and gold, and plumes white as the wings of seraphim; they had set it up on the altar, where the pictures of Christ had stood. All about him blazed a host of tall candles; the air quivered in the radiant light. The worthy Abbot of San-Lucar, in pontifical robes, with his mitre set with precious stones, his rochet and golden crosier, sat enthroned in imperial state among his clergy in the choir. Rows of impassive aged faces, silver-haired old men clad in fine linen albs, were grouped about him, as the saints who confessed Christ on earth are set by painters, each in his place, about the throne of God in heaven. The precentor and the dignitaries of the chapter, adorned with the gorgeous insignia of ecclesiastical vanity, came and went through the clouds of incense, like stars upon their courses in the firmament.

When the hour of triumph arrived, the bells awoke the echoes far and wide, and the whole vast crowd raised to God the first cry of praise that begins the *Te Deum*. A sublime cry! High, pure notes, the voices of women in ecstasy, mingled in it with the sterner and deeper voices of men; thousands of voices sent up a volume of sound so mighty, that the straining, groaning organ-pipes could not dominate that harmony. But the shrill sound of children's singing among the choristers, the reverberation of deep bass notes, awakened gracious associations, visions of childhood, and of man in his strength, and rose above that entrancing harmony of human voices blended in one sentiment of love.

Te Deum laudamus!

The chant went up from the black masses of men and women kneeling in the cathedral, like a sudden breaking out of light in darkness, and the silence was shattered as by a peal of thunder. The voices floated up with the clouds of incense that had begun to cast thin bluish veils over the fanciful marvels of the architecture, and the aisles were filled with splendor and perfume and light and melody. Even at the moment when that music of love and thanksgiving soared up to the altar, Don Juan, too well bred not to express his acknowledgments, too witty not to understand how to take a jest, bridled up in his reliquary, and responded with an appalling burst of laughter. Then the Devil having put him in mind of the risk he was running of being taken for an ordinary man, a saint, a Boniface, a Pantaleone, he interrupted the melody of love by a yell, the thousand voices of hell joined in it. Earth blessed, Heaven banned. The church was shaken to its ancient foundations.

Te Deum laudamus! cried the many voices.

"Go to the devil, brute beasts that you are! *Dios! Dios! Garajos demonios!* Idiots! What fools you are with your dotard God!" and a torrent of imprecations poured forth like a stream of red-hot lava from the mouth of Vesuvius.

"*Deus Sabaoth! . . . Sabaoth!*" cried the believers.

"You are insulting the majesty of Hell," shouted Don Juan, gnashing his teeth. In another moment the living arm struggled out of the reliquary, and was brandished over the assembly in mockery and despair.

"The saint is blessing us," cried the old women, children, lovers, and the credulous among the crowd.

And note how often we are deceived in the homage we pay; the great man scoffs at those who praise him, and pays compliments now and again to those whom he laughs at in the depths of his heart.

Just as the Abbot, prostrate before the altar, was chanting *"Sancte Johannes, ora pro noblis!"* he heard a voice exclaim sufficiently distinctly: *"O coglione!"*

"What can be going on up there?" cried the Sub-prior, as he saw the reliquary move.

"The saint is playing the devil," replied the Abbot.

Even as he spoke the living head tore itself away from the lifeless body, and dropped upon the sallow cranium of the officiating priest.

"Remember Dona Elvira!" cried the thing, with its teeth set fast in the Abbot's head.

The Abbot's horror-stricken shriek disturbed the ceremony; all the ecclesiastics hurried up and crowded about their chief.

"Idiot, tell us now if there is a God!" the voice cried, as the Abbot, bitten through the brain, drew his last breath.

THE FALL OF THE HOUSE OF USHER

Edgar Allan Poe

Son coeur est un luth suspendu;
Sitôt qu'on le touche il résonne.
—De Beranger

During the whole of a dull, dark, and soundless day in the autumn of the year, when the clouds hung oppressively low in the heavens, I had been passing alone, on horseback, through a singularly dreary tract of country; and at length found myself, as the shades of the evening drew on, within view of the melancholy House of Usher. I know not how it was—but, with the first glimpse of the building, a sense of insufferable gloom pervaded my spirit. I say insufferable; for the feeling was unrelieved by any of that half-pleasurable, because poetic, sentiment, with which the mind usually receives even the sternest natural images of the desolate or terrible. I looked upon the scene before me—upon the mere house, and the simple landscape features of the domain—upon the bleak walls—upon the vacant eye-like windows—upon a few rank sedges—and upon a few white trunks of decayed trees—with an utter depression of soul which I can compare to no earthly sensation more properly than to the after-dream of the reveller upon opium—the bitter lapse into everyday life—the hideous dropping off of the veil. There was an iciness, a sinking, a sickening of the heart—an unredeemed dreariness of thought which no goading of the imagination could torture into aught of the sublime. What was it—I paused to think—what was it that so unnerved me in the contemplation of the House of Usher? It was a mystery all insoluble; nor could I grapple with the shadowy fancies that crowded upon me as I pondered. I was forced to fall back upon the unsatisfactory conclusion, that while, beyond doubt, there *are* combinations of very simple natural objects which have the power of thus affecting us, still the analysis of this power lies among considerations beyond our depth. It was possible, I reflected, that a mere different arrangement of the particulars of the scene, of the details of the picture, would be sufficient to modify, or perhaps to annihilate its capacity for sorrowful impression; and, acting upon this idea, I reined my horse to the precipitous brink of a black and lurid tarn that lay in unruffled lustre by the dwelling, and gazed down—but with a shudder even more thrilling than before—upon the remodelled and inverted images of the gray sedge, and the ghastly tree-stems, and the vacant and eye-like windows.

Nevertheless, in this mansion of gloom I now proposed to myself a sojourn of some weeks. Its proprietor, Roderick Usher, had been one of my boon companions in boyhood; but many years had elapsed since our last meeting. A letter, however, had lately reached me in a distant part of the country—a letter from him—which, in its wildly importunate nature, had admitted of no other than a personal reply. The MS. gave evidence of nervous agitation. The writer spoke of acute bodily illness—of a mental disorder which oppressed him—and of an earnest desire to see me, as his best, and indeed his only personal friend, with a view of attempting, by the cheerfulness of my society, some alleviation of his malady. It was the manner in which all this, and much more, was said—it was the apparent *heart* that went with his request—which allowed me no room for hesitation; and I accordingly obeyed forthwith what I still considered a very singular summons.

Although, as boys, we had been even intimate associates, yet I really knew little of my friend. His reserve had been always excessive and habitual. I was aware, however, that his very ancient family had been noted, time out of mind, for a peculiar sensibility of temperament, displaying itself, through long ages, in many works of exalted art, and manifested, of late, in repeated deeds of munificent yet unobtrusive charity, as well as in a passionate devotion to the intricacies, perhaps even more than to the orthodox and easily recognisable beauties, of musical science. I had learned, too, the very remarkable fact, that the stem of the Usher race, all time-honored as it was, had put forth, at no period, any enduring branch; in other words, that the entire family lay in the direct line of descent, and had always, with very trifling and very temporary variation, so lain. It was this deficiency, I considered, while running over in thought the perfect keeping of the character of the premises with the accredited character of the people, and while speculating upon the possible influence which the one, in the long lapse of centuries, might have exercised upon the other—it was this deficiency, perhaps, of collateral issue, and the consequent undeviating transmission, from sire to son, of the patrimony with the name, which had, at length, so identified the two as to merge the original title of the estate in the quaint and equivocal appellation of the "House of Usher"—an appellation which seemed to include, in the minds of the peasantry who used it, both the family and the family mansion.

I have said that the sole effect of my somewhat childish experiment—that of looking down within the tarn—had been to deepen the first singular impression. There can be no doubt that the consciousness of the rapid increase of my superstition—for why should I not so term it?—served mainly to accelerate the increase itself. Such, I have long known, is the paradoxical law of all sentiments having terror as a basis. And it might have been for this reason only, that, when I again uplifted my eyes to the house itself, from its image in the pool, there grew in my mind a strange fancy—a fancy so ridiculous, indeed, that I but mention it to show the vivid force of the sensations which oppressed me. I had so worked upon my imagination as really to believe that about the whole mansion and domain there hung an atmosphere peculiar to themselves and their immediate vicinity—an atmosphere which had no affinity with the air of heaven, but which had reeked up from the decayed trees, and the gray wall, and the silent tarn—a pestilent and mystic vapor, dull, sluggish, faintly discernible, and leaden-hued.

Shaking off from my spirit what must have been a dream, I scanned more narrowly the real aspect of the building. Its principal feature seemed to be that of an excessive antiquity. The discoloration of ages had been great. Minute fungi overspread the whole exterior, hanging in a fine tangled web-work from the eaves. Yet all this was apart from any extraordinary dilapidation. No portion of the masonry had fallen; and there appeared to be a wild inconsistency between its still perfect adaptation of parts, and the crumbling condition of the individual stones. In this there was much that reminded me of the specious totality of old wood-work which has rotted for long years in some neglected vault, with no disturbance from the breath of the external air. Beyond this indication of extensive decay, however, the fabric gave little token of instability. Perhaps the eye of a scrutinizing observer might have discovered a barely perceptible fissure, which, extending from the roof of the building in front, made its way down the wall in a zigzag direction, until it became lost in the sullen waters of the tarn.

Noticing these things, I rode over a short causeway to the house. A servant in waiting took my horse, and I entered the Gothic archway of the hall. A valet, of stealthy step, thence conducted me, in silence, through many dark and intricate passages in my progress to the *studio* of his master. Much that I encountered on the way contributed, I know not how, to heighten the vague sentiments of which I have already spoken. While the objects around me—while the carvings of the ceilings, the sombre tapestries of the walls, the ebon blackness of the floors, and the phantasmagoric armorial trophies which rattled as I strode, were but matters to which, or to such as which, I had been accustomed from my infancy—while I hesitated not to acknowledge how familiar was all this—I still wondered to find how unfamiliar were the fancies which ordinary images were stirring up. On one of the staircases, I met the physician of the family. His countenance, I thought, wore a mingled expression of low cunning and perplexity. He accosted me with trepidation and passed on. The valet now threw open a door and ushered me into the presence of his master.

The room in which I found myself was very large and lofty. The windows were long, narrow, and pointed, and at so vast a distance from the black oaken floor as to be altogether inaccessible from within. Feeble gleams of encrimsoned light made their way through the trellissed panes, and served to render sufficiently distinct the more prominent objects around; the eye, however, struggled in vain to reach the remoter angles of the chamber, or the recesses of the vaulted and fretted ceiling. Dark draperies hung upon the walls. The general furniture was profuse, comfortless, antique, and tattered. Many books and musical instruments lay scattered about, but failed to give any vitality to the scene. I felt that I breathed an atmosphere of sorrow. An air of stern, deep, and irredeemable gloom hung over and pervaded all.

Upon my entrance, Usher arose from a sofa on which he had been lying at full length, and greeted me with a vivacious warmth which had much in it, I at first thought, of an overdone cordiality—of the constrained effort of the *ennuye*; man of the world. A glance, however, at his countenance, convinced me of his perfect sincerity. We sat down; and for some moments, while he spoke not, I gazed upon him with a feeling half of pity, half of awe. Surely, man had never before so terribly altered, in so brief a period, as had Roderick Usher! It was with difficulty that I could bring myself to admit the identity of the wan being before me with the companion of my early boyhood. Yet the character of his face had been at all times remarkable. A cadaverousness of complexion; an eye large, liquid, and luminous beyond comparison; lips somewhat thin and very pallid, but of a surpassingly beautiful curve; a nose of a delicate Hebrew model, but with a breadth of nostril unusual in similar formations; a finely moulded chin, speaking, in its want of prominence, of a want of moral energy; hair of a more than web-like softness and tenuity; these features, with an inordinate expansion above the regions of the temple, made up altogether a countenance not easily to be forgotten. And now in the mere exaggeration of the prevailing character of these features, and of the expression they were wont to convey, lay so much of change that I doubted to whom I spoke. The now ghastly pallor of the skin, and the now miraculous lustre of the eye, above all things startled and even awed me. The silken hair, too, had been suffered to grow all unheeded, and as, in its wild gossamer texture, it floated rather than fell about the face, I could not, even with effort, connect its Arabesque expression with any idea of simple humanity.

In the manner of my friend I was at once struck with an incoherence—an inconsistency; and I soon found this to arise from a series of feeble and futile struggles to overcome an habitual trepidancy—an excessive nervous agitation. For something of this nature I had indeed been prepared, no less by his letter, than by reminiscences of certain boyish traits, and by conclusions deduced from his peculiar physical conformation and temperament. His action was alternately vivacious and sullen. His voice varied rapidly from a tremulous indecision (when the animal spirits seemed utterly in abeyance) to that species of energetic concision—that abrupt, weighty, unhurried, and hollow-sounding enunciation—that leaden, self-balanced and perfectly modulated guttural utterance, which may be observed in the lost drunkard, or the irreclaimable eater of opium, during the periods of his most intense excitement.

It was thus that he spoke of the object of my visit, of his earnest desire to see me, and of the solace he expected me to afford him. He entered, at some length, into what he conceived to be the nature of his malady. It was, he said, a constitutional and a family evil, and one for which he despaired to find a remedy—a mere nervous affection, he immediately added, which would undoubtedly soon pass off. It displayed itself in a host of unnatural sensations. Some of these, as he detailed them, interested and bewildered me; although, perhaps, the terms, and the general manner of the narration had their weight. He suffered much from a morbid acuteness of the senses; the most insipid food was alone endurable; he could wear only garments of certain texture; the odors of all flowers were oppressive; his eyes were tortured by even a faint light; and there were but peculiar sounds, and these from stringed instruments, which did not inspire him with horror.

To an anomalous species of terror I found him a bounden slave. "I shall perish," said he, "I *must* perish in this deplorable folly. Thus, thus, and not otherwise, shall I be lost. I dread the events of the future, not in themselves, but in their results. I shudder at the thought of any, even the most trivial, incident, which may operate upon this intolerable agitation of soul. I have, indeed, no abhorrence of danger, except in its absolute effect—in terror. In this unnerved—in this pitiable condition—I feel that the period will sooner or later arrive when I must abandon life and reason together, in some struggle with the grim phantasm, *fear*."

I learned, moreover, at intervals, and through broken and equivocal hints, another singular feature of his mental condition. He was enchained by certain superstitious impressions in regard to the dwelling which he tenanted, and whence, for many years, he had never ventured forth—in regard to an influence whose supposititious force was conveyed in terms too shadowy here to be re-stated—an influence which some peculiarities in the mere form and substance of his family mansion, had, by dint of long sufferance, he said, obtained over his spirit—an effect which the *physique* of the gray walls and turrets, and of the dim tarn into which they all looked down, had, at length, brought about upon the *morale* of his existence.

He admitted, however, although with hesitation, that much of the peculiar gloom which thus afflicted him could be traced to a more natural and far more palpable origin—to the severe and long-continued illness—indeed to the evidently approaching dissolution—of a tenderly beloved sister—his sole companion for long years—his last and only relative on earth. "Her decease," he said, with a bitterness which I can never forget, "would leave him (him the hopeless and the frail) the last of the ancient race of the Ushers." While he spoke, the Lady Madeline (for so was she called) passed slowly through a remote portion of the apartment, and, without having noticed my presence, disappeared. I regarded her with an utter astonishment not unmingled with dread—and yet I found it impossible to account for such feelings. A sensation of stupor oppressed me, as my eyes followed her retreating steps. When a door, at length, closed upon her, my glance sought instinctively and eagerly the countenance of the brother—but he had buried his face in his hands, and I could only perceive that a far more than ordinary wanness had overspread the emaciated fingers through which trickled many passionate tears.

The disease of the Lady Madeline had long baffled the skill of her physicians. A settled apathy, a gradual wasting away of the person, and frequent although transient affections of a partially cataleptical character, were the unusual diagnosis. Hitherto she had steadily borne up against the pressure of her malady, and had not betaken herself finally to bed; but, on the closing in of the evening of my arrival at the house, she succumbed (as her brother told me at night with inexpressible agitation) to the prostrating power of the destroyer; and I learned that the glimpse I had obtained of her person would thus probably be the last I should obtain—that the lady, at least while living, would be seen by me no more.

For several days ensuing, her name was unmentioned by either Usher or myself: and during this period I was busied in earnest endeavors to alleviate the melancholy of my friend. We painted and read together; or I listened, as if in a dream, to the wild improvisations of his speaking guitar. And thus, as a closer and still closer intimacy admitted me more unreservedly into the recesses of his spirit, the more bitterly did I perceive the futility of all attempt at cheering a mind from which darkness, as if an inherent positive quality, poured forth upon all objects of the moral and physical universe, in one unceasing radiation of gloom.

I shall ever bear about me a memory of the many solemn hours I thus spent alone with the master of the House of Usher. Yet I should fail in any attempt to convey an idea of the exact character of the studies, or of the occupations, in which he involved me, or led me the way. An excited and highly distempered ideality threw a sulphureous lustre over all. His long improvised dirges will ring forever in my ears. Among other things, I hold painfully in mind a certain singular perversion and amplification of the wild air of the last waltz of Von Weber. From the paintings over which his elaborate fancy brooded, and which grew, touch by touch, into vaguenesses at which I shuddered the more thrillingly, because I shuddered knowing not why—from these paintings (vivid as their images now are before me) I would in vain endeavor to educe more than a small portion which should lie within the compass of merely written words. By the utter simplicity, by the nakedness of his designs, he arrested and overawed attention. If ever mortal painted an idea, that mortal was Roderick Usher. For me at least—in the circumstances then surrounding me—there arose out of the pure abstractions which the hypochondriac contrived to throw upon his canvass, an intensity of intolerable awe, no shadow of which felt I ever yet in the contemplation of the certainly glowing yet too concrete reveries of Fuseli.

One of the phantasmagoric conceptions of my friend, partaking not so rigidly of the spirit of abstraction, may be shadowed forth, although feebly, in words. A small picture presented the interior of an immensely long and rectangular vault or tunnel, with low walls, smooth, white, and without interruption or device. Certain accessory points of the design served well to convey the idea that this excavation lay at an exceeding depth below the surface of the earth. No outlet was observed in any portion of its vast extent, and no torch, or other artificial source of light was discernible; yet a flood of intense rays rolled throughout, and bathed the whole in a ghastly and inappropriate splendor.

I have just spoken of that morbid condition of the auditory nerve which rendered all music intolerable to the sufferer, with the exception of certain effects of stringed instruments. It was, perhaps, the narrow limits to which he thus confined himself upon the guitar, which gave birth, in great measure, to the fantastic character of his performances. But the fervid *facility* of his *impromptus* could not be so accounted for. They must have been, and were, in the notes, as well as in the words of his wild fantasias (for he not unfrequently accompanied himself with rhymed verbal improvisations), the result of that intense mental collectedness and concentration to which I have previously alluded as observable only in particular moments of the highest artificial excitement. The words of one of these rhapsodies I have easily remembered. I was, perhaps, the more forcibly impressed with it, as he gave it, because, in the under or mystic current of its meaning, I fancied that I perceived, and for the first time, a full consciousness on the part of Usher, of the tottering of his lofty reason upon her throne. The verses, which were entitled "The Haunted Palace," ran very nearly, if not accurately, thus:

I

In the greenest of our valleys,
  By good angels tenanted,
Once a fair and stately palace—
  Radiant palace—reared its head.
In the monarch Thought's dominion—
  It stood there!
Never seraph spread a pinion
  Over fabric half so fair.

II

Banners yellow, glorious, golden,
  On its roof did float and flow;
(This—all this—was in the olden
  Time long ago)
And every gentle air that dallied,
  In that sweet day,
Along the ramparts plumed and pallid,
  A winged odor went away.

III

Wanderers in that happy valley
  Through two luminous windows saw
Spirits moving musically
  To a lute's well-tuned law,
Round about a throne, where sitting
  (Porphyrogene!)
In state his glory well befitting,
  The ruler of the realm was seen.

IV

And all with pearl and ruby glowing
  Was the fair palace door,
Through which came flowing, flowing, flowing,
  And sparkling evermore,
A troop of Echoes whose sweet duty
  Was but to sing,
In voices of surpassing beauty,
  The wit and wisdom of their king.

V

But evil things, in robes of sorrow,
    Assailed the monarch's high estate;
(Ah, let us mourn, for never morrow
    Shall dawn upon him, desolate!)
And, round about his home, the glory
    That blushed and bloomed
Is but a dim-remembered story
    Of the old time entombed.

VI

And travellers now within that valley,
    Through the red-litten windows, see
Vast forms that move fantastically
    To a discordant melody;
While, like a rapid ghastly river,
    Through the pale door,
A hideous throng rush out forever,
    And laugh—but smile no more.

I well remember that suggestions arising from this ballad, led us into a train of thought wherein there became manifest an opinion of Usher's which I mention not so much on account of its novelty (for other men have thought thus), as on account of the pertinacity with which he maintained it. This opinion, in its general form, was that of the sentience of all vegetable things. But, in his disordered fancy, the idea had assumed a more daring character, and trespassed, under certain conditions, upon the kingdom of inorganization. I lack words to express the full extent, or the earnest *abandon* of his persuasion. The belief, however, was connected (as I have previously hinted) with the gray stones of the home of his forefathers. The conditions of the sentience had been here, he imagined, fulfilled in the method of collocation of these stones—in the order of their arrangement, as well as in that of the many *fungi* which overspread them, and of the decayed trees which stood around—above all, in the long undisturbed endurance of this arrangement, and in its reduplication in the still waters of the tarn. Its evidence—the evidence of the sentience—was to be seen, he said (and I here started as he spoke), in the gradual yet certain condensation of an atmosphere of their own about the waters and the walls. The result was discoverable, he added, in that silent, yet importunate and terrible influence which for centuries had moulded the destinies of his family, and which made *him* what I now saw him—what he was. Such opinions need no comment, and I will make none.

Our books—the books which, for years, had formed no small portion of the mental existence of the invalid—were, as might be supposed, in strict keeping with this character of phantasm. We pored together over such works as the Ververt et Chartreuse of Gresset; the Belphegor of Machiavelli; the Heaven and Hell of Swedenborg; the Subterranean Voyage of Nicholas Klimm by Holberg; the Chiromancy of Robert Flud, of Jean D'Indagine, and of De la Chambre; the Journey into the Blue Distance of Tieck; and the City of the Sun of Campanella. One favorite volume was a small octavo edition of the *Directorium Inquisitorium*, by the Dominican Eymeric de Gironne; and there were passages in Pomponius Mela, about the old African Satyrs and Oegipans, over which Usher would sit dreaming for hours. His chief delight, however, was found in the perusal of an exceedingly rare and curious book in quarto Gothic—the manual of a forgotten church—the *Vigiliae Mortuorum secundum Chorum Ecclesiae Maguntinae.*

I could not help thinking of the wild ritual of this work, and of its probable influence upon the hypochondriac, when, one evening, having informed me abruptly that the Lady Madeline was no more, he stated his intention of preserving her corpse for a fortnight (previously to its final interment), in one of the numerous vaults within the main walls of the building. The worldly reason, however, assigned for this singular proceeding, was one which I did not feel at liberty to dispute. The brother had been led to his resolution (so he told me) by consideration of the unusual character of the malady of the deceased, of certain obtrusive and eager inquiries on the part of her medical men, and of the remote and exposed situation of the burial-ground of the family. I will not deny that when I called to mind the sinister countenance of the person whom I met upon the staircase, on the day of my arrival at the house, I had no desire to oppose what I regarded as at best but a harmless, and by no means an unnatural, precaution.

At the request of Usher, I personally aided him in the arrangements for the temporary entombment. The body having been encoffined, we two alone bore it to its rest. The vault in which we placed it (and which had been so long unopened that our torches, half smothered in its oppressive atmosphere, gave us little opportunity for investigation) was small, damp, and entirely without means of admission for light; lying, at great depth, immediately beneath that portion of the building in which was my own sleeping apartment. It had been used, apparently, in remote feudal times, for the worst purposes of a donjon-keep, and, in later days, as a place of deposit for powder, or some other highly combustible substance, as a portion of its floor, and the whole interior of a long archway through which we reached it, were carefully sheathed with copper. The door, of massive iron, had been, also, similarly protected. Its immense weight caused an unusually sharp grating sound, as it moved upon its hinges.

Having deposited our mournful burden upon tressels within this region of horror, we partially turned aside the yet unscrewed lid of the coffin, and looked upon the face of the tenant. A striking similitude between the brother and sister now first arrested my attention; and Usher, divining, perhaps, my thoughts, murmured out some few words from which I learned that the deceased and himself had been twins, and that sympathies of a scarcely intelligible nature had always existed between them. Our glances, however, rested not long upon the dead—for we could not regard her unawed. The disease which had thus entombed the lady in the maturity of youth, had left, as usual in all maladies of a strictly cataleptical character, the mockery of a faint blush upon the bosom and the face, and that suspiciously lingering smile upon the lip which is so terrible in death. We replaced and screwed down the lid, and, having secured the door of iron, made our way, with toil, into the scarcely less gloomy apartments of the upper portion of the house.

And now, some days of bitter grief having elapsed, an observable change came over the features of the mental disorder of my friend. His ordinary manner had vanished. His ordinary occupations were neglected or forgotten. He roamed from chamber to chamber with hurried, unequal, and objectless step. The pallor of his countenance had assumed, if possible, a more ghastly hue—but the luminousness of his eye had utterly gone out. The once occasional huskiness of his tone was heard no more; and a tremulous quaver, as if of extreme terror, habitually characterized his utterance. There were times, indeed, when I thought his unceasingly agitated mind was laboring with some oppressive secret, to divulge which he struggled for the necessary courage. At times, again, I was obliged to resolve all into the mere inexplicable vagaries of madness, for I beheld him gazing upon vacancy for long hours, in an attitude of the profoundest attention, as if listening to some imaginary sound. It was no wonder that his condition terrified—that it infected me. I felt creeping upon me, by slow yet certain degrees, the wild influences of his own fantastic yet impressive superstitions.

It was, especially, upon retiring to bed late in the night of the seventh or eighth day after the placing of the Lady Madeline within the donjon, that I experienced the full power of such feelings. Sleep came not near my couch—while the hours waned and waned away. I struggled to reason off the nervousness which had dominion over me. I endeavored to believe that much, if not all of what I felt, was due to the bewildering influence of the gloomy furniture of the room—of the dark and tattered draperies, which, tortured into motion by the breath of a rising tempest, swayed fitfully to and fro upon the walls, and rustled uneasily about the decorations of the bed. But my efforts were fruitless. An irrepressible tremor gradually pervaded my frame; and, at length, there sat upon my very heart an incubus of utterly causeless alarm. Shaking this off with a gasp and a struggle, I uplifted myself upon the pillows, and, peering earnestly within the intense darkness of the chamber, harkened—I know not why, except that an instinctive spirit prompted me—to certain low and indefinite sounds which came, through the pauses of the storm, at long intervals, I knew not whence. Overpowered by an intense sentiment of horror, unaccountable yet unendurable, I threw on my clothes with haste (for I felt that I should sleep no more during the night), and endeavored to arouse myself from the pitiable condition into which I had fallen, by pacing rapidly to and fro through the apartment.

I had taken but few turns in this manner, when a light step on an adjoining staircase arrested my attention. I presently recognised it as that of Usher. In an instant afterward he rapped, with a gentle touch, at my door, and entered, bearing a lamp. His countenance was, as usual, cadaverously wan—but, moreover, there was a species of mad hilarity in his eyes—an evidently restrained hysteria in his whole demeanor. His air appalled me—but anything was preferable to the solitude which I had so long endured, and I even welcomed his presence as a relief.

"And you have not seen it?" he said abruptly, after having stared about him for some moments in silence—"you have not then seen it?—but, stay! you shall." Thus speaking, and having carefully shaded his lamp, he hurried to one of the casements, and threw it freely open to the storm.

The impetuous fury of the entering gust nearly lifted us from our feet. It was, indeed, a tempestuous yet sternly beautiful night, and one wildly singular in its terror and its beauty. A whirlwind had apparently collected its force in our vicinity; for there were frequent and violent alterations in the direction of the wind; and the exceeding density of the clouds (which hung so low as to press upon the turrets of the house) did not prevent our perceiving the life-like velocity with which they flew careering from all points against each other, without passing away into the distance. I say that even their exceeding density did not prevent our perceiving this—yet we had no glimpse of the moon or stars—nor was there any flashing forth of the lightning. But the under surfaces of the huge masses of agitated vapor, as well as all terrestrial objects immediately around us, were glowing in the unnatural light of a faintly luminous and distinctly visible gaseous exhalation which hung about and enshrouded the mansion.

"You must not—you shall not behold this!" said I, shudderingly, to Usher, as I led him, with a gentle violence, from the window to a seat. "These appearances, which bewilder you, are merely electrical phenomena not uncommon—or it may be that they have their ghastly origin in the rank miasma of the tarn. Let us close this casement—the air is chilling and dangerous to your frame. Here is one of your favorite romances. I will read, and you shall listen—and so we will pass away this terrible night together."

The antique volume which I had taken up was the "Mad Trist" of Sir Launcelot Canning; but I had called it a favorite of Usher's more in sad jest than in earnest; for, in truth, there is little in its uncouth and unimaginative prolixity which could have had interest for the lofty and spiritual ideality of my friend. It was, however, the only book immediately at hand; and I indulged a vague hope that the excitement which now agitated the hypochondriac, might find relief (for the history of mental disorder is full of similar anomalies) even in the extremeness of the folly which I should read. Could I have judged, indeed, by the wild overstrained air of vivacity with which he harkened, or apparently harkened, to the words of the tale, I might well have congratulated myself upon the success of my design.

I had arrived at that well-known portion of the story where Ethelred, the hero of the Trist, having sought in vain for peaceable admission into the dwelling of the hermit, proceeds to make good an entrance by force. Here, it will be remembered, the words of the narrative run thus:

"And Ethelred, who was by nature of a doughty heart, and who was now mighty withal, on account of the powerfulness of the wine which he had drunken, waited no longer to hold parley with the hermit, who, in sooth, was of an obstinate and maliceful turn, but, feeling the rain upon his shoulders, and fearing the rising of the tempest, uplifted his mace outright, and, with blows, made quickly room in the plankings of the door for his gauntleted hand; and now pulling therewith sturdily, he so cracked, and ripped, and tore all asunder, that the noise of the dry and hollow-sounding wood alarummed and reverberated throughout the forest."

At the termination of this sentence I started, and for a moment, paused; for it appeared to me (although I at once concluded that my excited fancy had deceived me)—it appeared to me that, from some very remote portion of the mansion, there came, indistinctly, to my ears, what might have been, in its exact similarity of character, the echo (but a stifled and dull one certainly) of the very cracking and ripping sound which Sir Launcelot had so particularly described. It was, beyond doubt, the coincidence alone which had arrested my attention; for, amid the rattling of the sashes of the casements, and the ordinary commingled noises of the still increasing storm, the sound, in itself, had nothing, surely, which should have interested or disturbed me. I continued the story:

"But the good champion Ethelred, now entering within the door, was sore enraged and amazed to perceive no signal of the maliceful hermit; but, in the stead thereof, a dragon of a scaly and prodigious demeanor, and of a fiery tongue, which sate in guard before a palace of gold, with a floor of silver; and upon the wall there hung a shield of shining brass with this legend enwritten:

> *Who entereth herein, a conqueror hath bin;*
> *Who slayeth the dragon, the shield he shall win;*

And Ethelred uplifted his mace, and struck upon the head of the dragon, which fell before him, and gave up his pesty breath, with a shriek so horrid and harsh, and withal so piercing, that Ethelred had fain to close his ears with his hands against the dreadful noise of it, the like whereof was never before heard."

Here again I paused abruptly, and now with a feeling of wild amazement—for there could be no doubt whatever that, in this instance, I did actually hear (although from what direction it proceeded I found it impossible to say) a low and apparently distant, but harsh, protracted, and most unusual screaming or grating sound—the exact counterpart of what my fancy had already conjured up for the dragon's unnatural shriek as described by the romancer.

Oppressed, as I certainly was, upon the occurrence of this second and most extraordinary coincidence, by a thousand conflicting sensations, in which wonder and extreme terror were predominant, I still retained sufficient presence of mind to avoid exciting, by any observation, the sensitive nervousness of my companion. I was by no means certain that he had noticed the sounds in question; although, assuredly, a strange alteration had, during the last few minutes, taken place in his demeanor. From a position fronting my own, he had gradually brought round his chair, so as to sit with his face to the door of the chamber; and thus I could but partially perceive his features, although I saw that his lips trembled as if he were murmuring inaudibly. His head had dropped upon his breast—yet I knew that he was not asleep, from the wide and rigid opening of the eye as I caught a glance of it in profile. The motion of his body, too, was at variance with this idea—for he rocked from side to side with a gentle yet constant and uniform sway. Having rapidly taken notice of all this, I resumed the narrative of Sir Launcelot, which thus proceeded:

"And now, the champion, having escaped from the terrible fury of the dragon, bethinking himself of the brazen shield, and of the breaking up of the enchantment which was upon it, removed the carcass from out of the way before him, and approached valorously over the silver pavement of the castle to where the shield was upon the wall; which in sooth the feet upon the silver floor, with a mighty great and terrible ringing sound."

No sooner had these syllables passed my lips, than—as if a shield of brass had indeed, at the moment, fallen heavily upon a floor of silver—I became aware of a distinct, hollow, metallic, and clangorous, yet apparently muffled reverberation. Completely unnerved, I leaped to my feet; but the measured rocking movement of Usher was undisturbed. I rushed to the chair in which he sat. His eyes were bent fixedly before him, and throughout his whole countenance there reigned a stony rigidity. But, as I placed my hand upon his shoulder, there came a strong shudder over his whole person; a sickly smile quivered about his lips; and I saw that he spoke in a low, hurried, and gibbering murmur, as if unconscious of my presence. Bending closely over him, I at length drank in the hideous import of his words.

"Not hear it?—yes, I hear it, and have heard it. Long—long—long—many minutes, many hours, many days, have I heard it—yet I dared not—oh, pity me, miserable wretch that I am!—I dared not—I dared not speak! *We have put her living in the tomb!* Said I not that my senses were acute? I now tell you that I heard her first feeble movements in the hollow coffin. I heard them—many, many days ago—yet I dared not—*I dared not speak!* And now—to-night—Ethelred—ha! ha!—the breaking of the hermit's door, and the death-cry of the dragon, and the clangor of the shield!—say, rather, the rending of her coffin, and the grating of the iron hinges of her prison, and her struggles within the coppered archway of the vault! Oh whither shall I fly? Will she not be here anon? Is she not hurrying to upbraid me for my haste? Have I not heard her footstep on the stair? Do I not distinguish that heavy and horrible beating of her heart? Madman!"—here he sprang furiously to his feet, and shrieked out his syllables, as if in the effort he were giving up his soul—"*Madman! I tell you that she now stands without the door!*"

As if in the superhuman energy of his utterance there had been found the potency of a spell—the huge antique panels to which the speaker pointed, threw slowly back, upon the instant, their ponderous and ebony jaws. It was the work of the rushing gust—but then without those doors there *did* stand the lofty and enshrouded figure of the Lady Madeline of Usher. There was blood upon her white robes, and the evidence of some bitter struggle upon every portion of her emaciated frame. For a moment she remained trembling and reeling to and fro upon the threshold—then, with a low moaning cry, fell heavily inward upon the person of her brother, and in her violent and now final death-agonies, bore him to the floor a corpse, and a victim to the terrors he had anticipated.

From that chamber, and from that mansion, I fled aghast. The storm was still abroad in all its wrath as I found myself crossing the old causeway. Suddenly there shot along the path a wild light, and I turned to see whence a gleam so unusual could have issued; for the vast house and its shadows were alone behind me. The radiance was that of the full, setting, and blood-red moon, which now shone vividly through that once barely-discernible fissure, of which I have before spoken as extending from the roof of the building, in a zigzag direction, to the base. While I gazed, this fissure rapidly widened—there came a fierce breath of the whirlwind—the entire orb of the satellite burst at once upon my sight—my brain reeled as I saw the mighty walls rushing asunder—there was a long tumultuous shouting sound like the voice of a thousand waters—and the deep and dank tarn at my feet closed sullenly and silently over the fragments of the "House of Usher."

THE CASE OF LADY SANNOX

Arthur Conan Doyle

The relations between Douglas Stone and the notorious Lady Sannox were very well known both among the fashionable circles of which she was a brilliant member, and the scientific bodies which numbered him among their most illustrious confreres. There was naturally, therefore, a very widespread interest when it was announced one morning that the lady had absolutely and for ever taken the veil, and that the world would see her no more. When, at the very tail of this rumour, there came the assurance that the celebrated operating surgeon, the man of steel nerves, had been found in the morning by his valet, seated on one side of his bed, smiling pleasantly upon the universe, with both legs jammed into one side of his breeches and his great brain about as valuable as a cap full of porridge, the matter was strong enough to give quite a little thrill of interest to folk who had never hoped that their jaded nerves were capable of such a sensation.

Douglas Stone in his prime was one of the most remarkable men in England. Indeed, he could hardly be said to have ever reached his prime, for he was but nine-and-thirty at the time of this little incident. Those who knew him best were aware that famous as he was as a surgeon, he might have succeeded with even greater rapidity in any of a dozen lines of life. He could have cut his way to fame as a soldier, struggled to it as an explorer, bullied for it in the courts, or built it out of stone and iron as an engineer. He was born to be great, for he could plan what another man dare not do, and he could do what another man dare not plan. In surgery none could follow him. His nerve, his judgement, his intuition, were things apart. Again and again his knife cut away death, but grazed the very springs of life in doing it, until his assistants were as white as the patient. His energy, his audacity, his full-blooded self-confidence—does not the memory of them still linger to the south of Marylebone Road and the north of Oxford Street?

His vices were as magnificent as his virtues, and infinitely more picturesque. Large as was his income, and it was the third largest of all professional men in London, it was far beneath the luxury of his living. Deep in his complex nature lay a rich vein of sensualism, at the sport of which he placed all the prizes of his life. The eye, the ear, the touch, the palate, all were his masters. The bouquet of old vintages, the scent of rare exotics, the curves and tints of the daintiest potteries of Europe, it was to these that the quick-running stream of gold was transformed. And then there came his sudden mad passion for

Lady Sannox, when a single interview with two challenging glances and a whispered word set him ablaze. She was the loveliest woman in London and the only one to him. He was one of the handsomest men in London, but not the only one to her. She had a liking for new experiences, and was gracious to most men who wooed her. It may have been cause or it may have been effect that Lord Sannox looked fifty, though he was but six-and-thirty.

He was a quiet, silent, neutral-tinted man, this lord, with thin lips and heavy eyelids, much given to gardening, and full of home-like habits. He had at one time been fond of acting, had even rented a theatre in London, and on its boards had first seen Miss Marion Dawson, to whom he had offered his hand, his title, and the third of a county. Since his marriage his early hobby had become distasteful to him. Even in private theatricals it was no longer possible to persuade him to exercise the talent which he had often showed that he possessed. He was happier with a spud and a watering-can among his orchids and chrysanthemums.

It was quite an interesting problem whether he was absolutely devoid of sense, or miserably wanting in spirit. Did he know his lady's ways and condone them, or was he a mere blind, doting fool? It was a point to be discussed over the teacups in snug little drawing-rooms, or with the aid of a cigar in the bow windows of clubs. Bitter and plain were the comments among men upon his conduct. There was but one who had a good word to say for him, and he was the most silent member in the smoking-room. He had seen him break in a horse at the University, and it seemed to have left an impression upon his mind.

But when Douglas Stone became the favourite all doubts as to Lord Sannox's knowledge or ignorance were set for ever at rest. There was no subterfuge about Stone. In his high-handed, impetuous fashion, he set all caution and discretion at defiance. The scandal became notorious. A learned body intimated that his name had been struck from the list of its vice-presidents. Two friends implored him to consider his professional credit. He cursed them all three, and spent forty guineas on a bangle to take with him to the lady. He was at her house every evening, and she drove in his carriage in the afternoons. There was not an attempt on either side to conceal their relations; but there came at last a little incident to interrupt them.

It was a dismal winter's night, very cold and gusty, with the wind whooping in the chimneys and blustering against the window-panes. A thin spatter of rain tinkled on the glass with each fresh sough of the gale, drowning for the instant the dull gurgle and drip from the eaves. Douglas Stone had finished his dinner, and sat by his fire in the study, a glass of rich port upon the malachite table at his elbow. As he raised it to his lips, he held it up against the lamplight, and watched with the eye of a connoisseur the tiny scales of beeswing which floated in its rich ruby depths. The fire, as it spurted up, threw fitful lights upon his bald, clear-cut face, with its widely-opened grey eyes, its thick and yet firm lips, and the deep, square jaw, which had something Roman in its strength and its animalism. He smiled from time to time as he nestled back in his luxurious chair. Indeed, he had a right to feel well pleased, for, against the advice of six colleagues, he had performed an operation that day of which only two cases were on record, and the result had been brilliant beyond all expectation. No other man in London would have had the daring to plan, or the skill to execute, such a heroic measure.

But he had promised Lady Sannox to see her that evening and it was already half-past eight. His hand was outstretched to the bell to order the carriage when he heard the dull thud of the knocker. An instant later there was the shuffling of feet in the hall, and the sharp closing of a door.

"A patient to see you, sir, in the consulting room," said the butler.

"About himself?"

"No, sir; I think he wants you to go out."

"It is too late," cried Douglas Stone peevishly. "I won't go."

"This is his card, sir."

The butler presented it upon the gold salver which had been given to his master by the wife of a Prime Minister.

"'Hamil Ali, Smyrna.' Hum! The fellow is a Turk, I suppose."

"Yes, sir. He seems as if he came from abroad, sir. And he's in a terrible way."

"Tut, tut! I have an engagement. I must go somewhere else. But I'll see him. Show him in here, Pim."

A few moments later the butler swung open the door and ushered in a small and decrepit man, who walked with a bent back and with the forward push of the face and blink of the eyes which goes with extreme short sight. His face was swarthy, and his hair and beard of the deepest black. In one hand he held a turban of white muslin striped with red, in the other a small chamois-leather bag.

"Good evening," said Douglas Stone, when the butler had closed the door. "You speak English, I presume?"

"Yes, sir. I am from Asia Minor, but I speak English when I speak slow."

"You wanted me to go out, I understand?"

"Yes, sir. I wanted very much that you should see my wife."

"I could come in the morning, but I have an engagement which prevents me from seeing your wife tonight."

The Turk's answer was a singular one. He pulled the string which closed the mouth of the chamois-leather bag, and poured a flood of gold on to the table.

"There are one hundred pounds there," said he, "and I promise you that it will not take you an hour. I have a cab ready at the door."

Douglas Stone glanced at his watch. An hour would not make it too late to visit Lady Sannox. He had been there later. And the fee was an extraordinarily high one. He had been pressed by his creditors lately, and he could not afford to let such a chance pass. He would go.

"What is the case?" he asked.

"Oh, it is so sad a one! So sad a one! You have not, perhaps heard of the daggers of the Almohades?"

"Never."

"Ah, they are Eastern daggers of a great age and of a singular shape, with the hilt like what you call a stirrup. I am a curiosity dealer, you understand, and that is why I have come to England from Smyrna, but next week I go back once more. Many things I brought with me, and I have a few things left, but among them, to my sorrow, is one of these daggers."

"You will remember that I have an appointment, sir," said the surgeon, with some irritation; "pray confine yourself to the necessary details."

"You will see that it is necessary. Today my wife fell down in a faint in the room in which I keep my wares, and she cut her lower lip upon this cursed dagger of Almohades."

"I see," said Douglas Stone, rising. "And you wish me to dress the wound?"

"No, no, it is worse than that."

"What then?"

"These daggers are poisoned."

"Poisoned!"

"Yes, and there is no man, East or West, who can tell now what is the poison or what the cure. But all that is known I know, for my father was in this trade before me, and we have had much to do with these poisoned weapons."

"What are the symptoms?"

"Deep sleep, and death in thirty hours."

"And you say there is no cure. Why then should you pay me this considerable fee?"

"No drug can cure, but the knife may."

"And how?"

"The poison is slow of absorption. It remains for hours in the wound."

"Washing, then, might cleanse it?"

"No more than in a snake bite. It is too subtle and too deadly."

"Excision of the wound, then?"

"That is it. If it be on the finger, take the finger off. So said my father always. But think of where this wound is, and that it is my wife. It is dreadful!"

But familiarity with such grim matters may take the finer edge from a man's sympathy. To Douglas Stone this was already an interesting case, and he brushed aside as irrelevant the feeble objections of the husband.

"It appears to be that or nothing," said he brusquely. "It is better to lose a lip than a life."

"Ah, yes, I know that you are right. Well, well, it is kismet, and it must be faced. I have the cab, and you will come with me and do this thing."

Douglas Stone took his case of bistouries from a drawer, and placed it with a roll of bandage and a compress of lint in his pocket. He must waste no more time if he were to see Lady Sannox.

"I am ready," said he, pulling on his overcoat. "Will you take a glass of wine before you go out into this cold air?"

His visitor shrank away, with a protesting hand upraised.

"You forget that I am a Mussulman, and a true follower of the Prophet," said he. "But tell me what is the bottle of green glass which you have placed in your pocket?"

"It is chloroform."

"Ah, that also is forbidden to us. It is a spirit, and we make no use of such things."

"What! You would allow your wife to go through an operation without an anaesthetic?"

"Ah! she will feel nothing, poor soul. The deep sleep has already come on, which is the first working of the poison. And then I have given her of our Smyrna opium. Come, sir, for already an hour has passed."

As they stepped out into the darkness, a sheet of rain was driven in upon their faces, and the hall lamp, which dangled from the arm of a marble Caryatid, went out with a fluff. Pim, the butler, pushed the heavy door to, straining hard with his shoulder against the wind, while the two men groped their way towards the yellow glare which showed where the cab was waiting. An instant later they were rattling upon their journey.

"Is it far?" asked Douglas Stone.

"Oh, no. We have a very little quiet place off the Euston Road."

The surgeon pressed the spring of his repeater and listened to the little tings which told him the hour. It was a quarter past nine. He calculated the distances, and the short time which it would take him to perform so trivial an operation. He ought to reach Lady Sannox by ten o'clock. Through the fogged windows he saw the blurred gas lamps dancing past, with occasionally the broader glare of a shop front. The rain was pelting and rattling upon the leathern top of the carriage, and the wheels swashed as they rolled through puddle and mud. Opposite to him the white headgear of his companion gleamed faintly through the obscurity. The surgeon felt in his pockets and arranged his needles, his ligatures and his safety-pins, that no time might be wasted when they arrived. He chafed with impatience and drummed his foot upon the floor.

But the cab slowed down at last and pulled up. In an instant Douglas Stone was out, and the Smyrna merchant's toe was at his very heel.

"You can wait," said he to the driver.

It was a mean-looking house in a narrow and sordid street. The surgeon, who knew his London well, cast a swift glance into the shadows, but there was nothing distinctive—no shop, no movement, nothing but a double line of dull, flat-faced houses, a double stretch of wet flagstones which gleamed in the lamplight, and a double rush of water in the gutters which swirled and gurgled towards the sewer gratings. The door which faced them was blotched and discoloured, and a faint light in the fan pane above, it served to show the dust and the grime which covered it. Above in one of the bedroom windows, there was a dull yellow glimmer. The merchant knocked loudly, and, as he turned his dark face towards the light, Douglas Stone could see that it was contracted with anxiety. A bolt was drawn, and an elderly woman with a taper stood in the doorway, shielding the thin flame with her gnarled hand.

"Is all well?" gasped the merchant.

"She is as you left her, sir."

"She has not spoken?"

"No, she is in a deep sleep."

The merchant closed the door, and Douglas Stone walked down the narrow passage, glancing about him in some surprise as he did so. There was no oil-cloth, no mat, no hat-rack. Deep grey dust and heavy festoons of cobwebs met his eyes everywhere. Following the old woman up the winding stair, his firm footfall echoed harshly through the silent house. There was no carpet.

The bedroom was on the second landing. Douglas Stone followed the old nurse into it, with the merchant at his heels. Here, at least, there was furniture and to spare. The floor was littered and the corners piled with Turkish cabinets, inlaid tables, coats of chain mail, strange pipes, and grotesque weapons. A single small lamp stood upon a bracket on the wall. Douglas Stone took it down, and picking his way among the lumber, walked over to a couch in the corner, on which lay a woman dressed in the Turkish fashion, with yashmak and veil. The lower part of the face was exposed, and the surgeon saw a jagged cut which zigzagged along the border of the under lip.

"You will forgive the yashmak," said the Turk. "You know our views about women in the East."

But the surgeon was not thinking about the yashmak. This was no longer a woman to him. It was a case. He stooped and examined the wound carefully.

"There are no signs of irritation," said he. "We might delay the operation until local symptoms develop."

The husband wrung his hands in uncontrollable agitation.

"Oh! sir, sir," he cried. "Do not trifle. You do not know. It is deadly. I know, and I give you my assurance that an operation is absolutely necessary. Only the knife can save her."

"And yet I am inclined to wait," said Douglas Stone.

"That is enough," the Turk cried, angrily. "Every minute is of importance, and I cannot stand here and see my wife allowed to sink. It only remains for me to give you my thanks for having come, and to call in some other surgeon before it is too late."

Douglas Stone hesitated. To refund that hundred pounds was no pleasant matter. But of course if he left the case he must return the money. And if the Turk were right and the woman died, his position before a coroner might be an embarrassing one.

"You have had personal experience of this poison?" he asked.

"I have."

"And you assure me that an operation is needful."

"I swear it by all that I hold sacred."

"The disfigurement will be frightful."

"I can understand that the mouth will not be a pretty one to kiss."

Douglas Stone turned fiercely upon the man. The speech was a brutal one. But the Turk has his own fashion of talk and of thought, and there was no time for wrangling. Douglas Stone drew a bistoury from his case, opened it and felt the keen straight edge with his forefinger. Then he held the lamp closer to the bed. Two dark eyes were gazing up at him through the slit in the yashmak. They were all iris, and the pupil was hardly to be seen.

"You have given her a very heavy dose of opium."

"Yes, she has had a good dose."

He glanced again at the dark eyes which looked straight at his own. They were dull and lustreless, but, even as he gazed, a little shifting sparkle came into them, and the lips quivered.

"She is not absolutely unconscious," said he.

"Would it not be well to use the knife while it will be painless?"

The same thought had crossed the surgeon's mind. He grasped the wounded lip with his forceps, and with two swift cuts he took out a broad V-shaped piece. The woman sprang up on the couch with a dreadful gurgling scream. Her covering was torn from her face. It was a face that he knew. In spite of that protruding upper lip and that slobber of blood, it was a face that he knew. She kept on putting her hand up to the gap and screaming. Douglas Stone sat down at the foot of the couch with his knife and his forceps. The room was whirling round, and he had felt something go like a ripping seam behind his ear. A bystander would have said that his face was the more ghastly of the two. As in a dream, or as if he had been looking at something at the play, he was conscious that the Turk's hair and beard lay upon the table, and that Lord Sannox was leaning against the wall with his hand to his side, laughing silently. The screams had died away now, and the dreadful head had dropped back again upon the pillow, but Douglas Stone still sat motionless, and Lord Sannox still chuckled quietly to himself.

"It was really very necessary for Marion, this operation," said he, "not physically, but morally, you know, morally."

Douglas Stone stooped for yards and began to play with the fringe of the coverlet. His knife tinkled down upon the ground, but he still held the forceps and something more.

"I had long intended to make a little example," said Lord Sannox, suavely. "Your note of Wednesday miscarried, and I have it here in my pocket-book. I took some pains in carrying out my idea. The wound, by the way, was from nothing more dangerous than my signet ring."

He glanced keenly at his silent companion, and cocked the small revolver which he held in his coat pocket. But Douglas Stone was still picking at the coverlet.

"You see you have kept your appointment after all," said Lord Sannox.

And at that Douglas Stone began to laugh. He laughed long and loudly. But Lord Sannox did not laugh now. Something like fear sharpened and hardened his features. He walked from the room, and he walked on tiptoe. The old woman was waiting outside.

"Attend to your mistress when she awakes," said Lord Sannox.

Then he went down to the street. The cab was at the door, and the driver raised his hand to his hat.

"John," said Lord Sannox, "you will take the doctor home first. He will want leading downstairs, I think. Tell his butler that he has been taken ill at a case."

"Very good, sir."

"Then you can take Lady Sannox home."

"And how about yourself, sir?"

"Oh, my address for the next few months will be Hotel di Roma, Venice. Just see that the letters are sent on. And tell Stevens to exhibit all the purple chrysanthemums next Monday, and to wire me the result."

YOUNG GOODMAN BROWN

Nathaniel Hawthorne

Young Goodman Brown came forth at sunset into the street at Salem village; but put his head back, after crossing the threshold, to exchange a parting kiss with his young wife. And Faith, as the wife was aptly named, thrust her own pretty head into the street, letting the wind play with the pink ribbons of her cap while she called to Goodman Brown.

"Dearest heart," whispered she, softly and rather sadly, when her lips were close to his ear, "prithee put off your journey until sunrise and sleep in your own bed to-night. A lone woman is troubled with such dreams and such thoughts that she's afeard of herself sometimes. Pray tarry with me this night, dear husband, of all nights in the year."

"My love and my Faith," replied young Goodman Brown, "of all nights in the year, this one night must I tarry away from thee. My journey, as thou callest it, forth and back again, must needs be done 'twixt now and sunrise. What, my sweet, pretty wife, dost thou doubt me already, and we but three months married?"

"Then God bless you!" said Faith, with the pink ribbons; "and may you find all well when you come back."

"Amen!" cried Goodman Brown. "Say thy prayers, dear Faith, and go to bed at dusk, and no harm will come to thee."

So they parted; and the young man pursued his way until, being about to turn the corner by the meeting-house, he looked back and saw the head of Faith still peeping after him with a melancholy air, in spite of her pink ribbons.

"Poor little Faith!" thought he, for his heart smote him. "What a wretch am I to leave her on such an errand! She talks of dreams, too. Methought as she spoke there was trouble in her face, as if a dream had warned her what work is to be done tonight. But no, no; 't would kill her to think it. Well, she's a blessed angel on earth; and after this one night I'll cling to her skirts and follow her to heaven."

With this excellent resolve for the future, Goodman Brown felt himself justified in making more haste on his present evil purpose. He had taken a dreary road, darkened by all the gloomiest trees of the forest, which barely stood aside to let the narrow path creep through, and closed immediately behind. It was all as lonely as could be; and there is this peculiarity in such a solitude, that the traveller knows not who may be concealed by the innumerable trunks and the thick boughs overhead; so that with lonely footsteps he may yet be passing through an unseen multitude.

"There may be a devilish Indian behind every tree," said Goodman Brown to himself; and he glanced fearfully behind him as he added, "What if the devil himself should be at my very elbow!"

His head being turned back, he passed a crook of the road, and, looking forward again, beheld the figure of a man, in grave and decent attire, seated at the foot of an old tree. He arose at Goodman Brown's approach and walked onward side by side with him.

"You are late, Goodman Brown," said he. "The clock of the Old South was striking as I came through Boston, and that is full fifteen minutes agone."

"Faith kept me back a while," replied the young man, with a tremor in his voice, caused by the sudden appearance of his companion, though not wholly unexpected.

It was now deep dusk in the forest, and deepest in that part of it where these two were journeying. As nearly as could be discerned, the second traveller was about fifty years old, apparently in the same rank of life as Goodman Brown, and bearing a considerable resemblance to him, though perhaps more in expression than features. Still they might have been taken for father and son. And yet, though the elder person was as simply clad as the younger, and as simple in manner too, he had an indescribable air of one who knew the world, and who would not have felt abashed at the governor's dinner table or in King William's court, were it possible that his affairs should call him thither. But the only thing about him that could be fixed upon as remarkable was his staff, which bore the likeness of a great black snake, so curiously wrought that it might almost be seen to twist and wriggle itself like a living serpent. This, of course, must have been an ocular deception, assisted by the uncertain light.

"Come, Goodman Brown," cried his fellow-traveller, "this is a dull pace for the beginning of a journey. Take my staff, if you are so soon weary."

"Friend," said the other, exchanging his slow pace for a full stop, "having kept covenant by meeting thee here, it is my purpose now to return whence I came. I have scruples touching the matter thou wot'st of."

"Sayest thou so?" replied he of the serpent, smiling apart. "Let us walk on, nevertheless, reasoning as we go; and if I convince thee not thou shalt turn back. We are but a little way in the forest yet."

"Too far! too far!" exclaimed the goodman, unconsciously resuming his walk. "My father never went into the woods on such an errand, nor his father before him. We have been a race of honest men and good Christians since the days of the martyrs; and shall I be the first of the name of Brown that ever took this path and kept—"

"Such company, thou wouldst say," observed the elder person, interpreting his pause. "Well said, Goodman Brown! I have been as well acquainted with your family as with ever a one among the Puritans; and that's no trifle to say. I helped your grandfather, the constable, when he lashed the Quaker woman so smartly through the streets of Salem; and it was I that brought your father a pitch-pine knot, kindled at my own hearth, to set fire to an Indian village, in King Philip's war. They were my good friends, both; and many a pleasant walk have we had along this path, and returned merrily after midnight. I would fain be friends with you for their sake."

"If it be as thou sayest," replied Goodman Brown, "I marvel they never spoke of these matters; or, verily, I marvel not, seeing that the least rumor of the sort would have driven them from New England. We are a people of prayer, and good works to boot, and abide no such wickedness."

"Wickedness or not," said the traveller with the twisted staff, "I have a very general acquaintance here in New England. The deacons of many a church have drunk the communion wine with me; the selectmen of divers towns make me their chairman; and a majority of the Great and General Court are firm supporters of my interest. The governor and I, too—But these are state secrets."

"Can this be so?" cried Goodman Brown, with a stare of amazement at his undisturbed companion. "Howbeit, I have nothing to do with the governor and council; they have their own ways, and are no rule for a simple husbandman like me. But, were I to go on with thee, how should I meet the eye of that good old man, our minister, at Salem village? Oh, his voice would make me tremble both Sabbath day and lecture day."

Thus far the elder traveller had listened with due gravity; but now burst into a fit of irrepressible mirth, shaking himself so violently that his snake-like staff actually seemed to wriggle in sympathy.

"Ha! ha! ha!" shouted he again and again; then composing himself, "Well, go on, Goodman Brown, go on; but, prithee, don't kill me with laughing."

"Well, then, to end the matter at once," said Goodman Brown, considerably nettled, "there is my wife, Faith. It would break her dear little heart; and I'd rather break my own."

"Nay, if that be the case," answered the other, "e'en go thy ways, Goodman Brown. I would not for twenty old women like the one hobbling before us that Faith should come to any harm."

As he spoke he pointed his staff at a female figure on the path, in whom Goodman Brown recognized a very pious and exemplary dame, who had taught him his catechism in youth, and was still his moral and spiritual adviser, jointly with the minister and Deacon Gookin.

"A marvel, truly, that Goody Cloyse should be so far in the wilderness at nightfall," said he. "But with your leave, friend, I shall take a cut through the woods until we have left this Christian woman behind. Being a stranger to you, she might ask whom I was consorting with and whither I was going."

"Be it so," said his fellow-traveller. "Betake you to the woods, and let me keep the path."

Accordingly the young man turned aside, but took care to watch his companion, who advanced softly along the road until he had come within a staff's length of the old dame. She, meanwhile, was making the best of her way, with singular speed for so aged a woman, and mumbling some indistinct words—a prayer, doubtless—as she went. The traveller put forth his staff and touched her withered neck with what seemed the serpent's tail.

"The devil!" screamed the pious old lady.

"Then Goody Cloyse knows her old friend?" observed the traveller, confronting her and leaning on his writhing stick.

"Ah, forsooth, and is it your worship indeed?" cried the good dame. "Yea, truly is it, and in the very image of my old gossip, Goodman Brown, the grandfather of the silly fellow that now is. But—would your worship believe it?—my broomstick hath strangely disappeared, stolen, as I suspect, by that unhanged witch, Goody Cory, and that, too, when I was all anointed with the juice of smallage, and cinquefoil, and wolf's bane."

"Mingled with fine wheat and the fat of a new-born babe," said the shape of old Goodman Brown.

"Ah, your worship knows the recipe," cried the old lady, cackling aloud. "So, as I was saying, being all ready for the meeting, and no horse to ride on, I made up my mind to foot it; for they tell me there is a nice young man to be taken into communion to-night. But now your good worship will lend me your arm, and we shall be there in a twinkling."

"That can hardly be," answered her friend. "I may not spare you my arm, Goody Cloyse; but here is my staff, if you will."

So saying, he threw it down at her feet, where, perhaps, it assumed life, being one of the rods which its owner had formerly lent to the Egyptian magi. Of this fact, however, Goodman Brown could not take cognizance. He had cast up his eyes in astonishment, and, looking down again, beheld neither Goody Cloyse nor the serpentine staff, but his fellow-traveller alone, who waited for him as calmly as if nothing had happened.

"That old woman taught me my catechism," said the young man; and there was a world of meaning in this simple comment.

They continued to walk onward, while the elder traveller exhorted his companion to make good speed and persevere in the path, discoursing so aptly that his arguments seemed rather to spring up in the bosom of his auditor than to be suggested by himself. As they went, he plucked a branch of maple to serve for a walking stick, and began to strip it of the twigs and little boughs, which were wet with evening dew. The moment his fingers touched them they became strangely withered and dried up as with a week's sunshine. Thus the pair proceeded, at a good free pace, until suddenly, in a gloomy hollow of the road, Goodman Brown sat himself down on the stump of a tree and refused to go any farther.

"Friend," said he, stubbornly, "my mind is made up. Not another step will I budge on this errand. What if a wretched old woman do choose to go to the devil when I thought she was going to heaven: is that any reason why I should quit my dear Faith and go after her?"

"You will think better of this by and by," said his acquaintance, composedly. "Sit here and rest yourself a while; and when you feel like moving again, there is my staff to help you along."

Without more words, he threw his companion the maple stick, and was as speedily out of sight as if he had vanished into the deepening gloom. The young man sat a few moments by the roadside, applauding himself greatly, and thinking with how clear a conscience he should meet the minister in his morning walk, nor shrink from the eye of good old Deacon Gookin. And what calm sleep would be his that very night, which was to have been spent so wickedly, but so purely and sweetly now, in the arms of Faith! Amidst these pleasant and praiseworthy meditations, Goodman Brown heard the tramp of horses along the road, and deemed it advisable to conceal himself within the verge of the forest, conscious of the guilty purpose that had brought him thither, though now so happily turned from it.

On came the hoof tramps and the voices of the riders, two grave old voices, conversing soberly as they drew near. These mingled sounds appeared to pass along the road, within a few yards of the young man's hiding-place; but, owing doubtless to the depth of the gloom at that particular spot, neither the travellers nor their steeds were visible. Though their figures brushed the small boughs by the wayside, it could not be seen that they intercepted, even for a moment, the faint gleam from the strip of bright sky athwart which they must have passed. Goodman Brown alternately crouched and stood on tiptoe, pulling aside the branches and thrusting forth his head as far as he durst without discerning so much as a shadow. It vexed him the more, because he could have sworn, were such a thing possible, that he recognized the voices of the minister and Deacon Gookin, jogging along quietly, as they were wont to do, when bound to some ordination or ecclesiastical council. While yet within hearing, one of the riders stopped to pluck a switch.

"Of the two, reverend sir," said the voice like the deacon's, "I had rather miss an ordination dinner than to-night's meeting. They tell me that some of our community are to be here from Falmouth and beyond, and others from

Connecticut and Rhode Island, besides several of the Indian powwows, who, after their fashion, know almost as much deviltry as the best of us. Moreover, there is a goodly young woman to be taken into communion."

"Mighty well, Deacon Gookin!" replied the solemn old tones of the minister. "Spur up, or we shall be late. Nothing can be done, you know, until I get on the ground."

The hoofs clattered again; and the voices, talking so strangely in the empty air, passed on through the forest, where no church had ever been gathered or solitary Christian prayed. Whither, then, could these holy men be journeying so deep into the heathen wilderness? Young Goodman Brown caught hold of a tree for support, being ready to sink down on the ground, faint and overburdened with the heavy sickness of his heart. He looked up to the sky, doubting whether there really was a heaven above him. Yet there was the blue arch, and the stars brightening in it.

"With heaven above and Faith below, I will yet stand firm against the devil!" cried Goodman Brown.

While he still gazed upward into the deep arch of the firmament and had lifted his hands to pray, a cloud, though no wind was stirring, hurried across the zenith and hid the brightening stars. The blue sky was still visible, except directly overhead, where this black mass of cloud was sweeping swiftly northward. Aloft in the air, as if from the depths of the cloud, came a confused and doubtful sound of voices. Once the listener fancied that he could distinguish the accents of towns-people of his own, men and women, both pious and ungodly, many of whom he had met at the communion table, and had seen others rioting at the tavern. The next moment, so indistinct were the sounds, he doubted whether he had heard aught but the murmur of the old forest, whispering without a wind. Then came a stronger swell of those familiar tones, heard daily in the sunshine at Salem village, but never until now from a cloud of night. There was one voice of a young woman, uttering lamentations, yet with an uncertain sorrow, and entreating for some favor, which, perhaps, it would grieve her to obtain; and all the unseen multitude, both saints and sinners, seemed to encourage her onward.

"Faith!" shouted Goodman Brown, in a voice of agony and desperation; and the echoes of the forest mocked him, crying, "Faith! Faith!" as if bewildered wretches were seeking her all through the wilderness.

The cry of grief, rage, and terror was yet piercing the night, when the unhappy husband held his breath for a response. There was a scream, drowned immediately in a louder murmur of voices, fading into far-off laughter, as the dark cloud swept away, leaving the clear and silent sky above Goodman Brown. But something fluttered lightly down through the air and caught on the branch of a tree. The young man seized it, and beheld a pink ribbon.

"My Faith is gone!" cried he, after one stupefied moment. "There is no good on earth; and sin is but a name. Come, devil; for to thee is this world given."

And, maddened with despair, so that he laughed loud and long, did Goodman Brown grasp his staff and set forth again, at such a rate that he seemed to fly along the forest path rather than to walk or run. The road grew wilder and drearier and more faintly traced, and vanished at length, leaving him in the heart of the dark wilderness, still rushing onward with the instinct that guides mortal man to evil. The whole forest was peopled with frightful sounds—the creaking of the trees, the howling of wild beasts, and the yell of Indians; while sometimes the wind tolled like a distant church bell, and sometimes gave a broad roar around the traveller, as if all Nature were laughing him to scorn. But he was himself the chief horror of the scene, and shrank not from its other horrors.

"Ha! ha! ha!" roared Goodman Brown when the wind laughed at him. "Let us hear which will laugh loudest. Think not to frighten me with your deviltry. Come witch, come wizard, come Indian powwow, come devil himself, and here comes Goodman Brown. You may as well fear him as he fear you."

In truth, all through the haunted forest there could be nothing more frightful than the figure of Goodman Brown. On he flew among the black pines, brandishing his staff with frenzied gestures, now giving vent to an inspiration of horrid blasphemy, and now shouting forth such laughter as set all the echoes of the forest laughing like demons around him. The fiend in his own shape is less hideous than when he rages in the breast of man. Thus sped the demoniac on his course, until, quivering among the trees, he saw a red light before him, as when the felled trunks and branches of a clearing have been set on fire, and throw up their lurid blaze against the sky, at the hour of midnight. He paused, in a lull of the tempest that had driven him onward, and heard the swell of what seemed a hymn, rolling solemnly from a distance with the weight of many voices. He knew the tune; it was a familiar one in the choir of the village meeting-house. The verse died heavily away, and was lengthened by a chorus, not of human voices, but of all the sounds of the benighted wilderness pealing in awful harmony together. Goodman Brown cried out, and his cry was lost to his own ear by its unison with the cry of the desert.

In the interval of silence he stole forward until the light glared full upon his eyes. At one extremity of an open space, hemmed in by the dark wall of the forest, arose a rock, bearing some rude, natural resemblance either to an altar or a pulpit, and surrounded by four blazing pines, their tops aflame, their stems untouched, like candles at an evening meeting. The mass of foliage that had overgrown the summit of the rock was all on fire, blazing high into the night and fitfully illuminating the whole field. Each pendent twig and leafy festoon was in a blaze. As the red light arose and fell, a numerous congregation alternately shone forth, then disappeared in shadow, and again grew, as it were, out of the darkness, peopling the heart of the solitary woods at once.

"A grave and dark-clad company," quoth Goodman Brown.

In truth they were such. Among them, quivering to and fro between gloom and splendor, appeared faces that would be seen next day at the council board of the province, and others which, Sabbath after Sabbath, looked devoutly heavenward, and benignantly over the crowded pews, from the holiest pulpits in the land. Some affirm that the lady of the governor was there. At least there were high dames well known to her, and wives of honored husbands, and widows, a great multitude, and ancient maidens, all of excellent repute, and fair young girls, who trembled lest their mothers should espy them. Either the sudden gleams of light flashing over the obscure field bedazzled Goodman Brown, or he recognized a score of the church members of Salem village famous for their especial sanctity. Good old Deacon Gookin had arrived, and waited at the skirts of that venerable saint, his revered pastor. But, irreverently consorting with these grave, reputable, and pious people, these elders of the church, these chaste dames and dewy virgins, there were men of dissolute lives and women of spotted fame, wretches given over to all mean and filthy vice, and suspected even of horrid crimes. It was strange to see that the good shrank not from the wicked, nor were the sinners abashed by the saints. Scattered also among their pale-faced enemies were the Indian priests, or powwows, who had often scared their native forest with more hideous incantations than any known to English witchcraft.

"But where is Faith?" thought Goodman Brown; and, as hope came into his heart, he trembled.

Another verse of the hymn arose, a slow and mournful strain, such as the pious love, but joined to words which expressed all that our nature can conceive of sin, and darkly hinted at far more. Unfathomable to mere mortals is the lore of fiends. Verse after verse was sung; and still the chorus of the desert swelled between like the deepest tone of a mighty organ; and with the final peal of that dreadful anthem there came a sound, as if the roaring wind, the rushing streams, the howling beasts, and every other voice of the unconcerted wilderness were mingling and according with the voice of guilty man in homage to the prince of all. The four blazing pines threw up a loftier flame, and obscurely discovered shapes and visages of horror on the smoke wreaths above the impious assembly. At the same moment the fire on the rock shot redly forth and formed a glowing arch above its base, where now appeared a figure. With reverence be it spoken, the figure bore no slight similitude, both in garb and manner, to some grave divine of the New England churches.

"Bring forth the converts!" cried a voice that echoed through the field and rolled into the forest.

At the word, Goodman Brown stepped forth from the shadow of the trees and approached the congregation, with whom he felt a loathful brotherhood by the sympathy of all that was wicked in his heart. He could have well-nigh sworn that the shape of his own dead father beckoned him to advance, looking downward from a smoke wreath, while a woman, with dim features of despair, threw out her hand to warn him back. Was it his mother? But he had no power to retreat one step, nor to resist, even in thought, when the minister and good old Deacon Gookin seized his arms and led him to the blazing rock. Thither came also the slender form of a veiled female, led between Goody Cloyse, that pious teacher of the catechism, and Martha Carrier, who had received the devil's promise to be queen of hell. A rampant hag was she. And there stood the proselytes beneath the canopy of fire.

"Welcome, my children," said the dark figure, "to the communion of your race. Ye have found thus young your nature and your destiny. My children, look behind you!"

They turned; and flashing forth, as it were, in a sheet of flame, the fiend worshippers were seen; the smile of welcome gleamed darkly on every visage.

"There," resumed the sable form, "are all whom ye have reverenced from youth. Ye deemed them holier than yourselves, and shrank from your own sin, contrasting it with their lives of righteousness and prayerful aspirations heavenward. Yet here are they all in my worshipping assembly. This night it shall be granted you to know their secret deeds: how hoary-bearded elders of the church have whispered wanton words to the young maids of their households; how many a woman, eager for widows' weeds, has given her husband a drink at bedtime and let him sleep his last sleep in her bosom; how beardless youths have made haste to inherit their fathers' wealth; and how fair damsels—blush not, sweet ones—have dug little graves in the garden, and bidden me, the sole guest to an infant's funeral. By the sympathy of your human hearts for sin ye shall scent out all the places—whether in church, bedchamber, street, field, or forest—where crime has been committed, and shall exult to behold the whole earth one stain of guilt, one mighty blood spot. Far more than this. It shall be yours to penetrate, in every bosom, the deep mystery of sin, the fountain of all wicked arts, and which inexhaustibly supplies more evil impulses than human power—than my power at its utmost—can make manifest in deeds. And now, my children, look upon each other."

They did so; and, by the blaze of the hell-kindled torches, the wretched man beheld his Faith, and the wife her husband, trembling before that unhallowed altar.

"Lo, there ye stand, my children," said the figure, in a deep and solemn tone, almost sad with its despairing awfulness, as if his once angelic nature could yet mourn for our miserable race. "Depending upon one another's hearts, ye had still hoped that virtue were not all a dream. Now are ye undeceived. Evil is the nature of mankind. Evil must be your only happiness. Welcome again, my children, to the communion of your race."

"Welcome," repeated the fiend worshippers, in one cry of despair and triumph.

And there they stood, the only pair, as it seemed, who were yet hesitating on the verge of wickedness in this dark world. A basin was hollowed, naturally, in the rock. Did it contain water, reddened by the lurid light? or was it blood? or, perchance, a liquid flame? Herein did the shape of evil dip his hand and prepare to lay the mark of baptism upon their foreheads, that they might be partakers of the mystery of sin, more conscious of the secret guilt of others, both in deed and thought, than they could now be of their own. The husband cast one look at his pale wife, and Faith at him. What polluted wretches would the next glance show them to each other, shuddering alike at what they disclosed and what they saw!

"Faith! Faith!" cried the husband, "look up to heaven, and resist the wicked one."

Whether Faith obeyed he knew not. Hardly had he spoken when he found himself amid calm night and solitude, listening to a roar of the wind which died heavily away through the forest. He staggered against the rock, and felt it chill and damp; while a hanging twig, that had been all on fire, besprinkled his cheek with the coldest dew.

The next morning young Goodman Brown came slowly into the street of Salem village, staring around him like a bewildered man. The good old minister was taking a walk along the graveyard to get an appetite for breakfast and meditate his sermon, and bestowed a blessing, as he passed, on Goodman Brown. He shrank from the venerable saint as if to avoid an anathema. Old Deacon Gookin was at domestic worship, and the holy words of his prayer were heard through the open window. "What God doth the wizard pray to?" quoth Goodman Brown. Goody Cloyse, that excellent old Christian, stood in the early sunshine at her own lattice, catechizing a little girl who had brought her a pint of morning's milk. Goodman Brown snatched away the child as from the grasp of the fiend himself. Turning the corner by the meeting-house, he spied the head of Faith, with the pink ribbons, gazing anxiously forth, and bursting into such joy at sight of him that she skipped along the street and almost kissed her husband before the whole village. But Goodman Brown looked sternly and sadly into her face, and passed on without a greeting.

Had Goodman Brown fallen asleep in the forest and only dreamed a wild dream of a witch-meeting?

Be it so if you will; but, alas! it was a dream of evil omen for young Goodman Brown. A stern, a sad, a darkly meditative, a distrustful, if not a desperate man did he become from the night of that fearful dream. On the Sabbath day, when the congregation were singing a holy psalm, he could not listen because an anthem of sin rushed loudly upon his ear and drowned all the blessed strain. When the minister spoke from the pulpit with power and fervid eloquence, and, with his hand on the open Bible, of the sacred truths of our religion, and of saint-like lives and triumphant deaths, and of future bliss or misery unutterable, then did Goodman Brown turn pale, dreading lest the roof should thunder down upon the gray blasphemer and his hearers. Often, waking suddenly at midnight, he shrank from the bosom of Faith; and at morning or eventide, when the family knelt down at prayer, he scowled and muttered to himself, and gazed sternly at his wife, and turned away. And when he had lived long, and was borne to his grave a hoary corpse, followed by Faith, an aged woman, and children and grandchildren, a goodly procession, besides neighbors not a few, they carved no hopeful verse upon his tombstone, for his dying hour was gloom.

THE TURN OF THE SCREW

Henry James

The story had held us, round the fire, sufficiently breathless, but except the obvious remark that it was gruesome, as, on Christmas Eve in an old house, a strange tale should essentially be, I remember no comment uttered till somebody happened to say that it was the only case he had met in which such a visitation had fallen on a child. The case, I may mention, was that of an apparition in just such an old house as had gathered us for the occasion—an appearance, of a dreadful kind, to a little boy sleeping in the room with his mother and waking her up in the terror of it; waking her not to dissipate his dread and soothe him to sleep again, but to encounter also, herself, before she had succeeded in doing so, the same sight that had shaken him. It was this observation that drew from Douglas—not immediately, but later in the evening—a reply that had the interesting consequence to which I call attention. Someone else told a story not particularly effective, which I saw he was not following. This I took for a sign that he had himself something to produce and that we should only have to wait. We waited in fact till two nights later; but that same evening, before we scattered, he brought out what was in his mind.

"I quite agree—in regard to Griffin's ghost, or whatever it was—that its appearing first to the little boy, at so tender an age, adds a particular touch. But it's not the first occurrence of its charming kind that I know to have involved a child. If the child gives the effect another turn of the screw, what do you say to *two* children—?"

"We say, of course," somebody exclaimed, "that they give two turns! Also that we want to hear about them."

I can see Douglas there before the fire, to which he had got up to present his back, looking down at his interlocutor with his hands in his pockets. "Nobody but me, till now, has ever heard. It's quite too horrible." This, naturally, was declared by several voices to give the thing the utmost price, and our friend, with quiet art, prepared his triumph by turning his eyes over the rest of us and going on: "It's beyond everything. Nothing at all that I know touches it."

"For sheer terror?" I remember asking.

He seemed to say it was not so simple as that; to be really at a loss how to qualify it. He passed his hand over his eyes, made a little wincing grimace. "For dreadful—dreadfulness!"

"Oh, how delicious!" cried one of the women.

He took no notice of her; he looked at me, but as if, instead of me, he saw what he spoke of. "For general uncanny ugliness and horror and pain."

"Well then," I said, "just sit right down and begin."

He turned round to the fire, gave a kick to a log, watched it an instant. Then as he faced us again: "I can't begin. I shall have to send to town." There was a unanimous groan at this, and much reproach; after which, in his preoccupied way, he explained. "The story's written. It's in a locked drawer—it has not been out for years. I could write to my man and enclose the key; he could send down the packet as he finds it." It was to me in particular that he appeared to propound this—appeared almost to appeal for aid not to hesitate. He had broken a thickness of ice, the formation of many a winter; had had his reasons for a long silence. The others resented postponement, but it was just his scruples that charmed me. I adjured him to write by the first post and to agree with us for an early hearing; then I asked him if the experience in question had been his own. To this his answer was prompt. "Oh, thank God, no!"

"And is the record yours? You took the thing down?"

"Nothing but the impression. I took that *here*"—he tapped his heart. "I've never lost it."

"Then your manuscript—?"

"Is in old, faded ink, and in the most beautiful hand." He hung fire again. "A woman's. She has been dead these twenty years. She sent me the pages in question before she died." They were all listening now, and of course there was somebody to be arch, or at any rate to draw the inference. But if he put the inference by without a smile it was also without irritation. "She was a most charming person, but she was ten years older than I. She was my sister's governess," he quietly said. "She was the most agreeable woman I've ever known in her position; she would have been worthy of any whatever. It was long ago, and this episode was long before. I was at Trinity, and I found her at home on my coming down the second summer. I was much there that year—it was a beautiful one; and we had, in her off-hours, some strolls and talks in the garden—talks in which she struck me as awfully clever and nice. Oh yes; don't grin: I liked her extremely and am glad to this day to think she liked me, too. If she hadn't she wouldn't have told me. She had never told anyone. It wasn't simply that she said so, but that I knew she hadn't. I was sure; I could see. You'll easily judge why when you hear."

"Because the thing had been such a scare?"

He continued to fix me. "You'll easily judge," he repeated: "You will."

I fixed him, too. "I see. She was in love."

He laughed for the first time. "You *are* acute. Yes, she was in love. That is, she had been. That came out—she couldn't tell her story without its coming out. I saw it, and she saw I saw it; but neither of us spoke of it. I remember the time and the place—the corner of the lawn, the shade of the great beeches and the long, hot summer afternoon. It wasn't a scene for a shudder; but oh—!" He quitted the fire and dropped back into his chair.

"You'll receive the packet Thursday morning?" I inquired.

"Probably not till the second post."

"Well then; after dinner—"

"You'll all meet me here?" He looked us round again. "Isn't anybody going?" It was almost the tone of hope.

"Everybody will stay!"

"*I* will"—and "I will!" cried the ladies whose departure had been fixed. Mrs. Griffin, however, expressed the need for a little more light. "Who was it she was in love with?"

"The story will tell," I took upon myself to reply.

"Oh, I can't wait for the story!"

"The story *won't* tell," said Douglas; "not in any literal, vulgar way."

"More's the pity, then. That's the only way I ever understand."

"Won't *you* tell, Douglas?" somebody else inquired.

He sprang to his feet again. "Yes—tomorrow. Now I must go to bed. Good night." And quickly catching up a candlestick, he left us slightly bewildered. From our end of the great brown hall we heard his step on the stair; whereupon Mrs. Griffin spoke. "Well, if I don't know who she was in love with, I know who *he* was."

"She was ten years older," said her husband.

"Raison de plus—at that age! But it's rather nice, his long reticence."

"Forty years!" Griffin put in.

"With this outbreak at last."

"The outbreak," I returned, "will make a tremendous occasion of Thursday night"; and everyone so agreed with me that, in the light of it, we lost all attention for everything else. The last story, however incomplete and like the mere opening of a serial, had been told; we handshook and "candlestuck," as somebody said, and went to bed.

I knew the next day that a letter containing the key had, by the first post, gone off to his London apartments; but in spite of—or perhaps just on account of—the eventual diffusion of this knowledge we quite let him alone till after dinner, till such an hour of the evening, in fact, as might best accord with the kind of emotion on which our hopes were fixed. Then he became as communicative as we could desire and indeed gave us his best reason for being so. We had it from him again before the fire in the hall, as we had had our mild wonders of the previous night. It appeared that the narrative he had promised to read us really required for a proper intelligence a few words of prologue. Let me say here distinctly, to have done with it, that this narrative, from an exact transcript of my own made much later, is what I shall presently give. Poor Douglas, before his death—when it was in sight—committed to me the manuscript that reached him on the third of these days and that, on the same spot, with immense effect, he began to read to our hushed little circle on the night of the fourth. The departing ladies who had said they would stay didn't, of course, thank heaven, stay: they departed, in consequence of arrangements made, in a rage of curiosity, as they professed, produced by the touches with which he had already worked us up. But that only made his little final auditory more compact and select, kept it, round the hearth, subject to a common thrill.

The first of these touches conveyed that the written statement took up the tale at a point after it had, in a manner, begun. The fact to be in possession of was therefore that his old friend, the youngest of several daughters of a poor country parson, had, at the age of twenty, on taking service for the first time in the schoolroom, come up to London, in trepidation, to answer in person an advertisement that had already placed her in brief correspondence with the advertiser. This person proved, on her presenting herself, for judgment, at a house in Harley Street, that impressed her as vast and imposing—this prospective patron proved a gentleman, a bachelor in the prime of life, such a figure as had never risen, save in a dream or an old novel, before a fluttered, anxious girl out of a Hampshire vicarage. One could easily fix his type; it never, happily, dies out. He was handsome and bold and pleasant, offhand and gay and kind. He struck her, inevitably, as gallant and splendid, but what took her most of all and gave her the courage she afterward showed was that he put the whole thing to her as a kind of favor, an obligation he should gratefully incur. She conceived him as rich, but as fearfully extravagant—saw him all in a glow of high fashion, of good looks, of expensive habits, of charming ways with women. He had for his own town residence a big house filled with the spoils of travel and the trophies of the chase; but it was to his country home, an old family place in Essex, that he wished her immediately to proceed.

He had been left, by the death of their parents in India, guardian to a small nephew and a small niece, children of a younger, a military brother, whom he had lost two years before. These children were, by the strangest of chances for a man in his position—a lone man without the right sort of experience or a grain of patience—very heavily on his hands. It had all been a great worry and, on his own part doubtless, a series of blunders, but he immensely pitied the poor chicks and had done all he could; had in particular sent them down to his other house, the proper place for them being of course the country, and kept them there, from the first, with the best people he could find to look after them, parting even with his own servants to wait on them and going down himself, whenever he might, to see how they were doing. The awkward thing was that they had practically no other relations and that his own affairs took up all his time. He had put them in possession of Bly, which was healthy and secure, and had placed at the head of their little establishment—but below stairs only—an excellent woman, Mrs. Grose, whom he was sure his visitor would like and who had formerly been maid to his mother. She was now housekeeper and was also acting for the time as superintendent to the little girl, of whom, without children of her own, she was, by good luck, extremely fond. There were plenty of people to help, but of course the young lady who should go down as governess would be in supreme authority. She would also have, in holidays, to look after the small boy, who had been for a term at school—young as he was to be sent, but what else could be done?—and who, as the holidays were about to begin, would be back from one day to the other. There had been for the two children at first a young lady whom they had had the misfortune to lose. She had done for them quite beautifully—she was a most respectable person—till her death, the great awkwardness of which had, precisely, left no alternative but the school for little Miles. Mrs. Grose, since then, in the way of manners and things, had done as she could for Flora; and there were, further, a cook, a housemaid, a dairywoman, an old pony, an old groom, and an old gardener, all likewise thoroughly respectable.

So far had Douglas presented his picture when someone put a question. "And what did the former governess die of?—of so much respectability?"

Our friend's answer was prompt. "That will come out. I don't anticipate."

"Excuse me—I thought that was just what you *are* doing."

"In her successor's place," I suggested, "I should have wished to learn if the office brought with it—"

"Necessary danger to life?" Douglas completed my thought. "She did wish to learn, and she did learn. You shall hear tomorrow what she learned. Meanwhile, of course, the prospect struck her as slightly grim. She was young, untried, nervous: it was a vision of serious duties and little company, of really great loneliness. She hesitated—took a couple of days to consult and consider. But the salary offered much exceeded her modest measure, and on a second interview she faced the music, she engaged." And Douglas, with this, made a pause that, for the benefit of the company, moved me to throw in—

"The moral of which was of course the seduction exercised by the splendid young man. She succumbed to it."

He got up and, as he had done the night before, went to the fire, gave a stir to a log with his foot, then stood a moment with his back to us. "She saw him only twice."

"Yes, but that's just the beauty of her passion."

A little to my surprise, on this, Douglas turned round to me. "It *was* the beauty of it. There were others," he went on, "who hadn't succumbed. He told her frankly all his difficulty—that for several applicants the conditions had been prohibitive. They were, somehow, simply afraid. It sounded dull—it sounded strange; and all the more so because of his main condition."

"Which was—?"

"That she should never trouble him—but never, never: neither appeal nor complain nor write about anything; only meet all questions herself, receive all moneys from his solicitor, take the whole thing over and let him alone. She promised to do this, and she mentioned to me that when, for a moment, disburdened, delighted, he held her hand, thanking her for the sacrifice, she already felt rewarded."

"But was that all her reward?" one of the ladies asked.

"She never saw him again."

"Oh!" said the lady; which, as our friend immediately left us again, was the only other word of importance contributed to the subject till, the next night, by the corner of the hearth, in the best chair, he opened the faded red cover of a thin old-fashioned gilt-edged album. The whole thing took indeed more nights than one, but on the first occasion the same lady put another question. "What is your title?"

"I haven't one."

"Oh, *I* have!" I said. But Douglas, without heeding me, had begun to read with a fine clearness that was like a rendering to the ear of the beauty of his author's hand.

I

I remember the whole beginning as a succession of flights and drops, a little seesaw of the right throbs and the wrong. After rising, in town, to meet his appeal, I had at all events a couple of very bad days—found myself doubtful again, felt indeed sure I had made a mistake. In this state of mind I spent the long hours of bumping, swinging coach that carried me to the stopping place at which I was to be met by a vehicle from the house. This convenience, I was told, had been ordered, and I found, toward the close of the June afternoon, a commodious fly in waiting for me. Driving at that hour, on a lovely day, through a country to which the summer sweetness seemed to offer me a friendly welcome, my fortitude mounted afresh and, as we turned into the avenue, encountered a reprieve that was probably but a proof of the point to which it had sunk. I suppose I had expected, or had dreaded, something so melancholy that what greeted me was a good surprise. I remember as a most pleasant impression the broad, clear front, its open windows and fresh curtains and the pair of maids looking out; I remember the lawn and the bright flowers and the crunch of my wheels on the gravel and the clustered treetops over which the rooks circled and cawed in the golden sky. The scene had a greatness that made it a different affair from my own scant home, and there immediately appeared at the door, with a little girl in her hand, a civil person who dropped me as decent a curtsy as if I had been the mistress or a distinguished visitor. I had received in Harley Street a narrower notion of the place, and that, as I recalled it, made me think the proprietor still more of a gentleman, suggested that what I was to enjoy might be something beyond his promise.

I had no drop again till the next day, for I was carried triumphantly through the following hours by my introduction to the younger of my pupils. The little girl who accompanied Mrs. Grose appeared to me on the spot a creature so charming as to make it a great fortune to have to do with her. She was the most beautiful child I had ever seen, and I afterward wondered that my employer had not told me more of her. I slept little that night—I was too much excited; and this astonished me, too, I recollect, remained with me, adding to my sense of the liberality with which I was treated. The large, impressive room, one of the best in the house, the great state bed, as I almost felt it, the full, figured draperies, the long glasses in which, for the first time, I could see myself from head to foot, all struck me—like the extraordinary charm of my small charge—as so many things thrown in. It was thrown in as well, from the first moment, that I should get on with Mrs. Grose in a relation over which, on my way, in the coach, I fear I had rather brooded. The only thing indeed that in this early outlook might have made me shrink again was the clear circumstance of her being so glad to see me. I perceived within half an hour that she was so glad—stout, simple, plain, clean, wholesome woman—as to be positively on her guard against showing it too much. I wondered even then a little why she should wish not to show it, and that, with reflection, with suspicion, might of course have made me uneasy.

But it was a comfort that there could be no uneasiness in a connection with anything so beatific as the radiant image of my little girl, the vision of whose angelic beauty had probably more than anything else to do with the restlessness that, before morning, made me several times rise and wander about my room to take in the whole picture and prospect; to watch, from my open window, the faint summer dawn, to look at such portions of the rest of the house as I could catch, and to listen, while, in the fading dusk, the first birds began to twitter, for the possible recurrence of a sound or two, less natural and not without, but within, that I had fancied I heard. There had been a moment when I believed I recognized, faint and far, the cry of a child; there had been another when I found myself just consciously starting as at the passage, before my door, of a light footstep. But these fancies were not marked enough not to be thrown off, and it is only in the light, or the gloom, I should rather say, of other and subsequent matters that they now come back to me. To watch, teach, "form" little Flora would too evidently be the making of a happy and useful life. It had been agreed between us downstairs that after this first occasion I should have her as a matter of course at night, her small white bed being already arranged, to that end, in my room. What I had undertaken was the whole care of her, and she had remained, just this last time, with Mrs. Grose only as an effect of our consideration for my inevitable strangeness and her natural timidity. In spite of this timidity—which the child herself, in the oddest way in the world, had been perfectly frank and brave about, allowing it, without a sign of uncomfortable consciousness, with the deep, sweet serenity indeed of one of Raphael's holy infants, to be discussed, to be imputed to her, and to determine us—I feel quite sure she would presently like me. It was part of what I already liked Mrs. Grose herself for, the pleasure I could see her feel in my admiration and wonder as I sat at supper with four tall candles and with my pupil, in a high chair and a bib, brightly facing me, between them, over bread and milk. There were naturally things that in Flora's presence could pass between us only as prodigious and gratified looks, obscure and roundabout allusions.

"And the little boy—does he look like her? Is he too so very remarkable?"

One wouldn't flatter a child. "Oh, miss, *most* remarkable. If you think well of this one!"—and she stood there with a plate in her hand, beaming at our companion, who looked from one of us to the other with placid heavenly eyes that contained nothing to check us.

"Yes; if I do—?"

"You *will* be carried away by the little gentleman!"

"Well, that, I think, is what I came for—to be carried away. I'm afraid, however," I remember feeling the impulse to add, "I'm rather easily carried away. I was carried away in London!"

I can still see Mrs. Grose's broad face as she took this in. "In Harley Street?"

"In Harley Street."

"Well, miss, you're not the first—and you won't be the last."

"Oh, I've no pretension," I could laugh, "to being the only one. My other pupil, at any rate, as I understand, comes back tomorrow?"

"Not tomorrow—Friday, miss. He arrives, as you did, by the coach, under care of the guard, and is to be met by the same carriage."

I forthwith expressed that the proper as well as the pleasant and friendly thing would be therefore that on the arrival of the public conveyance I should be in waiting for him with his little sister; an idea in which Mrs. Grose concurred so heartily that I somehow took her manner as a kind of comforting pledge—never falsified, thank heaven!—that we should on every question be quite at one. Oh, she was glad I was there!

What I felt the next day was, I suppose, nothing that could be fairly called a reaction from the cheer of my arrival; it was probably at the most only a slight oppression produced by a fuller measure of the scale, as I walked round them, gazed up at them, took them in, of my new circumstances. They had, as it were, an extent and mass for which I had not been prepared and in the presence of which I found myself, freshly, a little scared as well as a little proud. Lessons, in this agitation, certainly suffered some delay; I reflected that my first duty was, by the gentlest arts I could contrive, to win the child into the sense of knowing me. I spent the day with her out-of-doors; I arranged with her, to her great satisfaction, that it should be she, she only, who might show me the place. She showed it step by step and room by room and secret by secret, with droll, delightful, childish talk about it and with the result, in half an hour, of our becoming immense friends. Young as she was, I was struck, throughout our little tour, with her confidence and courage with the way, in empty chambers and dull corridors, on crooked staircases that made me pause and even on the summit of an old machicolated square tower that made me dizzy, her morning music, her disposition to tell me so many more things than she asked, rang out and led me on. I have not seen Bly since the day I left it, and I daresay that to my older and more informed eyes it would now appear sufficiently contracted. But as my little conductress, with her hair of gold and her frock of blue, danced before me round corners and pattered down passages, I had the view of a castle of romance inhabited by a rosy sprite, such a place as would somehow, for diversion of the young idea, take all color out of storybooks and fairytales. Wasn't it just a storybook over which I had fallen adoze and adream? No; it was a big, ugly, antique, but convenient house, embodying a few features of a building still older, half-replaced and half-utilized, in which I had the fancy of our being almost as lost as a handful of passengers in a great drifting ship. Well, I was, strangely, at the helm!

II

This came home to me when, two days later, I drove over with Flora to meet, as Mrs. Grose said, the little gentleman; and all the more for an incident that, presenting itself the second evening, had deeply disconcerted me. The first day had been, on the whole, as I have expressed, reassuring; but I was to see it wind up in keen apprehension. The postbag, that evening—it came late—contained a letter for me, which, however, in the hand of my employer, I found to be composed but of a few words enclosing another, addressed to himself, with a seal still unbroken. "This, I recognize, is from the headmaster, and the headmaster's an awful bore. Read him, please; deal with him; but mind you don't report. Not a word. I'm off!" I broke the seal with a great effort—so great a one that I was a long time coming to it; took the unopened missive at last up to my room and only attacked it just before going to bed. I had better have let it wait till morning, for it gave me a second sleepless night. With no counsel to take, the next day, I was full of distress; and it finally got so the better of me that I determined to open myself at least to Mrs. Grose.

"What does it mean? The child's dismissed his school."

She gave me a look that I remarked at the moment; then, visibly, with a quick blankness, seemed to try to take it back. "But aren't they all—?"

"Sent home—yes. But only for the holidays. Miles may never go back at all."

Consciously, under my attention, she reddened. "They won't take him?"

"They absolutely decline."

At this she raised her eyes, which she had turned from me; I saw them fill with good tears. "What has he done?"

I hesitated; then I judged best simply to hand her my letter—which, however, had the effect of making her, without taking it, simply put her hands behind her. She shook her head sadly. "Such things are not for me, miss."

My counselor couldn't read! I winced at my mistake, which I attenuated as I could, and opened my letter again to repeat it to her; then, faltering in the act and folding it up once more, I put it back in my pocket. "Is he really *bad*?"

The tears were still in her eyes. "Do the gentlemen say so?"

"They go into no particulars. They simply express their regret that it should be impossible to keep him. That can have only one meaning." Mrs. Grose listened with dumb emotion; she forbore to ask me what this meaning might be; so that, presently, to put the thing with some coherence and with the mere aid of her presence to my own mind, I went on: "That he's an injury to the others."

At this, with one of the quick turns of simple folk, she suddenly flamed up. "Master Miles! *Him* an injury?"

There was such a flood of good faith in it that, though I had not yet seen the child, my very fears made me jump to the absurdity of the idea. I found myself, to meet my friend the better, offering it, on the spot, sarcastically. "To his poor little innocent mates!"

"It's too dreadful," cried Mrs. Grose, "to say such cruel things! Why, he's scarce ten years old."

"Yes, yes; it would be incredible."

She was evidently grateful for such a profession. "See him, miss, first. *Then* believe it!" I felt forthwith a new impatience to see him; it was the beginning of a curiosity that, for all the next hours, was to deepen almost to pain. Mrs. Grose was aware, I could judge, of what she had produced in me, and she followed it up with assurance. "You might as well believe it of the little lady. Bless her," she added the next moment—"*look* at her!"

I turned and saw that Flora, whom, ten minutes before, I had established in the schoolroom with a sheet of white paper, a pencil, and a copy of nice "round o's," now presented herself to view at the open door. She expressed in her little way an extraordinary detachment from disagreeable duties, looking to me, however, with a great childish light that seemed to offer it as a mere result of the affection she had conceived for my person, which had rendered necessary that she should follow me. I needed nothing more than this to feel the full force of Mrs. Grose's comparison, and, catching my pupil in my arms, covered her with kisses in which there was a sob of atonement.

Nonetheless, the rest of the day I watched for further occasion to approach my colleague, especially as, toward evening, I began to fancy she rather sought to avoid me. I overtook her, I remember, on the staircase; we went down together, and at the bottom I detained her, holding her there with a hand on her arm. "I take what you said to me at noon as a declaration that you've never known him to be bad."

She threw back her head; she had clearly, by this time, and very honestly, adopted an attitude. "Oh, never known him—I don't pretend *that!*"

I was upset again. "Then you *have* known him—?"

"Yes indeed, miss, thank God!"

On reflection I accepted this. "You mean that a boy who never is—?"

"Is no boy for *me!*"

I held her tighter. "You like them with the spirit to be naughty?" Then, keeping pace with her answer, "So do I!" I eagerly brought out. "But not to the degree to contaminate—"

"To contaminate?"—my big word left her at a loss. I explained it. "To corrupt."

She stared, taking my meaning in; but it produced in her an odd laugh. "Are you afraid he'll corrupt *you*?" She put the question with such a fine bold humor that, with a laugh, a little silly doubtless, to match her own, I gave way for the time to the apprehension of ridicule.

But the next day, as the hour for my drive approached, I cropped up in another place. "What was the lady who was here before?"

"The last governess? She was also young and pretty—almost as young and almost as pretty, miss, even as you."

"Ah, then, I hope her youth and her beauty helped her!" I recollect throwing off. "He seems to like us young and pretty!"

"Oh, he *did*," Mrs. Grose assented: "it was the way he liked everyone!" She had no sooner spoken indeed than she caught herself up. "I mean that's *his* way—the master's."

I was struck. "But of whom did you speak first?"

She looked blank, but she colored. "Why, of *him*."

"Of the master?"

"Of who else?"

There was so obviously no one else that the next moment I had lost my impression of her having accidentally said more than she meant; and I merely asked what I wanted to know. "Did *she* see anything in the boy—?"

"That wasn't right? She never told me."

I had a scruple, but I overcame it. "Was she careful—particular?"

Mrs. Grose appeared to try to be conscientious. "About some things—yes."

"But not about all?"

Again she considered. "Well, miss—she's gone. I won't tell tales."

"I quite understand your feeling," I hastened to reply; but I thought it, after an instant, not opposed to this concession to pursue: "Did she die here?"

"No—she went off."

I don't know what there was in this brevity of Mrs. Grose's that struck me as ambiguous. "Went off to die?" Mrs. Grose looked straight out of the window, but I felt that, hypothetically, I had a right to know what young persons engaged for Bly were expected to do. "She was taken ill, you mean, and went home?"

"She was not taken ill, so far as appeared, in this house. She left it, at the end of the year, to go home, as she said, for a short holiday, to which the time she had put in had certainly given her a right. We had then a young woman—a nursemaid who had stayed on and who was a good girl and clever; and *she* took the children altogether for the interval. But our young lady never came back, and at the very moment I was expecting her I heard from the master that she was dead."

I turned this over. "But of what?"

"He never told me! But please, miss," said Mrs. Grose, "I must get to my work."

III

Her thus turning her back on me was fortunately not, for my just preoccupations, a snub that could check the growth of our mutual esteem. We met, after I had brought home little Miles, more intimately than ever on the ground of my stupefaction, my general emotion: so monstrous was I then ready to pronounce it that such a child as had now been revealed to me should be under an interdict. I was a little late on the scene, and I felt, as he stood wistfully looking out for me before the door of the inn at which the coach had put him down, that I had seen him, on the instant, without and within, in the great glow of freshness, the same positive fragrance of purity, in which I had, from the first moment, seen his little sister. He was incredibly beautiful, and Mrs. Grose had put her finger on it: everything but a sort of passion of tenderness for him was swept away by his presence. What I then and there took him to my heart for was something divine that I have never found to the same degree in any child—his indescribable little air of knowing nothing in the world but love. It would have been impossible to carry a bad name with a greater sweetness of innocence, and by the time I had got back to Bly with him I remained merely bewildered—so far, that is, as I was not outraged—by the sense of the horrible letter locked up in my room, in a drawer. As soon as I could compass a private word with Mrs. Grose I declared to her that it was grotesque.

She promptly understood me. "You mean the cruel charge—?"

"It doesn't live an instant. My dear woman, *look* at him!"

She smiled at my pretention to have discovered his charm. "I assure you, miss, I do nothing else! What will you say, then?" she immediately added.

"In answer to the letter?" I had made up my mind. "Nothing."

"And to his uncle?"

I was incisive. "Nothing."

"And to the boy himself?"

I was wonderful. "Nothing."

She gave with her apron a great wipe to her mouth. "Then I'll stand by you. We'll see it out."

"We'll see it out!" I ardently echoed, giving her my hand to make it a vow.

She held me there a moment, then whisked up her apron again with her detached hand. "Would you mind, miss, if I used the freedom—"

"To kiss me? No!" I took the good creature in my arms and, after we had embraced like sisters, felt still more fortified and indignant.

This, at all events, was for the time: a time so full that, as I recall the way it went, it reminds me of all the art I now need to make it a little distinct. What I look back at with amazement is the situation I accepted. I had undertaken, with my companion, to see it out, and I was under a charm, apparently, that could smooth away the extent and the far and difficult connections of such an effort. I was lifted aloft on a great wave of infatuation and pity. I found it simple, in my ignorance, my confusion, and perhaps my conceit, to assume that I could deal with a boy whose education for the world was all on the point of beginning. I am unable even to remember at this day what proposal I framed for the end of his holidays and the resumption of his studies. Lessons with me, indeed, that charming summer, we all had a theory that he was to have; but I now feel that, for weeks, the lessons must have been rather my own. I learned something—at first, certainly—that had not been one of the teachings of my small, smothered life; learned to be amused, and even amusing, and not to think for the morrow. It was the first time, in a manner, that I had known space and air and freedom, all the music of summer and all the mystery of nature. And then there was consideration—and consideration was sweet. Oh, it was a trap—not designed, but deep—to my imagination, to my delicacy, perhaps to my vanity; to whatever, in me, was most excitable. The best way to picture it all is to say that I was off my guard. They gave me so little trouble—they were of a gentleness so extraordinary. I used to speculate—but even this with a dim disconnectedness—as to how the rough future (for all futures are rough!) would handle them and might bruise them. They had the bloom of health and happiness; and yet, as if I had been in charge of a pair of little grandees, of princes of the blood, for whom everything, to be right, would have to be enclosed and protected, the only form that, in my fancy, the afteryears could take for them was that of a romantic, a really royal extension of the garden and the park. It may be, of course, above all, that what suddenly broke into this gives the previous time a charm of stillness—that hush in which something gathers or crouches. The change was actually like the spring of a beast.

In the first weeks the days were long; they often, at their finest, gave me what I used to call my own hour, the hour when, for my pupils, teatime and bedtime having come and gone, I had, before my final retirement, a small interval alone. Much as I liked my companions, this hour was the thing in the day I liked most; and I liked it best of all when, as the light faded—or rather, I should say, the day lingered and the last calls of the last birds sounded, in a flushed sky, from the old trees—I could take a turn into the grounds and enjoy, almost with a sense of property that amused and flattered me, the beauty and dignity of the place. It was a pleasure at these moments to feel myself tranquil and justified; doubtless, perhaps, also to reflect that by my discretion, my quiet good sense and general high propriety, I was giving pleasure—if he ever thought of it!—to the person to whose pressure I had responded. What I was doing was what he had earnestly hoped and directly asked of me, and that I *could*, after all, do it proved even a greater joy than I had expected. I daresay I fancied myself, in short, a remarkable young woman and took comfort in the faith that this would more publicly appear. Well, I needed to be remarkable to offer a front to the remarkable things that presently gave their first sign.

It was plump, one afternoon, in the middle of my very hour: the children were tucked away, and I had come out for my stroll. One of the thoughts that, as I don't in the least shrink now from noting, used to be with me in these wanderings was that it would be as charming as a charming story suddenly to meet someone. Someone would appear there at the turn of a path and would stand before me and smile and approve. I didn't ask more than that—I only asked that he should *know*; and the only way to be sure he knew would be to see it, and the kind light of it, in his handsome face. That was exactly present to me—by which I mean the face was—when, on the first of these occasions, at the end of a long June day, I stopped short on emerging from one of the plantations and coming into view of the house. What arrested me on the spot—and with a shock much greater than any vision had allowed for—was the sense that my imagination had, in a flash, turned real. He did stand there!—but high up, beyond the lawn and at the very top of the tower to which, on that first morning, little Flora had conducted me. This tower was one of a pair—square, incongruous, crenelated structures—that were distinguished, for some reason, though I could see little difference, as the new and the old. They flanked opposite ends of the house and were probably architectural absurdities, redeemed in a measure indeed by not being wholly disengaged nor of a height too pretentious, dating, in their gingerbread antiquity, from a romantic revival that was already a respectable past. I admired them, had fancies about them, for we could all profit in a degree, especially when they loomed through the dusk, by the grandeur of their actual battlements; yet it was not at such an elevation that the figure I had so often invoked seemed most in place.

It produced in me, this figure, in the clear twilight, I remember, two distinct gasps of emotion, which were, sharply, the shock of my first and that of my second surprise. My second was a violent perception of the mistake of my first: the man who met my eyes was not the person I had precipitately supposed. There came to me thus a bewilderment of vision of which, after these years, there is no living view that I can hope to give. An unknown man in a lonely place is a permitted object of fear to a young woman privately bred; and the figure that faced me was—a few more seconds assured me—as little anyone else I knew as it was the image that had been in my mind. I had not seen it in Harley Street—I had not seen it anywhere. The place, moreover, in the strangest way in the world, had, on the instant, and by the very fact of its appearance, become a solitude. To me at least, making my statement here with a deliberation with which I have never made it, the whole feeling of the moment returns. It was as if, while I took in—what I did take in—all the rest of the scene had been stricken with death. I can hear again, as I write, the intense hush in which the sounds of evening dropped. The rooks stopped cawing in the golden sky, and the friendly hour lost, for the minute, all its voice. But there was no other change in nature, unless indeed it were a change that I saw with a stranger sharpness. The gold was still in the sky, the clearness in the air, and the man who looked at me over the battlements was as definite as a picture in a frame. That's how I thought, with extraordinary quickness, of each person that he might have been and that he was not. We were confronted across our distance quite long enough for me to ask myself with intensity who then he was and to feel, as an effect of my inability to say, a wonder that in a few instants more became intense.

The great question, or one of these, is, afterward, I know, with regard to certain matters, the question of how long they have lasted. Well, this matter of mine, think what you will of it, lasted while I caught at a dozen possibilities, none of which made a difference for the better, that I could see, in there having been in the house—and for how long, above all?—a person of whom I was in ignorance. It lasted while I just bridled a little with the sense that my office demanded that there should be no such ignorance and no such person. It lasted while this visitant, at all events—and there was a touch of the strange freedom, as I remember, in the sign of familiarity of his wearing no hat—seemed to fix me, from his position, with just the question, just the scrutiny through the fading light, that his own presence provoked. We were too far apart to call to each other, but there was a moment at which, at shorter range, some challenge between us, breaking the hush, would have been the right result of our straight mutual stare. He was in one of the angles, the one away from the house, very erect, as it struck me, and with both hands on the ledge. So I saw him as I see the letters I form on this page; then, exactly, after a minute, as if to add to the spectacle, he slowly changed his place—passed, looking at me hard all the while, to the opposite corner of the platform. Yes, I had the sharpest sense that during this transit he never took his eyes from me, and I can see at this moment the way his hand, as he went, passed from one of the crenelations to the next. He stopped at the other corner, but less long, and even as he turned away still markedly fixed me. He turned away; that was all I knew.

IV

It was not that I didn't wait, on this occasion, for more, for I was rooted as deeply as I was shaken. Was there a "secret" at Bly—a mystery of Udolpho or an insane, an unmentionable relative kept in unsuspected confinement? I can't say how long I turned it over, or how long, in a confusion of curiosity and dread, I remained where I had had my collision; I only recall that when I re-entered the house darkness had quite closed in. Agitation, in the interval, certainly had held me and driven me, for I must, in circling about the place, have walked three miles; but I was to be, later on, so much more overwhelmed that this mere dawn of alarm was a comparatively human chill. The most singular part of it, in fact—singular as the rest had been—was the part I became, in the hall, aware of in meeting Mrs. Grose. This picture comes back to me in the general train—the impression, as I received it on my return, of the wide white panelled space, bright in the lamplight and with its portraits and red carpet, and of the good surprised look of my friend, which immediately told me she had missed me. It came to me straightway, under her contact, that, with plain heartiness, mere relieved anxiety at my appearance, she knew nothing whatever that could bear upon the incident I had there ready for her. I had not suspected in advance that her comfortable face would pull me up, and I somehow measured the importance of what I had seen by my thus finding myself hesitate to mention it. Scarce anything in the whole history seems to me so odd as this fact that my real beginning of fear was one, as I may say, with the instinct of sparing my companion. On the spot, accordingly, in the pleasant hall and with her eyes on me, I, for a reason that I couldn't then have phrased, achieved an inward resolution—offered a vague pretext for my lateness and, with the plea of the beauty of the night and of the heavy dew and wet feet, went as soon as possible to my room.

Here it was another affair; here, for many days after, it was a queer affair enough. There were hours, from day to day—or at least there were moments, snatched even from clear duties—when I had to shut myself up to think. It was not so much yet that I was more nervous than I could bear to be as that I was remarkably afraid of becoming so; for the truth I had now to turn over was, simply and clearly, the truth that I could arrive at no account whatever of the visitor with whom I had been so inexplicably and yet, as it seemed to me, so intimately concerned. It took little time to see that I could sound without forms of inquiry and without exciting remark any domestic complications. The shock I had suffered must have sharpened all my senses; I felt sure, at the end of three days and as the result of mere closer attention, that I had not been practiced upon by the servants nor made the object of any "game." Of whatever it was that I knew, nothing was known around me. There was but one sane inference: someone had taken a liberty rather gross. That was what, repeatedly, I dipped into my room and locked the door to say to myself. We had been, collectively, subject to an intrusion; some unscrupulous traveler, curious in old houses, had made his way in unobserved, enjoyed the prospect from the best point of view, and then stolen out as he came. If he had given me such a bold hard stare, that was but a part of his indiscretion. The good thing, after all, was that we should surely see no more of him.

This was not so good a thing, I admit, as not to leave me to judge that what, essentially, made nothing else much signify was simply my charming work. My charming work was just my life with Miles and Flora, and through nothing could I so like it as through feeling that I could throw myself into it in trouble. The attraction of my small charges was a constant joy, leading me to wonder afresh at the vanity of my original fears, the distaste I had begun by entertaining for the probable gray prose of my office. There was to be no gray prose, it appeared, and no long grind; so how could work not be charming that presented itself as daily beauty? It was all the romance of the nursery and the poetry of the schoolroom. I don't mean by this, of course, that we studied only fiction and verse; I mean I can express no otherwise the sort of interest my companions inspired. How can I describe that except by saying that instead of growing used to them—and it's a marvel for a governess: I call the sisterhood to witness!—I made constant fresh discoveries. There was one direction, assuredly, in which these discoveries stopped: deep obscurity continued to cover the region of the boy's conduct at school. It had been promptly given me, I have noted, to face that mystery without a pang. Perhaps even it would be nearer the truth to say that—without a word—he himself had cleared it up. He had made the whole charge absurd. My conclusion bloomed there with the real rose flush of his innocence: he was only too fine and fair for the little horrid, unclean school world, and he had paid a price for it. I reflected acutely that the sense of such differences, such superiorities of quality, always, on the part of the majority—which could include even stupid, sordid headmasters—turn infallibly to the vindictive.

Both the children had a gentleness (it was their only fault, and it never made Miles a muff) that kept them—how shall I express it?—almost impersonal and certainly quite unpunishable. They were like the cherubs of the anecdote, who had—morally, at any rate—nothing to whack! I remember feeling with Miles in especial as if he had had, as it were, no history. We expect of a small child a scant one, but there was in this beautiful little boy something extraordinarily sensitive, yet extraordinarily happy, that, more than in any creature of his age I have seen, struck me as beginning anew each day. He had never for a second suffered. I took this as a direct disproof of his having really been chastised. If he had been wicked he would have "caught" it, and I should have caught it by the rebound—I should have found the trace. I found nothing at all, and he was therefore an angel. He never spoke of his school, never mentioned a comrade or a master; and I, for my part, was quite too much disgusted to allude to them. Of course I was under the spell, and the wonderful part is that, even at the time, I perfectly knew I was. But I gave myself up to it; it was an antidote to any pain, and I had more pains than one. I was in receipt in these days of disturbing letters from home, where things were not going well. But with my children, what things in the world mattered? That was the question I used to put to my scrappy retirements. I was dazzled by their loveliness.

There was a Sunday—to get on—when it rained with such force and for so many hours that there could be no procession to church; in consequence of which, as the day declined, I had arranged with Mrs. Grose that, should the evening show improvement, we would attend together the late service. The rain happily stopped, and I prepared for our walk, which, through the park and by the good road to the village, would be a matter of twenty minutes. Coming downstairs to meet my colleague in the hall, I remembered a pair of gloves that had required three stitches and that had received them—with a publicity perhaps not edifying—while I sat with the children at their tea, served on Sundays, by exception, in that cold, clean temple of mahogany and brass, the "grown-up" dining room. The gloves had been dropped there, and I turned in to recover them. The day was gray enough, but the afternoon light still lingered, and it enabled me, on crossing the threshold, not only to recognize, on a chair near the wide window, then closed, the articles I wanted, but to become aware of a person on the other side of the window and looking straight in. One step into the room had sufficed; my vision was instantaneous; it was all there. The person looking straight in was the person who had already appeared to me. He appeared thus again with I won't say greater distinctness, for that was impossible, but with a nearness that represented a forward stride in our intercourse and made me, as I met him, catch my breath and turn cold. He was the same—he was the same, and seen, this time, as he had been seen before, from the waist up, the window, though the dining room was on the ground floor, not going down to the terrace on which he stood. His face was close to the glass, yet the effect of this better view was, strangely, only to show me how intense the former had been. He remained but a few seconds—long enough to convince me he also saw and recognized; but it was as if I had been looking at him for years and had known him always. Something, however, happened this time that had not happened before; his stare into my face, through the glass and across the room, was as deep and hard as then, but it quitted me for a moment during which I could still watch it, see it fix successively several other things. On the spot there came to me the added shock of a certitude that it was not for me he had come there. He had come for someone else.

The flash of this knowledge—for it was knowledge in the midst of dread—produced in me the most extraordinary effect, started as I stood there, a sudden vibration of duty and courage. I say courage because I was beyond all doubt already far gone. I bounded straight out of the door again, reached that of the house, got, in an instant, upon the drive, and, passing along the terrace as fast as I could rush, turned a corner and came full in sight. But it was in sight of nothing now—my visitor had vanished. I stopped, I almost dropped, with the real relief of this; but I took in the whole scene—I gave him time to reappear. I call it time, but how long was it? I can't speak to the purpose today of the duration of these things. That kind of measure must have left me: they couldn't have lasted as they actually appeared to me to last. The terrace and the whole place, the lawn and the garden beyond it, all I could see of the park, were empty with a great emptiness. There were shrubberies and big trees, but I remember the clear assurance I felt that none of them concealed him. He was there or was not there: not there if I didn't see him. I got hold of this; then, instinctively, instead of returning as I had come, went to the window. It was confusedly present to me that I ought to place myself where he had stood. I did so; I applied my face to the pane and looked, as he had looked, into the room. As if, at this moment, to show me exactly what his range had been, Mrs. Grose, as I had done for himself just before, came in from the hall. With this I had the full image of a repetition of what had already occurred. She saw me as I had seen my own visitant; she pulled up short as I had done; I gave her something of the shock that I had received. She turned white, and this made me ask myself if I had blanched as much. She stared, in short, and retreated on just *my* lines, and I knew she had then passed out and come round to me and that I should presently meet her. I remained where I was, and while I waited I thought of more things than one. But there's only one I take space to mention. I wondered why *she* should be scared.

V

Oh, she let me know as soon as, round the corner of the house, she loomed again into view. "What in the name of goodness is the matter—?" She was now flushed and out of breath.

I said nothing till she came quite near. "With me?" I must have made a wonderful face. "Do I show it?"

"You're as white as a sheet. You look awful."

I considered; I could meet on this, without scruple, any innocence. My need to respect the bloom of Mrs. Grose's had dropped, without a rustle, from my shoulders, and if I wavered for the instant it was not with what I kept back. I put out my hand to her and she took it; I held her hard a little, liking to feel her close to me. There was a kind of support in the shy heave of her surprise. "You came for me for church, of course, but I can't go."

"Has anything happened?"

"Yes. You must know now. Did I look very queer?"

"Through this window? Dreadful!"

"Well," I said, "I've been frightened." Mrs. Grose's eyes expressed plainly that *she* had no wish to be, yet also that she knew too well her place not to be ready to share with me any marked inconvenience. Oh, it was quite settled that she *must* share! "Just what you saw from the dining room a minute ago was the effect of that. What I saw—just before—was much worse."

Her hand tightened. "What was it?"

"An extraordinary man. Looking in."

"What extraordinary man?"

"I haven't the least idea."

Mrs. Grose gazed round us in vain. "Then where is he gone?"

"I know still less."

"Have you seen him before?"

"Yes—once. On the old tower."

She could only look at me harder. "Do you mean he's a stranger?"

"Oh, very much!"

"Yet you didn't tell me?"

"No—for reasons. But now that you've guessed—"

Mrs. Grose's round eyes encountered this charge. "Ah, I haven't guessed!" she said very simply. "How can I if *you* don't imagine?"

"I don't in the very least."

"You've seen him nowhere but on the tower?"

"And on this spot just now."

Mrs. Grose looked round again. "What was he doing on the tower?"

"Only standing there and looking down at me."

She thought a minute. "Was he a gentleman?"

I found I had no need to think. "No." She gazed in deeper wonder. "No."

"Then nobody about the place? Nobody from the village?"

"Nobody—nobody. I didn't tell you, but I made sure."

She breathed a vague relief: this was, oddly, so much to the good. It only went indeed a little way. "But if he isn't a gentleman—"

"What *is* he? He's a horror."

"A horror?"

"He's—God help me if I know what he is!"

Mrs. Grose looked round once more; she fixed her eyes on the duskier distance, then, pulling herself together, turned to me with abrupt inconsequence. "It's time we should be at church."

"Oh, I'm not fit for church!"

"Won't it do you good?"

"It won't do *them*—!" I nodded at the house.

"The children?"

"I can't leave them now."

"You're afraid—?"

I spoke boldly. "I'm afraid of *him*."

Mrs. Grose's large face showed me, at this, for the first time, the faraway faint glimmer of a consciousness more acute: I somehow made out in it the delayed dawn of an idea I myself had not given her and that was as yet quite obscure to me. It comes back to me that I thought instantly of this as something I could get from her; and I felt it to be connected with the desire she presently showed to know more. "When was it—on the tower?"

"About the middle of the month. At this same hour."

"Almost at dark," said Mrs. Grose.

"Oh, no, not nearly. I saw him as I see you."

"Then how did he get in?"

"And how did he get out?" I laughed. "I had no opportunity to ask him! This evening, you see," I pursued, "he has not been able to get in."

"He only peeps?"

"I hope it will be confined to that!" She had now let go my hand; she turned away a little. I waited an instant; then I brought out: "Go to church. Goodbye. I must watch."

Slowly she faced me again. "Do you fear for them?"

We met in another long look. "Don't *you*?" Instead of answering she came nearer to the window and, for a minute, applied her face to the glass. "You see how he could see," I meanwhile went on.

She didn't move. "How long was he here?"

"Till I came out. I came to meet him."

Mrs. Grose at last turned round, and there was still more in her face. "I couldn't have come out."

"Neither could I!" I laughed again. "But I did come. I have my duty."

"So have I mine," she replied; after which she added: "What is he like?"

"I've been dying to tell you. But he's like nobody."

"Nobody?" she echoed.

"He has no hat." Then seeing in her face that she already, in this, with a deeper dismay, found a touch of picture, I quickly added stroke to stroke. "He has red hair, very red, close-curling, and a pale face, long in shape, with straight, good features and little, rather queer whiskers that are as red as his hair. His eyebrows are, somehow, darker; they look particularly arched and as if they might move a good deal. His eyes are sharp, strange—awfully; but I only know clearly that they're rather small and very fixed. His mouth's wide, and his lips are thin, and except for his little whiskers he's quite clean-shaven. He gives me a sort of sense of looking like an actor."

"An actor!" It was impossible to resemble one less, at least, than Mrs. Grose at that moment.

"I've never seen one, but so I suppose them. He's tall, active, erect," I continued, "but never—no, never!—a gentleman."

My companion's face had blanched as I went on; her round eyes started and her mild mouth gaped. "A gentleman?" she gasped, confounded, stupefied: "a gentleman *he*?"

"You know him then?"

She visibly tried to hold herself. "But he *is* handsome?"

I saw the way to help her. "Remarkably!"

"And dressed—?"

"In somebody's clothes."

"They're smart, but they're not his own."

She broke into a breathless affirmative groan: "They're the master's!"

I caught it up. "You *do* know him?"

She faltered but a second. "Quint!" she cried.

"Quint?"

"Peter Quint—his own man, his valet, when he was here!"

"When the master was?"

Gaping still, but meeting me, she pieced it all together. "He never wore his hat, but he did wear—well, there were waistcoats missed. They were both here—last year. Then the master went, and Quint was alone."

I followed, but halting a little. "Alone?"

"Alone with *us*." Then, as from a deeper depth, "In charge," she added.

"And what became of him?"

She hung fire so long that I was still more mystified. "He went, too," she brought out at last.

"Went where?"

Her expression, at this, became extraordinary. "God knows where! He died."

"Died?" I almost shrieked.

She seemed fairly to square herself, plant herself more firmly to utter the wonder of it. "Yes. Mr. Quint is dead."

VI

It took of course more than that particular passage to place us together in presence of what we had now to live with as we could—my dreadful liability to impressions of the order so vividly exemplified, and my companion's knowledge, henceforth—a knowledge half consternation and half compassion—of that liability. There had been, this evening, after the revelation left me, for an hour, so prostrate—there had been, for either of us, no attendance on any service but a little service of tears and vows, of prayers and promises, a climax to the series of mutual challenges and pledges that had straightway ensued on our retreating together to the schoolroom and shutting ourselves up there to have everything out. The result of our having everything out was simply to reduce our situation to the last rigor of its elements. She herself had seen nothing, not the shadow of a shadow, and nobody in the house but the governess was in the governess's plight; yet she accepted without directly impugning my sanity the truth as I gave it to her, and ended by showing me, on this ground, an awestricken tenderness, an expression of the sense of my more than questionable privilege, of which the very breath has remained with me as that of the sweetest of human charities.

What was settled between us, accordingly, that night, was that we thought we might bear things together; and I was not even sure that, in spite of her exemption, it was she who had the best of the burden. I knew at this hour, I think, as well as I knew later, what I was capable of meeting to shelter my pupils; but it took me some time to be wholly sure of what my honest ally was prepared for to keep terms with so compromising a contract. I was queer company enough—quite as queer as the company I received; but as I trace over what we went through I see how much common ground we must have found in the one idea that, by good fortune, *could* steady us. It was the idea, the second movement, that led me straight out, as I may say, of the inner chamber of my dread. I could take the air in the court, at least, and there Mrs. Grose could join me. Perfectly can I recall now the particular way strength came to me before we separated for the night. We had gone over and over every feature of what I had seen.

"He was looking for someone else, you say—someone who was not you?"

"He was looking for little Miles." A portentous clearness now possessed me. "That's whom he was looking for."

"But how do you know?"

"I know, I know, I know!" My exaltation grew. "And you know, my dear!"

She didn't deny this, but I required, I felt, not even so much telling as that. She resumed in a moment, at any rate: "What if he should see him?"

"Little Miles? That's what he wants!"

She looked immensely scared again. "The child?"

"Heaven forbid! The man. He wants to appear to *them*." That he might was an awful conception, and yet, somehow, I could keep it at bay; which, moreover, as we lingered there, was what I succeeded in practically proving. I had an absolute certainty that I should see again what I had already seen, but something within me said that by offering myself bravely as the sole subject of such experience, by accepting, by inviting, by surmounting it all, I should serve as an expiatory victim and guard the tranquility of my companions.

The children, in especial, I should thus fence about and absolutely save. I recall one of the last things I said that night to Mrs. Grose.

"It does strike me that my pupils have never mentioned—"

She looked at me hard as I musingly pulled up. "His having been here and the time they were with him?"

"The time they were with him, and his name, his presence, his history, in any way."

"Oh, the little lady doesn't remember. She never heard or knew."

"The circumstances of his death?" I thought with some intensity. "Perhaps not. But Miles would remember—Miles would know."

"Ah, don't try him!" broke from Mrs. Grose.

I returned her the look she had given me. "Don't be afraid." I continued to think. "It *is* rather odd."

"That he has never spoken of him?"

"Never by the least allusion. And you tell me they were 'great friends'?"

"Oh, it wasn't *him!*" Mrs. Grose with emphasis declared. "It was Quint's own fancy. To play with him, I mean—to spoil him." She paused a moment; then she added: "Quint was much too free."

This gave me, straight from my vision of his face—such a face!—a sudden sickness of disgust. "Too free with *my* boy?"

"Too free with everyone!"

I forbore, for the moment, to analyze this description further than by the reflection that a part of it applied to several of the members of the household, of the half-dozen maids and men who were still of our small colony. But there was everything, for our apprehension, in the lucky fact that no discomfortable legend, no perturbation of scullions, had ever, within anyone's memory attached to the kind old place. It had neither bad name nor ill fame, and Mrs. Grose, most apparently, only desired to cling to me and to quake in silence. I even put her, the very last thing of all, to the test. It was when, at midnight, she had her hand on the schoolroom door to take leave. "I have it from you then—for it's of great importance—that he was definitely and admittedly bad?"

"Oh, not admittedly. I knew it—but the master didn't."

"And you never told him?"

"Well, he didn't like tale-bearing—he hated complaints. He was terribly short with anything of that kind, and if people were all right to *him*—"

"He wouldn't be bothered with more?" This squared well enough with my impressions of him: he was not a trouble-loving gentleman, nor so very particular perhaps about some of the company *he* kept. All the same, I pressed my interlocutress. "I promise you I would have told!"

She felt my discrimination. "I daresay I was wrong. But, really, I was afraid."

"Afraid of what?"

"Of things that man could do. Quint was so clever—he was so deep."

I took this in still more than, probably, I showed. "You weren't afraid of anything else? Not of his effect—?"

"His effect?" she repeated with a face of anguish and waiting while I faltered.

"On innocent little precious lives. They were in your charge."

"No, they were not in mine!" she roundly and distressfully returned. "The master believed in him and placed him here because he was supposed not to be well and the country air so good for him. So he had everything to say. Yes"—she let me have it—"even about *them*."

"Them—that creature?" I had to smother a kind of howl. "And you could bear it!"

"No. I couldn't—and I can't now!" And the poor woman burst into tears.

A rigid control, from the next day, was, as I have said, to follow them; yet how often and how passionately, for a week, we came back together to the subject! Much as we had discussed it that Sunday night, I was, in the immediate later hours in especial—for it may be imagined whether I slept—still haunted with the shadow of something she had not told me. I myself had kept back nothing, but there was a word Mrs. Grose had kept back. I was sure, moreover, by morning, that this was not from a failure of frankness, but because on every side there were fears. It seems to me indeed, in retrospect, that by the time the morrow's sun was high I had restlessly read into the fact before us almost all the meaning they were to receive from subsequent and more cruel occurrences. What they gave me above all was just the sinister figure of the living man—the dead one would keep awhile!—and of the months he had continuously passed at Bly, which, added up, made a formidable stretch. The limit of this evil time had arrived only when, on the dawn of a winter's morning, Peter Quint was found, by a laborer going to early work, stone dead on the road from the village: a catastrophe explained—superficially at least—by a visible wound to his head; such a wound as might have been produced—and as, on the final evidence, *had* been—by a fatal slip, in the dark and after leaving the public house, on the steepish icy slope, a wrong path altogether, at the bottom of which he lay. The icy slope, the turn mistaken at night and in liquor, accounted for much—practically, in the end and after the inquest and boundless chatter, for everything; but there had been matters in his life—strange passages and perils, secret disorders, vices more than suspected—that would have accounted for a good deal more.

I scarce know how to put my story into words that shall be a credible picture of my state of mind; but I was in these days literally able to find a joy in the extraordinary flight of heroism the occasion demanded of me. I now saw that I had been asked for a service admirable and difficult; and there would be a greatness in letting it be seen—oh, in the right quarter!—that I could succeed where many another girl might have failed. It was an immense help to me—I confess I rather applaud myself as I look back!—that I saw my service so strongly and so simply. I was there to protect and defend the little creatures in the world the most bereaved and the most lovable, the appeal of whose helplessness had suddenly become only too explicit, a deep, constant ache of one's own committed heart. We were cut off, really, together; we were united in our danger. They had nothing but me, and I—well, I *had* them. It was in short a magnificent chance. This chance presented itself to me in an image richly material. I was a screen—I was to stand before them. The more I saw, the less they would. I began to watch them in a stifled suspense, a disguised excitement that might well, had it continued too long, have turned to something like madness. What saved me, as I now see, was that it turned to something else altogether. It didn't last as suspense—it was superseded by horrible proofs. Proofs, I say, yes—from the moment I really took hold.

This moment dated from an afternoon hour that I happened to spend in the grounds with the younger of my pupils alone. We had left Miles indoors, on the red cushion of a deep window seat; he had wished to finish a book, and I had been glad to encourage a purpose so laudable in a young man whose only defect was an occasional excess of the restless. His sister, on the contrary, had been alert to come out, and I strolled with her half an hour, seeking the shade, for the sun was still high and the day exceptionally warm. I was aware afresh, with her, as we went, of how, like her brother, she contrived—it was the charming thing in both children—to let me alone without appearing to drop me and to accompany me without appearing to surround. They were never importunate and yet never listless. My attention to them all really went to seeing them amuse themselves immensely without me: this was a spectacle they seemed actively to prepare and that engaged me as an active admirer. I walked in a world of their invention—they had no occasion whatever to draw upon mine; so that my time was taken only with being, for them, some remarkable person or thing that the game of the moment required and that was merely, thanks to my superior, my exalted stamp, a happy and highly distinguished sinecure. I forget what I was on the present occasion; I only remember that I was something very important and very quiet and that Flora was playing very hard. We were on the edge of the lake, and, as we had lately begun geography, the lake was the Sea of Azof.

Suddenly, in these circumstances, I became aware that, on the other side of the Sea of Azof, we had an interested spectator. The way this knowledge gathered in me was the strangest thing in the world—the strangest, that is, except the very much stranger in which it quickly merged itself. I had sat down with a piece of work—for I was something or other that could sit—on the old stone bench which overlooked the pond; and in this position I began to take in with certitude, and yet without direct vision, the presence, at a distance, of a third person. The old trees, the thick shrubbery, made a great and pleasant shade, but it was all suffused with the brightness of the hot, still hour. There was no ambiguity in anything; none whatever, at least, in the conviction I from one moment to another found myself forming as to what I should see straight before me and across the lake as a consequence of raising my eyes. They were attached at this juncture to the stitching in which I was engaged, and I can feel once more the spasm of my effort not to move them till I should so have steadied myself as to be able to make up my mind what to do. There was an alien object in view—a figure whose right of presence I instantly, passionately questioned. I recollect counting over perfectly the possibilities, reminding myself that nothing was more natural, for instance, then the appearance of one of the men about the place, or even of a messenger, a postman, or a tradesman's boy, from the village. That reminder had as little effect on my practical certitude as I was conscious—still even without looking—of its having upon the character and attitude of our visitor. Nothing was more natural than that these things should be the other things that they absolutely were not.

Of the positive identity of the apparition I would assure myself as soon as the small clock of my courage should have ticked out the right second; meanwhile, with an effort that was already sharp enough, I transferred my eyes straight to little Flora, who, at the moment, was about ten yards away. My heart had stood still for an instant with the wonder and terror of the question whether she too would see; and I held my breath while I waited for what a cry from her, what some sudden innocent sign either of interest or of alarm, would tell me. I waited, but nothing came; then, in the first place—and there is something more dire in this, I feel, than in anything I have to relate—I was determined by a sense that, within a minute, all sounds from her had previously dropped; and, in the second, by the circumstance that, also within the minute, she had, in her play, turned her back to the water. This was her attitude when I at last looked at her—looked with the confirmed conviction that we were still, together, under direct personal notice. She had picked up a small flat piece of wood, which happened to have in it a little hole that had evidently suggested to her the idea of sticking in another fragment that might figure as a mast and make the thing a boat. This second morsel, as I watched her, she was very markedly and intently attempting to tighten in its place. My apprehension of what she was doing sustained me so that after some seconds I felt I was ready for more. Then I again shifted my eyes—I faced what I had to face.

VII

I got hold of Mrs. Grose as soon after this as I could; and I can give no intelligible account of how I fought out the interval. Yet I still hear myself cry as I fairly threw myself into her arms: "They know—it's too monstrous: they know, they *know!*"

"And what on earth—?" I felt her incredulity as she held me.

"Why, all that we know—and heaven knows what else besides!" Then, as she released me, I made it out to her, made it out perhaps only now with full coherency even to myself. "Two hours ago, in the garden"—I could scarce articulate—"Flora *saw!*"

Mrs. Grose took it as she might have taken a blow in the stomach. "She has told you?" she panted.

"Not a word—that's the horror. She kept it to herself! The child of eight, *that* child!" Unutterable still, for me, was the stupefaction of it.

Mrs. Grose, of course, could only gape the wider. "Then how do you know?"

"I was there—I saw with my eyes: saw that she was perfectly aware."

"Do you mean aware of *him*?"

"No—of *her*." I was conscious as I spoke that I looked prodigious things, for I got the slow reflection of them in my companion's face. "Another person—this time; but a figure of quite as unmistakable horror and evil: a woman in black, pale and dreadful—with such an air also, and such a face!—on the other side of the lake. I was there with the child—quiet for the hour; and in the midst of it she came."

"Came how—from where?"

"From where they come from! She just appeared and stood there—but not so near."

"And without coming nearer?"

"Oh, for the effect and the feeling, she might have been as close as you!"

My friend, with an odd impulse, fell back a step. "Was she someone you've never seen?"

"Yes. But someone the child has. Someone *you* have." Then, to show how I had thought it all out: "My predecessor—the one who died."

"Miss Jessel?"

"Miss Jessel. You don't believe me?" I pressed.

She turned right and left in her distress. "How can you be sure?"

This drew from me, in the state of my nerves, a flash of impatience. "Then ask Flora—*she's* sure!" But I had no sooner spoken than I caught myself up. "No, for God's sake, *don't!* She'll say she isn't—she'll lie!"

Mrs. Grose was not too bewildered instinctively to protest. "Ah, how *can* you?"

"Because I'm clear. Flora doesn't want me to know."

"It's only then to spare you."

"No, no—there are depths, depths! The more I go over it, the more I see in it, and the more I see in it, the more I fear. I don't know what I *don't* see—what I *don't* fear!"

Mrs. Grose tried to keep up with me. "You mean you're afraid of seeing her again?"

"Oh, no; that's nothing—now!" Then I explained. "It's of not *seeing* her."

But my companion only looked wan. "I don't understand you."

"Why, it's that the child may keep it up—and that the child assuredly *will*—without my knowing it."

At the image of this possibility Mrs. Grose for a moment collapsed, yet presently to pull herself together again, as if from the positive force of the sense of what, should we yield an inch, there would really be to give way to. "Dear, dear—we must keep our heads! And after all, if she doesn't mind it—!" She even tried a grim joke. "Perhaps she likes it!"

"Likes *such* things—a scrap of an infant!"

"Isn't it just a proof of her blessed innocence?" my friend bravely inquired.

She brought me, for the instant, almost round. "Oh, we must clutch at *that*—we must cling to it! If it isn't a proof of what you say, it's a proof of—God knows what! For the woman's a horror of horrors."

Mrs. Grose, at this, fixed her eyes a minute on the ground; then at last raising them, "Tell me how you know," she said.

"Then you admit it's what she was?" I cried.

"Tell me how you know," my friend simply repeated.

"Know? By seeing her! By the way she looked."

"At you, do you mean—so wickedly?"

"Dear me, no—I could have borne that. She gave me never a glance. She only fixed the child."

Mrs. Grose tried to see it. "Fixed her?"

"Ah, with such awful eyes!"

She stared at mine as if they might really have resembled them. "Do you mean of dislike?"

"God help us, no. Of something much worse."

"Worse than dislike?"—this left her indeed at a loss.

"With a determination—indescribable. With a kind of fury of intention."

I made her turn pale. "Intention?"

"To get hold of her." Mrs. Grose—her eyes just lingering on mine—gave a shudder and walked to the window; and while she stood there looking out I completed my statement. "*That's* what Flora knows."

After a little she turned round. "The person was in black, you say?"

"In mourning—rather poor, almost shabby. But—yes—with extraordinary beauty." I now recognized to what I had at last, stroke by stroke, brought the victim of my confidence, for she quite visibly weighed this. "Oh, handsome—very, very," I insisted; "wonderfully handsome. But infamous."

She slowly came back to me. "Miss Jessel—was infamous." She once more took my hand in both her own, holding it as tight as if to fortify me against the increase of alarm I might draw from this disclosure. "They were both infamous," she finally said.

So, for a little, we faced it once more together; and I found absolutely a degree of help in seeing it now so straight. "I appreciate," I said, "the great decency of your not having hitherto spoken; but the time has certainly come to give me the whole thing." She appeared to assent to this, but still only in silence; seeing which I went on: "I must have it now. Of what did she die? Come, there was something between them."

"There was everything."

"In spite of the difference—?"

"Oh, of their rank, their condition"—she brought it woefully out. "She was a lady."

I turned it over; I again saw. "Yes—she was a lady."

"And he so dreadfully below," said Mrs. Grose.

I felt that I doubtless needn't press too hard, in such company, on the place of a servant in the scale; but there was nothing to prevent an acceptance of my companion's own measure of my predecessor's abasement. There was a way to deal with that, and I dealt; the more readily for my full vision—on the evidence—of our employer's late clever, good-looking "own" man; impudent, assured, spoiled, depraved. "The fellow was a hound."

Mrs. Grose considered as if it were perhaps a little a case for a sense of shades. "I've never seen one like him. He did what he wished."

"With *her*?"

"With them all."

It was as if now in my friend's own eyes Miss Jessel had again appeared. I seemed at any rate, for an instant, to see their evocation of her as distinctly as I had seen her by the pond; and I brought out with decision: "It must have been also what she wished!"

Mrs. Grose's face signified that it had been indeed, but she said at the same time: "Poor woman—she paid for it!"

"Then you do know what she died of?" I asked.

"No—I know nothing. I wanted not to know; I was glad enough I didn't; and I thanked heaven she was well out of this!"

"Yet you had, then, your idea—"

"Of her real reason for leaving? Oh, yes—as to that. She couldn't have stayed. Fancy it here—for a governess! And afterward I imagined—and I still imagine. And what I imagine is dreadful."

"Not so dreadful as what *I* do," I replied; on which I must have shown her—as I was indeed but too conscious—a front of miserable defeat. It brought out again all her compassion for me, and at the renewed touch of her kindness my power to resist broke down. I burst, as I had, the other time, made her burst, into tears; she took me to her motherly breast, and my lamentation overflowed. "I don't do it!" I sobbed in despair; "I don't save or shield them! It's far worse than I dreamed—they're lost!"

VIII

What I had said to Mrs. Grose was true enough: there were in the matter I had put before her depths and possibilities that I lacked resolution to sound; so that when we met once more in the wonder of it we were of a common mind about the duty of resistance to extravagant fancies. We were to keep our heads if we should keep nothing else—difficult indeed as that might be in the face of what, in our prodigious experience, was least to be questioned. Late that night, while the house slept, we had another talk in my room, when she went all the way with me as to its being beyond doubt that I had seen exactly what I had seen. To hold her perfectly in the pinch of that, I found I had only to ask her how, if I had "made it up," I came to be able to give, of each of the persons appearing to me, a picture disclosing, to the last detail, their special marks—a portrait on the exhibition of which she had instantly recognized and named them. She wished of course—small blame to her!—to sink the whole subject; and I was quick to assure her that my own interest in it had now violently taken the form of a search for the way to escape from it. I encountered her on the ground of a probability that with recurrence—for recurrence we took for granted—I should get used to my danger, distinctly professing that my personal exposure had suddenly become the least of my discomforts. It was my new suspicion that was intolerable; and yet even to this complication the later hours of the day had brought a little ease.

On leaving her, after my first outbreak, I had of course returned to my pupils, associating the right remedy for my dismay with that sense of their charm which I had already found to be a thing I could positively cultivate and which had never failed me yet. I had simply, in other words, plunged afresh into Flora's special society and there become aware—it was almost a luxury!—that she could put her little conscious hand straight upon the spot that ached. She had looked at me in sweet speculation and then had accused me to my face of having "cried." I had supposed I had brushed away the ugly signs: but I could literally—for the time, at all events—rejoice, under this fathomless charity, that they had not entirely disappeared. To gaze into the depths of blue of the child's eyes and pronounce their loveliness a trick of premature cunning was to be guilty of a cynicism in preference to which I naturally preferred to abjure my judgment and, so far as might be, my agitation. I couldn't abjure for merely wanting to, but I could repeat to Mrs. Grose—as I did there, over and over, in the small hours—that with their voices in the air, their pressure on one's heart, and their fragrant faces against one's cheek, everything fell to the ground but their incapacity and their beauty. It was a pity that, somehow, to settle this once for all, I had equally to re-enumerate the signs of subtlety that, in the afternoon, by the lake had made a miracle of my show of self-possession. It was a pity to be obliged to reinvestigate the certitude of the moment itself and repeat how it had come to me as a revelation that the inconceivable communion I then surprised was a matter, for either party, of habit. It was a pity that I should have had to quaver out again the reasons for my not having, in my delusion, so much as questioned that the little girl saw our visitant even as I actually saw Mrs. Grose herself, and that she wanted, by just so much as she did thus see, to make me suppose she didn't, and at the same time, without showing anything, arrive at a guess as to whether I myself did! It was a pity that I needed once more to describe the portentous little activity by which she sought to divert my attention—the perceptible increase of movement, the greater intensity of play, the singing, the gabbling of nonsense, and the invitation to romp.

Yet if I had not indulged, to prove there was nothing in it, in this review, I should have missed the two or three dim elements of comfort that still remained to me. I should not for instance have been able to asseverate to my friend that I was certain—which was so much to the good—that I at least had not betrayed myself. I should not have been prompted, by stress of need, by desperation of mind—I scarce know what to call it—to invoke such further aid to intelligence as might spring from pushing my colleague fairly to the wall. She had told me, bit by bit, under pressure, a great deal; but a small shifty spot on the wrong side of it all still sometimes brushed my brow like the wing of a bat; and I remember how on this occasion—for the sleeping house and the concentration alike of our danger and our watch seemed to help—I felt the importance of giving the last jerk to the curtain. "I don't believe anything so horrible," I recollect saying; "no, let us put it definitely, my dear, that I don't. But if I did, you know, there's a thing I should require now, just without sparing you the least bit more—oh, not a scrap, come!—to get out of you. What was it you had in mind when, in our distress, before Miles came back, over the letter from his school, you said, under my insistence, that you didn't pretend for him that he had not literally ever been 'bad'? He has not literally 'ever,' in these weeks that I myself have lived with him and so closely watched him; he has been an imperturbable little prodigy of delightful, lovable goodness. Therefore you might perfectly have made the claim for him if you had not, as it happened, seen an exception to take. What was your exception, and to what passage in your personal observation of him did you refer?"

It was a dreadfully austere inquiry, but levity was not our note, and, at any rate, before the gray dawn admonished us to separate I had got my answer. What my friend had had in mind proved to be immensely to the purpose. It was neither more nor less than the circumstance that for a period of several months Quint and the boy had been perpetually together. It was in fact the very appropriate truth that she had ventured to criticize the propriety, to hint at the incongruity, of so close an alliance, and even to go so far on the subject as a frank overture to Miss Jessel. Miss Jessel had, with a most strange manner, requested her to mind her business, and the good woman had, on this, directly approached little Miles. What she had said to him, since I pressed, was that she liked to see young gentlemen not forget their station.

I pressed again, of course, at this. "You reminded him that Quint was only a base menial?"

"As you might say! And it was his answer, for one thing, that was bad."

"And for another thing?" I waited. "He repeated your words to Quint?"

"No, not that. It's just what he *wouldn't!*" she could still impress upon me. "I was sure, at any rate," she added, "that he didn't. But he denied certain occasions."

"What occasions?"

"When they had been about together quite as if Quint were his tutor—and a very grand one—and Miss Jessel only for the little lady. When he had gone off with the fellow, I mean, and spent hours with him."

"He then prevaricated about it—he said he hadn't?" Her assent was clear enough to cause me to add in a moment: "I see. He lied."

"Oh!" Mrs. Grose mumbled. This was a suggestion that it didn't matter; which indeed she backed up by a further remark. "You see, after all, Miss Jessel didn't mind. She didn't forbid him."

I considered. "Did he put that to you as a justification?"

At this she dropped again. "No, he never spoke of it."

"Never mentioned her in connection with Quint?"

She saw, visibly flushing, where I was coming out. "Well, he didn't show anything. He denied," she repeated; "he denied."

Lord, how I pressed her now! "So that you could see he knew what was between the two wretches?"

"I don't know—I don't know!" the poor woman groaned.

"You do know, you dear thing," I replied; "only you haven't my dreadful boldness of mind, and you keep back, out of timidity and modesty and delicacy, even the impression that, in the past, when you had, without my aid, to flounder about in silence, most of all made you miserable. But I shall get it out of you yet! There was something in the boy that suggested to you," I continued, "that he covered and concealed their relation."

"Oh, he couldn't prevent—"

"Your learning the truth? I daresay! But, heavens," I fell, with vehemence, athinking, "what it shows that they must, to that extent, have succeeded in making of him!"

"Ah, nothing that's not nice *now!*" Mrs. Grose lugubriously pleaded.

"I don't wonder you looked queer," I persisted, "when I mentioned to you the letter from his school!"

"I doubt if I looked as queer as you!" she retorted with homely force. "And if he was so bad then as that comes to, how is he such an angel now?"

"Yes, indeed—and if he was a fiend at school! How, how, how? Well," I said in my torment, "you must put it to me again, but I shall not be able to tell you for some days. Only, put it to me again!" I cried in a way that made my friend stare. "There are directions in which I must not for the present let myself go." Meanwhile I returned to her first example—the one to which she had just previously referred—of the boy's happy capacity for an occasional slip. "If Quint—on your remonstrance at the time you speak of—was a base menial, one of the things Miles said to you, I find myself guessing, was that you were another." Again her admission was so adequate that I continued: "And you forgave him that?"

"Wouldn't *you*?"

"Oh, yes!" And we exchanged there, in the stillness, a sound of the oddest amusement. Then I went on: "At all events, while he was with the man—"

"Miss Flora was with the woman. It suited them all!"

It suited me, too, I felt, only too well; by which I mean that it suited exactly the particularly deadly view I was in the very act of forbidding myself to entertain. But I so far succeeded in checking the expression of this view that I will throw, just here, no further light on it than may be offered by the mention of my final observation to Mrs. Grose. "His having lied and been impudent are, I confess, less engaging specimens than I had hoped to have from you of the outbreak in him of the little natural man. Still," I mused, "They must do, for they make me feel more than ever that I must watch."

It made me blush, the next minute, to see in my friend's face how much more unreservedly she had forgiven him than her anecdote struck me as presenting to my own tenderness an occasion for doing. This came out when, at the schoolroom door, she quitted me. "Surely you don't accuse *him*—"

"Of carrying on an intercourse that he conceals from me? Ah, remember that, until further evidence, I now accuse nobody." Then, before shutting her out to go, by another passage, to her own place, "I must just wait," I wound up.

IX

I waited and waited, and the days, as they elapsed, took something from my consternation. A very few of them, in fact, passing, in constant sight of my pupils, without a fresh incident, sufficed to give to grievous fancies and even to odious memories a kind of brush of the sponge. I have spoken of the surrender to their extraordinary childish grace as a thing I could actively cultivate, and it may be imagined if I neglected now to address myself to this source for whatever it would yield. Stranger than I can express, certainly, was the effort to struggle against my new lights; it would doubtless have been, however, a greater tension still had it not been so frequently successful. I used to wonder how my little charges could help guessing that I thought strange things about them; and the circumstances that these things only made them more interesting was not by itself a direct aid to keeping them in the dark. I trembled lest they should see that they were so immensely more interesting. Putting things at the worst, at all events, as in meditation I so often did, any clouding of their innocence could only be—blameless and foredoomed as they were—a reason the more for taking risks. There were moments when, by an irresistible impulse, I found myself catching them up and pressing them to my heart. As soon as I had done so I used to say to myself: "What will they think of that? Doesn't it betray too much?" It would have been easy to get into a sad, wild tangle about how much I might betray; but the real account, I feel, of the hours of peace that I could still enjoy was that the immediate charm of my companions was a beguilement still effective even under the shadow of the possibility that it was studied. For if it occurred to me that I might occasionally excite suspicion by the little outbreaks of my sharper passion for them, so too I remember wondering if I mightn't see a queerness in the traceable increase of their own demonstrations.

They were at this period extravagantly and preternaturally fond of me; which, after all, I could reflect, was no more than a graceful response in children perpetually bowed over and hugged. The homage of which they were so lavish succeeded, in truth, for my nerves, quite as well as if I never appeared to myself, as I may say, literally to catch them at a purpose in it. They had never, I think, wanted to do so many things for their poor protectress; I mean—though they got their lessons better and better, which was naturally what would please her most—in the way of diverting, entertaining, surprising her; reading her passages, telling her stories, acting her charades, pouncing out at her, in disguises, as animals and historical characters, and above all astonishing her by the "pieces" they had secretly got by heart and could interminably recite. I should never get to the bottom—were I to let myself go even now—of the prodigious private commentary, all under still more private correction, with which, in these days, I overscored their full hours. They had shown me from the first a facility for everything, a general faculty which, taking a fresh start, achieved remarkable flights. They got their little tasks as if they loved them, and indulged, from the mere exuberance of the gift, in the most unimposed little miracles of memory. They not only popped out at me as tigers and as Romans, but as Shakespeareans, astronomers, and navigators. This was so singularly the case that it had presumably much to do with the fact as to which, at the present day, I am at a loss for a different explanation: I allude to my unnatural composure on the subject of another school for Miles. What I remember is that I was content not, for the time, to open the question, and that contentment must have sprung from the sense of his perpetually striking show of cleverness. He was too clever for a bad governess, for a parson's daughter, to spoil; and the strangest if not the brightest thread in the pensive embroidery I just spoke of was the impression I might have got, if I had dared to work it out, that he was under some influence operating in his small intellectual life as a tremendous incitement.

If it was easy to reflect, however, that such a boy could postpone school, it was at least as marked that for such a boy to have been "kicked out" by a schoolmaster was a mystification without end. Let me add that in their company now—and I was careful almost never to be out of it—I could follow no scent very far. We lived in a cloud of music and love and success and private theatricals. The musical sense in each of the children was of the quickest, but the elder in especial had a marvelous knack of catching and repeating. The schoolroom piano broke into all gruesome fancies; and when that failed there were confabulations in corners, with a sequel of one of them going out in the highest spirits in order to "come in" as something new. I had had brothers myself, and it was no revelation to me that little girls could be slavish idolaters of little boys. What surpassed everything was that there was a little boy in the world who could have for the inferior age, sex, and intelligence so fine a consideration. They were extraordinarily at one, and to say that they never either quarreled or complained is to make the note of praise coarse for their quality of sweetness. Sometimes, indeed, when I dropped into coarseness, I perhaps came across traces of little understandings between them by which one of them should keep me occupied while the other slipped away. There is a naive side, I suppose, in all diplomacy; but if my pupils practiced upon me, it was surely with the minimum of grossness. It was all in the other quarter that, after a lull, the grossness broke out.

I find that I really hang back; but I must take my plunge. In going on with the record of what was hideous at Bly, I not only challenge the most liberal faith—for which I little care; but—and this is another matter—I renew what I myself suffered, I again push my way through it to the end. There came suddenly an hour after which, as I look back, the affair seems to me to have been all pure suffering; but I have at least reached the heart of it, and the straightest road out is doubtless to advance. One evening—with nothing to lead up or to prepare it—I felt the cold touch of the impression that had breathed on me the night of my arrival and which, much lighter then, as I have mentioned, I should probably have made little of in memory had my subsequent sojourn been less agitated. I had not gone to bed; I sat reading by a couple of candles. There was a roomful of old books at Bly—last-century fiction, some of it, which, to the extent of a distinctly deprecated renown, but never to so much as that of a stray specimen, had reached the sequestered home and appealed to the unavowed curiosity of my youth. I remember that the book I had in my hand was Fielding's *Amelia*; also that I was wholly awake. I recall further both a general conviction that it was horribly late and a particular objection to looking at my watch. I figure, finally, that the white curtain draping, in the fashion of those days, the head of Flora's little bed, shrouded, as I had assured myself long before, the perfection of childish rest. I recollect in short that, though I was deeply interested in my author, I found myself, at the turn of a page and with his spell all scattered, looking straight up from him and hard at the door of my room. There was a moment during which I listened, reminded of the faint sense I had had, the first night, of there being something undefinably astir in the house, and noted the soft breath of the open casement just move the half-drawn blind. Then, with all the marks of a deliberation that must have seemed magnificent had there been anyone to admire it, I laid down my book, rose to my feet, and, taking a candle, went straight out of the room and, from the passage, on which my light made little impression, noiselessly closed and locked the door.

I can say now neither what determined nor what guided me, but I went straight along the lobby, holding my candle high, till I came within sight of the tall window that presided over the great turn of the staircase. At this point I precipitately found myself aware of three things. They were practically simultaneous, yet they had flashes of succession. My candle, under a bold flourish, went out, and I perceived, by the uncovered window, that the yielding dusk of earliest morning rendered it unnecessary. Without it, the next instant, I saw that there was someone on the stair. I speak of sequences, but I required no lapse of seconds to stiffen myself for a third encounter with Quint. The apparition had reached the landing halfway up and was therefore on the spot nearest the window, where at sight of me, it stopped short and fixed me exactly as it had fixed me from the tower and from the garden. He knew me as well as I knew him; and so, in the cold, faint twilight, with a glimmer in the high glass and another on the polish of the oak stair below, we faced each other in our common intensity. He was absolutely, on this occasion, a living, detestable, dangerous presence. But that was not the wonder of wonders; I reserve this distinction for quite another circumstance: the circumstance that dread had unmistakably quitted me and that there was nothing in me there that didn't meet and measure him.

I had plenty of anguish after that extraordinary moment, but I had, thank God, no terror. And he knew I had not—I found myself at the end of an instant magnificently aware of this. I felt, in a fierce rigor of confidence, that if I stood my ground a minute I should cease—for the time, at least—to have him to reckon with; and during the minute, accordingly, the thing was as human and hideous as a real interview: hideous just because it was human, as human as to have met alone, in the small hours, in a sleeping house, some enemy, some adventurer, some criminal. It was the dead silence of our long gaze at such close quarters that gave the whole horror, huge as it was, its only note of the unnatural. If I had met a murderer in such a place and at such an hour, we still at least would have spoken. Something would have passed, in life, between us; if nothing had passed, one of us would have moved. The moment was so prolonged that it would have taken but little more to make me doubt if even I were in life. I can't express what followed it save by saying that the silence itself—which was indeed in a manner an attestation of my strength—became the element into which I saw the figure disappear; in which I definitely saw it turn as I might have seen the low wretch to which it had once belonged turn on receipt of an order, and pass, with my eyes on the villainous back that no hunch could have more disfigured, straight down the staircase and into the darkness in which the next bend was lost.

X

I remained awhile at the top of the stair, but with the effect presently of understanding that when my visitor had gone, he had gone: then I returned to my room. The foremost thing I saw there by the light of the candle I had left burning was that Flora's little bed was empty; and on this I caught my breath with all the terror that, five minutes before, I had been able to resist. I dashed at the place in which I had left her lying and over which (for the small silk counterpane and the sheets were disarranged) the white curtains had been deceivingly pulled forward; then my step, to my unutterable relief, produced an answering sound: I perceived an agitation of the window blind, and the child, ducking down, emerged rosily from the other side of it. She stood there in so much of her candor and so little of her nightgown, with her pink bare feet and the golden glow of her curls. She looked intensely grave, and I had never had such a sense of losing an advantage acquired (the thrill of which had just been so prodigious) as on my consciousness that she addressed me with a reproach. "You naughty: where have you been?"—instead of challenging her own irregularity I found myself arraigned and explaining. She herself explained, for that matter, with the loveliest, eagerest simplicity. She had known suddenly, as she lay there, that I was out of the room, and had jumped up to see what had become of me. I had dropped, with the joy of her reappearance, back into my chair—feeling then, and then only, a little faint; and she had pattered straight over to me, thrown herself upon my knee, given herself to be held with the flame of the candle full in the wonderful little face that was still flushed with sleep. I remember closing my eyes an instant, yieldingly, consciously, as before the excess of something beautiful that shone out of the blue of her own. "You were looking for me out of the window?" I said. "You thought I might be walking in the grounds?"

"Well, you know, I thought someone was"—she never blanched as she smiled out that at me.

Oh, how I looked at her now! "And did you see anyone?"

"Ah, *no*!" she returned, almost with the full privilege of childish inconsequence, resentfully, though with a long sweetness in her little drawl of the negative.

At that moment, in the state of my nerves, I absolutely believed she lied; and if I once more closed my eyes it was before the dazzle of the three or four possible ways in which I might take this up. One of these, for a moment, tempted me with such singular intensity that, to withstand it, I must have gripped my little girl with a spasm that, wonderfully, she submitted to without a cry or a sign of fright. Why not break out at her on the spot and have it all over?—give it to her straight in her lovely little lighted face? "You see, you see, you *know* that you do and that you already quite suspect I believe it; therefore, why not frankly confess it to me, so that we may at least live with it together and learn perhaps, in the strangeness of our fate, where we are and what it means?" This solicitation dropped, alas, as it came: if I could immediately have succumbed to it I might have spared myself—well, you'll see what. Instead of succumbing I sprang again to my feet, looked at her bed, and took a helpless middle way. "Why did you pull the curtain over the place to make me think you were still there?"

Flora luminously considered; after which, with her little divine smile: "Because I don't like to frighten you!"

"But if I had, by your idea, gone out—?"

She absolutely declined to be puzzled; she turned her eyes to the flame of the candle as if the question were as irrelevant, or at any rate as impersonal, as Mrs. Marcet or nine-times-nine. "Oh, but you know," she quite adequately answered, "that you might come back, you dear, and that you *have!*" And after a little, when she had got into bed, I had, for a long time, by almost sitting on her to hold her hand, to prove that I recognized the pertinence of my return.

You may imagine the general complexion, from that moment, of my nights. I repeatedly sat up till I didn't know when; I selected moments when my roommate unmistakably slept, and, stealing out, took noiseless turns in the passage and even pushed as far as to where I had last met Quint. But I never met him there again; and I may as well say at once that I on no other occasion saw him in the house. I just missed, on the staircase, on the other hand, a different adventure. Looking down it from the top I once recognized the presence of a woman seated on one of the lower steps with her back presented to me, her body half-bowed and her head, in an attitude of woe, in her hands. I had been there but an instant, however, when she vanished without looking round at me. I knew, nonetheless, exactly what dreadful face she had to show; and I wondered whether, if instead of being above I had been below, I should have had, for going up, the same nerve I had lately shown Quint. Well, there continued to be plenty of chance for nerve. On the eleventh night after my latest encounter with that gentleman—they were all numbered now—I had an alarm that perilously skirted it and that indeed, from the particular quality of its unexpectedness, proved quite my sharpest shock. It was precisely the first night during this series that, weary with watching, I had felt that I might again without laxity lay myself down at my old hour. I slept immediately and, as I afterward knew, till about one o'clock; but when I woke it was to sit straight up, as completely roused as if a hand had shook me. I had left a light burning, but it was now out, and I felt an instant certainty that Flora had extinguished it. This brought me to my feet and straight, in the darkness, to her bed, which I found she had left. A glance at the window enlightened me further, and the striking of a match completed the picture.

The child had again got up—this time blowing out the taper, and had again, for some purpose of observation or response, squeezed in behind the blind and was peering out into the night. That she now saw—as she had not, I had satisfied myself, the previous time—was proved to me by the fact that she was disturbed neither by my reillumination nor by the haste I made to get into slippers and into a wrap. Hidden, protected, absorbed, she evidently rested on the sill—the casement opened forward—and gave herself up. There was a great still moon to help her, and this fact had counted in my quick decision. She was face to face with the apparition we had met at the lake, and could now communicate with it as she had not then been able to do. What I, on my side, had to care for was, without disturbing her, to reach, from the corridor, some other window in the same quarter. I got to the door without her hearing me; I got out of it, closed it, and listened, from the other side, for some sound from her. While I stood in the passage I had my eyes on her brother's door, which was but ten steps off and which, indescribably, produced in me a renewal of the strange impulse that I lately spoke of as my temptation. What if I should go straight in and march to *his* window?—what if, by risking to his boyish bewilderment a revelation of my motive, I should throw across the rest of the mystery the long halter of my boldness?

This thought held me sufficiently to make me cross to his threshold and pause again. I preternaturally listened; I figured to myself what might portentously be; I wondered if his bed were also empty and he too were secretly at watch. It was a deep, soundless minute, at the end of which my impulse failed. He was quiet; he might be innocent; the risk was hideous; I turned away. There was a figure in the grounds—a figure prowling for a sight, the visitor with whom Flora was engaged; but it was not the visitor most concerned with my boy. I hesitated afresh, but on other grounds and only for a few seconds; then I had made my choice. There were empty rooms at Bly, and it was only a question of choosing the right one. The right one suddenly presented itself to me as the lower one—though high above the gardens—in the solid corner of the house that I have spoken of as the old tower. This was a large, square chamber, arranged with some state as a bedroom, the extravagant size of which made it so inconvenient that it had not for years, though kept by Mrs. Grose in exemplary order, been occupied. I had often admired it and I knew my way about in it; I had only, after just faltering at the first chill gloom of its disuse, to pass across it and unbolt as quietly as I could one of the shutters. Achieving this transit, I uncovered the glass without a sound and, applying my face to the pane, was able, the darkness without being much less than within, to see that I commanded the right direction. Then I saw something more. The moon made the night extraordinarily penetrable and showed me on the lawn a person, diminished by distance, who stood there motionless and as if fascinated, looking up to where I had appeared—looking, that is, not so much straight at me as at something that was apparently above me. There was clearly another person above me—there was a person on the tower; but the presence on the lawn was not in the least what I had conceived and had confidently hurried to meet. The presence on the lawn—I felt sick as I made it out—was poor little Miles himself.

XI

It was not till late next day that I spoke to Mrs. Grose; the rigor with which I kept my pupils in sight making it often difficult to meet her privately, and the more as we each felt the importance of not provoking—on the part of the servants quite as much as on that of the children—any suspicion of a secret flurry or that of a discussion of mysteries. I drew a great security in this particular from her mere smooth aspect. There was nothing in her fresh face to pass on to others my horrible confidences. She believed me, I was sure, absolutely: if she hadn't I don't know what would have become of me, for I couldn't have borne the business alone. But she was a magnificent monument to the blessing of a want of imagination, and if she could see in our little charges nothing but their beauty and amiability, their happiness and cleverness, she had no direct communication with the sources of my trouble. If they had been at all visibly blighted or battered, she would doubtless have grown, on tracing it back, haggard enough to match them; as matters stood, however, I could feel her, when she surveyed them, with her large white arms folded and the habit of serenity in all her look, thank the Lord's mercy that if they were ruined the pieces would still serve. Flights of fancy gave place, in her mind, to a steady fireside glow, and I had already begun to perceive how, with the development of the conviction that—as time went on without a public accident—our young things could, after all, look out for themselves, she addressed her greatest solicitude to the sad case presented by their instructress. That, for myself, was a sound simplification: I could engage that, to the world, my face should tell no tales, but it would have been, in the conditions, an immense added strain to find myself anxious about hers.

At the hour I now speak of she had joined me, under pressure, on the terrace, where, with the lapse of the season, the afternoon sun was now agreeable; and we sat there together while, before us, at a distance, but within call if we wished, the children strolled to and fro in one of their most manageable moods. They moved slowly, in unison, below us, over the lawn, the boy, as they went, reading aloud from a storybook and passing his arm round his sister to keep her quite in touch. Mrs. Grose watched them with positive placidity; then I caught the suppressed intellectual creak with which she conscientiously turned to take from me a view of the back of the tapestry. I had made her a receptacle of lurid things, but there was an odd recognition of my superiority—my accomplishments and my function—in her patience under my pain. She offered her mind to my disclosures as, had I wished to mix a witch's broth and proposed it with assurance, she would have held out a large clean saucepan. This had become thoroughly her attitude by the time that, in my recital of the events of the night, I reached the point of what Miles had said to me when, after seeing him, at such a monstrous hour, almost on the very spot where he happened now to be, I had gone down to bring him in; choosing then, at the window, with a concentrated need of not alarming the house, rather that method than a signal more resonant. I had left her meanwhile in little doubt of my small hope of representing with success even to her actual sympathy my sense of the real splendor of the little inspiration with which, after I had got him into the house, the boy met my final articulate challenge. As soon as I appeared in the moonlight on the terrace, he had come to me as straight as possible; on which I had taken his hand without a word and led him, through the dark spaces, up the staircase where Quint had so hungrily hovered for him, along the lobby where I had listened and trembled, and so to his forsaken room.

Not a sound, on the way, had passed between us, and I had wondered—oh, how I had wondered!—if he were groping about in his little mind for something plausible and not too grotesque. It would tax his invention, certainly, and I felt, this time, over his real embarrassment, a curious thrill of triumph. It was a sharp trap for the inscrutable! He couldn't play any longer at innocence; so how the deuce would he get out of it? There beat in me indeed, with the passionate throb of this question an equal dumb appeal as to how the deuce *I* should. I was confronted at last, as never yet, with all the risk attached even now to sounding my own horrid note. I remember in fact that as we pushed into his little chamber, where the bed had not been slept in at all and the window, uncovered to the moonlight, made the place so clear that there was no need of striking a match—I remember how I suddenly dropped, sank upon the edge of the bed from the force of the idea that he must know how he really, as they say, "had" me. He could do what he liked, with all his cleverness to help him, so long as I should continue to defer to the old tradition of the criminality of those caretakers of the young who minister to superstitions and fears. He "had" me indeed, and in a cleft stick; for who would ever absolve me, who would consent that I should go unhung, if, by the faintest tremor of an overture, I were the first to introduce into our perfect intercourse an element so dire? No, no: it was useless to attempt to convey to Mrs. Grose, just as it is scarcely less so to attempt to suggest here, how, in our short, stiff brush in the dark, he fairly shook me with admiration. I was of course thoroughly kind and merciful; never, never yet had I placed on his little shoulders hands of such tenderness as those with which, while I rested against the bed, I held him there well under fire. I had no alternative but, in form at least, to put it to him.

"You must tell me now—and all the truth. What did you go out for? What were you doing there?"

I can still see his wonderful smile, the whites of his beautiful eyes, and the uncovering of his little teeth shine to me in the dusk. "If I tell you why, will you understand?" My heart, at this, leaped into my mouth. *Would* he tell me why? I found no sound on my lips to press it, and I was aware of replying only with a vague, repeated, grimacing nod. He was gentleness itself, and while I wagged my head at him he stood there more than ever a little fairy prince. It was his brightness indeed that gave me a respite. Would it be so great if he were really going to tell me? "Well," he said at last, "just exactly in order that you should do this."

"Do what?"

"Think me—for a change—*bad!*" I shall never forget the sweetness and gaiety with which he brought out the word, nor how, on top of it, he bent forward and kissed me. It was practically the end of everything. I met his kiss and I had to make, while I folded him for a minute in my arms, the most stupendous effort not to cry. He had given exactly the account of himself that permitted least of my going behind it, and it was only with the effect of confirming my acceptance of it that, as I presently glanced about the room, I could say—

"Then you didn't undress at all?"

He fairly glittered in the gloom. "Not at all. I sat up and read."

"And when did you go down?"

"At midnight. When I'm bad I *am* bad!"

"I see, I see—it's charming. But how could you be sure I would know it?"

"Oh, I arranged that with Flora." His answers rang out with a readiness! "She was to get up and look out."

"Which is what she did do." It was I who fell into the trap!

"So she disturbed you, and, to see what she was looking at, you also looked—you saw."

"While you," I concurred, "caught your death in the night air!"

He literally bloomed so from this exploit that he could afford radiantly to assent. "How otherwise should I have been bad enough?" he asked. Then, after another embrace, the incident and our interview closed on my recognition of all the reserves of goodness that, for his joke, he had been able to draw upon.

XII

The particular impression I had received proved in the morning light, I repeat, not quite successfully presentable to Mrs. Grose, though I reinforced it with the mention of still another remark that he had made before we separated. "It all lies in half a dozen words," I said to her, "words that really settle the matter. 'Think, you know, what I might do!' He threw that off to show me how good he is. He knows down to the ground what he 'might' do. That's what he gave them a taste of at school."

"Lord, you do change!" cried my friend.

"I don't change—I simply make it out. The four, depend upon it, perpetually meet. If on either of these last nights you had been with either child, you would clearly have understood. The more I've watched and waited the more I've felt that if there were nothing else to make it sure it would be made so by the systematic silence of each. *Never*, by a slip of the tongue, have they so much as alluded to either of their old friends, any more than Miles has alluded to his expulsion. Oh, yes, we may sit here and look at them, and they may show off to us there to their fill; but even while they pretend to be lost in their fairytale they're steeped in their vision of the dead restored. He's not reading to her," I declared; "they're talking of *them*—they're talking horrors! I go on, I know, as if I were crazy; and it's a wonder I'm not. What I've seen would have made you so; but it has only made me more lucid, made me get hold of still other things."

My lucidity must have seemed awful, but the charming creatures who were victims of it, passing and repassing in their interlocked sweetness, gave my colleague something to hold on by; and I felt how tight she held as, without stirring in the breath of my passion, she covered them still with her eyes. "Of what other things have you got hold?"

"Why, of the very things that have delighted, fascinated, and yet, at bottom, as I now so strangely see, mystified and troubled me. Their more than earthly beauty, their absolutely unnatural goodness. It's a game," I went on; "it's a policy and a fraud!"

"On the part of little darlings—?"

"As yet mere lovely babies? Yes, mad as that seems!" The very act of bringing it out really helped me to trace it—follow it all up and piece it all together. "They haven't been good—they've only been absent. It has been easy to live with them, because they're simply leading a life of their own. They're not mine—they're not ours. They're his and they're hers!"

"Quint's and that woman's?"

"Quint's and that woman's. They want to get to them."

Oh, how, at this, poor Mrs. Grose appeared to study them! "But for what?"

"For the love of all the evil that, in those dreadful days, the pair put into them. And to ply them with that evil still, to keep up the work of demons, is what brings the others back."

"Laws!" said my friend under her breath. The exclamation was homely, but it revealed a real acceptance of my further proof of what, in the bad time—for there had been a worse even than this!—must have occurred. There could have been no such justification for me as the plain assent of her experience to whatever depth of depravity I found credible in our brace of scoundrels. It was in obvious submission of memory that she brought out after a moment: "They *were* rascals! But what can they now do?" she pursued.

"Do?" I echoed so loud that Miles and Flora, as they passed at their distance, paused an instant in their walk and looked at us. "Don't they do enough?" I demanded in a lower tone, while the children, having smiled and nodded and kissed hands to us, resumed their exhibition. We were held by it a minute; then I answered: "They can destroy them!" At this my companion did turn, but the inquiry she launched was a silent one, the effect of which was to make me more explicit. "They don't know, as yet, quite how—but they're trying hard. They're seen only across, as it were, and beyond—in strange places and on high places, the top of towers, the roof of houses, the outside of windows, the further edge of pools; but there's a deep design, on either side, to shorten the distance and overcome the obstacle; and the success of the tempters is only a question of time. They've only to keep to their suggestions of danger."

"For the children to come?"

"And perish in the attempt!" Mrs. Grose slowly got up, and I scrupulously added: "Unless, of course, we can prevent!"

Standing there before me while I kept my seat, she visibly turned things over. "Their uncle must do the preventing. He must take them away."

"And who's to make him?"

She had been scanning the distance, but she now dropped on me a foolish face. "You, miss."

"By writing to him that his house is poisoned and his little nephew and niece mad?"

"But if they *are*, miss?"

"And if I am myself, you mean? That's charming news to be sent him by a governess whose prime undertaking was to give him no worry."

Mrs. Grose considered, following the children again. "Yes, he do hate worry. That was the great reason—"

"Why those fiends took him in so long? No doubt, though his indifference must have been awful. As I'm not a fiend, at any rate, I shouldn't take him in."

My companion, after an instant and for all answer, sat down again and grasped my arm. "Make him at any rate come to you."

I stared. "To *me*?" I had a sudden fear of what she might do. " 'Him'?"

"He ought to *be* here—he ought to help."

I quickly rose, and I think I must have shown her a queerer face than ever yet. "You see me asking him for a visit?" No, with her eyes on my face she evidently couldn't. Instead of it even—as a woman reads another—she could see what I myself saw: his derision, his amusement, his contempt for the breakdown of my resignation at being left alone and for the fine machinery I had set in motion to attract his attention to my slighted charms. She didn't know—no one knew—how proud I had been to serve him and to stick to our terms; yet she nonetheless took the measure, I think, of the warning I now gave her. "If you should so lose your head as to appeal to him for me—"

She was really frightened. "Yes, miss?"

"I would leave, on the spot, both him and you."

XIII

It was all very well to join them, but speaking to them proved quite as much as ever an effort beyond my strength—offered, in close quarters, difficulties as insurmountable as before. This situation continued a month, and with new aggravations and particular notes, the note above all, sharper and sharper, of the small ironic consciousness on the part of my pupils. It was not, I am as sure today as I was sure then, my mere infernal imagination: it was absolutely traceable that they were aware of my predicament and that this strange relation made, in a manner, for a long time, the air in which we moved. I don't mean that they had their tongues in their cheeks or did anything vulgar, for that was not one of their dangers: I do mean, on the other hand, that the element of the unnamed and untouched became, between us, greater than any other, and that so much avoidance could not have been so successfully effected without a great deal of tacit arrangement. It was as if, at moments, we were perpetually coming into sight of subjects before which we must stop short, turning suddenly out of alleys that we perceived to be blind, closing with a little bang that made us look at each other—for, like all bangs, it was something louder than we had intended—the doors we had indiscreetly opened. All roads lead to Rome, and there were times when it might have struck us that almost every branch of study or subject of conversation skirted forbidden ground. Forbidden ground was the question of the return of the dead in general and of whatever, in especial, might survive, in memory, of the friends little children had lost. There were days when I could have sworn that one of them had, with a small invisible nudge, said to the other: "She thinks she'll do it this time—but she *won't!*" To "do it" would have been to indulge for instance—and for once in a way—in some direct reference to the lady who had prepared them for my discipline. They had a delightful endless appetite for passages in my own history, to which I had again and again treated them; they were in possession of everything that had ever happened to me, had had, with every circumstance the story of my smallest adventures and of those of my brothers and sisters and of the cat and the dog at home, as well as many particulars of the eccentric nature of my father, of the furniture and arrangement of our house, and of the conversation of the old women of our village. There were things enough, taking one with another, to chatter about, if one went very fast and knew by instinct when to go round. They pulled with an art of their own the strings of my invention and my memory; and nothing else perhaps, when I thought of such occasions afterward, gave me so the suspicion of being watched from under cover. It was in any case over my life, my past, and my friends alone that we could take anything like our ease—a state of affairs that led them sometimes without the least pertinence to break out into sociable reminders. I was invited—with no visible connection—to repeat afresh Goody Gosling's celebrated mot or to confirm the details already supplied as to the cleverness of the vicarage pony.

It was partly at such junctures as these and partly at quite different ones that, with the turn my matters had now taken, my predicament, as I have called it, grew most sensible. The fact that the days passed for me without another encounter ought, it would have appeared, to have done something toward soothing my nerves. Since the light brush, that second night on the upper landing, of the presence of a woman at the foot of the stair, I had seen nothing, whether in or out of the house, that one had better not have seen. There was many a corner round which I expected to come upon Quint, and many a situation that, in a merely sinister way, would have favored the appearance of Miss Jessel. The summer had turned, the summer had gone; the autumn had dropped upon Bly and had blown out half our lights. The place, with its gray sky and withered garlands, its bared spaces and scattered dead leaves, was like a theater after the performance—all strewn with crumpled playbills. There were exactly states of the air, conditions of sound and of stillness, unspeakable impressions of the *kind* of ministering moment, that brought back to me, long enough to catch it, the feeling of the medium in which, that June evening out of doors, I had had my first sight of Quint, and in which, too, at those other instants, I had, after seeing him through the window, looked for him in vain in the circle of shrubbery. I recognized the signs, the portents—I recognized the moment, the spot. But they remained unaccompanied and empty, and I continued unmolested; if unmolested one could call a young woman whose sensibility had, in the most extraordinary fashion, not declined but deepened. I had said in my talk with Mrs. Grose on that horrid scene of Flora's by the lake—and had perplexed her by so saying—that it would from that moment distress me much more to lose my power than to keep it. I had then expressed what was vividly in my mind: the truth that, whether the children really saw or not—since, that is, it was not yet definitely proved—I greatly preferred, as a safeguard, the fullness of my own exposure. I was ready to know the very worst that was to be known. What I had then had an ugly glimpse of was that my eyes might be sealed just while theirs were most opened. Well, my eyes *were* sealed, it appeared, at present—a consummation for which it seemed blasphemous not to thank God. There was, alas, a difficulty about that: I would have thanked him with all my soul had I not had in a proportionate measure this conviction of the secret of my pupils.

How can I retrace today the strange steps of my obsession? There were times of our being together when I would have been ready to swear that, literally, in my presence, but with my direct sense of it closed, they had visitors who were known and were welcome. Then it was that, had I not been deterred by the very chance that such an injury might prove greater than the injury to be averted, my exultation would have broken out. "They're here, they're here, you little wretches," I would have cried, "and you can't deny it now!" The little wretches denied it with all the added volume of their sociability and their tenderness, in just the crystal depths of which—like the flash of a fish in a stream—the mockery of their advantage peeped up. The shock, in truth, had sunk into me still deeper than I knew on the night when, looking out to see either Quint or Miss Jessel under the stars, I had beheld the boy over whose rest I watched and who had immediately brought in with him—had straightway, there, turned it on me—the lovely upward look with which, from the battlements above me, the hideous apparition of Quint had played. If it was a question of a scare, my discovery on this occasion had scared me more than any other, and it was in the condition of nerves produced by it that I made my actual inductions. They harassed me so that sometimes, at odd moments, I shut myself up audibly to rehearse—it was at once a fantastic relief and a renewed despair—the manner in which I might come to the point. I approached it from one side and the other while, in my room, I flung myself about, but I always broke down in the monstrous utterance of names. As they died away on my lips, I said to myself that I should indeed help them to represent something infamous, if, by pronouncing them, I should violate as rare a little case of instinctive delicacy as any schoolroom, probably, had ever known. When I said to myself: "*They* have the manners to be silent, and you, trusted as you are, the baseness to speak!" I felt myself crimson and I covered my face with my hands. After these secret scenes I chattered more than ever, going on volubly enough till one of our prodigious, palpable hushes occurred—I can call them nothing else—the strange, dizzy lift or swim (I try for terms!) into a stillness, a pause of all life, that had nothing to do with the more or less noise that at the moment we might be engaged in making and that I could hear through any deepened exhilaration or quickened recitation or louder strum of the piano. Then it was that the others, the outsiders, were there. Though they were not angels, they "passed," as the French say, causing me, while they stayed, to tremble with the fear of their addressing to their younger victims some yet more infernal message or more vivid image than they had thought good enough for myself.

What it was most impossible to get rid of was the cruel idea that, whatever I had seen, Miles and Flora saw more—things terrible and unguessable and that sprang from dreadful passages of intercourse in the past. Such things naturally left on the surface, for the time, a chill which we vociferously denied that we felt; and we had, all three, with repetition, got into such splendid training that we went, each time, almost automatically, to mark the close of the incident, through the very same movements. It was striking of the children, at all events, to kiss me inveterately with a kind of wild irrelevance and never to fail—one or the other—of the precious question that had helped us through many a peril. "When do you think he *will* come? Don't you think we ought to write?"—there was nothing like that inquiry, we found by experience, for carrying off an awkwardness. "He" of course was their uncle in Harley Street; and we lived in much profusion of theory that he might at any moment arrive to mingle in our circle. It was impossible to have given less encouragement than he had done to such a doctrine, but if we had not had the doctrine to fall back upon we should have deprived each other of some of our finest exhibitions. He never wrote to them—that may have been selfish, but it was a part of the flattery of his trust of me; for the way in which a man pays his highest tribute to a woman is apt to be but by the more festal celebration of one of the sacred laws of his comfort; and I held that I carried out the spirit of the pledge given not to appeal to him when I let my charges understand that their own letters were but charming literary exercises. They were too beautiful to be posted; I kept them myself; I have them all to this hour. This was a rule indeed which only added to the satiric effect of my being plied with the supposition that he might at any moment be among us. It was exactly as if my charges knew how almost more awkward than anything else that might be for me. There appears to me, moreover, as I look back, no note in all this more extraordinary than the mere fact that, in spite of my tension and of their triumph, I never lost patience with them. Adorable they must in truth have been, I now reflect, that I didn't in these days hate them! Would exasperation, however, if relief had longer been postponed, finally have betrayed me? It little matters, for relief arrived. I call it relief, though it was only the relief that a snap brings to a strain or the burst of a thunderstorm to a day of suffocation. It was at least change, and it came with a rush.

XIV

Walking to church a certain Sunday morning, I had little Miles at my side and his sister, in advance of us and at Mrs. Grose's, well in sight. It was a crisp, clear day, the first of its order for some time; the night had brought a touch of frost, and the autumn air, bright and sharp, made the church bells almost gay. It was an odd accident of thought that I should have happened at such a moment to be particularly and very gratefully struck with the obedience of my little charges. Why did they never resent my inexorable, my perpetual society? Something or other had brought nearer home to me that I had all but pinned the boy to my shawl and that, in the way our companions were marshaled before me, I might have appeared to provide against some danger of rebellion. I was like a gaoler with an eye to possible surprises and escapes. But all this belonged—I mean their magnificent little surrender—just to the special array of the facts that were most abysmal. Turned out for Sunday by his uncle's tailor, who had had a free hand and a notion of pretty waistcoats and of his grand little air, Miles's whole title to independence, the rights of his sex and situation, were so stamped upon him that if he had suddenly struck for freedom I should have had nothing to say. I was by the strangest of chances wondering how I should meet him when the revolution unmistakably occurred. I call it a revolution because I now see how, with the word he spoke, the curtain rose on the last act of my dreadful drama, and the catastrophe was precipitated. "Look here, my dear, you know," he charmingly said, "when in the world, please, am I going back to school?"

Transcribed here the speech sounds harmless enough, particularly as uttered in the sweet, high, casual pipe with which, at all interlocutors, but above all at his eternal governess, he threw off intonations as if he were tossing roses. There was something in them that always made one "catch," and I caught, at any rate, now so effectually that I stopped as short as if one of the trees of the park had fallen across the road. There was something new, on the spot, between us, and he was perfectly aware that I recognized it, though, to enable me to do so, he had no need to look a whit less candid and charming than usual. I could feel in him how he already, from my at first finding nothing to reply, perceived the advantage he had gained. I was so slow to find anything that he had plenty of time, after a minute, to continue with his suggestive but inconclusive smile: "You know, my dear, that for a fellow to be with a lady *always*—!" His "my dear" was constantly on his lips for me, and nothing could have expressed more the exact shade of the sentiment with which I desired to inspire my pupils than its fond familiarity. It was so respectfully easy.

But, oh, how I felt that at present I must pick my own phrases! I remember that, to gain time, I tried to laugh, and I seemed to see in the beautiful face with which he watched me how ugly and queer I looked. "And always with the same lady?" I returned.

He neither blanched nor winked. The whole thing was virtually out between us. "Ah, of course, she's a jolly, 'perfect' lady; but, after all, I'm a fellow, don't you see? that's—well, getting on."

I lingered there with him an instant ever so kindly. "Yes, you're getting on." Oh, but I felt helpless!

I have kept to this day the heartbreaking little idea of how he seemed to know that and to play with it. "And you can't say I've not been awfully good, can you?"

I laid my hand on his shoulder, for, though I felt how much better it would have been to walk on, I was not yet quite able. "No, I can't say that, Miles."

"Except just that one night, you know—!"

"That one night?" I couldn't look as straight as he.

"Why, when I went down—went out of the house."

"Oh, yes. But I forget what you did it for."

"You forget?"—he spoke with the sweet extravagance of childish reproach. "Why, it was to show you I could!"

"Oh, yes, you could."

"And I can again."

I felt that I might, perhaps, after all, succeed in keeping my wits about me. "Certainly. But you won't."

"No, not *that* again. It was nothing."

"It was nothing," I said. "But we must go on."

He resumed our walk with me, passing his hand into my arm. "Then when am I going back?"

I wore, in turning it over, my most responsible air. "Were you very happy at school?"

He just considered. "Oh, I'm happy enough anywhere!"

"Well, then," I quavered, "if you're just as happy here—!"

"Ah, but that isn't everything! Of course *you* know a lot—"

"But you hint that you know almost as much?" I risked as he paused.

"Not half I want to!" Miles honestly professed. "But it isn't so much that."

"What is it, then?"

"Well—I want to see more life."

"I see; I see." We had arrived within sight of the church and of various persons, including several of the household of Bly, on their way to it and clustered about the door to see us go in. I quickened our step; I wanted to get there before the question between us opened up much further; I reflected hungrily that, for more than an hour, he would have to be silent; and I thought with envy of the comparative dusk of the pew and of the almost spiritual help of the hassock on which I might bend my knees. I seemed literally to be running a race with some confusion to which he was about to reduce me, but I felt that he had got in first when, before we had even entered the churchyard, he threw out—

"I want my own sort!"

It literally made me bound forward. "There are not many of your own sort, Miles!" I laughed. "Unless perhaps dear little Flora!"

"You really compare me to a baby girl?"

This found me singularly weak. "Don't you, then, *love* our sweet Flora?"

"If I didn't—and you, too; if I didn't—!" he repeated as if retreating for a jump, yet leaving his thought so unfinished that, after we had come into the gate, another stop, which he imposed on me by the pressure of his arm, had become inevitable. Mrs. Grose and Flora had passed into the church, the other worshippers had followed, and we were, for the minute, alone among the old, thick graves. We had paused, on the path from the gate, by a low, oblong, tablelike tomb.

"Yes, if you didn't—?"

He looked, while I waited, at the graves. "Well, you know what!" But he didn't move, and he presently produced something that made me drop straight down on the stone slab, as if suddenly to rest. "Does my uncle think what you think?"

I markedly rested. "How do you know what I think?"

"Ah, well, of course I don't; for it strikes me you never tell me. But I mean does *he* know?"

"Know what, Miles?"

"Why, the way I'm going on."

I perceived quickly enough that I could make, to this inquiry, no answer that would not involve something of a sacrifice of my employer. Yet it appeared to me that we were all, at Bly, sufficiently sacrificed to make that venial. "I don't think your uncle much cares."

Miles, on this, stood looking at me. "Then don't you think he can be made to?"

"In what way?"

"Why, by his coming down."

"But who'll get him to come down?"

"*I* will!" the boy said with extraordinary brightness and emphasis. He gave me another look charged with that expression and then marched off alone into church.

XV

The business was practically settled from the moment I never followed him. It was a pitiful surrender to agitation, but my being aware of this had somehow no power to restore me. I only sat there on my tomb and read into what my little friend had said to me the fullness of its meaning; by the time I had grasped the whole of which I had also embraced, for absence, the pretext that I was ashamed to offer my pupils and the rest of the congregation such an example of delay. What I said to myself above all was that Miles had got something out of me and that the proof of it, for him, would be just this awkward collapse. He had got out of me that there was something I was much afraid of and that he should probably be able to make use of my fear to gain, for his own purpose, more freedom. My fear was of having to deal with the intolerable question of the grounds of his dismissal from school, for that was really but the question of the horrors gathered behind. That his uncle should arrive to treat with me of these things was a solution that, strictly speaking, I ought now to have desired to bring on; but I could so little face the ugliness and the pain of it that I simply procrastinated and lived from hand to mouth. The boy, to my deep discomposure, was immensely in the right, was in a position to say to me: "Either you clear up with my guardian the mystery of this interruption of my studies, or you cease to expect me to lead with you a life that's so unnatural for a boy." What was so unnatural for the particular boy I was concerned with was this sudden revelation of a consciousness and a plan.

That was what really overcame me, what prevented my going in. I walked round the church, hesitating, hovering; I reflected that I had already, with him, hurt myself beyond repair. Therefore I could patch up nothing, and it was too extreme an effort to squeeze beside him into the pew: he would be so much more sure than ever to pass his arm into mine and make me sit there for an hour in close, silent contact with his commentary on our talk. For the first minute since his arrival I wanted to get away from him. As I paused beneath the high east window and listened to the sounds of worship, I was taken with an impulse that might master me, I felt, completely should I give it the least encouragement. I might easily put an end to my predicament by getting away altogether. Here was my chance; there was no one to stop me; I could give the whole thing up—turn my back and retreat. It was only a question of hurrying again, for a few preparations, to the house which the attendance at church of so many of the servants would practically have left unoccupied. No one, in short, could blame me if I should just drive desperately off. What was it to get away if I got away only till dinner? That would be in a couple of hours, at the end of which—I had the acute prevision—my little pupils would play at innocent wonder about my nonappearance in their train.

"What *did* you do, you naughty, bad thing? Why in the world, to worry us so—and take our thoughts off, too, don't you know?—did you desert us at the very door?" I couldn't meet such questions nor, as they asked them, their false little lovely eyes; yet it was all so exactly what I should have to meet that, as the prospect grew sharp to me, I at last let myself go.

I got, so far as the immediate moment was concerned, away; I came straight out of the churchyard and, thinking hard, retraced my steps through the park. It seemed to me that by the time I reached the house I had made up my mind I would fly. The Sunday stillness both of the approaches and of the interior, in which I met no one, fairly excited me with a sense of opportunity. Were I to get off quickly, this way, I should get off without a scene, without a word. My quickness would have to be remarkable, however, and the question of a conveyance was the great one to settle. Tormented, in the hall, with difficulties and obstacles, I remember sinking down at the foot of the staircase—suddenly collapsing there on the lowest step and then, with a revulsion, recalling that it was exactly where more than a month before, in the darkness of night and just so bowed with evil things, I had seen the specter of the most horrible of women. At this I was able to straighten myself; I went the rest of the way up; I made, in my bewilderment, for the schoolroom, where there were objects belonging to me that I should have to take. But I opened the door to find again, in a flash, my eyes unsealed. In the presence of what I saw I reeled straight back upon my resistance.

Seated at my own table in clear noonday light I saw a person whom, without my previous experience, I should have taken at the first blush for some housemaid who might have stayed at home to look after the place and who, availing herself of rare relief from observation and of the schoolroom table and my pens, ink, and paper, had applied herself to the considerable effort of a letter to her sweetheart. There was an effort in the way that, while her arms rested on the table, her hands with evident weariness supported her head; but at the moment I took this in I had already become aware that, in spite of my entrance, her attitude strangely persisted. Then it was—with the very act of its announcing itself—that her identity flared up in a change of posture. She rose, not as if she had heard me, but with an indescribable grand melancholy of indifference and detachment, and, within a dozen feet of me, stood there as my vile predecessor. Dishonored and tragic, she was all before me; but even as I fixed and, for memory, secured it, the awful image passed away. Dark as midnight in her black dress, her haggard beauty and her unutterable woe, she had looked at me long enough to appear to say that her right to sit at my table was as good as mine to sit at hers. While these instants lasted, indeed, I had the extraordinary chill of feeling that it was I who was the intruder. It was as a wild protest against it that, actually addressing her—

"You terrible, miserable woman!"—I heard myself break into a sound that, by the open door, rang through the long passage and the empty house. She looked at me as if she heard me, but I had recovered myself and cleared the air. There was nothing in the room the next minute but the sunshine and a sense that I must stay.

XVI

I had so perfectly expected that the return of my pupils would be marked by a demonstration that I was freshly upset at having to take into account that they were dumb about my absence. Instead of gaily denouncing and caressing me, they made no allusion to my having failed them, and I was left, for the time, on perceiving that she too said nothing, to study Mrs. Grose's odd face. I did this to such purpose that I made sure they had in some way bribed her to silence; a silence that, however, I would engage to break down on the first private opportunity. This opportunity came before tea: I secured five minutes with her in the housekeeper's room, where, in the twilight, amid a smell of lately baked bread, but with the place all swept and garnished, I found her sitting in pained placidity before the fire. So I see her still, so I see her best: facing the flame from her straight chair in the dusky, shining room, a large clean image of the "put away"—of drawers closed and locked and rest without a remedy.

"Oh, yes, they asked me to say nothing; and to please them—so long as they were there—of course I promised. But what had happened to you?"

"I only went with you for the walk," I said. "I had then to come back to meet a friend."

She showed her surprise. "A friend—*you*?"

"Oh, yes, I have a couple!" I laughed. "But did the children give you a reason?"

"For not alluding to your leaving us? Yes; they said you would like it better. Do you like it better?"

My face had made her rueful. "No, I like it worse!" But after an instant I added: "Did they say why I should like it better?"

"No; Master Miles only said, 'We must do nothing but what she likes!'"

"I wish indeed he would. And what did Flora say?"

"Miss Flora was too sweet. She said, 'Oh, of course, of course!'—and I said the same."

I thought a moment. "You were too sweet, too—I can hear you all. But nonetheless, between Miles and me, it's now all out."

"All out?" My companion stared. "But what, miss?"

"Everything. It doesn't matter. I've made up my mind. I came home, my dear," I went on, "for a talk with Miss Jessel."

I had by this time formed the habit of having Mrs. Grose literally well in hand in advance of my sounding that note; so that even now, as she bravely blinked under the signal of my word, I could keep her comparatively firm. "A talk! Do you mean she spoke?"

"It came to that. I found her, on my return, in the schoolroom."

"And what did she say?" I can hear the good woman still, and the candor of her stupefaction.

"That she suffers the torments—!"

It was this, of a truth, that made her, as she filled out my picture, gape. "Do you mean," she faltered, "—of the lost?"

"Of the lost. Of the damned. And that's why, to share them—" I faltered myself with the horror of it.

But my companion, with less imagination, kept me up. "To share them—?"

"She wants Flora." Mrs. Grose might, as I gave it to her, fairly have fallen away from me had I not been prepared. I still held her there, to show I was. "As I've told you, however, it doesn't matter."

"Because you've made up your mind? But to what?"

"To everything."

"And what do you call 'everything'?"

"Why, sending for their uncle."

"Oh, miss, in pity do," my friend broke out. "ah, but I will, I *will!* I see it's the only way. What's 'out,' as I told you, with Miles is that if he thinks I'm afraid to—and has ideas of what he gains by that—he shall see he's mistaken. Yes, yes; his uncle shall have it here from me on the spot (and before the boy himself, if necessary) that if I'm to be reproached with having done nothing again about more school—"

"Yes, miss—" my companion pressed me.

"Well, there's that awful reason."

There were now clearly so many of these for my poor colleague that she was excusable for being vague. "But—a—which?"

"Why, the letter from his old place."

"You'll show it to the master?"

"I ought to have done so on the instant."

"Oh, no!" said Mrs. Grose with decision.

"I'll put it before him," I went on inexorably, "that I can't undertake to work the question on behalf of a child who has been expelled—"

"For we've never in the least known what!" Mrs. Grose declared.

"For wickedness. For what else—when he's so clever and beautiful and perfect? Is he stupid? Is he untidy? Is he infirm? Is he ill-natured? He's exquisite—so it can be only *that;* and that would open up the whole thing. After all," I said, "it's their uncle's fault. If he left here such people—!"

"He didn't really in the least know them. The fault's mine." She had turned quite pale.

"Well, you shan't suffer," I answered.

"The children shan't!" she emphatically returned.

I was silent awhile; we looked at each other. "Then what am I to tell him?"

"You needn't tell him anything. *I'll* tell him."

I measured this. "Do you mean you'll write—?" Remembering she couldn't, I caught myself up. "How do you communicate?"

"I tell the bailiff. *He* writes."

"And should you like him to write our story?"

My question had a sarcastic force that I had not fully intended, and it made her, after a moment, inconsequently break down. The tears were again in her eyes. "Ah, miss, you write!"

"Well—tonight," I at last answered; and on this we separated.

XVII

I went so far, in the evening, as to make a beginning. The weather had changed back, a great wind was abroad, and beneath the lamp, in my room, with Flora at peace beside me, I sat for a long time before a blank sheet of paper and listened to the lash of the rain and the batter of the gusts. Finally I went out, taking a candle; I crossed the passage and listened a minute at Miles's door. What, under my endless obsession, I had been impelled to listen for was some betrayal of his not being at rest, and I presently caught one, but not in the form I had expected. His voice tinkled out. "I say, you there—come in." It was a gaiety in the gloom!

I went in with my light and found him, in bed, very wide awake, but very much at his ease. "Well, what are *you* up to?" he asked with a grace of sociability in which it occurred to me that Mrs. Grose, had she been present, might have looked in vain for proof that anything was "out."

I stood over him with my candle. "How did you know I was there?"

"Why, of course I heard you. Did you fancy you made no noise? You're like a troop of cavalry!" he beautifully laughed.

"Then you weren't asleep?"

"Not much! I lie awake and think."

I had put my candle, designedly, a short way off, and then, as he held out his friendly old hand to me, had sat down on the edge of his bed. "What is it," I asked, "that you think of?"

"What in the world, my dear, but you?"

"Ah, the pride I take in your appreciation doesn't insist on that! I had so far rather you slept."

"Well, I think also, you know, of this queer business of ours."

I marked the coolness of his firm little hand. "Of what queer business, Miles?"

"Why, the way you bring me up. And all the rest!"

I fairly held my breath a minute, and even from my glimmering taper there was light enough to show how he smiled up at me from his pillow. "What do you mean by all the rest?"

"Oh, you know, you know!"

I could say nothing for a minute, though I felt, as I held his hand and our eyes continued to meet, that my silence had all the air of admitting his charge and that nothing in the whole world of reality was perhaps at that moment so fabulous as our actual relation. "Certainly you shall go back to school," I said, "if it be that that troubles you. But not to the old place—we must find another, a better. How could I know it did trouble you, this question, when you never told me so, never spoke of it at all?" His clear, listening face, framed in its smooth whiteness, made him for the minute as appealing as some wistful patient in a children's hospital; and I would have given, as the resemblance came to me, all I possessed on earth really to be the nurse or the sister of charity who might have helped to cure him. Well, even as it was, I perhaps might help! "Do you know you've never said a word to me about your school—I mean the old one; never mentioned it in any way?"

He seemed to wonder; he smiled with the same loveliness. But he clearly gained time; he waited, he called for guidance. "Haven't I?" It wasn't for *me* to help him—it was for the thing I had met!

Something in his tone and the expression of his face, as I got this from him, set my heart aching with such a pang as it had never yet known; so unutterably touching was it to see his little brain puzzled and his little resources taxed to play, under the spell laid on him, a part of innocence and consistency. "No, never—from the hour you came back. You've never mentioned to me one of your masters, one of your comrades, nor the least little thing that ever happened to you at school. Never, little Miles—no, never—have you given me an inkling of anything that *may* have happened there. Therefore you can fancy how much I'm in the dark. Until you came out, that way, this morning, you had, since the first hour I saw you, scarce even made a reference to anything in your previous life. You seemed so perfectly to accept the present." It was extraordinary how my absolute conviction of his secret precocity (or whatever I might call the poison of an influence that I dared but half to phrase) made him, in spite of the faint breath of his inward trouble, appear as accessible as an older person—imposed him almost as an intellectual equal. "I thought you wanted to go on as you are."

It struck me that at this he just faintly colored. He gave, at any rate, like a convalescent slightly fatigued, a languid shake of his head. "I don't—I don't. I want to get away."

"You're tired of Bly?"

"Oh, no, I like Bly."

"Well, then—?"

"Oh, *you* know what a boy wants!"

I felt that I didn't know so well as Miles, and I took temporary refuge. "You want to go to your uncle?"

Again, at this, with his sweet ironic face, he made a movement on the pillow. "Ah, you can't get off with that!"

I was silent a little, and it was I, now, I think, who changed color. "My dear, I don't want to get off!"

"You can't, even if you do. You can't, you can't!"—he lay beautifully staring. "My uncle must come down, and you must completely settle things."

"If we do," I returned with some spirit, "you may be sure it will be to take you quite away."

"Well, don't you understand that that's exactly what I'm working for? You'll have to tell him—about the way you've let it all drop: you'll have to tell him a tremendous lot!"

The exultation with which he uttered this helped me somehow, for the instant, to meet him rather more. "And how much will you, Miles, have to tell him? There are things he'll ask you!"

He turned it over. "Very likely. But what things?"

"The things you've never told me. To make up his mind what to do with you. He can't send you back—"

"Oh, I don't want to go back!" he broke in. "I want a new field."

He said it with admirable serenity, with positive unimpeachable gaiety; and doubtless it was that very note that most evoked for me the poignancy, the unnatural childish tragedy, of his probable reappearance at the end of three months with all this bravado and still more dishonor. It overwhelmed me now that I should never be able to bear that, and it made me let myself go. I threw myself upon him and in the tenderness of my pity I embraced him. "Dear little Miles, dear little Miles—!"

My face was close to his, and he let me kiss him, simply taking it with indulgent good humor. "Well, old lady?"

"Is there nothing—nothing at all that you want to tell me?"

He turned off a little, facing round toward the wall and holding up his hand to look at as one had seen sick children look. "I've told you—I told you this morning."

Oh, I was sorry for him! "That you just want me not to worry you?"

He looked round at me now, as if in recognition of my understanding him; then ever so gently, "To let me alone," he replied.

There was even a singular little dignity in it, something that made me release him, yet, when I had slowly risen, linger beside him. God knows I never wished to harass him, but I felt that merely, at this, to turn my back on him was to abandon or, to put it more truly, to lose him. "I've just begun a letter to your uncle," I said.

"Well, then, finish it!"

I waited a minute. "What happened before?"

He gazed up at me again. "Before what?"

"Before you came back. And before you went away."

For some time he was silent, but he continued to meet my eyes. "What happened?"

It made me, the sound of the words, in which it seemed to me that I caught for the very first time a small faint quaver of consenting consciousness—it made me drop on my knees beside the bed and seize once more the chance of possessing him. "Dear little Miles, dear little Miles, if you knew how I want to help you! It's only that, it's nothing but that, and I'd rather die than give you a pain or do you a wrong—I'd rather die than hurt a hair of you. Dear little Miles"—oh, I brought it out now even if I *should* go too far—"I just want you to help me to save you!" But I knew in a moment after this that I had gone too far. The answer to my appeal was instantaneous, but it came in the form of an extraordinary blast and chill, a gust of frozen air, and a shake of the room as great as if, in the wild wind, the casement had crashed in. The boy gave a loud, high shriek, which, lost in the rest of the shock of sound, might have seemed, indistinctly, though I was so close to him, a note either of jubilation or of terror. I jumped to my feet again and was conscious of darkness. So for a moment we remained, while I stared about me and saw that the drawn curtains were unstirred and the window tight. "Why, the candle's out!" I then cried.

"It was I who blew it, dear!" said Miles.

XVIII

The next day, after lessons, Mrs. Grose found a moment to say to me quietly: "Have you written, miss?"

"Yes—I've written." But I didn't add—for the hour—that my letter, sealed and directed, was still in my pocket. There would be time enough to send it before the messenger should go to the village. Meanwhile there had been, on the part of my pupils, no more brilliant, more exemplary morning. It was exactly as if they had both had at heart to gloss over any recent little friction.

They performed the dizziest feats of arithmetic, soaring quite out of my feeble range, and perpetrated, in higher spirits than ever, geographical and historical jokes. It was conspicuous of course in Miles in particular that he appeared to wish to show how easily he could let me down. This child, to my memory, really lives in a setting of beauty and misery that no words can translate; there was a distinction all his own in every impulse he revealed; never was a small natural creature, to the uninitiated eye all frankness and freedom, a more ingenious, a more extraordinary little gentleman. I had perpetually to guard against the wonder of contemplation into which my initiated view betrayed me; to check the irrelevant gaze and discouraged sigh in which I constantly both attacked and renounced the enigma of what such a little gentleman could have done that deserved a penalty. Say that, by the dark prodigy I knew, the imagination of all evil *had* been opened up to him: all the justice within me ached for the proof that it could ever have flowered into an act.

He had never, at any rate, been such a little gentleman as when, after our early dinner on this dreadful day, he came round to me and asked if I shouldn't like him, for half an hour, to play to me. David playing to Saul could never have shown a finer sense of the occasion. It was literally a charming exhibition of tact, of magnanimity, and quite tantamount to his saying outright: "The true knights we love to read about never push an advantage too far. I know what you mean now: you mean that—to be let alone yourself and not followed up—you'll cease to worry and spy upon me, won't keep me so close to you, will let me go and come. Well, I 'come,' you see—but I don't go! There'll be plenty of time for that. I do really delight in your society, and I only want to show you that I contended for a principle." It may be imagined whether I resisted this appeal or failed to accompany him again, hand in hand, to the schoolroom. He sat down at the old piano and played as he had never played; and if there are those who think he had better have been kicking a football I can only say that I wholly agree with them. For at the end of a time that under his influence I had quite ceased to measure, I started up with a strange sense of having literally slept at my post. It was after luncheon, and by the schoolroom fire, and yet I hadn't really, in the least, slept: I had only done something much worse—I had forgotten. Where, all this time, was Flora? When I put the question to Miles, he played on a minute before answering and then could only say: "Why, my dear, how do *I* know?"—breaking moreover into a happy laugh which, immediately after, as if it were a vocal accompaniment, he prolonged into incoherent, extravagant song.

I went straight to my room, but his sister was not there; then, before going downstairs, I looked into several others. As she was nowhere about she would surely be with Mrs. Grose, whom, in the comfort of that theory, I accordingly proceeded in quest of. I found her where I had found her the evening before, but she met my quick challenge with blank, scared ignorance. She had only supposed that, after the repast, I had carried off both the children; as to which she was quite in her right, for it was the very first time I had allowed the little girl out of my sight without some special provision. Of course now indeed she might be with the maids, so that the immediate thing was to look for her without an air of alarm. This we promptly arranged between us; but when, ten minutes later and in pursuance of our arrangement, we met in the hall, it was only to report on either side that after guarded inquiries we had altogether failed to trace her. For a minute there, apart from observation, we exchanged mute alarms, and I could feel with what high interest my friend returned me all those I had from the first given her.

"She'll be above," she presently said—"in one of the rooms you haven't searched."

"No; she's at a distance." I had made up my mind. "She has gone out."

Mrs. Grose stared. "Without a hat?"

I naturally also looked volumes. "Isn't that woman always without one?"

"She's with *her?"*

"She's with *her!"* I declared. "We must find them."

My hand was on my friend's arm, but she failed for the moment, confronted with such an account of the matter, to respond to my pressure. She communed, on the contrary, on the spot, with her uneasiness. "And where's Master Miles?"

"Oh, *he's* with Quint. They're in the schoolroom."

"Lord, miss!" My view, I was myself aware—and therefore I suppose my tone—had never yet reached so calm an assurance.

"The trick's played," I went on; "they've successfully worked their plan. He found the most divine little way to keep me quiet while she went off."

"'Divine'?" Mrs. Grose bewilderedly echoed.

"Infernal, then!" I almost cheerfully rejoined. "He has provided for himself as well. But come!"

She had helplessly gloomed at the upper regions. "You leave him—?"

"So long with Quint? Yes—I don't mind that now."

She always ended, at these moments, by getting possession of my hand, and in this manner she could at present still stay me. But after gasping an instant at my sudden resignation, "Because of your letter?" she eagerly brought out.

I quickly, by way of answer, felt for my letter, drew it forth, held it up, and then, freeing myself, went and laid it on the great hall table. "Luke will take it," I said as I came back. I reached the house door and opened it; I was already on the steps.

My companion still demurred: the storm of the night and the early morning had dropped, but the afternoon was damp and gray. I came down to the drive while she stood in the doorway. "You go with nothing on?"

"What do I care when the child has nothing? I can't wait to dress," I cried, "and if you must do so, I leave you. Try meanwhile, yourself, upstairs."

"With them?" Oh, on this, the poor woman promptly joined me!

XIX

We went straight to the lake, as it was called at Bly, and I daresay rightly called, though I reflect that it may in fact have been a sheet of water less remarkable than it appeared to my untraveled eyes. My acquaintance with sheets of water was small, and the pool of Bly, at all events on the few occasions of my consenting, under the protection of my pupils, to affront its surface in the old flat-bottomed boat moored there for our use, had impressed me both with its extent and its agitation. The usual place of embarkation was half a mile from the house, but I had an intimate conviction that, wherever Flora might be, she was not near home. She had not given me the slip for any small adventure, and, since the day of the very great one that I had shared with her by the pond, I had been aware, in our walks, of the quarter to which she most inclined. This was why I had now given to Mrs. Grose's steps so marked a direction—a direction that made her, when she perceived it, oppose a resistance that showed me she was freshly mystified. "You're going to the water, Miss?—you think she's *in*—?"

"She may be, though the depth is, I believe, nowhere very great. But what I judge most likely is that she's on the spot from which, the other day, we saw together what I told you."

"When she pretended not to see—?"

"With that astounding self-possession? I've always been sure she wanted to go back alone. And now her brother has managed it for her."

Mrs. Grose still stood where she had stopped. "You suppose they really *talk* of them?"

"I could meet this with a confidence! They say things that, if we heard them, would simply appall us."

"And if she *is* there—"

"Yes?"

"Then Miss Jessel is?"

"Beyond a doubt. You shall see."

"Oh, thank you!" my friend cried, planted so firm that, taking it in, I went straight on without her. By the time I reached the pool, however, she was close behind me, and I knew that, whatever, to her apprehension, might befall me, the exposure of my society struck her as her least danger. She exhaled a moan of relief as we at last came in sight of the greater part of the water without a sight of the child. There was no trace of Flora on that nearer side of the bank where my observation of her had been most startling, and none on the opposite edge, where, save for a margin of some twenty yards, a thick copse came down to the water. The pond, oblong in shape, had a width so scant compared to its length that, with its ends out of view, it might have been taken for a scant river. We looked at the empty expanse, and then I felt the suggestion of my friend's eyes. I knew what she meant and I replied with a negative headshake.

"No, no; wait! She has taken the boat."

My companion stared at the vacant mooring place and then again across the lake. "Then where is it?"

"Our not seeing it is the strongest of proofs. She has used it to go over, and then has managed to hide it."

"All alone—that child?"

"She's not alone, and at such times she's not a child: she's an old, old woman." I scanned all the visible shore while Mrs. Grose took again, into the queer element I offered her, one of her plunges of submission; then I pointed out that the boat might perfectly be in a small refuge formed by one of the recesses of the pool, an indentation masked, for the hither side, by a projection of the bank and by a clump of trees growing close to the water.

"But if the boat's there, where on earth's *she*?" my colleague anxiously asked.

"That's exactly what we must learn." And I started to walk further.

"By going all the way round?"

"Certainly, far as it is. It will take us but ten minutes, but it's far enough to have made the child prefer not to walk. She went straight over."

"Laws!" cried my friend again; the chain of my logic was ever too much for her. It dragged her at my heels even now, and when we had got halfway round—a devious, tiresome process, on ground much broken and by a path choked with overgrowth—I paused to give her breath. I sustained her with a grateful arm, assuring her that she might hugely help me; and this started us afresh, so that in the course of but few minutes more we reached a point from which we found the boat to be where I had supposed it. It had been intentionally left as much as possible out of sight and was tied to one of the stakes of a fence that came, just there, down to the brink and that had been an assistance to disembarking. I recognized, as I looked at the pair of short, thick oars, quite safely drawn up, the prodigious character of the feat for a little girl; but I had lived, by this time, too long among wonders and had panted to too many livelier measures. There was a gate in the fence, through which we passed, and that brought us, after a trifling interval, more into the open. Then, "There she is!" we both exclaimed at once.

Flora, a short way off, stood before us on the grass and smiled as if her performance was now complete. The next thing she did, however, was to stoop straight down and pluck—quite as if it were all she was there for—a big, ugly spray of withered fern. I instantly became sure she had just come out of the copse. She waited for us, not herself taking a step, and I was conscious of the rare solemnity with which we presently approached her. She smiled and smiled, and we met; but it was all done in a silence by this time flagrantly ominous. Mrs. Grose was the first to break the spell: she threw herself on her knees and, drawing the child to her breast, clasped in a long embrace the little tender, yielding body. While this dumb convulsion lasted I could only watch it—which I did the more intently when I saw Flora's face peep at me over our companion's shoulder. It was serious now—the flicker had left it; but it strengthened the pang with which I at that moment envied Mrs. Grose the simplicity of *her* relation. Still, all this while, nothing more passed between us save that Flora had let her foolish fern again drop to the ground. What she and I had virtually said to each other was that pretexts were useless now. When Mrs. Grose finally got up she kept the child's hand, so that the two were still before me; and the singular reticence of our communion was even more marked in the frank look she launched me. "I'll be hanged," it said, "if *I'll* speak!"

It was Flora who, gazing all over me in candid wonder, was the first. She was struck with our bareheaded aspect. "Why, where are your things?"

"Where yours are, my dear!" I promptly returned.

She had already got back her gaiety, and appeared to take this as an answer quite sufficient. "And where's Miles?" she went on.

There was something in the small valor of it that quite finished me: these three words from her were, in a flash like the glitter of a drawn blade, the jostle of the cup that my hand, for weeks and weeks, had held high and full to the brim that now, even before speaking, I felt overflow in a deluge. "I'll tell you if you'll tell *me*—" I heard myself say, then heard the tremor in which it broke.

"Well, what?"

Mrs. Grose's suspense blazed at me, but it was too late now, and I brought the thing out handsomely. "Where, my pet, is Miss Jessel?"

XX

Just as in the churchyard with Miles, the whole thing was upon us. Much as I had made of the fact that this name had never once, between us, been sounded, the quick, smitten glare with which the child's face now received it fairly likened my breach of the silence to the smash of a pane of glass. It added to the interposing cry, as if to stay the blow, that Mrs. Grose, at the same instant, uttered over my violence—the shriek of a creature scared, or rather wounded, which, in turn, within a few seconds, was completed by a gasp of my own. I seized my colleague's arm. "She's there, she's there!"

Miss Jessel stood before us on the opposite bank exactly as she had stood the other time, and I remember, strangely, as the first feeling now produced in me, my thrill of joy at having brought on a proof. She was there, and I was justified; she was there, and I was neither cruel nor mad. She was there for poor scared Mrs. Grose, but she was there most for Flora; and no moment of my monstrous time was perhaps so extraordinary as that in which I consciously threw out to her—with the sense that, pale and ravenous demon as she was, she would catch and understand it—an inarticulate message of gratitude. She rose erect on the spot my friend and I had lately quitted, and there was not, in all the long reach of her desire, an inch of her evil that fell short. This first vividness of vision and emotion were things of a few seconds, during which Mrs. Grose's dazed blink across to where I pointed struck me as a sovereign sign that she too at last saw, just as it carried my own eyes precipitately to the child. The revelation then of the manner in which Flora was affected startled me, in truth, far more than it would have done to find her also merely agitated, for direct dismay was of course not what I had expected. Prepared and on her guard as our pursuit had actually made her, she would repress every betrayal; and I was therefore shaken, on the spot, by my first glimpse of the particular one for which I had not allowed. To see her, without a convulsion of her small pink face, not even feign to glance in the direction of the prodigy I announced, but only, instead of that, turn at me an expression of hard, still gravity, an expression absolutely new and unprecedented and that appeared to read and accuse and judge me—this was a stroke that somehow converted the little girl herself into the very presence that could make me quail. I quailed even though my certitude that she thoroughly saw was never greater than at that instant, and in the immediate need to defend myself I called it passionately to witness. "She's there, you little unhappy thing—there, there, *there*, and you see her as well as you see me!" I had said shortly before to Mrs. Grose that she was not at these times a child, but an old, old woman, and that description of her could not have been more strikingly confirmed than in the way in which, for all answer to this, she simply showed me, without a concession, an admission, of her eyes, a countenance of deeper and deeper, of indeed suddenly quite fixed, reprobation. I was by this time—if I can put the whole thing at all together—more appalled at what I may properly call her manner than at anything else, though it was simultaneously with this that I became aware of having Mrs. Grose also, and very formidably, to reckon with. My elder companion, the next moment, at any rate, blotted out everything but her own flushed face and her loud, shocked protest, a burst of high disapproval. "What a dreadful turn, to be sure, miss! Where on earth do you see anything?"

I could only grasp her more quickly yet, for even while she spoke the hideous plain presence stood undimmed and undaunted. It had already lasted a minute, and it lasted while I continued, seizing my colleague, quite thrusting her at it and presenting her to it, to insist with my pointing hand. "You don't see her exactly as *we* see?—you mean to say you don't now—*now*? She's as big as a blazing fire! Only look, dearest woman, *look*—!" She looked, even as I did, and gave me, with her deep groan of negation, repulsion, compassion—the mixture with her pity of her relief at her exemption—a sense, touching to me even then, that she would have backed me up if she could. I might well have needed that, for with this hard blow of the proof that her eyes were hopelessly sealed I felt my own situation horribly crumble, I felt—I saw—my livid predecessor press, from her position, on my defeat, and I was conscious, more than all, of what I should have from this instant to deal with in the astounding little attitude of Flora. Into this attitude Mrs. Grose immediately and violently entered, breaking, even while there pierced through my sense of ruin a prodigious private triumph, into breathless reassurance.

"She isn't there, little lady, and nobody's there—and you never see nothing, my sweet! How can poor Miss Jessel—when poor Miss Jessel's dead and buried? We know, don't we, love?"—and she appealed, blundering in, to the child. "It's all a mere mistake and a worry and a joke—and we'll go home as fast as we can!"

Our companion, on this, had responded with a strange, quick primness of propriety, and they were again, with Mrs. Grose on her feet, united, as it were, in pained opposition to me. Flora continued to fix me with her small mask of reprobation, and even at that minute I prayed God to forgive me for seeming to see that, as she stood there holding tight to our friend's dress, her incomparable childish beauty had suddenly failed, had quite vanished. I've said it already—she was literally, she was hideously, hard; she had turned common and almost ugly. "I don't know what you mean. I see nobody. I see nothing. I never have. I think you're cruel. I don't like you!" Then, after this deliverance, which might have been that of a vulgarly pert little girl in the street, she hugged Mrs. Grose more closely and buried in her skirts the dreadful little face. In this position she produced an almost furious wail. "Take me away, take me away—oh, take me away from *her*!"

"From *me*?" I panted.

"From you—from you!" she cried.

Even Mrs. Grose looked across at me dismayed, while I had nothing to do but communicate again with the figure that, on the opposite bank, without a movement, as rigidly still as if catching, beyond the interval, our voices, was as vividly there for my disaster as it was not there for my service. The wretched child had spoken exactly as if she had got from some outside source each of her stabbing little words, and I could therefore, in the full despair of all I had to accept, but sadly shake my head at her. "If I had ever doubted, all my doubt would at present have gone. I've been living with the miserable truth, and now it has only too much closed round me. Of course I've lost you: I've interfered, and you've seen—under *her* dictation"—with which I faced, over the pool again, our infernal witness—"the easy and perfect way to meet it. I've done my best, but I've lost you. Goodbye." For Mrs. Grose I had an imperative, an almost frantic "Go, go!" before which, in infinite distress, but mutely possessed of the little girl and clearly convinced, in spite of her blindness, that something awful had occurred and some collapse engulfed us, she retreated, by the way we had come, as fast as she could move.

Of what first happened when I was left alone I had no subsequent memory. I only knew that at the end of, I suppose, a quarter of an hour, an odorous dampness and roughness, chilling and piercing my trouble, had made me understand that I must have thrown myself, on my face, on the ground and given way to a wildness of grief. I must have lain there long and cried and sobbed, for when I raised my head the day was almost done. I got up and looked a moment, through the twilight, at the gray pool and its blank, haunted edge, and then I took, back to the house, my dreary and difficult course. When I reached the gate in the fence the boat, to my surprise, was gone, so that I had a fresh reflection to make on Flora's extraordinary command of the situation. She passed that night, by the most tacit, and I should add, were not the word so grotesque a false note, the happiest of arrangements, with Mrs. Grose. I saw neither of them on my return, but, on the other hand, as by an ambiguous compensation, I saw a great deal of Miles. I saw—I can use no other phrase—so much of him that it was as if it were more than it had ever been. No evening I had passed at Bly had the portentous quality of this one; in spite of which—and in spite also of the deeper depths of consternation that had opened beneath my feet—there was literally, in the ebbing actual, an extraordinarily sweet sadness. On reaching the house I had never so much as looked for the boy; I had simply gone straight to my room to change what I was wearing and to take in, at a glance, much material testimony to Flora's rupture. Her little belongings had all been removed. When later, by the schoolroom fire, I was served with tea by the usual maid, I indulged, on the article of my other pupil, in no inquiry whatever. He had his freedom now—he might have it to the end! Well, he did have it; and it consisted—in part at least—of his coming in at about eight o'clock and sitting down with me in silence. On the removal of the tea things I had blown out the candles and drawn my chair closer: I was conscious of a mortal coldness and felt as if I should never again be warm. So, when he appeared, I was sitting in the glow with my thoughts. He paused a moment by the door as if to look at me; then—as if to share them—came to the other side of the hearth and sank into a chair. We sat there in absolute stillness; yet he wanted, I felt, to be with me.

XXI

Before a new day, in my room, had fully broken, my eyes opened to Mrs. Grose, who had come to my bedside with worse news. Flora was so markedly feverish that an illness was perhaps at hand; she had passed a night of extreme unrest, a night agitated above all by fears that had for their subject not in the least her former, but wholly her present, governess. It was not against the possible re-entrance of Miss Jessel on the scene that she protested—it was conspicuously and passionately against mine. I was promptly on my feet of course, and with an immense deal to ask; the more that my friend had discernibly now girded her loins to meet me once more. This I felt as soon as I had put to her the question of her sense of the child's sincerity as against my own. "She persists in denying to you that she saw, or has ever seen, anything?"

My visitor's trouble, truly, was great. "Ah, miss, it isn't a matter on which I can push her! Yet it isn't either, I must say, as if I much needed to. It has made her, every inch of her, quite old."

"Oh, I see her perfectly from here. She resents, for all the world like some high little personage, the imputation on her truthfulness and, as it were, her respectability. 'Miss Jessel indeed—she!' Ah, she's 'respectable,' the chit! The impression she gave me there yesterday was, I assure you, the very strangest of all; it was quite beyond any of the others. I *did* put my foot in it! She'll never speak to me again."

Hideous and obscure as it all was, it held Mrs. Grose briefly silent; then she granted my point with a frankness which, I made sure, had more behind it. "I think indeed, miss, she never will. She do have a grand manner about it!"

"And that manner"—I summed it up—"is practically what's the matter with her now!"

Oh, that manner, I could see in my visitor's face, and not a little else besides! "She asks me every three minutes if I think you're coming in."

"I see—I see." I, too, on my side, had so much more than worked it out. "Has she said to you since yesterday—except to repudiate her familiarity with anything so dreadful—a single other word about Miss Jessel?"

"Not one, miss. And of course you know," my friend added, "I took it from her, by the lake, that, just then and there at least, there was nobody."

"Rather! and, naturally, you take it from her still."

"I don't contradict her. What else can I do?"

"Nothing in the world! You've the cleverest little person to deal with. They've made them—their two friends, I mean—still cleverer even than nature did; for it was wondrous material to play on! Flora has now her grievance, and she'll work it to the end."

"Yes, miss; but to *what* end?"

"Why, that of dealing with me to her uncle. She'll make me out to him the lowest creature—!"

I winced at the fair show of the scene in Mrs. Grose's face; she looked for a minute as if she sharply saw them together. "And him who thinks so well of you!"

"He has an odd way—it comes over me now," I laughed, "—of proving it! But that doesn't matter. What Flora wants, of course, is to get rid of me."

My companion bravely concurred. "Never again to so much as look at you."

"So that what you've come to me now for," I asked, "is to speed me on my way?" Before she had time to reply, however, I had her in check. "I've a better idea—the result of my reflections. My going *would* seem the right thing, and on Sunday I was terribly near it. Yet that won't do. It's *you* who must go. You must take Flora."

My visitor, at this, did speculate. "But where in the world—?"

"Away from here. Away from *them*. Away, even most of all, now, from me. Straight to her uncle."

"Only to tell on you—?"

"No, not 'only'! To leave me, in addition, with my remedy."

She was still vague. "And what *is* your remedy?"

"Your loyalty, to begin with. And then Miles's."

She looked at me hard. "Do you think he—?"

"Won't, if he has the chance, turn on me? Yes, I venture still to think it. At all events, I want to try. Get off with his sister as soon as possible and leave me with him alone." I was amazed, myself, at the spirit I had still in reserve, and therefore perhaps a trifle the more disconcerted at the way in which, in spite of this fine example of it, she hesitated. "There's one thing, of course," I went on: "they mustn't, before she goes, see each other for three seconds." Then it came over me that, in spite of Flora's presumable sequestration from the instant of her return from the pool, it might already be too late. "Do you mean," I anxiously asked, "that they *have* met?"

At this she quite flushed. "Ah, miss, I'm not such a fool as that! If I've been obliged to leave her three or four times, it has been each time with one of the maids, and at present, though she's alone, she's locked in safe. And yet—and yet!" There were too many things.

"And yet what?"

"Well, are you so sure of the little gentleman?"

"I'm not sure of anything but *you*. But I have, since last evening, a new hope. I think he wants to give me an opening. I do believe that—poor little exquisite wretch!—he wants to speak. Last evening, in the firelight and the silence, he sat with me for two hours as if it were just coming."

Mrs. Grose looked hard, through the window, at the gray, gathering day. "And did it come?"

"No, though I waited and waited, I confess it didn't, and it was without a breach of the silence or so much as a faint allusion to his sister's condition and absence that we at last kissed for good night. All the same," I continued, "I can't, if her uncle sees her, consent to his seeing her brother without my having given the boy—and most of all because things have got so bad—a little more time."

My friend appeared on this ground more reluctant than I could quite understand. "What do you mean by more time?"

"Well, a day or two—really to bring it out. He'll then be on my side—of which you see the importance. If nothing comes, I shall only fail, and you will, at the worst, have helped me by doing, on your arrival in town, whatever you may have found possible." So I put it before her, but she continued for a little so inscrutably embarrassed that I came again to her aid. "Unless, indeed," I wound up, "you really want *not* to go."

I could see it, in her face, at last clear itself; she put out her hand to me as a pledge. "I'll go—I'll go. I'll go this morning."

I wanted to be very just. "If you should wish still to wait, I would engage she shouldn't see me."

"No, no: it's the place itself. She must leave it." She held me a moment with heavy eyes, then brought out the rest. "Your idea's the right one. I myself, miss—"

"Well?"

"I can't stay."

The look she gave me with it made me jump at possibilities. "You mean that, since yesterday, you *have* seen—?"

She shook her head with dignity. "I've *heard*—!"

"Heard?"

"From that child—horrors! There!" she sighed with tragic relief. "On my honor, miss, she says things—!" But at this evocation she broke down; she dropped, with a sudden sob, upon my sofa and, as I had seen her do before, gave way to all the grief of it.

It was quite in another manner that I, for my part, let myself go. "Oh, thank God!"

She sprang up again at this, drying her eyes with a groan. "'Thank God'?"

"It so justifies me!"

"It does that, miss!"

I couldn't have desired more emphasis, but I just hesitated. "She's so horrible?"

I saw my colleague scarce knew how to put it. "Really shocking."

"And about me?"

"About you, miss—since you must have it. It's beyond everything, for a young lady; and I can't think wherever she must have picked up—"

"The appalling language she applied to me? I can, then!" I broke in with a laugh that was doubtless significant enough.

It only, in truth, left my friend still more grave. "Well, perhaps I ought to also—since I've heard some of it before! Yet I can't bear it," the poor woman went on while, with the same movement, she glanced, on my dressing table, at the face of my watch. "But I must go back."

I kept her, however. "Ah, if you can't bear it—!"

"How can I stop with her, you mean? Why, just for that: to get her away. Far from this," she pursued, "far from *them*—"

"She may be different? She may be free?" I seized her almost with joy. "Then, in spite of yesterday, you *believe*—"

"In such doings?" Her simple description of them required, in the light of her expression, to be carried no further, and she gave me the whole thing as she had never done. "I believe."

Yes, it was a joy, and we were still shoulder to shoulder: if I might continue sure of that I should care but little what else happened. My support in the presence of disaster would be the same as it had been in my early need of confidence, and if my friend would answer for my honesty, I would answer for all the rest. On the point of taking leave of her, nonetheless, I was to some extent embarrassed. "There's one thing, of course—it occurs to me—to remember. My letter, giving the alarm, will have reached town before you."

I now perceived still more how she had been beating about the bush and how weary at last it had made her. "Your letter won't have got there. Your letter never went."

"What then became of it?"

"Goodness knows! Master Miles—"

"Do you mean he took it?" I gasped.

She hung fire, but she overcame her reluctance. "I mean that I saw yesterday, when I came back with Miss Flora, that it wasn't where you had put it. Later in the evening I had the chance to question Luke, and he declared that he had neither noticed nor touched it." We could only exchange, on this, one of our deeper mutual soundings, and it was Mrs. Grose who first brought up the plumb with an almost elated "You see!"

"Yes, I see that if Miles took it instead he probably will have read it and destroyed it."

"And don't you see anything else?"

I faced her a moment with a sad smile. "It strikes me that by this time your eyes are open even wider than mine."

They proved to be so indeed, but she could still blush, almost, to show it. "I make out now what he must have done at school." And she gave, in her simple sharpness, an almost droll disillusioned nod. "He stole!"

I turned it over—I tried to be more judicial. "Well—perhaps."

She looked as if she found me unexpectedly calm. "He stole *letters!*"

She couldn't know my reasons for a calmness after all pretty shallow; so I showed them off as I might. "I hope then it was to more purpose than in this case! The note, at any rate, that I put on the table yesterday," I pursued, "will have given him so scant an advantage—for it contained only the bare demand for an interview—that he is already much ashamed of having gone so far for so little, and that what he had on his mind last evening was precisely the need of confession." I seemed to myself, for the instant, to have mastered it, to see it all. "Leave us, leave us"—I was already, at the door, hurrying her off. "I'll get it out of him. He'll meet me—he'll confess. If he confesses, he's saved. And if he's saved—"

"Then you are?" The dear woman kissed me on this, and I took her farewell. "I'll save you without him!" she cried as she went.

XXII

Yet it was when she had got off—and I missed her on the spot—that the great pinch really came. If I had counted on what it would give me to find myself alone with Miles, I speedily perceived, at least, that it would give me a measure. No hour of my stay in fact was so assailed with apprehensions as that of my coming down to learn that the carriage containing Mrs. Grose and my younger pupil had already rolled out of the gates. Now I was, I said to myself, face to face with the elements, and for much of the rest of the day, while I fought my weakness, I could consider that I had been supremely rash. It was a tighter place still than I had yet turned round in; all the more that, for the first time, I could see in the aspect of others a confused reflection of the crisis. What had happened naturally caused them all to stare; there was too little of the explained, throw out whatever we might, in the suddenness of my colleague's act. The maids and the men looked blank; the effect of which on my nerves was an aggravation until I saw the necessity of making it a positive aid. It was precisely, in short, by just clutching the helm that I avoided total wreck; and I dare say that, to bear up at all, I became, that morning, very grand and very dry. I welcomed the consciousness that I was charged with much to do, and I caused it to be known as well that, left thus to myself, I was quite remarkably firm. I wandered with that manner, for the next hour or two, all over the place and looked, I have no doubt, as if I were ready for any onset. So, for the benefit of whom it might concern, I paraded with a sick heart.

The person it appeared least to concern proved to be, till dinner, little Miles himself. My perambulations had given me, meanwhile, no glimpse of him, but they had tended to make more public the change taking place in our relation as a consequence of his having at the piano, the day before, kept me, in Flora's interest, so beguiled and befooled. The stamp of publicity had of course been fully given by her confinement and departure, and the change itself was now ushered in by our nonobservance of the regular custom of the schoolroom. He had already disappeared when, on my way down, I pushed open his door, and I learned below that he had breakfasted—in the presence of a couple of the maids—with Mrs. Grose and his sister. He had then gone out, as he said, for a stroll; than which nothing, I reflected, could better have expressed his frank view of the abrupt transformation of my office. What he would not permit this office to consist of was yet to be settled: there was a queer relief, at all events—I mean for myself in especial—in the renouncement of one pretension. If so much had sprung to the surface, I scarce put it too strongly in saying that what had perhaps sprung highest was the absurdity of our prolonging the fiction that I had anything more to teach him. It sufficiently stuck out that, by tacit little tricks in which even more than myself he carried out the care for my dignity, I had had to appeal to him to let me off straining to meet him on the ground of his true capacity. He had at any rate his freedom now; I was never to touch it again; as I had amply shown, moreover, when, on his joining me in the schoolroom the previous night, I had uttered, on the subject of the interval just concluded, neither challenge nor hint. I had too much, from this moment, my other ideas. Yet when he at last arrived, the difficulty of applying them, the accumulations of my problem, were brought straight home to me by the beautiful little presence on which what had occurred had as yet, for the eye, dropped neither stain nor shadow.

To mark, for the house, the high state I cultivated I decreed that my meals with the boy should be served, as we called it, downstairs; so that I had been awaiting him in the ponderous pomp of the room outside of the window of which I had had from Mrs. Grose, that first scared Sunday, my flash of something it would scarce have done to call light. Here at present I felt afresh—for I had felt it again and again—how my equilibrium depended on the success of my rigid will, the will to shut my eyes as tight as possible to the truth that what I had to deal with was, revoltingly, against nature. I could only get on at all by taking "nature" into my confidence and my account, by treating my monstrous ordeal as a push in a direction unusual, of course, and unpleasant, but demanding, after all, for a fair front, only another turn of the screw of ordinary human virtue. No attempt, nonetheless, could well require more tact than just this attempt to supply, one's self, all the nature. How could I put even a little of that article into a suppression of reference to what had occurred? How, on the other hand, could I make reference without a new plunge into the hideous obscure? Well, a sort of answer, after a time, had come to me, and it was so far confirmed as that I was met, incontestably, by the quickened vision of what was rare in my little companion. It was indeed as if he had found even now—as he had so often found at lessons—still some other delicate way to ease me off. Wasn't there light in the fact which, as we shared our solitude, broke out with a specious glitter it had never yet quite worn?—the fact that (opportunity aiding, precious opportunity which had now come) it would be preposterous, with a child so endowed, to forego the help one might wrest from absolute intelligence? What had his intelligence been given him for but to save him? Mightn't one, to reach his mind, risk the stretch of an angular arm over his character? It was as if, when we were face to face in the dining room, he had literally shown me the way. The roast mutton was on the table, and I had dispensed with attendance. Miles, before he sat down, stood a moment with his hands in his pockets and looked at the joint, on which he seemed on the point of passing some humorous judgment. But what he presently produced was: "I say, my dear, is she really very awfully ill?"

"Little Flora? Not so bad but that she'll presently be better. London will set her up. Bly had ceased to agree with her. Come here and take your mutton."

He alertly obeyed me, carried the plate carefully to his seat, and, when he was established, went on. "Did Bly disagree with her so terribly suddenly?"

"Not so suddenly as you might think. One had seen it coming on."

"Then why didn't you get her off before?"

"Before what?"

"Before she became too ill to travel."

I found myself prompt. "She's *not* too ill to travel: she only might have become so if she had stayed. This was just the moment to seize. The journey will dissipate the influence"—oh, I was grand!—"and carry it off."

"I see, I see"—Miles, for that matter, was grand, too. He settled to his repast with the charming little "table manner" that, from the day of his arrival, had relieved me of all grossness of admonition. Whatever he had been driven from school for, it was not for ugly feeding. He was irreproachable, as always, today; but he was unmistakably more conscious. He was discernibly trying to take for granted more things than he found, without assistance, quite easy; and he dropped into peaceful silence while he felt his situation. Our meal was of the briefest—mine a vain pretense, and I had the things immediately removed. While this was done Miles stood again with his hands in his little pockets and his back to me—stood and looked out of the wide window through which, that other day, I had seen what pulled me up. We continued silent while the maid was with us—as silent, it whimsically occurred to me, as some young couple who, on their wedding journey, at the inn, feel shy in the presence of the waiter. He turned round only when the waiter had left us. "Well—so we're alone!"

XXIII

"Oh, more or less." I fancy my smile was pale. "Not absolutely. We shouldn't like that!" I went on.

"No—I suppose we shouldn't. Of course we have the others."

"We have the others—we have indeed the others," I concurred.

"Yet even though we have them," he returned, still with his hands in his pockets and planted there in front of me, "they don't much count, do they?"

I made the best of it, but I felt wan. "It depends on what you call 'much'!"

"Yes"—with all accommodation—"everything depends!" On this, however, he faced to the window again and presently reached it with his vague, restless, cogitating step. He remained there awhile, with his forehead against the glass, in contemplation of the stupid shrubs I knew and the dull things of November. I had always my hypocrisy of "work," behind which, now, I gained the sofa. Steadying myself with it there as I had repeatedly done at those moments of torment that I have described as the moments of my knowing the children to be given to something from which I was barred, I sufficiently obeyed my habit of being prepared for the worst. But an extraordinary impression dropped on me as I extracted a meaning from the boy's embarrassed back—none other than the impression that I was not barred now. This inference grew in a few minutes to sharp intensity and seemed bound up with the direct perception that it was positively *he* who was. The frames and squares of the great window were a kind of image, for him, of a kind of failure. I felt that I saw him, at any rate, shut in or shut out. He was admirable, but not comfortable: I took it in with a throb of hope. Wasn't he looking, through the haunted pane, for something he couldn't see?—and wasn't it the first time in the whole business that he had known such a lapse? The first, the very first: I found it a splendid portent. It made him anxious, though he watched himself; he had been anxious all day and, even while in his usual sweet little manner he sat at table, had needed all his small strange genius to give it a gloss. When he at last turned round to meet me, it was almost as if this genius had succumbed. "Well, I think I'm glad Bly agrees with me!"

"You would certainly seem to have seen, these twenty-four hours, a good deal more of it than for some time before. I hope," I went on bravely, "that you've been enjoying yourself."

"Oh, yes, I've been ever so far; all round about—miles and miles away. I've never been so free."

He had really a manner of his own, and I could only try to keep up with him. "Well, do you like it?"

He stood there smiling; then at last he put into two words—"Do *you*?"—more discrimination than I had ever heard two words contain. Before I had time to deal with that, however, he continued as if with the sense that this was an impertinence to be softened. "Nothing could be more charming than the way you take it, for of course if we're alone together now it's you that are alone most. But I hope," he threw in, "you don't particularly mind!"

"Having to do with you?" I asked. "My dear child, how can I help minding? Though I've renounced all claim to your company—you're so beyond me—I at least greatly enjoy it. What else should I stay on for?"

He looked at me more directly, and the expression of his face, graver now, struck me as the most beautiful I had ever found in it. "You stay on just for *that?*"

"Certainly. I stay on as your friend and from the tremendous interest I take in you till something can be done for you that may be more worth your while. That needn't surprise you." My voice trembled so that I felt it impossible to suppress the shake. "Don't you remember how I told you, when I came and sat on your bed the night of the storm, that there was nothing in the world I wouldn't do for you?"

"Yes, yes!" He, on his side, more and more visibly nervous, had a tone to master; but he was so much more successful than I that, laughing out through his gravity, he could pretend we were pleasantly jesting. "Only that, I think, was to get me to do something for *you*!"

"It was partly to get you to do something," I conceded. "But, you know, you didn't do it."

"Oh, yes," he said with the brightest superficial eagerness, "you wanted me to tell you something."

"That's it. Out, straight out. What you have on your mind, you know."

"Ah, then, is *that* what you've stayed over for?"

He spoke with a gaiety through which I could still catch the finest little quiver of resentful passion; but I can't begin to express the effect upon me of an implication of surrender even so faint. It was as if what I had yearned for had come at last only to astonish me. "Well, yes—I may as well make a clean breast of it, it was precisely for that."

He waited so long that I supposed it for the purpose of repudiating the assumption on which my action had been founded; but what he finally said was: "Do you mean now—here?"

"There couldn't be a better place or time." He looked round him uneasily, and I had the rare—oh, the queer!—impression of the very first symptom I had seen in him of the approach of immediate fear. It was as if he were suddenly afraid of me—which struck me indeed as perhaps the best thing to make him. Yet in the very pang of the effort I felt it vain to try sternness, and I heard myself the next instant so gentle as to be almost grotesque. "You want so to go out again?"

"Awfully!" He smiled at me heroically, and the touching little bravery of it was enhanced by his actually flushing with pain. He had picked up his hat, which he had brought in, and stood twirling it in a way that gave me, even as I was just nearly reaching port, a perverse horror of what I was doing. To do it in *any* way was an act of violence, for what did it consist of but the obtrusion of the idea of grossness and guilt on a small helpless creature who had been for me a revelation of the possibilities of beautiful intercourse? Wasn't it base to create for a being so exquisite a mere alien awkwardness? I suppose I now read into our situation a clearness it couldn't have had at the time, for I seem to see our poor eyes already lighted with some spark of a prevision of the anguish that was to come. So we circled about, with terrors and scruples, like fighters not daring to close. But it was for each other we feared! That kept us a little longer suspended and unbruised. "I'll tell you everything," Miles said—"I mean I'll tell you anything you like. You'll stay on with me, and we shall both be all right, and I *will* tell you—I *will*. But not now."

"Why not now?"

My insistence turned him from me and kept him once more at his window in a silence during which, between us, you might have heard a pin drop. Then he was before me again with the air of a person for whom, outside, someone who had frankly to be reckoned with was waiting. "I have to see Luke."

I had not yet reduced him to quite so vulgar a lie, and I felt proportionately ashamed. But, horrible as it was, his lies made up my truth. I achieved thoughtfully a few loops of my knitting. "Well, then, go to Luke, and I'll wait for what you promise. Only, in return for that, satisfy, before you leave me, one very much smaller request."

He looked as if he felt he had succeeded enough to be able still a little to bargain. "Very much smaller—?"

"Yes, a mere fraction of the whole. Tell me"—oh, my work preoccupied me, and I was offhand!—"if, yesterday afternoon, from the table in the hall, you took, you know, my letter."

XXIV

My sense of how he received this suffered for a minute from something that I can describe only as a fierce split of my attention—a stroke that at first, as I sprang straight up, reduced me to the mere blind movement of getting hold of him, drawing him close, and, while I just fell for support against the nearest piece of furniture, instinctively keeping him with his back to the window. The appearance was full upon us that I had already had to deal with here: Peter Quint had come into view like a sentinel before a prison. The next thing I saw was that, from outside, he had reached the window, and then I knew that, close to the glass and glaring in through it, he offered once more to the room his white face of damnation. It represents but grossly what took place within me at the sight to say that on the second my decision was made; yet I believe that no woman so overwhelmed ever in so short a time recovered her grasp of the *act*. It came to me in the very horror of the immediate presence that the act would be, seeing and facing what I saw and faced, to keep the boy himself unaware. The inspiration—I can call it by no other name—was that I felt how voluntarily, how transcendently, I *might*. It was like fighting with a demon for a human soul, and when I had fairly so appraised it I saw how the human soul—held out, in the tremor of my hands, at arm's length—had a perfect dew of sweat on a lovely childish forehead. The face that was close to mine was as white as the face against the glass, and out of it presently came a sound, not low nor weak, but as if from much further away, that I drank like a waft of fragrance.

"Yes—I took it."

At this, with a moan of joy, I enfolded, I drew him close; and while I held him to my breast, where I could feel in the sudden fever of his little body the tremendous pulse of his little heart, I kept my eyes on the thing at the window and saw it move and shift its posture. I have likened it to a sentinel, but its slow wheel, for a moment, was rather the prowl of a baffled beast. My present quickened courage, however, was such that, not too much to let it through, I had to shade, as it were, my flame. Meanwhile the glare of the face was again at the window, the scoundrel fixed as if to watch and wait. It was the very confidence that I might now defy him, as well as the positive certitude, by this time, of the child's unconsciousness, that made me go on. "What did you take it for?"

"To see what you said about me."

"You opened the letter?"

"I opened it."

My eyes were now, as I held him off a little again, on Miles's own face, in which the collapse of mockery showed me how complete was the ravage of uneasiness. What was prodigious was that at last, by my success, his sense was sealed and his communication stopped: he knew that he was in presence, but knew not of what, and knew still less that I also was and that I did know. And what did this strain of trouble matter when my eyes went back to the window only to see that the air was clear again and—by my personal triumph—the influence quenched? There was nothing there. I felt that the cause was mine and that I should surely get *all.* "And you found nothing!"—I let my elation out.

He gave the most mournful, thoughtful little headshake. "Nothing."

"Nothing, nothing!" I almost shouted in my joy.

"Nothing, nothing," he sadly repeated.

I kissed his forehead; it was drenched. "So what have you done with it?"

"I've burned it."

"Burned it?" It was now or never. "Is that what you did at school?"

Oh, what this brought up! "At school?"

"Did you take letters?—or other things?"

"Other things?" He appeared now to be thinking of something far off and that reached him only through the pressure of his anxiety. Yet it did reach him. "Did I *steal?*"

I felt myself redden to the roots of my hair as well as wonder if it were more strange to put to a gentleman such a question or to see him take it with allowances that gave the very distance of his fall in the world. "Was it for that you mightn't go back?"

The only thing he felt was rather a dreary little surprise. "Did you know I mightn't go back?"

"I know everything."

He gave me at this the longest and strangest look. "Everything?"

"Everything. Therefore *did* you—?" But I couldn't say it again.

Miles could, very simply. "No. I didn't steal."

My face must have shown him I believed him utterly; yet my hands—but it was for pure tenderness—shook him as if to ask him why, if it was all for nothing, he had condemned me to months of torment. "What then did you do?"

He looked in vague pain all round the top of the room and drew his breath, two or three times over, as if with difficulty. He might have been standing at the bottom of the sea and raising his eyes to some faint green twilight. "Well—I said things."

"Only that?"

"They thought it was enough!"

"To turn you out for?"

Never, truly, had a person "turned out" shown so little to explain it as this little person! He appeared to weigh my question, but in a manner quite detached and almost helpless. "Well, I suppose I oughtn't."

"But to whom did you say them?"

He evidently tried to remember, but it dropped—he had lost it. "I don't know!"

He almost smiled at me in the desolation of his surrender, which was indeed practically, by this time, so complete that I ought to have left it there. But I was infatuated—I was blind with victory, though even then the very effect that was to have brought him so much nearer was already that of added separation. "Was it to everyone?" I asked.

"No; it was only to—" But he gave a sick little headshake. "I don't remember their names."

"Were they then so many?"

"No—only a few. Those I liked."

Those he liked? I seemed to float not into clearness, but into a darker obscure, and within a minute there had come to me out of my very pity the appalling alarm of his being perhaps innocent. It was for the instant confounding and bottomless, for if he *were* innocent, what then on earth was *I?* Paralyzed, while it lasted, by the mere brush of the question, I let him go a little, so that, with a deep-drawn sigh, he turned away from me again; which, as he faced toward the clear window, I suffered, feeling that I had nothing now there to keep him from. "And did they repeat what you said?" I went on after a moment.

He was soon at some distance from me, still breathing hard and again with the air, though now without anger for it, of being confined against his will. Once more, as he had done before, he looked up at the dim day as if, of what had hitherto sustained him, nothing was left but an unspeakable anxiety. "Oh, yes," he nevertheless replied—"they must have repeated them. To those *they* liked," he added.

There was, somehow, less of it than I had expected; but I turned it over. "And these things came round—?"

"To the masters? Oh, yes!" he answered very simply. "But I didn't know they'd tell."

"The masters? They didn't—they've never told. That's why I ask you."

He turned to me again his little beautiful fevered face. "Yes, it was too bad."

"Too bad?"

"What I suppose I sometimes said. To write home."

I can't name the exquisite pathos of the contradiction given to such a speech by such a speaker; I only know that the next instant I heard myself throw off with homely force: "Stuff and nonsense!" But the next after that I must have sounded stern enough. "What were these things?"

My sternness was all for his judge, his executioner; yet it made him avert himself again, and that movement made *me*, with a single bound and an irrepressible cry, spring straight upon him. For there again, against the glass, as if to blight his confession and stay his answer, was the hideous author of our woe—the white face of damnation. I felt a sick swim at the drop of my victory and all the return of my battle, so that the wildness of my veritable leap only served as a great betrayal. I saw him, from the midst of my act, meet it with a divination, and on the perception that even now he only guessed, and that the window was still to his own eyes free, I let the impulse flame up to convert the climax of his dismay into the very proof of his liberation. "No more, no more, no more!" I shrieked, as I tried to press him against me, to my visitant.

"Is she *here*?" Miles panted as he caught with his sealed eyes the direction of my words. Then as his strange "she" staggered me and, with a gasp, I echoed it, "Miss Jessel, Miss Jessel!" he with a sudden fury gave me back.

I seized, stupefied, his supposition—some sequel to what we had done to Flora, but this made me only want to show him that it was better still than that. "It's not Miss Jessel! But it's at the window—straight before us. It's *there*—the coward horror, there for the last time!"

At this, after a second in which his head made the movement of a baffled dog's on a scent and then gave a frantic little shake for air and light, he was at me in a white rage, bewildered, glaring vainly over the place and missing wholly, though it now, to my sense, filled the room like the taste of poison, the wide, overwhelming presence. "It's *he?*"

I was so determined to have all my proof that I flashed into ice to challenge him. "Whom do you mean by 'he'?"

"Peter Quint—you devil!" His face gave again, round the room, its convulsed supplication. "*Where?*"

They are in my ears still, his supreme surrender of the name and his tribute to my devotion. "What does he matter now, my own?—what will he *ever* matter? I have you," I launched at the beast, "but he has lost you forever!" Then, for the demonstration of my work, "There, *there!*" I said to Miles.

But he had already jerked straight round, stared, glared again, and seen but the quiet day. With the stroke of the loss I was so proud of he uttered the cry of a creature hurled over an abyss, and the grasp with which I recovered him might have been that of catching him in his fall. I caught him, yes, I held him—it may be imagined with what a passion; but at the end of a minute I began to feel what it truly was that I held. We were alone with the quiet day, and his little heart, dispossessed, had stopped.

THE WILLOWS

Algernon Blackwood

I

After leaving Vienna, and long before you come to Budapest, the Danube enters a region of singular loneliness and desolation, where its waters spread away on all sides regardless of a main channel, and the country becomes a swamp for miles upon miles, covered by a vast sea of low willow-bushes. On the big maps this deserted area is painted in a fluffy blue, growing fainter in color as it leaves the banks, and across it may be seen in large straggling letters the word *Sümpfe*, meaning marshes.

In high flood this great acreage of sand, shingle-beds, and willow-grown islands is almost topped by the water, but in normal seasons the bushes bend and rustle in the free winds, showing their silver leaves to the sunshine in an ever-moving plain of bewildering beauty. These willows never attain to the dignity of trees; they have no rigid trunks; they remain humble bushes, with rounded tops and soft outline, swaying on slender stems that answer to the least pressure of the wind; supple as grasses, and so continually shifting that they somehow give the impression that the entire plain is moving and alive. For the wind sends waves rising and falling over the whole surface, waves of leaves instead of waves of water, green swells like the sea, too, until the branches turn and lift, and then silvery white as their underside turns to the sun.

Happy to slip beyond the control of the stern banks, the Danube here wanders about at will among the intricate network of channels intersecting the islands everywhere with broad avenues down which the waters pour with a shouting sound; making whirlpools, eddies, and foaming rapids; tearing at the sandy banks; carrying away masses of shore and willow-clumps; and forming new islands innumerably which shift daily in size and shape and possess at best an impermanent life, since the flood-time obliterates their very existence.

Properly speaking, this fascinating part of the river's life begins soon after leaving Pressburg, and we, in our Canadian canoe, with gipsy tent and frying-pan on board, reached it on the crest of a rising flood about mid-July. That very same morning, when the sky was reddening before sunrise, we had slipped swiftly through still-sleeping Vienna, leaving it a couple of hours later a mere patch of smoke against the blue hills of the Wienerwald on the horizon; we had breakfasted below Fischeramend under a grove of birch trees roaring in the wind; and had then swept on the tearing current past Orth, Hainburg, Petronell (the old Roman Carnuntum of Marcus Aurelius), and so under the frowning heights of Thelsen on a spur of the Carpathians, where the March steals in quietly from the left and the frontier is crossed between Austria and Hungary.

Racing along at twelve kilometers an hour soon took us well into Hungary, and the muddy waters—sure sign of flood—sent us aground on many a shingle-bed, and twisted us like a cork in many a sudden belching whirlpool before the towers of Pressburg (Hungarian, Poszony) showed against the sky; and then the canoe, leaping like a spirited horse, flew at top speed under the grey walls, negotiated safely the sunken chain of the Fliegende Brucke ferry, turned the corner sharply to the left, and plunged on yellow foam into the wilderness of islands, sandbanks, and swamp-land beyond—the land of the willows.

The change came suddenly, as when a series of bioscope pictures snaps down on the streets of a town and shifts without warning into the scenery of lake and forest. We entered the land of desolation on wings, and in less than half an hour there was neither boat nor fishing-hut nor red roof, nor any single sign of human habitation and civilization within sight. The sense of remoteness from the world of humankind, the utter isolation, the fascination of this singular world of willows, winds, and waters, instantly laid its spell upon us both, so that we allowed laughingly to one another that we ought by rights to have held some special kind of passport to admit us, and that we had, somewhat audaciously, come without asking leave into a separate little kingdom of wonder and magic—a kingdom that was reserved for the use of others who had a right to it, with everywhere unwritten warnings to trespassers for those who had the imagination to discover them.

Though still early in the afternoon, the ceaseless buffetings of a most tempestuous wind made us feel weary, and we at once began casting about for a suitable camping-ground for the night. But the bewildering character of the islands made landing difficult; the swirling flood carried us in shore and then swept us out again; the willow branches tore our hands as we seized them to stop the canoe, and we pulled many a yard of sandy bank into the water before at length we shot with a great sideways blow from the wind into a backwater and managed to beach the bows in a cloud of spray. Then we lay panting and laughing after our exertions on the hot yellow sand, sheltered from the wind, and in the full blaze of a scorching sun, a cloudless blue sky above, and an immense army of dancing, shouting willow bushes, closing in from all sides, shining with spray and clapping their thousand little hands as though to applaud the success of our efforts.

"What a river!" I said to my companion, thinking of all the way we had traveled from the source in the Black Forest, and how he had often been obliged to wade and push in the upper shallows at the beginning of June.

"Won't stand much nonsense now, will it?" he said, pulling the canoe a little farther into safety up the sand, and then composing himself for a nap.

I lay by his side, happy and peaceful in the bath of the elements—water, wind, sand, and the great fire of the sun—thinking of the long journey that lay behind us, and of the great stretch before us to the Black Sea, and how lucky I was to have such a delightful and charming traveling companion as my friend, the Swede.

We had made many similar journeys together, but the Danube, more than any other river I knew, impressed us from the very beginning with its aliveness. From its tiny bubbling entry into the world among the pinewood gardens of Donaueschingen, until this moment when it began to play the great river-game of losing itself among the deserted swamps, unobserved, unrestrained, it had seemed to us like following the growth of some living creature. Sleepy at first, but later developing violent desires as it became conscious of its deep soul, it rolled, like some huge fluid being, through all the countries we had passed, holding our little craft on its mighty shoulders, playing roughly with us sometimes, yet always friendly and well-meaning, till at length we had come inevitably to regard it as a Great Personage.

How, indeed, could it be otherwise, since it told us so much of its secret life? At night we heard it singing to the moon as we lay in our tent, uttering that odd sibilant note peculiar to itself and said to be caused by the rapid tearing of the pebbles along its bed, so great is its hurrying speed. We knew, too, the voice of its gurgling whirlpools, suddenly bubbling up on a surface previously quite calm; the roar of its shallows and swift rapids; its constant steady thundering below all mere surface sounds; and that ceaseless tearing of its icy waters at the banks. How it stood up and shouted when the rains fell flat upon its face! And how its laughter roared out when the wind blew up-stream and tried to stop its growing speed! We knew all its sounds and voices, its tumblings and foamings, its unnecessary splashing against the bridges; that self-conscious chatter when there were hills to look on; the affected dignity of its speech when it passed through the little towns, far too important to laugh; and all these faint, sweet whisperings when the sun caught it fairly in some slow curve and poured down upon it till the steam rose.

It was full of tricks, too, in its early life before the great world knew it. There were places in the upper reaches among the Swabian forests, when yet the first whispers of its destiny had not reached it, where it elected to disappear through holes in the ground, to appear again on the other side of the porous limestone hills and start a new river with another name; leaving, too, so little water in its own bed that we had to climb out and wade and push the canoe through miles of shallows.

And a chief pleasure, in those early days of its irresponsible youth, was to lie low, like Brer Fox, just before the little turbulent tributaries came to join it from the Alps, and to refuse to acknowledge them when in, but to run for miles side by side, the dividing line well marked, the very levels different, the Danube utterly declining to recognize the newcomer. Below Passau, however, it gave up this particular trick, for there the Inn comes in with a thundering power impossible to ignore, and so pushes and incommodes the parent river that there is hardly room for them in the long twisting gorge that follows, and the Danube is shoved this way and that against the cliffs, and forced to hurry itself with great waves and much dashing to and fro in order to get through in time. And during the fight our canoe slipped down from its shoulder to its breast, and had the time of its life among the struggling waves. But the Inn taught the old river a lesson, and after Passau it no longer pretended to ignore new arrivals.

This was many days back, of course, and since then we had come to know other aspects of the great creature, and across the Bavarian wheat plain of Straubing she wandered so slowly under the blazing June sun that we could well imagine only the surface inches were water, while below there moved, concealed as by a silken mantle, a whole army of Undines, passing silently and unseen down to the sea, and very leisurely too, lest they be discovered.

Much, too, we forgave her because of her friendliness to the birds and animals that haunted the shores. Cormorants lined the banks in lonely places in rows like short black palings; grey crows crowded the shingle-beds; storks stood fishing in the vistas of shallower water that opened up between the islands, and hawks, swans, and marsh birds of all sorts filled the air with glinting wings and singing, petulant cries. It was impossible to feel annoyed with the river's vagaries after seeing a deer leap with a splash into the water at sunrise and swim past the bows of the canoe; and often we saw fawns peering at us from the underbrush, or looked straight into the brown eyes of a stag as we charged full tilt round a corner and entered another reach of the river. Foxes, too, everywhere haunted the banks, tripping daintily among the driftwood and disappearing so suddenly that it was impossible to see how they managed it.

But now, after leaving Pressburg, everything changed a little, and the Danube became more serious. It ceased trifling. It was half-way to the Black Sea, within seeming distance almost of other, stranger countries where no tricks would be permitted or understood. It became suddenly grown-up, and claimed our respect and even our awe. It broke out into three arms, for one thing, that only met again a hundred kilometers farther down, and for a canoe there were no indications which one was intended to be followed.

"If you take a side channel," said the Hungarian officer we met in the Pressburg shop while buying provisions, "you may find yourselves, when the flood subsides, forty miles from anywhere, high and dry, and you may easily starve. There are no people, no farms, no fishermen. I warn you not to continue. The river, too, is still rising, and this wind will increase."

The rising river did not alarm us in the least, but the matter of being left high and dry by a sudden subsidence of the waters might be serious, and we had consequently laid in an extra stock of provisions. For the rest, the officer's prophecy held true, and the wind, blowing down a perfectly clear sky, increased steadily till it reached the dignity of a westerly gale.

It was earlier than usual when we camped, for the sun was a good hour or two from the horizon, and leaving my friend still asleep on the hot sand, I wandered about in desultory examination of our hotel. The island, I found, was less than an acre in extent, a mere sandy bank standing some two or three feet above the level of the river. The far end, pointing into the sunset, was covered with flying spray which the tremendous wind drove off the crests of the broken waves. It was triangular in shape, with the apex up stream.

I stood there for several minutes, watching the impetuous crimson flood bearing down with a shouting roar, dashing in waves against the bank as though to sweep it bodily away, and then swirling by in two foaming streams on either side. The ground seemed to shake with the shock and rush, while the furious movement of the willow bushes as the wind poured over them increased the curious illusion that the island itself actually moved. Above, for a mile or two, I could see the great river descending upon me; it was like looking up the slope of a sliding hill, white with foam, and leaping up everywhere to show itself to the sun.

The rest of the island was too thickly grown with willows to make walking pleasant, but I made the tour, nevertheless. From the lower end the light, of course, changed, and the river looked dark and angry. Only the backs of the flying waves were visible, streaked with foam, and pushed forcibly by the great puffs of wind that fell upon them from behind. For a short mile it was visible, pouring in and out among the islands, and then disappearing with a huge sweep into the willows, which closed about it like a herd of monstrous antediluvian creatures crowding down to drink. They made me think of gigantic sponge-like growths that sucked the river up into themselves. They caused it to vanish from sight. They herded there together in such overpowering numbers.

Altogether it was an impressive scene, with its utter loneliness, its bizarre suggestion; and as I gazed, long and curiously, a singular emotion began to stir somewhere in the depths of me. Midway in my delight of the wild beauty, there crept, unbidden and unexplained, a curious feeling of disquietude, almost of alarm.

A rising river, perhaps, always suggests something of the ominous; many of the little islands I saw before me would probably have been swept away by the morning; this resistless, thundering flood of water touched the sense of awe. Yet I was aware that my uneasiness lay deeper far than the emotions of awe and wonder. It was not that I felt. Nor had it directly to do with the power of the driving wind—this shouting hurricane that might almost carry up a few acres of willows into the air and scatter them like so much chaff over the landscape. The wind was simply enjoying itself, for nothing rose out of the flat landscape to stop it, and I was conscious of sharing its great game with a kind of pleasurable excitement. Yet this novel emotion had nothing to do with the wind. Indeed, so vague was the sense of distress I experienced, that it was impossible to trace it to its source and deal with it accordingly, though I was aware somehow that it had to do with my realization of our utter insignificance before this unrestrained power of the elements about me. The huge-grown river had something to do with it too—a vague, unpleasant idea that we had somehow trifled with these great elemental forces in whose power we lay helpless every hour of the day and night. For here, indeed, they were gigantically at play together, and the sight appealed to the imagination.

But my emotion, so far as I could understand it, seemed to attach itself more particularly to the willow bushes, to these acres and acres of willows, crowding, so thickly growing there, swarming everywhere the eye could reach, pressing upon the river as though to suffocate it, standing in dense array mile after mile beneath the sky, watching, waiting, listening. And, apart quite from the elements, the willows connected themselves subtly with my malaise, attacking the mind insidiously somehow by reason of their vast numbers, and contriving in some way or other to represent to the imagination a new and mighty power, a power, moreover, not altogether friendly to us.

Great revelations of nature, of course, never fail to impress in one way or another, and I was no stranger to moods of the kind. Mountains overawe and oceans terrify, while the mystery of great forests exercises a spell peculiarly its own. But all these, at one point or another, somewhere link on intimately with human life and human experience. They stir comprehensible, even if alarming, emotions. They tend on the whole to exalt.

With this multitude of willows, however, it was something far different, I felt. Some essence emanated from them that besieged the heart. A sense of awe awakened, true, but of awe touched somewhere by a vague terror. Their serried ranks, growing everywhere darker about me as the shadows deepened, moving furiously yet softly in the wind, woke in me the curious and unwelcome suggestion that we had trespassed here upon the borders of an alien world, a world where we were intruders, a world where we were not wanted or invited to remain—where we ran grave risks perhaps!

The feeling, however, though it refused to yield its meaning entirely to analysis, did not at the time trouble me by passing into menace. Yet it never left me quite, even during the very practical business of putting up the tent in a hurricane of wind and building a fire for the stew-pot. It remained, just enough to bother and perplex, and to rob a most delightful camping-ground of a good portion of its charm. To my companion, however, I said nothing, for he was a man I considered devoid of imagination. In the first place, I could never have explained to him what I meant, and in the second, he would have laughed stupidly at me if I had.

There was a slight depression in the center of the island, and here we pitched the tent. The surrounding willows broke the wind a bit.

"A poor camp," observed the imperturbable Swede when at last the tent stood upright, "no stones and precious little firewood. I'm for moving on early tomorrow—eh? This sand won't hold anything."

But the experience of a collapsing tent at midnight had taught us many devices, and we made the cozy gipsy house as safe as possible, and then set about collecting a store of wood to last till bed-time. Willow bushes drop no branches, and driftwood was our only source of supply. We hunted the shores pretty thoroughly. Everywhere the banks were crumbling as the rising flood tore at them and carried away great portions with a splash and a gurgle.

"The island's much smaller than when we landed," said the accurate Swede. "It won't last long at this rate. We'd better drag the canoe close to the tent, and be ready to start at a moment's notice. I shall sleep in my clothes."

He was a little distance off, climbing along the bank, and I heard his rather jolly laugh as he spoke.

"By Jove!" I heard him call, a moment later, and turned to see what had caused his exclamation. But for the moment he was hidden by the willows, and I could not find him.

"What in the world's this?" I heard him cry again, and this time his voice had become serious.

I ran up quickly and joined him on the bank. He was looking over the river, pointing at something in the water.

"Good heavens, it's a man's body!" he cried excitedly. "Look!"

A black thing, turning over and over in the foaming waves, swept rapidly past. It kept disappearing and coming up to the surface again. It was about twenty feet from the shore, and just as it was opposite to where we stood it lurched round and looked straight at us. We saw its eyes reflecting the sunset, and gleaming an odd yellow as the body turned over. Then it gave a swift, gulping plunge, and dived out of sight in a flash.

"An otter, by gad!" we exclaimed in the same breath, laughing.

It was an otter, alive, and out on the hunt; yet it had looked exactly like the body of a drowned man turning helplessly in the current. Far below it came to the surface once again, and we saw its black skin, wet and shining in the sunlight.

Then, too, just as we turned back, our arms full of driftwood, another thing happened to recall us to the river bank. This time it really was a man, and what was more, a man in a boat. Now a small boat on the Danube was an unusual sight at any time, but here in this deserted region, and at flood time, it was so unexpected as to constitute a real event. We stood and stared.

Whether it was due to the slanting sunlight, or the refraction from the wonderfully illumined water, I cannot say, but, whatever the cause, I found it difficult to focus my sight properly upon the flying apparition. It seemed, however, to be a man standing upright in a sort of flat-bottomed boat, steering with a long oar, and being carried down the opposite shore at a tremendous pace. He apparently was looking across in our direction, but the distance was too great and the light too uncertain for us to make out very plainly what he was about. It seemed to me that he was gesticulating and making signs at us. His voice came across the water to us shouting something furiously, but the wind drowned it so that no single word was audible. There was something curious about the whole appearance—man, boat, signs, voice—that made an impression on me out of all proportion to its cause.

"He's crossing himself!" I cried. "Look, he's making the sign of the Cross!"

"I believe you're right," the Swede said, shading his eyes with his hand and watching the man out of sight. He seemed to be gone in a moment, melting away down there into the sea of willows where the sun caught them in the bend of the river and turned them into a great crimson wall of beauty. Mist, too, had begun to ruse, so that the air was hazy.

"But what in the world is he doing at nightfall on this flooded river?" I said, half to myself. "Where is he going at such a time, and what did he mean by his signs and shouting? D'you think he wished to warn us about something?"

"He saw our smoke, and thought we were spirits probably," laughed my companion. "These Hungarians believe in all sorts of rubbish; you remember the shopwoman at Pressburg warning us that no one ever landed here because it belonged to some sort of beings outside man's world! I suppose they believe in fairies and elementals, possibly demons, too. That peasant in the boat saw people on the islands for the first time in his life," he added, after a slight pause, "and it scared him, that's all."

The Swede's tone of voice was not convincing, and his manner lacked something that was usually there. I noted the change instantly while he talked, though without being able to label it precisely.

"If they had enough imagination," I laughed loudly—I remember trying to make as much noise as I could—"they might well people a place like this with the old gods of antiquity. The Romans must have haunted all this region more or less with their shrines and sacred groves and elemental deities."

The subject dropped and we returned to our stew-pot, for my friend was not given to imaginative conversation as a rule. Moreover, just then I remember feeling distinctly glad that he was not imaginative; his stolid, practical nature suddenly seemed to me welcome and comforting. It was an admirable temperament, I felt; he could steer down rapids like a red Indian, shoot dangerous bridges and whirlpools better than any white man I ever saw in a canoe. He was a grand fellow for an adventurous trip, a tower of strength when untoward things happened. I looked at his strong face and light curly hair as he staggered along under his pile of driftwood (twice the size of mine!), and I experienced a feeling of relief. Yes, I was distinctly glad just then that the Swede was—what he was, and that he never made remarks that suggested more than they said.

"The river's still rising, though," he added, as if following out some thoughts of his own, and dropping his load with a gasp. "This island will be under water in two days if it goes on."

"I wish the wind would go down," I said. "I don't care a fig for the river."

The flood, indeed, had no terrors for us; we could get off at ten minutes' notice, and the more water the better we liked it. It meant an increasing current and the obliteration of the treacherous shingle-beds that so often threatened to tear the bottom out of our canoe.

Contrary to our expectations, the wind did not go down with the sun. It seemed to increase with the darkness, howling overhead and shaking the willows round us like straws. Curious sounds accompanied it sometimes, like the explosion of heavy guns, and it fell upon the water and the island in great flat blows of immense power. It made me think of the sounds a planet must make, could we only hear it, driving along through space.

But the sky kept wholly clear of clouds, and soon after supper the full moon rose up in the east and covered the river and the plain of shouting willows with a light like the day.

We lay on the sandy patch beside the fire, smoking, listening to the noises of the night round us, and talking happily of the journey we had already made, and of our plans ahead. The map lay spread in the door of the tent, but the high wind made it hard to study, and presently we lowered the curtain and extinguished the lantern. The firelight was enough to smoke and see each other's faces by, and the sparks flew about overhead like fireworks. A few yards beyond, the river gurgled and hissed, and from time to time a heavy splash announced the falling away of further portions of the bank.

Our talk, I noticed, had to do with the faraway scenes and incidents of our first camps in the Black Forest, or of other subjects altogether remote from the present setting, for neither of us spoke of the actual moment more than was necessary—almost as though we had agreed tacitly to avoid discussion of the camp and its incidents. Neither the otter nor the boatman, for instance, received the honor of a single mention, though ordinarily these would have furnished discussion for the greater part of the evening. They were, of course, distinct events in such a place.

The scarcity of wood made it a business to keep the fire going, for the wind, that drove the smoke in our faces wherever we sat, helped at the same time to make a forced draught. We took it in turn to make some foraging expeditions into the darkness, and the quantity the Swede brought back always made me feel that he took an absurdly long time finding it; for the fact was I did not care much about being left alone, and yet it always seemed to be my turn to grub about among the bushes or scramble along the slippery banks in the moonlight. The long day's battle with wind and water—such wind and such water!—had tired us both, and an early bed was the obvious program. Yet neither of us made the move for the tent. We lay there, tending the fire, talking in desultory fashion, peering about us into the dense willow bushes, and listening to the thunder of wind and river. The loneliness of the place had entered our very bones, and silence seemed natural, for after a bit the sound of our voices became a trifle unreal and forced; whispering would have been the fitting mode of communication, I felt, and the human voice, always rather absurd amid the roar of the elements, now carried with it something almost illegitimate. It was like talking out loud in church, or in some place where it was not lawful, perhaps not quite safe, to be overheard.

The eeriness of this lonely island, set among a million willows, swept by a hurricane, and surrounded by hurrying deep waters, touched us both, I fancy. Untrodden by man, almost unknown to man, it lay there beneath the moon, remote from human influence, on the frontier of another world, an alien world, a world tenanted by willows only and the souls of willows. And we, in our rashness, had dared to invade it, even to make use of it! Something more than the power of its mystery stirred in me as I lay on the sand, feet to fire, and peered up through the leaves at the stars. For the last time I rose to get firewood.

"When this has burnt up," I said firmly, "I shall turn in," and my companion watched me lazily as I moved off into the surrounding shadows.

For an unimaginative man I thought he seemed unusually receptive that night, unusually open to suggestion of things other than sensory. He too was touched by the beauty and loneliness of the place. I was not altogether pleased, I remember, to recognize this slight change in him, and instead of immediately collecting sticks, I made my way to the far point of the island where the moonlight on plain and river could be seen to better advantage. The desire to be alone had come suddenly upon me; my former dread returned in force; there was a vague feeling in me I wished to face and probe to the bottom.

When I reached the point of sand jutting out among the waves, the spell of the place descended upon me with a positive shock. No mere "scenery" could have produced such an effect. There was something more here, something to alarm.

I gazed across the waste of wild waters; I watched the whispering willows; I heard the ceaseless beating of the tireless wind; and, one and all, each in its own way, stirred in me this sensation of a strange distress. But the willows especially; for ever they went on chattering and talking among themselves, laughing a little, shrilly crying out, sometimes sighing—but what it was they made so much to-do about belonged to the secret life of the great plain they inhabited. And it was utterly alien to the world I knew, or to that of the wild yet kindly elements. They made me think of a host of beings from another plane of life, another evolution altogether, perhaps, all discussing a mystery known only to themselves. I watched them moving busily together, oddly shaking their big bushy heads, twirling their myriad leaves even when there was no wind. They moved of their own will as though alive, and they touched, by some incalculable method, my own keen sense of the horrible.

There they stood in the moonlight, like a vast army surrounding our camp, shaking their innumerable silver spears defiantly, formed all ready for an attack.

The psychology of places, for some imaginations at least, is very vivid; for the wanderer, especially, camps have their "note" either of welcome or rejection. At first it may not always be apparent, because the busy preparations of tent and cooking prevent, but with the first pause—after supper usually—it comes and announces itself. And the note of this willow-camp now became unmistakably plain to me; we were interlopers, trespassers; we were not welcomed. The sense of unfamiliarity grew upon me as I stood there watching. We touched the frontier of a region where our presence was resented. For a night's lodging we might perhaps be tolerated; but for a prolonged and inquisitive stay—No! by all the gods of the trees and wilderness, no! We were the first human influences upon this island, and we were not wanted. The willows were against us.

Strange thoughts like these, bizarre fancies, borne I know not whence, found lodgment in my mind as I stood listening. What, I thought, if, after all, these crouching willows proved to be alive; if suddenly they should rise up, like a swarm of living creatures, marshaled by the gods whose territory we had invaded, sweep towards us off the vast swamps, booming overhead in the night—and then settle down! As I looked it was so easy to imagine they actually moved, crept nearer, retreated a little, huddled together in masses, hostile, waiting for the great wind that should finally start them a-running. I could have sworn their aspect changed a little, and their ranks deepened and pressed more closely together.

The melancholy shrill cry of a night-bird sounded overhead, and suddenly I nearly lost my balance as the piece of bank I stood upon fell with a great splash into the river, undermined by the flood. I stepped back just in time, and went on hunting for firewood again, half laughing at the odd fancies that crowded so thickly into my mind and cast their spell upon me. I recalled the Swede's remark about moving on next day, and I was just thinking that I fully agreed with him, when I turned with a start and saw the subject of my thoughts standing immediately in front of me. He was quite close. The roar of the elements had covered his approach.

II

"You've been gone so long," he shouted above the wind, "I thought something must have happened to you."

But there was that in his tone, and a certain look in his face as well, that conveyed to me more than his usual words, and in a flash I understood the real reason for his coming. It was because the spell of the place had entered his soul too, and he did not like being alone.

"River still rising," he cried, pointing to the flood in the moonlight, "and the wind's simply awful."

He always said the same things, but it was the cry for companionship that gave the real importance to his words.

"Lucky," I cried back, "our tent's in the hollow. I think it'll hold all right." I added something about the difficulty of finding wood, in order to explain my absence, but the wind caught my words and flung them across the river, so that he did not hear, but just looked at me through the branches, nodding his head.

"Lucky if we get away without disaster!" he shouted, or words to that effect; and I remember feeling half angry with him for putting the thought into words, for it was exactly what I felt myself. There was disaster impending somewhere, and the sense of presentiment lay unpleasantly upon me.

We went back to the fire and made a final blaze, poking it up with our feet. We took a last look round. But for the wind the heat would have been unpleasant. I put this thought into words, and I remember my friend's reply struck me oddly: that he would rather have the heat, the ordinary July weather, than this "diabolical wind."

Everything was snug for the night; the canoe lying turned over beside the tent, with both yellow paddles beneath her; the provision sack hanging from a willow-stem, and the washed-up dishes removed to a safe distance from the fire, all ready for the morning meal.

We smothered the embers of the fire with sand, and then turned in. The flap of the tent door was up, and I saw the branches and the stars and the white moonlight. The shaking willows and the heavy buffetings of the wind against our taut little house were the last things I remembered as sleep came down and covered all with its soft and delicious forgetfulness.

Suddenly I found myself lying awake, peering from my sandy mattress through the door of the tent. I looked at my watch pinned against the canvas, and saw by the bright moonlight that it was past twelve o'clock—the threshold of a new day—and I had therefore slept a couple of hours. The Swede was asleep still beside me; the wind howled as before; something plucked at my heart and made me feel afraid. There was a sense of disturbance in my immediate neighborhood.

I sat up quickly and looked out. The trees were swaying violently to and fro as the gusts smote them, but our little bit of green canvas lay snugly safe in the hollow, for the wind passed over it without meeting enough resistance to make it vicious. The feeling of disquietude did not pass, however, and I crawled quietly out of the tent to see if our belongings were safe. I moved carefully so as not to waken my companion. A curious excitement was on me.

I was half-way out, kneeling on all fours, when my eye first took in that the tops of the bushes opposite, with their moving tracery of leaves, made shapes against the sky. I sat back on my haunches and stared. It was incredible, surely, but there, opposite and slightly above me, were shapes of some indeterminate sort among the willows, and as the branches swayed in the wind they seemed to group themselves about these shapes, forming a series of monstrous outlines that shifted rapidly beneath the moon. Close, about fifty feet in front of me, I saw these things.

My first instinct was to waken my companion, that he too might see them, but something made me hesitate—the sudden realization, probably, that I should not welcome corroboration; and meanwhile I crouched there staring in amazement with smarting eyes. I was wide awake. I remember saying to myself that I was not dreaming.

They first became properly visible, these huge figures, just within the tops of the bushes—immense, bronze-colored, moving, and wholly independent of the swaying of the branches. I saw them plainly and noted, now I came to examine them more calmly, that they were very much larger than human, and indeed that something in their appearance proclaimed them to be not human at all. Certainly they were not merely the moving tracery of the branches against the moonlight. They shifted independently. They rose upwards in a continuous stream from earth to sky, vanishing utterly as soon as they reached the dark of the sky. They were interlaced one with another, making a great column, and I saw their limbs and huge bodies melting in and out of each other, forming this serpentine line that bent and swayed and twisted spirally with the contortions of the wind-tossed trees. They were nude, fluid shapes, passing up the bushes, within the leaves almost—rising up in a living column into the heavens. Their faces I never could see. Unceasingly they poured upwards, swaying in great bending curves, with a hue of dull bronze upon their skins.

I stared, trying to force every atom of vision from my eyes. For a long time I thought they must every moment disappear and resolve themselves into the movements of the branches and prove to be an optical illusion. I searched everywhere for a proof of reality, when all the while I understood quite well that the standard of reality had changed. For the longer I looked the more certain I became that these figures were real and living, though perhaps not according to the standards that the camera and the biologist would insist upon.

Far from feeling fear, I was possessed with a sense of awe and wonder such as I have never known. I seemed to be gazing at the personified elemental forces of this haunted and primeval region. Our intrusion had stirred the powers of the place into activity. It was we who were the cause of the disturbance, and my brain filled to bursting with stories and legends of the spirits and deities of places that have been acknowledged and worshipped by men in all ages of the world's history. But, before I could arrive at any possible explanation, something impelled me to go farther out, and I crept forward on the sand and stood upright. I felt the ground still warm under my bare feet; the wind tore at my hair and face; and the sound of the river burst upon my ears with a sudden roar. These things, I knew, were real, and proved that my senses were acting normally. Yet the figures still rose from earth to heaven, silent, majestically, in a great spiral of grace and strength that overwhelmed me at length with a genuine deep emotion of worship. I felt that I must fall down and worship—absolutely worship.

Perhaps in another minute I might have done so, when a gust of wind swept against me with such force that it blew me sideways, and I nearly stumbled and fell. It seemed to shake the dream violently out of me. At least it gave me another point of view somehow. The figures still remained, still ascended into heaven from the heart of the night, but my reason at last began to assert itself. It must be a subjective experience, I argued—none the less real for that, but still subjective. The moonlight and the branches combined to work out these pictures upon the mirror of my imagination, and for some reason I projected them outwards and made them appear objective. I knew this must be the case, of course. I took courage, and began to move forward across the open patches of sand. By Jove, though, was it all hallucination? Was it merely subjective? Did not my reason argue in the old futile way from the little standard of the known?

I only know that great column of figures ascended darkly into the sky for what seemed a very long period of time, and with a very complete measure of reality as most men are accustomed to gauge reality. Then suddenly they were gone!

And, once they were gone and the immediate wonder of their great presence had passed, fear came down upon me with a cold rush. The esoteric meaning of this lonely and haunted region suddenly flamed up within me, and I began to tremble dreadfully. I took a quick look round—a look of horror that came near to panic—calculating vainly ways of escape; and then, realizing how helpless I was to achieve anything really effective, I crept back silently into the tent and lay down again upon my sandy mattress, first lowering the door-curtain to shut out the sight of the willows in the moonlight, and then burying my head as deeply as possible beneath the blankets to deaden the sound of the terrifying wind.

As though further to convince me that I had not been dreaming, I remember that it was a long time before I fell again into a troubled and restless sleep; and even then only the upper crust of me slept, and underneath there was something that never quite lost consciousness, but lay alert and on the watch.

But this second time I jumped up with a genuine start of terror. It was neither the wind nor the river that woke me, but the slow approach of something that caused the sleeping portion of me to grow smaller and smaller till at last it vanished altogether, and I found myself sitting bolt upright—listening.

Outside there was a sound of multitudinous little patterings. They had been coming, I was aware, for a long time, and in my sleep they had first become audible. I sat there nervously wide awake as though I had not slept at all. It seemed to me that my breathing came with difficulty, and that there was a great weight upon the surface of my body. In spite of the hot night, I felt clammy with cold and shivered. Something surely was pressing steadily against the sides of the tent and weighing down upon it from above. Was it the body of the wind? Was this the pattering rain, the dripping of the leaves? The spray blown from the river by the wind and gathering in big drops? I thought quickly of a dozen things.

Then suddenly the explanation leaped into my mind: a bough from the poplar, the only large tree on the island, had fallen with the wind. Still half caught by the other branches, it would fall with the next gust and crush us, and meanwhile its leaves brushed and tapped upon the tight canvas surface of the tent. I raised a loose flap and rushed out, calling to the Swede to follow.

But when I got out and stood upright I saw that the tent was free. There was no hanging bough; there was no rain or spray; nothing approached.

A cold, grey light filtered down through the bushes and lay on the faintly gleaming sand. Stars still crowded the sky directly overhead, and the wind howled magnificently, but the fire no longer gave out any glow, and I saw the east reddening in streaks through the trees. Several hours must have passed since I stood there before watching the ascending figures, and the memory of it now came back to me horribly, like an evil dream. Oh, how tired it made me feel, that ceaseless raging wind! Yet, though the deep lassitude of a sleepless night was on me, my nerves were tingling with the activity of an equally tireless apprehension, and all idea of repose was out of the question. The river I saw had risen further. Its thunder filled the air, and a fine spray made itself felt through my thin sleeping shirt.

Yet nowhere did I discover the slightest evidence of anything to cause alarm. This deep, prolonged disturbance in my heart remained wholly unaccounted for.

My companion had not stirred when I called him, and there was no need to waken him now. I looked about me carefully, noting everything; the turned-over canoe; the yellow paddles—two of them, I'm certain; the provision sack and the extra lantern hanging together from the tree; and, crowding everywhere about me, enveloping all, the willows, those endless, shaking willows. A bird uttered its morning cry, and a string of duck passed with whirring flight overhead in the twilight. The sand whirled, dry and stinging, about my bare feet in the wind.

I walked round the tent and then went out a little way into the bush, so that I could see across the river to the farther landscape, and the same profound yet indefinable emotion of distress seized upon me again as I saw the interminable sea of bushes stretching to the horizon, looking ghostly and unreal in the wan light of dawn. I walked softly here and there, still puzzling over that odd sound of infinite pattering, and of that pressure upon the tent that had wakened me. It must have been the wind, I reflected—the wind bearing upon the loose, hot sand, driving the dry particles smartly against the taut canvas—the wind dropping heavily upon our fragile roof.

Yet all the time my nervousness and malaise increased appreciably.

I crossed over to the farther shore and noted how the coast-line had altered in the night, and what masses of sand the river had torn away. I dipped my hands and feet into the cool current, and bathed my forehead. Already there was a glow of sunrise in the sky and the exquisite freshness of coming day. On my way back I passed purposely beneath the very bushes where I had seen the column of figures rising into the air, and midway among the clumps I suddenly found myself overtaken by a sense of vast terror. From the shadows a large figure went swiftly by. Someone passed me, as sure as ever man did . . .

It was a great staggering blow from the wind that helped me forward again, and once out in the more open space, the sense of terror diminished strangely. The winds were about and walking, I remember saying to myself, for the winds often move like great presences under the trees. And altogether the fear that hovered about me was such an unknown and immense kind of fear, so unlike anything I had ever felt before, that it woke a sense of awe and wonder in me that did much to counteract its worst effects; and when I reached a high point in the middle of the island from which I could see the wide stretch of river, crimson in the sunrise, the whole magical beauty of it all was so overpowering that a sort of wild yearning woke in me and almost brought a cry up into the throat.

But this cry found no expression, for as my eyes wandered from the plain beyond to the island round me and noted our little tent half hidden among the willows, a dreadful discovery leaped out at me, compared to which my terror of the walking winds seemed as nothing at all.

For a change, I thought, had somehow come about in the arrangement of the landscape. It was not that my point of vantage gave me a different view, but that an alteration had apparently been effected in the relation of the tent to the willows, and of the willows to the tent. Surely the bushes now crowded much closer—unnecessarily, unpleasantly close. They had moved nearer.

Creeping with silent feet over the shifting sands, drawing imperceptibly nearer by soft, unhurried movements, the willows had come closer during the night. But had the wind moved them, or had they moved of themselves? I recalled the sound of infinite small patterings and the pressure upon the tent and upon my own heart that caused me to wake in terror. I swayed for a moment in the wind like a tree, finding it hard to keep my upright position on the sandy hillock. There was a suggestion here of personal agency, of deliberate intention, of aggressive hostility, and it terrified me into a sort of rigidity.

Then the reaction followed quickly. The idea was so bizarre, so absurd, that I felt inclined to laugh. But the laughter came no more readily than the cry, for the knowledge that my mind was so receptive to such dangerous imaginings brought the additional terror that it was through our minds and not through our physical bodies that the attack would come, and was coming.

The wind buffeted me about, and, very quickly it seemed, the sun came up over the horizon, for it was after four o'clock, and I must have stood on that little pinnacle of sand longer than I knew, afraid to come down to close quarters with the willows. I returned quietly, creepily, to the tent, first taking another exhaustive look round and—yes, I confess it—making a few measurements. I paced out on the warm sand the distances between the willows and the tent, making a note of the shortest distance particularly.

I crawled stealthily into my blankets. My companion, to all appearances, still slept soundly, and I was glad that this was so. Provided my experiences were not corroborated, I could find strength somehow to deny them, perhaps. With the daylight I could persuade myself that it was all a subjective hallucination, a fantasy of the night, a projection of the excited imagination.

Nothing further came in to disturb me, and I fell asleep almost at once, utterly exhausted, yet still in dread of hearing again that weird sound of multitudinous pattering, or of feeling the pressure upon my heart that had made it difficult to breathe.

The sun was high in the heavens when my companion woke me from a heavy sleep and announced that the porridge was cooked and there was just time to bathe. The grateful smell of frizzling bacon entered the tent door.

"River still rising," he said, "and several islands out in mid-stream have disappeared altogether. Our own island's much smaller."

"Any wood left?" I asked sleepily.

"The wood and the island will finish tomorrow in a dead heat," he laughed, "but there's enough to last us till then."

I plunged in from the point of the island, which had indeed altered a lot in size and shape during the night, and was swept down in a moment to the landing-place opposite the tent. The water was icy, and the banks flew by like the country from an express train. Bathing under such conditions was an exhilarating operation, and the terror of the night seemed cleansed out of me by a process of evaporation in the brain. The sun was blazing hot; not a cloud showed itself anywhere; the wind, however, had not abated one little jot.

Quite suddenly then the implied meaning of the Swede's words flashed across me, showing that he no longer wished to leave post-haste, and had changed his mind. "Enough to last till tomorrow"—he assumed we should stay on the island another night. It struck me as odd. The night before he was so positive the other way. How had the change come about?

Great crumblings of the banks occurred at breakfast, with heavy splashings and clouds of spray which the wind brought into our frying-pan, and my fellow-traveler talked incessantly about the difficulty the Vienna-Pesth steamers must have to find the channel in flood. But the state of his mind interested and impressed me far more than the state of the river or the difficulties of the steamers. He had changed somehow since the evening before. His manner was different—a trifle excited, a trifle shy, with a sort of suspicion about his voice and gestures. I hardly know how to describe it now in cold blood, but at the time I remember being quite certain of one thing—that he had become frightened!

He ate very little breakfast, and for once omitted to smoke his pipe. He had the map spread open beside him, and kept studying its markings.

"We'd better get off sharp in an hour," I said presently, feeling for an opening that must bring him indirectly to a partial confession at any rate. And his answer puzzled me uncomfortably: "Rather! If they'll let us."

"Who'll let us? The elements?" I asked quickly, with affected indifference.

"The powers of this awful place, whoever they are," he replied, keeping his eyes on the map. "The gods are here, if they are anywhere at all in the world."

"The elements are always the true immortals," I replied, laughing as naturally as I could manage, yet knowing quite well that my face reflected my true feelings when he looked up gravely at me and spoke across the smoke:

"We shall be fortunate if we get away without further disaster."

This was exactly what I had dreaded, and I screwed myself up to the point of the direct question. It was like agreeing to allow the dentist to extract the tooth; it had to come anyhow in the long run, and the rest was all pretence.

"Further disaster! Why, what's happened?"

"For one thing—the steering paddle's gone," he said quietly.

"The steering paddle gone!" I repeated, greatly excited, for this was our rudder, and the Danube in flood without a rudder was suicide. "But what—"

"And there's a tear in the bottom of the canoe," he added, with a genuine little tremor in his voice.

I continued staring at him, able only to repeat the words in his face somewhat foolishly. There, in the heat of the sun, and on this burning sand, I was aware of a freezing atmosphere descending round us. I got up to follow him, for he merely nodded his head gravely and led the way towards the tent a few yards on the other side of the fireplace. The canoe still lay there as I had last seen her in the night, ribs uppermost, the paddles, or rather, the paddle, on the sand beside her.

"There's only one," he said, stooping to pick it up. "And here's the rent in the base-board."

It was on the tip of my tongue to tell him that I had clearly noticed two paddles a few hours before, but a second impulse made me think better of it, and I said nothing. I approached to see.

There was a long, finely made tear in the bottom of the canoe where a little slither of wood had been neatly taken clean out; it looked as if the tooth of a sharp rock or snag had eaten down her length, and investigation showed that the hole went through. Had we launched out in her without observing it we must inevitably have foundered. At first the water would have made the wood swell so as to close the hole, but once out in mid-stream the water must have poured in, and the canoe, never more than two inches above the surface, would have filled and sunk very rapidly.

"There, you see an attempt to prepare a victim for the sacrifice," I heard him saying, more to himself than to me, "two victims rather," he added as he bent over and ran his fingers along the slit.

I began to whistle—a thing I always do unconsciously when utterly nonplussed—and purposely paid no attention to his words. I was determined to consider them foolish.

"It wasn't there last night," he said presently, straightening up from his examination and looking anywhere but at me.

"We must have scratched her in landing, of course," I stopped whistling to say. "The stones are very sharp."

I stopped abruptly, for at that moment he turned round and met my eye squarely. I knew just as well as he did how impossible my explanation was. There were no stones, to begin with.

"And then there's this to explain too," he added quietly, handing me the paddle and pointing to the blade.

A new and curious emotion spread freezingly over me as I took and examined it. The blade was scraped down all over, beautifully scraped, as though someone had sand-papered it with care, making it so thin that the first vigorous stroke must have snapped it off at the elbow.

"One of us walked in his sleep and did this thing," I said feebly, "or—or it has been filed by the constant stream of sand particles blown against it by the wind, perhaps."

"Ah," said the Swede, turning away, laughing a little, "you can explain everything."

"The same wind that caught the steering paddle and flung it so near the bank that it fell in with the next lump that crumbled," I called out after him, absolutely determined to find an explanation for everything he showed me.

"I see," he shouted back, turning his head to look at me before disappearing among the willow bushes.

Once alone with these perplexing evidences of personal agency, I think my first thoughts took the form of "One of us must have done this thing, and it certainly was not I." But my second thought decided how impossible it was to suppose, under all the circumstances, that either of us had done it. That my companion, the trusted friend of a dozen similar expeditions, could have knowingly had a hand in it, was a suggestion not to be entertained for a moment. Equally absurd seemed the explanation that this imperturbable and densely practical nature had suddenly become insane and was busied with insane purposes.

Yet the fact remained that what disturbed me most, and kept my fear actively alive even in this blaze of sunshine and wild beauty, was the clear certainty that some curious alteration had come about in his mind—that he was nervous, timid, suspicious, aware of goings on he did not speak about, watching a series of secret and hitherto unmentionable events—waiting, in a word, for a climax that he expected, and, I thought, expected very soon. This grew up in my mind intuitively—I hardly knew how.

I made a hurried examination of the tent and its surroundings, but the measurements of the night remained the same. There were deep hollows formed in the sand I now noticed for the first time, basin-shaped and of various depths and sizes, varying from that of a tea-cup to a large bowl. The wind, no doubt, was responsible for these miniature craters, just as it was for lifting the paddle and tossing it towards the water. The rent in the canoe was the only thing that seemed quite inexplicable; and, after all, it was conceivable that a sharp point had caught it when we landed. The examination I made of the shore did not assist this theory, but all the same I clung to it with that diminishing portion of my intelligence which I called my "reason." An explanation of some kind was an absolute necessity, just as some working explanation of the universe is necessary—however absurd—to the happiness of every individual who seeks to do his duty in the world and face the problems of life. The simile seemed to me at the time an exact parallel.

I at once set the pitch melting, and presently the Swede joined me at the work, though under the best conditions in the world the canoe could not be safe for traveling till the following day. I drew his attention casually to the hollows in the sand.

"Yes," he said, "I know. They're all over the island. But you can explain them, no doubt!"

"Wind, of course," I answered without hesitation. "Have you never watched those little whirlwinds in the street that twist and twirl everything into a circle? This sand's loose enough to yield, that's all."

He made no reply, and we worked on in silence for a bit. I watched him surreptitiously all the time, and I had an idea he was watching me. He seemed, too, to be always listening attentively to something I could not hear, or perhaps for something that he expected to hear, for he kept turning about and staring into the bushes, and up into the sky, and out across the water where it was visible through the openings among the willows. Sometimes he even put his hand to his ear and held it there for several minutes. He said nothing to me, however, about it, and I asked no questions. And meanwhile, as he mended that torn canoe with the skill and address of a red Indian, I was glad to notice his absorption in the work, for there was a vague dread in my heart that he would speak of the changed aspect of the willows. And, if he had noticed that, my imagination could no longer be held a sufficient explanation of it.

III

At length, after a long pause, he began to talk.

"Queer thing," he added in a hurried sort of voice, as though he wanted to say something and get it over. "Queer thing. I mean, about that otter last night."

I had expected something so totally different that he caught me with surprise, and I looked up sharply.

"Shows how lonely this place is. Otters are awfully shy things—"

"I don't mean that, of course," he interrupted. "I mean—do you think—did you think it really was an otter?"

"What else, in the name of Heaven, what else?"

"You know, I saw it before you did, and at first it seemed—so much bigger than an otter."

"The sunset as you looked up-stream magnified it, or something," I replied.

He looked at me absently a moment, as though his mind were busy with other thoughts.

"It had such extraordinary yellow eyes," he went on half to himself.

"That was the sun too," I laughed, a trifle boisterously. "I suppose you'll wonder next if that fellow in the boat—"

I suddenly decided not to finish the sentence. He was in the act again of listening, turning his head to the wind, and something in the expression of his face made me halt. The subject dropped, and we went on with our caulking. Apparently he had not noticed my unfinished sentence. Five minutes later, however, he looked at me across the canoe, the smoking pitch in his hand, his face exceedingly grave.

"I did rather wonder, if you want to know," he said slowly, "what that thing in the boat was. I remember thinking at the time it was not a man. The whole business seemed to rise quite suddenly out of the water."

I laughed again boisterously in his face, but this time there was impatience, and a strain of anger too, in my feeling.

"Look here now," I cried, "this place is quite queer enough without going out of our way to imagine things! That boat was an ordinary boat, and the man in it was an ordinary man, and they were both going down-stream as fast as they could lick. And that otter was an otter, so don't let's play the fool about it!"

He looked steadily at me with the same grave expression. He was not in the least annoyed. I took courage from his silence.

"And, for Heaven's sake," I went on, "don't keep pretending you hear things, because it only gives me the jumps, and there's nothing to hear but the river and this cursed old thundering wind."

"You fool!" he answered in a low, shocked voice, "you utter fool. That's just the way all victims talk. As if you didn't understand just as well as I do!" he sneered with scorn in his voice, and a sort of resignation. "The best thing you can do is to keep quiet and try to hold your mind as firm as possible. This feeble attempt at self-deception only makes the truth harder when you're forced to meet it."

My little effort was over, and I found nothing more to say, for I knew quite well his words were true, and that I was the fool, not he. Up to a certain stage in the adventure he kept ahead of me easily, and I think I felt annoyed to be out of it, to be thus proved less psychic, less sensitive than himself to these extraordinary happenings, and half ignorant all the time of what was going on under my very nose. He knew from the very beginning, apparently. But at the moment I wholly missed the point of his words about the necessity of there being a victim, and that we ourselves were destined to satisfy the want. I dropped all pretence thenceforward, but thenceforward likewise my fear increased steadily to the climax.

"But you're quite right about one thing," he added, before the subject passed, "and that is that we're wiser not to talk about it, or even to think about it, because what one thinks finds expression in words, and what one says, happens."

That afternoon, while the canoe dried and hardened, we spent trying to fish, testing the leak, collecting wood, and watching the enormous flood of rising water. Masses of driftwood swept near our shores sometimes, and we fished for them with long willow branches. The island grew perceptibly smaller as the banks were torn away with great gulps and splashes. The weather kept brilliantly fine till about four o'clock, and then for the first time for three days the wind showed signs of abating. Clouds began to gather in the south-west, spreading thence slowly over the sky.

This lessening of the wind came as a great relief, for the incessant roaring, banging, and thundering had irritated our nerves. Yet the silence that came about five o'clock with its sudden cessation was in a manner quite as oppressive. The booming of the river had everything in its own way then; it filled the air with deep murmurs, more musical than the wind noises, but infinitely more monotonous. The wind held many notes, rising, falling always beating out some sort of great elemental tune; whereas the river's song lay between three notes at most—dull pedal notes, that held a lugubrious quality foreign to the wind, and somehow seemed to me, in my then nervous state, to sound wonderfully well the music of doom.

It was extraordinary, too, how the withdrawal suddenly of bright sunlight took everything out of the landscape that made for cheerfulness; and since this particular landscape had already managed to convey the suggestion of something sinister, the change of course was all the more unwelcome and noticeable. For me, I know, the darkening outlook became distinctly more alarming, and I found myself more than once calculating how soon after sunset the full moon would get up in the east, and whether the gathering clouds would greatly interfere with her lighting of the little island.

With this general hush of the wind—though it still indulged in occasional brief gusts—the river seemed to me to grow blacker, the willows to stand more densely together. The latter, too, kept up a sort of independent movement of their own, rustling among themselves when no wind stirred, and shaking oddly from the roots upwards. When common objects in this way become charged with the suggestion of horror, they stimulate the imagination far more than things of unusual appearance; and these bushes, crowding huddled about us, assumed for me in the darkness a bizarre grotesquerie of appearance that lent to them somehow the aspect of purposeful and living creatures. Their very ordinariness, I felt, masked what was malignant and hostile to us. The forces of the region drew nearer with the coming of night. They were focusing upon our island, and more particularly upon ourselves. For thus, somehow, in the terms of the imagination, did my really indescribable sensations in this extraordinary place present themselves.

I had slept a good deal in the early afternoon, and had thus recovered somewhat from the exhaustion of a disturbed night, but this only served apparently to render me more susceptible than before to the obsessing spell of the haunting. I fought against it, laughing at my feelings as absurd and childish, with very obvious physiological explanations, yet, in spite of every effort, they gained in strength upon me so that I dreaded the night as a child lost in a forest must dread the approach of darkness.

The canoe we had carefully covered with a waterproof sheet during the day, and the one remaining paddle had been securely tied by the Swede to the base of a tree, lest the wind should rob us of that too. From five o'clock onwards I busied myself with the stew-pot and preparations for dinner, it being my turn to cook that night. We had potatoes, onions, bits of bacon fat to add flavor, and a general thick residue from former stews at the bottom of the pot; with black bread broken up into it the result was most excellent, and it was followed by a stew of plums with sugar and a brew of strong tea with dried milk. A good pile of wood lay close at hand, and the absence of wind made my duties easy. My companion sat lazily watching me, dividing his attentions between cleaning his pipe and giving useless advice—an admitted privilege of the off-duty man. He had been very quiet all the afternoon, engaged in re-caulking the canoe, strengthening the tent ropes, and fishing for driftwood while I slept. No more talk about undesirable things had passed between us, and I think his only remarks had to do with the gradual destruction of the island, which he declared was not fully a third smaller than when we first landed.

The pot had just begun to bubble when I heard his voice calling to me from the bank, where he had wandered away without my noticing. I ran up.

"Come and listen," he said, "and see what you make of it." He held his hand cupwise to his ear, as so often before.

"Now do you hear anything?" he asked, watching me curiously.

We stood there, listening attentively together. At first I heard only the deep note of the water and the hissings rising from its turbulent surface. The willows, for once, were motionless and silent. Then a sound began to reach my ears faintly, a peculiar sound—something like the humming of a distant gong. It seemed to come across to us in the darkness from the waste of swamps and willows opposite. It was repeated at regular intervals, but it was certainly neither the sound of a bell nor the hooting of a distant steamer. I can liken it to nothing so much as to the sound of an immense gong, suspended far up in the sky, repeating incessantly its muffled metallic note, soft and musical, as it was repeatedly struck. My heart quickened as I listened.

"I've heard it all day," said my companion. "While you slept this afternoon it came all round the island. I hunted it down, but could never get near enough to see—to localize it correctly. Sometimes it was overhead, and sometimes it seemed under the water. Once or twice, too, I could have sworn it was not outside at all, but within myself—you know—the way a sound in the fourth dimension is supposed to come."

I was too much puzzled to pay much attention to his words. I listened carefully, striving to associate it with any known familiar sound I could think of, but without success. It changed in the direction, too, coming nearer, and then sinking utterly away into remote distance. I cannot say that it was ominous in quality, because to me it seemed distinctly musical, yet I must admit it set going a distressing feeling that made me wish I had never heard it.

"The wind blowing in those sand-funnels," I said determined to find an explanation, "or the bushes rubbing together after the storm perhaps."

"It comes off the whole swamp," my friend answered. "It comes from everywhere at once." He ignored my explanations. "It comes from the willow bushes somehow—"

"But now the wind has dropped," I objected. "The willows can hardly make a noise by themselves, can they?"

His answer frightened me, first because I had dreaded it, and secondly, because I knew intuitively it was true.

"It is because the wind has dropped we now hear it. It was drowned before. It is the cry, I believe, of the—"

I dashed back to my fire, warned by the sound of bubbling that the stew was in danger, but determined at the same time to escape further conversation. I was resolute, if possible, to avoid the exchanging of views. I dreaded, too, that he would begin about the gods, or the elemental forces, or something else disquieting, and I wanted to keep myself well in hand for what might happen later. There was another night to be faced before we escaped from this distressing place, and there was no knowing yet what it might bring forth.

"Come and cut up bread for the pot," I called to him, vigorously stirring the appetizing mixture. That stew-pot held sanity for us both, and the thought made me laugh.

He came over slowly and took the provision sack from the tree, fumbling in its mysterious depths, and then emptying the entire contents upon the ground-sheet at his feet.

"Hurry up!" I cried; "it's boiling."

The Swede burst out into a roar of laughter that startled me. It was forced laughter, not artificial exactly, but mirthless.

"There's nothing here!" he shouted, holding his sides.

"Bread, I mean."

"It's gone. There is no bread. They've taken it!"

I dropped the long spoon and ran up. Everything the sack had contained lay upon the ground-sheet, but there was no loaf.

The whole dead weight of my growing fear fell upon me and shook me. Then I burst out laughing too. It was the only thing to do: and the sound of my laughter also made me understand his. The stain of psychical pressure caused it—this explosion of unnatural laughter in both of us; it was an effort of repressed forces to seek relief; it was a temporary safety-valve. And with both of us it ceased quite suddenly.

"How criminally stupid of me!" I cried, still determined to be consistent and find an explanation. "I clean forgot to buy a loaf at Pressburg. That chattering woman put everything out of my head, and I must have left it lying on the counter or—"

"The oatmeal, too, is much less than it was this morning," the Swede interrupted.

Why in the world need he draw attention to it? I thought angrily.

"There's enough for tomorrow," I said, stirring vigorously, "and we can get lots more at Komorn or Gran. In twenty-four hours we shall be miles from here."

"I hope so—to God," he muttered, putting the things back into the sack, "unless we're claimed first as victims for the sacrifice," he added with a foolish laugh. He dragged the sack into the tent, for safety's sake, I suppose, and I heard him mumbling to himself, but so indistinctly that it seemed quite natural for me to ignore his words.

Our meal was beyond question a gloomy one, and we ate it almost in silence, avoiding one another's eyes, and keeping the fire bright. Then we washed up and prepared for the night, and, once smoking, our minds unoccupied with any definite duties, the apprehension I had felt all day long became more and more acute. It was not then active fear, I think, but the very vagueness of its origin distressed me far more than if I had been able to ticket and face it squarely. The curious sound I have likened to the note of a gong became now almost incessant, and filled the stillness of the night with a faint, continuous ringing rather than a series of distinct notes. At one time it was behind and at another time in front of us. Sometimes I fancied it came from the bushes on our left, and then again from the clumps on our right. More often it hovered directly overhead like the whirring of wings. It was really everywhere at once, behind, in front, at our sides and over our heads, completely surrounding us. The sound really defies description. But nothing within my knowledge is like that ceaseless muffled humming rising off the deserted world of swamps and willows.

We sat smoking in comparative silence, the strain growing every minute greater. The worst feature of the situation seemed to me that we did not know what to expect, and could therefore make no sort of preparation by way of defense. We could anticipate nothing. My explanations made in the sunshine, moreover, now came to haunt me with their foolish and wholly unsatisfactory nature, and it was more and more clear to us that some kind of plain talk with my companion was inevitable, whether I liked it or not. After all, we had to spend the night together, and to sleep in the same tent side by side. I saw that I could not get along much longer without the support of his mind, and for that, of course, plain talk was imperative. As long as possible, however, I postponed this little climax, and tried to ignore or laugh at the occasional sentences he flung into the emptiness.

Some of these sentences, moreover, were confoundedly disquieting to me, coming as they did to corroborate much that I felt myself; corroboration, too—which made it so much more convincing—from a totally different point of view. He composed such curious sentences, and hurled them at me in such an inconsequential sort of way, as though his main line of thought was secret to himself, and these fragments were mere bits he found it impossible to digest. He got rid of them by uttering them. Speech relieved him. It was like being sick.

"There are things about us, I'm sure, that make for disorder, disintegration, destruction, our destruction," he said once, while the fire blazed between us. "We've strayed out of a safe line somewhere."

And, another time, when the gong sounds had come nearer, ringing much louder than before, and directly over our heads, he said as though talking to himself:

"I don't think a gramophone would show any record of that. The sound doesn't come to me by the ears at all. The vibrations reach me in another manner altogether, and seem to be within me, which is precisely how a fourth dimensional sound might be supposed to make itself heard."

I purposely made no reply to this, but I sat up a little closer to the fire and peered about me into the darkness. The clouds were massed all over the sky, and no trace of moonlight came through. Very still, too, everything was, so that the river and the frogs had things all their own way.

"It has that about it," he went on, "which is utterly out of common experience. It is unknown. Only one thing describes it really; it is a non-human sound; I mean a sound outside humanity."

Having rid himself of this indigestible morsel, he lay quiet for a time, but he had so admirably expressed my own feeling that it was a relief to have the thought out, and to have confined it by the limitation of words from dangerous wandering to and fro in the mind.

The solitude of that Danube camping-place, can I ever forget it? The feeling of being utterly alone on an empty planet! My thoughts ran incessantly upon cities and the haunts of men. I would have given my soul, as the saying is, for the "feel" of those Bavarian villages we had passed through by the score; for the normal, human commonplaces; peasants drinking beer, tables beneath the trees, hot sunshine, and a ruined castle on the rocks behind the red-roofed church. Even the tourists would have been welcome.

Yet what I felt of dread was no ordinary ghostly fear. It was infinitely greater, stranger, and seemed to arise from some dim ancestral sense of terror more profoundly disturbing than anything I had known or dreamed of. We had "strayed," as the Swede put it, into some region or some set of conditions where the risks were great, yet unintelligible to us; where the frontiers of some unknown world lay close about us. It was a spot held by the dwellers in some outer space, a sort of peep-hole whence they could spy upon the earth, themselves unseen, a point where the veil between had worn a little thin. As the final result of too long a sojourn here, we should be carried over the border and deprived of what we called "our lives," yet by mental, not physical, processes. In that sense, as he said, we should be the victims of our adventure—a sacrifice.

It took us in different fashion, each according to the measure of his sensitiveness and powers of resistance. I translated it vaguely into a personification of the mightily disturbed elements, investing them with the horror of a deliberate and malefic purpose, resentful of our audacious intrusion into their breeding-place; whereas my friend threw it into the unoriginal form at first of a trespass on some ancient shrine, some place where the old gods still held sway, where the emotional forces of former worshippers still clung, and the ancestral portion of him yielded to the old pagan spell.

At any rate, here was a place unpolluted by men, kept clean by the winds from coarsening human influences, a place where spiritual agencies were within reach and aggressive. Never, before or since, have I been so attacked by indescribable suggestions of a "beyond region," of another scheme of life, another revolution not parallel to the human. And in the end our minds would succumb under the weight of the awful spell, and we should be drawn across the frontier into their world.

Small things testified to the amazing influence of the place, and now in the silence round the fire they allowed themselves to be noted by the mind. The very atmosphere had proved itself a magnifying medium to distort every indication: the otter rolling in the current, the hurrying boatman making signs, the shifting willows, one and all had been robbed of its natural character, and revealed in something of its other aspect—as it existed across the border to that other region. And this changed aspect I felt was now not merely to me, but to the race. The whole experience whose verge we touched was unknown to humanity at all. It was a new order of experience, and in the true sense of the word unearthly.

"It's the deliberate, calculating purpose that reduces one's courage to zero," the Swede said suddenly, as if he had been actually following my thoughts. "Otherwise imagination might count for much. But the paddle, the canoe, the lessening food—"

"Haven't I explained all that once?" I interrupted viciously.

"You have," he answered dryly; "you have indeed."

He made other remarks too, as usual, about what he called the "plain determination to provide a victim"; but, having now arranged my thoughts better, I recognized that this was simply the cry of his frightened soul against the knowledge that he was being attacked in a vital part, and that he would be somehow taken or destroyed. The situation called for a courage and calmness of reasoning that neither of us could compass, and I have never before been so clearly conscious of two persons in me—the one that explained everything, and the other that laughed at such foolish explanations, yet was horribly afraid.

Meanwhile, in the pitchy night the fire died down and the wood pile grew small. Neither of us moved to replenish the stock, and the darkness consequently came up very close to our faces. A few feet beyond the circle of firelight it was inky black. Occasionally a stray puff of wind set the willows shivering about us, but apart from this not very welcome sound a deep and depressing silence reigned, broken only by the gurgling of the river and the humming in the air overhead.

We both missed, I think, the shouting company of the winds.

At length, at a moment when a stray puff prolonged itself as though the wind were about to rise again, I reached the point for me of saturation, the point where it was absolutely necessary to find relief in plain speech, or else to betray myself by some hysterical extravagance that must have been far worse in its effect upon both of us. I kicked the fire into a blaze, and turned to my companion abruptly. He looked up with a start.

"I can't disguise it any longer," I said; "I don't like this place, and the darkness, and the noises, and the awful feelings I get. There's something here that beats me utterly. I'm in a blue funk, and that's the plain truth. If the other shore was—different, I swear I'd be inclined to swim for it!"

The Swede's face turned very white beneath the deep tan of sun and wind. He stared straight at me and answered quietly, but his voice betrayed his huge excitement by its unnatural calmness. For the moment, at any rate, he was the strong man of the two. He was more phlegmatic, for one thing.

"It's not a physical condition we can escape from by running away," he replied, in the tone of a doctor diagnosing some grave disease; "we must sit tight and wait. There are forces close here that could kill a herd of elephants in a second as easily as you or I could squash a fly. Our only chance is to keep perfectly still. Our insignificance perhaps may save us."

I put a dozen questions into my expression of face, but found no words. It was precisely like listening to an accurate description of a disease whose symptoms had puzzled me.

"I mean that so far, although aware of our disturbing presence, they have not found us—not 'located' us, as the Americans say," he went on. "They're blundering about like men hunting for a leak of gas. The paddle and canoe and provisions prove that. I think they feel us, but cannot actually see us. We must keep our minds quiet—it's our minds they feel. We must control our thoughts, or it's all up with us."

"Death, you mean?" I stammered, icy with the horror of his suggestion.

"Worse—by far," he said. "Death, according to one's belief, means either annihilation or release from the limitations of the senses, but it involves no change of character. You don't suddenly alter just because the body's gone. But this means a radical alteration, a complete change, a horrible loss of oneself by substitution—far worse than death, and not even annihilation. We happen to have camped in a spot where their region touches ours, where the veil between has worn thin"—horrors! he was using my very own phrase, my actual words—"so that they are aware of our being in their neighborhood."

"But who are aware?" I asked.

I forgot the shaking of the willows in the windless calm, the humming overhead, everything except that I was waiting for an answer that I dreaded more than I can possibly explain.

He lowered his voice at once to reply, leaning forward a little over the fire, an indefinable change in his face that made me avoid his eyes and look down upon the ground.

"All my life," he said, "I have been strangely, vividly conscious of another region—not far removed from our own world in one sense, yet wholly different in kind—where great things go on unceasingly, where immense and terrible personalities hurry by, intent on vast purposes compared to which earthly affairs, the rise and fall of nations, the destinies of empires, the fate of armies and continents, are all as dust in the balance; vast purposes, I mean, that deal directly with the soul, and not indirectly with more expressions of the soul—"

"I suggest just now—" I began, seeking to stop him, feeling as though I was face to face with a madman. But he instantly overbore me with his torrent that had to come.

"You think," he said, "it is the spirit of the elements, and I thought perhaps it was the old gods. But I tell you now it is—neither. These would be comprehensible entities, for they have relations with men, depending upon them for worship or sacrifice, whereas these beings who are now about us have absolutely nothing to do with mankind, and it is mere chance that their space happens just at this spot to touch our own."

The mere conception, which his words somehow made so convincing, as I listened to them there in the dark stillness of that lonely island, set me shaking a little all over. I found it impossible to control my movements.

"And what do you propose?" I began again.

"A sacrifice, a victim, might save us by distracting them until we could get away," he went on, "just as the wolves stop to devour the dogs and give the sleigh another start. But—I see no chance of any other victim now."

I stared blankly at him. The gleam in his eye was dreadful. Presently he continued.

IV

"It's the willows, of course. The willows mask the others, but the others are feeling about for us. If we let our minds betray our fear, we're lost, lost utterly."

He looked at me with an expression so calm, so determined, so sincere, that I no longer had any doubts as to his sanity. He was as sane as any man ever was. "If we can hold out through the night," he added, "we may get off in the daylight unnoticed, or rather, undiscovered."

"But you really think a sacrifice would—"

That gong-like humming came down very close over our heads as I spoke, but it was my friend's scared face that really stopped my mouth.

"Hush!" he whispered, holding up his hand. "Do not mention them more than you can help. Do not refer to them by name. To name is to reveal; it is the inevitable clue, and our only hope lies in ignoring them, in order that they may ignore us."

"Even in thought?" He was extraordinarily agitated.

"Especially in thought. Our thoughts make spirals in their world. We must keep them out of our minds at all costs if possible."

I raked the fire together to prevent the darkness having everything its own way. I never longed for the sun as I longed for it then in the awful blackness of that summer night.

"Were you awake all last night?" he went on suddenly.

"I slept badly a little after dawn," I replied evasively, trying to follow his instructions, which I knew instinctively were true, "but the wind, of course—"

"I know. But the wind won't account for all the noises."

"Then you heard it too?"

"The multiplying countless little footsteps I heard," he said, adding, after a moment's hesitation, "and that other sound—"

"You mean above the tent, and the pressing down upon us of something tremendous, gigantic?"

He nodded significantly.

"It was like the beginning of a sort of inner suffocation?" I said.

"Partly, yes. It seemed to me that the weight of the atmosphere had been altered—had increased enormously, so that we should have been crushed."

"And that," I went on, determined to have it all out, pointing upwards where the gong-like note hummed ceaselessly, rising and falling like wind. "What do you make of that?"

"It's their sound," he whispered gravely. "It's the sound of their world, the humming in their region. The division here is so thin that it leaks through somehow. But, if you listen carefully, you'll find it's not above so much as around us. It's in the willows. It's the willows themselves humming, because here the willows have been made symbols of the forces that are against us."

I could not follow exactly what he meant by this, yet the thought and idea in my mind were beyond question the thought and idea in his. I realized what he realized, only with less power of analysis than his. It was on the tip of my tongue to tell him at last about my hallucination of the ascending figures and the moving bushes, when he suddenly thrust his face again close into mine across the firelight and began to speak in a very earnest whisper. He amazed me by his calmness and pluck, his apparent control of the situation. This man I had for years deemed unimaginative, stolid!

"Now listen," he said. "The only thing for us to do is to go on as though nothing had happened, follow our usual habits, go to bed, and so forth; pretend we feel nothing and notice nothing. It is a question wholly of the mind, and the less we think about them the better our chance of escape. Above all, don't think, for what you think happens!"

"All right," I managed to reply, simply breathless with his words and the strangeness of it all; "all right, I'll try, but tell me one more thing first. Tell me what you make of those hollows in the ground all about us, those sand-funnels?"

"No!" he cried, forgetting to whisper in his excitement. "I dare not, simply dare not, put the thought into words. If you have not guessed I am glad. Don't try to. They have put it into my mind; try your hardest to prevent their putting it into yours."

He sank his voice again to a whisper before he finished, and I did not press him to explain. There was already just about as much horror in me as I could hold. The conversation came to an end, and we smoked our pipes busily in silence.

Then something happened, something unimportant apparently, as the way is when the nerves are in a very great state of tension, and this small thing for a brief space gave me an entirely different point of view. I chanced to look down at my sand-shoe—the sort we used for the canoe—and something to do with the hole at the toe suddenly recalled to me the London shop where I had bought them, the difficulty the man had in fitting me, and other details of the uninteresting but practical operation. At once, in its train, followed a wholesome view of the modern skeptical world I was accustomed to move in at home. I thought of roast beef, and ale, motor-cars, policemen, brass bands, and a dozen other things that proclaimed the soul of ordinariness or utility. The effect was immediate and astonishing even to myself. Psychologically, I suppose, it was simply a sudden and violent reaction after the strain of living in an atmosphere of things that to the normal consciousness must seem impossible and incredible. But, whatever the cause, it momentarily lifted the spell from my heart, and left me for the short space of a minute feeling free and utterly unafraid. I looked up at my friend opposite.

"You damned old pagan!" I cried, laughing aloud in his face. "You imaginative idiot! You superstitious idolater! You—"

I stopped in the middle, seized anew by the old horror. I tried to smother the sound of my voice as something sacrilegious. The Swede, of course, heard it too—the strange cry overhead in the darkness—and that sudden drop in the air as though something had come nearer.

He had turned ashen white under the tan. He stood bolt upright in front of the fire, stiff as a rod, staring at me.

"After that," he said in a sort of helpless, frantic way, "we must go! We can't stay now; we must strike camp this very instant and go on—down the river."

He was talking, I saw, quite wildly, his words dictated by abject terror—the terror he had resisted so long, but which had caught him at last.

"In the dark?" I exclaimed, shaking with fear after my hysterical outburst, but still realizing our position better than he did. "Sheer madness! The river's in flood, and we've only got a single paddle. Besides, we only go deeper into their country! There's nothing ahead for fifty miles but willows, willows, willows!"

He sat down again in a state of semi-collapse. The positions, by one of those kaleidoscopic changes nature loves, were suddenly reversed, and the control of our forces passed over into my hands. His mind at last had reached the point where it was beginning to weaken.

"What on earth possessed you to do such a thing?" he whispered with the awe of genuine terror in his voice and face.

I crossed round to his side of the fire. I took both his hands in mine, kneeling down beside him and looking straight into his frightened eyes.

"We'll make one more blaze," I said firmly, "and then turn in for the night. At sunrise we'll be off full speed for Komorn. Now, pull yourself together a bit, and remember your own advice about not thinking fear!"

He said no more, and I saw that he would agree and obey. In some measure, too, it was a sort of relief to get up and make an excursion into the darkness for more wood. We kept close together, almost touching, groping among the bushes and along the bank. The humming overhead never ceased, but seemed to me to grow louder as we increased our distance from the fire. It was shivery work!

We were grubbing away in the middle of a thickish clump of willows where some driftwood from a former flood had caught high among the branches, when my body was seized in a grip that made me half drop upon the sand. It was the Swede. He had fallen against me, and was clutching me for support. I heard his breath coming and going in short gasps.

"Look! By my soul!" he whispered, and for the first time in my experience I knew what it was to hear tears of terror in a human voice. He was pointing to the fire, some fifty feet away. I followed the direction of his finger, and I swear my heart missed a beat.

There, in front of the dim glow, something was moving.

I saw it through a veil that hung before my eyes like the gauze drop-curtain used at the back of a theater—hazily a little. It was neither a human figure nor an animal. To me it gave the strange impression of being as large as several animals grouped together, like horses, two or three, moving slowly. The Swede, too, got a similar result, though expressing it differently, for he thought it was shaped and sized like a clump of willow bushes, rounded at the top, and moving all over upon its surface—"coiling upon itself like smoke," he said afterwards.

"I watched it settle downwards through the bushes," he sobbed at me. "Look, by God! It's coming this way! Oh, oh!"—he gave a kind of whistling cry. "They've found us."

I gave one terrified glance, which just enabled me to see that the shadowy form was swinging towards us through the bushes, and then I collapsed backwards with a crash into the branches. These failed, of course, to support my weight, so that with the Swede on top of me we fell in a struggling heap upon the sand. I really hardly knew what was happening. I was conscious only of a sort of enveloping sensation of icy fear that plucked the nerves out of their fleshly covering, twisted them this way and that, and replaced them quivering. My eyes were tightly shut; something in my throat choked me; a feeling that my consciousness was expanding, extending out into space, swiftly gave way to another feeling that I was losing it altogether, and about to die.

An acute spasm of pain passed through me, and I was aware that the Swede had hold of me in such a way that he hurt me abominably. It was the way he caught at me in falling.

But it was the pain, he declared afterwards, that saved me; it caused me to forget them and think of something else at the very instant when they were about to find me. It concealed my mind from them at the moment of discovery, yet just in time to evade their terrible seizing of me. He himself, he says, actually swooned at the same moment, and that was what saved him.

I only know that at a later date, how long or short is impossible to say, I found myself scrambling up out of the slippery network of willow branches, and saw my companion standing in front of me holding out a hand to assist me. I stared at him in a dazed way, rubbing the arm he had twisted for me. Nothing came to me to say, somehow.

"I lost consciousness for a moment or two," I heard him say. "That's what saved me. It made me stop thinking about them."

"You nearly broke my arm in two," I said, uttering my only connected thought at the moment. A numbness came over me.

"That's what saved you!" he replied. "Between us, we've managed to set them off on a false tack somewhere. The humming has ceased. It's gone—for the moment at any rate!"

A wave of hysterical laughter seized me again, and this time spread to my friend too—great healing gusts of shaking laughter that brought a tremendous sense of relief in their train. We made our way back to the fire and put the wood on so that it blazed at once. Then we saw that the tent had fallen over and lay in a tangled heap upon the ground.

We picked it up, and during the process tripped more than once and caught our feet in sand.

"It's those sand-funnels," exclaimed the Swede, when the tent was up again and the firelight lit up the ground for several yards about us. "And look at the size of them!"

All round the tent and about the fireplace where we had seen the moving shadows there were deep funnel-shaped hollows in the sand, exactly similar to the ones we had already found over the island, only far bigger and deeper, beautifully formed, and wide enough in some instances to admit the whole of my foot and leg.

Neither of us said a word. We both knew that sleep was the safest thing we could do, and to bed we went accordingly without further delay, having first thrown sand on the fire and taken the provision sack and the paddle inside the tent with us. The canoe, too, we propped in such a way at the end of the tent that our feet touched it, and the least motion would disturb and wake us.

In case of emergency, too, we again went to bed in our clothes, ready for a sudden start.

It was my firm intention to lie awake all night and watch, but the exhaustion of nerves and body decreed otherwise, and sleep after a while came over me with a welcome blanket of oblivion. The fact that my companion also slept quickened its approach. At first he fidgeted and constantly sat up, asking me if I "heard this" or "heard that." He tossed about on his cork mattress, and said the tent was moving and the river had risen over the point of the island, but each time I went out to look I returned with the report that all was well, and finally he grew calmer and lay still. Then at length his breathing became regular and I heard unmistakable sounds of snoring—the first and only time in my life when snoring has been a welcome and calming influence.

This, I remember, was the last thought in my mind before dozing off.

A difficulty in breathing woke me, and I found the blanket over my face. But something else besides the blanket was pressing upon me, and my first thought was that my companion had rolled off his mattress on to my own in his sleep. I called to him and sat up, and at the same moment it came to me that the tent was surrounded. That sound of multitudinous soft pattering was again audible outside, filling the night with horror.

I called again to him, louder than before. He did not answer, but I missed the sound of his snoring, and also noticed that the flap of the tent was down. This was the unpardonable sin. I crawled out in the darkness to hook it back securely, and it was then for the first time I realized positively that the Swede was not here. He had gone.

I dashed out in a mad run, seized by a dreadful agitation, and the moment I was out I plunged into a sort of torrent of humming that surrounded me completely and came out of every quarter of the heavens at once. It was that same familiar humming—gone mad! A swarm of great invisible bees might have been about me in the air. The sound seemed to thicken the very atmosphere, and I felt that my lungs worked with difficulty.

But my friend was in danger, and I could not hesitate.

The dawn was just about to break, and a faint whitish light spread upwards over the clouds from a thin strip of clear horizon. No wind stirred. I could just make out the bushes and river beyond, and the pale sandy patches. In my excitement I ran frantically to and fro about the island, calling him by name, shouting at the top of my voice the first words that came into my head. But the willows smothered my voice, and the humming muffled it, so that the sound only traveled a few feet round me. I plunged among the bushes, tripping headlong, tumbling over roots, and scraping my face as I tore this way and that among the preventing branches.

Then, quite unexpectedly, I came out upon the island's point and saw a dark figure outlined between the water and the sky. It was the Swede. And already he had one foot in the river! A moment more and he would have taken the plunge.

I threw myself upon him, flinging my arms about his waist and dragging him shorewards with all my strength. Of course he struggled furiously, making a noise all the time just like that cursed humming, and using the most outlandish phrases in his anger about "going inside to Them," and "taking the way of the water and the wind," and God only knows what more besides, that I tried in vain to recall afterwards, but which turned me sick with horror and amazement as I listened. But in the end I managed to get him into the comparative safety of the tent, and flung him breathless and cursing upon the mattress where I held him until the fit had passed.

I think the suddenness with which it all went and he grew calm, coinciding as it did with the equally abrupt cessation of the humming and pattering outside—I think this was almost the strangest part of the whole business perhaps. For he had just opened his eyes and turned his tired face up to me so that the dawn threw a pale light upon it through the doorway, and said, for all the world just like a frightened child:

"My life, old man—it's my life I owe you. But it's all over now anyhow. They've found a victim in our place!"

Then he dropped back upon his blankets and went to sleep literally under my eyes. He simply collapsed, and began to snore again as healthily as though nothing had happened and he had never tried to offer his own life as a sacrifice by drowning. And when the sunlight woke him three hours later—hours of ceaseless vigil for me—it became so clear to me that he remembered absolutely nothing of what he had attempted to do, that I deemed it wise to hold my peace and ask no dangerous questions.

He woke naturally and easily, as I have said, when the sun was already high in a windless hot sky, and he at once got up and set about the preparation of the fire for breakfast. I followed him anxiously at bathing, but he did not attempt to plunge in, merely dipping his head and making some remark about the extra coldness of the water.

"River's falling at last," he said, "and I'm glad of it."

"The humming has stopped too," I said.

He looked up at me quietly with his normal expression. Evidently he remembered everything except his own attempt at suicide.

"Everything has stopped," he said, "because—"

He hesitated. But I knew some reference to that remark he had made just before he fainted was in his mind, and I was determined to know it.

"Because 'They've found another victim'?" I said, forcing a little laugh.

"Exactly," he answered, "exactly! I feel as positive of it as though—as though—I feel quite safe again, I mean," he finished.

He began to look curiously about him. The sunlight lay in hot patches on the sand. There was no wind. The willows were motionless. He slowly rose to feet.

"Come," he said; "I think if we look, we shall find it."

He started off on a run, and I followed him. He kept to the banks, poking with a stick among the sandy bays and caves and little back-waters, myself always close on his heels.

"Ah!" he exclaimed presently, "ah!"

The tone of his voice somehow brought back to me a vivid sense of the horror of the last twenty-four hours, and I hurried up to join him. He was pointing with his stick at a large black object that lay half in the water and half on the sand. It appeared to be caught by some twisted willow roots so that the river could not sweep it away. A few hours before the spot must have been under water.

"See," he said quietly, "the victim that made our escape possible!"

And when I peered across his shoulder I saw that his stick rested on the body of a man. He turned it over. It was the corpse of a peasant, and the face was hidden in the sand. Clearly the man had been drowned, but a few hours before, and his body must have been swept down upon our island somewhere about the hour of the dawn—at the very time the fit had passed.

"We must give it a decent burial, you know."

"I suppose so," I replied. I shuddered a little in spite of myself, for there was something about the appearance of that poor drowned man that turned me cold.

The Swede glanced up sharply at me, an undecipherable expression on his face, and began clambering down the bank. I followed him more leisurely. The current, I noticed, had torn away much of the clothing from the body, so that the neck and part of the chest lay bare.

Halfway down the bank my companion suddenly stopped and held up his hand in warning; but either my foot slipped, or I had gained too much momentum to bring myself quickly to a halt, for I bumped into him and sent him forward with a sort of leap to save himself. We tumbled together on to the hard sand so that our feet splashed into the water. And, before anything could be done, we had collided a little heavily against the corpse.

The Swede uttered a sharp cry. And I sprang back as if I had been shot.

At the moment we touched the body there rose from its surface the loud sound of humming—the sound of several hummings—which passed with a vast commotion as of winged things in the air about us and disappeared upwards into the sky, growing fainter and fainter till they finally ceased in the distance. It was exactly as though we had disturbed some living yet invisible creatures at work.

My companion clutched me, and I think I clutched him, but before either of us had time properly to recover from the unexpected shock, we saw that a movement of the current was turning the corpse round so that it became released from the grip of the willow roots. A moment later it had turned completely over, the dead face uppermost, staring at the sky. It lay on the edge of the main stream. In another moment it would be swept away.

The Swede started to save it, shouting again something I did not catch about a "proper burial"—and then abruptly dropped upon his knees on the sand and covered his eyes with his hands. I was beside him in an instant.

I saw what he had seen.

For just as the body swung round to the current the face and the exposed chest turned full towards us, and showed plainly how the skin and flesh were indented with small hollows, beautifully formed, and exactly similar in shape and kind to the sand-funnels that we had found all over the island.

"Their mark!" I heard my companion mutter under his breath. "Their awful mark!"

And when I turned my eyes again from his ghastly face to the river, the current had done its work, and the body had been swept away into mid-stream and was already beyond our reach and almost out of sight, turning over and over on the waves like an otter.

THE SHUNNED HOUSE

H. P. Lovecraft

I

From even the greatest of horrors irony is seldom absent. Sometimes it enters directly into the composition of the events, while sometimes it relates only to their fortuitous position among persons and places. The latter sort is splendidly exemplified by a case in the ancient city of Providence, where in the late forties Edgar Allan Poe used to sojourn often during his unsuccessful wooing of the gifted poetess, Mrs. Whitman. Poe generally stopped at the Mansion House in Benefit Street—the renamed Golden Ball Inn whose roof has sheltered Washington, Jefferson, and Lafayette—and his favorite walk led northward along the same street to Mrs. Whitman's home and the neighboring hillside churchyard of St. John's, whose hidden expanse of eighteenth-century gravestones had for him a peculiar fascination.

Now the irony is this. In this walk, so many times repeated, the world's greatest master of the terrible and the bizarre was obliged to pass a particular house on the eastern side of the street; a dingy, antiquated structure perched on the abruptly rising side hill, with a great unkempt yard dating from a time when the region was partly open country. It does not appear that he ever wrote or spoke of it, nor is there any evidence that he even noticed it. And yet that house, to the two persons in possession of certain information, equals or outranks in horror the wildest fantasy of the genius who so often passed it unknowingly, and stands starkly leering as a symbol of all that is unutterably hideous.

The house was—and for that matter still is—of a kind to attract the attention of the curious. Originally a farm or semi-farm building, it followed the average New England colonial lines of the middle eighteenth century—the prosperous peaked-roof sort, with two stories and dormerless attic, and with the Georgian doorway and interior panelling dictated by the progress of taste at that time. It faced south, with one gable end buried to the lower windows in the eastward rising hill, and the other exposed to the foundations toward the street. Its construction, over a century and a half ago, had followed the grading and straightening of the road in that especial vicinity; for Benefit Street—at first called Back Street—was laid out as a lane winding amongst the graveyards of the first settlers, and straightened only when the removal of the bodies to the North Burial Ground made it decently possible to cut through the old family plots.

At the start, the western wall had lain some twenty feet up a precipitous lawn from the roadway; but a widening of the street at about the time of the Revolution sheared off most of the intervening space, exposing the foundations so that a brick basement wall had to be made, giving the deep cellar a street frontage with door and one window above ground, close to the new line of public travel. When the sidewalk was laid out a century ago the last of the intervening space was removed; and Poe in his walks must have seen only a sheer ascent of dull gray brick flush with the sidewalk and surmounted at a height of ten feet by the antique shingled bulk of the house proper.

The farm-like ground extended back very deeply up the hill, almost to Wheaton Street. The space south of the house, abutting on Benefit Street, was of course greatly above the existing sidewalk level, forming a terrace bounded by a high bank wall of damp, mossy stone pierced by a steep flight of narrow steps which led inward between canyon-like surfaces to the upper region of mangy lawn, rheumy brick walks, and neglected gardens whose dismantled cement urns, rusted kettles fallen from tripods of knotty sticks, and similar paraphernalia set off the weather-beaten front door with its broken fanlight, rotting Ionic pilasters, and wormy triangular pediment.

* * * * *

What I heard in my youth about the shunned house was merely that people died there in alarmingly great numbers. That, I was told, was why the original owners had moved out some twenty years after building the place. It was plainly unhealthy, perhaps because of the dampness and fungous growths in the cellar, the general sickish smell, the drafts of the hallways, or the quality of the well and pump water. These things were bad enough, and these were all that gained belief among the persons whom I knew. Only the notebooks of my antiquarian uncle, Doctor Elihu Whipple, revealed to me at length the darker, vaguer surmises which formed an undercurrent of folklore among old-time servants and humble folk; surmises which never travelled far, and which were largely forgotten when Providence grew to be a metropolis with a shifting modern population.

The general fact is, that the house was never regarded by the solid part of the community as in any real sense "haunted." There were no widespread tales of rattling chains, cold currents of air, extinguished lights, or faces at the window. Extremists sometimes said the house was "unlucky," but that is as far as even they went. What was really beyond dispute is that a frightful proportion of persons died there; or more accurately, had died there, since after some peculiar happenings over sixty years ago the building had become deserted through the sheer impossibility of renting it. These persons were not all cut off suddenly by any one cause; rather did it seem that their vitality was insidiously sapped, so that each one died the sooner from whatever tendency to weakness he may have naturally had. And those who did not die displayed in varying degree a type of anemia or consumption, and sometimes a decline of the mental faculties, which spoke ill for the salubriousness of the building. Neighboring houses, it must be added, seemed entirely free from the noxious quality.

This much I knew before my insistent questioning led my uncle to show me the notes which finally embarked us both on our hideous investigation. In my childhood the shunned house was vacant, with barren, gnarled and terrible old trees, long, queerly pale grass and nightmarishly misshapen weeds in the high terraced yard where birds never lingered. We boys used to overrun the place, and I can still recall my youthful terror not only at the morbid strangeness of this sinister vegetation, but at the eldritch atmosphere and odor of the dilapidated house, whose unlocked front door was often entered in quest of shudders. The small-paned windows were largely broken, and a nameless air of desolation hung round the precarious panelling, shaky interior shutters, peeling wallpaper, falling plaster, rickety staircases, and such fragments of battered furniture as still remained. The dust and cobwebs added their touch of the fearful; and brave indeed was the boy who would voluntarily ascend the ladder to the attic, a vast raftered length lighted only by small blinking windows in the gable ends, and filled with a massed wreckage of chests, chairs, and spinning-wheels which infinite years of deposit had shrouded and festooned into monstrous and hellish shapes.

But after all, the attic was not the most terrible part of the house. It was the dank, humid cellar which somehow exerted the strongest repulsion on us, even though it was wholly above ground on the street side, with only a thin door and window-pierced brick wall to separate it from the busy sidewalk. We scarcely knew whether to haunt it in spectral fascination, or to shun it for the sake of our souls and our sanity. For one thing, the bad odor of the house was strongest there; and for another thing, we did not like the white fungous growths which occasionally sprang up in rainy summer weather from the hard earth floor. Those fungi, grotesquely like the vegetation in the yard outside, were truly horrible in their outlines; detestable parodies of toadstools and Indian-pipes, whose like we had never seen in any other situation. They rotted quickly, and at one stage became slightly phosphorescent; so that nocturnal passers-by sometimes spoke of witch-fires glowing behind the broken panes of the fetor-spreading windows.

We never—even in our wildest Halloween moods—visited this cellar by night, but in some of our daytime visits could detect the phosphorescence, especially when the day was dark and wet. There was also a subtler thing we often thought we detected—a very strange thing which was, however, merely suggestive at most. I refer to a sort of cloudy whitish pattern on the dirt floor—a vague, shifting deposit of mold or niter which we sometimes thought we could trace amidst the sparse fungous growths near the huge fireplace of the basement kitchen. Once in a while it struck us that this patch bore an uncanny resemblance to a doubled-up human figure, though generally no such kinship existed, and often there was no whitish deposit whatever.

On a certain rainy afternoon when this illusion seemed phenomenally strong, and when, in addition, I had fancied I glimpsed a kind of thin, yellowish, shimmering exhalation rising from the nitrous pattern toward the yawning fireplace, I spoke to my uncle about the matter. He smiled at this odd conceit, but it seemed that his smile was tinged with reminiscence. Later I heard that a similar notion entered into some of the wild ancient tales of the common folk—a notion likewise alluding to ghoulish, wolfish shapes taken by smoke from the great chimney, and queer contours assumed by certain of the sinuous tree-roots that thrust their way into the cellar through the loose foundation-stones.

II

Not till my adult years did my uncle set before me the notes and data which he had collected concerning the shunned house. Doctor Whipple was a sane, conservative physician of the old school, and for all his interest in the place was not eager to encourage young thoughts toward the abnormal. His own view, postulating simply a building and location of markedly unsanitary qualities, had nothing to do with abnormality; but he realized that the very picturesqueness which aroused his own interest would in a boy's fanciful mind take on all manner of gruesome imaginative associations.

The doctor was a bachelor; a white-haired, clean-shaven, old-fashioned gentleman, and a local historian of note, who had often broken a lance with such controversial guardians of tradition as Sidney S. Rider and Thomas W. Bicknell. He lived with one man-servant in a Georgian homestead with knocker and iron-railed steps, balanced eerily on the steep ascent of North Court Street beside the ancient brick court and colony house where his grandfather—a cousin of that celebrated privateersman, Captain Whipple, who burnt His Majesty's armed schooner *Gaspee* in 1772—had voted in the legislature on May 4, 1776, for the independence of the Rhode Island Colony. Around him in the damp, low-ceiled library with the musty white panelling, heavy carved overmantel and small-paned, vine-shaded windows, were the relics and records of his ancient family, among which were many dubious allusions to the shunned house in Benefit Street. That pest spot lies not far distant—for Benefit runs ledgewise just above the court house along the precipitous hill up which the first settlement climbed.

When, in the end, my insistent pestering and maturing years evoked from my uncle the hoarded lore I sought, there lay before me a strange enough chronicle. Long-winded, statistical, and drearily genealogical as some of the matter was, there ran through it a continuous thread of brooding, tenacious horror and preternatural malevolence which impressed me even more than it had impressed the good doctor. Separate events fitted together uncannily, and seemingly irrelevant details held mines of hideous possibilities. A new and burning curiosity grew in me, compared to which my boyish curiosity was feeble and inchoate.

The first revelation led to an exhaustive research, and finally to that shuddering quest which proved so disastrous to myself and mine. For at the last my uncle insisted on joining the search I had commenced, and after a certain night in that house he did not come away with me. I am lonely without that gentle soul whose long years were filled only with honor, virtue, good taste, benevolence, and learning. I have reared a marble urn to his memory in St. John's churchyard—the place that Poe loved—the hidden grove of giant willows on the hill, where tombs and headstones huddle quietly between the hoary bulk of the church and the houses and bank walls of Benefit Street.

The history of the house, opening amidst a maze of dates, revealed no trace of the sinister either about its construction or about the prosperous and honorable family who built it. Yet from the first a taint of calamity, soon increased to boding significance, was apparent. My uncle's carefully compiled record began with the building of the structure in 1763, and followed the theme with an unusual amount of detail. The shunned house, it seems, was first inhabited by William Harris and his wife Rhoby Dexter, with their children, Elkanah, born in 1755, Abigail, born in 1757, William, Jr., born in 1759, and Ruth, born in 1761. Harris was a substantial merchant and seaman in the West India trade, connected with the firm of Obadiah Brown and his nephews. After Brown's death in 1761, the new firm of Nicholas Brown & Company made him master of the brig *Prudence*, Providence-built, of 120 tons, thus enabling him to erect the new homestead he had desired ever since his marriage.

The site he had chosen—a recently straightened part of the new and fashionable Back Street, which ran along the side of the hill above crowded Cheapside—was all that could be wished, and the building did justice to the location. It was the best that moderate means could afford, and Harris hastened to move in before the birth of a fifth child which the family expected.

That child, a boy, came in December; but was still-born. Nor was any child to be born alive in that house for a century and a half.

The next April, sickness occurred among the children, and Abigail and Ruth died before the month was over. Doctor Job Ives diagnosed the trouble as some infantile fever, though others declared it was more of a mere wasting-away or decline. It seemed, in any event, to be contagious; for Hannah Bowen, one of the two servants, died of it in the following June. Eli Lideason, the other servant, constantly complained of weakness; and would have returned to his father's farm in Rehoboth but for a sudden attachment for Mehitabel Pierce, who was hired to succeed Hannah. He died the next year—a sad year indeed, since it marked the death of William Harris himself, enfeebled as he was by the climate of Martinique, where his occupation had kept him for considerable periods during the preceding decade.

The widowed Rhoby Harris never recovered from the shock of her husband's death, and the passing of her first-born Elkanah two years later was the final blow to her reason. In 1768 she fell victim to a mild form of insanity, and was thereafter confined to the upper part of the house; her elder maiden sister, Mercy Dexter, having moved in to take charge of the family. Mercy was a plain, raw-boned woman of great strength; but her health visibly declined from the time of her advent. She was greatly devoted to her unfortunate sister, and had an especial affection for her only surviving nephew William, who from a sturdy infant had become a sickly, spindling lad. In this year the servant Mehitabel died, and the other servant, Preserved Smith, left without coherent explanation—or at least, with only some wild tales and a complaint that he disliked the smell of the place. For a time Mercy could secure no more help, since the seven deaths and case of madness, all occurring within five years' space, had begun to set in motion the body of fireside rumor which later became so bizarre. Ultimately, however, she obtained new servants from out of town; Ann White, a morose woman from that part of North Kingstown now set off as the township of Exeter, and a capable Boston man named Zenas Low.

* * * * *

It was Ann White who first gave definite shape to the sinister idle talk. Mercy should have known better than to hire anyone from the Nooseneck Hill country, for that remote bit of backwoods was then, as now, a seat of the most uncomfortable superstitions. As lately as 1892 an Exeter community exhumed a dead body and ceremoniously burnt its heart in order to prevent certain alleged visitations injurious to the public health and peace, and one may imagine the point of view of the same section in 1768. Ann's tongue was perniciously active, and within a few months Mercy discharged her, filling her place with a faithful and amiable Amazon from Newport, Maria Robbins.

Meanwhile poor Rhoby Harris, in her madness, gave voice to dreams and imaginings of the most hideous sort. At times her screams became insupportable, and for long periods she would utter shrieking horrors which necessitated her son's temporary residence with his cousin, Peleg Harris, in Presbyterian Lane near the new college building. The boy would seem to improve after these visits, and had Mercy been as wise as she was well-meaning, she would have let him live permanently with Peleg. Just what Mrs. Harris cried out in her fits of violence, tradition hesitates to say; or rather, presents such extravagant accounts that they nullify themselves through sheer absurdity. Certainly it sounds absurd to hear that a woman educated only in the rudiments of French often shouted for hours in a coarse and idiomatic form of that language, or that the same person, alone and guarded, complained wildly of a staring thing which bit and chewed at her. In 1772 the servant Zenas died, and when Mrs. Harris heard of it she laughed with a shocking delight utterly foreign to her. The next year she herself died, and was laid to rest in the North Burial Ground beside her husband.

Upon the outbreak of trouble with Great Britain in 1775, William Harris, despite his scant sixteen years and feeble constitution, managed to enlist in the Army of Observation under General Greene; and from that time on enjoyed a steady rise in health and prestige. In 1780, as a captain in the Rhode Island forces in New Jersey under Colonel Angell, he met and married Phebe Hetfield of Elizabethtown, whom he brought to Providence upon his honorable discharge in the following year.

The young soldier's return was not a thing of unmitigated happiness. The house, it is true, was still in good condition; and the street had been widened and changed in name from Back Street to Benefit Street. But Mercy Dexter's once robust frame had undergone a sad and curious decay, so that she was now a stooped and pathetic figure with hollow voice and disconcerting pallor—qualities shared to a singular degree by the one remaining servant Maria. In the autumn of 1782 Phebe Harris gave birth to a still-born daughter, and on the fifteenth of the next May Mercy Dexter took leave of a useful, austere, and virtuous life.

William Harris, at last thoroughly convinced of the radically unhealthful nature of his abode, now took steps toward quitting it and closing it for ever. Securing temporary quarters for himself and his wife at the newly opened Golden Ball Inn, he arranged for the building of a new and finer house in Westminster Street, in the growing part of the town across the Great Bridge. There, in 1785, his son Dutee was born; and there the family dwelt till the encroachments of commerce drove them back across the river and over the hill to Angell Street, in the newer East Side residence district, where the late Archer Harris built his sumptuous but hideous French-roofed mansion in 1876. William and Phebe both succumbed to the yellow fever epidemic of 1797, but Dutee was brought up by his cousin Rathbone Harris, Peleg's son.

Rathbone was a practical man, and rented the Benefit Street house despite William's wish to keep it vacant. He considered it an obligation to his ward to make the most of all the boy's property, nor did he concern himself with the deaths and illnesses which caused so many changes of tenants, or the steadily growing aversion with which the house was generally regarded. It is likely that he felt only vexation when, in 1804, the town council ordered him to fumigate the place with sulfur, tar, and gum camphor on account of the much-discussed deaths of four persons, presumably caused by the then diminishing fever epidemic. They said the place had a febrile smell.

Dutee himself thought little of the house, for he grew up to be a privateersman, and served with distinction on the *Vigilant* under Captain Cahoone in the War of 1812. He returned unharmed, married in 1814, and became a father on that memorable night of September 23, 1815, when a great gale drove the waters of the bay over half the town, and floated a tall sloop well up Westminster Street so that its masts almost tapped the Harris windows in symbolic affirmation that the new boy, Welcome, was a seaman's son.

Welcome did not survive his father, but lived to perish gloriously at Fredericksburg in 1862. Neither he nor his son Archer knew of the shunned house as other than a nuisance almost impossible to rent—perhaps on account of the mustiness and sickly odor of unkempt old age. Indeed, it never was rented after a series of deaths culminating in 1861, which the excitement of the war tended to throw into obscurity. Carrington Harris, last of the male line, knew it only as a deserted and somewhat picturesque center of legend until I told him my experience. He had meant to tear it down and build an apartment house on the site, but after my account decided to let it stand, install plumbing, and rent it. Nor has he yet had any difficulty in obtaining tenants. The horror has gone.

III

It may well be imagined how powerfully I was affected by the annals of the Harrises. In this continuous record there seemed to me to brood a persistent evil beyond anything in nature as I had known it; an evil clearly connected with the house and not with the family. This impression was confirmed by my uncle's less systematic array of miscellaneous data—legends transcribed from servant gossip, cuttings from the papers, copies of death certificates by fellow-physicians, and the like. All of this material I cannot hope to give, for my uncle was a tireless antiquarian and very deeply interested in the shunned house; but I may refer to several dominant points which earn notice by their recurrence through many reports from diverse sources. For example, the servant gossip was practically unanimous in attributing to the fungous and malodorous *cellar* of the house a vast supremacy in evil influence. There had been servants—Ann White especially—who would not use the cellar kitchen, and at least three well-defined legends bore upon the queer quasi-human or diabolic outlines assumed by tree-roots and patches of mold in that region. These latter narratives interested me profoundly, on account of what I had seen in my boyhood, but I felt that most of the significance had in each case been largely obscured by additions from the common stock of local ghost lore.

Ann White, with her Exeter superstition, had promulgated the most extravagant and at the same time most consistent tale; alleging that there must lie buried beneath the house one of those vampires—the dead who retain their bodily form and live on the blood or breath of the living—whose hideous legions send their preying shapes or spirits abroad by night. To destroy a vampire one must, the grandmothers say, exhume it and burn its heart, or at least drive a stake through that organ; and Ann's dogged insistence on a search under the cellar had been prominent in bringing about her discharge.

Her tales, however, commanded a wide audience, and were the more readily accepted because the house indeed stood on land once used for burial purposes. To me their interest depended less on this circumstance than on the peculiarly appropriate way in which they dovetailed with certain other things—the complaint of the departing servant Preserved Smith, who had preceded Ann and never heard of her, that something "sucked his breath" at night; the death-certificates of the fever victims of 1804, issued by Doctor Chad Hopkins, and showing the four deceased persons all unaccountably lacking in blood; and the obscure passages of poor Rhoby Harris's ravings, where she complained of the sharp teeth of a glassy-eyed, half-visible presence.

Free from unwarranted superstition though I am, these things produced in me an odd sensation, which was intensified by a pair of widely separated newspaper cuttings relating to deaths in the shunned house—one from the *Providence Gazette and Country-Journal* of April 12, 1815, and the other from the *Daily Transcript and Chronicle* of October 27, 1845—each of which detailed an appallingly grisly circumstance whose duplication was remarkable. It seems that in both instances the dying person, in 1815 a gentle old lady named Stafford and in 1845 a schoolteacher of middle age named Eleazar Durfee, became transfigured in a horrible way, glaring glassily and attempting to bite the throat of the attending physician. Even more puzzling, though, was the final case which put an end to the renting of the house—a series of anemia deaths preceded by progressive madnesses wherein the patient would craftily attempt the lives of his relatives by incisions in the neck or wrist.

This was in 1860 and 1861, when my uncle had just begun his medical practise; and before leaving for the front he heard much of it from his elder professional colleagues. The really inexplicable thing was the way in which the victims—ignorant people, for the ill-smelling and widely shunned house could now be rented to no others—would babble maledictions in French, a language they could not possibly have studied to any extent. It made one think of poor Rhoby Harris nearly a century before, and so moved my uncle that he commenced collecting historical data on the house after listening, some time subsequent to his return from the war, to the first-hand account of Doctors Chase and Whitmarsh. Indeed, I could see that my uncle had thought deeply on the subject, and that he was glad of my own interest—an open-minded and sympathetic interest which enabled him to discuss with me matters at which others would merely have laughed. His fancy had not gone so far as mine, but he felt that the place was rare in its imaginative potentialities, and worthy of note as an inspiration in the field of the grotesque and macabre.

For my part, I was disposed to take the whole subject with profound seriousness, and began at once not only to review the evidence, but to accumulate as much more as I could. I talked with the elderly Archer Harris, then owner of the house, many times before his death in 1916; and obtained from him and his still surviving maiden sister Alice an authentic corroboration of all the family data my uncle had collected. When, however, I asked them what connection with France or its language the house could have, they confessed themselves as frankly baffled and ignorant as I. Archer knew nothing, and all that Miss Harris could say was that an old allusion her grandfather, Dutee Harris, had heard of might have shed a little light. The old seaman, who had survived his son Welcome's death in battle by two years, had not himself known the legend, but recalled that his earliest nurse, the ancient Maria Robbins, seemed darkly aware of something that might have lent a weird significance to the French raving of Rhoby Harris, which she had so often heard during the last days of that hapless woman. Maria had been at the shunned house from 1769 till the removal of the family in 1783, and had seen Mercy Dexter die. Once she hinted to the child Dutee of a somewhat peculiar circumstance in Mercy's last moments, but he had soon forgotten all about it save that it was something peculiar. The granddaughter, moreover, recalled even this much with difficulty. She and her brother were not so much interested in the house as was Archer's son Carrington, the present owner, with whom I talked after my experience.

* * * * *

Having exhausted the Harris family of all the information it could furnish, I turned my attention to early town records and deeds with a zeal more penetrating than that which my uncle had occasionally shown in the same work. What I wished was a comprehensive history of the site from its very settlement in 1636—or even before, if any Narragansett Indian legend could be unearthed to supply the data. I found, at the start, that the land had been part of the long strip of home lot granted originally to John Throckmorton; one of many similar strips beginning at the Town Street beside the river and extending up over the hill to a line roughly corresponding with the modern Hope Street. The Throckmorton lot had later, of course, been much subdivided; and I became very assiduous in tracing that section through which Back or Benefit Street was later run. It had, as rumor indeed said, been the Throckmorton graveyard; but as I examined the records more carefully, I found that the graves had all been transferred at an early date to the North Burial Ground on the Pawtucket West Road.

Then suddenly I came—by a rare piece of chance, since it was not in the main body of records and might easily have been missed—upon something which aroused my keenest eagerness, fitting in as it did with several of the queerest phases of the affair. It was the record of a lease, in 1697, of a small tract of ground to an Etienne Roulet and wife. At last the French element had appeared—that, and another deeper element of horror which the name conjured up from the darkest recesses of my weird and heterogeneous reading—and I feverishly studied the platting of the locality as it had been before the cutting through and partial straightening of Back Street between 1747 and 1758. I found what I had half expected, that where the shunned house now stood the Roulets had laid out their graveyard behind a one-story and attic cottage, and that no record of any transfer of graves existed. The document, indeed, ended in much confusion; and I was forced to ransack both the Rhode Island Historical Society and Shepley Library before I could find a local door which the name of Etienne Roulet would unlock. In the end I did find something; something of such vague but monstrous import that I set about at once to examine the cellar of the shunned house itself with a new and excited minuteness.

The Roulets, it seemed, had come in 1696 from East Greenwich, down the west shore of Narragansett Bay. They were Huguenots from Caude, and had encountered much opposition before the Providence selectmen allowed them to settle in the town. Unpopularity had dogged them in East Greenwich, whither they had come in 1686, after the revocation of the Edict of Nantes, and rumor said that the cause of dislike extended beyond mere racial and national prejudice, or the land disputes which involved other French settlers with the English in rivalries which not even Governor Andros could quell. But their ardent Protestantism—too ardent, some whispered—and their evident distress when virtually driven from the village down the bay, had moved the sympathy of the town fathers. Here the strangers had been granted a haven; and the swarthy Etienne Roulet, less apt at agriculture than at reading queer books and drawing queer diagrams, was given a clerical post in the warehouse at Pardon Tillinghast's wharf, far south in Town Street. There had, however, been a riot of some sort later on—perhaps forty years later, after old Roulet's death—and no one seemed to hear of the family after that.

For a century and more, it appeared, the Roulets had been well remembered and frequently discussed as vivid incidents in the quiet life of a New England seaport. Etienne's son Paul, a surly fellow whose erratic conduct had probably provoked the riot which wiped out the family, was particularly a source of speculation; and though Providence never shared the witchcraft panics of her Puritan neighbors, it was freely intimated by old wives that his prayers were neither uttered at the proper time nor directed toward the proper object. All this had undoubtedly formed the basis of the legend known by old Maria Robbins. What relation it had to the French ravings of Rhoby Harris and other inhabitants of the shunned house, imagination or future discovery alone could determine. I wondered how many of those who had known the legends realized that additional link with the terrible which my wider reading had given me; that ominous item in the annals of morbid horror which tells of the creature Jacques Roulet, of Caude, who in 1598 was condemned to death as a demoniac but afterward saved from the stake by the Paris parliament and shut in a madhouse. He had been found covered with blood and shreds of flesh in a wood, shortly after the killing and rending of a boy by a pair of wolves. One wolf was seen to lope away unhurt. Surely a pretty hearthside tale, with a queer significance as to name and place; but I decided that the Providence gossips could not have generally known of it. Had they known, the coincidence of names would have brought some drastic and frightened action—indeed, might not its limited whispering have precipitated the final riot which erased the Roulets from the town?

* * * * *

I now visited the accursed place with increased frequency; studying the unwholesome vegetation of the garden, examining all the walls of the building, and poring over every inch of the earthen cellar floor. Finally, with Carrington Harris's permission, I fitted a key to the disused door opening from the cellar directly upon Benefit Street, preferring to have a more immediate access to the outside world than the dark stairs, ground-floor hall, and front door could give. There, where morbidity lurked most thickly, I searched and poked during long afternoons when the sunlight filtered in through the cobwebbed above-ground windows, and a sense of security glowed from the unlocked door which placed me only a few feet from the placid sidewalk outside. Nothing new rewarded my efforts—only the same depressing mustiness and faint suggestions of noxious odors and nitrous outlines on the floor—and I fancy that many pedestrians must have watched me curiously through the broken panes.

At length, upon a suggestion of my uncle's, I decided to try the spot nocturnally; and one stormy midnight ran the beams of an electric torch over the moldy floor with its uncanny shapes and distorted, half-phosphorescent fungi. The place had dispirited me curiously that evening, and I was almost prepared when I saw—or thought I saw—amidst the whitish deposits a particularly sharp definition of the "huddled form" I had suspected from boyhood. Its clearness was astonishing and unprecedented—and as I watched I seemed to see again the thin, yellowish, shimmering exhalation which had startled me on that rainy afternoon so many years before.

Above the anthropomorphic patch of mold by the fireplace it rose; a subtle, sickish, almost luminous vapor which as it hung trembling in the dampness seemed to develop vague and shocking suggestions of form, gradually trailing off into nebulous decay and passing up into the blackness of the great chimney with a fetor in its wake. It was truly horrible, and the more so to me because of what I knew of the spot. Refusing to flee, I watched it fade—and as I watched I felt that it was in turn watching me greedily with eyes more imaginable than visible. When I told my uncle about it he was greatly aroused; and after a tense hour of reflection, arrived at a definite and drastic decision. Weighing in his mind the importance of the matter, and the significance of our relation to it, he insisted that we both test—and if possible destroy—the horror of the house by a joint night or nights of aggressive vigil in that musty and fungus-cursed cellar.

IV

On Wednesday, June 25, 1919, after a proper notification of Carrington Harris which did not include surmises as to what we expected to find, my uncle and I conveyed to the shunned house two camp chairs and a folding camp cot, together with some scientific mechanism of greater weight and intricacy. These we placed in the cellar during the day, screening the windows with paper and planning to return in the evening for our first vigil. We had locked the door from the cellar to the ground floor; and having a key to the outside cellar door, were prepared to leave our expensive and delicate apparatus—which we had obtained secretly and at great cost—as many days as our vigils might be protracted. It was our design to sit up together till very late, and then watch singly till dawn in two-hour stretches, myself first and then my companion; the inactive member resting on the cot.

The natural leadership with which my uncle procured the instruments from the laboratories of Brown University and the Cranston Street Armory, and instinctively assumed direction of our venture, was a marvelous commentary on the potential vitality and resilience of a man of eighty-one. Elihu Whipple had lived according to the hygienic laws he had preached as a physician, and but for what happened later would be here in full vigor today. Only two persons suspected what did happen—Carrington Harris and myself. I had to tell Harris because he owned the house and deserved to know what had gone out of it. Then too, we had spoken to him in advance of our quest; and I felt after my uncle's going that he would understand and assist me in some vitally necessary public explanations. He turned very pale, but agreed to help me, and decided that it would now be safe to rent the house.

To declare that we were not nervous on that rainy night of watching would be an exaggeration both gross and ridiculous. We were not, as I have said, in any sense childishly superstitious, but scientific study and reflection had taught us that the known universe of three dimensions embraces the merest fraction of the whole cosmos of substance and energy. In this case an overwhelming preponderance of evidence from numerous authentic sources pointed to the tenacious existence of certain forces of great power and, so far as the human point of view is concerned, exceptional malignancy. To say that we actually believed in vampires or werewolves would be a carelessly inclusive statement. Rather must it be said that we were not prepared to deny the possibility of certain unfamiliar and unclassified modifications of vital force and attenuated matter; existing very infrequently in three-dimensional space because of its more intimate connection with other spatial units, yet close enough to the boundary of our own to furnish us occasional manifestations which we, for lack of a proper vantage-point, may never hope to understand.

In short, it seemed to my uncle and me that an incontrovertible array of facts pointed to some lingering influence in the shunned house; traceable to one or another of the ill-favored French settlers of two centuries before, and still operative through rare and unknown laws of atomic and electronic motion. That the family of Roulet had possessed an abnormal affinity for outer circles of entity—dark spheres which for normal folk hold only repulsion and terror—their recorded history seemed to prove. Had not, then, the riots of those bygone seventeen-thirties set moving certain kinetic patterns in the morbid brain of one or more of them—notably the sinister Paul Roulet—which obscurely survived the bodies murdered and buried by the mob, and continued to function in some multiple-dimensioned space along the original lines of force determined by a frantic hatred of the encroaching community?

Such a thing was surely not a physical or biochemical impossibility in the light of a newer science which includes the theories of relativity and intra-atomic action. One might easily imagine an alien nucleus of substance or energy, formless or otherwise, kept alive by imperceptible or immaterial subtractions from the life-force or bodily tissue and fluids of other and more palpably living things into which it penetrates and with whose fabric it sometimes completely merges itself. It might be actively hostile, or it might be dictated merely by blind motives of self-preservation. In any case such a monster must of necessity be in our scheme of things an anomaly and an intruder, whose extirpation forms a primary duty with every man not an enemy to the world's life, health, and sanity.

What baffled us was our utter ignorance of the aspect in which we might encounter the thing. No sane person had ever seen it, and few had ever felt it definitely. It might be pure energy—a form ethereal and outside the realm of substance—or it might be partly material; some unknown and equivocal mass of plasticity, capable of changing at will to nebulous approximations of the solid, liquid, gaseous, or tenuously unparticled states. The anthropomorphic patch of mold on the floor, the form of the yellowish vapor, and the curvature of the tree-roots in some of the old tales, all argued at least a remote and reminiscent connection with the human shape; but how representative or permanent that similarity might be, none could say with any kind of certainty.

* * * * *

We had devised two weapons to fight it; a large and specially fitted Crookes tube operated by powerful storage batteries and provided with peculiar screens and reflectors, in case it proved intangible and opposable only by vigorously destructive ether radiations, and a pair of military flame-throwers of the sort used in the World War, in case it proved partly material and susceptible of mechanical destruction—for like the superstitious Exeter rustics, we were prepared to burn the thing's heart out if heart existed to burn. All this aggressive mechanism we set in the cellar in positions carefully arranged with reference to the cot and chairs, and to the spot before the fireplace where the mold had taken strange shapes. That suggestive patch, by the way, was only faintly visible when we placed our furniture and instruments, and when we returned that evening for the actual vigil. For a moment I half doubted that I had ever seen it in the more definitely limned form—but then I thought of the legends.

Our cellar vigil began at ten p.m., daylight saving time, and as it continued we found no promise of pertinent developments. A weak, filtered glow from the rain-harassed street-lamps outside, and a feeble phosphorescence from the detestable fungi within, showed the dripping stone of the walls, from which all traces of whitewash had vanished; the dank, fetid and mildew-tainted hard earth floor with its obscene fungi; the rotting remains of what had been stools, chairs, and tables, and other more shapeless furniture; the heavy planks and massive beams of the ground floor overhead; the decrepit plank door leading to bins and chambers beneath other parts of the house; the crumbling stone staircase with ruined wooden hand-rail; and the crude and cavernous fireplace of blackened brick where rusted iron fragments revealed the past presence of hooks, andirons, spit, crane, and a door to the Dutch oven—these things, and our austere cot and camp chairs, and the heavy and intricate destructive machinery we had brought.

We had, as in my own former explorations, left the door to the street unlocked; so that a direct and practical path of escape might lie open in case of manifestations beyond our power to deal with. It was our idea that our continued nocturnal presence would call forth whatever malign entity lurked there; and that being prepared, we could dispose of the thing with one or the other of our provided means as soon as we had recognized and observed it sufficiently. How long it might require to evoke and extinguish the thing, we had no notion. It occurred to us, too, that our venture was far from safe; for in what strength the thing might appear no one could tell. But we deemed the game worth the hazard, and embarked on it alone and unhesitatingly; conscious that the seeking of outside aid would only expose us to ridicule and perhaps defeat our entire purpose. Such was our frame of mind as we talked—far into the night, till my uncle's growing drowsiness made me remind him to lie down for his two-hour sleep.

Something like fear chilled me as I sat there in the small hours alone—I say alone, for one who sits by a sleeper is indeed alone; perhaps more alone than he can realize. My uncle breathed heavily, his deep inhalations and exhalations accompanied by the rain outside, and punctuated by another nerve-racking sound of distant dripping water within—for the house was repulsively damp even in dry weather, and in this storm positively swamp-like. I studied the loose, antique masonry of the walls in the fungus-light and the feeble rays which stole in from the street through the screened window; and once, when the noisome atmosphere of the place seemed about to sicken me, I opened the door and looked up and down the street, feasting my eyes on familiar sights and my nostrils on wholesome air. Still nothing occurred to reward my watching; and I yawned repeatedly, fatigue getting the better of apprehension.

Then the stirring of my uncle in his sleep attracted my notice. He had turned restlessly on the cot several times during the latter half of the first hour, but now he was breathing with unusual irregularity, occasionally heaving a sigh which held more than a few of the qualities of a choking moan.

I turned my electric flashlight on him and found his face averted; so rising and crossing to the other side of the cot, I again flashed the light to see if he seemed in any pain. What I saw unnerved me most surprisingly, considering its relative triviality. It must have been merely the association of any odd circumstance with the sinister nature of our location and mission, for surely the circumstance was not in itself frightful or unnatural. It was merely that my uncle's facial expression, disturbed no doubt by the strange dreams which our situation prompted, betrayed considerable agitation, and seemed not at all characteristic of him. His habitual expression was one of kindly and well-bred calm, whereas now a variety of emotions seemed struggling within him. I think, on the whole, that it was this *variety* which chiefly disturbed me. My uncle, as he gasped and tossed in increasing perturbation and with eyes that had now started open, seemed not one but many men, and suggested a curious quality of alienage from himself.

* * * * *

All at once he commenced to mutter, and I did not like the look of his mouth and teeth as he spoke. The words were at first indistinguishable, and then—with a tremendous start—I recognized something about them which filled me with icy fear till I recalled the breadth of my uncle's education and the interminable translations he had made from anthropological and antiquarian articles in the *Revue des Deux Mondes*. For the venerable Elihu Whipple was muttering *in French*, and the few phrases I could distinguish seemed connected with the darkest myths he had ever adapted from the famous Paris magazine.

Suddenly a perspiration broke out on the sleeper's forehead, and he leaped abruptly up, half awake. The jumble of French changed to a cry in English, and the hoarse voice shouted excitedly, "My breath, my breath!" Then the awakening became complete, and with a subsidence of facial expression to the normal state my uncle seized my hand and began to relate a dream whose nucleus of significance I could only surmise with a kind of awe.

He had, he said, floated off from a very ordinary series of dream-pictures into a scene whose strangeness was related to nothing he had ever read. It was of this world, and yet not of it—a shadowy geometrical confusion in which could be seen elements of familiar things in most unfamiliar and perturbing combinations. There was a suggestion of queerly disordered pictures superimposed one upon another; an arrangement in which the essentials of time as well as of space seemed dissolved and mixed in the most illogical fashion. In this kaleidoscopic vortex of phantasmal images were occasional snap-shots, if one might use the term, of singular clearness but unaccountable heterogeneity.

Once my uncle thought he lay in a carelessly dug open pit, with a crowd of angry faces framed by straggling locks and three-cornered hats frowning down on him. Again he seemed to be in the interior of a house—an old house, apparently—but the details and inhabitants were constantly changing, and he could never be certain of the faces or the furniture, or even of the room itself, since doors and windows seemed in just as great a state of flux as the presumably more mobile objects. It was queer—damnably queer—and my uncle spoke almost sheepishly, as if half expecting not to be believed, when he declared that of the strange faces many had unmistakably borne the features of the Harris family. And all the while there was a personal sensation of choking, as if some pervasive presence had spread itself through his body and sought to possess itself of his vital processes.

I shuddered at the thought of those vital processes, worn as they were by eighty-one years of continuous functioning, in conflict with unknown forces of which the youngest and strongest system might well be afraid; but in another moment reflected that dreams are only dreams, and that these uncomfortable visions could be, at most, no more than my uncle's reaction to the investigations and expectations which had lately filled our minds to the exclusion of all else.

Conversation, also, soon tended to dispel my sense of strangeness; and in time I yielded to my yawns and took my turn at slumber. My uncle seemed now very wakeful, and welcomed his period of watching even though the nightmare had aroused him far ahead of his allotted two hours.

Sleep seized me quickly, and I was at once haunted with dreams of the most disturbing kind. I felt, in my visions, a cosmic and abysmal loneness; with hostility surging from all sides upon some prison where I lay confined. I seemed bound and gagged, and taunted by the echoing yells of distant multitudes who thirsted for my blood. My uncle's face came to me with less pleasant association than in waking hours, and I recall many futile struggles and attempts to scream. It was not a pleasant sleep, and for a second I was not sorry for the echoing shriek which clove through the barriers of dream and flung me to a sharp and startled awakeness in which every actual object before my eyes stood out with more than natural clearness and reality.

V

I had been lying with my face away from my uncle's chair, so that in this sudden flash of awakening I saw only the door to the street, the window, and the wall and floor and ceiling toward the north of the room, all photographed with morbid vividness on my brain in a light brighter than the glow of the fungi or the rays from the street outside. It was not a strong or even a fairly strong light; certainly not nearly strong enough to read an average book by. But it cast a shadow of myself and the cot on the floor, and had a yellowish, penetrating force that hinted at things more potent than luminosity. This I perceived with unhealthy sharpness despite the fact that two of my other senses were violently assailed. For on my ears rang the reverberations of that shocking scream, while my nostrils revolted at the stench which filled the place. My mind, as alert as my senses, recognized the gravely unusual; and almost automatically I leaped up and turned about to grasp the destructive instruments which we had left trained on the moldy spot before the fireplace. As I turned, I dreaded what I was to see; for the scream had been in my uncle's voice, and I knew not against what menace I should have to defend him and myself.

Yet after all, the sight was worse than I had dreaded. There are horrors beyond horrors, and this was one of those nuclei of all dreamable hideousness which the cosmos saves to blast an accursed and unhappy few. Out of the fungus-ridden earth steamed up a vaporous corpse-light, yellow and diseased, which bubbled and lapped to a gigantic height in vague outlines half human and half monstrous, through which I could see the chimney and fireplace beyond. It was all eyes—wolfish and mocking—and the rugose insect-like head dissolved at the top to a thin stream of mist which curled putridly about and finally vanished up the chimney. I say that I saw this thing, but it is only in conscious retrospection that I ever definitely traced its damnable approach to form. At the time, it was to me only a seething, dimly phosphorescent cloud of fungous loathsomeness, enveloping and dissolving to an abhorrent plasticity the one object on which all my attention was focussed. That object was my uncle—the venerable Elihu Whipple—who with blackening and decaying features leered and gibbered at me, and reached out dripping claws to rend me in the fury which this horror had brought.

It was a sense of routine which kept me from going mad. I had drilled myself in preparation for the crucial moment, and blind training saved me. Recognizing the bubbling evil as no substance reachable by matter or material chemistry, and therefore ignoring the flame-thrower which loomed on my left, I threw on the current of the Crookes tube apparatus, and focussed toward that scene of immortal blasphemousness the strongest ether radiations which man's art can arouse from the spaces and fluids of nature. There was a bluish haze and a frenzied sputtering, and the yellowish phosphorescence grew dimmer to my eyes. But I saw the dimness was only that of contrast, and that the waves from the machine had no effect whatever.

Then, in the midst of that demoniac spectacle, I saw a fresh horror which brought cries to my lips and sent me fumbling and staggering toward that unlocked door to the quiet street, careless of what abnormal terrors I loosed upon the world, or what thoughts or judgments of men I brought down upon my head. In that dim blend of blue and yellow the form of my uncle had commenced a nauseous liquefaction whose essence eludes all description, and in which there played across his vanishing face such changes of identity as only madness can conceive. He was at once a devil and a multitude, a charnel-house and a pageant. Lit by the mixed and uncertain beams, that gelatinous face assumed a dozen—a score—a hundred—aspects; grinning, as it sank to the ground on a body that melted like tallow, in the caricatured likeness of legions strange and yet not strange.

I saw the features of the Harris line, masculine and feminine, adult and infantile, and other features old and young, coarse and refined, familiar and unfamiliar. For a second there flashed a degraded counterfeit of a miniature of poor mad Rhoby Harris that I had seen in the School of Design museum, and another time I thought I caught the raw-boned image of Mercy Dexter as I recalled her from a painting in Carrington Harris's house. It was frightful beyond conception; toward the last, when a curious blend of servant and baby visages flickered close to the fungous floor where a pool of greenish grease was spreading, it seemed as though the shifting features fought against themselves and strove to form contours like those of my uncle's kindly face. I like to think that he existed at that moment, and that he tried to bid me farewell. It seems to me I hiccupped a farewell from my own parched throat as I lurched out into the street; a thin stream of grease following me through the door to the rain-drenched sidewalk.

* * * * *

The rest is shadowy and monstrous. There was no one in the soaking street, and in all the world there was no one I dared tell. I walked aimlessly south past College Hill and the Athenaeum, down Hopkins Street, and over the bridge to the business section where tall buildings seemed to guard me as modern material things guard the world from ancient and unwholesome wonder. Then gray dawn unfolded wetly from the east, silhouetting the archaic hill and its venerable steeples, and beckoning me to the place where my terrible work was still unfinished. And in the end I went, wet, hatless, and dazed in the morning light, and entered that awful door in Benefit Street which I had left ajar, and which still swung cryptically in full sight of the early householders to whom I dared not speak.

The grease was gone, for the moldy floor was porous. And in front of the fireplace was no vestige of the giant doubled-up form traced in niter. I looked at the cot, the chairs, the instruments, my neglected hat, and the yellowed straw hat of my uncle. Dazedness was uppermost, and I could scarcely recall what was dream and what was reality. Then thought trickled back, and I knew that I had witnessed things more horrible than I had dreamed.

Sitting down, I tried to conjecture as nearly as sanity would let me just what had happened, and how I might end the horror, if indeed it had been real. Matter it seemed not to be, nor ether, nor anything else conceivable by mortal mind. What, then, but some exotic *emanation*; some vampirish vapor such as Exeter rustics tell of as lurking over certain churchyards? This I felt was the clue, and again I looked at the floor before the fireplace where the mold and niter had taken strange forms.

In ten minutes my mind was made up, and taking my hat I set out for home, where I bathed, ate, and gave by telephone an order for a pickax, a spade, a military gas-mask, and six carboys of sulfuric acid, all to be delivered the next morning at the cellar door of the shunned house in Benefit Street. After that I tried to sleep; and failing, passed the hours in reading and in the composition of inane verses to counteract my mood.

At eleven a. m. the next day I commenced digging. It was sunny weather, and I was glad of that. I was still alone, for as much as I feared the unknown horror I sought, there was more fear in the thought of telling anybody. Later I told Harris only through sheer necessity, and because he had heard odd tales from old people which disposed him ever so little toward belief. As I turned up the stinking black earth in front of the fireplace, my spade causing a viscous yellow ichor to ooze from the white fungi which it severed, I trembled at the dubious thoughts of what I might uncover. Some secrets of inner earth are not good for mankind, and this seemed to me one of them.

My hand shook perceptibly, but still I delved; after a while standing in the large hole I had made. With the deepening of the hole, which was about six feet square, the evil smell increased; and I lost all doubt of my imminent contact with the hellish thing whose emanations had cursed the house for over a century and a half. I wondered what it would look like—what its form and substance would be, and how big it might have waxed through long ages of life-sucking. At length I climbed out of the hole and dispersed the heaped-up dirt, then arranging the great carboys of acid around and near two sides, so that when necessary I might empty them all down the aperture in quick succession. After that I dumped earth only along the other two sides;

working more slowly and donning my gas-mask as the smell grew. I was nearly unnerved at my proximity to a nameless thing at the bottom of a pit.

Suddenly my spade struck something softer than earth. I shuddered, and made a motion as if to climb out of the hole, which was now as deep as my neck. Then courage returned, and I scraped away more dirt in the light of the electric torch I had provided. The surface I uncovered was fishy and glassy—a kind of semi-putrid congealed jelly with suggestions of translucency. I scraped further, and saw that it had form. There was a rift where a part of the substance was folded over. The exposed area was huge and roughly cylindrical; like a mammoth soft blue-white stovepipe doubled in two, its largest part some two feet in diameter. Still more I scraped, and then abruptly I leaped out of the hole and away from the filthy thing; frantically unstopping and tilting the heavy carboys, and precipitating their corrosive contents one after another down that charnel gulf and upon the unthinkable abnormality whose titan *elbow* I had seen.

* * * * *

The blinding maelstrom of greenish-yellow vapor which surged tempestuously up from that hole as the floods of acid descended, will never leave my memory. All along the hill people tell of the yellow day, when virulent and horrible fumes arose from the factory waste dumped in the Providence River, but I know how mistaken they are as to the source. They tell, too, of the hideous roar which at the same time came from some disordered water-pipe or gas main underground—but again I could correct them if I dared. It was unspeakably shocking, and I do not see how I lived through it. I did faint after emptying the fourth carboy, which I had to handle after the fumes had begun to penetrate my mask; but when I recovered I saw that the hole was emitting no fresh vapors.

The two remaining carboys I emptied down without particular result, and after a time I felt it safe to shovel the earth back into the pit. It was twilight before I was done, but fear had gone out of the place. The dampness was less fetid, and all the strange fungi had withered to a kind of harmless grayish powder which blew ash-like along the floor. One of earth's nethermost terrors had perished for ever; and if there be a hell, it had received at last the demon soul of an unhallowed thing. And as I patted down the last spadeful of mold, I shed the first of the many tears with which I have paid unaffected tribute to my beloved uncle's memory.

The next spring no more pale grass and strange weeds came up in the shunned house's terraced garden, and shortly afterward Carrington Harris rented the place. It is still spectral, but its strangeness fascinates me, and I shall find mixed with my relief a queer regret when it is torn down to make way for a tawdry shop or vulgar apartment building. The barren old trees in the yard have begun to bear small, sweet apples, and last year the birds nested in their gnarled boughs.

THE PIT AND THE PENDULUM

Edgar Allan Poe

Impia tortorum longos hic turba furores
Sanguinis innocui, non satiata, aluit.
Sospite nunc patria, fracto nunc funeris antro,
Mors ubi dira fuit vita salusque patent.
[Quatrain composed for the gates of a market to be erected
upon the site of the Jacobin Club House at Paris.]

I was sick—sick unto death with that long agony; and when they at length unbound me, and I was permitted to sit, I felt that my senses were leaving me. The sentence—the dread sentence of death—was the last of distinct accentuation which reached my ears. After that, the sound of the inquisitorial voices seemed merged in one dreamy indeterminate hum. It conveyed to my soul the idea of *revolution*—perhaps from its association in fancy with the burr of a mill wheel. This only for a brief period; for presently I heard no more. Yet, for a while, I saw; but with how terrible an exaggeration! I saw the lips of the black-robed judges. They appeared to me white—whiter than the sheet upon which I trace these words—and thin even to grotesqueness; thin with the intensity of their expression of firmness—of immoveable resolution—of stern contempt of human torture. I saw that the decrees of what to me was Fate, were still issuing from those lips. I saw them writhe with a deadly locution. I saw them fashion the syllables of my name; and I shuddered because no sound succeeded. I saw, too, for a few moments of delirious horror, the soft and nearly imperceptible waving of the sable draperies which enwrapped the walls of the apartment. And then my vision fell upon the seven tall candles upon the table. At first they wore the aspect of charity, and seemed white and slender angels who would save me; but then, all at once, there came a most deadly nausea over my spirit, and I felt every fibre in my frame thrill as if I had touched the wire of a galvanic battery, while the angel forms became meaningless spectres, with heads of flame, and I saw that from them there would be no help. And then there stole into my fancy, like a rich musical note, the thought of what sweet rest there must be in the grave. The thought came gently and stealthily, and it seemed long before it attained full appreciation; but just as my spirit came at length properly to feel and entertain it, the figures of the judges vanished, as if magically, from before me; the tall candles sank into nothingness; their flames went out utterly; the blackness of darkness supervened; all sensations appeared swallowed up in a mad rushing descent as of the soul into Hades. Then silence, and stillness, night were the universe.

I had swooned; but still will not say that all of consciousness was lost. What of it there remained I will not attempt to define, or even to describe; yet all was not lost. In the deepest slumber—no! In delirium—no! In a swoon—no! In death—no! Even in the grave all *is not* lost. Else there is no immortality for man. Arousing from the most profound of slumbers, we break the gossamer web of some dream. Yet in a second afterward (so frail may that web have been), we remember not that we have dreamed. In the return to life from the swoon there are two stages; first, that of the sense of mental or spiritual; secondly, that of the sense of physical, existence. It seems probable that if, upon reaching the second stage, we could recall the impressions of the first, we should find these impressions eloquent in memories of the gulf beyond. And that gulf is—what? How at least shall we distinguish its shadows from those of the tomb? But if the impressions of what I have termed the first stage, are not, at will, recalled, yet, after long interval, do they not come unbidden, while we marvel whence they come? He who has never swooned, is not he who finds strange palaces and wildly familiar faces in coals that glow; is not he who beholds floating in mid-air the sad visions that the many may not view; is not he who ponders over the perfume of some novel flower—is not he whose brain grows bewildered with the meaning of some musical cadence which has never before arrested his attention.

Amid frequent and thoughtful endeavors to remember; amid earnest struggles to regather some token of the state of seeming nothingness into which my soul had lapsed, there have been moments when I have dreamed of success; there have been brief, very brief periods when I have conjured up remembrances which the lucid reason of a later epoch assures me could have had reference only to that condition of seeming unconsciousness. These shadows of memory tell, indistinctly, of tall figures that lifted and bore me in silence down—down—still down—till a hideous dizziness oppressed me at the mere idea of the interminableness of the descent. They tell also of a vague horror at my heart, on account of that heart's unnatural stillness. Then comes a sense of sudden motionlessness throughout all things; as if those who bore me (a ghastly train!) had outrun, in their descent, the limits of the limitless, and paused from the wearisomeness of their toil. After this I call to mind flatness and dampness; and then all is madness—the madness of a memory which busies itself among forbidden things.

Very suddenly there came back to my soul motion and sound—the tumultuous motion of the heart, and, in my ears, the sound of its beating. Then a pause in which all is blank. Then again sound, and motion, and touch—a tingling sensation pervading my frame. Then the mere consciousness of existence, without thought—a condition which lasted long. Then, very suddenly, thought, and shuddering terror, and earnest endeavor to comprehend my true state. Then a strong desire to lapse into insensibility. Then a rushing revival of soul and a successful effort to move. And now a full memory of the trial, of the judges, of the sable draperies, of the sentence, of the sickness, of the swoon. Then entire forgetfulness of all that followed; of all that a later day and much earnestness of endeavor have enabled me vaguely to recall.

So far, I had not opened my eyes. I felt that I lay upon my back, unbound. I reached out my hand, and it fell heavily upon something damp and hard. There I suffered it to remain for many minutes, while I strove to imagine where and what I could be. I longed, yet dared not to employ my vision. I dreaded the first glance at objects around me. It was not that I feared to look upon things horrible, but that I grew aghast lest there should be *nothing* to see. At length, with a wild desperation at heart, I quickly unclosed my eyes. My worst thoughts, then, were confirmed. The blackness of eternal night encompassed me. I struggled for breath. The intensity of the darkness seemed to oppress and stifle me. The atmosphere was intolerably close. I still lay quietly, and made effort to exercise my reason. I brought to mind the inquisitorial proceedings, and attempted from that point to deduce my real condition. The sentence had passed; and it appeared to me that a very long interval of time had since elapsed. Yet not for a moment did I suppose myself actually dead. Such a supposition, notwithstanding what we read in fiction, is altogether inconsistent with real existence;—but where and in what state was I? The condemned to death, I knew, perished usually at the *autos-da-fé*, and one of these had been held on the very night of the day of my trial. Had I been remanded to my dungeon, to await the next sacrifice, which would not take place for many months? This I at once saw could not be. Victims had been in immediate demand. Moreover, my dungeon, as well as all the condemned cells at Toledo, had stone floors, and light was not altogether excluded.

A fearful idea now suddenly drove the blood in torrents upon my heart, and for a brief period, I once more relapsed into insensibility. Upon recovering, I at once started to my feet, trembling convulsively in every fibre. I thrust my arms wildly above and around me in all directions. I felt nothing; yet dreaded to move a step, lest I should be impeded by the walls of a *tomb*. Perspiration burst from every pore, and stood in cold big beads upon my forehead. The agony of suspense grew at length intolerable, and I cautiously moved forward, with my arms extended, and my eyes straining from their sockets, in the hope of catching some faint ray of light. I proceeded for many paces; but still all was blackness and vacancy. I breathed more freely. It seemed evident that mine was not, at least, the most hideous of fates.

And now, as I still continued to step cautiously onward, there came thronging upon my recollection a thousand vague rumors of the horrors of Toledo. Of the dungeons there had been strange things narrated—fables I had always deemed them—but yet strange, and too ghastly to repeat, save in a whisper. Was I left to perish of starvation in this subterranean world of darkness; or what fate, perhaps even more fearful, awaited me? That the result would be death, and a death of more than customary bitterness, I knew too well the character of my judges to doubt. The mode and the hour were all that occupied or distracted me.

My outstretched hands at length encountered some solid obstruction. It was a wall, seemingly of stone masonry—very smooth, slimy, and cold. I followed it up; stepping with all the careful distrust with which certain antique narratives had inspired me. This process, however, afforded me no means of ascertaining the dimensions of my dungeon; as I might make its circuit, and return to the point whence I set out, without being aware of the fact; so perfectly uniform seemed the wall. I therefore sought the knife which had been in my pocket, when led into the inquisitorial chamber; but it was gone; my clothes had been exchanged for a wrapper of coarse serge. I had thought of forcing the blade in some minute crevice of the masonry, so as to identify my point of departure. The difficulty, nevertheless, was but trivial; although, in the disorder of my fancy, it seemed at first insuperable. I tore a part of the hem from the robe and placed the fragment at full length, and at right angles to the wall. In groping my way around the prison, I could not fail to encounter this rag upon completing the circuit. So, at least I thought: but I had not counted upon the extent of the dungeon, or upon my own weakness. The ground was moist and slippery. I staggered onward for some time, when I stumbled and fell. My excessive fatigue induced me to remain prostrate; and sleep soon overtook me as I lay.

Upon awaking, and stretching forth an arm, I found beside me a loaf and a pitcher with water. I was too much exhausted to reflect upon this circumstance, but ate and drank with avidity. Shortly afterward, I resumed my tour around the prison, and with much toil came at last upon the fragment of the serge. Up to the period when I fell I had counted fifty-two paces, and upon resuming my walk, I had counted forty-eight more;—when I arrived at the rag. There were in all, then, a hundred paces; and, admitting two paces to the yard, I presumed the dungeon to be fifty yards in circuit. I had met, however, with many angles in the wall, and thus I could form no guess at the shape of the vault; for vault I could not help supposing it to be.

I had little object—certainly no hope these researches; but a vague curiosity prompted me to continue them. Quitting the wall, I resolved to cross the area of the enclosure. At first I proceeded with extreme caution, for the floor, although seemingly of solid material, was treacherous with slime. At length, however, I took courage, and did not hesitate to step firmly; endeavoring to cross in as direct a line as possible. I had advanced some ten or twelve paces in this manner, when the remnant of the torn hem of my robe became entangled between my legs. I stepped on it, and fell violently on my face.

In the confusion attending my fall, I did not immediately apprehend a somewhat startling circumstance, which yet, in a few seconds afterward, and while I still lay prostrate, arrested my attention. It was this—my chin rested upon the floor of the prison, but my lips and the upper portion of my head, although seemingly at a less elevation than the chin, touched nothing. At the same time my forehead seemed bathed in a clammy vapor, and the peculiar smell of decayed fungus arose to my nostrils. I put forward my arm, and shuddered to find that I had fallen at the very brink of a circular pit, whose extent, of course, I had no means of ascertaining at the moment. Groping about the masonry just below the margin, I succeeded in dislodging a small fragment, and let it fall into the abyss. For many seconds I hearkened to its reverberations as it dashed against the sides of the chasm in its descent; at length there was a sullen plunge into water, succeeded by loud echoes. At the same moment there came a sound resembling the quick opening, and as rapid closing of a door overhead, while a faint gleam of light flashed suddenly through the gloom, and as suddenly faded away.

I saw clearly the doom which had been prepared for me, and congratulated myself upon the timely accident by which I had escaped. Another step before my fall, and the world had seen me no more. And the death just avoided, was of that very character which I had regarded as fabulous and frivolous in the tales respecting the Inquisition. To the victims of its tyranny, there was the choice of death with its direst physical agonies, or death with its most hideous moral horrors. I had been reserved for the latter. By long suffering my nerves had been unstrung, until I trembled at the sound of my own voice, and had become in every respect a fitting subject for the species of torture which awaited me.

Shaking in every limb, I groped my way back to the wall; resolving there to perish rather than risk the terrors of the wells, of which my imagination now pictured many in various positions about the dungeon. In other conditions of mind I might have had courage to end my misery at once by a plunge into one of these abysses; but now I was the veriest of cowards. Neither could I forget what I had read of these pits—that the sudden extinction of life formed no part of their most horrible plan.

Agitation of spirit kept me awake for many long hours; but at length I again slumbered. Upon arousing, I found by my side, as before, a loaf and a pitcher of water. A burning thirst consumed me, and I emptied the vessel at a draught. It must have been drugged; for scarcely had I drunk, before I became irresistibly drowsy. A deep sleep fell upon me—a sleep like that of death. How long it lasted of course, I know not; but when, once again, I unclosed my eyes, the objects around me were visible. By a wild sulphurous lustre, the origin of which I could not at first determine, I was enabled to see the extent and aspect of the prison.

In its size I had been greatly mistaken. The whole circuit of its walls did not exceed twenty-five yards. For some minutes this fact occasioned me a world of vain trouble; vain indeed! for what could be of less importance, under the terrible circumstances which environed me, then the mere dimensions of my dungeon? But my soul took a wild interest in trifles, and I busied myself in endeavors to account for the error I had committed in my measurement. The truth at length flashed upon me. In my first attempt at exploration I had counted fifty-two paces, up to the period when I fell; I must then have been within a pace or two of the fragment of serge; in fact, I had nearly performed the circuit of the vault. I then slept, and upon awaking, I must have returned upon my steps—thus supposing the circuit nearly double what it actually was. My confusion of mind prevented me from observing that I began my tour with the wall to the left, and ended it with the wall to the right.

I had been deceived, too, in respect to the shape of the enclosure. In feeling my way I had found many angles, and thus deduced an idea of great irregularity; so potent is the effect of total darkness upon one arousing from lethargy or sleep! The angles were simply those of a few slight depressions, or niches, at odd intervals. The general shape of the prison was square. What I had taken for masonry seemed now to be iron, or some other metal, in huge plates, whose sutures or joints occasioned the depression. The entire surface of this metallic enclosure was rudely daubed in all the hideous and repulsive devices to which the charnel superstition of the monks has given rise. The figures of fiends in aspects of menace, with skeleton forms, and other more really fearful images, overspread and disfigured the walls. I observed that the outlines of these monstrosities were sufficiently distinct, but that the colors seemed faded and blurred, as if from the effects of a damp atmosphere. I now noticed the floor, too, which was of stone. In the centre yawned the circular pit from whose jaws I had escaped; but it was the only one in the dungeon.

All this I saw indistinctly and by much effort: for my personal condition had been greatly changed during slumber. I now lay upon my back, and at full length, on a species of low framework of wood. To this I was securely bound by a long strap resembling a surcingle. It passed in many convolutions about my limbs and body, leaving at liberty only my head, and my left arm to such extent that I could, by dint of much exertion, supply myself with food from an earthen dish which lay by my side on the floor. I saw, to my horror, that the pitcher had been removed. I say to my horror; for I was consumed with intolerable thirst. This thirst it appeared to be the design of my persecutors to stimulate: for the food in the dish was meat pungently seasoned.

Looking upward, I surveyed the ceiling of my prison. It was some thirty or forty feet overhead, and constructed much as the side walls. In one of its panels a very singular figure riveted my whole attention. It was the painted figure of Time as he is commonly represented, save that, in lieu of a scythe, he held what, at a casual glance, I supposed to be the pictured image of a huge pendulum such as we see on antique clocks. There was something, however, in the appearance of this machine which caused me to regard it more attentively. While I gazed directly upward at it (for its position was immediately over my own) I fancied that I saw it in motion. In an instant afterward the fancy was confirmed. Its sweep was brief, and of course slow. I watched it for some minutes, somewhat in fear, but more in wonder. Wearied at length with observing its dull movement, I turned my eyes upon the other objects in the cell.

A slight noise attracted my notice, and, looking to the floor, I saw several enormous rats traversing it. They had issued from the well, which lay just within view to my right. Even then, while I gazed, they came up in troops, hurriedly, with ravenous eyes, allured by the scent of the meat. From this it required much effort and attention to scare them away.

It might have been half an hour, perhaps even an hour (for I could take but imperfect note of time), before I again cast my eyes upward. What I then saw confounded and amazed me. The sweep of the pendulum had increased in extent by nearly a yard. As a natural consequence, its velocity was also much greater. But what mainly disturbed me was the idea that had perceptibly descended. I now observed—with what horror it is needless to say—that its nether extremity was formed of a crescent of glittering steel, about a foot in length from horn to horn; the horns upward, and the under edge evidently as keen as that of a razor. Like a razor also, it seemed massy and heavy, tapering from the edge into a solid and broad structure above. It was appended to a weighty rod of brass, and the whole hissed as it swung through the air.

I could no longer doubt the doom prepared for me by monkish ingenuity in torture. My cognizance of the pit had become known to the inquisitorial agents—the pit whose horrors had been destined for so bold a recusant as myself—*the pit*, typical of hell, and regarded by rumor as the Ultima Thule of all their punishments. The plunge into this pit I had avoided by the merest of accidents, I knew that surprise, or entrapment into torment, formed an important portion of all the grotesquerie of these dungeon deaths. Having failed to fall, it was no part of the demon plan to hurl me into the abyss; and thus (there being no alternative) a different and a milder destruction awaited me. Milder! I half smiled in my agony as I thought of such application of such a term.

What boots it to tell of the long, long hours of horror more than mortal, during which I counted the rushing vibrations of the steel! Inch by inch—line by line—with a descent only appreciable at intervals that seemed ages—down and still down it came! Days passed—it might have been that many days passed—ere it swept so closely over me as to fan me with its acrid breath. The odor of the sharp steel forced itself into my nostrils. I prayed—I wearied heaven with my prayer for its more speedy descent. I grew frantically mad, and struggled to force myself upward against the sweep of the fearful scimitar. And then I fell suddenly calm, and lay smiling at the glittering death, as a child at some rare bauble.

There was another interval of utter insensibility; it was brief; for, upon again lapsing into life there had been no perceptible descent in the pendulum. But it might have been long; for I knew there were demons who took note of my swoon, and who could have arrested the vibration at pleasure. Upon my recovery, too, I felt very—oh, inexpressibly sick and weak, as if through long inanition. Even amid the agonies of that period, the human nature craved food. With painful effort I outstretched my left arm as far as my bonds permitted, and took possession of the small remnant which had been spared me by the rats. As I put a portion of it within my lips, there rushed to my mind a half formed thought of joy—of hope. Yet what business had I with hope? It was, as I say, a half formed thought—man has many such which are never completed. I felt that it was of joy—of hope; but felt also that it had perished in its formation. In vain I struggled to perfect—to regain it. Long suffering had nearly annihilated all my ordinary powers of mind. I was an imbecile—an idiot.

The vibration of the pendulum was at right angles to my length. I saw that the crescent was designed to cross the region of the heart. It would fray the serge of my robe—it would return and repeat its operations—again—and again. Notwithstanding terrifically wide sweep (some thirty feet or more) and the hissing vigor of its descent, sufficient to sunder these very walls of iron, still the fraying of my robe would be all that, for several minutes, it would accomplish. And at this thought I paused. I dared not go farther than this reflection. I dwelt upon it with a pertinacity of attention—as if, in so dwelling, I could arrest here the descent of the steel. I forced myself to ponder upon the sound of the crescent as it should pass across the garment—upon the peculiar thrilling sensation which the friction of cloth produces on the nerves. I pondered upon all this frivolity until my teeth were on edge.

Down—steadily down it crept. I took a frenzied pleasure in contrasting its downward with its lateral velocity. To the right—to the left—far and wide—with the shriek of a damned spirit; to my heart with the stealthy pace of the tiger! I alternately laughed and howled as the one or the other idea grew predominant.

Down—certainly, relentlessly down! It vibrated within three inches of my bosom! I struggled violently, furiously, to free my left arm. This was free only from the elbow to the hand. I could reach the latter, from the platter beside me, to my mouth, with great effort, but no farther. Could I have broken the fastenings above the elbow, I would have seized and attempted to arrest the pendulum. I might as well have attempted to arrest an avalanche!

Down—still unceasingly—still inevitably down! I gasped and struggled at each vibration. I shrunk convulsively at its every sweep. My eyes followed its outward or upward whirls with the eagerness of the most unmeaning despair; they closed themselves spasmodically at the descent, although death would have been a relief, oh! how unspeakable! Still I quivered in every nerve to think how slight a sinking of the machinery would precipitate that keen, glistening axe upon my bosom. It was hope that prompted the nerve to quiver—the frame to shrink. It was hope—the hope that triumphs on the rack—that whispers to the death-condemned even in the dungeons of the Inquisition.

I saw that some ten or twelve vibrations would bring the steel in actual contact with my robe, and with this observation there suddenly came over my spirit all the keen, collected calmness of despair. For the first time during many hours—or perhaps days—I *thought.* It now occurred to me that the bandage, or surcingle, which enveloped me, was *unique.* I was tied by no separate cord. The first stroke of the razorlike crescent athwart any portion of the band, would so detach it that it might be unwound from my person by means of my left hand. But how fearful, in that case, the proximity of the steel! The result of the slightest struggle how deadly! Was it likely, moreover, that the minions of the torturer had not foreseen and provided for this possibility! Was it probable that the bandage crossed my bosom in the track of the pendulum? Dreading to find my faint, and, as it seemed, in last hope frustrated, I so far elevated my head as to obtain a distinct view of my breast. The surcingle enveloped my limbs and body close in all directions—*save in the path of the destroying crescent.*

Scarcely had I dropped my head back into its original position, when there flashed upon my mind what I cannot better describe than as the unformed half of that idea of deliverance to which I have previously alluded, and of which a moiety only floated indeterminately through my brain when I raised food to my burning lips. The whole thought was now present—feeble, scarcely sane, scarcely definite—but still entire. I proceeded at once, with the nervous energy of despair, to attempt its execution.

For many hours the immediate vicinity of the low framework upon which I lay, had been literally swarming with rats. They were wild, bold, ravenous; their red eyes glaring upon me as if they waited but for motionlessness on my part to make me their prey. "To what food," I thought, "have they been accustomed in the well?"

They had devoured, in spite of all my efforts to prevent them, all but a small remnant of the contents of the dish. I had fallen into an habitual see-saw, or wave of the hand about the platter: and, at length, the unconscious uniformity of the movement deprived it of effect. In their voracity the vermin frequently fastened their sharp fangs in my fingers. With the particles of the oily and spicy viand which now remained, I thoroughly rubbed the bandage wherever I could reach it; then, raising my hand from the floor, I lay breathlessly still.

At first the ravenous animals were startled and terrified at the change—at the cessation of movement. They shrank alarmedly back; many sought the well. But this was only for a moment. I had not counted in vain upon their voracity. Observing that I remained without motion, one or two of the boldest leaped upon the frame-work, and smelt at the surcingle. This seemed the signal for a general rush. Forth from the well they hurried in fresh troops. They clung to the wood—they overran it, and leaped in hundreds upon my person. The measured movement of the pendulum disturbed them not at all. Avoiding its strokes they busied themselves with the anointed bandage. They pressed—they swarmed upon me in ever accumulating heaps. They writhed upon my throat; their cold lips sought my own; I was half stifled by their thronging pressure; disgust, for which the world has no name, swelled my bosom, and chilled, with a heavy clamminess, my heart. Yet one minute, and I felt that the struggle would be over. Plainly I perceived the loosening of the bandage. I knew that in more than one place it must be already severed. With a more than human resolution I lay still.

Nor had I erred in my calculations—nor had I endured in vain. I at length felt that I was free. The surcingle hung in ribands from my body. But the stroke of the pendulum already pressed upon my bosom. It had divided the serge of the robe. It had cut through the linen beneath. Twice again it swung, and a sharp sense of pain shot through every nerve. But the moment of escape had arrived. At a wave of my hand my deliverers hurried tumultuously away. With a steady movement—cautious, sidelong, shrinking, and slow—I slid from the embrace of the bandage and beyond the reach of the scimitar. For the moment, at least, *I was free.*

Free!—and in the grasp of the Inquisition! I had scarcely stepped from my wooden bed of horror upon the stone floor of the prison, when the motion of the hellish machine ceased and I beheld it drawn up, by some invisible force, through the ceiling. This was a lesson which I took desperately to heart. My every motion was undoubtedly watched. Free!—I had but escaped death in one form of agony, to be delivered unto worse than death in some other. With that thought I rolled my eves nervously around on the barriers of iron that hemmed me in. Something unusual—some change which, at first, I could not appreciate distinctly—it was obvious, had taken place in the apartment. For many minutes of a dreamy and trembling abstraction, I busied myself in vain, unconnected conjecture. During this period, I became aware, for the first time, of the origin of the sulphurous light which illumined the cell. It proceeded from a fissure, about half an inch in width, extending entirely around the prison at the base of the walls, which thus appeared, and were, completely separated from the floor. I endeavored, but of course in vain, to look through the aperture.

As I arose from the attempt, the mystery of the alteration in the chamber broke at once upon my understanding. I have observed that, although the outlines of the figures upon the walls were sufficiently distinct, yet the colors seemed blurred and indefinite. These colors had now assumed, and were momentarily assuming, a startling and most intense brilliancy, that gave to the spectral and fiendish portraitures an aspect that might have thrilled even firmer nerves than my own. Demon eyes, of a wild and ghastly vivacity, glared upon me in a thousand directions, where none had been visible before, and gleamed with the lurid lustre of a fire that I could not force my imagination to regard as unreal.

Unreal!—Even while I breathed there came to my nostrils the breath of the vapour of heated iron! A suffocating odour pervaded the prison! A deeper glow settled each moment in the eyes that glared at my agonies! A richer tint of crimson diffused itself over the pictured horrors of blood. I panted! I gasped for breath! There could be no doubt of the design of my tormentors—oh! most unrelenting! oh! most demoniac of men! I shrank from the glowing metal to the centre of the cell. Amid the thought of the fiery destruction that impended, the idea of the coolness of the well came over my soul like balm. I rushed to its deadly brink. I threw my straining vision below. The glare from the enkindled roof illumined its inmost recesses. Yet, for a wild moment, did my spirit refuse to comprehend the meaning of what I saw. At length it forced—it wrestled its way into my soul—it burned itself in upon my shuddering reason.—Oh! for a voice to speak!—oh! horror!—oh! any horror but this! With a shriek, I rushed from the margin, and buried my face in my hands—weeping bitterly.

The heat rapidly increased, and once again I looked up, shuddering as with a fit of the ague. There had been a second change in the cell—and now the change was obviously in the form. As before, it was in vain that I, at first, endeavoured to appreciate or understand what was taking place. But not long was I left in doubt. The Inquisitorial vengeance had been hurried by my two-fold escape, and there was to be no more dallying with the King of Terrors. The room had been square. I saw that two of its iron angles were now acute—two, consequently, obtuse. The fearful difference quickly increased with a low rumbling or moaning sound. In an instant the apartment had shifted its form into that of a lozenge. But the alteration stopped not here—I neither hoped nor desired it to stop. I could have clasped the red walls to my bosom as a garment of eternal peace. "Death," I said, "any death but that of the pit!" Fool! Might I have not known that *into the pit* it was the object of the burning iron to urge me? Could I resist its glow? Or, if even that, could I withstand its pressure? And now, flatter and flatter grew the lozenge, with a rapidity that left me no time for contemplation. Its centre, and of course, its greatest width, came just over the yawning gulf. I shrank back—but the closing walls pressed me resistlessly onward. At length for my seared and writhing body there was no longer an inch of foothold on the firm floor of the prison. I struggled no more, but the agony of my soul found vent in one loud, long, and final scream of despair. I felt that I tottered upon the brink—I averted my eyes—

There was a discordant hum of human voices! There was a loud blast as of many trumpets! There was a harsh grating as of a thousand thunders! The fiery walls rushed back! An outstretched arm caught my own as I fell, fainting, into the abyss. It was that of General Lasalle. The French army had entered Toledo. The Inquisition was in the hands of its enemies.

THE VAMPYRE

John William Polidori

It happened that in the midst of the dissipations attendant upon a London winter, there appeared at the various parties of the leaders of the *ton* a nobleman, more remarkable for his singularities, than his rank. He gazed upon the mirth around him, as if he could not participate therein. Apparently, the light laughter of the fair only attracted his attention, that he might by a look quell it, and throw fear into those breasts where thoughtlessness reigned. Those who felt this sensation of awe, could not explain whence it arose: some attributed it to the dead grey eye, which, fixing upon the object's face, did not seem to penetrate, and at one glance to pierce through to the inward workings of the heart; but fell upon the cheek with a leaden ray that weighed upon the skin it could not pass. His peculiarities caused him to be invited to every house; all wished to see him, and those who had been accustomed to violent excitement, and now felt the weight of ennui, were pleased at having something in their presence capable of engaging their attention. In spite of the deadly hue of his face, which never gained a warmer tint, either from the blush of modesty, or from the strong emotion of passion, though its form and outline were beautiful, many of the female hunters after notoriety attempted to win his attentions, and gain, at least, some marks of what they might term affection: Lady Mercer, who had been the mockery of every monster shewn in drawing-rooms since her marriage, threw herself in his way, and did all but put on the dress of a mountebank, to attract his notice—though in vain—when she stood before him, though his eyes were apparently fixed upon hers, still it seemed as if they were unperceived—even her unappalled impudence was baffled, and she left the field. But though the common adultress could not influence even the guidance of his eyes, it was not that the female sex was indifferent to him: yet such was the apparent caution with which he spoke to the virtuous wife and innocent daughter, that few knew he ever addressed himself to females. He had, however, the reputation of a winning tongue; and whether it was that it even overcame the dread of his singular character, or that they were moved by his apparent hatred of vice, he was as often among those females who form the boast of their sex from their domestic virtues, as among those who sully it by their vices.

About the same time, there came to London a young gentleman of the name of Aubrey: he was an orphan left with an only sister in the possession of great wealth, by parents who died while he was yet in childhood. Left also to himself by guardians, who thought it their duty merely to take care of his fortune, while they relinquished the more important charge of his mind to the care of mercenary subalterns, he cultivated more his imagination than his judgment. He had, hence, that high romantic feeling of honour and candour, which daily ruins so many milliners' apprentices. He believed all to sympathise with virtue, and thought that vice was thrown in by Providence merely for the picturesque effect of the scene, as we see in romances: he thought that the misery of a cottage merely consisted in the vesting of clothes, which were as warm, but which were better adapted to the painter's eye by their irregular folds and various coloured patches. He thought, in fine, that the dreams of poets were the realities of life. He was handsome, frank, and rich: for these reasons, upon his entering into the gay circles, many mothers surrounded him, striving which should describe with least truth their languishing or romping favourites: the daughters at the same time, by their brightening countenances when he approached, and by their sparkling eyes, when he opened his lips, soon led him into false notions of his talents and his merit. Attached as he was to the romance of his solitary hours, he was startled at finding, that, except in the tallow and wax candles that flickered, not from the presence of a ghost, but from want of snuffing, there was no foundation in real life for any of that congeries of pleasing pictures and descriptions contained in those volumes, from which he had formed his study. Finding, however, some compensation in his gratified vanity, he was about to relinquish his dreams, when the extraordinary being we have above described, crossed him in his career.

He watched him; and the very impossibility of forming an idea of the character of a man entirely absorbed in himself, who gave few other signs of his observation of external objects, than the tacit assent to their existence, implied by the avoidance of their contact: allowing his imagination to picture every thing that flattered its propensity to extravagant ideas, he soon formed this object into the hero of a romance, and determined to observe the offspring of his fancy, rather than the person before him. He became acquainted with him, paid him attentions, and so far advanced upon his notice, that his presence was always recognised. He gradually learnt that Lord Ruthven's affairs were embarrassed, and soon found, from the notes of preparation in —— Street, that he was about to travel. Desirous of gaining some information respecting this singular character, who, till now, had only whetted his curiosity, he hinted to his guardians, that it was time for him to perform the tour, which for many generations has been thought necessary to enable the young to take some rapid steps in the career of vice towards putting themselves upon an equality with the aged, and not allowing them to appear as if fallen from the skies, whenever scandalous intrigues are mentioned as the subjects of pleasantry or of praise, according to the degree of skill shewn in carrying them on. They consented: and Aubrey immediately mentioning his intentions to Lord Ruthven, was surprised to receive from him a proposal to join him. Flattered by such a mark of esteem from him, who, apparently, had nothing in common with other men, he gladly accepted it, and in a few days they had passed the circling waters.

Hitherto, Aubrey had had no opportunity of studying Lord Ruthven's character, and now he found, that, though many more of his actions were exposed to his view, the results offered different conclusions from the apparent motives to his conduct. His companion was profuse in his liberality—the idle, the vagabond, and the beggar, received from his hand more than enough to relieve their immediate wants. But Aubrey could not avoid remarking, that it was not upon the virtuous, reduced to indigence by the misfortunes attendant even upon virtue, that he bestowed his alms;—these were sent from the door with hardly suppressed sneers; but when the profligate came to ask something, not to relieve his wants, but to allow him to wallow in his lust, or to sink him still deeper in his iniquity, he was sent away with rich charity. This was, however, attributed by him to the greater importunity of the vicious, which generally prevails over the retiring bashfulness of the virtuous indigent. There was one circumstance about the charity of his Lordship, which was still more impressed upon his mind: all those upon whom it was bestowed, inevitably found that there was a curse upon it, for they were all either led to the scaffold, or sunk to the lowest and the most abject misery. At Brussels and other towns through which they passed, Aubrey was surprized at the apparent eagerness with which his companion sought for the centres of all fashionable vice; there he entered into all the spirit of the faro table: he betted, and always gambled with success, except where the known sharper was his antagonist, and then he lost even more than he gained; but it was always with the same unchanging face, with which he generally watched the society around: it was not, however, so when he encountered the rash youthful novice, or the luckless father of a numerous family; then his very wish seemed fortune's law—this apparent abstractedness of mind was laid aside, and his eyes sparkled with more fire than that of the cat whilst dallying with the half-dead mouse. In every town, he left the formerly affluent youth, torn from the circle he adorned, cursing, in the solitude of a dungeon, the fate that had drawn him within the reach of this fiend; whilst many a father sat frantic, amidst the speaking looks of mute hungry children, without a single farthing of his late immense wealth, wherewith to buy even sufficient to satisfy their present craving. Yet he took no money from the gambling table; but immediately lost, to the ruiner of many, the last gilder he had just snatched from the convulsive grasp of the innocent: this might but be the result of a certain degree of knowledge, which was not, however, capable of combating the cunning of the more experienced. Aubrey often wished to represent this to his friend, and beg him to resign that charity and pleasure which proved the ruin of all, and did not tend to his own profit;—but he delayed it—for each day he hoped his friend would give him some opportunity of speaking frankly and openly to him; however, this never occurred. Lord Ruthven in his carriage, and amidst the various wild and rich scenes of nature, was always the same: his eye spoke less than his lip; and though Aubrey was near the object of his curiosity, he obtained no greater gratification from it than the constant excitement of vainly wishing to break that mystery, which to his exalted imagination began to assume the appearance of something supernatural.

They soon arrived at Rome, and Aubrey for a time lost sight of his companion; he left him in daily attendance upon the morning circle of an Italian countess, whilst he went in search of the memorials of another almost deserted city. Whilst he was thus engaged, letters arrived from England, which he opened with eager impatience; the first was from his sister, breathing nothing but affection; the others were from his guardians, the latter astonished him; if it had before entered into his imagination that there was an evil power resident in his companion, these seemed to give him sufficient reason for the belief. His guardians insisted upon his immediately leaving his friend, and urged, that his character was dreadfully vicious, for that the possession of irresistible powers of seduction, rendered his licentious habits more dangerous to society. It had been discovered, that his contempt for the adultress had not originated in hatred of her character; but that he had required, to enhance his gratification, that his victim, the partner of his guilt, should be hurled from the pinnacle of unsullied virtue, down to the lowest abyss of infamy and degradation: in fine, that all those females whom he had sought, apparently on account of their virtue, had, since his departure, thrown even the mask aside, and had not scrupled to expose the whole deformity of their vices to the public gaze.

Aubrey determined upon leaving one, whose character had not yet shown a single bright point on which to rest the eye. He resolved to invent some plausible pretext for abandoning him altogether, purposing, in the mean while, to watch him more closely, and to let no slight circumstances pass by unnoticed. He entered into the same circle, and soon perceived, that his Lordship was endeavouring to work upon the inexperience of the daughter of the lady whose house he chiefly frequented. In Italy, it is seldom that an unmarried female is met with in society; he was therefore obliged to carry on his plans in secret; but Aubrey's eye followed him in all his windings, and soon discovered that an assignation had been appointed, which would most likely end in the ruin of an innocent, though thoughtless girl. Losing no time, he entered the apartment of Lord Ruthven, and abruptly asked him his intentions with respect to the lady, informing him at the same time that he was aware of his being about to meet her that very night. Lord Ruthven answered, that his intentions were such as he supposed all would have upon such an occasion; and upon being pressed whether he intended to marry her, merely laughed. Aubrey retired; and, immediately writing a note, to say, that from that moment he must decline accompanying his Lordship in the remainder of their proposed tour, he ordered his servant to seek other apartments, and calling upon the mother of the lady, informed her of all he knew, not only with regard to her daughter, but also concerning the character of his Lordship. The assignation was prevented. Lord Ruthven next day merely sent his servant to notify his complete assent to a separation; but did not hint any suspicion of his plans having been foiled by Aubrey's interposition.

Having left Rome, Aubrey directed his steps towards Greece, and crossing the Peninsula, soon found himself at Athens. He then fixed his residence in the house of a Greek; and soon occupied himself in tracing the faded records of ancient glory upon monuments that apparently, ashamed of chronicling the deeds of freemen only before slaves, had hidden themselves beneath the sheltering soil or many coloured lichen. Under the same roof as himself, existed a being, so beautiful and delicate, that she might have formed the model for a painter, wishing; to pourtray on canvass the promised hope of the faithful in Mahomet's paradise, save that her eyes spoke too much mind for any one to think she could belong to those who had no souls. As she danced upon the plain, or tripped along the mountain's side, one would have thought the gazelle a poor type of her beauties; for who would have exchanged her eye, apparently the eye of animated nature, for that sleepy luxurious look of the animal suited but to the taste of an epicure. The light step of Ianthe often accompanied Aubrey in his search after antiquities, and often would the unconscious girl, engaged in the pursuit of a Kashmere butterfly, show the whole beauty of her form, floating as it were upon the wind, to the eager gaze of him, who forgot the letters he had just decyphered upon an almost effaced tablet, in the contemplation of her sylph-like figure. Often would her tresses falling, as she flitted around, exhibit in the sun's ray such delicately brilliant and swiftly fading hues, its might well excuse the forgetfulness of the antiquary, who let escape from his mind the very object he had before thought of vital importance to the proper interpretation of a passage in Pausanias. But why attempt to describe charms which all feel, but none can appreciate? It was innocence, youth, and beauty, unaffected by crowded drawing-rooms and stifling balls. Whilst he drew those remains of which he wished to preserve a memorial for his future hours, she would stand by, and watch the magic effects of his pencil, in tracing the scenes of her native place; she would then describe to him the circling dance upon the open plain, would paint, to him in all the glowing colours of youthful memory, the marriage pomp she remembered viewing in her infancy; and then, turning to subjects that had evidently made a greater impression upon her mind, would tell him all the supernatural tales of her nurse. Her earnestness and apparent belief of what she narrated, excited the interest even of Aubrey; and often as she told him the tale of the living vampyre, who had passed years amidst his friends, and dearest ties, forced every year, by feeding upon the life of a lovely female to prolong his existence for the ensuing months, his blood would run cold, whilst he attempted to laugh her out of such idle and horrible fantasies; but Ianthe cited to him the names of old men, who had at last detected one living among themselves, after several of their near relatives and children had been found marked with the stamp of the fiend's appetite; and when she found him so incredulous, she begged of him to believe her, for it had been remarked that those who had dared to question their existence, always had some proof given, which obliged them, with grief and heartbreaking, to confess it was true. She detailed to him the traditional appearance of these monsters, and his horror was increased, by hearing a pretty accurate description of Lord Ruthven; he, however, still persisted in persuading her, that there could be no truth in her fears, though at the same time he wondered at the many coincidences which had all tended to excite a belief in the supernatural power of Lord Ruthven.

Aubrey began to attach himself more and more to Ianthe; her innocence, so contrasted with all the affected virtues of the women among whom he had sought for his vision of romance, won his heart; and while he ridiculed the idea of a young man of English habits, marrying an uneducated Greek girl, still he found himself more and more attached to the almost fairy form before him. He would tear himself at times from her, and, forming a plan for some antiquarian research, he would depart, determined not to return until his object was attained; but he always found it impossible to fix his attention upon the ruins around him, whilst in his mind he retained an image that seemed alone the rightful possessor of his thoughts. Ianthe was unconscious of his love, and was ever the same frank infantile being he had first known. She always seemed to part from him with reluctance; but it was because she had no longer any one with whom she could visit her favourite haunts, whilst her guardian was occupied in sketching or uncovering some fragment which had yet escaped the destructive hand of time. She had appealed to her parents on the subject of Vampyres, and they both, with several present, affirmed their existence, pale with horror at the very name. Soon after, Aubrey determined to proceed upon one of his excursions, which was to detain him for a few hours; when they heard the name of the place, they all at once begged of him not to return at night, as he must necessarily pass through a wood, where no Greek would ever remain, after the day had closed, upon any consideration. They described it as the resort of the vampyres in their nocturnal orgies, and denounced the most heavy evils as impending upon him who dared to cross their path. Aubrey made light of their representations, and tried to laugh them out of the idea; but when he saw them shudder at his daring thus to mock a superior, infernal power, the very name of which apparently made their blood freeze, he was silent.

Next morning Aubrey set off upon his excursion unattended; he was surprised to observe the melancholy face of his host, and was concerned to find that his words, mocking the belief of those horrible fiends, had inspired them with such terror. When he was about to depart, Ianthe came to the side of his horse, and earnestly begged of him to return, ere night allowed the power of these beings to be put in action—he promised. He was, however, so occupied in his research, that he did not perceive that day-light would soon end, and that in the horizon there was one of those specks which, in the warmer climates, so rapidly gather into a tremendous mass, and pour all their rage upon the devoted country. He at last, however, mounted his horse, determined to make up by speed for his delay: but it was too late. Twilight, in these southern climates, is almost unknown; immediately the sun sets, night begins: and ere he had advanced far, the power of the storm was above—its echoing thunders had scarcely an interval of rest—its thick heavy rain forced its way through the canopying foliage, whilst the blue forked lightning seemed to fall and radiate at his very feet. Suddenly his horse took fright, and he was carried with dreadful rapidity through the entangled forest. The animal at last, through fatigue, stopped, and he found, by the glare of lightning, that he was in the neighbourhood of a hovel that hardly lifted itself up from the masses of dead leaves and brushwood which surrounded it. Dismounting, he approached, hoping to find some one to guide him to the town, or at least trusting to obtain shelter from the pelting of the storm. As he approached, the thunders, for a moment silent, allowed him to hear the dreadful shrieks of a woman mingling with the stifled, exultant mockery of a laugh, continued in one almost unbroken sound;—he was startled: but, roused by the thunder which again rolled over his head, he, with a sudden effort, forced open the door of the hut. He found himself in utter darkness: the sound, however, guided him. He was apparently unperceived; for, though he called, still the sounds continued, and no notice was taken of him. He found himself in contact with some one, whom he immediately seized; when a voice cried, "Again baffled!" to which a loud laugh succeeded; and he felt himself grappled by one whose strength seemed superhuman: determined to sell his life as dearly as he could, he struggled; but it was in vain: he was lifted from his feet and hurled with enormous force against the ground—his enemy threw himself upon him, and kneeling upon his breast, had placed his hands upon his throat—when the glare of many torches penetrating through the hole that gave light in the day, disturbed him—he instantly rose, and, leaving his prey, rushed through the door, and in a moment the crashing of the branches, as he broke through the wood, was no longer heard. The storm was now still; and Aubrey, incapable of moving, was soon heard by those without. They entered; the light of their torches fell upon the mud walls, and the thatch loaded on every individual straw with heavy flakes of soot. At the desire of Aubrey they searched for her who had attracted him by her cries; he was again left in darkness; but what was his horror, when the light of the torches once more burst upon him, to perceive the airy form of his fair conductress brought in a lifeless corse. He shut his eyes, hoping that it was but a vision arising from his disturbed imagination; but he again saw the same form, when he unclosed them, stretched by his side. There was no colour upon her cheek, not even upon her lip; yet there was a stillness about her face that seemed almost as attaching as the life that once dwelt there—upon her neck and breast was blood, and upon her throat were the marks of teeth having opened the vein—to this the men pointed, crying, simultaneously struck with horror, "A Vampyre! a Vampyre!" A litter was quickly formed, and Aubrey was laid by the side of her who had lately been to him the object of so many bright and fairy visions, now fallen with the flower of life that had died within her. He knew not what his thoughts were—his mind was benumbed and seemed to shun reflection, and take refuge in vacancy—he held almost unconsciously in his hand a naked dagger of a particular construction, which had been found in the hut. They were soon met by different parties who had been engaged in the search of her whom a mother had missed. Their lamentable cries, as they approached the city, forewarned the parents of some dreadful catastrophe. To describe their grief would be impossible; but when they ascertained the cause of their child's death, they looked at Aubrey, and pointed to the corse. They were inconsolable; both died broken-hearted.

Aubrey being put to bed was seized with a most violent fever, and was often delirious; in these intervals he would call upon Lord Ruthven and upon Ianthe—by some unaccountable combination he seemed to beg of his former companion to spare the being he loved. At other times he would imprecate maledictions upon his head, and curse him as her destroyer. Lord Ruthven, chanced at this time to arrive at Athens, and, from whatever motive, upon hearing of the state of Aubrey, immediately placed himself in the same house, and became his constant attendant. When the latter recovered from his delirium, he was horrified and startled at the sight of him whose image he had now combined with that of a Vampyre; but Lord Ruthven, by his kind words, implying almost repentance for the fault that had caused their separation, and still more by the attention, anxiety, and care which he showed, soon reconciled him to his presence. His lordship seemed quite changed; he no longer appeared that apathetic being who had so astonished Aubrey; but as soon as his convalescence began to be rapid, he again gradually retired into the same state of mind, and Aubrey perceived no difference from the former man, except that at times he was surprised to meet his gaze fixed intently upon him, with a smile of malicious exultation playing upon his lips: he knew not why, but this smile haunted him. During the last stage of the invalid's recovery, Lord Ruthven was apparently engaged in watching the tideless waves raised by the cooling breeze, or in marking the progress of those orbs, circling, like our world, the moveless sun—indeed, he appeared to wish to avoid the eyes of all.

Aubrey's mind, by this shock, was much weakened, and that elasticity of spirit which had once so distinguished him now seemed to have fled for ever. He was now as much a lover of solitude and silence as Lord Ruthven; but much as he wished for solitude, his mind could not find it in the neighbourhood of Athens; if he sought it amidst the ruins he had formerly frequented, Ianthe's form stood by his side—if he sought it in the woods, her light step would appear wandering amidst the underwood, in quest of the modest violet; then suddenly turning round, would show, to his wild imagination, her pale face and wounded throat, with a meek smile upon her lips. He determined to fly scenes, every feature of which created such bitter associations in his mind. He proposed to Lord Ruthven, to whom he held himself bound by the tender care he had taken of him during his illness, that they should visit those parts of Greece neither had yet seen. They travelled in every direction, and sought every spot to which a recollection could be attached: but though they thus hastened from place to place, yet they seemed not to heed what they gazed upon. They heard much of robbers, but they gradually began to slight these reports, which they imagined were only the invention of individuals, whose interest it was to excite the generosity of those whom they defended from pretended dangers. In consequence of thus neglecting the advice of the inhabitants, on one occasion they travelled with only a few guards, more to serve as guides than as a defence. Upon entering, however, a narrow defile, at the bottom of which was the bed of a torrent, with large masses of rock brought down from the neighbouring precipices, they had reason to repent their negligence; for scarcely were the whole of the party engaged in the narrow pass, when they were startled by the whistling of bullets close to their heads, and by the echoed report of several guns. In an instant their guards had left them, and, placing themselves behind rocks, had begun to fire in the direction whence the report came. Lord Ruthven and Aubrey, imitating their example, retired for a moment behind the sheltering turn of the defile: but ashamed of being thus detained by a foe, who with insulting shouts bade them advance, and being exposed to unresisting slaughter, if any of the robbers should climb above and take them in the rear, they determined at once to rush forward in search of the enemy. Hardly had they lost the shelter of the rock, when Lord Ruthven received a shot in the shoulder, which brought him to the ground. Aubrey hastened to his assistance; and, no longer heeding the contest or his own peril, was soon surprised by seeing the robbers' faces around him—his guards having, upon Lord Ruthven's being wounded, immediately thrown up their arms and surrendered.

By promises of great reward, Aubrey soon induced them to convey his wounded friend to a neighbouring cabin; and having agreed upon a ransom, he was no more disturbed by their presence—they being content merely to guard the entrance till their comrade should return with the promised sum, for which he had an order. Lord Ruthven's strength rapidly decreased; in two days mortification ensued, and death seemed advancing with hasty steps. His conduct and appearance had not changed; he seemed as unconscious of pain as he had been of the objects about him: but towards the close of the last evening, his mind became apparently uneasy, and his eye often fixed upon Aubrey, who was induced to offer his assistance with more than usual earnestness—"Assist me! you may save me—you may do more than that—I mean not my life, I heed the death of my existence as little as that of the passing day; but you may save my honour, your friend's honour."—"How? tell me how? I would do any thing," replied Aubrey. "I need but little—my life ebbs apace—I cannot explain the whole—but if you would conceal all you know of me, my honour were free from stain in the world's mouth—and if my death were unknown for some time in England—I—I—but life."—"It shall not be known."—"Swear!" cried the dying man, raising himself with exultant violence, "Swear by all your soul reveres, by all your nature fears, swear that, for a year and a day you will not impart your knowledge of my crimes or death to any living being in any way, whatever may happen, or whatever you may see." His eyes seemed bursting from their sockets: "I swear!" said Aubrey; he sunk laughing upon his pillow, and breathed no more.

Aubrey retired to rest, but did not sleep; the many circumstances attending his acquaintance with this man rose upon his mind, and he knew not why; when he remembered his oath a cold shivering came over him, as if from the presentiment of something horrible awaiting him. Rising early in the morning, he was about to enter the hovel in which he had left the corpse, when a robber met him, and informed him that it was no longer there, having been conveyed by himself and comrades, upon his retiring, to the pinnacle of a neighbouring mount, according to a promise they had given his lordship, that it should be exposed to the first cold ray of the moon that rose after his death. Aubrey astonished, and taking several of the men, determined to go and bury it upon the spot where it lay. But, when he had mounted to the summit he found no trace of either the corpse or the clothes, though the robbers swore they pointed out the identical rock on which they had laid the body. For a time his mind was bewildered in conjectures, but he at last returned, convinced that they had buried the corpse for the sake of the clothes.

Weary of a country in which he had met with such terrible misfortunes, and in which all apparently conspired to heighten that superstitious melancholy that had seized upon his mind, he resolved to leave it, and soon arrived at Smyrna. While waiting for a vessel to convey him to Otranto, or to Naples, he occupied himself in arranging those effects he had with him belonging to Lord Ruthven. Amongst other things there was a case containing several weapons of offence, more or less adapted to ensure the death of the victim. There were several daggers and ataghans. Whilst turning them over, and examining their curious forms, what was his surprise at finding a sheath apparently ornamented in the same style as the dagger discovered in the fatal hut—he shuddered—hastening to gain further proof, he found the weapon, and his horror may be imagined when he discovered that it fitted, though peculiarly shaped, the sheath he held in his hand. His eyes seemed to need no further certainty—they seemed gazing to be bound to the dagger; yet still he wished to disbelieve; but the particular form, the same varying tints upon the haft and sheath were alike in splendour on both, and left no room for doubt; there were also drops of blood on each.

He left Smyrna, and on his way home, at Rome, his first inquiries were concerning the lady he had attempted to snatch from Lord Ruthven's seductive arts. Her parents were in distress, their fortune ruined, and she had not been heard of since the departure of his lordship. Aubrey's mind became almost broken under so many repeated horrors; he was afraid that this lady had fallen a victim to the destroyer of Ianthe. He became morose and silent; and his only occupation consisted in urging the speed of the postilions, as if he were going to save the life of some one he held dear. He arrived at Calais; a breeze, which seemed obedient to his will, soon wafted him to the English shores; and he hastened to the mansion of his fathers, and there, for a moment, appeared to lose, in the embraces and caresses of his sister, all memory of the past. If she before, by her infantine caresses, had gained his affection, now that the woman began to appear, she was still more attaching as a companion.

Miss Aubrey had not that winning grace which gains the gaze and applause of the drawing-room assemblies. There was none of that light brilliancy which only exists in the heated atmosphere of a crowded apartment. Her blue eye was never lit up by the levity of the mind beneath. There was a melancholy charm about it which did not seem to arise from misfortune, but from some feeling within, that appeared to indicate a soul conscious of a brighter realm. Her step was not that light footing, which strays where'er a butterfly or a colour may attract—it was sedate and pensive. When alone, her face was never brightened by the smile of joy; but when her brother breathed to her his affection, and would in her presence forget those griefs she knew destroyed his rest, who would have exchanged her smile for that of the voluptuary? It seemed as if those eyes,—that face were then playing in the light of their own native sphere. She was yet only eighteen, and had not been presented to the world, it having been thought by her guardians more fit that her presentation should be delayed until her brother's return from the continent, when he might be her protector. It was now, therefore, resolved that the next drawing-room, which was fast approaching, should be the epoch of her entry into the "busy scene." Aubrey would rather have remained in the mansion of his fathers, and fed upon the melancholy which overpowered him. He could not feel interest about the frivolities of fashionable strangers, when his mind had been so torn by the events he had witnessed; but he determined to sacrifice his own comfort to the protection of his sister. They soon arrived in town, and prepared for the next day, which had been announced as a drawing-room.

The crowd was excessive—a drawing-room had not been held for a long time, and all who were anxious to bask in the smile of royalty, hastened thither. Aubrey was there with his sister. While he was standing in a corner by himself, heedless of all around him, engaged in the remembrance that the first time he had seen Lord Ruthven was in that very place—he felt himself suddenly seized by the arm, and a voice he recognized too well, sounded in his ear—"Remember your oath." He had hardly courage to turn, fearful of seeing a spectre that would blast him, when he perceived, at a little distance, the same figure which had attracted his notice on this spot upon his first entry into society. He gazed till his limbs almost refusing to bear their weight, he was obliged to take the arm of a friend, and forcing a passage through the crowd, he threw himself into his carriage, and was driven home. He paced the room with hurried steps, and fixed his hands upon his head, as if he were afraid his thoughts were bursting from his brain. Lord Ruthven again before him—circumstances started up in dreadful array—the dagger—his oath.—He roused himself, he could not believe it possible—the dead rise again!—He thought his imagination had conjured up the image, his mind was resting upon. It was impossible that it could be real—he determined, therefore, to go again into society; for though he attempted to ask concerning Lord

Ruthven, the name hung upon his lips, and he could not succeed in gaining information. He went a few nights after with his sister to the assembly of a near relation. Leaving her under the protection of a matron, he retired into a recess, and there gave himself up to his own devouring thoughts. Perceiving, at last, that many were leaving, he roused himself, and entering another room, found his sister surrounded by several, apparently in earnest conversation; he attempted to pass and get near her, when one, whom he requested to move, turned round, and revealed to him those features he most abhorred. He sprang forward, seized his sister's arm, and, with hurried step, forced her towards the street: at the door he found himself impeded by the crowd of servants who were waiting for their lords; and while he was engaged in passing them, he again heard that voice whisper close to him—"Remember your oath!"—He did not dare to turn, but, hurrying his sister, soon reached home.

Aubrey became almost distracted. If before his mind had been absorbed by one subject, how much more completely was it engrossed, now that the certainty of the monster's living again pressed upon his thoughts. His sister's attentions were now unheeded, and it was in vain that she intreated him to explain to her what had caused his abrupt conduct. He only uttered a few words, and those terrified her. The more he thought, the more he was bewildered. His oath startled him;—was he then to allow this monster to roam, bearing ruin upon his breath, amidst all he held dear, and not avert its progress? His very sister might have been touched by him. But even if he were to break his oath, and disclose his suspicions, who would believe him? He thought of employing his own hand to free the world from such a wretch; but death, he remembered, had been already mocked. For days he remained in this state; shut up in his room, he saw no one, and eat only when his sister came, who, with eyes streaming with tears, besought him, for her sake, to support nature. At last, no longer capable of bearing stillness and solitude, he left his house, roamed from street to street, anxious to fly that image which haunted him. His dress became neglected, and he wandered, as often exposed to the noon-day sun as to the midnight damps. He was no longer to be recognized; at first he returned with the evening to the house; but at last he laid him down to rest wherever fatigue overtook him. His sister, anxious for his safety, employed people to follow him; but they were soon distanced by him who fled from a pursuer swifter than any—from thought. His conduct, however, suddenly changed. Struck with the idea that he left by his absence the whole of his friends, with a fiend amongst them, of whose presence they were unconscious, he determined to enter again into society, and watch him closely, anxious to forewarn, in spite of his oath, all whom Lord Ruthven approached with intimacy. But when he entered into a room, his haggard and suspicious looks were so striking, his inward shudderings so visible, that his sister was at last obliged to beg of him to abstain from seeking, for her sake, a society which affected him so strongly. When, however, remonstrance proved unavailing, the guardians thought proper to interpose, and, fearing that his mind was becoming alienated, they thought it high time to resume again that trust which had been before imposed upon them by Aubrey's parents.

Desirous of saving him from the injuries and sufferings he had daily encountered in his wanderings, and of preventing him from exposing to the general eye those marks of what they considered folly, they engaged a physician to reside in the house, and take constant care of him. He hardly appeared to notice it, so completely was his mind absorbed by one terrible subject. His incoherence became at last so great, that he was confined to his chamber. There he would often lie for days, incapable of being roused. He had become emaciated, his eyes had attained a glassy lustre—the only sign of affection and recollection remaining displayed itself upon the entry of his sister; then he would sometimes start, and, seizing her hands, with looks that severely afflicted her, he would desire her not to touch him. "Oh, do not touch him—if your love for me is aught, do not go near him!" When, however, she inquired to whom he referred, his only answer was, "True! true!" and again he sank into a state, whence not even she could rouse him. This lasted many months: gradually, however, as the year was passing, his incoherences became less frequent, and his mind threw off a portion of its gloom, whilst his guardians observed, that several times in the day he would count upon his fingers a definite number, and then smile.

The time had nearly elapsed, when, upon the last day of the year, one of his guardians entering his room, began to converse with his physician upon the melancholy circumstance of Aubrey's being in so awful a situation, when his sister was going next day to be married. Instantly Aubrey's attention was attracted; he asked anxiously to whom. Glad of this mark of returning intellect, of which they feared he had been deprived, they mentioned the name of the Earl of Marsden. Thinking this was a young Earl whom he had met with in society, Aubrey seemed pleased, and astonished them still more by his expressing his intention to be present at the nuptials, and desiring to see his sister. They answered not, but in a few minutes his sister was with him. He was apparently again capable of being affected by the influence of her lovely smile; for he pressed her to his breast, and kissed her cheek, wet with tears, flowing at the thought of her brother's being once more alive to the feelings of affection. He began to speak with all his wonted warmth, and to congratulate her upon her marriage with a person so distinguished for rank and every accomplishment; when he suddenly perceived a locket upon her breast; opening it, what was his surprise at beholding the features of the monster who had so long influenced his life. He seized the portrait in a paroxysm of rage, and trampled it under foot. Upon her asking him why he thus destroyed the resemblance of her future husband, he looked as if he did not understand her—then seizing her hands, and gazing on her with a frantic expression of countenance, he bade her swear that she would never wed this monster, for he—

But he could not advance—it seemed as if that voice again bade him remember his oath—he turned suddenly round, thinking Lord Ruthven was near him but saw no one. In the meantime the guardians and physician, who had heard the whole, and thought this was but a return of his disorder, entered, and forcing him from Miss Aubrey, desired her to leave him. He fell upon his knees to them, he implored, he begged of them to delay but for one day. They, attributing this to the insanity they imagined had taken possession of his mind, endeavoured to pacify him, and retired.

Lord Ruthven had called the morning after the drawing-room, and had been refused with every one else. When he heard of Aubrey's ill health, he readily understood himself to be the cause of it; but when he learned that he was deemed insane, his exultation and pleasure could hardly be concealed from those among whom he had gained this information. He hastened to the house of his former companion, and, by constant attendance, and the pretence of great affection for the brother and interest in his fate, he gradually won the ear of Miss Aubrey. Who could resist his power? His tongue had dangers and toils to recount—could speak of himself as of an individual having no sympathy with any being on the crowded earth, save with her to whom he addressed himself;—could tell how, since he knew her, his existence, had begun to seem worthy of preservation, if it were merely that he might listen to her soothing accents;—in fine, he knew so well how to use the serpent's art, or such was the will of fate, that he gained her affections. The title of the elder branch falling at length to him, he obtained an important embassy, which served as an excuse for hastening the marriage (in spite of her brother's deranged state), which was to take place the very day before his departure for the continent.

Aubrey, when he was left by the physician and his guardians, attempted to bribe the servants, but in vain. He asked for pen and paper; it was given him; he wrote a letter to his sister, conjuring her, as she valued her own happiness, her own honour, and the honour of those now in the grave, who once held her in their arms as their hope and the hope of their house, to delay but for a few hours that marriage, on which he denounced the most heavy curses. The servants promised they would deliver it; but giving it to the physician, he thought it better not to harass any more the mind of Miss Aubrey by, what he considered, the ravings of a maniac. Night passed on without rest to the busy inmates of the house; and Aubrey heard, with a horror that may more easily be conceived than described, the notes of busy preparation. Morning came, and the sound of carriages broke upon his ear. Aubrey grew almost frantic. The curiosity of the servants at last overcame their vigilance, they gradually stole away, leaving him in the custody of an helpless old woman. He seized the opportunity, with one bound was out of the room, and in a moment found himself in the apartment where all were nearly assembled. Lord Ruthven was the first to perceive him: he immediately approached, and, taking his arm by force, hurried him from the room, speechless with rage. When on the staircase, Lord Ruthven whispered in his ear—"Remember your oath, and know, if not my bride to day, your sister is dishonoured. Women are frail!" So saying, he pushed him towards his attendants, who, roused by the old woman, had come in search of him. Aubrey could no longer support himself; his rage not finding vent, had broken a blood-vessel, and he was conveyed to bed. This was not mentioned to his sister, who was not present when he entered, as the physician was afraid of agitating her. The marriage was solemnized, and the bride and bridegroom left London.

Aubrey's weakness increased; the effusion of blood produced symptoms of the near approach of death. He desired his sister's guardians might be called, and when the midnight hour had struck, he related composedly what the reader has perused—he died immediately after.

The guardians hastened to protect Miss Aubrey; but when they arrived, it was too late. Lord Ruthven had disappeared, and Aubrey's sister had glutted the thirst of a *Vampyre!*

ONE SUMMER NIGHT

Ambrose Bierce

The fact that Henry Armstrong was buried did not seem to him to prove that he was dead: he had always been a hard man to convince. That he really was buried, the testimony of his senses compelled him to admit. His posture—flat upon his back, with his hands crossed upon his stomach and tied with something that he easily broke without profitably altering the situation—the strict confinement of his entire person, the black darkness and profound silence, made a body of evidence impossible to controvert and he accepted it without cavil. But dead—no; he was only very, very ill. He had, withal, the invalid's apathy and did not greatly concern himself about the uncommon fate that had been allotted to him. No philosopher was he—just a plain, commonplace person gifted, for the time being, with a pathological indifference: the organ that he feared consequences with was torpid. So, with no particular apprehension for his immediate future, he fell asleep and all was peace with Henry Armstrong. But something was going on overhead. It was a dark summer night, shot through with infrequent shimmers of lightning silently firing a cloud lying low in the west and portending a storm. These brief, stammering illuminations brought out with ghastly distinctness the monuments and headstones of the cemetery and seemed to set them dancing. It was not a night in which any credible witness was likely to be straying about a cemetery, so the three men who were there, digging into the grave of Henry Armstrong, felt reasonably secure. Two of them were young students from a medical college a few miles away; the third was a gigantic negro known as Jess. For many years Jess had been employed about the cemetery as a man-of-all-work and it was his favourite pleasantry that he knew "every soul in the place." From the nature of what he was now doing it was inferable that the place was not so populous as its register may have shown it to be. Outside the wall, at the part of the grounds farthest from the public road, were a horse and a light wagon, waiting. The work of excavation was not difficult: the earth with which the grave had been loosely filled a few hours before offered little resistance and was soon thrown out. Removal of the casket from its box was less easy, but it was taken out, for it was a perquisite of Jess, who carefully unscrewed the cover and laid it aside, exposing the body in black trousers and white shirt. At that instant the air sprang to flame, a cracking shock of thunder shook the stunned world and Henry Armstrong tranquilly sat up. With inarticulate cries the men fled in terror, each in a different direction. For nothing on earth could two of them have been persuaded to return. But Jess was of another breed. In the grey of the morning the two students, pallid and haggard from anxiety and with the terror of their adventure still beating tumultuously in their blood, met at the medical college. "You saw it?" cried one. "God! yes—what are we to do?" They went around to the rear of the building, where they saw a horse, attached to a light wagon, hitched to a gatepost near the door of the dissecting-room. Mechanically they entered the room. On a bench in the obscurity sat the negro Jess. He rose, grinning, all eyes and teeth. "I'm waiting for my pay," he said. Stretched naked on a long table lay the body of Henry Armstrong, the head defiled with blood and clay from a blow with a spade.

FOR THE BLOOD IS THE LIFE

F. Marion Crawford

We had dined at sunset on the broad roof of the old tower, because it was cooler there during the great heat of summer. Besides, the little kitchen was built at one corner of the great square platform, which made it more convenient than if the dishes had to be carried down the steep stone steps, broken in places and everywhere worn with age. The tower was one of those built all down the west coast of Calabria by the Emperor Charles V early in the sixteenth century, to keep off the Barbary pirates, when the unbelievers were allied with Francis I against the Emperor and the Church. They have gone to ruin, a few still stand intact, and mine is one of the largest. How it came into my possession ten years ago, and why I spend a part of each year in it, are matters which do not concern this tale. The tower stands in one of the loneliest spots in Southern Italy, at the extremity of a curving rocky promontory, which forms a small but safe natural harbour at the southern extremity of the Gulf of Policastro, and just north of Cape Scalea, the birthplace of Judas Iscariot, according to the old local legend. The tower stands alone on this hooked spur of the rock, and there is not a house to be seen within three miles of it. When I go there I take a couple of sailors, one of whom is a fair cook, and when I am away it is in charge of a gnome-like little being who was once a miner and who attached himself to me long ago.

My friend, who sometimes visits me in my summer solitude, is an artist by profession, a Scandinavian by birth, and a cosmopolitan by force of circumstances. We had dined at sunset; the sunset glow had reddened and faded again, and the evening purple steeped the vast chain of the mountains that embrace the deep gulf to eastward and rear themselves higher and higher toward the south. It was hot, and we sat at the landward corner of the platform, waiting for the night breeze to come down from the lower hills. The colour sank out of the air, there was a little interval of deep-grey twilight, and a lamp sent a yellow streak from the open door of the kitchen, where the men were getting their supper.

Then the moon rose suddenly above the crest of the promontory, flooding the platform and lighting up every little spur of rock and knoll of grass below us, down to the edge of the motionless water. My friend lighted his pipe and sat looking at a spot on the hillside. I knew that he was looking at it, and for a long time past I had wondered whether he would ever see anything there that would fix his attention. I knew that spot well. It was clear that he was interested at last, though it was a long time before he spoke. Like most painters, he trusts to his own eyesight, as a lion trusts his strength and a stag his speed, and he is always disturbed when he cannot reconcile what he sees with what he believes that he ought to see.

"It's strange," he said. "Do you see that little mound just on this side of the boulder?"

"Yes," I said, and I guessed what was coming.

"It looks like a grave," observed Holger.

"Very true. It does look like a grave."

"Yes," continued my friend, his eyes still fixed on the spot. "But the strange thing is that I see the body lying on the top of it. Of course," continued Holger, turning his head on one side as artists do, "it must be an effect of light. In the first place, it is not a grave at all. Secondly, if it were, the body would be inside and not outside. Therefore, it's an effect of the moonlight. Don't you see it?"

"Perfectly; I always see it on moonlight nights."

"It doesn't seem to interest you much," said Holger.

"On the contrary, it does interest me, though I am used to it. You're not so far wrong, either. The mound is really a grave."

"Nonsense!" cried Holger, incredulously. "I suppose you'll tell me what I see lying on it is really a corpse!"

"No," I answered, "it's not. I know, because I have taken the trouble to go down and see."

"Then what is it?" asked Holger.

"It's nothing."

"You mean that it's an effect of light, I suppose?"

"Perhaps it is. But the inexplicable part of the matter is that it makes no difference whether the moon is rising or setting, or waxing or waning. If there's any moonlight at all, from east or west or overhead, so long as it shines on the grave you can see the outline of the body on top."

Holger stirred up his pipe with the point of his knife, and then used his finger for a stopper. When the tobacco burned well he rose from his chair.

"If you don't mind," he said, "I'll go down and take a look at it."

He left me, crossed the roof, and disappeared down the dark steps. I did not move, but sat looking down until he came out of the tower below. I heard him humming an old Danish song as he crossed the open space in the bright moonlight, going straight to the mysterious mound. When he was ten paces from it, Holger stopped short, made two steps forward, and then three or four backward, and then stopped again. I know what that meant. He had reached the spot where the Thing ceased to be visible—where, as he would have said, the effect of light changed.

Then he went on till he reached the mound and stood upon it. I could see the Thing still, but it was no longer lying down; it was on its knees now, winding its white arms round Holger's body and looking up into his face. A cool breeze stirred my hair at that moment, as the night wind began to come down from the hills, but it felt like a breath from another world.

The Thing seemed to be trying to climb to its feet, helping itself up by Holger's body while he stood upright, quite unconscious of it and apparently looking toward the tower, which is very picturesque when the moonlight falls upon it on that side.

"Come along!" I shouted. "Don't stay there all night!"

It seemed to me that he moved reluctantly as he stepped from the mound, or else with difficulty. That was it. The Thing's arms were still round his waist, but its feet could not leave the grave. As he came slowly forward it was drawn and lengthened like a wreath of mist, thin and white, till I saw distinctly that Holger shook himself, as a man does who feels a chill. At the same instant a little wail of pain came to me on the breeze—it might have been the cry of the small owl that lives among the rocks—and the misty presence floated swiftly back from Holger's advancing figure and lay once more at its length upon the mound.

Again I felt the cool breeze in my hair, and this time an icy thrill of dread ran down my spine. I remembered very well that I had once gone down there alone in the moonlight; that presently, being near, I had seen nothing; that, like Holger, I had gone and had stood upon the mound; and I remembered how, when I came back, sure that there was nothing there, I had felt the sudden conviction that there was something after all if I would only look behind me. I remembered the strong temptation to look back, a temptation I had resisted as unworthy of a man of sense, until, to get rid of it, I had shaken myself just as Holger did.

And now I knew that those white, misty arms had been round me too; I knew it in a flash, and I shuddered as I remembered that I had heard the night owl then too. But it had not been the night owl. It was the cry of the Thing.

I refilled my pipe and poured out a cup of strong southern wine; in less than a minute Holger was seated beside me again.

"Of course there's nothing there," he said, "but it's creepy, all the same. Do you know, when I was coming back I was so sure that there was something behind me that I wanted to turn round and look? It was an effort not to."

He laughed a little, knocked the ashes out of his pipe, and poured himself out some wine. For a while neither of us spoke, and the moon rose higher, and we both looked at the Thing that lay on the mound.

"You might make a story about that," said Holger after a long time.

"There is one," I answered. "If you're not sleepy, I'll tell it to you."

"Go ahead," said Holger, who likes stories.

* * * * *

Old Alario was dying up there in the village behind the hill. You remember him, I have no doubt. They say that he made his money by selling sham jewellery in South America, and escaped with his gains when he was found out. Like all those fellows, if they bring anything back with them, he at once set to work to enlarge his house, and as there are no masons here, he sent all the way to Paola for two workmen. They were a rough-looking pair of scoundrels—a Neapolitan who had lost one eye and a Sicilian with an old scar half an inch deep across his left cheek. I often saw them, for on Sundays they used to come down here and fish off the rocks. When Alario caught the fever that killed him the masons were still at work. As he had agreed that part of their pay should be their board and lodging, he made them sleep in the house. His wife was dead, and he had an only son called Angelo, who was a much better sort than himself. Angelo was to marry the daughter of the richest man in the village, and, strange to say, though the marriage was arranged by their parents, the young people were said to be in love with each other.

For that matter, the whole village was in love with Angelo, and among the rest a wild, good-looking creature called Cristina, who was more like a gipsy than any girl I ever saw about here. She had very red lips and very black eyes, she was built like a greyhound, and had the tongue of the devil. But Angelo did not care a straw for her. He was rather a simple-minded fellow, quite different from his old scoundrel of a father, and under what I should call normal circumstances I really believe that he would never have looked at any girl except the nice plump little creature, with a fat dowry, whom his father meant him to marry. But things turned up which were neither normal nor natural.

On the other hand, a very handsome young shepherd from the hills above Maratea was in love with Cristina, who seems to have been quite indifferent to him. Cristina had no regular means of subsistence, but she was a good girl and willing to do any work or go on errands to any distance for the sake of a loaf of bread or a mess of beans, and permission to sleep under cover. She was especially glad when she could get something to do about the house of Angelo's father. There is no doctor in the village, and when the neighbours saw that old Alario was dying they sent Cristina to Scalea to fetch one. That was late in the afternoon, and if they had waited so long, it was because the dying miser refused to allow any such extravagance while he was able to speak. But while Cristina was gone matters grew rapidly worse, the priest was brought to the bedside, and when he had done what he could he gave it as his opinion to the bystanders that the old man was dead, and left the house.

You know these people. They have a physical horror of death. Until the priest spoke, the room had been full of people. The words were hardly out of his mouth before it was empty. It was night now. They hurried down the dark steps and out into the street.

Angelo, as I have said, was away, Cristina had not come back—the simple woman-servant who had nursed the sick man fled with the rest, and the body was left alone in the flickering light of the earthen oil lamp.

Five minutes later two men looked in cautiously and crept forward toward the bed. They were the one-eyed Neapolitan mason and his Sicilian companion. They knew what they wanted. In a moment they had dragged from under the bed a small but heavy iron-bound box, and long before any one thought of coming back to the dead man they had left the house and the village under cover of the darkness. It was easy enough, for Alario's house is the last toward the gorge which leads down here, and the thieves merely went out by the back door, got over the stone wall, and had nothing to risk after that except the possibility of meeting some belated countryman, which was very small indeed, since few of the people use that path. They had a mattock and shovel, and they made their way here without accident.

I am telling you this story as it must have happened, for, of course, there were no witnesses to this part of it. The men brought the box down by the gorge, intending to bury it until they should be able to come back and take it away in a boat. They must have been clever enough to guess that some of the money would be in paper notes, for they would otherwise have buried it on the beach in the wet sand, where it would have been much safer. But the paper would have rotted if they had been obliged to leave it there long, so they dug their hole down there, close to that boulder. Yes, just where the mound is now.

Cristina did not find the doctor in Scalea, for he had been sent for from a place up the valley, halfway to San Domenico. If she had found him, he would have come on his mule by the upper road, which is smoother but much longer. But Cristina took the short cut by the rocks, which passes about fifty feet above the mound, and goes round that corner. The men were digging when she passed, and she heard them at work. It would not have been like her to go by without finding out what the noise was, for she was never afraid of anything in her life, and, besides, the fishermen sometimes come ashore here at night to get a stone for an anchor or to gather sticks to make a little fire. The night was dark, and Cristina probably came close to the two men before she could see what they were doing. She knew them, of course, and they knew her, and understood instantly that they were in her power. There was only one thing to be done for their safety, and they did it. They knocked her on the head, they dug the hole deep, and they buried her quickly with the iron-bound chest. They must have understood that their only chance of escaping suspicion lay in getting back to the village before their absence was noticed, for they returned immediately, and were found half an hour later gossiping quietly with the man who was making Alario's coffin. He was a crony of theirs, and had been working at the repairs in the old man's house. So far as I have been able to make out, the only persons who were supposed to know where Alario kept his treasure were Angelo and the one woman-servant I have mentioned. Angelo was away; it was the woman who discovered the theft.

It is easy enough to understand why no one else knew where the money was. The old man kept his door locked and the key in his pocket when he was out, and did not let the woman enter to clean the place unless he was there himself. The whole village knew that he had money somewhere, however, and the masons had probably discovered the whereabouts of the chest by climbing in at the window in his absence. If the old man had not been delirious until he lost consciousness, he would have been in frightful agony of mind for his riches. The faithful woman-servant forgot their existence only for a few moments when she fled with the rest, overcome by the horror of death. Twenty minutes had not passed before she returned with the two hideous old hags who are always called in to prepare the dead for burial. Even then she had not at first the courage to go near the bed with them, but she made a pretence of dropping something, went down on her knees as if to find it, and looked under the bedstead. The walls of the room were newly whitewashed down to the floor, and she saw at a glance that the chest was gone. It had been there in the afternoon, it had therefore been stolen in the short interval since she had left the room.

There are no carabineers stationed in the village; there is not so much as a municipal watchman, for there is no municipality. There never was such a place, I believe. Scalea is supposed to look after it in some mysterious way, and it takes a couple of hours to get anybody from there. As the old woman had lived in the village all her life, it did not even occur to her to apply to any civil authority for help. She simply set up a howl and ran through the village in the dark, screaming out that her dead master's house had been robbed. Many of the people looked out, but at first no one seemed inclined to help her. Most of them, judging her by themselves, whispered to each other that she had probably stolen the money herself. The first man to move was the father of the girl whom Angelo was to marry; having collected his household, all of whom felt a personal interest in the wealth which was to have come into the family, he declared it to be his opinion that the chest had been stolen by the two journeyman masons who lodged in the house. He headed a search for them, which naturally began in Alario's house and ended in the carpenter's workshop, where the thieves were found discussing a measure of wine with the carpenter over the half-finished coffin, by the light of one earthen lamp filled with oil and tallow. The search party at once accused the delinquents of the crime, and threatened to lock them up in the cellar till the carabineers could be fetched from Scalea. The two men looked at each other for one moment, and then without the slightest hesitation they put out the single light, seized the unfinished coffin between them, and using it as a sort of battering ram, dashed upon their assailants in the dark. In a few moments they were beyond pursuit.

That is the end of the first part of the story. The treasure had disappeared, and as no trace of it could be found the people naturally supposed that the thieves had succeeded in carrying it off. The old man was buried, and when Angelo came back at last he had to borrow money to pay for the miserable funeral, and had some difficulty in doing so. He hardly needed to be told that in losing his inheritance he had lost his bride. In this part of the world marriages are made on strictly business principles, and if the promised cash is not forthcoming on the appointed day the bride or the bridegroom whose parents have failed to produce it may as well take themselves off, for there will be no wedding. Poor Angelo knew that well enough. His father had been possessed of hardly any land, and now that the hard cash which he had brought from South America was gone, there was nothing left but debts for the building materials that were to have been used for enlarging and improving the old house. Angelo was beggared, and the nice plump little creature who was to have been his turned up her nose at him in the most approved fashion. As for Cristina, it was several days before she was missed, for no one remembered that she had been sent to Scalea for the doctor, who had never come. She often disappeared in the same way for days together, when she could find a little work here and there at the distant farms among the hills. But when she did not come back at all, people began to wonder, and at last made up their minds that she had connived with the masons and had escaped with them.

* * * * *

I paused and emptied my glass.

"That sort of thing could not happen anywhere else," observed Holger, filling his everlasting pipe again. "It is wonderful what a natural charm there is about murder and sudden death in a romantic country like this. Deeds that would be simply brutal and

disgusting anywhere else become dramatic and mysterious because this is Italy and we are living in a genuine tower of Charles V built against genuine Barbary pirates."

"There's something in that," I admitted. Holger is the most romantic man in the world inside of himself, but he always thinks it necessary to explain why he feels anything.

"I suppose they found the poor girl's body with the box," he said presently.

"As it seems to interest you," I answered, "I'll tell you the rest of the story."

The moon had risen high by this time; the outline of the Thing on the mound was clearer to our eyes than before.

* * * * *

The village very soon settled down to its small, dull life. No one missed old Alario, who had been away so much on his voyages to South America that he had never been a familiar figure in his native place. Angelo lived in the half-finished house, and because he had no money to pay the old woman-servant she would not stay with him, but once in a long time she would come and wash a shirt for him for old acquaintance' sake. Besides the house, he had inherited a small patch of ground at some distance from the village; he tried to cultivate it, but he had no heart in the work, for he knew he could never pay the taxes on it and on the house, which would certainly be confiscated by the Government, or seized for the debt of the building material, which the man who had supplied it refused to take back.

Angelo was very unhappy. So long as his father had been alive and rich, every girl in the village had been in love with him; but that was all changed now. It had been pleasant to be admired and courted, and invited to drink wine by fathers who had girls to marry. It was hard to be stared at coldly, and sometimes laughed at because he had been robbed of his inheritance. He cooked his miserable meals for himself, and from being sad became melancholy and morose.

At twilight, when the day's work was done, instead of hanging about in the open space before the church with young fellows of his own age, he took to wandering in lonely places on the outskirts of the village till it was quite dark. Then he slunk home and went to bed to save the expense of a light. But in those lonely twilight hours he began to have strange waking dreams. He was not always alone, for often when he sat on the stump of a tree, where the narrow path turns down the gorge, he was sure that a woman came up noiselessly over the rough stones, as if her feet were bare; and she stood under a clump of chestnut trees only half a dozen yards down the path, and beckoned to him without speaking. Though she was in the shadow he knew that her lips were red, and that when they parted a little and smiled at him she showed two small sharp teeth. He knew this at first rather than saw it, and he knew that it was Cristina, and that she was dead. Yet he was not afraid; he only wondered whether it was a dream, for he thought that if he had been awake he should have been frightened.

Besides, the dead woman had red lips, and that could only happen in a dream. Whenever he went near the gorge after sunset she was already there waiting for him, or else she very soon appeared, and he began to be sure that she came a little nearer to him every day. At first he had only been sure of her blood-red mouth, but now each feature grew distinct, and the pale face looked at him with deep and hungry eyes.

It was the eyes that grew dim. Little by little he came to know that some day the dream would not end when he turned away to go home, but would lead him down the gorge out of which the vision rose. She was nearer now when she beckoned to him. Her cheeks were not livid like those of the dead, but pale with starvation, with the furious and unappeased physical hunger of her eyes that devoured him. They feasted on his soul and cast a spell over him, and at last they were close to his own and held him. He could not tell whether her breath was as hot as fire or as cold as ice; he could not tell whether her red lips burned his or froze them, or whether her five fingers on his wrists seared scorching scars or bit his flesh like frost; he could not tell whether he was awake or asleep, whether she was alive or dead, but he knew that she loved him, she alone of all creatures, earthly or unearthly, and her spell had power over him.

When the moon rose high that night the shadow of that Thing was not alone down there upon the mound.

Angelo awoke in the cool dawn, drenched with dew and chilled through flesh, and blood, and bone. He opened his eyes to the faint grey light, and saw the stars still shining overhead. He was very weak, and his heart was beating so slowly that he was almost like a man fainting. Slowly he turned his head on the mound, as on a pillow, but the other face was not there. Fear seized him suddenly, a fear unspeakable and unknown; he sprang to his feet and fled up the gorge, and he never looked behind him until he reached the door of the house on the outskirts of the village. Drearily he went to his work that day, and wearily the hours dragged themselves after the sun, till at last he touched the sea and sank, and the great sharp hills above Maratea turned purple against the dove-coloured eastern sky.

Angelo shouldered his heavy hoe and left the field. He felt less tired now than in the morning when he had begun to work, but he promised himself that he would go home without lingering by the gorge, and eat the best supper he could get himself, and sleep all night in his bed like a Christian man. Not again would he be tempted down the narrow way by a shadow with red lips and icy breath; not again would he dream that dream of terror and delight.

He was near the village now; it was half an hour since the sun had set, and the cracked church bell sent little discordant echoes across the rocks and ravines to tell all good people that the day was done. Angelo stood still a moment where the path forked, where it led toward the village on the left, and down to the gorge on the right, where a clump of chestnut trees overhung the narrow way. He stood still a minute, lifting his battered hat from his head and gazing at the fast-fading sea westward, and his lips moved as he silently repeated the familiar evening prayer. His lips moved, but the words that followed them in his brain lost their meaning and turned into others, and ended in a name that he spoke aloud—Cristina! With the name, the tension of his will relaxed suddenly, reality went out and the dream took him again, and bore him on swiftly and surely like a man walking in his sleep, down, down, by the steep path in the gathering darkness. And as she glided beside him, Cristina whispered strange, sweet things in his ear, which somehow, if he had been awake, he knew that he could not quite have understood; but now they were the most wonderful words he had ever heard in his life. And she kissed him also, but not upon his mouth. He felt her sharp kisses upon his white throat, and he knew that her lips were red. So the wild dream sped on through twilight and darkness and moonrise, and all the glory of the summer's night. But in the chilly dawn he lay as one half dead upon the mound down there, recalling and not recalling, drained of his blood, yet strangely longing to give those red lips more. Then came the fear, the awful nameless panic, the mortal horror that guards the confines of the world we see not, neither know of as we know of other things, but which we feel when its icy chill freezes our bones and stirs our hair with the touch of a ghostly hand. Once more Angelo sprang from the mound and fled up the gorge in the breaking day, but his step was less sure this time, and he panted for breath as he ran; and when he came to the bright spring of water that rises halfway up the hillside, he dropped upon his knees and hands and plunged his whole face in and drank as he had never drunk before—for it was the thirst of the wounded man who has lain bleeding all night long upon the battle-field.

She had him fast now, and he could not escape her, but would come to her every evening at dusk until she had drained him of his last drop of blood. It was in vain that when the day was done he tried to take another turning and to go home by a path that did not lead near the gorge. It was in vain that he made promises to himself each morning at dawn when he climbed the lonely way up from the shore to the village. It was all in vain, for when the sun sank burning into the sea, and the coolness of the evening stole out as from a hiding-place to delight the weary world, his feet turned toward the old way, and she was waiting for him in the shadow under the chestnut trees; and then all happened as before, and she fell to kissing his white throat even as she flitted lightly down the way, winding one arm about him. And as his blood failed, she grew more hungry and more thirsty every day, and every day when he awoke in the early dawn it was harder to rouse himself to the effort of climbing the steep path to the village; and when he went to his work his feet dragged painfully, and there was hardly strength in his arms to wield the heavy hoe. He scarcely spoke to any one now, but the people said he was "consuming himself" for love of the girl he was to have married when he lost his inheritance; and they laughed heartily at the thought, for this is not a very romantic country. At this time, Antonio, the man who stays here to look after the tower, returned from a visit to his people, who live near Salerno. He had been away all the time since before Alario's death and knew nothing of what had happened. He has told me that he came back late in the afternoon and shut himself up in the tower to eat and sleep, for he was very tired. It was past midnight when he awoke, and when he looked out the waning moon was rising over the shoulder of the hill. He looked out toward the mound, and he saw something, and he did not sleep again that night. When he went out again in the morning it was broad daylight, and there was nothing to be seen on the mound but loose stones and driven sand. Yet he did not go very near it; he went straight up the path to the village and directly to the house of the old priest.

"I have seen an evil thing this night," he said; "I have seen how the dead drink the blood of the living. And the blood is the life."

"Tell me what you have seen," said the priest in reply.

Antonio told him everything he had seen.

"You must bring your book and your holy water to-night," he added. "I will be here before sunset to go down with you, and if it pleases your reverence to sup with me while we wait, I will make ready."

"I will come," the priest answered, "for I have read in old books of these strange beings which are neither quick nor dead, and which lie ever fresh in their graves, stealing out in the dusk to taste life and blood."

Antonio cannot read, but he was glad to see that the priest understood the business; for, of course, the books must have instructed him as to the best means of quieting the half-living Thing for ever.

So Antonio went away to his work, which consists largely in sitting on the shady side of the tower, when he is not perched upon a rock with a fishing-line catching nothing. But on that day he went twice to look at the mound in the bright sunlight, and he searched round and round it for some hole through which the being might get in and out; but he found none. When the sun began to sink and the air was cooler in the shadows, he went up to fetch the old priest, carrying a little wicker basket with him; and in this they placed a bottle of holy water, and the basin, and sprinkler, and the stole which the priest would need; and they came down and waited in the door of the tower till it should be dark. But while the light still lingered very grey and faint, they saw something moving, just there, two figures, a man's that walked, and a woman's that flitted beside him, and while her head lay on his shoulder she kissed his throat. The priest has told me that, too, and that his teeth chattered and he grasped Antonio's arm. The vision passed and disappeared into the shadow. Then Antonio got the leathern flask of strong liquor, which he kept for great occasions, and poured such a draught as made the old man feel almost young again; and he got the lantern, and his pick and shovel, and gave the priest his stole to put on and the holy water to carry, and they went out together toward the spot where the work was to be done. Antonio says that in spite of the rum his own knees shook together, and the priest stumbled over his Latin. For when they were yet a few yards from the mound the flickering light of the lantern fell upon Angelo's white face, unconscious as if in sleep, and on his upturned throat, over which a very thin red line of blood trickled down into his collar; and the flickering light of the lantern played upon another face that looked up from the feast—upon two deep, dead eyes that saw in spite of death—upon parted lips redder than life itself—upon two gleaming teeth on which glistened a rosy drop. Then the priest, good old man, shut his eyes tight and showered holy water before him, and his cracked voice rose almost to a scream; and then Antonio, who is no coward after all, raised his pick in one hand and the lantern in the other, as he sprang forward, not knowing what the end should be; and then he swears that he heard a woman's cry, and the Thing was gone, and Angelo lay alone on the mound unconscious, with the red line on his throat and the beads of deathly sweat on his cold forehead. They lifted him, half-dead as he was, and laid him on the ground close by; then Antonio went to work, and the priest helped him, though he was old and could not do much; and they dug deep, and at last Antonio, standing in the grave, stooped down with his lantern to see what he might see.

His hair used to be dark brown, with grizzled streaks about the temples; in less than a month from that day he was as grey as a badger. He was a miner when he was young, and most of these fellows have seen ugly sights now and then, when accidents have happened, but he had never seen what he saw that night—that Thing which is neither alive nor dead, that Thing that will abide neither above ground nor in the grave. Antonio had brought something with him which the priest had not noticed. He had made it that afternoon—a sharp stake shaped from a piece of tough old driftwood. He had it with him now, and he had his heavy pick, and he had taken the lantern down into the grave. I don't think any power on earth could make him speak of what happened then, and the old priest was too frightened to look in. He says he heard Antonio breathing like a wild beast, and moving as if he were fighting with something almost as strong as himself; and he heard an evil sound also, with blows, as of something violently driven through flesh and bone; and then the most awful sound of all—a woman's shriek, the unearthly scream of a woman neither dead nor alive, but buried deep for many days. And he, the poor old priest, could only rock himself as he knelt there in the sand, crying aloud his prayers and exorcisms to drown these dreadful sounds. Then suddenly a small iron-bound chest was thrown up and rolled over against the old man's knee, and in a moment more Antonio was beside him, his face as white as tallow in the flickering light of the lantern, shovelling the sand and pebbles into the grave with furious haste, and looking over the edge till the pit was half full; and the priest said that there was much fresh blood on Antonio's hands and on his clothes.

* * * * *

I had come to the end of my story. Holger finished his wine and leaned back in his chair.

"So Angelo got his own again," he said. "Did he marry the prim and plump young person to whom he had been betrothed?"

"No; he had been badly frightened. He went to South America, and has not been heard of since."

"And that poor thing's body is there still, I suppose," said Holger. "Is it quite dead yet, I wonder?"

I wonder, too. But whether it be dead or alive, I should hardly care to see it, even in broad daylight. Antonio is as grey as a badger, and he has never been quite the same man since that night.

COUNT MAGNUS

M. R. James

By what means the papers out of which I have made a connected story came into my hands is the last point which the reader will learn from these pages. But it is necessary to prefix to my extracts from them a statement of the form in which I possess them.

They consist, then, partly of a series of collections for a book of travels, such a volume as was a common product of the forties and fifties. Horace Marryat's *Journal of a Residence in Jutland and the Danish Isles* is a fair specimen of the class to which I allude. These books usually treated of some unknown district on the Continent. They were illustrated with woodcuts or steel plates. They gave details of hotel accommodation and of means of communication, such as we now expect to find in any well-regulated guide-book, and they dealt largely in reported conversations with intelligent foreigners, racy innkeepers, and garrulous peasants. In a word, they were chatty.

Begun with the idea of furnishing material for such a book, my papers as they progressed assumed the character of a record of one single personal experience, and this record was continued up to the very eve, almost, of its termination.

The writer was a Mr. Wraxall. For my knowledge of him I have to depend entirely on the evidence his writings afford, and from these I deduce that he was a man past middle age, possessed of some private means, and very much alone in the world. He had, it seems, no settled abode in England, but was a denizen of hotels and boarding-houses. It is probable that he entertained the idea of settling down at some future time which never came; and I think it also likely that the Pantechnicon fire in the early seventies must have destroyed a great deal that would have thrown light on his antecedents, for he refers once or twice to property of his that was warehoused at that establishment.

It is further apparent that Mr. Wraxall had published a book, and that it treated of a holiday he had once taken in Brittany. More than this I cannot say about his work, because a diligent search in bibliographical works has convinced me that it must have appeared either anonymously or under a pseudonym.

As to his character, it is not difficult to form some superficial opinion. He must have been an intelligent and cultivated man. It seems that he was near being a Fellow of his college at Oxford—Brasenose, as I judge from the Calendar. His besetting fault was pretty clearly that of over-inquisitiveness, possibly a good fault in a traveller, certainly a fault for which this traveller paid dearly enough in the end.

On what proved to be his last expedition, he was plotting another book. Scandinavia, a region not widely known to Englishmen forty years ago, had struck him as an interesting field. He must have alighted on some old books of Swedish history or memoirs, and the idea had struck him that there was room for a book descriptive of travel in Sweden, interspersed with episodes from the history of some of the great Swedish families. He procured letters of introduction, therefore, to some persons of quality in Sweden, and set out thither in the early summer of 1863.

Of his travels in the North there is no need to speak, nor of his residence of some weeks in Stockholm. I need only mention that some *savant* resident there put him on the track of an important collection of family papers belonging to the proprietors of an ancient manor-house in Vestergothland, and obtained for him permission to examine them.

The manor-house, or *herrgard*, in question is to be called Råbäck (pronounced something like Roebeck), though that is not its name. It is one of the best buildings of its kind in all the country, and the picture of it in Dahlenberg's *Suecia antiqua et moderna*, engraved in 1694, shows it very much as the tourist may see it today. It was built soon after 1600, and is, roughly speaking, very much like an English house of that period in respect of material—red-brick with stone facings—and style. The man who built it was a scion of the great house of De la Gardie, and his descendants possess it still. De la Gardie is the name by which I will designate them when mention of them becomes necessary.

They received Mr. Wraxall with great kindness and courtesy, and pressed him to stay in the house as long as his researches lasted. But, preferring to be independent, and mistrusting his powers of conversing in Swedish, he settled himself at the village inn, which turned out quite sufficiently comfortable, at any rate during the summer months. This arrangement would entail a short walk daily to and from the manor-house of something under a mile. The house itself stood in a park, and was protected—we should say grown up—with large old timber. Near it you found the walled garden, and then entered a close wood fringing one of the small lakes with which the whole country is pitted. Then came the wall of the demesne, and you climbed a steep knoll—a knob of rock lightly covered with soil—and on the top of this stood the church, fenced in with tall dark trees. It was a curious building to English eyes. The nave and aisles were low, and filled with pews and galleries. In the western gallery stood the handsome old organ, gaily painted, and with silver pipes. The ceiling was flat, and had been adorned by a seventeenth-century artist with a strange and hideous "Last Judgement," full of lurid flames, falling cities, burning ships, crying souls, and brown and smiling demons. Handsome brass coronae hung from the roof; the pulpit was like a doll's-house covered with little painted wooden cherubs and saints; a stand with three hour-glasses was hinged to the preacher's desk. Such sights as these may be seen in many a church in Sweden now, but what distinguished this one was an addition to the original building. At the eastern end of the north aisle the builder of the manor-house had erected a mausoleum for himself and his family. It was a largish eight-sided building, lighted by a series of oval windows, and it had a domed roof, topped by a kind of pumpkin-shaped object rising into a spire, a form in which Swedish architects greatly delighted. The roof was of copper externally, and was painted black, while the walls, in common with those of the church, were staringly white. To this mausoleum there was no access from the church. It had a portal and steps of its own on the northern side.

Past the churchyard the path to the village goes, and not more than three or four minutes bring you to the inn door.

On the first day of his stay at Råbäck Mr. Wraxall found the church door open, and made these notes of the interior which I have epitomized. Into the mausoleum, however, he could not make his way. He could by looking through the keyhole just descry that there were fine marble effigies and sarcophagi of copper, and a wealth of armorial ornament, which made him very anxious to spend some time in investigation.

The papers he had come to examine at the manor-house proved to be of just the kind he wanted for his book. There were family correspondence, journals, and account-books of the earliest owners of the estate, very carefully kept and clearly written, full of amusing and picturesque detail. The first De la Gardie appeared in them as a strong and capable man. Shortly after the building of the mansion there had been a period of distress in the district, and the peasants had risen and attacked several châteaux and done some damage. The owner of Råbäck took a leading part in supressing trouble, and there was reference to executions of ring-leaders and severe punishments inflicted with no sparing hand.

The portrait of this Magnus de la Gardie was one of the best in the house, and Mr. Wraxall studied it with no little interest after his day's work. He gives no detailed description of it, but I gather that the face impressed him rather by its power than by its beauty or goodness; in fact, he writes that Count Magnus was an almost phenomenally ugly man.

On this day Mr. Wraxall took his supper with the family, and walked back in the late but still bright evening.

"I must remember," he writes, "to ask the sexton if he can let me into the mausoleum at the church. He evidently has access to it himself, for I saw him tonight standing on the steps, and, as I thought, locking or unlocking the door."

I find that early on the following day Mr. Wraxall had some conversation with his landlord. His setting it down at such length as he does surprised me at first; but I soon realized that the papers I was reading were, at least in their beginning, the materials for the book he was meditating, and that it was to have been one of those quasi-journalistic productions which admit of the introduction of an admixture of conversational matter.

His object, he says, was to find out whether any traditions of Count Magnus de la Gardie lingered on in the scenes of that gentleman's activity, and whether the popular estimate of him were favourable or not. He found that the Count was decidedly not a favourite. If his tenants came late to their work on the days which they owed to him as Lord of the Manor, they were set on the wooden horse, or flogged and branded in the manor-house yard. One or two cases there were of men who had occupied lands which encroached on the lord's domain, and whose houses had been mysteriously burnt on a winter's night, with the whole family inside. But what seemed to dwell on the innkeeper's mind most—for he returned to the subject more than once—was that the Count had been on the Black Pilgrimage, and had brought something or someone back with him.

You will naturally inquire, as Mr. Wraxall did, what the Black Pilgrimage may have been. But your curiosity on the point must remain unsatisfied for the time being, just as his did. The landlord was evidently unwilling to give a full answer, or indeed any answer, on the point, and, being called out for a moment, trotted out with obvious alacrity, only putting his head in at the door a few minutes afterwards to say that he was called away to Skara, and should not be back till evening.

So Mr. Wraxall had to go unsatisfied to his day's work at the manor-house. The papers on which he was just then engaged soon put his thoughts into another channel, for he had to occupy himself with glancing over the correspondence between Sophia Albertina in Stockholm and her married cousin Ulrica Leonora at Råbäck in the years 1705–10. The letters were of exceptional interest from the light they threw upon the culture of that period in Sweden, as anyone can testify who has read the full edition of them in the publications of the Swedish Historical Manuscripts Commission.

In the afternoon he had done with these, and after returning the boxes in which they were kept to their places on the shelf, he proceeded, very naturally, to take down some of the volumes nearest to them, in order to determine which of them had best be his principal subject of investigation next day. The shelf he had hit upon was occupied mostly by a collection of account-books in the writing of the first Count Magnus. But one among them was not an account-book, but a book of alchemical and other tracts in another sixteenth-century hand. Not being very familiar with alchemical literature, Mr. Wraxall spends much space which he might have spared in setting out the names and beginnings of the various treatises: The book of the Phoenix, book of the Thirty Words, book of the Toad, book of Miriam, Turba philosophorum, and so forth; and then he announces with a good deal of circumstance his delight at finding, on a leaf originally left blank near the middle of the book, some writing of Count Magnus himself headed "Liber nigrae peregrinationis." It is true that only a few lines were written, but there was quite enough to show that the landlord had that morning been referring to a belief at least as old as the time of Count Magnus, and probably shared by him. This is the English of what was written:

"If any man desires to obtain a long life, if he would obtain a faithful messenger and see the blood of his enemies, it is necessary that he should first go into the city of Chorazin, and there salute the prince . . ." Here there was an erasure of one word, not very thoroughly done, so that Mr. Wraxall felt pretty sure that he was right in reading it as aeris ("of the air"). But there was no more of the text copied, only a line in Latin: *Quaere reliqua hujus materiei inter secretiora.* (See the rest of this matter among the more private things.)

It could not be denied that this threw a rather lurid light upon the tastes and beliefs of the Count; but to Mr. Wraxall, separated from him by nearly three centuries, the thought that he might have added to his general forcefulness alchemy, and to alchemy something like magic, only made him a more picturesque figure, and when, after a rather prolonged contemplation of his picture in the hall, Mr. Wraxall set out on his homeward way, his mind was full of the thought of Count Magnus. He had no eyes for his surroundings, no perception of the evening scents of the woods or the evening light on the lake; and when all of a sudden he pulled up short, he was astonished to find himself already at the gate of the churchyard, and within a few minutes of his dinner. His eyes fell on the mausoleum.

"Ah," he said, "Count Magnus, there you are. I should dearly like to see you."

"Like many solitary men," he writes, "I have a habit of talking to myself aloud; and, unlike some of the Greek and Latin particles, I do not expect an answer. Certainly, and perhaps fortunately in this case, there was neither voice nor any that regarded: only the woman who, I suppose, was cleaning up the church, dropped some metallic object on the floor, whose clang startled me. Count Magnus, I think, sleeps sound enough."

That same evening the landlord of the inn, who had heard Mr. Wraxall say that he wished to see the clerk or deacon (as he would be called in Sweden) of the parish, introduced him to that official in the inn parlour. A visit to the De la Gardie tomb-house was soon arranged for the next day, and a little general conversation ensued.

Mr. Wraxall, remembering that one function of Scandinavian deacons is to teach candidates for Confirmation, thought he would refresh his own memory on a Biblical point.

"Can you tell me," he said, "anything about Chorazin?"

The deacon seemed startled, but readily reminded him how that village had once been denounced.

"To be sure," said Mr. Wraxall; "it is, I suppose, quite a ruin now?"

"So I expect," replied the deacon. "I have heard some of our old priests say that Antichrist is to be born there; and there are tales—"

"Ah! what tales are those?" Mr. Wraxall put in.

"Tales, I was going to say, which I have forgotten," said the deacon; and soon after that he said good night.

The landlord was now alone, and at Mr. Wraxall's mercy; and that inquirer was not inclined to spare him.

"Herr Nielsen," he said, "I have found out something about the Black Pilgrimage. You may as well tell me what you know. What did the Count bring back with him?"

Swedes are habitually slow, perhaps, in answering, or perhaps the landlord was an exception. I am not sure; but Mr. Wraxall notes that the landlord spent at least one minute in looking at him before he said anything at all. Then he came close up to his guest, and with a good deal of effort he spoke:

"Mr. Wraxall, I can tell you this one little tale, and no more—not any more. You must not ask anything when I have done. In my grandfather's time—that is, ninety-two years ago—there were two men who said: "The Count is dead; we do not care for him. We will go tonight and have a free hunt in his wood"—the long wood on the hill that you have seen behind Råbäck. Well, those that heard them say this, they said: "No, do not go; we are sure you will meet with persons walking who should not be walking. They should be resting, not walking." These men laughed. There were no forestmen to keep the wood, because no one wished to live there. The family were not here at the house. These men could do what they wished.

"Very well, they go to the wood that night. My grandfather was sitting here in this room. It was the summer, and a light night. With the window open, he could see out to the wood, and hear.

"So he sat there, and two or three men with him, and they listened. At first they hear nothing at all; then they hear someone—you know how far away it is—they hear someone scream, just as if the most inside part of his soul was twisted out of him. All of them in the room caught hold of each other, and they sat so for three-quarters of an hour. Then they hear someone else, only about three hundred ells off. They hear him laugh out loud: it was not one of those two men that laughed, and, indeed, they have all of them said that it was not any man at all. After that they hear a great door shut.

"Then, when it was just light with the sun, they all went to the priest. They said to him:

" 'Father, put on your gown and your ruff, and come to bury these men, Anders Bjornsen and Hans Thorbjorn."

"You understand that they were sure these men were dead. So they went to the wood—my grandfather never forgot this. He said they were all like so many dead men themselves. The priest, too, he was in a white fear. He said when they came to him:

"I heard one cry in the night, and I heard one laugh afterwards. If I cannot forget that, I shall not be able to sleep again."

"So they went to the wood, and they found these men on the edge of the wood. Hans Thorbjorn was standing with his back against a tree, and all the time he was pushing with his hands—pushing something away from him which was not there. So he was not dead. And they led him away, and took him to the house at Nykjoping, and he died before the winter; but he went on pushing with his hands. Also Anders Bjornsen was there; but he was dead. And I tell you this about Anders Bjornsen, that he was once a beautiful man, but now his face was not there, because the flesh of it was sucked away off the bones. You understand that? My grandfather did not forget that. And they laid him on the bier which they brought, and they put a cloth over his head, and the priest walked before; and they began to sing the psalm for the dead as well as they could. So, as they were singing the end of the first verse, one fell down, who was carrying the head of the bier, and the others looked back, and they saw that the cloth had fallen off, and the eyes of Anders Bjornsen were looking up, because there was nothing to close over them. And this they could not bear. Therefore the priest laid the cloth upon him, and sent for a spade, and they buried him in that place."

The next day Mr. Wraxall records that the deacon called for him soon after his breakfast, and took him to the church and mausoleum. He noticed that the key of the latter was hung on a nail just by the pulpit, and it occurred to him that, as the church door seemed to be left unlocked as a rule, it would not be difficult for him to pay a second and more private visit to the monuments if there proved to be more of interest among them than could be digested at first. The building, when he entered it, he found not unimposing. The monuments, mostly large erections of the seventeenth and eighteenth centuries, were dignified if luxuriant, and the epitaphs and heraldry were copious. The central space of the domed room was occupied by three copper sarcophagi, covered with finely-engraved ornament. Two of them had, as is commonly the case in Denmark and Sweden, a large metal crucifix on the lid. The third, that of Count Magnus, as it appeared, had, instead of that, a full-length effigy engraved upon it, and round the edge were several bands of similar ornament representing various scenes. One was a battle, with cannon belching out smoke, and walled towns, and troops of pikemen. Another showed an execution. In a third, among trees, was a man running at full speed, with flying hair and outstretched hands. After him followed a strange form; it would be hard to say whether the artist had intended it for a man, and was unable to give the requisite similitude, or whether it was intentionally made as monstrous as it looked. In view of the skill with which the rest of the drawing was done, Mr. Wraxall felt inclined to adopt the latter idea. The figure was unduly short, and was for the most part muffled in a hooded garment which swept the ground. The only part of the form which projected from that shelter was not shaped like any hand or arm. Mr. Wraxall compares it to the tentacle of a devil-fish, and continues: "On seeing this, I said to myself, 'This, then, which is evidently an allegorical representation of some kind—a fiend pursuing a hunted soul—may be the origin of the story of Count Magnus and his mysterious companion. Let us see how the huntsman is pictured: doubtless it will be a demon blowing his horn.'" But, as it turned out, there was no such sensational figure, only the semblance of a cloaked man on a hillock, who stood leaning on a stick, and watching the hunt with an interest which the engraver had tried to express in his attitude.

Mr. Wraxall noted the finely-worked and massive steel padlocks—three in number—which secured the sarcophagus. One of them, he saw, was detached, and lay on the pavement. And then, unwilling to delay the deacon longer or to waste his own working-time, he made his way onward to the manor-house.

"It is curious," he notes, "how, on retracing a familiar path, one's thoughts engross one to the absolute exclusion of surrounding objects. Tonight, for the second time, I had entirely failed to notice where I was going (I had planned a private visit to the tomb-house to copy the epitaphs), when I suddenly, as it were, awoke to consciousness, and found myself (as before) turning in at the churchyard gate, and, I believe, singing or chanting some such words as, 'Are you awake, Count Magnus? Are you asleep, Count Magnus?' and then something more which I have failed to recollect. It seemed to me that I must have been behaving in this nonsensical way for some time."

He found the key of the mausoleum where he had expected to find it, and copied the greater part of what he wanted; in fact, he stayed until the light began to fail him.

"I must have been wrong," he writes, "in saying that one of the padlocks of my Count's sarcophagus was unfastened; I see tonight that two are loose.

I picked both up, and laid them carefully on the window-ledge, after trying unsuccessfully to close them. The remaining one is still firm, and, though I take it to be a spring lock, I cannot guess how it is opened. Had I succeeded in undoing it, I am almost afraid I should have taken the liberty of opening the sarcophagus. It is strange, the interest I feel in the personality of this, I fear, somewhat ferocious and grim old noble."

The day following was, as it turned out, the last of Mr. Wraxall's stay at Råbäck. He received letters connected with certain investments which made it desirable that he should return to England; his work among the papers was practically done, and travelling was slow. He decided, therefore, to make his farewells, put some finishing touches to his notes, and be off.

These finishing touches and farewells, as it turned out, took more time than he had expected. The hospitable family insisted on his staying to dine with them—they dined at three—and it was verging on half past six before he was outside the iron gates of Råbäck. He dwelt on every step of his walk by the lake, determined to saturate himself, now that he trod it for the last time, in the sentiment of the place and hour. And when he reached the summit of the churchyard knoll, he lingered for many minutes, gazing at the limitless prospect of woods near and distant, all dark beneath a sky of liquid green. When at last he turned to go, the thought struck him that surely he must bid farewell to Count Magnus as well as the rest of the De la Gardies. The church was but twenty yards away, and he knew where the key of the mausoleum hung. It was not long before he was standing over the great copper coffin, and, as usual, talking to himself aloud: "You may have been a bit of a rascal in your time, Magnus," he was saying, "but for all that I should like to see you, or, rather—"

"Just at that instant," he says, "I felt a blow on my foot. Hastily enough I drew it back, and something fell on the pavement with a clash. It was the third, the last of the three padlocks which had fastened the sarcophagus. I stooped to pick it up, and—Heaven is my witness that I am writing only the bare truth—before I had raised myself there was a sound of metal hinges creaking, and I distinctly saw the lid shifting upwards. I may have behaved like a coward, but I could not for my life stay for one moment. I was outside that dreadful building in less time than I can write—almost as quickly as I could have said—the words; and what frightens me yet more, I could not turn the key in the lock. As I sit here in my room noting these facts, I ask myself (it was not twenty minutes ago) whether that noise of creaking metal continued, and I cannot tell whether it did or not. I only know that there was something more than I have written that alarmed me, but whether it was sound or sight I am not able to remember. What is this that I have done?"

* * * * *

Poor Mr. Wraxall! He set out on his journey to England on the next day, as he had planned, and he reached England in safety; and yet, as I gather from his changed hand and inconsequent jottings, a broken man. One of the several small note-books that have come to me with his papers gives, not a key to, but a kind of inkling of, his experiences. Much of his journey was made by canal-boat, and I find not less than six painful attempts to enumerate and describe his fellow-passengers. The entries are of this kind:

24. Pastor of village in Skane. Usual black coat and soft black hat.
25. Commercial traveller from Stockholm going to Trollhättan. Black cloak, brown hat.
26. Man in long black cloak, broad-leafed hat, very old-fashioned.

This entry is lined out, and a note added: "Perhaps identical with No. 13. Have not yet seen his face." On referring to No. 13, I find that he is a Roman priest in a cassock.

The net result of the reckoning is always the same. Twenty-eight people appear in the enumeration, one being always a man in a long black cloak and broad hat, and another a "short figure in dark cloak and hood." On the other hand, it is always noted that only twenty-six passengers appear at meals, and that the man in the cloak is perhaps absent, and the short figure is certainly absent.

On reaching England, it appears that Mr. Wraxall landed at Harwich, and that he resolved at once to put himself out of the reach of some person or persons whom he never specifies, but whom he had evidently come to regard as his pursuers. Accordingly he took a vehicle—it was a closed fly—not trusting the railway and drove across country to the village of Belchamp St. Paul. It was about nine o'clock on a moonlight August night when he neared the place. He was sitting forward, and looking out of the window at the fields and thickets—there was little else to be seen—racing past him. Suddenly he came to a cross-road. At the corner two figures were standing motionless; both were in dark cloaks; the taller one wore a hat, the shorter a hood. He had no time to see their faces, nor did they make any motion that he could discern. Yet the horse shied violently and broke into a gallop, and Mr. Wraxall sank back into his seat in something like desperation. He had seen them before.

Arrived at Belchamp St. Paul, he was fortunate enough to find a decent furnished lodging, and for the next twenty-four hours he lived, comparatively speaking, in peace. His last notes were written on this day. They are too disjointed and ejaculatory to be given here in full, but the substance of them is clear enough. He is expecting a visit from his pursuers—how or when he knows not—and his constant cry is "What has he done?" and "Is there no hope?" Doctors, he knows, would call him mad, policemen would laugh at him. The parson is away. What can he do but lock his door and cry to God?

People still remember last year at Belchamp St. Paul how a strange gentleman came one evening in August years back; and how the next morning but one he was found dead, and there was an inquest; and the jury that viewed the body fainted, seven of 'em did, and none of 'em wouldn't speak to what they see, and the verdict was visitation of God; and how the people as kep' the 'ouse moved out that same week, and went away from that part. But they do not, I think, know that any glimmer of light has ever been thrown, or could be thrown, on the mystery. It so happened that last year the little house came into my hands as part of a legacy. It had stood empty since 1863, and there seemed no prospect of letting it; so I had it pulled down, and the papers of which I have given you an abstract were found in a forgotten cupboard under the window in the best bedroom.

THE BODY-SNATCHER

Robert Louis Stevenson

Every night in the year, four of us sat in the small parlour of the George at Debenham—the undertaker, and the landlord, and Fettes, and myself. Sometimes there would be more; but blow high, blow low, come rain or snow or frost, we four would be each planted in his own particular arm-chair. Fettes was an old drunken Scotchman, a man of education obviously, and a man of some property, since he lived in idleness. He had come to Debenham years ago, while still young, and by a mere continuance of living had grown to be an adopted townsman. His blue camlet cloak was a local antiquity, like the church-spire. His place in the parlour at the George, his absence from church, his old, crapulous, disreputable vices, were all things of course in Debenham. He had some vague Radical opinions and some fleeting infidelities, which he would now and again set forth and emphasise with tottering slaps upon the table. He drank rum—five glasses regularly every evening; and for the greater portion of his nightly visit to the George sat, with his glass in his right hand, in a state of melancholy alcoholic saturation. We called him the Doctor, for he was supposed to have some special knowledge of medicine, and had been known, upon a pinch, to set a fracture or reduce a dislocation; but beyond these slight particulars, we had no knowledge of his character and antecedents.

One dark winter night—it had struck nine some time before the landlord joined us—there was a sick man in the George, a great neighbouring proprietor suddenly struck down with apoplexy on his way to Parliament; and the great man's still greater London doctor had been telegraphed to his bedside. It was the first time that such a thing had happened in Debenham, for the railway was but newly open, and we were all proportionately moved by the occurrence.

"He's come," said the landlord, after he had filled and lighted his pipe.

"He?" said I. "Who?—not the doctor?"

"Himself," replied our host.

"What is his name?"

"Doctor Macfarlane," said the landlord.

Fettes was far through his third tumbler, stupidly fuddled, now nodding over, now staring mazily around him; but at the last word he seemed to awaken, and repeated the name "Macfarlane" twice, quietly enough the first time, but with sudden emotion at the second.

"Yes," said the landlord, "that's his name, Doctor Wolfe Macfarlane."

Fettes became instantly sober; his eyes awoke, his voice became clear, loud, and steady, his language forcible and earnest. We were all startled by the transformation, as if a man had risen from the dead.

"I beg your pardon," he said, "I am afraid I have not been paying much attention to your talk. Who is this Wolfe Macfarlane?" And then, when he had heard the landlord out, "It cannot be, it cannot be," he added; "and yet I would like well to see him face to face."

"Do you know him, Doctor?" asked the undertaker, with a gasp.

"God forbid!" was the reply. "And yet the name is a strange one; it were too much to fancy two. Tell me, landlord, is he old?"

"Well," said the host, "he's not a young man, to be sure, and his hair is white; but he looks younger than you."

"He is older, though; years older. But," with a slap upon the table, "it's the rum you see in my face—rum and sin. This man, perhaps, may have an easy conscience and a good digestion. Conscience! Hear me speak. You would think I was some good, old, decent Christian, would you not? But no, not I; I never canted. Voltaire might have canted if he'd stood in my shoes; but the brains"—with a rattling fillip on his bald head—"the brains were clear and active, and I saw and made no deductions."

"If you know this doctor," I ventured to remark, after a somewhat awful pause, "I should gather that you do not share the landlord's good opinion."

Fettes paid no regard to me.

"Yes," he said, with sudden decision, "I must see him face to face."

There was another pause, and then a door was closed rather sharply on the first floor, and a step was heard upon the stair.

"That's the doctor," cried the landlord. "Look sharp, and you can catch him."

It was but two steps from the small parlour to the door of the old George Inn; the wide oak staircase landed almost in the street; there was room for a Turkey rug and nothing more between the threshold and the last round of the descent; but this little space was every evening brilliantly lit up, not only by the light upon the stair and the great signal-lamp below the sign, but by the warm radiance of the bar-room window. The George thus brightly advertised itself to passers-by in the cold street. Fettes walked steadily to the spot, and we, who were hanging behind, beheld the two men meet, as one of them had phrased it, face to face. Dr. Macfarlane was alert and vigorous. His white hair set off his pale and placid, although energetic, countenance. He was richly dressed in the finest of broadcloth and the whitest of linen, with a great gold watch-chain, and studs and spectacles of the same precious material. He wore a broad-folded tie, white and speckled with lilac, and he carried on his arm a comfortable driving-coat of fur. There was no doubt but he became his years, breathing, as he did, of wealth and consideration; and it was a surprising contrast to see our parlour sot—bald, dirty, pimpled, and robed in his old camlet cloak—confront him at the bottom of the stairs.

"Macfarlane!" he said somewhat loudly, more like a herald than a friend.

The great doctor pulled up short on the fourth step, as though the familiarity of the address surprised and somewhat shocked his dignity.

"Toddy Macfarlane!" repeated Fettes.

The London man almost staggered. He stared for the swiftest of seconds at the man before him, glanced behind him with a sort of scare, and then in a startled whisper, "Fettes!" he said, "You!"

"Ay," said the other, "me! Did you think I was dead too? We are not so easy shut of our acquaintance."

"Hush, hush!" exclaimed the doctor. "Hush, hush! this meeting is so unexpected—I can see you are unmanned. I hardly knew you, I confess, at first; but I am overjoyed—overjoyed to have this opportunity. For the present it must be how-d'ye-do and good-bye in one, for my fly is waiting, and I must not fail the train; but you shall—let me see—yes—you shall give me your address, and you can count on early news of me. We must do something for you, Fettes. I fear you are out at elbows; but we must see to that for auld lang syne, as once we sang at suppers."

"Money!" cried Fettes; "money from you! The money that I had from you is lying where I cast it in the rain."

Dr. Macfarlane had talked himself into some measure of superiority and confidence, but the uncommon energy of this refusal cast him back into his first confusion.

A horrible, ugly look came and went across his almost venerable countenance. "My dear fellow," he said, "be it as you please; my last thought is to offend you. I would intrude on none. I will leave you my address, however—"

"I do not wish it—I do not wish to know the roof that shelters you," interrupted the other. "I heard your name; I feared it might be you; I wished to know if, after all, there were a God; I know now that there is none. Begone!"

He still stood in the middle of the rug, between the stair and doorway; and the great London physician, in order to escape, would be forced to step to one side. It was plain that he hesitated before the thought of this humiliation. White as he was, there was a dangerous glitter in his spectacles; but while he still paused uncertain, he became aware that the driver of his fly was peering in from the street at this unusual scene and caught a glimpse at the same time of our little body from the parlour, huddled by the corner of the bar. The presence of so many witnesses decided him at once to flee. He crouched together, brushing on the wainscot, and made a dart like a serpent, striking for the door. But his tribulation was not yet entirely at an end, for even as he was passing Fettes clutched him by the arm and these words came in a whisper, and yet painfully distinct, "Have you seen it again?"

The great rich London doctor cried out aloud with a sharp, throttling cry; he dashed his questioner across the open space, and, with his hands over his head, fled out of the door like a detected thief. Before it had occurred to one of us to make a movement the fly was already rattling toward the station. The scene was over like a dream, but the dream had left proofs and traces of its passage. Next day the servant found the fine gold spectacles broken on the threshold, and that very night we were all standing breathless by the bar-room window, and Fettes at our side, sober, pale, and resolute in look.

"God protect us, Mr. Fettes!" said the landlord, coming first into possession of his customary senses. "What in the universe is all this? These are strange things you have been saying."

Fettes turned toward us; he looked us each in succession in the face. "See if you can hold your tongues," said he. "That man Macfarlane is not safe to cross; those that have done so already have repented it too late."

And then, without so much as finishing his third glass, far less waiting for the other two, he bade us good-bye and went forth, under the lamp of the hotel, into the black night.

We three turned to our places in the parlour, with the big red fire and four clear candles; and as we recapitulated what had passed, the first chill of our surprise soon changed into a glow of curiosity. We sat late; it was the latest session I have known in the old George. Each man, before we parted, had his theory that he was bound to prove; and none of us had any nearer business in this world than to track out the past of our condemned companion, and surprise the secret that he shared with the great London doctor. It is no great boast, but I believe I was a better hand at worming out a story than either of my fellows at the George; and perhaps there is now no other man alive who could narrate to you the following foul and unnatural events.

In his young days Fettes studied medicine in the schools of Edinburgh. He had talent of a kind, the talent that picks up swiftly what it hears and readily retails it for its own. He worked little at home; but he was civil, attentive, and intelligent in the presence of his masters. They soon picked him out as a lad who listened closely and remembered well; nay, strange as it seemed to me when I first heard it, he was in those days well favoured, and pleased by his exterior. There was, at that period, a certain extramural teacher of anatomy, whom I shall here designate by the letter K. His name was subsequently too well known. The man who bore it skulked through the streets of Edinburgh in disguise, while the mob that applauded at the execution of Burke called loudly for the blood of his employer. But Mr. K— was then at the top of his vogue; he enjoyed a popularity due partly to his own talent and address, partly to the incapacity of his rival, the university professor. The students, at least, swore by his name, and Fettes believed himself, and was believed by others, to have laid the foundations of success when he had acquired the favour of this meteorically famous man. Mr. K— was a bon vivant as well as an accomplished teacher; he liked a sly illusion no less than a careful preparation. In both capacities Fettes enjoyed and deserved his notice, and by the second year of his attendance he held the half-regular position of second demonstrator or sub-assistant in his class.

In this capacity the charge of the theatre and lecture-room devolved in particular upon his shoulders. He had to answer for the cleanliness of the premises and the conduct of the other students, and it was a part of his duty to supply, receive, and divide the various subjects. It was with a view to this last—at that time very delicate—affair that he was lodged by Mr. K— in the same wynd, and at last in the same building, with the dissecting-rooms. Here, after a night of turbulent pleasures, his hand still tottering, his sight still misty and confused, he would be called out of bed in the black hours before the winter dawn by the unclean and desperate interlopers who supplied the table. He would open the door to these men, since infamous throughout the land. He would help them with their tragic burden, pay them their sordid price, and remain alone, when they were gone, with the unfriendly relics of humanity. From such a scene he would return to snatch another hour or two of slumber, to repair the abuses of the night, and refresh himself for the labours of the day.

Few lads could have been more insensible to the impressions of a life thus passed among the ensigns of mortality. His mind was closed against all general considerations. He was incapable of interest in the fate and fortunes of another, the slave of his own desires and low ambitions. Cold, light, and selfish in the last resort, he had that modicum of prudence, miscalled morality, which keeps a man from inconvenient drunkenness or punishable theft. He coveted, besides, a measure of consideration from his masters and his fellow-pupils, and he had no desire to fail conspicuously in the external parts of life. Thus he made it his pleasure to gain some distinction in his studies, and day after day rendered unimpeachable eye-service to his employer, Mr. K—. For his day of work he indemnified himself by nights of roaring, blackguardly enjoyment; and when that balance had been struck, the organ that he called his conscience declared itself content.

The supply of subjects was a continual trouble to him as well as to his master. In that large and busy class, the raw material of the anatomists kept perpetually running out; and the business thus rendered necessary was not only unpleasant in itself, but threatened dangerous consequences to all who were concerned. It was the policy of Mr. K— to ask no questions in his dealings with the trade. "They bring the body, and we pay the price," he used to say, dwelling on the alliteration—"*quid pro quo.*" And, again, and somewhat profanely, "Ask no questions," he would tell his assistants, "for conscience' sake." There was no understanding that the subjects were provided by the crime of murder. Had that idea been broached to him in words, he would have recoiled in horror; but the lightness of his speech upon so grave a matter was, in itself, an offence against good manners, and a temptation to the men with whom he dealt. Fettes, for instance, had often remarked to himself upon the singular freshness of the bodies. He had been struck again and again by the hang-dog, abominable looks of the ruffians who came to him before the dawn; and putting things together clearly in his private thoughts, he perhaps attributed a meaning too immoral and too categorical to the unguarded counsels of his master. He understood his duty, in short, to have three branches: to take what was brought, to pay the price, and to avert the eye from any evidence of crime.

One November morning this policy of silence was put sharply to the test. He had been awake all night with a racking toothache—pacing his room like a caged beast or throwing himself in fury on his bed—and had fallen at last into that profound, uneasy slumber that so often follows on a night of pain, when he was awakened by the third or fourth angry repetition of the concerted signal. There was a thin, bright moonshine; it was bitter cold, windy, and frosty; the town had not yet awakened, but an indefinable stir already preluded the noise and business of the day. The ghouls had come later than usual, and they seemed more than usually eager to be gone. Fettes, sick with sleep, lighted them upstairs. He heard their grumbling Irish voices through a dream; and as they stripped the sack from their sad merchandise he leaned dozing, with his shoulder propped against the wall; he had to shake himself to find the men their money. As he did so his eyes lighted on the dead face. He started; he took two steps nearer, with the candle raised.

"God Almighty!" he cried. "That is Jane Galbraith!"

The men answered nothing, but they shuffled nearer the door.

"I know her, I tell you," he continued. "She was alive and hearty yesterday. It's impossible she can be dead; it's impossible you should have got this body fairly."

"Sure, sir, you're mistaken entirely," said one of the men.

But the other looked Fettes darkly in the eyes, and demanded the money on the spot.

It was impossible to misconceive the threat or to exaggerate the danger. The lad's heart failed him. He stammered some excuses, counted out the sum, and saw his hateful visitors depart. No sooner were they gone than he hastened to confirm his doubts. By a dozen unquestionable marks he identified the girl he had jested with the day before. He saw, with horror, marks upon her body that might well betoken violence. A panic seized him, and he took refuge in his room. There he reflected at length over the discovery that he had made; considered soberly the bearing of Mr. K—'s instructions and the danger to himself of interference in so serious a business, and at last, in sore perplexity, determined to wait for the advice of his immediate superior, the class assistant.

This was a young doctor, Wolfe Macfarlane, a high favourite among all the reckless students, clever, dissipated, and unscrupulous to the last degree. He had travelled and studied abroad. His manners were agreeable and a little forward. He was an authority on the stage, skilful on the ice or the links with skate or golf-club; he dressed with nice audacity, and, to put the finishing touch upon his glory, he kept a gig and a strong trotting-horse. With Fettes he was on terms of intimacy; indeed, their relative positions called for some community of life; and when subjects were scarce the pair would drive far into the country in Macfarlane's gig, visit and desecrate some lonely graveyard, and return before dawn with their booty to the door of the dissecting-room.

On that particular morning Macfarlane arrived somewhat earlier than his wont. Fettes heard him, and met him on the stairs, told him his story, and showed him the cause of his alarm. Macfarlane examined the marks on her body.

"Yes," he said with a nod, "it looks fishy."

"Well, what should I do?" asked Fettes.

"Do?" repeated the other. "Do you want to do anything? Least said soonest mended, I should say."

"Some one else might recognise her," objected Fettes. "She was as well known as the Castle Rock."

"We'll hope not," said Macfarlane, "and if anybody does—well, you didn't, don't you see, and there's an end. The fact is, this has been going on too long. Stir up the mud, and you'll get K— into the most unholy trouble; you'll be in a shocking box yourself. So will I, if you come to that. I should like to know how any one of us would look, or what the devil we should have to say for ourselves, in any Christian witness-box. For me, you know there's one thing certain—that, practically speaking, all our subjects have been murdered."

"Macfarlane!" cried Fettes.

"Come now!" sneered the other. "As if you hadn't suspected it yourself!"

"Suspecting is one thing—"

"And proof another. Yes, I know; and I'm as sorry as you are this should have come here," tapping the body with his cane. "The next best thing for me is not to recognise it; and," he added coolly, "I don't. You may, if you please. I don't dictate, but I think a man of the world would do as I do; and I may add, I fancy that is what K— would look for at our hands. The question is, Why did he choose us two for his assistants? And I answer, because he didn't want old wives."

This was the tone of all others to affect the mind of a lad like Fettes. He agreed to imitate Macfarlane. The body of the unfortunate girl was duly dissected, and no one remarked or appeared to recognise her.

One afternoon, when his day's work was over, Fettes dropped into a popular tavern and found Macfarlane sitting with a stranger. This was a small man, very pale and dark, with coal-black eyes. The cut of his features gave a promise of intellect and refinement which was but feebly realised in his manners, for he proved, upon a nearer acquaintance, coarse, vulgar, and stupid. He exercised, however, a very remarkable control over Macfarlane; issued orders like the Great Bashaw; became inflamed at the least discussion or delay, and commented rudely on the servility with which he was obeyed. This most offensive person took a fancy to Fettes on the spot, plied him with drinks, and honoured him with unusual confidences on his past career. If a tenth part of what he confessed were true, he was a very loathsome rogue; and the lad's vanity was tickled by the attention of so experienced a man.

"I'm a pretty bad fellow myself," the stranger remarked, "but Macfarlane is the boy—Toddy Macfarlane I call him. Toddy, order your friend another glass." Or it might be, "Toddy, you jump up and shut the door." "Toddy hates me," he said again. "Oh yes, Toddy, you do!"

"Don't you call me that confounded name," growled Macfarlane.

"Hear him! Did you ever see the lads play knife? He would like to do that all over my body," remarked the stranger.

"We medicals have a better way than that," said Fettes. "When we dislike a dead friend of ours, we dissect him."

Macfarlane looked up sharply, as though this jest were scarcely to his mind.

The afternoon passed. Gray, for that was the stranger's name, invited Fettes to join them at dinner, ordered a feast so sumptuous that the tavern was thrown into commotion, and when all was done commanded Macfarlane to settle the bill. It was late before they separated; the man Gray was incapably drunk. Macfarlane, sobered by his fury, chewed the cud of the money he had been forced to squander and the slights he had been obliged to swallow. Fettes, with various liquors singing in his head, returned home with devious footsteps and a mind entirely in abeyance. Next day Macfarlane was absent from the class, and Fettes smiled to himself as he imagined him still squiring the intolerable Gray from tavern to tavern. As soon as the hour of liberty had struck he posted from place to place in quest of his last night's companions.

He could find them, however, nowhere; so returned early to his rooms, went early to bed, and slept the sleep of the just.

At four in the morning he was awakened by the well-known signal. Descending to the door, he was filled with astonishment to find Macfarlane with his gig, and in the gig one of those long and ghastly packages with which he was so well acquainted.

"What?" he cried. "Have you been out alone? How did you manage?"

But Macfarlane silenced him roughly, bidding him turn to business. When they had got the body upstairs and laid it on the table, Macfarlane made at first as if he were going away. Then he paused and seemed to hesitate; and then, "You had better look at the face," said he, in tones of some constraint. "You had better," he repeated, as Fettes only stared at him in wonder.

"But where, and how, and when did you come by it?" cried the other.

"Look at the face," was the only answer.

Fettes was staggered; strange doubts assailed him. He looked from the young doctor to the body, and then back again. At last, with a start, he did as he was bidden. He had almost expected the sight that met his eyes, and yet the shock was cruel. To see, fixed in the rigidity of death and naked on that coarse layer of sackcloth, the man whom he had left well clad and full of meat and sin upon the threshold of a tavern, awoke, even in the thoughtless Fettes, some of the terrors of the conscience. It was a *cras tibi* which re-echoed in his soul, that two whom he had known should have come to lie upon these icy tables. Yet these were only secondary thoughts. His first concern regarded Wolfe. Unprepared for a challenge so momentous, he knew not how to look his comrade in the face. He durst not meet his eye, and he had neither words nor voice at his command.

It was Macfarlane himself who made the first advance. He came up quietly behind and laid his hand gently but firmly on the other's shoulder.

"Richardson," said he, "may have the head."

Now Richardson was a student who had long been anxious for that portion of the human subject to dissect. There was no answer, and the murderer resumed: "Talking of business, you must pay me; your accounts, you see, must tally."

Fettes found a voice, the ghost of his own: "Pay you!" he cried. "Pay you for that?"

"Why, yes, of course you must. By all means and on every possible account, you must," returned the other. "I dare not give it for nothing, you dare not take it for nothing; it would compromise us both. This is another case like Jane Galbraith's. The more things are wrong the more we must act as if all were right. Where does old K— keep his money?"

"There," answered Fettes hoarsely, pointing to a cupboard in the corner.

"Give me the key, then," said the other, calmly, holding out his hand.

There was an instant's hesitation, and the die was cast. Macfarlane could not suppress a nervous twitch, the infinitesimal mark of an immense relief, as he felt the key between his fingers. He opened the cupboard, brought out pen and ink and a paper-book that stood in one compartment, and separated from the funds in a drawer a sum suitable to the occasion.

"Now, look here," he said, "there is the payment made—first proof of your good faith: first step to your security. You have now to clinch it by a second. Enter the payment in your book, and then you for your part may defy the devil."

The next few seconds were for Fettes an agony of thought; but in balancing his terrors it was the most immediate that triumphed. Any future difficulty seemed almost welcome if he could avoid a present quarrel with Macfarlane. He set down the candle which he had been carrying all this time, and with a steady hand entered the date, the nature, and the amount of the transaction.

"And now," said Macfarlane, "it's only fair that you should pocket the lucre. I've had my share already. By the bye, when a man of the world falls into a bit of luck, has a few shillings extra in his pocket—I'm ashamed to speak of it, but there's a rule of conduct in the case. No treating, no purchase of expensive class-books, no squaring of old debts; borrow, don't lend."

"Macfarlane," began Fettes, still somewhat hoarsely, "I have put my neck in a halter to oblige you."

"To oblige me?" cried Wolfe. "Oh, come! You did, as near as I can see the matter, what you downright had to do in self-defence. Suppose I got into trouble, where would you be? This second little matter flows clearly from the first. Mr. Gray is the continuation of Miss Galbraith. You can't begin and then stop. If you begin, you must keep on beginning; that's the truth. No rest for the wicked."

A horrible sense of blackness and the treachery of fate seized hold upon the soul of the unhappy student.

"My God!" he cried, "but what have I done? and when did I begin? To be made a class assistant—in the name of reason, where's the harm in that? Service wanted the position; Service might have got it. Would he have been where I am now?"

"My dear fellow," said Macfarlane, "what a boy you are! What harm has come to you? What harm can come to you if you hold your tongue? Why, man, do you know what this life is? There are two squads of us—the lions and the lambs. If you're a lamb, you'll come to lie upon these tables like Gray or Jane Galbraith; if you're a lion, you'll live and drive a horse like me, like K—, like all the world with any wit or courage. You're staggered at the first. But look at K—! My dear fellow, you're clever, you have pluck. I like you, and K— likes you. You were born to lead the hunt; and I tell you, on my honour and my experience of life, three days from now you'll laugh at all these scarecrows like a High School boy at a farce."

And with that Macfarlane took his departure and drove off up the wynd in his gig to get under cover before daylight. Fettes was thus left alone with his regrets. He saw the miserable peril in which he stood involved. He saw, with inexpressible dismay, that there was no limit to his weakness, and that, from concession to concession, he had fallen from the arbiter of Macfarlane's destiny to his paid and helpless accomplice. He would have given the world to have been a little braver at the time, but it did not occur to him that he might still be brave. The secret of Jane Galbraith and the cursed entry in the day-book closed his mouth.

Hours passed; the class began to arrive; the members of the unhappy Gray were dealt out to one and to another, and received without remark. Richardson was made happy with the head; and before the hour of freedom rang Fettes trembled with exultation to perceive how far they had already gone toward safety.

For two days he continued to watch, with increasing joy, the dreadful process of disguise.

On the third day Macfarlane made his appearance. He had been ill, he said; but he made up for lost time by the energy with which he directed the students. To Richardson in particular he extended the most valuable assistance and advice, and that student, encouraged by the praise of the demonstrator, burned high with ambitious hopes, and saw the medal already in his grasp.

Before the week was out Macfarlane's prophecy had been fulfilled. Fettes had outlived his terrors and had forgotten his baseness. He began to plume himself upon his courage, and had so arranged the story in his mind that he could look back on these events with an unhealthy pride. Of his accomplice he saw but little. They met, of course, in the business of the class; they received their orders together from Mr. K—. At times they had a word or two in private, and Macfarlane was from first to last particularly kind and jovial. But it was plain that he avoided any reference to their common secret; and even when Fettes whispered to him that he had cast in his lot with the lions and foresworn the lambs, he only signed to him smilingly to hold his peace.

At length an occasion arose which threw the pair once more into a closer union. Mr. K— was again short of subjects; pupils were eager, and it was a part of this teacher's pretensions to be always well supplied. At the same time there came the news of a burial in the rustic graveyard of Glencorse. Time has little changed the place in question. It stood then, as now, upon a cross road, out of call of human habitations, and buried fathom deep in the foliage of six cedar trees. The cries of the sheep upon the neighbouring hills, the streamlets upon either hand, one loudly singing among pebbles, the other dripping furtively from pond to pond, the stir of the wind in mountainous old flowering chestnuts, and once in seven days the voice of the bell and the old tunes of the precentor, were the only sounds that disturbed the silence around the rural church. The Resurrection Man—to use a byname of the period—was not to be deterred by any of the sanctities of customary piety. It was part of his trade to despise and desecrate the scrolls and trumpets of old tombs, the paths worn by the feet of worshippers and mourners, and the offerings and the inscriptions of bereaved affection. To rustic neighbourhoods, where love is more than commonly tenacious, and where some bonds of blood or fellowship unite the entire society of a parish, the body-snatcher, far from being repelled by natural respect, was attracted by the ease and safety of the task. To bodies that had been laid in earth, in joyful expectation of a far different awakening, there came that hasty, lamp-lit, terror-haunted resurrection of the spade and mattock. The coffin was forced, the cerements torn, and the melancholy relics, clad in sackcloth, after being rattled for hours on moonless byways, were at length exposed to uttermost indignities before a class of gaping boys.

Somewhat as two vultures may swoop upon a dying lamb, Fettes and Macfarlane were to be let loose upon a grave in that green and quiet resting-place. The wife of a farmer, a woman who had lived for sixty years, and been known for nothing but good butter and a godly conversation, was to be rooted from her grave at midnight and carried, dead and naked, to that far-away city that she had always honoured with her Sunday's best; the place beside her family was to be empty till the crack of doom; her innocent and almost venerable members to be exposed to that last curiosity of the anatomist.

Late one afternoon the pair set forth, well wrapped in cloaks and furnished with a formidable bottle. It rained without remission—a cold, dense, lashing rain. Now and again there blew a puff of wind, but these sheets of falling water kept it down. Bottle and all, it was a sad and silent drive as far as Penicuik, where they were to spend the evening. They stopped once, to hide their implements in a thick bush not far from the churchyard, and once again at the Fisher's Tryst, to have a toast before the kitchen fire and vary their nips of whisky with a glass of ale. When they reached their journey's end the gig was housed, the horse was fed and comforted, and the two young doctors in a private room sat down to the best dinner and the best wine the house afforded. The lights, the fire, the beating rain upon the window, the cold, incongruous work that lay before them, added zest to their enjoyment of the meal. With every glass their cordiality increased. Soon Macfarlane handed a little pile of gold to his companion.

"A compliment," he said. "Between friends these little d—d accommodations ought to fly like pipe-lights."

Fettes pocketed the money, and applauded the sentiment to the echo. "You are a philosopher," he cried. "I was an ass till I knew you. You and K— between you, by the Lord Harry! but you'll make a man of me."

"Of course we shall," applauded Macfarlane. "A man? I tell you, it required a man to back me up the other morning. There are some big, brawling, forty-year-old cowards who would have turned sick at the look of the d—d thing; but not you—you kept your head. I watched you."

"Well, and why not?" Fettes thus vaunted himself. "It was no affair of mine. There was nothing to gain on the one side but disturbance, and on the other I could count on your gratitude, don't you see?" And he slapped his pocket till the gold pieces rang.

Macfarlane somehow felt a certain touch of alarm at these unpleasant words. He may have regretted that he had taught his young companion so successfully, but he had no time to interfere, for the other noisily continued in this boastful strain:—

"The great thing is not to be afraid. Now, between you and me, I don't want to hang—that's practical; but for all cant, Macfarlane, I was born with a contempt. Hell, God, Devil, right, wrong, sin, crime, and all the old gallery of curiosities—they may frighten boys, but men of the world, like you and me, despise them. Here's to the memory of Gray!"

It was by this time growing somewhat late. The gig, according to order, was brought round to the door with both lamps brightly shining, and the young men had to pay their bill and take the road. They announced that they were bound for Peebles, and drove in that direction till they were clear of the last houses of the town; then, extinguishing the lamps, returned upon their course, and followed a by-road toward Glencorse. There was no sound but that of their own passage, and the incessant, strident pouring of the rain. It was pitch dark; here and there a white gate or a white stone in the wall guided them for a short space across the night; but for the most part it was at a foot pace, and almost groping, that they picked their way through that resonant blackness to their solemn and isolated destination. In the sunken woods that traverse the neighbourhood of the burying-ground the last glimmer failed them, and it became necessary to kindle a match and re-illumine one of the lanterns of the gig. Thus, under the dripping trees, and environed by huge and moving shadows, they reached the scene of their unhallowed labours.

They were both experienced in such affairs, and powerful with the spade; and they had scarce been twenty minutes at their task before they were rewarded by a dull rattle on the coffin lid. At the same moment Macfarlane, having hurt his hand upon a stone, flung it carelessly above his head. The grave, in which they now stood almost to the shoulders, was close to the edge of the plateau of the graveyard; and the gig lamp had been propped, the better to illuminate their labours, against a tree, and on the immediate verge of the steep bank descending to the stream. Chance had taken a sure aim with the stone. Then came a clang of broken glass; night fell upon them; sounds alternately dull and ringing announced the bounding of the lantern down the bank, and its occasional collision with the trees. A stone or two, which it had dislodged in its descent, rattled behind it into the profundities of the glen; and then silence, like night, resumed its sway; and they might bend their hearing to its utmost pitch, but naught was to be heard except the rain, now marching to the wind, now steadily falling over miles of open country.

They were so nearly at an end of their abhorred task that they judged it wisest to complete it in the dark. The coffin was exhumed and broken open; the body inserted in the dripping sack and carried between them to the gig; one mounted to keep it in its place, and the other, taking the horse by the mouth, groped along by wall and bush until they reached the wider road by the Fisher's Tryst. Here was a faint, diffused radiancy, which they hailed like daylight; by that they pushed the horse to a good pace and began to rattle along merrily in the direction of the town.

They had both been wetted to the skin during their operations, and now, as the gig jumped among the deep ruts, the thing that stood propped between them fell now upon one and now upon the other. At every repetition of the horrid contact each instinctively repelled it with the greater haste; and the process, natural although it was, began to tell upon the nerves of the companions. Macfarlane made some ill-favoured jest about the farmer's wife, but it came hollowly from his lips, and was allowed to drop in silence. Still their unnatural burden bumped from side to side; and now the head would be laid, as if in confidence, upon their shoulders, and now the drenching sack-cloth would flap icily about their faces. A creeping chill began to possess the soul of Fettes. He peered at the bundle, and it seemed somehow larger than at first. All over the country-side, and from every degree of distance, the farm dogs accompanied their passage with tragic ululations; and it grew and grew upon his mind that some unnatural miracle had been accomplished, that some nameless change had befallen the dead body, and that it was in fear of their unholy burden that the dogs were howling.

"For God's sake," said he, making a great effort to arrive at speech, "for God's sake, let's have a light!"

Seemingly Macfarlane was affected in the same direction; for, though he made no reply, he stopped the horse, passed the reins to his companion, got down, and proceeded to kindle the remaining lamp. They had by that time got no farther than the cross-road down to Auchenclinny. The rain still poured as though the deluge were returning, and it was no easy matter to make a light in such a world of wet and darkness. When at last the flickering blue flame had been transferred to the wick and began to expand and clarify, and shed a wide circle of misty brightness round the gig, it became possible for the two young men to see each other and the thing they had along with them. The rain had moulded the rough sacking to the outlines of the body underneath; the head was distinct from the trunk, the shoulders plainly modelled; something at once spectral and human riveted their eyes upon the ghastly comrade of their drive.

For some time Macfarlane stood motionless, holding up the lamp. A nameless dread was swathed, like a wet sheet, about the body, and tightened the white skin upon the face of Fettes; a fear that was meaningless, a horror of what could not be, kept mounting to his brain. Another beat of the watch, and he had spoken. But his comrade forestalled him.

"That is not a woman," said Macfarlane, in a hushed voice.

"It was a woman when we put her in," whispered Fettes.

"Hold that lamp," said the other. "I must see her face."

And as Fettes took the lamp his companion untied the fastenings of the sack and drew down the cover from the head. The light fell very clear upon the dark, well-moulded features and smooth-shaven cheeks of a too familiar countenance, often beheld in dreams of both of these young men. A wild yell rang up into the night; each leaped from his own side into the roadway: the lamp fell, broke, and was extinguished; and the horse, terrified by this unusual commotion, bounded and went off toward Edinburgh at a gallop, bearing along with it, sole occupant of the gig, the body of the dead and long-dissected Gray.

SREDNI VASHTAR

Saki

Conradin was ten years old, and the doctor had pronounced his professional opinion that the boy would not live another five years. The doctor was silky and effete, and counted for little, but his opinion was endorsed by Mrs. De Ropp, who counted for nearly everything. Mrs. De Ropp was Conradin's cousin and guardian, and in his eyes she represented those three-fifths of the world that are necessary and disagreeable and real; the other two-fifths, in perpetual antagonism to the foregoing, were summed up in himself and his imagination. One of these days Conradin supposed he would succumb to the mastering pressure of wearisome necessary things—such as illnesses and coddling restrictions and drawn-out dullness. Without his imagination, which was rampant under the spur of loneliness, he would have succumbed long ago.

Mrs. De Ropp would never, in her honestest moments, have confessed to herself that she disliked Conradin, though she might have been dimly aware that thwarting him "for his good" was a duty which she did not find particularly irksome. Conradin hated her with a desperate sincerity which he was perfectly able to mask. Such few pleasures as he could contrive for himself gained an added relish from the likelihood that they would be displeasing to his guardian, and from the realm of his imagination she was locked out—an unclean thing, which should find no entrance.

In the dull, cheerless garden, overlooked by so many windows that were ready to open with a message not to do this or that, or a reminder that medicines were due, he found little attraction. The few fruit-trees that it contained were set jealously apart from his plucking, as though they were rare specimens of their kind blooming in an arid waste; it would probably have been difficult to find a market-gardener who would have offered ten shillings for their entire yearly produce. In a forgotten corner, however, almost hidden behind a dismal shrubbery, was a disused tool-shed of respectable proportions, and within its walls Conradin found a haven, something that took on the varying aspects of a playroom and a cathedral. He had peopled it with a legion of familiar phantoms, evoked partly from fragments of history and partly from his own brain, but it also boasted two inmates of flesh and blood. In one corner lived a ragged-plumaged Houdan hen, on which the boy lavished an affection that had scarcely another outlet. Further back in the gloom stood a large hutch, divided into two compartments, one of which was fronted with close iron bars. This was the abode of a large polecat-ferret, which a friendly butcher-boy had once smuggled, cage and all, into its present quarters, in exchange for a long-secreted hoard of small silver. Conradin was dreadfully afraid of the lithe, sharp-fanged beast, but it was his most treasured possession. Its very presence in the tool-shed was a secret and fearful joy, to be kept scrupulously from the knowledge of the Woman, as he privately dubbed his cousin. And one day, out of Heaven knows what material, he spun the beast a wonderful name, and from that moment it grew into a god and a religion. The Woman indulged in religion once a week at a church near by, and took Conradin with her, but to him the church service was an alien rite in the House of Rimmon. Every Thursday, in the dim and musty silence of the tool-shed, he worshipped with mystic and elaborate ceremonial before the wooden hutch where dwelt Sredni Vashtar, the great ferret. Red flowers in their season and scarlet berries in the winter-time were offered at his shrine, for he was a god who laid some special stress on the fierce impatient side of things, as opposed to the Woman's religion, which, as far as Conradin could observe, went to great lengths in the contrary direction. And on great festivals powdered nutmeg was strewn in front of his hutch, an important feature of the offering being that the nutmeg had to be stolen. These festivals were of irregular occurrence, and were chiefly appointed to celebrate some passing event. On one occasion, when Mrs. De Ropp suffered from acute toothache for three days, Conradin kept up the festival during the entire three days, and almost succeeded in persuading himself that Sredni Vashtar was personally responsible for the toothache. If the malady had lasted for another day the supply of nutmeg would have given out.

The Houdan hen was never drawn into the cult of Sredni Vashtar. Conradin had long ago settled that she was an Anabaptist. He did not pretend to have the remotest knowledge as to what an Anabaptist was, but he privately hoped that it was dashing and not very respectable. Mrs. De Ropp was the ground plan on which he based and detested all respectability.

After a while Conradin's absorption in the tool-shed began to attract the notice of his guardian. "It is not good for him to be pottering down there in all weathers," she promptly decided, and at breakfast one morning she announced that the Houdan hen had been sold and taken away overnight. With her short-sighted eyes she peered at Conradin, waiting for an outbreak of rage and sorrow, which she was ready to rebuke with a flow of excellent precepts and reasoning. But Conradin said nothing: there was nothing to be said. Something perhaps in his white set face gave her a momentary qualm, for at tea that afternoon there was toast on the table, a delicacy which she usually banned on the ground that it was bad for him; also because the making of it "gave trouble," a deadly offence in the middle-class feminine eye.

"I thought you liked toast," she exclaimed, with an injured air, observing that he did not touch it.

"Sometimes," said Conradin.

In the shed that evening there was an innovation in the worship of the hutch-god. Conradin had been wont to chant his praises, to-night he asked a boon.

"Do one thing for me, Sredni Vashtar."

The thing was not specified. As Sredni Vashtar was a god he must be supposed to know. And choking back a sob as he looked at that other empty corner, Conradin went back to the world he so hated.

And every night, in the welcome darkness of his bedroom, and every evening in the dusk of the tool-shed, Conradin's bitter litany went up: "Do one thing for me, Sredni Vashtar."

Mrs. De Ropp noticed that the visits to the shed did not cease, and one day she made a further journey of inspection.

"What are you keeping in that locked hutch?" she asked. "I believe it's guinea-pigs. I'll have them all cleared away."

Conradin shut his lips tight, but the Woman ransacked his bedroom till she found the carefully hidden key, and forthwith marched down to the shed to complete her discovery. It was a cold afternoon, and Conradin had been bidden to keep to the house. From the furthest window of the dining-room the door of the shed could just be seen beyond the corner of the shrubbery, and there Conradin stationed himself. He saw the Woman enter, and then he imagined her opening the door of the sacred hutch and peering down with her short-sighted eyes into the thick straw bed where his god lay hidden. Perhaps she would prod at the straw in her clumsy impatience. And Conradin fervently breathed his prayer for the last time. But he knew as he prayed that he did not believe. He knew that the Woman would come out presently with that pursed smile he loathed so well on her face, and that in an hour or two the gardener would carry away his wonderful god, a god no longer, but a simple brown ferret in a hutch. And he knew that the Woman would triumph always as she triumphed now, and that he would grow ever more sickly under her pestering and domineering and superior wisdom, till one day nothing would matter much more with him, and the doctor would be proved right. And in the sting and misery of his defeat, he began to chant loudly and defiantly the hymn of his threatened idol:

Sredni Vashtar went forth,
His thoughts were red thoughts and his teeth were white.
His enemies called for peace, but he brought them death.
Sredni Vashtar the Beautiful.

And then of a sudden he stopped his chanting and drew closer to the window-pane. The door of the shed still stood ajar as it had been left, and the minutes were slipping by. They were long minutes, but they slipped by nevertheless. He watched the starlings running and flying in little parties across the lawn; he counted them over and over again, with one eye always on that swinging door. A sour-faced maid came in to lay the table for tea, and still Conradin stood and waited and watched. Hope had crept by inches into his heart, and now a look of triumph began to blaze in his eyes that had only known the wistful patience of defeat. Under his breath, with a furtive exultation, he began once again the paean of victory and devastation. And presently his eyes were rewarded: out through that doorway came a long, low, yellow-and-brown beast, with eyes a-blink at the waning daylight, and dark wet stains around the fur of jaws and throat. Conradin dropped on his knees. The great polecat-ferret made its way down to a small brook at the foot of the garden, drank for a moment, then crossed a little plank bridge and was lost to sight in the bushes. Such was the passing of Sredni Vashtar.

"Tea is ready," said the sour-faced maid; "where is the mistress?"

"She went down to the shed some time ago," said Conradin.

And while the maid went to summon her mistress to tea, Conradin fished a toasting-fork out of the sideboard drawer and proceeded to toast himself a piece of bread. And during the toasting of it and the buttering of it with much butter and the slow enjoyment of eating it, Conradin listened to the noises and silences which fell in quick spasms beyond the dining-room door. The loud foolish screaming of the maid, the answering chorus of wondering ejaculations from the kitchen region, the scuttering footsteps and hurried embassies for outside help, and then, after a lull, the scared sobbings and the shuffling tread of those who bore a heavy burden into the house.

"Whoever will break it to the poor child? I couldn't for the life of me!" exclaimed a shrill voice. And while they debated the matter among themselves, Conradin made himself another piece of toast.

THE HORLA

Guy de Maupassant

Translated by Jonathan Sturges

May 8th.

What a magnificent day! I spent the whole morning stretched on the grass, before my house, under the great plane-tree which entirely covers, shelters, and shades it. I love this country, and I love to live here, because here I have my roots, those deep, fine roots which attach a man to the soil where his forefathers were born and buried, which attach him to what is thought there and to what is eaten, to its customs as to its dishes, to its localisms of speech, to the peculiar intonation of its peasants, to the smell of its earth, of its villages, of its very air.

I love the house where I have grown up. From my windows I see the Seine, flowing by my garden; on the other side of the road, almost on my own property: the great, wide Seine that goes to Havre from Rouen, covered with the passing boats.

To the left, down there, Rouen the great city of blue roofs swarming far and wide below a crowd of pointed Gothic bell-towers. These, ponderous or slender, are innumerable, overtowered by the cathedral's cast-iron spire, and filled with bells which ring in the blue air on fine mornings. Their sweet and distant iron humming, their brazen chant, reaches out to me, brought by the breeze, and now louder, now lower, as the breeze now wakes, now drowses.

How fine it was this morning!

About eleven o'clock, I remember, a long tow of ships defiled past my garden railings. They were pulled by a tug the size of a fly; it groaned and vomited forth a thick, black smoke.

Just behind two English schooners, whose red flag waved against the sky, came a superb Brazilian three-master, quite white, admirably clean and shining. This ship gave me so much pleasure that I saluted her, I don't know why.

May 12th.

For some days I have had a little fever; I feel unwell, or rather, properly speaking, I feel depressed.

Whence come these mysterious influences which change our happiness into discouragement and our confidence into distress? One would almost say that the air, the invisible air, was full of unknowable Powers, to whose mysterious proximity we submit. I awake full of gayety, with desires to sing in my throat. Why? I go down to the waterside, and suddenly, after a short walk, return distressed, as though some misfortune awaited me at home. Why? Is it a shiver of cold which, brushing across my skin, has unsettled my nerves and darkened my soul? Is it the shapes of the clouds, or the colors of the day, or the changeable colors of things which have passed in through my eyes, and have troubled my thoughts? Do we know? Everything about us, everything which we see without observing, everything which we brush against without recognizing, everything which we touch without feeling, everything which we encounter without clearly distinguishing, may have upon us, upon our senses, and, through them, upon our minds and upon our hearts, instant effects which are wonderful and not to be explained.

Ah! but it is deep, this mystery of the Invisible! No, we may not sound it with our wretched senses, with our eyes which can perceive neither what is too small nor too great, nor too near nor too far, nor the inhabitants of a planet nor the inhabitants of a drop of water. And we may not sound it with our ears which deceive us, transmitting air-waves in the form of sonorous notes. They are the fairies who perform the miracle of changing movement into sound, and by this metamorphosis they give birth to music and to Nature's dumb agitation the power of singing. No, we may not sound it with our sense of smell feebler than that of the dog; nor with our taste which can hardly discern the age of wine!

Ah, if we had only other organs which would perform in our favor other miracles like that miracle of music, what new things we should discover all about our lives!

May 16th.

I am certainly ill. Last month I was so well! I have a fever, a dreadful fever, or rather a feeling of feverish enervation which causes my mind to suffer as much as my body. I experience that awful sense of some menacing danger, that apprehension of coming misfortune or approaching death, that curious presentiment which is no doubt really the stroke of a still unrecognized sickness germinating in body and in blood.

May 18th.

I have just been to consult my physician, for I was not able to sleep. He found my pulse rapid, my eye dilated, my nerves disturbed, but no alarming symptoms. I must take shower-baths and drink a little bromide of potassium.

May 25th.

No change. My condition is truly curious. With the approach of evening a strange anxiety invades me, as if the night concealed for me some dreadful menace. I dine quickly, then try to read, but I do not comprehend the words. I barely distinguish the letters. Then I pace my drawing-room backward and forward, under the oppression of a confused and resistless fear, the fear of sleep and the fear of my bed.

Towards ten o'clock I go up-stairs to my room. As soon as I get inside the door I double-lock it and I push the bolts; I am afraid . . . of what? . . . Hitherto I feared nothing . . . I open my closets, I look under my bed; I listen . . . I listen for what? . . . Is it not strange that a simple indisposition, a difficulty in the circulation perhaps, an irritated nerve, a slight congestion, a little disturbance of the works of my delicate, imperfect human machinery, can out of a merry man make a melancholy one out of a brave man make a coward? Then I go to bed, and I await sleep as one might await an executioner. I wait with terror for its coming. And my heart beats, and my limbs quiver, and my whole body trembles under the warmth of the bedclothes, until the moment when I fall suddenly into slumber, as a man might fall, to drown himself, into a gulf of stagnant water. I do not feel sleep coming in the way I used to feel it coming calmly. For this sleep, hidden somewhere near me, is perfidious, and it watches and will soon seize me by the head, and close my eyes, and destroy me.

I sleep long two or three hours then a dream—no, a nightmare grips me in its arms. I feel that I am in bed and that I am sleeping . . . I feel it and I know it . . . and I also feel that some one approaches me, looks at me, touches me, mounts upon my bed, kneels upon my breast, seizes my neck in his hands and presses . . . presses . . . with all his force, to strangle me.

I writhe, bound fast by that awful powerlessness which paralyzes us in dreams. I desire to shout, I cannot; to move, I cannot; I try, with fearful efforts, panting, to turn myself, to throw off this being who is crushing and suffocating me; I cannot.

And suddenly I awake, wild, covered with perspiration. I light a candle. I am alone.

After this crisis, which recurs every night, I sleep at last calmly until dawn.

June 2d.

My condition is still worse. What is the matter with me? The bromide has no effect; the shower-baths have no effect. Just now, in order to tire myself out (though Heaven knows I am languid enough already!) I went to walk in the forest of Roumare. I thought at first that the fresh, buoyant, balmy air, full of the perfume of herbs and leaves, was pouring new blood into my veins, new energy into my heart. I took a wide glade. Then I turned towards La Bouille, along a narrow *allée*, between two armies of great trees which built a thick, green, almost black roof between the sky and myself.

Suddenly a shiver seized me not a shiver of cold, but a strange shiver of anguish.

I quickened my pace, uneasy at being alone in the wood, terrified without reason, stupidly, by the profound loneliness. All at once it seemed to me that I was being followed, that some one was treading on my heels, on the point—on the point—on the point of touching me.

I turned abruptly. I was alone. I saw behind me only the straight, wide glade empty, high, fearfully empty; and in front of me also it stretched out of sight just the same dreadful!

I closed my eyes. Why? And I began to turn round and round on my heel, quickly, like a top. I came near falling. I opened my eyes again; the trees danced; the earth swam; I was obliged to sit down. Then, of course, I no longer knew from which direction I had come! Fantastic thought! Strange! Fantastic thought! I set off to the right, and happened into the same avenue which had led me to the middle of the forest.

June 3d.

The night was horrible. I shall go away for a few weeks. A little journey will no doubt set me on my feet again.

July 2d.

At home again. I am cured; and, besides that, I have made a charming trip. I have visited Mont Saint Michel, where I had never been.

What a vision, when one arrives, as I did, at Avranches towards the end of the day! The city is on a little hill; a guide took me to the public garden at the end of the town. A great bay stretched away before me out of sight, between two lonely shores which lost themselves far off in the mists; and in the midst of this immense yellow bay, beneath a golden and glittering sky, rose, sombre and pointed, a strange mount in the midst of the sands. The sun had just disappeared, and against the still flaming horizon there was designed the profile of that fantastic rock which bears upon its summit a fantastic monument.

By daybreak I was on my way towards it. The tide was low, as yesterday at evening, and I watched that wonder-arousing abbey growing taller and taller before me as I approached. After several hours of walking I reached the enormous block of stones which bears the little town dominated by the great church. Having ascended the narrow and steep street, I entered the most admirable Gothic dwelling which has ever been constructed for God on earth, vast as a city, full of low passages borne down by heavy arches, of high galleries borne up by slender columns. I entered that gigantic granite jewel, light as a bit of lace, covered with towers and with slender belfries linked one to the other by fine-carved arches. They are climbed by twisting stair-ways, and they dart into the blue sky of day and into the black sky of night, their fantastic heads bristling with chimeras, with Devils, and with strange Beasts.

When I reached the top I said to the monk who accompanied me, "Father, you must be well off here."

He answered: "There's a great deal of wind, Monsieur"; and we fell into conversation while we watched the rising sea spread over the sand and cover it with a steely cuirass.

And the monk told me stories—all the old stories of the place—legends, always legends.

One of them impressed me very strongly. The country people, those of the mount, pretend that talking is heard on the sands by night, then the bleating of two goats, the one with a voice which is high, the other with a voice which is deep. Unbelievers maintain it is the sea-birds' crying, which resembles now a bleat, and now a human wail; but belated fishermen swear that they have met, wandering on the sands, between two tides, about the little city cast out so far from the rest of the world, an old shepherd whose head, shrouded in a cloak, is always invisible, and who leads behind him a he-goat with the face of a man, and a she-goat with the face of a woman. They have long white hair, and they talk incessantly, quarrelling together in an unknown tongue; then suddenly they cease crying and begin to bleat with all their might.

I said to the monk: "Do you believe it?"

He murmured: "I do not know."

I continued: "If there really existed on the earth any other beings beside ourselves, how is it possible that we should not have known them long ago? How should you have seen them, you? How should I not have seen them, I?"

He answered: "Do we see the hundred-thousandth part of what exists? For instance, take the wind, which is the greatest force in nature, which knocks down men, lays low buildings, tears up trees by the roots, heaps the sea into mountains of water, destroys coasts, and hurls great ships upon the breakers, the wind which kills, which whistles, which moans, which roars, have you ever seen it? Can you see it? It exists, nevertheless."

I was silent before this simple reasoning. This man was a wise man or perhaps a fool. I could not have decided which; but I was silent. What he had just said I had often thought.

July 3d.

I have slept badly; there is certainly something feverish in the air here, for my coachman suffers from the same complaint as myself. On my return yesterday I noticed that he was looking curiously pale. I asked him: "What is the matter, Jean?"

"It is that I cannot sleep, Monsieur; my nights eat up my days. Since Monsieur went away, it holds me like a charm."

The other servants, however, are well; but I myself am in great fear of a relapse.

July 4th.

Yes, I have had a relapse. My old nightmares have returned. Last night I felt some one squatting on my chest with his mouth to mine, drinking my life out through my lips. Yes, like a leech he drew it out of my throat. Then when he was satiated he arose, and I, I awoke, so nearly murdered, so exhausted, so broken, that I had no longer power to move. If this continues many days more I shall certainly go away again.

July 5th.

Have I lost my reason? That which has happened, that which I saw last night, is so strange that my head turns when I think of it!

I had, as I now do every evening, locked my door; then, being thirsty, I drank half a glass of water, and I noticed by mere chance that the water-bottle was full up to the glass stopper.

After that I went to bed and fell into one of my dreadful slumbers, from which, two hours later, I was drawn by a shock more awful yet.

Imagine a man who sleeps, who is being murdered, and who awakes with a knife in his breast, and who groans covered with blood, and who cannot breathe, and who is dying, and who does not understand. It was like that!

Having at last recovered my reason, I again felt thirsty; I lit a candle and I went to the table where the water-bottle stood. I raised it, tipping it over the glass; nothing came out. It was empty! It was completely empty! At first I did not understand; then, all at once, I experienced so terrible an emotion that I had to sit down, or rather that I simply fell, upon a chair! Then, with a start, I jumped to my feet, and looked about me! Then, again, I sat down, dazed with astonishment and with fear, before the transparent glass! I glared at it with staring eyes, trying to understand. My hands trembled! Had some one really drunk that water? Who—I? I, without a doubt. It could only be I. Then I was a somnambulist, I was living, without knowing it, that mysterious double life which makes us wonder whether we are in ourselves two beings, or whether some strange being, unknowable and invisible, may not animate, at moments when our will is weak, our bodies captive and more obedient to this stranger than to us.

Ah! who will understand my abominable anguish? Who will understand the emotion of a man, perfectly sane, well educated, full of reason, and yet contemplating in terror, through the glass of a water-bottle, the disappearance, while he slept, of a little water! And I remained there until morning, not daring to go back to bed.

July 6th.

I am going mad. The water was again drunk by some one last night; or, rather, I drank it!

But, is it—is it I? Who should it be? Who? Oh, my God! I am going mad. Who shall save me?

July 10th.
I have just established the most wonder-arousing proofs.

Yes, I am mad! And yet?

On the 6th of July, before going to bed, I placed some wine, some milk, some water, some bread, and some strawberries on my table.

Some one drank—I drank—all the water, and a little milk. The wine, the bread, and the strawberries were not touched.

On the 7th of July I made the same experiment, with the same result.

On the 8th of July I suppressed the water and the milk. Nothing was touched at all.

Finally, on the 9th of July, I put only the milk and the water on my table, being careful to wrap up the bottles in cloths of white muslin and to tie down the stoppers. Then I rubbed my lips, my beard, my hands, with black-lead, and I retired.

The invincible slumber seized me, soon followed by the dreadful awaking. I had not stirred; my very sheets bore no stains. I rushed to the table. The cloths covering the bottles were immaculate. I untied the cords, trembling with fear. Some one had drunk all the water! Some one had drunk all the milk! Oh, my God! . . .

I leave to-day for Paris.

July 12th.
Paris. I must have lost my head completely these last days. I have been undoubtedly the plaything of a nervous imagination, unless, that is, I am really a somnambulist, or that I have been subjected to one of those influences admitted but not yet explained, which are called "suggestions." In any case my perturbation came near insanity, and twenty-four hours of Paris have sufficed to put me on my feet again.

Yesterday, after taking a drive and making some visits which caused a new revivifying air to pass into my soul, I finished the evening at the Theatre Franais. They were playing a piece by Alexandre Dumas *fils;* and that strong alert spirit completed my cure. Solitude is certainly dangerous for an active intelligence. We need around us men who think and talk. When we are long alone, we people the void with phantoms.

I returned to the hotel in great good spirits, along the boulevards. Reminded by the jostling of the crowd, I thought, not without irony, of my terrors and imaginings of last week, when I believed, yes, really believed, that an invisible being was dwelling under my roof. How easily we lose our heads, how weakly and quickly we become wild with fear the moment we encounter some little incident which cannot be explained!

Instead of concluding with the words: "The reason I do not understand is that the cause as yet escapes me," we immediately proceed to imagine some dreadful mystery, some supernatural power.

July 14th.

Fête de la République. I took a walk in the streets. The flags and the fireworks amused me like a child. Nevertheless, it is simply an absurdity—this being joyous on a fixed date, by Government decree. The people is an imbecile herd, now stupidly patient, now ferociously rebellious. Some one says to it: "Make merry." It makes merry. Some one says to it: "Go and fight with your neighbors." It goes and fights. Some one says to it: "Vote for the Emperor." It votes for the Emperor. Then some one says to it: "Vote for the Republic." And it votes for the Republic.

Those who give it these orders are fools, also, but instead of obeying men, they obey principles, things whose stupidity, whose barrenness, whose falsity appears in the very name Principles! Ideas supposed certain and immutable in this world where one is sure of nothing, where even light, even sound are illusions, merely states in the brain, merely states in the brain!

July 16th.

Yesterday I saw something which disturbed me very much.

I was dining with my cousin Mme. Sablé, whose husband commands the 76th Chasseurs at Limoges. At dinner there were two young ladies, and the husband of one of them, a Doctor Parent, a nerve-specialist, much interested in the extraordinary developments brought to light by the experiments now making in Hypnotism and Suggestion.

He gave us a long account of the prodigious results obtained by English scientists and by the physicians of the school at Nancy.

The facts which he advanced appeared to me so extremely fantastic that I declared myself entirely sceptical.

"We are," he maintained, "on the point of discovering one of Nature's most important secrets—I mean to say, one of her most important terrestrial secrets; since, of course, she hides forever others quite as important up there in the stars. Ever since Man has been able to think, ever since he has been able to speak and write his thoughts, he has from time to time felt brushing against him the touch of a mystery which is impenetrable to his gross, imperfect senses; and he has tried to supplement this weakness of his bodily organs by an effort of his mind. While his intelligence remained in the rudimentary state this notion of phenomena, all about him, yet invisible, took on shapes of the most vulgar terror. From it were born popular beliefs in the supernatural, legends of wandering spirits, of fairies, of gnomes, of ghosts—I might even add, the vulgar idea of God; for the ordinary conception of a workman-creator, in whatever religion it springs up, is, of all the inventions of the human brain, the most common, the most stupid, the most unacceptable. Nothing is truer than Voltaire's epigram: 'God made man in his own image, and man has returned the compliment.'

"But about a century ago people began to have dim forebodings of something new. Mesmer and several others started us on an unexpected track, and now, and especially in the last three or four years, we have arrived at wonderful results."

My cousin, as unbelieving as myself, smiled. Doctor Parent said to her: "May I try to hypnotize you, madame?"

"Certainly you may."

She seated herself in an arm-chair, and, trying to fascinate her gaze, he looked at her fixedly. As for me, I felt suddenly troubled—my heart beating, a choking in my throat. I saw the eyes of Mme. Sablé droop, her mouth work, her breast heave. At the end of ten minutes she slept.

"Put yourself behind her," said the physician.

And I seated myself behind her. In her hands he placed a visiting-card, saying: "This is a mirror; what do you see in it?"

She answered: "I see my cousin."

"What is he doing?"

"He is twisting his mustache."

"What now?"

"He is taking a photograph out of his pocket."

"A photograph of whom?"

"Of himself."

It was true! And the photograph had been sent home only that evening to my hotel.

"How does he look in the photograph?"

"He is standing up, with his hat in his hand."

So then she saw in this card, in this white card, as well as she would have seen in a glass!

The young ladies, very much frightened, cried: "Enough! Enough! Enough!"

But the doctor gave her an order: "You will rise at eight o'clock to-morrow morning; and you will go to find your cousin at his hotel; and you will beg him to lend you five thousand francs, which your husband has said he needs, and hopes to get from you when he comes up shortly to town."

Then he awoke her.

While returning to the hotel I meditated on this curious séance, and I was assailed by doubts, not of the absolute, the indubitable good faith of my cousin, whom I have known like a sister from childhood up, but of a possible trick on the part of the doctor. Might he not, at the same time with his visiting-card, have held before the sleeping lady a mirror hidden in his hand? Professional prestidigitators perform equally extraordinary feats.

So I went home and to bed.

But this morning, about half after eight, I was awaked by my man, who said: "It is Mme. Sablé. She asks to speak with you, sir, immediately."

I dressed in all haste, and I bid him show her in.

Very much embarrassed, she sat down, lowering her eyes, not lifting her veil; and she said: "My dear cousin, I have to ask you for a great favor."

"What is it, cousin?"

"I hate to ask you, and yet I must. I need—I need five thousand francs; I need it very much."

"Oh, come now! You?"

"Yes, I. Or, rather, my husband. He says I must get the money for him somehow."

I was so stupefied that I stammered. I asked myself if this were not a joke on me which she was playing with Doctor Parent; if this were not a simple farce rehearsed in advance, and very well acted.

But, when I looked at her carefully, all my doubts vanished. She trembled with anguish, the proceeding was so painful for her; and I saw that her throat was full of sobs.

I knew she was very rich, and I continued: "What! Your husband has not five thousand francs at his disposal? Come! Think a little. Are you sure he told you to ask me for it?"

For some seconds she hesitated as though making a great effort to remember, then she answered: "Yes . . . Yes . . . I am sure of it."

"Has he written?"

Again she hesitated, reflecting. I divined how she was tortured by the working of her thoughts. She did not know. She knew simply that she must borrow from me, for her husband, five thousand francs. But she gained the courage to lie.

"Yes, he wrote to me."

"When, then? You said nothing to me of it yesterday."

"I got the letter this morning."

"Can you show it me?"

"No . . . no . . . no . . . it had private matters in it . . . too personal . . . I . . . I burnt it."

"Oh I suppose then he's been getting into debt."

Again she hesitated; then murmured: "I do not know."

I announced, abruptly: "The fact is at the moment I haven't five thousand francs to my hand, cousin."

She uttered a kind of suffering cry.

"Oh, oh! I beg you, I beg you to get it somehow, somehow."

She grew excited, clasped her hands before me as though she were praying! I heard her voice change tone; she wept and stammered; she was tormented, overpowered, dominated by the irresistible order which had been laid upon her.

"Oh, oh! I beg you . . . if you knew how I suffer . . . I must have it to-day."

I took pity on her.

"You shall have it, and very soon, I promise."

"Oh, thank you! thank you! You are good."

I continued: "Do you remember what happened at your house last night?"

"Yes."

"Do you remember that Doctor Parent put you to sleep?"

"Yes."

"Well, he ordered you to come to me this morning, and borrow five thousand francs. And at this moment you are obeying his suggestion."

She reflected for a few seconds, and answered:

"But it's my husband who wants it."

For an hour I tried in vain to convince her.

As soon as she had gone, I hurried to the Doctor. He was on the point of going out; and he listened to me with a smile. Then he said: "Do you believe now?"

"Yes, I must."

"Let us go to your cousin."

She was already dozing in a long chair, exhausted with fatigue. The physician felt her pulse, looked at her for a time, his raised hand pointing towards her eyes. Little by little she closed them, submitting to the resistless strength of the magnetic power.

When she slumbered:

"Your husband has no longer any need of five thousand francs. You will therefore forget that you have asked your cousin to lend you them; and if he speaks to you of it, you will not understand him."

Then he awoke her. I drew out a pocket-book.

"Here, my dear cousin, here is what you asked me for this morning."

She was so surprised that I did not dare to insist. Nevertheless, I tried to arouse her memory; but she denied everything with vehemence, thought I was making fun of her, and at last came near being angry.

* * * * *

There it is! I have just returned; and I was so disturbed by this experience that at luncheon I could eat nothing.

July 19th.
Several people to whom I have related this adventure have made fun of me. I do not know what to think. The wise man says: "It may be."

July 21st.
I've been to dine at Bougival; afterwards I went to the Watermen's Ball. Decidedly everything depends on circumstance and place. To believe in the supernatural on the island of La Grenouilliere would be the height of folly indeed . . . But on the top of Mont St. Michel? . . . But in the Far East? We are subject fearsomely to the influence of what surrounds us. Next week I shall go home.

July 30th.
I arrived yesterday. All well.

August 2d.
Nothing new. Beautiful weather. I pass my days watching the Seine flow.

August 4th.
Quarrels among the servants. They say that some one breaks the glass at night in the closets. My man accuses the cook, who accuses the laundress, who accuses the two maids. Which one is guilty? It would take a wise man to say.

August 6th.
This time I am not mad. I have seen . . . I have seen! . . . I have seen! . . . I can doubt no more . . . I have seen! . . . I am still chilled to my very finger-nails . . . I am still afraid to the very marrow . . . I have seen! . . .

I was taking a walk about two o'clock, in broad daylight, in my rose-garden . . . along a row of autumn roses which are already beginning to bloom.

Pausing to look at a Géant des Batailles, which bore three magnificent buds, I saw, I distinctly saw, quite near me the stem of one of these roses bend as though twisted by an invisible hand, then break, as though that hand had plucked it! Then the flower lifted itself, following the curve which would have been described by an arm carrying it to a mouth; and it remained hanging in the empty air, alone, motionless, a terrifying red stain three paces from my eyes.

Maddened, I threw myself forward to seize it! I found nothing; it had disappeared. Then I was overcome with violent anger against myself, since a man who is serious and reasonable should not allow himself to have such hallucinations as this.

But was it really an hallucination? I turned to look for the stem, and I discovered it almost immediately, on the plant, freshly broken, between the two other roses which remained upon the tree.

So I went back to the house with a troubled soul; for now I am certain that near me there exists an invisible being who lives on milk and on water; who can touch objects; can take them up and change their places; whose nature, therefore, though imperceptible to our sense, is material, and who, like myself, dwells under my roof . . .

August 7th.

I slept quietly. He drank all the water in my bottle, but did not disturb my sleep.

I ask myself if I am mad. While walking just now along the river, doubts about my reason came to me; not vague doubts such as I have hitherto experienced, but doubts precise and absolute. I have seen lunatics, I have known some who remained intelligent, clear-headed, lucid on every subject save one. They talked clearly, easily, profoundly, then suddenly their intelligence, striking on the rock of their monomania, there ground itself to pieces, was broken up and foundered in that terrible, furious sea, full of heaving waves and mists and squalls, the sea which we call "Madness."

I should certainly believe that I was mad, quite mad, if I were not so entirely self-conscious, if I did not recognize my condition so perfectly, if I were not always sounding it by an analysis which is so completely clear. I am, then, only a man who suffers from an hallucination, but who is in full possession of his reason? Some trouble has occurred in my brain, one of those troubles which psychologists nowadays endeavor to note and particularize? And this trouble has induced a profound lapse in my intellect, in the order and logic of my thoughts? A similar phenomenon occurs in dreams, where we are led through the most improbable of phantasmagoria without feeling a shadow of surprise, simply for the reason that the verifying apparatus, our sense of control, is asleep, while our imaginative faculty wakes and is active. May it not be, therefore, that one of the invisible keys of my cerebral piano is paralyzed? People very often, in consequence of an accident, lose their memory of proper names, or of verbs, or of figures, or simply of dates. That the various little bundles of thought are specially localized is now considered proved. Hence what is there surprising if my power of controlling the unreality of certain hallucinations finds itself at the present moment torpid? I pondered on all this as I followed the bank of the river. The sun covered the stream with radiance, made the earth delicious, filled my eyes with love for life, for the swallows whose swift motions are a joy to look at, for the grasses by the water's edge whose rustling is a joy to me when I listen. Little by little, however, I was penetrated by a strange uneasiness. It seemed to me that a force, an occult force, benumbed me, checked me, prevented me from going farther, called me back. I experienced a mournful feeling that I must return, a feeling like that which oppresses us when, having left at home some sick person whom we love, we are suddenly seized by a presentiment that she is worse.

So I turned back, against my will, certain that I should find bad news at home, a letter, or a telegram. There was nothing, and I remained more surprised and uneasy than if I had again seen some fantastic vision.

August 8th.
I passed a dreadful evening yesterday. He no longer makes his presence evident, but I feel him near me, spying, watching, penetrating me, dominating me, more terrible while thus concealed than if he manifested by supernatural phenomena his invisible and constant presence.

I slept, however.

August 9th.
Nothing. But I am afraid.

August 10th.
Nothing. What will happen to-morrow?

August 11th.
Still nothing; I cannot stay at home any longer with this fear and these thoughts in my soul; I shall go away.

August 12th: 10 p.m.
All day I have wanted to be off; I could not go. I wished to perform an act of free-will, very easy and very simple: going out of my door getting into my carriage driving to Rouen. I was not able. Why?

August 13th.
When one is attacked by certain maladies all the powers of the physical being seem broken, all the energies destroyed, all the muscles relaxed, the bones becoming soft as flesh and the flesh liquid as water. I experience this in my moral state after a strange and appalling fashion. I have no longer any strength, courage, self-control, no power to put in motion my own will. I can no longer will; but some one wills for me, and I obey.

August 14th.
I am lost! Some one is in possession of my soul and governs it. Some one orders all my acts, all my movements, all my thoughts. I am no longer anything in myself; I am nothing but an enslaved and terrified spectator of the things

which I accomplish. I desire to go out; I cannot he does not wish it, and I remain, frightened, trembling, in the arm-chair where he holds me seated. I desire simply to rise, to get up, so as to prove that I am still my own master. I cannot! I am riveted to my seat, and my seat adheres to the ground with such force that no power could lift us up.

Then, on a sudden, I must, I must, I must go to the end of the garden and pick some strawberries and eat them. And I go. I pick the berries and I eat them. Oh, my God! my God! If there be a God, deliver me, save me, help me! Pardon! Pity! Grace! Save me! Oh, what suffering! what torture! what horror!

August 15th.

Yes, this is the way in which my poor cousin was possessed and dominated when she came to me to borrow five thousand francs. She submitted to a strange will which had entered into her like a new soul—like a new parasite and dominant soul. Is the world ending?

But this being who governs me—what is he, this invisible? Who is he, this unknowable, this prowler of a supernatural race?

And so the Invisibles exist! How is it, then, that since the beginning of the world they have never manifested themselves as they have to me? I never read of any such things as have happened here in my house. Oh, if I could leave it! If I could go away—flee and never return—I should be saved! But I cannot.

August 16th.

I was able to make my escape to-day for two hours, like a prisoner who finds the door of his dungeon, by chance, open. I suddenly felt that I was free, and that he was far away. I ordered the carriage instantly, and I got as far as Rouen. Oh, what joy to say to a man who obeys you—"Go to Rouen."

I had myself driven to the library, and I took out Hermann Herestauss's great treatise, *The Unrecognized Inhabitants of the Ancient and Modern World.*

Then, as I was getting back into my brougham I wanted to say: "To the station!" but cried—I did not say, I shouted—with a voice so loud that the people in the street turned round—"Home!" and I fell, mad with despair, on the cushions of the carriage. He had found and captured me again.

August 17th.

Ah! what a night! what a night! And yet it occurs to me that I ought to rejoice. I read till one o'clock in the morning. Hermann Herestauss is a doctor of philosophy and of theogony; he has written a complete history of the manifestations of those beings which wander mostly invisible about mankind, or are imagined by him as so doing; he treats exhaustively of their origin, of their domain, of the power which they exercise; and not one of them resembles the one who haunts me. One would say that ever since man could think he has had dim forebodings and fears of a new being, stronger than himself, his successor in the world; and that, feeling him near at hand, and being unable to foresee the real nature of this new master, he has in terror created all that fantastic crowd of occult beings vague phantoms born of fear.

But to continue. Having read till one o'clock, I went and seated myself at an open window to refresh brow and brain in the calm air of darkness.

The night was gentle and warm. How I should have loved this kind of a night long ago!

No moon. The stars at the back of the black sky glittered and trembled. Who dwell in those worlds up there? What forms? what living things? what animals? what plants? That which thinks in those distant universes, what knows it more than we? What power has it more than we? What sees it that we know not? And some day or another will not one of those beings, traversing space, appear upon the earth and conquer it, just as the Normans of old crossed the sea to subdue more feeble races?

We are so weak, so defenseless, so ignorant, so little, we here on this revolving speck of mud and water.

Thus dozing in the fresh evening breeze, I drowsed off.

But after I had slept about forty minutes, I opened my eyes, making no other movement, awoke by some confused fantastical emotion. At first I saw nothing; then, on a sudden, it seemed to me that a page of the open book lying on my table had just turned by itself. No breath of air came through the window. I was surprised, and I waited. At the end of about four minutes I saw, I saw, yes, I saw with my eyes another page lift itself and fold over down on the preceding one as though a finger had turned it. My arm-chair was empty, seemed empty; but I understood that he was there, he, seated in my place, and that he was reading. With one furious leap, with the bound of a beast who has rebelled at last, and fallen on his master to tear him open, I crossed the room to seize, to grip him in my hands, to kill him! . . . But my chair, before I had reached it, was overturned, as though someone fled before me . . . my table tottered, my lamp fell and was extinguished, and my window shut itself as though a detected thief had leaped out into the night by catching both the sashes in his hands.

So, he fled! He was afraid, he was afraid of me!

Then . . . then . . . to-morrow . . . or the day after . . . or some day . . . I shall be able to get him down under my hands, and to crush him against the earth! Do not dogs sometimes bite and throttle their masters?

August 18th.

I have reflected all day. Oh yes, I shall obey him, follow his suggestions, accomplish all his desires, appear humble, submissive, cowardly! He is the strongest. But an hour will come . . .

August 19th.

I know . . . I know . . . I know all! I have read as follows in the *Revue du Monde Scientifique:* "Information of a curious nature comes to us from Rio de Janeiro. An epidemic of madness, comparable to those contagious crazes which attacked the European peoples during the Middle Ages, is, it seems, at present, raging in the Province of San Paulo. The inhabitants are leaving their houses in dismay, deserting their villages, and abandoning their crops, maintaining that they are being pursued, taken possession of, governed like a human herd of cattle, by certain invisible but tangible beings, resembling vampires, who suck upon their life-blood during their sleep, and who, besides that, take water and milk, but no other nourishment.

"Professor Don Pedro Henriquez, accompanied by several other scientists of the medical profession, is on his way to the province of San Paulo, to study on the spot the causes and the manifestations of this curious mania; he will then propose to the Emperor whatever measures he decides best for recalling these unhappy lunatics to their reason."

Ah! Ah! I remember, I remember the beautiful Brazilian three-master which passed up the Seine under my windows on the 8th of last May! I thought it so beautiful, so white, so gay! The Being was aboard it, coming from that distant country where his race was born! And he saw me! He saw that my dwelling was white, likewise; and he leaped from the ship to the river-banks. Oh, my God!

And now, I know, I divine. The kingdom of man is ended.

He has come. He whom primitive peoples dreaded with a naive terror, He who was exorcised by anxious priests, He whom sorcerers invoked in vain on sombre nights, He to whom the forebodings of man, the transitory master of the earth, have given the monstrous or gracious forms of gnomes and ghosts, of genii, of fairies, and of familiar spirits. After the vulgar conceptions of primitive fear came the clearer presentations of more highly developed minds. Mesmer first divined Him; and the doctors, as long as ten years ago, discovered the exact nature of His power before He himself had ever used it. They have played with this weapon of the new Lord, this domination of a mysterious will over a human soul made captive. They have called it magnetism, hypnotism, suggestion . . . what not? I have seen them, like careless children, amusing themselves with that dreadful power! Woe to us! Woe to Man! He is come, the . . . the . . . how calls he himself . . . the . . . it seems to me that he is crying out his name, and that I cannot hear it . . . the . . . yes . . . he is crying it . . . I am listening . . . I cannot . . . I repeat . . . the . . . Horla . . . I heard . . . the Horla . . . it is he . . . the Horla . . . he has come! . . .

Ah! the vulture has devoured the dove, and the wolf has devoured the sheep, the lion has devoured the buffalo with the pointed horns; and the man has slain the lion by arrows and by his knife and by powder. But the Horla will make of man what man has made of the horse, and of the ox: his thing, his servant, his food, by the sole power of his will. Woe unto us!

Nevertheless, the animal sometimes revolts and kills his master . . . and I, too, I wish . . . I shall be able . . . but I must first know what he is like, I must touch him, see him! Scientists say that the eyes of animals are different from ours, and do not distinguish things as ours do . . . Just so my eyes cannot distinguish this new-comer who oppresses me.

Why? Oh! now I remember the word; of the monk of Mont St. Michel: "Do we see the hundred-thousandth part of what exists? For instance, take the wind, which is the greatest force in nature, which knocks down men, lays low buildings, tears up trees by the roots, heaps the sea into mountains of water, destroys coasts, and hurls great ships upon the breakers, the wind which kills, which whistles, which moans, which roars, have you ever seen it? Can you see it? It exists, nevertheless."

And I continued to reflect: "My eye is so feeble, so imperfect, that it does not even distinguish solid bodies, if they are transparent such as glass! . . . And if a mirror without a quicksilver back bars the way, my eye allows me to throw myself up against it like a bird which, straying into a room, dashes its head to pieces against the window-panes. A thousand things beside deceive and confuse it. Then what wonder if it cannot see this new transparent body?"

A new being! Why not? Inevitably he must have arisen! Why should we be the last? We cannot see him as we do other beings created before ourselves? That is simply because his nature is more perfect, because his body is more subtilely and highly developed than ours, than ours so feeble, than ours conceived so roughly, encumbered with organs like over-complex springs, always fatigued, and always straining. For our body lives like a plant and like a beast, gaining a painful sustenance from air, from grasses, and from flesh. A living machine, the prey to sickness, to deformity, and to decay, it is of dust; a work at once coarse and delicate, irregular, pitifully simple, fantastic, and ill-made ingeniously; the first rough sketch of a being which might sometime be developed into something intelligent and perfect.

There are, after all, from the oyster up to the man, so few of us here on the earth. Why not one more, once the period which separates the appearances of different successive species has been accomplished?

Why not one more? Why not other trees with immense flowers dazzling and suffusing entire regions with their perfume? Why not other elements besides Fire, Air, Earth, and Water? They are four, only four, these nursing fathers of being! What a pity! Why are they not forty, four hundred, four thousand?

How poor, how mean, how wretched is everything! Granted, but not freely; conceived, but without genius; executed, but with no lightness of touch! The elephant, forsooth, the hippopotamus, how graceful! The camel, how elegant!

But what say you of the butterfly, that flying flower? I dream of one large as a hundred worlds, with wings whose shape, whose beauty, whose color, and whose manner of motion I cannot even describe. But I see it . . . it is going from star to star refreshing and perfuming each with the light and harmonious breathing of its course! . . . And whole peoples, high up there, watch, in ecstasy and ravishment, its passing! . . .

* * * * *

What is the matter with me? It is he, he, the Horla, who haunts me and makes me dream such follies! He is within me. He has become my soul; I shall kill him!

August 20th.

I shall kill him. I have seen him. I sat down last night at my table, and I pretended to be absorbed in writing. I knew very well that he would come and prowl round me, very near, so near that perhaps I should be able to touch him, to seize him. And then! . . . then I should have the strength of desperation; I should have hands and knees, breast, and brow, and teeth, to strangle, to crush, to bite, to tear.

And, straining every sense, I watched for him.

I had lit my two lamps and the eight candles on my mantel, exactly as though the light would help me to discover him!

Before me was my bed, an old oak bedstead with columns. On my right the chimney-piece. On my left the door, which I had carefully shut, after leaving it open for a while in order to attract him. Behind me, a tall wardrobe, with a looking-glass which I used every day for shaving and for dressing, and in which, every time I passed it, I had a habit of looking myself over from head to foot.

So I pretended to write in order to deceive him; for he, too, was watching. And suddenly I felt, I was certain, that he was reading over my shoulder, that he was there almost brushing my ear.

I jumped up with out-stretched hands, and turned round so quickly that I almost fell. Well? In my chamber it was as light as day, but I did not see myself in the glass! . . . It was empty, clear, deep, full of light! My image was not in it . . . and I stood there right in front of it, I! The great glass was clear from top to bottom. And with wild eyes I stared at this thing; and I did not dare to advance, I did not dare to move, feeling indeed that he was there, but that he would escape me, he, whose invisible body had absorbed the reflection of mine.

What fear I suffered! Then, all of a sudden, I began to perceive myself in a mist at the back of the mirror, in a mist as though through a sheet of water; and it seemed to me that this water glided from left to right, slowly, making my figure clearer, from second to second. It was like the ending of an eclipse. That which concealed me did not appear to possess sharp outlines, but merely a kind of opaque transparence, rarefying itself little by little.

At last I could distinguish my whole figure, just as I do each day when I look.

I had seen him! The terror of it remains still on me, causing me still to shiver.

August 21st.

Kill him? How? Since I cannot reach him? Poison? But he would see me mixing it in the water; and, besides, would our poisons have any effect on his supersensual body? No . . . no . . . of course not . . . What then? . . . what then?

August 22d.

I have had up a locksmith from Rouen, and I have ordered for my room some iron shutters like those which certain private houses in Paris have on the ground-floor as a protection against robbers. He is also to make me an iron door. I am appearing like a great coward, but at that I laugh! . . .

Sept. 10th.

Rouen. Hôtel Continental. It is accomplished . . . it is accomplished . . . but is he dead? My soul is overwhelmed by what I have seen.

Yesterday the locksmith, having fitted my shutters and my iron door, I left everything open until midnight, although it began to be very cold.

All of a sudden I felt that he was there, and a joy, a mad joy seized me. I rose gently, and I walked up and down for a long time in order to put him off his guard. Then I carelessly took off my boots and put on my slippers. Then I closed my iron shutters, and, returning tranquilly to the door, I closed that also and double-locked it. Again returning to the window, I secured the shutter with a padlock, and put the key in my pocket.

All of a sudden I understood that he was stirring anxiously round me; that, in his turn now, he was afraid; that he was commanding me to open. I came near yielding; I did not yield, but, setting my back against the door, I opened it on a crack just wide enough for me to pass through backward; and as I am very tall, my head touched the lintel. I was sure that he could not have escaped, and I shut him in all alone—all alone! What happiness! I had him fast! Then I went downstairs, running. In the drawing-room under my bedchamber I took the two lamps, and I poured oil over the carpet, over the furniture, over everything; then I set fire to it and I escaped from the house after having double-locked on the outside the great hall door.

And I hid myself at the bottom of the garden in a thicket of laurels. How long it was! How long it was! All remained black, silent, immobile; not a breath of air, not a star in the great mountains of clouds which I could not see, but which rested on my soul so heavily, so heavily.

I watched my house and I waited. How long it was! I had begun to think that the fire had gone out of itself, or that he had extinguished it. Then one of the windows on the ground-floor cracked under the pressure of the inner conflagration, and a tongue of flame—a great tongue of red and yellow flame—long and soft and caressing, climbed up along the white wall and kissed the very roof. A glow ran over the trees, the branches, the leaves, and a shiver—a shiver of fear also! The birds awoke; a dog began to howl; it seemed to me that the day itself was getting up! Soon two other windows burst open, and I saw that the whole ground-floor of my house was nothing but a dreadful brazier. But a cry—an awful cry—sharp, heart-rending—a woman's shriek—came out into the night, and two windows in the garret opened! I had forgotten my servants! I saw their wild faces, their waving arms! . . .

Then, mad with horror, I set off running to the village, shouting "Help! help! Fire! fire!" I met people already hastening to the scene, and I returned with them to look!

The house was now simply a horrible and magnificent stake—a monstrous stake—illuminating all the country—a stake at which men were burning, and at which he burned also—He, He, my prisoner, the new Being, the new master, the Horla!

Suddenly the entire roof fell in between the walls, and a volcano of flame shot upward to the sky. Through the windows open upon the furnace I saw the fiery vat, and I thought: he is there in that burning oven—dead . . .

Dead? Perhaps . . . But his body? His body, which the light of day could pass through, is it not perhaps indestructible by such means as destroy our bodies?

What if he be not dead? . . . Time alone, perhaps, has power over the Being Invisible, the Being Terrible. Why a transparent body? why an imperceptible body? why the body of a Spirit, if he too must fear misfortunes, wounds, infirmities, premature destruction?

Premature destruction? All human terror springs from the idea of that. After Man, the Horla. After him who can die any day, any hour, any moment, by any accident, has come He who shall die only on his appointed day, at his appointed hour, at his appointed minute, having touched the appointed limit of existence!

No . . . no . . . there is no doubt, there is no doubt . . . I have not killed him . . . Then . . . then . . . I see . . . it is plain . . . yes, it is plain that I must . . . kill . . . myself!

THE RAVEN

Edgar Allan Poe

Once upon a midnight dreary, while I pondered, weak and weary,
Over many a quaint and curious volume of forgotten lore,
While I nodded, nearly napping, suddenly there came a tapping,
As of some one gently rapping, rapping at my chamber door.
" 'Tis some visiter," I muttered, "tapping at my chamber door—
Only this, and nothing more."

Ah, distinctly I remember it was in the bleak December,
And each separate dying ember wrought its ghost upon the floor.
Eagerly I wished the morrow;—vainly I had sought to borrow
From my books surcease of sorrow—sorrow for the lost Lenore—
For the rare and radiant maiden whom the angels name Lenore—
Nameless here for evermore.

And the silken sad uncertain rustling of each purple curtain
Thrilled me—filled me with fantastic terrors never felt before;
So that now, to still the beating of my heart, I stood repeating
" 'Tis some visiter entreating entrance at my chamber door—
Some late visiter entreating entrance at my chamber door;—
This it is, and nothing more."

Presently my soul grew stronger; hesitating then no longer,
"Sir," said I, "or Madam, truly your forgiveness I implore;
But the fact is I was napping, and so gently you came rapping,
And so faintly you came tapping, tapping at my chamber door,
That I scarce was sure I heard you"—here I opened wide the door;—
Darkness there and nothing more.

Deep into that darkness peering, long I stood there wondering, fearing,
Doubting, dreaming dreams no mortal ever dared to dream before;
But the silence was unbroken, and the darkness gave no token,
And the only word there spoken was the whispered word, "Lenore!"
This I whispered, and an echo murmured back the word, "Lenore!"—
Merely this, and nothing more.

Back into the chamber turning, all my soul within me burning,
Soon I heard again a tapping somewhat louder than before.
"Surely," said I, "surely that is something at my window lattice;
Let me see, then, what thereat is, and this mystery explore—
Let my heart be still a moment and this mystery explore;—
'Tis the wind and nothing more!"

Open here I flung the shutter, when, with many a flirt and flutter,
In there stepped a stately raven of the saintly days of yore;
Not the least obeisance made he; not an instant stopped or stayed he;
But, with mien of lord or lady, perched above my chamber door—
Perched upon a bust of Pallas just above my chamber door—
Perched, and sat, and nothing more.

Then this ebony bird beguiling my sad fancy into smiling,
By the grave and stern decorum of the countenance it wore,
"Though thy crest be shorn and shaven, thou," I said, "art sure no craven,
Ghastly grim and ancient raven wandering from the Nightly shore—
Tell me what thy lordly name is on the Night's Plutonian shore!"
Quoth the raven, "Nevermore."

Much I marvelled this ungainly fowl to hear discourse so plainly,
Though its answer little meaning—little relevancy bore;
For we cannot help agreeing that no living human being
Ever yet was blessed with seeing bird above his chamber door—
Bird or beast upon the sculptured bust above his chamber door,
With such name as "Nevermore."

But the raven, sitting lonely on the placid bust, spoke only
That one word, as if his soul in that one word he did outpour.
Nothing farther then he uttered—not a feather then he fluttered—
Till I scarcely more than muttered "Other friends have flown before—
On the morrow he will leave me, as my hopes have flown before."
Then the bird said, "Nevermore."

Startled at the stillness broken by reply so aptly spoken,
"Doubtless," said I, "what it utters is its only stock and store
Caught from some unhappy master whom unmerciful Disaster
Followed fast and followed faster till his songs one burden bore—
Till the dirges of his Hope that melancholy burden bore
Of "Never—nevermore."

But the raven still beguiling all my sad soul into smiling,
Straight I wheeled a cushioned seat in front of bird, and bust and door;
Then, upon the velvet sinking, I betook myself to linking
Fancy unto fancy, thinking what this ominous bird of yore—
What this grim, ungainly, ghastly, gaunt and ominous bird of yore
Meant in croaking "Nevermore."

This I sat engaged in guessing, but no syllable expressing
To the fowl whose fiery eyes now burned into my bosom's core;
This and more I sat divining, with my head at ease reclining
On the cushion's velvet lining that the lamplght gloated o'er,
But whose velvet violet lining with the lamplight gloating o'er,
She shall press, ah, nevermore!

Then, methought, the air grew denser, perfumed from an unseen censer
Swung by Angels whose faint foot-falls tinkled on the tufted floor.
"Wretch," I cried, "thy God hath lent thee—by these angels he hath sent thee
Respite—respite and nepenthe from thy memories of Lenore;
Quaff, oh quaff this kind nepenthe and forget this lost Lenore!"
Quoth the raven, "Nevermore."

"Prophet!" said I, "thing of evil!—prophet still, if bird or devil!—
Whether Tempter sent, or whether tempest tossed thee here ashore,
Desolate yet all undaunted, on this desert land enchanted—
On this home by Horror haunted—tell me truly, I implore—
Is there—is there balm in Gilead?—tell me—tell me, I implore!"
Quoth the raven, "Nevermore."

"Prophet!" said I, "thing of evil—prophet still, if bird or devil!
By that Heaven that bends above us—by that God we both adore—
Tell this soul with sorrow laden if, within the distant Aidenn,
It shall clasp a sainted maiden whom the angels name Lenore—
Clasp a rare and radiant maiden whom the angels name Lenore."
Quoth the raven, "Nevermore."

"Be that word our sign of parting, bird or fiend!" I shrieked, upstarting—
"Get thee back into the tempest and the Night's Plutonian shore!
Leave no black plume as a token of that lie thy soul hath spoken!
Leave my loneliness unbroken!—quit the bust above my door!
Take thy beak from out my heart, and take thy form from off my door!"
Quoth the raven, "Nevermore."

And the raven, never flitting, still is sitting, still is sitting
On the pallid bust of Pallas just above my chamber door;
And his eyes have all the seeming of a demon's that is dreaming,
And the lamp-light o'er him streaming throws his shadow on the floor;
And my soul from out that shadow that lies floating on the floor
Shall be lifted—nevermore!

THE MAN WHO FOUND OUT

Algernon Blackwood

I

Professor Mark Ebor, the scientist, led a double life, and the only persons who knew it were his assistant, Dr. Laidlaw, and his publishers. But a double life need not always be a bad one, and, as Dr. Laidlaw and the gratified publishers well knew, the parallel lives of this particular man were equally good, and indefinitely produced would certainly have ended in a heaven somewhere that can suitably contain such strangely opposite characteristics as his remarkable personality combined.

For Mark Ebor, F.R.S., etc., etc., was that unique combination hardly ever met with in actual life, a man of science and a mystic.

As the first, his name stood in the gallery of the great, and as the second—but there came the mystery! For under the pseudonym of "Pilgrim" (the author of that brilliant series of books that appealed to so many), his identity was as well concealed as that of the anonymous writer of the weather reports in a daily newspaper. Thousands read the sanguine, optimistic, stimulating little books that issued annually from the pen of "Pilgrim," and thousands bore their daily burdens better for having read; while the Press generally agreed that the author, besides being an incorrigible enthusiast and optimist, was also—a woman; but no one ever succeeded in penetrating the veil of anonymity and discovering that "Pilgrim" and the biologist were one and the same person.

Mark Ebor, as Dr. Laidlaw knew him in his laboratory, was one man; but Mark Ebor, as he sometimes saw him after work was over, with rapt eyes and ecstatic face, discussing the possibilities of "union with God" and the future of the human race, was quite another.

"I have always held, as you know," he was saying one evening as he sat in the little study beyond the laboratory with his assistant and intimate, "that Vision should play a large part in the life of the awakened man—not to be regarded as infallible, of course, but to be observed and made use of as a guide-post to possibilities—"

"I am aware of your peculiar views, sir," the young doctor put in deferentially, yet with a certain impatience.

"For Visions come from a region of the consciousness where observation and experiment are out of the question," pursued the other with enthusiasm, not noticing the interruption, "and, while they should be checked by reason afterwards, they should not be laughed at or ignored. All inspiration, I hold, is of the nature of interior Vision, and all our best knowledge has come—such is my confirmed belief—as a sudden revelation to the brain prepared to receive it—"

"Prepared by hard work first, by concentration, by the closest possible study of ordinary phenomena," Dr. Laidlaw allowed himself to observe.

"Perhaps," sighed the other; "but by a process, none the less, of spiritual illumination. The best match in the world will not light a candle unless the wick be first suitably prepared."

It was Laidlaw's turn to sigh. He knew so well the impossibility of arguing with his chief when he was in the regions of the mystic, but at the same time the respect he felt for his tremendous attainments was so sincere that he always listened with attention and deference, wondering how far the great man would go and to what end this curious combination of logic and "illumination" would eventually lead him.

"Only last night," continued the elder man, a sort of light coming into his rugged features, "the vision came to me again—the one that has haunted me at intervals ever since my youth, and that will not be denied."

Dr. Laidlaw fidgeted in his chair.

"About the Tablets of the Gods, you mean—and that they lie somewhere hidden in the sands," he said patiently. A sudden gleam of interest came into his face as he turned to catch the professor's reply.

"And that I am to be the one to find them, to decipher them, and to give the great knowledge to the world—"

"Who will not believe," laughed Laidlaw shortly, yet interested in spite of his thinly-veiled contempt.

"Because even the keenest minds, in the right sense of the word, are hopelessly—unscientific," replied the other gently, his face positively aglow with the memory of his vision. "Yet what is more likely," he continued after a moment's pause, peering into space with rapt eyes that saw things too wonderful for exact language to describe, "than that there should have been given to man in the first ages of the world some record of the purpose and problem that had been set him to solve? In a word," he cried, fixing his shining eyes upon the face of his perplexed assistant, "that God's messengers in the far-off ages should have given to His creatures some full statement of the secret of the world, of the secret of the soul, of the meaning of life and death—the explanation of our being here, and to what great end we are destined in the ultimate fullness of things?"

Dr. Laidlaw sat speechless. These outbursts of mystical enthusiasm he had witnessed before. With any other man he would not have listened to a single sentence, but to Professor Ebor, man of knowledge and profound investigator, he listened with respect, because he regarded this condition as temporary and pathological, and in some sense a reaction from the intense strain of the prolonged mental concentration of many days.

He smiled, with something between sympathy and resignation as he met the other's rapt gaze.

"But you have said, sir, at other times, that you consider the ultimate secrets to be screened from all possible—"

"The ultimate secrets, yes," came the unperturbed reply; "but that there lies buried somewhere an indestructible record of the secret meaning of life, originally known to men in the days of their pristine innocence, I am convinced. And, by this strange vision so often vouchsafed to me, I am equally sure that one day it shall be given to me to announce to a weary world this glorious and terrific message."

And he continued at great length and in glowing language to describe the species of vivid dream that had come to him at intervals since earliest childhood, showing in detail how he discovered these very Tablets of the Gods, and proclaimed their splendid contents—whose precise nature was always, however, withheld from him in the vision—to a patient and suffering humanity.

"The Scrutator, sir, well described 'Pilgrim' as the Apostle of Hope," said the young doctor gently, when he had finished; "and now, if that reviewer could hear you speak and realize from what strange depths comes your simple faith—"

The professor held up his hand, and the smile of a little child broke over his face like sunshine in the morning.

"Half the good my books do would be instantly destroyed," he said sadly; "they would say that I wrote with my tongue in my cheek. But wait," he added significantly; "wait till I find these Tablets of the Gods! Wait till I hold the solutions of the old world-problems in my hands! Wait till the light of this new revelation breaks upon confused humanity, and it wakes to find its bravest hopes justified! Ah, then, my dear Laidlaw—"

He broke off suddenly; but the doctor, cleverly guessing the thought in his mind, caught him up immediately.

"Perhaps this very summer," he said, trying hard to make the suggestion keep pace with honesty; "in your explorations in Assyria—your digging in the remote civilization of what was once Chaldea, you may find—what you dream of—"

The professor held up his hand, and the smile of a fine old face.

"Perhaps," he murmured softly, "perhaps!"

And the young doctor, thanking the gods of science that his leader's aberrations were of so harmless a character, went home strong in the certitude of his knowledge of externals, proud that he was able to refer his visions to self-suggestion, and wondering complaisantly whether in his old age he might not after all suffer himself from visitations of the very kind that afflicted his respected chief.

And as he got into bed and thought again of his master's rugged face, and finely shaped head, and the deep lines traced by years of work and self-discipline, he turned over on his pillow and fell asleep with a sigh that was half of wonder, half of regret.

II

It was in February, nine months later, when Dr. Laidlaw made his way to Charing Cross to meet his chief after his long absence of travel and exploration. The vision about the so-called Tablets of the Gods had meanwhile passed almost entirely from his memory.

There were few people in the train, for the stream of traffic was now running the other way, and he had no difficulty in finding the man he had come to meet. The shock of white hair beneath the low-crowned felt hat was alone enough to distinguish him by easily.

"Here I am at last!" exclaimed the professor, somewhat wearily, clasping his friend's hand as he listened to the young doctor's warm greetings and questions. "Here I am—a little older, and much dirtier than when you last saw me!" He glanced down laughingly at his travel-stained garments.

"And much wiser," said Laidlaw, with a smile, as he bustled about the platform for porters and gave his chief the latest scientific news.

At last they came down to practical considerations.

"And your luggage—where is that? You must have tons of it, I suppose?" said Laidlaw.

"Hardly anything," Professor Ebor answered. "Nothing, in fact, but what you see."

"Nothing but this hand-bag?" laughed the other, thinking he was joking.

"And a small portmanteau in the van," was the quiet reply. "I have no other luggage."

"You have no other luggage?" repeated Laidlaw, turning sharply to see if he were in earnest.

"Why should I need more?" the professor added simply.

Something in the man's face, or voice, or manner—the doctor hardly knew which—suddenly struck him as strange. There was a change in him, a change so profound—so little on the surface, that is—that at first he had not become aware of it. For a moment it was as though an utterly alien personality stood before him in that noisy, bustling throng. Here, in all the homely, friendly turmoil of a Charing Cross crowd, a curious feeling of cold passed over his heart, touching his life with icy finger, so that he actually trembled and felt afraid.

He looked up quickly at his friend, his mind working with startled and unwelcome thoughts.

"Only this?" he repeated, indicating the bag. "But where's all the stuff you went away with? And—have you brought nothing home—no treasures?"

"This is all I have," the other said briefly. The pale smile that went with the words caused the doctor a second indescribable sensation of uneasiness. Something was very wrong, something was very queer; he wondered now that he had not noticed it sooner.

"The rest follows, of course, by slow freight," he added tactfully, and as naturally as possible. "But come, sir, you must be tired and in want of food after your long journey. I'll get a taxi at once, and we can see about the other luggage afterwards."

It seemed to him he hardly knew quite what he was saying; the change in his friend had come upon him so suddenly and now grew upon him more and more distressingly. Yet he could not make out exactly in what it consisted. A terrible suspicion began to take shape in his mind, troubling him dreadfully.

"I am neither very tired, nor in need of food, thank you," the professor said quietly. "And this is all I have. There is no luggage to follow. I have brought home nothing—nothing but what you see."

His words conveyed finality. They got into a taxi, tipped the porter, who had been staring in amazement at the venerable figure of the scientist, and were conveyed slowly and noisily to the house in the north of London where the laboratory was, the scene of their labours of years.

And the whole way Professor Ebor uttered no word, nor did Dr. Laidlaw find the courage to ask a single question.

It was only late that night, before he took his departure, as the two men were standing before the fire in the study—that study where they had discussed so many problems of vital and absorbing interest—that Dr. Laidlaw at last found strength to come to the point with direct questions. The professor had been giving him a superficial and desultory account of his travels, of his journeys by camel, of his encampments among the mountains and in the desert, and of his explorations among the buried temples, and, deeper, into the waste of the pre-historic sands, when suddenly the doctor came to the desired point with a kind of nervous rush, almost like a frightened boy.

"And you found—" he began stammering, looking hard at the other's dreadfully altered face, from which every line of hope and cheerfulness seemed to have been obliterated as a sponge wipes markings from a slate—"you found—"

"I found," replied the other, in a solemn voice, and it was the voice of the mystic rather than the man of science—"I found what I went to seek. The vision never once failed me. It led me straight to the place like a star in the heavens. I found—the Tablets of the Gods."

Dr. Laidlaw caught his breath, and steadied himself on the back of a chair. The words fell like particles of ice upon his heart. For the first time the professor had uttered the well-known phrase without the glow of light and wonder in his face that always accompanied it.

"You have—brought them?" he faltered.

"I have brought them home," said the other, in a voice with a ring like iron; "and I have—deciphered them."

Profound despair, the bloom of outer darkness, the dead sound of a hopeless soul freezing in the utter cold of space seemed to fill in the pauses between the brief sentences. A silence followed, during which Dr. Laidlaw saw nothing but the white face before him alternately fade and return. And it was like the face of a dead man.

"They are, alas, indestructible," he heard the voice continue, with its even, metallic ring.

"Indestructible," Laidlaw repeated mechanically, hardly knowing what he was saying.

Again a silence of several minutes passed, during which, with a creeping cold about his heart, he stood and stared into the eyes of the man he had known and loved so long—aye, and worshipped, too; the man who had first opened his own eyes when they were blind, and had led him to the gates of knowledge, and no little distance along the difficult path beyond; the man who, in another direction, had passed on the strength of his faith into the hearts of thousands by his books.

"I may see them?" he asked at last, in a low voice he hardly recognized as his own. "You will let me know—their message?"

Professor Ebor kept his eyes fixedly upon his assistant's face as he answered with a smile that was more like the grin of death than a living human smile.

"When I am gone," he whispered; "when I have passed away. Then you shall find them and read the translation I have made. And then, too, in your turn, you must try, with the latest resources of science at your disposal to aid you, to compass their utter destruction." He paused a moment, and his face grew pale as the face of a corpse. "Until that time," he added presently without looking up, "I must ask you not to refer to the subject again—and to keep my confidence meanwhile—*ab—so—lute—ly.*"

III

A year passed slowly by, and at the end of it Dr. Laidlaw had found it necessary to sever his working connexion with his friend and one-time leader. Professor Ebor was no longer the same man. The light had gone out of his life; the laboratory was closed; he no longer put pen to paper or applied his mind to a single problem. In the short space of a few months he had passed from a hale and hearty man of late middle life to the condition of old age—a man collapsed and on the edge of dissolution. Death, it was plain, lay waiting for him in the shadows of any day—and he knew it.

To describe faithfully the nature of this profound alteration in his character and temperament is not easy, but Dr. Laidlaw summed it up to himself in three words: *Loss of Hope.* The splendid mental powers remained indeed undimmed, but the incentive to use them—to use them for the help of others—had gone. The character still held to its fine and unselfish habits of years, but the far goal to which they had been the leading strings had faded away. The desire for knowledge—knowledge for its own sake—had died, and the passionate hope which hitherto had animated with tireless energy the heart and brain of this splendidly equipped intellect had suffered total eclipse. The central fires had gone out. Nothing was worth doing, thinking, working for. There was nothing to work for any longer!

The professor's first step was to recall as many of his books as possible; his second to close his laboratory and stop all research. He gave no explanation, he invited no questions. His whole personality crumbled away, so to speak, till his daily life became a mere mechanical process of clothing the body, feeding the body, keeping it in good health so as to avoid physical discomfort, and, above all, doing nothing that could interfere with sleep. The professor did everything he could to lengthen the hours of sleep, and therefore of forgetfulness.

It was all clear enough to Dr. Laidlaw. A weaker man, he knew, would have sought to lose himself in one form or another of sensual indulgence—sleeping-draughts, drink, the first pleasures that came to hand. Self-destruction would have been the method of a little bolder type; and deliberate evil-doing, poisoning with his awful knowledge all he could, the means of still another kind of man. Mark Ebor was none of these. He held himself under fine control, facing silently and without complaint the terrible facts he honestly believed himself to have been unfortunate enough to discover. Even to his intimate friend and assistant, Dr. Laidlaw, he vouchsafed no word of true explanation or lament. He went straight forward to the end, knowing well that the end was not very far away.

And death came very quietly one day to him, as he was sitting in the arm-chair of the study, directly facing the doors of the laboratory—the doors that no longer opened. Dr. Laidlaw, by happy chance, was with him at the time, and just able to reach his side in response to the sudden painful efforts for breath; just in time, too, to catch the murmured words that fell from the pallid lips like a message from the other side of the grave.

"Read them, if you must; and, if you can—destroy. But"—his voice sank so low that Dr. Laidlaw only just caught the dying syllables—"but—never, never—give them to the world."

And like a grey bundle of dust loosely gathered up in an old garment the professor sank back into his chair and expired.

But this was only the death of the body. His spirit had died two years before.

IV

The estate of the dead man was small and uncomplicated, and Dr. Laidlaw, as sole executor and residuary legatee, had no difficulty in settling it up. A month after the funeral he was sitting alone in his upstairs library, the last sad duties completed, and his mind full of poignant memories and regrets for the loss of a friend he had revered and loved, and to whom his debt was so incalculably great. The last two years, indeed, had been for him terrible. To watch the swift decay of the greatest combination of heart and brain he had ever known, and to realize he was powerless to help, was a source of profound grief to him that would remain to the end of his days.

At the same time an insatiable curiosity possessed him. The study of dementia was, of course, outside his special province as a specialist, but he knew enough of it to understand how small a matter might be the actual cause of how great an illusion, and he had been devoured from the very beginning by a ceaseless and increasing anxiety to know what the professor had found in the sands of "Chaldea," what these precious Tablets of the Gods might be, and particularly—for this was the real cause that had sapped the man's sanity and hope—what the inscription was that he had believed to have deciphered thereon.

The curious feature of it all to his own mind was, that whereas his friend had dreamed of finding a message of glorious hope and comfort, he had apparently found (so far as he had found anything intelligible at all, and not invented the whole thing in his dementia) that the secret of the world, and the meaning of life and death, was of so terrible a nature that it robbed the heart of courage and the soul of hope. What, then, could be the contents of the little brown parcel the professor had bequeathed to him with his pregnant dying sentences?

Actually his hand was trembling as he turned to the writing-table and began slowly to unfasten a small old-fashioned desk on which the small gilt initials "M.E." stood forth as a melancholy memento. He put the key into the lock and half turned it. Then, suddenly, he stopped and looked about him. Was that a sound at the back of the room? It was just as though someone had laughed and then tried to smother the laugh with a cough. A slight shiver ran over him as he stood listening.

"This is absurd," he said aloud; "too absurd for belief—that I should be so nervous! It's the effect of curiosity unduly prolonged." He smiled a little sadly and his eyes wandered to the blue summer sky and the plane trees swaying in the wind below his window. "It's the reaction," he continued. "The curiosity of two years to be quenched in a single moment! The nervous tension, of course, must be considerable."

He turned back to the brown desk and opened it without further delay. His hand was firm now, and he took out the paper parcel that lay inside without a tremor. It was heavy. A moment later there lay on the table before him a couple of weather-worn plaques of grey stone—they looked like stone, although they felt like metal—on which he saw markings of a curious character that might have been the mere tracings of natural forces through the ages, or, equally well, the half-obliterated hieroglyphics cut upon their surface in past centuries by the more or less untutored hand of a common scribe.

He lifted each stone in turn and examined it carefully. It seemed to him that a faint glow of heat passed from the substance into his skin, and he put them down again suddenly, as with a gesture of uneasiness.

"A very clever, or a very imaginative man," he said to himself, "who could squeeze the secrets of life and death from such broken lines as those!"

Then he turned to a yellow envelope lying beside them in the desk, with the single word on the outside in the writing of the professor—the word *Translation.*

"Now," he thought, taking it up with a sudden violence to conceal his nervousness, "now for the great solution. Now to learn the meaning of the worlds, and why mankind was made, and why discipline is worth while, and sacrifice and pain the true law of advancement."

There was the shadow of a sneer in his voice, and yet something in him shivered at the same time. He held the envelope as though weighing it in his hand, his mind pondering many things. Then curiosity won the day, and he suddenly tore it open with the gesture of an actor who tears open a letter on the stage, knowing there is no real writing inside at all.

A page of finely written script in the late scientist's handwriting lay before him. He read it through from beginning to end, missing no word, uttering each syllable distinctly under his breath as he read.

The pallor of his face grew ghastly as he neared the end. He began to shake all over as with ague. His breath came heavily in gasps. He still gripped the sheet of paper, however, and deliberately, as by an intense effort of will, read it through a second time from beginning to end. And this time, as the last syllable dropped from his lips, the whole face of the man flamed with a sudden and terrible anger. His skin became deep, deep red, and he clenched his teeth. With all the strength of his vigorous soul he was struggling to keep control of himself.

For perhaps five minutes he stood there beside the table without stirring a muscle. He might have been carved out of stone. His eyes were shut, and only the heaving of the chest betrayed the fact that he was a living being. Then, with a strange quietness, he lit a match and applied it to the sheet of paper he held in his hand. The ashes fell slowly about him, piece by piece, and he blew them from the window-sill into the air, his eyes following them as they floated away on the summer wind that breathed so warmly over the world.

He turned back slowly into the room. Although his actions and movements were absolutely steady and controlled, it was clear that he was on the edge of violent action. A hurricane might burst upon the still room any moment. His muscles were tense and rigid. Then, suddenly, he whitened, collapsed, and sank backwards into a chair, like a tumbled bundle of inert matter. He had fainted.

In less than half an hour he recovered consciousness and sat up. As before, he made no sound. Not a syllable passed his lips. He rose quietly and looked about the room.

Then he did a curious thing.

Taking a heavy stick from the rack in the corner he approached the mantlepiece, and with a heavy shattering blow he smashed the clock to pieces. The glass fell in shivering atoms.

"Cease your lying voice for ever," he said, in a curiously still, even tone. "There is no such thing as time!"

He took the watch from his pocket, swung it round several times by the long gold chain, smashed it into smithereens against the wall with a single blow, and then walked into his laboratory next door, and hung its broken body on the bones of the skeleton in the corner of the room.

"Let one damned mockery hang upon another," he said smiling oddly. "Delusions, both of you, and cruel as false!"

He slowly moved back to the front room. He stopped opposite the bookcase where stood in a row the "Scriptures of the World," choicely bound and exquisitely printed, the late professor's most treasured possession, and next to them several books signed "Pilgrim."

One by one he took them from the shelf and hurled them through the open window.

"A devil's dreams! A devil's foolish dreams!" he cried, with a vicious laugh.

Presently he stopped from sheer exhaustion. He turned his eyes slowly to the wall opposite, where hung a weird array of Eastern swords and daggers, scimitars and spears, the collections of many journeys. He crossed the room and ran his finger along the edge. His mind seemed to waver.

"No," he muttered presently; "not that way. There are easier and better ways than that."

He took his hat and passed downstairs into the street.

V

It was five o'clock, and the June sun lay hot upon the pavement. He felt the metal door-knob burn the palm of his hand.

"Ah, Laidlaw, this is well met," cried a voice at his elbow; "I was in the act of coming to see you. I've a case that will interest you, and besides, I remembered that you flavoured your tea with orange leaves!—and I admit—"

It was Alexis Stephen, the great hypnotic doctor.

"I've had no tea to-day," Laidlaw said, in a dazed manner, after staring for a moment as though the other had struck him in the face. A new idea had entered his mind.

"What's the matter?" asked Dr. Stephen quickly. "Something's wrong with you. It's this sudden heat, or overwork. Come, man, let's go inside."

A sudden light broke upon the face of the younger man, the light of a heaven-sent inspiration. He looked into his friend's face, and told a direct lie.

"Odd," he said, "I myself was just coming to see you. I have something of great importance to test your confidence with. But in your house, please," as Stephen urged him towards his own door—"in your house. It's only round the corner, and I—I cannot go back there—to my rooms—till I have told you.

"I'm your patient—for the moment," he added stammeringly as soon as they were seated in the privacy of the hypnotist's sanctum, "and I want—er—"

"My dear Laidlaw," interrupted the other, in that soothing voice of command which had suggested to many a suffering soul that the cure for its pain lay in the powers of its own reawakened will, "I am always at your service, as you know. You have only to tell me what I can do for you, and I will do it." He showed every desire to help him out. His manner was indescribably tactful and direct.

Dr. Laidlaw looked up into his face.

"I surrender my will to you," he said, already calmed by the other's healing presence, "and I want you to treat me hypnotically—and at once. I want you to suggest to me"—his voice became very tense—"that I shall forget—forget till I die—everything that has occurred to me during the last two hours; till I die, mind," he added, with solemn emphasis, "till I die."

He floundered and stammered like a frightened boy. Alexis Stephen looked at him fixedly without speaking.

"And further," Laidlaw continued, "I want you to ask me no questions. I wish to forget for ever something I have recently discovered—something so terrible and yet so obvious that I can hardly understand why it is not patent to every mind in the world—for I have had a moment of absolute *clear vision*—of merciless clairvoyance. But I want no one else in the whole world to know what it is—least of all, old friend, yourself."

He talked in utter confusion, and hardly knew what he was saying. But the pain on his face and the anguish in his voice were an instant passport to the other's heart.

"Nothing is easier," replied Dr. Stephen, after a hesitation so slight that the other probably did not even notice it. "Come into my other room where we shall not be disturbed. I can heal you. Your memory of the last two hours shall be wiped out as though it had never been. You can trust me absolutely."

"I know I can," Laidlaw said simply, as he followed him in.

VI

An hour later they passed back into the front room again. The sun was already behind the houses opposite, and the shadows began to gather.

"I went off easily?" Laidlaw asked.

"You were a little obstinate at first. But though you came in like a lion, you went out like a lamb. I let you sleep a bit afterwards."

Dr. Stephen kept his eyes rather steadily upon his friend's face.

"What were you doing by the fire before you came here?" he asked, pausing, in a casual tone, as he lit a cigarette and handed the case to his patient.

"I? Let me see. Oh, I know; I was worrying my way through poor old Ebor's papers and things. I'm his executor, you know. Then I got weary and came out for a whiff of air." He spoke lightly and with perfect naturalness. Obviously he was telling the truth. "I prefer specimens to papers," he laughed cheerily.

"I know, I know," said Dr. Stephen, holding a lighted match for the cigarette. His face wore an expression of content. The experiment had been a complete success. The memory of the last two hours was wiped out utterly. Laidlaw was already chatting gaily and easily about a dozen other things that interested him. Together they went out into the street, and at his door Dr. Stephen left him with a joke and a wry face that made his friend laugh heartily.

"Don't dine on the professor's old papers by mistake," he cried, as he vanished down the street.

Dr. Laidlaw went up to his study at the top of the house. Half way down he met his housekeeper, Mrs. Fewings. She was flustered and excited, and her face was very red and perspiring.

"There've been burglars here," she cried excitedly, "or something funny! All your things is just any'ow, sir. I found everything all about everywhere!" She was very confused. In this orderly and very precise establishment it was unusual to find a thing out of place.

"Oh, my specimens!" cried the doctor, dashing up the rest of the stairs at top speed. "Have they been touched or—"

He flew to the door of the laboratory. Mrs. Fewings panted up heavily behind him.

"The labatry ain't been touched," she explained, breathlessly, "but they smashed the libry clock and they've 'ung your gold watch, sir, on the skelinton's hands. And the books that weren't no value they flung out er the window just like so much rubbish. They must have been wild drunk, Dr. Laidlaw, sir!"

The young scientist made a hurried examination of the rooms. Nothing of value was missing. He began to wonder what kind of burglars they were. He looked up sharply at Mrs. Fewings standing in the doorway. For a moment he seemed to cast about in his mind for something.

"Odd," he said at length. "I only left here an hour ago and everything was all right then."

"Was it, sir? Yes, sir." She glanced sharply at him. Her room looked out upon the courtyard, and she must have seen the books come crashing down, and also have heard her master leave the house a few minutes later.

"And what's this rubbish the brutes have left?" he cried, taking up two slabs of worn gray stone, on the writing-table. "Bath brick, or something, I do declare."

He looked very sharply again at the confused and troubled housekeeper.

"Throw them on the dust heap, Mrs. Fewings, and—and let me know if anything is missing in the house, and I will notify the police this evening."

When she left the room he went into the laboratory and took his watch off the skeleton's fingers. His face wore a troubled expression, but after a moment's thought it cleared again. His memory was a complete blank.

"I suppose I left it on the writing-table when I went out to take the air," he said. And there was no one present to contradict him.

He crossed to the window and blew carelessly some ashes of burned paper from the sill, and stood watching them as they floated away lazily over the tops of the trees.

LA GRANDE BRETÈCHE

Honoré de Balzac

Translated by Ellen Marriage
and Clara Bell

"Ah! madame," replied the doctor, "I have some appalling stories in my collection. But each one has its proper hour in a conversation—you know the pretty jest recorded by Chamfort, and said to the Duc de Fronsac: 'Between your sally and the present moment lie ten bottles of champagne.'"

"But it is two in the morning, and the story of Rosina has prepared us," said the mistress of the house.

"Tell us, Monsieur Bianchon!" was the cry on every side.

The obliging doctor bowed, and silence reigned.

"At about a hundred paces from Vendome, on the banks of the Loir," said he, "stands an old brown house, crowned with very high roofs, and so completely isolated that there is nothing near it, not even a fetid tannery or a squalid tavern, such as are commonly seen outside small towns. In front of this house is a garden down to the river, where the box shrubs, formerly clipped close to edge the walks, now straggle at their own will. A few willows, rooted in the stream, have grown up quickly like an enclosing fence, and half hide the house. The wild plants we call weeds have clothed the bank with their beautiful luxuriance. The fruit-trees, neglected for these ten years past, no longer bear a crop, and their suckers have formed a thicket. The espaliers are like a copse. The paths, once graveled, are overgrown with purslane; but, to be accurate there is no trace of a path.

"Looking down from the hilltop, to which cling the ruins of the old castle of the Dukes of Vendome, the only spot whence the eye can see into this enclosure, we think that at a time, difficult now to determine, this spot of earth must have been the joy of some country gentleman devoted to roses and tulips, in a word, to horticulture, but above all a lover of choice fruit. An arbor is visible, or rather the wreck of an arbor, and under it a table still stands not entirely destroyed by time. At the aspect of this garden that is no more, the negative joys of the peaceful life of the provinces may be divined as we divine the history of a worthy tradesman when we read the epitaph on his tomb. To complete the mournful and tender impressions which seize the soul, on one of the walls there is a sundial graced with this homely Christian motto, '*Ultimam cogita.*'

"The roof of this house is dreadfully dilapidated; the outside shutters are always closed; the balconies are hung with swallows' nests; the doors are for ever shut. Straggling grasses have outlined the flagstones of the steps with green; the ironwork is rusty. Moon and sun, winter, summer, and snow have eaten into the wood, warped the boards, peeled off the paint. The dreary silence is broken only by birds and cats, polecats, rats, and mice, free to scamper round, and fight, and eat each other. An invisible hand has written over it all: 'Mystery.'

"If, prompted by curiosity, you go to look at this house from the street, you will see a large gate, with a round-arched top; the children have made many holes in it. I learned later that this door had been blocked for ten years. Through these irregular breaches you will see that the side towards the courtyard is in perfect harmony with the side towards the garden. The same ruin prevails. Tufts of weeds outline the paving-stones; the walls are scored by enormous cracks, and the blackened coping is laced with a thousand festoons of pellitory. The stone steps are disjointed; the bell-cord is rotten; the gutter-spouts broken. What fire from heaven could have fallen there? By what decree has salt been sown on this dwelling? Has God been mocked here? Or was France betrayed? These are the questions we ask ourselves. Reptiles crawl over it, but give no reply. This empty and deserted house is a vast enigma of which the answer is known to none.

"It was formerly a little domain, held in fief, and is known as La Grande Bretèche. During my stay at Vendome, where Despleins had left me in charge of a rich patient, the sight of this strange dwelling became one of my keenest pleasures. Was it not far better than a ruin? Certain memories of indisputable authenticity attach themselves to a ruin; but this house, still standing, though being slowly destroyed by an avenging hand, contained a secret, an unrevealed thought. At the very least, it testified to a caprice. More than once in the evening I boarded the hedge, run wild, which surrounded the enclosure. I braved scratches, I got into this ownerless garden, this plot which was no longer public or private; I lingered there for hours gazing at the disorder. I would not, as the price of the story to which this strange scene no doubt was due, have asked a single question of any gossiping native. On that spot I wove delightful romances, and abandoned myself to little debauches of melancholy which enchanted me. If I had known the reason—perhaps quite commonplace—of this neglect, I should have lost the unwritten poetry which intoxicated me. To me this refuge represented the most various phases of human life, shadowed by misfortune; sometimes the peace of the graveyard without the dead, who speak in the language of epitaphs; one day I saw in it the home of lepers; another, the house of the Atridae; but, above all, I found there provincial life, with its contemplative ideas, its hour-glass existence. I often wept there, I never laughed.

"More than once I felt involuntary terrors as I heard overhead the dull hum of the wings of some hurrying wood-pigeon. The earth is dank; you must be on the watch for lizards, vipers, and frogs, wandering about with the wild freedom of nature; above all, you must have no fear of cold, for in a few moments you feel an icy cloak settle on your shoulders, like the Commendatore's hand on Don Giovanni's neck.

"One evening I felt a shudder; the wind had turned an old rusty weathercock, and the creaking sounded like a cry from the house, at the very moment when I was finishing a gloomy drama to account for this monumental embodiment of woe. I returned to my inn, lost in gloomy thoughts. When I had supped, the hostess came into my room with an air of mystery, and said, 'Monsieur, here is Monsieur Regnault.'

"'Who is Monsieur Regnault?'

"'What, sir, do you not know Monsieur Regnault?—Well, that's odd,' said she, leaving the room.

"On a sudden I saw a man appear, tall, slim, dressed in black, hat in hand, who came in like a ram ready to butt his opponent, showing a receding forehead, a small pointed head, and a colorless face of the hue of a glass of dirty water. You would have taken him for an usher. The stranger wore an old coat, much worn at the seams; but he had a diamond in his shirt frill, and gold rings in his ears.

"'Monsieur,' said I, 'whom have I the honor of addressing?'—He took a chair, placed himself in front of my fire, put his hat on my table, and answered while he rubbed his hands: 'Dear me, it is very cold.—Monsieur, I am Monsieur Regnault.'

"I was encouraging myself by saying to myself, '*Il bondo cani!* Seek!'

"'I am,' he went on, 'notary at Vendome.'

"'I am delighted to hear it, monsieur,' I exclaimed. 'But I am not in a position to make a will for reasons best known to myself.'

"'One moment!' said he, holding up his hand as though to gain silence. 'Allow me, monsieur, allow me! I am informed that you sometimes go to walk in the garden of la Grande Bretèche.'

"'Yes, monsieur.'

"'One moment!' said he, repeating his gesture. 'That constitutes a misdemeanor. Monsieur, as executor under the will of the late Comtesse de Merret, I come in her name to beg you to discontinue the practice. One moment! I am not a Turk, and do not wish to make a crime of it. And besides, you are free to be ignorant of the circumstances which compel me to leave the finest mansion in Vendome to fall into ruin. Nevertheless, monsieur, you must be a man of education, and you should know that the laws forbid, under heavy penalties, any trespass on enclosed property. A hedge is the same as a wall. But, the state in which the place is left may be an excuse for your curiosity. For my part, I should be quite content to make you free to come and go in the house; but being bound to respect the will of the testatrix, I have the honor, monsieur, to beg that you will go into the garden no more. I myself, monsieur, since the will was read, have never set foot in the house, which, as I had the honor of informing you, is part of the estate of the late Madame de Merret. We have done nothing there but verify the number of doors and windows to assess the taxes I have to pay annually out of the funds left for that purpose by the late Madame de Merret. Ah! my dear sir, her will made a great commotion in the town.'

"The good man paused to blow his nose. I respected his volubility, perfectly understanding that the administration of Madame de Merret's estate had been the most important event of his life, his reputation, his glory, his Restoration. As I was forced to bid farewell to my beautiful reveries and romances, I was to reject learning the truth on official authority.

"'Monsieur,' said I, 'would it be indiscreet if I were to ask you the reasons for such eccentricity?'

"At these words an expression, which revealed all the pleasure which men feel who are accustomed to ride a hobby, overspread the lawyer's countenance. He pulled up the collar of his shirt with an air, took out his snuffbox, opened it, and offered me a pinch; on my refusing, he took a large one. He was happy! A man who has no hobby does not know all the good to be got out of life. A hobby is the happy medium between a passion and a monomania. At this moment I understood the whole bearing of Sterne's charming passion, and had a perfect idea of the delight with which my uncle Toby, encouraged by Trim, bestrode his hobby-horse.

"'Monsieur,' said Monsieur Regnault, 'I was head-clerk in Monsieur Roguin's office, in Paris. A first-rate house, which you may have heard mentioned? No! An unfortunate bankruptcy made it famous.—Not having money enough to purchase a practice in Paris at the price to which they were run up in 1816, I came here and bought my predecessor's business. I had relations in Vendome; among others, a wealthy aunt, who allowed me to marry her daughter.—Monsieur,' he went on after a little pause, 'three months after being licensed by the Keeper of the Seals, one evening, as I was going to bed—it was before my marriage—I was sent for by Madame la Comtesse de Merret, to her Chateau of Merret. Her maid, a good girl, who is now a servant in this inn, was waiting at my door with the Countess' own carriage. Ah! one moment! I ought to tell you that Monsieur le Comte de Merret had gone to Paris to die two months before I came here. He came to a miserable end, flinging himself into every kind of dissipation. You understand?

"'On the day when he left, Madame la Comtesse had quitted la Grand Bretèche, having dismantled it. Some people even say that she had burnt all the furniture, the hangings—in short, all the chattels and furniture whatever used in furnishing the premises now let by the said M.—(Dear, what am I saying? I beg your pardon, I thought I was dictating a lease.)—In short, that she burnt everything in the meadow at Merret. Have you been to Merret, monsieur?—No,' said he, answering himself, 'Ah, it is a very fine place.'

"'For about three months previously,' he went on, with a jerk of his head, 'the Count and Countess had lived in a very eccentric way; they admitted no visitors; Madame lived on the ground-floor, and Monsieur on the first floor. When the Countess was left alone, she was never seen excepting at church. Subsequently, at home, at the chateau, she refused to see the friends, whether gentlemen or ladies, who went to call on her. She was already very much altered when she left la Grande Bretèche to go to Merret. That dear lady—I say dear lady, for it was she who gave me this diamond, but indeed I saw her but once—that kind lady was very ill; she had, no doubt, given up all hope, for she died without choosing to send for a doctor; indeed, many of our ladies fancied she was not quite right in her head. Well, sir, my curiosity was strangely excited by hearing that Madame de Merret had need of my services. Nor was I the only person who took an interest in the affair. That very night, though it was already late, all the town knew that I was going to Merret.

"'The waiting-woman replied but vaguely to the questions I asked her on the way; nevertheless, she told me that her mistress had received the Sacrament in the course of the day at the hands of the Cure of Merret, and seemed unlikely to live through the night. It was about eleven when I reached the chateau. I went up the great staircase. After crossing some large, lofty, dark rooms, diabolically cold and damp, I reached the state bedroom where the Countess lay. From the rumors that were current concerning this lady (monsieur, I should never end if I were to repeat all the tales that were told about her), I had imagined her a coquette. Imagine, then, that I had great difficulty in seeing her in the great bed where she was lying. To be sure, to light this enormous room, with old-fashioned heavy cornices, and so thick with dust that merely to see it was enough to make you sneeze, she had only an old Argand lamp. Ah! but you have not been to Merret. Well, the bed is one of those old world beds, with a high tester hung with flowered chintz. A small table stood by the bed, on which I saw an "Imitation of Christ," which, by the way, I bought for my wife, as well as the lamp. There were also a deep armchair for her confidential maid, and two small chairs. There was no fire. That was all the furniture, not enough to fill ten lines in an inventory.

"'My dear sir, if you had seen, as I then saw, that vast room, papered and hung with brown, you would have felt yourself transported into a scene of a romance. It was icy, nay more, funereal,' and he lifted his hand with a theatrical gesture and paused.

"'By dint of seeking, as I approached the bed, at last I saw Madame de Merret, under the glimmer of the lamp, which fell on the pillows. Her face was as yellow as wax, and as narrow as two folded hands. The Countess had a lace cap showing her abundant hair, but as white as linen thread. She was sitting up in bed, and seemed to keep upright with great difficulty. Her large black eyes, dimmed by fever, no doubt, and half-dead already, hardly moved under the bony arch of her eyebrows.—There,' he added, pointing to his own brow. 'Her forehead was clammy; her fleshless hands were like bones covered with soft skin; the veins and muscles were perfectly visible. She must have been very handsome; but at this moment I was startled into an indescribable emotion at the sight. Never, said those who wrapped her in her shroud, had any living creature been so emaciated and lived. In short, it was awful to behold! Sickness so consumed that woman, that she was no more than a phantom. Her lips, which were pale violet, seemed to me not to move when she spoke to me.

"'Though my profession has familiarized me with such spectacles, by calling me not infrequently to the bedside of the dying to record their last wishes, I confess that families in tears and the agonies I have seen were as nothing in comparison with this lonely and silent woman in her vast chateau. I heard not the least sound, I did not perceive the movement which the sufferer's breathing ought to have given to the sheets that covered her, and I stood motionless, absorbed in looking at her in a sort of stupor. In fancy I am there still. At last her large eyes moved; she tried to raise her right hand, but it fell back on the bed, and she uttered these words, which came like a breath, for her voice was no longer a voice: "I have waited for you with the greatest impatience." A bright flush rose to her cheeks. It was a great effort to her to speak.

"'Madame,' I began. She signed to me to be silent. At that moment the old housekeeper rose and said in my ear, 'Do not speak; Madame la Comtesse is not in a state to bear the slightest noise, and what you say might agitate her.'

"'I sat down. A few instants after, Madame de Merret collected all her remaining strength to move her right hand, and slipped it, not without infinite difficulty, under the bolster; she then paused a moment. With a last effort she withdrew her hand; and when she brought out a sealed paper, drops of perspiration rolled from her brow. "I place my will in your hands—Oh! God! Oh!" and that was all. She clutched a crucifix that lay on the bed, lifted it hastily to her lips, and died.

"'The expression of her eyes still makes me shudder as I think of it. She must have suffered much! There was joy in her last glance, and it remained stamped on her dead eyes.

"'I brought away the will, and when it was opened I found that Madame de Merret had appointed me her executor. She left the whole of her property to the hospital at Vendome excepting a few legacies. But these were her instructions as relating to la Grande Bretèche: She ordered me to leave the place, for fifty years counting from the day of her death, in the state in which it might be at the time of her death, forbidding any one, whoever he might be, to enter the apartments, prohibiting any repairs whatever, and even settling a salary to pay watchmen if it were needful to secure the absolute fulfilment of her intentions. At the expiration of that term, if the will of the testatrix has been duly carried out, the house is to become the property of my heirs, for, as you know, a notary cannot take a bequest. Otherwise la Grande reverts to the heirs-at-law, but on condition of fulfilling certain conditions set forth in a codicil to the will, which is not to be opened till the expiration of the said term of fifty years. The will has not been disputed, so—' And without finishing his sentence, the lanky notary looked at me with an air of triumph; I made him quite happy by offering him my congratulations.

"'Monsieur,' I said in conclusion, 'you have so vividly impressed me that I fancy I see the dying woman whiter than her sheets; her glittering eyes frighten me; I shall dream of her to-night.—But you must have formed some idea as to the instructions contained in that extraordinary will.'

"'Monsieur,' said he, with comical reticence, 'I never allow myself to criticise the conduct of a person who honors me with the gift of a diamond.'

"However, I soon loosened the tongue of the discreet notary of Vendome, who communicated to me, not without long digressions, the opinions of the deep politicians of both sexes whose judgments are law in Vendome. But these opinions were so contradictory, so diffuse, that I was near falling asleep in spite of the interest I felt in this authentic history. The notary's ponderous voice and monotonous accent, accustomed no doubt to listen to himself and to make himself listened to by his clients or fellow-townsmen, were too much for my curiosity. Happily, he soon went away.

"'Ah, ha, monsieur,' said he on the stairs, 'a good many persons would be glad to live five-and-forty years longer; but—one moment!' and he laid the first finger of his right hand to his nostril with a cunning look, as much as to say, 'Mark my words!—To last as long as that—as long as that,' said he, 'you must not be past sixty now.'

"I closed my door, having been roused from my apathy by this last speech, which the notary thought very funny; then I sat down in my armchair, with my feet on the fire-dogs. I had lost myself in a romance a la Radcliffe, constructed on the juridical base given me by Monsieur Regnault, when the door, opened by a woman's cautious hand, turned on the hinges. I saw my landlady come in, a buxom, florid dame, always good-humored, who had missed her calling in life. She was a Fleming, who ought to have seen the light in a picture by Teniers.

"'Well, monsieur,' said she, 'Monsieur Regnault has no doubt been giving you his history of la Grande Bretèche?'

"'Yes, Madame Lepas.'

"'And what did he tell you?'

"I repeated in a few words the creepy and sinister story of Madame de Merret. At each sentence my hostess put her head forward, looking at me with an innkeeper's keen scrutiny, a happy compromise between the instinct of a police constable, the astuteness of a spy, and the cunning of a dealer.

"'My good Madame Lepas,' said I as I ended, 'you seem to know more about it. Heh? If not, why have you come up to me?'

"'On my word, as an honest woman—'

"'Do not swear; your eyes are big with a secret. You knew Monsieur de Merret; what sort of man was he?'

"'Monsieur de Merret—well, you see he was a man you never could see the top of, he was so tall! A very good gentleman, from Picardy, and who had, as we say, his head close to his cap. He paid for everything down, so as never to have difficulties with any one. He was hot-tempered, you see! All our ladies liked him very much.'

"'Because he was hot-tempered?' I asked her.

"'Well, may be,' said she; 'and you may suppose, sir, that a man had to have something to show for a figurehead before he could marry Madame de Merret, who, without any reflection on others, was the handsomest and richest heiress in our parts. She had about twenty thousand francs a year. All the town was at the wedding; the bride was pretty and sweet-looking, quite a gem of a woman. Oh, they were a handsome couple in their day!'

"'And were they happy together?'

"'Hm, hm! so-so—so far as can be guessed, for, as you may suppose, we of the common sort were not hail-fellow-well-met with them.—Madame de Merret was a kind woman and very pleasant, who had no doubt sometimes to put up with her husband's tantrums. But though he was rather haughty, we were fond of him. After all, it was his place to behave so. When a man is a born nobleman, you see—'

"'Still, there must have been some catastrophe for Monsieur and Madame de Merret to part so violently?'

"'I did not say there was any catastrophe, sir. I know nothing about it.'

"'Indeed. Well, now, I am sure you know everything.'

"'Well, sir, I will tell you the whole story.—When I saw Monsieur Regnault go up to see you, it struck me that he would speak to you about Madame de Merret as having to do with la Grande Bretèche. That put it into my head to ask your advice, sir, seeming to me that you are a man of good judgment and incapable of playing a poor woman like me false—for I never did any one a wrong, and yet I am tormented by my conscience. Up to now I have never dared to say a word to the people of these parts; they are all chatter-mags, with tongues like knives. And never till now, sir, have I had any traveler here who stayed so long in the inn as you have, and to whom I could tell the history of the fifteen thousand francs—'

"'My dear Madame Lepas, if there is anything in your story of a nature to compromise me,' I said, interrupting the flow of her words, 'I would not hear it for all the world.'

"'You need have no fears,' said she; 'you will see.'

"Her eagerness made me suspect that I was not the only person to whom my worthy landlady had communicated the secret of which I was to be the sole possessor, but I listened.

"'Monsieur,' said she, 'when the Emperor sent the Spaniards here, prisoners of war and others, I was required to lodge at the charge of the Government a young Spaniard sent to Vendome on parole. Notwithstanding his parole, he had to show himself every day to the sub-prefect. He was a Spanish grandee—neither more nor less. He had a name in *os* and *dia*, something like Bagos de Feredia. I wrote his name down in my books, and you may see it if you like. Ah! he was a handsome young fellow for a Spaniard, who are all ugly they say. He was not more than five feet two or three in height, but so well made; and he had little hands that he kept so beautifully! Ah! you should have seen them. He had as many brushes for his hands as a woman has for her toilet. He had thick, black hair, a flame in his eye, a somewhat coppery complexion, but which I admired all the same. He wore the finest linen I have ever seen, though I have had princesses to lodge here, and, among others, General Bertrand, the Duc and Duchesse d'Abrantes, Monsieur Descazes, and the King of Spain. He did not eat much, but he had such polite and amiable ways that it was impossible to owe him a grudge for that. Oh! I was very fond of him, though he did not say four words to me in a day, and it was impossible to have the least bit of talk with him; if he was spoken to, he did not answer; it is a way, a mania they all have, it would seem.

"'He read his breviary like a priest, and went to mass and all the services quite regularly. And where did he post himself?—we found this out later.—Within two yards of Madame de Merret's chapel. As he took that place the very first time he entered the church, no one imagined that there was any purpose in it. Besides, he never raised his nose above his book, poor young man! And then, monsieur, of an evening he went for a walk on the hill among the ruins of the old castle. It was his only amusement, poor man; it reminded him of his native land. They say that Spain is all hills!

"'One evening, a few days after he was sent here, he was out very late. I was rather uneasy when he did not come in till just on the stroke of midnight; but we all got used to his whims; he took the key of the door, and we never sat up for him. He lived in a house belonging to us in the Rue des Casernes. Well, then, one of our stable-boys told us one evening that, going down to wash the horses in the river, he fancied he had seen the Spanish Grandee swimming some little way off, just like a fish. When he came in, I told him to be careful of the weeds, and he seemed put out at having been seen in the water.

"'At last, monsieur, one day, or rather one morning, we did not find him in his room; he had not come back. By hunting through his things, I found a written paper in the drawer of his table, with fifty pieces of Spanish gold of the kind they call doubloons, worth about five thousand francs; and in a little sealed box ten thousand francs worth of diamonds. The paper said that in case he should not return, he left us this money and these diamonds in trust to found masses to thank God for his escape and for his salvation.

"'At that time I still had my husband, who ran off in search of him. And this is the queer part of the story: he brought back the Spaniard's clothes, which he had found under a big stone on a sort of breakwater along the river bank, nearly opposite la Grande Bretèche. My husband went so early that no one saw him. After reading the letter, he burnt the clothes, and, in obedience to Count Feredia's wish, we announced that he had escaped.

"'The sub-prefect set all the constabulary at his heels; but, pshaw! he was never caught. Lepas believed that the Spaniard had drowned himself. I, sir, have never thought so; I believe, on the contrary, that he had something to do with the business about Madame de Merret, seeing that Rosalie told me that the crucifix her mistress was so fond of that she had it buried with her, was made of ebony and silver; now in the early days of his stay here, Monsieur Feredia had one of ebony and silver which I never saw later.—And now, monsieur, do not you say that I need have no remorse about the Spaniard's fifteen thousand francs? Are they not really and truly mine?'

"'Certainly.—But have you never tried to question Rosalie?' said I.

"'Oh, to be sure I have, sir. But what is to be done? That girl is like a wall. She knows something, but it is impossible to make her talk.'

"After chatting with me for a few minutes, my hostess left me a prey to vague and sinister thoughts, to romantic curiosity, and a religious dread, not unlike the deep emotion which comes upon us when we go into a dark church at night and discern a feeble light glimmering under a lofty vault—a dim figure glides across—the sweep of a gown or of a priest's cassock is audible—and we shiver! La Grande Bretèche, with its rank grasses, its shuttered windows, its rusty iron-work, its locked doors, its deserted rooms, suddenly rose before me in fantastic vividness. I tried to get into the mysterious dwelling to search out the heart of this solemn story, this drama which had killed three persons.

"Rosalie became in my eyes the most interesting being in Vendome. As I studied her, I detected signs of an inmost thought, in spite of the blooming health that glowed in her dimpled face. There was in her soul some element of truth or of hope; her manner suggested a secret, like the expression of devout souls who pray in excess, or of a girl who has killed her child and for ever hears its last cry. Nevertheless, she was simple and clumsy in her ways; her vacant smile had nothing criminal in it, and you would have pronounced her innocent only from seeing the large red and blue checked kerchief that covered her stalwart bust, tucked into the tight-laced bodice of a lilac- and white-striped gown. 'No,' said I to myself, 'I will not quit Vendome without knowing the whole history of la Grande Bretèche. To achieve this end, I will make love to Rosalie if it proves necessary.'

"'Rosalie!' said I one evening.

"'Your servant, sir?'

"'You are not married?' She started a little.

"'Oh! there is no lack of men if ever I take a fancy to be miserable!' she replied, laughing. She got over her agitation at once; for every woman, from the highest lady to the inn-servant inclusive, has a native presence of mind.

"'Yes; you are fresh and good-looking enough never to lack lovers! But tell me, Rosalie, why did you become an inn-servant on leaving Madame de Merret? Did she not leave you some little annuity?'

"'Oh yes, sir. But my place here is the best in all the town of Vendome.'

"This reply was such an one as judges and attorneys call evasive. Rosalie, as it seemed to me, held in this romantic affair the place of the middle square of the chess-board: she was at the very centre of the interest and of the truth; she appeared to me to be tied into the knot of it. It was not a case for ordinary love-making; this girl contained the last chapter of a romance, and from that moment all my attentions were devoted to Rosalie. By dint of studying the girl, I observed in her, as in every woman whom we make our ruling thought, a variety of good qualities; she was clean and neat; she was handsome, I need not say; she soon was possessed of every charm that desire can lend to a woman in whatever rank of life. A fortnight after the notary's visit, one evening, or rather one morning, in the small hours, I said to Rosalie:

"'Come, tell me all you know about Madame de Merret.'

"'Oh!' she said, 'I will tell you; but keep the secret carefully.'

"'All right, my child; I will keep all your secrets with a thief's honor, which is the most loyal known.'

"'If it is all the same to you,' said she, 'I would rather it should be with your own.'

"Thereupon she set her head-kerchief straight, and settled herself to tell the tale; for there is no doubt a particular attitude of confidence and security is necessary to the telling of a narrative. The best tales are told at a certain hour—just as we are all here at table. No one ever told a story well standing up, or fasting.

"If I were to reproduce exactly Rosalie's diffuse eloquence, a whole volume would scarcely contain it. Now, as the event of which she gave me a confused account stands exactly midway between the notary's gossip and that of Madame Lepas, as precisely as the middle term of a rule-of-three sum stands between the first and third, I have only to relate it in as few words as may be. I shall therefore be brief.

"The room at la Grande Bretèche in which Madame de Merret slept was on the ground floor; a little cupboard in the wall, about four feet deep, served her to hang her dresses in. Three months before the evening of which I have to relate the events, Madame de Merret had been seriously ailing, so much so that her husband had left her to herself, and had his own bedroom on the first floor. By one of those accidents which it is impossible to foresee, he came in that evening two hours later than usual from the club, where he went to read the papers and talk politics with the residents in the neighborhood. His wife supposed him to have come in, to be in bed and asleep. But the invasion of France had been the subject of a very animated discussion; the game of billiards had waxed vehement; he had lost forty francs, an enormous sum at Vendome, where everybody is thrifty, and where social habits are restrained within the bounds of a simplicity worthy of all praise, and the foundation perhaps of a form of true happiness which no Parisian would care for.

"For some time past Monsieur de Merret had been satisfied to ask Rosalie whether his wife was in bed; on the girl's replying always in the affirmative, he at once went to his own room, with the good faith that comes of habit and confidence. But this evening, on coming in, he took it into his head to go to see Madame de Merret, to tell her of his ill-luck, and perhaps to find consolation. During dinner he had observed that his wife was very becomingly dressed; he reflected as he came home from the club that his wife was certainly much better, that convalescence had improved her beauty, discovering it, as husbands discover everything, a little too late. Instead of calling Rosalie, who was in the kitchen at the moment watching the cook and the coachman playing a puzzling hand at cards, Monsieur de Merret made his way to his wife's room by the light of his lantern, which he set down at the lowest step of the stairs. His step, easy to recognize, rang under the vaulted passage.

"At the instant when the gentleman turned the key to enter his wife's room, he fancied he heard the door shut of the closet of which I have spoken; but when he went in, Madame de Merret was alone, standing in front of the fireplace. The unsuspecting husband fancied that Rosalie was in the cupboard; nevertheless, a doubt, ringing in his ears like a peal of bells, put him on his guard; he looked at his wife, and read in her eyes an indescribably anxious and haunted expression.

"'You are very late,' said she.—Her voice, usually so clear and sweet, struck him as being slightly husky.

"Monsieur de Merret made no reply, for at this moment Rosalie came in. This was like a thunder-clap. He walked up and down the room, going from one window to another at a regular pace, his arms folded.

"'Have you had bad news, or are you ill?' his wife asked him timidly, while Rosalie helped her to undress. He made no reply.

"'You can go, Rosalie,' said Madame de Merret to her maid; 'I can put in my curl-papers myself.'—She scented disaster at the mere aspect of her husband's face, and wished to be alone with him. As soon as Rosalie was gone, or supposed to be gone, for she lingered a few minutes in the passage, Monsieur de Merret came and stood facing his wife, and said coldly, 'Madame, there is some one in your cupboard!' She looked at her husband calmly, and replied quite simply, 'No, monsieur.'

"This 'No' wrung Monsieur de Merret's heart; he did not believe it; and yet his wife had never appeared purer or more saintly than she seemed to be at this moment. He rose to go and open the closet door. Madame de Merret took his hand, stopped him, looked at him sadly, and said in a voice of strange emotion, 'Remember, if you should find no one there, everything must be at an end between you and me.'

"The extraordinary dignity of his wife's attitude filled him with deep esteem for her, and inspired him with one of those resolves which need only a grander stage to become immortal.

"'No, Josephine,' he said, 'I will not open it. In either event we should be parted for ever. Listen; I know all the purity of your soul, I know you lead a saintly life, and would not commit a deadly sin to save your life.'—At these words Madame de Merret looked at her husband with a haggard stare.—'See, here is your crucifix,' he went on. 'Swear to me before God that there is no one in there; I will believe you—I will never open that door.'

"Madame de Merret took up the crucifix and said, 'I swear it.'

"'Louder,' said her husband; 'and repeat: "I swear before God that there is nobody in that closet."' She repeated the words without flinching.

"'That will do,' said Monsieur de Merret coldly. After a moment's silence: 'You have there a fine piece of work which I never saw before,' said he, examining the crucifix of ebony and silver, very artistically wrought.

"'I found it at Duvivier's; last year when that troop of Spanish prisoners came through Vendome, he bought it of a Spanish monk.'

"'Indeed,' said Monsieur de Merret, hanging the crucifix on its nail; and he rang the bell.

"He had to wait for Rosalie. Monsieur de Merret went forward quickly to meet her, led her into the bay of the window that looked on to the garden, and said to her in an undertone:

"'I know that Gorenflot wants to marry you, that poverty alone prevents your setting up house, and that you told him you would not be his wife till he found means to become a master mason.—Well, go and fetch him; tell him to come here with his trowel and tools. Contrive to wake no one in his house but himself. His reward will be beyond your wishes. Above all, go out without saying a word—or else!' and he frowned.

"Rosalie was going, and he called her back. 'Here, take my latch-key,' said he.

"'Jean!' Monsieur de Merret called in a voice of thunder down the passage. Jean, who was both coachman and confidential servant, left his cards and came.

"'Go to bed, all of you,' said his master, beckoning him to come close; and the gentleman added in a whisper, 'When they are all asleep—mind, asleep—you understand?—come down and tell me.'

"Monsieur de Merret, who had never lost sight of his wife while giving his orders, quietly came back to her at the fireside, and began to tell her the details of the game of billiards and the discussion at the club. When Rosalie returned she found Monsieur and Madame de Merret conversing amiably.

"Not long before this Monsieur de Merret had had new ceilings made to all the reception-rooms on the ground floor. Plaster is very scarce at Vendome; the price is enhanced by the cost of carriage; the gentleman had therefore had a considerable quantity delivered to him, knowing that he could always find purchasers for what might be left. It was this circumstance which suggested the plan he carried out.

"'Gorenflot is here, sir,' said Rosalie in a whisper.

"'Tell him to come in,' said her master aloud.

"Madame de Merret turned paler when she saw the mason.

"'Gorenflot,' said her husband, 'go and fetch some bricks from the coach-house; bring enough to wall up the door of this cupboard; you can use the plaster that is left for cement.' Then, dragging Rosalie and the workman close to him—'Listen, Gorenflot,' said he, in a low voice, 'you are to sleep here to-night; but to-morrow morning you shall have a passport to take you abroad to a place I will tell you of. I will give you six thousand francs for your journey. You must live in that town for ten years; if you find you do not like it, you may settle in another, but it must be in the same country. Go through Paris and wait there till I join you. I will there give you an agreement for six thousand francs more, to be paid to you on your return, provided you have carried out the conditions of the bargain. For that price you are to keep perfect silence as to what you have to do this night. To you, Rosalie, I will secure ten thousand francs, which will not be paid to you till your wedding day, and on condition of your marrying Gorenflot; but, to get married, you must hold your tongue. If not, no wedding gift!'

"'Rosalie,' said Madame de Merret, 'come and brush my hair.'

"Her husband quietly walked up and down the room, keeping an eye on the door, on the mason, and on his wife, but without any insulting display of suspicion. Gorenflot could not help making some noise. Madame de Merret seized a moment when he was unloading some bricks, and when her husband was at the other end of the room to say to Rosalie: 'My dear child, I will give you a thousand francs a year if only you will tell Gorenflot to leave a crack at the bottom.' Then she added aloud quite coolly: 'You had better help him.'

"Monsieur and Madame de Merret were silent all the time while Gorenflot was walling up the door. This silence was intentional on the husband's part; he did not wish to give his wife the opportunity of saying anything with a double meaning. On Madame de Merret's side it was pride or prudence. When the wall was half built up the cunning mason took advantage of his master's back being turned to break one of the two panes in the top of the door with a blow of his pick. By this Madame de Merret understood that Rosalie had spoken to Gorenflot. They all three then saw the face of a dark, gloomy-looking man, with black hair and flaming eyes.

"Before her husband turned round again the poor woman had nodded to the stranger, to whom the signal was meant to convey, 'Hope.'

"At four o'clock, as the day was dawning, for it was the month of September, the work was done. The mason was placed in charge of Jean, and Monsieur de Merret slept in his wife's room.

"Next morning when he got up he said with apparent carelessness, 'Oh, by the way, I must go to the Maire for the passport.' He put on his hat, took two or three steps towards the door, paused, and took the crucifix. His wife was trembling with joy.

"'He will go to Duvivier's,' thought she.

"As soon as he had left, Madame de Merret rang for Rosalie, and then in a terrible voice she cried: 'The pick! Bring the pick! and set to work. I saw how Gorenflot did it yesterday; we shall have time to make a gap and build it up again.'

"In an instant Rosalie had brought her mistress a sort of cleaver; she, with a vehemence of which no words can give an idea, set to work to demolish the wall. She had already got out a few bricks, when, turning to deal a stronger blow than before, she saw behind her Monsieur de Merret. She fainted away.

"'Lay madame on her bed,' said he coldly.

"Foreseeing what would certainly happen in his absence, he had laid this trap for his wife; he had merely written to the Maire and sent for Duvivier. The jeweler arrived just as the disorder in the room had been repaired.

"'Duvivier,' asked Monsieur de Merret, 'did not you buy some crucifixes of the Spaniards who passed through the town?'

"'No, monsieur.'

"'Very good; thank you,' said he, flashing a tiger's glare at his wife. 'Jean,' he added, turning to his confidential valet, 'you can serve my meals here in Madame de Merret's room. She is ill, and I shall not leave her till she recovers.'

"The cruel man remained in his wife's room for twenty days. During the earlier time, when there was some little noise in the closet, and Josephine wanted to intercede for the dying man, he said, without allowing her to utter a word, 'You swore on the Cross that there was no one there.'"

After this story all the ladies rose from table, and thus the spell under which Bianchon had held them was broken. But there were some among them who had almost shivered at the last words.

THE TERROR OF BLUE JOHN GAP

Arthur Conan Doyle

The following narrative was found among the papers of Dr. James Hardcastle, who died of phthisis on February 4th, 1908, at 36, Upper Coventry Flats, South Kensington. Those who knew him best, while refusing to express an opinion upon this particular statement, are unanimous in asserting that he was a man of a sober and scientific turn of mind, absolutely devoid of imagination, and most unlikely to invent any abnormal series of events. The paper was contained in an envelope, which was docketed, "A Short Account of the Circumstances which occurred near Miss Allerton's Farm in North-West Derbyshire in the Spring of Last Year." The envelope was sealed, and on the other side was written in pencil—

"Dear Seaton,—

"It may interest, and perhaps pain you, to know that the incredulity with which you met my story has prevented me from ever opening my mouth upon the subject again. I leave this record after my death, and perhaps strangers may be found to have more confidence in me than my friend."

Inquiry has failed to elicit who this Seaton may have been. I may add that the visit of the deceased to Allerton's Farm, and the general nature of the alarm there, apart from his particular explanation, have been absolutely established. With this foreword I append his account exactly as he left it. It is in the form of a diary, some entries in which have been expanded, while a few have been erased.

April 17.—Already I feel the benefit of this wonderful upland air. The farm of the Allertons lies fourteen hundred and twenty feet above sea-level, so it may well be a bracing climate. Beyond the usual morning cough I have very little discomfort, and, what with the fresh milk and the home-grown mutton, I have every chance of putting on weight. I think Saunderson will be pleased.

The two Miss Allertons are charmingly quaint and kind, two dear little hard-working old maids, who are ready to lavish all the heart which might have gone out to husband and to children upon an invalid stranger. Truly, the old maid is a most useful person, one of the reserve forces of the community. They talk of the superfluous woman, but what would the poor superfluous man do without her kindly presence? By the way, in their simplicity they very quickly let out the reason why Saunderson recommended their farm. The Professor rose from the ranks himself, and I believe that in his youth he was not above scaring crows in these very fields.

It is a most lonely spot, and the walks are picturesque in the extreme. The farm consists of grazing land lying at the bottom of an irregular valley. On each side are the fantastic limestone hills, formed of rock so soft that you can break it away with your hands. All this country is hollow. Could you strike it with some gigantic hammer it would boom like a drum, or possibly cave in altogether and expose some huge subterranean sea. A great sea there must surely be, for on all sides the streams run into the mountain itself, never to reappear. There are gaps everywhere amid the rocks, and when you pass through them you find yourself in great caverns, which wind down into the bowels of the earth. I have a small bicycle lamp, and it is a perpetual joy to me to carry it into these weird solitudes, and to see the wonderful silver and black effect when I throw its light upon the stalactites which drape the lofty roofs. Shut off the lamp, and you are in the blackest darkness. Turn it on, and it is a scene from the Arabian Nights.

But there is one of these strange openings in the earth which has a special interest, for it is the handiwork, not of nature, but of man. I had never heard of Blue John when I came to these parts. It is the name given to a peculiar mineral of a beautiful purple shade, which is only found at one or two places in the world. It is so rare that an ordinary vase of Blue John would be valued at a great price. The Romans, with that extraordinary instinct of theirs, discovered that it was to be found in this valley, and sank a horizontal shaft deep into the mountain side. The opening of their mine has been called Blue John Gap, a clean-cut arch in the rock, the mouth all overgrown with bushes. It is a goodly passage which the Roman miners have cut, and it intersects some of the great water-worn caves, so that if you enter Blue John Gap you would do well to mark your steps and to have a good store of candles, or you may never make your way back to the daylight again. I have not yet gone deeply into it, but this very day I stood at the mouth of the arched tunnel, and peering down into the black recesses beyond, I vowed that when my health returned I would devote some holiday to exploring those mysterious depths and finding out for myself how far the Roman had penetrated into the Derbyshire hills.

Strange how superstitious these countrymen are! I should have thought better of young Armitage, for he is a man of some education and character, and a very fine fellow for his station in life. I was standing at the Blue John Gap when he came across the field to me.

"Well, doctor," said he, "you're not afraid, anyhow."

"Afraid!" I answered. "Afraid of what?"

"Of it," said he, with a jerk of his thumb towards the black vault, "of the Terror that lives in the Blue John Cave."

How absurdly easy it is for a legend to arise in a lonely countryside! I examined him as to the reasons for his weird belief. It seems that from time to time sheep have been missing from the fields, carried bodily away, according to Armitage. That they could have wandered away of their own accord and disappeared among the mountains was an explanation to which he would not listen. On one occasion a pool of blood had been found, and some tufts of wool. That also, I pointed out, could be explained in a perfectly natural way. Further, the nights upon which sheep disappeared were invariably very dark, cloudy nights with no moon. This I met with the obvious retort that those were the nights which a commonplace sheep-stealer would naturally choose for his work. On one occasion a gap had been made in a wall, and some of the stones scattered for a considerable distance. Human agency again, in my opinion. Finally, Armitage clinched all his arguments by telling me that he had actually heard the Creature—indeed, that anyone could hear it who remained long enough at the Gap. It was a distant roaring of an immense volume. I could not but smile at this, knowing, as I do, the strange reverberations which come out of an underground water system running amid the chasms of a limestone formation. My incredulity annoyed Armitage so that he turned and left me with some abruptness.

And now comes the queer point about the whole business. I was still standing near the mouth of the cave turning over in my mind the various statements of Armitage, and reflecting how readily they could be explained away, when suddenly, from the depth of the tunnel beside me, there issued a most extraordinary sound. How shall I describe it? First of all, it seemed to be a great distance away, far down in the bowels of the earth. Secondly, in spite of this suggestion of distance, it was very loud. Lastly, it was not a boom, nor a crash, such as one would associate with falling water or tumbling rock, but it was a high whine, tremulous and vibrating, almost like the whinnying of a horse. It was certainly a most remarkable experience, and one which for a moment, I must admit, gave a new significance to Armitage's words. I waited by the Blue John Gap for half an hour or more, but there was no return of the sound, so at last I wandered back to the farmhouse, rather mystified by what had occurred. Decidedly I shall explore that cavern when my strength is restored. Of course, Armitage's explanation is too absurd for discussion, and yet that sound was certainly very strange. It still rings in my ears as I write.

April 20.—In the last three days I have made several expeditions to the Blue John Gap, and have even penetrated some short distance, but my bicycle lantern is so small and weak that I dare not trust myself very far. I shall do the thing more systematically. I have heard no sound at all, and could almost believe that I had been the victim of some hallucination suggested, perhaps, by Armitage's conversation. Of course, the whole idea is absurd, and yet I must confess that those bushes at the entrance of the cave do present an appearance as if some heavy creature had forced its way through them. I begin to be keenly interested. I have said nothing to the Miss Allertons, for they are quite superstitious enough already, but I have bought some candles, and mean to investigate for myself.

I observed this morning that among the numerous tufts of sheep's wool which lay among the bushes near the cavern there was one which was smeared with blood. Of course, my reason tells me that if sheep wander into such rocky places they are likely to injure themselves, and yet somehow that splash of crimson gave me a sudden shock, and for a moment I found myself shrinking back in horror from the old Roman arch. A fetid breath seemed to ooze from the black depths into which I peered. Could it indeed be possible that some nameless thing, some dreadful presence, was lurking down yonder? I should have been incapable of such feelings in the days of my strength, but one grows more nervous and fanciful when one's health is shaken.

For the moment I weakened in my resolution, and was ready to leave the secret of the old mine, if one exists, for ever unsolved. But tonight my interest has returned and my nerves grown more steady. Tomorrow I trust that I shall have gone more deeply into this matter.

April 22.—Let me try and set down as accurately as I can my extraordinary experience of yesterday. I started in the afternoon, and made my way to the Blue John Gap. I confess that my misgivings returned as I gazed into its depths, and I wished that I had brought a companion to share my exploration. Finally, with a return of resolution, I lit my candle, pushed my way through the briars, and descended into the rocky shaft.

It went down at an acute angle for some fifty feet, the floor being covered with broken stone. Thence there extended a long, straight passage cut in the solid rock. I am no geologist, but the lining of this corridor was certainly of some harder material than limestone, for there were points where I could actually see the tool-marks which the old miners had left in their excavation, as fresh as if they had been done yesterday. Down this strange, old-world corridor I stumbled, my feeble flame throwing a dim circle of light around me, which made the shadows beyond the more threatening and obscure. Finally, I came to a spot where the Roman tunnel opened into a water-worn cavern—a huge hall, hung with long white icicles of lime deposit. From this central chamber I could dimly perceive that a number of passages worn by the subterranean streams wound away into the depths of the earth. I was standing there wondering whether I had better return, or whether I dare venture farther into this dangerous labyrinth, when my eyes fell upon something at my feet which strongly arrested my attention.

The greater part of the floor of the cavern was covered with boulders of rock or with hard incrustations of lime, but at this particular point there had been a drip from the distant roof, which had left a patch of soft mud. In the very centre of this there was a huge mark—an ill-defined blotch, deep, broad and irregular, as if a great boulder had fallen upon it. No loose stone lay near, however, nor was there anything to account for the impression. It was far too large to be caused by any possible animal, and besides, there was only the one, and the patch of mud was of such a size that no reasonable stride could have covered it. As I rose from the examination of that singular mark and then looked round into the black shadows which hemmed me in, I must confess that I felt for a moment a most unpleasant sinking of my heart, and that, do what I could, the candle trembled in my outstretched hand.

I soon recovered my nerve, however, when I reflected how absurd it was to associate so huge and shapeless a mark with the track of any known animal. Even an elephant could not have produced it. I determined, therefore, that I would not be scared by vague and senseless fears from carrying out my exploration. Before proceeding, I took good note of a curious rock formation in the wall by which I could recognize the entrance of the Roman tunnel. The precaution was very necessary, for the great cave, so far as I could see it, was intersected by passages. Having made sure of my position, and reassured myself by examining my spare candles and my matches, I advanced slowly over the rocky and uneven surface of the cavern.

And now I come to the point where I met with such sudden and desperate disaster. A stream, some twenty feet broad, ran across my path, and I walked for some little distance along the bank to find a spot where I could cross dry-shod. Finally, I came to a place where a single flat boulder lay near the centre, which I could reach in a stride. As it chanced, however, the rock had been cut away and made top-heavy by the rush of the stream, so that it tilted over as I landed on it and shot me into the ice-cold water. My candle went out, and I found myself floundering about in utter and absolute darkness.

I staggered to my feet again, more amused than alarmed by my adventure. The candle had fallen from my hand, and was lost in the stream, but I had two others in my pocket, so that it was of no importance. I got one of them ready, and drew out my box of matches to light it. Only then did I realize my position. The box had been soaked in my fall into the river. It was impossible to strike the matches.

A cold hand seemed to close round my heart as I realized my position. The darkness was opaque and horrible. It was so utter one put one's hand up to one's face as if to press off something solid. I stood still, and by an effort I steadied myself. I tried to reconstruct in my mind a map of the floor of the cavern as I had last seen it. Alas! the bearings which had impressed themselves upon my mind were high on the wall, and not to be found by touch. Still, I remembered in a general way how the sides were situated, and I hoped that by groping my way along them I should at last come to the opening of the Roman tunnel. Moving very slowly, and continually striking against the rocks, I set out on this desperate quest.

But I very soon realized how impossible it was. In that black, velvety darkness one lost all one's bearings in an instant. Before I had made a dozen paces, I was utterly bewildered as to my whereabouts. The rippling of the stream, which was the one sound audible, showed me where it lay, but the moment that I left its bank I was utterly lost. The idea of finding my way back in absolute darkness through that limestone labyrinth was clearly an impossible one.

I sat down upon a boulder and reflected upon my unfortunate plight. I had not told anyone that I proposed to come to the Blue John mine, and it was unlikely that a search party would come after me. Therefore I must trust to my own resources to get clear of the danger. There was only one hope, and that was that the matches might dry. When I fell into the river, only half of me had got thoroughly wet. My left shoulder had remained above the water. I took the box of matches, therefore, and put it into my left armpit. The moist air of the cavern might possibly be counteracted by the heat of my body, but even so, I knew that I could not hope to get a light for many hours. Meanwhile there was nothing for it but to wait.

By good luck I had slipped several biscuits into my pocket before I left the farm-house. These I now devoured, and washed them down with a draught from that wretched stream which had been the cause of all my misfortunes. Then I felt about for a comfortable seat among the rocks, and, having discovered a place where I could get a support for my back, I stretched out my legs and settled myself down to wait. I was wretchedly damp and cold, but I tried to cheer myself with the reflection that modern science prescribed open windows and walks in all weather for my disease. Gradually, lulled by the monotonous gurgle of the stream, and by the absolute darkness, I sank into an uneasy slumber.

How long this lasted I cannot say. It may have been for an hour, it may have been for several. Suddenly I sat up on my rock couch, with every nerve thrilling and every sense acutely on the alert. Beyond all doubt I had heard a sound—some sound very distinct from the gurgling of the waters. It had passed, but the reverberation of it still lingered in my ear. Was it a search party? They would most certainly have shouted, and vague as this sound was which had wakened me, it was very distinct from the human voice. I sat palpitating and hardly daring to breathe. There it was again! And again! Now it had become continuous. It was a tread—yes, surely it was the tread of some living creature. But what a tread it was! It gave one the impression of enormous weight carried upon sponge-like feet, which gave forth a muffled but ear-filling sound. The darkness was as complete as ever, but the tread was regular and decisive. And it was coming beyond all question in my direction.

My skin grew cold, and my hair stood on end as I listened to that steady and ponderous footfall. There was some creature there, and surely by the speed of its advance, it was one which could see in the dark. I crouched low on my rock and tried to blend myself into it. The steps grew nearer still, then stopped, and presently I was aware of a loud lapping and gurgling. The creature was drinking at the stream. Then again there was silence, broken by a succession of long sniffs and snorts of tremendous volume and energy. Had it caught the scent of me? My own nostrils were filled by a low fetid odour, mephitic and abominable. Then I heard the steps again. They were on my side of the stream now. The stones rattled within a few yards of where I lay. Hardly daring to breathe, I crouched upon my rock. Then the steps drew away. I heard the splash as it returned across the river, and the sound died away into the distance in the direction from which it had come.

For a long time I lay upon the rock, too much horrified to move. I thought of the sound which I had heard coming from the depths of the cave, of Armitage's fears, of the strange impression in the mud, and now came this final and absolute proof that there was indeed some inconceivable monster, something utterly unearthly and dreadful, which lurked in the hollow of the mountain. Of its nature or form I could frame no conception, save that it was both light-footed and gigantic. The combat between my reason, which told me that such things could not be, and my senses, which told me that they were, raged within me as I lay. Finally, I was almost ready to persuade myself that this experience had been part of some evil dream, and that my abnormal condition might have conjured up an hallucination. But there remained one final experience which removed the last possibility of doubt from my mind.

I had taken my matches from my armpit and felt them. They seemed perfectly hard and dry. Stooping down into a crevice of the rocks, I tried one of them. To my delight it took fire at once. I lit the candle, and, with a terrified backward glance into the obscure depths of the cavern, I hurried in the direction of the Roman passage. As I did so I passed the patch of mud on which I had seen the huge imprint. Now I stood astonished before it, for there were three similar imprints upon its surface, enormous in size, irregular in outline, of a depth which indicated the ponderous weight which had left them. Then a great terror surged over me. Stooping and shading my candle with my hand, I ran in a frenzy of fear to the rocky archway, hastened up it, and never stopped until, with weary feet and panting lungs, I rushed up the final slope of stones, broke through the tangle of briars, and flung myself exhausted upon the soft grass under the peaceful light of the stars. It was three in the morning when I reached the farm-house, and today I am all unstrung and quivering after my terrific adventure. As yet I have told no one. I must move warily in the matter. What would the poor lonely women, or the uneducated yokels here think of it if I were to tell them my experience? Let me go to someone who can understand and advise.

April 25.—I was laid up in bed for two days after my incredible adventure in the cavern. I use the adjective with a very definite meaning, for I have had an experience since which has shocked me almost as much as the other. I have said that I was looking round for someone who could advise me. There is a Dr. Mark Johnson who practices some few miles away, to whom I had a note of recommendation from Professor Saunderson. To him I drove, when I was strong enough to get about, and I recounted to him my whole strange experience. He listened intently, and then carefully examined me, paying special attention to my reflexes and to the pupils of my eyes. When he had finished, he refused to discuss my adventure, saying that it was entirely beyond him, but he gave me the card of a Mr. Picton at Castleton, with the advice that I should instantly go to him and tell him the story exactly as I had done to himself. He was, according to my adviser, the very man who was pre-eminently suited to help me. I went on to the station, therefore, and made my way to the little town, which is some ten miles away. Mr. Picton appeared to be a man of importance, as his brass plate was displayed upon the door of a considerable building on the outskirts of the town. I was about to ring his bell, when some misgiving came into my mind, and, crossing to a neighbouring shop, I asked the man behind the counter if he could tell me anything of Mr. Picton. "Why," said he, "he is the best mad doctor in Derbyshire, and yonder is his asylum." You can imagine that it was not long before I had shaken the dust of Castleton from my feet and returned to the farm, cursing all unimaginative pedants who cannot conceive that there may be things in creation which have never yet chanced to come across their mole's vision. After all, now that I am cooler, I can afford to admit that I have been no more sympathetic to Armitage than Dr. Johnson has been to me.

April 27.—When I was a student I had the reputation of being a man of courage and enterprise. I remember that when there was a ghost-hunt at Coltbridge it was I who sat up in the haunted house. Is it advancing years (after all, I am only thirty-five), or is it this physical malady which has caused degeneration? Certainly my heart quails when I think of that horrible cavern in the hill, and the certainty that it has some monstrous occupant. What shall I do? There is not an hour in the day that I do not debate the question. If I say nothing, then the mystery remains unsolved. If I do say anything, then I have the alternative of mad alarm over the whole countryside, or of absolute incredulity which may end in consigning me to an asylum. On the whole, I think that my best course is to wait, and to prepare for some expedition which shall be more deliberate and better thought out than the last. As a first step I have been to Castleton and obtained a few essentials—a large acetylene lantern for one thing, and a good double-barrelled sporting rifle for another. The latter I have hired, but I have bought a dozen heavy game cartridges, which would bring down a rhinoceros. Now I am ready for my troglodyte friend. Give me better health and a little spate of energy, and I shall try conclusions with him yet. But who and what is he? Ah! there is the question which stands between me and my sleep. How many theories do I form, only to discard each in turn! It is all so utterly unthinkable. And yet the cry, the footmark, the tread in the cavern—no reasoning can get past these I think of the old-world legends of dragons and of other monsters. Were they, perhaps, not such fairy-tales as we have thought? Can it be that there is some fact which underlies them, and am I, of all mortals, the one who is chosen to expose it?

May 3.—For several days I have been laid up by the vagaries of an English spring, and during those days there have been developments, the true and sinister meaning of which no one can appreciate save myself. I may say that we have had cloudy and moonless nights of late, which according to my information were the seasons upon which sheep disappeared. Well, sheep have disappeared. Two of Miss Allerton's, one of old Pearson's of the Cat Walk, and one of Mrs. Moulton's. Four in all during three nights. No trace is left of them at all, and the countryside is buzzing with rumours of gipsies and of sheep-stealers.

But there is something more serious than that. Young Armitage has disappeared also. He left his moorland cottage early on Wednesday night and has never been heard of since. He was an unattached man, so there is less sensation than would otherwise be the case. The popular explanation is that he owes money, and has found a situation in some other part of the country, whence he will presently write for his belongings. But I have grave misgivings. Is it not much more likely that the recent tragedy of the sheep has caused him to take some steps which may have ended in his own destruction? He may, for example, have lain in wait for the creature and been carried off by it into the recesses of the mountains. What an inconceivable fate for a civilized Englishman of the twentieth century! And yet I feel that it is possible and even probable. But in that case, how far am I answerable both for his death and for any other mishap which may occur? Surely with the knowledge I already possess it must be my duty to see that something is done, or if necessary to do it myself. It must be the latter, for this morning I went down to the local police-station and told my story. The inspector entered it all in a large book and bowed me out with commendable gravity, but I heard a burst of laughter before I had got down his garden path. No doubt he was recounting my adventure to his family.

June 10.—I am writing this, propped up in bed, six weeks after my last entry in this journal. I have gone through a terrible shock both to mind and body, arising from such an experience as has seldom befallen a human being before. But I have attained my end. The danger from the Terror which dwells in the Blue John Gap has passed never to return. Thus much at least I, a broken invalid, have done for the common good. Let me now recount what occurred as clearly as I may.

The night of Friday, May 3rd, was dark and cloudy—the very night for the monster to walk. About eleven o'clock I went from the farm-house with my lantern and my rifle, having first left a note upon the table of my bedroom in which I said that, if I were missing, search should be made for me in the direction of the Gap. I made my way to the mouth of the Roman shaft, and, having perched myself among the rocks close to the opening, I shut off my lantern and waited patiently with my loaded rifle ready to my hand.

It was a melancholy vigil. All down the winding valley I could see the scattered lights of the farm-houses, and the church clock of Chapel-le-Dale tolling the hours came faintly to my ears. These tokens of my fellow-men served only to make my own position seem the more lonely, and to call for a greater effort to overcome the terror which tempted me continually to get back to the farm, and abandon for ever this dangerous quest. And yet there lies deep in every man a rooted self-respect which makes it hard for him to turn back from that which he has once undertaken. This feeling of personal pride was my salvation now, and it was that alone which held me fast when every instinct of my nature was dragging me away. I am glad now that I had the strength. In spite of all that is has cost me, my manhood is at least above reproach.

Twelve o'clock struck in the distant church, then one, then two. It was the darkest hour of the night. The clouds were drifting low, and there was not a star in the sky. An owl was hooting somewhere among the rocks, but no other sound, save the gentle sough of the wind, came to my ears. And then suddenly I heard it! From far away down the tunnel came those muffled steps, so soft and yet so ponderous. I heard also the rattle of stones as they gave way under that giant tread. They drew nearer. They were close upon me. I heard the crashing of the bushes round the entrance, and then dimly through the darkness I was conscious of the loom of some enormous shape, some monstrous inchoate creature, passing swiftly and very silently out from the tunnel. I was paralysed with fear and amazement. Long as I had waited, now that it had actually come I was unprepared for the shock. I lay motionless and breathless, whilst the great dark mass whisked by me and was swallowed up in the night.

But now I nerved myself for its return. No sound came from the sleeping countryside to tell of the horror which was loose. In no way could I judge how far off it was, what it was doing, or when it might be back. But not a second time should my nerve fail me, not a second time should it pass unchallenged. I swore it between my clenched teeth as I laid my cocked rifle across the rock.

And yet it nearly happened. There was no warning of approach now as the creature passed over the grass. Suddenly, like a dark, drifting shadow, the huge bulk loomed up once more before me, making for the entrance of the cave. Again came that paralysis of volition which held my crooked forefinger impotent upon the trigger. But with a desperate effort I shook it off. Even as the brushwood rustled, and the monstrous beast blended with the shadow of the Gap, I fired at the retreating form. In the blaze of the gun I caught a glimpse of a great shaggy mass, something with rough and bristling hair of a withered grey colour, fading away to white in its lower parts, the huge body supported upon short, thick, curving legs. I had just that glance, and then I heard the rattle of the stones as the creature tore down into its burrow. In an instant, with a triumphant revulsion of feeling, I had cast my fears to the wind, and uncovering my powerful lantern, with my rifle in my hand, I sprang down from my rock and rushed after the monster down the old Roman shaft.

My splendid lamp cast a brilliant flood of vivid light in front of me, very different from the yellow glimmer which had aided me down the same passage only twelve days before. As I ran, I saw the great beast lurching along before me, its huge bulk filling up the whole space from wall to wall. Its hair looked like coarse faded oakum, and hung down in long, dense masses which swayed as it moved. It was like an enormous unclipped sheep in its fleece, but in size it was far larger than the largest elephant, and its breadth seemed to be nearly as great as its height. It fills me with amazement now to think that I should have dared to follow such a horror into the bowels of the earth, but when one's blood is up, and when one's quarry seems to be flying, the old primeval hunting-spirit awakes and prudence is cast to the wind. Rifle in hand, I ran at the top of my speed upon the trail of the monster.

I had seen that the creature was swift. Now I was to find out to my cost that it was also very cunning. I had imagined that it was in panic flight, and that I had only to pursue it. The idea that it might turn upon me never entered my excited brain. I have already explained that the passage down which I was racing opened into a great central cave. Into this I rushed, fearful lest I should lose all trace of the beast. But he had turned upon his own traces, and in a moment we were face to face.

That picture, seen in the brilliant white light of the lantern, is etched for ever upon my brain. He had reared up on his hind legs as a bear would do, and stood above me, enormous, menacing—such a creature as no nightmare had ever brought to my imagination. I have said that he reared like a bear, and there was something bear-like—if one could conceive a bear which was tenfold the bulk of any bear seen upon earth—in his whole pose and attitude, in his great crooked forelegs with their ivory-white claws, in his rugged skin, and in his red, gaping mouth, fringed with monstrous fangs. Only in one point did he differ from the bear, or from any other creature which walks the earth, and even at that supreme moment a shudder of horror passed over me as I observed that the eyes which glistened in the glow of my lantern were huge, projecting bulbs, white and sightless. For a moment his great paws swung over my head. The next he fell forward upon me, I and my broken lantern crashed to the earth, and I remember no more.

When I came to myself I was back in the farm-house of the Allertons. Two days had passed since my terrible adventure in the Blue John Gap. It seems that I had lain all night in the cave insensible from concussion of the brain, with my left arm and two ribs badly fractured. In the morning my note had been found, a search party of a dozen farmers assembled, and I had been tracked down and carried back to my bedroom, where I had lain in high delirium ever since. There was, it seems, no sign of the creature, and no bloodstain which would show that my bullet had found him as he passed. Save for my own plight and the marks upon the mud, there was nothing to prove that what I said was true.

Six weeks have now elapsed, and I am able to sit out once more in the sunshine. Just opposite me is the steep hillside, grey with shaly rock, and yonder on its flank is the dark cleft which marks the opening of the Blue John Gap. But it is no longer a source of terror. Never again through that ill-omened tunnel shall any strange shape flit out into the world of men. The educated and the scientific, the Dr. Johnsons and the like, may smile at my narrative, but the poorer folk of the countryside had never a doubt as to its truth. On the day after my recovering consciousness they assembled in their hundreds round the Blue John Gap. As the *Castleton Courier* said:

"It was useless for our correspondent, or for any of the adventurous gentlemen who had come from Matlock, Buxton, and other parts, to offer to descend, to explore the cave to the end, and to finally test the extraordinary narrative of Dr. James Hardcastle. The country people had taken the matter into their own hands, and from an early hour of the morning they had worked hard in stopping up the entrance of the tunnel. There is a sharp slope where the shaft begins, and great boulders, rolled along by many willing hands, were thrust down it until the Gap was absolutely sealed. So ends the episode which has caused such excitement throughout the country. Local opinion is fiercely divided upon the subject.

On the one hand are those who point to Dr. Hardcastle's impaired health, and to the possibility of cerebral lesions of tubercular origin giving rise to strange hallucinations. Some *idée fixe*, according to these gentlemen, caused the doctor to wander down the tunnel, and a fall among the rocks was sufficient to account for his injuries. On the other hand, a legend of a strange creature in the Gap has existed for some months back, and the farmers look upon Dr. Hardcastle's narrative and his personal injuries as a final corroboration. So the matter stands, and so the matter will continue to stand, for no definite solution seems to us to be now possible. It transcends human wit to give any scientific explanation which could cover the alleged facts."

Perhaps before the *Courier* published these words they would have been wise to send their representative to me. I have thought the matter out, as no one else has occasion to do, and it is possible that I might have removed some of the more obvious difficulties of the narrative and brought it one degree nearer to scientific acceptance. Let me then write down the only explanation which seems to me to elucidate what I know to my cost to have been a series of facts. My theory may seem to be wildly improbable, but at least no one can venture to say that it is impossible.

My view is—and it was formed, as is shown by my diary, before my personal adventure—that in this part of England there is a vast subterranean lake or sea, which is fed by the great number of streams which pass down through the limestone. Where there is a large collection of water there must also be some evaporation, mists or rain, and a possibility of vegetation. This in turn suggests that there may be animal life, arising, as the vegetable life would also do, from those seeds and types which had been introduced at an early period of the world's history, when communication with the outer air was more easy. This place had then developed a fauna and flora of its own, including such monsters as the one which I had seen, which may well have been the old cave-bear, enormously enlarged and modified by its new environment. For countless aeons the internal and the external creation had kept apart, growing steadily away from each other. Then there had come some rift in the depths of the mountain which had enabled one creature to wander up and, by means of the Roman tunnel, to reach the open air. Like all subterranean life, it had lost the power of sight, but this had no doubt been compensated for by nature in other directions. Certainly it had some means of finding its way about, and of hunting down the sheep upon the hillside. As to its choice of dark nights, it is part of my theory that light was painful to those great white eyeballs, and that it was only a pitch-black world which it could tolerate. Perhaps, indeed, it was the glare of my lantern which saved my life at that awful moment when we were face to face. So I read the riddle. I leave these facts behind me, and if you can explain them, do so; or if you choose to doubt them, do so. Neither your belief nor your incredulity can alter them, nor affect one whose task is nearly over.

So ended the strange narrative of Dr. James Hardcastle.

THE YELLOW WALLPAPER

Charlotte Perkins Gilman

It is very seldom that mere ordinary people like John and myself secure ancestral halls for the summer.

A colonial mansion, a hereditary estate, I would say a haunted house, and reach the height of romantic felicity—but that would be asking too much of fate!

Still I will proudly declare that there is something queer about it.

Else, why should it be let so cheaply? And why have stood so long untenanted?

John laughs at me, of course, but one expects that in marriage.

John is practical in the extreme. He has no patience with faith, an intense horror of superstition, and he scoffs openly at any talk of things not to be felt and seen and put down in figures.

John is a physician, and *perhaps*—(I would not say it to a living soul, of course, but this is dead paper and a great relief to my mind)—*perhaps* that is one reason I do not get well faster.

You see he does not believe I am sick!

And what can one do?

If a physician of high standing, and one's own husband, assures friends and relatives that there is really nothing the matter with one but temporary nervous depression—a slight hysterical tendency—what is one to do?

My brother is also a physician, and also of high standing, and he says the same thing.

So I take phosphates or phosphites—whichever it is, and tonics, and journeys, and air, and exercise, and am absolutely forbidden to "work" until I am well again.

Personally, I disagree with their ideas.

Personally, I believe that congenial work, with excitement and change, would do me good.

But what is one to do?

I did write for a while in spite of them; but it does exhaust me a good deal—having to be so sly about it, or else meet with heavy opposition.

I sometimes fancy that in my condition if I had less opposition and more society and stimulus—but John says the very worst thing I can do is to think about my condition, and I confess it always makes me feel bad.

So I will let it alone and talk about the house.

The most beautiful place! It is quite alone, standing well back from the road, quite three miles from the village. It makes me think of English places that you read about, for there are hedges and walls and gates that lock, and lots of separate little houses for the gardeners and people.

There is a delicious garden! I never saw such a garden—large and shady, full of box-bordered paths, and lined with long grape-covered arbors with seats under them.

There were greenhouses, too, but they are all broken now.

There was some legal trouble, I believe, something about the heirs and coheirs; anyhow, the place has been empty for years.

That spoils my ghostliness, I am afraid, but I don't care—there is something strange about the house—I can feel it.

I even said so to John one moonlight evening, but he said what I felt was a draught, and shut the window.

I get unreasonably angry with John sometimes. I'm sure I never used to be so sensitive. I think it is due to this nervous condition.

But John says if I feel so, I shall neglect proper self-control; so I take pains to control myself—before him, at least, and that makes me very tired.

I don't like our room a bit. I wanted one downstairs that opened on the piazza and had roses all over the window, and such pretty old-fashioned chintz hangings! but John would not hear of it.

He said there was only one window and not room for two beds, and no near room for him if he took another.

He is very careful and loving, and hardly lets me stir without special direction.

I have a schedule prescription for each hour in the day; he takes all care from me, and so I feel basely ungrateful not to value it more.

He said we came here solely on my account, that I was to have perfect rest and all the air I could get. "Your exercise depends on your strength, my dear," said he, "and your food somewhat on your appetite; but air you can absorb all the time." So we took the nursery at the top of the house.

It is a big, airy room, the whole floor nearly, with windows that look all ways, and air and sunshine galore. It was nursery first and then playroom and gymnasium, I should judge; for the windows are barred for little children, and there are rings and things in the walls.

The paint and paper look as if a boys' school had used it. It is stripped off—the paper—in great patches all around the head of my bed, about as far as I can reach, and in a great place on the other side of the room low down. I never saw a worse paper in my life.

One of those sprawling flamboyant patterns committing every artistic sin.

It is dull enough to confuse the eye in following, pronounced enough to constantly irritate and provoke study, and when you follow the lame uncertain curves for a little distance they suddenly commit suicide—plunge off at outrageous angles, destroy themselves in unheard of contradictions.

The color is repellent, almost revolting; a smouldering unclean yellow, strangely faded by the slow-turning sunlight.

It is a dull yet lurid orange in some places, a sickly sulphur tint in others.

No wonder the children hated it! I should hate it myself if I had to live in this room long.

There comes John, and I must put this away,—he hates to have me write a word.

We have been here two weeks, and I haven't felt like writing before, since that first day.

I am sitting by the window now, up in this atrocious nursery, and there is nothing to hinder my writing as much as I please, save lack of strength.

John is away all day, and even some nights when his cases are serious.

I am glad my case is not serious!

But these nervous troubles are dreadfully depressing.

John does not know how much I really suffer. He knows there is no reason to suffer, and that satisfies him.

Of course it is only nervousness. It does weigh on me so not to do my duty in any way!

I meant to be such a help to John, such a real rest and comfort, and here I am a comparative burden already!

Nobody would believe what an effort it is to do what little I am able,—to dress and entertain, and order things.

It is fortunate Mary is so good with the baby. Such a dear baby!

And yet I cannot be with him, it makes me so nervous.

I suppose John never was nervous in his life. He laughs at me so about this wallpaper!

At first he meant to repaper the room, but afterwards he said that I was letting it get the better of me, and that nothing was worse for a nervous patient than to give way to such fancies.

He said that after the wallpaper was changed it would be the heavy bedstead, and then the barred windows, and then that gate at the head of the stairs, and so on.

"You know the place is doing you good," he said, "and really, dear, I don't care to renovate the house just for a three months' rental."

"Then do let us go downstairs," I said, "there are such pretty rooms there."

Then he took me in his arms and called me a blessed little goose, and said he would go down to the cellar, if I wished, and have it whitewashed into the bargain.

But he is right enough about the beds and windows and things.

It is an airy and comfortable room as any one need wish, and, of course, I would not be so silly as to make him uncomfortable just for a whim.

I'm really getting quite fond of the big room, all but that horrid paper.

Out of one window I can see the garden, those mysterious deepshaded arbors, the riotous old-fashioned flowers, and bushes and gnarly trees.

Out of another I get a lovely view of the bay and a little private wharf belonging to the estate. There is a beautiful shaded lane that runs down there from the house. I always fancy I see people walking in these numerous paths and arbors, but John has cautioned me not to give way to fancy in the least. He says that with my imaginative power and habit of story-making, a nervous weakness like mine is sure to lead to all manner of excited fancies, and that I ought to use my will and good sense to check the tendency. So I try.

I think sometimes that if I were only well enough to write a little it would relieve the press of ideas and rest me.

But I find I get pretty tired when I try.

It is so discouraging not to have any advice and companionship about my work. When I get really well, John says we will ask Cousin Henry and Julia down for a long visit; but he says he would as soon put fireworks in my pillow-case as to let me have those stimulating people about now.

I wish I could get well faster.

But I must not think about that. This paper looks to me as if it knew what a vicious influence it had!

There is a recurrent spot where the pattern lolls like a broken neck and two bulbous eyes stare at you upside down.

I get positively angry with the impertinence of it and the everlastingness. Up and down and sideways they crawl, and those absurd, unblinking eyes are everywhere. There is one place where two breadths didn't match, and the eyes go all up and down the line, one a little higher than the other.

I never saw so much expression in an inanimate thing before, and we all know how much expression they have! I used to lie awake as a child and get more entertainment and terror out of blank walls and plain furniture than most children could find in a toy store.

I remember what a kindly wink the knobs of our big, old bureau used to have, and there was one chair that always seemed like a strong friend.

I used to feel that if any of the other things looked too fierce I could always hop into that chair and be safe.

The furniture in this room is no worse than inharmonious, however, for we had to bring it all from downstairs. I suppose when this was used as a playroom they had to take the nursery things out, and no wonder! I never saw such ravages as the children have made here.

The wallpaper, as I said before, is torn off in spots, and it sticketh closer than a brother—they must have had perseverance as well as hatred.

Then the floor is scratched and gouged and splintered, the plaster itself is dug out here and there, and this great heavy bed which is all we found in the room, looks as if it had been through the wars.

But I don't mind it a bit—only the paper.

There comes John's sister. Such a dear girl as she is, and so careful of me! I must not let her find me writing.

She is a perfect and enthusiastic housekeeper, and hopes for no better profession. I verily believe she thinks it is the writing which made me sick!

But I can write when she is out, and see her a long way off from these windows.

There is one that commands the road, a lovely shaded winding road, and one that just looks off over the country. A lovely country, too, full of great elms and velvet meadows.

This wallpaper has a kind of sub-pattern in a different shade, a particularly irritating one, for you can only see it in certain lights, and not clearly then.

But in the places where it isn't faded and where the sun is just so—I can see a strange, provoking, formless sort of figure, that seems to skulk about behind that silly and conspicuous front design.

There's sister on the stairs!

Well, the Fourth of July is over! The people are gone and I am tired out. John thought it might do me good to see a little company, so we just had mother and Nellie and the children down for a week.

Of course I didn't do a thing. Jennie sees to everything now.

But it tired me all the same.

John says if I don't pick up faster he shall send me to Weir Mitchell in the fall.

But I don't want to go there at all. I had a friend who was in his hands once, and she says he is just like John and my brother, only more so!

Besides, it is such an undertaking to go so far.

I don't feel as if it was worth while to turn my hand over for anything, and I'm getting dreadfully fretful and querulous.

I cry at nothing, and cry most of the time.

Of course I don't when John is here, or anybody else, but when I am alone.

And I am alone a good deal just now. John is kept in town very often by serious cases, and Jennie is good and lets me alone when I want her to.

So I walk a little in the garden or down that lovely lane, sit on the porch under the roses, and lie down up here a good deal.

I'm getting really fond of the room in spite of the wallpaper. Perhaps *because* of the wallpaper.

It dwells in my mind so!

I lie here on this great immovable bed—it is nailed down, I believe—and follow that pattern about by the hour. It is as good as gymnastics, I assure you. I start, we'll say, at the bottom, down in the corner over there where it has not been touched, and I determine for the thousandth time that I will follow that pointless pattern to some sort of a conclusion.

I know a little of the principle of design, and I know this thing was not arranged on any laws of radiation, or alternation, or repetition, or symmetry, or anything else that I ever heard of.

It is repeated, of course, by the breadths, but not otherwise.

Looked at in one way each breadth stands alone, the bloated curves and flourishes—a kind of "debased Romanesque" with delirium tremens—go waddling up and down in isolated columns of fatuity.

But, on the other hand, they connect diagonally, and the sprawling outlines run off in great slanting waves of optic horror, like a lot of wallowing seaweeds in full chase.

The whole thing goes horizontally, too, at least it seems so, and I exhaust myself in trying to distinguish the order of its going in that direction.

They have used a horizontal breadth for a frieze, and that adds wonderfully to the confusion.

There is one end of the room where it is almost intact, and there, when the crosslights fade and the low sun shines directly upon it, I can almost fancy radiation after all,—the interminable grotesques seem to form around a common centre and rush off in headlong plunges of equal distraction.

It makes me tired to follow it. I will take a nap I guess.

I don't know why I should write this.

I don't want to.

I don't feel able.

And I know John would think it absurd. But I must say what I feel and think in some way—it is such a relief!

But the effort is getting to be greater than the relief.

Half the time now I am awfully lazy, and lie down ever so much.

John says I musn't lose my strength, and has me take cod liver oil and lots of tonics and things, to say nothing of ale and wine and rare meat.

Dear John! He loves me very dearly, and hates to have me sick. I tried to have a real earnest reasonable talk with him the other day, and tell him how I wish he would let me go and make a visit to Cousin Henry and Julia.

But he said I wasn't able to go, nor able to stand it after I got there; and I did not make out a very good case for myself, for I was crying before I had finished.

It is getting to be a great effort for me to think straight. Just this nervous weakness I suppose.

And dear John gathered me up in his arms, and just carried me upstairs and laid me on the bed, and sat by me and read to me till it tired my head.

He said I was his darling and his comfort and all he had, and that I must take care of myself for his sake, and keep well.

He says no one but myself can help me out of it, that I must use my will and self-control and not let any silly fancies run away with me.

There's one comfort, the baby is well and happy, and does not have to occupy this nursery with the horrid wallpaper.

If we had not used it, that blessed child would have! What a fortunate escape! Why, I wouldn't have a child of mine, an impressionable little thing, live in such a room for worlds.

I never thought of it before, but it is lucky that John kept me here after all, I can stand it so much easier than a baby, you see.

Of course I never mention it to them any more—I am too wise—but I keep watch of it all the same.

There are things in that paper that nobody knows but me, or ever will.

Behind that outside pattern the dim shapes get clearer every day.

It is always the same shape, only very numerous.

And it is like a woman stooping down and creeping about behind that pattern. I don't like it a bit. I wonder—I begin to think—I wish John would take me away from here!

It is so hard to talk with John about my case, because he is so wise, and because he loves me so.

But I tried it last night.

It was moonlight. The moon shines in all around just as the sun does.

I hate to see it sometimes, it creeps so slowly, and always comes in by one window or another.

John was asleep and I hated to waken him, so I kept still and watched the moonlight on that undulating wallpaper till I felt creepy.

The faint figure behind seemed to shake the pattern, just as if she wanted to get out.

I got up softly and went to feel and see if the paper *did* move, and when I came back John was awake.

"What is it, little girl?" he said. "Don't go walking about like that—you'll get cold."

I thought it was a good time to talk, so I told him that I really was not gaining here, and that I wished he would take me away.

"Why darling!" said he, "our lease will be up in three weeks, and I can't see how to leave before.

"The repairs are not done at home, and I cannot possibly leave town just now. Of course if you were in any danger, I could and would, but you really are better, dear, whether you can see it or not. I am a doctor, dear, and I know. You are gaining flesh and color, your appetite is better, I feel really much easier about you."

"I don't weigh a bit more," said I, "nor as much; and my appetite may be better in the evening when you are here, but it is worse in the morning when you are away!"

"Bless her little heart!" said he with a big hug, "she shall be as sick as she pleases! But now let's improve the shining hours by going to sleep, and talk about it in the morning!"

"And you won't go away?" I asked gloomily.

"Why, how can I, dear? It is only three weeks more and then we will take a nice little trip of a few days while Jennie is getting the house ready. Really dear you are better!"

"Better in body perhaps—" I began, and stopped short, for he sat up straight and looked at me with such a stern, reproachful look that I could not say another word.

"My darling," said he, "I beg of you, for my sake and for our child's sake, as well as for your own, that you will never for one instant let that idea enter your mind! There is nothing so dangerous, so fascinating, to a temperament like yours. It is a false and foolish fancy. Can you not trust me as a physician when I tell you so?"

So of course I said no more on that score, and we went to sleep before long. He thought I was asleep first, but I wasn't, and lay there for hours trying to decide whether that front pattern and the back pattern really did move together or separately.

On a pattern like this, by daylight, there is a lack of sequence, a defiance of law, that is a constant irritant to a normal mind.

The color is hideous enough, and unreliable enough, and infuriating enough, but the pattern is torturing.

You think you have mastered it, but just as you get well underway in following, it turns a back-somersault and there you are. It slaps you in the face, knocks you down, and tramples upon you. It is like a bad dream.

The outside pattern is a florid arabesque, reminding one of a fungus. If you can imagine a toadstool in joints, an interminable string of toadstools, budding and sprouting in endless convolutions—why, that is something like it.

That is, sometimes!

There is one marked peculiarity about this paper, a thing nobody seems to notice but myself, and that is that it changes as the light changes.

When the sun shoots in through the east window—I always watch for that first long, straight ray—it changes so quickly that I never can quite believe it.

That is why I watch it always.

By moonlight—the moon shines in all night when there is a moon—I wouldn't know it was the same paper.

At night in any kind of light, in twilight, candle light, lamplight, and worst of all by moonlight, it becomes bars! The outside pattern I mean, and the woman behind it is as plain as can be.

I didn't realize for a long time what the thing was that showed behind, that dim sub-pattern, but now I am quite sure it is a woman.

By daylight she is subdued, quiet. I fancy it is the pattern that keeps her so still. It is so puzzling. It keeps me quiet by the hour.

I lie down ever so much now. John says it is good for me, and to sleep all I can.

Indeed he started the habit by making me lie down for an hour after each meal.

It is a very bad habit I am convinced, for you see I don't sleep.

And that cultivates deceit, for I don't tell them I'm awake—O no!

The fact is I am getting a little afraid of John.

He seems very queer sometimes, and even Jennie has an inexplicable look.

It strikes me occasionally, just as a scientific hypothesis,—that perhaps it is the paper!

I have watched John when he did not know I was looking, and come into the room suddenly on the most innocent excuses, and I've caught him several times looking at the paper! And Jennie too. I caught Jennie with her hand on it once.

She didn't know I was in the room, and when I asked her in a quiet, a very quiet voice, with the most restrained manner possible, what she was doing with the paper—she turned around as if she had been caught stealing, and looked quite angry—asked me why I should frighten her so!

Then she said that the paper stained everything it touched, that she had found yellow smooches on all my clothes and John's, and she wished we would be more careful!

Did not that sound innocent? But I know she was studying that pattern, and I am determined that nobody shall find it out but myself!

Life is very much more exciting now than it used to be. You see I have something more to expect, to look forward to, to watch. I really do eat better, and am more quiet than I was.

John is so pleased to see me improve! He laughed a little the other day, and said I seemed to be flourishing in spite of my wallpaper.

I turned it off with a laugh. I had no intention of telling him it was *because* of the wallpaper—he would make fun of me. He might even want to take me away.

I don't want to leave now until I have found it out. There is a week more, and I think that will be enough.

I'm feeling ever so much better! I don't sleep much at night, for it is so interesting to watch developments; but I sleep a good deal in the daytime.

In the daytime it is tiresome and perplexing.

There are always new shoots on the fungus, and new shades of yellow all over it. I cannot keep count of them, though I have tried conscientiously.

It is the strangest yellow, that wallpaper! It makes me think of all the yellow things I ever saw—not beautiful ones like buttercups, but old foul, bad yellow things.

But there is something else about that paper—the smell! I noticed it the moment we came into the room, but with so much air and sun it was not bad. Now we have had a week of fog and rain, and whether the windows are open or not, the smell is here.

It creeps all over the house.

I find it hovering in the dining-room, skulking in the parlor, hiding in the hall, lying in wait for me on the stairs.

It gets into my hair.

Even when I go to ride, if I turn my head suddenly and surprise it—there is that smell!

Such a peculiar odor, too! I have spent hours in trying to analyze it, to find what it smelled like.

It is not bad—at first, and very gentle, but quite the subtlest, most enduring odor I ever met.

In this damp weather it is awful, I wake up in the night and find it hanging over me.

It used to disturb me at first. I thought seriously of burning the house—to reach the smell.

But now I am used to it. The only thing I can think of that it is like is the *color* of the paper! A yellow smell.

There is a very funny mark on this wall, low down, near the mopboard. A streak that runs round the room. It goes behind every piece of furniture, except the bed, a long, straight, even smooch, as if it had been rubbed over and over.

I wonder how it was done and who did it, and what they did it for. Round and round and round—round and round and round—it makes me dizzy!

I really have discovered something at last.

Through watching so much at night, when it changes so, I have finally found out.

The front pattern *does* move—and no wonder! The woman behind shakes it!

Sometimes I think there are a great many women behind, and sometimes only one, and she crawls around fast, and her crawling shakes it all over.

Then in the very bright spots she keeps still, and in the very shady spots she just takes hold of the bars and shakes them hard.

And she is all the time trying to climb through. But nobody could climb through that pattern—it strangles so; I think that is why it has so many heads.

They get through, and then the pattern strangles them off and turns them upside down, and makes their eyes white!

If those heads were covered or taken off it would not be half so bad.

I think that woman gets out in the daytime!

And I'll tell you why—privately—I've seen her!

I can see her out of every one of my windows!

It is the same woman, I know, for she is always creeping, and most women do not creep by daylight.

I see her on that long road under the trees, creeping along, and when a carriage comes she hides under the blackberry vines.

I don't blame her a bit. It must be very humiliating to be caught creeping by daylight!

I always lock the door when I creep by daylight. I can't do it at night, for I know John would suspect something at once.

And John is so queer now, that I don't want to irritate him. I wish he would take another room! Besides, I don't want anybody to get that woman out at night but myself.

I often wonder if I could see her out of all the windows at once.

But, turn as fast as I can, I can only see out of one at one time.

And though I always see her, she *may* be able to creep faster than I can turn!

I have watched her sometimes away off in the open country, creeping as fast as a cloud shadow in a high wind.

If only that top pattern could be gotten off from the under one! I mean to try it, little by little.

I have found out another funny thing, but I shan't tell it this time! It does not do to trust people too much.

There are only two more days to get this paper off, and I believe John is beginning to notice. I don't like the look in his eyes.

And I heard him ask Jennie a lot of professional questions about me. She had a very good report to give.

She said I slept a good deal in the daytime.

John knows I don't sleep very well at night, for all I'm so quiet!

He asked me all sorts of questions, too, and pretended to be very loving and kind.

As if I couldn't see through him!

Still, I don't wonder he acts so, sleeping under this paper for three months.

It only interests me, but I feel sure John and Jennie are secretly affected by it.

Hurrah! This is the last day, but it is enough. John is to stay in town over night, and won't be out until this evening.

Jennie wanted to sleep with me—the sly thing! but I told her I should undoubtedly rest better for a night all alone.

That was clever, for really I wasn't alone a bit! As soon as it was moonlight and that poor thing began to crawl and shake the pattern, I got up and ran to help her.

I pulled and she shook, I shook and she pulled, and before morning we had peeled off yards of that paper.

A strip about as high as my head and half around the room.

And then when the sun came and that awful pattern began to laugh at me, I declared I would finish it to-day!

We go away to-morrow, and they are moving all my furniture down again to leave things as they were before.

Jennie looked at the wall in amazement, but I told her merrily that I did it out of pure spite at the vicious thing.

She laughed and said she wouldn't mind doing it herself, but I must not get tired.

How she betrayed herself that time!

But I am here, and no person touches this paper but me—not *alive!*

She tried to get me out of the room—it was too patent! But I said it was so quiet and empty and clean now that I believed I would lie down again and sleep all I could; and not to wake me even for dinner—I would call when I woke.

So now she is gone, and the servants are gone, and the things are gone, and there is nothing left but that great bedstead nailed down, with the canvas mattress we found on it.

We shall sleep downstairs to-night, and take the boat home to-morrow.

I quite enjoy the room, now it is bare again.

How those children did tear about here!

This bedstead is fairly gnawed!

But I must get to work.

I have locked the door and thrown the key down into the front path.

I don't want to go out, and I don't want to have anybody come in, till John comes.

I want to astonish him.

I've got a rope up here that even Jennie did not find. If that woman does get out, and tries to get away, I can tie her!

But I forgot I could not reach far without anything to stand on!

This bed will not move!

I tried to lift and push it until I was lame, and then I got so angry I bit off a little piece at one corner—but it hurt my teeth.

Then I peeled off all the paper I could reach standing on the floor. It sticks horribly and the pattern just enjoys it! All those strangled heads and bulbous eyes and waddling fungus growths just shriek with derision!

I am getting angry enough to do something desperate. To jump out of the window would be admirable exercise, but the bars are too strong even to try.

Besides I wouldn't do it. Of course not. I know well enough that a step like that is improper and might be misconstrued.

I don't like to look out of the windows even—there are so many of those creeping women, and they creep so fast.

I wonder if they all come out of that wallpaper as I did?

But I am securely fastened now by my well-hidden rope—you don't get me out in the road there!

I suppose I shall have to get back behind the pattern when it comes night, and that is hard!

It is so pleasant to be out in this great room and creep around as I please!

I don't want to go outside. I won't, even if Jennie asks me to.

For outside you have to creep on the ground, and everything is green instead of yellow.

But here I can creep smoothly on the floor, and my shoulder just fits in that long smooch around the wall, so I cannot lose my way.

Why there's John at the door!

It is no use, young man, you can't open it!

How he does call and pound!

Now he's crying for an axe.

It would be a shame to break down that beautiful door!

"John dear!" said I in the gentlest voice, "the key is down by the front steps, under a plantain leaf!"

That silenced him for a few moments.

Then he said—very quietly indeed, "Open the door, my darling!"

"I can't," said I. "The key is down by the front door under a plantain leaf!"

And then I said it again, several times, very gently and slowly, and said it so often that he had to go and see, and he got it of course, and came in. He stopped short by the door.

"What is the matter?" he cried. "For God's sake, what are you doing!"

I kept on creeping just the same, but I looked at him over my shoulder.

"I've got out at last," said I, "in spite of you and Jane. And I've pulled off most of the paper, so you can't put me back!"

Now why should that man have fainted? But he did, and right across my path by the wall, so that I had to creep over him every time!

THE MASQUE OF THE RED DEATH

Edgar Allan Poe

The "Red Death" had long devastated the country. No pestilence had ever been so fatal, or so hideous. Blood was its Avatar and its seal—the redness and the horror of blood. There were sharp pains, and sudden dizziness, and then profuse bleeding at the pores, with dissolution. The scarlet stains upon the body and especially upon the face of the victim, were the pest ban which shut him out from the aid and from the sympathy of his fellow-men. And the whole seizure, progress and termination of the disease, were the incidents of half an hour.

But the Prince Prospero was happy and dauntless and sagacious. When his dominions were half depopulated, he summoned to his presence a thousand hale and light-hearted friends from among the knights and dames of his court, and with these retired to the deep seclusion of one of his castellated abbeys. This was an extensive and magnificent structure, the creation of the prince's own eccentric yet august taste. A strong and lofty wall girdled it in. This wall had gates of iron. The courtiers, having entered, brought furnaces and massy hammers and welded the bolts. They resolved to leave means neither of ingress or egress to the sudden impulses of despair or of frenzy from within. The abbey was amply provisioned. With such precautions the courtiers might bid defiance to contagion. The external world could take care of itself. In the meantime it was folly to grieve, or to think. The prince had provided all the appliances of pleasure. There were buffoons, there were improvisatori, there were ballet-dancers, there were musicians, there was Beauty, there was wine. All these and security were within. Without was the "Red Death."

It was toward the close of the fifth or sixth month of his seclusion, and while the pestilence raged most furiously abroad, that the Prince Prospero entertained his thousand friends at a masked ball of the most unusual magnificence.

It was a voluptuous scene, that masquerade. But first let me tell of the rooms in which it was held. There were seven—an imperial suite. In many palaces, however, such suites form a long and straight vista, while the folding doors slide back nearly to the walls on either hand, so that the view of the whole extent is scarcely impeded. Here the case was very different; as might have been expected from the duke's love of the bizarre. The apartments were so irregularly disposed that the vision embraced but little more than one at a time. There was a sharp turn at every twenty or thirty yards, and at each turn a novel effect. To the right and left, in the middle of each wall, a tall and narrow Gothic window looked out upon a closed corridor which pursued the windings of the suite. These windows were of stained glass whose color varied in accordance with the prevailing hue of the decorations of the chamber into which it opened. That at the eastern extremity was hung, for example, in blue—and vividly blue were its windows. The second chamber was purple in its ornaments and tapestries, and here the panes were purple. The third was green throughout, and so were the casements. The fourth was furnished and lighted with orange—the fifth with white—the sixth with violet. The seventh apartment was closely shrouded in black velvet tapestries that hung all over the ceiling and down the walls, falling in heavy folds upon a carpet of the same material and hue. But in this chamber only, the color of the windows failed to correspond with the decorations. The panes here were scarlet—a deep blood color. Now in no one of the seven apartments was there any lamp or candelabrum, amid the profusion of golden ornaments that lay scattered to and fro or depended from the roof. There was no light of any kind emanating from lamp or candle within the suite of chambers. But in the corridors that followed the suite, there stood, opposite to each window, a heavy tripod, bearing a brazier of fire that protected its rays through the tinted glass and so glaringly illumined the room. And thus were produced a multitude of gaudy and fantastic appearances. But in the western or black chamber the effect of the fire-light that streamed upon the dark hangings through the blood-tinted panes, was ghastly in the extreme, and produced so wild a look upon the countenances of those who entered, that there were few of the company bold enough to set foot within its precincts at all.

It was in this apartment, also, that there stood against the western wall, a gigantic clock of ebony. Its pendulum swung to and fro with a dull, heavy, monotonous clang; and when the minute-hand made the circuit of the face, and the hour was to be stricken, there came from the brazen lungs of the clock a sound which was clear and loud and deep and exceedingly musical, but of so peculiar a note and emphasis that, at each lapse of an hour, the musicians of the orchestra were constrained to pause, momentarily, in their performance, to hearken to the sound; and thus the waltzers perforce ceased their evolutions; and there was a brief disconcert of the whole gay company; and, while the chimes of the clock yet rang, it was observed that the giddiest grew pale, and the more aged and sedate passed their hands over their brows as if in confused reverie or meditation. But when the echoes had fully ceased, a light laughter at once pervaded the assembly; the musicians looked at each other and smiled as if at their own nervousness and folly, and made whispering vows, each to the other, that the next chiming of the clock should produce in them no similar emotion; and then, after the lapse of sixty minutes (which embrace three thousand and six hundred seconds of the Time that flies), there came yet another chiming of the clock, and then were the same disconcert and tremulousness and meditation as before.

But, in spite of these things, it was a gay and magnificent revel. The tastes of the duke were peculiar. He had a fine eye for colors and effects. He disregarded the decora of mere fashion. His plans were bold and fiery, and his conceptions glowed with barbaric lustre. There are some who would have thought him mad. His followers felt that he was not. It was necessary to hear and see and touch him to be sure that he was not.

He had directed, in great part, the moveable embellishments of the seven chambers, upon occasion of this great fête; and it was his own guiding taste which had given character to the masqueraders. Be sure they were grotesque. There were much glare and glitter and piquancy and phantasm—much of what has been since seen in Hernani. There were arabesque figures with unsuited limbs and appointments. There were delirious fancies such as the madman fashions. There was much of the beautiful, much of the wanton, much of the bizarre, something of the terrible, and not a little of that which might have excited disgust. To and fro in the seven chambers there stalked, in fact, a multitude of dreams. And these—the dreams—writhed in and about, taking hue from the rooms, and causing the wild music of the orchestra to seem as the echo of their steps. And, anon, there strikes the ebony clock which stands in the hall of the velvet. And then, for a moment, all is still, and all is silent save the voice of the clock. The dreams are stiff-frozen as they stand. But the echoes of the chime die away—they have endured but an instant—and a light, half-subdued laughter floats after them as they depart. And now again the music swells, and the dreams live, and writhe to and fro more merrily than ever, taking hue from the many-tinted windows through which stream the rays from the tripods. But to the chamber which lies most westwardly of the seven, there are now none of the maskers who venture; for the night is waning away; and there flows a ruddier light through the blood-colored panes; and the blackness of the sable drapery appals; and to him whose foot falls upon the sable carpet, there comes from the near clock of ebony a muffled peal more solemnly emphatic than any which reaches their ears who indulge in the more remote gaieties of the other apartments.

But these other apartments were densely crowded, and in them beat feverishly the heart of life. And the revel went whirlingly on, until at length there commenced the sounding of midnight upon the clock. And then the music ceased, as I have told; and the evolutions of the waltzers were quieted; and there was an uneasy cessation of all things as before. But now there were twelve strokes to be sounded by the bell of the clock; and thus it happened, perhaps, that more of thought crept, with more of time, into the meditations of the thoughtful among those who revelled. And thus, too, it happened, perhaps, that before the last echoes of the last chime had utterly sunk into silence, there were many individuals in the crowd who had found leisure to become aware of the presence of a masked figure which had arrested the attention of no single individual before. And the rumor of this new presence having spread itself whisperingly around, there arose at length from the whole company a buzz, or murmur, expressive of disapprobation and surprise—then, finally, of terror, of horror, and of disgust.

In an assembly of phantasms such as I have painted, it may well be supposed that no ordinary appearance could have excited such sensation. In truth the masquerade license of the night was nearly unlimited; but the figure in question had out-Heroded Herod, and gone beyond the bounds of even the prince's indefinite decorum. There are chords in the hearts of the most reckless which cannot be touched without emotion. Even with the utterly lost, to whom life and death are equally jests, there are matters of which no jest can be made. The whole company, indeed, seemed now deeply to feel that in the costume and bearing of the stranger neither wit nor propriety existed. The figure was tall and gaunt, and shrouded from head to foot in the habiliments of the grave. The mask which concealed the visage was made so nearly to resemble the countenance of a stiffened corpse that the closest scrutiny must have had difficulty in detecting the cheat. And yet all this might have been endured, if not approved, by the mad revellers around. But the mummer had gone so far as to assume the type of the Red Death. His vesture was dabbled in *blood*—and his broad brow, with all the features of the face, was besprinkled with the scarlet horror.

When the eyes of Prince Prospero fell upon this spectral image (which with a slow and solemn movement, as if more fully to sustain its role, stalked to and fro among the waltzers) he was seen to be convulsed, in the first moment with a strong shudder either of terror or distaste; but, in the next, his brow reddened with rage.

"Who dares?" he demanded hoarsely of the courtiers who stood near him—"who dares insult us with this blasphemous mockery? Seize him and unmask him—that we may know whom we have to hang at sunrise, from the battlements!"

It was in the eastern or blue chamber in which stood the Prince Prospero as he uttered these words. They rang throughout the seven rooms loudly and clearly—for the prince was a bold and robust man, and the music had become hushed at the waving of his hand.

It was in the blue room where stood the prince, with a group of pale courtiers by his side. At first, as he spoke, there was a slight rushing movement of this group in the direction of the intruder, who at the moment was also near at hand, and now, with deliberate and stately step, made closer approach to the speaker. But from a certain nameless awe with which the mad assumptions of the mummer had inspired the whole party, there were found none who put forth hand to seize him; so that, unimpeded, he passed within a yard of the prince's person; and, while the vast assembly, as if with one impulse, shrank from the centres of the rooms to the walls, he made his way uninterruptedly, but with the same solemn and measured step which had distinguished him from the first, through the blue chamber to the purple—through the purple to the green—through the green to the orange—through this again to the white—and even thence to the violet, ere a decided movement had been made to arrest him. It was then, however, that the Prince Prospero, maddening with rage and the shame of his own momentary cowardice, rushed hurriedly through the six chambers, while none followed him on account of a deadly terror that had seized upon all. He bore aloft a drawn dagger, and had approached, in rapid impetuosity, to within three or four feet of the retreating figure, when the latter, having attained the extremity of the velvet apartment, turned suddenly and confronted his pursuer. There was a sharp cry—and the dagger dropped gleaming upon the sable carpet, upon which, instantly afterwards, fell prostrate in death the Prince Prospero. Then, summoning the wild courage of despair, a throng of the revellers at once threw themselves into the black apartment, and, seizing the mummer, whose tall figure stood erect and motionless within the shadow of the ebony clock, gasped in unutterable horror at finding the grave-cerements and corpse-like mask which they handled with so violent a rudeness, untenanted by any tangible form.

And now was acknowledged the presence of the Red Death. He had come like a thief in the night. And one by one dropped the revellers in the blood-bedewed halls of their revel, and died each in the despairing posture of his fall. And the life of the ebony clock went out with that of the last of the gay. And the flames of the tripods expired. And Darkness and Decay and the Red Death held illimitable dominion over all.

THE METAMORPHOSIS

Franz Kafka

Translated by David Wyllie

I

One morning, when Gregor Samsa woke from troubled dreams, he found himself transformed in his bed into a horrible vermin. He lay on his armor-like back, and if he lifted his head a little he could see his brown belly, slightly domed and divided by arches into stiff sections. The bedding was hardly able to cover it and seemed ready to slide off any moment. His many legs, pitifully thin compared with the size of the rest of him, waved about helplessly as he looked.

"What's happened to me?" he thought. It wasn't a dream. His room, a proper human room although a little too small, lay peacefully between its four familiar walls. A collection of textile samples lay spread out on the table—Samsa was a traveling salesman—and above it there hung a picture that he had recently cut out of an illustrated magazine and housed in a nice, gilded frame. It showed a lady fitted out with a fur hat and fur boa who sat upright, raising a heavy fur muff that covered the whole of her lower arm towards the viewer.

Gregor then turned to look out the window at the dull weather. Drops of rain could be heard hitting the pane, which made him feel quite sad. "How about if I sleep a little bit longer and forget all this nonsense," he thought, but that was something he was unable to do because he was used to sleeping on his right, and in his present state couldn't get into that position. However hard he threw himself onto his right, he always rolled back to where he was. He must have tried it a hundred times, shut his eyes so that he wouldn't have to look at the floundering legs, and only stopped when he began to feel a mild, dull pain there that he had never felt before.

"Oh, God," he thought, "what a strenuous career it is that I've chosen! Traveling day in and day out. Doing business like this takes much more effort than doing your own business at home, and on top of that there's the curse of travelling, worries about making train connections, bad and irregular food, contact with different people all the time so that you can never get to know anyone or become friendly with them. It can all go to Hell!" He felt a slight itch up on his belly; pushed himself slowly up on his back towards the headboard so that he could lift his head better; found where the itch was, and saw that it was covered with lots of little white spots which he didn't know what to make of; and when he tried to feel the place with one of his legs he drew it quickly back because as soon as he touched it he was overcome by a cold shudder.

He slid back into his former position. "Getting up early all the time," he thought, "it makes you stupid. You've got to get enough sleep. Other traveling salesmen live a life of luxury. For instance, whenever I go back to the guest house during the morning to copy out the contract, these gentlemen are always still sitting there eating their breakfasts. I ought to just try that with my boss; I'd get kicked out on the spot. But who knows, maybe that would be the best thing for me. If I didn't have my parents to think about I'd have given in my notice a long time ago, I'd have gone up to the boss and told him just what I think, tell him everything I would, let him know just what I feel. He'd fall right off his desk! And it's a funny sort of business to be sitting up there at your desk, talking down at your subordinates from up there, especially when you have to go right up close because the boss is hard of hearing. Well, there's still some hope; once I've got the money together to pay off my parents' debt to him—another five or six years I suppose—that's definitely what I'll do. That's when I'll make the big change. First of all though, I've got to get up, my train leaves at five."

And he looked over at the alarm clock, ticking on the chest of drawers. "God in Heaven!" he thought. It was half past six and the hands were quietly moving forwards, it was even later than half past, more like quarter to seven. Had the alarm clock not rung? He could see from the bed that it had been set for four o'clock as it should have been; it certainly must have rung. Yes, but was it possible to quietly sleep through that furniture-rattling noise? True, he had not slept peacefully, but probably all the more deeply because of that. What should he do now? The next train went at seven; if he were to catch that he would have to rush like mad and the collection of samples was still not packed, and he did not at all feel particularly fresh and lively. And even if he did catch the train he would not avoid his boss's anger as the office assistant would have been there to see the five o'clock train go, he would have put in his report about Gregor's not being there a long time ago. The office assistant was the boss's man, spineless, and with no understanding. What about if he reported sick? But that would be extremely strained and suspicious as in fifteen years of service Gregor had never once yet been ill. His boss would certainly come round with the doctor from the medical insurance company, accuse his parents of having a lazy son, and accept the doctor's recommendation not to make any claim as the doctor believed that no one was ever ill but that many were workshy. And what's more, would he have been entirely wrong in this case? Gregor did in fact, apart from excessive sleepiness after sleeping for so long, feel completely well and even felt much hungrier than usual.

He was still hurriedly thinking all this through, unable to decide to get out of the bed, when the clock struck quarter to seven. There was a cautious knock at the door near his head. "Gregor," somebody called—it was his mother—"it's quarter to seven. Didn't you want to go somewhere?" That gentle voice! Gregor was shocked when he heard his own voice answering, it could hardly be recognized as the voice he had had before. As if from deep inside him, there was a painful and uncontrollable squeaking mixed in with it, the words could be made out at first but then there was a sort of echo which made them unclear, leaving the hearer unsure whether he had heard properly or not. Gregor had wanted to give a full answer and explain everything, but in the circumstances contented himself with saying: "Yes, mother, yes, thank you, I'm getting up now." The change in Gregor's voice probably could not be noticed outside through the wooden door, as his mother was satisfied with this explanation and shuffled away. But this short conversation made the other members of the family aware that Gregor, against their expectations was still at home, and soon his father came knocking at one of the side doors, gently, but with his fist. "Gregor, Gregor," he called, "what's wrong?" And after a short while he called again with a warning deepness in his voice: "Gregor! Gregor!" At the other side door his sister came plaintively: "Gregor? Aren't you well? Do you need anything?" Gregor answered to both sides: "I'm ready, now," making an effort to remove all the strangeness from his voice by enunciating very carefully and putting long pauses between each individual word. His father went back to his breakfast, but his sister whispered: "Gregor, open the door, I beg of you." Gregor, however, had no thought of opening the door, and instead congratulated himself for his cautious habit, acquired from his traveling, of locking all doors at night even when he was at home.

The first thing he wanted to do was to get up in peace without being disturbed, to get dressed, and most of all to have his breakfast. Only then would he consider what to do next, as he was well aware that he would not bring his thoughts to any sensible conclusions by lying in bed. He remembered that he had often felt a slight pain in bed, perhaps caused by lying awkwardly, but that had always turned out to be pure imagination and he wondered how his imaginings would slowly resolve themselves today. He did not have the slightest doubt that the change in his voice was nothing more than the first sign of a serious cold, which was an occupational hazard for traveling salesmen.

It was a simple matter to throw off the covers; he only had to blow himself up a little and they fell off by themselves. But it became difficult after that, especially as he was so exceptionally broad. He would have used his arms and his hands to push himself up; but instead of them he only had all those little legs continuously moving in different directions, and which he was moreover unable to control. If he wanted to bend one of them, then that was the first one that would stretch itself out; and if he finally managed to do what he wanted with that leg, all the others seemed to be set free and would move about painfully. "This is something that can't be done in bed," Gregor said to himself, "so don't keep trying to do it."

The first thing he wanted to do was get the lower part of his body out of the bed, but he had never seen this lower part, and could not imagine what it looked like; it turned out to be too hard to move; it went so slowly; and finally, almost in a frenzy, when he carelessly shoved himself forwards with all the force he could gather, he chose the wrong direction, hit hard against the lower bedpost, and learned from the burning pain he felt that the lower part of his body might well, at present, be the most sensitive.

So then he tried to get the top part of his body out of the bed first, carefully turning his head to the side. This he managed quite easily, and despite its breadth and its weight, the bulk of his body eventually followed slowly in the direction of the head. But when he had at last got his head out of the bed and into the fresh air it occurred to him that if he let himself fall it would be a miracle if his head were not injured, so he became afraid to carry on pushing himself forward the same way. And he could not knock himself out now at any price; better to stay in bed than lose consciousness.

It took just as much effort to get back to where he had been earlier, but when he lay there sighing, and was once more watching his legs as they struggled against each other even harder than before, if that was possible, he could think of no way of bringing peace and order to this chaos. He told himself once more that it was not possible for him to stay in bed and that the most sensible thing to do would be to get free of it in whatever way he could at whatever sacrifice. At the same time, though, he did not forget to remind himself that calm consideration was much better than rushing to desperate conclusions. At times like this he would direct his eyes to the window and look out as clearly as he could, but unfortunately, even the other side of the narrow street was enveloped in morning fog and the view had little confidence or cheer to offer him. "Seven o'clock, already," he said to himself when the clock struck again, "seven o'clock, and there's still a fog like this." And he lay there quietly a while longer, breathing lightly as if he perhaps expected the total stillness to bring things back to their real and natural state.

But then he said to himself: "Before it strikes quarter past seven I'll definitely have to have got properly out of bed. And by then somebody will have come round from work to ask what's happened to me as well, as they open up at work before seven o'clock." And so he set himself to the task of swinging the entire length of his body out of the bed all at the same time. If he succeeded in falling out of bed in this way and kept his head raised as he did so he could probably avoid injuring it. His back seemed to be quite hard, and probably nothing would happen to it falling onto the carpet. His main concern was for the loud noise he was bound to make, and which even through all the doors would probably raise concern if not alarm. But it was something that had to be risked.

When Gregor was already sticking half way out of the bed—the new method was more of a game than an effort, all he had to do was rock back and forth—it occurred to him how simple everything would be if somebody came to help him. Two strong people—he had his father and the maid in mind—would have been more than enough; they would only have to push their arms under the dome of his back, peel him away from the bed, bend down with the load and then be patient and careful as he swang over onto the floor, where, hopefully, the little legs would find a use. Should he really call for help though, even apart from the fact that all the doors were locked? Despite all the difficulty he was in, he could not suppress a smile at this thought.

After a while he had already moved so far across that it would have been hard for him to keep his balance if he rocked too hard. The time was now ten past seven and he would have to make a final decision very soon. Then there was a ring at the door of the flat. "That'll be someone from work," he said to himself, and froze very still, although his little legs only became all the more lively as they danced around. For a moment everything remained quiet. "They're not opening the door," Gregor said to himself, caught in some nonsensical hope. But then of course, the maid's firm steps went to the door as ever and opened it. Gregor only needed to hear the visitor's first words of greeting and he knew who it was—the chief clerk himself. Why did Gregor have to be the only one condemned to work for a company where they immediately became highly suspicious at the slightest shortcoming? Were all employees, every one of them, louts, was there not one of them who was faithful and devoted who would go so mad with pangs of conscience that he couldn't get out of bed if he didn't spend at least a couple of hours in the morning on company business? Was it really not enough to let one of the trainees make enquiries—assuming enquiries were even necessary—did the chief clerk have to come himself, and did they have to show the whole, innocent family that this was so suspicious that only the chief clerk could be trusted to have the wisdom to investigate it? And more because these thoughts had made him upset than through any proper decision, he swang himself with all his force out of the bed. There was a loud thump, but it wasn't really a loud noise. His fall was softened a little by the carpet, and

Gregor's back was also more elastic than he had thought, which made the sound muffled and not too noticeable. He had not held his head carefully enough, though, and hit it as he fell; annoyed and in pain, he turned it and rubbed it against the carpet.

"Something's fallen down in there," said the chief clerk in the room on the left. Gregor tried to imagine whether something of the sort that had happened to him today could ever happen to the chief clerk too; you had to concede that it was possible. But as if in gruff reply to this question, the chief clerk's firm footsteps in his highly polished boots could now be heard in the adjoining room. From the room on his right, Gregor's sister whispered to him to let him know: "Gregor, the chief clerk is here." "Yes, I know," said Gregor to himself; but without daring to raise his voice loud enough for his sister to hear him.

"Gregor," said his father now from the room to his left, "the chief clerk has come round and wants to know why you didn't leave on the early train. We don't know what to say to him. And anyway, he wants to speak to you personally. So please open up this door. I'm sure he'll be good enough to forgive the untidiness of your room." Then the chief clerk called "Good morning, Mr. Samsa." "He isn't well," said his mother to the chief clerk, while his father continued to speak through the door. "He isn't well, please believe me. Why else would Gregor have missed a train! The lad only ever thinks about the business. It nearly makes me cross the way he never goes out in the evenings; he's been in town for a week now but stayed home every evening. He sits with us in the kitchen and just reads the paper or studies train timetables. His idea of relaxation is working with his fretsaw. He's made a little frame, for instance, it only took him two or three evenings, you'll be amazed how nice it is; it's hanging up in his room; you'll see it as soon as Gregor opens the door. Anyway, I'm glad you're here; we wouldn't have been able to get Gregor to open the door by ourselves; he's so stubborn; and I'm sure he isn't well, he said this morning that he is, but he isn't." "I'll be there in a moment," said Gregor slowly and thoughtfully, but without moving so that he would not miss any word of the conversation. "Well I can't think of any other way of explaining it, Mrs. Samsa," said the chief clerk, "I hope it's nothing serious. But on the other hand, I must say that if we people in commerce ever become slightly unwell then, fortunately or unfortunately as you like, we simply have to overcome it because of business considerations." "Can the chief clerk come in to see you now then?" asked his father impatiently, knocking at the door again. "No," said Gregor. In the room on his right there followed a painful silence; in the room on his left his sister began to cry.

So why did his sister not go and join the others? She had probably only just got up and had not even begun to get dressed. And why was she crying? Was it because he had not got up, and had not let the chief clerk in, because he was in danger of losing his job and if that happened his boss would once more pursue their parents with the same demands as before? There was no need to worry about things like that yet. Gregor was still there and had not the slightest intention of abandoning his family. For the time being he just lay there on the carpet, and no one who knew the condition he was in would seriously have expected him to let the chief clerk in. It was only a minor discourtesy, and a suitable excuse could easily be found for it later on, it was not something for which Gregor could be sacked on the spot. And it seemed to Gregor much more sensible to leave him now in peace instead of disturbing him with talking at him and crying. But the others didn't know what was happening, they were worried, that would excuse their behavior.

The chief clerk now raised his voice, "Mr. Samsa," he called to him, "what is wrong? You barricade yourself in your room, give us no more than yes or no for an answer, you are causing serious and unnecessary concern to your parents and you fail—and I mention this just by the way—you fail to carry out your business duties in a way that is quite unheard of. I'm speaking here on behalf of your parents and of your employer, and really must request a clear and immediate explanation. I am astonished, quite astonished. I thought I knew you as a calm and sensible person, and now you suddenly seem to be showing off with peculiar whims. This morning, your employer did suggest a possible reason for your failure to appear, it's true—it had to do with the money that was recently entrusted to you—but I came near to giving him my word of honor that that could not be the right explanation. But now that I see your incomprehensible stubbornness I no longer feel any wish whatsoever to intercede on your behalf. And nor is your position all that secure. I had originally intended to say all this to you in private, but since you cause me to waste my time here for no good reason I don't see why your parents should not also learn of it. Your turnover has been very unsatisfactory of late; I grant you that it's not the time of year to do especially good business, we recognize that; but there simply is no time of year to do no business at all, Mr. Samsa, we cannot allow there to be."

"But Sir," called Gregor, beside himself and forgetting all else in the excitement, "I'll open up immediately, just a moment. I'm slightly unwell, an attack of dizziness, I haven't been able to get up. I'm still in bed now. I'm quite fresh again now, though. I'm just getting out of bed. Just a moment. Be patient! It's not quite as easy as I'd thought. I'm quite alright now, though. It's shocking, what can suddenly happen to a person! I was quite alright last night, my parents know about it, perhaps better than me, I had a small symptom of it last night already. They must have noticed it. I don't know why I didn't let you know at work! But you always think you can get over an illness without staying at home. Please, don't make my parents suffer! There's no basis for any of the accusations you're making; nobody's ever said a word to me about any of these things. Maybe you haven't read the latest contracts I sent in. I'll set off with the eight o'clock train, as well, these few hours of rest have given me strength. You don't need to wait, sir; I'll be in the office soon after you, and please be so good as to tell that to the boss and recommend me to him!"

And while Gregor gushed out these words, hardly knowing what he was saying, he made his way over to the chest of drawers—this was easily done, probably because of the practice he had already had in bed—where he now tried to get himself upright. He really did want to open the door, really did want to let them see him and to speak with the chief clerk; the others were being so insistent, and he was curious to learn what they would say when they caught sight of him. If they were shocked then it would no longer be Gregor's responsibility and he could rest. If, however, they took everything calmly he would still have no reason to be upset, and if he hurried he really could be at the station for eight o'clock. The first few times he tried to climb up on the smooth chest of drawers he just slid down again, but he finally gave himself one last swing and stood there upright; the lower part of his body was in serious pain but he no longer gave any attention to it. Now he let himself fall against the back of a nearby chair and held tightly to the edges of it with his little legs. By now he had also calmed down, and kept quiet so that he could listen to what the chief clerk was saying.

"Did you understand a word of all that?" the chief clerk asked his parents, "surely he's not trying to make fools of us." "Oh, God!" called his mother, who was already in tears, "he could be seriously ill and we're making him suffer. Grete! Grete!" she then cried. "Mother?" his sister called from the other side. They communicated across Gregor's room. "You'll have to go for the doctor straight away. Gregor is ill. Quick, get the doctor. Did you hear the way Gregor spoke just now?" "That was the voice of an animal," said the chief clerk, with a calmness that was in contrast with his mother's screams. "Anna! Anna!" his father called into the kitchen through the entrance hall, clapping his hands, "get a locksmith here, now!" And the two girls, their skirts swishing, immediately ran out through the hall, wrenching open the front door of the flat as they went. How had his sister managed to get dressed so quickly? There was no sound of the door banging shut again; they must have left it open; people often do in homes where something awful has happened.

Gregor, in contrast, had become much calmer. So they couldn't understand his words any more, although they seemed clear enough to him, clearer than before—perhaps his ears had become used to the sound. They had realized, though, that there was something wrong with him, and were ready to help.

The first response to his situation had been confident and wise, and that made him feel better. He felt that he had been drawn back in among people, and from the doctor and the locksmith he expected great and surprising achievements—although he did not really distinguish one from the other. Whatever was said next would be crucial, so, in order to make his voice as clear as possible, he coughed a little, but taking care to do this not too loudly as even this might well sound different from the way that a human coughs and he was no longer sure he could judge this for himself. Meanwhile, it had become very quiet in the next room. Perhaps his parents were sat at the table whispering with the chief clerk, or perhaps they were all pressed against the door and listening.

Gregor slowly pushed his way over to the door with the chair. Once there he let go of it and threw himself onto the door, holding himself upright against it using the adhesive on the tips of his legs. He rested there a little while to recover from the effort involved and then set himself to the task of turning the key in the lock with his mouth. He seemed, unfortunately, to have no proper teeth—how was he, then, to grasp the key?—but the lack of teeth was, of course, made up for with a very strong jaw; using the jaw, he really was able to start the key turning, ignoring the fact that he must have been causing some kind of damage as a brown fluid came from his mouth, flowed over the key and dripped onto the floor. "Listen," said the chief clerk in the next room, "he's turning the key." Gregor was greatly encouraged by this; but they all should have been calling to him, his father and his mother too: "Well done, Gregor," they should have cried, "keep at it, keep hold of the lock!" And with the idea that they were all excitedly following his efforts, he bit on the key with all his strength, paying no attention to the pain he was causing himself. As the key turned round he turned around the lock with it, only holding himself upright with his mouth, and hung onto the key or pushed it down again with the whole weight of his body as needed. The clear sound of the lock as it snapped back was Gregor's sign that he could break his concentration, and as he regained his breath he said to himself: "So, I didn't need the locksmith after all." Then he lay his head on the handle of the door to open it completely.

Because he had to open the door in this way, it was already wide open before he could be seen. He had first to slowly turn himself around one of the double doors, and he had to do it very carefully if he did not want to fall flat on his back before entering the room. He was still occupied with this difficult movement, unable to pay attention to anything else, when he heard the chief clerk exclaim a loud "Oh!" which sounded like the soughing of the wind. Now he also saw him—he was the nearest to the door—his hand pressed against his open mouth and slowly retreating as if driven by a steady and invisible force. Gregor's mother, her hair still disheveled from bed despite the chief clerk's being there, looked at his father. Then she unfolded her arms, took two steps forward towards Gregor and sank down onto the floor into her skirts that spread themselves out around her as her head disappeared down onto her breast. His father looked hostile, and clenched his fists as if wanting to knock Gregor back into his room. Then he looked uncertainly round the living room, covered his eyes with his hands and wept so that his powerful chest shook.

So Gregor did not go into the room, but leant against the inside of the other door which was still held bolted in place. In this way only half of his body could be seen, along with his head above it which he leant over to one side as he peered out at the others. Meanwhile the day had become much lighter; part of the endless, gray-black building on the other side of the street—which was a hospital—could be seen quite clearly with the austere and regular line of windows piercing its facade; the rain was still falling, now throwing down large, individual droplets which hit the ground one at a time. The washing up from breakfast lay on the table; there was so much of it because, for Gregor's father, breakfast was the most important meal of the day and he would stretch it out for several hours as he sat reading a number of different newspapers. On the wall exactly opposite there was a photograph of Gregor when he was a lieutenant in the army, his sword in his hand and a carefree smile on his face as he called forth respect for his uniform and bearing. The door to the entrance hall was open and as the front door of the flat was also open he could see onto the landing and the stairs where they began their way down below.

"Now, then," said Gregor, well aware that he was the only one to have kept calm, "I'll get dressed straight away now, pack up my samples and set off. Will you please just let me leave? You can see," he said to the chief clerk, "that I'm not stubborn and I like to do my job; being a commercial traveler is arduous but without traveling I couldn't earn my living. So where are you going, in to the office? Yes? Will you report everything accurately, then? It's quite possible for someone to be temporarily unable to work, but that's just the right time to remember what's been achieved in the past and consider that later on, once the difficulty has been removed, he will certainly work with all the more diligence and concentration. You're well aware that I'm seriously in debt to our employer as well as having to look after my parents and my sister, so that I'm trapped in a difficult situation, but I will work my way out of it again. Please don't make things any harder for me than they are already, and don't take sides against me at the office. I know that nobody likes the travelers. They think we earn an enormous wage as well as having a soft time of it. That's just prejudice but they have no particular reason to think better of it. But you, sir, you have a better overview than the rest of the staff, in fact, if I can say this in confidence, a better overview than the boss himself—it's very easy for a businessman like him to make mistakes about his employees and judge them more harshly than he should. And you're also well aware that we travelers spend almost the whole year away from the office, so that we can very easily fall victim to gossip and chance and groundless complaints, and it's almost impossible to defend yourself from that sort of thing, we don't usually even hear about them, or if at all it's when we arrive back home exhausted from a trip, and that's when we feel the harmful effects of what's been going on without even knowing what caused them. Please, don't go away, at least first say something to show that you grant that I'm at least partly right!"

But the chief clerk had turned away as soon as Gregor had started to speak, and, with protruding lips, only stared back at him over his trembling shoulders as he left. He did not keep still for a moment while Gregor was speaking, but moved steadily towards the door without taking his eyes off him. He moved very gradually, as if there had been some secret prohibition on leaving the room. It was only when he had reached the entrance hall that he made a sudden movement, drew his foot from the living room, and rushed forward in a panic. In the hall, he stretched his right hand far out towards the stairway as if out there, there were some supernatural force waiting to save him.

Gregor realized that it was out of the question to let the chief clerk go away in this mood if his position in the firm was not to be put into extreme danger. That was something his parents did not understand very well; over the years, they had become convinced that this job would provide for Gregor for his entire life, and besides, they had so much to worry about at present that they had lost sight of any thought for the future. Gregor, though, did think about the future. The chief clerk had to be held back, calmed down, convinced and finally won over; the future of Gregor and his family depended on it! If only his sister were here! She was clever; she was already in tears while Gregor was still lying peacefully on his back. And the chief clerk was a lover of women, surely she could persuade him; she would close the front door in the entrance hall and talk him out of his shocked state. But his sister was not there, Gregor would have to do the job himself. And without considering that he still was not familiar with how well he could move about in his present state, or that his speech still might not—or probably would not—be understood, he let go of the door; pushed himself through the opening; tried to reach the chief clerk on the landing who, ridiculously, was holding on to the banister with both hands; but Gregor fell immediately over and, with a little scream as he sought something to hold onto, landed on his numerous little legs. Hardly had that happened than, for the first time that day, he began to feel alright with his body; the little legs had the solid ground under them; to his pleasure, they did exactly as he told them; they were even making the effort to carry him where he wanted to go; and he was soon believing that all his sorrows would soon be finally at an end. He held back the urge to move but swayed from side to side as he crouched there on the floor. His mother was not far away in front of him and seemed, at first, quite engrossed in herself, but then she suddenly jumped up with her arms outstretched and her fingers spread shouting: "Help, for pity's sake, Help!" The way she held her head suggested she wanted to see Gregor better, but the unthinking way she was hurrying backwards showed that she did not; she had forgotten that the table was behind her with all the breakfast things on it; when she reached the table she sat quickly down on it without knowing what she was doing; without even seeming to notice that the coffee pot had been knocked over and a gush of coffee was pouring down onto the carpet.

"Mother, mother," said Gregor gently, looking up at her. He had completely forgotten the chief clerk for the moment, but could not help himself snapping in the air with his jaws at the sight of the flow of coffee. That set his mother screaming anew, she fled from the table and into the arms of his father as he rushed towards her. Gregor, though, had no time to spare for his parents now; the chief clerk had already reached the stairs; with his chin on the banister, he looked back for the last time. Gregor made a run for him; he wanted to be sure of reaching him; the chief clerk must have expected something, as he leapt down several steps at once and disappeared; his shouts resounding all around the staircase. The flight of the chief clerk seemed, unfortunately, to put Gregor's father into a panic as well. Until then he had been relatively self controlled, but now, instead of running after the chief clerk himself, or at least not impeding Gregor as he ran after him, Gregor's father seized the chief clerk's stick in his right hand (the chief clerk had left it behind on a chair, along with his hat and overcoat), picked up a large newspaper from the table with his left, and used them to drive Gregor back into his room, stamping his foot at him as he went. Gregor's appeals to his father were of no help, his appeals were simply not understood, however much he humbly turned his head his father merely stamped his foot all the harder. Across the room, despite the chilly weather, Gregor's mother had pulled open a window, leant far out of it and pressed her hands to her face. A strong draught of air flew in from the street towards the stairway, the curtains flew up, the newspapers on the table fluttered and some of them were blown onto the floor. Nothing would stop Gregor's father as he drove him back, making hissing noises at him like a wild man. Gregor had never had any practice in moving backwards and was only able to go very slowly. If Gregor had only been allowed to turn round he would have been back in his room straight away, but he was afraid that if he took the time to do that his father would become impatient, and there was the threat of a lethal blow to his back or head from the stick in his father's hand any moment. Eventually, though, Gregor realized that he had no choice as he saw, to his disgust, that he was quite incapable of going backwards in a straight line; so he began, as quickly as possible and with frequent anxious glances at his father, to turn himself round. It went very slowly, but perhaps his father was able to see his good intentions as he did nothing to hinder him, in fact now and then he used the tip of his stick to give directions from a distance as to which way to turn. If only his father would stop that unbearable hissing! It was making Gregor quite confused. When he had nearly finished turning round, still listening to that hissing, he made a mistake and turned himself back a little the way he had just come. He was pleased when he finally had his head in front of the doorway, but then saw that it was too narrow, and his body was too broad to get through it without further difficulty. In his present mood, it obviously did not occur to his father to open the other of the double doors so that Gregor would have enough space to get through. He was merely fixed on the idea that Gregor should be got back into his room as quickly as possible. Nor would he ever have allowed Gregor the time to get himself upright as preparation for getting through the doorway. What he did, making more noise than ever, was to drive Gregor forwards all the harder as if there had been nothing in the way; it sounded to Gregor as if there was now more than one father behind him; it was not a pleasant experience, and Gregor pushed himself into the doorway without regard for what might happen. One side of his body lifted itself, he lay at an angle in the doorway, one flank scraped on the white door and was painfully injured, leaving vile brown flecks on it, soon he was stuck fast and would not have been able to move at all by himself, the little legs along one side hung quivering in the air while those on the other side were pressed painfully against the ground. Then his father gave him a hefty shove from behind which released him from where he was held and sent him flying, and heavily bleeding, deep into his room. The door was slammed shut with the stick, then, finally, all was quiet.

II

It was not until it was getting dark that evening that Gregor awoke from his deep and coma-like sleep. He would have woken soon afterwards anyway even if he hadn't been disturbed, as he had had enough sleep and felt fully rested. But he had the impression that some hurried steps and the sound of the door leading into the front room being carefully shut had woken him. The light from the electric street lamps shone palely here and there onto the ceiling and tops of the furniture, but down below, where Gregor was, it was dark. He pushed himself over to the door, feeling his way clumsily with his antennae—of which he was now beginning to learn the value—in order to see what had been happening there. The whole of his left side seemed like one painfully stretched scar, and he limped badly on his two rows of legs. One of the legs had been badly injured in the events of that morning—it was nearly a miracle that only one of them had been—and dragged along lifelessly.

It was only when he had reached the door that he realized what it actually was that had drawn him over to it; it was the smell of something to eat. By the door there was a dish filled with sweetened milk with little pieces of white bread floating in it. He was so pleased he almost laughed, as he was even hungrier than he had been that morning, and immediately dipped his head into the milk, nearly covering his eyes with it. But he soon drew his head back again in disappointment; not only did the pain in his tender left side make it difficult to eat the food—he was only able to eat if his whole body worked together as a snuffling whole—but the milk did not taste at all nice. Milk like this was normally his favorite drink, and his sister had certainly left it there for him because of that, but he turned, almost against his own will, away from the dish and crawled back into the center of the room.

Through the crack in the door, Gregor could see that the gas had been lit in the living room. His father at this time would normally be sat with his evening paper, reading it out in a loud voice to Gregor's mother, and sometimes to his sister, but there was now not a sound to be heard. Gregor's sister would often write and tell him about this reading, but maybe his father had lost the habit in recent times. It was so quiet all around too, even though there must have been somebody in the flat. "What a quiet life it is the family lead," said Gregor to himself, and, gazing into the darkness, felt a great pride that he was able to provide a life like that in such a nice home for his sister and parents. But what now, if all this peace and wealth and comfort should come to a horrible and frightening end? That was something that Gregor did not want to think about too much, so he started to move about, crawling up and down the room.

Once during that long evening, the door on one side of the room was opened very slightly and hurriedly closed again; later on the door on the other side did the same; it seemed that someone needed to enter the room but thought better of it. Gregor went and waited immediately by the door, resolved either to bring the timorous visitor into the room in some way or at least to find out who it was; but the door was opened no more that night and Gregor waited in vain. The previous morning while the doors were locked everyone had wanted to get in there to him, but now, now that he had opened up one of the doors and the other had clearly been unlocked some time during the day, no one came, and the keys were in the other sides.

It was not until late at night that the gaslight in the living room was put out, and now it was easy to see that his parents and sister had stayed awake all that time, as they all could be distinctly heard as they went away together on tip-toe. It was clear that no one would come into Gregor's room any more until morning; that gave him plenty of time to think undisturbed about how he would have to re-arrange his life. For some reason, the tall, empty room where he was forced to remain made him feel uneasy as he lay there flat on the floor, even though he had been living in it for five years. Hardly aware of what he was doing other than a slight feeling of shame, he hurried under the couch. It pressed down on his back a little, and he was no longer able to lift his head, but he nonetheless felt immediately at ease and his only regret was that his body was too broad to get it all underneath.

He spent the whole night there. Some of the time he passed in a light sleep, although he frequently woke from it in alarm because of his hunger, and some of the time was spent in worries and vague hopes which, however, always led to the same conclusion: for the time being he must remain calm, he must show patience and the greatest consideration so that his family could bear the unpleasantness that he, in his present condition, was forced to impose on them.

Gregor soon had the opportunity to test the strength of his decisions, as early the next morning, almost before the night had ended, his sister, nearly fully dressed, opened the door from the front room and looked anxiously in. She did not see him straight away, but when she did notice him under the couch—he had to be somewhere, for God's sake, he couldn't have flown away—she was so shocked that she lost control of herself and slammed the door shut again from outside. But she seemed to regret her behavior, as she opened the door again straight away and came in on tip-toe as if entering the room of someone seriously ill or even of a stranger. Gregor had pushed his head forward, right to the edge of the couch, and watched her. Would she notice that he had left the milk as it was, realize that it was not from any lack of hunger and bring him in some other food that was more suitable? If she didn't do it herself he would rather go hungry than draw her attention to it, although he did feel a terrible urge to rush forward from under the couch, throw himself at his sister's feet and beg her for something good to eat. However, his sister noticed the full dish immediately and looked at it and the few drops of milk splashed around it with some surprise. She immediately picked it up—using a rag, not her bare hands—and carried it out. Gregor was extremely curious as to what she would bring in its place, imagining the wildest possibilities, but he never could have guessed what his sister, in her goodness, actually did bring. In order to test his taste, she brought him a whole selection of things, all spread out on an old newspaper. There were old, half-rotten vegetables; bones from the evening meal, covered in white sauce that had gone hard; a few raisins and almonds; some cheese that Gregor had declared inedible two days before; a dry roll and some bread spread with butter and salt. As well as all that she had poured some water into the dish, which had probably been permanently set aside for Gregor's use, and placed it beside them. Then, out of consideration for Gregor's feelings, as she knew that he would not eat in front of her, she hurried out again and even turned the key in the lock so that Gregor would know he could make things as comfortable for himself as he liked. Gregor's little legs whirred, at last he could eat. What's more, his injuries must already have completely healed as he found no difficulty in moving. This amazed him, as more than a month earlier he had cut his finger slightly with a knife, he thought of how his finger had still hurt the day before yesterday. "Am I less sensitive than I used to be, then?" he thought, and was already sucking greedily at the cheese which had immediately, almost compellingly, attracted him much more than the other foods on the newspaper. Quickly one after another, his eyes watering with pleasure, he consumed the cheese, the vegetables and the sauce; the fresh foods, on the other hand, he didn't like at all, and even dragged the things he did want to eat a little way away from them because he couldn't stand the smell. Long after he had finished eating and lay lethargic in the same place, his sister slowly turned the key in the lock as a sign to him that he should withdraw. He was immediately startled, although he had been half asleep, and he hurried back under the couch. But he needed great self-control to stay there even for the short time that his sister was in the room, as eating so much food had rounded out his body a little and he could hardly breathe in that narrow space. Half suffocating, he watched with bulging eyes as his sister unselfconsciously took a broom and swept up the left-overs, mixing them in with the food he had not even touched at all as if it could not be used any more. She quickly dropped it all into a bin, closed it with its wooden lid, and carried everything out. She had hardly turned her back before Gregor came out again from under the couch and stretched himself.

This was how Gregor received his food each day now, once in the morning while his parents and the maid were still asleep, and the second time after everyone had eaten their meal at midday as his parents would sleep for a little while then as well, and Gregor's sister would send the maid away on some errand. Gregor's father and mother certainly did not want him to starve either, but perhaps it would have been more than they could stand to have any more experience of his feeding than being told about it, and perhaps his sister wanted to spare them what distress she could as they were indeed suffering enough.

It was impossible for Gregor to find out what they had told the doctor and the locksmith that first morning to get them out of the flat. As nobody could understand him, nobody, not even his sister, thought that he could understand them, so he had to be content to hear his sister's sighs and appeals to the saints as she moved about his room. It was only later, when she had become a little more used to everything—there was, of course, no question of her ever becoming fully used to the situation—that Gregor would sometimes catch a friendly comment, or at least a comment that could be construed as friendly. "He's enjoyed his dinner today," she might say when he had diligently cleared away all the food left for him, or if he left most of it, which slowly became more and more frequent, she would often say, sadly, "Now everything's just been left there again."

Although Gregor wasn't able to hear any news directly he did listen to much of what was said in the next rooms, and whenever he heard anyone speaking he would scurry straight to the appropriate door and press his whole body against it. There was seldom any conversation, especially at first, that was not about him in some way, even if only in secret. For two whole days, all the talk at every mealtime was about what they should do now; but even between meals they spoke about the same subject as there were always at least two members of the family at home—nobody wanted to be at home by themselves and it was out of the question to leave the flat entirely empty. And on the very first day the maid had fallen to her knees and begged Gregor's mother to let her go without delay. It was not very clear how much she knew of what had happened but she left within a quarter of an hour, tearfully thanking Gregor's mother for her dismissal as if she had done her an enormous service. She even swore emphatically not to tell anyone the slightest about what had happened, even though no one had asked that of her.

Now Gregor's sister also had to help his mother with the cooking; although that was not so much bother as no one ate very much. Gregor often heard how one of them would unsuccessfully urge another to eat, and receive no more answer than "No thanks, I've had enough" or something similar. No one drank very much either. His sister would sometimes ask his father whether he would like a beer, hoping for the chance to go and fetch it herself. When his father then said nothing she would add, so that he would not feel selfish, that she could send the housekeeper for it, but then his father would close the matter with a big, loud "No," and no more would be said.

Even before the first day had come to an end, his father had explained to Gregor's mother and sister what their finances and prospects were. Now and then he stood up from the table and took some receipt or document from the little cash box he had saved from his business when it had collapsed five years earlier. Gregor heard how he opened the complicated lock and then closed it again after he had taken the item he wanted. What he heard his father say was some of the first good news that Gregor heard since he had first been incarcerated in his room. He had thought that nothing at all remained from his father's business, at least he had never told him anything different, and Gregor had never asked him about it anyway. Their business misfortune had reduced the family to a state of total despair, and Gregor's only concern at that time had been to arrange things so that they could all forget about it as quickly as possible. So then he started working especially hard, with a fiery vigor that raised him from a junior salesman to a traveling representative almost overnight, bringing with it the chance to earn money in quite different ways. Gregor converted his success at work straight into cash that he could lay on the table at home for the benefit of his astonished and delighted family. They had been good times and they had never come again, at least not with the same splendor, even though Gregor had later earned so much that he was in a position to bear the costs of the whole family, and did bear them. They had even got used to it, both Gregor and the family, they took the money with gratitude and he was glad to provide it, although there was no longer much warm affection given in return. Gregor only remained close to his sister now. Unlike him, she was very fond of music and a gifted and expressive violinist, it was his secret plan to send her to the conservatory next year even though it would cause great expense that would have to be made up for in some other way. During Gregor's short periods in town, conversation with his sister would often turn to the conservatory but it was only ever mentioned as a lovely dream that could never be realized. Their parents did not like to hear this innocent talk, but Gregor thought about it quite hard and decided he would let them know what he planned with a grand announcement of it on Christmas day.

That was the sort of totally pointless thing that went through his mind in his present state, pressed upright against the door and listening. There were times when he simply became too tired to continue listening, when his head would fall wearily against the door and he would pull it up again with a start, as even the slightest noise he caused would be heard next door and they would all go silent. "What's that he's doing now," his father would say after a while, clearly having gone over to the door, and only then would the interrupted conversation slowly be taken up again.

When explaining things, his father repeated himself several times, partly because it was a long time since he had been occupied with these matters himself and partly because Gregor's mother did not understand everything the first time. From these repeated explanations Gregor learned, to his pleasure, that despite all their misfortunes there was still some money available from the old days. It was not a lot, but it had not been touched in the meantime and some interest had accumulated. Besides that, they had not been using up all the money that Gregor had been bringing home every month, keeping only a little for himself, so that that, too, had been accumulating. Behind the door, Gregor nodded with enthusiasm in his pleasure at this unexpected thrift and caution. He could actually have used this surplus money to reduce his father's debt to his boss, and the day when he could have freed himself from that job would have come much closer, but now it was certainly better the way his father had done things.

This money, however, was certainly not enough to enable the family to live off the interest; it was enough to maintain them for, perhaps, one or two years, no more. That's to say, it was money that should not really be touched but set aside for emergencies; money to live on had to be earned. His father was healthy but old, and lacking in self confidence. During the five years that he had not been working—the first holiday in a life that had been full of strain and no success—he had put on a lot of weight and become very slow and clumsy. Would Gregor's elderly mother now have to go and earn money? She suffered from asthma and it was a strain for her just to move about the home, every other day would be spent struggling for breath on the sofa by the open window. Would his sister have to go and earn money? She was still a child of seventeen, her life up till then had been very enviable, consisting of wearing nice clothes, sleeping late, helping out in the business, joining in with a few modest pleasures and most of all playing the violin. Whenever they began to talk of the need to earn money, Gregor would always first let go of the door and then throw himself onto the cool leather sofa next to it, as he became quite hot with shame and regret.

He would often lie there the whole night through, not sleeping a wink but scratching at the leather for hours on end. Or he might go to all the effort of pushing a chair to the window, climbing up onto the sill and, propped up in the chair, leaning on the window to stare out of it. He had used to feel a great sense of freedom from doing this, but doing it now was obviously something more remembered than experienced, as what he actually saw in this way was becoming less distinct every day, even things that were quite near; he had used to curse the ever-present view of the hospital across the street, but now he could not see it at all, and if he had not known that he lived in Charlottenstrasse, which was a quiet street despite being in the middle of the city, he could have thought that he was looking out the window at a barren waste where the gray sky and the gray earth mingled inseparably. His observant sister only needed to notice the chair twice before she would always push it back to its exact position by the window after she had tidied up the room, and even left the inner pane of the window open from then on.

If Gregor had only been able to speak to his sister and thank her for all that she had to do for him it would have been easier for him to bear it; but as it was it caused him pain. His sister, naturally, tried as far as possible to pretend there was nothing burdensome about it, and the longer it went on, of course, the better she was able to do so, but as time went by Gregor was also able to see through it all so much better. It had even become very unpleasant for him, now, whenever she entered the room. No sooner had she come in than she would quickly close the door as a precaution so that no one would have to suffer the view into Gregor's room, then she would go straight to the window and pull it hurriedly open almost as if she were suffocating. Even if it was cold, she would stay at the window breathing deeply for a little while. She would alarm Gregor twice a day with this running about and noise making; he would stay under the couch shivering the whole while, knowing full well that she would certainly have liked to spare him this ordeal, but it was impossible for her to be in the same room with him with the windows closed.

One day, about a month after Gregor's transformation when his sister no longer had any particular reason to be shocked at his appearance, she came into the room a little earlier than usual and found him still staring out the window, motionless, and just where he would be most horrible. In itself, his sister's not coming into the room would have been no surprise for Gregor as it would have been difficult for her to immediately open the window while he was still there, but not only did she not come in, she went straight back and closed the door behind her, a stranger would have thought he had threatened her and tried to bite her. Gregor went straight to hide himself under the couch, of course, but he had to wait until midday before his sister came back and she seemed much more uneasy than usual. It made him realize that she still found his appearance unbearable and would continue to do so, she probably even had to overcome the urge to flee when she saw the little bit of him that protruded from under the couch. One day, in order to spare her even this sight, he spent four hours carrying the bedsheet over to the couch on his back and arranged it so that he was completely covered and his sister would not be able to see him even if she bent down. If she did not think this sheet was necessary then all she had to do was take it off again, as it was clear enough that it was no pleasure for Gregor to cut himself off so completely. She left the sheet where it was. Gregor even thought he glimpsed a look of gratitude one time when he carefully looked out from under the sheet to see how his sister liked the new arrangement.

For the first fourteen days, Gregor's parents could not bring themselves to come into the room to see him. He would often hear them say how they appreciated all the new work his sister was doing even though, before, they had seen her as a girl who was somewhat useless and frequently been annoyed with her. But now the two of them, father and mother, would often both wait outside the door of Gregor's room while his sister tidied up in there, and as soon as she went out again she would have to tell them exactly how everything looked, what Gregor had eaten, how he had behaved this time and whether, perhaps, any slight improvement could be seen. His mother also wanted to go in and visit Gregor relatively soon but his father and sister at first persuaded her against it. Gregor listened very closely to all this, and approved fully. Later, though, she had to be held back by force, which made her call out: "Let me go and see Gregor, he is my unfortunate son! Can't you understand I have to see him?" and Gregor would think to himself that maybe it would be better if his mother came in, not every day of course, but one day a week, perhaps; she could understand everything much better than his sister who, for all her courage, was still just a child after all, and really might not have had an adult's appreciation of the burdensome job she had taken on.

Gregor's wish to see his mother was soon realized. Out of consideration for his parents, Gregor wanted to avoid being seen at the window during the day, the few square meters of the floor did not give him much room to crawl about, it was hard to just lie quietly through the night, his food soon stopped giving him any pleasure at all, and so, to entertain himself, he got into the habit of crawling up and down the walls and ceiling. He was especially fond of hanging from the ceiling; it was quite different from lying on the floor; he could breathe more freely; his body had a light swing to it; and up there, relaxed and almost happy, it might happen that he would surprise even himself by letting go of the ceiling and landing on the floor with a crash. But now, of course, he had far better control of his body than before and, even with a fall as great as that, caused himself no damage. Very soon his sister noticed Gregor's new way of entertaining himself—he had, after all, left traces of the adhesive from his feet as he crawled about—and got it into her head to make it as easy as possible for him by removing the furniture that got in his way, especially the chest of drawers and the desk. Now, this was not something that she would be able to do by herself; she did not dare to ask for help from her father; the sixteen year old maid had carried on bravely since the cook had left but she certainly would not have helped in this, she had even asked to be allowed to keep the kitchen locked at all times and never to have to open the door unless it was especially important; so his sister had no choice but to choose some time when Gregor's father was not there and fetch his mother to help her. As she approached the room, Gregor could hear his mother express her joy, but once at the door she went silent.

First, of course, his sister came in and looked round to see that everything in the room was alright; and only then did she let her mother enter. Gregor had hurriedly pulled the sheet down lower over the couch and put more folds into it so that everything really looked as if it had just been thrown down by chance. Gregor also refrained, this time, from spying out from under the sheet; he gave up the chance to see his mother until later and was simply glad that she had come. "You can come in, he can't be seen," said his sister, obviously leading her in by the hand. The old chest of drawers was too heavy for a pair of feeble women to be heaving about, but Gregor listened as they pushed it from its place, his sister always taking on the heaviest part of the work for herself and ignoring her mother's warnings that she would strain herself. This lasted a very long time. After labouring at it for fifteen minutes or more his mother said it would be better to leave the chest where it was, for one thing it was too heavy for them to get the job finished before Gregor's father got home and leaving it in the middle of the room it would be in his way even more, and for another thing it wasn't even sure that taking the furniture away would really be any help to him. She thought just the opposite; the sight of the bare walls saddened her right to her heart; and why wouldn't Gregor feel the same way about it, he'd been used to this furniture in his room for a long time and it would make him feel abandoned to be in an empty room like that. Then, quietly, almost whispering as if wanting Gregor (whose whereabouts she did not know) to hear not even the tone of her voice, as she was convinced that he did not understand her words, she added, "And by taking the furniture away, won't it seem like we're showing that we've given up all hope of improvement and we're abandoning him to cope for himself? I think it'd be best to leave the room exactly the way it was before so that when Gregor comes back to us again he'll find everything unchanged and he'll be able to forget the time in between all the easier."

Hearing these words from his mother made Gregor realize that the lack of any direct human communication, along with the monotonous life led by the family during these two months, must have made him confused—he could think of no other way of explaining to himself why he had seriously wanted his room emptied out. Had he really wanted to transform his room into a cave, a warm room fitted out with the nice furniture he had inherited? That would have let him crawl around unimpeded in any direction, but it would also have let him quickly forget his past when he had still been human. He had come very close to forgetting, and it had only been the voice of his mother, unheard for so long, that had shaken him out of it. Nothing should be removed; everything had to stay; he could not do without the good influence the furniture had on his condition; and if the furniture made it difficult for him to crawl about mindlessly that was not a loss but a great advantage.

His sister, unfortunately, did not agree; she had become used to the idea, not without reason, that she was Gregor's spokesman to his parents about the things that concerned him. This meant that his mother's advice now was sufficient reason for her to insist on removing not only the chest of drawers and the desk, as she had thought at first, but all the furniture apart from the all-important couch. It was more than childish perversity, of course, or the unexpected confidence she had recently acquired, that made her insist; she had indeed noticed that Gregor needed a lot of room to crawl about in, whereas the furniture, as far as anyone could see, was of no use to him at all. Girls of that age, though, do become enthusiastic about things and feel they must get their way whenever they can. Perhaps this was what tempted Grete to make Gregor's situation seem even more shocking than it was so that she could do even more for him. Grete would probably be the only one who would dare enter a room dominated by Gregor crawling about the bare walls by himself.

So she refused to let her mother dissuade her. Gregor's mother already looked uneasy in his room, she soon stopped speaking and helped Gregor's sister to get the chest of drawers out with what strength she had. The chest of drawers was something that Gregor could do without if he had to, but the writing desk had to stay. Hardly had the two women pushed the chest of drawers, groaning, out of the room than Gregor poked his head out from under the couch to see what he could do about it. He meant to be as careful and considerate as he could, but, unfortunately, it was his mother who came back first while Grete in the next room had her arms round the chest, pushing and pulling at it from side to side by herself without, of course, moving it an inch. His mother was not used to the sight of Gregor, he might have made her ill, so Gregor hurried backwards to the far end of the couch. In his startlement, though, he was not able to prevent the sheet at its front from moving a little. It was enough to attract his mother's attention. She stood very still, remained there a moment, and then went back out to Grete.

Gregor kept trying to assure himself that nothing unusual was happening, it was just a few pieces of furniture being moved after all, but he soon had to admit that the women going to and fro, their little calls to each other, the scraping of the furniture on the floor, all these things made him feel as if he were being assailed from all sides. With his head and legs pulled in against him and his body pressed to the floor, he was forced to admit to himself that he could not stand all of this much longer. They were emptying his room out; taking away everything that was dear to him; they had already taken out the chest containing his fretsaw and other tools; now they threatened to remove the writing desk with its place clearly worn into the floor, the desk where he had done his homework as a business trainee, at high school, even while he had been at infant school—he really could not wait any longer to see whether the two women's intentions were good. He had nearly forgotten they were there anyway, as they were now too tired to say anything while they worked and he could only hear their feet as they stepped heavily on the floor.

So, while the women were leant against the desk in the other room catching their breath, he sallied out, changed direction four times not knowing what he should save first before his attention was suddenly caught by the picture on the wall—which was already denuded of everything else that had been on it—of the lady dressed in copious fur. He hurried up onto the picture and pressed himself against its glass, it held him firmly and felt good on his hot belly. This picture at least, now totally covered by Gregor, would certainly be taken away by no one. He turned his head to face the door into the living room so that he could watch the women when they came back.

They had not allowed themselves a long rest and came back quite soon; Grete had put her arm around her mother and was nearly carrying her. "What shall we take now, then?" said Grete and looked around. Her eyes met those of Gregor on the wall. Perhaps only because her mother was there, she remained calm, bent her face to her so that she would not look round and said, albeit hurriedly and with a tremor in her voice: "Come on, let's go back in the living room for a while?" Gregor could see what Grete had in mind, she wanted to take her mother somewhere safe and then chase him down from the wall. Well, she could certainly try it! He sat unyielding on his picture. He would rather jump at Grete's face.

But Grete's words had made her mother quite worried, she stepped to one side, saw the enormous brown patch against the flowers of the wallpaper, and before she even realised it was Gregor that she saw screamed: "Oh God, oh God!" Arms outstretched, she fell onto the couch as if she had given up everything and stayed there immobile. "Gregor!" shouted his sister, glowering at him and shaking her fist.

That was the first word she had spoken to him directly since his transformation. She ran into the other room to fetch some kind of smelling salts to bring her mother out of her faint; Gregor wanted to help too—he could save his picture later, although he stuck fast to the glass and had to pull himself off by force; then he, too, ran into the next room as if he could advise his sister like in the old days; but he had to just stand behind her doing nothing; she was looking into various bottles, he startled her when she turned round; a bottle fell to the ground and broke; a splinter cut Gregor's face, some kind of caustic medicine splashed all over him; now, without delaying any longer, Grete took hold of all the bottles she could and ran with them in to her mother; she slammed the door shut with her foot. So now Gregor was shut out from his mother, who, because of him, might be near to death;

he could not open the door if he did not want to chase his sister away, and she had to stay with his mother; there was nothing for him to do but wait; and, oppressed with anxiety and self-reproach, he began to crawl about, he crawled over everything, walls, furniture, ceiling, and finally in his confusion as the whole room began to spin around him he fell down into the middle of the dinner table.

He lay there for a while, numb and immobile, all around him it was quiet, maybe that was a good sign. Then there was someone at the door. The maid, of course, had locked herself in her kitchen so that Grete would have to go and answer it. His father had arrived home. "What's happened?" were his first words; Grete's appearance must have made everything clear to him. She answered him with subdued voice, and openly pressed her face into his chest: "Mother's fainted, but she's better now. Gregor got out." "Just as I expected," said his father, "just as I always said, but you women wouldn't listen, would you." It was clear to Gregor that Grete had not said enough and that his father took it to mean that something bad had happened, that he was responsible for some act of violence. That meant Gregor would now have to try to calm his father, as he did not have the time to explain things to him even if that had been possible. So he fled to the door of his room and pressed himself against it so that his father, when he came in from the hall, could see straight away that Gregor had the best intentions and would go back into his room without delay, that it would not be necessary to drive him back but that they had only to open the door and he would disappear.

His father, though, was not in the mood to notice subtleties like that; "Ah!" he shouted as he came in, sounding as if he were both angry and glad at the same time. Gregor drew his head back from the door and lifted it towards his father. He really had not imagined his father the way he stood there now; of late, with his new habit of crawling about, he had neglected to pay attention to what was going on the rest of the flat the way he had done before. He really ought to have expected things to have changed, but still, still, was that really his father? The same tired man as used to be laying there entombed in his bed when Gregor came back from his business trips, who would receive him sitting in the armchair in his nightgown when he came back in the evenings; who was hardly even able to stand up but, as a sign of his pleasure, would just raise his arms and who, on the couple of times a year when they went for a walk together on a Sunday or public holiday wrapped up tightly in his overcoat between Gregor and his mother, would always labor his way forward a little more slowly than them, who were already walking slowly for his sake; who would place his stick down carefully and, if he wanted to say something would invariably stop and gather his companions around him. He was standing up straight enough now; dressed in a smart blue uniform with gold buttons, the sort worn by the employees at the banking institute; above the high, stiff collar of the coat his strong double-chin emerged; under the bushy eyebrows, his piercing, dark eyes looked out fresh and alert; his normally unkempt white hair was combed down painfully close to his scalp. He took his cap, with its gold monogram from, probably, some bank, and threw it in an arc right across the room onto the sofa, put his hands in his trouser pockets, pushing back the bottom of his long uniform coat, and, with look of determination, walked towards Gregor. He probably did not even know himself what he had in mind, but nonetheless lifted his feet unusually high. Gregor was amazed at the enormous size of the soles of his boots, but wasted no time with that—he knew full well, right from the first day of his new life, that his father thought it necessary to always be extremely strict with him. And so he ran up to his father, stopped when his father stopped, scurried forwards again when he moved, even slightly. In this way they went round the room several times without anything decisive happening, without even giving the impression of a chase as everything went so slowly. Gregor remained all this time on the floor, largely because he feared his father might see it as especially provoking if he fled onto the wall or ceiling. Whatever he did, Gregor had to admit that he certainly would not be able to keep up this running about for long, as for each step his father took he had to carry out countless movements. He became noticeably short of breath, even in his earlier life his lungs had not been very reliable. Now, as he lurched about in his efforts to muster all the strength he could for running he could hardly keep his eyes open; his thoughts became too slow for him to think of any other way of saving himself than running; he almost forgot that the walls were there for him to use although, here, they were concealed behind carefully carved furniture full of notches and protrusions—then, right beside him, lightly tossed, something flew down and rolled in front of him. It was an apple; then another one immediately flew at him; Gregor froze in shock; there was no longer any point in running as his father had decided to bombard him. He had filled his pockets with fruit from the bowl on the sideboard and now, without even taking the time for careful aim, threw one apple after another. These little, red apples rolled about on the floor, knocking into each other as if they had electric motors. An apple thrown without much force glanced against Gregor's back and slid off without doing any harm. Another one however, immediately following it, hit squarely and lodged in his back; Gregor wanted to drag himself away, as if he could remove the surprising, the incredible pain by changing his position; but he felt as if nailed to the spot and spread himself out, all his senses in confusion. The last thing he saw was the door of his room being pulled open, his sister was screaming, his mother ran out in front of her in her blouse (as his sister had taken off some of her clothes after she had fainted to make it easier for her to breathe), she ran to his father, her skirts unfastened and sliding one after another to the ground, stumbling over the skirts she pushed herself to his father, her arms around him, uniting herself with him totally—now Gregor lost his ability to see anything—her hands behind his father's head begging him to spare Gregor's life.

III

No one dared to remove the apple lodged in Gregor's flesh, so it remained there as a visible reminder of his injury. He had suffered it there for more than a month, and his condition seemed serious enough to remind even his father that Gregor, despite his current sad and revolting form, was a family member who could not be treated as an enemy. On the contrary, as a family there was a duty to swallow any revulsion for him and to be patient, just to be patient.

Because of his injuries, Gregor had lost much of his mobility—probably permanently. He had been reduced to the condition of an ancient invalid and it took him long, long minutes to crawl across his room—crawling over the ceiling was out of the question—but this deterioration in his condition was fully (in his opinion) made up for by the door to the living room being left open every evening.

He got into the habit of closely watching it for one or two hours before it was opened and then, lying in the darkness of his room where he could not be seen from the living room, he could watch the family in the light of the dinner table and listen to their conversation—with everyone's permission, in a way, and thus quite differently from before.

They no longer held the lively conversations of earlier times, of course, the ones that Gregor always thought about with longing when he was tired and getting into the damp bed in some small hotel room.

All of them were usually very quiet nowadays. Soon after dinner, his father would go to sleep in his chair; his mother and sister would urge each other to be quiet; his mother, bent deeply under the lamp, would sew fancy underwear for a fashion shop; his sister, who had taken a sales job, learned shorthand and French in the evenings so that she might be able to get a better position later on. Sometimes his father would wake up and say to Gregor's mother "you're doing so much sewing again today!" as if he did not know that he had been dozing—and then he would go back to sleep again while mother and sister would exchange a tired grin.

With a kind of stubbornness, Gregor's father refused to take his uniform off even at home; while his nightgown hung unused on its peg Gregor's father would slumber where he was, fully dressed, as if always ready to serve and expecting to hear the voice of his superior even here. The uniform had not been new to start with, but as a result of this it slowly became even shabbier despite the efforts of Gregor's mother and sister to look after it. Gregor would often spend the whole evening looking at all the stains on this coat, with its gold buttons always kept polished and shiny, while the old man in it would sleep, highly uncomfortable but peaceful.

As soon as it struck ten, Gregor's mother would speak gently to his father to wake him and try to persuade him to go to bed, as he couldn't sleep properly where he was and he really had to get his sleep if he was to be up at six to get to work. But since he had been in work he had become more obstinate and would always insist on staying longer at the table, even though he regularly fell asleep and it was then harder than ever to persuade him to exchange the chair for his bed. Then, however much mother and sister would importune him with little reproaches and warnings he would keep slowly shaking his head for a quarter of an hour with his eyes closed and refusing to get up. Gregor's mother would tug at his sleeve, whisper endearments into his ear, Gregor's sister would leave her work to help her mother, but nothing would have any effect on him. He would just sink deeper into his chair. Only when the two women took him under the arms he would abruptly open his eyes, look at them one after the other and say: "What a life! This is what peace I get in my old age!" And supported by the two women he would lift himself up carefully as if he were carrying the greatest load himself, let the women take him to the door, send them off and carry on by himself while Gregor's mother would throw down her needle and his sister her pen so that they could run after his father and continue being of help to him.

Who, in this tired and overworked family, would have had time to give more attention to Gregor than was absolutely necessary? The household budget became even smaller; so now the maid was dismissed; an enormous, thick-boned charwoman with white hair that flapped around her head came every morning and evening to do the heaviest work; everything else was looked after by Gregor's mother on top of the large amount of sewing work she did. Gregor even learned, listening to the evening conversation about what price they had hoped for, that several items of jewelry belonging to the family had been sold, even though both mother and sister had been very fond of wearing them at functions and celebrations. But the loudest complaint was that although the flat was much too big for their present circumstances, they could not move out of it, there was no imaginable way of transferring Gregor to the new address. He could see quite well, though, that there were more reasons than consideration for him that made it difficult for them to move, it would have been quite easy to transport him in any suitable crate with a few air holes in it; the main thing holding the family back from their decision to move was much more to do with their total despair, and the thought that they had been struck with a misfortune unlike anything experienced by anyone else they knew or were related to. They carried out absolutely everything that the world expects from poor people, Gregor's father brought bank employees their breakfast, his mother sacrificed herself by washing clothes for strangers, his sister ran back and forth behind her desk at the behest of the customers, but they just did not have the strength to do any more. And the injury in Gregor's back began to hurt as much as when it was new. After they had come back from taking his father to bed Gregor's mother and sister would now leave their work where it was and sit close together, cheek to cheek; his mother would point to Gregor's room and say, "Close that door, Grete," and then, when he was in the dark again, they would sit in the next room and their tears would mingle, or they would simply sit there staring dry-eyed at the table.

Gregor hardly slept at all, either night or day. Sometimes he would think of taking over the family's affairs, just like before, the next time the door was opened; he had long forgotten about his boss and the chief clerk, but they would appear again in his thoughts, the salesmen and the apprentices, that stupid teaboy, two or three friends from other businesses, one of the chambermaids from a provincial hotel, a tender memory that appeared and disappeared again, a cashier from a hat shop for whom his attention had been serious but too slow—all of them appeared to him, mixed together with strangers and others he had forgotten, but instead of helping him and his family they were all of them inaccessible, and he was glad when they disappeared. Other times he was not at all in the mood to look after his family, he was filled with simple rage about the lack of attention he was shown, and although he could think of nothing he would have wanted, he made plans of how he could get into the pantry where he could take all the things he was entitled to, even if he was not hungry. Gregor's sister no longer thought about how she could please him but would hurriedly push some food or other into his room with her foot before she rushed out to work in the morning and at midday, and in the evening she would sweep it away again with the broom, indifferent as to whether it had been eaten or—more often than not—had been left totally untouched. She still cleared up the room in the evening, but now she could not have been any quicker about it. Smears of dirt were left on the walls, here and there were little balls of dust and filth. At first, Gregor went into one of the worst of these places when his sister arrived as a reproach to her, but he could have stayed there for weeks without his sister doing anything about it; she could see the dirt as well as he could but she had simply decided to leave him to it. At the same time she became touchy in a way that was quite new for her and which everyone in the family understood—cleaning up Gregor's room was for her and her alone. Gregor's mother did once thoroughly clean his room, and needed to use several bucketfuls of water to do it—although that much dampness also made Gregor ill and he lay flat on the couch, bitter and immobile. But his mother was to be punished still more for what she had done, as hardly had his sister arrived home in the evening than she noticed the change in Gregor's room and, highly aggrieved, ran back into the living room where, despite her mother's raised and imploring hands, she broke into convulsive tears. Her father, of course, was startled out of his chair and the two parents looked on astonished and helpless; then they, too, became agitated; Gregor's father, standing to the right of his mother, accused her of not leaving the cleaning of Gregor's room to his sister; from her left, Gregor's sister screamed at her that she was never to clean Gregor's room again; while his mother tried to draw his father, who was beside himself with anger, into the bedroom; his sister, quaking with tears, thumped on the table with her small fists; and Gregor hissed in anger that no one had even thought of closing the door to save him the sight of this and all its noise.

Gregor's sister was exhausted from going out to work, and looking after Gregor as she had done before was even more work for her, but even so his mother ought certainly not to have taken her place. Gregor, on the other hand, ought not to be neglected. Now, though, the charwoman was here. This elderly widow, with a robust bone structure that made her able to withstand the hardest of things in her long life, wasn't really repelled by Gregor. Just by chance one day, rather than any real curiosity, she opened the door to Gregor's room and found herself face to face with him. He was taken totally by surprise, no one was chasing him but he began to rush to and fro while she just stood there in amazement with her hands crossed in front of her. From then on she never failed to open the door slightly every evening and morning and look briefly in on him. At first she would call to him as she did so with words that she probably considered friendly, such as "Come on then, you old dung-beetle!" or "Look at the old dung-beetle there!" Gregor never responded to being spoken to in that way, but just remained where he was without moving as if the door had never even been opened. If only they had told this charwoman to clean up his room every day instead of letting her disturb him for no reason whenever she felt like it! One day, early in the morning while a heavy rain struck the windowpanes, perhaps indicating that spring was coming, she began to speak to him in that way once again. Gregor was so resentful of it that he started to move toward her, he was slow and infirm, but it was like a kind of attack. Instead of being afraid, the charwoman just lifted up one of the chairs from near the door and stood there with her mouth open, clearly intending not to close her mouth until the chair in her hand had been slammed down into Gregor's back. "Aren't you coming any closer, then?" she asked when Gregor turned round again, and she calmly put the chair back in the corner.

Gregor had almost entirely stopped eating. Only if he happened to find himself next to the food that had been prepared for him he might take some of it into his mouth to play with it, leave it there a few hours and then, more often than not, spit it out again. At first he thought it was distress at the state of his room that stopped him eating, but he had soon got used to the changes made there. They had got into the habit of putting things into this room that they had no room for anywhere else, and there were now many such things as one of the rooms in the flat had been rented out to three gentlemen. These earnest gentlemen—all three of them had full beards, as Gregor learned peering through the crack in the door one day—were painfully insistent on things being tidy. This meant not only in their own room but, since they had taken a room in this establishment, in the entire flat and especially in the kitchen. Unnecessary clutter was something they could not tolerate, especially if it was dirty. They had moreover brought most of their own furnishings and equipment with them. For this reason, many things had become superfluous which, although they could not be sold, the family did not wish to discard. All these things found their way into Gregor's room. The dustbins from the kitchen found their way in there too. The charwoman was always in a hurry, and anything she couldn't use for the time being she would just chuck in there. He, fortunately, would usually see no more than the object and the hand that held it. The woman most likely meant to fetch the things back out again when she had time and the opportunity, or to throw everything out in one go, but what actually happened was that they were left where they landed when they had first been thrown unless Gregor made his way through the junk and moved it somewhere else. At first he moved it because, with no other room free where he could crawl about, he was forced to, but later on he came to enjoy it although moving about in that way left him sad and tired to death and he would remain immobile for hours afterwards.

The gentlemen who rented the room would sometimes take their evening meal at home in the living room that was used by everyone, and so the door to this room was often kept closed in the evening. But Gregor found it easy to give up having the door open, he had, after all, often failed to make use of it when it was open and, without the family having noticed it, lain in his room in its darkest corner. One time, though, the charwoman left the door to the living room slightly open, and it remained open when the gentlemen who rented the room came in in the evening and the light was put on. They sat up at the table where, formerly, Gregor had taken his meals with his father and mother, they unfolded the serviettes and picked up their knives and forks. Gregor's mother immediately appeared in the doorway with a dish of meat and soon behind her came his sister with a dish piled high with potatoes. The food was steaming, and filled the room with its smell. The gentlemen bent over the dishes set in front of them as if they wanted to test the food before eating it, and the gentleman in the middle, who seemed to count as an authority for the other two, did indeed cut off a piece of meat while it was still in its dish, clearly wishing to establish whether it was sufficiently cooked or whether it should be sent back to the kitchen. It was to his satisfaction, and Gregor's mother and sister, who had been looking on anxiously, began to breathe again and smiled.

The family themselves ate in the kitchen. Nonetheless, Gregor's father came into the living room before he went into the kitchen, bowed once with his cap in his hand and did his round of the table. The gentlemen stood as one, and mumbled something into their beards.

Then, once they were alone, they ate in near perfect silence. It seemed remarkable to Gregor that above all the various noises of eating their chewing teeth could still be heard, as if they had wanted to show Gregor that you need teeth in order to eat and it was not possible to perform anything with jaws that are toothless however nice they might be. "I'd like to eat something," said Gregor anxiously, "but not anything like they're eating. They do feed themselves. And here I am, dying!"

Throughout all this time, Gregor could not remember having heard the violin being played, but this evening it began to be heard from the kitchen. The three gentlemen had already finished their meal, the one in the middle had produced a newspaper, given a page to each of the others, and now they leant back in their chairs reading them and smoking. When the violin began playing they became attentive, stood up and went on tip-toe over to the door of the hallway where they stood pressed against each other. Someone must have heard them in the kitchen, as Gregor's father called out: "Is the playing perhaps unpleasant for the gentlemen? We can stop it straight away." "On the contrary," said the middle gentleman, "would the young lady not like to come in and play for us here in the room, where it is, after all, much more cozy and comfortable?" "Oh yes, we'd love to," called back Gregor's father as if he had been the violin player himself. The gentlemen stepped back into the room and waited. Gregor's father soon appeared with the music stand, his mother with the music and his sister with the violin. She calmly prepared everything for her to begin playing; his parents, who had never rented a room out before and therefore showed an exaggerated courtesy towards the three gentlemen, did not even dare to sit on their own chairs; his father leant against the door with his right hand pushed in between two buttons on his uniform coat; his mother, though, was offered a seat by one of the gentlemen and sat—leaving the chair where the gentleman happened to have placed it—out of the way in a corner.

His sister began to play; father and mother paid close attention, one on each side, to the movements of her hands. Drawn in by the playing, Gregor had dared to come forward a little and already had his head in the living room. Before, he had taken great pride in how considerate he was but now it hardly occurred to him that he had become so thoughtless about the others. What's more, there was now all the more reason to keep himself hidden as he was covered in the dust that lay everywhere in his room and flew up at the slightest movement; he carried threads, hairs, and remains of food about on his back and sides; he was much too indifferent to everything now to lay on his back and wipe himself on the carpet like he had used to do several times a day. And despite this condition, he was not too shy to move forward a little onto the immaculate floor of the living room.

No one noticed him, though. The family was totally preoccupied with the violin playing; at first, the three gentlemen had put their hands in their pockets and come up far too close behind the music stand to look at all the notes being played, and they must have disturbed Gregor's sister, but soon, in contrast with the family, they withdrew back to the window with their heads sunk and talking to each other at half volume, and they stayed by the window while Gregor's father observed them anxiously. It really now seemed very obvious that they had expected to hear some beautiful or entertaining violin playing but had been disappointed, that they had had enough of the whole performance and it was only now out of politeness that they allowed their peace to be disturbed. It was especially unnerving, the way they all blew the smoke from their cigarettes upwards from their mouth and noses. Yet Gregor's sister was playing so beautifully. Her face was leant to one side, following the lines of music with a careful and melancholy expression. Gregor crawled a little further forward, keeping his head close to the ground so that he could meet her eyes if the chance came. Was he an animal if music could captivate him so? It seemed to him that he was being shown the way to the unknown nourishment he had been yearning for. He was determined to make his way forward to his sister and tug at her skirt to show her she might come into his room with her violin, as no one appreciated her playing here as much as he would. He never wanted to let her out of his room, not while he lived, anyway; his shocking appearance should, for once, be of some use to him; he wanted to be at every door of his room at once to hiss and spit at the attackers; his sister should not be forced to stay with him, though, but stay of her own free will; she would sit beside him on the couch with her ear bent down to him while he told her how he had always intended to send her to the conservatory, how he would have told everyone about it last Christmas—had

Christmas really come and gone already?—if this misfortune hadn't got in the way, and refuse to let anyone dissuade him from it. On hearing all this, his sister would break out in tears of emotion, and Gregor would climb up to her shoulder and kiss her neck, which, since she had been going out to work, she had kept free without any necklace or collar.

"Mr. Samsa!" shouted the middle gentleman to Gregor's father, pointing, without wasting any more words, with his forefinger at Gregor as he slowly moved forward. The violin went silent, the middle of the three gentlemen first smiled at his two friends, shaking his head, and then looked back at Gregor. His father seemed to think it more important to calm the three gentlemen before driving Gregor out, even though they were not at all upset and seemed to think Gregor was more entertaining than the violin playing had been. He rushed up to them with his arms spread out and attempted to drive them back into their room at the same time as trying to block their view of Gregor with his body. Now they did become a little annoyed, and it was not clear whether it was his father's behavior that annoyed them or the dawning realization that they had had a neighbor like Gregor in the next room without knowing it. They asked Gregor's father for explanations, raised their arms like he had, tugged excitedly at their beards and moved back towards their room only very slowly. Meanwhile Gregor's sister had overcome the despair she had fallen into when her playing was suddenly interrupted. She had let her hands drop and let violin and bow hang limply for a while but continued to look at the music as if still playing, but then she suddenly pulled herself together, lay the instrument on her mother's lap who still sat laboriously struggling for breath where she was, and ran into the next room which, under pressure from her father, the three gentlemen were more quickly moving toward. Under his sister's experienced hand, the pillows and covers on the beds flew up and were put into order and she had already finished making the beds and slipped out again before the three gentlemen had reached the room. Gregor's father seemed so obsessed with what he was doing that he forgot all the respect he owed to his tenants. He urged them and pressed them until, when he was already at the door of the room, the middle of the three gentlemen shouted like thunder and stamped his foot and thereby brought Gregor's father to a halt. "I declare here and now," he said, raising his hand and glancing at Gregor's mother and sister to gain their attention too, "that with regard to the repugnant conditions that prevail in this flat and with this family"—here he looked briefly but decisively at the floor—"I give immediate notice on my room. For the days that I have been living here I will, of course, pay nothing at all, on the contrary I will consider whether to proceed with some kind of action for damages from you, and believe me it would be very easy to set out the grounds for such an action." He was silent and looked straight ahead as if waiting for something. And indeed, his two friends joined in with the words: "And we also give immediate notice." With that, he took hold of the door handle and slammed the door.

Gregor's father staggered back to his seat, feeling his way with his hands, and fell into it; it looked as if he was stretching himself out for his usual evening nap but from the uncontrolled way his head kept nodding it could be seen that he was not sleeping at all. Throughout all this, Gregor had lain still where the three gentlemen had first seen him. His disappointment at the failure of his plan, and perhaps also because he was weak from hunger, made it impossible for him to move. He was sure that everyone would turn on him any moment, and he waited. He was not even startled out of this state when the violin on his mother's lap fell from her trembling fingers and landed loudly on the floor.

"Father, Mother," said his sister, hitting the table with her hand as introduction, "we can't carry on like this. Maybe you can't see it, but I can. I don't want to call this monster my brother, all I can say is: we have to try and get rid of it. We've done all that's humanly possible to look after it and be patient, I don't think anyone could accuse us of doing anything wrong."

"She's absolutely right," said Gregor's father to himself. His mother, who still had not had time to catch her breath, began to cough dully, her hand held out in front of her and a deranged expression in her eyes.

Gregor's sister rushed to his mother and put her hand on her forehead. Her words seemed to give Gregor's father some more definite ideas. He sat upright, played with his uniform cap between the plates left by the three gentlemen after their meal, and occasionally looked down at Gregor as he lay there immobile.

"We have to try and get rid of it," said Gregor's sister, now speaking only to her father, as her mother was too occupied with coughing to listen, "it'll be the death of both of you, I can see it coming. We can't all work as hard as we have to and then come home to be tortured like this, we can't endure it. I can't endure it any more." And she broke out so heavily in tears that they flowed down the face of her mother, and she wiped them away with mechanical hand movements.

"My child," said her father with sympathy and obvious understanding, "what are we to do?"

His sister just shrugged her shoulders as a sign of the helplessness and tears that had taken hold of her, displacing her earlier certainty.

"If he could just understand us," said his father almost as a question; his sister shook her hand vigorously through her tears as a sign that of that there was no question.

"If he could just understand us," repeated Gregor's father, closing his eyes in acceptance of his sister's certainty that that was quite impossible, "then perhaps we could come to some kind of arrangement with him. But as it is . . ."

"It's got to go," shouted his sister, "that's the only way, Father. You've got to get rid of the idea that that's Gregor. We've only harmed ourselves by believing it for so long. How can that be Gregor? If it were Gregor he would have seen long ago that it's not possible for human beings to live with an animal like that and he would have gone of his own free will. We wouldn't have a brother any more, then, but we could carry on with our lives and remember him with respect. As it is this animal is persecuting us, it's driven out our tenants, it obviously wants to take over the whole flat and force us to sleep on the streets. Father, look, just look," she suddenly screamed, "he's starting again!"

In her alarm, which was totally beyond Gregor's comprehension, his sister even abandoned his mother as she pushed herself vigorously out of her chair as if more willing to sacrifice her own mother than stay anywhere near Gregor. She rushed over to behind her father, who had become excited merely because she was and stood up half raising his hands in front of Gregor's sister as if to protect her.

But Gregor had had no intention of frightening anyone, least of all his sister. All he had done was begin to turn round so that he could go back into his room, although that was in itself quite startling as his pain-wracked condition meant that turning round required a great deal of effort and he was using his head to help himself do it, repeatedly raising it and striking it against the floor. He stopped and looked round. They seemed to have realized his good intention and had only been alarmed briefly. Now they all looked at him in unhappy silence. His mother lay in her chair with her legs stretched out and pressed against each other, her eyes nearly closed with exhaustion; his sister sat next to his father with her arms around his neck.

"Maybe now they'll let me turn round," thought Gregor and went back to work. He could not help panting loudly with the effort and had sometimes to stop and take a rest. No one was making him rush any more, everything was left up to him. As soon as he had finally finished turning round he began to move straight ahead. He was amazed at the great distance that separated him from his room, and could not understand how he had covered that distance in his weak state a little while before and almost without noticing it. He concentrated on crawling as fast as he could and hardly noticed that there was not a word, not any cry, from his family to distract him. He did not turn his head until he had reached the doorway. He did not turn it all the way round as he felt his neck becoming stiff, but it was nonetheless enough to see that nothing behind him had changed, only his sister had stood up. With his last glance he saw that his mother had now fallen completely asleep.

He was hardly inside his room before the door was hurriedly shut, bolted and locked. The sudden noise behind Gregor so startled him that his little legs collapsed under him. It was his sister who had been in so much of a rush. She had been standing there waiting and sprung forward lightly, Gregor had not heard her coming at all, and as she turned the key in the lock she said loudly to her parents "At last!"

"What now, then?" Gregor asked himself as he looked round in the darkness. He soon made the discovery that he could no longer move at all. This was no surprise to him, it seemed rather that being able to actually move around on those spindly little legs until then was unnatural. He also felt relatively comfortable. It is true that his entire body was aching, but the pain seemed to be slowly getting weaker and weaker and would finally disappear altogether. He could already hardly feel the decayed apple in his back or the inflamed area around it, which was entirely covered in white dust. He thought back of his family with emotion and love. If it was possible, he felt that he must go away even more strongly than his sister. He remained in this state of empty and peaceful rumination until he heard the clock tower strike three in the morning. He watched as it slowly began to get light everywhere outside the window too. Then, without his willing it, his head sank down completely, and his last breath flowed weakly from his nostrils.

When the cleaner came in early in the morning—they'd often asked her not to keep slamming the doors but with her strength and in her hurry she still did, so that everyone in the flat knew when she'd arrived and from then on it was impossible to sleep in peace—she made her usual brief look in on Gregor and at first found nothing special. She thought he was laying there so still on purpose, playing the martyr; she attributed all possible understanding to him. She happened to be holding the long broom in her hand, so she tried to tickle Gregor with it from the doorway. When she had no success with that she tried to make a nuisance of herself and poked at him a little, and only when she found she could shove him across the floor with no resistance at all did she start to pay attention. She soon realized what had really happened, opened her eyes wide, whistled to herself, but did not waste time to yank open the bedroom doors and shout loudly into the darkness of the bedrooms: "Come and 'ave a look at this, it's dead, just lying there, stone dead!"

Mr. and Mrs. Samsa sat upright there in their marriage bed and had to make an effort to get over the shock caused by the cleaner before they could grasp what she was saying. But then, each from his own side, they hurried out of bed. Mr. Samsa threw the blanket over his shoulders, Mrs. Samsa just came out in her nightdress; and that is how they went into Gregor's room. On the way they opened the door to the living room where Grete had been sleeping since the three gentlemen had moved in; she was fully dressed as if she had never been asleep, and the paleness of her face seemed to confirm this. "Dead?" asked Mrs. Samsa, looking at the charwoman enquiringly, even though she could have checked for herself and could have known it even without checking. "That's what I said," replied the cleaner, and to prove it she gave Gregor's body another shove with the broom, sending it sideways across the floor. Mrs. Samsa made a movement as if she wanted to hold back the broom, but did not complete it. "Now then," said Mr. Samsa, "let's give thanks to God for that." He crossed himself, and the three women followed his example. Grete, who had not taken her eyes from the corpse, said: "Just look how thin he was. He didn't eat anything for so long. The food came out again just the same as when it went in." Gregor's body was indeed completely dried up and flat, they had not seen it until then, but now he was not lifted up on his little legs, nor did he do anything to make them look away.

"Grete, come with us in here for a little while," said Mrs. Samsa with a pained smile, and Grete followed her parents into the bedroom but not without looking back at the body. The cleaner shut the door and opened the window wide. Although it was still early in the morning the fresh air had something of warmth mixed in with it. It was already the end of March, after all.

The three gentlemen stepped out of their room and looked round in amazement for their breakfasts; they had been forgotten about. "Where is our breakfast?" the middle gentleman asked the cleaner irritably. She just put her finger on her lips and made a quick and silent sign to the men that they might like to come into Gregor's room. They did so, and stood around Gregor's corpse with their hands in the pockets of their well-worn coats. It was now quite light in the room.

Then the door of the bedroom opened and Mr. Samsa appeared in his uniform with his wife on one arm and his daughter on the other. All of them had been crying a little; Grete now and then pressed her face against her father's arm.

"Leave my home. Now!" said Mr. Samsa, indicating the door and without letting the women from him. "What do you mean?" asked the middle of the three gentlemen somewhat disconcerted, and he smiled sweetly. The other two held their hands behind their backs and continually rubbed them together in gleeful anticipation of a loud quarrel which could only end in their favor. "I mean just what I said," answered Mr. Samsa, and, with his two companions, went in a straight line towards the man. At first, he stood there still, looking at the ground as if the contents of his head were rearranging themselves into new positions. "Alright, we'll go then," he said, and looked up at Mr. Samsa as if he had been suddenly overcome with humility and wanted permission again from Mr. Samsa for his decision. Mr. Samsa merely opened his eyes wide and briefly nodded to him several times. At that, and without delay, the man actually did take long strides into the front hallway; his two friends had stopped rubbing their hands some time before and had been listening to what was being said. Now they jumped off after their friend as if taken with a sudden fear that Mr. Samsa might go into the hallway in front of them and break the connection with their leader. Once there, all three took their hats from the stand, took their sticks from the holder, bowed without a word and left the premises. Mr. Samsa and the two women followed them out onto the landing; but they had had no reason to mistrust the men's intentions and as they leaned over the landing they saw how the three gentlemen made slow but steady progress down the many steps. As they turned the corner on each floor they disappeared and would reappear a few moments later; the further down they went, the more that the Samsa family lost interest in them; when a butcher's boy, proud of posture with his tray on his head, passed them on his way up and came nearer than they were, Mr. Samsa and the women came away from the landing and went, as if relieved, back into the flat.

They decided the best way to make use of that day was for relaxation and to go for a walk; not only had they earned a break from work but they were in serious need of it. So they sat at the table and wrote three letters of excusal, Mr. Samsa to his employers, Mrs. Samsa to her contractor and Grete to her principal. The cleaner came in while they were writing to tell them she was going, she'd finished her work for that morning. The three of them at first just nodded without looking up from what they were writing, and it was only when the cleaner still did not seem to want to leave that they looked up in irritation. "Well?" asked Mr. Samsa. The charwoman stood in the doorway with a smile on her face as if she had some tremendous good news to report, but would only do it if she was clearly asked to. The almost vertical little ostrich feather on her hat, which had been a source of irritation to Mr. Samsa all the time she had been working for them, swayed gently in all directions. "What is it you want then?" asked Mrs. Samsa, whom the cleaner had the most respect for. "Yes," she answered, and broke into a friendly laugh that made her unable to speak straight away, "well then, that thing in there, you needn't worry about how you're going to get rid of it. That's all been sorted out."

Mrs. Samsa and Grete bent down over their letters as if intent on continuing with what they were writing; Mr. Samsa saw that the cleaner wanted to start describing everything in detail but, with outstretched hand, he made it quite clear that she was not to. So, as she was prevented from telling them all about it, she suddenly remembered what a hurry she was in and, clearly peeved, called out, "Cheerio then, everyone," turned round sharply and left, slamming the door terribly as she went.

"Tonight she gets sacked," said Mr. Samsa, but he received no reply from either his wife or his daughter as the charwoman seemed to have destroyed the peace they had only just gained. They got up and went over to the window where they remained with their arms around each other. Mr. Samsa twisted round in his chair to look at them and sat there watching for a while. Then he called out: "Come here, then. Let's forget about all that old stuff, shall we. Come and give me a bit of attention." The two women immediately did as he said, hurrying over to him where they kissed him and hugged him and then they quickly finished their letters.

After that, the three of them left the flat together, which was something they had not done for months, and took the tram out to the open country outside the town. They had the tram, filled with warm sunshine, all to themselves. Leant back comfortably on their seats, they discussed their prospects and found that on closer examination they were not at all bad—until then they had never asked each other about their work but all three had jobs which were very good and held particularly good promise for the future. The greatest improvement for the time being, of course, would be achieved quite easily by moving house; what they needed now was a flat that was smaller and cheaper than the current one which had been chosen by Gregor, one that was in a better location and, most of all, more practical. All the time, Grete was becoming livelier. With all the worry they had been having of late her cheeks had become pale, but, while they were talking, Mr. and Mrs. Samsa were struck, almost simultaneously, with the thought of how their daughter was blossoming into a well built and beautiful young lady. They became quieter. Just from each other's glance and almost without knowing it they agreed that it would soon be time to find a good man for her. And, as if in confirmation of their new dreams and good intentions, as soon as they reached their destination Grete was the first to get up and stretch out her young body.

THE OUTSIDER

H. P. Lovecraft

That night the Baron dreamt of many a woe;
And all his warrior-guests, with shade and form
Of witch, and demon, and large coffin-worm,
Were long be-nightmared.

—Keats

Unhappy is he to whom the memories of childhood bring only fear and sadness. Wretched is he who looks back upon lone hours in vast and dismal chambers with brown hangings and maddening rows of antique books, or upon awed watches in twilight groves of grotesque, gigantic, and vine-encumbered trees that silently wave twisted branches far aloft. Such a lot the gods gave to me—to me, the dazed, the disappointed; the barren, the broken. And yet I am strangely content, and cling desperately to those sere memories, when my mind momentarily threatens to reach beyond to the other.

I know not where I was born, save that the castle was infinitely old and infinitely horrible; full of dark passages and having high ceilings where the eye could find only cobwebs and shadows. The stones in the crumbling corridors seemed always hideously damp, and there was an accursed smell everywhere, as of the piled-up corpses of dead generations. It was never light, so that I used sometimes to light candles and gaze steadily at them for relief; nor was there any sun outdoors, since the terrible trees grew high above the topmost accessible tower. There was one black tower which reached above the trees into the unknown outer sky, but that was partly ruined and could not be ascended save by a well-nigh impossible climb up the sheer wall, stone by stone.

I must have lived years in this place, but I cannot measure the time. Beings must have cared for my needs, yet I cannot recall any person except myself; or anything alive but the noiseless rats and bats and spiders. I think that whoever nursed me must have been shockingly aged, since my first conception of a living person was that of something mockingly like myself, yet distorted, shrivelled, and decaying like the castle. To me there was nothing grotesque in the bones and skeletons that strowed some of the stone crypts deep down among the foundations. I fantastically associated these things with every-day events, and thought them more natural than the coloured pictures of living beings which I found in many of the mouldy books. From such books I learned all that I know. No teacher urged or guided me, and I do not recall hearing any human voice in all those years—not even my own; for although I had read of speech, I had never thought to try to speak aloud. My aspect was a matter equally unthought of, for there were no mirrors in the castle, and I merely regarded myself by instinct as akin to the youthful figures I saw drawn and painted in the books. I felt conscious of youth because I remembered so little.

Outside, across the putrid moat and under the dark mute trees, I would often lie and dream for hours about what I read in the books; and would longingly picture myself amidst gay crowds in the sunny world beyond the endless forest. Once I tried to escape from the forest, but as I went farther from the castle the shade grew denser and the air more filled with brooding fear; so that I ran frantically back lest I lose my way in a labyrinth of nighted silence.

So through endless twilights I dreamed and waited, though I knew not what I waited for. Then in the shadowy solitude my longing for light grew so frantic that I could rest no more, and I lifted entreating hands to the single black ruined tower that reached above the forest into the unknown outer sky. And at last I resolved to scale that tower, fall though I might; since it were better to glimpse the sky and perish, than to live without ever beholding day.

In the dank twilight I climbed the worn and aged stone stairs till I reached the level where they ceased, and thereafter clung perilously to small footholds leading upward. Ghastly and terrible was that dead, stairless cylinder of rock; black, ruined, and deserted, and sinister with startled bats whose wings made no noise. But more ghastly and terrible still was the slowness of my progress; for climb as I might, the darkness overhead grew no thinner, and a new chill as of haunted and venerable mould assailed me. I shivered as I wondered why I did not reach the light, and would have looked down had I dared. I fancied that night had come suddenly upon me, and vainly groped with one free hand for a window embrasure, that I might peer out and above, and try to judge the height I had attained.

All at once, after an infinity of awesome, sightless crawling up that concave and desperate precipice, I felt my head touch a solid thing, and I knew I must have gained the roof, or at least some kind of floor. In the darkness I raised my free hand and tested the barrier, finding it stone and immovable. Then came a deadly circuit of the tower, clinging to whatever holds the slimy wall could give; till finally my testing hand found the barrier yielding, and I turned upward again, pushing the slab or door with my head as I used both hands in my fearful ascent. There was no light revealed above, and as my hands went higher I knew that my climb was for the nonce ended; since the slab was the trap-door of an aperture leading to a level stone surface of greater circumference than the lower tower, no doubt the floor of some lofty and capacious observation chamber. I crawled through carefully, and tried to prevent the heavy slab from falling back into place; but failed in the latter attempt. As I lay exhausted on the stone floor I heard the eerie echoes of its fall, but hoped when necessary to pry it open again.

Believing I was now at a prodigious height, far above the accursed branches of the wood, I dragged myself up from the floor and fumbled about for windows, that I might look for the first time upon the sky, and the moon and stars of which I had read. But on every hand I was disappointed; since all that I found were vast shelves of marble, bearing odious oblong boxes of disturbing size. More and more I reflected, and wondered what hoary secrets might abide in this high apartment so many aeons cut off from the castle below. Then unexpectedly my hands came upon a doorway, where hung a portal of stone, rough with strange chiselling. Trying it, I found it locked; but with a supreme burst of strength I overcame all obstacles and dragged it open inward. As I did so there came to me the purest ecstasy I have ever known; for shining tranquilly through an ornate grating of iron, and down a short stone passageway of steps that ascended from the newly found doorway, was the radiant full moon, which I had never before seen save in dreams and in vague visions I dared not call memories.

Fancying now that I had attained the very pinnacle of the castle, I commenced to rush up the few steps beyond the door; but the sudden veiling of the moon by a cloud caused me to stumble, and I felt my way more slowly in the dark. It was still very dark when I reached the grating—which I tried carefully and found unlocked, but which I did not open for fear of falling from the amazing height to which I had climbed. Then the moon came out.

Most daemoniacal of all shocks is that of the abysmally unexpected and grotesquely unbelievable. Nothing I had before undergone could compare in terror with what I now saw; with the bizarre marvels that sight implied. The sight itself was as simple as it was stupefying, for it was merely this: instead of a dizzying prospect of treetops seen from a lofty eminence, there stretched around me on a level through the grating nothing less than the solid ground, decked and diversified by marble slabs and columns, and overshadowed by an ancient stone church, whose ruined spire gleamed spectrally in the moonlight.

Half unconscious, I opened the grating and staggered out upon the white gravel path that stretched away in two directions. My mind, stunned and chaotic as it was, still held the frantic craving for light; and not even the fantastic wonder which had happened could stay my course. I neither knew nor cared whether my experience was insanity, dreaming, or magic; but was determined to gaze on brilliance and gaiety at any cost. I knew not who I was or what I was, or what my surroundings might be; though as I continued to stumble along I became conscious of a kind of fearsome latent memory that made my progress not wholly fortuitous. I passed under an arch out of that region of slabs and columns, and wandered through the open country; sometimes following the visible road, but sometimes leaving it curiously to tread across meadows where only occasional ruins bespoke the ancient presence of a forgotten road. Once I swam across a swift river where crumbling, mossy masonry told of a bridge long vanished.

Over two hours must have passed before I reached what seemed to be my goal, a venerable ivied castle in a thickly wooded park; maddeningly familiar, yet full of perplexing strangeness to me. I saw that the moat was filled in, and that some of the well-known towers were demolished; whilst new wings existed to confuse the beholder. But what I observed with chief interest and delight were the open windows—gorgeously ablaze with light and sending forth sound of the gayest revelry. Advancing to one of these I looked in and saw an oddly dressed company, indeed; making merry, and speaking brightly to one another. I had never, seemingly, heard human speech before; and could guess only vaguely what was said. Some of the faces seemed to hold expressions that brought up incredibly remote recollections; others were utterly alien.

I now stepped through the low window into the brilliantly lighted room, stepping as I did so from my single bright moment of hope to my blackest convulsion of despair and realisation. The nightmare was quick to come; for as I entered, there occurred immediately one of the most terrifying demonstrations I had ever conceived. Scarcely had I crossed the sill when there descended upon the whole company a sudden and unheralded fear of hideous intensity, distorting every face and evoking the most horrible screams from nearly every throat. Flight was universal, and in the clamour and panic several fell in a swoon and were dragged away by their madly fleeing companions. Many covered their eyes with their hands, and plunged blindly and awkwardly in their race to escape; overturning furniture and stumbling against the walls before they managed to reach one of the many doors.

The cries were shocking; and as I stood in the brilliant apartment alone and dazed, listening to their vanishing echoes, I trembled at the thought of what might be lurking near me unseen. At a casual inspection the room seemed deserted, but when I moved toward one of the alcoves I thought I detected a presence there—a hint of motion beyond the golden-arched doorway leading to another and somewhat similar room. As I approached the arch I began to perceive the presence more clearly; and then, with the first and last sound I ever uttered—a ghastly ululation that revolted me almost as poignantly as its noxious cause—I beheld in full, frightful vividness the inconceivable, indescribable, and unmentionable monstrosity which had by its simple appearance changed a merry company to a herd of delirious fugitives.

I cannot even hint what it was like, for it was a compound of all that is unclean, uncanny, unwelcome, abnormal, and detestable. It was the ghoulish shade of decay, antiquity, and desolation; the putrid, dripping eidolon of unwholesome revelation; the awful baring of that which the merciful earth should always hide. God knows it was not of this world—or no longer of this world—yet to my horror I saw in its eaten-away and bone-revealing outlines a leering, abhorrent travesty on the human shape; and in its mouldy, disintegrating apparel an unspeakable quality that chilled me even more.

I was almost paralysed, but not too much so to make a feeble effort toward flight; a backward stumble which failed to break the spell in which the nameless, voiceless monster held me. My eyes, bewitched by the glassy orbs which stared loathsomely into them, refused to close; though they were mercifully blurred, and shewed the terrible object but indistinctly after the first shock. I tried to raise my hand to shut out the sight, yet so stunned were my nerves that my arm could not fully obey my will. The attempt, however, was enough to disturb my balance; so that I had to stagger forward several steps to avoid falling. As I did so I became suddenly and agonisingly aware of the nearness of the carrion thing, whose hideous hollow breathing I half fancied I could hear. Nearly mad, I found myself yet able to throw out a hand to ward off the foetid apparition which pressed so close; when in one cataclysmic second of cosmic nightmarishness and hellish accident *my fingers touched the rotting outstretched paw of the monster beneath the golden arch.*

I did not shriek, but all the fiendish ghouls that ride the night-wind shrieked for me as in that same second there crashed down upon my mind a single and fleeting avalanche of soul-annihilating memory. I knew in that second all that had been; I remembered beyond the frightful castle and the trees, and recognised the altered edifice in which I now stood; I recognised, most terrible of all, the unholy abomination that stood leering before me as I withdrew my sullied fingers from its own.

But in the cosmos there is balm as well as bitterness, and that balm is nepenthe. In the supreme horror of that second I forgot what had horrified me, and the burst of black memory vanished in a chaos of echoing images. In a dream I fled from that haunted and accursed pile, and ran swiftly and silently in the moonlight. When I returned to the churchyard place of marble and went down the steps I found the stone trap-door immovable; but I was not sorry, for I had hated the antique castle and the trees. Now I ride with the mocking and friendly ghouls on the night-wind, and play by day amongst the catacombs of Nephren-Ka in the sealed and unknown valley of Hadoth by the Nile. I know that light is not for me, save that of the moon over the rock tombs of Neb, nor any gaiety save the unnamed feasts of Nitokris beneath the Great Pyramid; yet in my new wildness and freedom I almost welcome the bitterness of alienage.

For although nepenthe has calmed me, I know always that I am an outsider; a stranger in this century and among those who are still men. This I have known ever since I stretched out my fingers to the abomination within that great gilded frame; stretched out my fingers and touched *a cold and unyielding surface of polished glass.*

THE MONKEY'S PAW

W. W. Jacobs

I

Without, the night was cold and wet, but in the small parlour of Laburnam Villa the blinds were drawn and the fire burned brightly. Father and son were at chess, the former, who possessed ideas about the game involving radical changes, putting his king into such sharp and unnecessary perils that it even provoked comment from the white-haired old lady knitting placidly by the fire.

"Hark at the wind," said Mr. White, who, having seen a fatal mistake after it was too late, was amiably desirous of preventing his son from seeing it.

"I'm listening," said the latter, grimly surveying the board as he stretched out his hand. "Check."

"I should hardly think that he'd come to-night," said his father, with his hand poised over the board.

"Mate," replied the son.

"That's the worst of living so far out," bawled Mr. White, with sudden and unlooked-for violence; "of all the beastly, slushy, out-of-the-way places to live in, this is the worst. Pathway's a bog, and the road's a torrent. I don't know what people are thinking about. I suppose because only two houses in the road are let, they think it doesn't matter."

"Never mind, dear," said his wife, soothingly; "perhaps you'll win the next one."

Mr. White looked up sharply, just in time to intercept a knowing glance between mother and son. The words died away on his lips, and he hid a guilty grin in his thin grey beard.

"There he is," said Herbert White, as the gate banged too loudly and heavy footsteps came toward the door.

The old man rose with hospitable haste, and opening the door, was heard condoling with the new arrival. The new arrival also condoled with himself, so that Mrs. White said, "Tut, tut!" and coughed gently as her husband entered the room, followed by a tall, burly man, beady of eye and rubicund of visage.

"Sergeant-Major Morris," he said, introducing him.

The sergeant-major shook hands, and taking the proffered seat by the fire, watched contentedly while his host got out whiskey and tumblers and stood a small copper kettle on the fire.

At the third glass his eyes got brighter, and he began to talk, the little family circle regarding with eager interest this visitor from distant parts, as he squared his broad shoulders in the chair and spoke of wild scenes and doughty deeds; of wars and plagues and strange peoples.

"Twenty-one years of it," said Mr. White, nodding at his wife and son. "When he went away he was a slip of a youth in the warehouse. Now look at him."

"He don't look to have taken much harm," said Mrs. White, politely.

"I'd like to go to India myself," said the old man, "just to look round a bit, you know."

"Better where you are," said the sergeant-major, shaking his head. He put down the empty glass, and sighing softly, shook it again.

"I should like to see those old temples and fakirs and jugglers," said the old man. "What was that you started telling me the other day about a monkey's paw or something, Morris?"

"Nothing," said the soldier, hastily. "Leastways nothing worth hearing."

"Monkey's paw?" said Mrs. White, curiously.

"Well, it's just a bit of what you might call magic, perhaps," said the sergeant-major, offhandedly.

His three listeners leaned forward eagerly. The visitor absent-mindedly put his empty glass to his lips and then set it down again. His host filled it for him.

"To look at," said the sergeant-major, fumbling in his pocket, "it's just an ordinary little paw, dried to a mummy."

He took something out of his pocket and proffered it. Mrs. White drew back with a grimace, but her son, taking it, examined it curiously.

"And what is there special about it?" inquired Mr. White as he took it from his son, and having examined it, placed it upon the table.

"It had a spell put on it by an old fakir," said the sergeant-major, "a very holy man. He wanted to show that fate ruled people's lives, and that those who interfered with it did so to their sorrow. He put a spell on it so that three separate men could each have three wishes from it."

His manner was so impressive that his hearers were conscious that their light laughter jarred somewhat.

"Well, why don't you have three, sir?" said Herbert White, cleverly.

The soldier regarded him in the way that middle age is wont to regard presumptuous youth. "I have," he said, quietly, and his blotchy face whitened.

"And did you really have the three wishes granted?" asked Mrs. White.

"I did," said the sergeant-major, and his glass tapped against his strong teeth.

"And has anybody else wished?" persisted the old lady.

"The first man had his three wishes. Yes," was the reply; "I don't know what the first two were, but the third was for death. That's how I got the paw."

His tones were so grave that a hush fell upon the group.

"If you've had your three wishes, it's no good to you now, then, Morris," said the old man at last. "What do you keep it for?"

The soldier shook his head. "Fancy, I suppose," he said, slowly. "I did have some idea of selling it, but I don't think I will. It has caused enough mischief already. Besides, people won't buy. They think it's a fairy tale; some of them, and those who do think anything of it want to try it first and pay me afterward."

"If you could have another three wishes," said the old man, eyeing him keenly, "would you have them?"

"I don't know," said the other. "I don't know."

He took the paw, and dangling it between his forefinger and thumb, suddenly threw it upon the fire. White, with a slight cry, stooped down and snatched it off.

"Better let it burn," said the soldier, solemnly.

"If you don't want it, Morris," said the other, "give it to me."

"I won't," said his friend, doggedly. "I threw it on the fire. If you keep it, don't blame me for what happens. Pitch it on the fire again like a sensible man."

The other shook his head and examined his new possession closely. "How do you do it?" he inquired.

"Hold it up in your right hand and wish aloud," said the sergeant-major, "but I warn you of the consequences."

"Sounds like the *Arabian Nights*," said Mrs. White, as she rose and began to set the supper. "Don't you think you might wish for four pairs of hands for me?"

Her husband drew the talisman from pocket, and then all three burst into laughter as the sergeant-major, with a look of alarm on his face, caught him by the arm.

"If you must wish," he said, gruffly, "wish for something sensible."

Mr. White dropped it back in his pocket, and placing chairs, motioned his friend to the table. In the business of supper the talisman was partly forgotten, and afterward the three sat listening in an enthralled fashion to a second instalment of the soldier's adventures in India.

"If the tale about the monkey's paw is not more truthful than those he has been telling us," said Herbert, as the door closed behind their guest, just in time for him to catch the last train, "we sha'nt make much out of it."

"Did you give him anything for it, father?" inquired Mrs. White, regarding her husband closely.

"A trifle," said he, colouring slightly. "He didn't want it, but I made him take it. And he pressed me again to throw it away."

"Likely," said Herbert, with pretended horror. "Why, we're going to be rich, and famous and happy. Wish to be an emperor, father, to begin with; then you can't be henpecked."

He darted round the table, pursued by the maligned Mrs. White armed with an antimacassar.

Mr. White took the paw from his pocket and eyed it dubiously. "I don't know what to wish for, and that's a fact," he said, slowly. "It seems to me I've got all I want."

"If you only cleared the house, you'd be quite happy, wouldn't you?" said Herbert, with his hand on his shoulder. "Well, wish for two hundred pounds, then; that'll just do it."

His father, smiling shamefacedly at his own credulity, held up the talisman, as his son, with a solemn face, somewhat marred by a wink at his mother, sat down at the piano and struck a few impressive chords.

"I wish for two hundred pounds," said the old man distinctly.

A fine crash from the piano greeted the words, interrupted by a shuddering cry from the old man. His wife and son ran toward him.

"It moved," he cried, with a glance of disgust at the object as it lay on the floor.

"As I wished, it twisted in my hand like a snake."

"Well, I don't see the money," said his son as he picked it up and placed it on the table, "and I bet I never shall."

"It must have been your fancy, father," said his wife, regarding him anxiously.

He shook his head. "Never mind, though; there's no harm done, but it gave me a shock all the same."

They sat down by the fire again while the two men finished their pipes. Outside, the wind was higher than ever, and the old man started nervously at the sound of a door banging upstairs. A silence unusual and depressing settled upon all three, which lasted until the old couple rose to retire for the night.

"I expect you'll find the cash tied up in a big bag in the middle of your bed," said Herbert, as he bade them good-night, "and something horrible squatting up on top of the wardrobe watching you as you pocket your ill-gotten gains."

He sat alone in the darkness, gazing at the dying fire, and seeing faces in it. The last face was so horrible and so simian that he gazed at it in amazement. It got so vivid that, with a little uneasy laugh, he felt on the table for a glass containing a little water to throw over it. His hand grasped the monkey's paw, and with a little shiver he wiped his hand on his coat and went up to bed.

II

In the brightness of the wintry sun next morning as it streamed over the breakfast table he laughed at his fears. There was an air of prosaic wholesomeness about the room which it had lacked on the previous night, and the dirty, shrivelled little paw was pitched on the sideboard with a carelessness which betokened no great belief in its virtues.

"I suppose all old soldiers are the same," said Mrs. White. "The idea of our listening to such nonsense! How could wishes be granted in these days? And if they could, how could two hundred pounds hurt you, father?"

"Might drop on his head from the sky," said the frivolous Herbert.

"Morris said the things happened so naturally," said his father, "that you might if you so wished attribute it to coincidence."

"Well, don't break into the money before I come back," said Herbert as he rose from the table. "I'm afraid it'll turn you into a mean, avaricious man, and we shall have to disown you."

His mother laughed, and following him to the door, watched him down the road; and returning to the breakfast table, was very happy at the expense of her husband's credulity. All of which did not prevent her from scurrying to the door at the postman's knock, nor prevent her from referring somewhat shortly to retired sergeant-majors of bibulous habits when she found that the post brought a tailor's bill.

"Herbert will have some more of his funny remarks, I expect, when he comes home," she said, as they sat at dinner.

"I dare say," said Mr. White, pouring himself out some beer; "but for all that, the thing moved in my hand; that I'll swear to."

"You thought it did," said the old lady soothingly.

"I say it did," replied the other. "There was no thought about it; I had just—what's the matter?"

His wife made no reply. She was watching the mysterious movements of a man outside, who, peering in an undecided fashion at the house, appeared to be trying to make up his mind to enter. In mental connection with the two hundred pounds, she noticed that the stranger was well dressed, and wore a silk hat of glossy newness. Three times he paused at the gate, and then walked on again. The fourth time he stood with his hand upon it, and then with sudden resolution flung it open and walked up the path. Mrs. White at the same moment placed her hands behind her, and hurriedly unfastening the strings of her apron, put that useful article of apparel beneath the cushion of her chair.

She brought the stranger, who seemed ill at ease, into the room. He gazed at her furtively, and listened in a preoccupied fashion as the old lady apologized for the appearance of the room, and her husband's coat, a garment which he usually reserved for the garden. She then waited as patiently as her sex would permit, for him to broach his business, but he was at first strangely silent.

"I—was asked to call," he said at last, and stooped and picked a piece of cotton from his trousers. "I come from 'Maw and Meggins.'"

The old lady started. "Is anything the matter?" she asked, breathlessly. "Has anything happened to Herbert? What is it? What is it?"

Her husband interposed. "There, there, mother," he said, hastily. "Sit down, and don't jump to conclusions. You've not brought bad news, I'm sure, sir"; and he eyed the other wistfully.

"I'm sorry—" began the visitor.

"Is he hurt?" demanded the mother, wildly.

The visitor bowed in assent. "Badly hurt," he said, quietly, "but he is not in any pain."

"Oh, thank God!" said the old woman, clasping her hands. "Thank God for that! Thank—"

She broke off suddenly as the sinister meaning of the assurance dawned upon her and she saw the awful confirmation of her fears in the other's averted face. She caught her breath, and turning to her slower-witted husband, laid her trembling old hand upon his. There was a long silence.

"He was caught in the machinery," said the visitor at length in a low voice.

"Caught in the machinery," repeated Mr. White, in a dazed fashion, "yes."

He sat staring blankly out at the window, and taking his wife's hand between his own, pressed it as he had been wont to do in their old courting-days nearly forty years before.

"He was the only one left to us," he said, turning gently to the visitor. "It is hard."

The other coughed, and rising, walked slowly to the window. "The firm wished me to convey their sincere sympathy with you in your great loss," he said, without looking round. "I beg that you will understand I am only their servant and merely obeying orders."

There was no reply; the old woman's face was white, her eyes staring, and her breath inaudible; on the husband's face was a look such as his friend the sergeant might have carried into his first action.

"I was to say that 'Maw and Meggins' disclaim all responsibility," continued the other. "They admit no liability at all, but in consideration of your son's services, they wish to present you with a certain sum as compensation."

Mr. White dropped his wife's hand, and rising to his feet, gazed with a look of horror at his visitor. His dry lips shaped the words, "How much?"

"Two hundred pounds," was the answer.

Unconscious of his wife's shriek, the old man smiled faintly, put out his hands like a sightless man, and dropped, a senseless heap, to the floor.

III

In the huge new cemetery, some two miles distant, the old people buried their dead, and came back to a house steeped in shadow and silence. It was all over so quickly that at first they could hardly realize it, and remained in a state of expectation as though of something else to happen—something else which was to lighten this load, too heavy for old hearts to bear.

But the days passed, and expectation gave place to resignation—the hopeless resignation of the old, sometimes miscalled, apathy. Sometimes they hardly exchanged a word, for now they had nothing to talk about, and their days were long to weariness.

It was about a week after that the old man, waking suddenly in the night, stretched out his hand and found himself alone. The room was in darkness, and the sound of subdued weeping came from the window. He raised himself in bed and listened.

"Come back," he said, tenderly. "You will be cold."

"It is colder for my son," said the old woman, and wept afresh.

The sound of her sobs died away on his ears. The bed was warm, and his eyes heavy with sleep. He dozed fitfully, and then slept until a sudden wild cry from his wife awoke him with a start.

"The paw!" she cried wildly. "The monkey's paw!"

He started up in alarm. "Where? Where is it? What's the matter?"

She came stumbling across the room toward him. "I want it," she said, quietly. "You've not destroyed it?"

"It's in the parlour, on the bracket," he replied, marvelling. "Why?"

She cried and laughed together, and bending over, kissed his cheek.

"I only just thought of it," she said, hysterically. "Why didn't I think of it before? Why didn't you think of it?"

"Think of what?" he questioned.

"The other two wishes," she replied, rapidly. "We've only had one."

"Was not that enough?" he demanded, fiercely.

"No," she cried, triumphantly; "we'll have one more. Go down and get it quickly, and wish our boy alive again."

The man sat up in bed and flung the bedclothes from his quaking limbs. "Good God, you are mad!" he cried, aghast.

"Get it," she panted; "get it quickly, and wish—Oh, my boy, my boy!"

Her husband struck a match and lit the candle. "Get back to bed," he said, unsteadily. "You don't know what you are saying."

"We had the first wish granted," said the old woman, feverishly; "why not the second?"

"A coincidence," stammered the old man.

"Go and get it and wish," cried his wife, quivering with excitement.

The old man turned and regarded her, and his voice shook. "He has been dead ten days, and besides he—I would not tell you else, but—I could only recognize him by his clothing. If he was too terrible for you to see then, how now?"

"Bring him back," cried the old woman, and dragged him toward the door. "Do you think I fear the child I have nursed?"

He went down in the darkness, and felt his way to the parlour, and then to the mantelpiece. The talisman was in its place, and a horrible fear that the unspoken wish might bring his mutilated son before him ere he could escape from the room seized upon him, and he caught his breath as he found that he had lost the direction of the door. His brow cold with sweat, he felt his way round the table, and groped along the wall until he found himself in the small passage with the unwholesome thing in his hand.

Even his wife's face seemed changed as he entered the room. It was white and expectant, and to his fears seemed to have an unnatural look upon it. He was afraid of her.

"Wish!" she cried, in a strong voice.

"It is foolish and wicked," he faltered.

"Wish!" repeated his wife.

He raised his hand. "I wish my son alive again."

The talisman fell to the floor, and he regarded it fearfully. Then he sank trembling into a chair as the old woman, with burning eyes, walked to the window and raised the blind.

He sat until he was chilled with the cold, glancing occasionally at the figure of the old woman peering through the window. The candle-end, which had burned below the rim of the china candlestick, was throwing pulsating shadows on the ceiling and walls, until, with a flicker larger than the rest, it expired. The old man, with an unspeakable sense of relief at the failure of the talisman, crept back to his bed, and a minute or two afterward the old woman came silently and apathetically beside him.

Neither spoke, but lay silently listening to the ticking of the clock. A stair creaked, and a squeaky mouse scurried noisily through the wall. The darkness was oppressive, and after lying for some time screwing up his courage, he took the box of matches, and striking one, went downstairs for a candle.

At the foot of the stairs the match went out, and he paused to strike another; and at the same moment a knock, so quiet and stealthy as to be scarcely audible, sounded on the front door.

The matches fell from his hand and spilled in the passage. He stood motionless, his breath suspended until the knock was repeated. Then he turned and fled swiftly back to his room, and closed the door behind him. A third knock sounded through the house.

"What's that?" cried the old woman, starting up.

"A rat," said the old man in shaking tones—"a rat. It passed me on the stairs."

His wife sat up in bed listening. A loud knock resounded through the house.

"It's Herbert!" she screamed. "It's Herbert!"

She ran to the door, but her husband was before her, and catching her by the arm, held her tightly.

"What are you going to do?" he whispered hoarsely.

"It's my boy; it's Herbert!" she cried, struggling mechanically. "I forgot it was two miles away. What are you holding me for? Let go. I must open the door."

"For God's sake don't let it in," cried the old man, trembling.

"You're afraid of your own son," she cried, struggling. "Let me go. I'm coming, Herbert; I'm coming."

There was another knock, and another. The old woman with a sudden wrench broke free and ran from the room. Her husband followed to the landing, and called after her appealingly as she hurried downstairs. He heard the chain rattle back and the bottom bolt drawn slowly and stiffly from the socket. Then the old woman's voice, strained and panting.

"The bolt," she cried, loudly. "Come down. I can't reach it."

But her husband was on his hands and knees groping wildly on the floor in search of the paw. If he could only find it before the thing outside got in. A perfect fusillade of knocks reverberated through the house, and he heard the scraping of a chair as his wife put it down in the passage against the door. He heard the creaking of the bolt as it came slowly back, and at the same moment he found the monkey's paw, and frantically breathed his third and last wish.

The knocking ceased suddenly, although the echoes of it were still in the house. He heard the chair drawn back, and the door opened. A cold wind rushed up the staircase, and a long loud wail of disappointment and misery from his wife gave him courage to run down to her side, and then to the gate beyond. The street lamp flickering opposite shone on a quiet and deserted road.

CANON ALBERIC'S SCRAP-BOOK

M. R. James

St. Bertrand de Comminges is a decayed town on the spurs of the Pyrenees, not very far from Toulouse, and still nearer to Bagnères-de-Luchon. It was the site of a bishopric until the Revolution, and has a cathedral which is visited by a certain number of tourists. In the spring of 1883 an Englishman arrived at this old-world place—I can hardly dignify it with the name of city, for there are not a thousand inhabitants. He was a Cambridge man, who had come specially from Toulouse to see St. Bertrand's Church, and had left two friends, who were less keen archaeologists than himself, in their hotel at Toulouse, under promise to join him on the following morning. Half an hour at the church would satisfy *them*, and all three could then pursue their journey in the direction of Auch. But our Englishman had come early on the day in question, and proposed to himself to fill a note-book and to use several dozens of plates in the process of describing and photographing every corner of the wonderful church that dominates the little hill of Comminges. In order to carry out this design satisfactorily, it was necessary to monopolize the verger of the church for the day. The verger or sacristan (I prefer the latter appellation, inaccurate as it may be) was accordingly sent for by the somewhat brusque lady who keeps the inn of the Chapeau Rouge; and when he came, the Englishman found him an unexpectedly interesting object of study. It was not in the personal appearance of the little, dry, wizened old man that the interest lay, for he was precisely like dozens of other church-guardians in France, but in a curious furtive or rather hunted and oppressed air which he had. He was perpetually half glancing behind him; the muscles of his back and shoulders seemed to be hunched in a continual nervous contraction, as if he were expecting every moment to find himself in the clutch of an enemy. The Englishman hardly knew whether to put him down as a man haunted by a fixed delusion, or as one oppressed by a guilty conscience, or as an unbearably henpecked husband. The probabilities, when reckoned up, certainly pointed to the last idea; but, still, the impression conveyed was that of a more formidable persecutor even than a termagant wife.

However, the Englishman (let us call him Dennistoun) was soon too deep in his note-book and too busy with his camera to give more than an occasional glance to the sacristan. Whenever he did look at him, he found him at no great distance, either huddling himself back against the wall or crouching in one of the gorgeous stalls. Dennistoun became rather fidgety after a time. Mingled suspicions that he was keeping the old man from his *déjeuner*, that he was regarded as likely to make away with St. Bertrand's ivory crozier, or with the dusty stuffed crocodile that hangs over the font, began to torment him.

"Won't you go home?" he said at last; "I'm quite well able to finish my notes alone; you can lock me in if you like. I shall want at least two hours more here, and it must be cold for you, isn't it?"

"Good heavens!" said the little man, whom the suggestion seemed to throw into a state of unaccountable terror, "such a thing cannot be thought of for a moment. Leave monsieur alone in the church? No, no; two hours, three hours, all will be the same to me. I have breakfasted, I am not at all cold, with many thanks to monsieur."

"Very well, my little man," quoth Dennistoun to himself: "you have been warned, and you must take the consequences."

Before the expiration of the two hours, the stalls, the enormous dilapidated organ, the choir-screen of Bishop John de Mauléon, the remnants of glass and tapestry, and the objects in the treasure-chamber had been well and truly examined; the sacristan still keeping at Dennistoun's heels, and every now and then whipping round as if he had been stung, when one or other of the strange noises that trouble a large empty building fell on his ear. Curious noises they were, sometimes.

"Once," Dennistoun said to me, "I could have sworn I heard a thin metallic voice laughing high up in the tower. I darted an inquiring glance at my sacristan. He was white to the lips. "It is he—that is—it is no one; the door is locked," was all he said, and we looked at each other for a full minute."

Another little incident puzzled Dennistoun a good deal. He was examining a large dark picture that hangs behind the altar, one of a series illustrating the miracles of St. Bertrand. The composition of the picture is well-nigh indecipherable, but there is a Latin legend below, which runs thus:

Qualiter S. Bertrandus liberavit hominem quem diabolus diu volebat strangulare. (How St. Bertrand delivered a man whom the Devil long sought to strangle.)

Dennistoun was turning to the sacristan with a smile and a jocular remark of some sort on his lips, but he was confounded to see the old man on his knees, gazing at the picture with the eye of a suppliant in agony, his hands tightly clasped, and a rain of tears on his cheeks. Dennistoun naturally pretended to have noticed nothing, but the question would not go away from him, "Why should a daub of this kind affect anyone so strongly?" He seemed to himself to be getting some sort of clue to the reason of the strange look that had been puzzling him all the day: the man must be a monomaniac; but what was his monomania?

It was nearly five o'clock; the short day was drawing in, and the church began to fill with shadows, while the curious noises—the muffled footfalls and distant talking voices that had been perceptible all day—seemed, no doubt because of the fading light and the consequently quickened sense of hearing, to become more frequent and insistent.

The sacristan began for the first time to show signs of hurry and impatience. He heaved a sigh of relief when camera and note-book were finally packed up and stowed away, and hurriedly beckoned Dennistoun to the western door of the church, under the tower. It was time to ring the Angelus. A few pulls at the reluctant rope, and the great bell Bertrande, high in the tower, began to speak, and swung her voice up among the pines and down to the valleys, loud with mountain-streams, calling the dwellers on those lonely hills to remember and repeat the salutation of the angel to her whom he called Blessed among women. With that a profound quiet seemed to fall for the first time that day upon the little town, and Dennistoun and the sacristan went out of the church.

On the doorstep they fell into conversation.

"Monsieur seemed to interest himself in the old choir-books in the sacristy."

"Undoubtedly. I was going to ask you if there were a library in the town."

"No, monsieur; perhaps there used to be one belonging to the Chapter, but it is now such a small place—" Here came a strange pause of irresolution, as it seemed; then, with a sort of plunge, he went on: "But if monsieur is *amateur des vieux livres*, I have at home something that might interest him. It is not a hundred yards."

At once all Dennistoun's cherished dreams of finding priceless manuscripts in untrodden corners of France flashed up, to die down again the next moment. It was probably a stupid missal of Plantin's printing, about 1580. Where was the likelihood that a place so near Toulouse would not have been ransacked long ago by collectors? However, it would be foolish not to go; he would reproach himself for ever after if he refused. So they set off. On the way the curious irresolution and sudden determination of the sacristan recurred to Dennistoun, and he wondered in a shamefaced way whether he was being decoyed into some purlieu to be made away with as a supposed rich Englishman. He contrived, therefore, to begin talking with his guide, and to drag in, in a rather clumsy fashion, the fact that he expected two friends to join him early the next morning. To his surprise, the announcement seemed to relieve the sacristan at once of some of the anxiety that oppressed him.

"That is well," he said quite brightly—"that is very well. Monsieur will travel in company with his friends: they will be always near him. It is a good thing to travel thus in company—sometimes."

The last word appeared to be added as an afterthought and to bring with it a relapse into gloom for the poor little man.

They were soon at the house, which was one rather larger than its neighbours, stone-built, with a shield carved over the door, the shield of Alberic de Mauléon, a collateral descendant, Dennistoun tells me, of Bishop John de Mauléon. This Alberic was a Canon of Comminges from 1680 to 1701. The upper windows of the mansion were boarded up, and the whole place bore, as does the rest of Comminges, the aspect of decaying age.

Arrived on his doorstep, the sacristan paused a moment.

"Perhaps," he said, "perhaps, after all, monsieur has not the time?"

"Not at all—lots of time—nothing to do till tomorrow. Let us see what it is you have got."

The door was opened at this point, and a face looked out, a face far younger than the sacristan's, but bearing something of the same distressing look: only here it seemed to be the mark, not so much of fear for personal safety as of acute anxiety on behalf of another. Plainly the owner of the face was the sacristan's daughter; and, but for the expression I have described, she was a handsome girl enough. She brightened up considerably on seeing her father accompanied by an able-bodied stranger. A few remarks passed between father and daughter of which Dennistoun only caught these words, said by the sacristan: "He was laughing in the church," words which were answered only by a look of terror from the girl.

But in another minute they were in the sitting-room of the house, a small, high chamber with a stone floor, full of moving shadows cast by a wood-fire that flickered on a great hearth. Something of the character of an oratory was imparted to it by a tall crucifix, which reached almost to the ceiling on one side; the figure was painted of the natural colours, the cross was black. Under this stood a chest of some age and solidity, and when a lamp had been brought, and chairs set, the sacristan went to this chest, and produced therefrom, with growing excitement and nervousness, as Dennistoun thought, a large book, wrapped in a white cloth, on which cloth a cross was rudely embroidered in red thread. Even before the wrapping had been removed, Dennistoun began to be interested by the size and shape of the volume. "Too large for a missal," he thought, "and not the shape of an antiphoner; perhaps it may be something good, after all." The next moment the book was open, and Dennistoun felt that he had at last lit upon something better than good. Before him lay a large folio, bound, perhaps, late in the seventeenth century, with the arms of Canon Alberic de Mauléon stamped in gold on the sides. There may have been a hundred and fifty leaves of paper in the book, and on almost every one of them was fastened a leaf from an illuminated manuscript. Such a collection Dennistoun had hardly dreamed of in his wildest moments. Here were ten leaves from a copy of Genesis, illustrated with pictures, which could not be later than A.D. 700. Further on was a complete set of pictures from a Psalter, of English execution, of the very finest kind that the thirteenth century could produce; and, perhaps best of all, there were twenty leaves of uncial writing in Latin, which, as a few words seen here and there told him at once, must belong to some very early unknown patristic treatise. Could it possibly be a fragment of the copy of Papias "On the Words of Our Lord," which was known to have existed as late as the twelfth century at Nimes?* In any case, his mind was made up; that book must return to Cambridge with him, even if he had to draw the whole of his balance from the bank and stay at St. Bertrand till the money came. He glanced up at the sacristan to see if his face yielded any hint that the book was for sale. The sacristan was pale, and his lips were working.

"If monsieur will turn on to the end," he said.

So monsieur turned on, meeting new treasures at every rise of a leaf; and at the end of the book he came upon two sheets of paper, of much more recent date than anything he had seen yet, which puzzled him considerably. They must be contemporary, he decided, with the unprincipled Canon Alberic, who had doubtless plundered the Chapter library of St. Bertrand to form this priceless scrap-book. On the first of the paper sheets was a plan, carefully drawn and instantly recognizable by a person who knew the ground, of the south aisle and cloisters of St. Bertrand's. There were curious signs looking like planetary symbols, and a few Hebrew words in the corners; and in the north-west angle of the cloister was a cross drawn in gold paint. Below the plan were some lines of writing in Latin, which ran thus:

> *Responsa 12(mi) Dec. 1694. Interrogatum est: Inveniamne? Responsum est: Invenies. Fiamne dives? Fies. Vivamne invidendus? Vives. Moriarne in lecto meo? Ita.*
>
> (Answers of the 12th of December, 1694. It was asked: Shall I find it? Answer: Thou shalt. Shall I become rich? Thou wilt. Shall I live an object of envy? Thou wilt. Shall I die in my bed? Thou wilt.)

"A good specimen of the treasure-hunter's record—quite reminds one of Mr. Minor-Canon Quatremain in *Old St. Paul's*," was Dennistoun's comment, and he turned the leaf.

What he then saw impressed him, as he has often told me, more than he could have conceived any drawing or picture capable of impressing him. And, though the drawing he saw is no longer in existence, there is a photograph of it (which I possess) which fully bears out that statement. The picture in question was a sepia drawing at the end of the seventeenth century, representing, one would say at first sight, a Biblical scene; for the architecture (the picture represented an interior) and the figures had that

* We now know that these leaves did contain a considerable fragment of that work, if not of that actual copy of it.

semi-classical flavour about them which the artists of two hundred years ago thought appropriate to illustrations of the Bible. On the right was a king on his throne, the throne elevated on twelve steps, a canopy overhead, soldiers on either side—evidently King Solomon. He was bending forward with outstretched sceptre, in attitude of command; his face expressed horror and disgust, yet there was in it also the mark of imperious command and confident power. The left half of the picture was the strangest, however. The interest plainly centred there.

On the pavement before the throne were grouped four soldiers, surrounding a crouching figure which must be described in a moment. A fifth soldier lay dead on the pavement, his neck distorted, and his eye-balls starting from his head. The four surrounding guards were looking at the King. In their faces, the sentiment of horror was intensified; they seemed, in fact, only restrained from flight by their implicit trust in their master. All this terror was plainly excited by the being that crouched in their midst.

I entirely despair of conveying by any words the impression which this figure makes upon anyone who looks at it. I recollect once showing the photograph of the drawing to a lecturer on morphology—a person of, I was going to say, abnormally sane and unimaginative habits of mind. He absolutely refused to be alone for the rest of that evening, and he told me afterwards that for many nights he had not dared to put out his light before going to sleep. However, the main traits of the figure I can at least indicate.

At first you saw only a mass of coarse, matted black hair; presently it was seen that this covered a body of fearful thinness, almost a skeleton, but with the muscles standing out like wires. The hands were of a dusky pallor, covered, like the body, with long, coarse hairs, and hideously taloned. The eyes, touched in with a burning yellow, had intensely black pupils, and were fixed upon the throned King with a look of beast-like hate. Imagine one of the awful bird-catching spiders of South America translated into human form, and endowed with intelligence just less than human, and you will have some faint conception of the terror inspired by the appalling effigy. One remark is universally made by those to whom I have shown the picture: "It was drawn from the life."

As soon as the first shock of his irresistible fright had subsided, Dennistoun stole a look at his hosts. The sacristan's hands were pressed upon his eyes; his daughter, looking up at the cross on the wall, was telling her beads feverishly.

At last the question was asked: "Is this book for sale?"

There was the same hesitation, the same plunge of determination that he had noticed before, and then came the welcome answer: "If monsieur pleases."

"How much do you ask for it?"

"I will take two hundred and fifty francs."

This was confounding. Even a collector's conscience is sometimes stirred, and Dennistoun's conscience was tenderer than a collector's.

"My good man!" he said again and again, "your book is worth far more than two hundred and fifty francs. I assure you—far more."

But the answer did not vary: "I will take two hundred and fifty francs—not more."

There was really no possibility of refusing such a chance. The money was paid, the receipt signed, a glass of wine drunk over the transaction, and then the sacristan seemed to become a new man. He stood upright, he ceased to throw those suspicious glances behind him, he actually laughed or tried to laugh. Dennistoun rose to go.

"I shall have the honour of accompanying monsieur to his hotel?" said the sacristan.

"Oh, no, thanks! it isn't a hundred yards. I know the way perfectly, and there is a moon."

The offer was pressed three or four times and refused as often.

"Then, monsieur will summon me if—if he finds occasion; he will keep the middle of the road, the sides are so rough."

"Certainly, certainly," said Dennistoun, who was impatient to examine his prize by himself; and he stepped out into the passage with his book under his arm.

Here he was met by the daughter; she, it appeared, was anxious to do a little business on her own account; perhaps, like Gehazi, to "take somewhat" from the foreigner whom her father had spared.

"A silver crucifix and chain for the neck; monsieur would perhaps be good enough to accept it?"

Well, really, Dennistoun hadn't much use for these things. What did mademoiselle want for it?

"Nothing—nothing in the world. Monsieur is more than welcome to it."

The tone in which this and much more was said was unmistakably genuine, so that Dennistoun was reduced to profuse thanks, and submitted to have the chain put round his neck. It really seemed as if he had rendered the father and daughter some service which they hardly knew how to repay. As he set off with his book they stood at the door looking after him, and they were still looking when he waved them a last good night from the steps of the Chapeau Rouge.

Dinner was over, and Dennistoun was in his bedroom, shut up alone with his acquisition. The landlady had manifested a particular interest in him since he had told her that he had paid a visit to the sacristan and bought an old book from him. He thought, too, that he had heard a hurried dialogue between her and the said sacristan in the passage outside the *salle à manger*; some words to the effect that "Pierre and Bertrand would be sleeping in the house" had closed the conversation.

All this time a growing feeling of discomfort had been creeping over him—nervous reaction, perhaps, after the delight of his discovery. Whatever it was, it resulted in a conviction that there was someone behind him, and that he was far more comfortable with his back to the wall. All this, of course, weighed light in the balance as against the obvious value of the collection he had acquired. And now, as I said, he was alone in his bedroom, taking stock of Canon Alberic's treasures, in which every moment revealed something more charming.

"Bless Canon Alberic!" said Dennistoun, who had an inveterate habit of talking to himself. "I wonder where he is now? Dear me! I wish that landlady would learn to laugh in a more cheering manner; it makes one feel as if there was someone dead in the house. Half a pipe more, did you say? I think perhaps you are right. I wonder what that crucifix is that the young woman insisted on giving me? Last century, I suppose. Yes, probably. It is rather a nuisance of a thing to have round one's neck—just too heavy. Most likely her father has been wearing it for years. I think I might give it a clean up before I put it away."

He had taken the crucifix off, and laid it on the table, when his attention was caught by an object lying on the red cloth just by his left elbow. Two or three ideas of what it might be flitted through his brain with their own incalculable quickness.

A penwiper? No, no such thing in the house. A rat? No, too black. A large spider? I trust to goodness not—no. Good God! a hand like the hand in that picture!

In another infinitesimal flash he had taken it in. Pale, dusky skin, covering nothing but bones and tendons of appalling strength; coarse black hairs, longer than ever grew on a human hand; nails rising from the ends of the fingers and curving sharply down and forward, grey, horny, and wrinkled.

He flew out of his chair with deadly, inconceivable terror clutching at his heart. The shape, whose left hand rested on the table, was rising to a standing posture behind his seat, its right hand crooked above his scalp. There was black and tattered drapery about it; the coarse hair covered it as in the drawing. The lower jaw was thin—what can I call it?—shallow, like a beast's; teeth showed behind the black lips; there was no nose; the eyes, of a fiery yellow, against which the pupils showed black and intense, and the exulting hate and thirst to destroy life which shone there, were the most horrifying features in the whole vision. There was intelligence of a kind in them—intelligence beyond that of a beast, below that of a man.

The feelings which this horror stirred in Dennistoun were the intensest physical fear and the most profound mental loathing. What did he do? What could he do? He has never been quite certain what words he said, but he knows that he spoke, that he grasped blindly at the silver crucifix, that he was conscious of a movement towards him on the part of the demon, and that he screamed with the voice of an animal in hideous pain.

Pierre and Bertrand, the two sturdy little serving-men, who rushed in, saw nothing, but felt themselves thrust aside by something that passed out between them, and found Dennistoun in a swoon. They sat up with him that night, and his two friends were at St. Bertrand by nine o'clock next morning. He himself, though still shaken and nervous, was almost himself by that time, and his story found credence with them, though not until they had seen the drawing and talked with the sacristan.

Almost at dawn the little man had come to the inn on some pretence, and had listened with the deepest interest to the story retailed by the landlady. He showed no surprise.

"It is he—it is he! I have seen him myself," was his only comment; and to all questionings but one reply was vouchsafed: "Deux fois je l'ai vu: mille fois je l'ai senti." He would tell them nothing of the provenance of the book, nor any details of his experiences. "I shall soon sleep, and my rest will be sweet. Why should you trouble me?" he said.*

We shall never know what he or Canon Alberic de Mauléon suffered. At the back of that fateful drawing were some lines of writing which may be supposed to throw light on the situation:

> *Contradictio Salomonis cum demonio nocturno. Albericus de Mauléone delineavit. V. Deus in adiutorium. Ps. Qui habitat. Sancte Bertrande, demoniorum effugator, intercede pro me miserrimo. Primum uidi nocte 12(mi) Dec. 1694: uidebo mox ultimum. Peccaui et passus sum, plura adhuc passurus. Dec. 29, 1701.*†

The "Gallia Christiana" gives the date of the Canon's death as December 31, 1701, "in bed, of a sudden seizure." Details of this kind are not common in the great work of the Sammarthani.

I have never quite understood what was Dennistoun's view of the events I have narrated. He quoted to me once a text from Ecclesiasticus: "Some spirits there be that are created for vengeance, and in their fury lay on sore strokes." On another occasion he said: "Isaiah was a very sensible man; doesn't he say

* He died that summer; his daughter married, and settled at St. Papoul. She never understood the circumstances of her father's "obsession."

† The Dispute of Solomon with a demon of the night. Drawn by Alberic de Mauléon. Versicle. O Lord, make haste to help me. Psalm. Whoso dwelleth xci. Saint Bertrand, who puttest devils to flight, pray for me most unhappy. I saw it first on the night of Dec. 12, 1694: soon I shall see it for the last time. I have sinned and suffered, and have more to suffer yet. Dec. 29, 1701.

something about night monsters living in the ruins of Babylon? These things are rather beyond us at present."

Another confidence of his impressed me rather, and I sympathized with it. We had been, last year, to Comminges, to see Canon Alberic's tomb. It is a great marble erection with an effigy of the Canon in a large wig and soutane, and an elaborate eulogy of his learning below. I saw Dennistoun talking for some time with the Vicar of St. Bertrand's, and as we drove away he said to me: "I hope it isn't wrong: you know I am a Presbyterian—but I—I believe there will be 'saying of Mass and singing of dirges' for Alberic de Mauléon's rest. Then he added, with a touch of the Northern British in his tone, "I had no notion they came so dear."

* * * * *

The book is in the Wentworth Collection at Cambridge. The drawing was photographed and then burnt by Dennistoun on the day when he left Comminges on the occasion of his first visit.

PRESENT AT A HANGING

Ambrose Bierce

An old man named Daniel Baker, living near Lebanon, Iowa, was suspected by his neighbors of having murdered a peddler who had obtained permission to pass the night at his house. This was in 1853, when peddling was more common in the Western country than it is now, and was attended with considerable danger. The peddler with his pack traversed the country by all manner of lonely roads, and was compelled to rely upon the country people for hospitality. This brought him into relation with queer characters, some of whom were not altogether scrupulous in their methods of making a living, murder being an acceptable means to that end. It occasionally occurred that a peddler with diminished pack and swollen purse would be traced to the lonely dwelling of some rough character and never could be traced beyond. This was so in the case of "old man Baker," as he was always called. (Such names are given in the western "settlements" only to elderly persons who are not esteemed; to the general disrepute of social unworth is affixed the special reproach of age.) A peddler came to his house and none went away—that is all that anybody knew. Seven years later the Rev. Mr. Cummings, a Baptist minister well known in that part of the country, was driving by Baker's farm one night. It was not very dark: there was a bit of moon somewhere above the light veil of mist that lay along the earth. Mr. Cummings, who was at all times a cheerful person, was whistling a tune, which he would occasionally interrupt to speak a word of friendly encouragement to his horse. As he came to a little bridge across a dry ravine he saw the figure of a man standing upon it, clearly outlined against the gray background of a misty forest. The man had something strapped on his back and carried a heavy stick—obviously an itinerant peddler. His attitude had in it a suggestion of abstraction, like that of a sleepwalker. Mr. Cummings reined in his horse when he arrived in front of him, gave him a pleasant salutation and invited him to a seat in the vehicle—"if you are going my way," he added. The man raised his head, looked him full in the face, but neither answered nor made any further movement. The minister, with good-natured persistence, repeated his invitation. At this the man threw his right hand forward from his side and pointed downward as he stood on the extreme edge of the bridge. Mr. Cummings looked past him, over into the ravine, saw nothing unusual and withdrew his eyes to address the man again. He had disappeared. The horse, which all this time had been uncommonly restless, gave at the same moment a snort of terror and started to run away. Before he had regained control of the animal the minister was at the crest of the hill a hundred yards along. He looked back and saw the figure again, at the same place and in the same attitude as when he had first observed it. Then for the first time he was conscious of a sense of the supernatural and drove home as rapidly as his willing horse would go. On arriving at home he related his adventure to his family, and early the next morning, accompanied by two neighbors, John White Corwell and Abner Raiser, returned to the spot. They found the body of old man Baker hanging by the neck from one of the beams of the bridge, immediately beneath the spot where the apparition had stood. A thick coating of dust, slightly dampened by the mist, covered the floor of the bridge, but the only footprints were those of Mr. Cummings' horse. In taking down the body the men disturbed the loose, friable earth of the slope below it, disclosing human bones already nearly uncovered by the action of water and frost. They were identified as those of the lost peddler. At the double inquest the coroner's jury found that Daniel Baker died by his own hand while suffering from temporary insanity, and that Samuel Morritz was murdered by some person or persons to the jury unknown.

THE ROOM IN THE TOWER

E. F. Benson

It is probable that everybody who is at all a constant dreamer has had at least one experience of an event or a sequence of circumstances which have come to his mind in sleep being subsequently realized in the material world. But, in my opinion, so far from this being a strange thing, it would be far odder if this fulfilment did not occasionally happen, since our dreams are, as a rule, concerned with people whom we know and places with which we are familiar, such as might very naturally occur in the awake and daylit world. True, these dreams are often broken into by some absurd and fantastic incident, which puts them out of court in regard to their subsequent fulfilment, but on the mere calculation of chances, it does not appear in the least unlikely that a dream imagined by anyone who dreams constantly should occasionally come true. Not long ago, for instance, I experienced such a fulfilment of a dream which seems to me in no way remarkable and to have no kind of psychical significance. The manner of it was as follows.

A certain friend of mine, living abroad, is amiable enough to write to me about once in a fortnight. Thus, when fourteen days or thereabouts have elapsed since I last heard from him, my mind, probably, either consciously or subconsciously, is expectant of a letter from him. One night last week I dreamed that as I was going upstairs to dress for dinner I heard, as I often heard, the sound of the postman's knock on my front door, and diverted my direction downstairs instead. There, among other correspondence, was a letter from him. Thereafter the fantastic entered, for on opening it I found inside the ace of diamonds, and scribbled across it in his well-known handwriting, "I am sending you this for safe custody, as you know it is running an unreasonable risk to keep aces in Italy." The next evening I was just preparing to go upstairs to dress when I heard the postman's knock, and did precisely as I had done in my dream. There, among other letters, was one from my friend. Only it did not contain the ace of diamonds. Had it done so, I should have attached more weight to the matter, which, as it stands, seems to me a perfectly ordinary coincidence. No doubt I consciously or subconsciously expected a letter from him, and this suggested to me my dream. Similarly, the fact that my friend had not written to me for a fortnight suggested to him that he should do so. But occasionally it is not so easy to find such an explanation, and for the following story I can find no explanation at all. It came out of the dark, and into the dark it has gone again.

All my life I have been a habitual dreamer: the nights are few, that is to say, when I do not find on awaking in the morning that some mental experience has been mine, and sometimes, all night long, apparently, a series of the most dazzling adventures befall me. Almost without exception these adventures are pleasant, though often merely trivial. It is of an exception that I am going to speak.

It was when I was about sixteen that a certain dream first came to me, and this is how it befell. It opened with my being set down at the door of a big red-brick house, where, I understood, I was going to stay. The servant who opened the door told me that tea was being served in the garden, and led me through a low dark-panelled hall, with a large open fireplace, on to a cheerful green lawn set round with flower beds. There were grouped about the tea-table a small party of people, but they were all strangers to me except one, who was a schoolfellow called Jack Stone, clearly the son of the house, and he introduced me to his mother and father and a couple of sisters. I was, I remember, somewhat astonished to find myself here, for the boy in question was scarcely known to me, and I rather disliked what I knew of him; moreover, he had left school nearly a year before. The afternoon was very hot, and an intolerable oppression reigned. On the far side of the lawn ran a red-brick wall, with an iron gate in its center, outside which stood a walnut tree. We sat in the shadow of the house opposite a row of long windows, inside which I could see a table with cloth laid, glimmering with glass and silver. This garden front of the house was very long, and at one end of it stood a tower of three stories, which looked to me much older than the rest of the building.

Before long, Mrs. Stone, who, like the rest of the party, had sat in absolute silence, said to me, "Jack will show you your room: I have given you the room in the tower."

Quite inexplicably my heart sank at her words. I felt as if I had known that I should have the room in the tower, and that it contained something dreadful and significant. Jack instantly got up, and I understood that I had to follow him. In silence we passed through the hall, and mounted a great oak staircase with many corners, and arrived at a small landing with two doors set in it. He pushed one of these open for me to enter, and without coming in himself, closed it after me. Then I knew that my conjecture had been right: there was something awful in the room, and with the terror of nightmare growing swiftly and enveloping me, I awoke in a spasm of terror.

Now that dream or variations on it occurred to me intermittently for fifteen years. Most often it came in exactly this form, the arrival, the tea laid out on the lawn, the deadly silence succeeded by that one deadly sentence, the mounting with Jack Stone up to the room in the tower where horror dwelt, and it always came to a close in the nightmare of terror at that which was in the room, though I never saw what it was. At other times I experienced variations on this same theme. Occasionally, for instance, we would be sitting at dinner in the dining-room, into the windows of which I had looked on the first night when the dream of this house visited me, but wherever we were, there was the same silence, the same sense of dreadful oppression and foreboding. And the silence I knew would always be broken by Mrs. Stone saying to me, "Jack will show you your room: I have given you the room in the tower." Upon which (this was invariable) I had to follow him up the oak staircase with many corners, and enter the place that I dreaded more and more each time that I visited it in sleep. Or, again, I would find myself playing cards still in silence in a drawing-room lit with immense chandeliers, that gave a blinding illumination. What the game was I have no idea; what I remember, with a sense of miserable anticipation, was that soon Mrs. Stone would get up and say to me, "Jack will show you your room: I have given you the room in the tower." This drawing-room where we played cards was next to the dining-room, and, as I have said, was always brilliantly illuminated, whereas the rest of the house was full of dusk and shadows. And yet, how often, in spite of those bouquets of lights, have I not pored over the cards that were dealt me, scarcely able for some reason to see them. Their designs, too, were strange: there were no red suits, but all were black, and among them there were certain cards which were black all over. I hated and dreaded those.

As this dream continued to recur, I got to know the greater part of the house. There was a smoking-room beyond the drawing-room, at the end of a passage with a green baize door. It was always very dark there, and as often as I went there I passed somebody whom I could not see in the doorway coming out. Curious developments, too, took place in the characters that peopled the dream as might happen to living persons. Mrs. Stone, for instance, who, when I first saw her, had been black-haired, became gray, and instead of rising briskly, as she had done at first when she said, "Jack will show you your room: I have given you the room in the tower," got up very feebly, as if the strength was leaving her limbs. Jack also grew up, and became a rather ill-looking young man, with a brown moustache, while one of the sisters ceased to appear, and I understood she was married.

Then it so happened that I was not visited by this dream for six months or more, and I began to hope, in such inexplicable dread did I hold it, that it had passed away for good. But one night after this interval I again found myself being shown out onto the lawn for tea, and Mrs. Stone was not there, while the others were all dressed in black. At once I guessed the reason, and my heart leaped at the thought that perhaps this time I should not have to sleep in the room in the tower, and though we usually all sat in silence, on this occasion the sense of relief made me talk and laugh as I had never yet done. But even then matters were not altogether comfortable, for no one else spoke, but they all looked secretly at each other. And soon the foolish stream of my talk ran dry, and gradually an apprehension worse than anything I had previously known gained on me as the light slowly faded.

Suddenly a voice which I knew well broke the stillness, the voice of Mrs. Stone, saying, "Jack will show you your room: I have given you the room in the tower." It seemed to come from near the gate in the red-brick wall that bounded the lawn, and looking up, I saw that the grass outside was sown thick with gravestones. A curious greyish light shone from them, and I could read the lettering on the grave nearest me, and it was, "In evil memory of Julia Stone." And as usual Jack got up, and again I followed him through the hall and up the staircase with many corners. On this occasion it was darker than usual, and when I passed into the room in the tower I could only just see the furniture, the position of which was already familiar to me. Also there was a dreadful odor of decay in the room, and I woke screaming.

The dream, with such variations and developments as I have mentioned, went on at intervals for fifteen years. Sometimes I would dream it two or three nights in succession; once, as I have said, there was an intermission of six months, but taking a reasonable average, I should say that I dreamed it quite as often as once in a month. It had, as is plain, something of nightmare about it, since it always ended in the same appalling terror, which so far from getting less, seemed to me to gather fresh fear every time that I experienced it. There was, too, a strange and dreadful consistency about it. The characters in it, as I have mentioned, got regularly older, death and marriage visited this silent family, and I never in the dream, after Mrs. Stone had died, set eyes on her again. But it was always her voice that told me that the room in the tower was prepared for me, and whether we had tea out on the lawn, or the scene was laid in one of the rooms overlooking it, I could always see her gravestone standing just outside the iron gate. It was the same, too, with the married daughter; usually she was not present, but once or twice she returned again, in company with a man, whom I took to be her husband. He, too, like the rest of them, was always silent. But, owing to the constant repetition of the dream, I had ceased to attach, in my waking hours, any significance to it. I never met Jack Stone again during all those years, nor did I ever see a house that resembled this dark house of my dream. And then something happened.

I had been in London in this year, up till the end of the July, and during the first week in August went down to stay with a friend in a house he had taken for the summer months, in the Ashdown Forest district of Sussex. I left London early, for John Clinton was to meet me at Forest Row Station, and we were going to spend the day golfing, and go to his house in the evening. He had his motor with him, and we set off, about five of the afternoon, after a thoroughly delightful day, for the drive, the distance being some ten miles. As it was still so early we did not have tea at the club house, but waited till we should get home. As we drove, the weather, which up till then had been, though hot, deliciously fresh, seemed to me to alter in quality, and become very stagnant and oppressive, and I felt that indefinable sense of ominous apprehension that I am accustomed to before thunder. John, however, did not share my views, attributing my loss of lightness to the fact that I had lost both my matches. Events proved, however, that I was right, though I do not think that the thunderstorm that broke that night was the sole cause of my depression.

Our way lay through deep high-banked lanes, and before we had gone very far I fell asleep, and was only awakened by the stopping of the motor. And with a sudden thrill, partly of fear but chiefly of curiosity, I found myself standing in the doorway of my house of dream. We went, I half wondering whether or not I was dreaming still, through a low oak-panelled hall, and out onto the lawn, where tea was laid in the shadow of the house. It was set in flower beds, a red-brick wall, with a gate in it, bounded one side, and out beyond that was a space of rough grass with a walnut tree. The facade of the house was very long, and at one end stood a three-storied tower, markedly older than the rest.

Here for the moment all resemblance to the repeated dream ceased. There was no silent and somehow terrible family, but a large assembly of exceedingly cheerful persons, all of whom were known to me. And in spite of the horror with which the dream itself had always filled me, I felt nothing of it now that the scene of it was thus reproduced before me. But I felt intensest curiosity as to what was going to happen.

Tea pursued its cheerful course, and before long Mrs. Clinton got up. And at that moment I think I knew what she was going to say. She spoke to me, and what she said was:

"Jack will show you your room: I have given you the room in the tower."

At that, for half a second, the horror of the dream took hold of me again. But it quickly passed, and again I felt nothing more than the most intense curiosity. It was not very long before it was amply satisfied.

John turned to me.

"Right up at the top of the house," he said, "but I think you'll be comfortable. We're absolutely full up. Would you like to go and see it now? By Jove, I believe that you are right, and that we are going to have a thunderstorm. How dark it has become."

I got up and followed him. We passed through the hall, and up the perfectly familiar staircase. Then he opened the door, and I went in. And at that moment sheer unreasoning terror again possessed me. I did not know what I feared: I simply feared. Then like a sudden recollection, when one remembers a name which has long escaped the memory, I knew what I feared. I feared Mrs. Stone, whose grave with the sinister inscription, "In evil memory," I had so often seen in my dream, just beyond the lawn which lay below my window. And then once more the fear passed so completely that I wondered what there was to fear, and I found myself, sober and quiet and sane, in the room in the tower, the name of which I had so often heard in my dream, and the scene of which was so familiar.

I looked around it with a certain sense of proprietorship, and found that nothing had been changed from the dreaming nights in which I knew it so well. Just to the left of the door was the bed, lengthways along the wall, with the head of it in the angle. In a line with it was the fireplace and a small bookcase; opposite the door the outer wall was pierced by two lattice-paned windows, between which stood the dressing-table, while ranged along the fourth wall was the washing-stand and a big cupboard. My luggage had already been unpacked, for the furniture of dressing and undressing lay orderly on the wash-stand and toilet-table, while my dinner clothes were spread out on the coverlet of the bed. And then, with a sudden start of unexplained dismay, I saw that there were two rather conspicuous objects which I had not seen before in my dreams: one a life-sized oil painting of Mrs. Stone, the other a black-and-white sketch of Jack Stone, representing him as he had appeared to me only a week before in the last of the series of these repeated dreams, a rather secret and evil-looking man of about thirty. His picture hung between the windows, looking straight across the room to the other portrait, which hung at the side of the bed. At that I looked next, and as I looked I felt once more the horror of nightmare seize me.

It represented Mrs. Stone as I had seen her last in my dreams: old and withered and white-haired. But in spite of the evident feebleness of body, a dreadful exuberance and vitality shone through the envelope of flesh, an exuberance wholly malign, a vitality that foamed and frothed with unimaginable evil. Evil beamed from the narrow, leering eyes; it laughed in the demon-like mouth. The whole face was instinct with some secret and appalling mirth; the hands, clasped together on the knee, seemed shaking with suppressed and nameless glee. Then I saw also that it was signed in the left-hand bottom corner, and wondering who the artist could be, I looked more closely, and read the inscription, "Julia Stone by Julia Stone."

There came a tap at the door, and John Clinton entered.

"Got everything you want?" he asked.

"Rather more than I want," said I, pointing to the picture.

He laughed.

"Hard-featured old lady," he said. "By herself, too, I remember. Anyhow she can't have flattered herself much."

"But don't you see?" said I. "It's scarcely a human face at all. It's the face of some witch, of some devil."

He looked at it more closely.

"Yes; it isn't very pleasant," he said. "Scarcely a bedside manner, eh? Yes; I can imagine getting the nightmare if I went to sleep with that close by my bed. I'll have it taken down if you like."

"I really wish you would," I said. He rang the bell, and with the help of a servant we detached the picture and carried it out onto the landing, and put it with its face to the wall.

"By Jove, the old lady is a weight," said John, mopping his forehead. "I wonder if she had something on her mind."

The extraordinary weight of the picture had struck me too. I was about to reply, when I caught sight of my own hand. There was blood on it, in considerable quantities, covering the whole palm.

"I've cut myself somehow," said I.

John gave a little startled exclamation.

"Why, I have too," he said.

Simultaneously the footman took out his handkerchief and wiped his hand with it. I saw that there was blood also on his handkerchief.

John and I went back into the tower room and washed the blood off; but neither on his hand nor on mine was there the slightest trace of a scratch or cut. It seemed to me that, having ascertained this, we both, by a sort of tacit consent, did not allude to it again. Something in my case had dimly occurred to me that I did not wish to think about. It was but a conjecture, but I fancied that I knew the same thing had occurred to him.

The heat and oppression of the air, for the storm we had expected was still undischarged, increased very much after dinner, and for some time most of the party, among whom were John Clinton and myself, sat outside on the path bounding the lawn, where we had had tea. The night was absolutely dark, and no twinkle of star or moon ray could penetrate the pall of cloud that overset the sky. By degrees our assembly thinned, the women went up to bed, men dispersed to the smoking or billiard room, and by eleven o'clock my host and I were the only two left. All the evening I thought that he had something on his mind, and as soon as we were alone he spoke.

"The man who helped us with the picture had blood on his hand, too, did you notice?" he said.

"I asked him just now if he had cut himself, and he said he supposed he had, but that he could find no mark of it. Now where did that blood come from?"

By dint of telling myself that I was not going to think about it, I had succeeded in not doing so, and I did not want, especially just at bedtime, to be reminded of it.

"I don't know," said I, "and I don't really care so long as the picture of Mrs. Stone is not by my bed."

He got up.

"But it's odd," he said. "Ha! Now you'll see another odd thing."

A dog of his, an Irish terrier by breed, had come out of the house as we talked. The door behind us into the hall was open, and a bright oblong of light shone across the lawn to the iron gate which led on to the rough grass outside, where the walnut tree stood. I saw that the dog had all his hackles up, bristling with rage and fright; his lips were curled back from his teeth, as if he was ready to spring at something, and he was growling to himself. He took not the slightest notice of his master or me, but stiffly and tensely walked across the grass to the iron gate. There he stood for a moment, looking through the bars and still growling. Then of a sudden his courage seemed to desert him: he gave one long howl, and scuttled back to the house with a curious crouching sort of movement.

"He does that half-a-dozen times a day." said John. "He sees something which he both hates and fears."

I walked to the gate and looked over it. Something was moving on the grass outside, and soon a sound which I could not instantly identify came to my ears. Then I remembered what it was: it was the purring of a cat. I lit a match, and saw the purrer, a big blue Persian, walking round and round in a little circle just outside the gate, stepping high and ecstatically, with tail carried aloft like a banner. Its eyes were bright and shining, and every now and then it put its head down and sniffed at the grass.

I laughed.

"The end of that mystery, I am afraid." I said. "Here's a large cat having Walpurgis night all alone."

"Yes, that's Darius," said John. "He spends half the day and all night there. But that's not the end of the dog mystery, for Toby and he are the best of friends, but the beginning of the cat mystery. What's the cat doing there? And why is Darius pleased, while Toby is terror-stricken?"

At that moment I remembered the rather horrible detail of my dreams when I saw through the gate, just where the cat was now, the white tombstone with the sinister inscription. But before I could answer the rain began, as suddenly and heavily as if a tap had been turned on, and simultaneously the big cat squeezed through the bars of the gate, and came leaping across the lawn to the house for shelter. Then it sat in the doorway, looking out eagerly into the dark. It spat and struck at John with its paw, as he pushed it in, in order to close the door.

Somehow, with the portrait of Julia Stone in the passage outside, the room in the tower had absolutely no alarm for me, and as I went to bed, feeling very sleepy and heavy, I had nothing more than interest for the curious incident about our bleeding hands, and the conduct of the cat and dog. The last thing I looked at before I put out my light was the square empty space by my bed where the portrait had been. Here the paper was of its original full tint of dark red: over the rest of the walls it had faded. Then I blew out my candle and instantly fell asleep.

My awaking was equally instantaneous, and I sat bolt upright in bed under the impression that some bright light had been flashed in my face, though it was now absolutely pitch dark. I knew exactly where I was, in the room which I had dreaded in dreams, but no horror that I ever felt when asleep approached the fear that now invaded and froze my brain. Immediately after a peal of thunder crackled just above the house, but the probability that it was only a flash of lightning which awoke me gave no reassurance to my galloping heart. Something I knew was in the room with me, and instinctively I put out my right hand, which was nearest the wall, to keep it away. And my hand touched the edge of a picture-frame hanging close to me.

I sprang out of bed, upsetting the small table that stood by it, and I heard my watch, candle, and matches clatter onto the floor. But for the moment there was no need of light, for a blinding flash leaped out of the clouds, and showed me that by my bed again hung the picture of Mrs. Stone. And instantly the room went into blackness again. But in that flash I saw another thing also, namely a figure that leaned over the end of my bed, watching me. It was dressed in some close-clinging white garment, spotted and stained with mold, and the face was that of the portrait.

Overhead the thunder cracked and roared, and when it ceased and the deathly stillness succeeded, I heard the rustle of movement coming nearer me, and, more horrible yet, perceived an odor of corruption and decay. And then a hand was laid on the side of my neck, and close beside my ear I heard quick-taken, eager breathing. Yet I knew that this thing, though it could be perceived by touch, by smell, by eye and by ear, was still not of this earth, but something that had passed out of the body and had power to make itself manifest. Then a voice, already familiar to me, spoke.

"I knew you would come to the room in the tower," it said. "I have been long waiting for you. At last you have come. Tonight I shall feast; before long we will feast together."

And the quick breathing came closer to me; I could feel it on my neck.

At that the terror, which I think had paralyzed me for the moment, gave way to the wild instinct of self-preservation. I hit wildly with both arms, kicking out at the same moment, and heard a little animal-squeal, and something soft dropped with a thud beside me. I took a couple of steps forward, nearly tripping up over whatever it was that lay there, and by the merest good-luck found the handle of the door. In another second I ran out on the landing, and had banged the door behind me. Almost at the same moment I heard a door open somewhere below, and John Clinton, candle in hand, came running upstairs.

"What is it?" he said. "I sleep just below you, and heard a noise as if—Good heavens, there's blood on your shoulder."

I stood there, so he told me afterwards, swaying from side to side, white as a sheet, with the mark on my shoulder as if a hand covered with blood had been laid there.

"It's in there," I said, pointing. "She, you know. The portrait is in there, too, hanging up on the place we took it from."

At that he laughed.

"My dear fellow, this is mere nightmare," he said.

He pushed by me, and opened the door, I standing there simply inert with terror, unable to stop him, unable to move.

"Phew! What an awful smell," he said.

Then there was silence; he had passed out of my sight behind the open door. Next moment he came out again, as white as myself, and instantly shut it.

"Yes, the portrait's there," he said, "and on the floor is a thing—a thing spotted with earth, like what they bury people in. Come away, quick, come away."

How I got downstairs I hardly know. An awful shuddering and nausea of the spirit rather than of the flesh had seized me, and more than once he had to place my feet upon the steps, while every now and then he cast glances of terror and apprehension up the stairs. But in time we came to his dressing-room on the floor below, and there I told him what I have here described.

The sequel can be made short; indeed, some of my readers have perhaps already guessed what it was, if they remember that inexplicable affair of the churchyard at West Fawley, some eight years ago, where an attempt was made three times to bury the body of a certain woman who had committed suicide. On each occasion the coffin was found in the course of a few days again protruding from the ground. After the third attempt, in order that the thing should not be talked about, the body was buried elsewhere in unconsecrated ground. Where it was buried was just outside the iron gate of the garden belonging to the house where this woman had lived. She had committed suicide in a room at the top of the tower in that house. Her name was Julia Stone.

Subsequently the body was again secretly dug up, and the coffin was found to be full of blood.

THE TRIAL FOR MURDER

Charles Dickens

I have always noticed a prevalent want of courage, even among persons of superior intelligence and culture, as to imparting their own psychological experiences when those have been of a strange sort. Almost all men are afraid that what they could relate in such wise would find no parallel or response in a listener's internal life, and might be suspected or laughed at. A truthful traveller, who should have seen some extraordinary creature in the likeness of a sea-serpent, would have no fear of mentioning it; but the same traveller, having had some singular presentiment, impulse, vagary of thought, vision (so-called), dream, or other remarkable mental impression, would hesitate considerably before he would own to it. To this reticence I attribute much of the obscurity in which such subjects are involved. We do not habitually communicate our experiences of these subjective things as we do our experiences of objective creation. The consequence is, that the general stock of experience in this regard appears exceptional, and really is so, in respect of being miserably imperfect.

In what I am going to relate, I have no intention of setting up, opposing, or supporting, any theory whatever. I know the history of the Bookseller of Berlin, I have studied the case of the wife of a late Astronomer Royal as related by Sir David Brewster, and I have followed the minutest details of a much more remarkable case of Spectral Illusion occurring within my private circle of friends. It may be necessary to state as to this last, that the sufferer (a lady) was in no degree, however distant, related to me. A mistaken assumption on that head might suggest an explanation of a part of my own case—but only a part—which would be wholly without foundation. It cannot be referred to my inheritance of any developed peculiarity, nor had I ever before any at all similar experience, nor have I ever had any at all similar experience since.

It does not signify how many years ago, or how few, a certain murder was committed in England, which attracted great attention. We hear more than enough of murderers as they rise in succession to their atrocious eminence, and I would bury the memory of this particular brute, if I could, as his body was buried, in Newgate Jail. I purposely abstain from giving any direct clue to the criminal's individuality.

When the murder was first discovered, no suspicion fell—or I ought rather to say, for I cannot be too precise in my facts, it was nowhere publicly hinted that any suspicion fell—on the man who was afterwards brought to trial. As no reference was at that time made to him in the newspapers, it is obviously impossible that any description of him can at that time have been given in the newspapers. It is essential that this fact be remembered.

Unfolding at breakfast my morning paper, containing the account of that first discovery, I found it to be deeply interesting, and I read it with close attention. I read it twice, if not three times. The discovery had been made in a bedroom, and, when I laid down the paper, I was aware of a flash—rush—flow—I do not know what to call it,—no word I can find is satisfactorily descriptive,—in which I seemed to see that bedroom passing through my room, like a picture impossibly painted on a running river. Though almost instantaneous in its passing, it was perfectly clear; so clear that I distinctly, and with a sense of relief, observed the absence of the dead body from the bed.

It was in no romantic place that I had this curious sensation, but in chambers in Piccadilly, very near to the corner of St. James's Street. It was entirely new to me. I was in my easy-chair at the moment, and the sensation was accompanied with a peculiar shiver which started the chair from its position. (But it is to be noted that the chair ran easily on castors.) I went to one of the windows (there are two in the room, and the room is on the second floor) to refresh my eyes with the moving objects down in Piccadilly. It was a bright autumn morning, and the street was sparkling and cheerful. The wind was high. As I looked out, it brought down from the Park a quantity of fallen leaves, which a gust took, and whirled into a spiral pillar. As the pillar fell and the leaves dispersed, I saw two men on the opposite side of the way, going from West to East. They were one behind the other. The foremost man often looked back over his shoulder. The second man followed him, at a distance of some thirty paces, with his right hand menacingly raised. First, the singularity and steadiness of this threatening gesture in so public a thoroughfare attracted my attention; and next, the more remarkable circumstance that nobody heeded it. Both men threaded their way among the other passengers with a smoothness hardly consistent even with the action of walking on a pavement; and no single creature, that I could see, gave them place, touched them, or looked after them. In passing before my windows, they both stared up at me. I saw their two faces very distinctly, and I knew that I could recognise them anywhere. Not that I had consciously noticed anything very remarkable in either face, except that the man who went first had an unusually lowering appearance, and that the face of the man who followed him was of the colour of impure wax.

I am a bachelor, and my valet and his wife constitute my whole establishment. My occupation is in a certain Branch Bank, and I wish that my duties as head of a Department were as light as they are popularly supposed to be. They kept me in town that autumn, when I stood in need of change. I was not ill, but I was not well. My reader is to make the most that can be reasonably made of my feeling jaded, having a depressing sense upon me of a monotonous life, and being "slightly dyspeptic." I am assured by my renowned doctor that my real state of health at that time justifies no stronger description, and I quote his own from his written answer to my request for it.

As the circumstances of the murder, gradually unravelling, took stronger and stronger possession of the public mind, I kept them away from mine by knowing as little about them as was possible in the midst of the universal excitement. But I knew that a verdict of Wilful Murder had been found against the suspected murderer, and that he had been committed to Newgate for trial. I also knew that his trial had been postponed over one Sessions of the Central Criminal Court, on the ground of general prejudice and want of time for the preparation of the defence. I may further have known, but I believe I did not, when, or about when, the Sessions to which his trial stood postponed would come on.

My sitting-room, bedroom, and dressing-room, are all on one floor. With the last there is no communication but through the bedroom. True, there is a door in it, once communicating with the staircase; but a part of the fitting of my bath has been—and had then been for some years—fixed across it. At the same period, and as a part of the same arrangement,—the door had been nailed up and canvased over.

I was standing in my bedroom late one night, giving some directions to my servant before he went to bed. My face was towards the only available door of communication with the dressing-room, and it was closed. My servant's back was towards that door. While I was speaking to him, I saw it open, and a man look in, who very earnestly and mysteriously beckoned to me. That man was the man who had gone second of the two along Piccadilly, and whose face was of the colour of impure wax.

The figure, having beckoned, drew back, and closed the door. With no longer pause than was made by my crossing the bedroom, I opened the dressing-room door, and looked in. I had a lighted candle already in my hand. I felt no inward expectation of seeing the figure in the dressing-room, and I did not see it there.

Conscious that my servant stood amazed, I turned round to him, and said: "Derrick, could you believe that in my cool senses I fancied I saw a—" As I there laid my hand upon his breast, with a sudden start he trembled violently, and said, "O Lord, yes, sir! A dead man beckoning!"

Now I do not believe that this John Derrick, my trusty and attached servant for more than twenty years, had any impression whatever of having seen any such figure, until I touched him. The change in him was so startling, when I touched him, that I fully believe he derived his impression in some occult manner from me at that instant.

I bade John Derrick bring some brandy, and I gave him a dram, and was glad to take one myself. Of what had preceded that night's phenomenon, I told him not a single word. Reflecting on it, I was absolutely certain that I had never seen that face before, except on the one occasion in Piccadilly. Comparing its expression when beckoning at the door with its expression when it had stared up at me as I stood at my window, I came to the conclusion that on the first occasion it had sought to fasten itself upon my memory, and that on the second occasion it had made sure of being immediately remembered.

I was not very comfortable that night, though I felt a certainty, difficult to explain, that the figure would not return. At daylight I fell into a heavy sleep, from which I was awakened by John Derrick's coming to my bedside with a paper in his hand.

This paper, it appeared, had been the subject of an altercation at the door between its bearer and my servant. It was a summons to me to serve upon a Jury at the forthcoming Sessions of the Central Criminal Court at the Old Bailey. I had never before been summoned on such a Jury, as John Derrick well knew. He believed—I am not certain at this hour whether with reason or otherwise—that that class of Jurors were customarily chosen on a lower qualification than mine, and he had at first refused to accept the summons. The man who served it had taken the matter very coolly. He had said that my attendance or non-attendance was nothing to him; there the summons was; and I should deal with it at my own peril, and not at his.

For a day or two I was undecided whether to respond to this call, or take no notice of it. I was not conscious of the slightest mysterious bias, influence, or attraction, one way or other. Of that I am as strictly sure as of every other statement that I make here. Ultimately I decided, as a break in the monotony of my life, that I would go.

The appointed morning was a raw morning in the month of November. There was a dense brown fog in Piccadilly, and it became positively black and in the last degree oppressive East of Temple Bar. I found the passages and staircases of the Court-House flaringly lighted with gas, and the Court itself similarly illuminated. I think that, until I was conducted by officers into the Old Court and saw its crowded state, I did not know that the Murderer was to be tried that day. I think that, until I was so helped into the Old Court with considerable difficulty, I did not know into which of the two Courts sitting my summons would take me. But this must not be received as a positive assertion, for I am not completely satisfied in my mind on either point.

I took my seat in the place appropriated to Jurors in waiting, and I looked about the Court as well as I could through the cloud of fog and breath that was heavy in it. I noticed the black vapour hanging like a murky curtain outside the great windows, and I noticed the stifled sound of wheels on the straw or tan that was littered in the street; also, the hum of the people gathered there, which a shrill whistle, or a louder song or hail than the rest, occasionally pierced. Soon afterwards the Judges, two in number, entered, and took their seats. The buzz in the Court was awfully hushed. The direction was given to put the Murderer to the bar. He appeared there. And in that same instant I recognised in him the first of the two men who had gone down Piccadilly.

If my name had been called then, I doubt if I could have answered to it audibly. But it was called about sixth or eighth in the panel, and I was by that time able to say, "Here!" Now, observe. As I stepped into the box, the prisoner, who had been looking on attentively, but with no sign of concern, became violently agitated, and beckoned to his attorney. The prisoner's wish to challenge me was so manifest, that it occasioned a pause, during which the attorney, with his hand upon the dock, whispered with his client, and shook his head. I afterwards had it from that gentleman, that the prisoner's first affrighted words to him were, *"At all hazards, challenge that man!"* But that, as he would give no reason for it, and admitted that he had not even known my name until he heard it called and I appeared, it was not done.

Both on the ground already explained, that I wish to avoid reviving the unwholesome memory of that Murderer, and also because a detailed account of his long trial is by no means indispensable to my narrative, I shall confine myself closely to such incidents in the ten days and nights during which we, the Jury, were kept together, as directly bear on my own curious personal experience. It is in that, and not in the Murderer, that I seek to interest my reader. It is to that, and not to a page of the Newgate Calendar, that I beg attention.

I was chosen Foreman of the Jury. On the second morning of the trial, after evidence had been taken for two hours (I heard the church clocks strike), happening to cast my eyes over my brother jurymen, I found an inexplicable difficulty in counting them. I counted them several times, yet always with the same difficulty. In short, I made them one too many.

I touched the brother jurymen whose place was next me, and I whispered to him, "Oblige me by counting us." He looked surprised by the request, but turned his head and counted. "Why," says he, suddenly, "we are thirt—; but no, it's not possible. No. We are twelve."

According to my counting that day, we were always right in detail, but in the gross we were always one too many. There was no appearance—no figure—to account for it; but I had now an inward foreshadowing of the figure that was surely coming.

The Jury were housed at the London Tavern. We all slept in one large room on separate tables, and we were constantly in the charge and under the eye of the officer sworn to hold us in safe-keeping. I see no reason for suppressing the real name of that officer. He was intelligent, highly polite, and obliging, and (I was glad to hear) much respected in the City. He had an agreeable presence, good eyes, enviable black whiskers, and a fine sonorous voice. His name was Mr. Harker.

When we turned into our twelve beds at night, Mr. Harker's bed was drawn across the door. On the night of the second day, not being disposed to lie down, and seeing Mr. Harker sitting on his bed, I went and sat beside him, and offered him a pinch of snuff. As Mr. Harker's hand touched mine in taking it from my box, a peculiar shiver crossed him, and he said, "Who is this?"

Following Mr. Harker's eyes, and looking along the room, I saw again the figure I expected,—the second of the two men who had gone down Piccadilly. I rose, and advanced a few steps; then stopped, and looked round at Mr. Harker. He was quite unconcerned, laughed, and said in a pleasant way, "I thought for a moment we had a thirteenth juryman, without a bed. But I see it is the moonlight."

Making no revelation to Mr. Harker, but inviting him to take a walk with me to the end of the room, I watched what the figure did. It stood for a few moments by the bedside of each of my eleven brother jurymen, close to the pillow. It always went to the right-hand side of the bed, and always passed out crossing the foot of the next bed. It seemed, from the action of the head, merely to look down pensively at each recumbent figure. It took no notice of me, or of my bed, which was that nearest to Mr. Harker's. It seemed to go out where the moonlight came in, through a high window, as by an aërial flight of stairs.

Next morning at breakfast, it appeared that everybody present had dreamed of the murdered man last night, except myself and Mr. Harker.

I now felt as convinced that the second man who had gone down Piccadilly was the murdered man (so to speak), as if it had been borne into my comprehension by his immediate testimony. But even this took place, and in a manner for which I was not at all prepared.

On the fifth day of the trial, when the case for the prosecution was drawing to a close, a miniature of the murdered man, missing from his bedroom upon the discovery of the deed, and afterwards found in a hiding-place where the Murderer had been seen digging, was put in evidence. Having been identified by the witness under examination, it was handed up to the Bench, and thence handed down to be inspected by the Jury. As an officer in a black gown was making his way with it across to me, the figure of the second man who had gone down Piccadilly impetuously started from the crowd, caught the miniature from the officer, and gave it to me with his own hands, at the same time saying, in a low and hollow tone,—before I saw the miniature, which was in a locket,—"*I was younger then, and my face was not then drained of blood.*" It also came between me and the brother juryman to whom I would have given the miniature, and between him and the brother juryman to whom he would have given it, and so passed it on through the whole of our number, and back into my possession. Not one of them, however, detected this.

At table, and generally when we were shut up together in Mr. Harker's custody, we had from the first naturally discussed the day's proceedings a good deal. On that fifth day, the case for the prosecution being closed, and we having that side of the question in a completed shape before us, our discussion was more animated and serious. Among our number was a vestryman,—the densest idiot I have ever seen at large,—who met the plainest evidence with the most preposterous objections, and who was sided with by two flabby parochial parasites; all the three impanelled from a district so delivered over to Fever that they ought to have been upon their own trial for five hundred Murders. When these mischievous blockheads were at their loudest, which was towards midnight, while some of us were already preparing for bed, I again saw the murdered man. He stood grimly behind them, beckoning to me. On my going towards them, and striking into the conversation, he immediately retired. This was the beginning of a separate series of appearances, confined to that long room in which we were confined. Whenever a knot of my brother jurymen laid their heads together, I saw the head of the murdered man among theirs. Whenever their comparison of notes was going against him, he would solemnly and irresistibly beckon to me.

It will be borne in mind that down to the production of the miniature, on the fifth day of the trial, I had never seen the Appearance in Court. Three changes occurred now that we entered on the case for the defence. Two of them I will mention together, first. The figure was now in Court continually, and it never there addressed itself to me, but always to the person who was speaking at the time. For instance: the throat of the murdered man had been cut straight across. In the opening speech for the defence, it was suggested that the deceased might have cut his own throat. At that very moment, the figure, with its throat in the dreadful condition referred to (this it had concealed before), stood at the speaker's elbow, motioning across and across its windpipe, now with the right hand, now with the left, vigorously suggesting to the speaker himself the impossibility of such a wound having been self-inflicted by either hand. For another instance: a witness to character, a woman, deposed to the prisoner's being the most amiable of mankind. The figure at that instant stood on the floor before her, looking her full in the face, and pointing out the prisoner's evil countenance with an extended arm and an outstretched finger.

The third change now to be added impressed me strongly as the most marked and striking of all. I do not theorise upon it; I accurately state it, and there leave it. Although the Appearance was not itself perceived by those whom it addressed, its coming close to such persons was invariably attended by some trepidation or disturbance on their part. It seemed to me as if it were prevented, by laws to which I was not amenable, from fully revealing itself to others, and yet as if it could invisibly, dumbly, and darkly overshadow their minds. When the leading counsel for the defence suggested that hypothesis of suicide, and the figure stood at the learned gentleman's elbow, frightfully sawing at its severed throat, it is undeniable that the counsel faltered in his speech, lost for a few seconds the thread of his ingenious discourse, wiped his forehead with his handkerchief, and turned extremely pale. When the witness to character was confronted by the Appearance, her eyes most certainly did follow the direction of its pointed finger, and rest in great hesitation and trouble upon the prisoner's face. Two additional illustrations will suffice. On the eighth day of the trial, after the pause which was every day made early in the afternoon for a few minutes' rest and refreshment, I came back into Court with the rest of the Jury some little time before the return of the Judges. Standing up in the box and looking about me, I thought the figure was not there, until, chancing to raise my eyes to the gallery, I saw it bending forward, and leaning over a very decent woman, as if to assure itself whether the Judges had resumed their seats or not. Immediately afterwards that woman screamed, fainted, and was carried out. So with the venerable, sagacious, and patient Judge who conducted the trial. When the case was over, and he settled himself and his papers to sum up, the murdered man, entering by the Judges' door, advanced to his Lordship's desk, and looked eagerly over his shoulder at the pages of his notes which he was turning. A change came over his Lordship's face; his hand stopped; the peculiar shiver, that I knew so well, passed over him; he faltered, "Excuse me, gentlemen, for a few moments. I am somewhat oppressed by the vitiated air"; and did not recover until he had drunk a glass of water.

Through all the monotony of six of those interminable ten days,—the same Judges and others on the bench, the same Murderer in the dock, the same lawyers at the table, the same tones of question and answer rising to the roof of the court, the same scratching of the Judge's pen, the same ushers going in and out, the same lights kindled at the same hour when there had been any natural light of day, the same foggy curtain outside the great windows when it was foggy, the same rain pattering and dripping when it was rainy, the same footmarks of turnkeys and prisoner day after day on the same sawdust, the same keys locking and unlocking the same heavy doors,—through all the wearisome monotony which made me feel as if I had been Foreman of the Jury for a vast period of time, and Piccadilly had flourished coevally with Babylon, the murdered man never lost one trace of his distinctness in my eyes, nor was he at any moment less distinct than anybody else. I must not omit, as a matter of fact, that I never once saw the Appearance which I call by the name of the murdered man look at the Murderer. Again and again I wondered, "Why does he not?" But he never did.

Nor did he look at me, after the production of the miniature, until the last closing minutes of the trial arrived. We retired to consider, at seven minutes before ten at night. The idiotic vestryman and his two parochial parasites gave us so much trouble that we twice returned into Court to beg to have certain extracts from the Judge's notes re-read. Nine of us had not the smallest doubt about those passages, neither, I believe, had any one in the Court; the dunder-headed triumvirate, having no idea but obstruction, disputed them for that very reason. At length we prevailed, and finally the Jury returned into Court at ten minutes past twelve.

The murdered man at that time stood directly opposite the Jury-box, on the other side of the Court. As I took my place, his eyes rested on me with great attention; he seemed satisfied, and slowly shook a great gray veil, which he carried on his arm for the first time, over his head and whole form. As I gave in our verdict, "Guilty," the veil collapsed, all was gone, and his place was empty. The Murderer, being asked by the Judge, according to usage, whether he had anything to say before sentence of Death should be passed upon him, indistinctly muttered something which was described in the leading newspapers of the following day as "a few rambling, incoherent, and half-audible words, in which he was understood to complain that he had not had a fair trial, because the Foreman of the Jury was prepossessed against him."

The remarkable declaration that he really made was this: "*My Lord, I knew I was a doomed man, when the Foreman of my Jury came into the box. My Lord, I knew he would never let me off, because, before I was taken, he somehow got to my bedside in the night, woke me, and put a rope round my neck.*"

WILLIAM WILSON

Edgar Allan Poe

What say of it? what say of conscience *grim,*
That spectre in my path?
—CHAMBERLAYNE'S *Pharronida*

Let me call myself, for the present, William Wilson. The fair page now lying before me need not be sullied with my real appellation. This has been already too much an object for the scorn—for the horror—for the detestation of my race. To the uttermost regions of the globe have not the indignant winds bruited its unparalleled infamy? Oh, outcast of all outcasts most abandoned!—to the earth art thou not forever dead? to its honors, to its flowers, to its golden aspirations?—and a cloud, dense, dismal, and limitless, does it not hang eternally between thy hopes and heaven?

I would not, if I could, here or to-day, embody a record of my later years of unspeakable misery, and unpardonable crime. This epoch—these later years—took unto themselves a sudden elevation in turpitude, whose origin alone it is my present purpose to assign. Men usually grow base by degrees. From me, in an instant, all virtue dropped bodily as a mantle. From comparatively trivial wickedness I passed, with the stride of a giant, into more than the enormities of an Elah-Gabalus. What chance—what one event brought this evil thing to pass, bear with me while I relate. Death approaches; and the shadow which foreruns him has thrown a softening influence over my spirit. I long, in passing through the dim valley, for the sympathy—I had nearly said for the pity—of my fellow men. I would fain have them believe that I have been, in some measure, the slave of circumstances beyond human control. I would wish them to seek out for me, in the details I am about to give, some little oasis of *fatality* amid a wilderness of error. I would have them allow—what they cannot refrain from allowing—that, although temptation may have erewhile existed as great, man was never *thus*, at least, tempted before—certainly, never *thus* fell. And is it therefore that he has never thus suffered? Have I not indeed been living in a dream? And am I not now dying a victim to the horror and the mystery of the wildest of all sublunary visions?

I am the descendant of a race whose imaginative and easily excitable temperament has at all times rendered them remarkable; and, in my earliest infancy, I gave evidence of having fully inherited the family character. As

I advanced in years it was more strongly developed; becoming, for many reasons, a cause of serious disquietude to my friends, and of positive injury to myself. I grew self-willed, addicted to the wildest caprices, and a prey to the most ungovernable passions. Weak-minded, and beset with constitutional infirmities akin to my own, my parents could do but little to check the evil propensities which distinguished me. Some feeble and ill-directed efforts resulted in complete failure on their part, and, of course, in total triumph on mine. Thenceforward my voice was a household law; and at an age when few children have abandoned their leading-strings, I was left to the guidance of my own will, and became, in all but name, the master of my own actions.

My earliest recollections of a school-life, are connected with a large, rambling, Elizabethan house, in a misty-looking village of England, where were a vast number of gigantic and gnarled trees, and where all the houses were excessively ancient. In truth, it was a dream-like and spirit-soothing place, that venerable old town. At this moment, in fancy, I feel the refreshing chilliness of its deeply-shadowed avenues, inhale the fragrance of its thousand shrubberies, and thrill anew with undefinable delight, at the deep hollow note of the church-bell, breaking, each hour, with sullen and sudden roar, upon the stillness of the dusky atmosphere in which the fretted Gothic steeple lay imbedded and asleep.

It gives me, perhaps, as much of pleasure as I can now in any manner experience, to dwell upon minute recollections of the school and its concerns. Steeped in misery as I am—misery, alas! only too real—I shall be pardoned for seeking relief, however slight and temporary, in the weakness of a few rambling details. These, moreover, utterly trivial, and even ridiculous in themselves, assume, to my fancy, adventitious importance, as connected with a period and a locality when and where I recognise the first ambiguous monitions of the destiny which afterwards so fully overshadowed me. Let me then remember.

The house, I have said, was old and irregular. The grounds were extensive, and a high and solid brick wall, topped with a bed of mortar and broken glass, encompassed the whole. This prison-like rampart formed the limit of our domain; beyond it we saw but thrice a week—once every Saturday afternoon, when, attended by two ushers, we were permitted to take brief walks in a body through some of the neighbouring fields—and twice during Sunday, when we were paraded in the same formal manner to the morning and evening service in the one church of the village. Of this church the principal of our school was pastor. With how deep a spirit of wonder and perplexity was I wont to regard him from our remote pew in the gallery, as, with step solemn and slow, he ascended the pulpit! This reverend man, with countenance so demurely benign, with robes so glossy and so clerically flowing, with wig so minutely powdered, so rigid and so vast—could this be he who, of late, with sour visage, and in snuffy habiliments, administered, ferule in hand, the Draconian laws of the academy? Oh, gigantic paradox, too utterly monstrous for solution!

At an angle of the ponderous wall frowned a more ponderous gate. It was riveted and studded with iron bolts, and surmounted with jagged iron spikes. What impressions of deep awe did it inspire! It was never opened save for the three periodical egressions and ingressions already mentioned; then, in every creak of its mighty hinges, we found a plenitude of mystery—a world of matter for solemn remark, or for more solemn meditation.

The extensive enclosure was irregular in form, having many capacious recesses. Of these, three or four of the largest constituted the playground. It was level, and covered with fine hard gravel. I well remember it had no trees, nor benches, nor anything similar within it. Of course it was in the rear of the house. In front lay a small parterre, planted with box and other shrubs; but through this sacred division we passed only upon rare occasions indeed—such as a first advent to school or final departure thence, or perhaps, when a parent or friend having called for us, we joyfully took our way home for the Christmas or Midsummer holy-days.

But the house!—how quaint an old building was this!—to me how veritably a palace of enchantment! There was really no end to its windings—to its incomprehensible subdivisions. It was difficult, at any given time, to say with certainty upon which of its two stories one happened to be. From each room to every other there were sure to be found three or four steps either in ascent or descent. Then the lateral branches were innumerable—inconceivable—and so returning in upon themselves, that our most exact ideas in regard to the whole mansion were not very far different from those with which we pondered upon infinity. During the five years of my residence here, I was never able to ascertain with precision, in what remote locality lay the little sleeping apartment assigned to myself and some eighteen or twenty other scholars.

The school-room was the largest in the house—I could not help thinking, in the world. It was very long, narrow, and dismally low, with pointed Gothic windows and a ceiling of oak. In a remote and terror-inspiring angle was a square enclosure of eight or ten feet, comprising the sanctum, "during hours," of our principal, the Reverend Dr. Bransby. It was a solid structure, with massy door, sooner than open which in the absence of the "Dominic," we would all have willingly perished by the peine forte et dure. In other angles were two other similar boxes, far less reverenced, indeed, but still greatly matters of awe. One of these was the pulpit of the "classical" usher, one of the "English and mathematical." Interspersed about the room, crossing and recrossing in endless irregularity, were innumerable benches and desks, black, ancient, and time-worn, piled desperately with much-bethumbed books, and so beseamed with initial letters, names at full length, grotesque figures, and other multiplied efforts of the knife, as to have entirely lost what little of original form might have been their portion in days long departed. A huge bucket with water stood at one extremity of the room, and a clock of stupendous dimensions at the other.

Encompassed by the massy walls of this venerable academy, I passed, yet not in tedium or disgust, the years of the third lustrum of my life. The teeming brain of childhood requires no external world of incident to occupy or amuse it; and the apparently dismal monotony of a school was replete with more intense excitement than my riper youth has derived from luxury, or my full manhood from crime. Yet I must believe that my first mental development had in it much of the uncommon—even much of the outre. Upon mankind at large the events of very early existence rarely leave in mature age any definite impression. All is gray shadow—a weak and irregular remembrance—an indistinct regathering of feeble pleasures and phantasmagoric pains. With me this is not so. In childhood I must have felt with the energy of a man what I now find stamped upon memory in lines as vivid, as deep, and as durable as the *exergues* of the Carthaginian medals.

Yet in fact—in the fact of the world's view—how little was there to remember! The morning's awakening, the nightly summons to bed; the connings, the recitations; the periodical half-holidays, and perambulations; the play-ground, with its broils, its pastimes, its intrigues;—these, by a mental sorcery long forgotten, were made to involve a wilderness of sensation, a world of rich incident, an universe of varied emotion, of excitement the most passionate and spirit-stirring. *"Oh, le bon temps, que ce siècle de fer!"*

In truth, the ardor, the enthusiasm, and the imperiousness of my disposition, soon rendered me a marked character among my schoolmates, and by slow, but natural gradations, gave me an ascendancy over all not greatly older than myself;—over all with a single exception. This exception was found in the person of a scholar, who, although no relation, bore the same Christian and surname as myself;—a circumstance, in fact, little remarkable; for, notwithstanding a noble descent, mine was one of those everyday appellations which seem, by prescriptive right, to have been, time out of mind, the common property of the mob. In this narrative I have therefore designated myself as William Wilson,—a fictitious title not very dissimilar to the real. My namesake alone, of those who in school phraseology constituted "our set," presumed to compete with me in the studies of the class—in the sports and broils of the play-ground—to refuse implicit belief in my assertions, and submission to my will—indeed, to interfere with my arbitrary dictation in any respect whatsoever. If there is on earth a supreme and unqualified despotism, it is the despotism of a master mind in boyhood over the less energetic spirits of its companions.

Wilson's rebellion was to me a source of the greatest embarrassment—the more so as, in spite of the bravado with which in public I made a point of treating him and his pretensions, I secretly felt that I feared him, and could not help thinking the equality which he maintained so easily with myself, a proof of his true superiority; since not to be overcome cost me a perpetual struggle. Yet this superiority—even this equality—was in truth acknowledged by no one but myself; our associates, by some unaccountable blindness, seemed not even to suspect it. Indeed, his competition, his resistance, and especially his impertinent and dogged interference with my purposes, were not more pointed than private. He appeared to be destitute alike of the ambition which urged, and of the passionate energy of mind which enabled me to excel. In his rivalry he might have been supposed actuated solely by a whimsical desire to thwart, astonish, or mortify myself; although there were times when I could not help observing, with a feeling made up of wonder, abasement, and pique, that he mingled with his injuries, his insults, or his contradictions, a certain most inappropriate, and assuredly most unwelcome affectionateness of manner. I could only conceive this singular behavior to arise from a consummate self-conceit assuming the vulgar airs of patronage and protection.

Perhaps it was this latter trait in Wilson's conduct, conjoined with our identity of name, and the mere accident of our having entered the school upon the same day, which set afloat the notion that we were brothers, among the senior classes in the academy. These do not usually inquire with much strictness into the affairs of their juniors. I have before said, or should have said, that Wilson was not, in the most remote degree, connected with my family. But assuredly if we had been brothers we must have been twins; for, after leaving Dr. Bransby's, I casually learned that my namesake was born on the nineteenth of January, 1813—and this is a somewhat remarkable coincidence; for the day is precisely that of my own nativity.

It may seem strange that in spite of the continual anxiety occasioned me by the rivalry of Wilson, and his intolerable spirit of contradiction, I could not bring myself to hate him altogether. We had, to be sure, nearly every day a quarrel in which, yielding me publicly the palm of victory, he, in some manner, contrived to make me feel that it was he who had deserved it; yet a sense of pride on my part, and a veritable dignity on his own, kept us always upon what are called "speaking terms," while there were many points of strong congeniality in our tempers, operating to awake me in a sentiment which our position alone, perhaps, prevented from ripening into friendship. It is difficult, indeed, to define, or even to describe, my real feelings towards him. They formed a motley and heterogeneous admixture;—some petulant animosity, which was not yet hatred, some esteem, more respect, much fear, with a world of uneasy curiosity. To the moralist it will be unnecessary to say, in addition, that Wilson and myself were the most inseparable of companions.

It was no doubt the anomalous state of affairs existing between us, which turned all my attacks upon him (and they were many, either open or covert) into the channel of banter or practical joke (giving pain while assuming the aspect of mere fun) rather than into a more serious and determined hostility. But my endeavours on this head were by no means uniformly successful, even when my plans were the most wittily concocted; for my namesake had much about him, in character, of that unassuming and quiet austerity which, while enjoying the poignancy of its own jokes, has no heel of Achilles in itself, and absolutely refuses to be laughed at. I could find, indeed, but one vulnerable point, and that, lying in a personal peculiarity, arising, perhaps, from constitutional disease, would have been spared by any antagonist less at his wit's end than myself;—my rival had a weakness in the faucal or guttural organs, which precluded him from raising his voice at any time *above a very low whisper*. Of this defect I did not fail to take what poor advantage lay in my power.

Wilson's retaliations in kind were many; and there was one form of his practical wit that disturbed me beyond measure. How his sagacity first discovered at all that so petty a thing would vex me, is a question I never could solve; but, having discovered, he habitually practised the annoyance. I had always felt aversion to my uncourtly patronymic, and its very common, if not plebeian praenomen. The words were venom in my ears; and when, upon the day of my arrival, a second William Wilson came also to the academy, I felt angry with him for bearing the name, and doubly disgusted with the name because a stranger bore it, who would be the cause of its twofold repetition, who would be constantly in my presence, and whose concerns, in the ordinary routine of the school business, must inevitably, on account of the detestable coincidence, be often confounded with my own.

The feeling of vexation thus engendered grew stronger with every circumstance tending to show resemblance, moral or physical, between my rival and myself. I had not then discovered the remarkable fact that we were of the same age; but I saw that we were of the same height, and I perceived that we were even singularly alike in general contour of person and outline of feature. I was galled, too, by the rumor touching a relationship, which had grown current in the upper forms. In a word, nothing could more seriously disturb me (although I scrupulously concealed such disturbance), than any allusion to a similarity of mind, person, or condition existing between us. But, in truth, I had no reason to believe that (with the exception of the matter of relationship, and in the case of Wilson himself), this similarity had ever been made a subject of comment, or even observed at all by our schoolfellows. That he observed it in all its bearings, and as fixedly as I, was apparent; but that he could discover in such circumstances so fruitful a field of annoyance, can only be attributed, as I said before, to his more than ordinary penetration.

His cue, which was to perfect an imitation of myself, lay both in words and in actions; and most admirably did he play his part. My dress it was an easy matter to copy; my gait and general manner were, without difficulty, appropriated; in spite of his constitutional defect, even my voice did not escape him. My louder tones were, of course, unattempted, but then the key, it was identical; *and his singular whisper, it grew the very echo of my own.*

How greatly this most exquisite portraiture harassed me (for it could not justly be termed a caricature), I will not now venture to describe. I had but one consolation—in the fact that the imitation, apparently, was noticed by myself alone, and that I had to endure only the knowing and strangely sarcastic smiles of my namesake himself. Satisfied with having produced in my bosom the intended effect, he seemed to chuckle in secret over the sting he had inflicted, and was characteristically disregardful of the public applause which the success of his witty endeavours might have so easily elicited. That the school, indeed, did not feel his design, perceive its accomplishment, and participate in his sneer, was, for many anxious months, a riddle I could not resolve. Perhaps the gradation of his copy rendered it not so readily perceptible; or, more possibly, I owed my security to the master air of the copyist, who, disdaining the letter (which in a painting is all the obtuse can see), gave but the full spirit of his original for my individual contemplation and chagrin.

I have already more than once spoken of the disgusting air of patronage which he assumed toward me, and of his frequent officious interference with my will. This interference often took the ungracious character of advice; advice not openly given, but hinted or insinuated. I received it with a repugnance which gained strength as I grew in years. Yet, at this distant day, let me do him the simple justice to acknowledge that I can recall no occasion when the suggestions of my rival were on the side of those errors or follies so usual to his immature age and seeming inexperience; that his moral sense, at least, if not his general talents and worldly wisdom, was far keener than my own; and that I might, to-day, have been a better, and thus a happier man, had

I less frequently rejected the counsels embodied in those meaning whispers which I then but too cordially hated and too bitterly despised.

As it was, I at length grew restive in the extreme under his distasteful supervision, and daily resented more and more openly what I considered his intolerable arrogance. I have said that, in the first years of our connexion as schoolmates, my feelings in regard to him might have been easily ripened into friendship: but, in the latter months of my residence at the academy, although the intrusion of his ordinary manner had, beyond doubt, in some measure, abated, my sentiments, in nearly similar proportion, partook very much of positive hatred. Upon one occasion he saw this, I think, and afterwards avoided, or made a show of avoiding me.

It was about the same period, if I remember aright, that, in an altercation of violence with him, in which he was more than usually thrown off his guard, and spoke and acted with an openness of demeanor rather foreign to his nature, I discovered, or fancied I discovered, in his accent, his air, and general appearance, a something which first startled, and then deeply interested me, by bringing to mind dim visions of my earliest infancy—wild, confused and thronging memories of a time when memory herself was yet unborn. I cannot better describe the sensation which oppressed me than by saying that I could with difficulty shake off the belief of my having been acquainted with the being who stood before me, at some epoch very long ago—some point of the past even infinitely remote. The delusion, however, faded rapidly as it came; and I mention it at all but to define the day of the last conversation I there held with my singular namesake.

The huge old house, with its countless subdivisions, had several large chambers communicating with each other, where slept the greater number of the students. There were, however (as must necessarily happen in a building so awkwardly planned), many little nooks or recesses, the odds and ends of the structure; and these the economic ingenuity of Dr. Bransby had also fitted up as dormitories; although, being the merest closets, they were capable of accommodating but a single individual. One of these small apartments was occupied by Wilson.

One night, about the close of my fifth year at the school, and immediately after the altercation just mentioned, finding every one wrapped in sleep, I arose from bed, and, lamp in hand, stole through a wilderness of narrow passages from my own bedroom to that of my rival. I had long been plotting one of those ill-natured pieces of practical wit at his expense in which I had hitherto been so uniformly unsuccessful. It was my intention, now, to put my scheme in operation, and I resolved to make him feel the whole extent of the malice with which I was imbued. Having reached his closet, I noiselessly entered, leaving the lamp, with a shade over it, on the outside. I advanced a step, and listened to the sound of his tranquil breathing. Assured of his being asleep, I returned, took the light, and with it again approached the bed. Close curtains were around it, which, in the prosecution of my plan, I slowly and quietly withdrew, when the bright rays fell vividly upon the sleeper, and my eyes, at the same moment, upon his countenance. I looked;—and a numbness, an iciness of feeling instantly pervaded my frame. My breast heaved, my knees tottered, my whole spirit became possessed with an objectless yet intolerable horror. Gasping for breath, I lowered the lamp in still nearer proximity to the face. Were these—these the lineaments of William Wilson? I saw, indeed, that they were his, but I shook as if with a fit of the ague in fancying they were not. What was there about them to confound me in this manner? I gazed;—while my brain reeled with a multitude of incoherent thoughts. Not thus he appeared—assuredly not thus—in the vivacity of his waking hours. The same name! the same contour of person! the same day of arrival at the academy! And then his dogged and meaningless imitation of my gait, my voice, my habits, and my manner! Was it, in truth, within the bounds of human possibility, that what I now saw was the result, merely, of the habitual practice of this sarcastic imitation? Awe-stricken, and with a creeping shudder, I extinguished the lamp, passed silently from the chamber, and left, at once, the halls of that old academy, never to enter them again.

After a lapse of some months, spent at home in mere idleness, I found myself a student at Eton. The brief interval had been sufficient to enfeeble my remembrance of the events at Dr. Bransby's, or at least to effect a material change in the nature of the feelings with which I remembered them. The truth—the tragedy—of the drama was no more. I could now find room to doubt the evidence of my senses; and seldom called up the subject at all but with wonder at extent of human credulity, and a smile at the vivid force of the imagination which I hereditarily possessed. Neither was this species of scepticism likely to be diminished by the character of the life I led at Eton. The vortex of thoughtless folly into which I there so immediately and so recklessly plunged, washed away all but the froth of my past hours, engulfed at once every solid or serious impression, and left to memory only the veriest levities of a former existence.

I do not wish, however, to trace the course of my miserable profligacy here—a profligacy which set at defiance the laws, while it eluded the vigilance of the institution. Three years of folly, passed without profit, had but given me rooted habits of vice, and added, in a somewhat unusual degree, to my bodily stature, when, after a week of soulless dissipation, I invited a small party of the most dissolute students to a secret carousal in my chambers. We met at a late hour of the night; for our debaucheries were to be faithfully protracted until morning. The wine flowed freely, and there were not wanting other and perhaps more dangerous seductions; so that the gray dawn had already faintly appeared in the east, while our delirious extravagance was at its height. Madly flushed with cards and intoxication, I was in the act of insisting upon a toast of more than wonted profanity, when my attention was suddenly diverted by the violent, although partial unclosing of the door of the apartment, and by the eager voice of a servant from without. He said that some person, apparently in great haste, demanded to speak with me in the hall.

Wildly excited with wine, the unexpected interruption rather delighted than surprised me. I staggered forward at once, and a few steps brought me to the vestibule of the building. In this low and small room there hung no lamp; and now no light at all was admitted, save that of the exceedingly feeble dawn which made its way through the semicircular window. As I put my foot over the threshold, I became aware of the figure of a youth about my own height, and habited in a white kerseymere morning frock, cut in the novel fashion of the one I myself wore at the moment. This the faint light enabled me to perceive; but the features of his face I could not distinguish. Upon my entering he strode hurriedly up to me, and, seizing me by the arm with a gesture of petulant impatience, whispered the words "William Wilson!" in my ear.

I grew perfectly sober in an instant. There was that in the manner of the stranger, and in the tremulous shake of his uplifted finger, as he held it between my eyes and the light, which filled me with unqualified amazement; but it was not this which had so violently moved me. It was the pregnancy of solemn admonition in the singular, low, hissing utterance; and, above all, it was the character, the tone, the key, of those few, simple, and familiar, yet whispered syllables, which came with a thousand thronging memories of bygone days, and struck upon my soul with the shock of a galvanic battery. Ere I could recover the use of my senses he was gone.

Although this event failed not of a vivid effect upon my disordered imagination, yet was it evanescent as vivid. For some weeks, indeed, I busied myself in earnest inquiry, or was wrapped in a cloud of morbid speculation. I did not pretend to disguise from my perception the identity of the singular individual who thus perseveringly interfered with my affairs, and harassed me with his insinuated counsel. But who and what was this Wilson?—and whence came he?—and what were his purposes? Upon neither of these points could I be satisfied; merely ascertaining, in regard to him, that a sudden accident in his family had caused his removal from Dr. Bransby's academy on the afternoon of the day in which I myself had eloped. But in a brief period I ceased to think upon the subject; my attention being all absorbed in a contemplated departure for Oxford. Thither I soon went; the uncalculating vanity of my parents furnishing me with an outfit and annual establishment, which would enable me to indulge at will in the luxury already so dear to my heart,—to vie in profuseness of expenditure with the haughtiest heirs of the wealthiest earldoms in Great Britain.

Excited by such appliances to vice, my constitutional temperament broke forth with redoubled ardor, and I spurned even the common restraints of decency in the mad infatuation of my revels. But it were absurd to pause in the detail of my extravagance. Let it suffice, that among spendthrifts I out-Heroded Herod, and that, giving name to a multitude of novel follies, I added no brief appendix to the long catalogue of vices then usual in the most dissolute university of Europe.

It could hardly be credited, however, that I had, even here, so utterly fallen from the gentlemanly estate, as to seek acquaintance with the vilest arts of the gambler by profession, and, having become an adept in his despicable science, to practise it habitually as a means of increasing my already enormous income at the expense of the weak-minded among my fellow-collegians. Such, nevertheless, was the fact. And the very enormity of this offence against all manly and honourable sentiment proved, beyond doubt, the main if not the sole reason of the impunity with which it was committed. Who, indeed, among my most abandoned associates, would not rather have disputed the clearest evidence of his senses, than have suspected of such courses, the gay, the frank, the generous William Wilson—the noblest and most commoner at Oxford—him whose follies (said his parasites) were but the follies of youth and unbridled fancy—whose errors but inimitable whim—whose darkest vice but a careless and dashing extravagance?

I had been now two years successfully busied in this way, when there came to the university a young parvenu nobleman, Glendinning—rich, said report, as Herodes Atticus—his riches, too, as easily acquired. I soon found him of weak intellect, and, of course, marked him as a fitting subject for my skill. I frequently engaged him in play, and contrived, with the gambler's usual art, to let him win considerable sums, the more effectually to entangle him in my snares. At length, my schemes being ripe, I met him (with the full intention that this meeting should be final and decisive) at the chambers of a fellow-commoner (Mr. Preston), equally intimate with both, but who, to do him justice, entertained not even a remote suspicion of my design. To give to this a better colouring, I had contrived to have assembled a party of some eight or ten, and was solicitously careful that the introduction of cards should appear accidental, and originate in the proposal of my contemplated dupe himself. To be brief upon a vile topic, none of the low finesse was omitted, so customary upon similar occasions that it is a just matter for wonder how any are still found so besotted as to fall its victim.

We had protracted our sitting far into the night, and I had at length effected the manoeuvre of getting Glendinning as my sole antagonist. The game, too, was my favorite *ecarte!* The rest of the company, interested in the extent of our play, had abandoned their own cards, and were standing around us as spectators. The *parvenu*, who had been induced by my artifices in the early part of the evening, to drink deeply, now shuffled, dealt, or played, with a wild nervousness of manner for which his intoxication, I thought, might partially, but could not altogether account. In a very short period he had become my debtor to a large amount, when, having taken a long draught of port, he did precisely what I had been coolly anticipating—he proposed to double our already extravagant stakes. With a well-feigned show of reluctance, and not until after my repeated refusal had seduced him into some angry words which gave a color of pique to my compliance, did I finally comply. The result, of course, did but prove how entirely the prey was in my toils; in less than an hour he had quadrupled his debt. For some time his countenance had been losing the florid tinge lent it by the wine; but now, to my astonishment, I perceived that it had grown to a pallor truly fearful. I say to my astonishment. Glendinning had been represented to my eager inquiries as immeasurably wealthy; and the sums which he had as yet lost, although in themselves vast, could not, I supposed, very seriously annoy, much less so violently affect him. That he was overcome by the wine just swallowed, was the idea which most readily presented itself; and, rather with a view to the preservation of my own character in the eyes of my associates, than from any less interested motive, I was about to insist, peremptorily, upon a discontinuance of the play, when some expressions at my elbow from among the company, and an ejaculation evincing utter despair on the part of Glendinning, gave me to understand that I had effected his total ruin under circumstances which, rendering him an object for the pity of all, should have protected him from the ill offices even of a fiend.

What now might have been my conduct it is difficult to say. The pitiable condition of my dupe had thrown an air of embarrassed gloom over all; and, for some moments, a profound silence was maintained, during which I could not help feeling my cheeks tingle with the many burning glances of scorn or reproach cast upon me by the less abandoned of the party. I will even own that an intolerable weight of anxiety was for a brief instant lifted from my bosom by the sudden and extraordinary interruption which ensued. The wide, heavy folding doors of the apartment were all at once thrown open, to their full extent, with a vigorous and rushing impetuosity that extinguished, as if by magic, every candle in the room. Their light, in dying, enabled us just to perceive that a stranger had entered, about my own height, and closely muffled in a cloak. The darkness, however, was now total; and we could only feel that he was standing in our midst. Before any one of us could recover from the extreme astonishment into which this rudeness had thrown all, we heard the voice of the intruder.

"Gentlemen," he said, in a low, distinct, and never-to-be-forgotten whisper which thrilled to the very marrow of my bones, "Gentlemen, I make no apology for this behaviour, because in thus behaving, I am but fulfilling a duty. You are, beyond doubt, uninformed of the true character of the person who has to-night won at *écarté* a large sum of money from Lord Glendinning. I will therefore put you upon an expeditious and decisive plan of obtaining this very necessary information. Please to examine, at your leisure, the inner linings of the cuff of his left sleeve, and the several little packages which may be found in the somewhat capacious pockets of his embroidered morning wrapper."

While he spoke, so profound was the stillness that one might have heard a pin drop upon the floor. In ceasing, he departed at once, and as abruptly as he had entered. Can I—shall I describe my sensations?—must I say that I felt all the horrors of the damned? Most assuredly I had little time given for reflection. Many hands roughly seized me upon the spot, and lights were immediately reprocured. A search ensued. In the lining of my sleeve were found all the court cards essential in *écarté*, and, in the pockets of my wrapper, a number of packs, facsimiles of those used at our sittings, with the single exception that mine were of the species called, technically, *arrondees;* the honours being slightly convex at the ends, the lower cards slightly convex at the sides. In this disposition, the dupe who cuts, as customary, at the length of the pack, will invariably find that he cuts his antagonist an honor; while the gambler, cutting at the breadth, will, as certainly, cut nothing for his victim which may count in the records of the game.

Any burst of indignation upon this discovery would have affected me less than the silent contempt, or the sarcastic composure, with which it was received.

"Mr. Wilson," said our host, stooping to remove from beneath his feet an exceedingly luxurious cloak of rare furs, "Mr. Wilson, this is your property." (The weather was cold; and, upon quitting my own room, I had thrown a cloak over my dressing wrapper, putting it off upon reaching the scene of play.) "I presume it is supererogatory to seek here (eyeing the folds of the garment with a bitter smile) for any farther evidence of your skill. Indeed, we have had enough. You will see the necessity, I hope, of quitting Oxford—at all events, of quitting instantly my chambers."

Abased, humbled to the dust as I then was, it is probable that I should have resented this galling language by immediate personal violence, had not my whole attention been at the moment arrested by a fact of the most startling character. The cloak which I had worn was of a rare description of fur; how rare, how extravagantly costly, I shall not venture to say. Its fashion, too, was of my own fantastic invention; for I was fastidious to an absurd degree of coxcombry, in matters of this frivolous nature. When, therefore, Mr. Preston reached me that which he had picked up upon the floor, and near the folding doors of the apartment, it was with an astonishment nearly bordering upon terror, that I perceived my own already hanging on my arm (where I had no doubt unwittingly placed it), and that the one presented me was but its exact counterpart in every, in even the minutest possible particular. The singular being who had so disastrously exposed me, had been muffled, I remembered, in a cloak; and none had been worn at all by any of the members of our party with the exception of myself. Retaining some presence of mind, I took the one offered me by Preston; placed it, unnoticed, over my own; left the apartment with a resolute scowl of defiance; and, next morning ere dawn of day, commenced a hurried journey from Oxford to the continent, in a perfect agony of horror and of shame.

I fled in vain. My evil destiny pursued me as if in exultation, and proved, indeed, that the exercise of its mysterious dominion had as yet only begun. Scarcely had I set foot in Paris ere I had fresh evidence of the detestable interest taken by this Wilson in my concerns. Years flew, while I experienced no relief. Villain!—at Rome, with how untimely, yet with how spectral an officiousness, stepped he in between me and my ambition! At Vienna, too—at Berlin—and at Moscow! Where, in truth, had I not bitter cause to curse him within my heart? From his inscrutable tyranny did I at length flee, panic-stricken, as from a pestilence; and to the very ends of the earth *I fled in vain.*

And again, and again, in secret communion with my own spirit, would I demand the questions "Who is he?—whence came he?—and what are his objects?" But no answer was there found. And then I scrutinized, with a minute scrutiny, the forms, and the methods, and the leading traits of his impertinent supervision. But even here there was very little upon which to base a conjecture. It was noticeable, indeed, that, in no one of the multiplied instances in which he had of late crossed my path, had he so crossed it except to frustrate those schemes, or to disturb those actions, which, if fully carried out, might have resulted in bitter mischief. Poor justification this, in truth, for an authority so imperiously assumed! Poor indemnity for natural rights of self-agency so pertinaciously, so insultingly denied!

I had also been forced to notice that my tormentor, for a very long period of time (while scrupulously and with miraculous dexterity maintaining his whim of an identity of apparel with myself), had so contrived it, in the execution of his varied interference with my will, that I saw not, at any moment, the features of his face. Be Wilson what he might, this, at least, was but the veriest of affectation, or of folly. Could he, for an instant, have supposed that, in my admonisher at Eton—in the destroyer of my honor at Oxford,—in him who thwarted my ambition at Rome, my revenge at Paris, my passionate love at Naples, or what he falsely termed my avarice in Egypt,—that in this, my arch-enemy and evil genius, could fail to recognise the William Wilson of my school boy days,—the namesake, the companion, the rival—the hated and dreaded rival at Dr. Bransby's? Impossible!—But let me hasten to the last eventful scene of the drama.

Thus far I had succumbed supinely to this imperious domination. The sentiment of deep awe with which I habitually regarded the elevated character, the majestic wisdom, the apparent omnipresence and omnipotence of Wilson, added to a feeling of even terror, with which certain other traits in his nature and assumptions inspired me, had operated, hitherto, to impress me with an idea of my own utter weakness and helplessness, and to suggest an implicit, although bitterly reluctant submission to his arbitrary will. But, of late days, I had given myself up entirely to wine; and its maddening influence upon my hereditary temper rendered me more and more impatient of control. I began to murmur,—to hesitate,—to resist. And was it only fancy which induced me to believe that, with the increase of my own firmness, that of my tormentor underwent a proportional diminution? Be this as it may, I now began to feel the inspiration of a burning hope, and at length nurtured in my secret thoughts a stern and desperate resolution that I would submit no longer to be enslaved.

It was at Rome, during the Carnival of 18—, that I attended a masquerade in the palazzo of the Neapolitan Duke Di Broglio. I had indulged more freely than usual in the excesses of the wine-table; and now the suffocating atmosphere of the crowded rooms irritated me beyond endurance. The difficulty, too, of forcing my way through the mazes of the company contributed not a little to the ruffling of my temper; for I was anxiously seeking (let me not say with what unworthy motive) the young, the gay, the beautiful wife of the aged and doting Di Broglio. With a too unscrupulous confidence she had previously communicated to me the secret of the costume in which she would be habited, and now, having caught a glimpse of her person, I was hurrying to make my way into her presence.—At this moment I felt a light hand placed upon my shoulder, and that ever-remembered, low, damnable *whisper* within my ear.

In an absolute phrenzy of wrath, I turned at once upon him who had thus interrupted me, and seized him violently by the collar. He was attired, as I had expected, in a costume altogether similar to my own; wearing a Spanish cloak of blue velvet, begirt about the waist with a crimson belt sustaining a rapier. A mask of black silk entirely covered his face.

"Scoundrel!" I said, in a voice husky with rage, while every syllable I uttered seemed as new fuel to my fury, "scoundrel! impostor! accursed villain! you shall not—you shall not dog me unto death! Follow me, or I stab you where you stand!"—and I broke my way from the ballroom into a small antechamber adjoining—dragging him unresistingly with me as I went.

Upon entering, I thrust him furiously from me. He staggered against the wall, while I closed the door with an oath, and commanded him to draw. He hesitated but for an instant; then, with a slight sigh, drew in silence, and put himself upon his defence.

The contest was brief indeed. I was frantic with every species of wild excitement, and felt within my single arm the energy and power of a multitude. In a few seconds I forced him by sheer strength against the wainscoting, and thus, getting him at mercy, plunged my sword, with brute ferocity, repeatedly through and through his bosom.

At that instant some person tried the latch of the door. I hastened to prevent an intrusion, and then immediately returned to my dying antagonist. But what human language can adequately portray that astonishment, that horror which possessed me at the spectacle then presented to view? The brief moment in which I averted my eyes had been sufficient to produce, apparently, a material change in the arrangements at the upper or farther end of the room. A large mirror,—so at first it seemed to me in my confusion—now stood where none had been perceptible before; and, as I stepped up to it in extremity of terror, mine own image, but with features all pale and dabbled in blood, advanced to meet me with a feeble and tottering gait.

Thus it appeared, I say, but was not. It was my antagonist—it was Wilson, who then stood before me in the agonies of his dissolution. His mask and cloak lay, where he had thrown them, upon the floor. Not a thread in all his raiment—not a line in all the marked and singular lineaments of his face which was not, even in the most absolute identity, mine own!

It was Wilson; but he spoke no longer in a whisper, and I could have fancied that I myself was speaking while he said:

"*You have conquered, and I yield. Yet, henceforward art thou also dead—dead to the World, to Heaven and to Hope! In me didst thou exist—and, in my death, see by this image, which is thine own, how utterly thou hast murdered thyself.*"

AFTERWARD

Edith Wharton

I

"Oh, there is one, of course, but you'll never know it."

The assertion, laughingly flung out six months earlier in a bright June garden, came back to Mary Boyne with a sharp perception of its latent significance as she stood, in the December dusk, waiting for the lamps to be brought into the library.

The words had been spoken by their friend Alida Stair, as they sat at tea on her lawn at Pangbourne, in reference to the very house of which the library in question was the central, the pivotal "feature." Mary Boyne and her husband, in quest of a country place in one of the southern or southwestern counties, had, on their arrival in England, carried their problem straight to Alida Stair, who had successfully solved it in her own case; but it was not until they had rejected, almost capriciously, several practical and judicious suggestions that she threw it out: "Well, there's Lyng, in Dorsetshire. It belongs to Hugo's cousins, and you can get it for a song."

The reasons she gave for its being obtainable on these terms—its remoteness from a station, its lack of electric light, hot-water pipes, and other vulgar necessities—were exactly those pleading in its favor with two romantic Americans perversely in search of the economic drawbacks which were associated, in their tradition, with unusual architectural felicities.

"I should never believe I was living in an old house unless I was thoroughly uncomfortable," Ned Boyne, the more extravagant of the two, had jocosely insisted; "the least hint of 'convenience' would make me think it had been bought out of an exhibition, with the pieces numbered, and set up again." And they had proceeded to enumerate, with humorous precision, their various suspicions and exactions, refusing to believe that the house their cousin recommended was *really* Tudor till they learned it had no heating system, or that the village church was literally in the grounds till she assured them of the deplorable uncertainty of the water-supply.

"It's too uncomfortable to be true!" Edward Boyne had continued to exult as the avowal of each disadvantage was successively wrung from her; but he had cut short his rhapsody to ask, with a sudden relapse to distrust: "And the ghost? You've been concealing from us the fact that there is no ghost!"

Mary, at the moment, had laughed with him, yet almost with her laugh, being possessed of several sets of independent perceptions, had noted a sudden flatness of tone in Alida's answering hilarity.

"Oh, Dorsetshire's full of ghosts, you know."

"Yes, yes; but that won't do. I don't want to have to drive ten miles to see somebody else's ghost. I want one of my own on the premises. *Is* there a ghost at Lyng?"

His rejoinder had made Alida laugh again, and it was then that she had flung back tantalizingly: "Oh, there is one, of course, but you'll never know it."

"Never know it?" Boyne pulled her up. "But what in the world constitutes a ghost except the fact of its being known for one?"

"I can't say. But that's the story."

"That there's a ghost, but that nobody knows it's a ghost?"

"Well—not till afterward, at any rate."

"Till afterward?"

"Not till long, long afterward."

"But if it's once been identified as an unearthly visitant, why hasn't its *signalement* been handed down in the family? How has it managed to preserve its incognito?"

Alida could only shake her head. "Don't ask me. But it has."

"And then suddenly—" Mary spoke up as if from some cavernous depth of divination—"suddenly, long afterward, one says to one's self, '*That was it?*' "

She was oddly startled at the sepulchral sound with which her question fell on the banter of the other two, and she saw the shadow of the same surprise flit across Alida's clear pupils. "I suppose so. One just has to wait."

"Oh, hang waiting!" Ned broke in. "Life's too short for a ghost who can only be enjoyed in retrospect. Can't we do better than that, Mary?"

But it turned out that in the event they were not destined to, for within three months of their conversation with Mrs. Stair they were established at Lyng, and the life they had yearned for to the point of planning it out in all its daily details had actually begun for them.

It was to sit, in the thick December dusk, by just such a wide-hooded fireplace, under just such black oak rafters, with the sense that beyond the mullioned panes the downs were darkening to a deeper solitude: it was for the ultimate indulgence in such sensations that Mary Boyne had endured for nearly fourteen years the soul-deadening ugliness of the Middle West, and that Boyne had ground on doggedly at his engineering till, with a suddenness that still made her blink, the prodigious windfall of the Blue Star Mine had put them at a stroke in possession of life and the leisure to taste it. They had never for a moment meant their new state to be one of idleness; but they meant to give themselves only to harmonious activities. She had her vision of painting and gardening (against a background of gray walls), he dreamed of the production of his long-planned book on the "Economic Basis of Culture"; and with such absorbing work ahead no existence could be too sequestered; they could not get far enough from the world, or plunge deep enough into the past.

Dorsetshire had attracted them from the first by a semblance of remoteness out of all proportion to its geographical position. But to the Boynes it was one of the ever-recurring wonders of the whole incredibly compressed island—a nest of counties, as they put it—that for the production of its effects so little of a given quality went so far: that so few miles made a distance, and so short a distance a difference.

"It's that," Ned had once enthusiastically explained, "that gives such depth to their effects, such relief to their least contrasts. They've been able to lay the butter so thick on every exquisite mouthful."

The butter had certainly been laid on thick at Lyng: the old gray house, hidden under a shoulder of the downs, had almost all the finer marks of commerce with a protracted past. The mere fact that it was neither large nor exceptional made it, to the Boynes, abound the more richly in its special sense—the sense of having been for centuries a deep, dim reservoir of life. The life had probably not been of the most vivid order: for long periods, no doubt, it had fallen as noiselessly into the past as the quiet drizzle of autumn fell, hour after hour, into the green fish-pond between the yews; but these back-waters of existence sometimes breed, in their sluggish depths, strange acuities of emotion, and Mary Boyne had felt from the first the occasional brush of an intenser memory.

The feeling had never been stronger than on the December afternoon when, waiting in the library for the belated lamps, she rose from her seat and stood among the shadows of the hearth. Her husband had gone off, after luncheon, for one of his long tramps on the downs. She had noticed of late that he preferred to be unaccompanied on these occasions; and, in the tried security of their personal relations, had been driven to conclude that his book was bothering him, and that he needed the afternoons to turn over in solitude the problems left from the morning's work. Certainly the book was not going as smoothly as she had imagined it would, and the lines of perplexity between his eyes had never been there in his engineering days. Then he had often looked fagged to the verge of illness, but the native demon of "worry" had never branded his brow. Yet the few pages he had so far read to her—the introduction, and a synopsis of the opening chapter—gave evidences of a firm possession of his subject, and a deepening confidence in his powers.

The fact threw her into deeper perplexity, since, now that he had done with "business" and its disturbing contingencies, the one other possible element of anxiety was eliminated. Unless it were his health, then? But physically he had gained since they had come to Dorsetshire, grown robuster, ruddier, and fresher-eyed. It was only within a week that she had felt in him the undefinable change that made her restless in his absence, and as tongue-tied in his presence as though it were *she* who had a secret to keep from him!

The thought that there was a secret somewhere between them struck her with a sudden smart rap of wonder, and she looked about her down the dim, long room.

"Can it be the house?" she mused.

The room itself might have been full of secrets. They seemed to be piling themselves up, as evening fell, like the layers and layers of velvet shadow dropping from the low ceiling, the dusky walls of books, the smoke-blurred sculpture of the hooded hearth.

"Why, of course—the house is haunted!" she reflected.

The ghost—Alida's imperceptible ghost—after figuring largely in the banter of their first month or two at Lyng, had been gradually discarded as too ineffectual for imaginative use. Mary had, indeed, as became the tenant of a haunted house, made the customary inquiries among her few rural neighbors, but, beyond a vague, "They do say so, Ma'am," the villagers had nothing to impart. The elusive specter had apparently never had sufficient identity for a legend to crystallize about it, and after a time the Boynes had laughingly set the matter down to their profit-and-loss account, agreeing that Lyng was one of the few houses good enough in itself to dispense with supernatural enhancements.

"And I suppose, poor, ineffectual demon, that's why it beats its beautiful wings in vain in the void," Mary had laughingly concluded.

"Or, rather," Ned answered, in the same strain, "why, amid so much that's ghostly, it can never affirm its separate existence as *the* ghost." And thereupon their invisible housemate had finally dropped out of their references, which were numerous enough to make them promptly unaware of the loss.

Now, as she stood on the hearth, the subject of their earlier curiosity revived in her with a new sense of its meaning—a sense gradually acquired through close daily contact with the scene of the lurking mystery. It was the house itself, of course, that possessed the ghost-seeing faculty, that communed visually but secretly with its own past; and if one could only get into close enough communion with the house, one might surprise its secret, and acquire the ghost-sight on one's own account. Perhaps, in his long solitary hours in this very room, where she never trespassed till the afternoon, her husband had acquired it already, and was silently carrying the dread weight of whatever it had revealed to him. Mary was too well-versed in the code of the spectral world not to know that one could not talk about the ghosts one saw: to do so was almost as great a breach of good-breeding as to name a lady in a club. But this explanation did not really satisfy her. "What, after all, except for the fun of the *frisson*," she reflected, "would he really care for any of their old ghosts?" And thence she was thrown back once more on the fundamental dilemma: the fact that one's greater or less susceptibility to spectral influences had no particular bearing on the case, since, when one *did* see a ghost at Lyng, one did not know it.

"Not till long afterward," Alida Stair had said. Well, supposing Ned *had* seen one when they first came, and had known only within the last week what had happened to him? More and more under the spell of the hour, she threw back her searching thoughts to the early days of their tenancy, but at first only to recall a gay confusion of unpacking, settling, arranging of books, and calling to each other from remote corners of the house as treasure after treasure of their habitation revealed itself to them. It was in this particular connection that she presently recalled a certain soft afternoon of the previous October, when, passing from the first rapturous flurry of exploration to a detailed inspection of the old house, she had pressed (like a novel heroine) a panel that opened at her touch, on a narrow flight of stairs leading to an unsuspected flat ledge of the roof—the roof which, from below, seemed to slope away on all sides too abruptly for any but practised feet to scale.

The view from this hidden coign was enchanting, and she had flown down to snatch Ned from his papers and give him the freedom of her discovery. She remembered still how, standing on the narrow ledge, he had passed his arm about her while their gaze flew to the long, tossed horizon-line of the downs, and then dropped contentedly back to trace the arabesque of yew hedges about the fish-pond, and the shadow of the cedar on the lawn.

"And now the other way," he had said, gently turning her about within his arm; and closely pressed to him, she had absorbed, like some long, satisfying draft, the picture of the gray-walled court, the squat lions on the gates, and the lime-avenue reaching up to the highroad under the downs.

It was just then, while they gazed and held each other, that she had felt his arm relax, and heard a sharp "Hullo!" that made her turn to glance at him.

Distinctly, yes, she now recalled she had seen, as she glanced, a shadow of anxiety, of perplexity, rather, fall across his face; and, following his eyes, had beheld the figure of a man—a man in loose, grayish clothes, as it appeared to her—who was sauntering down the lime-avenue to the court with the tentative gait of a stranger seeking his way. Her short-sighted eyes had given her but a blurred impression of slightness and grayness, with something foreign, or at least unlocal, in the cut of the figure or its garb; but her husband had apparently seen more—seen enough to make him push past her with a sharp "Wait!" and dash down the twisting stairs without pausing to give her a hand for the descent.

A slight tendency to dizziness obliged her, after a provisional clutch at the chimney against which they had been leaning, to follow him down more cautiously; and when she had reached the attic landing she paused again for a less definite reason, leaning over the oak banister to strain her eyes through the silence of the brown, sun-flecked depths below. She lingered there till, somewhere in those depths, she heard the closing of a door; then, mechanically impelled, she went down the shallow flights of steps till she reached the lower hall.

The front door stood open on the mild sunlight of the court, and hall and court were empty. The library door was open, too, and after listening in vain for any sound of voices within, she quickly crossed the threshold, and found her husband alone, vaguely fingering the papers on his desk.

He looked up, as if surprised at her precipitate entrance, but the shadow of anxiety had passed from his face, leaving it even, as she fancied, a little brighter and clearer than usual.

"What was it? Who was it?" she asked.

"Who?" he repeated, with the surprise still all on his side.

"The man we saw coming toward the house." Boyne shrugged his shoulders. "So I thought; but he must have got up steam in the interval. What do you say to our trying a scramble up Meldon Steep before sunset?"

That was all. At the time the occurrence had been less than nothing, had, indeed, been immediately obliterated by the magic of their first vision from Meldon Steep, a height which they had dreamed of climbing ever since they had first seen its bare spine heaving itself above the low roof of Lyng. Doubtless it was the mere fact of the other incident's having occurred on the very day of their ascent to Meldon that had kept it stored away in the unconscious fold of association from which it now emerged; for in itself it had no mark of the portentous. At the moment there could have been nothing more natural than that Ned should dash himself from the roof in the pursuit of dilatory tradesmen. It was the period when they were always on the watch for one or the other of the specialists employed about the place; always lying in wait for them, and dashing out at them with questions, reproaches, or reminders. And certainly in the distance the gray figure had looked like Peters.

Yet now, as she reviewed the rapid scene, she felt her husband's explanation of it to have been invalidated by the look of anxiety on his face. Why had the familiar appearance of Peters made him anxious? Why, above all, if it was of such prime necessity to confer with that authority on the subject of the stable-drains, had the failure to find him produced such a look of relief? Mary could not say that any one of these considerations had occurred to her at the time, yet, from the promptness with which they now marshaled themselves at her summons, she had a sudden sense that they must all along have been there, waiting their hour.

II

Weary with her thoughts, she moved toward the window. The library was now completely dark, and she was surprised to see how much faint light the outer world still held.

As she peered out into it across the court, a figure shaped itself in the tapering perspective of bare lines: it looked a mere blot of deeper gray in the grayness, and for an instant, as it moved toward her, her heart thumped to the thought, "It's the ghost!"

She had time, in that long instant, to feel suddenly that the man of whom, two months earlier, she had a brief distant vision from the roof was now, at his predestined hour, about to reveal himself as not having been Peters; and her spirit sank under the impending fear of the disclosure. But almost with the next tick of the clock the ambiguous figure, gaining substance and character, showed itself even to her weak sight as her husband's; and she turned away to meet him, as he entered, with the confession of her folly.

"It's really too absurd," she laughed out from the threshold, "but I never can remember!"

"Remember what?" Boyne questioned as they drew together.

"That when one sees the Lyng ghost one never knows it."

Her hand was on his sleeve, and he kept it there, but with no response in his gesture or in the lines of his fagged, preoccupied face.

"Did you think you'd seen it?" he asked, after an appreciable interval.

"Why, I actually took *you* for it, my dear, in my mad determination to spot it!"

"Me—just now?" His arm dropped away, and he turned from her with a faint echo of her laugh. "Really, dearest, you'd better give it up, if that's the best you can do."

"Yes, I give it up—I give it up. Have *you*?" she asked, turning round on him abruptly.

The parlor-maid had entered with letters and a lamp, and the light struck up into Boyne's face as he bent above the tray she presented.

"Have you?" Mary perversely insisted, when the servant had disappeared on her errand of illumination.

"Have I what?" he rejoined absently, the light bringing out the sharp stamp of worry between his brows as he turned over the letters.

"I never tried," he said, tearing open the wrapper of a newspaper.

"Well, of course," Mary persisted, "the exasperating thing is that there's no use trying, since one can't be sure till so long afterward."

He was unfolding the paper as if he had hardly heard her; but after a pause, during which the sheets rustled spasmodically between his hands, he lifted his head to say abruptly, "Have you any idea how long?"

Mary had sunk into a low chair beside the fireplace. From her seat she looked up, startled, at her husband's profile, which was darkly projected against the circle of lamplight.

"No; none. Have you?" she retorted, repeating her former phrase with an added keenness of intention.

Boyne crumpled the paper into a bunch, and then inconsequently turned back with it toward the lamp.

"Lord, no! I only meant," he explained, with a faint tinge of impatience, "is there any legend, any tradition, as to that?"

"Not that I know of," she answered; but the impulse to add, "What makes you ask?" was checked by the reappearance of the parlor-maid with tea and a second lamp.

With the dispersal of shadows, and the repetition of the daily domestic office, Mary Boyne felt herself less oppressed by that sense of something mutely imminent which had darkened her solitary afternoon. For a few moments she gave herself silently to the details of her task, and when she looked up from it she was struck to the point of bewilderment by the change in her husband's face. He had seated himself near the farther lamp, and was absorbed in the perusal of his letters; but was it something he had found in them, or merely the shifting of her own point of view, that had restored his features to their normal aspect? The longer she looked, the more definitely the change affirmed itself. The lines of painful tension had vanished, and such traces of fatigue as lingered were of the kind easily attributable to steady mental effort. He glanced up, as if drawn by her gaze, and met her eyes with a smile.

"I'm dying for my tea, you know; and here's a letter for you," he said.

She took the letter he held out in exchange for the cup she proffered him, and, returning to her seat, broke the seal with the languid gesture of the reader whose interests are all inclosed in the circle of one cherished presence.

Her next conscious motion was that of starting to her feet, the letter falling to them as she rose, while she held out to her husband a long newspaper clipping.

"Ned! What's this? What does it mean?"

He had risen at the same instant, almost as if hearing her cry before she uttered it; and for a perceptible space of time he and she studied each other, like adversaries watching for an advantage, across the space between her chair and his desk.

"What's what? You fairly made me jump!" Boyne said at length, moving toward her with a sudden, half-exasperated laugh. The shadow of apprehension was on his face again, not now a look of fixed foreboding, but a shifting vigilance of lips and eyes that gave her the sense of his feeling himself invisibly surrounded.

Her hand shook so that she could hardly give him the clipping.

"This article—from the *Waukesha Sentinel*—that a man named Elwell has brought suit against you—that there was something wrong about the Blue Star Mine. I can't understand more than half."

They continued to face each other as she spoke, and to her astonishment, she saw that her words had the almost immediate effect of dissipating the strained watchfulness of his look.

"Oh, that!" He glanced down the printed slip, and then folded it with the gesture of one who handles something harmless and familiar. "What's the matter with you this afternoon, Mary? I thought you'd got bad news."

She stood before him with her undefinable terror subsiding slowly under the reassuring touch of his composure.

"You knew about this, then—it's all right?"

"Certainly I knew about it; and it's all right."

"But what is it? I don't understand. What does this man accuse you of?"

"Oh, pretty nearly every crime in the calendar." Boyne had tossed the clipping down, and thrown himself comfortably into an arm-chair near the fire. "Do you want to hear the story? It's not particularly interesting—just a squabble over interests in the Blue Star."

"But who is this Elwell? I don't know the name."

"Oh, he's a fellow I put into it—gave him a hand up. I told you all about him at the time."

"I daresay. I must have forgotten." Vainly she strained back among her memories. "But if you helped him, why does he make this return?"

"Oh, probably some shyster lawyer got hold of him and talked him over. It's all rather technical and complicated. I thought that kind of thing bored you."

His wife felt a sting of compunction. Theoretically, she deprecated the American wife's detachment from her husband's professional interests, but in practice she had always found it difficult to fix her attention on Boyne's report of the transactions in which his varied interests involved him Besides, she had felt from the first that, in a community where the amenities of living could be obtained only at the cost of efforts as arduous as her husband's professional labors, such brief leisure as they could command should be used as an escape from immediate preoccupations, a flight to the life they always dreamed of living. Once or twice, now that this new life had actually drawn its magic circle about them, she had asked herself if she had done right; but hitherto such conjectures had been no more than the retrospective excursions of an active fancy. Now, for the first time, it startled her a little to find how little she knew of the material foundation on which her happiness was built.

She glanced again at her husband, and was reassured by the composure of his face; yet she felt the need of more definite grounds for her reassurance.

"But doesn't this suit worry you? Why have you never spoken to me about it?"

He answered both questions at once: "I didn't speak of it at first because it *did* worry me—annoyed me, rather. But it's all ancient history now. Your correspondent must have got hold of a back number of the *Sentinel.*"

She felt a quick thrill of relief. "You mean it's over? He's lost his case?"

There was a just perceptible delay in Boyne's reply. "The suit's been withdrawn—that's all."

But she persisted, as if to exonerate herself from the inward charge of being too easily put off. "Withdrawn because he saw he had no chance?"

"Oh, he had no chance," Boyne answered.

She was still struggling with a dimly felt perplexity at the back of her thoughts.

"How long ago was it withdrawn?"

He paused, as if with a slight return of his former uncertainty. "I've just had the news now; but I've been expecting it."

"Just now—in one of your letters?"

"Yes; in one of my letters."

She made no answer, and was aware only, after a short interval of waiting, that he had risen, and strolling across the room, had placed himself on the sofa at her side. She felt him, as he did so, pass an arm about her, she felt his hand seek hers and clasp it, and turning slowly, drawn by the warmth of his cheek, she met the smiling clearness of his eyes.

"It's all right—it's all right?" she questioned, through the flood of her dissolving doubts; and "I give you my word it never was righter!" he laughed back at her, holding her close.

III

One of the strangest things she was afterward to recall out of all the next day's incredible strangeness was the sudden and complete recovery of her sense of security.

It was in the air when she woke in her low-ceilinged, dusky room; it accompanied her down-stairs to the breakfast-table, flashed out at her from the fire, and re-duplicated itself brightly from the flanks of the urn and the sturdy flutings of the Georgian teapot. It was as if, in some roundabout way, all her diffused apprehensions of the previous day, with their moment of sharp concentration about the newspaper article,—as if this dim questioning of the future, and startled return upon the past,—had between them liquidated the arrears of some haunting moral obligation. If she had indeed been careless of her husband's affairs, it was, her new state seemed to prove, because her faith in him instinctively justified such carelessness; and his right to her faith had overwhelmingly affirmed itself in the very face of menace and suspicion. She had never seen him more untroubled, more naturally and unconsciously in possession of himself, than after the cross-examination to which she had subjected him: it was almost as if he had been aware of her lurking doubts, and had wanted the air cleared as much as she did.

It was as clear, thank Heaven! as the bright outer light that surprised her almost with a touch of summer when she issued from the house for her daily round of the gardens. She had left Boyne at his desk, indulging herself, as she passed the library door, by a last peep at his quiet face, where he bent, pipe in his mouth, above his papers, and now she had her own morning's task to perform. The task involved on such charmed winter days almost as much delighted loitering about the different quarters of her demesne as if spring were already at work on shrubs and borders. There were such inexhaustible possibilities still before her, such opportunities to bring out the latent graces of the old place, without a single irreverent touch of alteration, that the winter months were all too short to plan what spring and autumn executed. And her recovered sense of safety gave, on this particular morning, a peculiar zest to her progress through the sweet, still place. She went first to the kitchen-garden, where the espaliered pear-trees drew complicated patterns on the walls, and pigeons were fluttering and preening about the silvery-slated roof of their cot. There was something wrong about the piping of the hothouse, and she was expecting an authority from Dorchester, who was to drive out between trains and make a diagnosis of the boiler. But when she dipped into the damp heat of the greenhouses, among the spiced scents and waxy pinks and reds of old-fashioned exotics,—even the flora of Lyng was in the note!—she learned that the great man had not arrived, and the day being too rare to waste in an artificial atmosphere, she came out again and paced slowly along the springy turf of the bowling-green to the gardens behind the house. At their farther end rose a grass terrace, commanding, over the fish-pond and the yew hedges, a view of the long house-front, with its twisted chimney-stacks and the blue shadows of its roof angles, all drenched in the pale gold moisture of the air.

Seen thus, across the level tracery of the yews, under the suffused, mild light, it sent her, from its open windows and hospitably smoking chimneys, the look of some warm human presence, of a mind slowly ripened on a sunny wall of experience. She had never before had so deep a sense of her intimacy with it, such a conviction that its secrets were all beneficent, kept, as they said to children, "for one's good," so complete a trust in its power to gather up her life and Ned's into the harmonious pattern of the long, long story it sat there weaving in the sun.

She heard steps behind her, and turned, expecting to see the gardener, accompanied by the engineer from Dorchester. But only one figure was in sight, that of a youngish, slightly built man, who, for reasons she could not on the spot have specified, did not remotely resemble her preconceived notion of an authority on hot-house boilers. The new-comer, on seeing her, lifted his hat, and paused with the air of a gentleman—perhaps a traveler—desirous of having it immediately known that his intrusion is involuntary. The local fame of Lyng occasionally attracted the more intelligent sight-seer, and Mary half-expected to see the stranger dissemble a camera, or justify his presence by producing it. But he made no gesture of any sort, and after a moment she asked, in a tone responding to the courteous deprecation of his attitude: "Is there any one you wish to see?"

"I came to see Mr. Boyne," he replied. His intonation, rather than his accent, was faintly American, and Mary, at the familiar note, looked at him more closely. The brim of his soft felt hat cast a shade on his face, which, thus obscured, wore to her short-sighted gaze a look of seriousness, as of a person arriving "on business," and civilly but firmly aware of his rights.

Past experience had made Mary equally sensible to such claims; but she was jealous of her husband's morning hours, and doubtful of his having given any one the right to intrude on them.

"Have you an appointment with Mr. Boyne?" she asked.

He hesitated, as if unprepared for the question.

"Not exactly an appointment," he replied.

"Then I'm afraid, this being his working-time, that he can't receive you now. Will you give me a message, or come back later?"

The visitor, again lifting his hat, briefly replied that he would come back later, and walked away, as if to regain the front of the house. As his figure receded down the walk between the yew hedges, Mary saw him pause and look up an instant at the peaceful house-front bathed in faint winter sunshine; and it struck her, with a tardy touch of compunction, that it would have been more humane to ask if he had come from a distance, and to offer, in that case, to inquire if her husband could receive him. But as the thought occurred to her he passed out of sight behind a pyramidal yew, and at the same moment her attention was distracted by the approach of the gardener, attended by the bearded pepper-and-salt figure of the boiler-maker from Dorchester.

The encounter with this authority led to such far-reaching issues that they resulted in his finding it expedient to ignore his train, and beguiled Mary into spending the remainder of the morning in absorbed confabulation among the greenhouses. She was startled to find, when the colloquy ended, that it was nearly luncheon-time, and she half expected, as she hurried back to the house, to see her husband coming out to meet her. But she found no one in the court but an under-gardener raking the gravel, and the hall, when she entered it, was so silent that she guessed Boyne to be still at work behind the closed door of the library.

Not wishing to disturb him, she turned into the drawing-room, and there, at her writing-table, lost herself in renewed calculations of the outlay to which the morning's conference had committed her. The knowledge that she could permit herself such follies had not yet lost its novelty; and somehow, in contrast to the vague apprehensions of the previous days, it now seemed an element of her recovered security, of the sense that, as Ned had said, things in general had never been "righter."

She was still luxuriating in a lavish play of figures when the parlor-maid, from the threshold, roused her with a dubiously worded inquiry as to the expediency of serving luncheon. It was one of their jokes that Trimmle announced luncheon as if she were divulging a state secret, and Mary, intent upon her papers, merely murmured an absent-minded assent.

She felt Trimmle wavering expressively on the threshold as if in rebuke of such offhand acquiescence; then her retreating steps sounded down the passage, and Mary, pushing away her papers, crossed the hall, and went to the library door. It was still closed, and she wavered in her turn, disliking to disturb her husband, yet anxious that he should not exceed his normal measure of work. As she stood there, balancing her impulses, the esoteric Trimmle returned with the announcement of luncheon, and Mary, thus impelled, opened the door and went into the library.

Boyne was not at his desk, and she peered about her, expecting to discover him at the book-shelves, somewhere down the length of the room; but her call brought no response, and gradually it became clear to her that he was not in the library.

She turned back to the parlor-maid.

"Mr. Boyne must be up-stairs. Please tell him that luncheon is ready."

The parlor-maid appeared to hesitate between the obvious duty of obeying orders and an equally obvious conviction of the foolishness of the injunction laid upon her. The struggle resulted in her saying doubtfully, "If you please, Madam, Mr. Boyne's not up-stairs."

"Not in his room? Are you sure?"

"I'm sure, Madam."

Mary consulted the clock. "Where is he, then?"

"He's gone out," Trimmle announced, with the superior air of one who has respectfully waited for the question that a well-ordered mind would have first propounded.

Mary's previous conjecture had been right, then. Boyne must have gone to the gardens to meet her, and since she had missed him, it was clear that he had taken the shorter way by the south door, instead of going round to the court. She crossed the hall to the glass portal opening directly on the yew garden, but the parlor-maid, after another moment of inner conflict, decided to bring out recklessly, "Please, Madam, Mr. Boyne didn't go that way."

Mary turned back. "Where *did* he go? And when?"

"He went out of the front door, up the drive, Madam." It was a matter of principle with Trimmle never to answer more than one question at a time.

"Up the drive? At this hour?" Mary went to the door herself, and glanced across the court through the long tunnel of bare limes. But its perspective was as empty as when she had scanned it on entering the house.

"Did Mr. Boyne leave no message?" she asked.

Trimmle seemed to surrender herself to a last struggle with the forces of chaos.

"No, Madam. He just went out with the gentleman."

"The gentleman? What gentleman?" Mary wheeled about, as if to front this new factor.

"The gentleman who called, Madam," said Trimmle, resignedly.

"When did a gentleman call? Do explain yourself, Trimmle!"

Only the fact that Mary was very hungry, and that she wanted to consult her husband about the greenhouses, would have caused her to lay so unusual an injunction on her attendant; and even now she was detached enough to note in Trimmle's eye the dawning defiance of the respectful subordinate who has been pressed too hard.

"I couldn't exactly say the hour, Madam, because I didn't let the gentleman in," she replied, with the air of magnanimously ignoring the irregularity of her mistress's course.

"You didn't let him in?"

"No, Madam. When the bell rang I was dressing, and Agnes—"

"Go and ask Agnes, then," Mary interjected. Trimmle still wore her look of patient magnanimity. "Agnes would not know, Madam, for she had unfortunately burnt her hand in trying the wick of the new lamp from town—" Trimmle, as Mary was aware, had always been opposed to the new lamp—"and so Mrs. Dockett sent the kitchen-maid instead."

Mary looked again at the clock. "It's after two! Go and ask the kitchen-maid if Mr. Boyne left any word."

She went into luncheon without waiting, and Trimmle presently brought her there the kitchen-maid's statement that the gentleman had called about one o'clock, that Mr. Boyne had gone out with him without leaving any message. The kitchen-maid did not even know the caller's name, for he had written it on a slip of paper, which he had folded and handed to her, with the injunction to deliver it at once to Mr. Boyne.

Mary finished her luncheon, still wondering, and when it was over, and Trimmle had brought the coffee to the drawing-room, her wonder had deepened to a first faint tinge of disquietude. It was unlike Boyne to absent himself without explanation at so unwonted an hour, and the difficulty of identifying the visitor whose summons he had apparently obeyed made his disappearance the more unaccountable. Mary Boyne's experience as the wife of a busy engineer, subject to sudden calls and compelled to keep irregular hours, had trained her to the philosophic acceptance of surprises; but since Boyne's withdrawal from business he had adopted a Benedictine regularity of life. As if to make up for the dispersed and agitated years, with their "stand-up" lunches and dinners rattled down to the joltings of the dining-car, he cultivated the last refinements of punctuality and monotony, discouraging his wife's fancy for the unexpected; and declaring that to a delicate taste there were infinite gradations of pleasure in the fixed recurrences of habit.

Still, since no life can completely defend itself from the unforeseen, it was evident that all Boyne's precautions would sooner or later prove unavailable, and Mary concluded that he had cut short a tiresome visit by walking with his caller to the station, or at least accompanying him for part of the way.

This conclusion relieved her from farther preoccupation, and she went out herself to take up her conference with the gardener. Thence she walked to the village post-office, a mile or so away; and when she turned toward home, the early twilight was setting in.

She had taken a foot-path across the downs, and as Boyne, meanwhile, had probably returned from the station by the highroad, there was little likelihood of their meeting on the way. She felt sure, however, of his having reached the house before her; so sure that, when she entered it herself, without even pausing to inquire of Trimmle, she made directly for the library. But the library was still empty, and with an unwonted precision of visual memory she immediately observed that the papers on her husband's desk lay precisely as they had lain when she had gone in to call him to luncheon.

Then of a sudden she was seized by a vague dread of the unknown. She had closed the door behind her on entering, and as she stood alone in the long, silent, shadowy room, her dread seemed to take shape and sound, to be there audibly breathing and lurking among the shadows. Her short-sighted eyes strained through them, half-discerning an actual presence, something aloof, that watched and knew; and in the recoil from that intangible propinquity she threw herself suddenly on the bell-rope and gave it a desperate pull.

The long, quavering summons brought Trimmle in precipitately with a lamp, and Mary breathed again at this sobering reappearance of the usual.

"You may bring tea if Mr. Boyne is in," she said, to justify her ring.

"Very well, Madam. But Mr. Boyne is not in," said Trimmle, putting down the lamp.

"Not in? You mean he's come back and gone out again?"

"No, Madam. He's never been back."

The dread stirred again, and Mary knew that now it had her fast.

"Not since he went out with—the gentleman?"

"Not since he went out with the gentleman."

"But who was the gentleman?" Mary gasped out, with the sharp note of some one trying to be heard through a confusion of meaningless noises.

"That I couldn't say, Madam." Trimmle, standing there by the lamp, seemed suddenly to grow less round and rosy, as though eclipsed by the same creeping shade of apprehension.

"But the kitchen-maid knows—wasn't it the kitchen-maid who let him in?"

"She doesn't know either, Madam, for he wrote his name on a folded paper."

Mary, through her agitation, was aware that they were both designating the unknown visitor by a vague pronoun, instead of the conventional formula which, till then, had kept their allusions within the bounds of custom. And at the same moment her mind caught at the suggestion of the folded paper.

"But he must have a name! Where is the paper?"

She moved to the desk, and began to turn over the scattered documents that littered it. The first that caught her eye was an unfinished letter in her husband's hand, with his pen lying across it, as though dropped there at a sudden summons.

"My dear Parvis,"—who was Parvis?—"I have just received your letter announcing Elwell's death, and while I suppose there is now no farther risk of trouble, it might be safer—"

She tossed the sheet aside, and continued her search; but no folded paper was discoverable among the letters and pages of manuscript which had been swept together in a promiscuous heap, as if by a hurried or a startled gesture.

"But the kitchen-maid saw him. Send her here," she commanded, wondering at her dullness in not thinking sooner of so simple a solution.

Trimmle, at the behest, vanished in a flash, as if thankful to be out of the room, and when she reappeared, conducting the agitated underling, Mary had regained her self-possession, and had her questions pat.

The gentleman was a stranger, yes—that she understood. But what had he said? And, above all, what had he looked like? The first question was easily enough answered, for the disconcerting reason that he had said so little—had merely asked for Mr. Boyne, and, scribbling something on a bit of paper, had requested that it should at once be carried in to him.

"Then you don't know what he wrote? You're not sure it was his name?"

The kitchen-maid was not sure, but supposed it was, since he had written it in answer to her inquiry as to whom she should announce.

"And when you carried the paper in to Mr. Boyne, what did he say?"

The kitchen-maid did not think that Mr. Boyne had said anything, but she could not be sure, for just as she had handed him the paper and he was opening it, she had become aware that the visitor had followed her into the library, and she had slipped out, leaving the two gentlemen together.

"But then, if you left them in the library, how do you know that they went out of the house?"

This question plunged the witness into momentary inarticulateness, from which she was rescued by Trimmle, who, by means of ingenious circumlocutions, elicited the statement that before she could cross the hall to the back passage she had heard the gentlemen behind her, and had seen them go out of the front door together.

"Then, if you saw the gentleman twice, you must be able to tell me what he looked like."

But with this final challenge to her powers of expression it became clear that the limit of the kitchen-maid's endurance had been reached. The obligation of going to the front door to "show in" a visitor was in itself so subversive of the fundamental order of things that it had thrown her faculties into hopeless disarray, and she could only stammer out, after various panting efforts at evocation, "His hat, mum, was different-like, as you might say—"

"Different? How different?" Mary flashed out at her, her own mind, in the same instant, leaping back to an image left on it that morning, but temporarily lost under layers of subsequent impressions.

"His hat had a wide brim, you mean? and his face was pale—a youngish face?" Mary pressed her, with a white-lipped intensity of interrogation. But if the kitchen-maid found any adequate answer to this challenge, it was swept away for her listener down the rushing current of her own convictions. The stranger—the stranger in the garden! Why had Mary not thought of him before? She needed no one now to tell her that it was he who had called for her husband and gone away with him. But who was he, and why had Boyne obeyed his call?

IV

It leaped out at her suddenly, like a grin out of the dark, that they had often called England so little—"such a confoundedly hard place to get lost in."

A confoundedly hard place to get lost in! That had been her husband's phrase. And now, with the whole machinery of official investigation sweeping its flash-lights from shore to shore, and across the dividing straits; now, with Boyne's name blazing from the walls of every town and village, his portrait (how that wrung her!) hawked up and down the country like the image of a hunted criminal; now the little compact, populous island, so policed, surveyed, and administered, revealed itself as a Sphinx-like guardian of abysmal mysteries, staring back into his wife's anguished eyes as if with the malicious joy of knowing something they would never know!

In the fortnight since Boyne's disappearance there had been no word of him, no trace of his movements. Even the usual misleading reports that raise expectancy in tortured bosoms had been few and fleeting. No one but the bewildered kitchen-maid had seen him leave the house, and no one else had seen "the gentleman" who accompanied him. All inquiries in the neighborhood failed to elicit the memory of a stranger's presence that day in the neighborhood of Lyng. And no one had met Edward Boyne, either alone or in company, in any of the neighboring villages, or on the road across the downs, or at either of the local railway-stations. The sunny English noon had swallowed him as completely as if he had gone out into Cimmerian night.

Mary, while every external means of investigation was working at its highest pressure, had ransacked her husband's papers for any trace of antecedent complications, of entanglements or obligations unknown to her, that might throw a faint ray into the darkness. But if any such had existed in the background of Boyne's life, they had disappeared as completely as the slip of paper on which the visitor had written his name. There remained no possible thread of guidance except—if it were indeed an exception—the letter which Boyne had apparently been in the act of writing when he received his mysterious summons. That letter, read and reread by his wife, and submitted by her to the police, yielded little enough for conjecture to feed on.

"I have just heard of Elwell's death, and while I suppose there is now no farther risk of trouble, it might be safer—" That was all. The "risk of trouble" was easily explained by the newspaper clipping which had apprised Mary of the suit brought against her husband by one of his associates in the Blue Star enterprise. The only new information conveyed in the letter was the fact of its showing Boyne, when he wrote it, to be still apprehensive of the results of the suit, though he had assured his wife that it had been withdrawn, and though the letter itself declared that the plaintiff was dead. It took several weeks of exhaustive cabling to fix the identity of the "Parvis" to whom the fragmentary communication was addressed, but even after these inquiries had shown him to be a Waukesha lawyer, no new facts concerning the Elwell suit were elicited. He appeared to have had no direct concern in it, but to have been conversant with the facts merely as an acquaintance, and possible intermediary; and he declared himself unable to divine with what object Boyne intended to seek his assistance.

This negative information, sole fruit of the first fortnight's feverish search, was not increased by a jot during the slow weeks that followed. Mary knew that the investigations were still being carried on, but she had a vague sense of their gradually slackening, as the actual march of time seemed to slacken. It was as though the days, flying horror-struck from the shrouded image of the one inscrutable day, gained assurance as the distance lengthened, till at last they fell back into their normal gait. And so with the human imaginations at work on the dark event. No doubt it occupied them still, but week by week and hour by hour it grew less absorbing, took up less space, was slowly but inevitably crowded out of the foreground of consciousness by the new problems perpetually bubbling up from the vaporous caldron of human experience.

Even Mary Boyne's consciousness gradually felt the same lowering of velocity. It still swayed with the incessant oscillations of conjecture; but they were slower, more rhythmical in their beat. There were moments of overwhelming lassitude when, like the victim of some poison which leaves the brain clear, but holds the body motionless, she saw herself domesticated with the Horror, accepting its perpetual presence as one of the fixed conditions of life.

These moments lengthened into hours and days, till she passed into a phase of stolid acquiescence. She watched the familiar routine of life with the incurious eye of a savage on whom the meaningless processes of civilization make but the faintest impression. She had come to regard herself as part of the routine, a spoke of the wheel, revolving with its motion; she felt almost like the furniture of the room in which she sat, an insensate object to be dusted and pushed about with the chairs and tables. And this deepening apathy held her fast at Lyng, in spite of the urgent entreaties of friends and the usual medical recommendation of "change." Her friends supposed that her refusal to move was inspired by the belief that her husband would one day return to the spot from which he had vanished, and a beautiful legend grew up about this imaginary state of waiting. But in reality she had no such belief: the depths of anguish inclosing her were no longer lighted by flashes of hope. She was sure that Boyne would never come back, that he had gone out of her sight as completely as if Death itself had waited that day on the threshold. She had even renounced, one by one, the various theories as to his disappearance which had been advanced by the press, the police, and her own agonized imagination. In sheer lassitude her mind turned from these alternatives of horror, and sank back into the blank fact that he was gone.

No, she would never know what had become of him—no one would ever know. But the house knew; the library in which she spent her long, lonely evenings knew. For it was here that the last scene had been enacted, here that the stranger had come, and spoken the word which had caused Boyne to rise and follow him. The floor she trod had felt his tread; the books on the shelves had seen his face; and there were moments when the intense consciousness of the old, dusky walls seemed about to break out into some audible revelation of their secret. But the revelation never came, and she knew it would never come. Lyng was not one of the garrulous old houses that betray the secrets intrusted to them. Its very legend proved that it had always been the mute accomplice, the incorruptible custodian of the mysteries it had surprised. And Mary Boyne, sitting face to face with its portentous silence, felt the futility of seeking to break it by any human means.

V

"I don't say it wasn't straight, yet don't say it was straight. It was business."

Mary, at the words, lifted her head with a start, and looked intently at the speaker.

When, half an hour before, a card with "Mr. Parvis" on it had been brought up to her, she had been immediately aware that the name had been a part of her consciousness ever since she had read it at the head of Boyne's unfinished letter. In the library she had found awaiting her a small neutral-tinted man with a bald head and gold eye-glasses, and it sent a strange tremor through her to know that this was the person to whom her husband's last known thought had been directed.

Parvis, civilly, but without vain preamble,—in the manner of a man who has his watch in his hand,—had set forth the object of his visit. He had "run over" to England on business, and finding himself in the neighborhood of Dorchester, had not wished to leave it without paying his respects to Mrs. Boyne; without asking her, if the occasion offered, what she meant to do about Bob Elwell's family.

The words touched the spring of some obscure dread in Mary's bosom. Did her visitor, after all, know what Boyne had meant by his unfinished phrase? She asked for an elucidation of his question, and noticed at once that he seemed surprised at her continued ignorance of the subject. Was it possible that she really knew as little as she said?

"I know nothing—you must tell me," she faltered out; and her visitor thereupon proceeded to unfold his story. It threw, even to her confused perceptions, and imperfectly initiated vision, a lurid glare on the whole hazy episode of the Blue Star Mine. Her husband had made his money in that brilliant speculation at the cost of "getting ahead" of some one less alert to seize the chance; the victim of his ingenuity was young Robert Elwell, who had "put him on" to the Blue Star scheme.

Parvis, at Mary's first startled cry, had thrown her a sobering glance through his impartial glasses.

"Bob Elwell wasn't smart enough, that's all; if he had been, he might have turned round and served Boyne the same way. It's the kind of thing that happens every day in business. I guess it's what the scientists call the survival of the fittest," said Mr. Parvis, evidently pleased with the aptness of his analogy.

Mary felt a physical shrinking from the next question she tried to frame; it was as though the words on her lips had a taste that nauseated her.

"But then—you accuse my husband of doing something dishonorable?"

Mr. Parvis surveyed the question dispassionately. "Oh, no, I don't. I don't even say it wasn't straight." He glanced up and down the long lines of books, as if one of them might have supplied him with the definition he sought. "I don't say it wasn't straight, and yet I don't say it was straight. It was business." After all, no definition in his category could be more comprehensive than that.

Mary sat staring at him with a look of terror. He seemed to her like the indifferent, implacable emissary of some dark, formless power.

"But Mr. Elwell's lawyers apparently did not take your view, since I suppose the suit was withdrawn by their advice."

"Oh, yes, they knew he hadn't a leg to stand on, technically. It was when they advised him to withdraw the suit that he got desperate. You see, he'd borrowed most of the money he lost in the Blue Star, and he was up a tree. That's why he shot himself when they told him he had no show."

The horror was sweeping over Mary in great, deafening waves.

"He shot himself? He killed himself because of *that?*"

"Well, he didn't kill himself, exactly. He dragged on two months before he died." Parvis emitted the statement as unemotionally as a gramophone grinding out its "record."

"You mean that he tried to kill himself, and failed? And tried again?"

"Oh, he didn't have to try again," said Parvis, grimly.

They sat opposite each other in silence, he swinging his eye-glass thoughtfully about his finger, she, motionless, her arms stretched along her knees in an attitude of rigid tension.

"But if you knew all this," she began at length, hardly able to force her voice above a whisper, "how is it that when I wrote you at the time of my husband's disappearance you said you didn't understand his letter?"

Parvis received this without perceptible discomfiture. "Why, I didn't understand it—strictly speaking. And it wasn't the time to talk about it, if I had. The Elwell business was settled when the suit was withdrawn. Nothing I could have told you would have helped you to find your husband."

Mary continued to scrutinize him. "Then why are you telling me now?"

Still Parvis did not hesitate. "Well, to begin with, I supposed you knew more than you appear to—I mean about the circumstances of Elwell's death. And then people are talking of it now; the whole matter's been raked up again. And I thought, if you didn't know, you ought to."

She remained silent, and he continued: "You see, it's only come out lately what a bad state Elwell's affairs were in. His wife's a proud woman, and she fought on as long as she could, going out to work, and taking sewing at home, when she got too sick—something with the heart, I believe. But she had his bedridden mother to look after, and the children, and she broke down under it, and finally had to ask for help. That attracted attention to the case, and the papers took it up, and a subscription was started. Everybody out there liked Bob Elwell, and most of the prominent names in the place are down on the list, and people began to wonder why—"

Parvis broke off to fumble in an inner pocket. "Here," he continued, "here's an account of the whole thing from the *Sentinel*—a little sensational, of course. But I guess you'd better look it over."

He held out a newspaper to Mary, who unfolded it slowly, remembering, as she did so, the evening when, in that same room, the perusal of a clipping from the *Sentinel* had first shaken the depths of her security.

As she opened the paper, her eyes, shrinking from the glaring head-lines, "Widow of Boyne's Victim Forced to Appeal for Aid," ran down the column of text to two portraits inserted in it. The first was her husband's, taken from a photograph made the year they had come to England. It was the picture of him that she liked best, the one that stood on the writing-table up-stairs in her bedroom. As the eyes in the photograph met hers, she felt it would be impossible to read what was said of him, and closed her lids with the sharpness of the pain.

"I thought if you felt disposed to put your name down—" she heard Parvis continue.

She opened her eyes with an effort, and they fell on the other portrait. It was that of a youngish man, slightly built, in rough clothes, with features somewhat blurred by the shadow of a projecting hat-brim. Where had she seen that outline before? She stared at it confusedly, her heart hammering in her throat and ears. Then she gave a cry.

"This is the man—the man who came for my husband!"

She heard Parvis start to his feet, and was dimly aware that she had slipped backward into the corner of the sofa, and that he was bending above her in alarm. With an intense effort she straightened herself, and reached out for the paper, which she had dropped.

"It's the man! I should know him anywhere!" she cried in a voice that sounded in her own ears like a scream.

Parvis's voice seemed to come to her from far off, down endless, fog-muffled windings.

"Mrs. Boyne, you're not very well. Shall I call somebody? Shall I get a glass of water?"

"No, no, no!" She threw herself toward him, her hand frantically clenching the newspaper. "I tell you, it's the man! I know him! He spoke to me in the garden!"

Parvis took the journal from her, directing his glasses to the portrait. "It can't be, Mrs. Boyne. It's Robert Elwell."

"Robert Elwell?" Her white stare seemed to travel into space. "Then it was Robert Elwell who came for him."

"Came for Boyne? The day he went away?" Parvis's voice dropped as hers rose. He bent over, laying a fraternal hand on her, as if to coax her gently back into her seat. "Why, Elwell was dead! Don't you remember?"

Mary sat with her eyes fixed on the picture, unconscious of what he was saying.

"Don't you remember Boyne's unfinished letter to me—the one you found on his desk that day? It was written just after he'd heard of Elwell's death." She noticed an odd shake in Parvis's unemotional voice. "Surely you remember that!" he urged her.

Yes, she remembered: that was the profoundest horror of it. Elwell had died the day before her husband's disappearance; and this was Elwell's portrait; and it was the portrait of the man who had spoken to her in the garden. She lifted her head and looked slowly about the library. The library could have borne witness that it was also the portrait of the man who had come in that day to call Boyne from his unfinished letter. Through the misty surgings of her brain she heard the faint boom of half-forgotten words—words spoken by Alida Stair on the lawn at Pangbourne before Boyne and his wife had ever seen the house at Lyng, or had imagined that they might one day live there.

"This was the man who spoke to me," she repeated.

She looked again at Parvis. He was trying to conceal his disturbance under what he imagined to be an expression of indulgent commiseration; but the edges of his lips were blue. "He thinks me mad; but I'm not mad," she reflected; and suddenly there flashed upon her a way of justifying her strange affirmation.

She sat quiet, controlling the quiver of her lips, and waiting till she could trust her voice to keep its habitual level; then she said, looking straight at Parvis: "Will you answer me one question, please? When was it that Robert Elwell tried to kill himself?"

"When—when?" Parvis stammered.

"Yes; the date. Please try to remember."

She saw that he was growing still more afraid of her. "I have a reason," she insisted gently.

"Yes, yes. Only I can't remember. About two months before, I should say."

"I want the date," she repeated.

Parvis picked up the newspaper. "We might see here," he said, still humoring her. He ran his eyes down the page. "Here it is. Last October—the—"

She caught the words from him. "The 20th, wasn't it?" With a sharp look at her, he verified. "Yes, the 20th. Then you *did* know?"

"I know now." Her white stare continued to travel past him. "Sunday, the 20th—that was the day he came first."

Parvis's voice was almost inaudible. "Came *here* first?"

"Yes."

"You saw him twice, then?"

"Yes, twice." She breathed it at him with dilated eyes. "He came first on the 20th of October. I remember the date because it was the day we went up Meldon Steep for the first time." She felt a faint gasp of inward laughter at the thought that but for that she might have forgotten.

Parvis continued to scrutinize her, as if trying to intercept her gaze.

"We saw him from the roof," she went on. "He came down the lime-avenue toward the house. He was dressed just as he is in that picture. My husband saw him first. He was frightened, and ran down ahead of me; but there was no one there. He had vanished."

"Elwell had vanished?" Parvis faltered.

"Yes." Their two whispers seemed to grope for each other. "I couldn't think what had happened. I see now. He *tried* to come then; but he wasn't dead enough—he couldn't reach us. He had to wait for two months; and then he came back again—and Ned went with him."

She nodded at Parvis with the look of triumph of a child who has successfully worked out a difficult puzzle. But suddenly she lifted her hands with a desperate gesture, pressing them to her bursting temples.

"Oh, my God! I sent him to Ned—I told him where to go! I sent him to this room!" she screamed out.

She felt the walls of the room rush toward her, like inward falling ruins;

and she heard Parvis, a long way off, as if through the ruins, crying to her, and struggling to get at her. But she was numb to his touch, she did not know what he was saying. Through the tumult she heard but one clear note, the voice of Alida Stair, speaking on the lawn at Pangbourne.

"You won't know till afterward," it said. "You won't know till long, long afterward."

THE SUCCUBUS

Honoré de Balzac

Translated by Jacques Le Clercq

Prologue

A number of persons of the noble country of Touraine, considerably edified by the warm search which the author is making into the antiquities, adventures, good jokes, and pretty tales of that blessed land, and believing for certain that he should know everything, have asked him (after drinking with him of course understood), if he had discovered the etymological reason, concerning which all the ladies of the town are so curious, and from which a certain street in Tours is called the Rue Chaude. By him it was replied, that he was much astonished to see that the ancient inhabitants had forgotten the great number of convents situated in this street, where the severe continence of the monks and nuns might have caused the walls to be made so hot that some woman of position should increase in size from walking too slowly along them to vespers. A troublesome fellow, wishing to appear learned, declared that formerly all the scandalmongers of the neighbourhood were wont to meet in this place. Another entangled himself in the minute suffrages of science, and poured forth golden words without being understood, qualifying words, harmonising the melodies of the ancient and modern, congregating customs, distilling verbs, alchemising all languages since the Deluge, of the Hebrew, Chaldeans, Egyptians, Greeks, Latins, and of Turnus, the ancient founder of Tours; and the good man finished by declaring that chaude or chaulde with the exception of the H and the L, came from Cauda, and that there was a tail in the affair, but the ladies only understood the end of it. An old man observed that in this same place was formerly a source of thermal water, of which his great great grandfather had drunk. In short, in less time than it takes a fly to embrace its sweetheart, there had been a pocketful of etymologies, in which the truth of the matter had been less easily found than a louse in the filthy beard of a Capuchin friar. But a man well learned and well informed, through having left his footprint in many monasteries, consumed much midnight oil, and manured his brain with many a volume—himself more encumbered with pieces, dyptic fragments, boxes, charters, and registers concerning the history of Touraine than is a gleaner with stalks of straw in the month of

August—this man, old, infirm, and gouty, who had been drinking in his corner without saying a word, smiled the smile of a wise man and knitted his brows, the said smile finally resolving itself into a pish! well articulated, which the Author heard and understood it to be big with an adventure historically good, the delights of which he would be able to unfold in this sweet collection.

To be brief, on the morrow this gouty old fellow said to him, "By your poem, which is called 'The Venial Sin,' you have forever gained my esteem, because everything therein is true from head to foot—which I believe to be a precious superabundance in such matters. But doubtless you do not know what became of the Moor placed in religion by the said knight, Bruyn de la Roche-Corbon. I know very well. Now if this etymology of the street harass you, and also the Egyptian nun, I will lend you a curious and antique parchment, found by me in the Olim of the episcopal palace, of which the libraries were a little knocked about at a period when none of us knew if he would have the pleasure of his head's society on the morrow. Now will not this yield you a perfect contentment?"

"Good!" said the author.

Then this worthy collector of truths gave certain rare and dusty parchments to the author, the which he has, not without great labour, translated into French, and which were fragments of a most ancient ecclesiastical process. He has believed that nothing would be more amusing than the actual resurrection of this antique affair, wherein shines forth the illiterate simplicity of the good old times. Now, then, give ear. This is the order in which were the manuscripts, of which the author has made use in his own fashion, because the language was devilishly difficult.

I

What the Succubus Was

In nomine Patris, et Filii, et Spiritus Sancti. Amen.

In the year of our Lord, one thousand two hundred and seventy-one, before me, Hierome Cornille, grand inquisitor and ecclesiastical judge (thereto commissioned by the members of the chapter of Saint Maurice, the cathedral of Tours, having of this deliberated in the presence of our Lord Jean de Montsoreau, archbishop—namely, the grievances and complaints of the inhabitants of the said town, whose request is here subjoined), have appeared certain noblemen, citizens, and inhabitants of the diocese, who have stated the following facts concerning a demon suspected of having taken the features of a woman, who has much afflicted the minds of the diocese, and is at present a prisoner in the jail of the chapter; and in order to arrive at the truth of the said charge we have opened the present court, this Monday, the eleventh day of December, after mass, to communicate the evidence of each witness to the said demon, to interrogate her upon the said crimes to her imputed, and to judge her according to the laws enforced *contra demonios.*

In this inquiry has assisted me to write the evidence therein given, Guillaume Tournebouche, rubrican of the chapter, a learned man.

Firstly has come before us one Jehan, surnamed Tortebras, a citizen of Tours, keeping by licence the hostelry of La Cigoyne, situated on the Place du Pont, and who has sworn by the salvation of his soul, his hand upon the holy Evangelists, to state no other thing than that which by himself hath been seen and heard.

He hath stated as here followeth:—

"I declare that about two years before the feast of St. Jehan, upon which are the grand illuminations, a gentleman, at first unknown to me, but belonging without doubt to our lord the King, and at that time returned to our country from the Holy Land, came to me with the proposition that I should let to him at rental a certain country-house by me built, in the quit rent of the chapter over against the place called of St. Etienne, and the which I let to him for nine years, for the consideration of three besans of fine gold. In the said house was placed by the said knight a fair wench having the appearance of a woman, dressed in the strange fashion of the Saracens Mohammedans, whom he would allow by none to be seen or to be approached within a bow-shot, but whom I have seen with mine own eyes, weird feathers upon her head, and eyes so flaming that I cannot adequately describe them, and from which gleamed forth a fire of hell. The defunct knight having threatened with death whoever should appear to spy about the said house, I have by reason of great fear left the said house, and I have until this day secretly kept to my mind certain presumptions and doubts concerning the bad appearance of the said foreigner, who was more strange than any woman, her equal not having as yet by me been seen.

"Many persons of all conditions having at the time believed the said knight to be dead, but kept upon his feet by virtue of the said charms, philters, spells, and diabolical sorceries of this seeming woman, who wished to settle in our country, I declare that I have always seen the said knight so ghastly pale that I can only compare his face to the wax of a Paschal candle, and to the knowledge of all the people of the hostelry of La Cigoyne, this knight was interred nine days after his first coming. According to the statement of his groom, the defunct had been chalorously coupled with the said Moorish woman during seven whole days shut up in my house, without coming out from her, the which I heard him horribly avow upon his deathbed. Certain persons at the present time have accused this she-devil of holding the said gentleman in her clutches by her long hair, the which was furnished with certain warm properties by means of which are communicated to Christians the flames of hell in the form of love, which work in them until their souls are by this means drawn from their bodies and possessed by Satan. But I declare that I have seen nothing of this excepting the said dead knight, bowelless, emaciated, wishing, in spite of his confessor, still to go to this wench; and then he has been recognized as the lord de Bueil, who was a crusader, and who was, according to certain persons of the town, under the spell of a demon whom he had met in the Asiatic country of Damascus or elsewhere.

"Afterwards I have let my house to the said unknown lady, according to the clauses of the deed of lease. The said lord of Bueil, being defunct, I had nevertheless been into my house in order to learn from the said foreign woman if she wished to remain in my dwelling, and after great trouble was led before her by a strange, half-naked black man, whose eyes were white.

"Then I have seen the said Moorish woman in a little room, shining with gold and jewels, lighted with strange lights, upon an Asiatic carpet, where she was seated, lightly attired, with another gentleman, who was there imperiling his soul; and I had not the heart bold enough to look upon her, seeing that her eyes would have incited me immediately to yield myself up to her, for already her voice thrilled into my very belly, filled my brain, and debauched my mind. Finding this, from the fear of God, and also of hell, I have departed with swift feet, leaving my house to her as long as she liked to retain it, so dangerous was it to behold that Moorish complexion from which radiated diabolical heats, besides a foot smaller than it was lawful in a real woman to possess; and to hear her voice, which pierced into one's heart! And from that day I have lacked the courage to enter my house from great fear of falling into hell. I have said my say."

To the said Tortebras we have then shown an Abyssinian, Nubian or Ethiopian, who, black from head to foot, had been found wanting in certain virile properties with which all good Christians are usually furnished, who, having persevered in his silence, after having been tormented and tortured many times, not without much moaning, has persisted in being unable to speak the language of our country. And the said Tortebras has recognized the said Abyss heretic as having been in his house in company with the said demoniacal spirit, and is suspected of having lent his aid to her sorcery.

And the said Tortebras has confessed his great faith in the Catholic religion, and declared no other things to be within his knowledge save certain rumours which were known to every one, of which he had been in no way a witness except in the hearing of them.

In obedience to the citations served upon him, has appeared then, Matthew, surname Cognefestu, a day-labourer of St. Etienne, whom, after having sworn by the holy Evangelists to speak the truth, has confessed to us always to have seen a bright light in the dwelling of the said foreign woman, and heard much wild and diabolical laughter on the days and nights of feasts and fasts, notably during the days of the holy and Christmas weeks, as if a great number of people were in the house. And he has sworn to have seen by the windows of the said dwellings, green buds of all kinds in the winter, growing as if by magic, especially roses in a time of frost, and other things for which there was a need of a great heat; but of this he was in no way astonished, seeing that the said foreigner threw out so much heat that when she walked in the evening by the side of his wall he found on the morrow his salad grown; and on certain occasions she had by the touching of her petticoats, caused the trees to put forth leaves and hasten the buds. Finally, the said, Cognefestu has declared to us to know no more, because he worked from early morning, and went to bed at the same hour as the fowls.

Afterwards the wife of the aforesaid Cognefestu has by us been required to state also upon oath the things come to her cognisance in this process, and has avowed naught save praises of the said foreigner, because since her coming her man had treated her better in consequence of the neighborhood of this good lady, who filled the air with love, as the sun did light, and other incongruous nonsense, which we have not committed to writing.

To the said Cognefestu and to his wife we have shown the said unknown African, who has been seen by them in the gardens of the house, and is stated by them for certain to belong to the said demon. In the third place, has advanced Harduin V, lord of Maille, who being by us reverentially begged to enlighten the religion of the church, has expressed his willingness so to do, and has, moreover, engaged his word, as a gallant knight, to say no other thing than that which he has seen. Then he has testified to have known in the army of the Crusades the demon in question, and in the town of Damascus to have seen the knight of Bueil, since defunct, fight at close quarters to be her sole possessor. The above-mentioned wench, or demon, belonged at that time to the knight Geoffroy IV, Lord of Roche-Pozay, by whom she was said to have been brought from Touraine, although she was a Saracen; concerning which the knights of France marvelled much, as well as at her beauty, which made a great noise and a thousand scandalous ravages in the camp. During the voyage this wench was the cause of many deaths, seeing that Roche-

Pozay had already discomfited certain Crusaders, who wished to keep her to themselves, because she shed, according to certain knights petted by her in secret, joys around her comparable to none others. But in the end the knight of Bueil, having killed Geoffroy de la Roche-Pozay, became lord and master of this young murderess, and placed her in a convent, or harem, according to the Saracen custom. About this time one used to see her and hear her chattering as entertainment many foreign dialects, such as the Greek or the Latin empire, Moorish, and, above all, French better than any of those who knew the language of France best in the Christian host, from which sprang the belief that she was demoniacal.

The said knight Harduin has confessed to us not to have tilted for her in the Holy Land, not from fear, coldness or other cause, so much as that he believed the time had arrived for him to bear away a portion of the true cross, and also he had belonging to him a noble lady of the Greek country, who saved him from this danger in denuding him of love, morning and night, seeing that she took all of it substantially from him, leaving him none in his heart or elsewhere for others.

And the said knight has assured us that the woman living in the country house of Tortebras, was really the said Saracen woman, come into the country from Syria, because he had been invited to a midnight feast at her house by the young Lord of Croixmare, who expired the seventh day afterwards, according to the statement of the Dame de Croixmare, his mother, ruined all points by the said wench, whose commerce with him had consumed his vital spirit, and whose strange phantasies had squandered his fortune.

Afterwards questioned in his quality of a man full of prudence, wisdom and authority in this country, upon the ideas entertained concerning the said woman, and summoned by us to open his conscience, seeing that it was a question of a most abominable case of Christian faith and divine justice, answer has been made by the said knight:—

That by certain of the host of Crusaders it has been stated to him that always this she-devil was a maid to him who embraced her, and that Mammon was for certain occupied in her, making for her a new virtue for each of her lovers, and a thousand other foolish sayings of drunken men, which were not of a nature to form a fifth gospel. But for a fact, he, an old knight on that turn of life, and knowing nothing more of the aforesaid, felt himself again a young man in that last supper with which he had been regaled by the lord of Croixmare; then the voice of this demon went straight to his heart before flowing into his ears, and had awakened so great a love in his body that his life was ebbing from the place whence it should flow, and that eventually, but for the assistance of Cyprus wine, which he had drunk to blind his sight, and his getting under the table in order no longer to gaze upon the fiery eyes of his diabolical hostess, and not to rend his heart from her, without doubt he would have fought the young Croixmare, in order to enjoy for a single moment this supernatural woman. Since then he had had absolution from his confessor for the wicked thought. Then, by advice from on high, he had carried back to his house his portion of the true Cross, and had remained in his own manor, where, in spite of his Christian precautions, the said voice still at certain times tickled his brain, and in the morning often had he in remembrance this demon, warm as brimstone; and because the look of this wench was so warm that it made him burn like a young man, be half dead, and because it cost him then many transshipments of the vital spirit, the said knight has requested us not to confront him with the empress of love to whom, if it were not the devil, God the Father had granted strange liberties with the minds of men. Afterwards, he retired, after reading over his statement, not without having first recognized the above-mentioned African to be the servant and page of the lady.

In the fourth place, upon the faith pledged in us in the name of the Chapter and of our Lord Archbishop, that he should not be tormented, tortured, nor harassed in any manner, nor further cited after his statement, in consequence of his commercial journeys, and upon the assurance that he should retire in perfect freedom, has come before us a Jew, Salomon al Rastchid, who, in spite of the infamy of his person and his Judaism, has been heard by us to this one end, to know everything concerning the conduct of the aforesaid demon. Thus he has not been required to take any oath this Salomon, seeing that he is beyond the pale of the Church, separated from us by the blood of our saviour (trucidatus Salvatore inter nos). Interrogated by us as to why he appeared without the green cap upon his head, and the yellow wheel in the apparent locality of the heart in his garment, according to the ecclesiastical and royal ordinances, the said de Rastchid has exhibited to us letters patent of the seneschal of Touraine and Poitou. Then the said Jew has declared to us to have done a large business for the lady dwelling in the house of the innkeeper Tortebras, to have sold to her golden chandeliers, with many branches, minutely engraved, plates of red silver, cups enriched with stones, emeralds and rubies; to have brought for her from the Levant a number of rare stuffs, Persian carpets, silks, and fine linen; in fact, things so magnificent that no queen in Christendom could say she was so well furnished with jewels and household goods; and that he had for his part received from her three hundred thousand pounds for the rarity of the purchases in which he had been employed, such as Indian flowers, poppingjays, birds' feathers, spices, Greek wines, and diamonds. Requested by us, the judge, to say if he had furnished certain ingredients of magical conjuration, the blood of new-born children, conjuring books, and things generally and whatsoever made use of by sorcerers, giving him licence to state his case without that thereupon he should be the subject to any further inquest or inquiry, the said al Rastchid has sworn by his Hebrew faith never to have had any such commerce; and has stated that he was involved in too high interests to give himself to such miseries, seeing that he was the agent of certain most powerful lords, such as the Marquis de Montferrat, the King of England, the King of Cyprus and Jerusalem, the Court of Provence, lords of Venice, and many German gentleman; to have belonging to him merchant galleys of all kinds, going into Egypt with the permission of the Sultan, and he trafficking in precious articles of silver and of gold, which took him often into the exchange of Tours. Moreover, he has declared that he considered the said lady, the subject of inquiry, to be a right royal and natural woman, with the sweetest limbs, and the smallest he has ever seen. That in consequence of her renown for a diabolical spirit, pushed by a wild imagination, and also because that he was smitten with her, he had heard once that she was husbandless, proposed to her to be her gallant, to which proposition she willingly acceded. Now, although from that night he felt his bones disjointed and his bowels crushed, he had not yet experienced, as certain persons say, that who once yielded was free no more; he went to his fate as lead into the crucible of the alchemist. Then the said Salomon, to whom we have granted his liberty according to the safe conduct, in spite of the statement, which proves abundantly his commerce with the devil, because he had been saved there where all Christians have succumbed, has admitted to us an agreement concerning the said demon. To make known that he had made an offer to the chapter of the cathedral to give for the said semblance of a woman such a ransom, if she were condemned to be burned alive, that the highest of the towers of the Church of St. Maurice, at present in course of construction, could therewith be finished.

The which we have noted to be deliberated upon at an opportune time by the assembled chapter. And the said Salomon has taken his departure without being willing to indicate his residence, and has told us that he can be informed of the deliberation of the chapter by a Jew of the synagogue of Tours, a name Tobias Nathaneus. The said Jew has before his departure been shown the African, and has recognised him as the page of the demon, and has stated the Saracens to have the custom of mutilating their slaves thus, to commit to them the task of guarding their women by an ancient usage, as it appears in the profane histories of Narsez, general of Constantinople, and others.

On the morrow after mass has appeared before us the most noble and illustrious lady of Croixmare. The same has worn her faith in the holy

Evangelists, and has related to us with tears how she had placed her eldest son beneath the earth, dead by reason of his extravagant amours with this female demon. The which noble gentleman was three-and-twenty years of age; of good complexion, very manly and well bearded like his defunct sire. Notwithstanding his great vigour, in ninety days he had little by little withered, ruined by his commerce with the succubus of the Rue Chaude, according to the statement of the common people; and her maternal authority over the son had been powerless. Finally in his latter days he appeared like a poor dried up worm, such as housekeepers meet with in a corner when they clean out the dwelling-rooms. And always, so long as he had the strength to go, he went to shorten his life with this cursed woman; where, also, he emptied his cash-box. When he was in his bed, and knew his last hour had come, he swore at, cursed, and threatened and heaped upon all—his sister, his brother, and upon her his mother—a thousand insults, rebelled in the face of the chaplain; denied God, and wished to die in damnation; at which were much afflicted the retainers of the family, who, to save his soul and pluck it from hell, have founded two annual masses in the cathedral. And in order to have him buried in consecrated ground, the house of Croixmare has undertaken to give to the chapter, during one hundred years, the wax candles for the chapels and the church, upon the day of the Paschal feast. And, in conclusion, saving the wicked words heard by the reverend person, Dom Loys Pot, a nun of Marmoustiers, who came to assist in his last hours the said Baron de Croixmaire affirms never to have heard any words offered by the defunct, touching the demon who had undone him.

And therewith has retired the noble and illustrious lady in deep mourning.

In the sixth place has appeared before us, after adjournment, Jacquette, called Vieux-Oing, a kitchen scullion, going to houses to wash dishes, residing at present in the Fishmarket, who, after having placed her word to say nothing she did not hold to be true, has declared as here follows:—Namely, that one day she, being come into the kitchen of the said demon, of whom she had no fear, because she was wont to regale herself only upon males, she had the opportunity of seeing in the garden this female demon, superbly attired, walking in company with a knight, with whom she was laughing, like a natural woman. Then she had recognised in this demon that true likeness of the Moorish woman placed as a nun in the convent of Notre Dame de l'Egrignolles by the defunct seneschal of Touraine and Poitou, Messire Bruyn, Count of Roche-Corbon, the which Moorish woman had been left in the situation and place of the image of our Lady the Virgin, the mother of our Blessed Saviour, stolen by the Egyptians about eighteen years since. Of this time, in consequence of the troubles come about in Touraine, no record has been kept. This girl, aged about twelve years, was saved from the stake at which she would have been burned by being baptised; and the said defunct and his wife had then been godfather and godmother to this child of hell. Being at that time laundress at the convent, she who bears witness has remembrance of the flight which the said Egyptian took twenty months after her entry into the convent, so subtilely that it has never been known how or by what means she escaped. At that time it was thought by all, that with the devil's aid she had flown away in the air, seeing that not withstanding much search, no trace of her flight was found in the convent, where everything remained in its accustomed order.

The African having been shown to the said scullion, she has declared not to have seen him before, although she was curious to do so, as he was commissioned to guard the place in which the Moorish woman combated with those whom she drained through the spigot.

In the seventh place has been brought before us Hugues de Fou, son of the Sieur de Bridore, who, aged twenty years, has been placed in the hands of his father, under caution of his estates, and by him is represented in this process, whom it concerns if should be duly attained and convicted of having, assisted by several unknown and bad young men, laid siege to the jail of the archbishop and of the chapter, and of having lent himself to disturb the force of ecclesiastical justice, by causing the escape of the demon now under consideration. In spite of the evil disposition we have commanded the said Hugues de Fou to testify truly, touching the things he should know concerning the said demon, with whom he is vehemently reputed to have had commerce, pointing out to him that it was a question of his salvation and of the life of the said demon. He, after having taken the oath, he said:—

"I swear by my eternal salvation, and by the holy Evangelists here present under my hand, to hold the woman suspected of being a demon to be an angel, a perfect woman, and even more so in mind than in body, living in all honesty, full of the migniard charms and delights of love, in no way wicked, but most generous, assisting greatly the poor and suffering. I declare that I have seen her weeping veritable tears for the death of my friend, the knight of Croixmare. And because on that day she had made a vow to our Lady the Virgin no more to receive the love of young noblemen too weak in her service; she has to me constantly and with great courage denied the enjoyment of her body, and has only granted to me love, and the possession of her heart, of which she has made sovereign. Since this gracious gift, in spite of my increasing flame I have remained alone in her dwelling, where I have spent the greater part of my days, happy in seeing and in hearing her. Oh! I would eat near her, partake of the air which entered into her lungs, of the light which shone in her sweet eyes, and found in this occupation more joy than have the lords of paradise. Elected by me to be forever my lady, chosen to be one day my dove, my wife, and only sweetheart, I, poor fool, have received from her no advances on the joys of the future, but, on the contrary, a thousand virtuous admonitions; such as that I should acquire renown as a good knight, become a strong man and a fine one, fear nothing except God; honour the ladies, serve but one and love them in memory of that one; that when I should be strengthened by the work of war, if her heart still pleased mine, at that time only would she be mine, because she would be able to wait for me, loving me so much."

So saying the young Sire Hugues wept, and weeping, added:—

"That thinking of this graceful and feeble woman, whose arms seemed scarcely large enough to sustain the light weight of her golden chains, he did not know how to contain himself while fancying the irons which would wound her, and the miseries with which she would traitorously be loaded, and from this cause came his rebellion. And that he had licence to express his sorrow before justice, because his life was so bound up with that of his delicious mistress and sweetheart that on the day when evil came to her he would surely die."

And the same young man has vociferated a thousand other praises of the said demon, which bear witness to the vehement sorcery practised upon him, and prove, moreover, the abominable, unalterable, and incurable life and the fraudulent witcheries to which he is at present subject, concerning which our lord the archbishop will judge, in order to save by exorcisms and penitences this young soul from the snares of hell, if the devil has not gained too strong a hold of it.

Then we have handed back the said young nobleman into the custody of the noble lord his father, after that by the said Hugues, the African has been recognised as the servant of the accused.

In the eighth place, before us, have the footguards of our lord the archbishop led in great state the *Most High and Reverend Lady Jacqueline de Champchevrier, Abbess of the Convent of Notre-Dame*, under the invocation of Mount Carmel, to whose control has been submitted by the late seneschal of Touraine, father of Monseigneur the Count of Roche-Corbon, present advocate of the said convent, the Egyptian, named at the baptismal font Blanche Bruyn.

To the said abbess we have shortly stated the present cause, in which is involved the holy church, the glory of God, and the eternal future of the people of the diocese afflicted with a demon, and also the life of a creature who it was possible might be quite innocent. Then the cause elaborated, we have requested the said noble abbess to testify that which was within her knowledge concerning the magical disappearance of her daughter in God, Blanche Bruyn, espoused by our Saviour under the name of Sister Clare.

Then has stated the very high, very noble, and very illustrious lady abbess as follows:—

"The Sister Clare, of origin to her unknown, but suspected to be of an heretic father and mother, people inimical to God, has truly been placed in religion in the convent of which the government had canonically come to her in spite of her unworthiness; that the said sister had properly concluded her noviciate, and made her vows according to the holy rule of the order. That the vows taken, she had fallen into great sadness, and had much drooped. Interrogated by her, the abbess, concerning her melancholy malady, the said sister had replied with tears that she herself did not know the cause. That one thousand and one tears engendered themselves in her at feeling no more her splendid hair upon her head; that besides this she thirsted for air, and could not resist her desire to jump up into the trees, to climb and tumble about according to her wont during her open air life; that she passed her nights in tears, dreaming of the forests under the leaves of which in other days she slept; and in remembrance of this she abhorred the quality of the air of the cloisters, which troubled her respiration; that in her inside she was troubled with evil vapours; that at times she was inwardly diverted in church by thoughts which made her lose countenance. Then I have repeated over and over again to the poor creature the holy directions of the church, have reminded her of the eternal happiness which women without seeing enjoy in paradise, and how transitory was life here below, and certain the goodness of God, who for first certain bitter pleasures lost, kept for us a love without end. In spite of this wise maternal advice the evil spirit has persisted in the said sister; and always would she gaze upon the leaves of the trees and grass of the meadows through the windows of the church during the offices and times of prayer; and persisted in becoming as white as linen in order that she might stay in her bed, and at certain times she would run about the cloisters like a goat broken loose from its fastening. Finally, she had grown thin, lost much of the great beauty, and shrunk away to nothing. While in this condition by us, the abbess her mother, was she placed in the sick-room, we daily expecting her to die. One winter's morning the said sister had fled, without leaving any trace of her steps, without breaking the door, forcing of locks, or opening of windows, nor any sign whatever of the manner of her passage; a frightful adventure which was believed to have taken place by the aid of the demon which has annoyed and tormented her. For the rest it was settled by the authorities of the metropolitan church that the mission of this daughter of hell was to divert the nuns from their holy ways, and blinded by their perfect lives, she had returned through the air on the wings of the sorcerer, who had left her for mockery of our holy religion in the place of our Virgin Mary."

The which having said, the lady abbess was, with great honour and according to the command of our lord the archbishop, accompanied as far as the convent of Carmel.

In the ninth place, before us has come, agreeably to the citation served upon him, Joseph, called Leschalopier, a money-changer, living on the bridge at the sign of the Besant d'Or, who, after having pledged his Catholic faith to say no other thing than the truth, and that known to him, touching the process before the ecclesiastical tribunal, has testified as follows:—

"I am a poor father, much afflicted by the sacred will of God. Before the coming of the Succubus of the Rue Chaude, I had, for all good, a son as handsome as a noble, learned as a clerk, and having made more than a dozen voyages into foreign lands; for the rest a good Catholic; keeping himself on guard against the needles of love, because he avoided marriage, knowing himself to be the support of my old days, the love for my eyes, and the constant delight of my heart. He was a son of whom the King of France might have been proud—a good and courageous man, the light on my commerce, the joy of my roof, and, above all, an inestimable blessing, seeing that I am alone in the world, having had the misfortune to lose my wife, and being too old to take another. Now, monseigneur, this treasure without equal has been taken from me, and cast into hell by the demon. Yes, my lord judge, directly he beheld this mischievous jade, this she-devil, in whom it is a whole workshop of perdition, a conjunction of pleasure and delectation, and whom nothing can satiate, my poor child stuck himself fast into the gluepot of love, and afterwards lived only between the columns of Venus, and there did not live long, because in that place like so great a heat that nothing can satisfy the thirst of this gulf, not even should you plunge therein the germs of the entire world. Alas! then, my poor boy—his fortune, his generative hopes, his eternal future, his entire self, more than himself, have been engulfed in this sewer, like a grain of corn in the jaws of a bull. By this means become an old orphan I, who speak, shall have no greater joy than to see burning, this demon, nourished with blood and gold. This Arachne who has drawn out and sucked more marriages, more families in the seed, more hearts, more Christians then there are lepers in all the lazar houses or Christendom. Burn, torment this fiend—this vampire who feeds on souls, this tigerish nature that drinks blood, this amorous lamp in which burns the venom of all the vipers. Close this abyss, the bottom of which no man can find . . . I offer my deniers to the chapter for the stake, and my arm to light the fire. Watch well, my lord judge, to surely guard this devil, seeing that she has a fire more flaming than all other terrestrial fires; she has all the fire of hell in her, the strength of Samson in her hair, and the sound of celestial music in her voice. She charms to kill the body and the soul at one stroke; she smiles to bite, she kisses to devour; in short, she would wheedle an angel, and make him deny his God. My son! my son! where is he at this hour? The flower of my life—a flower cut by this feminine needlecase as with scissors. Ha, lord! why have I been called? Who will give me back my son, whose soul has been absorbed by a womb which gives death to all, and life to none? The devil alone copulates, and engenders not. This is my evidence, which I pray Master Tournebouche to write without omitting one iota, and to grant me a schedule, that I may tell it to God every evening in my prayer, to this end to make the blood of the innocent cry aloud into His ears, and to obtain from His infinite mercy the pardon for my son."

Here followed twenty and seven other statements, of which the transcription in their true objectivity, in all their quality of space would be over-fastidious, would draw to a great length, and divert the thread of this curious process—a narrative which, according to ancient precepts, should go straight to the fact, like a bull to his principal office. Therefore, here is, in a few words, the substance of these testimonies.

A great number of good Christians, townsmen and townswomen, inhabitants of the noble town of Tours, testified the demon to have held every day wedding feasts and royal festivities, never to have been seen in any church, to have cursed God, to have mocked the priests, never to have crossed herself in any place; to have spoken all the languages of the earth—a gift which has only been granted by God to the blessed Apostles; to have been many times met in the fields, mounted upon an unknown animal who went before the clouds; not to grow old, and to have always a youthful face; to have received the father and the son on the same day, saying that her door sinned not; to have visible malign influences which flowed from her, for that a pastrycook, seated on a bench at her door, having perceived her one evening, received such a gust of warm love that, going in and getting to bed, he had with great passion embraced his wife, and was found dead on the morrow, that the old men of the town went to spend the remainder of their days and of their money with her, to taste the joys of the sins of their youth, and that they died like fleas on their bellies, and that certain of them, while dying, became as black as Moors; that this demon never allowed herself to be seen neither at dinner, nor at breakfast, nor at supper, but ate alone, because she lived upon human brains; that several had seen her during the night go to the cemeteries, and there embrace the young dead men, because she was not able to assuage otherwise the devil who worked in her entrails, and there raged like a tempest, and from that came the astringent biting, nitrous shooting, precipitant, and diabolical movements, squeezings, and writhings of love and voluptuousness, from which several men had emerged bruised, torn, bitten, pinched and crushed; and that since the coming of our Saviour, who had imprisoned the master devil in the bellies of the swine, no malignant beast had ever been seen in any portion of the earth so mischievous, venomous and so clutching; so much so that if one threw the town of Tours into this field of Venus, she would there transmute it into the grain of cities, and this demon would swallow it like a strawberry.

And a thousand other statements, sayings, and depositions, from which was evident in perfect clearness the infernal generation of this woman, daughter, sister, niece, spouse, or brother of the devil, beside abundant proofs of her evil doing, and of the calamity spread by her in all families. And if it were possible to put them here conformably with the catalogue preserved by the good man to whom he accused the discovery, it would seem like a sample of the horrible cries which the Egyptians gave forth on the day of the seventh plague. Also this examination has covered with great honour Messire Guillaume Tournebouche, by whom are quoted all the memoranda. In the tenth vacation was thus closed this inquest, arriving at a maturity of proof, furnished with authentic testimony and sufficiently engrossed with the particulars, plaints, interdicts, contradictions, charges, assignments, withdrawals, confessions public and private, oaths, adjournments, appearances and controversies, to which the said demon must reply. And the townspeople say everywhere if there were really a she-devil, and furnished with internal horns planted in her nature, with which she drank the men, and broke them, this woman might swim a long time in this sea of writing before being landed safe and sound in hell.

II

The Proceedings Taken Relative to This Female Vampire

In nomine Patris, et Filii, et Spiritus Sancti. Amen.

In the year of our Lord one thousand two hundred and seventy-one, before us, Hierome Cornille, grand penitentiary and ecclesiastical judge to this, canonically appointed, have appeared—

The Sire Philippe d'Idre, bailiff of the town and city of Tours and province of Touraine, living in his hotel in the Rue de la Rotisserie, in Chateauneuf; Master Jehan Ribou, provost of the brotherhood and company of drapers, residing on the Quay de Bretaingne, at the image of St. Pierre-es-liens; Messire Antoine Jehan, alderman and chief of the Brotherhood of Changers, residing in the Place du Pont, at the image of St. Mark-counting-tournoise-pounds; Master Martin Beaupertuys, captain of the archers of the town residing at the castle; Jehan Rabelais, a ships' painter and boat maker residing at the port at the isle of St. Jacques, treasurer of the brotherhood of the mariners of the Loire; Mark Hierome, called Maschefer, hosier, at the sign of Saint-Sebastian, president of the trades council; and Jacques, called de Villedomer, master tavern-keeper and vine dresser, residing in the High Street, at the Pomme de Pin; to the said Sire d'Idre, and to the said citizens, we have read the following petition by them, written, signed, and deliberated upon, to be brought under the notice of the ecclesiastical tribunal:—

PETITION

We, the undersigned, all citizens of Tours, are come into the hotel of his worship the Sire d'Idre, bailiff of Touraine, in the absence of our mayor, and have requested him to hear our plaints and statements concerning the following facts, which we intend to bring before the tribunal of the archbishop, the judge of ecclesiastical crimes, to whom should be deferred the conduct of the cause which we here expose:—

A long time ago there came into this town a wicked demon in the form of a woman, who lives in the parish of Saint-Etienne, in the house of the innkeeper Tortebras, situated in the quit-rent of the chapter, and under the temporal jurisdiction of the archiepiscopal domain. The which foreigner carries on the business of a gay woman in a prodigal and abusive manner, and with such increase of infamy that she threatens to ruin the Catholic faith in this town, because those who go to her come back again with their souls lost in every way, and refuse the assistance of the Church with a thousand scandalous discourses.

Now considering that a great number of those who yielded to her are dead, and that arrived in our town with no other wealth than her beauty, she has, according to public clamour, infinite riches and right royal treasure, the acquisition of which is vehemently attributed to sorcery, or at least to robberies committed by the aid of magical attractions and her supernaturally amorous person.

Considering that it is a question of the honour and security of our families, and that never before has been seen in this country a woman wild of body or a daughter of pleasure, carrying on with such mischief of vocation of light o' love, and menacing so openly and bitterly the life, the savings, the morals, chastity, religion, and the everything of the inhabitants of this town;

Considering that there is need of a inquiry into her person, her wealth and her deportment, in order to verify if these effects of love are legitimate, and to not proceed, as would seem indicated by her manners, from a bewitchment of Satan, who often visits Christianity under the form of a female, as appears in the holy books, in which it is stated that our blessed Saviour was carried away into a mountain, from which Lucifer or Astaroth showed him the fertile plains of Judea and that in many places have been seen succubi or demons, having the faces of women, who, not wishing to return to hell, and having with them an insatiable fire, attempt to refresh and sustain themselves by sucking in souls;

Considering that in the case of the said woman a thousand proofs of diablerie are met with, of which certain inhabitants speak openly, and that it is necessary for the repose of the said woman that the matter be sifted, in order that she shall not be attacked by certain people, ruined by the result of her wickedness;

For these causes we pray that it will please you to submit to our spiritual lord, father of this diocese, the most noble and blessed archbishop Jehan de Monsoreau, the troubles of his afflicted flock, to the end that he may advise upon them.

By doing so you will fulfil the duties of your office, as we do those of preservers of the security of this town, each one according to the things of which he has charge in his locality.

And we have signed the present, in the year of our Lord one thousand two hundred and seventy-one, of All Saints' Day, after mass.

Master Tournebouche having finished the reading of this petition, by us, Hierome Cornille, has it been said to the petitioners—

"Gentlemen, do you, at the present time, persist in these statements? have you proofs other than those come within your own knowledge, and do you undertake to maintain the truth of this before God, before man, and before the accused?"

All, with the exception of Master Jehan Rabelais, have persisted in their belief, and the aforesaid Rabelais has withdrawn from the process, saying that he considered the said Moorish woman to be a natural woman and a good wench who had no other fault than that of keeping up a very high temperature of love.

Then we, the judge appointed, have, after mature deliberation, found matter upon which to proceed in the petition of the aforesaid citizens, and have commanded that the woman at present in the jail of the chapter shall be proceeded against by all legal methods, as written in the canons and ordinances, *contra demonios*. The said ordinance, embodied in a writ, shall be published by the town-crier in all parts, and with the sound of the trumpet, in order to make it known to all, and that each witness may, according to his knowledge, be confronted with the said demon, and finally the said accused to be provided with a defender, according to custom, and the interrogations, and the process to be congruously conducted.

(Signed) HIEROME CORNILLE.

And, lower down.

TOURNEBOUCHE.

In nomine Patris, et Filii, et Spiritus Sancti. Amen.

In the year of our Lord one thousand two hundred and seventy-one, the 10th day of February, after mass, by command of us, Hierome Cornille, ecclesiastical judge, has been brought from the jail of the chapter and led before us the woman taken in the house of the innkeeper Tortebras, situated in the domains of the chapter and the cathedral of St. Maurice, and are subject to the temporal and seigneurial justice of the Archbishop of Tours; besides which, in consequence of the nature of the crimes imputed to her, she is liable to the tribunal and council of ecclesiastical justice, the which we have made known to her, to the end that she should not ignore it.

And after a serious reading, entirely at will understood by her, in the first place of the petition of the town, then of the statements, plaints, accusations, and proceedings which written in twenty-four quires by Master Tournebouche, and are above related, we have, with the invocation and assistance of God and the Church, resolved to ascertain the truth, first by interrogatories made to the said accused.

In the first interrogation we have requested the aforesaid to inform us in what land or town she had been born. By her who speaks was it answered: "In Mauritania."

We have then inquired: "If she had a father or mother, or any relations?" By her who speaks has it been replied: "That she had never known them." By us requested to declare her name. By her who speaks has been replied: "Zulma," in Arabian tongue.

By us has it been demanded: "Why she spoke our language?" By her who speaks has it been said: "Because she had come into this country." By us has it been asked: "At what time?" By her who speaks has it been replied: "About twelve years."

By us has it been asked: "What age she then was?" By her who speaks has it been answered: "Fifteen years or thereabout."

By us has it been said: "Then you acknowledge yourself to be twenty-seven years of age?" By her who speaks has it been replied: "Yes."

By us has it been said to her: "That she was then the Moorish child found in the niche of Madame the Virgin, baptised by the Archbishop, held at the font by the late Lord of Roche-Corbon and the Lady of Azay, his wife, afterwards by them placed in religion at the convent of Mount Carmel, where by her had been made vows of chastity, poverty, silence, and the love of God, under the divine assistance of St. Clare?" By her who speaks has been said: "That is true."

By us has it been asked her: "If, then, she allowed to be true the declarations of the very noble and illustrious lady the abbess of Mount Carmel, also the statements of Jacquette, called Vieux-Oing, being kitchen scullion?" By the accused has been answered: "These words are true in great measure."

Then by us has it been said to her: "Then you are a Christian?" And by her who speaks has been answered: "Yes, my father."

Then by us has she been requested to make the sign of the cross, and to take holy water from the brush placed by Master Tournebouche in her hand; the which having been done, and by us having been witnessed, it has been admitted as an indisputable fact, that Zulma, the Moorish woman, called in our country Blanche Bruyn, a nun of the convent under the invocation of Mount Carmel, there named Sister Clare, and suspected to be the false appearance of a woman under which is concealed a demon, has in our presence made act of religion and thus recognised the justice of the ecclesiastical tribunal.

Then by us have these words been said to her: "My daughter, you are vehemently suspected to have had recourse to the devil from the manner in which you left the convent, which was supernatural in every way." By her who speaks has it been stated, that she at that time gained naturally the fields by the street door after vespers, enveloped in the robes of Jehan de Marsilis, visitor of the convent, who had hidden her, the person speaking, in a little hovel belonging to him, situated in the Cupidon Lane, near a tower in the town. That there this said priest had to her then speaking, at great length, and most thoroughly taught the depths of love, of which she then speaking was before in all points ignorant, for which delights she had a great taste, finding them of great use. That the Sire d'Amboise having perceived her then speaking at the window of this retreat, had been smitten with a great love for her. That she loved him more heartily than the monk, and fled from the hovel where she was detained for profit of his pleasure by Don Marsilis. And then she had gone in great haste to Amboise, the castle of the said lord, where she had had a thousand pastimes, hunting, and dancing, and beautiful dresses fit for a queen. One day the Sire de la Roche-Pozay having been invited by the Sire d'Amboise to come and feast and enjoy himself, the Baron d'Amboise had allowed him to see her then speaking, as she came out naked from her bath. That at this sight the said Sire de la Roche-Pozay having fallen violently in love with her, had on the morrow discomfited in single combat the Sire d'Amboise, and by great violence, had, is spite of her tears, taken her to the Holy Land, where she who was speaking had lived the life of a woman well beloved, and had been held in great respect on account of her great beauty. That after numerous adventures, she who was speaking had returned into this country in spite of the apprehensions of misfortune, because such was the will of her lord and master, the Baron de Bueil, who was dying of grief in Asiatic lands, and desired to return to his patrimonial manor. Now he had promised her who was speaking to preserve her from peril. Now she who was speaking had faith and belief in him, the more so as she loved him very much; but on his arrival in this country, the Sire de Bueil was seized with an illness, and died deplorably, without taking any remedies, this spite of the fervent requests which she who was speaking had addressed to him, but without success, because he hated physicians, master surgeons, and apothecaries; and that this was the whole truth.

Then by us has it been said to the accused that she then held to be true the statements of the good Sire Harduin and of the innkeeper Tortebras. By her who speaks has it been replied, that she recognized as evidence the greater part, and also as malicious, calumnious, and imbecile certain portions.

Then by us has the accused been required to declare if she had had pleasure and carnal commerce with all the men, nobles, citizens, and others as set forth in the plaints and declarations of the inhabitants. To which her who speaks has it been answered with great effrontery: "Pleasure, yes! Commerce, I do not know."

By us has it been said to her, that all had died by her acts. By her who speaks has it been said that their deaths could not be the result of her acts, because she had always refused herself to them, and the more she fled from them the more they came and embraced her with infinite passion, and that when she who was speaking was taken by them she gave herself up to them with all her strength, by the grace of God, because she had in that more joy than in anything, and has stated, she who speaks, that she avows her secret sentiments solely because she had been requested by us to state the whole truth, and that she the speaker stood in great fear of the torments of the torturers.

Then by us has she been requested to answer, under pain of torture, in what state of mind she was when a young nobleman died in consequence of his commerce with her. Then by her speaking has it been replied, that she remained quite melancholy and wished to destroy herself; and prayed God, the Virgin, and the saints to receive her into Paradise, because never had she met with any but lovely and good hearts in which was no guile, and beholding them die she fell into a great sadness, fancying herself to be an evil creature or subject to an evil fate, which she communicated like the plague.

Then by us has she been requested to state where she paid her orisons.

By her speaking has it been said that she played in her oratory on her knees before God, who according to the Evangelists, sees and hears all things and resides in all places.

Then by us has it been demanded why she never frequented the churches, the offices, nor the feasts. To this by her speaking has it been answered, that those who came to love her had elected the feast days for that purpose, and that she speaking did all things to their liking.

By us has it been remonstrated that, by so doing, she was submissive to man rather than to the commandments of God.

Then by her speaking has it been stated, that for those who loved her well she speaking would have thrown herself into a flaming pile, never having followed in her love any course but that of nature, and that for the weight of the world in gold she would not have lent her body or her love to a king who did not love her with his heart, feet, hair, forehead, and all over. In short and moreover the speaker had never made an act of harlotry in selling one single grain of love to a man whom she had not chosen to be hers, and that he who held her in his arms one hour or kissed her on the mouth a little, possessed her for the remainder of her days.

Then by us has she been requested to state whence preceded the jewels, gold plate, silver, precious stones, regal furniture, carpets, et cetera, worth 200,000 doubloons, according to the inventory found in her residence and placed in the custody of the treasurer of the chapter. By the speaker answer has been made, that in us she placed all her hopes, even as much as in God, but that she dare not reply to this, because it involved the sweetest things of love upon which she had always lived. And interpellated anew, the speaker has said that if the judge knew with what fervour she held him she loved, with what obedience she followed him in good or evil ways, with what study she submitted to him, with what happiness she listened to his desires, and inhaled the sacred words with which his mouth gratified her, in what adoration she held his person, even we, an old judge, would believe with her well-beloved, that no sum could pay for this great affection which all the men ran after. After the speaker has declared never from any man loved by her, to have solicited any present or gift, and that she rested perfectly contented to live in their hearts, that she would there curl herself up with indestructible and ineffable pleasure, finding herself richer with this heart than with anything, and thinking of no other thing than to give them more pleasure and happiness than she received from them. But in spite of the iterated refusals of the speaker her lovers persisted in graciously rewarding her. At times one came to her with a necklace of pearls, saying, "This is to show my darling that the satin of her skin did not falsely appear to me whiter than pearls" and would put it on the speaker's neck, kissing her lovingly. The speaker would be angry at these follies, but could not refuse to keep a jewel that gave them pleasure to see it there where they placed it. Each one had a different fancy. At times another liked to tear the precious garments which the speaker wore to gratify him; another to deck out the speaker with sapphires on her arms, on her legs, on her neck, and in her hair; another to seat her on the carpet, clad in silk or black velvet, and to remain for days together in ecstasy at the perfections of the speaker the whom the things desired by her lovers gave infinite pleasure, because these things rendered them quite happy. And the speaker has said, that as we love nothing so much as our pleasure, and wish that everything should shine in beauty and harmonize, outside as well as inside the heart, so they all wished to see the place inhabited by the speaker adorned with handsome objects, and from this idea all her lovers were pleased as much as she was in spreading thereabout gold, silks and flowers. Now seeing that these lovely things spoil nothing, the speaker had no force or commandment by which to prevent a knight, or even a rich citizen beloved by her, having his will, and thus found herself constrained to receive rare perfumes and other satisfaction with which the speaker was loaded, and that such was the source of the gold, plate, carpets, and jewels seized at her house by the officers of justice. This terminates the first interrogation made to the said Sister Clare, suspected to be a demon, because we the judge and Guillaume Tournebouche, are greatly fatigued with having the voice of the aforesaid, in our ears, and finding our understanding in every way muddled.

By us the judge has the second interrogatory been appointed, three days from to-day, in order that the proofs of the possession and presence of the demon in the body of the aforesaid may be sought, and the accused, according to the order of the judge, has been taken back to the jail under the conduct of Master Guillaume Tournebouche.

In nomine Patris, et Filii, et Spiritus Sancti. Amen.

On the thirteenth day following of the said month of the February before us, Hierome Cornille, et cetera, has been produced the Sister Clare above-mentioned, in order to be interrogated upon the facts and deeds to her imputed, and of them to be convicted.

By us, the judge, has it been said to the accused that, looking at the divers responses by her given to the proceeding interrogatories, it was certain that it never had been in the power of a simple woman, even if she were authorised, if such licence were allowed to lead the life of a loose woman, to give pleasure to all, to cause so many deaths, and to accomplish sorceries so perfect, without the assistance of a special demon lodged in her body, and to whom her soul had been sold by an especial compact. That it had been clearly demonstrated that under her outward appearance lies and moves a demon, the author of these evils, and that she was now called upon to declare at what age she had received the demon, to vow the agreement existing between herself and him, and to tell the truth concerning their common evil doings. By the speaker was it replied that she would answer us, man, as to God, who would be judge of all of us. Then has the speaker pretended never to have seen the demon, neither to have spoken with him, nor in any way to desire to see him; never to have led the life of a courtesan, because she, the speaker, had never practised the various delights that love invents, other than those furnished by the pleasure which the Sovereign Creator has put in the thing, and to have always been incited more from the desire of being sweet and good to the dear lord loved by her, then by an incessantly raging desire. But if such had been her inclination, the speaker begged us to bear in mind that she was a poor African girl, in whom God had placed very hot blood, and in her brain so easy an understanding of the delights of love, that if a man only looked at her she felt greatly moved in her heart. That if from desire of acquaintance an amorous gentleman touched the speaker her on any portion of the body, there passing his hand, she was, in spite of everything, under his power, because her heart failed her instantly. By this touch, the apprehension and remembrance of all the sweet joys of love woke again in her breast, and there caused an intense heat, which mounted up, flamed in her veins, and made her love and joy from head to foot. And since the day when Don Marsilis had first awakened the understanding of the speaker concerning these things, she had never had any other thought, and thenceforth recognized love to be a thing so perfectly concordant with her nature, that it had since been proved to the speaker that in default of love and natural relief she would have died, withered at the said convent. As evidence of which, the speaker affirms as a certainty, that after her flight from the said convent she had not passed a single day or one particle of time in melancholy and sadness, but always was she joyous, and thus followed the sacred will of God, which she believed to have been diverted during the time lost by her in the convent.

To this was it objected by us, Hierome Cornille, to the said demon, that in this response she had openly blasphemed against God, because we had all been made to his greater glory, and placed in the world to honour and to serve Him, to have before our eyes His blessed commandments, and to live in sanctity, in order to gain eternal life, and not to be always in bed, doing that which even the beasts only do at a certain time. Then by the said sister, has answer been made, that she honoured God greatly, that in all countries she had taken care of the poor and suffering, giving them both money and raiment, and that at the last judgement-day she hoped to have around her a goodly company of holy works pleasant to God, which would intercede for her. That but for her humility, a fear of being reproached and of displeasing the gentlemen of the chapter, she would with joy have spent her wealth in finishing the cathedral of St. Maurice, and there have established foundations for the welfare of her soul—would have spared therein neither her pleasure nor her person, and that with this idea she would have taken double pleasure in her nights, because each one of her amours would have added a stone to the building of this basilic. Also the more this purpose, and for the eternal welfare of the speaker, would they have right heartily given their wealth.

Then by us has it been said to this demon that she could not justify the fact of her sterility, because in spite of so much commerce, no child had been born of her, the which proved the presence of a demon in her. Moreover, Astaroth alone, or an apostle, could speak all languages, and she spoke after the manner of all countries, the which proved the presence of the devil in her. Thereupon the speaker has asked: "In what consisted the said diversity of language?"—that of Greek she knew nothing but a Kyrie eleison, of which she made great use; of Latin, nothing, save Amen, which she said to God, wishing therewith to obtain her liberty. That for the rest the speaker had felt great sorrow, being without children, and if the good wives had them, she believed it was because they took so little pleasure in the business, and she, the speaker, a little too much. But that such was doubtless the will of God, who thought that from too great happiness, the world would be in danger of perishing. Taking this into consideration, and a thousand other reasons, which sufficiently establish the presence of the devil in the body of the sister, because the peculiar property of Lucifer is to always find arguments having the semblance of truth, we have ordered that in our presence the torture be applied to the said accused, and that she be well tormented in order to reduce the said demon by suffering to submit to the authority of the Church, and have requested to render us assistance one Francois de Hangest, master surgeon and doctor to the chapter, charging him by a codicil hereunder written to investigate the qualities of the feminine nature (*virtutes vulvae*) of the above-mentioned woman, to enlighten our religion on the methods employed by this demon to lay hold of souls in that way, and see if any article was there apparent.

Then the said Moorish women had wept bitterly, tortured in advance, and in spite of her irons, has knelt down imploring with cries and clamour the revocation of this order, objecting that her limbs were in such a feeble state, and her bones so tender, that they would break like glass; and finally, has offered to purchase her freedom from this by the gift all her goods to the chapter, and to quit incontinently the country.

Upon this, by us has she been required to voluntarily declare herself to be, and to have always been, demon of the nature of the Succubus, which is a female devil whose business it is to corrupt Christians by the blandishments and flagitious delights of love. To this the speaker has replied that the affirmation would be an abominable falsehood, seeing that she had always felt herself to be a most natural woman.

Then her irons being struck off by the torturer, the aforesaid has removed her dress, and has maliciously and with evil design bewildered and attacked our understandings with the sight of her body, the which, for a fact, exercises upon a man supernatural coercion.

Master Guillaume Tournebouche has, by reason of nature, quitted the pen at this period, and retired, objecting that he was unable, without incredible temptations, which worked in his brain, to be a witness of this torture, because he felt the devil violently gaining his person.

This finishes the second interrogatory; and as the apparitor and janitor of the chapter have stated Master Francois de Hangest to be in the country, the torture and interrogations are appointed for to-morrow at the hour of noon after mass.

This has been written verbally by me, Hierome, in the absence of Master Guillaume Tournebouche, on whose behalf it is signed.

HIEROME CORNILLE Grand Penitentiary.

PETITION

Today, the fourteenth day of the month of February, in the presence of me, Hierome Cornille, have appeared the said Masters Jehan Ribou, Antoine Jehan, Martin Beaupertuys, Hierome Maschefer, Jacques de Ville d'Omer, and the Sire d'Idre, in place of the mayor of the city of Tours, for the time absent. All plaintiffs designated in the act of process made at the Town Hall, to whom we have, at the request of Blanche Bruyn (now confessing herself a nun of the convent of Mount Carmel, under the name of Sister Clare), declared the appeal made to the Judgment of God by the said person accused of demonical possession, and her offer to pass through the ordeal of fire and water, in presence of the Chapter and of the town of Tours, in order to prove her reality as a woman and her innocence.

To this request have agreed for their parts, the said accusers, who, on condition that the town is security for it, have engaged to prepare a suitable place and a pile, to be approved by the godparents of the accused.

Then by us, the judge, has the first day of the new year been appointed for the day of the ordeal—which will be next Paschal Day—and we have indicated the hour of noon, after mass, each of the parties having acknowledged this delay to be sufficient.

And the present proclamation shall be cited, at the suit of each of them, in all the towns, boroughs, and castles of Touraine and the land of France, at their request and at their cost and suit.

HIEROME CORNILLE.

III

What the Succubus Did to Suck Out the Soul of the Old Judge, and What Came of the Diabolical Delectation

This the act of extreme confession made the first day of the month of March, in the year one thousand two hundred and seventy-one, after the coming of our blessed Saviour, by Hierome Cornille, priest, canon of the chapter of the cathedral of St. Maurice, grand penitentiary, of all acknowledging himself unworthy, who, finding his last hour to be come, and contrite of his sins, evil doings, forfeits, bad deeds, and wickednesses, has desired his avowal to be published to serve the preconisation of the truth, the glory of God, the justice of the tribunal, and to be an alleviation to him of his punishment, in the other world. The said Hierome Cornille being on his deathbed, there had been convoked to hear his declarations, Jehan de la Haye (de Hago), vicar of the church of St. Maurice; Pietro Guyard, treasurer of the chapter, appointed by our Lord Jean de Monsoreau, Archbishop, to write his words; and Dom Louis Pot, a monk of maius *Monasterium* (Marmoustier), chosen by him for a spiritual father and confessor; all three assisted by the great and illustrious Dr Guillaume de Censoris, Roman Archdeacon, at present sent into the diocese (legatus), by our Holy Father the Pope; and, finally, in the presence of a great number of Christians come to be witnesses of the death of the said Hierome Cornille, upon his known wish to make act of public repentance, seeing that he was fast sinking, and that his words might open the eyes of Christians about to fall into hell.

And before him, Hierome, who, by reason of his great weakness could not speak, has Dom Louis Pot read the following confession to the great agitation of the said company:—

"My brethren, until the seventy-first year of my age, which is the one in which I now am, with the exception of the little sins through which, all holy though he be, a Christian renders himself culpable before God, but which it is allowed to us to repurchase by penitence, I believe I led a Christian life, and merited the praise and renown bestowed upon me in this diocese, where I was raised to the high office of grand penitentiary, of which I am unworthy. Now, struck with the knowledge of the infinite glory of God, horrified at the agonies which await the wicked and prevaricators in hell, I have thought to lessen the enormity of my sins by the greatest penitence I can show in the extreme hour at which I am. Thus I have prayed of the Church, whom I have deceived and betrayed, whose rights and judicial renown I have sold, to grant me the opportunity of accusing myself publicly in the manner of ancient Christians. I hoped, in order to show my great repentance, to have still enough life in me to be reviled at the door of the cathedral by all my brethren, to remain there an entire day on my knees, holding a candle, a cord around my neck, and my feet naked, seeing that I had followed the way of hell with regard to the sacred instincts of the Church. But in this great shipwreck of my fragile virtue, which will be to you as a warning to fly from vice and the snares of the demon, and to take refuge in the Church, where all help is, I have been so bewitched by Lucifer that our Saviour Jesus Christ will take, by the intercession of all you whose help and prayers I request, pity on me, a poor abused Christian, whose eyes now stream with tears. So would I have another life to spend in works of penitence. Now then listen and tremble with great fear! Elected by the assembled Chapter to carry it out, instruct, and complete the process commenced against a demon, who had appeared in a feminine shape, in the person of a relapse nun—an abominable person, denying God, and bearing the name of Zulma in the infidel country whence she comes; the which devil is known in the diocese under that of Clare, of the convent of Mount Carmel, and has much afflicted the town by putting herself under an infinite number of men to gain their souls to Mammon, Astaroth, and Satan—princes of hell, by making them leave this world in a state of mortal sin, and causing their death where life has its source, I have, I the judge, fallen in my latter days into this snare, and have lost my senses, while acquitting myself traitorously of the functions committed with great confidence by the Chapter to my cold senility. Hear how subtle the demon is, and stand firm against her artifices. While listening to the first response of the aforesaid Succubus, I saw with horror that the irons placed upon her feet and hands left no mark there, and was astonished at her hidden strength and at her apparent weakness. Then my mind was troubled suddenly at the sight of the natural perfections with which the devil was endowed. I listened to the music of her voice, which warmed me from head to foot, and made me desire to be young, to give myself up to this demon, thinking that for an hour passed in her company my eternal salvation was but poor payment for the pleasure of love tasted in those slender arms. Then I lost that firmness with which all judges should be furnished. This demon by me questioned, reasoned with me in such a manner that at the second interrogatory I was firmly persuaded I should be committing a crime in fining and torturing a poor little creature who cried like an innocent child. Then warned by a voice from on high to do my duty, and that these golden words, the music of celestial appearance, were diabolical mummeries, that this body, so pretty, so infatuating, would transmute itself into a bristly beast with sharp claws, those eyes so soft into flames of hell, her behind into a scaly tail, the pretty rosebud mouth and gentle lips into the jaws of a crocodile, I came back to my intention of having the said Succubus tortured until she avowed her permission, as this practice had already been followed in Christianity. Now when this demon showed herself stripped to me, to be put to the torture, I was suddenly placed in her power by magical conjurations. I felt my old bones crack, my brain received a warm light, my heart transhipped young and boiling blood. I was light in myself, and by virtue of the magic philter thrown into my eyes the snows on my forehead melted away. I lost all conscience of my Christian life and found myself a schoolboy, running about the country, escaped from class and stealing apples. I had not the power to make the sign of the cross, neither did I remember the Church, God the Father, nor the sweet Saviour of men. A prey to this design, I went about the streets thinking over the delights of that voice, the abominable, pretty body of this demon, and saying a thousand wicked things to myself. Then pierced and drawn by a blow of the devil's fork, who had planted himself already in my head as a serpent in an oak, I was conducted by this sharp prong towards the jail, in spite of my guardian angel, who from time to time pulled me by the arm and defended me against these temptations, but in spite of his holy advice and his assistance I was dragged by a million claws stuck into my heart, and soon found myself in the jail. As soon as the door was opened to me I saw no longer any appearance of a prison, because the Succubus had there, with the assistance of evil genii or fays, constructed a pavilion of purple and silk, full of perfumes and flowers, where she was seated, superbly attired with neither irons on her neck nor chains on her feet. I allowed myself to be stripped of my ecclesiastical vestments, and was put into a scent bath. Then the demon covered me with a Saracen robe, entertained me with a repast of rare viands contained in precious vases, gold cups, Asiatic wines, songs and marvellous music, and a thousand sweet sounds that tickled my soul by means of my ears. At my side kept always the said Succubus, and her sweet, delectable embrace distilled new ardour into my members. My guardian angel quitted me. Then I lived only by the terrible light of the Moorish woman's eyes, coveted the warm embraces of the delicate body, wished always to feel her red lips, that I believed natural, and had no fear of the bite of those teeth which drew me to the bottom of hell, I delighted to feel the unequalled softness of her hands without thinking that they were unnatural claws. In short, I acted like husband desiring to go to his affianced without thinking that that spouse was everlasting death. I had no thought for the things of this world nor the interests of God, dreaming only of love, of the sweet breasts of this woman, who made me burn, and of the gate of hell in which I wished to cast myself. Alas! my brethren, during three days and three nights was I thus constrained to toil without being able to stop the stream which flowed from my reins, in which were plunged, like two pikes, the hands of the Succubus, which communicated to my poor old age and to my dried up bones, I know not what sweat of love. At first this demon, to draw me to her, caused to flow in my inside the softness of milk, then came poignant joys which pricked like a hundred needles my bones, my marrow, my brain, and my nerves. Then all this gone, all things became inflamed, my head, my blood, my nerves, my flesh, my bones, and then I burned with the real fire of hell, which caused me torments in my joints, and an incredible, intolerable, tearing voluptuousness which loosened the bonds of my life. The tresses of this demon, which enveloped my poor body, poured upon me a stream of flame, and I felt each lock like a bar of red iron. During this mortal delectation I saw the ardent face of the said Succubus, who laughed and addressed to me a thousand exciting words; such as that I was her knight, her lord, her lance, her day, her joy, her hero, her life, her good, her rider, and that she would like to clasp me even closer, wishing to be in my skin or have me in hers. Hearing which, under the prick of this tongue which sucked out my soul, I plunged and precipitated myself finally into hell without finding the bottom. And then when I had no more a drop of blood in my veins, when my heart no longer beat in my body, and I was ruined at all points, the demon, still fresh, white, rubicund, glowing, and laughing, said to me—

"'Poor fool, to think me a demon! Had I asked thee to sell thy soul for a kiss, wouldst thou not give it to me with all thy heart?'

"'Yes,' said I.

"'And if always to act thus it were necessary for thee to nourish thyself with the blood of new-born children in order always to have new life to spend in my arms, would you not imbibe it willingly?'

"'Yes,' said I.

"'And to be always my gallant horseman, gay as a man in his prime, feeling life, drinking pleasure, plunging to the depths of joy as a swimmer into the Loire, wouldst thou not deny God, wouldst thou not spit in the face of Jesus?'

"'Yes,' said I.

"Then I felt a hundred sharp claws which tore my diaphragm as if the beaks of a thousand birds there took their bellyfuls, shrieking. Then I was lifted suddenly above the earth upon the said Succubus, who had spread her wings, and cried to me—

"'Ride, ride, my gallant rider! Hold yourself firmly on the back of thy mule, by her mane, by her neck; and ride, ride, my gallant rider—everything rides!' And then I saw, as a thick fog, the cities of the earth, where by a special gift I perceived each one coupled with a female demon, and tossing about, and engendering in great concupiscence, all shrieking a thousand words of love and exclamations of all kinds, and all toiling away with ecstasy. Then my horse with the Moorish head pointed out to me, still flying and galloping beyond the clouds, the earth coupled with the sun in a conjunction, from which proceeded a germ of stars, and there each female world was embracing a male world; but in place of the words used by creatures, the worlds were giving forth the howls of tempests, throwing up lightnings and crying thunders. Then still rising, I saw overhead the female nature of all things in love with the Prince of Movement. Now, by way of mockery, the Succubus placed me in the centre of this horrible and perpetual conflict, where I was lost as a grain of sand in the sea. Then still cried my white mare to me, 'Ride, ride my gallant rider—all things ride!' Now, thinking how little was a priest in this torment of the seed of worlds, nature always clasped together, and metals, stones, waters, airs, thunders, fish, plants, animals, men, spirits, worlds and planets, all embracing with rage, I denied the Catholic faith. Then the Succubus, pointing out to me the great patch of stars seen in heavens, said to me, 'That way is a drop of celestial seed escaped from great flow of the worlds in conjunction.' Thereupon I instantly clasped the Succubus with passion by the light of a thousand million of stars, and I wished in clasping her to feel the nature of those thousand million creatures. Then by this great effort of love I fell impotent in every way, and heard a great infernal laugh. Then I found myself in my bed, surrounded by my servitors, who had had the courage to struggle with the demon, throwing into the bed where I was stretched a basin full of holy water, and saying fervent prayers to God. Then had I to sustain, in spite of this assistance, a horrible combat with the said Succubus, whose claws still clutched my heart, causing me infinite pains; still, while reanimated by the voice of my servitors, relations, and friends, I tried to make the sacred sign of the cross; the Succubus perched on my bed, on the bolster, at the foot, everywhere, occupying herself in distracting my nerves, laughing, grimacing, putting before my eyes a thousand obscene images, and causing me a thousand wicked desires. Nevertheless, taking pity on me, my lord the Archbishop caused the relics of St. Gatien to be brought, and the moment the shrine had touched my bed the said Succubus was obliged to depart, leaving an odour of sulphur and of hell, which made the throats of my servants, friends, and others sore for a whole day. Then the celestial light of God having enlightened my soul, I knew I was, through my sins and my combat with the evil spirit, in great danger of dying. Then did I implore the especial mercy, to live just a little time to render glory to God and his Church, objecting the infinite merits of Jesus dead upon the cross for the salvation of the Christians. By this prayer I obtained the favour of recovering sufficient strength to accuse myself of my sins, and to beg of the members of the Church of St. Maurice their aid and assistance to deliver me from purgatory, where I am about to atone for my faults by infinite agonies. Finally, I declare that my proclamation, wherein the said demon appeals the judgment of God by the ordeals of holy water and a fire, is a subterfuge due to an evil design suggested by the said demon, who would thus have had the power to escape the justice of the tribunal of the Archbishop and of the Chapter, seeing that she secretly confessed to me, to be able to make another demon accustomed to the ordeal appear in her place. And, in conclusion, I give and bequeath to the Chapter of the Church of St. Maurice my property of all kinds, to found a chapter in the said church, to build it and adorn it and put it under the invocation of St. Hierome and St. Gatien, of whom one is my patron and the other the saviour of my soul."

This, heard by all the company, has been brought to the notice of the ecclesiastical tribunal by Jehan to la Haye (Johannes de Haga).

We, Jehan de la Haye (Johannes de Haga), elected grand penitentiary of St. Maurice by the general assembly of the Chapter, according to the usage and custom of that church, and appointed to pursue afresh the trial of the demon Succubus, at present in the jail of the Chapter, have ordered a new inquest, at which will be heard all those of this diocese having cognisance of the facts relative thereto. We declared void the other proceedings, interrogations, and decrees, and annul them in the name of the members of the Church in general, and sovereign Chapter assembled, and declare that the appeal to God, traitorously made by the demon, shall not take place, in consequence of the notorious treachery of the devil in this affair. And the said judgment shall be cried by sound of trumpet in all parts of the diocese in which have been published the false edicts of the preceding month, all notoriously due to the instigation of the demon, according to the confession of the late Hierome Cornille.

Let all good Christians be of assistance to our Holy Church, and to her commandments.

JEHAN DE LA HAYE.

IV

How the Moorish Woman of the Rue Chaude Twisted About So Briskly that with Great Difficulty Was She Burned and Cooked Alive, to the Great Loss of the Infernal Regions

This was written in the month of May, of the year 1360, after the manner of a testament.

"My very dear and well-beloved son, when it shall be lawful for thee to read this I shall be, I thy father, reposing in the tomb, imploring thy prayers, and supplicating thee to conduct thyself in life as it will be commanded thee in this rescript, bequeathed for the good government of thy family, thy future, and safety; for I have done this at a period when I had my senses and understanding, still recently affected by the sovereign injustice of men. In my virile age I had a great ambition to raise myself in the Church, and therein to obtain the highest dignities, because no life appeared to me more splendid. Now with this earnest idea, I learned to read and write, and with great trouble became in a fit condition to enter the clergy. But because I had no protection, or good advice to superintend my training I had an idea of becoming the writer, tabellion, and rubrican of the Chapter of St. Maurice, in which were the highest and richest personages of Christendom, since the King of France is only therein a simple canon. Now there I should be able better than anywhere else to find services to render to certain lords, and thus to find a master or gain patronage, and by this assistance enter into religion, and be mitred and esconced in an archiepiscopal chair, somewhere or other. But this first vision was over credulous, and a little too ambitious, the which God caused me clearly to perceive by the sequel. In fact, Messire Jepan de Villedomer, who afterwards became cardinal, was given this appointment, and I was rejected, discomfited. Now in this unhappy hour I received an alleviation of my troubles, by the advice of the good old Hierome Cornille, of whom I have often spoken to you. This dear man induced me, by his kindness, to become penman to the Chapter of St. Maurice and the Archbishop of Tours, the which offer I accepted with joy, since I was reputed a scrivener. At the time I was about to enter into the presbytery commenced the famous process against the devil of the Rue Chaude, of which the old folk still talk, and which in its time, has been recounted in every home in France. Now, believing that it would be of great advantage to my ambition, and that for this assistance the Chapter would raise me to some dignity, my good master had me appointed for the purpose of writing all of that should be in this grave cause, subject to writing. At the very outset Monseigneur Hierome Cornille, a man approaching eighty years, of great sense, justice, and sound understanding, suspected some spitefulness in this cause, although he was not partial to immodest girls, and had never been involved with a woman in his life, and was holy and venerable, with a sanctity which had caused him to be selected as a judge, all this not withstanding. As soon as the depositions were completed, and the poor wench heard, it remained clear that although this merry doxy had broken her religious vows, she was innocent of all devilry, and that her great wealth was coveted by her enemies, and other persons, whom I must not name to thee for reasons of prudence. At this time every one believed her to be so well furnished with silver and gold that she could have bought the whole county of Touraine, if so it had pleased her. A thousand falsehoods and calumnious words concerning the girl, envied by all the honest women, were circulated and believed in as gospel. At this period Master Hierome Cornille, having ascertained that no demon other than that of love was in the girl, made her consent to remain in a convent for the remainder of her days. And having ascertained certain noble knights brave in war and rich in domains, that they would do everything to save her, he invited her secretly to demand of her accusers the judgment of God, at the same time giving her goods to the chapter, in order to silence mischievous tongues. By this means would be saved from the stake the most delicate flower that ever heaven has allowed to fall upon our earth; the which flower yielded only from excessive tenderness and amiability to the malady of love, cast by her eyes into the hearts of all her pursuers. But the real devil, under the form of a monk, mixed himself up in this affair; in this wise: great enemy of the virtue, wisdom, and sanctity of Monsignor Hierome Cornille, named Jehan de la Haye, having learned that in the jail, the poor girl was treated like a queen, wickedly accused the grand penitentiary of connivance with her and of being her servitor, because, said this wicked priest, she makes him young, amorous, and happy, from which the poor old man died of grief in one day, knowing by this that Jehan de la Haye had worn his ruin and coveted his dignities. In fact, our lord the archbishop visited the jail, and found the Moorish woman in a pleasant place, reposing comfortably, and without irons, because, having placed a diamond in a place when none could have believed she could have held it, she had purchased the clemency of her jailer. At the time certain persons said that this jailer was smitten with her, and that from love, or perhaps in great fear of the young barons, lovers of this woman, he had planned her escape. The good man Cornille being at the point of death, through the treachery of Jehan de la Haye, the Chapter thinking it necessary to make null and void the proceedings taken by the penitentiary, and also his decrees, the said Jehan de la Haye, at that time a simple vicar of the cathedral, pointed out that to do this it would be sufficient to obtain a public confession from the good man on his death-bed. Then was the moribund tortured and tormented by the gentleman of the Chapter, those of Saint Martin, those of Marmoustiers, by the archbishop and also by the Pope's legate, in order that he might recant to the advantage of the Church, to which the good man would not consent. But after a thousand ills, the public confession was prepared, at which the most noteworthy people of the town assisted, and the which spread more horror and consternation than I can describe. The churches of the diocese held public prayers for this calamity, and every one expected to see the devil tumble into his house by the chimney. But the truth of it is that the good Master Hierome had a fever, and saw cows in his room, and then was this recantation obtained of him. The access passed, the poor saint wept copiously on learning this trick from me. In fact, he died in my arms, assisted by his physicians, heartbroken at this mummery, telling us that he was going to the feet of God to pray to prevent the consummation of this deplorable iniquity. The poor Moorish woman had touched him much by her tears and repentance, seing that before making her demand for the judgment of God he had minutely confessed her, and by that means had disentangled the soul divine which was in the body, and of which he spoke as of a diamond worthy of adorning the holy crown of God, when she should have departed this life, after repenting her sins. Then, my dear son, knowing by the statements made in the town, and by the naive responses of this unhappy wretch, all the trickery of this affair, I determined by the advice of Master Francois de Hangest, physician of the chapter, to feign an illness and quit the service of the Church of St. Maurice and of the archbishopric, in order not to dip my hands in the innocent blood, which still cries and will continue to cry aloud unto God until the day of the last judgment. Then was the jailer dismissed, and in his place was put the second son of the torturer, who threw the Moorish woman into a dungeon, and inhumanly put upon her hands and feet chains weighing fifty pounds, besides a wooden waistband; and the jail were watched by the crossbowmen of the town and the people of the archbishop. The wench was tormented and tortured, and her bones were broken; conquered by sorrow, she made an avowal according to the wishes of Jehan de la Haye, and was instantly condemned to be burned in the enclosure of St. Etienne, having been previously placed in the portals of the church, attired in a chemise of sulphur, and her goods given over to the Chapter, et cetera. This order was the cause of great disturbances and fighting in the town, because three young knights of Touraine swore to die in the service of the poor girl, and to deliver her in all possible ways. Then they came into the town, accompanied by thousands of sufferers, labouring people, old soldiers, warriors, courtesans, and others, whom the said girls had succoured, saved from misfortune, from hunger and misery, and searched all the poor dwellings of the town where lay those to whom she had done good. Thus all were stirred up and called together to the plain of Mount-Louis under the protection of the soldiers of the said lords; they had for companions all the scape-graces of the said twenty leagues around, and came one morning to lay siege to the prison of the archbishop, demanding that the Moorish woman should be given up to them as though they would put her to death, but in fact to set her free, and to place her secretly upon a swift horse, that she might gain the open country, seeing that she rode like a groom. Then in this frightful tempest of men have we seen between the battlements of the archiepiscopal palace and the bridges, more than ten thousand men swarming, besides those who were perched upon the roofs of the houses and climbing on all the balconies to see the sedition; in short it was easy to hear the horrible cries of the Christians, who were terribly in earnest, and of those who surrounded the jail with the intention of setting the poor girl free, across the Loire, the other side of Saint Symphorien. The suffocation and squeezing of bodies was so great in this immense crowd, bloodthirsty for the poor creature at whose knees they would have fallen had they had the opportunity of seeing her, that seven children, eleven women, and eight citizens were crushed and smashed beyond all recognition, since they were like splodges of mud; in short, so wide open was the great mouth of this popular leviathan, this horrible monster, that the clamour was heard at Montils-les-Tours. All cried 'Death to the Succubus! Throw out the demon! Ha! I'd like a quarter! I'll have her skin! The foot for me, the mane for thee! The head for me! The something for me! Is it red? Shall we see? Will it be grilled? Death to her! death!' Each one had his say. But the cry, 'Largesse to God! Death to the Succubus!' was yelled at the same time by the crowd so hoarsely and so cruelly that one's ears and heart bled therefrom; and the other cries were scarcely heard in the houses. The archbishop decided, in order to calm this storm which threatened to overthrow everything, to come out with great pomp from the church, bearing the host, which would deliver the Chapter from ruin, since the wicked young men and the lords had sworn to destroy and burn the cloisters and all the canons. Now by this stratagem the crowd was obliged to break up, and from lack of provisions return to their houses. Then the monks of Touraine, the lords, and the citizens, in great apprehension of pillage on the morrow, held a nocturnal council, and accepted the advice of the Chapter. By their efforts the men-at-arms, archers, knights, and citizens, in a large number, kept watch, and killed a party of shepherds, road menders, and vagrants, who, knowing the disturbed state of Tours, came to swell the ranks of the malcontents. The Sire Harduin de Maille, an old nobleman, reasoned with the young knights, who were the champions of the Moorish woman, and argued sagely with them, asking them if for so small a woman they wished to put Touraine to fire and sword; that even if they were victorious they would be masters of the bad characters brought together by them; that these said freebooters, after having sacked the castles of their enemies, would turn to those of their chiefs. That the rebellion commenced had had no success in the first attack, because up to that time the place was untouched, could they have any over the church, which would invoke the aid of the king? And a thousand other arguments. To these reasons the young knights replied, that it was easy for the Chapter to aid the girl's escape in the night, and that thus the cause of the sedition would be removed. To this humane and wise requests replied Monseigneur de Censoris, the Pope's legate, that it was necessary that strength should remain with the religion of the Church. And thereupon the poor wench payed for all, since it was agreed that no inquiry should be made concerning this sedition.

"Then the Chapter had full licence to proceed to the penance of the girl, to which act and ecclesiastical ceremony the people came from twelve leagues around. So that on the day when, after divine satisfaction, the Succubus was to be delivered up to secular justice, in order to be publicly burnt at a stake, not for a gold pound would a lord or even an abbott have been found lodging in the town of Tours. The night before many camped outside the town in tents, or slept upon straw. Provisions were lacking, and many who came with their bellies full, returned with their bellies empty, having seen nothing but the reflection of the fire in the distance. And the bad characters did good strokes of business by the way.

"The poor courtesan was half dead; her hair had whitened. She was, to tell the truth, nothing but a skeleton, scarcely covered with flesh, and her chains weighed more than she did. If she had had joy in her life, she paid dearly for it at this moment. Those who saw her pass say that she wept and shrieked in a way that should have earned the pity of her hardest pursuers; and in the church there were compelled to put a piece of wood in her mouth, which she bit as a lizard bites a stick. Then the executioner tied her to a stake to sustain her, since she let herself roll at times and fell for want of strength. Then she suddenly recovered a vigorous handful, because, this notwithstanding, she was able, it is said to break her cords and escape into the church, where in remembrance of her old vocation, she climbed quickly into galleries above, flying like a bird along the little columns and small friezes. She was about to escape on to the roof when a soldier perceived her, and thrust his spear in the sole of her foot. In spite of her foot half cut through, the poor girl still ran along the church without noticing it, going along with her bones broken and her blood gushing out, so great fear had she of the flames of the stake. At last she was taken and bound, thrown into a tumbrel and led to the stake, without being afterwards heard to utter a cry. The account of her flight in the church assisted in making the common people believe that she was the devil, and some of them said that she had flown in the air. As soon as the executioner of the town threw her into the flames, she made two or three horrible leaps and fell down into the bottom of the pile, which burned day and night. On the following evening I went to see if anything remained of this gentle girl, so sweet, so loving, but I found nothing but a fragment of the 'os stomachal,' in which, is spite of this, there still remained some moisture, and which some say still trembled like a woman does in the same place. It is impossible to tell, my dear son, the sadnesses, without number and without equal, which for about ten years weighed upon me; always was I thinking of this angel burnt by wicked men, and always I beheld her with her eyes full of love. In short the supernatural gifts of this artless child were shining day and night before me, and I prayed for her in the church, where she had been martyred. At length I had neither the strength nor the courage to look without trembling upon the grand penitentiary Jehan de la Haye, who died eaten up by lice. Leprosy was his punishment. Fire burned his house and his wife; and all those who had a hand in the burning had their own hands singed.

"This, my well-beloved son, was the cause of a thousand ideas, which I have here put into writing to be forever the rule of conduct in our family.

"I quitted the service of the church, and espoused your mother, from whom I received infinite blessings, and with whom I shared my life, my goods, my soul, and all. And she agreed with me in following precepts—Firstly, that to live happily, it is necessary to keep far away from church people, to honour them much without giving them leave to enter your house, any more than to those who by right, just or unjust, are supposed to be superior to us. Secondly, to take a modest condition, and to keep oneself in it without wishing to appear in any way rich. To have a care to excite no envy, nor strike anyonesoever in any manner, because it is needful to be as strong as an oak, which kills the plants at its feet, to crush envious heads, and even then would one succumb, since human oaks are especially rare and that no Tournebouche should flatter himself that he is one, granting that he be a Tournebouche. Thirdly, never to spend more than one quarter of one's income, conceal one's wealth, hide one's goods and chattels, to undertake no office, to go to church like other people, and always keep one's thoughts to oneself, seeing that they belong to you and not to others, who twist them about, turn them after their own fashion, and make calumnies therefrom. Fourthly, always to remain in the condition of the Tournebouches, who are now and forever drapers. To marry your daughters to good drapers, send your sons to be drapers in other towns of France furnished with these wise precepts, and to bring them up to the honour of drapery, and without leaving any dream of ambition in their minds. A draper like a Tournebouche should be their glory, their arms, their name, their motto, their life. Thus by being always drapers, they will be always Tournebouches, and rub on like the good little insects, who, once lodged in the beam, made their dens, and go on with security to the end of their ball of thread. Fifthly never to speak any other language than that of drapery, and never to dispute concerning religion or government. And even though the government of the state, the province, religion, and God turn about, or have a fancy to go to the right or to the left, always in your quality of Tournebouche, stick to your cloth. Thus unnoticed by the others of the town, the Tournebouches will live in peace with their little Tournebouches—paying the tithes and taxes, and all that they are required by force to give, be it to God, or to the king, to the town or to the parish, with all of whom it is unwise to struggle. Also it is necessary to keep the patrimonial treasure, to have peace and to buy peace, never to owe anything, to have corn in the house, and enjoy yourselves with the doors and windows shut.

"By this means none will take from the Tournebouches, neither the state, nor the Church, nor the Lords, to whom should the case be that force is employed, you will lend a few crowns without cherishing the idea of ever seeing him again—I mean the crowns.

"Thus, in all seasons people will love the Tournebouches, will mock the Tournebouches as poor people—as the slow Tournebouches, as Tournebouches of no understanding. Let the know-nothings say on. The Tournebouches will neither be burned nor hanged, to the advantage of King or Church, or other people; and the wise Tournebouches will have secretly money in their pockets, and joy in their houses, hidden from all.

"Now, my dear son, follow this the counsel of a modest and middle-class life. Maintain this in thy family as a county charter; and when you die, let your successor maintain it as the sacred gospel of the Tournebouches, until God wills it that there be no longer Tournebouches in this world."

This letter has been found at the time of the inventory made in the house of Francois Tournebouche, lord of Veretz, chancellor to Monseigneur the Dauphin, and condemned at the time of the rebellion of the said lord against the King to lose his head, and have all his goods confiscated by order of the Parliament of Paris. The said letter has been handed to the Governor of Touraine as an historical curiosity, and joined to the pieces of the process in the archbishopric of Tours, by me, Pierre Gaultier, Sheriff, President of the Trades Council.

The author having finished the transcription and deciphering of these parchments, translating them from their strange language into French, the donor of them declared that the Rue Chaude at Tours was so called, according to certain people, because the sun remained there longer than in all other parts. But in spite of this version, people of lofty understanding will find, in the warm way of the said Succubus, the real origin of the said name. In which acquiesces the author. This teaches us not to abuse our body, but use it wisely in view of our salvation.

THE DAMNED THING

Ambrose Bierce

I

One Does Not Always Eat What Is on the Table

By the light of a tallow candle, which had been placed on one end of a rough table, a man was reading something written in a book. It was an old account book, greatly worn; and the writing was not, apparently, very legible, for the man sometimes held the page close to the flame of the candle to get a stronger light upon it. The shadow of the book would then throw into obscurity a half of the room, darkening a number of faces and figures; for besides the reader, eight other men were present. Seven of them sat against the rough log walls, silent and motionless, and, the room being small, not very far from the table. By extending an arm any one of them could have touched the eighth man, who lay on the table, face upward, partly covered by a sheet, his arms at his sides. He was dead.

The man with the book was not reading aloud, and no one spoke; all seemed to be waiting for something to occur; the dead man only was without expectation. From the blank darkness outside came in, through the aperture that served for a window, all the ever unfamiliar noises of night in the wilderness—the long, nameless note of a distant coyote; the stilly pulsing thrill of tireless insects in the trees; strange cries of night birds, so different from those of the birds of day; the drone of great blundering beetles and all that mysterious chorus of small sounds that seemed always to have been but half heard when they have suddenly ceased, as if conscious of an indiscretion. But nothing of all this was noted in that company; its members were not overmuch addicted to idle interest in matters of no practical importance; that was obvious in every line of their rugged faces—obvious even in the dim light of the single candle. They were evidently men of the vicinity—farmers and woodmen.

The person reading was a trifle different; one would have said of him that he was of the world, worldly, albeit there was that in his attire which attested a certain fellowship with the organisms of his environment. His coat would hardly have passed muster in San Francisco: his footgear was not of urban origin, and the hat that lay by him on the floor (he was the only one uncovered) was such that if one had considered it as an article of mere personal adornment he would have missed its meaning. In countenance the man was rather prepossessing, with just a hint of sternness; though that he may have assumed or cultivated, as appropriate to one in authority. For he was a coroner. It was by virtue of his office that he had possession of the book in which he was reading; it had been found among the dead man's effects—in his cabin, where the inquest was now taking place.

When the coroner had finished reading he put the book into his breast pocket. At that moment the door was pushed open and a young man entered. He, clearly, was not of mountain birth and breeding: he was clad as those who dwell in cities. His clothing was dusty, however, as from travel. He had, in fact, been riding hard to attend the inquest.

The coroner nodded; no one else greeted him.

"We have waited for you," said the coroner. "It is necessary to have done with this business to-night."

The young man smiled. "I am sorry to have kept you," he said, "I went away, not to evade your summons, but to post to my newspaper an account of what I suppose I am called back to relate."

The coroner smiled.

"The account that you posted to your newspaper," he said, "differs probably from that which you will give here under oath."

"That," replied the other, rather hotly and with a visible flush, "is as you choose. I used manifold paper and have a copy of what I sent. It was not written as news, for it is incredible, but as fiction. It may go as a part of my testimony under oath."

"But you say it is incredible."

"That is nothing to you, sir, if I also swear that it is true."

The coroner was apparently not greatly affected by the young man's manifest resentment. He was silent for some moments, his eyes upon the floor. The men about the sides of the cabin talked in whispers, but seldom withdrew their gaze from the face of the corpse. Presently the coroner lifted his eyes and said: "We will resume the inquest."

The men removed their hats. The witness was sworn.

"What is your name?" the coroner asked.

"William Harker."

"Age?"

"Twenty-seven."

"You knew the deceased, Hugh Morgan?"

"Yes."

"You were with him when he died?"

"Near him."

"How did that happen—your presence, I mean?"

"I was visiting him at his place to shoot and fish. A part of my purpose, however, was to study him, and his odd, solitary way of life. He seemed a good model for a character in fiction. I sometimes write stories."

"I sometimes read them."

"Thank you."

"Stories in general—not yours."

Some of the jurors laughed. Against a sombre background humour shows high lights. Soldiers in the intervals of battle laugh easily, and a jest in the death chamber conquers by surprise.

"Relate the circumstances of this man's death," said the coroner. "You may use any notes or memoranda that you please."

The witness understood. Pulling a manuscript from his breast pocket he held it near the candle, and turning the leaves until he found the passage that he wanted, began to read.

II

What May Happen in a Field of Wild Oats

". . . The sun had hardly risen when we left the house. We were looking for quail, each with a shot-gun, but we had only one dog. Morgan said that our best ground was beyond a certain ridge that he pointed out, and we crossed it by trail through the chaparral. On the other side was comparatively level ground, thickly covered with wild oats. As we emerged from the chaparral, Morgan was but a few yards in advance. Suddenly, we heard, at a little distance to our right, and partly in front, a noise as of some animal thrashing about in the bushes, which we could see were violently agitated.

"'We've started a deer,' I said. 'I wish we had brought a rifle.'

"Morgan, who had stopped and was intently watching the agitated chaparral, said nothing, but had cocked both barrels of his gun, and was holding it in readiness to aim. I thought him a trifle excited, which surprised me, for he had a reputation for exceptional coolness, even in moments of sudden and imminent peril.

"'O, come!' I said. 'You are not going to fill up a deer with quail-shot, are you?'

"Still he did not reply; but, catching a sight of his face as he turned it slightly toward me, I was struck by the pallor of it. Then I understood that we had serious business on hand, and my first conjecture was that we had 'jumped' a grizzly. I advanced to Morgan's side, cocking my piece as I moved.

"The bushes were now quiet, and the sounds had ceased, but Morgan was as attentive to the place as before.

" 'What is it? What the devil is it?' I asked.

" 'That Damned Thing!' he replied, without turning his head. His voice was husky and unnatural. He trembled visibly.

"I was about to speak further, when I observed the wild oats near the place of the disturbance moving in the most inexplicable way. I can hardly describe it. It seemed as if stirred by a streak of wind, which not only bent it, but pressed it down—crushed it so that it did not rise, and this movement was slowly prolonging itself directly toward us.

"Nothing that I had ever seen had affected me so strangely as this unfamiliar and unaccountable phenomenon, yet I am unable to recall any sense of fear. I remember—and tell it here because, singularly enough, I recollected it then—that once, in looking carelessly out of an open window, I momentarily mistook a small tree close at hand for one of a group of larger trees at a little distance away. It looked the same size as the others, but, being more distinctly and sharply defined in mass and details, seemed out of harmony with them. It was a mere falsification of the law of aerial perspective, but it startled, almost terrified me. We so rely upon the orderly operation of familar natural laws that any seeming suspension of them is noted as a menace to our safety, a warning of unthinkable calamity. So now the apparently causeless movement of the herbage, and the slow, undeviating approach of the line of disturbance were distinctly disquieting. My companion appeared actually frightened, and I could hardly credit my senses when I saw him suddenly throw his gun to his shoulders and fire both barrels at the agitated grass! Before the smoke of the discharge had cleared away I heard a loud savage cry—a scream like that of a wild animal—and, flinging his gun upon the ground, Morgan sprang away and ran swiftly from the spot. At the same instant I was thrown violently to the ground by the impact of something unseen in the smoke—some soft, heavy substance that seemed thrown against me with great force.

"Before I could get upon my feet and recover my gun, which seemed to have been struck from my hands, I heard Morgan crying out as if in mortal agony, and mingling with his cries were such hoarse, savage sounds as one hears from fighting dogs. Inexpressibly terrified, I struggled to my feet and looked in the direction of Morgan's retreat; and may heaven in mercy spare me from another sight like that! At a distance of less than thirty yards was my friend, down upon one knee, his head thrown back at a frightful angle, hatless, his long hair in disorder and his whole body in violent movement from side to side, backward and forward. His right arm was lifted and seemed to lack the hand—at least, I could see none. The other arm was invisible. At times, as my memory now reports this extraordinary scene, I could discern but a part of his body; it was as if he had been partly blotted out—I cannot otherwise express it—then a shifting of his position would bring it all into view again.

"All this must have occurred within a few seconds, yet in that time Morgan assumed all the postures of a determined wrestler vanquished by superior weight and strength. I saw nothing but him, and him not always distinctly. During the entire incident his shouts and curses were heard, as if through an enveloping uproar of such sounds of rage and fury as I had never heard from the throat of man or brute!

"For a moment only I stood irresolute, then throwing down my gun, I ran forward to my friend's assistance. I had a vague belief that he was suffering from a fit or some form of convulsion. Before I could reach his side he was down and quiet. All sounds had ceased, but, with a feeling of such terror as even these awful events had not inspired, I now saw the same mysterious movement of the wild oats prolonging itself from the trampled area about the prostrate man toward the edge of a wood. It was only when it had reached the wood that I was able to withdraw my eyes and look at my companion. He was dead."

III

A Man Though Naked May Be in Rags

The coroner rose from his seat and stood beside the dead man. Lifting an edge of the sheet he pulled it away, exposing the entire body, altogether naked and showing in the candle-light a clay-like yellow. It had, however, broad maculations of bluish-black, obviously caused by extravasated blood from contusions. The chest and sides looked as if they had been beaten with a bludgeon. There were dreadful lacerations; the skin was torn in strips and shreds.

The coroner moved round to the end of the table and undid a silk handkerchief, which had been passed under the chin and knotted on the top of the head. When the handkerchief was drawn away it exposed what had been the throat. Some of the jurors who had risen to get a better view repented their curiosity, and turned away their faces. Witness Harker went to the open window and leaned out across the sill, faint and sick. Dropping the handkerchief upon the dead man's neck, the coroner stepped to an angle of the room, and from a pile of clothing produced one garment after another, each of which he held up a moment for inspection. All were torn, and stiff with blood. The jurors did not make a closer inspection. They seemed rather uninterested. They had, in truth, seen all this before; the only thing that was new to them being Harker's testimony.

"Gentlemen," the coroner said, "we have no more evidence, I think. Your duty has been already explained to you; if there is nothing you wish to ask you may go outside and consider your verdict."

The foreman rose—a tall, bearded man of sixty, coarsely clad.

"I should like to ask one question, Mr. Coroner," he said. "What asylum did this yer last witness escape from?"

"Mr. Harker," said the coroner, gravely and tranquilly, "from what asylum did you last escape?"

Harker flushed crimson again, but said nothing, and the seven jurors rose and solemnly filed out of the cabin.

"If you have done insulting me, sir," said Harker, as soon as he and the officer were left alone with the dead man, "I suppose I am at liberty to go?"

"Yes."

Harker started to leave, but paused, with his hand on the door latch. The habit of his profession was strong in him—stronger than his sense of personal dignity. He turned about and said:

"The book that you have there—I recognise it as Morgan's diary. You seemed greatly interested in it; you read in it while I was testifying. May I see it? The public would like—"

"The book will cut no figure in this matter," replied the official, slipping it into his coat pocket; "all the entries in it were made before the writer's death."

As Harker passed out of the house the jury re-entered and stood about the table, on which the now covered corpse showed under the sheet with sharp definition. The foreman seated himself near the candle, produced from his breast pocket a pencil and scrap of paper, and wrote rather laboriously the following verdict, which with various degrees of effort all signed:

"We, the jury, do find that the remains come to their death at the hands of a mountain lion, but some of us thinks, all the same, they had fits."

IV

An Explanation from the Tomb

In the dairy of the late Hugh Morgan are certain interesting entries having, possibly, a scientific value as suggestions. At the inquest upon his body the book was not put in evidence; possibly the coroner thought it not worth while to confuse the jury. The date of the first of the entries mentioned cannot be ascertained; the upper part of the leaf is torn away; the part of the entry remaining is as follows:

". . . would run in a half circle, keeping his head turned always toward the centre and again he would stand still, barking furiously. At last he ran away into the brush as fast as he could go. I thought at first that he had gone mad, but on returning to the house found no other alteration in his manner than what was obviously due to fear of punishment.

"Can a dog see with his nose? Do odours impress some olfactory centre with images of the thing emitting them? . . .

"Sept. 2.—Looking at the stars last night as they rose above the crest of the ridge east of the house, I observed them successively disappear—from left to right. Each was eclipsed but an instant, and only a few at the same time, but along the entire length of the ridge all that were within a degree or two of the crest were blotted out. It was as if something had passed along between me and them; but I could not see it, and the stars were not thick enough to define its outline. Ugh! I don't like this . . ."

Several weeks' entries are missing, three leaves being torn from the book.

"Sept. 27.—It has been about here again—I find evidences of its presence every day. I watched again all of last night in the same cover, gun in hand, double-charged with buckshot. In the morning the fresh footprints were there, as before. Yet I would have sworn that I did not sleep—indeed, I hardly sleep at all. It is terrible, insupportable! If these amazing experiences are real I shall go mad; if they are fanciful I am mad already.

"Oct. 3.—I shall not go—it shall not drive me away. No, this is my house, my land. God hates a coward . . .

"Oct. 5.—I can stand it no longer; I have invited Harker to pass a few weeks with me—he has a level head. I can judge from his manner if he thinks me mad.

"Oct. 7.—I have the solution of the problem; it came to me last night—suddenly, as by revelation. How simple—how terribly simple!

"There are sounds that we cannot hear. At either end of the scale are notes that stir no chord of that imperfect instrument, the human ear. They are too high or too grave. I have observed a flock of blackbirds occupying an entire tree-top—the tops of several trees—and all in full song. Suddenly—in a moment—at absolutely the same instant—all spring into the air and fly away. How? They could not all see one another—whole tree-tops intervened. At no point could a leader have been visible to all. There must have been a signal of warning or command, high and shrill above the din, but by me unheard. I have observed, too, the same simultaneous flight when all were silent, among not only blackbirds, but other birds—quail, for example, widely separated by bushes—even on opposite sides of a hill.

"It is known to seamen that a school of whales basking or sporting on the surface of the ocean, miles apart, with the convexity of the earth between them, will sometimes dive at the same instant—all gone out of sight in a moment. The signal has been sounded—too grave for the ear of the sailor at the masthead and his comrades on the deck—who nevertheless feel its vibrations in the ship as the stones of a cathedral are stirred by the bass of the organ.

"As with sounds, so with colours. At each end of the solar spectrum the chemist can detect the presence of what are known as 'actinic' rays. They represent colours—integral colours in the composition of light—which we are unable to discern. The human eye is an imperfect instrument; its range is but a few octaves of the real 'chromatic scale.' I am not mad; there are colours that we cannot see.

"And, God help me! the Damned Thing is of such a colour!"

THE TREE

H. P. Lovecraft

"Fata viam invenient."

On a verdant slope of Mount Maenalus, in Arcadia, there stands an olive grove about the ruins of a villa. Close by is a tomb, once beautiful with the sublimest sculptures, but now fallen into as great decay as the house. At one end of that tomb, its curious roots displacing the time-stained blocks of Pentelic marble, grows an unnaturally large olive tree of oddly repellent shape; so like to some grotesque man, or death-distorted body of a man, that the country folk fear to pass it at night when the moon shines faintly through the crooked boughs. Mount Maenalus is a chosen haunt of dreaded Pan, whose queer companions are many, and simple swains believe that the tree must have some hideous kinship to these weird Panisci; but an old bee-keeper who lives in the neighbouring cottage told me a different story.

Many years ago, when the hillside villa was new and resplendent, there dwelt within it the two sculptors Kalos and Musides. From Lydia to Neapolis the beauty of their work was praised, and none dared say that the one excelled the other in skill. The Hermes of Kalos stood in a marble shrine in Corinth, and the Pallas of Musides surmounted a pillar in Athens, near the Parthenon. All men paid homage to Kalos and Musides, and marvelled that no shadow of artistic jealousy cooled the warmth of their brotherly friendship.

But though Kalos and Musides dwelt in unbroken harmony, their natures were not alike. Whilst Musides revelled by night amidst the urban gaieties of Tegea, Kalos would remain at home; stealing away from the sight of his slaves into the cool recesses of the olive grove. There he would meditate upon the visions that filled his mind, and there devise the forms of beauty which later became immortal in breathing marble. Idle folk, indeed, said that Kalos conversed with the spirits of the grove, and that his statues were but images of the fauns and dryads he met there—for he patterned his work after no living model.

So famous were Kalos and Musides, that none wondered when the Tyrant of Syracuse sent to them deputies to speak of the costly statue of Tyché which he had planned for his city. Of great size and cunning workmanship must the statue be, for it was to form a wonder of nations and a goal of travellers. Exalted beyond thought would be he whose work should gain acceptance, and for this honour Kalos and Musides were invited to compete.

Their brotherly love was well known, and the crafty Tyrant surmised that each, instead of concealing his work from the other, would offer aid and advice; this charity producing two images of unheard-of beauty, the lovelier of which would eclipse even the dreams of poets.

With joy the sculptors hailed the Tyrant's offer, so that in the days that followed their slaves heard the ceaseless blows of chisels. Not from each other did Kalos and Musides conceal their work, but the sight was for them alone. Saving theirs, no eyes beheld the two divine figures released by skilful blows from the rough blocks that had imprisoned them since the world began.

At night, as of yore, Musides sought the banquet halls of Tegea whilst Kalos wandered alone in the olive grove. But as time passed, men observed a want of gaiety in the once sparkling Musides. It was strange, they said amongst themselves, that depression should thus seize one with so great a chance to win art's loftiest reward. Many months passed, yet in the sour face of Musides came nothing of the sharp expectancy which the situation should arouse.

Then one day Musides spoke of the illness of Kalos, after which none marvelled again at his sadness, since the sculptors' attachment was known to be deep and sacred. Subsequently many went to visit Kalos, and indeed noticed the pallor of his face; but there was about him a happy serenity which made his glance more magical than the glance of Musides—who was clearly distracted with anxiety, and who pushed aside all the slaves in his eagerness to feed and wait upon his friend with his own hands. Hidden behind heavy curtains stood the two unfinished figures of Tyché, little touched of late by the sick man and his faithful attendant.

As Kalos grew inexplicably weaker and weaker despite the ministrations of puzzled physicians and of his assiduous friend, he desired to be carried often to the grove which he so loved. There he would ask to be left alone, as if wishing to speak with unseen things. Musides ever granted his requests, though his eyes filled with visible tears at the thought that Kalos should care more for the fauns and the dryads than for him. At last the end drew near, and Kalos discoursed of things beyond this life. Musides, weeping, promised him a sepulchre more lovely than the tomb of Mausolus; but Kalos bade him speak no more of marble glories. Only one wish now haunted the mind of the dying man; that twigs from certain olive trees in the grove be buried by his resting-place—close to his head. And one night, sitting alone in the darkness of the olive grove, Kalos died.

Beautiful beyond words was the marble sepulchre which stricken Musides carved for his beloved friend. None but Kalos himself could have fashioned such bas-reliefs, wherein were displayed all the splendours of Elysium. Nor did Musides fail to bury close to Kalos' head the olive twigs from the grove.

As the first violence of Musides' grief gave place to resignation, he laboured with diligence upon his figure of Tyché. All honour was now his, since the Tyrant of Syracuse would have the work of none save him or Kalos. His task proved a vent for his emotion, and he toiled more steadily each day, shunning the gaieties he once had relished. Meanwhile his evenings were spent beside the tomb of his friend, where a young olive tree had sprung up near the sleeper's head. So swift was the growth of this tree, and so strange was its form, that all who beheld it exclaimed in surprise; and Musides seemed at once fascinated and repelled.

Three years after the death of Kalos, Musides despatched a messenger to the Tyrant, and it was whispered in the agora at Tegea that the mighty statue was finished. By this time the tree by the tomb had attained amazing proportions, exceeding all other trees of its kind, and sending out a singularly heavy branch above the apartment in which Musides laboured. As many visitors came to view the prodigious tree, as to admire the art of the sculptor, so that Musides was seldom alone. But he did not mind his multitude of guests; indeed, he seemed to dread being alone now that his absorbing work was done. The bleak mountain wind, sighing through the olive grove and the tomb-tree, had an uncanny way of forming vaguely articulate sounds.

The sky was dark on the evening that the Tyrant's emissaries came to Tegea. It was definitely known that they had come to bear away the great image of Tyché and bring eternal honour to Musides, so their reception by the proxenoi was of great warmth. As the night wore on, a violent storm of wind broke over the crest of Maenalus, and the men from far Syracuse were glad that they rested snugly in the town. They talked of their illustrious Tyrant, and of the splendour of his capital; and exulted in the glory of the statue which Musides had wrought for him. And then the men of Tegea spoke of the goodness of Musides, and of his heavy grief for his friend; and how not even the coming laurels of art could console him in the absence of Kalos, who might have worn those laurels instead. Of the tree which grew by the tomb, near the head of Kalos, they also spoke. The wind shrieked more horribly, and both the Syracusans and the Arcadians prayed to Aiolos.

In the sunshine of the morning the proxenoi led the Tyrant's messengers up the slope to the abode of the sculptor, but the night-wind had done strange things. Slaves' cries ascended from a scene of desolation, and no more amidst the olive grove rose the gleaming colonnades of that vast hall wherein Musides had dreamed and toiled. Lone and shaken mourned the humble courts and the lower walls, for upon the sumptuous greater peristyle had fallen squarely the heavy overhanging bough of the strange new tree, reducing the stately poem in marble with odd completeness to a mound of unsightly ruins. Strangers and Tegeans stood aghast, looking from the wreckage to the great, sinister tree whose aspect was so weirdly human and whose roots reached so queerly into the sculptured sepulchre of Kalos. And their fear and dismay increased when they searched the fallen apartment; for of the gentle Musides, and of the marvellously fashioned image of Tyché, no trace could be discovered. Amidst such stupendous ruin only chaos dwelt, and the representatives of two cities left disappointed; Syracusans that they had no statue to bear home, Tegeans that they had no artist to crown. However, the Syracusans obtained after a while a very splendid statue in Athens, and the Tegeans consoled themselves by erecting in the agora a marble temple commemorating the gifts, virtues, and brotherly piety of Musides.

But the olive grove still stands, as does the tree growing out of the tomb of Kalos, and the old bee-keeper told me that sometimes the boughs whisper to one another in the night-wind, saying over and over again, *"Οἶδα! Οἶδα—I know! I know!"*

THE EMPTY HOUSE

Algernon Blackwood

Certain houses, like certain persons, manage somehow to proclaim at once their character for evil. In the case of the latter, no particular feature need betray them; they may boast an open countenance and an ingenuous smile; and yet a little of their company leaves the unalterable conviction that there is something radically amiss with their being: that they are evil. Willy nilly, they seem to communicate an atmosphere of secret and wicked thoughts which makes those in their immediate neighbourhood shrink from them as from a thing diseased.

And, perhaps, with houses the same principle is operative, and it is the aroma of evil deeds committed under a particular roof, long after the actual doers have passed away, that makes the gooseflesh come and the hair rise. Something of the original passion of the evil-doer, and of the horror felt by his victim, enters the heart of the innocent watcher, and he becomes suddenly conscious of tingling nerves, creeping skin, and a chilling of the blood. He is terror-stricken without apparent cause.

There was manifestly nothing in the external appearance of this particular house to bear out the tales of the horror that was said to reign within. It was neither lonely nor unkempt. It stood, crowded into a corner of the square, and looked exactly like the houses on either side of it. It had the same number of windows as its neighbours; the same balcony overlooking the gardens; the same white steps leading up to the heavy black front door; and, in the rear, there was the same narrow strip of green, with neat box borders, running up to the wall that divided it from the backs of the adjoining houses. Apparently, too, the number of chimney pots on the roof was the same; the breadth and angle of the eaves; and even the height of the dirty area railings.

And yet this house in the square, that seemed precisely similar to its fifty ugly neighbours, was as a matter of fact entirely different—horribly different.

Wherein lay this marked, invisible difference is impossible to say. It cannot be ascribed wholly to the imagination, because persons who had spent some time in the house, knowing nothing of the facts, had declared positively that certain rooms were so disagreeable they would rather die than enter them again, and that the atmosphere of the whole house produced in them symptoms of a genuine terror; while the series of innocent tenants who had tried to live in it and been forced to decamp at the shortest possible notice, was indeed little less than a scandal in the town.

When Shorthouse arrived to pay a "week-end" visit to his Aunt Julia in her little house on the sea-front at the other end of the town, he found her charged to the brim with mystery and excitement. He had only received her telegram that morning, and he had come anticipating boredom; but the moment he touched her hand and kissed her apple-skin wrinkled cheek, he caught the first wave of her electrical condition. The impression deepened when he learned that there were to be no other visitors, and that he had been telegraphed for with a very special object.

Something was in the wind, and the "something" would doubtless bear fruit; for this elderly spinster aunt, with a mania for psychical research, had brains as well as will power, and by hook or by crook she usually managed to accomplish her ends. The revelation was made soon after tea, when she sidled close up to him as they paced slowly along the sea-front in the dusk.

"I've got the keys," she announced in a delighted, yet half awesome voice. "Got them till Monday!"

"The keys of the bathing-machine, or—?" he asked innocently, looking from the sea to the town. Nothing brought her so quickly to the point as feigning stupidity.

"Neither," she whispered. "I've got the keys of the haunted house in the square—and I'm going there to-night."

Shorthouse was conscious of the slightest possible tremor down his back. He dropped his teasing tone. Something in her voice and manner thrilled him. She was in earnest.

"But you can't go alone—" he began.

"That's why I wired for you," she said with decision.

He turned to look at her. The ugly, lined, enigmatical face was alive with excitement. There was the glow of genuine enthusiasm round it like a halo. The eyes shone. He caught another wave of her excitement, and a second tremor, more marked than the first, accompanied it.

"Thanks, Aunt Julia," he said politely; "thanks awfully."

"I should not dare to go quite alone," she went on, raising her voice; "but with you I should enjoy it immensely. You're afraid of nothing, I know."

"Thanks so much," he said again. "Er—is anything likely to happen?"

"A great deal has happened," she whispered, "though it's been most cleverly hushed up. Three tenants have come and gone in the last few months, and the house is said to be empty for good now."

In spite of himself Shorthouse became interested. His aunt was so very much in earnest.

"The house is very old indeed," she went on, "and the story—an unpleasant one—dates a long way back. It has to do with a murder committed by a jealous stableman who had some affair with a servant in the house. One night he managed to secrete himself in the cellar, and when everyone was asleep, he crept upstairs to the servants' quarters, chased the girl down to the next landing, and before anyone could come to the rescue threw her bodily over the banisters into the hall below."

"And the stableman—?"

"Was caught, I believe, and hanged for murder; but it all happened a century ago, and I've not been able to get more details of the story."

Shorthouse now felt his interest thoroughly aroused; but, though he was not particularly nervous for himself, he hesitated a little on his aunt's account.

"On one condition," he said at length.

"Nothing will prevent my going," she said firmly; "but I may as well hear your condition."

"That you guarantee your power of self-control if anything really horrible happens. I mean—that you are sure you won't get too frightened."

"Jim," she said scornfully, "I'm not young, I know, nor are my nerves; but with you I should be afraid of nothing in the world!"

This, of course, settled it, for Shorthouse had no pretensions to being other than a very ordinary young man, and an appeal to his vanity was irresistible. He agreed to go.

Instinctively, by a sort of sub-conscious preparation, he kept himself and his forces well in hand the whole evening, compelling an accumulative reserve of control by that nameless inward process of gradually putting all the emotions away and turning the key upon them—a process difficult to describe, but wonderfully effective, as all men who have lived through severe trials of the inner man well understand. Later, it stood him in good stead.

But it was not until half-past ten, when they stood in the hall, well in the glare of friendly lamps and still surrounded by comforting human influences, that he had to make the first call upon this store of collected strength. For, once the door was closed, and he saw the deserted silent street stretching away white in the moonlight before them, it came to him clearly that the real test that night would be in dealing with *two fears* instead of one. He would have to carry his aunt's fear as well as his own. And, as he glanced down at her sphinx-like countenance and realised that it might assume no pleasant aspect in a rush of real terror, he felt satisfied with only one thing in the whole adventure—that he had confidence in his own will and power to stand against any shock that might come.

Slowly they walked along the empty streets of the town; a bright autumn moon silvered the roofs, casting deep shadows; there was no breath of wind; and the trees in the formal gardens by the sea-front watched them silently as they passed along. To his aunt's occasional remarks Shorthouse made no reply, realising that she was simply surrounding herself with mental buffers—saying ordinary things to prevent herself thinking of extra-ordinary things. Few windows showed lights, and from scarcely a single chimney came smoke or sparks. Shorthouse had already begun to notice everything, even the smallest details. Presently they stopped at the street corner and looked up at the name on the side of the house full in the moonlight, and with one accord, but without remark, turned into the square and crossed over to the side of it that lay in shadow.

"The number of the house is thirteen," whispered a voice at his side; and neither of them made the obvious reference, but passed across the broad sheet of moonlight and began to march up the pavement in silence.

It was about half-way up the square that Shorthouse felt an arm slipped quietly but significantly into his own, and knew then that their adventure had begun in earnest, and that his companion was already yielding imperceptibly to the influences against them. She needed support.

A few minutes later they stopped before a tall, narrow house that rose before them into the night, ugly in shape and painted a dingy white. Shutterless windows, without blinds, stared down upon them, shining here and there in the moonlight. There were weather streaks in the wall and cracks in the paint, and the balcony bulged out from the first floor a little unnaturally. But, beyond this generally forlorn appearance of an unoccupied house, there was nothing at first sight to single out this particular mansion for the evil character it had most certainly acquired.

Taking a look over their shoulders to make sure they had not been followed, they went boldly up the steps and stood against the huge black door that fronted them forbiddingly. But the first wave of nervousness was now upon them, and Shorthouse fumbled a long time with the key before he could fit it into the lock at all. For a moment, if truth were told, they both hoped it would not open, for they were a prey to various unpleasant emotions as they stood there on the threshold of their ghostly adventure. Shorthouse, shuffling with the key and hampered by the steady weight on his arm, certainly felt the solemnity of the moment. It was as if the whole world—for all experience seemed at that instant concentrated in his own consciousness—were listening to the grating noise of that key. A stray puff of wind wandering down the empty street woke a momentary rustling in the trees behind them, but otherwise this rattling of the key was the only sound audible; and at last it turned in the lock and the heavy door swung open and revealed a yawning gulf of darkness beyond.

With a last glance at the moonlit square, they passed quickly in, and the door slammed behind them with a roar that echoed prodigiously through empty halls and passages. But, instantly, with the echoes, another sound made itself heard, and Aunt Julia leaned suddenly so heavily upon him that he had to take a step backwards to save himself from falling.

A man had coughed close beside them—so close that it seemed they must have been actually by his side in the darkness.

With the possibility of practical jokes in his mind, Shorthouse at once swung his heavy stick in the direction of the sound; but it met nothing more solid than air. He heard his aunt give a little gasp beside him.

"There's someone here," she whispered; "I heard him."

"Be quiet!" he said sternly. "It was nothing but the noise of the front door."

"Oh! get a light—quick!" she added, as her nephew, fumbling with a box of matches, opened it upside down and let them all fall with a rattle on to the stone floor.

The sound, however, was not repeated; and there was no evidence of retreating footsteps. In another minute they had a candle burning, using an empty end of a cigar case as a holder; and when the first flare had died down he held the impromptu lamp aloft and surveyed the scene. And it was dreary enough in all conscience, for there is nothing more desolate in all the abodes of men than an unfurnished house dimly lit, silent, and forsaken, and yet tenanted by rumour with the memories of evil and violent histories.

They were standing in a wide hall-way; on their left was the open door of a spacious dining-room, and in front the hall ran, ever narrowing, into a long, dark passage that led apparently to the top of the kitchen stairs. The broad uncarpeted staircase rose in a sweep before them, everywhere draped in shadows, except for a single spot about half-way up where the moonlight came in through the window and fell on a bright patch on the boards. This shaft of light shed a faint radiance above and below it, lending to the objects within its reach a misty outline that was infinitely more suggestive and ghostly than complete darkness. Filtered moonlight always seems to paint faces on the surrounding gloom, and as Shorthouse peered up into the well of darkness and thought of the countless empty rooms and passages in the upper part of the old house, he caught himself longing again for the safety of the moonlit square, or the cosy, bright drawing-room they had left an hour before. Then realising that these thoughts were dangerous, he thrust them away again and summoned all his energy for concentration on the present.

"Aunt Julia," he said aloud, severely, "we must now go through the house from top to bottom and make a thorough search."

The echoes of his voice died away slowly all over the building, and in the intense silence that followed he turned to look at her. In the candle-light he saw that her face was already ghastly pale; but she dropped his arm for a moment and said in a whisper, stepping close in front of him—

"I agree. We must be sure there's no one hiding. That's the first thing."

She spoke with evident effort, and he looked at her with admiration.

"You feel quite sure of yourself? It's not too late—"

"I think so," she whispered, her eyes shifting nervously toward the shadows behind. "Quite sure, only one thing—"

"What's that?"

"You must never leave me alone for an instant."

"As long as you understand that any sound or appearance must be investigated at once, for to hesitate means to admit fear. That is fatal."

"Agreed," she said, a little shakily, after a moment's hesitation. "I'll try—"

Arm in arm, Shorthouse holding the dripping candle and the stick, while his aunt carried the cloak over her shoulders, figures of utter comedy to all but themselves, they began a systematic search.

Stealthily, walking on tip-toe and shading the candle lest it should betray their presence through the shutterless windows, they went first into the big dining-room. There was not a stick of furniture to be seen. Bare walls, ugly mantel-pieces and empty grates stared at them. Everything, they felt, resented their intrusion, watching them, as it were, with veiled eyes; whispers followed them; shadows flitted noiselessly to right and left; something seemed ever at their back, watching, waiting an opportunity to do them injury. There was the inevitable sense that operations which went on when the room was empty had been temporarily suspended till they were well out of the way again. The whole dark interior of the old building seemed to become a malignant Presence that rose up, warning them to desist and mind their own business; every moment the strain on the nerves increased.

Out of the gloomy dining-room they passed through large folding doors into a sort of library or smoking-room, wrapt equally in silence, darkness, and dust; and from this they regained the hall near the top of the back stairs.

Here a pitch black tunnel opened before them into the lower regions, and—it must be confessed—they hesitated. But only for a minute. With the worst of the night still to come it was essential to turn from nothing. Aunt Julia stumbled at the top step of the dark descent, ill lit by the flickering candle, and even Shorthouse felt at least half the decision go out of his legs.

"Come on!" he said peremptorily, and his voice ran on and lost itself in the dark, empty spaces below.

"I'm coming," she faltered, catching his arm with unnecessary violence.

They went a little unsteadily down the stone steps, a cold, damp air meeting them in the face, close and malodorous. The kitchen, into which the stairs led along a narrow passage, was large, with a lofty ceiling. Several doors opened out of it—some into cupboards with empty jars still standing on the shelves, and others into horrible little ghostly back offices, each colder and less inviting than the last. Black beetles scurried over the floor, and once, when they knocked against a deal table standing in a corner, something about the size of a cat jumped down with a rush and fled, scampering across the stone floor into the darkness. Everywhere there was a sense of recent occupation, an impression of sadness and gloom.

Leaving the main kitchen, they next went towards the scullery. The door was standing ajar, and as they pushed it open to its full extent Aunt Julia uttered a piercing scream, which she instantly tried to stifle by placing her hand over her mouth. For a second Shorthouse stood stock-still, catching his breath. He felt as if his spine had suddenly become hollow and someone had filled it with particles of ice.

Facing them, directly in their way between the doorposts, stood the figure of a woman. She had dishevelled hair and wildly staring eyes, and her face was terrified and white as death.

She stood there motionless for the space of a single second. Then the candle flickered and she was gone—gone utterly—and the door framed nothing but empty darkness.

"Only the beastly jumping candle-light," he said quickly, in a voice that sounded like someone else's and was only half under control. "Come on, aunt. There's nothing there."

He dragged her forward. With a clattering of feet and a great appearance of boldness they went on, but over his body the skin moved as if crawling ants covered it, and he knew by the weight on his arm that he was supplying the force of locomotion for two. The scullery was cold, bare, and empty; more like a large prison cell than anything else. They went round it, tried the door into the yard, and the windows, but found them all fastened securely. His aunt moved beside him like a person in a dream. Her eyes were tightly shut, and she seemed merely to follow the pressure of his arm. Her courage filled him with amazement. At the same time he noticed that a certain odd change had come over her face, a change which somehow evaded his power of analysis.

"There's nothing here, aunty," he repeated aloud quickly. "Let's go upstairs and see the rest of the house. Then we'll choose a room to wait up in."

She followed him obediently, keeping close to his side, and they locked the kitchen door behind them. It was a relief to get up again. In the hall there was more light than before, for the moon had travelled a little further down the stairs. Cautiously they began to go up into the dark vault of the upper house, the boards creaking under their weight.

On the first floor they found the large double drawing-rooms, a search of which revealed nothing. Here also was no sign of furniture or recent occupancy; nothing but dust and neglect and shadows. They opened the big folding doors between front and back drawing-rooms and then came out again to the landing and went on upstairs.

They had not gone up more than a dozen steps when they both simultaneously stopped to listen, looking into each other's eyes with a new apprehension across the flickering candle flame. From the room they had left hardly ten seconds before came the sound of doors quietly closing. It was beyond all question; they heard the booming noise that accompanies the shutting of heavy doors, followed by the sharp catching of the latch.

"We must go back and see," said Shorthouse briefly, in a low tone, and turning to go downstairs again.

Somehow she managed to drag after him, her feet catching in her dress, her face livid.

When they entered the front drawing-room it was plain that the folding doors had been closed—half a minute before. Without hesitation Shorthouse opened them. He almost expected to see someone facing him in the back room; but only darkness and cold air met him. They went through both rooms, finding nothing unusual. They tried in every way to make the doors close of themselves, but there was not wind enough even to set the candle flame flickering. The doors would not move without strong pressure. All was silent as the grave. Undeniably the rooms were utterly empty, and the house utterly still.

"It's beginning," whispered a voice at his elbow which he hardly recognised as his aunt's.

He nodded acquiescence, taking out his watch to note the time. It was fifteen minutes before midnight; he made the entry of exactly what had occurred in his notebook, setting the candle in its case upon the floor in order to do so. It took a moment or two to balance it safely against the wall.

Aunt Julia always declared that at this moment she was not actually watching him, but had turned her head towards the inner room, where she fancied she heard something moving; but, at any rate, both positively agreed that there came a sound of rushing feet, heavy and very swift—and the next instant the candle was out!

But to Shorthouse himself had come more than this, and he has always thanked his fortunate stars that it came to him alone and not to his aunt too. For, as he rose from the stooping position of balancing the candle, and before it was actually extinguished, a face thrust itself forward so close to his own that he could almost have touched it with his lips. It was a face working with passion; a man's face, dark, with thick features, and angry, savage eyes. It belonged to a common man, and it was evil in its ordinary normal expression, no doubt, but as he saw it, alive with intense, aggressive emotion, it was a malignant and terrible human countenance.

There was no movement of the air; nothing but the sound of rushing feet—stockinged or muffled feet; the apparition of the face; and the almost simultaneous extinguishing of the candle.

In spite of himself, Shorthouse uttered a little cry, nearly losing his balance as his aunt clung to him with her whole weight in one moment of real, uncontrollable terror. She made no sound, but simply seized him bodily. Fortunately, however, she had seen nothing, but had only heard the rushing feet, for her control returned almost at once, and he was able to disentangle himself and strike a match.

The shadows ran away on all sides before the glare, and his aunt stooped down and groped for the cigar case with the precious candle. Then they discovered that the candle had not been *blown* out at all; it had been *crushed* out. The wick was pressed down into the wax, which was flattened as if by some smooth, heavy instrument.

How his companion so quickly overcame her terror, Shorthouse never properly understood; but his admiration for her self-control increased tenfold, and at the same time served to feed his own dying flame—for which he was undeniably grateful. Equally inexplicable to him was the evidence of physical force they had just witnessed. He at once suppressed the memory of stories he had heard of "physical mediums" and their dangerous phenomena; for if these were true, and either his aunt or himself was unwittingly a physical medium, it meant that they were simply aiding to focus the forces of a haunted house already charged to the brim. It was like walking with unprotected lamps among uncovered stores of gun-powder.

So, with as little reflection as possible, he simply relit the candle and went up to the next floor. The arm in his trembled, it is true, and his own tread was often uncertain, but they went on with thoroughness, and after a search revealing nothing they climbed the last flight of stairs to the top floor of all.

Here they found a perfect nest of small servants' rooms, with broken pieces of furniture, dirty cane-bottomed chairs, chests of drawers, cracked mirrors, and decrepit bedsteads. The rooms had low sloping ceilings already hung here and there with cobwebs, small windows, and badly plastered walls—a depressing and dismal region which they were glad to leave behind.

It was on the stroke of midnight when they entered a small room on the third floor, close to the top of the stairs, and arranged to make themselves comfortable for the remainder of their adventure. It was absolutely bare, and was said to be the room—then used as a clothes closet—into which the infuriated groom had chased his victim and finally caught her. Outside, across the narrow landing, began the stairs leading up to the floor above, and the servants' quarters where they had just searched.

In spite of the chilliness of the night there was something in the air of this room that cried for an open window. But there was more than this. Shorthouse could only describe it by saying that he felt less master of himself here than in any other part of the house. There was something that acted directly on the nerves, tiring the resolution, enfeebling the will. He was conscious of this result before he had been in the room five minutes, and it was in the short time they stayed there that he suffered the wholesale depletion of his vital forces, which was, for himself, the chief horror of the whole experience.

They put the candle on the floor of the cupboard, leaving the door a few inches ajar, so that there was no glare to confuse the eyes, and no shadow to shift about on walls and ceiling. Then they spread the cloak on the floor and sat down to wait, with their backs against the wall.

Shorthouse was within two feet of the door on to the landing; his position commanded a good view of the main staircase leading down into the darkness, and also of the beginning of the servants' stairs going to the floor above; the heavy stick lay beside him within easy reach.

The moon was now high above the house. Through the open window they could see the comforting stars like friendly eyes watching in the sky. One by one the clocks of the town struck midnight, and when the sounds died away the deep silence of a windless night fell again over everything. Only the boom of the sea, far away and lugubrious, filled the air with hollow murmurs.

Inside the house the silence became awful; awful, he thought, because any minute now it might be broken by sounds portending terror. The strain of waiting told more and more severely on the nerves; they talked in whispers when they talked at all, for their voices aloud sounded queer and unnatural. A chilliness, not altogether due to the night air, invaded the room, and made them cold. The influences against them, whatever these might be, were slowly robbing them of self-confidence, and the power of decisive action; their forces were on the wane, and the possibility of real fear took on a new and terrible meaning. He began to tremble for the elderly woman by his side, whose pluck could hardly save her beyond a certain extent.

He heard the blood singing in his veins. It sometimes seemed so loud that he fancied it prevented his hearing properly certain other sounds that were beginning very faintly to make themselves audible in the depths of the house. Every time he fastened his attention on these sounds, they instantly ceased. They certainly came no nearer. Yet he could not rid himself of the idea that movement was going on somewhere in the lower regions of the house. The drawing-room floor, where the doors had been so strangely closed, seemed too near; the sounds were further off than that. He thought of the great kitchen, with the scurrying black-beetles, and of the dismal little scullery; but, somehow or other, they did not seem to come from there either. Surely they were not outside the house!

Then, suddenly, the truth flashed into his mind, and for the space of a minute he felt as if his blood had stopped flowing and turned to ice.

The sounds were not downstairs at all; they were upstairs—upstairs, somewhere among those horrid gloomy little servants' rooms with their bits of broken furniture, low ceilings, and cramped windows—upstairs where the victim had first been disturbed and stalked to her death.

And the moment he discovered where the sounds were, he began to hear them more clearly. It was the sound of feet, moving stealthily along the passage overhead, in and out among the rooms, and past the furniture.

He turned quickly to steal a glance at the motionless figure seated beside him, to note whether she had shared his discovery. The faint candle-light coming through the crack in the cupboard door, threw her strongly-marked face into vivid relief against the white of the wall. But it was something else that made him catch his breath and stare again. An extraordinary something had come into her face and seemed to spread over her features like a mask; it smoothed out the deep lines and drew the skin everywhere a little tighter so that the wrinkles disappeared; it brought into the face—with the sole exception of the old eyes—an appearance of youth and almost of childhood.

He stared in speechless amazement—amazement that was dangerously near to horror. It was his aunt's face indeed, but it was her face of forty years ago, the vacant innocent face of a girl. He had heard stories of that strange effect of terror which could wipe a human countenance clean of other emotions, obliterating all previous expressions; but he had never realised that it could be literally true, or could mean anything so simply horrible as what he now saw. For the dreadful signature of overmastering fear was written plainly in that utter vacancy of the girlish face beside him; and when, feeling his intense gaze, she turned to look at him, he instinctively closed his eyes tightly to shut out the sight.

Yet, when he turned a minute later, his feelings well in hand, he saw to his intense relief another expression; his aunt was smiling, and though the face was deathly white, the awful veil had lifted and the normal look was returning.

"Anything wrong?" was all he could think of to say at the moment. And the answer was eloquent, coming from such a woman.

"I feel cold—and a little frightened," she whispered.

He offered to close the window, but she seized hold of him and begged him not to leave her side even for an instant.

"It's upstairs, I know," she whispered, with an odd half laugh; "but I can't possibly go up."

But Shorthouse thought otherwise, knowing that in action lay their best hope of self-control.

He took the brandy flask and poured out a glass of neat spirit, stiff enough to help anybody over anything. She swallowed it with a little shiver. His only idea now was to get out of the house before her collapse became inevitable; but this could not safely be done by turning tail and running from the enemy. Inaction was no longer possible; every minute he was growing less master of himself, and desperate, aggressive measures were imperative without further delay. Moreover, the action must be taken towards the enemy, not away from it; the climax, if necessary and unavoidable, would have to be faced boldly. He could do it now; but in ten minutes he might not have the force left to act for himself, much less for both!

Upstairs, the sounds were meanwhile becoming louder and closer, accompanied by occasional creaking of the boards. Someone was moving stealthily about, stumbling now and then awkwardly against the furniture.

Waiting a few moments to allow the tremendous dose of spirits to produce its effect, and knowing this would last but a short time under the circumstances, Shorthouse then quietly got on his feet, saying in a determined voice—

"Now, Aunt Julia, we'll go upstairs and find out what all this noise is about. You must come too. It's what we agreed."

He picked up his stick and went to the cupboard for the candle. A limp form rose shakily beside him breathing hard, and he heard a voice say very faintly something about being "ready to come." The woman's courage amazed him; it was so much greater than his own; and, as they advanced, holding aloft the dripping candle, some subtle force exhaled from this trembling, white-faced old woman at his side that was the true source of his inspiration. It held something really great that shamed him and gave him the support without which he would have proved far less equal to the occasion.

They crossed the dark landing, avoiding with their eyes the deep black space over the banisters. Then they began to mount the narrow staircase to meet the sounds which, minute by minute, grew louder and nearer. About half-way up the stairs Aunt Julia stumbled and Shorthouse turned to catch her by the arm, and just at that moment there came a terrific crash in the servants' corridor overhead. It was instantly followed by a shrill, agonised scream that was a cry of terror and a cry for help melted into one.

Before they could move aside, or go down a single step, someone came rushing along the passage overhead, blundering horribly, racing madly, at full speed, three steps at a time, down the very staircase where they stood. The steps were light and uncertain; but close behind them sounded the heavier tread of another person, and the staircase seemed to shake.

Shorthouse and his companion just had time to flatten themselves against the wall when the jumble of flying steps was upon them, and two persons, with the slightest possible interval between them, dashed past at full speed. It was a perfect whirlwind of sound breaking in upon the midnight silence of the empty building.

The two runners, pursuer and pursued, had passed clean through them where they stood, and already with a thud the boards below had received first one, then the other. Yet they had seen absolutely nothing—not a hand, or arm, or face, or even a shred of flying clothing.

There came a second's pause. Then the first one, the lighter of the two, obviously the pursued one, ran with uncertain footsteps into the little room which Shorthouse and his aunt had just left. The heavier one followed. There was a sound of scuffling, gasping, and smothered screaming; and then out on to the landing came the step—of a single person *treading weightily*.

A dead silence followed for the space of half a minute, and then was heard a rushing sound through the air. It was followed by a dull, crashing thud in the depths of the house below—on the stone floor of the hall.

Utter silence reigned after. Nothing moved. The flame of the candle was steady. It had been steady the whole time, and the air had been undisturbed by any movement whatsoever. Palsied with terror, Aunt Julia, without waiting for her companion, began fumbling her way downstairs; she was crying gently to herself, and when Shorthouse put his arm round her and half carried her he felt that she was trembling like a leaf. He went into the little room and picked up the cloak from the floor, and, arm in arm, walking very slowly, without speaking a word or looking once behind them, they marched down the three flights into the hall.

In the hall they saw nothing, but the whole way down the stairs they were conscious that someone followed them; step by step; when they went faster *it* was left behind, and when they went more slowly *it* caught them up. But never once did they look behind to see; and at each turning of the staircase they lowered their eyes for fear of the following horror they might see upon the stairs above.

With trembling hands Shorthouse opened the front door, and they walked out into the moonlight and drew a deep breath of the cool night air blowing in from the sea.

THE BOTTLE IMP

Robert Louis Stevenson

Note.—Any student of that very unliterary product, the English drama of the early part of the century, will here recognise the name and the root idea of a piece once rendered popular by the redoubtable O. Smith. The root idea is there and identical, and yet I hope I have made it a new thing. And the fact that the tale has been designed and written for a Polynesian audience may lend it some extraneous interest nearer home.

—R. L. S.

There was a man of the Island of Hawaii, whom I shall call Keawe; for the truth is, he still lives, and his name must be kept secret; but the place of his birth was not far from Honaunau, where the bones of Keawe the Great lie hidden in a cave. This man was poor, brave, and active; he could read and write like a schoolmaster; he was a first-rate mariner besides, sailed for some time in the island steamers, and steered a whaleboat on the Hamakua coast. At length it came in Keawe's mind to have a sight of the great world and foreign cities, and he shipped on a vessel bound to San Francisco.

This is a fine town, with a fine harbour, and rich people uncountable; and, in particular, there is one hill which is covered with palaces. Upon this hill Keawe was one day taking a walk with his pocket full of money, viewing the great houses upon either hand with pleasure, "What fine houses these are!" he was thinking, "and how happy must those people be who dwell in them, and take no care for the morrow!" The thought was in his mind when he came abreast of a house that was smaller than some others, but all finished and beautified like a toy; the steps of that house shone like silver, and the borders of the garden bloomed like garlands, and the windows were bright like diamond; and Keawe stopped and wondered at the excellence of all he saw. So stopping, he was aware of a man that looked forth upon him through a window so clear that Keawe could see him as you see a fish in a pool upon the reef. The man was elderly, with a bald head and a black beard; and his face was heavy with sorrow, and he bitterly sighed. And the truth of it is, that as Keawe looked in upon the man, and the man looked out upon Keawe, each envied the other.

All of a sudden, the man smiled and nodded, and beckoned Keawe to enter, and met him at the door of the house.

"This is a fine house of mine," said the man, and bitterly sighed. "Would you not care to view the chambers?"

So he led Keawe all over it, from the cellar to the roof, and there was nothing there that was not perfect of its kind, and Keawe was astonished.

"Truly," said Keawe, "this is a beautiful house; if I lived in the like of it, I should be laughing all day long. How comes it, then, that you should be sighing?"

"There is no reason," said the man, "why you should not have a house in all points similar to this, and finer, if you wish. You have some money, I suppose?"

"I have fifty dollars," said Keawe; "but a house like this will cost more than fifty dollars."

The man made a computation. "I am sorry you have no more," said he, "for it may raise you trouble in the future; but it shall be yours at fifty dollars."

"The house?" asked Keawe.

"No, not the house," replied the man; "but the bottle. For, I must tell you, although I appear to you so rich and fortunate, all my fortune, and this house itself and its garden, came out of a bottle not much bigger than a pint. This is it."

And he opened a lockfast place, and took out a round-bellied bottle with a long neck; the glass of it was white like milk, with changing rainbow colours in the grain. Withinsides something obscurely moved, like a shadow and a fire.

"This is the bottle," said the man; and, when Keawe laughed, "You do not believe me?" he added. "Try, then, for yourself. See if you can break it."

So Keawe took the bottle up and dashed it on the floor till he was weary; but it jumped on the floor like a child's ball, and was not injured.

"This is a strange thing," said Keawe. "For by the touch of it, as well as by the look, the bottle should be of glass."

"Of glass it is," replied the man, sighing more heavily than ever; "but the glass of it was tempered in the flames of hell. An imp lives in it, and that is the shadow we behold there moving: or so I suppose. If any man buy this bottle the imp is at his command; all that he desires—love, fame, money, houses like this house, ay, or a city like this city—all are his at the word uttered. Napoleon had this bottle, and by it he grew to be the king of the world; but he sold it at the last, and fell. Captain Cook had this bottle, and by it he found his way to so many islands; but he, too, sold it, and was slain upon Hawaii. For, once it is sold, the power goes and the protection; and unless a man remain content with what he has, ill will befall him."

"And yet you talk of selling it yourself?" Keawe said.

"I have all I wish, and I am growing elderly," replied the man. "There is one thing the imp cannot do—he cannot prolong life; and, it would not be fair to conceal from you, there is a drawback to the bottle; for if a man die before he sells it, he must burn in hell forever."

"To be sure, that is a drawback and no mistake," cried Keawe. "I would not meddle with the thing. I can do without a house, thank God; but there is one thing I could not be doing with one particle, and that is to be damned."

"Dear me, you must not run away with things," returned the man. "All you have to do is to use the power of the imp in moderation, and then sell it to someone else, as I do to you, and finish your life in comfort."

"Well, I observe two things," said Keawe. "All the time you keep sighing like a maid in love, that is one; and, for the other, you sell this bottle very cheap."

"I have told you already why I sigh," said the man. "It is because I fear my health is breaking up; and, as you said yourself, to die and go to the devil is a pity for anyone. As for why I sell so cheap, I must explain to you there is a peculiarity about the bottle. Long ago, when the devil brought it first upon earth, it was extremely expensive, and was sold first of all to Prester John for many millions of dollars; but it cannot be sold at all, unless sold at a loss. If you sell it for as much as you paid for it, back it comes to you again like a homing pigeon. It follows that the price has kept falling in these centuries, and the bottle is now remarkably cheap. I bought it myself from one of my great neighbours on this hill, and the price I paid was only ninety dollars. I could sell it for as high as eighty-nine dollars and ninety-nine cents, but not a penny dearer, or back the thing must come to me. Now, about this there are two bothers. First, when you offer a bottle so singular for eighty odd dollars, people suppose you to be jesting. And second—but there is no hurry about that—and I need not go into it. Only remember it must be coined money that you sell it for."

"How am I to know that this is all true?" asked Keawe.

"Some of it you can try at once," replied the man. "Give me your fifty dollars, take the bottle, and wish your fifty dollars back into your pocket. If that does not happen, I pledge you my honour I will cry off the bargain and restore your money."

"You are not deceiving me?" said Keawe.

The man bound himself with a great oath.

"Well, I will risk that much," said Keawe, "for that can do no harm." And he paid over his money to the man, and the man handed him the bottle.

"Imp of the bottle," said Keawe, "I want my fifty dollars back." And sure enough he had scarce said the word before his pocket was as heavy as ever.

"To be sure this is a wonderful bottle," said Keawe.

"And now good-morning to you, my fine fellow, and the devil go with you for me!" said the man.

"Hold on," said Keawe, "I don't want any more of this fun. Here, take your bottle back."

"You have bought it for less than I paid for it," replied the man, rubbing his hands. "It is yours now; and, for my part, I am only concerned to see the back of you." And with that he rang for his Chinese servant, and had Keawe shown out of the house.

Now, when Keawe was in the street, with the bottle under his arm, he began to think. "If all is true about this bottle, I may have made a losing bargain," thinks he. "But perhaps the man was only fooling me." The first thing he did was to count his money; the sum was exact—forty-nine dollars American money, and one Chili piece. "That looks like the truth," said Keawe. "Now I will try another part."

The streets in that part of the city were as clean as a ship's decks, and though it was noon, there were no passengers. Keawe set the bottle in the gutter and walked away. Twice he looked back, and there was the milky, round-bellied bottle where he left it. A third time he looked back, and turned a corner; but he had scarce done so, when something knocked upon his elbow, and behold! it was the long neck sticking up; and as for the round belly, it was jammed into the pocket of his pilot-coat.

"And that looks like the truth," said Keawe.

The next thing he did was to buy a cork-screw in a shop, and go apart into a secret place in the fields. And there he tried to draw the cork, but as often as he put the screw in, out it came again, and the cork as whole as ever.

"This is some new sort of cork," said Keawe, and all at once he began to shake and sweat, for he was afraid of that bottle.

On his way back to the port-side, he saw a shop where a man sold shells and clubs from the wild islands, old heathen deities, old coined money, pictures from China and Japan, and all manner of things that sailors bring in their sea-chests. And here he had an idea. So he went in and offered the bottle for a hundred dollars. The man of the shop laughed at him at the first, and offered him five; but, indeed, it was a curious bottle—such glass was never blown in any human glassworks, so prettily the colours shone under the milky white, and so strangely the shadow hovered in the midst; so, after he had disputed awhile after the manner of his kind, the shop-man gave Keawe sixty silver dollars for the thing, and set it on a shelf in the midst of his window.

"Now," said Keawe, "I have sold that for sixty which I bought for fifty—or, to say truth, a little less, because one of my dollars was from Chili. Now I shall know the truth upon another point."

So he went back on board his ship, and, when he opened his chest, there was the bottle, and had come more quickly than himself. Now Keawe had a mate on board whose name was Lopaka.

"What ails you?" said Lopaka, "that you stare in your chest?"

They were alone in the ship's forecastle, and Keawe bound him to secrecy, and told all.

"This is a very strange affair," said Lopaka; "and I fear you will be in trouble about this bottle. But there is one point very clear—that you are sure of the trouble, and you had better have the profit in the bargain. Make up your mind what you want with it; give the order, and if it is done as you desire, I will buy the bottle myself; for I have an idea of my own to get a schooner, and go trading through the islands."

"That is not my idea," said Keawe; "but to have a beautiful house and garden on the Kona Coast, where I was born, the sun shining in at the door, flowers in the garden, glass in the windows, pictures on the walls, and toys and fine carpets on the tables, for all the world like the house I was in this day—only a storey higher, and with balconies all about like the King's palace; and to live there without care and make merry with my friends and relatives."

"Well," said Lopaka, "let us carry it back with us to Hawaii; and if all comes true, as you suppose, I will buy the bottle, as I said, and ask a schooner."

Upon that they were agreed, and it was not long before the ship returned to Honolulu, carrying Keawe and Lopaka, and the bottle. They were scarce come ashore when they met a friend upon the beach, who began at once to condole with Keawe.

"I do not know what I am to be condoled about," said Keawe.

"Is it possible you have not heard," said the friend, "your uncle—that good old man—is dead, and your cousin—that beautiful boy—was drowned at sea?"

Keawe was filled with sorrow, and, beginning to weep and to lament, he forgot about the bottle. But Lopaka was thinking to himself, and presently, when Keawe's grief was a little abated, "I have been thinking," said Lopaka. "Had not your uncle lands in Hawaii, in the district of Kau?"

"No," said Keawe, "not in Kau; they are on the mountain-side—a little way south of Hookena."

"These lands will now be yours?" asked Lopaka.

"And so they will," says Keawe, and began again to lament for his relatives.

"No," said Lopaka, "do not lament at present. I have a thought in my mind. How if this should be the doing of the bottle? For here is the place ready for your house."

"If this be so," cried Keawe, "it is a very ill way to serve me by killing my relatives. But it may be, indeed; for it was in just such a station that I saw the house with my mind's eye."

"The house, however, is not yet built," said Lopaka.

"No, nor like to be!" said Keawe; "for though my uncle has some coffee and ava and bananas, it will not be more than will keep me in comfort; and the rest of that land is the black lava."

"Let us go to the lawyer," said Lopaka; "I have still this idea in my mind."

Now, when they came to the lawyer's, it appeared Keawe's uncle had grown monstrous rich in the last days, and there was a fund of money.

"And here is the money for the house!" cried Lopaka.

"If you are thinking of a new house," said the lawyer, "here is the card of a new architect, of whom they tell me great things."

"Better and better!" cried Lopaka. "Here is all made plain for us. Let us continue to obey orders."

So they went to the architect, and he had drawings of houses on his table.

"You want something out of the way," said the architect. "How do you like this?" and he handed a drawing to Keawe.

Now, when Keawe set eyes on the drawing, he cried out aloud, for it was the picture of his thought exactly drawn.

"I am in for this house," thought he. "Little as I like the way it comes to me, I am in for it now, and I may as well take the good along with the evil."

So he told the architect all that he wished, and how he would have that house furnished, and about the pictures on the wall and the knick-knacks on the tables; and he asked the man plainly for how much he would undertake the whole affair.

The architect put many questions, and took his pen and made a computation; and when he had done he named the very sum that Keawe had inherited.

Lopaka and Keawe looked at one another and nodded.

"It is quite clear," thought Keawe, "that I am to have this house, whether or no. It comes from the devil, and I fear I will get little good by that; and of one thing I am sure, I will make no more wishes as long as I have this bottle. But with the house I am saddled, and I may as well take the good along with the evil."

So he made his terms with the architect, and they signed a paper; and Keawe and Lopaka took ship again and sailed to Australia; for it was concluded between them they should not interfere at all, but leave the architect and the bottle imp to build and to adorn that house at their own pleasure.

The voyage was a good voyage, only all the time Keawe was holding in his breath, for he had sworn he would utter no more wishes, and take no more favours from the devil. The time was up when they got back. The architect told them that the house was ready, and Keawe and Lopaka took a passage in the *Hall*, and went down Kona way to view the house, and see if all had been done fitly according to the thought that was in Keawe's mind.

Now the house stood on the mountain side, visible to ships. Above, the forest ran up into the clouds of rain; below, the black lava fell in cliffs, where the kings of old lay buried. A garden bloomed about that house with every hue of flowers; and there was an orchard of papaia on the one hand and an orchard of breadfruit on the other, and right in front, toward the sea, a ship's mast had been rigged up and bore a flag. As for the house, it was three storeys high, with great chambers and broad balconies on each. The windows were of glass, so excellent that it was as clear as water and as bright as day. All manner of furniture adorned the chambers. Pictures hung upon the wall in golden frames: pictures of ships, and men fighting, and of the most beautiful women, and of singular places; nowhere in the world are there pictures of so bright a colour as those Keawe found hanging in his house. As for the knick-knacks, they were extraordinary fine; chiming clocks and musical boxes, little men with nodding heads, books filled with pictures, weapons of price from all quarters of the world, and the most elegant puzzles to entertain the leisure of a solitary man. And as no one would care to live in such chambers, only to walk through and view them, the balconies were made so broad that a whole town might have lived upon them in delight; and Keawe knew not which to prefer, whether the back porch, where you got the land breeze, and looked upon the orchards and the flowers, or the front balcony, where you could drink the wind of the sea, and look down the steep wall of the mountain and see the *Hall* going by once a week or so between Hookena and the hills of Pele, or the schooners plying up the coast for wood and ava and bananas.

When they had viewed all, Keawe and Lopaka sat on the porch.

"Well," asked Lopaka, "is it all as you designed?"

"Words cannot utter it," said Keawe. "It is better than I dreamed, and I am sick with satisfaction."

"There is but one thing to consider," said Lopaka; "all this may be quite natural, and the bottle imp have nothing whatever to say to it. If I were to buy the bottle, and got no schooner after all, I should have put my hand in the fire for nothing. I gave you my word, I know; but yet I think you would not grudge me one more proof."

"I have sworn I would take no more favours," said Keawe. "I have gone already deep enough."

"This is no favour I am thinking of," replied Lopaka. "It is only to see the imp himself. There is nothing to be gained by that, and so nothing to be ashamed of; and yet, if I once saw him, I should be sure of the whole matter. So indulge me so far, and let me see the imp; and, after that, here is the money in my hand, and I will buy it."

"There is only one thing I am afraid of," said Keawe. "The imp may be very ugly to view; and if you once set eyes upon him you might be very undesirous of the bottle."

"I am a man of my word," said Lopaka. "And here is the money betwixt us."

"Very well," replied Keawe. "I have a curiosity myself. So come, let us have one look at you, Mr. Imp."

Now as soon as that was said, the imp looked out of the bottle, and in again, swift as a lizard; and there sat Keawe and Lopaka turned to stone. The night had quite come, before either found a thought to say or voice to say it with; and then Lopaka pushed the money over and took the bottle.

"I am a man of my word," said he, "and had need to be so, or I would not touch this bottle with my foot. Well, I shall get my schooner and a dollar or two for my pocket; and then I will be rid of this devil as fast as I can. For to tell you the plain truth, the look of him has cast me down."

"Lopaka," said Keawe, "do not you think any worse of me than you can help; I know it is night, and the roads bad, and the pass by the tombs an ill place to go by so late, but I declare since I have seen that little face, I cannot eat or sleep or pray till it is gone from me. I will give you a lantern and a basket to put the bottle in, and any picture or fine thing in all my house that takes your fancy;—and be gone at once, and go sleep at Hookena with Nahinu."

"Keawe," said Lopaka, "many a man would take this ill; above all, when I am doing you a turn so friendly, as to keep my word and buy the bottle; and for that matter, the night and the dark, and the way by the tombs, must be all tenfold more dangerous to a man with such a sin upon his conscience, and such a bottle under his arm. But for my part, I am so extremely terrified myself, I have not the heart to blame you. Here I go then; and I pray God you may be happy in your house, and I fortunate with my schooner, and both get to heaven in the end in spite of the devil and his bottle."

So Lopaka went down the mountain; and Keawe stood in his front balcony, and listened to the clink of the horse's shoes, and watched the lantern go shining down the path, and along the cliff of caves where the old dead are buried; and all the time he trembled and clasped his hands, and prayed for his friend, and gave glory to God that he himself was escaped out of that trouble.

But the next day came very brightly, and that new house of his was so delightful to behold that he forgot his terrors. One day followed another, and Keawe dwelt there in perpetual joy. He had his place on the back porch; it was there he ate and lived, and read the stories in the Honolulu newspapers; but when anyone came by they would go in and view the chambers and the pictures. And the fame of the house went far and wide; it was called *Ka-Hale Nui*—the Great House—in all Kona; and sometimes the Bright House, for Keawe kept a Chinaman, who was all day dusting and furbishing; and the glass, and the gilt, and the fine stuffs, and the pictures, shone as bright as the morning. As for Keawe himself, he could not walk in the chambers without singing, his heart was so enlarged; and when ships sailed by upon the sea, he would fly his colours on the mast.

So time went by, until one day Keawe went upon a visit as far as Kailua to certain of his friends. There he was well feasted; and left as soon as he could the next morning, and rode hard, for he was impatient to behold his beautiful house; and, besides, the night then coming on was the night in which the dead of old days go abroad in the sides of Kona; and having already meddled with the devil, he was the more chary of meeting with the dead. A little beyond Honaunau, looking far ahead, he was aware of a woman bathing in the edge of the sea; and she seemed a well-grown girl, but he thought no more of it. Then he saw her white shift flutter as she put it on, and then her red holoku; and by the time he came abreast of her she was done with her toilet, and had come up from the sea, and stood by the track-side in her red holoku, and she was all freshened with the bath, and her eyes shone and were kind. Now Keawe no sooner beheld her than he drew rein.

"I thought I knew everyone in this country," said he. "How comes it that I do not know you?"

"I am Kokua, daughter of Kiano," said the girl, "and I have just returned from Oahu. Who are you?"

"I will tell you who I am in a little," said Keawe, dismounting from his horse, "but not now. For I have a thought in my mind, and if you knew who I was, you might have heard of me, and would not give me a true answer. But tell me, first of all, one thing: Are you married?"

At this Kokua laughed out aloud. "It is you who ask questions," she said. "Are you married yourself?"

"Indeed, Kokua, I am not," replied Keawe, "and never thought to be until this hour. But here is the plain truth. I have met you here at the roadside, and I saw your eyes, which are like the stars, and my heart went to you as swift as a bird. And so now, if you want none of me, say so, and I will go on to my own place; but if you think me no worse than any other young man, say so, too, and I will turn aside to your father's for the night, and to-morrow I will talk with the good man."

Kokua said never a word, but she looked at the sea and laughed.

"Kokua," said Keawe, "if you say nothing, I will take that for the good answer; so let us be stepping to your father's door."

She went on ahead of him, still without speech; only sometimes she glanced back and glanced away again, and she kept the strings of her hat in her mouth.

Now, when they had come to the door, Kiano came out on his verandah, and cried out and welcomed Keawe by name. At that the girl looked over, for the fame of the great house had come to her ears; and, to be sure, it was a great temptation. All that evening they were very merry together; and the girl was as bold as brass under the eyes of her parents, and made a mock of Keawe, for she had a quick wit. The next day he had a word with Kiano, and found the girl alone.

"Kokua," said he, "you made a mock of me all the evening; and it is still time to bid me go. I would not tell you who I was, because I have so fine a house, and I feared you would think too much of that house and too little of the man that loves you. Now you know all, and if you wish to have seen the last of me, say so at once."

"No," said Kokua; but this time she did not laugh, nor did Keawe ask for more.

This was the wooing of Keawe; things had gone quickly; but so an arrow goes, and the ball of a rifle swifter still, and yet both may strike the target. Things had gone fast, but they had gone far also, and the thought of Keawe rang in the maiden's head; she heard his voice in the breach of the surf upon the lava, and for this young man that she had seen but twice she would have left father and mother and her native islands. As for Keawe himself, his horse flew up the path of the mountain under the cliff of tombs, and the sound of the hoofs, and the sound of Keawe singing to himself for pleasure, echoed in the caverns of the dead. He came to the Bright House, and still he was singing. He sat and ate in the broad balcony, and the Chinaman wondered at his master, to hear how he sang between the mouthfuls. The sun went down into the sea, and the night came; and Keawe walked the balconies by lamplight, high on the mountains, and the voice of his singing startled men on ships.

"Here am I now upon my high place," he said to himself. "Life may be no better; this is the mountain top; and all shelves about me toward the worse. For the first time I will light up the chambers, and bathe in my fine bath with the hot water and the cold, and sleep alone in the bed of my bridal chamber."

So the Chinaman had word, and he must rise from sleep and light the furnaces; and as he wrought below, beside the boilers, he heard his master singing and rejoicing above him in the lighted chambers. When the water began to be hot the Chinaman cried to his master; and Keawe went into the bathroom; and the Chinaman heard him sing as he filled the marble basin; and heard him sing, and the singing broken, as he undressed; until of a sudden, the song ceased. The Chinaman listened, and listened; he called up the house to Keawe to ask if all were well, and Keawe answered him "Yes," and bade him go to bed; but there was no more singing in the Bright House; and all night long, the Chinaman heard his master's feet go round and round the balconies without repose.

Now the truth of it was this: as Keawe undressed for his bath, he spied upon his flesh a patch like a patch of lichen on a rock, and it was then that he stopped singing. For he knew the likeness of that patch, and knew that he was fallen in the Chinese Evil.

Now, it is a sad thing for any man to fall into this sickness. And it would be a sad thing for anyone to leave a house so beautiful and so commodious, and depart from all his friends to the north coast of Molokai between the mighty cliff and the sea-breakers. But what was that to the case of the man Keawe, he who had met his love but yesterday, and won her but that morning, and now saw all his hopes break, in a moment, like a piece of glass?

Awhile he sat upon the edge of the bath; then sprang, with a cry, and ran outside; and to and fro, to and fro, along the balcony, like one despairing.

"Very willingly could I leave Hawaii, the home of my fathers," Keawe was thinking. "Very lightly could I leave my house, the high-placed, the many-windowed, here upon the mountains. Very bravely could I go to Molokai, to Kalaupapa by the cliffs, to live with the smitten and to sleep there, far from my fathers. But what wrong have I done, what sin lies upon my soul, that I should have encountered Kokua coming cool from the sea-water in the evening? Kokua, the soul ensnarer! Kokua, the light of my life! Her may I never wed, her may I look upon no longer, her may I no more handle with my loving hand; and it is for this, it is for you, O Kokua! that I pour my lamentations!"

Now you are to observe what sort of a man Keawe was, for he might have dwelt there in the Bright House for years, and no one been the wiser of his sickness; but he reckoned nothing of that, if he must lose Kokua. And again, he might have wed Kokua even as he was; and so many would have done, because they have the souls of pigs; but Keawe loved the maid manfully, and he would do her no hurt and bring her in no danger.

A little beyond the midst of the night, there came in his mind the recollection of that bottle. He went round to the back porch, and called to memory the day when the devil had looked forth; and at the thought ice ran in his veins.

"A dreadful thing is the bottle," thought Keawe, "and dreadful is the imp, and it is a dreadful thing to risk the flames of hell. But what other hope have I to cure my sickness or to wed Kokua? What!" he thought, "would I beard the devil once, only to get me a house, and not face him again to win Kokua?"

Thereupon he called to mind it was the next day the *Hall* went by on her return to Honolulu. "There must I go first," he thought, "and see Lopaka. For the best hope that I have now is to find that same bottle I was so pleased to be rid of."

Never a wink could he sleep; the food stuck in his throat; but he sent a letter to Kiano, and about the time when the steamer would be coming, rode down beside the cliff of the tombs. It rained; his horse went heavily; he looked up at the black mouths of the caves, and he envied the dead that slept there and were done with trouble; and called to mind how he had galloped by the day before, and was astonished. So he came down to Hookena, and there was all the country gathered for the steamer as usual. In the shed before the store they sat and jested and passed the news; but there was no matter of speech in Keawe's bosom, and he sat in their midst and looked without on the rain falling on the houses, and the surf beating among the rocks, and the sighs arose in his throat.

"Keawe of the Bright House is out of spirits," said one to another. Indeed, and so he was, and little wonder.

Then the *Hall* came, and the whaleboat carried him on board. The after-part of the ship was full of Haoles who had been to visit the volcano, as their custom is; and the midst was crowded with Kanakas, and the forepart with wild bulls from Hilo and horses from Kau; but Keawe sat apart from all in his sorrow, and watched for the house of Kiano. There it sat, low upon the shore in the black rocks, and shaded by the cocoa palms, and there by the door was a red holoku, no greater than a fly, and going to and fro with a fly's busyness. "Ah, queen of my heart," he cried, "I'll venture my dear soul to win you!"

Soon after, darkness fell, and the cabins were lit up, and the Haoles sat and played at the cards and drank whiskey as their custom is; but Keawe walked the deck all night; and all the next day, as they steamed under the lee of Maui or of Molokai, he was still pacing to and fro like a wild animal in a menagerie.

Towards evening they passed Diamond Head, and came to the pier of Honolulu. Keawe stepped out among the crowd and began to ask for Lopaka. It seemed he had become the owner of a schooner—none better in the islands—and was gone upon an adventure as far as Pola-Pola or Kahiki; so there was no help to be looked for from Lopaka. Keawe called to mind a friend of his, a lawyer in the town (I must not tell his name), and inquired of him. They said he was grown suddenly rich, and had a fine new house upon Waikiki shore; and this put a thought in Keawe's head, and he called a hack and drove to the lawyer's house.

The house was all brand new, and the trees in the garden no greater than walking-sticks, and the lawyer, when he came, had the air of a man well pleased.

"What can I do to serve you?" said the lawyer.

"You are a friend of Lopaka's," replied Keawe, "and Lopaka purchased from me a certain piece of goods that I thought you might enable me to trace."

The lawyer's face became very dark. "I do not profess to misunderstand you, Mr. Keawe," said he, "though this is an ugly business to be stirring in. You may be sure I know nothing, but yet I have a guess, and if you would apply in a certain quarter I think you might have news."

And he named the name of a man, which, again, I had better not repeat. So it was for days, and Keawe went from one to another, finding everywhere new clothes and carriages, and fine new houses and men everywhere in great contentment, although, to be sure, when he hinted at his business their faces would cloud over.

"No doubt I am upon the track," thought Keawe. "These new clothes and carriages are all the gifts of the little imp, and these glad faces are the faces of men who have taken their profit and got rid of the accursed thing in safety. When I see pale cheeks and hear sighing, I shall know that I am near the bottle."

So it befell at last that he was recommended to a Haole in Beritania Street. When he came to the door, about the hour of the evening meal, there were the usual marks of the new house, and the young garden, and the electric light shining in the windows; but when the owner came, a shock of hope and fear ran through Keawe; for here was a young man, white as a corpse, and black about the eyes, the hair shedding from his head, and such a look in his countenance as a man may have when he is waiting for the gallows.

"Here it is, to be sure," thought Keawe, and so with this man he noways veiled his errand. "I am come to buy the bottle," said he.

At the word, the young Haole of Beritania Street reeled against the wall.

"The bottle!" he gasped. "To buy the bottle!" Then he seemed to choke, and seizing Keawe by the arm carried him into a room and poured out wine in two glasses.

"Here is my respects," said Keawe, who had been much about with Haoles in his time. "Yes," he added, "I am come to buy the bottle. What is the price by now?"

At that word the young man let his glass slip through his fingers, and looked upon Keawe like a ghost.

"The price," says he; "the price! You do not know the price?"

"It is for that I am asking you," returned Keawe. "But why are you so much concerned? Is there anything wrong about the price?"

"It has dropped a great deal in value since your time, Mr. Keawe," said the young man stammering.

"Well, well, I shall have the less to pay for it," says Keawe. "How much did it cost you?"

The young man was as white as a sheet. "Two cents," said he.

"What?" cried Keawe, "two cents? Why, then, you can only sell it for one. And he who buys it—" The words died upon Keawe's tongue; he who bought it could never sell it again, the bottle and the bottle imp must abide with him until he died, and when he died must carry him to the red end of hell.

The young man of Beritania Street fell upon his knees. "For God's sake buy it!" he cried. "You can have all my fortune in the bargain. I was mad when I bought it at that price. I had embezzled money at my store; I was lost else; I must have gone to jail."

"Poor creature," said Keawe, "you would risk your soul upon so desperate an adventure, and to avoid the proper punishment of your own disgrace; and you think I could hesitate with love in front of me. Give me the bottle, and the change which I make sure you have all ready. Here is a five-cent piece."

It was as Keawe supposed; the young man had the change ready in a drawer; the bottle changed hands, and Keawe's fingers were no sooner clasped upon the stalk than he had breathed his wish to be a clean man. And, sure enough, when he got home to his room, and stripped himself before a glass, his flesh was whole like an infant's. And here was the strange thing: he had no sooner seen this miracle, than his mind was changed within him, and he cared naught for the Chinese Evil, and little enough for Kokua; and had but the one thought, that here he was bound to the bottle imp for time and for eternity, and had no better hope but to be a cinder for ever in the flames of hell. Away ahead of him he saw them blaze with his mind's eye, and his soul shrank, and darkness fell upon the light.

When Keawe came to himself a little, he was aware it was the night when the band played at the hotel. Thither he went, because he feared to be alone; and there, among happy faces, walked to and fro, and heard the tunes go up and down, and saw Berger beat the measure, and all the while he heard the flames crackle, and saw the red fire burning in the bottomless pit. Of a sudden the band played *Hiki-ao-ao*; that was a song that he had sung with Kokua, and at the strain courage returned to him.

"It is done now," he thought, "and once more let me take the good along with the evil."

So it befell that he returned to Hawaii by the first steamer, and as soon as it could be managed he was wedded to Kokua, and carried her up the mountain side to the Bright House.

Now it was so with these two, that when they were together, Keawe's heart was stilled; but so soon as he was alone he fell into a brooding horror, and heard the flames crackle, and saw the red fire burn in the bottomless pit. The girl, indeed, had come to him wholly; her heart leapt in her side at sight of him, her hand clung to his; and she was so fashioned from the hair upon her head to the nails upon her toes that none could see her without joy. She was pleasant in her nature. She had the good word always. Full of song she was, and went to and fro in the Bright House, the brightest thing in its three storeys, carolling like the birds. And Keawe beheld and heard her with delight, and then must shrink upon one side, and weep and groan to think upon the price that he had paid for her; and then he must dry his eyes, and wash his face, and go and sit with her on the broad balconies, joining in her songs, and, with a sick spirit, answering her smiles.

There came a day when her feet began to be heavy and her songs more rare; and now it was not Keawe only that would weep apart, but each would sunder from the other and sit in opposite balconies with the whole width of the Bright House betwixt. Keawe was so sunk in his despair, he scarce observed the change, and was only glad he had more hours to sit alone and brood upon his destiny, and was not so frequently condemned to pull a smiling face on a sick heart. But one day, coming softly through the house, he heard the sound of a child sobbing, and there was Kokua rolling her face upon the balcony floor, and weeping like the lost.

"You do well to weep in this house, Kokua," he said. "And yet I would give the head off my body that you (at least) might have been happy."

"Happy!" she cried. "Keawe, when you lived alone in your Bright House, you were the word of the island for a happy man; laughter and song were in your mouth, and your face was as bright as the sunrise. Then you wedded poor Kokua; and the good God knows what is amiss in her—but from that day you have not smiled. Oh!" she cried, "what ails me? I thought I was pretty, and I knew I loved him. What ails me that I throw this cloud upon my husband?"

"Poor Kokua," said Keawe. He sat down by her side, and sought to take her hand; but that she plucked away. "Poor Kokua," he said, again. "My poor child—my pretty. And I had thought all this while to spare you! Well, you shall know all. Then, at least, you will pity poor Keawe; then you will understand how much he loved you in the past—that he dared hell for your possession—and how much he loves you still (the poor condemned one), that he can yet call up a smile when he beholds you."

With that, he told her all, even from the beginning.

"You have done this for me?" she cried, "Ah, well, then what do I care!"—and she clasped and wept upon him.

"Ah, child!" said Keawe, "and yet, when I consider of the fire of hell, I care a good deal!"

"Never tell me," said she; "no man can be lost because he loved Kokua, and no other fault. I tell you, Keawe, I shall save you with these hands, or perish in your company. What! you loved me, and gave your soul, and you think I will not die to save you in return?"

"Ah, my dear! you might die a hundred times, and what difference would that make?" he cried, "except to leave me lonely till the time comes of my damnation?"

"You know nothing," said she. "I was educated in a school in Honolulu; I am no common girl. And I tell you, I shall save my lover. What is this you say about a cent? But all the world is not American. In England they have a piece they call a farthing, which is about half a cent. Ah! sorrow!" she cried, "that makes it scarcely better, for the buyer must be lost, and we shall find none so brave as my Keawe! But, then, there is France; they have a small coin there which they call a centime, and these go five to the cent or there-about. We could not do better. Come, Keawe, let us go to the French islands; let us go to Tahiti, as fast as ships can bear us. There we have four centimes, three centimes, two centimes, one centime; four possible sales to come and go on; and two of us to push the bargain. Come, my Keawe! kiss me, and banish care. Kokua will defend you."

"Gift of God!" he cried. "I cannot think that God will punish me for desiring aught so good! Be it as you will, then; take me where you please: I put my life and my salvation in your hands."

Early the next day Kokua was about her preparations. She took Keawe's chest that he went with sailoring; and first she put the bottle in a corner; and then packed it with the richest of their clothes and the bravest of the knick-knacks in the house. "For," said she, "we must seem to be rich folks, or who will believe in the bottle?" All the time of her preparation she was as gay as a bird; only when she looked upon Keawe, the tears would spring in her eye, and she must run and kiss him. As for Keawe, a weight was off his soul; now that he had his secret shared, and some hope in front of him, he seemed like a new man, his feet went lightly on the earth, and his breath was good to him again. Yet was terror still at his elbow; and ever and again, as the wind blows out a taper, hope died in him, and he saw the flames toss and the red fire burn in hell.

It was given out in the country they were gone pleasuring to the States, which was thought a strange thing, and yet not so strange as the truth, if any could have guessed it. So they went to Honolulu in the *Hall*, and thence in the *Umatilla* to San Francisco with a crowd of Haoles, and at San Francisco took their passage by the mail brigantine, the *Tropic Bird*, for Papeete, the chief place of the French in the south islands. Thither they came, after a pleasant voyage, on a fair day of the Trade Wind, and saw the reef with the surf breaking, and Motuiti with its palms, and the schooner riding within-side, and the white houses of the town low down along the shore among green trees, and overhead the mountains and the clouds of Tahiti, the wise island.

It was judged the most wise to hire a house, which they did accordingly, opposite the British Consul's, to make a great parade of money, and themselves conspicuous with carriages and horses. This it was very easy to do, so long as they had the bottle in their possession; for Kokua was more bold than Keawe, and, whenever she had a mind, called on the imp for twenty or a hundred dollars. At this rate they soon grew to be remarked in the town; and the strangers from Hawaii, their riding and their driving, the fine holokus and the rich lace of Kokua, became the matter of much talk.

They got on well after the first with the Tahitian language, which is indeed like to the Hawaiian, with a change of certain letters; and as soon as they had any freedom of speech, began to push the bottle. You are to consider it was not an easy subject to introduce; it was not easy to persuade people you were in earnest, when you offered to sell them for four centimes the spring of health and riches inexhaustible. It was necessary besides to explain the dangers of the bottle; and either people disbelieved the whole thing and laughed, or they thought the more of the darker part, became overcast with gravity, and drew away from Keawe and Kokua, as from persons who had dealings with the devil. So far from gaining ground, these two began to find they were avoided in the town; the children ran away from them screaming, a thing intolerable to Kokua; Catholics crossed themselves as they went by; and all persons began with one accord to disengage themselves from their advances.

Depression fell upon their spirits. They would sit at night in their new house, after a day's weariness, and not exchange one word, or the silence would be broken by Kokua bursting suddenly into sobs. Sometimes they would pray together; sometimes they would have the bottle out upon the floor, and sit all evening watching how the shadow hovered in the midst. At such times they would be afraid to go to rest. It was long ere slumber came to them, and, if either dozed off, it would be to wake and find the other silently weeping in the dark, or, perhaps, to wake alone, the other having fled from the house and the neighbourhood of that bottle, to pace under the bananas in the little garden, or to wander on the beach by moonlight.

One night it was so when Kokua awoke. Keawe was gone. She felt in the bed and his place was cold. Then fear fell upon her, and she sat up in bed. A little moonshine filtered through the shutters. The room was bright, and she could spy the bottle on the floor. Outside it blew high, the great trees of the avenue cried aloud, and the fallen leaves rattled in the verandah. In the midst of this Kokua was aware of another sound; whether of a beast or of a man she could scarce tell, but it was as sad as death, and cut her to the soul. Softly she arose, set the door ajar, and looked forth into the moonlit yard. There, under the bananas, lay Keawe, his mouth in the dust, and as he lay he moaned.

It was Kokua's first thought to run forward and console him; her second potently withheld her. Keawe had borne himself before his wife like a brave man; it became her little in the hour of weakness to intrude upon his shame. With the thought she drew back into the house.

"Heaven!" she thought, "how careless have I been—how weak! It is he, not I, that stands in this eternal peril; it was he, not I, that took the curse upon his soul. It is for my sake, and for the love of a creature of so little worth and such poor help, that he now beholds so close to him the flames of hell—ay, and smells the smoke of it, lying without there in the wind and moonlight. Am I so dull of spirit that never till now I have surmised my duty, or have I seen it before and turned aside? But now, at least, I take up my soul in both the hands of my affection; now I say farewell to the white steps of heaven and the waiting faces of my friends. A love for a love, and let mine be equalled with Keawe's! A soul for a soul, and be it mine to perish!"

She was a deft woman with her hands, and was soon apparelled. She took in her hands the change—the precious centimes they kept ever at their side; for this coin is little used, and they had made provision at a Government office. When she was forth in the avenue clouds came on the wind, and the moon was blackened. The town slept, and she knew not whither to turn till she heard one coughing in the shadow of the trees.

"Old man," said Kokua, "what do you here abroad in the cold night?"

The old man could scarce express himself for coughing, but she made out that he was old and poor, and a stranger in the island.

"Will you do me a service?" said Kokua. "As one stranger to another, and as an old man to a young woman, will you help a daughter of Hawaii?"

"Ah," said the old man. "So you are the witch from the eight islands, and even my old soul you seek to entangle. But I have heard of you, and defy your wickedness."

"Sit down here," said Kokua, "and let me tell you a tale." And she told him the story of Keawe from the beginning to the end.

"And now," said she, "I am his wife, whom he bought with his soul's welfare. And what should I do? If I went to him myself and offered to buy it, he would refuse. But if you go, he will sell it eagerly; I will await you here; you will buy it for four centimes, and I will buy it again for three. And the Lord strengthen a poor girl!"

"If you meant falsely," said the old man, "I think God would strike you dead."

"He would!" cried Kokua. "Be sure he would. I could not be so treacherous—God would not suffer it."

"Give me the four centimes and await me here," said the old man.

Now, when Kokua stood alone in the street, her spirit died. The wind roared in the trees, and it seemed to her the rushing of the flames of hell; the shadows tossed in the light of the street lamp, and they seemed to her the snatching hands of evil ones. If she had had the strength, she must have run away, and if she had had the breath she must have screamed aloud; but, in truth, she could do neither, and stood and trembled in the avenue, like an affrighted child.

Then she saw the old man returning, and he had the bottle in his hand.

"I have done your bidding," said he. "I left your husband weeping like a child; to-night he will sleep easy." And he held the bottle forth.

"Before you give it me," Kokua panted, "take the good with the evil—ask to be delivered from your cough."

"I am an old man," replied the other, "and too near the gate of the grave to take a favour from the devil. But what is this? Why do you not take the bottle? Do you hesitate?"

"Not hesitate!" cried Kokua. "I am only weak. Give me a moment. It is my hand resists, my flesh shrinks back from the accursed thing. One moment only!"

The old man looked upon Kokua kindly. "Poor child!" said he, "you fear; your soul misgives you. Well, let me keep it. I am old, and can never more be happy in this world, and as for the next—"

"Give it me!" gasped Kokua. "There is your money. Do you think I am so base as that? Give me the bottle."

"God bless you, child," said the old man.

Kokua concealed the bottle under her holoku, said farewell to the old man, and walked off along the avenue, she cared not whither. For all roads were now the same to her, and led equally to hell. Sometimes she walked, and sometimes ran; sometimes she screamed out loud in the night, and sometimes lay by the wayside in the dust and wept. All that she had heard of hell came back to her; she saw the flames blaze, and she smelt the smoke, and her flesh withered on the coals.

Near day she came to her mind again, and returned to the house. It was even as the old man said—Keawe slumbered like a child. Kokua stood and gazed upon his face.

"Now, my husband," said she, "it is your turn to sleep. When you wake it will be your turn to sing and laugh. But for poor Kokua, alas! that meant no evil—for poor Kokua no more sleep, no more singing, no more delight, whether in earth or heaven."

With that she lay down in the bed by his side, and her misery was so extreme that she fell in a deep slumber instantly.

Late in the morning her husband woke her and gave her the good news. It seemed he was silly with delight, for he paid no heed to her distress, ill though she dissembled it. The words stuck in her mouth, it mattered not; Keawe did the speaking. She ate not a bite, but who was to observe it? for Keawe cleared the dish. Kokua saw and heard him, like some strange thing in a dream; there were times when she forgot or doubted, and put her hands to her brow; to know herself doomed and hear her husband babble, seemed so monstrous.

All the while Keawe was eating and talking, and planning the time of their return, and thanking her for saving him, and fondling her, and calling her the true helper after all. He laughed at the old man that was fool enough to buy that bottle.

"A worthy old man he seemed," Keawe said. "But no one can judge by appearances. For why did the old reprobate require the bottle?"

"My husband," said Kokua, humbly, "his purpose may have been good."

Keawe laughed like an angry man.

"Fiddle-de-dee!" cried Keawe. "An old rogue, I tell you; and an old ass to boot. For the bottle was hard enough to sell at four centimes; and at three it will be quite impossible. The margin is not broad enough, the thing begins to smell of scorching—brrr!" said he, and shuddered. "It is true I bought it myself at a cent, when I knew not there were smaller coins. I was a fool for my pains; there will never be found another: and whoever has that bottle now will carry it to the pit."

"O my husband!" said Kokua. "Is it not a terrible thing to save oneself by the eternal ruin of another? It seems to me I could not laugh. I would be humbled. I would be filled with melancholy. I would pray for the poor holder."

Then Keawe, because he felt the truth of what she said, grew the more angry. "Heighty-teighty!" cried he. "You may be filled with melancholy if you please. It is not the mind of a good wife. If you thought at all of me, you would sit shamed."

Thereupon he went out, and Kokua was alone.

What chance had she to sell that bottle at two centimes? None, she perceived. And if she had any, here was her husband hurrying her away to a country where there was nothing lower than a cent. And here—on the morrow of her sacrifice—was her husband leaving her and blaming her.

She would not even try to profit by what time she had, but sat in the house, and now had the bottle out and viewed it with unutterable fear, and now, with loathing, hid it out of sight.

By-and-by, Keawe came back, and would have her take a drive.

"My husband, I am ill," she said. "I am out of heart. Excuse me, I can take no pleasure."

Then was Keawe more wroth than ever. With her, because he thought she was brooding over the case of the old man; and with himself, because he thought she was right, and was ashamed to be so happy.

"This is your truth," cried he, "and this your affection! Your husband is just saved from eternal ruin, which he encountered for the love of you—and you can take no pleasure! Kokua, you have a disloyal heart."

He went forth again furious, and wandered in the town all day. He met friends, and drank with them; they hired a carriage and drove into the country, and there drank again. All the time Keawe was ill at ease, because he was taking this pastime while his wife was sad, and because he knew in his heart that she was more right than he; and the knowledge made him drink the deeper.

Now there was an old brutal Haole drinking with him, one that had been a boatswain of a whaler, a runaway, a digger in gold mines, a convict in prisons. He had a low mind and a foul mouth; he loved to drink and to see others drunken; and he pressed the glass upon Keawe. Soon there was no more money in the company.

"Here, you!" says the boatswain, "you are rich, you have been always saying. You have a bottle or some foolishness."

"Yes," says Keawe, "I am rich; I will go back and get some money from my wife, who keeps it."

"That's a bad idea, mate," said the boatswain. "Never you trust a petticoat with dollars. They're all as false as water; you keep an eye on her."

Now, this word struck in Keawe's mind; for he was muddled with what he had been drinking.

"I should not wonder but she was false, indeed," thought he. "Why else should she be so cast down at my release? But I will show her I am not the man to be fooled. I will catch her in the act."

Accordingly, when they were back in town, Keawe bade the boatswain wait for him at the corner, by the old calaboose, and went forward up the avenue alone to the door of his house. The night had come again; there was a light within, but never a sound; and Keawe crept about the corner, opened the back door softly, and looked in.

There was Kokua on the floor, the lamp at her side; before her was a milk-white bottle, with a round belly and a long neck; and as she viewed it, Kokua wrung her hands.

A long time Keawe stood and looked in the doorway. At first he was struck stupid; and then fear fell upon him that the bargain had been made amiss, and the bottle had come back to him as it came at San Francisco; and at that his knees were loosened, and the fumes of the wine departed from his head like mists off a river in the morning. And then he had another thought; and it was a strange one, that made his cheeks to burn.

"I must make sure of this," thought he.

So he closed the door, and went softly round the corner again, and then came noisily in, as though he were but now returned. And, lo! by the time he opened the front door no bottle was to be seen; and Kokua sat in a chair and started up like one awakened out of sleep.

"I have been drinking all day and making merry," said Keawe. "I have been with good companions, and now I only come back for money, and return to drink and carouse with them again."

Both his face and voice were as stern as judgment, but Kokua was too troubled to observe.

"You do well to use your own, my husband," said she, and her words trembled.

"O, I do well in all things," said Keawe, and he went straight to the chest and took out money. But he looked besides in the corner where they kept the bottle, and there was no bottle there.

At that the chest heaved upon the floor like a sea-billow, and the house span about him like a wreath of smoke, for he saw he was lost now, and there was no escape. "It is what I feared," he thought. "It is she who has bought it."

And then he came to himself a little and rose up; but the sweat streamed on his face as thick as the rain and as cold as the well-water.

"Kokua," said he, "I said to you to-day what ill became me. Now I return to carouse with my jolly companions," and at that he laughed a little quietly. "I will take more pleasure in the cup if you forgive me."

She clasped his knees in a moment; she kissed his knees with flowing tears.

"O," she cried, "I asked but a kind word!"

"Let us never one think hardly of the other," said Keawe, and was gone out of the house.

Now, the money that Keawe had taken was only some of that store of centime pieces they had laid in at their arrival. It was very sure he had no mind to be drinking. His wife had given her soul for him, now he must give his for hers; no other thought was in the world with him.

At the corner, by the old calaboose, there was the boatswain waiting.

"My wife has the bottle," said Keawe, "and, unless you help me to recover it, there can be no more money and no more liquor to-night."

"You do not mean to say you are serious about that bottle?" cried the boatswain.

"There is the lamp," said Keawe. "Do I look as if I was jesting?"

"That is so," said the boatswain. "You look as serious as a ghost."

"Well, then," said Keawe, "here are two centimes; you must go to my wife in the house, and offer her these for the bottle, which (if I am not much mistaken) she will give you instantly. Bring it to me here, and I will buy it back from you for one; for that is the law with this bottle, that it still must be sold for a less sum. But whatever you do, never breathe a word to her that you have come from me."

"Mate, I wonder are you making a fool of me?" asked the boatswain.

"It will do you no harm if I am," returned Keawe.

"That is so, mate," said the boatswain.

"And if you doubt me," added Keawe, "you can try. As soon as you are clear of the house, wish to have your pocket full of money, or a bottle of the best rum, or what you please, and you will see the virtue of the thing."

"Very well, Kanaka," says the boatswain. "I will try; but if you are having your fun out of me, I will take my fun out of you with a belaying pin."

So the whaler-man went off up the avenue; and Keawe stood and waited. It was near the same spot where Kokua had waited the night before; but Keawe was more resolved, and never faltered in his purpose; only his soul was bitter with despair.

It seemed a long time he had to wait before he heard a voice singing in the darkness of the avenue. He knew the voice to be the boatswain's; but it was strange how drunken it appeared upon a sudden.

Next, the man himself came stumbling into the light of the lamp. He had the devil's bottle buttoned in his coat; another bottle was in his hand; and even as he came in view he raised it to his mouth and drank.

"You have it," said Keawe. "I see that."

"Hands off!" cried the boatswain, jumping back. "Take a step near me, and I'll smash your mouth. You thought you could make a cat's-paw of me, did you?"

"What do you mean?" cried Keawe.

"Mean?" cried the boatswain. "This is a pretty good bottle, this is; that's what I mean. How I got it for two centimes I can't make out; but I'm sure you shan't have it for one."

"You mean you won't sell?" gasped Keawe.

"No, sir!" cried the boatswain. "But I'll give you a drink of the rum, if you like."

"I tell you," said Keawe, "the man who has that bottle goes to hell."

"I reckon I'm going anyway," returned the sailor; "and this bottle's the best thing to go with I've struck yet. No, sir!" he cried again, "this is my bottle now, and you can go and fish for another."

"Can this be true?" Keawe cried. "For your own sake, I beseech you, sell it me!"

"I don't value any of your talk," replied the boatswain. "You thought I was a flat; now you see I'm not; and there's an end. If you won't have a swallow of the rum, I'll have one myself. Here's your health, and good-night to you!"

So off he went down the avenue towards town, and there goes the bottle out of the story.

But Keawe ran to Kokua light as the wind; and great was their joy that night; and great, since then, has been the peace of all their days in the Bright House.

THE SCREAMING SKULL

F. Marion Crawford

I have often heard it scream. No, I am not nervous, I am not imaginative, and I never believed in ghosts, unless that thing is one. Whatever it is, it hates me almost as much as it hated Luke Pratt, and it screams at me.

If I were you, I would never tell ugly stories about ingenious ways of killing people, for you never can tell but that some one at the table may be tired of his or her nearest and dearest. I have always blamed myself for Mrs. Pratt's death, and I suppose I was responsible for it in a way, though heaven knows I never wished her anything but long life and happiness. If I had not told that story she might be alive yet. That is why the thing screams at me, I fancy.

She was a good little woman, with a sweet temper, all things considered, and a nice gentle voice; but I remember hearing her shriek once when she thought her little boy was killed by a pistol that went off, though every one was sure that it was not loaded. It was the same scream; exactly the same, with a sort of rising quaver at the end; do you know what I mean? Unmistakable.

The truth is, I had not realised that the doctor and his wife were not on good terms. They used to bicker a bit now and then when I was here, and I often noticed that little Mrs. Pratt got very red and bit her lip hard to keep her temper, while Luke grew pale and said the most offensive things. He was that sort when he was in the nursery, I remember, and afterward at school. He was my cousin, you know; that is how I came by this house; after he died, and his boy Charley was killed in South Africa, there were no relations left. Yes, it's a pretty little property, just the sort of thing for an old sailor like me who has taken to gardening.

One always remembers one's mistakes much more vividly than one's cleverest things, doesn't one? I've often noticed it. I was dining with the Pratts one night, when I told them the story that afterwards made so much difference. It was a wet night in November, and the sea was moaning. Hush!—if you don't speak you will hear it now . . .

Do you hear the tide? Gloomy sound, isn't it? Sometimes, about this time of year—hallo!—there it is! Don't be frightened, man—it won't eat you—it's only a noise, after all! But I'm glad you've heard it, because there are always people who think it's the wind, or my imagination, or something. You won't hear it again to-night, I fancy, for it doesn't often come more than once. Yes—that's right. Put another stick on the fire, and a little more stuff into that weak mixture you're so fond of. Do you remember old Blauklot the carpenter, on that German ship that picked us up when the Clontarf went to the bottom? We were hove to in a howling gale one night, as snug as you please, with no land within five hundred miles, and the ship coming up and falling off as regularly as clockwork—"Biddy te boor beebles ashore tis night, poys!" old Blauklot sang out, as he went off to his quarters with the sail-maker. I often think of that, now that I'm ashore for good and all.

Yes, it was on a night like this, when I was at home for a spell, waiting to take the *Olympia* out on her first trip—it was on the next voyage that she broke the record, you remember—but that dates it. Ninety-two was the year, early in November.

The weather was dirty, Pratt was out of temper, and the dinner was bad, very bad indeed, which didn't improve matters, and cold, which made it worse. The poor little lady was very unhappy about it, and insisted on making a Welsh rarebit on the table to counteract the raw turnips and the half-boiled mutton. Pratt must have had a hard day. Perhaps he had lost a patient. At all events, he was in a nasty temper.

"My wife is trying to poison me, you see!" he said. "She'll succeed some day." I saw that she was hurt, and I made believe to laugh, and said that Mrs. Pratt was much too clever to get rid of her husband in such a simple way; and then I began to tell them about Japanese tricks with spun glass and chopped horsehair and the like.

Pratt was a doctor, and knew a lot more than I did about such things, but that only put me on my mettle, and I told a story about a woman in Ireland who did for three husbands before any one suspected foul play.

Did you never hear that tale? The fourth husband managed to keep awake and caught her, and she was hanged. How did she do it? She drugged them, and poured melted lead into their ears through a little horn funnel when they were asleep . . . No—that's the wind whistling. It's backing up to the southward again. I can tell by the sound. Besides, the other thing doesn't often come more than once in an evening even at this time of year—when it happened. Yes, it was in November. Poor Mrs. Pratt died suddenly in her bed not long after I dined here. I can fix the date, because I got the news in New York by the steamer that followed the *Olympia* when I took her out on her first trip. You had the *Leofric* the same year? Yes, I remember. What a pair of old buffers we are coming to be, you and I. Nearly fifty years since we were apprentices together on the *Clontarf*. Shall you ever forget old Blauklot? "Biddy te boor beebles ashore, poys!" Ha, ha! Take a little more, with all that water. It's the old Hulstkamp I found in the cellar when this house came to me, the same I brought Luke from Amsterdam five-and-twenty years ago. He had never touched a drop of it. Perhaps he's sorry now, poor fellow.

Where did I leave off? I told you that Mrs. Pratt died suddenly—yes. Luke must have been lonely here after she was dead, I should think; I came to see him now and then, and he looked worn and nervous, and told me that his practice was growing too heavy for him, though he wouldn't take an assistant on any account. Years went on, and his son was killed in South Africa, and after that he began to be queer. There was something about him not like other people. I believe he kept his senses in his profession to the end; there was no complaint of his having made bad mistakes in cases, or anything of that sort, but he had a look about him—

Luke was a red-headed man with a pale face when he was young, and he was never stout; in middle age he turned a sandy grey, and after his son died he grew thinner and thinner, till his head looked like a skull with parchment stretched over it very tight, and his eyes had a sort of glare in them that was very disagreeable to look at.

He had an old dog that poor Mrs. Pratt had been fond of, and that used to follow her everywhere. He was a bull-dog, and the sweetest tempered beast you ever saw, though he had a way of hitching his upper lip behind one of his fangs that frightened strangers a good deal. Sometimes, of an evening, Pratt and Bumble—that was the dog's name—used to sit and look at each other a long time, thinking about old times, I suppose, when Luke's wife used to sit in that chair you've got. That was always her place, and this was the doctor's, where I'm sitting. Bumble used to climb up by the footstool—he was old and fat by that time, and could not jump much, and his teeth were getting shaky. He would look steadily at Luke, and Luke looked steadily at the dog, his face growing more and more like a skull with two little coals for eyes; and after about five minutes or so, though it may have been less, old Bumble would suddenly begin to shake all over, and all on a sudden he would set up an awful howl, as if he had been shot, and tumble out of the easy-chair and trot away, and hide himself under the sideboard, and lie there making odd noises.

Considering Pratt's looks in those last months, the thing is not surprising, you know. I'm not nervous or imaginative, but I can quite believe he might have sent a sensitive woman into hysterics—his head looked so much like a skull in parchment.

At last I came down one day before Christmas, when my ship was in dock and I had three weeks off. Bumble was not about, and I said casually that I supposed the old dog was dead.

"Yes," Pratt answered, and I thought there was something odd in his tone even before he went on after a little pause. "I killed him," he said presently. "I could not stand it any longer."

I asked what it was that Luke could not stand, though I guessed well enough.

"He had a way of sitting in her chair and glaring at me, and then howling." Luke shivered a little. "He didn't suffer at all, poor old Bumble," he went on in a hurry, as if he thought I might imagine he had been cruel. "I put dionine into his drink to make him sleep soundly, and then I chloroformed him gradually, so that he could not have felt suffocated even if he was dreaming. It's been quieter since then."

I wondered what he meant, for the words slipped out as if he could not help saying them. I've understood since. He meant that he did not hear that noise so often after the dog was out of the way. Perhaps he thought at first that it was old Bumble in the yard howling at the moon, though it's not that kind of noise, is it? Besides, I know what it is, if Luke didn't. It's only a noise, after all, and a noise never hurt anybody yet. But he was much more imaginative than I am. No doubt there really is something about this place that I don't understand; but when I don't understand a thing, I call it a phenomenon, and I don't take it for granted that it's going to kill me, as he did. I don't understand everything, by long odds, nor do you, nor does any man who has been to sea. We used to talk of tidal waves, for instance, and we could not account for them; now we account for them by calling them submarine earthquakes, and we branch off into fifty theories, any one of which might make earthquakes quite comprehensible if we only knew what they are. I fell in with one of them once, and the inkstand flew straight up from the table against the ceiling of my cabin. The same thing happened to Captain Lecky—I dare say you've read about it in his "Wrinkles." Very good. If that sort of thing took place ashore, in this room for instance, a nervous person would talk about spirits and levitation and fifty things that mean nothing, instead of just quietly setting it down as a "phenomenon" that has not been explained yet. My view of that voice, you see.

Besides, what is there to prove that Luke killed his wife? I would not even suggest such a thing to any one but you. After all, there was nothing but the coincidence that poor little Mrs. Pratt died suddenly in her bed a few days after I told that story at dinner. She was not the only woman who ever died like that. Luke got the doctor over from the next parish, and they agreed that she had died of something the matter with her heart. Why not? It's common enough.

Of course, there was the ladle. I never told anybody about that, and it made me start when I found it in the cupboard in the bedroom. It was new, too—a little tinned iron ladle that had not been in the fire more than once or twice, and there was some lead in it that had been melted, and stuck to the bottom of the bowl, all grey, with hardened dross on it. But that proves nothing. A country doctor is generally a handy man, who does everything for himself, and Luke may have had a dozen reasons for melting a little lead in a ladle. He was fond of sea-fishing, for instance, and he may have cast a sinker for a night-line; perhaps it was a weight for the hall clock, or something like that. All the same, when I found it I had a rather queer sensation, because it looked so much like the thing I had described when I told them the story. Do you understand? It affected me unpleasantly, and I threw it away; it's at the bottom of the sea a mile from the Spit, and it will be jolly well rusted beyond recognising if it's ever washed up by the tide.

You see, Luke must have bought it in the village, years ago, for the man sells just such ladles still. I suppose they are used in cooking. In any case, there was no reason why an inquisitive housemaid should find such a thing lying about, with lead in it, and wonder what it was, and perhaps talk to the maid who heard me tell the story at dinner—for that girl married the plumber's son in the village, and may remember the whole thing.

You understand me, don't you? Now that Luke Pratt is dead and gone, and lies buried beside his wife, with an honest man's tombstone at his head, I should not care to stir up anything that could hurt his memory. They are both dead, and their son, too. There was trouble enough about Luke's death, as it was.

How? He was found dead on the beach one morning, and there was a coroner's inquest. There were marks on his throat, but he had not been robbed. The verdict was that he had come to his end "by the hands or teeth of some person or animal unknown," for half the jury thought it might have been a big dog that had thrown him down and gripped his windpipe, though the skin of his throat was not broken. No one knew at what time he had gone out, nor where he had been. He was found lying on his back above high-water mark, and an old cardboard bandbox that had belonged to his wife lay under his hand, open. The lid had fallen off. He seemed to have been carrying home a skull in the box—doctors are fond of collecting such things. It had rolled out and lay near his head, and it was a remarkably fine skull, rather small, beautifully shaped and very white, with perfect teeth. That is to say, the upper jaw was perfect, but there was no lower one at all, when I first saw it.

Yes, I found it here when I came. You see, it was very white and polished, like a thing meant to be kept under a glass case, and the people did not know where it came from, nor what to do with it; so they put it back into the bandbox and set it on the shelf of the cupboard in the best bedroom, and of course they showed it to me when I took possession. I was taken down to the beach, too, to be shown the place where Luke was found, and the old fisherman explained just how he was lying, and the skull beside him. The only point he could not explain was why the skull had rolled up the sloping sand toward Luke's head instead of rolling downhill to his feet. It did not seem odd to me at the time, but I have often thought of it since, for the place is rather steep. I'll take you there to-morrow if you like—I made a sort of cairn of stones there afterward.

When he fell down, or was thrown down—whichever happened—the bandbox struck the sand, and the lid came off, and the thing came out and ought to have rolled down. But it didn't. It was close to his head, almost touching it, and turned with the face toward it. I say it didn't strike me as odd when the man told me; but I could not help thinking about it afterward, again and again, till I saw a picture of it all when I closed my eyes; and then I began to ask myself why the plaguey thing had rolled up instead of down, and why it had stopped near Luke's head instead of anywhere else, a yard away, for instance.

You naturally want to know what conclusion I reached, don't you? None that at all explained the rolling, at all events. But I got something else into my head, after a time, that made me feel downright uncomfortable.

Oh, I don't mean as to anything supernatural! There may be ghosts, or there may not be. If there are, I'm not inclined to believe that they can hurt living people except by frightening them, and, for my part, I would rather face any shape of ghost than a fog in the Channel when it's crowded. No. What bothered me was just a foolish idea, that's all, and I cannot tell how it began, nor what made it grow till it turned into a certainty.

I was thinking about Luke and his poor wife one evening over my pipe and a dull book, when it occurred to me that the skull might possibly be hers, and I have never got rid of the thought since. You'll tell me there's no sense in it, no doubt; that Mrs. Pratt was buried like a Christian and is lying in the churchyard where they put her, and that it's perfectly monstrous to suppose her husband kept her skull in her old bandbox in his bedroom. All the same, in the face of reason, and common sense, and probability, I'm convinced that he did. Doctors do all sorts of queer things that would make men like you and me feel creepy, and those are just the things that don't seem probable, nor logical, nor sensible to us.

Then, don't you see?—if it really was her skull, poor woman, the only way of accounting for his having it is that he really killed her, and did it in that way, as the woman killed her husbands in the story, and that he was afraid there might be an examination some day which would betray him. You see, I told that too, and I believe it had really happened some fifty or sixty years ago. They dug up the three skulls, you know, and there was a small lump of lead rattling about in each one. That was what hanged the woman. Luke remembered that, I'm sure. I don't want to know what he did when he thought of it; my taste never ran in the direction of horrors, and I don't fancy you care for them either, do you? No. If you did, you might supply what is wanting to the story.

It must have been rather grim, eh? I wish I did not see the whole thing so distinctly, just as everything must have happened. He took it the night before she was buried, I'm sure, after the coffin had been shut, and when the servant girl was asleep. I would bet anything, that when he'd got it, he put something under the sheet in its place, to fill up and look like it. What do you suppose he put there, under the sheet?

I don't wonder you take me up on what I'm saying! First I tell you that I don't want to know what happened, and that I hate to think about horrors, and then I describe the whole thing to you as if I had seen it. I'm quite sure that it was her work-bag that he put there. I remember the bag very well, for she always used it of an evening; it was made of brown plush, and when it was stuffed full it was about the size of—you understand. Yes, there I am, at it again! You may laugh at me, but you don't live here alone, where it was done, and you didn't tell Luke the story about the melted lead. I'm not nervous, I tell you, but sometimes I begin to feel that I understand why some people are. I dwell on all this when I'm alone, and I dream of it, and when that thing screams—well, frankly, I don't like the noise any more than you do, though I should be used to it by this time.

I ought not to be nervous. I've sailed in a haunted ship. There was a Man in the Top, and two-thirds of the crew died of the West Coast fever inside of ten days after we anchored; but I was all right, then and afterward. I have seen some ugly sights, too, just as you have, and all the rest of us. But nothing ever stuck in my head in the way this does.

You see, I've tried to get rid of the thing, but it doesn't like that. It wants to be there in its place, in Mrs. Pratt's bandbox in the cupboard in the best bedroom. It's not happy anywhere else. How do I know that? Because I've tried it. You don't suppose that I've not tried, do you? As long as it's there it only screams now and then, generally at this time of year, but if I put it out of the house it goes on all night, and no servant will stay here twenty-four hours. As it is, I've often been left alone and have been obliged to shift for myself for a fortnight at a time. No one from the village would ever pass a night under the roof now, and as for selling the place, or even letting it, that's out of the question. The old women say that if I stay here I shall come to a bad end myself before long.

I'm not afraid of that. You smile at the mere idea that any one could take such nonsense seriously. Quite right. It's utterly blatant nonsense, I agree with you. Didn't I tell you that it's only a noise after all when you started and looked round as if you expected to see a ghost standing behind your chair?

I may be all wrong about the skull, and I like to think that I am—when I can. It may be just a fine specimen which Luke got somewhere long ago, and what rattles about inside when you shake it may be nothing but a pebble, or a bit of hard clay, or anything. Skulls that have lain long in the ground generally have something inside them that rattles, don't they? No, I've never tried to get it out, whatever it is; I'm afraid it might be lead, don't you see? And if it is, I don't want to know the fact, for I'd much rather not be sure. If it really is lead, I killed her quite as much as if I had done the deed myself. Anybody must see that, I should think. As long as I don't know for certain, I have the consolation of saying that it's all utterly ridiculous nonsense, that Mrs. Pratt died a natural death and that the beautiful skull belonged to Luke when he was a student in London. But if I were quite sure, I believe I should have to leave the house; indeed I do, most certainly. As it is, I had to give up trying to sleep in the best bedroom where the cupboard is.

You ask me why I don't throw it into the pond—yes, but please don't call it a "confounded bugbear"—it doesn't like being called names.

There! Lord, what a shriek! I told you so! You're quite pale, man. Fill up your pipe and draw your chair nearer to the fire, and take some more drink. Old Hollands never hurt anybody yet. I've seen a Dutchman in Java drink half a jug of Hulstkamp in a morning without turning a hair. I don't take much rum myself, because it doesn't agree with my rheumatism, but you are not rheumatic and it won't damage you. Besides, it's a very damp night outside. The wind is howling again, and it will soon be in the southwest; do you hear how the windows rattle? The tide must have turned too, by the moaning.

We should not have heard the thing again if you had not said that. I'm pretty sure we should not. Oh yes, if you choose to describe it as a coincidence, you are quite welcome, but I would rather that you should not call the thing names again, if you don't mind. It may be that the poor little woman hears, and perhaps it hurts her, don't you know? Ghost? No! You don't call anything a ghost that you can take in your hands and look at in broad daylight, and that rattles when you shake it. Do you, now? But it's something that hears and understands; there's no doubt about that.

I tried sleeping in the best bedroom when I first came to the house, just because it was the best and the most comfortable, but I had to give it up. It was their room, and there's the big bed she died in, and the cupboard is in the thickness of the wall, near the head, on the left. That's where it likes to be kept, in its bandbox. I only used the room for a fortnight after I came, and then I turned out and took the little room downstairs, next to the surgery, where Luke used to sleep when he expected to be called to a patient during the night.

I was always a good sleeper ashore; eight hours is my dose, eleven to seven when I'm alone, twelve to eight when I have a friend with me. But I could not sleep after three o'clock in the morning in that room—a quarter past, to be accurate—as a matter of fact, I timed it with my old pocket chronometer, which still keeps good time, and it was always at exactly seventeen minutes past three. I wonder whether that was the hour when she died?

It was not what you have heard. If it had been that I could not have stood it two nights. It was just a start and a moan and hard breathing for a few seconds in the cupboard, and it could never have waked me under ordinary circumstances, I'm sure. I suppose you are like me in that, and we are just like other people who have been to sea. No natural sounds disturb us at all, not all the racket of a square-rigger hove to in a heavy gale, or rolling on her beam ends before the wind. But if a lead pencil gets adrift and rattles in the drawer of your cabin table you are awake in a moment. Just so—you always understand. Very well, the noise in the cupboard was no louder than that, but it waked me instantly.

I said it was like a "start." I know what I mean, but it's hard to explain without seeming to talk nonsense. Of course you cannot exactly "hear" a person "start"; at the most, you might hear the quick drawing of the breath between the parted lips and closed teeth, and the almost imperceptible sound of clothing that moved suddenly though very slightly. It was like that.

You know how one feels what a sailing vessel is going to do, two or three seconds before she does it, when one has the wheel. Riders say the same of a horse, but that's less strange, because the horse is a live animal with feelings of its own, and only poets and landsmen talk about a ship being alive, and all that. But I have always felt somehow that besides being a steaming machine or a sailing machine for carrying weights, a vessel at sea is a sensitive instrument, and a means of communication between nature and man, and most particularly the man at the wheel, if she is steered by hand. She takes her impressions directly from wind and sea, tide and stream, and transmits them to the man's hand, just as the wireless telegraph picks up the interrupted currents aloft and turns them out below in the form of a message.

You see what I am driving at; I felt that something started in the cupboard, and I felt it so vividly that I heard it, though there may have been nothing to hear, and the sound inside my head waked me suddenly. But I really heard the other noise. It was as if it were muffled inside a box, as far away as if it came through a long-distance telephone; and yet I knew that it was inside the cupboard near the head of my bed. My hair did not bristle and my blood did not run cold that time. I simply resented being waked up by something that had no business to make a noise, any more than a pencil should rattle in the drawer of my cabin table on board ship. For I did not understand; I just supposed that the cupboard had some communication with the outside air, and that the wind had got in and was moaning through it with a sort of very faint screech. I struck a light and looked at my watch, and it was seventeen minutes past three. Then I turned over and went to sleep on my right ear. That's my good one; I'm pretty deaf with the other, for I struck the water with it when I was a lad in diving from the foretopsail yard. Silly thing to do, it was, but the result is very convenient when I want to go to sleep when there's a noise.

That was the first night, and the same thing happened again and several times afterward, but not regularly, though it was always at the same time, to a second; perhaps I was sometimes sleeping on my good ear, and sometimes not. I overhauled the cupboard and there was no way by which the wind could get in, or anything else, for the door makes a good fit, having been meant to keep out moths, I suppose; Mrs. Pratt must have kept her winter things in it, for it still smells of camphor and turpentine.

After about a fortnight I had had enough of the noises. So far I had said to myself that it would be silly to yield to it and take the skull out of the room. Things always look differently by daylight, don't they? But the voice grew louder—I suppose one may call it a voice—and it got inside my deaf ear, too, one night. I realised that when I was wide awake, for my good ear was jammed down on the pillow, and I ought not to have heard a fog-horn in that position. But I heard that, and it made me lose my temper, unless it scared me, for sometimes the two are not far apart. I struck a light and got up, and I opened the cupboard, grabbed the bandbox and threw it out of the window, as far as I could.

Then my hair stood on end. The thing screamed in the air, like a shell from a twelve-inch gun. It fell on the other side of the road. The night was very dark, and I could not see it fall, but I know it fell beyond the road. The window is just over the front door, it's fifteen yards to the fence, more or less, and the road is ten yards wide. There's a quickset hedge beyond, along the glebe that belongs to the vicarage.

I did not sleep much more that night. It was not more than half an hour after I had thrown the bandbox out when I heard a shriek outside—like what we've had to-night, but worse, more despairing, I should call it; and it may have been my imagination, but I could have sworn that the screams came nearer and nearer each time. I lit a pipe, and walked up and down for a bit, and then took a book and sat up reading, but I'll be hanged if I can remember what I read nor even what the book was, for every now and then a shriek came up that would have made a dead man turn in his coffin.

A little before dawn some one knocked at the front door. There was no mistaking that for anything else, and I opened my window and looked down, for I guessed that some one wanted the doctor, supposing that the new man had taken Luke's house. It was rather a relief to hear a human knock after that awful noise.

You cannot see the door from above, owing to the little porch. The knocking came again, and I called out, asking who was there, but nobody answered, though the knock was repeated. I sang out again, and said that the doctor did not live here any longer. There was no answer, but it occurred to me that it might be some old countryman who was stone deaf. So I took my candle and went down to open the door. Upon my word, I was not thinking of the thing yet, and I had almost forgotten the other noises. I went down convinced that I should find somebody outside, on the doorstep, with a message. I set the candle on the hall table, so that the wind should not blow it out when I opened. While I was drawing the old-fashioned bolt I heard the knocking again. It was not loud, and it had a queer, hollow sound, now that I was close to it, I remember, but I certainly thought it was made by some person who wanted to get in.

It wasn't. There was nobody there, but as I opened the door inward, standing a little on one side, so as to see out at once, something rolled across the threshold and stopped against my foot.

I drew back as I felt it, for I knew what it was before I looked down. I cannot tell you how I knew, and it seemed unreasonable, for I am still quite sure that I had thrown it across the road. It's a French window, that opens wide, and I got a good swing when I flung it out. Besides, when I went out early in the morning, I found the bandbox beyond the thickset hedge.

You may think it opened when I threw it, and that the skull dropped out; but that's impossible, for nobody could throw an empty cardboard box so far. It's out of the question; you might as well try to fling a ball of paper twenty-five yards, or a blown bird's egg.

To go back, I shut and bolted the hall door, picked the thing up carefully, and put it on the table beside the candle. I did that mechanically, as one instinctively does the right thing in danger without thinking at all—unless one does the opposite. It may seem odd, but I believe my first thought had been that somebody might come and find me there on the threshold while it was resting against my foot, lying a little on its side, and turning one hollow eye up at my face, as if it meant to accuse me. And the light and shadow from the candle played in the hollows of the eyes as it stood on the table, so that they seemed to open and shut at me. Then the candle went out quite unexpectedly, though the door was fastened and there was not the least draught; and I used up at least half a dozen matches before it would burn again.

I sat down rather suddenly, without quite knowing why. Probably I had been badly frightened, and perhaps you will admit there was no great shame in being scared. The thing had come home, and it wanted to go upstairs, back to its cupboard. I sat still and stared at it for a bit, till I began to feel very cold; then I took it and carried it up and set it in its place, and I remember that I spoke to it, and promised that it should have its bandbox again in the morning.

You want to know whether I stayed in the room till daybreak? Yes, but I kept a light burning, and sat up smoking and reading, most likely out of fright; plain, undeniable fear, and you need not call it cowardice either, for that's not the same thing. I could not have stayed alone with that thing in the cupboard; I should have been scared to death, though I'm not more timid than other people. Confound it all, man, it had crossed the road alone, and had got up the doorstep and had knocked to be let in.

When the dawn came, I put on my boots and went out to find the bandbox. I had to go a good way round, by the gate near the highroad, and I found the box open and hanging on the other side of the hedge. It had caught on the twigs by the string, and the lid had fallen off and was lying on the ground below it. That shows that it did not open till it was well over; and if it had not opened as soon as it left my hand, what was inside it must have gone beyond the road too.

That's all. I took the box upstairs to the cupboard, and put the skull back and locked it up. When the girl brought me my breakfast she said she was sorry, but that she must go, and she did not care if she lost her month's wages. I looked at her, and her face was a sort of greenish, yellowish white. I pretended to be surprised, and asked what was the matter; but that was of no use, for she just turned on me and wanted to know whether I meant to stay in a haunted house, and how long I expected to live if I did, for though she noticed I was sometimes a little hard of hearing, she did not believe that even I could sleep through those screams again—and if I could, why had I been moving about the house and opening and shutting the front door, between three and four in the morning? There was no answering that, since she had heard me, so off she went, and I was left to myself. I went down to the village during the morning and found a woman who was willing to come and do the little work there is and cook my dinner, on condition that she might go home every night. As for me, I moved downstairs that day, and I have never tried to sleep in the best bedroom since. After a little while I got a brace of middle-aged Scotch servants from London, and things were quiet enough for a long time. I began by telling them that the house was in a very exposed position, and that the wind whistled round it a good deal in the autumn and winter, which had given it a bad name in the village, the Cornish people being inclined to superstition and telling ghost stories. The two hard-faced, sandy-haired sisters almost smiled, and they answered with great contempt that they had no great opinion of any Southern bogey whatever, having been in service in two English haunted houses, where they had never seen so much as the Boy in Gray, whom they reckoned no very particular rarity in Forfarshire.

They stayed with me several months, and while they were in the house we had peace and quiet. One of them is here again now, but she went away with her sister within the year. This one—she was the cook—married the sexton, who works in my garden. That's the way of it. It's a small village and he has not much to do, and he knows enough about flowers to help me nicely, besides doing most of the hard work; for though I'm fond of exercise, I'm getting a little stiff in the hinges. He's a sober, silent sort of fellow, who minds his own business, and he was a widower when I came here—Trehearn is his name, James Trehearn. The Scotch sisters would not admit that there was anything wrong about the house, but when November came they gave me warning that they were going, on the ground that the chapel was such a long walk from here, being in the next parish, and that they could not possibly go to our church. But the younger one came back in the spring, and as soon as the banns could be published she was married to James Trehearn by the vicar, and she seems to have had no scruples about hearing him preach since then. I'm quite satisfied, if she is! The couple live in a small cottage that looks over the churchyard.

I suppose you are wondering what all this has to do with what I was talking about. I'm alone so much that when an old friend comes to see me, I sometimes go on talking just for the sake of hearing my own voice. But in this case there is really a connection of ideas. It was James Trehearn who buried poor Mrs. Pratt, and her husband after her in the same grave, and it's not far from the back of his cottage. That's the connection in my mind, you see. It's plain enough. He knows something; I'm quite sure that he does, by his manner, though he's such a reticent beggar.

Yes, I'm alone in the house at night now, for Mrs. Trehearn does everything herself, and when I have a friend the sexton's niece comes in to wait on the table. He takes his wife home every evening in winter, but in summer, when there's light, she goes by herself. She's not a nervous woman, but she's less sure than she used to be that there are no bogies in England worth a Scotchwoman's notice. Isn't it amusing, the idea that Scotland has a monopoly of the supernatural? Odd sort of national pride, I call that, don't you?

That's a good fire, isn't it? When driftwood gets started at last there's nothing like it, I think. Yes, we get lots of it, for I'm sorry to say there are still a great many wrecks about here. It's a lonely coast, and you may have all the wood you want for the trouble of bringing it in. Trehearn and I borrow a cart now and then, and load it between here and the Spit. I hate a coal fire when I can get wood of any sort. A log is company, even if it's only a piece of a deck-beam or timber sawn off, and the salt in it makes pretty sparks. See how they fly, like Japanese hand-fireworks! Upon my word, with an old friend and a good fire and a pipe, one forgets all about that thing upstairs, especially now that the wind has moderated. It's only a lull, though, and it will blow a gale before morning.

You think you would like to see the skull? I've no objection. There's no reason why you shouldn't have a look at it, and you never saw a more perfect one in your life, except that there are two front teeth missing in the lower jaw.

Oh yes—I had not told you about the jaw yet. Trehearn found it in the garden last spring when he was digging a pit for a new asparagus bed. You know we make asparagus beds six or eight feet deep here. Yes, yes—I had forgotten to tell you that. He was digging straight down, just as he digs a grave; if you want a good asparagus bed made, I advise you to get a sexton to make it for you. Those fellows have a wonderful knack at that sort of digging.

Trehearn had got down about three feet when he cut into a mass of white lime in the side of the trench. He had noticed that the earth was a little looser there, though he says it had not been disturbed for a number of years. I suppose he thought that even old lime might not be good for asparagus, so he broke it out and threw it up. It was pretty hard, he says, in biggish lumps, and out of sheer force of habit he cracked the lumps with his spade as they lay outside the pit beside him; the jawbone of a skull dropped out of one of the pieces. He thinks he must have knocked out the two front teeth in breaking up the lime, but he did not see them anywhere. He's a very experienced man in such things, as you may imagine, and he said at once that the jaw had probably belonged to a young woman, and that the teeth had been complete when she died. He brought it to me, and asked me if I wanted to keep it; if I did not, he said he would drop it into the next grave he made in the churchyard, as he supposed it was a Christian jaw, and ought to have decent burial, wherever the rest of the body might be. I told him that doctors often put bones into quicklime to whiten them nicely, and that I supposed Dr. Pratt had once had a little lime pit in the garden for that purpose, and had forgotten the jaw. Trehearn looked at me quietly.

"Maybe it fitted that skull that used to be in the cupboard upstairs, sir," he said. "Maybe Dr. Pratt had put the skull into the lime to clean it, or something, and when he took it out he left the lower jaw behind. There's some human hair sticking in the lime, sir."

I saw there was, and that was what Trehearn said. If he did not suspect something, why in the world should he have suggested that the jaw might fit the skull? Besides, it did. That's proof that he knows more than he cares to tell. Do you suppose he looked before she was buried? Or perhaps—when he buried Luke in the same grave—

Well, well, it's of no use to go over that, is it? I said I would keep the jaw with the skull, and I took it upstairs and fitted it into its place. There's not the slightest doubt about the two belonging together, and together they are.

Trehearn knows several things. We were talking about plastering the kitchen a while ago, and he happened to remember that it had not been done since the very week when Mrs. Pratt died. He did not say that the mason must have left some lime on the place, but he thought it, and that it was the very same lime he had found in the asparagus pit. He knows a lot. Trehearn is one of your silent beggars who can put two and two together. That grave is very near the back of his cottage, too, and he's one of the quickest men with a spade I ever saw. If he wanted to know the truth, he could, and no one else would ever be the wiser unless he chose to tell. In a quiet village like ours, people don't go and spend the night in the churchyard to see whether the sexton potters about by himself between ten o'clock and daylight.

What is awful to think of, is Luke's deliberation, if he did it; his cool certainty that no one would find him out; above all, his nerve, for that must have been extraordinary. I sometimes think it's bad enough to live in the place where it was done, if it really was done. I always put in the condition, you see, for the sake of his memory, and a little bit for my own sake, too.

I'll go upstairs and fetch the box in a minute. Let me light my pipe; there's no hurry! We had supper early, and it's only half-past nine o'clock. I never let a friend go to bed before twelve, or with less than three glasses—you may have as many more as you like, but you shan't have less, for the sake of old times.

It's breezing up again, do you hear? That was only a lull just now, and we are going to have a bad night.

A thing happened that made me start a little when I found that the jaw fitted exactly. I'm not very easily startled in that way myself, but I have seen people make a quick movement, drawing their breath sharply, when they had thought they were alone and suddenly turned and saw some one very near them. Nobody can call that fear. You wouldn't, would you? No. Well, just when I had set the jaw in its place under the skull, the teeth closed sharply on my finger. It felt exactly as if it were biting me hard, and I confess that I jumped before I realised that I had been pressing the jaw and the skull together with my other hand. I assure you I was not at all nervous. It was broad daylight, too, and a fine day, and the sun was streaming into the best bedroom. It would have been absurd to be nervous, and it was only a quick mistaken impression, but it really made me feel queer. Somehow it made me think of the funny verdict of the coroner's jury on Luke's death, "by the hand or teeth of some person or animal unknown." Ever since that I've wished I had seen those marks on his throat, though the lower jaw was missing then.

I have often seen a man do insane things with his hands that he does not realise at all. I once saw a man hanging on by an old awning stop with one hand, leaning backward, outboard, with all his weight on it, and he was just cutting the stop with the knife in his other hand when I got my arms round him. We were in mid-ocean, going twenty knots. He had not the smallest idea what he was doing; neither had I when I managed to pinch my finger between the teeth of that thing. I can feel it now. It was exactly as if it were alive and were trying to bite me. It would if it could, for I know it hates me, poor thing! Do you suppose that what rattles about inside is really a bit of lead? Well, I'll get the box down presently, and if whatever it is happens to drop out into your hands that's your affair. If it's only a clod of earth or a pebble, the whole matter would be off my mind, and I don't believe I should ever think of the skull again; but somehow I cannot bring myself to shake out the bit of hard stuff myself. The mere idea that it may be lead makes me confoundedly uncomfortable, yet I've got the conviction that I shall know before long. I shall certainly know. I'm sure Trehearn knows, but he's such a silent beggar.

I'll go upstairs now and get it. What? You had better go with me? Ha, ha! do you think I'm afraid of a bandbox and a noise? Nonsense!

Bother the candle, it won't light! As if the ridiculous thing understood what it's wanted for! Look at that—the third match. They light fast enough for my pipe. There, do you see? It's a fresh box, just out of the tin safe where I keep the supply on account of the dampness. Oh, you think the wick of the candle may be damp, do you? All right, I'll light the beastly thing in the fire. That won't go out, at all events. Yes, it sputters a bit, but it will keep lighted now. It burns just like any other candle, doesn't it? The fact is, candles are not very good about here. I don't know where they come from, but they have a way of burning low occasionally, with a greenish flame that spits tiny sparks, and I'm often annoyed by their going out of themselves. It cannot be helped, for it will be long before we have electricity in our village. It really is rather a poor light, isn't it?

You think I had better leave you the candle and take the lamp, do you? I don't like to carry lamps about, that's the truth. I never dropped one in my life, but I have always thought I might, and it's so confoundedly dangerous if you do. Besides, I am pretty well used to these rotten candles by this time.

You may as well finish that glass while I'm getting it, for I don't mean to let you off with less than three before you go to bed. You won't have to go upstairs, either, for I've put you in the old study next to the surgery—that's where I live myself. The fact is, I never ask a friend to sleep upstairs now. The last man who did was Crackenthorpe, and he said he was kept awake all night. You remember old Crack, don't you? He stuck to the Service, and they've just made him an admiral. Yes, I'm off now—unless the candle goes out. I couldn't help asking if you remembered Crackenthorpe. If any one had told us that the skinny little idiot he used to be was to turn out the most successful of the lot of us, we should have laughed at the idea, shouldn't we? You and I did not do badly, it's true—but I'm really going now. I don't mean to let you think that I've been putting it off by talking! As if there were anything to be afraid of! If I were scared, I should tell you so quite frankly, and get you to go upstairs with me.

* * * * *

Here's the box. I brought it down very carefully, so as not to disturb it, poor thing. You see, if it were shaken, the jaw might get separated from it again, and I'm sure it wouldn't like that. Yes, the candle went out as I was coming downstairs, but that was the draught from the leaky window on the landing. Did you hear anything? Yes, there was another scream. Am I pale, do you say? That's nothing. My heart is a little queer sometimes, and I went upstairs too fast. In fact, that's one reason why I really prefer to live altogether on the ground floor.

Wherever that shriek came from, it was not from the skull, for I had the box in my hand when I heard the noise, and here it is now; so we have proved definitely that the screams are produced by something else. I've no doubt I shall find out some day what makes them. Some crevice in the wall, of course, or a crack in a chimney, or a chink in the frame of a window. That's the way all ghost stories end in real life. Do you know, I'm jolly glad I thought of going up and bringing it down for you to see, for that last shriek settles the question. To think that I should have been so weak as to fancy that the poor skull could really cry out like a living thing!

Now I'll open the box, and we'll take it out and look at it under the bright light. It's rather awful to think that the poor lady used to sit there, in your chair, evening after evening, in just the same light, isn't it? But then—I've made up my mind that it's all rubbish from beginning to end, and that it's just an old skull that Luke had when he was a student; and perhaps he put it into the lime merely to whiten it, and could not find the jaw.

I made a seal on the string, you see, after I had put the jaw in its place, and I wrote on the cover. There's the old white label on it still, from the milliner's, addressed to Mrs. Pratt when the hat was sent to her, and as there was room I wrote on the edge: "A skull, once the property of the late Luke Pratt, M.D." I don't quite know why I wrote that, unless it was with the idea of explaining how the thing happened to be in my possession. I cannot help wondering sometimes what sort of hat it was that came in the bandbox. What colour was it, do you think? Was it a gay spring hat with a bobbing feather and pretty ribands? Strange that the very same box should hold the head that wore the finery—perhaps. No—we made up our minds that it just came from the hospital in London where Luke did his time. It's far better to look at it in that light, isn't it? There's no more connection between that skull and poor Mrs. Pratt than there was between my story about the lead and—

Good Lord! Take the lamp—don't let it go out, if you can help it—I'll have the window fastened again in a second—I say, what a gale! There, it's out! I told you so! Never mind, there's the firelight—I've got the window shut—the bolt was only half down. Was the box blown off the table? Where the deuce is it? There! That won't open again, for I've put up the bar. Good dodge, an old-fashioned bar—there's nothing like it. Now, you find the bandbox while I light the lamp. Confound those wretched matches! Yes, a pipe spill is better—it must light in the fire—I hadn't thought of it—thank you—there we are again. Now, where's the box? Yes, put it back on the table, and we'll open it.

That's the first time I have ever known the wind to burst that window open; but it was partly carelessness on my part when I last shut it. Yes, of course I heard the scream. It seemed to go all round the house before it broke in at the window. That proves that it's always been the wind and nothing else, doesn't it? When it was not the wind, it was my imagination. I've always been a very imaginative man: I must have been, though I did not know it. As we grow older we understand ourselves better, don't you know?

I'll have a drop of the Hulstkamp neat, by way of an exception, since you are filling up your glass. That damp gust chilled me, and with my rheumatic tendency I'm very much afraid of a chill, for the cold sometimes seems to stick in my joints all winter when it once gets in.

By George, that's good stuff! I'll just light a fresh pipe, now that everything is snug again, and then we'll open the box. I'm so glad we heard that last scream together, with the skull here on the table between us, for a thing cannot possibly be in two places at the same time, and the noise most certainly came from outside, as any noise the wind makes must. You thought you heard it scream through the room after the window was burst open? Oh yes, so did I, but that was natural enough when everything was open. Of course we heard the wind. What could one expect?

Look here, please. I want you to see that the seal is intact before we open the box together. Will you take my glasses? No, you have your own. All right. The seal is sound, you see, and you can read the words of the motto easily. "Sweet and low"—that's it—because the poem goes on "Wind of the Western sea," and says, "blow him again to me," and all that. Here is the seal on my watch-chain, where it's hung for more than forty years. My poor little wife gave it to me when I was courting, and I never had any other. It was just like her to think of those words—she was always fond of Tennyson.

It's of no use to cut the string, for it's fastened to the box, so I'll just break the wax and untie the knot, and afterward we'll seal it up again. You see, I like to feel that the thing is safe in its place, and that nobody can take it out. Not that I should suspect Trehearn of meddling with it, but I always feel that he knows a lot more than he tells.

You see, I've managed it without breaking the string, though when I fastened it I never expected to open the bandbox again. The lid comes off easily enough. There! Now look!

What? Nothing in it? Empty? It's gone, man, the skull is gone!

* * * * *

No, there's nothing the matter with me. I'm only trying to collect my thoughts. It's so strange. I'm positively certain that it was inside when I put on the seal last spring. I can't have imagined that: it's utterly impossible. If I ever took a stiff glass with a friend now and then, I would admit that I might have made some idiotic mistake when I had taken too much. But I don't, and I never did. A pint of ale at supper and half a go of rum at bedtime was the most I ever took in my good days. I believe it's always we sober fellows who get rheumatism and gout! Yet there was my seal, and there is the empty bandbox. That's plain enough.

I say, I don't half like this. It's not right. There's something wrong about it, in my opinion. You needn't talk to me about supernatural manifestations, for I don't believe in them, not a little bit! Somebody must have tampered with the seal and stolen the skull. Sometimes, when I go out to work in the garden in summer, I leave my watch and chain, on the table. Trehearn must have taken the seal then, and used it, for he would be quite sure that I should not come in for at least an hour.

If it was not Trehearn—oh, don't talk to me about the possibility that the thing has got out by itself! If it has, it must be somewhere about the house, in some out-of-the-way corner, waiting. We may come upon it anywhere, waiting for us, don't you know?—just waiting in the dark. Then it will scream at me; it will shriek at me in the dark, for it hates me, I tell you!

The bandbox is quite empty. We are not dreaming, either of us. There, I turn it upside down.

What's that? Something fell out as I turned it over. It's on the floor, it's near your feet, I know it is, and we must find it. Help me to find it, man. Have you got it? For God's sake, give it to me, quickly!

Lead! I knew it when I heard it fall. I knew it couldn't be anything else by the little thud it made on the hearth-rug. So it was lead after all, and Luke did it.

I feel a little bit shaken up—not exactly nervous, you know, but badly shaken up, that's the fact. Anybody would, I should think. After all, you cannot say that it's fear of the thing, for I went up and brought it down—at least, I believed I was bringing it down, and that's the same thing, and by George, rather than give in to such silly nonsense, I'll take the box upstairs again and put it back in its place. It's not that. It's the certainty that the poor little woman came to her end in that way, by my fault, because I told the story. That's what is so dreadful. Somehow, I had always hoped that I should never be quite sure of it, but there is no doubting it now. Look at that!

Look at it! That little lump of lead with no particular shape. Think of what it did, man! Doesn't it make you shiver? He gave her something to make her sleep, of course, but there must have been one moment of awful agony. Think of having boiling lead poured into your brain. Think of it. She was dead before she could scream, but only think of—oh! there it is again—it's just outside—I know it's just outside—I can't keep it out of my head!—oh!—oh!

* * * * *

You thought I had fainted? No, I wish I had, for it would have stopped sooner. It's all very well to say that it's only a noise, and that a noise never hurt anybody—you're as white as a shroud yourself. There's only one thing to be done, if we hope to close an eye to-night. We must find it and put it back into its bandbox and shut it up in the cupboard, where it likes to be. I don't know how it got out, but it wants to get in again. That's why it screams so awfully to-night—it was never so bad as this—never since I first—

Bury it? Yes, if we can find it, we'll bury it, if it takes us all night. We'll bury it six feet deep and ram down the earth over it, so that it shall never get out again, and if it screams, we shall hardly hear it so deep down. Quick, we'll get the lantern and look for it. It cannot be far away; I'm sure it's just outside—it was coming in when I shut the window, I know it.

Yes, you're quite right. I'm losing my senses, and I must get hold of myself. Don't speak to me for a minute or two; I'll sit quite still and keep my eyes shut and repeat something I know. That's the best way.

"Add together the altitude, the latitude, and the polar distance, divide by two and subtract the altitude from the half-sum; then add the logarithm of the secant of the latitude, the cosecant of the polar distance, the cosine of the half-sum and the sine of the half-sum minus the altitude"—there! Don't say that I'm out of my senses, for my memory is all right, isn't it?

Of course, you may say that it's mechanical, and that we never forget the things we learned when we were boys and have used almost every day for a lifetime. But that's the very point. When a man is going crazy, it's the mechanical part of his mind that gets out of order and won't work right; he remembers things that never happened, or he sees things that aren't real, or he hears noises when there is perfect silence. That's not what is the matter with either of us, is it?

Come, we'll get the lantern and go round the house. It's not raining—only blowing like old boots, as we used to say. The lantern is in the cupboard under the stairs in the hall, and I always keep it trimmed in case of a wreck.

No use to look for the thing? I don't see how you can say that. It was nonsense to talk of burying it, of course, for it doesn't want to be buried; it wants to go back into its bandbox and be taken upstairs, poor thing! Trehearn took it out, I know, and made the seal over again. Perhaps he took it to the churchyard, and he may have meant well. I daresay he thought that it would not scream any more if it were quietly laid in consecrated ground, near where it belongs. But it has come home. Yes, that's it. He's not half a bad fellow, Trehearn, and rather religiously inclined, I think. Does not that sound natural, and reasonable, and well meant? He supposed it screamed because it was not decently buried—with the rest. But he was wrong. How should he know that it screams at me because it hates me, and because it's my fault that there was that little lump of lead in it?

No use to look for it, anyhow? Nonsense! I tell you it wants to be found—Hark! what's that knocking? Do you hear it? Knock—knock—knock—three times, then a pause, and then again. It has a hollow sound, hasn't it?

It has come home. I've heard that knock before. It wants to come in and be taken upstairs, in its box. It's at the front door.

Will you come with me? We'll take it in. Yes, I own that I don't like to go alone and open the door. The thing will roll in and stop against my foot, just as it did before, and the light will go out. I'm a good deal shaken by finding that bit of lead, and, besides, my heart isn't quite right—too much strong tobacco, perhaps. Besides, I'm quite willing to own that I'm a bit nervous to-night, if I never was before in my life.

That's right, come along! I'll take the box with me, so as not to come back. Do you hear the knocking? It's not like any other knocking I ever heard. If you will hold this door open, I can find the lantern under the stairs by the light from this room without bringing the lamp into the hall—it would only go out.

The thing knows we are coming—hark! It's impatient to get in. Don't shut the door till the lantern is ready, whatever you do. There will be the usual trouble with the matches, I suppose—no, the first one, by Jove! I tell you it wants to get in, so there's no trouble. All right with that door now; shut it, please. Now come and hold the lantern, for it's blowing so hard outside that I shall have to use both hands. That's it, hold the light low. Do you hear the knocking still? Here goes—I'll open just enough with my foot against the bottom of the door—now!

Catch it! it's only the wind that blows it across the floor, that's all—there's half a hurricane outside, I tell you! Have you got it? The bandbox is on the table. One minute, and I'll have the bar up. There!

Why did you throw it into the box so roughly? It doesn't like that, you know.

What do you say? Bitten your hand? Nonsense, man! You did just what I did. You pressed the jaws together with your other hand and pinched yourself. Let me see. You don't mean to say you have drawn blood? You must have squeezed hard, by Jove, for the skin is certainly torn. I'll give you some carbolic solution for it before we go to bed, for they say a scratch from a skull's tooth may go bad and give trouble.

Come inside again and let me see it by the lamp. I'll bring the bandbox—never mind the lantern, it may just as well burn in the hall, for I shall need it presently when I go up the stairs. Yes, shut the door if you will; it makes it more cheerful and bright. Is your finger still bleeding? I'll get you the carbolic in an instant; just let me see the thing.

Ugh! There's a drop of blood on the upper jaw. It's on the eye-tooth. Ghastly, isn't it? When I saw it running along the floor of the hall, the strength almost went out of my hands, and I felt my knees bending; then I understood that it was the gale, driving it over the smooth boards. You don't blame me? No, I should think not! We were boys together, and we've seen a thing or two, and we may just as well own to each other that we were both in a beastly funk when it slid across the floor at you. No wonder you pinched your finger picking it up, after that, if I did the same thing out of sheer nervousness, in broad daylight, with the sun streaming in on me.

Strange that the jaw should stick to it so closely, isn't it? I suppose it's the dampness, for it shuts like a vice—I have wiped off the drop of blood, for it was not nice to look at. I'm not going to try to open the jaws, don't be afraid! I shall not play any tricks with the poor thing, but I'll just seal the box again, and we'll take it upstairs and put it away where it wants to be. The wax is on the writing-table by the window. Thank you. It will be long before I leave my seal lying about again, for Trehearn to use, I can tell you. Explain? I don't explain natural phenomena, but if you choose to think that Trehearn had hidden it somewhere in the bushes, and that the gale blew it to the house against the door, and made it knock, as if it wanted to be let in, you're not thinking the impossible, and I'm quite ready to agree with you.

Do you see that? You can swear that you've actually seen me seal it this time, in case anything of the kind should occur again. The wax fastens the strings to the lid, which cannot possibly be lifted, even enough to get in one finger. You're quite satisfied, aren't you? Yes. Besides, I shall lock the cupboard and keep the key in my pocket hereafter.

Now we can take the lantern and go upstairs. Do you know? I'm very much inclined to agree with your theory that the wind blew it against the house. I'll go ahead, for I know the stairs; just hold the lantern near my feet as we go up. How the wind howls and whistles! Did you feel the sand on the floor under your shoes as we crossed the hall?

Yes—this is the door of the best bedroom. Hold up the lantern, please. This side, by the head of the bed. I left the cupboard open when I got the box. Isn't it queer how the faint odour of women's dresses will hang about an old closet for years? This is the shelf. You've seen me set the box there, and now you see me turn the key and put it into my pocket. So that's done!

* * * * *

Good-night. Are you sure you're quite comfortable? It's not much of a room, but I daresay you would as soon sleep here as upstairs to-night. If you want anything, sing out; there's only a lath and plaster partition between us. There's not so much wind on this side by half. There's the Hollands on the table, if you'll have one more nightcap. No? Well, do as you please. Good-night again, and don't dream about that thing, if you can.

* * * * *

The following paragraph appeared in the *Penraddon News*, 23rd November, 1906:

"MYSTERIOUS DEATH OF A RETIRED SEA CAPTAIN

"The village of Tredcombe is much disturbed by the strange death of Captain Charles Braddock, and all sorts of impossible stories are circulating with regard to the circumstances, which certainly seem difficult of explanation. The retired captain, who had successfully commanded in his time the largest and fastest liners belonging to one of the principal transatlantic steamship companies, was found dead in his bed on Tuesday morning in his own cottage, a quarter of a mile from the village. An examination was made at once by the local practitioner, which revealed the horrible fact that the deceased had been bitten in the throat by a human assailant, with such amazing force as to crush the windpipe and cause death. The marks of the teeth of both jaws were so plainly visible on the skin that they could be counted, but the perpetrator of the deed had evidently lost the two lower middle incisors. It is hoped that this peculiarity may help to identify the murderer, who can only be a dangerous escaped maniac. The deceased, though over sixty-five years of age, is said to have been a hale man of considerable physical strength, and it is remarkable that no signs of any struggle were visible in the room, nor could it be ascertained how the murderer had entered the house. Warning has been sent to all the insane asylums in the United Kingdom, but as yet no information has been received regarding the escape of any dangerous patient.

"The coroner's jury returned the somewhat singular verdict that Captain Braddock came to his death 'by the hands or teeth of some person unknown.' The local surgeon is said to have expressed privately the opinion that the maniac is a woman, a view he deduces from the small size of the jaws, as shown by the marks of the teeth. The whole affair is shrouded in mystery. Captain Braddock was a widower, and lived alone. He leaves no children."

* * * * *

[Note.—Students of ghost lore and haunted houses will find the foundation of the foregoing story in the legends about a skull which is still preserved in the farm-house called Bettiscombe Manor, situated, I believe, on the Dorsetshire coast.]

THE JUDGE'S HOUSE

Bram Stoker

When the time for his examination drew near Malcolm Malcolmson made up his mind to go somewhere to read by himself. He feared the attractions of the seaside, and also he feared completely rural isolation, for of old he knew it charms, and so he determined to find some unpretentious little town where there would be nothing to distract him. He refrained from asking suggestions from any of his friends, for he argued that each would recommend some place of which he had knowledge, and where he had already acquaintances. As Malcolmson wished to avoid friends he had no wish to encumber himself with the attention of friends' friends, and so he determined to look out for a place for himself. He packed a portmanteau with some clothes and all the books he required, and then took ticket for the first name on the local time-table which he did not know.

When at the end of three hours' journey he alighted at Benchurch, he felt satisfied that he had so far obliterated his tracks as to be sure of having a peaceful opportunity of pursuing his studies. He went straight to the one inn which the sleepy little place contained, and put up for the night. Benchurch was a market town, and once in three weeks was crowded to excess, but for the remainder of the twenty-one days it was as attractive as a desert. Malcolmson looked around the day after his arrival to try to find quarters more isolated than even so quiet an inn as "The Good Traveller" afforded. There was only one place which took his fancy, and it certainly satisfied his wildest ideas regarding quiet; in fact, quiet was not the proper word to apply to it—desolation was the only term conveying any suitable idea of its isolation. It was an old rambling, heavy-built house of the Jacobean style, with heavy gables and windows, unusually small, and set higher than was customary in such houses, and was surrounded with a high brick wall massively built. Indeed, on examination, it looked more like a fortified house than an ordinary dwelling. But all these things pleased Malcolmson. "Here," he thought, "is the very spot I have been looking for, and if I can get opportunity of using it I shall be happy." His joy was increased when he realised beyond doubt that it was not at present inhabited.

From the post-office he got the name of the agent, who was rarely surprised at the application to rent a part of the old house. Mr. Carnford, the local lawyer and agent, was a genial old gentleman, and frankly confessed his delight at anyone being willing to live in the house.

"To tell you the truth," said he, "I should be only too happy, on behalf of the owners, to let anyone have the house rent free for a term of years if only to accustom the people here to see it inhabited. It has been so long empty that some kind of absurd prejudice has grown up about it, and this can be best put down by its occupation—if only," he added with a sly glance at Malcolmson, "by a scholar like yourself, who wants its quiet for a time."

Malcolmson thought it needless to ask the agent about the "absurd prejudice"; he knew he would get more information, if he should require it, on that subject from other quarters. He paid his three months' rent, got a receipt, and the name of an old woman who would probably undertake to "do" for him, and came away with the keys in his pocket. He then went to the landlady of the inn, who was a cheerful and most kindly person, and asked her advice as to such stores and provisions as he would be likely to require. She threw up her hands in amazement when he told her where he was going to settle himself.

"Not in the Judge's House!" she said, and grew pale as she spoke. He explained the locality of the house, saying that he did not know its name. When he had finished she answered:

"Aye, sure enough—sure enough the very place! It is the Judge's House sure enough." He asked her to tell him about the place, why so called, and what there was against it. She told him that it was so called locally because it had been many years before—how long she could not say, as she was herself from another part of the country, but she thought it must have been a hundred years or more—the abode of a judge who was held in great terror on account of his harsh sentences and his hostility to prisoners at Assizes. As to what there was against the house itself she could not tell. She had often asked, but no one could inform her; but there was a general feeling that there was something, and for her own part she would not take all the money in Drinkwater's Bank and stay in the house an hour by herself. Then she apologised to Malcolmson for her disturbing talk.

"It is too bad of me, sir, and you—and a young gentlemen, too—if you will pardon me saying it, going to live there all alone. If you were my boy—and you'll excuse me for saying it—you wouldn't sleep there a night, not if I had to go there myself and pull the big alarm bell that's on the roof!" The good creature was so manifestly in earnest, and was so kindly in her intentions, that Malcolmson, although amused, was touched. He told her kindly how much he appreciated her interest in him, and added:

"But, my dear Mrs. Witham, indeed you need not be concerned about me! A man who is reading for the Mathematical Tripos has too much to think of to be disturbed by any of these mysterious 'somethings,' and his work is of too exact and prosaic a kind to allow of his having any corner in his mind for mysteries of any kind. Harmonical Progression, Permutations and Combinations, and Elliptic Functions have sufficient mysteries for me!" Mrs. Witham kindly undertook to see after his commissions, and he went himself to look for the old woman who had been recommended to him. When he returned to the Judge's House with her, after an interval of a couple of hours, he found Mrs. Witham herself waiting with several men and boys carrying parcels, and an upholsterer's man with a bed in a car, for she said, though tables and chairs might be all very well, a bed that hadn't been aired for mayhap fifty years was not proper for young bones to lie on. She was evidently curious to see the inside of the house; and though manifestly so afraid of the "somethings" that at the slightest sound she clutched on to Malcolmson, whom she never left for a moment, went over the whole place.

After his examination of the house, Malcolmson decided to take up his abode in the great dining-room, which was big enough to serve for all his requirements; and Mrs. Witham, with the aid of the charwoman, Mrs. Dempster, proceeded to arrange matters. When the hampers were brought in and unpacked, Malcolmson saw that with much kind forethought she had sent from her own kitchen sufficient provisions to last for a few days. Before going she expressed all sorts of kind wishes; and at the door turned and said:

"And perhaps, sir, as the room is big and draughty it might be well to have one of those big screens put round your bed at night—though, truth to tell, I would die myself if I were to be so shut in with all kinds of—of 'things,' that put their heads round the sides, or over the top, and look on me!" The image which she had called up was too much for her nerves, and she fled incontinently.

Mrs. Dempster sniffed in a superior manner as the landlady disappeared, and remarked that for her own part she wasn't afraid of all the bogies in the kingdom.

"I'll tell you what it is, sir," she said; "bogies is all kinds and sorts of things—except bogies! Rats and mice, and beetles; and creaky doors, and loose slates, and broken panes, and stiff drawer handles, that stay out when you pull them and then fall down in the middle of the night. Look at the wainscot of the room! It is old—hundreds of years old! Do you think there's no rats and beetles there! And do you imagine, sir, that you won't see none of them? Rats is bogies, I tell you, and bogies is rats; and don't you get to think anything else!"

"Mrs. Dempster," said Malcolmson gravely, making her a polite bow, "you know more than a Senior Wrangler! And let me say, that, as a mark of esteem for your indubitable soundness of head and heart, I shall, when I go, give you possession of this house, and let you stay here by yourself for the last two months of my tenancy, for four weeks will serve my purpose."

"Thank you kindly, sir!" she answered, "but I couldn't sleep away from home a night. I am in Greenhow's Charity, and if I slept a night away from my rooms I should lose all I have got to live on. The rules is very strict; and there's too many watching for a vacancy for me to run any risks in the matter. Only for that, sir, I'd gladly come here and attend on you altogether during your stay."

"My good woman," said Malcolmson hastily, "I have come here on purpose to obtain solitude; and believe me that I am grateful to the late Greenhow for having so organised his admirable charity—whatever it is—that I am perforce denied the opportunity of suffering from such a form of temptation! Saint Anthony himself could not be more rigid on the point!"

The old woman laughed harshly. "Ah, you young gentlemen," she said, "you don't fear for naught; and belike you'll get all the solitude you want here." She set to work with her cleaning; and by nightfall, when Malcolmson returned from his walk—he always had one of his books to study as he walked—he found the room swept and tidied, a fire burning in the old hearth, the lamp lit, and the table spread for supper with Mrs. Witham's excellent fare. "This is comfort, indeed," he said, as he rubbed his hands.

When he had finished his supper, and lifted the tray to the other end of the great oak dining-table, he got out his books again, put fresh wood on the fire, trimmed his lamp, and set himself down to a spell of real hard work. He went on without pause till about eleven o'clock, when he knocked off for a bit to fix his fire and lamp, and to make himself a cup of tea. He had always been a tea-drinker, and during his college life had sat late at work and had taken tea late. The rest was a great luxury to him, and he enjoyed it with a sense of delicious, voluptuous ease. The renewed fire leaped and sparkled, and threw quaint shadows through the great old room; and as he sipped his hot tea he revelled in the sense of isolation from his kind. Then it was that he began to notice for the first time what a noise the rats were making.

"Surely," he thought, "they cannot have been at it all the time I was reading. Had they been, I must have noticed it!" Presently, when the noise increased, he satisfied himself that it was really new. It was evident that at first the rats had been frightened at the presence of a stranger, and the light of fire and lamp; but that as the time went on they had grown bolder and were now disporting themselves as was their wont.

How busy they were! and hark to the strange noises! Up and down behind the old wainscot, over the ceiling and under the floor they raced, and gnawed, and scratched! Malcolmson smiled to himself as he recalled to mind the saying of Mrs. Dempster, "Bogies is rats, and rats is bogies!" The tea began to have its effect of intellectual and nervous stimulus, he saw with joy another long spell of work to be done before the night was past, and in the sense of security which it gave him, he allowed himself the luxury of a good look round the room. He took his lamp in one hand, and went all around, wondering that so quaint and beautiful an old house had been so long neglected. The carving of the oak on the panels of the wainscot was fine, and on and round the doors and windows it was beautiful and of rare merit. There were some old pictures on the walls, but they were coated so thick with dust and dirt that he could not distinguish any detail of them, though he held his lamp as high as he could over his head. Here and there as he went round he saw some crack or hole blocked for a moment by the face of a rat with its bright eyes glittering in the light, but in an instant it was gone, and a squeak and a scamper followed. The thing that most struck him, however, was the rope of the great alarm bell on the roof, which hung down in a corner of the room on the right-hand side of the fireplace. He pulled up close to the hearth a great high-backed carved oak chair, and sat down to his last cup of tea. When this was done he made up the fire, and went back to his work, sitting at the corner of the table, having the fire to his left. For a little while the rats disturbed him somewhat with their perpetual scampering, but he got accustomed to the noise as one does to the ticking of a clock or to the roar of moving water; and he became so immersed in his work that everything in the world, except the problem which he was trying to solve, passed away from him.

He suddenly looked up, his problem was still unsolved, and there was in the air that sense of the hour before the dawn, which is so dread to doubtful life. The noise of the rats had ceased. Indeed it seemed to him that it must have ceased but lately and that it was the sudden cessation which had disturbed him. The fire had fallen low, but still it threw out a deep red glow. As he looked he started in spite of his sang froid.

There on the great high-backed carved oak chair by the right side of the fireplace sat an enormous rat, steadily glaring at him with baleful eyes. He made a motion to it as though to hunt it away, but it did not stir. Then he made the motion of throwing something. Still it did not stir, but showed its great white teeth angrily, and its cruel eyes shone in the lamplight with an added vindictiveness.

Malcolmson felt amazed, and seizing the poker from the hearth ran at it to kill it. Before, however, he could strike it, the rat, with a squeak that sounded like the concentration of hate, jumped upon the floor, and, running up the rope of the alarm bell, disappeared in the darkness beyond the range of the green-shaded lamp. Instantly, strange to say, the noisy scampering of the rats in the wainscot began again.

By this time Malcolmson's mind was quite off the problem; and as a shrill cock-crow outside told him of the approach of morning, he went to bed and to sleep.

He slept so sound that he was not even waked by Mrs. Dempster coming in to make up his room. It was only when she had tidied up the place and got his breakfast ready and tapped on the screen which closed in his bed that he woke. He was a little tired still after his night's hard work, but a strong cup of tea soon freshened him up and, taking his book, he went out for his morning walk, bringing with him a few sandwiches lest he should not care to return till dinner time. He found a quiet walk between high elms some way outside the town, and here he spent the greater part of the day studying his Laplace. On his return he looked in to see Mrs. Witham and to thank her for her kindness. When she saw him coming through the diamond-paned bay window of her sanctum she came out to meet him and asked him in. She looked at him searchingly and shook her head as she said:

"You must not overdo it, sir. You are paler this morning than you should be. Too late hours and too hard work on the brain isn't good for any man! But tell me, sir, how did you pass the night? Well, I hope? But my heart! sir, I was glad when Mrs. Dempster told me this morning that you were all right and sleeping sound when she went in."

"Oh, I was all right," he answered smiling, "the 'somethings' didn't worry me, as yet. Only the rats; and they had a circus, I tell you, all over the place. There was one wicked looking old devil that sat up on my own chair by the fire, and wouldn't go till I took the poker to him, and then he ran up the rope of the alarm bell and got to somewhere up the wall or the ceiling—I couldn't see where, it was so dark."

"Mercy on us," said Mrs. Witham, "an old devil, and sitting on a chair by the fireside! Take care, sir! take care! There's many a true word spoken in jest."

"How do you mean? 'Pon my word I don't understand."

"An old devil! The old devil, perhaps. There! sir, you needn't laugh," for Malcolmson had broken into a hearty peal. "You young folks thinks it easy to laugh at things that makes older ones shudder. Never mind, sir! never mind! Please God, you'll laugh all the time. It's what I wish you myself!" and the good lady beamed all over in sympathy with his enjoyment, her fears gone for a moment.

"Oh, forgive me!" said Malcolmson presently. "Don't think me rude; but the idea was too much for me—that the old devil himself was on the chair last night!" And at the thought he laughed again. Then he went home to dinner.

This evening the scampering of the rats began earlier; indeed it had been going on before his arrival, and only ceased whilst his presence by its freshness disturbed them. After dinner he sat by the fire for a while and had a smoke; and then, having cleared his table, began to work as before. Tonight the rats disturbed him more than they had done on the previous night. How they scampered up and down and under and over! How they squeaked, and scratched, and gnawed! How they, getting bolder by degrees, came to the mouths of their holes and to the chinks and cracks and crannies in the wainscoting till their eyes shone like tiny lamps as the firelight rose and fell. But to him, now doubtless accustomed to them, their eyes were not wicked; only their playfulness touched him. Sometimes the boldest of them made sallies out on the floor or along the mouldings of the wainscot. Now and again as they disturbed him Malcolmson made a sound to frighten them, smiting the table with his hand or giving a fierce "Hsh, hsh," so that they fled straightway to their holes.

And so the early part of the night wore on; and despite the noise Malcolmson got more and more immersed in his work.

All at once he stopped, as on the previous night, being overcome by a sudden sense of silence. There was not the faintest sound of gnaw, or scratch, or squeak. The silence was as of the grave. He remembered the odd occurrence of the previous night, and instinctively he looked at the chair standing close by the fireside. And then a very odd sensation thrilled through him.

There, on the great old high-backed carved oak chair beside the fireplace sat the same enormous rat, steadily glaring at him with baleful eyes.

Instinctively he took the nearest thing to his hand, a book of logarithms, and flung it at it. The book was badly aimed and the rat did not stir, so again the poker performance of the previous night was repeated; and again the rat, being closely pursued, fled up the rope of the alarm bell. Strangely too, the departure of this rat was instantly followed by the renewal of the noise made by the general rat community. On this occasion, as on the previous one, Malcolmson could not see at what part of the room the rat disappeared, for the green shade of his lamp left the upper part of the room in darkness, and the fire had burned low.

On looking at his watch he found it was close on midnight; and, not sorry for the divertissement, he made up his fire and made himself his nightly pot of tea. He had got through a good spell of work, and thought himself entitled to a cigarette; and so he sat on the great oak chair before the fire and enjoyed it. Whilst smoking he began to think that he would like to know where the rat disappeared to, for he had certain ideas for the morrow not entirely disconnected with a rat-trap. Accordingly he lit another lamp and placed it so that it would shine well into the right-hand corner of the wall by the fireplace. Then he got all the books he had with him, and placed them handy to throw at the vermin. Finally he lifted the rope of the alarm bell and placed the end of it on the table, fixing the extreme end under the lamp. As he handled it he could not help noticing how pliable it was, especially for so strong a rope, and one not in use. "You could hang a man with it," he thought to himself. When his preparations were made he looked around, and said complacently:

"There now, my friend, I think we shall learn something of you this time!" He began his work again, and though as before somewhat disturbed at first by the noise of the rats, soon lost himself in his propositions and problems.

Again he was called to his immediate surroundings suddenly. This time it might not have been the sudden silence only which took his attention; there was a slight movement of the rope, and the lamp moved. Without stirring, he looked to see if his pile of books was within range, and then cast his eye along the rope. As he looked he saw the great rat drop from the rope on the oak arm-chair and sit there glaring at him. He raised a book in his right hand, and taking careful aim, flung it at the rat. The latter, with a quick movement, sprang aside and dodged the missile. He then took another book, and a third, and flung them one after another at the rat, but each time unsuccessfully. At last, as he stood with a book poised in his hand to throw, the rat squeaked and seemed afraid. This made Malcolmson more than ever eager to strike, and the book flew and struck the rat a resounding blow. It gave a terrified squeak, and turning on his pursuer a look of terrible malevolence, ran up the chair-back and made a great jump to the rope of the alarm bell and ran up it like lightning. The lamp rocked under the sudden strain, but it was a heavy one and did not topple over. Malcolmson kept his eyes on the rat, and saw it by the light of the second lamp leap to a moulding of the wainscot and disappear through a hole in one of the great pictures which hung on the wall, obscured and invisible through its coating of dirt and dust.

"I shall look up my friend's habitation in the morning," said the student, as he went over to collect his books. "The third picture from the fireplace; I shall not forget." He picked up the books one by one, commenting on them as he lifted them. "*Conic Sections* he does not mind, nor *Cycloidal Oscillations*, nor the *Principia*, nor *Quaternions*, nor *Thermodynamics*. Now for the book that fetched him!" Malcolmson took it up and looked at it. As he did so he started, and a sudden pallor overspread his face. He looked round uneasily and shivered slightly, as he murmured to himself:

"The Bible my mother gave me! What an odd coincidence." He sat down to work again, and the rats in the wainscot renewed their gambols. They did not disturb him, however; somehow their presence gave him a sense of companionship. But he could not attend to his work, and after striving to master the subject on which he was engaged gave it up in despair, and went to bed as the first streak of dawn stole in through the eastern window.

He slept heavily but uneasily, and dreamed much; and when Mrs. Dempster woke him late in the morning he seemed ill at ease, and for a few minutes did not seem to realise exactly where he was. His first request rather surprised the servant.

"Mrs. Dempster, when I am out to-day I wish you would get the steps and dust or wash those pictures—specially that one the third from the fireplace—I want to see what they are."

Late in the afternoon Malcolmson worked at his books in the shaded walk, and the cheerfulness of the previous day came back to him as the day wore on, and he found that his reading was progressing well. He had worked out to a satisfactory conclusion all the problems which had as yet baffled him, and it was in a state of jubilation that he paid a visit to Mrs. Witham at "The Good Traveller." He found a stranger in the cosy sitting-room with the landlady, who was introduced to him as Dr. Thornhill. She was not quite at ease, and this, combined with the doctor's plunging at once into a series of questions, made Malcolmson come to the conclusion that his presence was not an accident, so without preliminary he said:

"Dr. Thornhill, I shall with pleasure answer you any question you may choose to ask me if you will answer me one question first."

The doctor seemed surprised, but he smiled and answered at once, "Done! What is it?"

"Did Mrs. Witham ask you to come here and see me and advise me?"

Dr. Thornhill for a moment was taken aback, and Mrs. Witham got fiery red and turned away; but the doctor was a frank and ready man, and he answered at once and openly.

"She did: but she didn't intend you to know it. I suppose it was my clumsy haste that made you suspect. She told me that she did not like the idea of your being in that house all by yourself, and that she thought you took too much strong tea. In fact, she wants me to advise you if possible to give up the tea and the very late hours. I was a keen student in my time, so I suppose I may take the liberty of a college man, and without offence, advise you not quite as a stranger."

Malcolmson with a bright smile held out his hand. "Shake! as they say in America," he said. "I must thank you for your kindness and Mrs. Witham too, and your kindness deserves a return on my part. I promise to take no more strong tea—no tea at all till you let me—and I shall go to bed tonight at one o'clock at latest. Will that do?"

"Capital," said the doctor. "Now tell us all that you noticed in the old house," and so Malcolmson then and there told in minute detail all that had happened in the last two nights. He was interrupted every now and then by some exclamation from Mrs. Witham, till finally when he told of the episode of the Bible the landlady's pent-up emotions found vent in a shriek; and it was not till a stiff glass of brandy and water had been administered that she grew composed again. Dr. Thornhill listened with a face of growing gravity, and when the narrative was complete and Mrs. Witham had been restored he asked:

"The rat always went up the rope of the alarm bell?"

"Always."

"I suppose you know," said the Doctor after a pause, "what the rope is?"

"No!"

"It is," said the Doctor slowly, "the very rope which the hangman used for all the victims of the Judge's judicial rancour!" Here he was interrupted by another scream from Mrs. Witham, and steps had to be taken for her recovery. Malcolmson having looked at his watch, and found that it was close to his dinner hour, had gone home before her complete recovery.

When Mrs. Witham was herself again she almost assailed the Doctor with angry questions as to what he meant by putting such horrible ideas into the poor young man's mind. "He has quite enough there already to upset him," she added. Dr. Thornhill replied:

"My dear madam, I had a distinct purpose in it! I wanted to draw his attention to the bell rope, and to fix it there. It may be that he is in a highly overwrought state, and has been studying too much, although I am bound to say that he seems as sound and healthy a young man, mentally and bodily, as ever I saw—but then the rats—and that suggestion of the devil." The doctor shook his head and went on. "I would have offered to go and stay the first night with him but that I felt sure it would have been a cause of offence. He may get in the night some strange fright or hallucination; and if he does I want him to pull that rope. All alone as he is it will give us warning, and we may reach him in time to be of service. I shall be sitting up pretty late tonight and shall keep my ears open. Do not be alarmed if Benchurch gets a surprise before morning."

"Oh, Doctor, what do you mean? What do you mean?"

"I mean this; that possibly—nay, more probably—we shall hear the great alarm bell from the Judge's House tonight," and the Doctor made about as effective an exit as could be thought of.

When Malcolmson arrived home he found that it was a little after his usual time, and Mrs. Dempster had gone away—the rules of Greenhow's Charity were not to be neglected. He was glad to see that the place was bright and tidy with a cheerful fire and a well-trimmed lamp. The evening was colder than might have been expected in April, and a heavy wind was blowing with such rapidly-increasing strength that there was every promise of a storm during the night. For a few minutes after his entrance the noise of the rats ceased; but so soon as they became accustomed to his presence they began again. He was glad to hear them, for he felt once more the feeling of companionship in their noise, and his mind ran back to the strange fact that they only ceased to manifest themselves when that other—the great rat with the baleful eyes—came upon the scene. The reading-lamp only was lit and its green shade kept the ceiling and the upper part of the room in darkness, so that the cheerful light from the hearth spreading over the floor and shining on the white cloth laid over the end of the table was warm and cheery. Malcolmson sat down to his dinner with a good appetite and a buoyant spirit. After his dinner and a cigarette he sat steadily down to work, determined not to let anything disturb him, for he remembered his promise to the doctor, and made up his mind to make the best of the time at his disposal.

For an hour or so he worked all right, and then his thoughts began to wander from his books. The actual circumstances around him, the calls on his physical attention, and his nervous susceptibility were not to be denied. By this time the wind had become a gale, and the gale a storm. The old house, solid though it was, seemed to shake to its foundations, and the storm roared and raged through its many chimneys and its queer old gables, producing strange, unearthly sounds in the empty rooms and corridors. Even the great alarm bell on the roof must have felt the force of the wind, for the rope rose and fell slightly, as though the bell were moved a little from time to time and the limber rope fell on the oak floor with a hard and hollow sound.

As Malcolmson listened to it he bethought himself of the doctor's words, "It is the rope which the hangman used for the victims of the Judge's judicial rancour," and he went over to the corner of the fireplace and took it in his hand to look at it. There seemed a sort of deadly interest in it, and as he stood there he lost himself for a moment in speculation as to who these victims were, and the grim wish of the Judge to have such a ghastly relic ever under his eyes. As he stood there the swaying of the bell on the roof still lifted the rope now and again; but presently there came a new sensation—a sort of tremor in the rope, as though something was moving along it.

Looking up instinctively Malcolmson saw the great rat coming slowly down towards him, glaring at him steadily. He dropped the rope and started back with a muttered curse, and the rat turning ran up the rope again and disappeared, and at the same instant Malcolmson became conscious that the noise of the rats, which had ceased for a while, began again.

All this set him thinking, and it occurred to him that he had not investigated the lair of the rat or looked at the pictures, as he had intended. He lit the other lamp without the shade, and, holding it up went and stood opposite the third picture from the fireplace on the right-hand side where he had seen the rat disappear on the previous night.

At the first glance he started back so suddenly that he almost dropped the lamp, and a deadly pallor overspread his face. His knees shook, and heavy drops of sweat came on his forehead, and he trembled like an aspen. But he was young and plucky, and pulled himself together, and after the pause of a few seconds stepped forward again, raised the lamp, and examined the picture which had been dusted and washed, and now stood out clearly.

It was of a judge dressed in his robes of scarlet and ermine. His face was strong and merciless, evil, crafty, and vindictive, with a sensual mouth, hooked nose of ruddy colour, and shaped like the beak of a bird of prey. The rest of the face was of a cadaverous colour. The eyes were of peculiar brilliance and with a terribly malignant expression. As he looked at them, Malcolmson grew cold, for he saw there the very counterpart of the eyes of the great rat. The lamp almost fell from his hand, he saw the rat with its baleful eyes peering out through the hole in the corner of the picture, and noted the sudden cessation of the noise of the other rats. However, he pulled himself together, and went on with his examination of the picture.

The Judge was seated in a great high-backed carved oak chair, on the right-hand side of a great stone fireplace where, in the corner, a rope hung down from the ceiling, its end lying coiled on the floor. With a feeling of something like horror, Malcolmson recognised the scene of the room as it stood, and gazed around him in an awestruck manner as though he expected to find some strange presence behind him. Then he looked over to the corner of the fireplace—and with a loud cry he let the lamp fall from his hand.

There, in the Judge's arm-chair, with the rope hanging behind, sat the rat with the Judge's baleful eyes, now intensified and with a fiendish leer. Save for the howling of the storm without there was silence.

The fallen lamp recalled Malcolmson to himself. Fortunately it was of metal, and so the oil was not spilt. However, the practical need of attending to it settled at once his nervous apprehensions. When he had turned it out, he wiped his brow and thought for a moment.

"This will not do," he said to himself. "If I go on like this I shall become a crazy fool. This must stop! I promised the doctor I would not take tea. Faith, he was pretty right! My nerves must have been getting into a queer state. Funny I did not notice it. I never felt better in my life. However, it is all right now, and I shall not be such a fool again."

Then he mixed himself a good stiff glass of brandy and water and resolutely sat down to his work.

It was nearly an hour when he looked up from his book, disturbed by the sudden stillness. Without, the wind howled and roared louder than ever, and the rain drove in sheets against the windows, beating like hail on the glass; but within there was no sound whatever save the echo of the wind as it roared in the great chimney, and now and then a hiss as a few raindrops found their way down the chimney in a lull of the storm. The fire had fallen low and had ceased to flame, though it threw out a red glow. Malcolmson listened attentively, and presently heard a thin, squeaking noise, very faint. It came from the corner of the room where the rope hung down, and he thought it was the creaking of the rope on the floor as the swaying of the bell raised and lowered it. Looking up, however, he saw in the dim light the great rat clinging to the rope and gnawing it. The rope was already nearly gnawed through—he could see the lighter colour where the strands were laid bare. As he looked the job was completed, and the severed end of the rope fell clattering on the oaken floor, whilst for an instant the great rat remained like a knob or tassel at the end of the rope, which now began to sway to and fro. Malcolmson felt for a moment another pang of terror as he thought that now the possibility of calling the outer world to his assistance was cut off, but an intense anger took its place, and seizing the book he was reading he hurled it at the rat. The blow was well aimed, but before the missile could reach him the rat dropped off and struck the floor with a soft thud. Malcolmson instantly rushed over towards him, but it darted away and disappeared in the darkness of the shadows of the room. Malcolmson felt that his work was over for the night, and determined then and there to vary the monotony of the proceedings by a hunt for the rat, and took off the green shade of the lamp so as to insure a wider spreading light. As he did so the gloom of the upper part of the room was relieved, and in the new flood of light, great by comparison with the previous darkness, the pictures on the wall stood out boldly. From where he stood, Malcolmson saw right opposite to him the third picture on the wall from the right of the fireplace. He rubbed his eyes in surprise, and then a great fear began to come upon him.

In the centre of the picture was a great irregular patch of brown canvas, as fresh as when it was stretched on the frame. The background was as before, with chair and chimney-corner and rope, but the figure of the Judge had disappeared.

Malcolmson, almost in a chill of horror, turned slowly round, and then he began to shake and tremble like a man in a palsy. His strength seemed to have left him, and he was incapable of action or movement, hardly even of thought. He could only see and hear.

There, on the great high-backed carved oak chair sat the Judge in his robes of scarlet and ermine, with his baleful eyes glaring vindictively, and a smile of triumph on the resolute, cruel mouth, as he lifted with his hands a *black cap*. Malcolmson felt as if the blood was running from his heart, as one does in moments of prolonged suspense. There was a singing in his ears. Without, he could hear the roar and howl of the tempest, and through it, swept on the storm, came the striking of midnight by the great chimes in the market place. He stood for a space of time that seemed to him endless still as a statue, and with wide-open, horror-struck eyes, breathless. As the clock struck, so the smile of triumph on the Judge's face intensified, and at the last stroke of midnight he placed the black cap on his head.

Slowly and deliberately the Judge rose from his chair and picked up the piece of the rope of the alarm bell which lay on the floor, drew it through his hands as if he enjoyed its touch, and then deliberately began to knot one end of it, fashioning it into a noose. This he tightened and tested with his foot, pulling hard at it till he was satisfied and then making a running noose of it, which he held in his hand. Then he began to move along the table on the opposite side to Malcolmson keeping his eyes on him until he had passed him, when with a quick movement he stood in front of the door. Malcolmson then began to feel that he was trapped, and tried to think of what he should do. There was some fascination in the Judge's eyes, which he never took off him, and he had, perforce, to look. He saw the Judge approach—still keeping between him and the door—and raise the noose and throw it towards him as if to entangle him. With a great effort he made a quick movement to one side, and saw the rope fall beside him, and heard it strike the oaken floor. Again the Judge raised the noose and tried to ensnare him, ever keeping his baleful eyes fixed on him, and each time by a mighty effort the student just managed to evade it. So this went on for many times, the Judge seeming never discouraged nor discomposed at failure, but playing as a cat does with a mouse. At last in despair, which had reached its climax, Malcolmson cast a quick glance round him. The lamp seemed to have blazed up, and there was a fairly good light in the room. At the many rat-holes and in the chinks and crannies of the wainscot he saw the rats' eyes; and this aspect, that was purely physical, gave him a gleam of comfort. He looked around and saw that the rope of the great alarm bell was laden with rats. Every inch of it was covered with them, and more and more were pouring through the small circular hole in the ceiling whence it emerged, so that with their weight the bell was beginning to sway.

Hark! it had swayed till the clapper had touched the bell. The sound was but a tiny one, but the bell was only beginning to sway, and it would increase.

At the sound the Judge, who had been keeping his eyes fixed on Malcolmson, looked up, and a scowl of diabolical anger overspread his face. His eyes fairly glowed like hot coals, and he stamped his foot with a sound that seemed to make the house shake. A dreadful peal of thunder broke overhead as he raised the rope again, whilst the rats kept running up and down the rope as though working against time. This time, instead of throwing it, he drew close to his victim, and held open the noose as he approached. As he came closer there seemed something paralysing in his very presence, and Malcolmson stood rigid as a corpse. He felt the Judge's icy fingers touch his throat as he adjusted the rope. The noose tightened—tightened. Then the Judge, taking the rigid form of the student in his arms, carried him over and placed him standing in the oak chair, and stepping up beside him, put his hand up and caught the end of the swaying rope of the alarm bell. As he raised his hand the rats fled squeaking, and disappeared through the hole in the ceiling. Taking the end of the noose which was round Malcolmson's neck he tied it to the hanging-bell rope, and then descending pulled away the chair.

* * * * *

When the alarm bell of the Judge's House began to sound a crowd soon assembled. Lights and torches of various kinds appeared, and soon a silent crowd was hurrying to the spot. They knocked loudly at the door, but there was no reply. Then they burst in the door, and poured into the great dining-room, the doctor at the head.

There at the end of the rope of the great alarm bell hung the body of the student, and on the face of the Judge in the picture was a malignant smile.

THE BLACK CAT

Edgar Allan Poe

For the most wild, yet most homely narrative which I am about to pen, I neither expect nor solicit belief. Mad indeed would I be to expect it, in a case where my very senses reject their own evidence. Yet, mad am I not—and very surely do I not dream. But tomorrow I die, and to-day I would unburthen my soul. My immediate purpose is to place before the world, plainly, succinctly, and without comment, a series of mere household events. In their consequences, these events have terrified—have tortured—have destroyed me. Yet I will not attempt to expound them. To me, they have presented little but Horror—to many they will seem less terrible than *baroques*. Hereafter, perhaps, some intellect may be found which will reduce my phantasm to the common-place—some intellect more calm, more logical, and far less excitable than my own, which will perceive, in the circumstances I detail with awe, nothing more than an ordinary succession of very natural causes and effects.

From my infancy I was noted for the docility and humanity of my disposition. My tenderness of heart was even so conspicuous as to make me the jest of my companions. I was especially fond of animals, and was indulged by my parents with a great variety of pets. With these I spent most of my time, and never was so happy as when feeding and caressing them. This peculiarity of character grew with my growth, and in my manhood, I derived from it one of my principal sources of pleasure. To those who have cherished an affection for a faithful and sagacious dog, I need hardly be at the trouble of explaining the nature or the intensity of the gratification thus derivable. There is something in the unselfish and self-sacrificing love of a brute, which goes directly to the heart of him who has had frequent occasion to test the paltry friendship and gossamer fidelity of mere Man.

I married early, and was happy to find in my wife a disposition not uncongenial with my own. Observing my partiality for domestic pets, she lost no opportunity of procuring those of the most agreeable kind. We had birds, gold-fish, a fine dog, rabbits, a small monkey, and *a cat.*

This latter was a remarkably large and beautiful animal, entirely black, and sagacious to an astonishing degree. In speaking of his intelligence, my wife, who at heart was not a little tinctured with superstition, made frequent allusion to the ancient popular notion, which regarded all black cats as witches in disguise. Not that she was ever *serious* upon this point—and I mention the matter at all for no better reason than that it happens, just now, to be remembered.

Pluto—this was the cat's name—was my favorite pet and playmate. I alone fed him, and he attended me wherever I went about the house. It was even with difficulty that I could prevent him from following me through the streets.

Our friendship lasted, in this manner, for several years, during which my general temperament and character—through the instrumentality of the Fiend Intemperance—had (I blush to confess it) experienced a radical alteration for the worse. I grew, day by day, more moody, more irritable, more regardless of the feelings of others. I suffered myself to use intemperate language to my wife. At length, I even offered her personal violence. My pets, of course, were made to feel the change in my disposition. I not only neglected, but ill-used them. For Pluto, however, I still retained sufficient regard to restrain me from maltreating him, as I made no scruple of maltreating the rabbits, the monkey, or even the dog, when by accident, or through affection, they came in my way. But my disease grew upon me—for what disease is like Alcohol!—and at length even Pluto, who was now becoming old, and consequently somewhat peevish—even Pluto began to experience the effects of my ill temper.

One night, returning home, much intoxicated, from one of my haunts about town, I fancied that the cat avoided my presence. I seized him; when, in his fright at my violence, he inflicted a slight wound upon my hand with his teeth. The fury of a demon instantly possessed me. I knew myself no longer. My original soul seemed, at once, to take its flight from my body and a more than fiendish malevolence, gin-nurtured, thrilled every fibre of my frame. I took from my waistcoat-pocket a pen-knife, opened it, grasped the poor beast by the throat, and deliberately cut one of its eyes from the socket! I blush, I burn, I shudder, while I pen the damnable atrocity.

When reason returned with the morning—when I had slept off the fumes of the night's debauch—I experienced a sentiment half of horror, half of remorse, for the crime of which I had been guilty; but it was, at best, a feeble and equivocal feeling, and the soul remained untouched. I again plunged into excess, and soon drowned in wine all memory of the deed.

In the meantime the cat slowly recovered. The socket of the lost eye presented, it is true, a frightful appearance, but he no longer appeared to suffer any pain. He went about the house as usual, but, as might be expected, fled in extreme terror at my approach. I had so much of my old heart left, as to be at first grieved by this evident dislike on the part of a creature which had once so loved me. But this feeling soon gave place to irritation. And then came, as if to my final and irrevocable overthrow, the spirit of *perverseness*. Of this spirit philosophy takes no account. Yet I am not more sure that my soul lives, than I am that perverseness is one of the primitive impulses of the human heart—one of the indivisible primary faculties, or sentiments, which give direction to the character of Man. Who has not, a hundred times, found himself committing a vile or a silly action, for no other reason than because he knows he should not? Have we not a perpetual inclination, in the teeth of our best judgment, to violate that which is *Law*, merely because we understand it to be such? This spirit of perverseness, I say, came to my final overthrow. It was this unfathomable longing of the soul *to vex itself*—to offer violence to its own nature—to do wrong for the wrong's sake only—that urged me to continue and finally to consummate the injury I had inflicted upon the unoffending brute. One morning, in cool blood, I slipped a noose about its neck and hung it to the limb of a tree;—hung it with the tears streaming from my eyes, and with the bitterest remorse at my heart;—hung it *because* I knew that it had loved me, and *because* I felt it had given me no reason of offence;—hung it *because* I knew that in so doing I was committing a sin—a deadly sin that would so jeopardize my immortal soul as to place it—if such a thing wore possible—even beyond the reach of the infinite mercy of the most merciful and most terrible God.

On the night of the day on which this cruel deed was done, I was aroused from sleep by the cry of fire. The curtains of my bed were in flames. The whole house was blazing. It was with great difficulty that my wife, a servant, and myself, made our escape from the conflagration. The destruction was complete. My entire worldly wealth was swallowed up, and I resigned myself thenceforward to despair.

I am above the weakness of seeking to establish a sequence of cause and effect, between the disaster and the atrocity. But I am detailing a chain of facts—and wish not to leave even a possible link imperfect. On the day succeeding the fire, I visited the ruins. The walls, with one exception, had fallen in. This exception was found in a compartment wall, not very thick, which stood about the middle of the house, and against which had rested the head of my bed. The plastering had here, in great measure, resisted the action of the fire—a fact which I attributed to its having been recently spread. About this wall a dense crowd were collected, and many persons seemed to be examining a particular portion of it with very minute and eager attention. The words "strange!" "singular!" and other similar expressions, excited my curiosity. I approached and saw, as if graven in *bas relief* upon the white surface, the figure of a gigantic *cat*. The impression was given with an accuracy truly marvellous. There was a rope about the animal's neck.

When I first beheld this apparition—for I could scarcely regard it as less—my wonder and my terror were extreme. But at length reflection came to my aid. The cat, I remembered, had been hung in a garden adjacent to the house. Upon the alarm of fire, this garden had been immediately filled by the crowd—by some one of whom the animal must have been cut from the tree and thrown, through an open window, into my chamber. This had probably been done with the view of arousing me from sleep. The falling of other walls had compressed the victim of my cruelty into the substance of the freshly-spread plaster; the lime of which, with the flames, and the *ammonia* from the carcass, had then accomplished the portraiture as I saw it.

Although I thus readily accounted to my reason, if not altogether to my conscience, for the startling fact just detailed, it did not the less fail to make a deep impression upon my fancy. For months I could not rid myself of the phantasm of the cat; and, during this period, there came back into my spirit a half-sentiment that seemed, but was not, remorse. I went so far as to regret the loss of the animal, and to look about me, among the vile haunts which I now habitually frequented, for another pet of the same species, and of somewhat similar appearance, with which to supply its place.

One night as I sat, half stupified, in a den of more than infamy, my attention was suddenly drawn to some black object, reposing upon the head of one of the immense hogsheads of Gin, or of Rum, which constituted the chief furniture of the apartment. I had been looking steadily at the top of this hogshead for some minutes, and what now caused me surprise was the fact that I had not sooner perceived the object thereupon. I approached it, and touched it with my hand. It was a black cat—a very large one—fully as large as Pluto, and closely resembling him in every respect but one. Pluto had not a white hair upon any portion of his body; but this cat had a large, although indefinite splotch of white, covering nearly the whole region of the breast.

Upon my touching him, he immediately arose, purred loudly, rubbed against my hand, and appeared delighted with my notice. This, then, was the very creature of which I was in search. I at once offered to purchase it of the landlord; but this person made no claim to it—knew nothing of it—had never seen it before.

I continued my caresses, and, when I prepared to go home, the animal evinced a disposition to accompany me. I permitted it to do so; occasionally stooping and patting it as I proceeded. When it reached the house it domesticated itself at once, and became immediately a great favorite with my wife.

For my own part, I soon found a dislike to it arising within me. This was just the reverse of what I had anticipated; but—I know not how or why it was—its evident fondness for myself rather disgusted and annoyed. By slow degrees, these feelings of disgust and annoyance rose into the bitterness of hatred. I avoided the creature; a certain sense of shame, and the remembrance of my former deed of cruelty, preventing me from physically abusing it. I did not, for some weeks, strike, or otherwise violently ill use it; but gradually—very gradually—I came to look upon it with unutterable loathing, and to flee silently from its odious presence, as from the breath of a pestilence.

What added, no doubt, to my hatred of the beast, was the discovery, on the morning after I brought it home, that, like Pluto, it also had been deprived of one of its eyes. This circumstance, however, only endeared it to my wife, who, as I have already said, possessed, in a high degree, that humanity of feeling which had once been my distinguishing trait, and the source of many of my simplest and purest pleasures.

With my aversion to this cat, however, its partiality for myself seemed to increase. It followed my footsteps with a pertinacity which it would be difficult to make the reader comprehend. Whenever I sat, it would crouch beneath my chair, or spring upon my knees, covering me with its loathsome caresses. If I arose to walk it would get between my feet and thus nearly throw me down, or, fastening its long and sharp claws in my dress, clamber, in this manner, to my breast. At such times, although I longed to destroy it with a blow, I was yet withheld from so doing, partly by a memory of my former crime, but chiefly—let me confess it at once—by absolute *dread* of the beast.

This dread was not exactly a dread of physical evil—and yet I should be at a loss how otherwise to define it. I am almost ashamed to own—yes, even in this felon's cell, I am almost ashamed to own—that the terror and horror with which the animal inspired me, had been heightened by one of the merest chimaeras it would be possible to conceive. My wife had called my attention, more than once, to the character of the mark of white hair, of which I have spoken, and which constituted the sole visible difference between the strange beast and the one I had destroyed. The reader will remember that this mark, although large, had been originally very indefinite; but, by slow degrees—degrees nearly imperceptible, and which for a long time my Reason struggled to reject as fanciful—it had, at length, assumed a rigorous distinctness of outline. It was now the representation of an object that I shudder to name—and for this, above all, I loathed, and dreaded, and would have rid myself of the monster *had I dared*—it was now, I say, the image of a hideous—of a ghastly thing—of the *gallows!*—oh, mournful and terrible engine of Horror and of Crime—of Agony and of Death!

And now was I indeed wretched beyond the wretchedness of mere Humanity. And a *brute beast*—whose fellow I had contemptuously destroyed—a *brute beast* to work out for *me*—for me a man, fashioned in the image of the High God—so much of insufferable wo! Alas! neither by day nor by night knew I the blessing of Rest any more! During the former the creature left me no moment alone; and, in the latter, I started, hourly, from dreams of unutterable fear, to find the hot breath of *the thing* upon my face, and its vast weight—an incarnate Night-Mare that I had no power to shake off—incumbent eternally upon my *heart!*

Beneath the pressure of torments such as these, the feeble remnant of the good within me succumbed. Evil thoughts became my sole intimates—the darkest and most evil of thoughts. The moodiness of my usual temper increased to hatred of all things and of all mankind; while, from the sudden, frequent, and ungovernable outbursts of a fury to which I now blindly abandoned myself, my uncomplaining wife, alas! was the most usual and the most patient of sufferers.

One day she accompanied me, upon some household errand, into the cellar of the old building which our poverty compelled us to inhabit. The cat followed me down the steep stairs, and, nearly throwing me headlong, exasperated me to madness. Uplifting an axe, and forgetting, in my wrath, the childish dread which had hitherto stayed my hand, I aimed a blow at the animal which, of course, would have proved instantly fatal had it descended as I wished. But this blow was arrested by the hand of my wife. Goaded, by the interference, into a rage more than demoniacal, I withdrew my arm from her grasp and buried the axe in her brain. She fell dead upon the spot, without a groan.

This hideous murder accomplished, I set myself forthwith, and with entire deliberation, to the task of concealing the body. I knew that I could not remove it from the house, either by day or by night, without the risk of being observed by the neighbors. Many projects entered my mind. At one period I thought of cutting the corpse into minute fragments, and destroying them by fire. At another, I resolved to dig a grave for it in the floor of the cellar. Again, I deliberated about casting it in the well in the yard—about packing it in a box, as if merchandize, with the usual arrangements, and so getting a porter to take it from the house. Finally I hit upon what I considered a far better expedient than either of these. I determined to wall it up in the cellar—as the monks of the middle ages are recorded to have walled up their victims.

For a purpose such as this the cellar was well adapted. Its walls were loosely constructed, and had lately been plastered throughout with a rough plaster, which the dampness of the atmosphere had prevented from hardening. Moreover, in one of the walls was a projection, caused by a false chimney, or fireplace, that had been filled up, and made to resemble the red of the cellar. I made no doubt that I could readily displace the bricks at this point, insert the corpse, and wall the whole up as before, so that no eye could detect any thing suspicious.

And in this calculation I was not deceived. By means of a crow-bar I easily dislodged the bricks, and, having carefully deposited the body against the inner wall, I propped it in that position, while, with little trouble, I re-laid the whole structure as it originally stood. Having procured mortar, sand, and hair, with every possible precaution, I prepared a plaster which could not be distinguished from the old, and with this I very carefully went over the new brickwork. When I had finished, I felt satisfied that all was right. The wall did not present the slightest appearance of having been disturbed. The rubbish on the floor was picked up with the minutest care. I looked around triumphantly, and said to myself—"Here at least, then, my labor has not been in vain."

My next step was to look for the beast which had been the cause of so much wretchedness; for I had, at length, firmly resolved to put it to death. Had I been able to meet with it, at the moment, there could have been no doubt of its fate; but it appeared that the crafty animal had been alarmed at the violence of my previous anger, and forebore to present itself in my present mood. It is impossible to describe, or to imagine, the deep, the blissful sense of relief which the absence of the detested creature occasioned in my bosom. It did not make its appearance during the night—and thus for one night at least, since its introduction into the house, I soundly and tranquilly slept; aye, slept even with the burden of murder upon my soul!

The second and the third day passed, and still my tormentor came not. Once again I breathed as a freeman. The monster, in terror, had fled the premises forever! I should behold it no more! My happiness was supreme! The guilt of my dark deed disturbed me but little. Some few inquiries had been made, but these had been readily answered. Even a search had been instituted—but of course nothing was to be discovered. I looked upon my future felicity as secured.

Upon the fourth day of the assassination, a party of the police came, very unexpectedly, into the house, and proceeded again to make rigorous investigation of the premises. Secure, however, in the inscrutability of my place of concealment, I felt no embarrassment whatever. The officers bade me accompany them in their search. They left no nook or corner unexplored. At length, for the third or fourth time, they descended into the cellar. I quivered not in a muscle. My heart beat calmly as that of one who slumbers in innocence. I walked the cellar from end to end. I folded my arms upon my bosom, and roamed easily to and fro. The police were thoroughly satisfied and prepared to depart. The glee at my heart was too strong to be restrained. I burned to say if but one word, by way of triumph, and to render doubly sure their assurance of my guiltlessness.

"Gentlemen," I said at last, as the party ascended the steps, "I delight to have allayed your suspicions. I wish you all health, and a little more courtesy. By the bye, gentlemen, this—this is a very well constructed house." (In the rabid desire to say something easily, I scarcely knew what I uttered at all.)—"I may say an *excellently* well constructed house. These walls—are you going, gentlemen?—these walls are solidly put together"; and here, through the mere phrenzy of bravado, I rapped heavily, with a cane which I held in my hand, upon that very portion of the brick-work behind which stood the corpse of the wife of my bosom.

But may God shield and deliver me from the fangs of the Arch-Fiend! No sooner had the reverberation of my blows sunk into silence, than I was answered by a voice from within the tomb!—by a cry, at first muffled and broken, like the sobbing of a child, and then quickly swelling into one long, loud, and continuous scream, utterly anomalous and inhuman—a howl—a wailing shriek, half of horror and half of triumph, such as might have arisen only out of hell, conjointly from the throats of the dammed in their agony and of the demons that exult in the damnation.

Of my own thoughts it is folly to speak. Swooning, I staggered to the opposite wall. For one instant the party upon the stairs remained motionless, through extremity of terror and of awe. In the next, a dozen stout arms were toiling at the wall. It fell bodily. The corpse, already greatly decayed and clotted with gore, stood erect before the eyes of the spectators. Upon its head, with red extended mouth and solitary eye of fire, sat the hideous beast whose craft had seduced me into murder, and whose informing voice had consigned me to the hangman. I had walled the monster up within the tomb!

THE OPEN WINDOW

Saki

"My aunt will be down presently, Mr. Nuttel," said a very self-possessed young lady of fifteen; "in the meantime you must try and put up with me."

Framton Nuttel endeavoured to say the correct something which should duly flatter the niece of the moment without unduly discounting the aunt that was to come. Privately he doubted more than ever whether these formal visits on a succession of total strangers would do much towards helping the nerve cure which he was supposed to be undergoing.

"I know how it will be," his sister had said when he was preparing to migrate to this rural retreat; "you will bury yourself down there and not speak to a living soul, and your nerves will be worse than ever from moping. I shall just give you letters of introduction to all the people I know there. Some of them, as far as I can remember, were quite nice."

Framton wondered whether Mrs. Sappleton, the lady to whom he was presenting one of the letters of introduction, came into the nice division.

"Do you know many of the people round here?" asked the niece, when she judged that they had had sufficient silent communion.

"Hardly a soul," said Framton. "My sister was staying here, at the rectory, you know, some four years ago, and she gave me letters of introduction to some of the people here."

He made the last statement in a tone of distinct regret.

"Then you know practically nothing about my aunt?" pursued the self-possessed young lady.

"Only her name and address," admitted the caller. He was wondering whether Mrs. Sappleton was in the married or widowed state. An undefinable something about the room seemed to suggest masculine habitation.

"Her great tragedy happened just three years ago," said the child; "that would be since your sister's time."

"Her tragedy?" asked Framton; somehow in this restful country spot tragedies seemed out of place.

"You may wonder why we keep that window wide open on an October afternoon," said the niece, indicating a large French window that opened on to a lawn.

"It is quite warm for the time of the year," said Framton; "but has that window got anything to do with the tragedy?"

"Out through that window, three years ago to a day, her husband and her two young brothers went off for their day's shooting. They never came back. In crossing the moor to their favourite snipe-shooting ground they were all three engulfed in a treacherous piece of bog. It had been that dreadful wet summer, you know, and places that were safe in other years gave way suddenly without warning. Their bodies were never recovered. That was the dreadful part of it." Here the child's voice lost its self-possessed note and became falteringly human. "Poor aunt always thinks that they will come back some day, they and the little brown spaniel that was lost with them, and walk in at that window just as they used to do. That is why the window is kept open every evening till it is quite dusk. Poor dear aunt, she has often told me how they went out, her husband with his white waterproof coat over his arm, and Ronnie, her youngest brother, singing 'Bertie, why do you bound?' as he always did to tease her, because she said it got on her nerves. Do you know, sometimes on still, quiet evenings like this, I almost get a creepy feeling that they will all walk in through that window—"

She broke off with a little shudder. It was a relief to Framton when the aunt bustled into the room with a whirl of apologies for being late in making her appearance.

"I hope Vera has been amusing you?" she said.

"She has been very interesting," said Framton.

"I hope you don't mind the open window," said Mrs. Sappleton briskly; "my husband and brothers will be home directly from shooting, and they always come in this way. They've been out for snipe in the marshes to-day, so they'll make a fine mess over my poor carpets. So like you men-folk, isn't it?"

She rattled on cheerfully about the shooting and the scarcity of birds, and the prospects for duck in the winter. To Framton it was all purely horrible. He made a desperate but only partially successful effort to turn the talk on to a less ghastly topic; he was conscious that his hostess was giving him only a fragment of her attention, and her eyes were constantly straying past him to the open window and the lawn beyond. It was certainly an unfortunate coincidence that he should have paid his visit on this tragic anniversary.

"The doctors agree in ordering me complete rest, an absence of mental excitement, and avoidance of anything in the nature of violent physical exercise," announced Framton, who laboured under the tolerably widespread delusion that total strangers and chance acquaintances are hungry for the least detail of one's ailments and infirmities, their cause and cure. "On the matter of diet they are not so much in agreement," he continued.

"No?" said Mrs. Sappleton, in a voice which only replaced a yawn at the last moment. Then she suddenly brightened into alert attention—but not to what Framton was saying.

"Here they are at last!" she cried. "Just in time for tea, and don't they look as if they were muddy up to the eyes!"

Framton shivered slightly and turned towards the niece with a look intended to convey sympathetic comprehension. The child was staring out through the open window with dazed horror in her eyes. In a chill shock of nameless fear Framton swung round in his seat and looked in the same direction.

In the deepening twilight three figures were walking across the lawn towards the window; they all carried guns under their arms, and one of them was additionally burdened with a white coat hung over his shoulders. A tired brown spaniel kept close at their heels. Noiselessly they neared the house, and then a hoarse young voice chanted out of the dusk: "I said, Bertie, why do you bound?"

Framton grabbed wildly at his stick and hat; the hall-door, the gravel-drive, and the front gate were dimly-noted stages in his headlong retreat. A cyclist coming along the road had to run into the hedge to avoid an imminent collision.

"Here we are, my dear," said the bearer of the white mackintosh, coming in through the window; "fairly muddy, but most of it's dry. Who was that who bolted out as we came up?"

"A most extraordinary man, a Mr. Nuttel," said Mrs. Sappleton; "could only talk about his illnesses, and dashed off without a word of good-bye or apology when you arrived. One would think he had seen a ghost."

"I expect it was the spaniel," said the niece calmly; "he told me he had a horror of dogs. He was once hunted into a cemetery somewhere on the banks of the Ganges by a pack of pariah dogs, and had to spend the night in a newly dug grave with the creatures snarling and grinning and foaming just above him. Enough to make anyone lose their nerve."

Romance at short notice was her speciality.

RAPPACCINI'S DAUGHTER

Nathaniel Hawthorne

(From the Writings of Aubepine.)

We do not remember to have seen any translated specimens of the productions of M. de l'Aubepine—a fact the less to be wondered at, as his very name is unknown to many of his own countrymen as well as to the student of foreign literature. As a writer, he seems to occupy an unfortunate position between the Transcendentalists (who, under one name or another, have their share in all the current literature of the world) and the great body of pen-and-ink men who address the intellect and sympathies of the multitude. If not too refined, at all events too remote, too shadowy, and unsubstantial in his modes of development to suit the taste of the latter class, and yet too popular to satisfy the spiritual or metaphysical requisitions of the former, he must necessarily find himself without an audience, except here and there an individual or possibly an isolated clique. His writings, to do them justice, are not altogether destitute of fancy and originality; they might have won him greater reputation but for an inveterate love of allegory, which is apt to invest his plots and characters with the aspect of scenery and people in the clouds, and to steal away the human warmth out of his conceptions. His fictions are sometimes historical, sometimes of the present day, and sometimes, so far as can be discovered, have little or no reference either to time or space. In any case, he generally contents himself with a very slight embroidery of outward manners,—the faintest possible counterfeit of real life,—and endeavors to create an interest by some less obvious peculiarity of the subject. Occasionally a breath of Nature, a raindrop of pathos and tenderness, or a gleam of humor, will find its way into the midst of his fantastic imagery, and make us feel as if, after all, we were yet within the limits of our native earth. We will only add to this very cursory notice that M. de l'Aubepine's productions, if the reader chance to take them in precisely the proper point of view, may amuse a leisure hour as well as those of a brighter man; if otherwise, they can hardly fail to look excessively like nonsense.

Our author is voluminous; he continues to write and publish with as much praiseworthy and indefatigable prolixity as if his efforts were crowned with the brilliant success that so justly attends those of Eugene Sue. His first appearance was by a collection of stories in a long series of volumes entitled "Contes deux fois racontées." The titles of some of his more recent works (we quote from memory) are as follows: "Le Voyage Céleste à Chemin de Fer," 3 tom., 1838; "Le nouveau Père Adam et la nouvelle Mère Eve," 2 tom., 1839; "Roderic; ou le Serpent à l'estomac," 2 tom., 1840; "Le Culte du Feu," a folio volume of ponderous research into the religion and ritual of the old Persian Ghebers, published in 1841; "La Soirée du Chateau en Espagne," 1 tom., 8vo, 1842; and "L'Artiste du Beau; ou le Papillon Mécanique," 5 tom., 4to, 1843. Our somewhat wearisome perusal of this startling catalogue of volumes has left behind it a certain personal affection and sympathy, though by no means admiration, for M. de l'Aubepine; and we would fain do the little in our power towards introducing him favorably to the American public. The ensuing tale is a translation of his "Beatrice; ou la Belle Empoisonneuse," recently published in "La Revue Anti-Aristocratique." This journal, edited by the Comte de Bearhaven, has for some years past led the defence of liberal principles and popular rights with a faithfulness and ability worthy of all praise.

A young man, named Giovanni Guasconti, came, very long ago, from the more southern region of Italy, to pursue his studies at the University of Padua. Giovanni, who had but a scanty supply of gold ducats in his pocket, took lodgings in a high and gloomy chamber of an old edifice which looked not unworthy to have been the palace of a Paduan noble, and which, in fact, exhibited over its entrance the armorial bearings of a family long since extinct. The young stranger, who was not unstudied in the great poem of his country, recollected that one of the ancestors of this family, and perhaps an occupant of this very mansion, had been pictured by Dante as a partaker of the immortal agonies of his Inferno. These reminiscences and associations, together with the tendency to heartbreak natural to a young man for the first time out of his native sphere, caused Giovanni to sigh heavily as he looked around the desolate and ill-furnished apartment.

"Holy Virgin, signor!" cried old Dame Lisabetta, who, won by the youth's remarkable beauty of person, was kindly endeavoring to give the chamber a habitable air, "what a sigh was that to come out of a young man's heart! Do you find this old mansion gloomy? For the love of Heaven, then, put your head out of the window, and you will see as bright sunshine as you have left in Naples."

Guasconti mechanically did as the old woman advised, but could not quite agree with her that the Paduan sunshine was as cheerful as that of southern Italy. Such as it was, however, it fell upon a garden beneath the window and expended its fostering influences on a variety of plants, which seemed to have been cultivated with exceeding care.

"Does this garden belong to the house?" asked Giovanni.

"Heaven forbid, signor, unless it were fruitful of better pot herbs than any that grow there now," answered old Lisabetta. "No; that garden is cultivated by the own hands of Signor Giacomo Rappaccini, the famous doctor, who, I warrant him, has been heard of as far as Naples. It is said that he distils these plants into medicines that are as potent as a charm. Oftentimes you may see the signor doctor at work, and perchance the signora, his daughter, too, gathering the strange flowers that grow in the garden."

The old woman had now done what she could for the aspect of the chamber; and, commending the young man to the protection of the saints, took her departure.

Giovanni still found no better occupation than to look down into the garden beneath his window. From its appearance, he judged it to be one of those botanic gardens which were of earlier date in Padua than elsewhere in Italy or in the world. Or, not improbably, it might once have been the pleasure-place of an opulent family; for there was the ruin of a marble fountain in the centre, sculptured with rare art, but so wofully shattered that it was impossible to trace the original design from the chaos of remaining fragments. The water, however, continued to gush and sparkle into the sunbeams as cheerfully as ever. A little gurgling sound ascended to the young man's window, and made him feel as if the fountain were an immortal spirit that sung its song unceasingly and without heeding the vicissitudes around it, while one century imbodied it in marble and another scattered the perishable garniture on the soil. All about the pool into which the water subsided grew various plants, that seemed to require a plentiful supply of moisture for the nourishment of gigantic leaves, and in some instances, flowers gorgeously magnificent. There was one shrub in particular, set in a marble vase in the midst of the pool, that bore a profusion of purple blossoms, each of which had the lustre and richness of a gem; and the whole together made a show so resplendent that it seemed enough to illuminate the garden, even had there been no sunshine. Every portion of the soil was peopled with plants and herbs, which, if less beautiful, still bore tokens of assiduous care, as if all had their individual virtues, known to the scientific mind that fostered them. Some were placed in urns, rich with old carving, and others in common garden pots; some crept serpent-like along the ground or climbed on high, using whatever means of ascent was offered them. One plant had wreathed itself round a statue of Vertumnus, which was thus quite veiled and shrouded in a drapery of hanging foliage, so happily arranged that it might have served a sculptor for a study.

While Giovanni stood at the window he heard a rustling behind a screen of leaves, and became aware that a person was at work in the garden. His figure soon emerged into view, and showed itself to be that of no common laborer, but a tall, emaciated, sallow, and sickly-looking man, dressed in a scholar's garb of black. He was beyond the middle term of life, with gray hair, a thin, gray beard, and a face singularly marked with intellect and cultivation, but which could never, even in his more youthful days, have expressed much warmth of heart.

Nothing could exceed the intentness with which this scientific gardener examined every shrub which grew in his path: it seemed as if he was looking into their inmost nature, making observations in regard to their creative essence, and discovering why one leaf grew in this shape and another in that, and wherefore such and such flowers differed among themselves in hue and perfume. Nevertheless, in spite of this deep intelligence on his part, there was no approach to intimacy between himself and these vegetable existences. On the contrary, he avoided their actual touch or the direct inhaling of their odors with a caution that impressed Giovanni most disagreeably; for the man's demeanor was that of one walking among malignant influences, such as savage beasts, or deadly snakes, or evil spirits, which, should he allow them one moment of license, would wreak upon him some terrible fatality. It was strangely frightful to the young man's imagination to see this air of insecurity in a person cultivating a garden, that most simple and innocent of human toils, and which had been alike the joy and labor of the unfallen parents of the race. Was this garden, then, the Eden of the present world? And this man, with such a perception of harm in what his own hands caused to grow,—was he the Adam?

The distrustful gardener, while plucking away the dead leaves or pruning the too luxuriant growth of the shrubs, defended his hands with a pair of thick gloves. Nor were these his only armor. When, in his walk through the garden, he came to the magnificent plant that hung its purple gems beside the marble fountain, he placed a kind of mask over his mouth and nostrils, as if all this beauty did but conceal a deadlier malice; but, finding his task still too dangerous, he drew back, removed the mask, and called loudly, but in the infirm voice of a person affected with inward disease, "Beatrice! Beatrice!"

"Here am I, my father. What would you?" cried a rich and youthful voice from the window of the opposite house—a voice as rich as a tropical sunset, and which made Giovanni, though he knew not why, think of deep hues of purple or crimson and of perfumes heavily delectable. "Are you in the garden?"

"Yes, Beatrice," answered the gardener, "and I need your help."

Soon there emerged from under a sculptured portal the figure of a young girl, arrayed with as much richness of taste as the most splendid of the flowers, beautiful as the day, and with a bloom so deep and vivid that one shade more would have been too much. She looked redundant with life, health, and energy; all of which attributes were bound down and compressed, as it were and girdled tensely, in their luxuriance, by her virgin zone. Yet Giovanni's fancy must have grown morbid while he looked down into the garden; for the impression which the fair stranger made upon him was as if here were another flower, the human sister of those vegetable ones, as beautiful as they, more beautiful than the richest of them, but still to be touched only with a glove, nor to be approached without a mask. As Beatrice came down the garden path, it was observable that she handled and inhaled the odor of several of the plants which her father had most sedulously avoided.

"Here, Beatrice," said the latter, "see how many needful offices require to be done to our chief treasure. Yet, shattered as I am, my life might pay the penalty of approaching it so closely as circumstances demand. Henceforth, I fear, this plant must be consigned to your sole charge."

"And gladly will I undertake it," cried again the rich tones of the young lady, as she bent towards the magnificent plant and opened her arms as if to embrace it. "Yes, my sister, my splendour, it shall be Beatrice's task to nurse and serve thee; and thou shalt reward her with thy kisses and perfumed breath, which to her is as the breath of life."

Then, with all the tenderness in her manner that was so strikingly expressed in her words, she busied herself with such attentions as the plant seemed to require; and Giovanni, at his lofty window, rubbed his eyes and almost doubted whether it were a girl tending her favorite flower, or one sister performing the duties of affection to another. The scene soon terminated. Whether Dr. Rappaccini had finished his labors in the garden, or that his watchful eye had caught the stranger's face, he now took his daughter's arm and retired. Night was already closing in; oppressive exhalations seemed to proceed from the plants and steal upward past the open window; and Giovanni, closing the lattice, went to his couch and dreamed of a rich flower and beautiful girl. Flower and maiden were different, and yet the same, and fraught with some strange peril in either shape.

But there is an influence in the light of morning that tends to rectify whatever errors of fancy, or even of judgment, we may have incurred during the sun's decline, or among the shadows of the night, or in the less wholesome glow of moonshine. Giovanni's first movement, on starting from sleep, was to throw open the window and gaze down into the garden which his dreams had made so fertile of mysteries. He was surprised and a little ashamed to find how real and matter-of-fact an affair it proved to be, in the first rays of the sun which gilded the dew-drops that hung upon leaf and blossom, and, while giving a brighter beauty to each rare flower, brought everything within the limits of ordinary experience. The young man rejoiced that, in the heart of the barren city, he had the privilege of overlooking this spot of lovely and luxuriant vegetation. It would serve, he said to himself, as a symbolic language to keep him in communion with Nature. Neither the sickly and thoughtworn Dr. Giacomo Rappaccini, it is true, nor his brilliant daughter, were now visible; so that Giovanni could not determine how much of the singularity which he attributed to both was due to their own qualities and how much to his wonder-working fancy; but he was inclined to take a most rational view of the whole matter.

In the course of the day he paid his respects to Signor Pietro Baglioni, professor of medicine in the university, a physician of eminent repute to whom Giovanni had brought a letter of introduction. The professor was an elderly personage, apparently of genial nature, and habits that might almost be called jovial. He kept the young man to dinner, and made himself very agreeable by the freedom and liveliness of his conversation, especially when warmed by a flask or two of Tuscan wine. Giovanni, conceiving that men of science, inhabitants of the same city, must needs be on familiar terms with one another, took an opportunity to mention the name of Dr. Rappaccini. But the professor did not respond with so much cordiality as he had anticipated.

"Ill would it become a teacher of the divine art of medicine," said Professor Pietro Baglioni, in answer to a question of Giovanni, "to withhold due and well-considered praise of a physician so eminently skilled as Rappaccini; but, on the other hand, I should answer it but scantily to my conscience were I to permit a worthy youth like yourself, Signor Giovanni, the son of an ancient friend, to imbibe erroneous ideas respecting a man who might hereafter chance to hold your life and death in his hands. The truth is, our worshipful Dr. Rappaccini has as much science as any member of the faculty—with perhaps one single exception—in Padua, or all Italy; but there are certain grave objections to his professional character."

"And what are they?" asked the young man.

"Has my friend Giovanni any disease of body or heart, that he is so inquisitive about physicians?" said the professor, with a smile. "But as for Rappaccini, it is said of him—and I, who know the man well, can answer for its truth—that he cares infinitely more for science than for mankind. His patients are interesting to him only as subjects for some new experiment. He would sacrifice human life, his own among the rest, or whatever else was dearest to him, for the sake of adding so much as a grain of mustard seed to the great heap of his accumulated knowledge."

"Methinks he is an awful man indeed," remarked Guasconti, mentally recalling the cold and purely intellectual aspect of Rappaccini. "And yet, worshipful professor, is it not a noble spirit? Are there many men capable of so spiritual a love of science?"

"God forbid," answered the professor, somewhat testily; "at least, unless they take sounder views of the healing art than those adopted by Rappaccini. It is his theory that all medicinal virtues are comprised within those substances which we term vegetable poisons. These he cultivates with his own hands, and is said even to have produced new varieties of poison, more horribly deleterious than Nature, without the assistance of this learned person, would ever have plagued the world withal. That the signor doctor does less mischief than might be expected with such dangerous substances is undeniable. Now and then, it must be owned, he has effected, or seemed to effect, a marvellous cure; but, to tell you my private mind, Signor Giovanni, he should receive little credit for such instances of success,—they being probably the work of chance,—but should be held strictly accountable for his failures, which may justly be considered his own work."

The youth might have taken Baglioni's opinions with many grains of allowance had he known that there was a professional warfare of long continuance between him and Dr. Rappaccini, in which the latter was generally thought to have gained the advantage. If the reader be inclined to judge for himself, we refer him to certain black-letter tracts on both sides, preserved in the medical department of the University of Padua.

"I know not, most learned professor," returned Giovanni, after musing on what had been said of Rappaccini's exclusive zeal for science,—"I know not how dearly this physician may love his art; but surely there is one object more dear to him. He has a daughter."

"Aha!" cried the professor, with a laugh. "So now our friend Giovanni's secret is out. You have heard of this daughter, whom all the young men in Padua are wild about, though not half a dozen have ever had the good hap to see her face. I know little of the Signora Beatrice save that Rappaccini is said to have instructed her deeply in his science, and that, young and beautiful as fame reports her, she is already qualified to fill a professor's chair. Perchance her father destines her for mine! Other absurd rumors there be, not worth talking about or listening to. So now, Signor Giovanni, drink off your glass of lachryma."

Guasconti returned to his lodgings somewhat heated with the wine he had quaffed, and which caused his brain to swim with strange fantasies in reference to Dr. Rappaccini and the beautiful Beatrice. On his way, happening to pass by a florist's, he bought a fresh bouquet of flowers.

Ascending to his chamber, he seated himself near the window, but within the shadow thrown by the depth of the wall, so that he could look down into the garden with little risk of being discovered. All beneath his eye was a solitude. The strange plants were basking in the sunshine, and now and then nodding gently to one another, as if in acknowledgment of sympathy and kindred. In the midst, by the shattered fountain, grew the magnificent shrub, with its purple gems clustering all over it; they glowed in the air, and gleamed back again out of the depths of the pool, which thus seemed to overflow with colored radiance from the rich reflection that was steeped in it. At first, as we have said, the garden was a solitude. Soon, however,—as Giovanni had half hoped, half feared, would be the case,—a figure appeared beneath the antique sculptured portal, and came down between the rows of plants, inhaling their various perfumes as if she were one of those beings of old classic fable that lived upon sweet odors. On again beholding Beatrice, the young man was even startled to perceive how much her beauty exceeded his recollection of it; so brilliant, so vivid, was its character, that she glowed amid the sunlight, and, as Giovanni whispered to himself, positively illuminated the more shadowy intervals of the garden path. Her face being now more revealed than on the former occasion, he was struck by its expression of simplicity and sweetness,—qualities that had not entered into his idea of her character, and which made him ask anew what manner of mortal she might be. Nor did he fail again to observe, or imagine, an analogy between the beautiful girl and the gorgeous shrub that hung its gemlike flowers over the fountain,—a resemblance which Beatrice seemed to have indulged a fantastic humor in heightening, both by the arrangement of her dress and the selection of its hues.

Approaching the shrub, she threw open her arms, as with a passionate ardor, and drew its branches into an intimate embrace—so intimate that her features were hidden in its leafy bosom and her glistening ringlets all intermingled with the flowers.

"Give me thy breath, my sister," exclaimed Beatrice; "for I am faint with common air. And give me this flower of thine, which I separate with gentlest fingers from the stem and place it close beside my heart."

With these words the beautiful daughter of Rappaccini plucked one of the richest blossoms of the shrub, and was about to fasten it in her bosom. But now, unless Giovanni's draughts of wine had bewildered his senses, a singular incident occurred. A small orange-colored reptile, of the lizard or chameleon species, chanced to be creeping along the path, just at the feet of Beatrice. It appeared to Giovanni,—but, at the distance from which he gazed, he could scarcely have seen anything so minute,—it appeared to him, however, that a drop or two of moisture from the broken stem of the flower descended upon the lizard's head. For an instant the reptile contorted itself violently, and then lay motionless in the sunshine. Beatrice observed this remarkable phenomenon and crossed herself, sadly, but without surprise; nor did she therefore hesitate to arrange the fatal flower in her bosom. There it blushed, and almost glimmered with the dazzling effect of a precious stone, adding to her dress and aspect the one appropriate charm which nothing else in the world could have supplied. But Giovanni, out of the shadow of his window, bent forward and shrank back, and murmured and trembled.

"Am I awake? Have I my senses?" said he to himself. "What is this being? Beautiful shall I call her, or inexpressibly terrible?"

Beatrice now strayed carelessly through the garden, approaching closer beneath Giovanni's window, so that he was compelled to thrust his head quite out of its concealment in order to gratify the intense and painful curiosity which she excited. At this moment there came a beautiful insect over the garden wall; it had, perhaps, wandered through the city, and found no flowers or verdure among those antique haunts of men until the heavy perfumes of Dr. Rappaccini's shrubs had lured it from afar. Without alighting on the flowers, this winged brightness seemed to be attracted by Beatrice, and lingered in the air and fluttered about her head. Now, here it could not be but that Giovanni Guasconti's eyes deceived him. Be that as it might, he fancied that, while Beatrice was gazing at the insect with childish delight, it grew faint and fell at her feet; its bright wings shivered; it was dead—from no cause that he could discern, unless it were the atmosphere of her breath. Again Beatrice crossed herself and sighed heavily as she bent over the dead insect.

An impulsive movement of Giovanni drew her eyes to the window. There she beheld the beautiful head of the young man—rather a Grecian than an Italian head, with fair, regular features, and a glistening of gold among his ringlets—gazing down upon her like a being that hovered in mid air. Scarcely knowing what he did, Giovanni threw down the bouquet which he had hitherto held in his hand.

"Signora," said he, "there are pure and healthful flowers. Wear them for the sake of Giovanni Guasconti."

"Thanks, signor," replied Beatrice, with her rich voice, that came forth as it were like a gush of music, and with a mirthful expression half childish and half woman-like. "I accept your gift, and would fain recompense it with this precious purple flower; but if I toss it into the air it will not reach you. So Signor Guasconti must even content himself with my thanks."

She lifted the bouquet from the ground, and then, as if inwardly ashamed at having stepped aside from her maidenly reserve to respond to a stranger's greeting, passed swiftly homeward through the garden. But few as the moments were, it seemed to Giovanni, when she was on the point of vanishing beneath the sculptured portal, that his beautiful bouquet was already beginning to wither in her grasp. It was an idle thought; there could be no possibility of distinguishing a faded flower from a fresh one at so great a distance.

For many days after this incident the young man avoided the window that looked into Dr. Rappaccini's garden, as if something ugly and monstrous would have blasted his eyesight had he been betrayed into a glance. He felt conscious of having put himself, to a certain extent, within the influence of an unintelligible power by the communication which he had opened with Beatrice. The wisest course would have been, if his heart were in any real danger, to quit his lodgings and Padua itself at once; the next wiser, to have accustomed himself, as far as possible, to the familiar and daylight view of Beatrice—thus bringing her rigidly and systematically within the limits of ordinary experience. Least of all, while avoiding her sight, ought Giovanni to have remained so near this extraordinary being that the proximity and possibility even of intercourse should give a kind of substance and reality to the wild vagaries which his imagination ran riot continually in producing. Guasconti had not a deep heart—or, at all events, its depths were not sounded now; but he had a quick fancy, and an ardent southern temperament, which rose every instant to a higher fever pitch. Whether or no Beatrice possessed those terrible attributes, that fatal breath, the affinity with those so beautiful and deadly flowers which were indicated by what Giovanni had witnessed, she had at least instilled a fierce and subtle poison into his system. It was not love, although her rich beauty was a madness to him; nor horror, even while he fancied her spirit to be imbued with the same baneful essence that seemed to pervade her physical frame; but a wild offspring of both love and horror that had each parent in it, and burned like one and shivered like the other. Giovanni knew not what to dread; still less did he know what to hope; yet hope and dread kept a continual warfare in his breast, alternately vanquishing one another and starting up afresh to renew the contest. Blessed are all simple emotions, be they dark or bright! It is the lurid intermixture of the two that produces the illuminating blaze of the infernal regions.

Sometimes he endeavored to assuage the fever of his spirit by a rapid walk through the streets of Padua or beyond its gates: his footsteps kept time with the throbbings of his brain, so that the walk was apt to accelerate itself to a race. One day he found himself arrested; his arm was seized by a portly personage, who had turned back on recognizing the young man and expended much breath in overtaking him.

"Signor Giovanni! Stay, my young friend!" cried he. "Have you forgotten me? That might well be the case if I were as much altered as yourself."

It was Baglioni, whom Giovanni had avoided ever since their first meeting, from a doubt that the professor's sagacity would look too deeply into his secrets. Endeavoring to recover himself, he stared forth wildly from his inner world into the outer one and spoke like a man in a dream.

"Yes; I am Giovanni Guasconti. You are Professor Pietro Baglioni. Now let me pass!"

"Not yet, not yet, Signor Giovanni Guasconti," said the professor, smiling, but at the same time scrutinizing the youth with an earnest glance. "What!

did I grow up side by side with your father? and shall his son pass me like a stranger in these old streets of Padua? Stand still, Signor Giovanni; for we must have a word or two before we part."

"Speedily, then, most worshipful professor, speedily," said Giovanni, with feverish impatience. "Does not your worship see that I am in haste?"

Now, while he was speaking there came a man in black along the street, stooping and moving feebly like a person in inferior health. His face was all overspread with a most sickly and sallow hue, but yet so pervaded with an expression of piercing and active intellect that an observer might easily have overlooked the merely physical attributes and have seen only this wonderful energy. As he passed, this person exchanged a cold and distant salutation with Baglioni, but fixed his eyes upon Giovanni with an intentness that seemed to bring out whatever was within him worthy of notice. Nevertheless, there was a peculiar quietness in the look, as if taking merely a speculative, not a human interest, in the young man.

"It is Dr. Rappaccini!" whispered the professor when the stranger had passed. "Has he ever seen your face before?"

"Not that I know," answered Giovanni, starting at the name.

"He has seen you! he must have seen you!" said Baglioni, hastily. "For some purpose or other, this man of science is making a study of you. I know that look of his! It is the same that coldly illuminates his face as he bends over a bird, a mouse, or a butterfly, which, in pursuance of some experiment, he has killed by the perfume of a flower; a look as deep as Nature itself, but without Nature's warmth of love. Signor Giovanni, I will stake my life upon it, you are the subject of one of Rappaccini's experiments!"

"Will you make a fool of me?" cried Giovanni, passionately. "*That*, signor professor, were an untoward experiment."

"Patience! patience!" replied the imperturbable professor. "I tell thee, my poor Giovanni, that Rappaccini has a scientific interest in thee. Thou hast fallen into fearful hands! And the Signora Beatrice,—what part does she act in this mystery?"

But Guasconti, finding Baglioni's pertinacity intolerable, here broke away, and was gone before the professor could again seize his arm. He looked after the young man intently and shook his head.

"This must not be," said Baglioni to himself. "The youth is the son of my old friend, and shall not come to any harm from which the arcana of medical science can preserve him. Besides, it is too insufferable an impertinence in Rappaccini, thus to snatch the lad out of my own hands, as I may say, and make use of him for his infernal experiments. This daughter of his! It shall be looked to. Perchance, most learned Rappaccini, I may foil you where you little dream of it!"

Meanwhile Giovanni had pursued a circuitous route, and at length found himself at the door of his lodgings. As he crossed the threshold he was met by old Lisabetta, who smirked and smiled, and was evidently desirous to attract his attention; vainly, however, as the ebullition of his feelings had momentarily subsided into a cold and dull vacuity. He turned his eyes full upon the withered face that was puckering itself into a smile, but seemed to behold it not. The old dame, therefore, laid her grasp upon his cloak.

"Signor! signor!" whispered she, still with a smile over the whole breadth of her visage, so that it looked not unlike a grotesque carving in wood, darkened by centuries. "Listen, signor! There is a private entrance into the garden!"

"What do you say?" exclaimed Giovanni, turning quickly about, as if an inanimate thing should start into feverish life. "A private entrance into Dr. Rappaccini's garden?"

"Hush! hush! not so loud!" whispered Lisabetta, putting her hand over his mouth. "Yes; into the worshipful doctor's garden, where you may see all his fine shrubbery. Many a young man in Padua would give gold to be admitted among those flowers."

Giovanni put a piece of gold into her hand.

"Show me the way," said he.

A surmise, probably excited by his conversation with Baglioni, crossed his mind, that this interposition of old Lisabetta might perchance be connected with the intrigue, whatever were its nature, in which the professor seemed to suppose that Dr. Rappaccini was involving him. But such a suspicion, though it disturbed Giovanni, was inadequate to restrain him. The instant that he was aware of the possibility of approaching Beatrice, it seemed an absolute necessity of his existence to do so. It mattered not whether she were angel or demon; he was irrevocably within her sphere, and must obey the law that whirled him onward, in ever-lessening circles, towards a result which he did not attempt to foreshadow; and yet, strange to say, there came across him a sudden doubt whether this intense interest on his part were not delusory; whether it were really of so deep and positive a nature as to justify him in now thrusting himself into an incalculable position; whether it were not merely the fantasy of a young man's brain, only slightly or not at all connected with his heart.

He paused, hesitated, turned half about, but again went on. His withered guide led him along several obscure passages, and finally undid a door, through which, as it was opened, there came the sight and sound of rustling leaves, with the broken sunshine glimmering among them. Giovanni stepped forth, and, forcing himself through the entanglement of a shrub that wreathed its tendrils over the hidden entrance, stood beneath his own window in the open area of Dr. Rappaccini's garden.

How often is it the case that, when impossibilities have come to pass and dreams have condensed their misty substance into tangible realities, we find ourselves calm, and even coldly self-possessed, amid circumstances which it would have been a delirium of joy or agony to anticipate! Fate delights to thwart us thus. Passion will choose his own time to rush upon the scene, and lingers sluggishly behind when an appropriate adjustment of events would seem to summon his appearance. So was it now with Giovanni. Day after day his pulses had throbbed with feverish blood at the improbable idea of an interview with Beatrice, and of standing with her, face to face, in this very garden, basking in the Oriental sunshine of her beauty, and snatching from her full gaze the mystery which he deemed the riddle of his own existence. But now there was a singular and untimely equanimity within his breast. He threw a glance around the garden to discover if Beatrice or her father were present, and, perceiving that he was alone, began a critical observation of the plants.

The aspect of one and all of them dissatisfied him; their gorgeousness seemed fierce, passionate, and even unnatural. There was hardly an individual shrub which a wanderer, straying by himself through a forest, would not have been startled to find growing wild, as if an unearthly face had glared at him out of the thicket. Several also would have shocked a delicate instinct by an appearance of artificialness indicating that there had been such commixture, and, as it were, adultery, of various vegetable species, that the production was no longer of God's making, but the monstrous offspring of man's depraved fancy, glowing with only an evil mockery of beauty. They were probably the result of experiment, which in one or two cases had succeeded in mingling plants individually lovely into a compound possessing the questionable and ominous character that distinguished the whole growth of the garden. In fine, Giovanni recognized but two or three plants in the collection, and those of a kind that he well knew to be poisonous. While busy with these contemplations he heard the rustling of a silken garment, and, turning, beheld Beatrice emerging from beneath the sculptured portal.

Giovanni had not considered with himself what should be his deportment; whether he should apologize for his intrusion into the garden, or assume that he was there with the privity at least, if not by the desire, of Dr. Rappaccini or his daughter; but Beatrice's manner placed him at his ease, though leaving him still in doubt by what agency he had gained admittance. She came lightly along the path and met him near the broken fountain. There was surprise in her face, but brightened by a simple and kind expression of pleasure.

"You are a connoisseur in flowers, signor," said Beatrice, with a smile, alluding to the bouquet which he had flung her from the window. "It is no marvel, therefore, if the sight of my father's rare collection has tempted you to take a nearer view. If he were here, he could tell you many strange and interesting facts as to the nature and habits of these shrubs; for he has spent a lifetime in such studies, and this garden is his world."

"And yourself, lady," observed Giovanni, "if fame says true,—you likewise are deeply skilled in the virtues indicated by these rich blossoms and these spicy perfumes. Would you deign to be my instructress, I should prove an apter scholar than if taught by Signor Rappaccini himself."

"Are there such idle rumors?" asked Beatrice, with the music of a pleasant laugh. "Do people say that I am skilled in my father's science of plants? What a jest is there! No; though I have grown up among these flowers, I know no more of them than their hues and perfume; and sometimes methinks I would fain rid myself of even that small knowledge. There are many flowers here, and those not the least brilliant, that shock and offend me when they meet my eye. But pray, signor, do not believe these stories about my science. Believe nothing of me save what you see with your own eyes."

"And must I believe all that I have seen with my own eyes?" asked Giovanni, pointedly, while the recollection of former scenes made him shrink. "No, signora; you demand too little of me. Bid me believe nothing save what comes from your own lips."

It would appear that Beatrice understood him. There came a deep flush to her cheek; but she looked full into Giovanni's eyes, and responded to his gaze of uneasy suspicion with a queenlike haughtiness.

"I do so bid you, signor," she replied. "Forget whatever you may have fancied in regard to me. If true to the outward senses, still it may be false in its essence; but the words of Beatrice Rappaccini's lips are true from the depths of the heart outward. Those you may believe."

A fervor glowed in her whole aspect and beamed upon Giovanni's consciousness like the light of truth itself; but while she spoke there was a fragrance in the atmosphere around her, rich and delightful, though evanescent, yet which the young man, from an indefinable reluctance, scarcely dared to draw into his lungs. It might be the odor of the flowers. Could it be Beatrice's breath which thus embalmed her words with a strange richness, as if by steeping them in her heart? A faintness passed like a shadow over Giovanni and flitted away; he seemed to gaze through the beautiful girl's eyes into her transparent soul, and felt no more doubt or fear.

The tinge of passion that had colored Beatrice's manner vanished; she became gay, and appeared to derive a pure delight from her communion with the youth not unlike what the maiden of a lonely island might have felt conversing with a voyager from the civilized world. Evidently her experience of life had been confined within the limits of that garden. She talked now about matters as simple as the daylight or summer clouds, and now asked questions in reference to the city, or Giovanni's distant home, his friends, his mother, and his sisters—questions indicating such seclusion, and such lack of familiarity with modes and forms, that Giovanni responded as if to an infant. Her spirit gushed out before him like a fresh rill that was just catching its first glimpse of the sunlight and wondering at the reflections of earth and sky which were flung into its bosom. There came thoughts, too, from a deep source, and fantasies of a gemlike brilliancy, as if diamonds and rubies sparkled upward among the bubbles of the fountain. Ever and anon there gleamed across the young man's mind a sense of wonder that he should be walking side by side with the being who had so wrought upon his imagination, whom he had idealized in such hues of terror, in whom he had positively witnessed such manifestations of dreadful attributes,—that he should be conversing with Beatrice like a brother, and should find her so human and so maidenlike. But such reflections were only momentary; the effect of her character was too real not to make itself familiar at once.

In this free intercourse they had strayed through the garden, and now, after many turns among its avenues, were come to the shattered fountain, beside which grew the magnificent shrub, with its treasury of glowing blossoms. A fragrance was diffused from it which Giovanni recognized as identical with that which he had attributed to Beatrice's breath, but incomparably more powerful. As her eyes fell upon it, Giovanni beheld her press her hand to her bosom as if her heart were throbbing suddenly and painfully.

"For the first time in my life," murmured she, addressing the shrub, "I had forgotten thee."

"I remember, signora," said Giovanni, "that you once promised to reward me with one of these living gems for the bouquet which I had the happy boldness to fling to your feet. Permit me now to pluck it as a memorial of this interview."

He made a step towards the shrub with extended hand; but Beatrice darted forward, uttering a shriek that went through his heart like a dagger. She caught his hand and drew it back with the whole force of her slender figure. Giovanni felt her touch thrilling through his fibres.

"Touch it not!" exclaimed she, in a voice of agony. "Not for thy life! It is fatal!"

Then, hiding her face, she fled from him and vanished beneath the sculptured portal. As Giovanni followed her with his eyes, he beheld the emaciated figure and pale intelligence of Dr. Rappaccini, who had been watching the scene, he knew not how long, within the shadow of the entrance.

No sooner was Guasconti alone in his chamber than the image of Beatrice came back to his passionate musings, invested with all the witchery that had been gathering around it ever since his first glimpse of her, and now likewise imbued with a tender warmth of girlish womanhood. She was human; her nature was endowed with all gentle and feminine qualities; she was worthiest to be worshipped; she was capable, surely, on her part, of the height and heroism of love. Those tokens which he had hitherto considered as proofs of a frightful peculiarity in her physical and moral system were now either forgotten, or, by the subtle sophistry of passion transmitted into a golden crown of enchantment, rendering Beatrice the more admirable by so much as she was the more unique. Whatever had looked ugly was now beautiful; or, if incapable of such a change, it stole away and hid itself among those shapeless half ideas which throng the dim region beyond the daylight of our perfect consciousness. Thus did he spend the night, nor fell asleep until the dawn had begun to awake the slumbering flowers in Dr. Rappaccini's garden, whither Giovanni's dreams doubtless led him. Up rose the sun in his due season, and, flinging his beams upon the young man's eyelids, awoke him to a sense of pain. When thoroughly aroused, he became sensible of a burning and tingling agony in his hand—in his right hand—the very hand which Beatrice had grasped in her own when he was on the point of plucking one of the gemlike flowers. On the back of that hand there was now a purple print like that of four small fingers, and the likeness of a slender thumb upon his wrist.

Oh, how stubbornly does love,—or even that cunning semblance of love which flourishes in the imagination, but strikes no depth of root into the heart,—how stubbornly does it hold its faith until the moment comes when it is doomed to vanish into thin mist! Giovanni wrapped a handkerchief about his hand and wondered what evil thing had stung him, and soon forgot his pain in a reverie of Beatrice.

After the first interview, a second was in the inevitable course of what we call fate. A third; a fourth; and a meeting with Beatrice in the garden was no longer an incident in Giovanni's daily life, but the whole space in which he might be said to live; for the anticipation and memory of that ecstatic hour made up the remainder. Nor was it otherwise with the daughter of Rappaccini. She watched for the youth's appearance, and flew to his side with confidence as unreserved as if they had been playmates from early infancy—as if they were such playmates still. If, by any unwonted chance, he failed to come at the appointed moment, she stood beneath the window and sent up the rich sweetness of her tones to float around him in his chamber and echo and reverberate throughout his heart: "Giovanni! Giovanni! Why tarriest thou? Come down!" And down he hastened into that Eden of poisonous flowers.

But, with all this intimate familiarity, there was still a reserve in Beatrice's demeanor, so rigidly and invariably sustained that the idea of infringing it scarcely occurred to his imagination. By all appreciable signs, they loved; they had looked love with eyes that conveyed the holy secret from the depths of one soul into the depths of the other, as if it were too sacred to be whispered by the way; they had even spoken love in those gushes of passion when their spirits darted forth in articulated breath like tongues of long-hidden flame; and yet there had been no seal of lips, no clasp of hands, nor any slightest caress such as love claims and hallows. He had never touched one of the gleaming ringlets of her hair; her garment—so marked was the physical barrier between them—had never been waved against him by a breeze. On the few occasions when Giovanni had seemed tempted to overstep the limit, Beatrice grew so sad, so stern, and withal wore such a look of desolate separation, shuddering at itself, that not a spoken word was requisite to repel him. At such times he was startled at the horrible suspicions that rose, monster-like, out of the caverns of his heart and stared him in the face; his love grew thin and faint as the morning mist, his doubts alone had substance. But, when Beatrice's face brightened again after the momentary shadow, she was transformed at once from the mysterious, questionable being whom he had watched with so much awe and horror; she was now the beautiful and unsophisticated girl whom he felt that his spirit knew with a certainty beyond all other knowledge.

A considerable time had now passed since Giovanni's last meeting with Baglioni. One morning, however, he was disagreeably surprised by a visit from the professor, whom he had scarcely thought of for whole weeks, and would willingly have forgotten still longer. Given up as he had long been to a pervading excitement, he could tolerate no companions except upon condition of their perfect sympathy with his present state of feeling. Such sympathy was not to be expected from Professor Baglioni.

The visitor chatted carelessly for a few moments about the gossip of the city and the university, and then took up another topic.

"I have been reading an old classic author lately," said he, "and met with a story that strangely interested me. Possibly you may remember it. It is of an Indian prince, who sent a beautiful woman as a present to Alexander the Great. She was as lovely as the dawn and gorgeous as the sunset; but what especially distinguished her was a certain rich perfume in her breath—richer than a garden of Persian roses. Alexander, as was natural to a youthful conqueror, fell in love at first sight with this magnificent stranger; but a certain sage physician, happening to be present, discovered a terrible secret in regard to her."

"And what was that?" asked Giovanni, turning his eyes downward to avoid those of the professor.

"That this lovely woman," continued Baglioni, with emphasis, "had been nourished with poisons from her birth upward, until her whole nature was so imbued with them that she herself had become the deadliest poison in existence. Poison was her element of life. With that rich perfume of her breath she blasted the very air. Her love would have been poison—her embrace death. Is not this a marvellous tale?"

"A childish fable," answered Giovanni, nervously starting from his chair. "I marvel how your worship finds time to read such nonsense among your graver studies."

"By the by," said the professor, looking uneasily about him, "what singular fragrance is this in your apartment? Is it the perfume of your gloves? It is faint, but delicious; and yet, after all, by no means agreeable. Were I to breathe it long, methinks it would make me ill. It is like the breath of a flower; but I see no flowers in the chamber."

"Nor are there any," replied Giovanni, who had turned pale as the professor spoke; "nor, I think, is there any fragrance except in your worship's imagination. Odors, being a sort of element combined of the sensual and the spiritual, are apt to deceive us in this manner. The recollection of a perfume, the bare idea of it, may easily be mistaken for a present reality."

"Ay; but my sober imagination does not often play such tricks," said Baglioni; "and, were I to fancy any kind of odor, it would be that of some vile apothecary drug, wherewith my fingers are likely enough to be imbued. Our worshipful friend Rappaccini, as I have heard, tinctures his medicaments with odors richer than those of Araby. Doubtless, likewise, the fair and learned Signora Beatrice would minister to her patients with draughts as sweet as a maiden's breath; but woe to him that sips them!"

Giovanni's face evinced many contending emotions. The tone in which the professor alluded to the pure and lovely daughter of Rappaccini was a torture to his soul; and yet the intimation of a view of her character opposite to his own, gave instantaneous distinctness to a thousand dim suspicions, which now grinned at him like so many demons. But he strove hard to quell them and to respond to Baglioni with a true lover's perfect faith.

"Signor professor," said he, "you were my father's friend; perchance, too, it is your purpose to act a friendly part towards his son. I would fain feel nothing towards you save respect and deference; but I pray you to observe, signor, that there is one subject on which we must not speak. You know not the Signora Beatrice. You cannot, therefore, estimate the wrong—the blasphemy, I may even say—that is offered to her character by a light or injurious word."

"Giovanni! my poor Giovanni!" answered the professor, with a calm expression of pity, "I know this wretched girl far better than yourself. You shall hear the truth in respect to the poisoner Rappaccini and his poisonous daughter; yes, poisonous as she is beautiful. Listen; for, even should you do violence to my gray hairs, it shall not silence me. That old fable of the Indian woman has become a truth by the deep and deadly science of Rappaccini and in the person of the lovely Beatrice."

Giovanni groaned and hid his face.

"Her father," continued Baglioni, "was not restrained by natural affection from offering up his child in this horrible manner as the victim of his insane zeal for science; for, let us do him justice, he is as true a man of science as ever distilled his own heart in an alembic. What, then, will be your fate? Beyond a doubt you are selected as the material of some new experiment. Perhaps the result is to be death; perhaps a fate more awful still. Rappaccini, with what he calls the interest of science before his eyes, will hesitate at nothing."

"It is a dream," muttered Giovanni to himself; "surely it is a dream."

"But," resumed the professor, "be of good cheer, son of my friend. It is not yet too late for the rescue. Possibly we may even succeed in bringing back this miserable child within the limits of ordinary nature, from which her father's madness has estranged her. Behold this little silver vase! It was wrought by the hands of the renowned Benvenuto Cellini, and is well worthy to be a love gift to the fairest dame in Italy. But its contents are invaluable. One little sip of this antidote would have rendered the most virulent poisons of the Borgias innocuous. Doubt not that it will be as efficacious against those of Rappaccini. Bestow the vase, and the precious liquid within it, on your Beatrice, and hopefully await the result."

Baglioni laid a small, exquisitely wrought silver vial on the table and withdrew, leaving what he had said to produce its effect upon the young man's mind.

"We will thwart Rappaccini yet," thought he, chuckling to himself, as he descended the stairs; "but, let us confess the truth of him, he is a wonderful man—a wonderful man indeed; a vile empiric, however, in his practice, and therefore not to be tolerated by those who respect the good old rules of the medical profession."

Throughout Giovanni's whole acquaintance with Beatrice, he had occasionally, as we have said, been haunted by dark surmises as to her character; yet so thoroughly had she made herself felt by him as a simple, natural, most affectionate, and guileless creature, that the image now held up by Professor Baglioni looked as strange and incredible as if it were not in accordance with his own original conception. True, there were ugly recollections connected with his first glimpses of the beautiful girl; he could not quite forget the bouquet that withered in her grasp, and the insect that perished amid the sunny air, by no ostensible agency save the fragrance of her breath. These incidents, however, dissolving in the pure light of her character, had no longer the efficacy of facts, but were acknowledged as mistaken fantasies, by whatever testimony of the senses they might appear to be substantiated. There is something truer and more real than what we can see with the eyes and touch with the finger. On such better evidence had Giovanni founded his confidence in Beatrice, though rather by the necessary force of her high attributes than by any deep and generous faith on his part. But now his spirit was incapable of sustaining itself at the height to which the early enthusiasm of passion had exalted it; he fell down, grovelling among earthly doubts, and defiled therewith the pure whiteness of Beatrice's image. Not that he gave her up; he did but distrust. He resolved to institute some decisive test that should satisfy him, once for all, whether there were those dreadful peculiarities in her physical nature which could not be supposed to exist without some corresponding monstrosity of soul. His eyes, gazing down afar, might have deceived him as to the lizard, the insect, and the flowers; but if he could witness, at the distance of a few paces, the sudden blight of one fresh and healthful flower in Beatrice's hand, there would be room for no further question. With this idea he hastened to the florist's and purchased a bouquet that was still gemmed with the morning dew-drops.

It was now the customary hour of his daily interview with Beatrice. Before descending into the garden, Giovanni failed not to look at his figure in the mirror,—a vanity to be expected in a beautiful young man, yet, as displaying itself at that troubled and feverish moment, the token of a certain shallowness of feeling and insincerity of character. He did gaze, however, and said to himself that his features had never before possessed so rich a grace, nor his eyes such vivacity, nor his cheeks so warm a hue of superabundant life.

"At least," thought he, "her poison has not yet insinuated itself into my system. I am no flower to perish in her grasp."

With that thought he turned his eyes on the bouquet, which he had never once laid aside from his hand. A thrill of indefinable horror shot through his frame on perceiving that those dewy flowers were already beginning to droop; they wore the aspect of things that had been fresh and lovely yesterday. Giovanni grew white as marble, and stood motionless before the mirror, staring at his own reflection there as at the likeness of something frightful. He remembered Baglioni's remark about the fragrance that seemed to pervade the chamber. It must have been the poison in his breath! Then he shuddered—shuddered at himself. Recovering from his stupor, he began to watch with curious eye a spider that was busily at work hanging its web from the antique cornice of the apartment, crossing and recrossing the artful system of interwoven lines—as vigorous and active a spider as ever dangled from an old ceiling. Giovanni bent towards the insect, and emitted a deep, long breath. The spider suddenly ceased its toil; the web vibrated with a tremor originating in the body of the small artisan. Again Giovanni sent forth a breath, deeper, longer, and imbued with a venomous feeling out of his heart: he knew not whether he were wicked, or only desperate. The spider made a convulsive gripe with his limbs and hung dead across the window.

"Accursed! accursed!" muttered Giovanni, addressing himself. "Hast thou grown so poisonous that this deadly insect perishes by thy breath?"

At that moment a rich, sweet voice came floating up from the garden.

"Giovanni! Giovanni! It is past the hour! Why tarriest thou? Come down!"

"Yes," muttered Giovanni again. "She is the only being whom my breath may not slay! Would that it might!"

He rushed down, and in an instant was standing before the bright and loving eyes of Beatrice. A moment ago his wrath and despair had been so fierce that he could have desired nothing so much as to wither her by a glance; but with her actual presence there came influences which had too real an existence to be at once shaken off: recollections of the delicate and benign power of her feminine nature, which had so often enveloped him in a religious calm; recollections of many a holy and passionate outgush of her heart, when the pure fountain had been unsealed from its depths and made visible in its transparency to his mental eye; recollections which, had Giovanni known how to estimate them, would have assured him that all this ugly mystery was but an earthly illusion, and that, whatever mist of evil might seem to have gathered over her, the real Beatrice was a heavenly angel. Incapable as he was of such high faith, still her presence had not utterly lost its magic. Giovanni's rage was quelled into an aspect of sullen insensibility. Beatrice, with a quick spiritual sense, immediately felt that there was a gulf of blackness between them which neither he nor she could pass. They walked on together, sad and silent, and came thus to the marble fountain and to its pool of water on the ground, in the midst of which grew the shrub that bore gem-like blossoms. Giovanni was affrighted at the eager enjoyment—the appetite, as it were—with which he found himself inhaling the fragrance of the flowers.

"Beatrice," asked he, abruptly, "whence came this shrub?"

"My father created it," answered she, with simplicity.

"Created it! created it!" repeated Giovanni. "What mean you, Beatrice?"

"He is a man fearfully acquainted with the secrets of Nature," replied Beatrice; "and, at the hour when I first drew breath, this plant sprang from the soil, the offspring of his science, of his intellect, while I was but his earthly child. Approach it not!" continued she, observing with terror that Giovanni was drawing nearer to the shrub. "It has qualities that you little dream of. But I, dearest Giovanni,—I grew up and blossomed with the plant and was nourished with its breath. It was my sister, and I loved it with a human affection; for, alas!—hast thou not suspected it?—there was an awful doom."

Here Giovanni frowned so darkly upon her that Beatrice paused and trembled. But her faith in his tenderness reassured her, and made her blush that she had doubted for an instant.

"There was an awful doom," she continued, "the effect of my father's fatal love of science, which estranged me from all society of my kind. Until Heaven sent thee, dearest Giovanni, oh, how lonely was thy poor Beatrice!"

"Was it a hard doom?" asked Giovanni, fixing his eyes upon her.

"Only of late have I known how hard it was," answered she, tenderly. "Oh, yes; but my heart was torpid, and therefore quiet."

Giovanni's rage broke forth from his sullen gloom like a lightning flash out of a dark cloud.

"Accursed one!" cried he, with venomous scorn and anger. "And, finding thy solitude wearisome, thou hast severed me likewise from all the warmth of life and enticed me into thy region of unspeakable horror!"

"Giovanni!" exclaimed Beatrice, turning her large bright eyes upon his face. The force of his words had not found its way into her mind; she was merely thunderstruck.

"Yes, poisonous thing!" repeated Giovanni, beside himself with passion. "Thou hast done it! Thou hast blasted me! Thou hast filled my veins with poison! Thou hast made me as hateful, as ugly, as loathsome and deadly a creature as thyself—a world's wonder of hideous monstrosity! Now, if our breath be happily as fatal to ourselves as to all others, let us join our lips in one kiss of unutterable hatred, and so die!"

"What has befallen me?" murmured Beatrice, with a low moan out of her heart. "Holy Virgin, pity me, a poor heart-broken child!"

"Thou—dost thou pray?" cried Giovanni, still with the same fiendish scorn. "Thy very prayers, as they come from thy lips, taint the atmosphere with death. Yes, yes; let us pray! Let us to church and dip our fingers in the holy water at the portal! They that come after us will perish as by a pestilence! Let us sign crosses in the air! It will be scattering curses abroad in the likeness of holy symbols!"

"Giovanni," said Beatrice, calmly, for her grief was beyond passion, "why dost thou join thyself with me thus in those terrible words? I, it is true, am the horrible thing thou namest me. But thou,—what hast thou to do, save with one other shudder at my hideous misery to go forth out of the garden and mingle with thy race, and forget there ever crawled on earth such a monster as poor Beatrice?"

"Dost thou pretend ignorance?" asked Giovanni, scowling upon her. "Behold! this power have I gained from the pure daughter of Rappaccini."

There was a swarm of summer insects flitting through the air in search of the food promised by the flower odors of the fatal garden. They circled round Giovanni's head, and were evidently attracted towards him by the same influence which had drawn them for an instant within the sphere of several of the shrubs. He sent forth a breath among them, and smiled bitterly at Beatrice as at least a score of the insects fell dead upon the ground.

"I see it! I see it!" shrieked Beatrice. "It is my father's fatal science! No, no, Giovanni; it was not I! Never! never! I dreamed only to love thee and be with thee a little time, and so to let thee pass away, leaving but thine image in mine heart; for, Giovanni, believe it, though my body be nourished with poison, my spirit is God's creature, and craves love as its daily food. But my father,—he has united us in this fearful sympathy. Yes; spurn me, tread upon me, kill me! Oh, what is death after such words as thine? But it was not I. Not for a world of bliss would I have done it."

Giovanni's passion had exhausted itself in its outburst from his lips. There now came across him a sense, mournful, and not without tenderness, of the intimate and peculiar relationship between Beatrice and himself. They stood, as it were, in an utter solitude, which would be made none the less solitary by the densest throng of human life. Ought not, then, the desert of humanity around them to press this insulated pair closer together? If they should be cruel to one another, who was there to be kind to them? Besides, thought Giovanni, might there not still be a hope of his returning within the limits of ordinary nature, and leading Beatrice, the redeemed Beatrice, by the hand? O, weak, and selfish, and unworthy spirit, that could dream of an earthly union and earthly happiness as possible, after such deep love had been so bitterly wronged as was Beatrice's love by Giovanni's blighting words! No, no; there could be no such hope. She must pass heavily, with that broken heart, across the borders of Time—she must bathe her hurts in some fount of paradise, and forget her grief in the light of immortality, and there be well.

But Giovanni did not know it.

"Dear Beatrice," said he, approaching her, while she shrank away as always at his approach, but now with a different impulse, "dearest Beatrice, our fate is not yet so desperate. Behold! there is a medicine, potent, as a wise physician has assured me, and almost divine in its efficacy. It is composed of ingredients the most opposite to those by which thy awful father has brought this calamity upon thee and me. It is distilled of blessed herbs. Shall we not quaff it together, and thus be purified from evil?"

"Give it me!" said Beatrice, extending her hand to receive the little silver vial which Giovanni took from his bosom. She added, with a peculiar emphasis, "I will drink; but do thou await the result."

She put Baglioni's antidote to her lips; and, at the same moment, the figure of Rappaccini emerged from the portal and came slowly towards the marble fountain. As he drew near, the pale man of science seemed to gaze with a triumphant expression at the beautiful youth and maiden, as might an artist who should spend his life in achieving a picture or a group of statuary and finally be satisfied with his success. He paused; his bent form grew erect with conscious power; he spread out his hands over them in the attitude of a father imploring a blessing upon his children; but those were the same hands that had thrown poison into the stream of their lives. Giovanni trembled. Beatrice shuddered nervously, and pressed her hand upon her heart.

"My daughter," said Rappaccini, "thou art no longer lonely in the world. Pluck one of those precious gems from thy sister shrub and bid thy bridegroom wear it in his bosom. It will not harm him now. My science and the sympathy between thee and him have so wrought within his system that he now stands apart from common men, as thou dost, daughter of my pride and triumph, from ordinary women. Pass on, then, through the world, most dear to one another and dreadful to all besides!"

"My father," said Beatrice, feebly,—and still as she spoke she kept her hand upon her heart,—"wherefore didst thou inflict this miserable doom upon thy child?"

"Miserable!" exclaimed Rappaccini. "What mean you, foolish girl? Dost thou deem it misery to be endowed with marvellous gifts against which no power nor strength could avail an enemy—misery, to be able to quell the mightiest with a breath—misery, to be as terrible as thou art beautiful? Wouldst thou, then, have preferred the condition of a weak woman, exposed to all evil and capable of none?"

"I would fain have been loved, not feared," murmured Beatrice, sinking down upon the ground. "But now it matters not. I am going, father, where the evil which thou hast striven to mingle with my being will pass away like a dream—like the fragrance of these poisonous flowers, which will no longer taint my breath among the flowers of Eden. Farewell, Giovanni! Thy words of hatred are like lead within my heart; but they, too, will fall away as I ascend. Oh, was there not, from the first, more poison in thy nature than in mine?"

To Beatrice,—so radically had her earthly part been wrought upon by Rappaccini's skill,—as poison had been life, so the powerful antidote was death; and thus the poor victim of man's ingenuity and of thwarted nature, and of the fatality that attends all such efforts of perverted wisdom, perished there, at the feet of her father and Giovanni. Just at that moment Professor Pietro Baglioni looked forth from the window, and called loudly, in a tone of triumph mixed with horror, to the thunderstricken man of science, "Rappaccini! Rappaccini! and is this the upshot of your experiment!"

SIR EDMUND ORME

Henry James

The statement appears to have been written, though the fragment is undated, long after the death of his wife, whom I take to have been one of the persons referred to. There is, however, nothing in the strange story to establish this point, which is, perhaps, not of importance. When I took possession of his effects I found these pages, in a locked drawer, among papers relating to the unfortunate lady's too brief career (she died in childbirth a year after her marriage), letters, memoranda, accounts, faded photographs, cards of invitation. That is the only connection I can point to, and you may easily and will probably say that the tale is too extravagant to have had a demonstrable origin. I cannot, I admit, vouch for his having intended it as a report of real occurrence—I can only vouch for his general veracity. In any case it was written for himself, not for others. I offer it to others—having full option—precisely because it is so singular. Let them, in respect to the form of the thing, bear in mind that it was written quite for himself. I have altered nothing but the names.

* * * * *

If there's a story in the matter I recognise the exact moment at which it began. This was on a soft, still Sunday noon in November, just after church, on the sunny Parade. Brighton was full of people; it was the height of the season, and the day was even more respectable than lovely—which helped to account for the multitude of walkers. The blue sea itself was decorous; it seemed to doze, with a gentle snore (if that be decorum), as if nature were preaching a sermon. After writing letters all the morning I had come out to take a look at it before luncheon. I was leaning over the rail which separates the King's Road from the beach, and I think I was smoking a cigarette, when I became conscious of an intended joke in the shape of a light walking-stick laid across my shoulders. The idea, I found, had been thrown off by Teddy Bostwick, of the Rifles, and was intended as a contribution to talk. Our talk came off as we strolled together—he always took your arm to show you he forgave your obtuseness about his humour—and looked at the people, and bowed to some of them, and wondered who others were, and differed in opinion as to the prettiness of the girls. About Charlotte Marden we agreed, however, as we saw her coming toward us with her mother; and there surely could have been no one who wouldn't have agreed with us. The Brighton air, of old, used to make plain girls pretty and pretty girls prettier still—I don't know whether it works the spell now. The place, at any rate, was rare for complexions, and Miss Marden's was one that made people turn round. It made us stop, heaven knows—at least, it was one of the things, for we already knew the ladies.

We turned with them, we joined them, we went where they were going. They were only going to the end and back—they had just come out of church. It was another manifestation of Teddy's humour that he got immediate possession of Charlotte, leaving me to walk with her mother. However, I was not unhappy; the girl was before me and I had her to talk about. We prolonged our walk, Mrs. Marden kept me, and presently she said she was tired and must sit down. We found a place on a sheltered bench—we gossiped as the people passed. It had already struck me, in this pair, that the resemblance between the mother and the daughter was wonderful even among such resemblances—the more so that it took so little account of a difference of nature. One often hears mature mothers spoken of as warnings—signposts, more or less discouraging, of the way daughters may go. But there was nothing deterrent in the idea that Charlotte, at fifty-five, should be as beautiful, even though it were conditioned on her being as pale and preoccupied, as Mrs. Marden. At twenty-two she had a kind of rosy blankness and she was admirably handsome. Her head had the charming shape of her mother's, and her features the same fine order. Then there were looks and movements and tones (moments when you could scarcely say whether it were aspect or sound), which, between the two personalities, were a reflection, a recall.

These ladies had a small fortune and a cheerful little house at Brighton, full of portraits and tokens and trophies (stuffed animals on the top of bookcases, and sallow, varnished fish under glass), to which Mrs. Marden professed herself attached by pious memories. Her husband had been "ordered" there in ill-health, to spend the last years of his life, and she had already mentioned to me that it was a place in which she felt herself still under the protection of his goodness. His goodness appeared to have been great, and she sometimes had the air of defending it against mysterious imputations. Some sense of protection, of an influence invoked and cherished, was evidently necessary to her; she had a dim wistfulness, a longing for security. She wanted friends and she had a good many. She was kind to me on our first meeting, and I never suspected her of the vulgar purpose of "making up" to me—a suspicion, of course, unduly frequent in conceited young men. It never struck me that she wanted me for her daughter, nor yet, like some unnatural mammas, for herself. It was as if they had had a common deep, shy need and had been ready to say: "Oh, be friendly to us and be trustful! Don't be afraid, you won't be expected to marry us."

"Of course there's something about mamma; that's really what makes her such a dear!" Charlotte said to me, confidentially, at an early stage of our acquaintance. She worshipped her mother's appearance. It was the only thing she was vain of; she accepted the raised eyebrows as a charming ultimate fact. "She looks as if she were waiting for the doctor, dear mamma," she said on another occasion. "Perhaps you're the doctor; do you think you are?" It appeared in the event that I had some healing power. At any rate when I learned, for she once dropped the remark, that Mrs. Marden also thought there was something "awfully strange" about Charlotte, the relation between the two ladies became extremely interesting. It was happy enough, at bottom; each had the other so much on her mind.

On the Parade the stream of strollers held its course, and Charlotte presently went by with Teddy Bostwick. She smiled and nodded and continued, but when she came back she stopped and spoke to us. Captain Bostwick positively declined to go in, he said the occasion was too jolly: might they therefore take another turn? Her mother dropped a "Do as you like," and the girl gave me an impertinent smile over her shoulder as they quitted us. Teddy looked at me with his glass in one eye; but I didn't mind that; it was only of Miss Marden I was thinking as I observed to my companion, laughing:

"She's a bit of a coquette, you know."

"Don't say that—don't say that!" Mrs. Marden murmured.

"The nicest girls always are—just a little," I was magnanimous enough to plead.

"Then why are they always punished?"

The intensity of the question startled me—it had come out in such a vivid flash. Therefore I had to think a moment before I inquired: "What do you know about it?"

"I was a bad girl myself."

"And were you punished?"

"I carry it through life," said Mrs. Marden, looking away from me. "Ah!" she suddenly panted, in the next breath, rising to her feet and staring at her daughter, who had reappeared again with Captain Bostwick. She stood a few seconds, with the queerest expression in her face; then she sank upon the seat again and I saw that she had blushed crimson. Charlotte, who had observed her movement, came straight up to her and, taking her hand with quick tenderness, seated herself on the other side of her. The girl had turned pale—she gave her mother a fixed, frightened look. Mrs. Marden, who had had some shock which escaped our detection, recovered herself; that is she sat quiet and inexpressive, gazing at the indifferent crowd, the sunny air, the slumbering sea. My eye happened to fall, however, on the interlocked hands of the two ladies, and I quickly guessed that the grasp of the elder one was violent. Bostwick stood before them, wondering what was the matter and asking me from his little vacant disk if *I* knew; which led Charlotte to say to him after a moment, with a certain irritation:

"Don't stand there that way, Captain Bostwick; go away—*please* go away."

I got up at this, hoping that Mrs. Marden wasn't ill; but she immediately begged that we would not go away, that we would particularly stay and that we would presently come home to lunch. She drew me down beside her and for a moment I felt her hand pressing my arm in a way that might have been an involuntary betrayal of distress and might have been a private signal. What she might have wished to point out to me I couldn't divine: perhaps she had seen somebody or something abnormal in the crowd. She explained to us in a few minutes that she was all right; that she was only liable to palpitations—they came as quickly as they went. It was time to move, and we moved. The incident was felt to be closed. Bostwick and I lunched with our sociable friends, and when I walked away with him he declared that he had never seen such dear kind creatures.

Mrs. Marden had made us promise to come back the next day to tea, and had exhorted us in general to come as often as we could. Yet the next day, when at five o'clock I knocked at the door of the pretty house, it was to learn that the ladies had gone up to town. They had left a message for us with the butler: he was to say that they had suddenly been called—were very sorry. They would be absent a few days. This was all I could extract from the dumb domestic. I went again three days later, but they were still away; and it was not till the end of a week that I got a note from Mrs. Marden, saying "We are back; do come and forgive us." It was on this occasion, I remember (the occasion of my going just after getting the note), that she told me she had intuitions. I don't know how many people there were in England at that time in that predicament, but there were very few who would have mentioned it; so that the announcement struck me as original, especially as her point was that some of these uncanny promptings were connected with me. There were other people present—idle Brighton folk, old women with frightened eyes and irrelevant interjections—and I had but a few minutes' talk with Charlotte; but the day after this I met them both at dinner and had the satisfaction of sitting next to Miss Marden. I recall that hour as the hour on which it first completely came over me that she was a beautiful, liberal creature. I had seen her personality in patches and gleams, like a song sung in snatches, but now it was before me in a large rosy glow, as if it had been a full volume of sound—I heard the whole of the air. It was sweet, fresh music—I was often to hum it over.

After dinner I had a few words with Mrs. Marden; it was at the moment, late in the evening, when tea was handed about. A servant passed near us with a tray, I asked her if she would have a cup, and, on her assenting, took one and handed it to her. She put out her hand for it and I gave it to her, safely as I supposed; but as she was in the act of receiving it she started and faltered, so that the cup and saucer dropped with a crash of porcelain and without, on the part of my interlocutress, the usual woman's movement to save her dress. I stooped to pick up the fragments and when I raised myself Mrs. Marden was looking across the room at her daughter, who looked back at her smiling, but with an anxious light in her eyes. "Dear mamma, what on earth is the matter with you?" the silent question seemed to say. Mrs. Marden coloured, just as she had done after her strange movement on the Parade the other week, and I was therefore surprised when she said to me with unexpected assurance: "You should really have a steadier hand!" I had begun to stammer a defence of my hand when I became aware that she had fixed her eyes upon me with an intense appeal. It was ambiguous at first and only added to my confusion; then suddenly I understood, as plainly as if she had murmured "Make believe it was you—make believe it was you." The servant came back to take the morsels of the cup and wipe up the spilt tea, and while I was in the midst of making believe Mrs. Marden abruptly brushed away from me and from her daughter's attention and went into another room. I noticed that she gave no heed to the state of her dress.

I saw nothing more of either of them that evening, but the next morning, in the King's Road, I met Miss Marden with a roll of music in her muff. She told me she had been a little way alone, to practise duets with a friend, and I asked her if she would go a little way further in company. She gave me leave to attend her to her door, and as we stood before it I inquired if I might go in. "No, not to-day—I don't want you," she said, candidly, though not roughly; while the words caused me to direct a wistful, disconcerted gaze at one of the windows of the house. It fell upon the white face of Mrs. Marden, who was looking out at us from the drawing-room. She stood there long enough for me to see that it was she and not an apparition, as I had thought for a second, and then she vanished before her daughter had observed her. The girl, during our walk, had said nothing about her. As I had been told they didn't want me I left them alone a little, after which circumstances supervened that kept us still longer apart. I finally went up to London, and while there I received a pressing invitation to come immediately down to Tranton, a pretty old place in Sussex belonging to a couple whose acquaintance I had lately made.

I went to Tranton from town, and on arriving found the Mardens, with a dozen other people, in the house. The first thing Mrs. Marden said was: "Will you forgive me?" and when I asked what I had to forgive she answered: "My throwing my tea over you." I replied that it had gone over herself; whereupon she said: "At any rate I was very rude; but some day I think you'll understand, and then you'll make allowances for me." The first day I was there she dropped two or three of these references (she had already indulged in more than one), to the mystic initiation that was in store for me; so that I began, as the phrase is, to chaff her about it, to say I would rather it were less wonderful and take it out at once. She answered that when it should come to me I would have to take it out—there would be little enough option. That it would come was privately clear to her, a deep presentiment, which was the only reason she had ever mentioned the matter. Didn't I remember she had told me she had intuitions? From the first time of her seeing me she had been sure there were things I should not escape knowing. Meanwhile there was nothing to do but wait and keep cool, not to be precipitate. She particularly wished not to be any more nervous than she was. And I was above all not to be nervous myself—one got used to everything. I declared that though I couldn't make out what she was talking about I was terribly frightened; the absence of a clue gave such a range to one's imagination. I exaggerated on purpose; for if Mrs. Marden was mystifying I can scarcely say she was alarming. I couldn't imagine what she meant, but I wondered more than I shuddered. I might have said to myself that she was a little wrong in the upper storey; but that never occurred to me. She struck me as hopelessly right.

There were other girls in the house, but Charlotte Marden was the most charming; which was so generally felt to be the case that she really interfered with the slaughter of ground game. There were two or three men, and I was of the number, who actually preferred her to the society of the beaters. In short she was recognised as a form of sport superior and exquisite. She was kind to all of us—she made us go out late and come in early. I don't know whether she flirted, but several other members of the party thought they did. Indeed, as regards himself, Teddy Bostwick, who had come over from Brighton, was visibly sure.

The third day I was at Tranton was a Sunday, and there was a very pretty walk to morning service over the fields. It was grey, windless weather, and the bell of the little old church that nestled in the hollow of the Sussex down sounded near and domestic. We were a straggling procession, in the mild damp air (which, as always at that season, gave one the feeling that after the trees were bare there was more of it—a larger sky), and I managed to fall a good way behind with Miss Marden. I remember entertaining, as we moved together over the turf, a strong impulse to say something intensely personal, something violent and important—important for me, such as that I had never seen her so lovely, or that that particular moment was the sweetest of my life. But always, in youth, such words have been on the lips many times before they are spoken; and I had the sense, not that I didn't know her well enough (I cared little for that), but that she didn't know me well enough. In the church, where there were old Tranton tombs and brasses, the big Tranton pew was full. Several of us were scattered, and I found a seat for Miss Marden, and another for myself beside it, at a distance from her mother and from most of our friends. There were two or three decent rustics on the bench, who moved in further to make room for us, and I took my place first, to cut off my companion from our neighbours. After she was seated there was still a space left, which remained empty till service was about half over.

This at least was the moment at which I became aware that another person had entered and had taken the seat. When I noticed him he had apparently been for some minutes in the pew, for he had settled himself and put down his hat beside him, and, with his hands crossed on the nob of his cane, was gazing before him at the altar. He was a pale young man in black, with the air of a gentleman. I was slightly startled on perceiving him, for Miss Marden had not attracted my attention to his entrance by moving to make room for him. After a few minutes, observing that he had no prayer-book, I reached across my neighbour and placed mine before him, on the ledge of the pew; a manoeuvre the motive of which was not unconnected with the possibility that, in my own destitution, Miss Marden would give me one side of her velvet volume to hold. The pretext, however, was destined to fail for at the moment I offered him the book the intruder—whose intrusion I had so condoned—rose from his place without thanking me, stepped noiselessly out of the pew (it had no door), and, so discreetly as to attract no attention, passed down the centre of the church. A few minutes had sufficed for his devotions. His behaviour was unbecoming, his early departure even more than his late arrival; but he managed so quietly that we were not incommoded, and I perceived, on turning a little to glance after him, that nobody was disturbed by his withdrawal. I only noticed, and with surprise, that Mrs. Marden had been so affected by it as to rise, involuntarily, an instant, in her place. She stared at him as he passed, but he passed very quickly, and she as quickly dropped down again, though not too soon to catch my eye across the church. Five minutes later I asked Miss Marden, in a low voice, if she would kindly pass me back my prayer-book—I had waited to see if she would spontaneously perform the act. She restored this aid to devotion, but had been so far from troubling herself about it that she could say to me as she did so: "Why on earth did you put it there?" I was on the point of answering her when she dropped on her knees, and I held my tongue. I had only been going to say: "To be decently civil."

After the benediction, as we were leaving our places, I was slightly surprised, again, to see that Mrs. Marden, instead of going out with her companions, had come up the aisle to join us, having apparently something to say to her daughter. She said it, but in an instant I observed that it was only a pretext—her real business was with me. She pushed Charlotte forward and suddenly murmured to me: "Did you see him?"

"The gentleman who sat down here? How could I help seeing him?"

"Hush!" she said, with the intensest excitement; "don't *speak* to her—don't tell her!" She slipped her hand into my arm, to keep me near her, to keep me, it seemed, away from her daughter. The precaution was unnecessary, for Teddy Bostwick had already taken possession of Miss Marden, and as they passed out of church in front of me I saw one of the other men close up on her other hand. It appeared to be considered that I had had my turn. Mrs. Marden withdrew her hand from my arm as soon as we got out, but not before I felt that she had really needed the support. "Don't speak to any one—don't tell any one!" she went on.

"I don't understand. Tell them what?"

"Why, that you saw him."

"Surely they saw him for themselves."

"Not one of them, not one of them." She spoke in a tone of such passionate decision that I glanced at her—she was staring straight before her. But she felt the challenge of my eyes and she stopped short, in the old brown timber porch of the church, with the others well in advance of us, and said, looking at me now and in a quite extraordinary manner: "You're the only person, the only person in the world."

"But you, dear madam?"

"Oh me—of course. That's my curse!" And with this she moved rapidly away from me to join the body of the party. I hovered on its outskirts on the way home, for I had food for rumination. Whom had I seen and why was the apparition—it rose before my mind's eye very vividly again—invisible to the others? If an exception had been made for Mrs. Marden, why did it constitute a curse, and why was I to share so questionable an advantage? This inquiry, carried on in my own locked breast, kept me doubtless silent enough during luncheon. After luncheon I went out on the old terrace to smoke a cigarette, but I had only taken a couple of turns when I perceived Mrs. Marden's moulded mask at the window of one of the rooms which opened on the crooked flags. It reminded me of the same flitting presence at the window at Brighton the day I met Charlotte and walked home with her. But this time my ambiguous friend didn't vanish; she tapped on the pane and motioned me to come in. She was in a queer little apartment, one of the many reception-rooms of which the ground-floor at Tranton consisted; it was known as the Indian room and had a decoration vaguely Oriental—bamboo lounges, lacquered screens, lanterns with long fringes and strange idols in cabinets, objects not held to conduce to sociability. The place was little used, and when I went round to her we had it to ourselves. As soon as I entered she said to me: "Please tell me this; are you in love with my daughter?"

I hesitated a moment. "Before I answer your question will you kindly tell me what gives you the idea? I don't consider that I have been very forward."

Mrs. Marden, contradicting me with her beautiful anxious eyes, gave me no satisfaction on the point I mentioned; she only went on strenuously: "Did you say nothing to her on the way to church?"

"What makes you think I said anything?"

"The fact that you saw him."

"Saw whom, dear Mrs. Marden?"

"Oh, you know," she answered, gravely, even a little reproachfully, as if I were trying to humiliate her by making her phrase the unphraseable.

"Do you mean the gentleman who formed the subject of your strange statement in church—the one who came into the pew?"

"You saw him, you saw him!" Mrs. Marden panted, with a strange mixture of dismay and relief.

"Of course I saw him; and so did you."

"It didn't follow. Did you feel it to be inevitable?"

I was puzzled again. "Inevitable?"

"That you *should* see him?"

"Certainly, since I'm not blind."

"You might have been; every one else is." I was wonderfully at sea, and I frankly confessed it to my interlocutress; but the case was not made clearer by her presently exclaiming: "I knew you would, from the moment you should be really in love with her! I knew it would be the test—what do I mean?—the proof."

"Are there such strange bewilderments attached to that high state?" I asked, smiling.

"You perceive there are. You see him, you see him!" Mrs. Marden announced, with tremendous exaltation. "You'll see him again."

"I've no objection; but I shall take more interest in him if you'll kindly tell me who he is."

She hesitated, looking down a moment; then she said, raising her eyes: "I'll tell you if you'll tell me first what you said to her on the way to church."

"Has she told you I said anything?"

"Do I need that?" smiled Mrs. Marden.

"Oh yes, I remember—your intuitions! But I'm sorry to see they're at fault this time; because I really said nothing to your daughter that was the least out of the way."

"Are you very sure?"

"On my honour, Mrs. Marden."

"Then you consider that you're not in love with her?"

"That's another affair!" I laughed.

"You are—you are! You wouldn't have seen him if you hadn't been."

"Who the deuce is he, then, madam?" I inquired with some irritation.

She would still only answer me with another question. "Didn't you at least want to say something to her—didn't you come very near it?"

The question was much to the point; it justified the famous intuitions. "Very near it—it was the turn of a hair. I don't know what kept me quiet."

"That was quite enough," said Mrs. Marden. "It isn't what you say that determines it; it's what you feel. *That's* what he goes by."

I was annoyed, at last, by her reiterated reference to an identity yet to be established, and I clasped my hands with an air of supplication which covered much real impatience, a sharper curiosity and even the first short throbs of a certain sacred dread. "I entreat you to tell me whom you're talking about."

She threw up her arms, looking away from me, as if to shake off both reserve and responsibility. "Sir Edmund Orme."

"And who is Sir Edmund Orme?"

At the moment I spoke she gave a start. "Hush, here they come." Then as, following the direction of her eyes, I saw Charlotte Marden on the terrace, at the window, she added, with an intensity of warning: "Don't notice him—*never!*"

Charlotte, who had had her hands beside her eyes, peering into the room and smiling, made a sign that she was to be admitted, on which I went and opened the long window. Her mother turned away, and the girl came in with a laughing challenge: "What plot in the world are you two hatching here?" Some plan—I forget what—was in prospect for the afternoon, as to which Mrs. Marden's participation or consent was solicited—*my* adhesion was taken for granted—and she had been half over the place in her quest. I was flurried, because I saw that Mrs. Marden was flurried (when she turned round to meet her daughter she covered it by a kind of extravagance, throwing herself on the girl's neck and embracing her), and to pass it off I said, fancifully, to Charlotte:

"I've been asking your mother for your hand."

"Oh, indeed, and has she given it?" Miss Marden answered, gayly.

"She was just going to when you appeared there."

"Well, it's only for a moment—I'll leave you free."

"Do you like him, Charlotte?" Mrs. Marden asked, with a candour I scarcely expected.

"It's difficult to say it *before* him isn't it?" the girl replied, entering into the humour of the thing, but looking at me as if she didn't like me.

She would have had to say it before another person as well, for at that moment there stepped into the room from the terrace (the window had been left open), a gentleman who had come into sight, at least into mine, only within the instant. Mrs. Marden had said "Here *they* come," but he appeared to have followed her daughter at a certain distance. I immediately recognised him as the personage who had sat beside us in church. This time I saw him better, saw that his face and his whole air were strange. I speak of him as a personage, because one felt, indescribably, as if a reigning prince had come into the room. He held himself with a kind of habitual majesty, as if he were different from us. Yet he looked fixedly and gravely at me, till I wondered what he expected of me. Did he consider that I should bend my knee or kiss his hand? He turned his eyes in the same way on Mrs. Marden, but she knew what to do. After the first agitation produced by his approach she took no notice of him whatever; it made me remember her passionate adjuration to me. I had to achieve a great effort to imitate her, for though I knew nothing about him but that he was Sir Edmund Orme I felt his presence as a strong appeal, almost as an oppression. He stood there without speaking—young, pale, handsome, clean-shaven, decorous, with extraordinary light blue eyes and something old-fashioned, like a portrait of years ago, in his head, his manner of wearing his hair. He was in complete mourning (one immediately felt that he was very well dressed), and he carried his hat in his hand. He looked again strangely hard at me, harder than any one in the world had ever looked before; and I remember feeling rather cold and wishing he would say something. No silence had ever seemed to me so soundless. All this was of course an impression intensely rapid; but that it had consumed some instants was proved to me suddenly by the aspect of Charlotte Marden, who stared from her mother to me and back again (he never looked at her, and she had no appearance of looking at him), and then broke out with: "What on earth is the matter with you? You've such odd faces!" I felt the colour come back to mine, and when she went on in the same tone: "One would think you had seen a ghost!" I was conscious that I had turned very red. Sir Edmund Orme never blushed, and I could see that he had no capacity for embarrassment. One had met people of that sort, but never any one with such a grand indifference.

"Don't be impertinent; and go and tell them all that I'll join them," said Mrs. Marden with much dignity, but with a quaver in her voice.

"And will you come—*you?*" the girl asked, turning away. I made no answer, taking the question, somehow, as meant for her companion. But he was more silent than I, and when she reached the door (she was going out that way), she stopped, with her hand on the knob, and looked at me, repeating it. I assented, springing forward to open the door for her, and as she passed out she exclaimed to me mockingly: "You haven't got your wits about you—you sha'n't have my hand!"

I closed the door and turned round to find that Sir Edmund Orme had during the moment my back was presented to him retired by the window. Mrs. Marden stood there and we looked at each other long. It had only then—as the girl flitted away—come home to me that her daughter was unconscious of what had happened. It was *that*, oddly enough, that gave me a sudden, sharp shake, and not my own perception of our visitor, which appeared perfectly natural. It made the fact vivid to me that she had been equally unaware of him in church, and the two facts together—now that they were over—set my heart more sensibly beating. I wiped my forehead, and Mrs. Marden broke out with a low distressful wail: "Now you know my life—now you know my life!"

"In God's name who is he—*what* is he?"

"He's a man I wronged."

"How did you wrong him?"

"Oh, awfully—years ago."

"Years ago? Why, he's very young."

"Young—young?" cried Mrs. Marden. "He was born before *I* was!"

"Then why does he look so?"

She came nearer to me, she laid her hand on my arm, and there was something in her face that made me shrink a little. "Don't you understand—don't you *feel?"* she murmured, reproachfully.

"I feel very queer!" I laughed; and I was conscious that my laugh betrayed it.

"He's dead!" said Mrs. Marden, from her white face.

"Dead?" I panted. "Then that gentleman was—?" I couldn't even say the word.

"Call him what you like—there are twenty vulgar names. He's a perfect presence."

"He's a splendid presence!" I cried. "The place is haunted—*haunted!"* I exulted in the word as if it represented the fulfilment of my dearest dream.

"It isn't the place—more's the pity! That has nothing to do with it!"

"Then it's you, dear lady?" I said, as if this were still better.

"No, nor me either—I wish it were!"

"Perhaps it's me," I suggested with a sickly smile.

"It's nobody but my child—my innocent, innocent child!" And with this Mrs. Marden broke down—she dropped into a chair and burst into tears. I stammered some question—I pressed on her some bewildered appeal, but she waved me off, unexpectedly and passionately. I persisted—couldn't I help her, couldn't I intervene? "You *have* intervened," she sobbed; "you're *in* it, you're *in* it."

"I'm very glad to be in anything so curious," I boldly declared.

"Glad or not, you can't get out of it."

"I don't want to get out of it—it's too interesting."

"I'm glad you like it. Go away."

"But I want to know more about it."

"You'll see all you want—go away!"

"But I want to understand what I see."

"How can you—when I don't understand myself?"

"We'll do so together—we'll make it out."

At this she got up, doing what she could to obliterate her tears. "Yes, it will be better together—that's why I've liked you."

"Oh, we'll see it through!" I declared.

"Then you must control yourself better."

"I will, I will—with practice."

"You'll get used to it," said Mrs. Marden, in a tone I never forgot. "But go and join them—I'll come in a moment."

I passed out to the terrace and I felt that I had a part to play. So far from dreading another encounter with the "perfect presence," as Mrs. Marden called it, I was filled with an excitement that was positively joyous. I desired a renewal of the sensation—I opened myself wide to the impression; I went round the house as quickly as if I expected to overtake Sir Edmund Orme. I didn't overtake him just then, but the day was not to close without my recognising that, as Mrs. Marden had said, I should see all I wanted of him.

We took, or most of us took, the collective sociable walk which, in the English country-house, is the consecrated pastime on Sunday afternoons. We were restricted to such a regulated ramble as the ladies were good for; the afternoons, moreover, were short, and by five o'clock we were restored to the fireside in the hall, with a sense, on my part at least, that we might have done a little more for our tea. Mrs. Marden had said she would join us, but she had not appeared; her daughter, who had seen her again before we went out, only explained that she was tired. She remained invisible all the afternoon, but this was a detail to which I gave as little heed as I had given to the circumstance of my not having Miss Marden to myself during all our walk. I was too much taken up with another emotion to care; I felt beneath my feet the threshold of the strange door, in my life, which had suddenly been thrown open and out of which unspeakable vibrations played up through me like a fountain. I had heard all my days of apparitions, but it was a different thing to have seen one and to know that I should in all probability see it familiarly, as it were, again. I was on the look-out for it, as a pilot for the flash of a revolving light, and I was ready to generalise on the sinister subject, to declare that ghosts were much less alarming and much more amusing than was commonly supposed. There is no doubt that I was extremely nervous. I couldn't get over the distinction conferred upon me—the exception (in the way of mystic enlargement of vision), made in my favour. At the same time I think I did justice to Mrs. Marden's absence; it was a commentary on what she had said to me—"Now you know my life." She had probably been seeing Sir Edmund Orme for years, and, not having my firm fibre, she had broken down under him. Her nerve was gone, though she had also been able to attest that, in a degree, one got used to him. She had got used to breaking down.

Afternoon tea, when the dusk fell early, was a friendly hour at Tranton; the firelight played into the wide, white last-century hall; sympathies almost confessed themselves, lingering together, before dressing, on deep sofas, in muddy boots, for last words, after walks; and even solitary absorption in the third volume of a novel that was wanted by some one else seemed a form of geniality. I watched my moment and went over to Charlotte Marden when I saw she was about to withdraw. The ladies had left the place one by one, and after I had addressed myself particularly to Miss Marden the three men who were near her gradually dispersed. We had a little vague talk—she appeared preoccupied, and heaven knows I was—after which she said she must go: she should be late for dinner. I proved to her by book that she had plenty of time, and she objected that she must at any rate go up to see her mother: she was afraid she was unwell.

"On the contrary, she's better than she has been for a long time—I'll guarantee that," I said. "She has found out that she can have confidence in me, and that has done her good." Miss Marden had dropped into her chair again. I was standing before her, and she looked up at me without a smile—with a dim distress in her beautiful eyes; not exactly as if I were hurting her, but as if she were no longer disposed to treat as a joke what had passed (whatever it was, it was at the same time difficult to be serious about it), between her mother and myself. But I could answer her inquiry in all kindness and candour, for I was really conscious that the poor lady had put off a part of her burden on me and was proportionately relieved and eased. "I'm sure she has slept all the afternoon as she hasn't slept for years," I went on. "You have only to ask her."

Charlotte got up again. "You make yourself out very useful."

"You've a good quarter of an hour," I said. "Haven't I a right to talk to you a little this way, alone, when your mother has given me your hand?"

"And is it your mother who has given me yours? I'm much obliged to her, but I don't want it. I think our hands are not our mothers'—they happen to be our own!" laughed the girl.

"Sit down, sit down and let me tell you!" I pleaded.

I still stood before her, urgently, to see if she wouldn't oblige me. She hesitated a moment, looking vaguely this way and that, as if under a compulsion that was slightly painful. The empty hall was quiet—we heard the loud ticking of the great clock. Then she slowly sank down and I drew a chair close to her. This made me face round to the fire again, and with the movement I perceived, disconcertedly, that we were not alone. The next instant, more strangely than I can say, my discomposure, instead of increasing, dropped, for the person before the fire was Sir Edmund Orme. He stood there as I had seen him in the Indian room, looking at me with the expressionless attention which borrowed its sternness from his sombre distinction. I knew so much more about him now that I had to check a movement of recognition, an acknowledgment of his presence. When once I was aware of it, and that it lasted, the sense that we had company, Charlotte and I, quitted me; it was impressed on me on the contrary that I was more intensely alone with Miss Marden. She evidently saw nothing to look at, and I made a tremendous and very nearly successful effort to conceal from her that my own situation was different. I say "very nearly," because she watched me an instant—while my words were arrested—in a way that made me fear she was going to say again, as she had said in the Indian room: "What on earth is the matter with you?"

What the matter with me was I quickly told her, for the full knowledge of it rolled over me with the touching spectacle of her unconsciousness. It was touching that she became, in the presence of this extraordinary portent. What was portended, danger or sorrow, bliss or bane, was a minor question; all I saw, as she sat there, was that, innocent and charming, she was close to a horror, as she might have thought it, that happened to be veiled from her but that might at any moment be disclosed. I didn't mind it now, as I found, but nothing was more possible than she should, and if it wasn't curious and interesting it might easily be very dreadful. If I didn't mind it for myself, as I afterwards saw, this was largely because I was so taken up with the idea of protecting her. My heart beat high with this idea, on the spot; I determined to do everything I could to keep her sense sealed. What I could do might have been very obscure to me if I had not, in all this, become more aware than of anything else that I loved her. The way to save her was to love her, and the way to love her was to tell her, now and here, that I did so. Sir Edmund Orme didn't prevent me, especially as after a moment he turned his back to us and stood looking discreetly at the fire. At the end of another moment he leaned his head on his arm, against the chimneypiece, with an air of gradual dejection, like a spirit still more weary than discreet. Charlotte Marden was startled by what I said to her, and she jumped up to escape it; but she took no offence—my tenderness was too real. She only moved about the room with a deprecating murmur, and I was so busy following up any little advantage that I might have obtained that I didn't notice in what manner Sir Edmund Orme disappeared. I only observed presently that he had gone. This made no difference—he had been so small a hindrance; I only remember being struck, suddenly, with something inexorable in the slow, sweet, sad headshake that Miss Marden gave me.

"I don't ask for an answer now," I said; "I only want you to be sure—to know how much depends on it."

"Oh, I don't want to give it to you, now or ever!" she replied. "I hate the subject, please—I wish one could be let alone." And then, as if I might have found something harsh in this irrepressible, artless cry of beauty beset, she added quickly, vaguely, kindly, as she left the room: "Thank you, thank you—thank you so much!"

At dinner I could be generous enough to be glad, for her, that I was placed on the same side of the table with her, where she couldn't see me. Her mother was nearly opposite to me, and just after we had sat down Mrs. Marden gave me one long, deep look, in which all our strange communion was expressed. It meant of course "She has told me," but it meant other things beside. At any rate I know what my answering look to her conveyed: "I've seen him again—I've seen him again!" This didn't prevent Mrs. Marden from treating her neighbours with her usual scrupulous blandness. After dinner, when, in the drawing-room, the men joined the ladies and I went straight up to her to tell her how I wished we could have some private conversation, she said immediately, in a low tone, looking down at her fan while she opened and shut it:

"He's here—he's here."

"Here?" I looked round the room, but I was disappointed.

"Look where *she* is," said Mrs. Marden, with just the faintest asperity. Charlotte was in fact not in the main saloon, but in an apartment into which it opened and which was known as the morning-room. I took a few steps and saw her, through a doorway, upright in the middle of the room, talking with three gentlemen whose backs were practically turned to me. For a moment my quest seemed vain; then I recognised that one of the gentlemen—the middle one—was Sir Edmund Orme. This time it was surprising that the others didn't see him. Charlotte seemed to be looking straight at him, addressing her conversation to him. She saw me after an instant, however, and immediately turned her eyes away. I went back to her mother with an annoyed sense that the girl would think I was watching her, which would be unjust. Mrs. Marden had found a small sofa—a little apart—and I sat down beside her. There were some questions I had so wanted to go into that I wished we were once more in the Indian room. I presently gathered, however, that our privacy was all-sufficient. We communicated so closely and completely now, and with such silent reciprocities, that it would in every circumstance be adequate.

"Oh, yes, he's there," I said; "and at about a quarter-past seven he was in the hall."

"I knew it at the time, and I was so glad!"

"So glad?"

"That it was your affair, this time, and not mine. It's a rest for me."

"Did you sleep all the afternoon?" I asked.

"As I haven't done for months. But how did you know that?"

"As you knew, I take it, that Sir Edmund was in the hall. We shall evidently each of us know things now—where the other is concerned."

"Where he is concerned," Mrs. Marden amended. "It's a blessing, the way you take it," she added, with a long, mild sigh.

"I take it as a man who's in love with your daughter."

"Of course—of course." Intense as I now felt my desire for the girl to be, I couldn't help laughing a little at the tone of these words; and it led my companion immediately to say: "Otherwise you wouldn't have seen him."

"But every one doesn't see him who's in love with her, or there would be dozens."

"They're not in love with her as you are."

"I can, of course, only speak for myself; and I found a moment, before dinner, to do so."

"She told me immediately."

"And have I any hope—any chance?"

"That's what I long for, what I pray for."

"Ah, how can I thank you enough?" I murmured.

"I believe it will all pass—if she loves you," Mrs. Marden continued.

"It will all pass?"

"We shall never see him again."

"Oh, if she loves me I don't care how often I see him!"

"Ah, you take it better than I could," said my companion. "You have the happiness not to know—not to understand."

"I don't indeed. What on earth does he want?"

"He wants to make me suffer." She turned her wan face upon me with this, and I saw now for the first time, fully, how perfectly, if this had been Sir Edmund Orme's purpose, he had succeeded. "For what I did to him," Mrs. Marden explained.

"And what did you do to him?"

She looked at me a moment. "I killed him." As I had seen him fifty yards away only five minutes before the words gave me a start. "Yes, I make you jump; be careful. He's there still, but he killed himself. I broke his heart—he thought me awfully bad. We were to have been married, but I broke it off—just at the last. I saw some one I liked better; I had no reason but that. It wasn't for interest, or money, or position, or anything of that sort. All those things were his. It was simply that I fell in love with Captain Marden. When I saw him I felt that I couldn't marry any one else. I wasn't in love with Edmund Orme—my mother, my elder sister had brought it about. But he did love me. I told him I didn't care—that I couldn't, that I *wouldn't*. I threw him over, and he took something, some abominable drug or draught that proved fatal. It was dreadful, it was horrible, he was found that way—he died in agony. I married Captain Marden, but not for five years. I was happy, perfectly happy; time obliterates. But when my husband died I began to see him."

I had listened intently, but I wondered. "To see your husband?"

"Never, never *that* way, thank God! To see *him*, with Chartie—always with Chartie. The first time it nearly killed me—about seven years ago, when she first came out. Never when I'm by myself—only with her. Sometimes not for months, then every day for a week. I've tried everything to break the spell—doctors and *régimes* and climates; I've prayed to God on my knees. That day at Brighton, on the Parade with you, when you thought I was ill, that was the first for an age. And then, in the evening, when I knocked my tea over you, and the day you were at the door with Charlotte and I saw you from the window—each time he was there."

"I see, I see." I was more thrilled than I could say. "It's an apparition like another."

"Like another? Have you ever seen another?"

"No, I mean the sort of thing one has heard of. It's tremendously interesting to encounter a case."

"Do you call me a 'case'?" Mrs. Marden asked, with exquisite resentment.

"I mean myself."

"Oh, you're the right one!" she exclaimed. "I was right when I trusted you."

"I'm devoutly grateful you did; but what made you do it?"

"I had thought the whole thing out—I had had time to in those dreadful years, while he was punishing me in my daughter."

"Hardly that," I objected, "if she never knew."

"That has been my terror, that she *will*, from one occasion to another. I've an unspeakable dread of the effect on her."

"She sha'n't, she sha'n't!" I declared, so loud that several people looked round. Mrs. Marden made me get up, and I had no more talk with her that evening. The next day I told her I must take my departure from Tranton—it was neither comfortable nor considerate to remain as a rejected suitor. She was disconcerted, but she accepted my reasons, only saying to me out of her mournful eyes: "You'll leave me alone then with my burden?" It was of course understood between us that for many weeks to come there would be no discretion in "worrying poor Charlotte": such were the terms in which, with odd feminine and maternal inconsistency, she alluded to an attitude on my part that she favoured. I was prepared to be heroically considerate, but it seemed to me that even this delicacy permitted me to say a word to Miss Marden before I went. I begged her, after breakfast, to take a turn with me on the terrace, and as she hesitated, looking at me distantly, I informed her that it was only to ask her a question and to say good-bye—I was leaving Tranton for *her*.

She came out with me, and we passed slowly round the house three or four times. Nothing is finer than this great airy platform, from which every look is a sweep of the country, with the sea on the furthest edge. It might have been that as we passed the windows we were conspicuous to our friends in the house, who would divine, sarcastically, why I was so significantly bolting. But I didn't care; I only wondered whether they wouldn't really this time make out Sir Edmund Orme, who joined us on one of our turns and strolled slowly on the other side of my companion. Of what transcendent essence he was composed I knew not; I have no theory about him (leaving that to others), any more than I have one about such or such another of my fellow-mortals whom I have elbowed in life. He was as positive, as individual, as ultimate a fact as any of these. Above all he was as respectable, as sensitive a fact; so that I should no more have thought of taking a liberty, of practising an experiment with him, of touching him, for instance, or speaking to him, since he set the example of silence, than I should have thought of committing any other social grossness. He had always, as I saw more fully later, the perfect propriety of his position—had always the appearance of being dressed and, in attitude and aspect, of comporting himself, as the occasion demanded. He looked strange, incontestably, but somehow he always looked *right*. I very soon came to attach an idea of beauty to his unmentionable presence, the beauty of an old story of love and pain. What I ended by feeling was that he was on my side, that he was watching over my interest, that he was looking to it that my heart shouldn't be broken. Oh, he had taken it seriously, his own catastrophe—he had certainly proved that in his day. If poor Mrs. Marden, as she told me, had thought it out, I also subjected the case to the finest analysis of which my intellect was capable. It was a case of retributive justice. The mother was to pay, in suffering, for the suffering she had inflicted, and as the disposition to jilt a lover might have been transmitted to the daughter, the daughter was to be watched, so that she might be made to suffer should she do an equal wrong. She might reproduce her mother in character as vividly as she did in face. On the day she should transgress, in other words, her eyes would be opened suddenly and unpitiedly to the "perfect presence," which she would have to work as she could into her conception of a young lady's universe. I had no great fear for her, because I didn't believe she was, in any cruel degree, a coquette. We should have a good deal of ground to get over before I, at least, should be in a position to be sacrificed by her. She couldn't throw me over before she had made a little more of me.

The question I asked her on the terrace that morning was whether I might continue, during the winter, to come to Mrs. Marden's house. I promised not to come too often and not to speak to her for three months of the question I had raised the day before. She replied that I might do as I liked, and on this we parted.

I carried out the vow I had made her; I held my tongue for my three months. Unexpectedly to myself there were moments of this time when she struck me as capable of playing with a man. I wanted so to make her like me that I became subtle and ingenious, wonderfully alert, patiently diplomatic. Sometimes I thought I had earned my reward, brought her to the point of saying: "Well, well, you're the best of them all—you may speak to me now." Then there was a greater blankness than ever in her beauty, and on certain days a mocking light in her eyes, of which the meaning seemed to be: "If you don't take care, I *will* accept you, to have done with you the more effectually." Mrs. Marden was a great help to me simply by believing in me, and I valued her faith all the more that it continued even though there was a sudden intermission of the miracle that had been wrought for me. After our visit to Tranton Sir Edmund Orme gave us a holiday, and I confess it was at first a disappointment to me. I felt less designated, less connected with Charlotte. "Oh, don't cry till you're out of the wood," her mother said; "he has let me off sometimes for six months. He'll break out again when you least expect it—he knows what he's about." For her these weeks were happy, and she was wise enough not to talk about me to the girl. She was so good as to assure me that I was taking the right way, that I looked as if I felt secure and that in the long run women give way to that. She had known them do it even when the man was a fool for looking so—or was a fool on any terms. For herself she felt it to be a good time, a sort of St Martin's summer of the soul. She was better than she had been for years, and she had me to thank for it. The sense of visitation was light upon her—she wasn't in anguish every time she looked round. Charlotte contradicted me very often, but she contradicted herself still more. That winter was a wonder of mildness, and we often sat out in the sun. I walked up and down with Charlotte, and Mrs. Marden, sometimes on a bench, sometimes in a bath-chair, waited for us and smiled at us as we passed. I always looked out for a sign in her face—"He's with you, he's with you" (she would see him before I should), but nothing came; the season had brought us also a sort of spiritual softness. Toward the end of April the air was so like June that, meeting my two friends one night at some Brighton sociability—an evening party with amateur music—I drew Miss Marden unresistingly out upon a balcony to which a window in one of the rooms stood open. The night was close and thick, the stars were dim, and below us, under the cliff, we heard the regular rumble of the sea. We listened to it a little and we heard mixed with it, from within the house, the sound of a violin accompanied by a piano—a performance which had been our pretext for passing out.

"Do you like me a little better?" I asked, abruptly, after a minute. "Could you listen to me again?"

I had no sooner spoken than she laid her hand quickly, with a certain force, on my arm. "Hush!—isn't there some one there?" She was looking into the gloom of the far end of the balcony. This balcony ran the whole width of the house, a width very great in the best of the old houses at Brighton. We were lighted a little by the open window behind us, but the other windows, curtained within, left the darkness undiminished, so that I made out but dimly the figure of a gentleman standing there and looking at us. He was in evening dress, like a guest—I saw the vague shine of his white shirt and the pale oval of his face—and he might perfectly have been a guest who had stepped out in advance of us to take the air. Miss Marden took him for one at first—then evidently, even in a few seconds, she saw that the intensity of his gaze was unconventional. What else she saw I couldn't determine; I was too taken up with my own impression to do more than feel the quick contact of her uneasiness. My own impression was in fact the strongest of sensations, a sensation of horror; for what could the thing mean but that the girl at last saw? I heard her give a sudden, gasping "Ah!" and move quickly into the house. It was only afterwards that I knew that I myself had had a totally new emotion—my horror passing into anger, and my anger into a stride along the balcony with a gesture of reprobation. The case was simplified to the vision of a frightened girl whom I loved. I advanced to vindicate her security, but I found nothing there to meet me. It was either all a mistake or Sir Edmund Orme had vanished.

I followed Miss Marden immediately, but there were symptoms of confusion in the drawing-room when I passed in. A lady had fainted, the music had stopped; there was a shuffling of chairs and a pressing forward. The lady was not Charlotte, as I feared, but Mrs. Marden, who had suddenly been taken ill. I remember the relief with which I learned this, for to see Charlotte stricken would have been anguish, and her mother's condition gave a channel to her agitation. It was of course all a matter for the people of the house and for the ladies, and I could have no share in attending to my friends or in conducting them to their carriage. Mrs. Marden revived and insisted on going home, after which I uneasily withdrew.

I called the next morning to ask about her and was informed that she was better, but when I asked if Miss Marden would see me the message sent down was that it was impossible. There was nothing for me to do all day but to roam about with a beating heart. But toward evening I received a line in pencil, brought by hand—"Please come; mother wishes you." Five minutes afterward I was at the door again and ushered into the drawing-room. Mrs. Marden lay upon the sofa, and as soon as I looked at her I saw the shadow of death in her face. But the first thing she said was that she was better, ever so much better; her poor old heart had been behaving queerly again, but now it was quiet. She gave me her hand and I bent over her with my eyes in hers, and in this way I was able to read what she didn't speak—"I'm really very ill, but appear to take what I say exactly as I say it." Charlotte stood there beside her, looking not frightened now, but intensely grave, and not meeting my eyes. "She has told me—she has told me!" her mother went on.

"She has told you?" I stared from one of them to the other, wondering if Mrs. Marden meant that the girl had spoken to her of the circumstances on the balcony.

"That you spoke to her again—that you're admirably faithful."

I felt a thrill of joy at this; it showed me that that memory had been uppermost, and also that Charlotte had wished to say the thing that would soothe her mother most, not the thing that would alarm her. Yet I now knew, myself, as well as if Mrs. Marden had told me, that she knew and had known at the moment what her daughter had seen. "I spoke—I spoke, but she gave me no answer," I said.

"She will now, won't you, Chartie? I want it so, I want it!" the poor lady murmured, with ineffable wistfulness.

"You're very good to me," Charlotte said to me, seriously and sweetly, looking fixedly on the carpet. There was something different in her, different from all the past. She had recognised something, she felt a coercion. I could see that she was trembling.

"Ah, if you would let me show you *how* good I can be!" I exclaimed, holding out my hands to her. As I uttered the words I was touched with the knowledge that something had happened. A form had constituted itself on the other side of the bed, and the form leaned over Mrs. Marden. My whole being went forth into a mute prayer that Charlotte shouldn't see it and that I should be able to betray nothing. The impulse to glance toward Mrs. Marden was even stronger than the involuntary movement of taking in Sir Edmund Orme; but I could resist even that, and Mrs. Marden was perfectly still. Charlotte got up to give me her hand, and with the definite act she saw. She gave, with a shriek, one stare of dismay, and another sound, like a wail of one of the lost, fell at the same instant on my ear. But I had already sprung toward the girl to cover her, to veil her face. She had already thrown herself into my arms. I held her there a moment—bending over her, given up to her, feeling each of her throbs with my own and not knowing which was which; then, all of a sudden, coldly, I gathered that we were alone. She released herself. The figure beside the sofa had vanished; but Mrs. Marden lay in her place with closed eyes, with something in her stillness that gave us both another terror. Charlotte expressed it in the cry of "Mother, mother!" with which she flung herself down. I fell on my knees beside her. Mrs. Marden had passed away.

Was the sound I heard when Chartie shrieked—the other and still more tragic sound I mean—the despairing cry of the poor lady's death-shock or the articulate sob (it was like a waft from a great tempest), of the exorcised and pacified spirit? Possibly the latter, for that was, mercifully, the last of Sir Edmund Orme.

A GHOST

Guy de Maupassant

Translated by M. Charles Sommer

We were speaking of sequestration, alluding to a recent lawsuit. It was at the close of a friendly evening in a very old mansion in the Rue de Grenelle, and each of the guests had a story to tell, which he assured us was true.

Then the old Marquis de la Tour-Samuel, eighty-two years of age, rose and came forward to lean on the mantelpiece. He told the following story in his slightly quavering voice.

"I, also, have witnessed a strange thing—so strange that it has been the nightmare of my life. It happened fifty-six years ago, and yet there is not a month when I do not see it again in my dreams. From that day I have borne a mark, a stamp of fear,—do you understand?

"Yes, for ten minutes I was a prey to terror, in such a way that ever since a constant dread has remained in my soul. Unexpected sounds chill me to the heart; objects which I can ill distinguish in the evening shadows make me long to flee. I am afraid at night.

"No! I would not have owned such a thing before reaching my present age. But now I may tell everything. One may fear imaginary dangers at eighty-two years old. But before actual danger I have never turned back, *mesdames.*

"That affair so upset my mind, filled me with such a deep, mysterious unrest that I never could tell it. I kept it in that inmost part, that corner where we conceal our sad, our shameful secrets, all the weaknesses of our life which cannot be confessed.

"I will tell you that strange happening just as it took place, with no attempt to explain it. Unless I went mad for one short hour it must be explainable, though. Yet I was not mad, and I will prove it to you. Imagine what you will. Here are the simple facts:

"It was in 1827, in July. I was quartered with my regiment in Rouen.

"One day, as I was strolling on the quay, I came across a man I believed I recognized, though I could not place him with certainty. I instinctively went more slowly, ready to pause. The stranger saw my impulse, looked at me, and fell into my arms.

"It was a friend of my younger days, of whom I had been very fond. He seemed to have become half a century older in the five years since I had seen him. His hair was white, and he stooped in his walk, as if he were exhausted. He understood my amazement and told me the story of his life.

"A terrible event had broken him down. He had fallen madly in love with a young girl and married her in a kind of dreamlike ecstasy. After a year of unalloyed bliss and unexhausted passion, she had died suddenly of heart disease, no doubt killed by love itself.

"He had left the country on the very day of her funeral, and had come to live in his hotel at Rouen. He remained there, solitary and desperate, grief slowly mining him, so wretched that he constantly thought of suicide.

" 'As I thus came across you again,' he said, 'I shall ask a great favor of you. I want you to go to my château and get some papers I urgently need. They are in the writing-desk of my room, of our room. I cannot send a servant or a lawyer, as the errand must be kept private. I want absolute silence.

" 'I shall give you the key of the room, which I locked carefully myself before leaving, and the key to the writing-desk. I shall also give you a note for the gardener, who will let you in.

" 'Come to breakfast with me to-morrow, and we'll talk the matter over.'

"I promised to render him that slight service. It would mean but a pleasant excursion for me, his home not being more than twenty-five miles from Rouen. I could go there in an hour on horseback.

"At ten o'clock the next day I was with him. We breakfasted alone together, yet he did not utter more than twenty words. He asked me to excuse him. The thought that I was going to visit the room where his happiness lay shattered, upset him, he said. Indeed, he seemed perturbed, worried, as if some mysterious struggle were taking place in his soul.

"At last he explained exactly what I was to do. It was very simple. I was to take two packages of letters and some papers, locked in the first drawer at the right of the desk of which I had the key. He added:

" 'I need not ask you not to glance at them.'

"I was almost hurt by his words, and told him so, rather sharply. He stammered:

" 'Forgive me. I suffer so much!'

"And tears came to his eyes.

"I left about one o'clock to accomplish my errand.

"The day was radiant, and I rushed through the meadows, listening to the song of the larks, and the rhythmical beat of my sword on my riding-boots.

"Then I entered the forest, and I set my horse to walking. Branches of the trees softly caressed my face, and now and then I would catch a leaf between my teeth and bite it with avidity, full of the joy of life, such as fills you without reason, with a tumultuous happiness almost indefinable, a kind of magical strength.

"As I neared the house I took out the letter for the gardener, and noted with surprise that it was sealed. I was so amazed and so annoyed that I almost turned back without fulfilling my mission. Then I thought that I should thus display over-sensitiveness and bad taste. My friend might have sealed it unconsciously, worried as he was.

"The manor looked as though it had been deserted the last twenty years. The gate, wide-open and rotten, held, one wondered how. Grass filled the paths; you could not tell the flower-beds from the lawn.

"At the noise I made kicking a shutter, an old man came out from a side-door and was apparently amazed to see me there. I dismounted from my horse and gave him the letter. He read it once or twice, turned it over, looked at me with suspicion, and asked:

" 'Well, what do you want?'

"I answered sharply:

" 'You must know it as you have read your master's orders. I want to get in the house.'

"He appeared overwhelmed. He said:

" 'So—you are going in—in his room?'

"I was getting impatient.

" '*Parbleu!* Do you intend to question me, by chance?'

"He stammered:

" 'No—monsieur—only—it has not been opened since—since the death. If you will wait five minutes, I will go in to see whether—'

"I interrupted angrily:

" 'See here, are you joking? You can't go in that room, as I have the key!'

"He no longer knew what to say.

" 'Then, monsieur, I will show you the way.'

" 'Show me the stairs and leave me alone. I can find it without your help.'

" 'But—still—monsieur—'

"Then I lost my temper.

" 'Now be quiet! Else you'll be sorry!'

"I roughly pushed him aside and went into the house.

"I first went through the kitchen, then crossed two small rooms occupied by the man and his wife. From there I stepped into a large hall. I went up the stairs, and I recognized the door my friend had described to me.

"I opened it with ease and went in.

"The room was so dark that at first I could not distinguish anything. I paused, arrested by that moldy and stale odor peculiar to deserted and condemned rooms, of dead rooms. Then gradually my eyes grew accustomed to the gloom, and I saw rather clearly a great room in disorder, a bed without sheets having still its mattresses and pillows, one of which bore the deep print of an elbow or a head, as if someone had just been resting on it.

"The chairs seemed all in confusion. I noticed that a door, probably that of a closet, had remained ajar.

"I first went to the window and opened it to get some light, but the hinges of the outside shutters were so rusted that I could not loosen them.

"I even tried to break them with my sword, but did not succeed. As those fruitless attempts irritated me, and as my eyes were by now adjusted to the dim light, I gave up hope of getting more light and went toward the writing-desk.

"I sat down in an arm-chair, folded back the top, and opened the drawer. It was full to the edge. I needed but three packages, which I knew how to distinguish, and I started looking for them.

"I was straining my eyes to decipher the inscriptions, when I thought I heard, or rather felt a rustle behind me. I took no notice, thinking a draft had lifted some curtain. But a minute later, another movement, almost indistinct, sent a disagreeable little shiver over my skin. It was so ridiculous to be moved thus even so slightly, that I would not turn round, being ashamed. I had just discovered the second package I needed, and was on the point of reaching for the third, when a great and sorrowful sigh, close to my shoulder, made me give a mad leap two yards away. In my spring I had turned round, my hand on the hilt of my sword, and surely had I not felt that, I should have fled like a coward.

"A tall woman, dressed in white, was facing me, standing behind the chair in which I had sat a second before.

"Such a shudder ran through me that I almost fell back! Oh, no one who has not felt them can understand those gruesome and ridiculous terrors! The soul melts; your heart seems to stop; your whole body becomes limp as a sponge, and your innermost parts seem collapsing.

"I do not believe in ghosts; and yet I broke down before the hideous fear of the dead; and I suffered, oh, I suffered more in a few minutes, in the irresistible anguish of supernatural dread, than I have suffered in all the rest of my life!

"If she had not spoken, I might have died. But she did speak; she spoke in a soft and plaintive voice which set my nerves vibrating. I could not say that I regained my self-control. No, I was past knowing what I did; but the kind of pride I have in me, as well as a military pride, helped me to maintain, almost in spite of myself, an honorable countenance. I was making a pose, a pose for myself, and for her, for her, whatever she was, woman, or phantom. I realized this later, for at the time of the apparition, I could think of nothing. I was afraid.

"She said:

" 'Oh, you can be of great help to me, monsieur!'

"I tried to answer, but I was unable to utter one word. A vague sound came from my throat.

"She continued:

" 'Will you? You can save me, cure me. I suffer terribly. I always suffer. I suffer, oh, I suffer!'

"And she sat down gently in my chair. She looked at me.

" 'Will you?'

"I nodded my head, being still paralyzed.

"Then she handed me a woman's comb of tortoise-shell, and murmured:

" 'Comb my hair! Oh, comb my hair! That will cure me. Look at my head—how I suffer! And my hair—how it hurts!'

"Her loose hair, very long, very black, it seemed to me, hung over the back of the chair, touching the floor.

"Why did I do it? Why did I, shivering, accept that comb, and why did I take between my hands her long hair, which left on my skin a ghastly impression of cold, as if I had handled serpents? I do not know.

"That feeling still clings about my fingers, and I shiver when I recall it.

"I combed her, I handled, I know not how, that hair of ice. I bound and unbound it; I plaited it as one plaits a horse's mane. She sighed, bent her head, seemed happy.

"Suddenly she said, 'Thank you!' tore the comb from my hands, and fled through the door which I had noticed was half opened.

"Left alone, I had for a few seconds the hazy feeling one feels in waking up from a nightmare. Then I recovered myself. I ran to the window and broke the shutters by my furious assault.

"A stream of light poured in. I rushed to the door through which that being had gone. I found it locked and immovable.

"Then a fever of flight seized on me, a panic, the true panic of battle. I quickly grasped the three packages of letters from the open desk; I crossed the room running, I took the steps of the stairway four at a time. I found myself outside, I don't know how, and seeing my horse close by, I mounted in one leap and left at a full gallop.

"I didn't stop till I reached Rouen and drew up in front of my house. Having thrown the reins to my orderly, I flew to my room and locked myself in to think.

"Then for an hour I asked myself whether I had not been the victim of an hallucination. Certainly I must have had one of those nervous shocks, one of those brain disorders such as give rise to miracles, to which the supernatural owes its strength.

"And I had almost concluded that it was a vision, an illusion of my senses, when I came near to the window. My eyes by chance looked down. My tunic was covered with hairs, long woman's hairs which had entangled themselves around the buttons!

"I took them off one by one and threw them out of the window with trembling fingers.

"I then called my orderly. I felt too perturbed, too moved, to go and see my friend on that day. Besides, I needed to think over what I should tell him.

"I had his letters delivered to him. He gave a receipt to the soldier. He inquired after me and was told that I was not well. I had had a sunstroke, or something. He seemed distressed.

"I went to see him the next day, early in the morning, bent on telling him the truth. He had gone out the evening before and had not come back.

"I returned the same day, but he had not been seen. I waited a week. He did not come back. I notified the police. They searched for him everywhere, but no one could find any trace of his passing or of his retreat.

"A careful search was made in the deserted manor. No suspicious clue was discovered.

"There was no sign that a woman had been concealed there.

"The inquest gave no result, and so the search went no further.

"And in fifty-six years I have learned nothing more. I never found out the truth."

IN THE PENAL COLONY

Franz Kafka

Translated by Ian Johnston

It's a peculiar apparatus," said the Officer to the Traveler, gazing with a certain admiration at the device, with which he was, of course, thoroughly familiar. It appeared that the Traveler had responded to the invitation of the Commandant only out of politeness, when he had been invited to attend the execution of a soldier condemned for disobeying and insulting his superior. Of course, interest in the execution was not very high, not even in the penal colony itself. At least, here in the small, deep, sandy valley, closed in on all sides by barren slopes, apart from the Officer and the Traveler there were present only the Condemned, a vacant-looking man with a broad mouth and dilapidated hair and face, and the Soldier, who held the heavy chain to which were connected the small chains which bound the Condemned Man by his feet and wrist bones, as well as by his neck, and which were also linked to each other by connecting chains. The Condemned Man had an expression of such dog-like resignation that it looked as if one could set him free to roam around the slopes and would only have to whistle at the start of the execution for him to return.

The Traveler had little interest in the apparatus and walked back and forth behind the Condemned Man, almost visibly indifferent, while the Officer took care of the final preparations. Sometimes he crawled under the apparatus, which was built deep into the earth, and sometimes he climbed up a ladder to inspect the upper parts. These were really jobs which could have been left to a mechanic, but the Officer carried them out with great enthusiasm, maybe because he was particularly fond of this apparatus or maybe because there was some other reason why one could not trust the work to anyone else. "It's all ready now!" he finally cried and climbed back down the ladder. He was unusually tired, breathing with his mouth wide open, and he had pushed two fine lady's handkerchiefs under the collar of his uniform.

"These uniforms are really too heavy for the tropics," the Traveler said, instead of asking some questions about the apparatus, as the Officer had expected. "That's true," said the Officer. He washed the oil and grease from his dirty hands in a bucket of water standing ready, "but they mean home, and we don't want to lose our homeland." "Now, have a look at this apparatus," he added immediately, drying his hands with a towel and pointing to the device. "Up to this point I had to do some work by hand, but from now on the apparatus should work entirely on its own." The Traveler nodded and followed the Officer. The latter tried to protect himself against all eventualities by saying, "Of course, breakdowns do happen. I really hope none will occur today, but we must be prepared for it. The apparatus is supposed to keep going for twelve hours without interruption. But if any breakdowns do occur, they'll only be very minor, and we'll deal with them right away."

"Don't you want to sit down?" he asked finally, as he pulled out a chair from a pile of cane chairs and offered it to the Traveler. The latter could not refuse. He sat on the edge of the pit, into which he cast a fleeting glance. It was not very deep. On one side of the hole the piled earth was heaped up into a wall; on the other side stood the apparatus. "I don't know," the officer said, "whether the Commandant has already explained the apparatus to you." The Traveler made a vague gesture with his hand. That was good enough for the Officer, for now he could explain the apparatus himself.

"This apparatus," he said, grasping a connecting rod and leaning against it, "is our previous Commandant's invention. I also worked with him on the very first tests and took part in all the work right up to its completion. However, the credit for the invention belongs to him alone. Have you heard of our previous Commandant? No? Well, I'm not claiming too much when I say that the organization of the entire penal colony is his work. We, his friends, already knew at the time of his death that the administration of the colony was so self-contained that even if his successor had a thousand new plans in mind, he would not be able to alter anything of the old plan, at least not for several years. And our prediction has held. The New Commandant has had to recognize that. It's a shame that you didn't know the previous Commandant!"

"However," the Officer said, interrupting himself, "I'm chattering, and his apparatus stands here in front of us. As you see, it consists of three parts. With the passage of time certain popular names have been developed for each of these parts. The one underneath is called the bed, the upper one is called the inscriber, and here in the middle, this moving part is called the harrow." "The harrow?" the Traveler asked. He had not been listening with full attention. The sun was excessively strong, trapped in the shadowless valley, and one could hardly collect one's thoughts. So the Officer appeared to him all the more admirable in his tight tunic weighed down with epaulettes and festooned with braid, ready to go on parade, as he explained the matter so eagerly and, while he was talking, adjusted screws here and there with a screwdriver.

The Soldier appeared to be in a state similar to the Traveler. He had wound the Condemned Man's chain around both his wrists and was supporting himself with his hand on his weapon, letting his head hang backward, not bothering about anything. The Traveler was not surprised at that, for the Officer spoke French, and clearly neither the Soldier nor the Condemned Man understood the language. So it was all the more striking that the Condemned Man, in spite of that, did what he could to follow the Officer's explanation. With a sort of sleepy persistence he kept directing his gaze to the place where the Officer had just pointed, and when the question from the Traveler interrupted the Officer, the Condemned Man looked at the Traveler, too, just as the Officer was doing.

"Yes, the harrow," said the Officer. "The name fits. The needles are arranged as in a harrow, and the whole thing is driven like a harrow, although it stays in one place and is, in principle, much more artistic. You'll understand in a moment. The condemned is laid out here on the bed. First, I'll describe the apparatus and only then let the procedure go to work. That way you'll be able to follow it better. Also a sprocket in the inscriber is excessively worn. It really squeaks. When it's in motion one can hardly make oneself understood. Unfortunately replacement parts are difficult to come by in this place. So, here is the bed, as I said. The whole thing is completely covered with a layer of cotton wool, the purpose of which you'll find out in a moment. The condemned man is laid out on his stomach on the cotton wool—naked, of course. There are straps for the hands here, for the feet here, and for the throat here, to tie him in securely. At the head of the bed here, where the man, as I have mentioned, first lies face down, is this small protruding lump of felt, which can easily be adjusted so that it presses right into the man's mouth. Its purpose is to prevent him screaming and biting his tongue to pieces. Of course, the man has to let the felt in his mouth—otherwise the straps around his throat would break his neck." "That's cotton wool?" asked the Traveler and bent down. "Yes, it is," said the Officer smiling, "feel it for yourself."

He took the Traveler's hand and led him over to the bed. "It's a specially prepared cotton wool. That's why it looks so unrecognizable. I'll get around to mentioning its purpose in a moment." The Traveler was already being won over a little to the apparatus. With his hand over his eyes to protect them from the sun, he looked at the apparatus in the hole. It was a massive construction. The bed and the inscriber were the same size and looked like two dark chests. The inscriber was set about two meters above the bed, and the two were joined together at the corners by four brass rods, which almost reflected the sun. The harrow hung between the chests on a band of steel.

The Officer had hardly noticed the earlier indifference of the Traveler, but he did have a sense now of how the latter's interest was being aroused for the first time. So he paused in his explanation in order to allow the Traveler time to observe the apparatus undisturbed. The Condemned Man imitated the Traveler, but since he could not put his hand over his eyes, he blinked upward with his eyes uncovered.

"So now the man is lying down," said the Traveler. He leaned back in his chair and crossed his legs.

"Yes," said the Officer, pushing his cap back a little and running his hand over his hot face. "Now, listen. Both the bed and the inscriber have their own electric batteries. The bed needs them for itself, and the inscriber for the harrow. As soon as the man is strapped in securely, the bed is set in motion. It quivers with tiny, very rapid oscillations from side to side and up and down simultaneously. You will have seen similar devices in mental hospitals. Only with our bed all movements are precisely calibrated, for they must be meticulously coordinated with the movements of the harrow. But it's the harrow which has the job of actually carrying out the sentence."

"What is the sentence?" the Traveler asked. "You don't even know that?" asked the Officer in astonishment and bit his lip. "Forgive me if my explanations are perhaps confused. I really do beg your pardon. Previously it was the Commandant's habit to provide such explanations. But the New Commandant has excused himself from this honorable duty. The fact that with such an eminent visitor"—the traveler tried to deflect the honor with both hands, but the officer insisted on the expression—"that with such an eminent visitor he didn't even once make him aware of the form of our sentencing is yet again something new, which . . ." He had a curse on his lips, but controlled himself and said merely: "I was not informed about it. It's not my fault. In any case, I am certainly the person best able to explain our style of sentencing, for here I am carrying"—he patted his breast pocket—"the relevant diagrams drawn by the previous Commandant."

"Diagrams made by the Commandant himself?" asked the Traveler. "Then was he in his own person a combination of everything? Was he soldier, judge, engineer, chemist, and draftsman?"

"He was indeed," said the Officer, nodding his head with a fixed and thoughtful expression. Then he looked at his hands, examining them. They didn't seem to him clean enough to handle the diagrams. So he went to the bucket and washed them again. Then he pulled out a small leather folder and said, "Our sentence does not sound severe. The law which a Condemned Man has violated is inscribed on his body with the harrow. This Condemned Man, for example," and the Officer pointed to the man, "will have inscribed on his body, 'Honor your superiors.'"

The Traveler had a quick look at the man. When the Officer was pointing at him, the man kept his head down and appeared to be directing all his energy into listening in order to learn something. But the movements of his thick pouting lips showed clearly that he was incapable of understanding anything. The Traveler wanted to raise various questions, but after looking at the Condemned Man he merely asked, "Does he know his sentence?" "No," said the Officer. He wished to get on with his explanation right away, but the Traveler interrupted him: "He doesn't know his own sentence?" "No," said the Officer once more. He then paused for a moment, as if he was asking the Traveler for a more detailed reason for his question, and said, "It would be useless to give him that information. He experiences it on his own body." The Traveler really wanted to keep quiet at this point, but he felt how the Condemned Man was gazing at him—he seemed to be asking whether he could approve of the process the Officer had described. So the Traveler, who had up to this point been leaning back, bent forward again and kept up his questions, "But does he nonetheless have some general idea that he's been condemned?" "Not that either," said the Officer, and he smiled at the Traveler, as if he was still waiting for some strange revelations from him. "No?" said the Traveler, wiping his forehead, "then does the man also not yet know how his defense was received?" "He has had no opportunity to defend himself," said the Officer and looked away, as if he was talking to himself and wished not to embarrass the Traveler with an explanation of matters so self-evident to him. "But he must have had a chance to defend himself," said the Traveler and stood up from his chair.

The Officer recognized that he was in danger of having his explanation of the apparatus held up for a long time. So he went to the Traveler, took him by the arm, pointed with his hand at the Condemned Man, who stood there stiffly now that the attention was so clearly directed at him—the Soldier was also pulling on his chain—and said, "The matter stands like this. Here in the penal colony I have been appointed judge. In spite of my youth. For I stood at the side of our Old Commandant in all matters of punishment, and I also know the most about the apparatus. The basic principle I use for my decisions is this: Guilt is always beyond a doubt. Other courts could not follow this principle, for they are made up of many heads and, in addition, have even higher courts above them. But that is not the case here, or at least it was not that way with the previous Commandant. It's true the New Commandant has already shown a desire to get mixed up in my court, but I've succeeded so far in fending him off. And I'll continue to be successful. You want this case explained. It's simple—just like all of them. This morning a captain laid a charge that this man, who is assigned to him as a servant and who sleeps before his door, had been sleeping on duty. For his task is to stand up every time the clock strikes the hour and salute in front of the captain's door. That's certainly not a difficult duty—and it's necessary, since he is supposed to remain fresh both for guarding and for service. Yesterday night the captain wanted to check whether his servant was fulfilling his duty. He opened the door on the stroke of two and found him curled up asleep. He got his horsewhip and hit him across the face. Now, instead of standing up and begging for forgiveness, the man grabbed his master by the legs, shook him, and cried out, 'Throw away that whip or I'll eat you up.' Those are the facts. The captain came to me an hour ago. I wrote up his statement and right after that the sentence. Then I had the man chained up. It was all very simple. If I had first summoned the man and interrogated him, the result would have been confusion. He would have lied, and if I had been successful in refuting his lies, he would have replaced them with new lies, and so forth. But now I have him, and I won't release him again. Now, does that clarify everything? But time is passing. We should be starting the execution, and I haven't finished explaining the apparatus yet."

He urged the Traveler to sit down in his chair, moved to the apparatus again, and started, "As you see, the shape of the harrow corresponds to the shape of a man. This is the harrow for the upper body, and here are the harrows for the legs. This small cutter is the only one designated for the head. Is that clear to you?" He leaned forward to the Traveler in a friendly way, ready to give the most comprehensive explanation.

The Traveler looked at the harrow with a wrinkled frown. The information about the judicial procedures had not satisfied him. However, he had to tell himself that here it was a matter of a penal colony, that in this place special regulations were necessary, and that one had to give precedence to military measures right down to the last detail. Beyond that, however, he had some hopes in the New Commandant, who obviously, although slowly, was intending to introduce a new procedure which the limited understanding of this Officer could not cope with.

Following this train of thought, the Traveler asked, "Will the Commandant be present at the execution?" "That is not certain," said the Officer, embarrassingly affected by the sudden question, and his friendly expression made a grimace. "That's why we need to hurry up. As much as I regret the fact, I'll have to make my explanation even shorter. But tomorrow, once the apparatus is clean again—the fact that it gets so very dirty is its only fault—I could add a detailed explanation. So now, only the most important things. When the man is lying on the bed and it starts quivering, the harrow sinks onto the body. It positions itself automatically in such a way that it touches the body only lightly with the needle tips. Once the machine is set in this position, this steel cable tightens up into a rod. And now the performance begins. Someone who is not an initiate sees no external difference among the punishments. The harrow seems to do its work uniformly. As it quivers, it sticks the tips of its needles into the body, which is also vibrating from the movement of the bed. Now, to enable someone to check on how the sentence is being carried out, the harrow is made of glass. That gave rise to certain technical difficulties with fastening the needles securely, but after several attempts we were successful. We didn't spare any efforts. And now, as the inscription is made on the body, everyone can see through the glass. Don't you want to come closer and see the needles for yourself."

The Traveler stood slowly, moved up, and bent over the harrow. "You see," the Officer said, "two sorts of needles in a multiple arrangement. Each long needle has a short one next to it. The long one inscribes, and the short one squirts water out to wash away the blood and keep the inscription always clear. The bloody water is then channeled here in small grooves and finally flows into these main gutters, and the outlet pipe takes it to the pit." The Officer pointed with his finger to the exact path which the bloody water had to take. As he began to demonstrate with both hands at the mouth of the outlet pipe, in order to make his account as clear as possible, the Traveler raised his head and, feeling behind him with his hand, wanted to return to his chair. Then he saw to his horror that the Condemned Man had also, like him, accepted the Officer's invitation to inspect the arrangement of the harrow up close. He had pulled the sleeping Soldier holding the chain a little forward and was also bending over the glass. One could see how with a confused gaze he also was looking for what the two gentlemen had just observed, but how he didn't succeed because he lacked the explanation. He leaned forward this way and that. He kept running his eyes over the glass again and again. The Traveler wanted to push him back, for what he was doing was probably punishable. But the Officer held the Traveler firmly with one hand, and with the other he took a lump of earth from the wall and threw it at the Soldier. The latter opened his eyes with a start, saw what the Condemned Man had dared to do, let his weapon fall, braced his heels in the earth, and pulled the Condemned Man back, so that he immediately collapsed. The Soldier looked down at him, as he writhed around, making his chain clink. "Stand him up," cried the Officer. Then he noticed that the Condemned Man was distracting the Traveler too much. The latter was even leaning out away from the harrow, without paying any attention to it, wanting to find out what was happening to the Condemned Man. "Handle him carefully," the Officer yelled again. He ran around the apparatus, personally grabbed the Condemned Man under the armpits and, with the help of the Soldier, stood the man, whose feet kept slipping, upright.

"Now I know all about it," said the Traveler, as the Officer turned back to him again. "Except the most important thing," said the latter, grabbing the Traveler by the arm and pointing up high. "There in the inscriber is the mechanism which determines the movement of the harrow, and this mechanism is arranged according to the diagram on which the sentence is set down. I still use the diagrams of the previous Commandant. Here they are." He pulled some pages out of the leather folder. "Unfortunately I can't hand them to you. They are the most cherished thing I possess. Sit down, and I'll show you them from this distance. Then you'll be able to see it all well." He showed the first sheet. The Traveler would have been happy to say something appreciative, but all he saw was a labyrinthine series of lines, criss-crossing each other in all sort of ways. These covered the paper so thickly that only with difficulty could one make out the white spaces in between. "Read it," said the Officer. "I can't," said the Traveler. "But it's clear," said the Officer. "It's very elaborate," said the Traveler evasively, "but I can't decipher it."

"Yes," said the Officer, smiling and putting the folder back again, "it's not calligraphy for school children. One has to read it a long time. You too will finally understand it clearly. Of course, it has to be a script that isn't simple. You see, it's not supposed to kill right away, but on average over a period of twelve hours. The turning point is set for the sixth hour. There must also be many, many embellishments surrounding the basic script. The essential script moves around the body only in a narrow belt. The rest of the body is reserved for decoration. Can you now appreciate the work of the harrow and the whole apparatus? Just look at it!" He jumped up the ladder, turned a wheel, and called down, "Watch out—move to the side!" Everything started moving. If the wheel had not squeaked, it would have been marvelous. The officer threatened the wheel with his fist, as if he was surprised by the disturbance it created. Then he spread his arms, apologizing to the traveler, and quickly clambered down, in order to observe the operation of the apparatus from below.

Something was still not working properly, something only he noticed. He clambered up again and reached with both hands into the inside of the inscriber. Then, in order to descend more quickly, instead of using the ladder, he slid down on one of the poles and, to make himself understandable through the noise, strained his voice to the limit as he yelled in the Traveler's ear, "Do you understand the process? The harrow is starting to write. When it's finished with the first part of the script on the man's back, the layer of cotton wool rolls and turns the body slowly onto its side to give the harrow a new area. Meanwhile those parts lacerated by the inscription are lying on the cotton wool which, because it has been specially treated, immediately stops the bleeding and prepares the script for a further deepening. Here, as the body continues to rotate, prongs on the edge of the harrow then pull the cotton wool from the wounds, throw it into the pit, and the harrow goes to work again. In this way it keeps making the inscription deeper for twelve hours. For the first six hours the Condemned Man goes on living almost as before. He suffers nothing but pain. After two hours, the felt is removed, for at that point the man has no more energy for screaming. Here at the head of the bed warm rice pudding is put in this electrically heated bowl. From this the man, if he feels like it, can help himself to what he can lap up with his tongue. No one passes up this opportunity. I don't know of a single one, and I have had a lot of experience. He first loses his pleasure in eating around the sixth hour. I usually kneel down at this point and observe the phenomenon. The man rarely swallows the last bit. He turns it around in his mouth and spits it into the pit. When he does that, I have to lean aside or else he'll get me in the face. But how quiet the man becomes around the sixth hour! The most stupid of them begin to understand. It starts around the eyes and spreads out from there. A look that could tempt one to lie down under the harrow. Nothing else happens. The man simply begins to decipher the inscription. He purses his lips, as if he is listening. You've seen that it's not easy to figure out the inscription with your eyes, but our man deciphers it with his wounds. True, it takes a lot of work. It requires six hours to complete. But then the harrow spits him right out and throws him into the pit, where he splashes down into the bloody water and cotton wool. Then the judgment is over, and we, the Soldier and I, quickly bury him."

The Traveler had leaned his ear towards the Officer and, with his hands in his coat pockets, was observing the machine at work. The Condemned Man was also watching, but without understanding. He bent forward a little and followed the moving needles, as the Soldier, after a signal from the Officer, cut through his shirt and trousers with a knife from the back, so that they fell off the Condemned Man. He wanted to grab the falling garments to cover his bare flesh, but the Soldier held him up and shook the last rags from him. The Officer turned the machine off, and in the silence which then ensued the Condemned Man was laid out under the harrow. The chains were taken off and the straps fastened in their place. For the Condemned Man it seemed at first glance to signify almost a relief. And now the harrow sunk down a stage lower, for the Condemned was a thin man. As the needle tips touched him, a shudder went over his skin. While the Soldier was busy with the right hand, the Condemned Man stretched out his left, with no sense of its direction. But it was pointing to where the Traveler was standing. The Officer kept looking at the Traveler from the side, without taking his eyes off him, as if he was trying to read from his face the impression he was getting of the execution, which he had now explained to him, at least superficially.

The strap meant to hold the wrist ripped off. The Soldier probably had pulled on it too hard. The Soldier showed the Officer the torn-off piece of strap, wanting him to help. So the Officer went over to him and said, with his face turned towards the Traveler, "The machine is very complicated. Now and then something has to tear or break. One shouldn't let that detract from one's overall opinion. Anyway, we have an immediate replacement for the strap. I'll use a chain—even though that will affect the sensitivity of the movements for the right arm." And while he put the chain in place, he kept talking, "Our resources for maintaining the machine are very limited at the moment. Under the previous Commandant, I had free access to a cash box specially set aside for this purpose. There was a store room here in which all possible replacement parts were kept. I admit I made almost extravagant use of it. I mean earlier, not now, as the New Commandant claims. For him everything serves only as a pretext to fight against the old arrangements. Now he keeps the cash box for machinery under his own control, and if I ask him for a new strap, he demands the torn one as a piece of evidence, the new one doesn't arrive for ten days, and it's an inferior brand, of not much use to me. But how I am supposed to get the machine to work in the meantime without a strap—no one's concerned about that."

The Traveler was thinking: it's always questionable to intervene decisively in strange circumstances. He was neither a citizen of the penal colony nor a citizen of the state to which it belonged. If he wanted to condemn the execution or even hinder it, people could say to him: You're a foreigner—keep quiet. He would have nothing in response to that, but could only add that he did not understand what he was doing on this occasion, for the purpose of his traveling was merely to observe and not to alter other people's judicial systems in any way. True, at this point the way things were turning out it was very tempting. The injustice of the process and the inhumanity of the execution were beyond doubt. No one could assume that the Traveler was acting out of any sense of his own self-interest, for the Condemned Man was a stranger to him, not a countryman and not someone who invited sympathy in any way. The Traveler himself had letters of reference from high officials and had been welcomed here with great courtesy. The fact that he had been invited to this execution even seemed to indicate that people were asking for his judgment of this trial. This was all the more likely since the Commandant, as he had now heard only too clearly, was no supporter of this process and maintained an almost hostile relationship with the Officer.

Then the Traveler heard a cry of rage from the Officer. He had just shoved the stub of felt in the Condemned Man's mouth, not without difficulty, when the Condemned Man, overcome by an irresistible nausea, shut his eyes and threw up. The Officer quickly yanked him up off the stump and wanted to turn his head aside toward the pit. But it was too late. The vomit was already flowing down onto the machine. "This is all the Commandant's fault!" cried the Officer and mindlessly rattled the brass rods at the front. "My machine's as filthy as a pigsty." With trembling hands he showed the Traveler what had happened. "Haven't I spent hours trying to make the Commandant understand that a day before the execution there should be no more food served. But the new lenient administration has a different opinion. Before the man is led away, the Commandant's women cram sugary things down his throat. His whole life he's fed himself on stinking fish, and now he has to eat sweets! But that would be all right—I'd have no objections—but why don't they get a new felt, the way I've been asking him for three months now? How can anyone take this felt into his mouth without feeling disgusted—something that a hundred men have sucked and bitten on it as they were dying?"

The Condemned Man had laid his head down and appeared peaceful. The Soldier was busy cleaning up the machine with the Condemned Man's shirt. The Officer went up to the Traveler, who, feeling some premonition, took a step backwards. But the Officer grasped him by the hand and pulled him aside. "I want to speak a few words to you in confidence," he said. "May I do that?" "Of course," said the Traveler and listened with his eyes lowered.

"This process and execution, which you now have an opportunity to admire, have no more open supporters in our colony. I am its only defender, just as I am the single advocate for the legacy of the Old Commandant. I can no longer think about a more extensive organization of the process—I'm using all my powers to maintain what there is at present. When the Old Commandant was alive, the colony was full of his supporters. I have something of the Old Commandant's power of persuasion, but I completely lack his power, and as a result the supporters have gone into hiding. There are still a lot of them, but no one admits to it. If you go into a tea house today—that is to say, on a day of execution—and keep your ears open, perhaps you'll hear nothing but ambiguous remarks. They are all supporters, but under the present Commandant, considering his present views, they are totally useless to me. And now I'm asking you: Should such a life's work," he pointed to the machine, "come to nothing because of this Commandant and the women influencing him? Should people let that happen? Even if one is a foreigner and only on our island for a couple of days? But there's no time to lose. People are already preparing something against my judicial proceedings. Discussions are already taking place in the Commandant's headquarters, to which I am not invited. Even your visit today seems to me typical of the whole situation. People are cowards and send you out—a foreigner. You should have seen the executions in earlier days! The entire valley was overflowing with people, even a day before the execution. They all came merely to watch. Early in the morning the Commandant appeared with his women. Fanfares woke up the entire campsite. I delivered the news that everything was ready. The whole society—and every high official had to attend—arranged itself around the machine. This pile of cane chairs is a sorry leftover from that time. The machine was freshly cleaned and glowed. For almost every execution I had new replacement parts. In front of hundreds of eyes—all the spectators stood on tip toe right up to the hills there—the Condemned Man was laid down under the harrow by the Commandant himself. What nowadays is done by a common soldier was then my work as the senior judge, and it was a honor for me. And then the execution began! No discordant note disturbed the work of the machine. Many people did not look any more at all, but lay down with closed eyes in the sand. They all knew: now justice was being carried out. In silence people listened to nothing but the groans of the Condemned Man, muffled by the felt. These days the machine no longer manages to squeeze a strong groan out of the Condemned Man—something the felt is not capable of smothering. But back then the needles which made the inscription dripped a caustic liquid which we are not permitted to use any more today. Well, then came the sixth hour. It was impossible to grant all the requests people made to be allowed to watch from up close. The Commandant, in his wisdom, arranged that the children should be taken care of before all the rest. Naturally, I was always allowed to stand close by, because of my official position. Often I crouched down there with two small children in my arms, on my right and left. How we all took in the expression of transfiguration on the martyred face! How we held our cheeks in the glow of this justice, finally attained and already passing away! What times we had, my friend!"

The Officer had obviously forgotten who was standing in front of him. He had put his arm around the Traveler and laid his head on his shoulder. The Traveler was extremely embarrassed. Impatiently he looked away over the Officer's head. The Soldier had ended his task of cleaning and had just shaken some rice pudding into the bowl from a tin. No sooner had the Condemned Man, who seemed to have fully recovered already, noticed this than his tongue began to lick at the pudding. The Soldier kept pushing him away, for the pudding was probably meant for a later time, but in any case it was not proper for the Soldier to reach in and grab some food with his dirty hands and eat it in front of the famished Condemned Man.

The Officer quickly collected himself. "I didn't want to upset you in any way," he said. "I know it is impossible to make someone understand those days now. Besides, the machine still works and operates on its own. It operates on its own even when it is standing alone in this valley. And at the end, the body still keeps falling in that incredibly soft flight into the pit, even if hundreds of people are not gathered like flies around the hole the way they used to be. Back then we had to erect a strong railing around the pit. It was pulled out long ago."

The Traveler wanted to turn his face away from the Officer and looked aimlessly around him. The Officer thought he was looking at the wasteland of the valley. So he grabbed his hands, turned him around in order to catch his gaze, and asked, "Do you see the shame of it?"

But the Traveler said nothing. The Officer left him alone for a while. With his legs apart and his hands on his hips, the Officer stood still and looked at the ground. Then he smiled at the Traveler cheerfully and said, "Yesterday I was nearby when the Commandant invited you. I heard the invitation. I know the Commandant. I understood right away what he intended with his invitation. Although his power might be sufficiently great to take action against me, he doesn't yet dare to. But my guess is that with you he is exposing me to the judgment of a respected foreigner. He calculates things with care. You are now in your second day on the island. You didn't know the Old Commandant and his way of thinking. You are trapped in a European way of seeing things. Perhaps you are fundamentally opposed to the death penalty in general and to this kind of mechanical style of execution in particular. Moreover, you see how the execution is a sad procedure, without any public participation, using a partially damaged machine. Now, if we take all this together (so the Commandant thinks) surely one could easily imagine that you would not consider my procedure proper? And if you didn't consider it right, you wouldn't keep quiet about it—I'm still speaking the mind of the Commandant—for you no doubt have faith that your tried-and-true convictions are correct. It's true that you have seen many peculiar things among many peoples and have learned to respect them. Thus, you will probably not speak out against the procedure with your full power, as you would perhaps in your own homeland. But the Commandant doesn't really need that. A casual word, merely a careless remark, is enough. It doesn't have to match your convictions at all, so long as it corresponds to his wishes. I'm certain he will use all his shrewdness to interrogate you. And his women will sit around in a circle and perk up their ears. You will say something like, 'Among us the judicial procedures are different,' or 'With us the accused is questioned before the verdict,' or 'We had torture only in the Middle Ages.' For you these observations appear as correct as they are self-evident—innocent remarks which do not impugn my procedure. But how will the Commandant take them? I see him, our excellent Commandant—the way he immediately pushes his stool aside and hurries out to the balcony—I see his women, how they stream after him. I hear his voice—the women call it a thunder voice. And now he's speaking: 'A great Western explorer who has been commissioned to inspect judicial procedures in all countries has just said that our process based on old customs is inhumane. After the verdict of such a personality it is, of course, no longer possible for me to tolerate this procedure. So from this day on I am ordering . . . and so forth.' You want to intervene—you didn't say what he is reporting—you didn't call my procedure inhumane; by contrast, in keeping with your deep insight, you consider it most humane and most worthy of human beings. You also admire this machinery. But it is too late. You don't even go onto the balcony, which is already filled with women. You want to attract attention. You want to cry out. But a lady's hand is covering your mouth, and I and the Old Commandant's work are lost."

The Traveler had to suppress a smile. So the work which he had considered so difficult was easy. He said evasively, "You're exaggerating my influence. The Commandant has read my letters of recommendation. He knows that I am no expert in judicial processes. If I were to express an opinion, it would be that of a lay person, no more significant than the opinion of anyone else, and in any case far less significant than the opinion of the Commandant, who, as I understand it, has very extensive powers in this penal colony. If his views of this procedure are as definite as you think they are, then I'm afraid the time has come for this procedure to end, without any need for my humble opinion."

Did the Officer understand by now? No, he did not yet get it. He shook his head vigorously, briefly looked back at the Condemned Man and the Soldier, who both flinched and stopped eating the rice, went up really close up to the Traveler, without looking into his face, but gazing at parts of his jacket, and said more gently than before: "You don't know the Commandant. Where he and all of us are concerned you are—forgive the expression—to a certain extent innocent. Your influence, believe me, cannot be overestimated. In fact, I was blissfully happy when I heard that you were to be present at the execution by yourself. This order of the Commandant was aimed at me, but now I'll turn it to my advantage. Without being distracted by false insinuations and disparaging looks—which could not have been avoided with a greater number of participants at the execution—you have listened to my explanation, looked at the machine, and are now about to view the execution. Your verdict is no doubt already fixed. If some small uncertainties remain, witnessing the execution will remove them. And now I'm asking you—help me with the Commandant!"

The Traveler did not let him go on talking. "How can I do that," he cried. "It's totally impossible. I can help you as little as I can harm you."

"You could do it," said the Officer. With some apprehension the Traveler observed that the Officer was clenching his fists. "You could do it," repeated the Officer, even more emphatically. "I have a plan which must succeed. You think your influence is insufficient. I know it will be enough. But assuming you're right, doesn't saving this whole procedure require one to try even those methods which may be inadequate? So listen to my plan. To carry it out, it's necessary, above all, for you to keep as quiet as possible today in the colony about your verdict on this procedure. Unless someone asks you directly, you should not express any view whatsoever. But what you do say must be short and vague. People should notice that it's difficult for you to speak about the subject, that you feel bitter, that, if you were to speak openly, you'd have to burst out cursing on the spot. I'm not asking you to lie, not at all. You should only give brief answers—something like, 'Yes, I've seen the execution' or 'Yes, I've heard the full explanation.' That's all—nothing further. For that will be enough of an indication for people to observe in you a certain bitterness, even if that's not what the Commandant will think. Naturally, he will completely misunderstand the issue and interpret it in his own way. My plan is based on that. Tomorrow a large meeting of all the higher administrative officials takes place at headquarters under the chairmanship of the Commandant. He, of course, understands how to turn such a meeting into a spectacle. A gallery has been built, which is always full of spectators. I'm compelled to take part in the discussions, though they fill me with disgust. In any case, you will certainly be invited to the meeting. If you follow my plan today and behave accordingly, the invitation will become an emphatic request. But should you for some inexplicable reason still not be invited, you must make sure you request an invitation. Then you'll receive one without question. Now, tomorrow you are sitting with the women in the Commandant's box. With frequent upward glances he reassures himself that you are there. After various trivial and ridiculous agenda items designed for the spectators—mostly harbor construction—always harbor construction—the judicial process comes up for discussion. If it's not raised by the Commandant himself or does not occur soon enough, I'll make sure that it comes up. I'll stand up and report on today's execution. Really briefly—just the report. Such a report is not really customary; however, I'll do it, nonetheless. The Commandant thanks me, as always, with a friendly smile. And now he cannot restrain himself. He seizes this excellent opportunity. 'The report of the execution,' he'll say, or something like that, 'has just been given. I would like to add to this report only the fact that this particular execution was attended by the great explorer whose visit confers such extraordinary honor on our colony, as you all know. Even the significance of our meeting today has been increased by his presence. Should we not now ask this great explorer for his appraisal of the execution based on old customs and of the process which preceded it?' Of course, there is the noise of applause everywhere, universal agreement. And I'm louder than anyone. The Commandant bows before you and says, 'Then in everyone's name, I'm putting the question to you.' And now you step up to the railing. Place your hands where everyone can see them. Otherwise the ladies will grab them and play with your fingers. And now finally come your remarks. I don't know how I'll bear the tension up to then. In your speech you mustn't hold back. Let truth resound. Lean over the railing and shout it out—yes, yes, roar your opinion at the Commandant, your unshakeable opinion. But perhaps you don't want to do that. It doesn't suit your character. Perhaps in your country people behave differently in such situations. That's all right. That's perfectly satisfactory. Don't stand up at all. Just say a couple of words. Whisper them so that only the officials underneath you can just hear them. That's enough. You don't even have to say anything at all about the lack of attendance at the execution or about the squeaky wheel, the torn strap, the disgusting felt. No. I'll take over all further details, and, believe me, if my speech doesn't chase him out of the room, it will force him to his knees, so he'll have to admit it: 'Old Commandant, I bow down before you.' That's my plan. Do you want to help me carry it out? But, of course, you want to. More than that—you have to."

And the officer gripped the traveler by both arms and looked at him, breathing heavily into his face. He had yelled the last sentences so loudly that even the Soldier and the Condemned Man were paying attention. Although they couldn't understand a thing, they stopped eating and looked over at the Traveler, still chewing.

From the start the Traveler had had no doubts about the answer he must give. He had experienced too much in his life to be able to waver here. Basically he was honest and unafraid. Still, with the Soldier and the Condemned Man looking at him, he hesitated a moment. But finally he said, as he had to, "No." The Officer's eyes blinked several times, but he did not take his eyes off the Traveler. "Would you like an explanation?" asked the Traveler. The Officer nodded dumbly. "I am opposed to this procedure," said the Traveler. "Even before you took me into your confidence—and, of course, I will never abuse your confidence under any circumstances—I was already thinking about whether I was entitled to intervene against this procedure and whether my intervention could have the smallest chance of success. And if that was the case, it was clear to me whom I had to turn to first of all—naturally, to the Commandant. You clarified the issue for me even more, but without reinforcing my decision in any way—quite the reverse. I find your conviction genuinely moving, even if it cannot deter me."

The Officer remained quiet, turned toward the machine, grabbed one of the brass rods, and then, leaning back a little, looked up at the inscriber, as if he was checking that everything was in order. The Soldier and the Condemned Man seemed to have made friends with each other. The Condemned Man was making signs to the Soldier, although, given the tight straps on him, this was difficult for him to do. The Soldier was leaning into him. The Condemned Man whispered something to him, and the Soldier nodded. The Traveler went over to the Officer and said, "You don't yet know what I'll do. Yes, I will tell the Commandant my opinion of the procedure—not in a meeting, but in private. In addition, I won't stay here long enough to be able to get called in to some meeting or other. Early tomorrow morning I leave, or at least I go on board ship." It didn't look as if the Officer had been listening. "So the process has not convinced you," he said to himself, smiling the way an old man smiles over the silliness of a child, concealing his own true thoughts behind that smile.

"Well then, it's time," he said finally and suddenly looked at the Traveler with bright eyes which contained some sort of demand, some appeal for participation. "Time for what?" asked the Traveler uneasily. But there was no answer.

"You are free," the Officer told the Condemned Man in his own language. At first the man did not believe him. "You are free now," said the Officer. For the first time the face of the Condemned Man showed signs of real life. Was it the truth? Was it only the Officer's mood, which could change? Had the foreign Traveler brought him a reprieve? What was it? That's what the man's face seemed to be asking. But not for long. Whatever the case might be, if he could he wanted to be truly free, and he began to shake back and forth, as much as the harrow permitted.

"You're tearing my straps," cried the Officer. "Be still! We'll undo them right away." And, giving a signal to the Soldier, he set to work with him. The Condemned Man said nothing and smiled slightly to himself. He turned his face to the Officer and then to the Soldier and then back again, without ignoring the Traveler.

"Pull him out," the Officer ordered the Soldier. This process required a certain amount of care because of the harrow. The Condemned Man already had a few small wounds on his back, thanks to his own impatience.

From this point on, however, the Officer paid him hardly any attention. He went up to the Traveler, pulled out the small leather folder once more, leafed through it, finally found the sheet he was looking for, and showed it to the Traveler. "Read that," he said. "I can't," said the Traveler. "I've already told you I can't read these pages." "But take a close look at the page," said the Officer, and moved up right next to the Traveler in order to read with him. When that didn't help, he raised his little finger high up over the paper, as if the page must not be touched under any circumstances, so that using this he might make the task of reading easier for the Traveler. The Traveler also made an effort so that at least he could satisfy the Officer, but it was impossible for him. Then the Officer began to spell out the inscription and then read out once again the joined up letters. "'Be just!' it states," he said. "Now you can read it." The Traveler bent so low over the paper that the Officer, afraid that he might touch it, moved it further away. The Traveler didn't say anything more, but it was clear that he was still unable to read anything. "'Be just!' it says," the Officer remarked once again.

"That could be," said the Traveler. "I do believe that's written there." "Good," said the Officer, at least partially satisfied. He climbed up the ladder, holding the paper. With great care he set the page in the inscriber and appeared to rotate the gear mechanism completely around. This was very tiring work. It must have required him to deal with extremely small wheels. He had to inspect the gears so closely that sometimes his head disappeared completely into the inscriber.

The Traveler followed this work from below without looking away. His neck grew stiff, and his eyes found the sunlight pouring down from the sky painful. The Soldier and the Condemned Man were keeping each other busy. With the tip of his bayonet the Soldier pulled out the Condemned Man's shirt and trousers which were lying in the hole. The shirt was horribly dirty, and the Condemned Man washed it in the bucket of water. When he was putting on his shirt and trousers, the Soldier and the Condemned Man had to laugh out loud, for the pieces of clothing were cut in two up the back. Perhaps the Condemned Man thought that it was his duty to amuse the Soldier. In his ripped-up clothes he circled around the Soldier, who crouched down on the ground, laughed, and slapped his knees. But they restrained themselves out of consideration for the two gentlemen present.

When the Officer was finally finished up on the machine, with a smile he looked over the whole thing and all its parts one more time, and this time closed the cover of the inscriber, which had been open up to this point. He climbed down, looked into the hole and then at the Condemned Man, observed with satisfaction that he had pulled out his clothes, then went to the bucket of water to wash his hands, recognized too late that it was disgustingly dirty, and was upset that now he couldn't wash his hands. Finally he pushed them into the sand. This option didn't satisfy him, but he had to do what he could in the circumstances. Then he stood up and began to unbutton the coat of his uniform. As he did this, the two lady's handkerchiefs, which he had pushed into the back of his collar, fell into his hands. "Here you have your handkerchiefs," he said and threw them over to the Condemned Man. And to the Traveler he said by way of an explanation, "Presents from the ladies."

In spite of the obvious speed with which he took off the coat of his uniform and then undressed himself completely, he handled each piece of clothing very carefully, even running his fingers over the silver braids on his tunic with special care and shaking a tassel into place. But in great contrast to this care, as soon he was finished handling an article of clothing, he immediately flung it angrily into the hole. The last items he had left were his short sword and its harness. He pulled the sword out of its scabbard, broke it in pieces, gathered up everything—the pieces of the sword, the scabbard, and the harness—and threw them away so forcefully that they rattled against each other down in the pit.

Now he stood there naked. The Traveler bit his lip and said nothing. For he was aware what would happen, but he had no right to hinder the Officer in any way. If the judicial process to which the officer clung was really so close to the point of being canceled—perhaps as a result of the intervention of the Traveler, something to which he for his part felt duty-bound—then the Officer was now acting in a completely correct manner. In his place, the Traveler would not have acted any differently.

The Soldier and the Condemned Man at first didn't understand a thing. To begin with they didn't look, not even once. The Condemned Man was extremely happy to get the handkerchiefs back, but he couldn't enjoy them very long, for the Soldier snatched them from him with a quick grab, which he had not anticipated. The Condemned Man then tried to pull the handkerchiefs out from the Soldier's belt, where he had put them for safe keeping, but the Soldier was too wary. So they were fighting, half in jest. Only when the Officer was fully naked did they start to pay attention. The Condemned Man especially seemed to be struck by a premonition of some sort of significant transformation. What had happened to him was now taking place with the Officer. Perhaps this time the procedure would play itself out to its conclusion. The foreign Traveler had probably given the order. So that was revenge. Without having suffered all the way to the end himself, nonetheless he would be completely revenged. A wide, silent laugh now appeared on his face and did not go away.

The Officer, however, had turned towards the machine. If earlier on it had already become clear that he understood the machine thoroughly, one might well get alarmed now at the way he handled it and how it obeyed. He only had to bring his hand near the harrow for it to rise and sink several times, until it had reached the correct position to make room for him. He only had to grasp the bed by the edges, and it already began to quiver. The stump of felt moved up to his mouth. One could see how the Officer really didn't want to accept it, but his hesitation was only momentary—he immediately submitted and took it in. Everything was ready, except that the straps still hung down on the sides. But they were clearly unnecessary. The Officer did not have to be strapped down. When the Condemned Man saw the loose straps, he thought the execution would be incomplete unless they were fastened. He waved eagerly to the Soldier, and they ran over to strap in the Officer. The latter had already stuck out his foot to kick the crank designed to set the inscriber in motion. Then he saw the two men coming. So he pulled his foot back and let himself be strapped in. But now he could no longer reach the crank. Neither the Soldier nor the Condemned Man would find it, and the Traveler was determined not to touch it. But that was unnecessary. Hardly were the straps attached when the machine already started working. The bed quivered, the needles danced on his skin, and the harrow swung up and down. The Traveler had already been staring for some time before he remembered that a wheel in the inscriber was supposed to squeak. But everything was quiet, without the slightest audible hum.

Because of its silent working, the machine did not really attract attention. The Traveler looked over at the Soldier and the Condemned Man. The Condemned Man was the livelier of the two. Everything in the machine interested him. At times he bent down—at other times he stretched up, all the time pointing with his forefinger in order to show something to the Soldier. For the Traveler it was embarrassing. He was determined to remain here until the end, but he could no longer endure the sight of the two men. "Go home," he said. The Soldier might have been ready to do that, but the Condemned Man took the order as a direct punishment. With his hands folded he begged and pleaded to be allowed to stay there. And when the Traveler shook his head and was unwilling to give in, he even knelt down. Seeing that orders were of no help here, the Traveler wanted to go over and chase the two away.

Then he heard a noise from up in the inscriber. He looked up. So was the gear wheel going out of alignment? But it was something else. The lid on the inscriber was lifting up slowly. Then it fell completely open. The teeth of a cog wheel were exposed and lifted up. Soon the entire wheel appeared. It was as if some huge force was compressing the inscriber, so that there was no longer sufficient room for this wheel. The wheel rolled all the way to the edge of the inscriber, fell down, rolled upright a bit in the sand, and then fell over and lay still. But already up on the inscriber another gear wheel was moving upwards. Several others followed—large ones, small ones, ones hard to distinguish. With each of them the same thing happened. One kept thinking that now the inscriber must surely be empty, but then a new cluster with lots of parts would move up, fall down, roll in the sand, and lie still. With all this going on, the Condemned Man totally forgot the Traveler's order. The gear wheels completely delighted him. He kept wanting to grab one, and at the same time he was urging the Soldier to help him. But he kept pulling his hand back startled, for immediately another wheel followed, which, at least in its initial rolling, surprised him.

The Traveler, by contrast, was very upset. Obviously the machine was breaking up. Its quiet operation had been an illusion. He felt as if he had to look after the Officer, now that the latter could no longer look after himself. But while the falling gear wheels were claiming all his attention, he had neglected to look at the rest of the machine. However, when he now bent over the harrow, once the last gear wheel had left the inscriber, he had a new, even more unpleasant surprise. The harrow was not writing but only stabbing, and the bed was not rolling the body, but lifting it, quivering, up into the needles. The Traveler wanted to reach in to stop the whole thing, if possible. This was not the torture the Officer wished to attain. It was murder, pure and simple. He stretched out his hands. But at that point the harrow was already moving upwards and to the side, with the skewered body—just as it did in other cases, but only in the twelfth hour. Blood flowed out in hundreds of streams, not mixed with water—the water tubes had also failed to work this time. Then one last thing went wrong: the body would not come loose from the needles. Its blood streamed out, but it hung over the pit without falling. The harrow wanted to move back to its original position, but, as if it realized that it could not free itself of its load, it remained over the hole.

"Help," the Traveler yelled out to the Soldier and the Condemned Man and grabbed the Officer's feet. He wanted to push against the feet himself and have the two others grab the Officer's head from the other side, so he could be slowly taken off the needles. But now the two men could not make up their mind whether to come or not. The Condemned Man turned away at once. The Traveler had to go over to him and drag him to the Officer's head by force. At this point, almost against his will, he looked at the face of the corpse. It was as it had been in his life. He could discover no sign of the promised transfiguration. What all the others had found in the machine, the Officer had not. His lips were pressed firmly together, his eyes were open and looked as they had when he was alive, his gaze was calm and convinced. The tip of a large iron needle had gone through his forehead.

* * * * *

As the Traveler, with the Soldier and the Condemned Man behind him, came to the first houses in the colony, the Soldier pointed to one and said, "That's the tea house."

On the ground floor of one of the houses was a deep, low room, like a cave, with smoke-covered walls and ceiling. On the street side it was open along its full width. Although there was little difference between the tea house and the rest of the houses in the colony, which were all very dilapidated, except for the

Commandant's palatial structure, the Traveler was struck by the impression of historical memory, and he felt the power of earlier times. Followed by his companions, he walked closer, going between the unoccupied tables, which stood in the street in front of the tea house, and took a breath of the cool, stuffy air which came from inside. "The old man is buried here," said the soldier; "a place in the cemetery was denied him by the chaplain. For a long time people were undecided where they should bury him. Finally they buried him here. Of course, the Officer explained none of that to you, for naturally he was the one most ashamed about it. A few times he even tried to dig up the old man at night, but he was always chased off." "Where is the grave?" asked the Traveler, who could not believe the Soldier. Instantly both men, the Soldier and the Condemned Man, ran in front of him and with hands outstretched pointed to the place where the grave was located. They led the Traveler to the back wall, where guests were sitting at a few tables. They were presumably dock workers, strong men with short, shiny, black beards. None of them wore coats, and their shirts were torn. They were poor, oppressed people. As the Traveler came closer, a few got up, leaned against the wall, and looked at him. A whisper went up around the Traveler—"It's a foreigner. He wants to look at the grave." They pushed one of the tables aside, under which there was a real grave stone. It was a simple stone, low enough for it to remain hidden under a table. It bore an inscription in very small letters. In order to read it the Traveler had to kneel down. It read, "Here rests the Old Commandant. His followers, who are now not permitted to have a name, buried him in this grave and erected this stone. There exists a prophecy that the Commandant will rise again after a certain number of years and from this house will lead his followers to a re-conquest of the colony. Have faith and wait!"

When the Traveler had read it and got up, he saw the men standing around him and smiling, as if they had read the inscription with him, found it ridiculous, and were asking him to share their opinion. The Traveler acted as if he hadn't noticed, distributed some coins among them, waited until the table was pushed back over the grave, left the tea house, and went to the harbor.

In the tea house the Soldier and the Condemned Man had come across some people they knew who detained them. However, they must have broken free of them soon, because by the time the Traveler found himself in the middle of a long staircase which led to the boats, they were already running after him. They probably wanted to force the Traveler at the last minute to take them with him. While the Traveler was haggling at the bottom of the stairs with a sailor about his passage out to the steamer, the two men were racing down the steps in silence, for they didn't dare cry out. But as they reached the bottom, the Traveler was already in the boat, and the sailor at once cast off from shore. They could still have jumped into the boat, but the Traveler picked up a heavy knotted rope from the boat bottom, threatened them with it, and thus prevented them from jumping in.

THE SIGNAL-MAN

Charles Dickens

"Halloa! Below there!"

When he heard a voice thus calling to him, he was standing at the door of his box, with a flag in his hand, furled round its short pole. One would have thought, considering the nature of the ground, that he could not have doubted from what quarter the voice came; but instead of looking up to where I stood on the top of the steep cutting nearly over his head, he turned himself about, and looked down the Line. There was something remarkable in his manner of doing so, though I could not have said for my life what. But I know it was remarkable enough to attract my notice, even though his figure was foreshortened and shadowed, down in the deep trench, and mine was high above him, so steeped in the glow of an angry sunset, that I had shaded my eyes with my hand before I saw him at all.

"Halloa! Below!"

From looking down the Line, he turned himself about again, and, raising his eyes, saw my figure high above him.

"Is there any path by which I can come down and speak to you?"

He looked up at me without replying, and I looked down at him without pressing him too soon with a repetition of my idle question. Just then there came a vague vibration in the earth and air, quickly changing into a violent pulsation, and an oncoming rush that caused me to start back, as though it had force to draw me down. When such vapour as rose to my height from this rapid train had passed me, and was skimming away over the landscape, I looked down again, and saw him refurling the flag he had shown while the train went by.

I repeated my inquiry. After a pause, during which he seemed to regard me with fixed attention, he motioned with his rolled-up flag towards a point on my level, some two or three hundred yards distant. I called down to him, "All right!" and made for that point. There, by dint of looking closely about me, I found a rough zigzag descending path notched out, which I followed.

The cutting was extremely deep, and unusually precipitate. It was made through a clammy stone, that became oozier and wetter as I went down. For these reasons, I found the way long enough to give me time to recall a singular air of reluctance or compulsion with which he had pointed out the path.

When I came down low enough upon the zigzag descent to see him again,

I saw that he was standing between the rails on the way by which the train had lately passed, in an attitude as if he were waiting for me to appear. He had his left hand at his chin, and that left elbow rested on his right hand, crossed over his breast. His attitude was one of such expectation and watchfulness that I stopped a moment, wondering at it.

I resumed my downward way, and stepping out upon the level of the railroad, and drawing nearer to him, saw that he was a dark, sallow man, with a dark beard and rather heavy eyebrows. His post was in as solitary and dismal a place as ever I saw. On either side, a dripping-wet wall of jagged stone, excluding all view but a strip of sky; the perspective one way only a crooked prolongation of this great dungeon; the shorter perspective in the other direction terminating in a gloomy red light, and the gloomier entrance to a black tunnel, in whose massive architecture there was a barbarous, depressing, and forbidding air. So little sunlight ever found its way to this spot, that it had an earthy, deadly smell; and so much cold wind rushed through it, that it struck chill to me, as if I had left the natural world.

Before he stirred, I was near enough to him to have touched him. Not even then removing his eyes from mine, he stepped back one step, and lifted his hand. This was a lonesome post to occupy (I said), and it had riveted my attention when I looked down from up yonder. A visitor was a rarity, I should suppose; not an unwelcome rarity, I hoped? In me, he merely saw a man who had been shut up within narrow limits all his life, and who, being at last set free, had a newly-awakened interest in these great works. To such purpose I spoke to him; but I am far from sure of the terms I used; for, besides that I am not happy in opening any conversation, there was something in the man that daunted me.

He directed a most curious look towards the red light near the tunnel's mouth, and looked all about it, as if something were missing from it, and then looked at me.

That light was part of his charge? Was it not?

He answered in a low voice: "Don't you know it is?"

The monstrous thought came into my mind, as I perused the fixed eyes and the saturnine face, that this was a spirit, not a man. I have speculated since, whether there may have been infection in his mind.

In my turn, I stepped back. But in making the action, I detected in his eyes some latent fear of me. This put the monstrous thought to flight.

"You look at me," I said, forcing a smile, "as if you had a dread of me."

"I was doubtful," he returned, "whether I had seen you before."

"Where?"

He pointed to the red light he had looked at.

"There?" I said.

Intently watchful of me, he replied (but without sound), "Yes."

"My good fellow, what should I do there? However, be that as it may, I never was there, you may swear."

"I think I may," he rejoined.

"Yes; I am sure I may."

His manner cleared, like my own. He replied to my remarks with readiness, and in well-chosen words. Had he much to do there? Yes; that was to say, he had enough responsibility to bear; but exactness and watchfulness were what was required of him, and of actual work—manual labour—he had next to none. To change that signal, to trim those lights, and to turn this iron handle now and then, was all he had to do under that head. Regarding those many long and lonely hours of which I seemed to make so much, he could only say that the routine of his life had shaped itself into that form, and he had grown used to it. He had taught himself a language down here,—if only to know it by sight, and to have formed his own crude ideas of its pronunciation, could be called learning it. He had also worked at fractions and decimals, and tried a little algebra; but he was, and had been as a boy, a poor hand at figures. Was it necessary for him when on duty always to remain in that channel of damp air, and could he never rise into the sunshine from between those high stone walls? Why, that depended upon times and circumstances. Under some conditions there would be less upon the Line than under others, and the same held good as to certain hours of the day and night. In bright weather, he did choose occasions for getting a little above these lower shadows; but, being at all times liable to be called by his electric bell, and at such times listening for it with redoubled anxiety, the relief was less than I would suppose.

He took me into his box, where there was a fire, a desk for an official book in which he had to make certain entries, a telegraphic instrument with its dial, face, and needles, and the little bell of which he had spoken. On my trusting that he would excuse the remark that he had been well educated, and (I hoped I might say without offence) perhaps educated above that station, he observed that instances of slight incongruity in such wise would rarely be found wanting among large bodies of men; that he had heard it was so in workhouses, in the police force, even in that last desperate resource, the army; and that he knew it was so, more or less, in any great railway staff. He had been, when young (if I could believe it, sitting in that hut,—he scarcely could), a student of natural philosophy, and had attended lectures; but he had run wild, misused his opportunities, gone down, and never risen again. He had no complaint to offer about that. He had made his bed, and he lay upon it. It was far too late to make another.

All that I have here condensed he said in a quiet manner, with his grave, dark regards divided between me and the fire. He threw in the word, "Sir," from time to time, and especially when he referred to his youth,—as though to request me to understand that he claimed to be nothing but what I found him. He was several times interrupted by the little bell, and had to read off messages, and send replies. Once he had to stand without the door, and display a flag as a train passed, and make some verbal communication to the driver. In the discharge of his duties, I observed him to be remarkably exact and vigilant, breaking off his discourse at a syllable, and remaining silent until what he had to do was done.

In a word, I should have set this man down as one of the safest of men to be employed in that capacity, but for the circumstance that while he was speaking to me he twice broke off with a fallen colour, turned his face towards the little bell when it did not ring, opened the door of the hut (which was kept shut to exclude the unhealthy damp), and looked out towards the red light near the mouth of the tunnel. On both of those occasions, he came back to the fire with the inexplicable air upon him which I had remarked, without being able to define, when we were so far asunder.

Said I, when I rose to leave him, "You almost make me think that I have met with a contented man."

(I am afraid I must acknowledge that I said it to lead him on.)

"I believe I used to be so," he rejoined, in the low voice in which he had first spoken; "but I am troubled, sir, I am troubled."

He would have recalled the words if he could. He had said them, however, and I took them up quickly.

"With what? What is your trouble?"

"It is very difficult to impart, sir. It is very, very difficult to speak of. If ever you make me another visit, I will try to tell you."

"But I expressly intend to make you another visit. Say, when shall it be?"

"I go off early in the morning, and I shall be on again at ten to-morrow night, sir."

"I will come at eleven."

He thanked me, and went out at the door with me. "I'll show my white light, sir," he said, in his peculiar low voice, "till you have found the way up. When you have found it, don't call out! And when you are at the top, don't call out!"

His manner seemed to make the place strike colder to me, but I said no more than, "Very well."

"And when you come down to-morrow night, don't call out! Let me ask you a parting question. What made you cry, 'Halloa! Below there!' to-night?"

"Heaven knows," said I. "I cried something to that effect—"

"Not to that effect, sir. Those were the very words. I know them well."

"Admit those were the very words. I said them, no doubt, because I saw you below."

"For no other reason?"

"What other reason could I possibly have?"

"You had no feeling that they were conveyed to you in any supernatural way?"

"No."

He wished me good-night, and held up his light. I walked by the side of the down line of rails (with a very disagreeable sensation of a train coming behind me) until I found the path. It was easier to mount than to descend, and I got back to my inn without any adventure.

Punctual to my appointment, I placed my foot on the first notch of the zigzag next night, as the distant clocks were striking eleven. He was waiting for me at the bottom, with his white light on. "I have not called out," I said, when we came close together; "may I speak now?"

"By all means, sir."

"Good-night, then, and here's my hand."

"Good-night, sir, and here's mine."

With that we walked side by side to his box, entered it, closed the door, and sat down by the fire.

"I have made up my mind, sir," he began, bending forward as soon as we were seated, and speaking in a tone but a little above a whisper, "that you shall not have to ask me twice what troubles me. I took you for some one else yesterday evening. That troubles me."

"That mistake?"

"No. That some one else."

"Who is it?"

"I don't know."

"Like me?"

"I don't know. I never saw the face. The left arm is across the face, and the right arm is waved,—violently waved. This way."

I followed his action with my eyes, and it was the action of an arm gesticulating, with the utmost passion and vehemence, "For God's sake, clear the way!"

"One moonlight night," said the man, "I was sitting here, when I heard a voice cry, 'Halloa! Below there!' I started up, looked from that door, and saw this some one else standing by the red light near the tunnel, waving as I just now showed you. The voice seemed hoarse with shouting, and it cried, 'Look out! Look out!' And then again, 'Halloa! Below there! Look out!' I caught up my lamp, turned it on red, and ran towards the figure, calling, 'What's wrong? What has happened? Where?' It stood just outside the blackness of the tunnel. I advanced so close upon it that I wondered at its keeping the sleeve across its eyes. I ran right up at it, and had my hand stretched out to pull the sleeve away, when it was gone."

"Into the tunnel?" said I.

"No. I ran on into the tunnel, five hundred yards. I stopped, and held my lamp above my head, and saw the figures of the measured distance, and saw the wet stains stealing down the walls and trickling through the arch. I ran out again faster than I had run in (for I had a mortal abhorrence of the place upon me), and I looked all round the red light with my own red light, and I went up the iron ladder to the gallery atop of it, and I came down again, and ran back here. I telegraphed both ways, 'An alarm has been given. Is anything wrong?' The answer came back, both ways, 'All well.'"

Resisting the slow touch of a frozen finger tracing out my spine, I showed him how that this figure must be a deception of his sense of sight; and how that figures, originating in disease of the delicate nerves that minister to the functions of the eye, were known to have often troubled patients, some of whom had become conscious of the nature of their affliction, and had even proved it by experiments upon themselves.

"As to an imaginary cry," said I, "do but listen for a moment to the wind in this unnatural valley while we speak so low, and to the wild harp it makes of the telegraph wires."

That was all very well, he returned, after we had sat listening for a while, and he ought to know something of the wind and the wires,—he who so often passed long winter nights there, alone and watching. But he would beg to remark that he had not finished.

I asked his pardon, and he slowly added these words, touching my arm:

"Within six hours after the Appearance, the memorable accident on this Line happened, and within ten hours the dead and wounded were brought along through the tunnel over the spot where the figure had stood."

A disagreeable shudder crept over me, but I did my best against it. It was not to be denied, I rejoined, that this was a remarkable coincidence, calculated deeply to impress his mind. But it was unquestionable that remarkable coincidences did continually occur, and they must be taken into account in dealing with such a subject. Though to be sure I must admit, I added (for I thought I saw that he was going to bring the objection to bear upon me), men of common sense did not allow much for coincidences in making the ordinary calculations of life.

He again begged to remark that he had not finished.

I again begged his pardon for being betrayed into interruptions.

"This," he said, again laying his hand upon my arm, and glancing over his shoulder with hollow eyes, "was just a year ago. Six or seven months passed, and I had recovered from the surprise and shock, when one morning, as the day was breaking, I, standing at the door, looked towards the red light, and saw the spectre again." He stopped, with a fixed look at me.

"Did it cry out?"

"No. It was silent."

"Did it wave its arm?"

"No. It leaned against the shaft of the light, with both hands before the face. Like this."

Once more I followed his action with my eyes. It was an action of mourning. I have seen such an attitude in stone figures on tombs.

"Did you go up to it?"

"I came in and sat down, partly to collect my thoughts, partly because it had turned me faint. When I went to the door again, daylight was above me, and the ghost was gone."

"But nothing followed? Nothing came of this?"

He touched me on the arm with his forefinger twice or thrice giving a ghastly nod each time:

"That very day, as a train came out of the tunnel, I noticed, at a carriage window on my side, what looked like a confusion of hands and heads, and something waved. I saw it just in time to signal the driver, Stop! He shut off, and put his brake on, but the train drifted past here a hundred and fifty yards or more. I ran after it, and, as I went along, heard terrible screams and cries. A beautiful young lady had died instantaneously in one of the compartments, and was brought in here, and laid down on this floor between us."

Involuntarily I pushed my chair back, as I looked from the boards at which he pointed to himself.

"True, sir. True. Precisely as it happened, so I tell it you."

I could think of nothing to say, to any purpose, and my mouth was very dry. The wind and the wires took up the story with a long lamenting wail.

He resumed. "Now, sir, mark this, and judge how my mind is troubled. The spectre came back a week ago. Ever since, it has been there, now and again, by fits and starts."

"At the light?"

"At the Danger-light."

"What does it seem to do?"

He repeated, if possible with increased passion and vehemence, that former gesticulation of, "For God's sake, clear the way!"

Then he went on. "I have no peace or rest for it. It calls to me, for many minutes together, in an agonised manner, 'Below there! Look out! Look out!' It stands waving to me. It rings my little bell—"

I caught at that. "Did it ring your bell yesterday evening when I was here, and you went to the door?"

"Twice."

"Why, see," said I, "how your imagination misleads you. My eyes were on the bell, and my ears were open to the bell, and if I am a living man, it did *not* ring at those times. No, nor at any other time, except when it was rung in the natural course of physical things by the station communicating with you."

He shook his head. "I have never made a mistake as to that yet, sir. I have never confused the spectre's ring with the man's. The ghost's ring is a strange vibration in the bell that it derives from nothing else, and I have not asserted that the bell stirs to the eye. I don't wonder that you failed to hear it. But I heard it."

"And did the spectre seem to be there, when you looked out?"

"It *was* there."

"Both times?"

He repeated firmly: "Both times."

"Will you come to the door with me, and look for it now?"

He bit his under lip as though he were somewhat unwilling, but arose. I opened the door, and stood on the step, while he stood in the doorway. There was the Danger-light. There was the dismal mouth of the tunnel. There were the high, wet stone walls of the cutting. There were the stars above them.

"Do you see it?" I asked him, taking particular note of his face. His eyes were prominent and strained, but not very much more so, perhaps, than my own had been when I had directed them earnestly towards the same spot.

"No," he answered. "It is not there."

"Agreed," said I.

We went in again, shut the door, and resumed our seats. I was thinking how best to improve this advantage, if it might be called one, when he took up the conversation in such a matter-of-course way, so assuming that there could be no serious question of fact between us, that I felt myself placed in the weakest of positions.

"By this time you will fully understand, sir," he said, "that what troubles me so dreadfully is the question, What does the spectre mean?"

I was not sure, I told him, that I did fully understand.

"What is its warning against?" he said, ruminating, with his eyes on the fire, and only by times turning them on me. "What is the danger? Where is the danger? There is danger overhanging somewhere on the Line. Some dreadful calamity will happen. It is not to be doubted this third time, after what has gone before. But surely this is a cruel haunting of me. What can I do?"

He pulled out his handkerchief, and wiped the drops from his heated forehead.

"If I telegraph Danger, on either side of me, or on both, I can give no reason for it," he went on, wiping the palms of his hands. "I should get into trouble, and do no good. They would think I was mad. This is the way it would work,—Message: 'Danger! Take care!' Answer: 'What Danger? Where?' Message: 'Don't know. But, for God's sake, take care!' They would displace me. What else could they do?"

His pain of mind was most pitiable to see. It was the mental torture of a conscientious man, oppressed beyond endurance by an unintelligible responsibility involving life.

"When it first stood under the Danger-light," he went on, putting his dark hair back from his head, and drawing his hands outward across and across his temples in an extremity of feverish distress, "why not tell me where that accident was to happen,—if it must happen? Why not tell me how it could be averted,—if it could have been averted? When on its second coming it hid its face, why not tell me, instead, 'She is going to die. Let them keep her at home'? If it came, on those two occasions, only to show me that its warnings were true, and so to prepare me for the third, why not warn me plainly now? And I, Lord help me! A mere poor signal-man on this solitary station! Why not go to somebody with credit to be believed, and power to act?"

When I saw him in this state, I saw that for the poor man's sake, as well as for the public safety, what I had to do for the time was to compose his mind. Therefore, setting aside all question of reality or unreality between us, I represented to him that whoever thoroughly discharged his duty must do well, and that at least it was his comfort that he understood his duty, though he did not understand these confounding Appearances. In this effort I succeeded far better than in the attempt to reason him out of his conviction. He became calm; the occupations incidental to his post as the night advanced began to make larger demands on his attention: and I left him at two in the morning. I had offered to stay through the night, but he would not hear of it.

That I more than once looked back at the red light as I ascended the pathway, that I did not like the red light, and that I should have slept but poorly if my bed had been under it, I see no reason to conceal. Nor did I like the two sequences of the accident and the dead girl. I see no reason to conceal that either.

But what ran most in my thoughts was the consideration how ought I to act, having become the recipient of this disclosure? I had proved the man to be intelligent, vigilant, painstaking, and exact; but how long might he remain so, in his state of mind? Though in a subordinate position, still he held a most important trust, and would I (for instance) like to stake my own life on the chances of his continuing to execute it with precision?

Unable to overcome a feeling that there would be something treacherous in my communicating what he had told me to his superiors in the Company, without first being plain with himself and proposing a middle course to him, I ultimately resolved to offer to accompany him (otherwise keeping his secret for the present) to the wisest medical practitioner we could hear of in those parts, and to take his opinion. A change in his time of duty would come round next night, he had apprised me, and he would be off an hour or two after sunrise, and on again soon after sunset. I had appointed to return accordingly.

Next evening was a lovely evening, and I walked out early to enjoy it. The sun was not yet quite down when I traversed the field-path near the top of the deep cutting. I would extend my walk for an hour, I said to myself, half an hour on and half an hour back, and it would then be time to go to my signal-man's box.

Before pursuing my stroll, I stepped to the brink, and mechanically looked down, from the point from which I had first seen him. I cannot describe the thrill that seized upon me, when, close at the mouth of the tunnel, I saw the appearance of a man, with his left sleeve across his eyes, passionately waving his right arm.

The nameless horror that oppressed me passed in a moment, for in a moment I saw that this appearance of a man was a man indeed, and that there was a little group of other men, standing at a short distance, to whom he seemed to be rehearsing the gesture he made. The Danger-light was not yet lighted. Against its shaft, a little low hut, entirely new to me, had been made of some wooden supports and tarpaulin. It looked no bigger than a bed.

With an irresistible sense that something was wrong,—with a flashing self-reproachful fear that fatal mischief had come of my leaving the man there, and causing no one to be sent to overlook or correct what he did,—I descended the notched path with all the speed I could make.

"What is the matter?" I asked the men.

"Signal-man killed this morning, sir."

"Not the man belonging to that box?"

"Yes, sir."

"Not the man I know?"

"You will recognise him, sir, if you knew him," said the man who spoke for the others, solemnly uncovering his own head, and raising an end of the tarpaulin, "for his face is quite composed."

"O, how did this happen, how did this happen?" I asked, turning from one to another as the hut closed in again.

"He was cut down by an engine, sir. No man in England knew his work better. But somehow he was not clear of the outer rail. It was just at broad day. He had struck the light, and had the lamp in his hand. As the engine came out of the tunnel, his back was towards her, and she cut him down. That man drove her, and was showing how it happened. Show the gentleman, Tom."

The man, who wore a rough dark dress, stepped back to his former place at the mouth of the tunnel.

"Coming round the curve in the tunnel, sir," he said, "I saw him at the end, like as if I saw him down a perspective-glass. There was no time to check speed, and I knew him to be very careful. As he didn't seem to take heed of the whistle, I shut it off when we were running down upon him, and called to him as loud as I could call."

"What did you say?"

"I said, 'Below there! Look out! Look out! For God's sake, clear the way!'"

I started.

"Ah! it was a dreadful time, sir. I never left off calling to him. I put this arm before my eyes not to see, and I waved this arm to the last; but it was no use."

* * * * *

Without prolonging the narrative to dwell on any one of its curious circumstances more than on any other, I may, in closing it, point out the coincidence that the warning of the Engine-Driver included, not only the words which the unfortunate Signal-man had repeated to me as haunting him, but also the words which I myself—not he—had attached, and that only in my own mind, to the gesticulation he had imitated.

LOST HEARTS

M. R. James

It was, as far as I can ascertain, in September of the year 1811 that a post-chaise drew up before the door of Aswarby Hall, in the heart of Lincolnshire. The little boy who was the only passenger in the chaise, and who jumped out as soon as it had stopped, looked about him with the keenest curiosity during the short interval that elapsed between the ringing of the bell and the opening of the hall door. He saw a tall, square, red-brick house, built in the reign of Anne; a stone-pillared porch had been added in the purer classical style of 1790; the windows of the house were many, tall and narrow, with small panes and thick white woodwork. A pediment, pierced with a round window, crowned the front. There were wings to right and left, connected by curious glazed galleries, supported by colonnades, with the central block. These wings plainly contained the stables and offices of the house. Each was surmounted by an ornamental cupola with a gilded vane.

An evening light shone on the building, making the window-panes glow like so many fires. Away from the Hall in front stretched a flat park studded with oaks and fringed with firs, which stood out against the sky. The clock in the church-tower, buried in trees on the edge of the park, only its golden weather-cock catching the light, was striking six, and the sound came gently beating down the wind. It was altogether a pleasant impression, though tinged with the sort of melancholy appropriate to an evening in early autumn, that was conveyed to the mind of the boy who was standing in the porch waiting for the door to open to him.

The post-chaise had brought him from Warwickshire, where, some six months before, he had been left an orphan. Now, owing to the generous offer of his elderly cousin, Mr. Abney, he had come to live at Aswarby. The offer was unexpected, because all who knew anything of Mr. Abney looked upon him as a somewhat austere recluse, into whose steady-going household the advent of a small boy would import a new and, it seemed, incongruous element. The truth is that very little was known of Mr. Abney's pursuits or temper. The Professor of Greek at Cambridge had been heard to say that no one knew more of the religious beliefs of the later pagans than did the owner of Aswarby. Certainly his library contained all the then available books bearing on the Mysteries, the Orphic poems, the worship of Mithras, and the Neo-Platonists. In the marble-paved hall stood a fine group of Mithras slaying a bull, which had been imported from the Levant at great expense by the owner. He had contributed a description of it to the *Gentleman's Magazine*, and he had written a remarkable series of articles in the *Critical Museum* on the superstitions of the Romans of the Lower Empire. He was looked upon, in fine, as a man wrapped up in his books, and it was a matter of great surprise among his neighbours that he should ever have heard of his orphan cousin, Stephen Elliott, much more that he should have volunteered to make him an inmate of Aswarby Hall.

Whatever may have been expected by his neighbours, it is certain that Mr. Abney—the tall, the thin, the austere—seemed inclined to give his young cousin a kindly reception. The moment the front-door was opened he darted out of his study, rubbing his hands with delight.

"How are you, my boy?—how are you? How old are you?" said he—"that is, you are not too much tired, I hope, by your journey to eat your supper?"

"No, thank you, sir," said Master Elliott; "I am pretty well."

"That's a good lad," said Mr. Abney. "And how old are you, my boy?"

It seemed a little odd that he should have asked the question twice in the first two minutes of their acquaintance.

"I'm twelve years old next birthday, sir," said Stephen.

"And when is your birthday, my dear boy? Eleventh of September, eh? That's well—that's very well. Nearly a year hence, isn't it? I like—ha, ha!—I like to get these things down in my book. Sure it's twelve? Certain?"

"Yes, quite sure, sir."

"Well, well! Take him to Mrs. Bunch's room, Parkes, and let him have his tea—supper—whatever it is."

"Yes, sir," answered the staid Mr. Parkes; and conducted Stephen to the lower regions.

Mrs. Bunch was the most comfortable and human person whom Stephen had as yet met at Aswarby. She made him completely at home; they were great friends in a quarter of an hour: and great friends they remained. Mrs. Bunch had been born in the neighbourhood some fifty-five years before the date of Stephen's arrival, and her residence at the Hall was of twenty years' standing. Consequently, if anyone knew the ins and outs of the house and the district, Mrs. Bunch knew them; and she was by no means disinclined to communicate her information.

Certainly there were plenty of things about the Hall and the Hall gardens which Stephen, who was of an adventurous and inquiring turn, was anxious to have explained to him. "Who built the temple at the end of the laurel walk? Who was the old man whose picture hung on the staircase, sitting at a table, with a skull under his hand?" These and many similar points were cleared up by the resources of Mrs. Bunch's powerful intellect.

There were others, however, of which the explanations furnished were less satisfactory.

One November evening Stephen was sitting by the fire in the housekeeper's room reflecting on his surroundings.

"Is Mr. Abney a good man, and will he go to heaven?" he suddenly asked, with the peculiar confidence which children possess in the ability of their elders to settle these questions, the decision of which is believed to be reserved for other tribunals.

"Good?—bless the child!" said Mrs. Bunch. "Master's as kind a soul as ever I see! Didn't I never tell you of the little boy as he took in out of the street, as you may say, this seven years back? and the little girl, two years after I first come here?"

"No. Do tell me all about them, Mrs. Bunch—now, this minute!"

"Well," said Mrs. Bunch, "the little girl I don't seem to recollect so much about. I know master brought her back with him from his walk one day, and give orders to Mrs. Ellis, as was housekeeper then, as she should be took every care with. And the pore child hadn't no one belonging to her—she telled me so her own self—and here she lived with us a matter of three weeks it might be; and then, whether she were somethink of a gipsy in her blood or what not, but one morning she out of her bed afore any of us had opened a eye, and neither track nor yet trace of her have I set eyes on since. Master was wonderful put about, and had all the ponds dragged; but it's my belief she was had away by them gipsies, for there was singing round the house for as much as an hour the night she went, and Parkes, he declare as he heard them a-calling in the woods all that afternoon. Dear, dear! a hodd child she was, so silent in her ways and all, but I was wonderful taken up with her, so domesticated she was—surprising."

"And what about the little boy?" said Stephen.

"Ah, that pore boy!" sighed Mrs. Bunch. "He were a foreigner—Jevanny he called hisself—and he come a-tweaking his 'urdy-gurdy round and about the drive one winter day, and master 'ad him in that minute, and ast all about where he came from, and how old he was, and how he made his way, and where was his relatives, and all as kind as heart could wish. But it went the same way with him. They're a hunruly lot, them foreign nations, I do suppose, and he was off one fine morning just the same as the girl. Why he went and what he done was our question for as much as a year after; for he never took his 'urdy-gurdy, and there it lays on the shelf."

The remainder of the evening was spent by Stephen in miscellaneous cross-examination of Mrs. Bunch and in efforts to extract a tune from the hurdy-gurdy.

That night he had a curious dream. At the end of the passage at the top of the house, in which his bedroom was situated, there was an old disused bathroom. It was kept locked, but the upper half of the door was glazed, and, since the muslin curtains which used to hang there had long been gone, you could look in and see the lead-lined bath affixed to the wall on the right hand, with its head towards the window.

On the night of which I am speaking, Stephen Elliott found himself, as he thought, looking through the glazed door. The moon was shining through the window, and he was gazing at a figure which lay in the bath.

His description of what he saw reminds me of what I once beheld myself in the famous vaults of St. Michan's Church in Dublin, which possesses the horrid property of preserving corpses from decay for centuries. A figure inexpressibly thin and pathetic, of a dusty leaden colour, enveloped in a shroud-like garment, the thin lips crooked into a faint and dreadful smile, the hands pressed tightly over the region of the heart.

As he looked upon it, a distant, almost inaudible moan seemed to issue from its lips, and the arms began to stir. The terror of the sight forced Stephen backwards and he awoke to the fact that he was indeed standing on the cold boarded floor of the passage in the full light of the moon. With a courage which I do not think can be common among boys of his age, he went to the door of the bathroom to ascertain if the figure of his dreams were really there. It was not, and he went back to bed.

Mrs. Bunch was much impressed next morning by his story, and went so far as to replace the muslin curtain over the glazed door of the bathroom. Mr. Abney, moreover, to whom he confided his experiences at breakfast, was greatly interested and made notes of the matter in what he called "his book."

The spring equinox was approaching, as Mr. Abney frequently reminded his cousin, adding that this had been always considered by the ancients to be a critical time for the young: that Stephen would do well to take care of himself, and to shut his bedroom window at night; and that Censorinus had some valuable remarks on the subject. Two incidents that occurred about this time made an impression upon Stephen's mind.

The first was after an unusually uneasy and oppressed night that he had passed—though he could not recall any particular dream that he had had.

The following evening Mrs. Bunch was occupying herself in mending his nightgown.

"Gracious me, Master Stephen!" she broke forth rather irritably, "how do you manage to tear your nightdress all to flinders this way? Look here, sir, what trouble you do give to poor servants that have to darn and mend after you!"

There was indeed a most destructive and apparently wanton series of slits or scorings in the garment, which would undoubtedly require a skilful needle to make good. They were confined to the left side of the chest—long, parallel slits about six inches in length, some of them not quite piercing the texture of the linen. Stephen could only express his entire ignorance of their origin: he was sure they were not there the night before.

"But," he said, "Mrs. Bunch, they are just the same as the scratches on the outside of my bedroom door: and I'm sure I never had anything to do with making them."

Mrs. Bunch gazed at him open-mouthed, then snatched up a candle, departed hastily from the room, and was heard making her way upstairs. In a few minutes she came down.

"Well," she said, "Master Stephen, it's a funny thing to me how them marks and scratches can 'a' come there—too high up for any cat or dog to 'ave made 'em, much less a rat: for all the world like a Chinaman's finger-nails, as my uncle in the tea-trade used to tell us of when we was girls together. I wouldn't say nothing to master, not if I was you, Master Stephen, my dear; and just turn the key of the door when you go to your bed."

"I always do, Mrs. Bunch, as soon as I've said my prayers."

"Ah, that's a good child: always say your prayers, and then no one can't hurt you."

Herewith Mrs. Bunch addressed herself to mending the injured nightgown, with intervals of meditation, until bed-time. This was on a Friday night in March, 1812.

On the following evening the usual duet of Stephen and Mrs. Bunch was augmented by the sudden arrival of Mr. Parkes, the butler, who as a rule kept himself rather to himself in his own pantry. He did not see that Stephen was there: he was, moreover, flustered and less slow of speech than was his wont.

"Master may get up his own wine, if he likes, of an evening," was his first remark. "Either I do it in the daytime or not at all, Mrs. Bunch. I don't know what it may be: very like it's the rats, or the wind got into the cellars; but I'm not so young as I was, and I can't go through with it as I have done."

"Well, Mr. Parkes, you know it is a surprising place for the rats, is the Hall."

"I'm not denying that, Mrs. Bunch; and, to be sure, many a time I've heard the tale from the men in the shipyards about the rat that could speak. I never laid no confidence in that before; but tonight, if I'd demeaned myself to lay my ear to the door of the further bin, I could pretty much have heard what they was saying."

"Oh, there, Mr. Parkes, I've no patience with your fancies! Rats talking in the wine-cellar indeed!"

"Well, Mrs. Bunch, I've no wish to argue with you: all I say is, if you choose to go to the far bin, and lay your ear to the door, you may prove my words this minute."

"What nonsense you do talk, Mr. Parkes—not fit for children to listen to! Why, you'll be frightening Master Stephen there out of his wits."

"What! Master Stephen?" said Parkes, awaking to the consciousness of the boy's presence. "Master Stephen knows well enough when I'm a-playing a joke with you, Mrs. Bunch."

In fact, Master Stephen knew much too well to suppose that Mr. Parkes had in the first instance intended a joke. He was interested, not altogether pleasantly, in the situation; but all his questions were unsuccessful in inducing the butler to give any more detailed account of his experiences in the wine-cellar.

* * * * *

We have now arrived at March 24, 1812. It was a day of curious experiences for Stephen: a windy, noisy day, which filled the house and the gardens with a restless impression. As Stephen stood by the fence of the grounds, and looked out into the park, he felt as if an endless procession of unseen people were sweeping past him on the wind, borne on resistlessly and aimlessly, vainly striving to stop themselves, to catch at something that might arrest their flight and bring them once again into contact with the living world of which they had formed a part. After luncheon that day Mr. Abney said:

"Stephen, my boy, do you think you could manage to come to me tonight as late as eleven o'clock in my study? I shall be busy until that time, and I wish to show you something connected with your future life which it is most important that you should know. You are not to mention this matter to Mrs. Bunch nor to anyone else in the house; and you had better go to your room at the usual time."

Here was a new excitement added to life: Stephen eagerly grasped at the opportunity of sitting up till eleven o'clock. He looked in at the library door on his way upstairs that evening, and saw a brazier, which he had often noticed in the corner of the room, moved out before the fire; an old silver-gilt cup stood on the table, filled with red wine, and some written sheets of paper lay near it. Mr. Abney was sprinkling some incense on the brazier from a round silver box as Stephen passed, but did not seem to notice his step.

The wind had fallen, and there was a still night and a full moon. At about ten o'clock Stephen was standing at the open window of his bedroom, looking out over the country. Still as the night was, the mysterious population of the distant moon-lit woods was not yet lulled to rest. From time to time strange cries as of lost and despairing wanderers sounded from across the mere. They might be the notes of owls or water-birds, yet they did not quite resemble either sound. Were not they coming nearer? Now they sounded from the nearer side of the water, and in a few moments they seemed to be floating about among the shrubberies. Then they ceased; but just as Stephen was thinking of shutting the window and resuming his reading of *Robinson Crusoe*, he caught sight of two figures standing on the gravelled terrace that ran along the garden side of the Hall—the figures of a boy and girl, as it seemed; they stood side by side, looking up at the windows. Something in the form of the girl recalled irresistibly his dream of the figure in the bath. The boy inspired him with more acute fear.

Whilst the girl stood still, half smiling, with her hands clasped over her heart, the boy, a thin shape, with black hair and ragged clothing, raised his arms in the air with an appearance of menace and of unappeasable hunger and longing. The moon shone upon his almost transparent hands, and Stephen saw that the nails were fearfully long and that the light shone through them. As he stood with his arms thus raised, he disclosed a terrifying spectacle. On the left side of his chest there opened a black and gaping rent; and there fell upon Stephen's brain, rather than upon his ear, the impression of one of those hungry and desolate cries that he had heard resounding over the woods of Aswarby all that evening. In another moment this dreadful pair had moved swiftly and noiselessly over the dry gravel, and he saw them no more.

Inexpressibly frightened as he was, he determined to take his candle and go down to Mr. Abney's study, for the hour appointed for their meeting was near at hand. The study or library opened out of the front-hall on one side, and Stephen, urged on by his terrors, did not take long in getting there. To effect an entrance was not so easy. It was not locked, he felt sure, for the key was on the outside of the door as usual. His repeated knocks produced no answer. Mr. Abney was engaged: he was speaking. What! why did he try to cry out? and why was the cry choked in his throat? Had he, too, seen the mysterious children? But now everything was quiet, and the door yielded to Stephen's terrified and frantic pushing.

* * * * *

On the table in Mr. Abney's study certain papers were found which explained the situation to Stephen Elliott when he was of an age to understand them. The most important sentences were as follows:

"It was a belief very strongly and generally held by the ancients—of whose wisdom in these matters I have had such experience as induces me to place confidence in their assertions—that by enacting certain processes, which to us moderns have something of a barbaric complexion, a very remarkable enlightenment of the spiritual faculties in man may be attained: that, for example, by absorbing the personalities of a certain number of his fellow-creatures, an individual may gain a complete ascendancy over those orders of spiritual beings which control the elemental forces of our universe.

"It is recorded of Simon Magus that he was able to fly in the air, to become invisible, or to assume any form he pleased, by the agency of the soul of a boy whom, to use the libellous phrase employed by the author of the *Clementine Recognitions*, he had "murdered." I find it set down, moreover, with considerable detail in the writings of Hermes Trismegistus, that similar happy results may be produced by the absorption of the hearts of not less than three human beings below the age of twenty-one years. To the testing of the truth of this receipt I have devoted the greater part of the last twenty years, selecting as the *corpora vilia* of my experiment such persons as could conveniently be removed without occasioning a sensible gap in society. The first step I effected by the removal of one Phoebe Stanley, a girl of gipsy extraction, on March 24, 1792. The second, by the removal of a wandering Italian lad, named Giovanni Paoli, on the night of March 23, 1805. The final "victim"—to employ a word repugnant in the highest degree to my feelings—must be my cousin, Stephen Elliott. His day must be this March 24, 1812.

"The best means of effecting the required absorption is to remove the heart from the *living* subject, to reduce it to ashes, and to mingle them with about a pint of some red wine, preferably port. The remains of the first two subjects, at least, it will be well to conceal: a disused bathroom or wine-cellar will be found convenient for such a purpose. Some annoyance may be experienced from the psychic portion of the subjects, which popular language dignifies with the name of ghosts. But the man of philosophic temperament—to whom alone the experiment is appropriate—will be little prone to attach importance to the feeble efforts of these beings to wreak their vengeance on him. I contemplate with the liveliest satisfaction the enlarged and emancipated existence which the experiment, if successful, will confer on me; not only placing me beyond the reach of human justice (so-called), but eliminating to a great extent the prospect of death itself."

* * * * *

Mr. Abney was found in his chair, his head thrown back, his face stamped with an expression of rage, fright, and mortal pain. In his left side was a terrible lacerated wound, exposing the heart. There was no blood on his hands, and a long knife that lay on the table was perfectly clean. A savage wild-cat might have inflicted the injuries. The window of the study was open, and it was the opinion of the coroner that Mr. Abney had met his death by the agency of some wild creature. But Stephen Elliott's study of the papers I have quoted led him to a very different conclusion.

AN INHABITANT OF CARCOSA

Ambrose Bierce

For there be divers sorts of death—some wherein the body remaineth; and in some it vanisheth quite away with the spirit. This commonly occurreth only in solitude (such is God's will) and, none seeing the end, we say the man is lost, or gone on a long journey—which indeed he hath; but sometimes it hath happened in sight of many, as abundant testimony showeth. In one kind of death the spirit also dieth, and this it hath been known to do while yet the body was in vigour for many years. Sometimes, as is veritably attested, it dieth with the body, but after a season is raised up again in that place where the body did decay.

Pondering these words of Hali (whom God rest) and questioning their full meaning, as one who, having an intimation, yet doubts if there be not something behind, other than that which he has discerned, I noted not whither I had strayed until a sudden chill wind striking my face revived in me a sense of my surroundings. I observed with astonishment that everything seemed unfamiliar. On every side of me stretched a bleak and desolate expanse of plain, covered with a tall overgrowth of sere grass, which rustled and whistled in the autumn wind with Heaven knows what mysterious and disquieting suggestion. Protruded at long intervals above it, stood strangely shaped and sombre-coloured rocks, which seemed to have an understanding with one another and to exchange looks of uncomfortable significance, as if they had reared their heads to watch the issue of some foreseen event. A few blasted trees here and there appeared as leaders in this malevolent conspiracy of silent expectation.

The day, I thought, must be far advanced, though the sun was invisible; and although sensible that the air was raw and chill my consciousness of that fact was rather mental than physical—I had no feeling of discomfort. Over all the dismal landscape a canopy of low, lead-coloured clouds hung like a visible curse. In all this there was a menace and a portent—a hint of evil, an intimation of doom. Bird, beast, or insect there was none. The wind sighed in the bare branches of the dead trees and the grey grass bent to whisper its dread secret to the earth; but no other sound nor motion broke the awful repose of that dismal place.

I observed in the herbage a number of weatherworn stones, evidently shaped with tools. They were broken, covered with moss and half sunken in the earth. Some lay prostrate, some leaned at various angles, none was vertical. They were obviously headstones of graves, though the graves themselves no longer existed as either mounds or depressions; the years had levelled all. Scattered here and there, more massive blocks showed where some pompous tomb or ambitious monument had once flung its feeble defiance at oblivion. So old seemed these relics, these vestiges of vanity and memorials of affection and piety, so battered and worn and stained—so neglected, deserted, forgotten the place, that I could not help thinking myself the discoverer of the burial-ground of a prehistoric race of men whose very name was long extinct.

Filled with these reflections, I was for some time heedless of the sequence of my own experiences, but soon I thought, "How came I hither?" A moment's reflection seemed to make this all clear and explain at the same time, though in a disquieting way, the singular character with which my fancy had invested all that I saw or heard. I was ill. I remembered now that I had been prostrated by a sudden fever, and that my family had told me that in my periods of delirium I had constantly cried out for liberty and air, and had been held in bed to prevent my escape out-of-doors. Now I had eluded the vigilance of my attendants and had wandered hither to—to where? I could not conjecture. Clearly I was at a considerable distance from the city where I dwelt—the ancient and famous city of Carcosa.

No signs of human life were anywhere visible nor audible; no rising smoke, no watch-dog's bark, no lowing of cattle, no shouts of children at play—nothing but that dismal burial-place, with its air of mystery and dread, due to my own disordered brain. Was I not becoming again delirious, there beyond human aid? Was it not indeed all an illusion of my madness? I called aloud the names of my wives and sons, reached out my hands in search of theirs, even as I walked among the crumbling stones and in the withered grass.

A noise behind me caused me to turn about. A wild animal—a lynx—was approaching. The thought came to me: if I break down here in the desert—if the fever return and I fail, this beast will be at my throat. I sprang toward it, shouting. It trotted tranquilly by within a hand's-breadth of me and disappeared behind a rock.

A moment later a man's head appeared to rise out of the ground a short distance away. He was ascending the farther slope of a low hill whose crest was hardly to be distinguished from the general level. His whole figure soon came into view against the background of grey cloud. He was half naked, half clad in skins. His hair was unkempt, his beard long and ragged. In one hand he carried a bow and arrow; the other held a blazing torch with a long trail of black smoke. He walked slowly and with caution, as if he feared falling into some open grave concealed by the tall grass. This strange apparition surprised but did not alarm, and taking such a course as to intercept him I met him almost face to face, accosting him with the familiar salutation, "God keep you."

He gave no heed, nor did he arrest his pace.

"Good stranger," I continued, "I am ill and lost. Direct me, I beseech you, to Carcosa."

The man broke into a barbarous chant in an unknown tongue, passing on and away.

An owl on the branch of a decayed tree hooted dismally and was answered by another in the distance. Looking upward, I saw through a sudden rift in the clouds Aldebaran and the Hyades! In all this there was a hint of night—the lynx, the man with the torch, the owl. Yet I saw—I saw even the stars in absence of the darkness. I saw, but was apparently not seen nor heard. Under what awful spell did I exist?

I seated myself at the root of a great tree, seriously to consider what it were best to do. That I was mad I could no longer doubt, yet recognized a ground of doubt in the conviction. Of fever I had no trace. I had, withal, a sense of exhilaration and vigour altogether unknown to me—a feeling of mental and physical exaltation. My senses seemed all alert; I could feel the air as a ponderous substance; I could hear the silence.

A great root of the giant tree against whose trunk I leaned as I sat held enclosed in its grasp a slab of stone, a part of which protruded into a recess formed by another root. The stone was thus partly protected from the weather, though greatly decomposed. Its edges were worn round, its corners eaten away, its surface deeply furrowed and scaled. Glittering particles of mica were visible in the earth about it—vestiges of its decomposition. This stone had apparently marked the grave out of which the tree had sprung ages ago. The tree's exacting roots had robbed the grave and made the stone a prisoner.

A sudden wind pushed some dry leaves and twigs from the uppermost face of the stone; I saw the low-relief letters of an inscription and bent to read it. God in heaven! *My* name in full!—the date of my birth!—the date of *my* death!

A level shaft of light illuminated the whole side of the tree as I sprang to my feet in terror. The sun was rising in the rosy east. I stood between the tree and his broad red disk—no shadow darkened the trunk!

A chorus of howling wolves saluted the dawn. I saw them sitting on their haunches, singly and in groups, on the summits of irregular mounds and tumuli filling a half of my desert prospect and extending to the horizon.

And then I knew that these were ruins of the ancient and famous city of Carcosa.

Such are the facts imparted to the medium Bayrolles by the spirit Hoseib Alar Robardin.

THE DAMNED

Algernon Blackwood

I

"I'm over forty, Frances, and rather set in my ways," I said good-naturedly, ready to yield if she insisted that our going together on the visit involved her happiness. "My work is rather heavy just now too, as you know. The question is, could I work there—with a lot of unassorted people in the house?"

"Mabel doesn't mention any other people, Bill," was my sister's rejoinder. "I gather she's alone—as well as lonely."

By the way she looked sideways out of the window at nothing, it was obvious she was disappointed, but to my surprise she did not urge the point; and as I glanced at Mrs. Franklyn's invitation lying upon her sloping lap, the neat, childish handwriting conjured up a mental picture of the banker's widow, with her timid, insignificant personality, her pale grey eyes and her expression as of a backward child. I thought, too, of the roomy country mansion her late husband had altered to suit his particular needs, and of my visit to it a few years ago when its barren spaciousness suggested a wing of Kensington Museum fitted up temporarily as a place to eat and sleep in. Comparing it mentally with the poky Chelsea flat where I and my sister kept impecunious house, I realized other points as well. Unworthy details flashed across me to entice: the fine library, the organ, the quiet work-room I should have, perfect service, the delicious cup of early tea, and hot baths at any moment of the day—without a geyser!

"It's a longish visit, a month—isn't it?" I hedged, smiling at the details that seduced me, and ashamed of my man's selfishness, yet knowing that Frances expected it of me. "There are points about it, I admit. If you're set on my going with you, I could manage it all right."

I spoke at length in this way because my sister made no answer. I saw her tired eyes gazing into the dreariness of Oakley Street and felt a pang strike through me. After a pause, in which again she said no word, I added: "So, when you write the letter, you might hint, perhaps, that I usually work all the morning, and—er—am not a very lively visitor! Then she'll understand, you see." And I half-rose to return to my diminutive study, where I was slaving, just then, at an absorbing article on Comparative Aesthetic Values in the Blind and Deaf.

But Frances did not move. She kept her grey eyes upon Oakley Street where the evening mist from the river drew mournful perspectives into view. It was late October. We heard the omnibuses thundering across the bridge. The monotony of that broad, characterless street seemed more than usually depressing. Even in June sunshine it was dead, but with autumn its melancholy soaked into every house between King's Road and the Embankment. It washed thought into the past, instead of inviting it hopefully towards the future. For me, its easy width was an avenue through which nameless slums across the river sent creeping messages of depression, and I always regarded it as Winter's main entrance into London—fog, slush, gloom trooped down it every November, waving their forbidding banners till March came to rout them.

Its one claim upon my love was that the south wind swept sometimes unobstructed up it, soft with suggestions of the sea. These lugubrious thoughts I naturally kept to myself, though I never ceased to regret the little flat whose cheapness had seduced us. Now, as I watched my sister's impassive face, I realized that perhaps she, too, felt as I felt, yet, brave woman, without betraying it.

"And, look here, Fanny," I said, putting a hand upon her shoulder as I crossed the room, "it would be the very thing for you. You're worn out with catering and housekeeping. Mabel is your oldest friend, besides, and you've hardly seen her since he died—"

"She's been abroad for a year, Bill, and only just came back," my sister interposed. "She came back rather unexpectedly, though I never thought she would go there to live—" She stopped abruptly. Clearly, she was only speaking half her mind. "Probably," she went on, "Mabel wants to pick up old links again."

"Naturally," I put in, "yourself chief among them." The veiled reference to the house I let pass.

It involved discussing the dead man for one thing.

"I feel I ought to go anyhow," she resumed, "and of course it would be jollier if you came too. You'd get in such a muddle here by yourself, and eat wrong things, and forget to air the rooms, and—oh, everything!" She looked up laughing. "Only," she added, "there's the British Museum—?"

"But there's a big library there," I answered, "and all the books of reference I could possibly want. It was of you I was thinking. You could take up your painting again; you always sell half of what you paint. It would be a splendid rest too, and Sussex is a jolly country to walk in. By all means, Fanny, I advise—"

Our eyes met, as I stammered in my attempts to avoid expressing the thought that hid in both our minds. My sister had a weakness for dabbling in the various "new" theories of the day, and Mabel, who before her marriage had belonged to foolish societies for investigating the future life to the neglect of the present one, had fostered this undesirable tendency. Her amiable, impressionable temperament was open to every psychic wind that blew. I deplored, detested the whole business. But even more than this I abhorred the later influence that Mr. Franklyn had steeped his wife in, capturing her body and soul in his somber doctrines. I had dreaded lest my sister also might be caught.

"Now that she is alone again—"

I stopped short. Our eyes now made pretence impossible, for the truth had slipped out inevitably, stupidly, although unexpressed in definite language. We laughed, turning our faces a moment to look at other things in the room. Frances picked up a book and examined its cover as though she had made an important discovery, while I took my case out and lit a cigarette I did not want to smoke. We left the matter there. I went out of the room before further explanation could cause tension. Disagreements grow into discord from such tiny things—wrong adjectives, or a chance inflection of the voice. Frances had a right to her views of life as much as I had. At least, I reflected comfortably, we had separated upon an agreement this time, recognized mutually, though not actually stated.

And this point of meeting was, oddly enough, our way of regarding some one who was dead.

For we had both disliked the husband with a great dislike, and during his three years' married life had only been to the house once—for a weekend visit; arriving late on Saturday, we had left after an early breakfast on Monday morning. Ascribing my sister's dislike to a natural jealousy at losing her old friend, I said merely that he displeased me. Yet we both knew that the real emotion lay much deeper. Frances, loyal, honorable creature, had kept silence; and beyond saying that house and grounds—he altered one and laid out the other—distressed her as an expression of his personality somehow ("distressed" was the word she used), no further explanation had passed her lips.

Our dislike of his personality was easily accounted for—up to a point, since both of us shared the artist's point of view that a creed, cut to measure and carefully dried, was an ugly thing, and that a dogma to which believers must subscribe or perish everlastingly was a barbarism resting upon cruelty. But while my own dislike was purely due to an abstract worship of Beauty, my sister's had another twist in it, for with her "new" tendencies, she believed that all religions were an aspect of truth and that no one, even the lowest wretch, could escape "heaven" in the long run.

Samuel Franklyn, the rich banker, was a man universally respected and admired, and the marriage, though Mabel was fifteen years his junior, won general applause; his bride was an heiress in her own right—breweries—and the story of her conversion at a revivalist meeting where Samuel Franklyn had spoken fervidly of heaven, and terrifyingly of sin, hell and damnation, even contained a touch of genuine romance. She was a brand snatched from the burning; his detailed eloquence had frightened her into heaven; salvation came in the nick of time; his words had plucked her from the edge of that lake of fire and brimstone where their worm dieth not and the fire is not quenched. She regarded him as a hero, sighed her relief upon his saintly shoulder, and accepted the peace he offered her with a grateful resignation.

For her husband was a "religious man" who successfully combined great riches with the glamour of winning souls. He was a portly figure, though tall, with masterful, big hands, his fingers rather thick and red; and his dignity, that just escaped being pompous, held in it something that was implacable. A convinced assurance, almost remorseless, gleamed in his eyes when he preached especially, and his threats of hell fire must have scared souls stronger than the timid, receptive Mabel whom he married. He clad himself in long frock-coats that buttoned unevenly, big square boots, and trousers that invariably bagged at the knee and were a little short; he wore low collars, spats occasionally, and a tall black hat that was not of silk. His voice was alternately hard and unctuous; and he regarded theaters, ballrooms, and racecourses as the vestibule of that brimstone lake of whose geography he was as positive as of his great banking offices in the City. A philanthropist up to the hilt, however, no one ever doubted his complete sincerity; his convictions were ingrained, his faith borne out by his life—as witness his name upon so many admirable Societies, as treasurer, patron, or heading the donation list. He bulked large in the world of doing good, a broad and stately stone in the rampart against evil. And his heart was genuinely kind and soft for others—who believed as he did.

Yet, in spite of this true sympathy with suffering and his desire to help, he was narrow as a telegraph wire and unbending as a church pillar; he was intensely selfish; intolerant as an officer of the Inquisition, his bourgeois soul constructed a revolting scheme of heaven that was reproduced in miniature in all he did and planned. Faith was the sine qua non of salvation, and by "faith" he meant belief in his own particular view of things—"which faith, except every one do keep whole and undefiled, without doubt he shall perish everlastingly." All the world but his own small, exclusive sect must be damned eternally—a pity, but alas, inevitable. He was right.

Yet he prayed without ceasing, and gave heavily to the poor—the only thing he could not give being big ideas to his provincial and suburban deity. Pettier than an insect, and more obstinate than a mule, he had also the superior, sleek humility of a "chosen one." He was churchwarden too. He read the lesson in a "place of worship," either chilly or overheated, where neither organ, vestments, nor lighted candles were permitted, but where the odor of hair-wash on the boys' heads in the back rows pervaded the entire building.

This portrait of the banker, who accumulated riches both on earth and in heaven, may possibly be overdrawn, however, because Frances and I were "artistic temperaments" that viewed the type with a dislike and distrust amounting to contempt. The majority considered Samuel Franklyn a worthy man and a good citizen. The majority, doubtless, held the saner view. A few years more, and he certainly would have been made a baronet. He relieved much suffering in the world, as assuredly as he caused many souls the agonies of torturing fear by his emphasis upon damnation.

Had there been one point of beauty in him, we might have been more lenient; only we found it not, and, I admit, took little pains to search. I shall never forget the look of dour forgiveness with which he heard our excuses for missing Morning Prayers that Sunday morning of our single visit to The Towers. My sister learned that a change was made soon afterwards, prayers being "conducted" after breakfast instead of before.

The Towers stood solemnly upon a Sussex hill amid park-like modern grounds, but the house cannot better be described—it would be so wearisome for one thing—than by saying that it was a cross between an overgrown, pretentious Norwood villa and one of those saturnine Institutes for cripples the train passes as it slinks ashamed through South London into Surrey. It was "wealthily" furnished and at first sight imposing, but on closer acquaintance revealed a meager personality, barren and austere. One looked for Rules and Regulations on the walls, all signed By Order. The place was a prison that shut out "the world." There was, of course, no billiard-room, no smoking-room, no room for play of any kind, and the great hall at the back, once a chapel, which might have been used for dancing, theatricals, or other innocent amusements, was consecrated in his day to meetings of various kinds, chiefly brigades, temperance or missionary societies. There was a harmonium at one end—on the level floor—a raised dais or platform at the other, and a gallery above for the servants, gardeners, and coachmen. It was heated with hot-water pipes, and hung with Doré's pictures, though these latter were soon removed and stored out of sight in the attics as being too unspiritual. In polished, shiny wood, it was a representation in miniature of that poky exclusive Heaven he took about with him, externalizing it in all he did and planned, even in the grounds about the house.

Changes in The Towers, Frances told me, had been made during Mabel's year of widowhood abroad—an organ put into the big hall, the library made livable and re-catalogued—when it was permissible to suppose she had found her soul again and returned to her normal, healthy views of life, which included enjoyment and play, literature, music and the arts, without, however, a touch of that trivial thoughtlessness usually termed worldliness. Mrs. Franklyn, as I remembered her, was a quiet little woman, shallow, perhaps, and easily influenced, but sincere as a dog and thorough in her faithful Friendship. Her tastes at heart were catholic, and that heart was simple and unimaginative. That she took up with the various movements of the day was sign merely that she was searching in her limited way for a belief that should bring her peace. She was, in fact, a very ordinary woman, her caliber a little less than that of Frances. I knew they used to discuss all kinds of theories together, but as these discussions never resulted in action, I had come to regard her as harmless. Still, I was not sorry when she married, and I did not welcome now a renewal of the former intimacy. The philanthropist she had given no children, or she would have made a good and sensible mother. No doubt she would marry again.

"Mabel mentions that she's been alone at The Towers since the end of August," Frances told me at teatime; "and I'm sure she feels out of it and lonely. It would be a kindness to go. Besides, I always liked her."

I agreed. I had recovered from my attack of selfishness. I expressed my pleasure.

"You've written to accept," I said, half statement and half question.

Frances nodded. "I thanked for you," she added quietly, "explaining that you were not free at the moment, but that later, if not inconvenient, you might come down for a bit and join me."

I stared. Frances sometimes had this independent way of deciding things. I was convicted, and punished into the bargain.

Of course there followed argument and explanation, as between brother and sister who were affectionate, but the recording of our talk could be of little interest. It was arranged thus, Frances and I both satisfied. Two days later she departed for The Towers, leaving me alone in the flat with everything planned for my comfort and good behavior—she was rather a tyrant in her quiet way—and her last words as I saw her off from Charing Cross rang in my head for a long time after she was gone:

"I'll write and let you know, Bill. Eat properly, mind, and let me know if anything goes wrong."

She waved her small gloved hand, nodded her head till the feather brushed the window, and was gone.

II

After the note announcing her safe arrival a week of silence passed, and then a letter came; there were various suggestions for my welfare, and the rest was the usual rambling information and description Frances loved, generously italicized.

". . . and we are quite alone," she went on in her enormous handwriting that seemed such a waste of space and labor, "though some others are coming presently, I believe. You could work here to your heart's content. Mabel *quite* understands, and says she would love to have you when you feel free to come. She has changed a bit—back to her old natural self: she never mentions *him*. The place has changed too in certain ways: it has more cheerfulness, I think. *She* has put it in, this cheerfulness, spaded it in, if you know what I mean; but it lies about uneasily and is not natural—quite. The organ is a beauty. She must be very rich now, but she's as gentle and sweet as ever. Do you know, Bill, I think he must have *frightened* her into marrying him. I get the impression she was afraid of him." This last sentence was inked out, I but I read it through the scratching; the letters being too big to hide. "He had an inflexible will beneath all that oily kindness which passed for spiritual. He was a real personality, I mean. I'm sure he'd have sent you and me cheerfully to the stake in another century—*for our own good.* Isn't it odd she never speaks of him, even to me?" This, again, was stroked through, though without the intention to obliterate—merely because it was repetition, probably. "The only reminder of him in the house now is a big copy of the presentation portrait that stands on the stairs of the Multitechnic Institute at Peckham—you know—that life-size one with his fat hand sprinkled with rings resting on a thick Bible and the other slipped between the buttons of a tight frock-coat. It hangs in the dining room and rather dominates our meals. I wish Mabel would take it down. I think she'd like to, if she *dared.* There's not a single photograph of him anywhere, even in her own room. Mrs. Marsh is here—you remember her, *his* housekeeper, the wife of the man who got penal servitude for killing a baby or something—*you* said she robbed him and justified her stealing because the story of the unjust steward was in the Bible! How we laughed over that! *She's* just the same too, gliding about all over the house and turning up when least expected."

Other reminiscences filled the next two sides of the letter, and ran, without a trace of punctuation, into instructions about a Salamander stove for heating my work-room in the flat; these were followed by things I was to tell the cook, and by requests for several articles she had forgotten and would like sent after her, two of them blouses, with descriptions so lengthy and contradictory that I sighed as I read them—"unless you come down soon, in which case perhaps you wouldn't mind bringing them; not the mauve one I wear in the evening sometimes, but the pale blue one with lace round the collar and the crinkly front. They're in the cupboard—or the drawer, I'm not sure which—of my bedroom. *Ask Annie* if you're in doubt. Thanks most *awfully*. Send a telegram, remember, and we'll meet you in the motor *any time.* I don't quite know if I shall stay the whole month—*alone*. It all depends . . ."

And she closed the letter, the italicized words increasing recklessly towards the end, with a repetition that Mabel would love to have me "for myself," as also to have a "man in the house," and that I only had to telegraph the day and the train . . . This letter, coming by the second post, interrupted me in a moment of absorbing work, and, having read it through to make sure there was nothing requiring instant attention, I threw it aside and went on with my notes and reading. Within five minutes, however, it was back at me again. That restless thing called "between the lines" fluttered about my mind. My interest in the Balkan States—political article that had been "ordered"—faded. Somewhere, somehow I felt disquieted, disturbed. At first I persisted in my work, forcing myself to concentrate, but soon found that a layer of new impressions floated between the article and my attention. It was like a shadow, though a shadow that dissolved upon inspection. Once or twice I glanced up, expecting to find some one in the room, that the door had opened unobserved and Annie was waiting for instructions. I heard the buses thundering across the bridge. I was aware of Oakley Street.

Montenegro and the blue Adriatic melted into the October haze along that depressing Embankment that aped a riverbank, and sentences from the letter flashed before my eyes and stung me. Picking it up and reading it through more carefully, I rang the bell and told Annie to find the blouses and pack them for the post, showing her finally the written description, and resenting the superior smile with which she at once interrupted. "I know them, sir," and disappeared.

But it was not the blouses: it was that exasperating thing "between the lines" that put an end to my work with its elusive teasing nuisance. The first sharp impression is alone of value in such a case, for once analysis begins the imagination constructs all kinds of false interpretation. The more I thought, the more I grew fuddled. The letter, it seemed to me, wanted to say another thing; instead the eight sheets conveyed it merely. It came to the edge of disclosure, then halted.

There was something on the writer's mind, and I felt uneasy. Studying the sentences brought, however, no revelation, but increased confusion only; for while the uneasiness remained, the first clear hint had vanished. In the end I closed my books and went out to look up another matter at the British Museum library. Perhaps I should discover it that way—by turning the mind in a totally new direction. I lunched at the Express Dairy in Oxford Street close by, and telephoned to Annie that I would be home to tea at five.

And at tea, tired physically and mentally after breathing the exhausted air of the Rotunda for five hours, my mind suddenly delivered up its original impression, vivid and clear-cut; no proof accompanied the revelation; it was mere presentiment, but convincing. Frances was disturbed in her mind, her orderly, sensible, housekeeping mind; she was uneasy, even perhaps afraid; something in the house distressed her, and she had need of me. Unless I went down, her time of rest and change, her quite necessary holiday, in fact, would be spoilt. She was too unselfish to say this, but it ran everywhere between the lines. I saw it clearly now. Mrs. Franklyn, moreover—and that meant Frances too—would like a "man in the house." It was a disagreeable phrase, a suggestive way of hinting something she dared not state definitely. The two women in that great, lonely barrack of a house were afraid.

My sense of duty, affection, unselfishness, whatever the composite emotion may be termed, was stirred; also my vanity. I acted quickly, lest reflection should warp clear, decent judgment.

"Annie," I said, when she answered the bell, "you need not send those blouses by the post. I'll take them down tomorrow when I go. I shall be away a week or two, possibly longer." And, having looked up a train, I hastened out to telegraph before I could change my fickle mind.

But no desire came that night to change my mind. I was doing the right, the necessary thing. I was even in something of a hurry to get down to The Towers as soon as possible. I chose an early afternoon train.

III

A telegram had told me to come to a town ten miles from the house, so I was saved the crawling train to the local station, and traveled down by an express. As soon as we left London the fog cleared off, and an autumn sun, though without heat in it, painted the landscape with golden browns and yellows. My spirits rose as I lay back in the luxurious motor and sped between the woods and hedges. Oddly enough, my anxiety of overnight had disappeared. It was due, no doubt, to that exaggeration of detail which reflection in loneliness brings. Frances and I had not been separated for over a year, and her letters from The Towers told so little. It had seemed unnatural to be deprived of those intimate particulars of mood and feeling I was accustomed to. We had such confidence in one another, and our affection was so deep. Though she was but five years younger than myself, I regarded her as a child. My attitude was fatherly.

In return, she certainly mothered me with a solicitude that never cloyed. I felt no desire to marry while she was still alive. She painted in watercolors with a reasonable success, and kept house for me; I wrote, reviewed books and lectured on aesthetics; we were a humdrum couple of quasi-artists, well satisfied with life, and all I feared for her was that she might become a suffragette or be taken captive by one of these wild theories that caught her imagination sometimes, and that Mabel, for one, had fostered. As for myself, no doubt she deemed me a trifle solid or stolid—I forget which word she preferred—but on the whole there was just sufficient difference of opinion to make intercourse suggestive without monotony, and certainly without quarrelling.

Drawing in deep draughts of the stinging autumn air, I felt happy and exhilarated. It was like going for a holiday, with comfort at the end of the journey instead of bargaining for centimes.

But my heart sank noticeably the moment the house came into view. The long drive, lined with hostile monkey trees and formal wellingtonias that were solemn and sedate, was mere extension of the miniature approach to a thousand semidetached suburban "residences"; and the appearance of The Towers, as we turned the corner with a rush, suggested a commonplace climax to a story that had begun interestingly, almost thrillingly. A villa had escaped from the shadow of the Crystal Palace, thumped its way down by night, grown suddenly monstrous in a shower of rich rain, and settled itself insolently to stay. Ivy climbed about the opulent red-brick walls, but climbed neatly and with disfiguring effect, sham as on a prison or—the simile made me smile—an orphan asylum. There was no hint of the comely roughness of untidy ivy on a ruin. Clipped, trained, and precise it was, as on a brand-new protestant church. I swear there was not a bird's nest nor a single earwig in it anywhere. About the porch it was particularly thick, smothering a seventeenth-century lamp with a contrast that was quite horrible. Extensive glass-houses spread away on the farther side of the house; the numerous towers to which the building owed its name seemed made to hold school bells; and the windowsills, thick with potted flowers, made me think of the desolate suburbs of Brighton or Bexhill. In a commanding position upon the crest of a hill, it overlooked miles of undulating, wooded country southwards to the Downs, but behind it, to the north, thick banks of ilex, holly, and privet protected it from the cleaner and more stimulating winds. Hence, though highly placed, it was shut in. Three years had passed since I last set eyes upon it, but the unsightly memory I had retained was justified by the reality. The place was deplorable.

It is my habit to express my opinions audibly sometimes, when impressions are strong enough to warrant it; but now I only sighed "Oh, dear," as I extricated my legs from many rugs and went into the house. A tall parlor-maid, with the bearing of a grenadier, received me, and standing behind her was Mrs. Marsh, the housekeeper, whom I remembered because her untidy back hair had suggested to me that it had been burnt. I went at once to my room, my hostess already dressing for dinner, but Frances came in to see me just as I was struggling with my black tie that had got tangled like a bootlace. She fastened it for me in a neat, effective bow, and while I held my chin up for the operation, staring blankly at the ceiling, the impression came—I wondered, was it her touch that caused it?—that something in her trembled. Shrinking perhaps is the truer word. Nothing in her face or manner betrayed it, nor in her pleasant, easy talk while she tidied my things and scolded my slovenly packing, as her habit was, questioning me about the servants at the flat. The blouses, though right, were crumpled, and my scolding was deserved. There was no impatience even. Yet somehow or other the suggestion of a shrinking reserve and holding back reached my mind. She had been lonely, of course, but it was more than that; she was glad that I had come, yet for some reason unstated she could have wished that I had stayed away. We discussed the news that had accumulated during our brief separation, and in doing so the impression, at best exceedingly slight, was forgotten. My chamber was large and beautifully furnished; the hall and dining room of our flat would have gone into it with a good remainder; yet it was not a place I could settle down in for work. It conveyed the idea of impermanence, making me feel transient as in a hotel bedroom. This, of course, was the fact. But some rooms convey a settled, lasting hospitality even in a hotel; this one did not; and as I was accustomed to work in the room I slept in, at least when visiting, a slight frown must have crept between my eyes.

"Mabel has fitted a work-room for you just out of the library," said the clairvoyant Frances.

"No one will disturb you there, and you'll have fifteen thousand books all catalogued within easy reach. There's a private staircase too. You can breakfast in your room and slip down in your dressing gown if you want to." She laughed. My spirits took a turn upwards as absurdly as they had gone down.

"And how are you?" I asked, giving her a belated kiss. "It's jolly to be together again. I did feel rather lost without you, I'll admit."

"That's natural," she laughed. "I'm so glad."

She looked well and had country color in her cheeks. She informed me that she was eating and sleeping well, going out for little walks with Mabel, painting bits of scenery again, and enjoying a complete change and rest; and yet, for all her brave description, the word somehow did not quite ring true. Those last words in particular did not ring true. There lay in her manner, just out of sight, I felt, this suggestion of the exact reverse—of unrest, shrinking, almost of anxiety. Certain small strings in her seemed over-tight. "Keyed-up" was the slang expression that crossed my mind. I looked rather searchingly into her face as she was telling me this.

"Only—the evenings," she added, noticing my query, yet rather avoiding my eyes, "the evenings are—well, rather heavy sometimes, and I find it difficult to keep awake."

"The strong air after London makes you drowsy," I suggested, "and you like to get early to bed."

Frances turned and looked at me for a moment steadily. "On the contrary, Bill, I dislike going to bed—here. And Mabel goes so early." She said it lightly enough, fingering the disorder upon my dressing table in such a stupid way that I saw her mind was working in another direction altogether. She looked up suddenly with a kind of nervousness from the brush and scissors.

"Billy," she said abruptly, lowering her voice, "isn't it odd, but I hate sleeping alone here? I can't make it out quite; I've never felt such a thing before in my life. Do you—think it's all nonsense?"

And she laughed, with her lips but not with her eyes; there was a note of defiance in her I failed to understand.

"Nothing a nature like yours feels strongly is nonsense, Frances," I replied soothingly.

But I, too, answered with my lips only, for another part of my mind was working elsewhere, and among uncomfortable things. A touch of bewilderment passed over me. I was not certain how best to continue. If I laughed she would tell me no more, yet if I took her too seriously the strings would tighten further. Instinctively, then, this flashed rapidly across me: that something of what she felt, I had also felt, though interpreting it differently. Vague it was, as the coming of rain or storm that announce themselves hours in advance with their hint of faint, unsettling excitement in the air. I had been but a short hour in the house—big, comfortable, luxurious house—but had experienced this sense of being unsettled, unfixed, fluctuating—a kind of impermanence that transient lodgers in hotels must feel, but that a guest in a friend's home ought not to feel, be the visit short or long. To Frances, an impressionable woman, the feeling had come in the terms of alarm. She disliked sleeping alone, while yet she longed to sleep. The precise idea in my mind evaded capture, merely brushing through me, three-quarters out of sight; I realized only that we both felt the same thing, and that neither of us could get at it clearly.

Degrees of unrest we felt, but the actual thing did not disclose itself. It did not happen.

I felt strangely at sea for a moment. Frances would interpret hesitation as endorsement, and encouragement might be the last thing that could help her.

"Sleeping in a strange house," I answered at length, "is often difficult at first, and one feels lonely. After fifteen months in our tiny flat one feels lost and uncared-for in a big house. It's an uncomfortable feeling—I know it well. And this is a barrack, isn't it? The masses of furniture only make it worse. One feels in storage somewhere underground—the furniture doesn't furnish. One must never yield to fancies, though—"

Frances looked away towards the windows; she seemed disappointed a little.

"After our thickly-populated Chelsea," I went on quickly, "it seems isolated here."

But she did not turn back, and clearly I was saying the wrong thing. A wave of pity rushed suddenly over me. Was she really frightened, perhaps? She was imaginative, I knew, but never moody; common sense was strong in her, though she had her times of hypersensitiveness. I caught the echo of some unreasoning, big alarm in her. She stood there, gazing across my balcony towards the sea of wooded country that spread dim and vague in the obscurity of the dusk. The deepening shadows entered the room, I fancied, from the grounds below. Following her abstracted gaze a moment, I experienced a curious sharp desire to leave, to escape. Out yonder was wind and space and freedom. This enormous building was oppressive, silent, still.

Great catacombs occurred to me, things beneath the ground, imprisonment and capture. I believe I even shuddered a little.

I touched her shoulder. She turned round slowly, and we looked with a certain deliberation into each other's eyes.

"Fanny," I asked, more gravely than I intended, "you are not frightened, are you? Nothing has happened, has it?"

She replied with emphasis, "Of course not! How could it—I mean, why should I?" She stammered, as though the wrong sentence flustered her a second. "It's simply—that I have this ter—this dislike of sleeping alone."

Naturally, my first thought was how easy it would be to cut our visit short. But I did not say this. Had it been a true solution, Frances would have said it for me long ago.

"Wouldn't Mabel double-up with you?" I said instead, "or give you an adjoining room, so that you could leave the door between you open? There's space enough, heaven knows."

And then, as the gong sounded in the hall below for dinner, she said, as with an effort, this thing:

"Mabel did ask me—on the third night—after I had told her. But I declined."

"You'd rather be alone than with her?" I asked, with a certain relief.

Her reply was so gravely given, a child would have known there was more behind it: "Not that; but that she did not really want it."

I had a moment's intuition and acted on it impulsively. "She feels it too, perhaps, but wishes to face it by herself—and get over it?"

My sister bowed her head, and the gesture made me realize of a sudden how grave and solemn our talk had grown, as though some portentous thing were under discussion. It had come of itself—indefinite as a gradual change of temperature. Yet neither of us knew its nature, for apparently neither of us could state it plainly. Nothing happened, even in our words.

"That was my impression," she said, "—that if she yields to it she encourages it. And a habit forms so easily. Just think," she added with a faint smile that was the first sign of lightness she had yet betrayed, "what a nuisance it would be—everywhere—if everybody was afraid of being alone—like that."

I snatched readily at the chance. We laughed a little, though it was a quiet kind of laughter that seemed wrong. I took her arm and led her towards the door.

"Disastrous, in fact," I agreed.

She raised her voice to its normal pitch again, as I had done. "No doubt it will pass," she said, "now that you have come. Of course, it's chiefly my imagination." Her tone was lighter, though nothing could convince me that the matter itself was light—just then. "And in any case," tightening her grip on my arm as we passed into the bright enormous corridor and caught sight of Mrs. Franklyn waiting in the cheerless hall below, "I'm very glad you're here, Bill, and Mabel, I know, is too."

"If it doesn't pass," I just had time to whisper with a feeble attempt at jollity, "I'll come at night and snore outside your door. After that you'll be so glad to get rid of me that you won't mind being alone."

"That's a bargain," said Frances.

I shook my hostess by the hand, made a banal remark about the long interval since last we met, and walked behind them into the great dining room, dimly lit by candles, wondering in my heart how long my sister and I should stay, and why in the world we had ever left our cozy little flat to enter this desolation of riches and false luxury at all. The unsightly picture of the late Samuel Franklyn, Esq., stared down upon me from the farther end of the room above the mighty mantelpiece.

He looked, I thought, like some pompous Heavenly Butler who denied to all the world, and to us in particular, the right of entry without presentation cards signed by his hand as proof that we belonged to his own exclusive set. The majority, to his deep grief, and in spite of all his prayers on their behalf, must burn and "perish everlastingly."

IV

With the instinct of the healthy bachelor I always try to make myself a nest in the place I live in, be it for long or short. Whether visiting, in lodging-house, or in hotel, the first essential is this nest—one's own things built into the walls as a bird builds in its feathers. It may look desolate and uncomfortable enough to others, because the central detail is neither bed nor wardrobe, sofa nor armchair, but a good solid writing-table that does not wriggle, and that has wide elbowroom.

And The Towers is vividly described for me by the single fact that I could not "nest" there.

I took several days to discover this, but the first impression of impermanence was truer than I knew. The feathers of the mind refused here to lie one way. They ruffled, pointed, and grew wild.

Luxurious furniture does not mean comfort; I might as well have tried to settle down in the sofa and armchair department of a big shop. My bedroom was easily managed; it was the private workroom, prepared especially for my reception, that made me feel alien and outcast.

Externally, it was all one could desire: an antechamber to the great library, with not one, but two generous oak tables, to say nothing of smaller ones against the walls with capacious drawers.

There were reading desks, mechanical devices for holding books, perfect light, quiet as in a church, and no approach but across the huge adjoining room. Yet it did not invite.

"I hope you'll be able to work here," said my little hostess the next morning, as she took me in—her only visit to it while I stayed in the house—and showed me the ten-volume Catalogue.

"It's absolutely quiet and no one will disturb you."

"If you can't, Bill, you're not much good," laughed Frances, who was on her arm. "Even I could write in a study like this!"

I glanced with pleasure at the ample tables, the sheets of thick blotting paper, the rulers, sealing wax, paper knives, and all the other immaculate paraphernalia. "It's perfect," I answered with a secret thrill, yet feeling a little foolish. This was for Gibbon or Carlyle, rather than for my potboiling insignificancies. "If I can't write masterpieces here, it's certainly not your fault," and I turned with gratitude to Mrs. Franklyn. She was looking straight at me, and there was a question in her small pale eyes I did not understand. Was she noting the effect upon me, I wondered?

"You'll write here—perhaps a story about the house," she said, "Thompson will bring you anything you want; you only have to ring." She pointed to the electric bell on the central table, the wire running neatly down the leg. "No one has ever worked here before, and the library has been hardly used since it was put in. So there's no previous atmosphere to affect your imagination—er—adversely."

We laughed. "Bill isn't that sort," said my sister; while I wished they would go out and leave me to arrange my little nest and set to work.

I thought, of course, it was the huge listening library that made me feel so inconsiderable—the fifteen thousand silent, staring books, the solemn aisles, the deep, eloquent shelves. But when the women had gone and I was alone, the beginning of the truth crept over me, and I felt that first hint of disconsolateness which later became an imperative No. The mind shut down, images ceased to rise and flow. I read, made copious notes, but I wrote no single line at The Towers.

Nothing completed itself there. Nothing happened.

The morning sunshine poured into the library through ten long narrow windows; birds were singing; the autumn air, rich with a faint aroma of November melancholy that stung the imagination pleasantly, filled my antechamber. I looked out upon the undulating wooded landscape, hemmed in by the sweep of distant Downs, and I tasted a whiff of the sea. Rooks cawed as they floated above the elms, and there were lazy cows in the nearer meadows. A dozen times I tried to make my nest and settle down to work, and a dozen times, like a turning fastidious dog upon a hearth rug, I rearranged my chair and books and papers. The temptation of the Catalogue and shelves, of course, was accountable for much, yet not, I felt, for all. That was a manageable seduction. My work, moreover, was not of the creative kind that requires absolute absorption; it was the mere readable presentation of data I had accumulated. My notebooks were charged with facts ready to tabulate—facts, too, that interested me keenly. A mere effort of the will was necessary, and concentration of no difficult kind. Yet, somehow, it seemed beyond me: something forever pushed the facts into disorder . . . and in the end I sat in the sunshine, dipping into a dozen books selected from the shelves outside, vexed with myself and only half-enjoying it. I felt restless. I wanted to be elsewhere.

And even while I read, attention wandered. Frances, Mabel, her late husband, the house and grounds, each in turn and sometimes all together, rose uninvited into the stream of thought, hindering any consecutive flow of work. In disconnected fashion came these pictures that interrupted concentration, yet presenting themselves as broken fragments of a bigger thing my mind already groped for unconsciously. They fluttered round this hidden thing of which they were aspects, fugitive interpretations, no one of them bringing complete revelation. There was no adjective, such as pleasant or unpleasant, that I could attach to what I felt, beyond that the result was unsettling. Vague as the atmosphere of a dream, it yet persisted, and I could not dissipate it.

Isolated words or phrases in the lines I read sent questions scouring across my mind, sure sign that the deeper part of me was restless and ill at ease.

Rather trivial questions too—half-foolish interrogations, as of a puzzled or curious child: Why was my sister afraid to sleep alone, and why did her friend feel a similar repugnance, yet seek to conquer it? Why was the solid luxury of the house without comfort, its shelter without the sense of permanence? Why had Mrs. Franklyn asked us to come, artists, unbelieving vagabonds, types at the farthest possible remove from the saved sheep of her husband's household? Had a reaction set in against the hysteria of her conversion? I had seen no signs of religious fervor in her; her atmosphere was that of an ordinary, high-minded woman, yet a woman of the world. Lifeless, though, a little, perhaps, now that I came to think about it: she had made no definite impression upon me of any kind. And my thoughts ran vaguely after this fragile clue.

Closing my book, I let them run. For, with this chance reflection came the discovery that I could not see her clearly—could not feel her soul, her personality. Her face, her small pale eyes, her dress and body and walk, all these stood before me like a photograph; but her Self evaded me. She seemed not there, lifeless, empty, a shadow—nothing. The picture was disagreeable, and I put it by. Instantly she melted out, as though light thought had conjured up a phantom that had no real existence. And at that very moment, singularly enough, my eye caught sight of her moving past the window, going silently along the gravel path. I watched her, a sudden new sensation gripping me. "There goes a prisoner," my thought instantly ran, "one who wishes to escape, but cannot."

What brought the outlandish notion, heaven only knows. The house was of her own choice, she was twice an heiress, and the world lay open at her feet. Yet she stayed—unhappy, frightened, caught. All this flashed over me, and made a sharp impression even before I had time to dismiss it as absurd. But a moment later explanation offered itself, though it seemed as far-fetched as the original impression. My mind, being logical, was obliged to provide something, apparently. For Mrs. Franklyn, while dressed to go out, with thick walking-boots, a pointed stick, and a motor-cap tied on with a veil as for the windy lanes, was obviously content to go no farther than the little garden paths. The costume was a sham and a pretence. It was this, and her lithe, quick movements that suggested a caged creature—a creature tamed by fear and cruelty that cloaked themselves in kindness—pacing up and down, unable to realize why it got no farther, but always met the same bars in exactly the same place. The mind in her was barred.

I watched her go along the paths and down the steps from one terrace to another, until the laurels hid her altogether; and into this mere imagining of a moment came a hint of something slightly disagreeable, for which my mind, search as it would, found no explanation at all. I remembered then certain other little things. They dropped into the picture of their own accord. In a mind not deliberately hunting for clues, pieces of a puzzle sometimes come together in this way, bringing revelation, so that for a second there flashed across me, vanishing instantly again before I could consider it, a large, distressing thought I can only describe vaguely as a Shadow.

Dark and ugly, oppressive certainly it might be described, with something torn and dreadful about the edges that suggested pain and strife and terror. The interior of a prison with two rows of occupied condemned cells, seen years ago in New York, sprang to memory after it—the connection between the two impossible to surmise even. But the "certain other little things" mentioned above were these: that Mrs. Franklyn, in last night's dinner talk, had always referred to "this house," but never called it "home"; and had emphasized unnecessarily, for a well-bred woman, our "great kindness" in coming down to stay so long with her. Another time, in answer to my futile compliment about the "stately rooms," she said quietly, "It is an enormous house for so small a party; but I stay here very little, and only till I get it straight again." The three of us were going up the great staircase to bed as this was said, and, not knowing quite her meaning, I dropped the subject. It edged delicate ground, I felt. Frances added no word of her own. It now occurred to me abruptly that "stay" was the word made use of, when "live" would have been more natural. How insignificant to recall! Yet why did they suggest themselves just at this moment . . . ?

And, on going to Frances's room to make sure she was not nervous or lonely, I realized abruptly, that Mrs. Franklyn, of course, had talked with her in a confidential sense that I, as a mere visiting brother, could not share. Frances had told me nothing. I might easily have wormed it out of her, had I not felt that for us to discuss further our hostess and her house merely because we were under the roof together, was not quite nice or loyal.

"I'll call you, Bill, if I'm scared," she had laughed as we parted, my room being just across the big corridor from her own. I had fallen asleep, thinking what in the world was meant by "getting it straight again."

And now in my antechamber to the library, on the second morning, sitting among piles of foolscap and sheets of spotless blotting-paper, all useless to me, these slight hints came back and helped to frame the big, vague Shadow I have mentioned. Up to the neck in this Shadow, almost drowned, yet just treading water, stood the figure of my hostess in her walking costume. Frances and I seemed swimming to her aid. The Shadow was large enough to include both house and grounds, but farther than that I could not see . . . Dismissing it, I fell to reading my purloined book again. Before I turned another page, however, another startling detail leaped out at me: the figure of Mrs. Franklyn in the Shadow was not living. It floated helplessly, like a doll or puppet that has no life in it. It was both pathetic and dreadful.

Any one who sits in reverie thus, of course, may see similar ridiculous pictures when the will no longer guides construction. The incongruities of dreams are thus explained. I merely record the picture as it came. That it remained by me for several days, just as vivid dreams do, is neither here nor there. I did not allow myself to dwell upon it. The curious thing, perhaps, is that from this moment I date my inclination, though not yet my desire, to leave. I purposely say "to leave."

I cannot quite remember when the word changed to that aggressive, frantic thing which is escape.

V

We were left delightfully to ourselves in this pretentious country mansion with the soul of a villa. Frances took up her painting again, and, the weather being propitious, spent hours out of doors, sketching flowers, trees and nooks of woodland, garden, even the house itself where bits of it peered suggestively across the orchards. Mrs. Franklyn seemed always busy about something or other, and never interfered with us except to propose motoring, tea in another part of the lawn, and so forth. She flitted everywhere, preoccupied, yet apparently doing nothing. The house engulfed her rather. No visitor called. For one thing, she was not supposed to be back from abroad yet; and for another, I think, the neighborhood—her husband's neighborhood—was puzzled by her sudden cessation from good works. Brigades and temperance societies did not ask to hold their meetings in the big hall, and the vicar arranged the school-treats in another's field without explanation. The full-length portrait in the dining room, and the presence of the housekeeper with the "burnt" back hair, indeed, were the only reminders of the man who once had lived here. Mrs. Marsh retained her place in silence, well-paid sinecure as it doubtless was, yet with no hint of that suppressed disapproval one might have expected from her. Indeed there was nothing positive to disapprove, since nothing "worldly" entered grounds or building. In her master's lifetime she had been another "brand snatched from the burning," and it had then been her custom to give vociferous "testimony" at the revival meetings where he adorned the platform and led in streams of prayer. I saw her sometimes on the stairs, hovering, wandering, half-watching and half-listening, and the idea came to me once that this woman somehow formed a link with the departed influence of her bigoted employer. She, alone among us, belonged to the house, and looked at home there. When I saw her talking—oh, with such correct and respectful mien—to Mrs. Franklyn, I had the feeling that for all her unaggressive attitude, she yet exerted some influence that sought to make her mistress stay in the building forever—live there. She would prevent her escape, prevent "getting it straight again," thwart somehow her will to freedom, if she could. The idea in me was of the most fleeting kind. But another time, when I came down late at night to get a book from the library antechamber, and found her sitting in the hall—alone—the impression left upon me was the reverse of fleeting. I can never forget the vivid, disagreeable effect it produced upon me. What was she doing there at half-past eleven at night, all alone in the darkness? She was sitting upright, stiff, in a big chair below the clock. It gave me a turn. It was so incongruous and odd. She rose quietly as I turned the corner of the stairs, and asked me respectfully, her eyes cast down as usual, whether I had finished with the library, so that she might lock up. There was no more to it than that; but the picture stayed with me—unpleasantly.

These various impressions came to me at odd moments, of course, and not in a single sequence as I now relate them. I was hard at work before three days were past, not writing, as explained, but reading, making notes, and gathering material from the library for future use. It was in chance moments that these curious flashes came, catching me unawares with a touch of surprise that sometimes made me start. For they proved that my under-mind was still conscious of the Shadow, and that far away out of sight lay the cause of it that left me with a vague unrest, unsettled, seeking to "nest" in a place that did not want me. Only when this deeper part knows harmony, perhaps, can good brainwork result, and my inability to write was thus explained.

Certainly, I was always seeking for something here I could not find—an explanation that continually evaded me. Nothing but these trivial hints offered themselves. Lumped together, however, they had the effect of defining the Shadow a little. I became more and more aware of its very real existence. And, if I have made little mention of Frances and my hostess in this connection, it is because they contributed at first little or nothing towards the discovery of what this story tries to tell. Our life was wholly external, normal, quiet, and uneventful; conversation banal—Mrs. Franklyn's conversation in particular. They said nothing that suggested revelation.

Both were in this Shadow, and both knew that they were in it, but neither betrayed by word or act a hint of interpretation. They talked privately, no doubt, but of that I can report no details.

And so it was that, after ten days of a very commonplace visit, I found myself looking straight into the face of a Strangeness that defied capture at close quarters. "There's something here that never happens," were the words that rose in my mind, "and that's why none of us can speak of it."

And as I looked out of the window and watched the vulgar blackbirds, with toes turned in, boring out their worms, I realized sharply that even they, as indeed everything large and small in the house and grounds, shared this strangeness, and were twisted out of normal appearance because of it. Life, as expressed in the entire place, was crumpled, dwarfed, emasculated. God's meanings here were crippled, His love of joy was stunted. Nothing in the garden danced or sang.

There was hate in it. "The Shadow," my thought hurried on to completion, "is a manifestation of hate; and hate is the Devil." And then I sat back frightened in my chair, for I knew that I had partly found the truth.

Leaving my books I went out into the open. The sky was overcast, yet the day by no means gloomy, for a soft, diffused light oozed through the clouds and turned all things warm and almost summery. But I saw the grounds now in their nakedness because I understood. Hate means strife, and the two together weave the robe that terror wears. Having no so-called religious beliefs myself, nor belonging to any set of dogmas called a creed, I could stand outside these feelings and observe. Yet they soaked into me sufficiently for me to grasp sympathetically what others, with more cabined souls (I flattered myself), might feel. That picture in the dining room stalked everywhere, hid behind every tree, peered down upon me from the peaked ugliness of the bourgeois towers, and left the impress of its powerful hand upon every bed of flowers. "You must not do this, you must not do that," went past me through the air. "You must not leave these narrow paths," said the rigid iron railings of black. "You shall not walk here," was written on the lawns. "Keep to the steps," "Don't pick the flowers; make no noise of laughter, singing, dancing," was placarded all over the rose-garden, and "Trespassers will be—not prosecuted but—destroyed" hung from the crest of monkey tree and holly. Guarding the ends of each artificial terrace stood gaunt, implacable policemen, warders, jailers. "Come with us," they chanted, "or be damned eternally."

I remember feeling quite pleased with myself that I had discovered this obvious explanation of the prison feeling the place breathed out. That the posthumous influence of heavy old Samuel Franklyn might be an inadequate solution did not occur to me. By "getting the place straight again," his widow, of course, meant forgetting the glamour of fear and foreboding his depressing creed had temporarily forced upon her; and Frances, delicately minded being, did not speak of it because it was the influence of the man her friend had loved. I felt lighter; a load was lifted from me. "To trace the unfamiliar to the familiar," came back a sentence I had read somewhere, "is to understand." It was a real relief. I could talk with Frances now, even with my hostess, no danger of treading clumsily. For the key was in my hands. I might even help to dissipate the Shadow, "to get it straight again." It seemed, perhaps, our long invitation was explained!

I went into the house laughing—at myself a little. "Perhaps after all the artist's outlook, with no hard and fast dogmas, is as narrow as the others! How small humanity is! And why is there no possible and true combination of all outlooks?"

The feeling of "unsettling" was very strong in me just then, in spite of my big discovery which was to clear everything up. And at the moment I ran into Frances on the stairs, with a portfolio of sketches under her arm.

It came across me then abruptly that, although she had worked a great deal since we came, she had shown me nothing. It struck me suddenly as odd, unnatural. The way she tried to pass me now confirmed my newborn suspicion that—well, that her results were hardly what they ought to be.

"Stand and deliver!" I laughed, stepping in front of her. "I've seen nothing you've done since you've been here, and as a rule you show me all your things. I believe they are atrocious and degrading!" Then my laughter froze.

She made a sly gesture to slip past me, and I almost decided to let her go, for the expression that flashed across her face shocked me. She looked uncomfortable and ashamed; the color came and went a moment in her cheeks, making me think of a child detected in some secret naughtiness. It was almost fear.

"It's because they're not finished then?" I said, dropping the tone of banter, "or because they're too good for me to understand?" For my criticism of painting, she told me, was crude and ignorant sometimes. "But you'll let me see them later, won't you?"

Frances, however, did not take the way of escape I offered. She changed her mind. She drew the portfolio from beneath her arm instead. "You can see them if you really want to, Bill," she said quietly, and her tone reminded me of a nurse who says to a boy just grown out of childhood, "you are old enough now to look upon horror and ugliness—only I don't advise it."

"I do want to," I said, and made to go downstairs with her. But, instead, she said in the same low voice as before, "Come up to my room, we shall be undisturbed there." So I guessed that she had been on her way to show the paintings to our hostess, but did not care for us all three to see them together. My mind worked furiously.

"Mabel asked me to do them," she explained in a tone of submissive horror, once the door was shut, "in fact, she begged it of me. You know how persistent she is in her quiet way. I—er—had to."

She flushed and opened the portfolio on the little table by the window, standing behind me as I turned the sketches over—sketches of the grounds and trees and garden. In the first moment of inspection, however, I did not take in clearly why my sister's sense of modesty had been offended. For my attention flashed a second elsewhere. Another bit of the puzzle had dropped into place, defining still further the nature of what I called "the Shadow." Mrs. Franklyn, I now remembered, had suggested to me in the library that I might perhaps write something about the place, and I had taken it for one of her banal sentences and paid no further attention. I realized now that it was said in earnest. She wanted our interpretations, as expressed in our respective "talents," painting and writing. Her invitation was explained. She left us to ourselves on purpose.

"I should like to tear them up," Frances was whispering behind me with a shudder, "only I promised—" She hesitated a moment.

"Promised not to?" I asked with a queer feeling of distress, my eyes glued to the papers.

"Promised always to show them to her first," she finished so low I barely caught it.

I have no intuitive, immediate grasp of the value of paintings; results come to me slowly, and though every one believes his own judgment to be good, I dare not claim that mine is worth more than that of any other layman, Frances had too often convicted me of gross ignorance and error. I can only say that I examined these sketches with a feeling of amazement that contained revulsion, if not actually horror and disgust. They were outrageous. I felt hot for my sister, and it was a relief to know she had moved across the room on some pretence or other, and did not examine them with me. Her talent, of course, is mediocre, yet she has her moments of inspiration—moments, that is to say, when a view of Beauty not normally her own flames divinely through her. And these interpretations struck me forcibly as being thus "inspired"—not her own. They were uncommonly well done; they were also atrocious. The meaning in them, however, was never more than hinted. There the unholy skill and power came in: they suggested so abominably, leaving most to the imagination. To find such significance in a bourgeois villa garden, and to interpret it with such delicate yet legible certainty, was a kind of symbolism that was sinister, even diabolical. The delicacy was her own, but the point of view was another's.

And the word that rose in my mind was not the gross description of "impure," but the more fundamental qualification—"un-pure."

In silence I turned the sketches over one by one, as a boy hurries through the pages of an evil book lest he be caught.

"What does Mabel do with them?" I asked presently in a low tone, as I neared the end. "Does she keep them?"

"She makes notes about them in a book and then destroys them," was the reply from the end of the room. I heard a sigh of relief. "I'm glad you've seen them, Bill. I wanted you to—but was afraid to show them. You understand?"

"I understand," was my reply, though it was not a question intended to be answered. All I understood really was that Mabel's mind was as sweet and pure as my sister's, and that she had some good reason for what she did. She destroyed the sketches, but first made notes! It was an interpretation of the place she sought. Brother-like, I felt resentment, though, that Frances should waste her time and talent, when she might be doing work that she could sell. Naturally, I felt other things as well . . .

"Mabel pays me five guineas for each one," I heard. "Absolutely insists."

I stared at her stupidly a moment, bereft of speech or wit. "I must either accept, or go away," she went on calmly, but a little white. "I've tried everything. There was a scene the third day I was here—when I showed her my first result. I wanted to write to you, but hesitated—"

"It's unintentional, then, on your part—forgive my asking it, Frances, dear?" I blundered, hardly knowing what to think or say. "Between the lines" of her letter came back to me. "I mean, you make the sketches in your ordinary way and—the result comes out of itself, so to speak?"

She nodded, throwing her hands out like a Frenchman. "We needn't keep the money for ourselves, Bill. We can give it away, but—I must either accept or leave," and she repeated the shrugging gesture. She sat down on the chair facing me, staring helplessly at the carpet.

"You say there was a scene?" I went on presently, "She insisted?"

"She begged me to continue," my sister replied very quietly. "She thinks—that is, she has an idea or theory that there's something about the place—something she can't get at quite." Frances stammered badly. She knew I did not encourage her wild theories.

"Something she feels—yes," I helped her, more than curious.

"Oh, you know what I mean, Bill," she said desperately. "That the place is saturated with some influence that she is herself too positive or too stupid to interpret. She's trying to make herself negative and receptive, as she calls it, but can't, of course, succeed. Haven't you noticed how dull and impersonal and insipid she seems, as though she had no personality? She thinks impressions will come to her that way. But they don't—"

"Naturally."

"So she's trying me—us—what she calls the sensitive and impressionable artistic temperament. She says that until she is sure exactly what this influence is, she can't fight it, turn it out, 'get the house straight,' as she phrases it."

Remembering my own singular impressions, I felt more lenient than I might otherwise have done. I tried to keep impatience out of my voice.

"And this influence, what—whose is it?"

We used the pronoun that followed in the same breath, for I answered my own question at the same moment as she did:

"His." Our heads nodded involuntarily towards the floor, the dining room being directly underneath.

And my heart sank, my curiosity died away on the instant; I felt bored. A commonplace haunted house was the last thing in the world to amuse or interest me. The mere thought exasperated, with its suggestions of imagination, overwrought nerves, hysteria, and the rest.

Mingled with my other feelings was certainly disappointment. To see a figure or feel a "presence," and report from day to day strange incidents to each other would be a form of weariness I could never tolerate.

"But really, Frances," I said firmly, after a moment's pause, "it's too far-fetched, this explanation. A curse, you know, belongs to the ghost stories of early Victorian days." And only my positive conviction that there was something after all worth discovering, and that it most certainly was not this, prevented my suggesting that we terminate our visit forthwith, or as soon as we decently could. "This is not a haunted house, whatever it is," I concluded somewhat vehemently, bringing my hand down upon her odious portfolio.

My sister's reply revived my curiosity sharply.

"I was waiting for you to say that. Mabel says exactly the same. He is in it—but it's something more than that alone, something far bigger and more complicated." Her sentence seemed to indicate the sketches, and though I caught the inference I did not take it up, having no desire to discuss them with her just then, indeed, if ever.

I merely stared at her and listened. Questions, I felt sure, would be of little use. It was better she should say her thought in her own way.

"He is one influence, the most recent," she went on slowly, and always very calmly, "but there are others—deeper layers, as it were—underneath. If his were the only one, something would happen. But nothing ever does happen. The others hinder and prevent—as though each were struggling to predominate."

I had felt it already myself. The idea was rather horrible. I shivered.

"That's what is so ugly about it—that nothing ever happens," she said. "There is this endless anticipation—always on the dry edge of a result that never materializes. It is torture. Mabel is at her wits' end, you see. And when she begged me—what I felt about my sketches—I mean—"

She stammered badly as before.

I stopped her. I had judged too hastily. That queer symbolism in her paintings, pagan and yet not innocent, was, I understood, the result of mixture. I did not pretend to understand, but at least I could be patient. I consequently held my peace. We did talk on a little longer, but it was more general talk that avoided successfully our hostess, the paintings, wild theories, and him—until at length the emotion Frances had hitherto so successfully kept under burst vehemently forth again.

It had hidden between her calm sentences, as it had hidden between the lines of her letter. It swept her now from head to foot, packed tight in the thing she then said.

"Then, Bill, if it is not an ordinary haunted house," she asked, "what is it?"

The words were commonplace enough. The emotion was in the tone of her voice that trembled; in the gesture she made, leaning forward and clasping both hands upon her knees, and in the slight blanching of her cheeks as her brave eyes asked the question and searched my own with anxiety that bordered upon panic. In that moment she put herself under my protection. I winced.

"And why," she added, lowering her voice to a still and furtive whisper, "does nothing ever happen? If only,"—this with great emphasis—"something would happen—break this awful tension—bring relief. It's the waiting I cannot stand." And she shivered all over as she said it, a touch of wildness in her eyes.

I would have given much to have made a true and satisfactory answer. My mind searched frantically for a moment, but in vain. There lay no sufficient answer in me. I felt what she felt, though with differences. No conclusive explanation lay within reach. Nothing happened. Eager as I was to shoot the entire business into the rubbish heap where ignorance and superstition discharge their poisonous weeds, I could not honestly accomplish this. To treat Frances as a child, and merely "explain away" would be to strain her confidence in my protection, so affectionately claimed. It would further be dishonest to myself—weak, besides—to deny that I had also felt the strain and tension even as she did. While my mind continued searching, I returned her stare in silence; and Frances then, with more honesty and insight than my own, gave suddenly the answer herself—an answer whose truth and adequacy, so far as they went, I could not readily gainsay:

"I think, Bill, because it is too big to happen here—to happen anywhere, indeed, all at once—and too awful!"

To have tossed the sentence aside as nonsense, argued it away, proved that it was really meaningless, would have been easy—at any other time or in any other place; and, had the past week brought me none of the vivid impressions it had brought me, this is doubtless what I should have done. My narrowness again was proved. We understand in others only what we have in ourselves. But her explanation, in a measure, I knew was true. It hinted at the strife and struggle that my notion of a Shadow had seemed to cover thinly.

"Perhaps," I murmured lamely, waiting in vain for her to say more. "But you said just now that you felt the thing was 'in layers,' as it were. Do you mean each one—each influence—fighting for the upper hand?"

I used her phraseology to conceal my own poverty. Terminology, after all, was nothing, provided we could reach the idea itself.

Her eyes said yes. She had her clear conception, arrived at independently, as was her way.

And, unlike her sex, she kept it clear, unsmothered by too many words.

"One set of influences gets at me, another gets at you. It's according to our temperaments, I think." She glanced significantly at the vile portfolio.

"Sometimes they are mixed—and therefore false. There has always been in me, more than in you, the pagan thing, perhaps, though never, thank God, like that."

The frank confession of course invited my own, as it was meant to do. Yet it was difficult to find the words.

"What I have felt in this place, Frances, I honestly can hardly tell you, because—er—my impressions have not arranged themselves in any definite form I can describe. The strife, the agony of vainly-sought escape, and the unrest—a sort of prison atmosphere—this I have felt at different times and with varying degrees of strength. But I find, as yet, no final label to attach. I couldn't say pagan, Christian, or anything like that, I mean, as you do. As with the blind and deaf, you may have an intensification of certain senses denied to me, or even another sense altogether in embryo—"

"Perhaps," she stopped me, anxious to keep to the point, "you feel it as Mabel does. She feels the whole thing complete."

"That also is possible," I said very slowly. I was thinking behind my words. Her odd remark that it was "big and awful" came back upon me as true. A vast sensation of distress and discomfort swept me suddenly. Pity was in it, and a fierce contempt, a savage, bitter anger as well. Fury against some sham authority was part of it.

"Frances," I said, caught unawares, and dropping all pretence, "what in the world can it be?" I looked hard at her. For some minutes neither of us spoke.

"Have you felt no desire to interpret it?" she asked presently, "Mabel did suggest my writing something about the house," was my reply, "but I've felt nothing imperative. That sort of writing is not my line, you know. My only feeling," I added, noticing that she waited for more, "is the impulse to explain, discover, get it out of me somehow, and so get rid of it. Not by writing, though—as yet." And again I repeated my former question:

"What in the world do you think it is?" My voice had become involuntarily hushed. There was awe in it. Her answer, given with slow emphasis, brought back all my reserve: the phraseology provoked me rather:—"Whatever it is, Bill, it is not of God."

I got up to go downstairs. I believe I shrugged my shoulders. "Would you like to leave, Frances? Shall we go back to town?" I suggested this at the door, and hearing no immediate reply, I turned back to look. Frances was sitting with her head bowed over and buried in her hands. The attitude horribly suggested tears. No woman, I realized, can keep back the pressure of strong emotion as long as Frances had done, without ending in a fluid collapse. I waited a moment uneasily, longing to comfort, yet afraid to act—and in this way discovered the existence of the appalling emotion in myself, hitherto but half guessed. At all costs a scene must be prevented: it would involve such exaggeration and overstatement. Brutally, such is the weakness of the ordinary man, I turned the handle to go out, but my sister then raised her head. The sunlight caught her face, framed untidily in its auburn hair, and I saw her wonderful expression with a start. Pity, tenderness, and sympathy shone in it like a flame. It was undeniable. There shone through all her features the imperishable love and yearning to sacrifice self for others which I have seen in only one type of human being. It was the great mother look.

"We must stay by Mabel and help her get it straight," she whispered, making the decision for us both.

I murmured agreement. Abashed and half ashamed, I stole softly from the room and went out into the grounds. And the first thing clearly realized when alone was this: that the long scene between us was without definite result. The exchange of confidence was really nothing but hints and vague suggestion. We had decided to stay, but it was a negative decision not to leave rather than a positive action. All our words and questions, our guesses, inferences, explanations, our most subtle allusions and insinuations, even the odious paintings themselves, were without definite result. Nothing had happened.

VI

And instinctively, once alone, I made for the places where she had painted her extraordinary pictures; I tried to see what she had seen. Perhaps, now that she had opened my mind to another view, I should be sensitive to some similar interpretation—and possibly by way of literary expression. If I were to write about the place, I asked myself, how should I treat it? I deliberately invited an interpretation in the way that came easiest to me—writing.

But in this case there came no such revelation. Looking closely at the trees and flowers, the bits of lawn and terrace, the rose-garden and corner of the house where the flaming creeper hung so thickly, I discovered nothing of the odious, unpure thing her color and grouping had unconsciously revealed. At first, that is, I discovered nothing. The reality stood there, commonplace and ugly, side by side with her distorted version of it that lay in my mind. It seemed incredible. I tried to force it, but in vain. My imagination, ploughed less deeply than hers, or to another pattern, grew different seed. Where I saw the gross soul of an overgrown suburban garden, inspired by the spirit of a vulgar, rich revivalist who loved to preach damnation, she saw this rush of pagan liberty and joy, this strange license of primitive flesh which, tainted by the other, produced the adulterated, vile result.

Certain things, however, gradually then became apparent, forcing themselves upon me, willy-nilly. They came slowly, but overwhelmingly. Not that facts had changed, or natural details altered in the grounds—this was impossible—but that I noticed for the first time various aspects I had not noticed before—trivial enough, yet for me, just then, significant. Some I remembered from previous days; others I saw now as I wandered to and fro, uneasy, uncomfortable,—almost, it seemed, watched by some one who took note of my impressions. The details were so foolish, the total result so formidable. I was half aware that others tried hard to make me see. It was deliberate.

My sister's phrase, "one layer got at me, another gets at you," flashed, undesired, upon me.

For I saw, as with the eyes of a child, what I can only call a goblin garden—house, grounds, trees, and flowers belonged to a goblin world that children enter through the pages of their fairy tales. And what made me first aware of it was the whisper of the wind behind me, so that I turned with a sudden start, feeling that something had moved closer. An old ash tree, ugly and ungainly, had been artificially trained to form an arbor at one end of the terrace that was a tennis lawn, and the leaves of it now went rustling together, swishing as they rose and fell. I looked at the ash tree, and felt as though I had passed that moment between doors into this goblin garden that crouched behind the real one. Below, at a deeper layer perhaps, lay hidden the one my sister had entered.

To deal with my own, however, I call it goblin, because an odd aspect of the quaint in it yet never quite achieved the picturesque. Grotesque, probably, is the truer word, for everywhere I noticed, and for the first time, this slight alteration of the natural due either to the exaggeration of some detail, or to its suppression, generally, I think, to the latter. Life everywhere appeared to me as blocked from the full delivery of its sweet and lovely message. Some counter influence stopped it—suppression; or sent it awry—exaggeration. The house itself, mere expression, of course, of a narrow, limited mind, was sheer ugliness; it required no further explanation. With the grounds and garden, so far as shape and general plan were concerned, this was also true; but that trees and flowers and other natural details should share the same deficiency perplexed my logical soul, and even dismayed it. I stood and stared, then moved about, and stood and stared again. Everywhere was this mockery of a sinister, unfinished aspect. I sought in vain to recover my normal point of view. My mind had found this goblin garden and wandered to and fro in it, unable to escape.

The change was in myself, of course, and so trivial were the details which illustrated it, that they sound absurd, thus mentioned one by one. For me, they proved it, is all I can affirm. The goblin touch lay plainly everywhere: in the forms of the trees, planted at neat intervals along the lawns; in this twisted ash that rustled just behind me; in the shadow of the gloomy wellingtonias, whose sweeping skirts obscured the grass; but especially, I noticed, in the tops and crests of them. For here, the delicate, graceful curves of last year's growth seemed to shrink back into themselves. None of them pointed upwards. Their life had failed and turned aside just when it should have become triumphant. The character of a tree reveals itself chiefly at the extremities, and it was precisely here that they all drooped and achieved this hint of goblin distortion—in the growth, that is, of the last few years. What ought to have been fairy, joyful, natural, was instead uncomely to the verge of the grotesque. Spontaneous expression was arrested. My mind perceived a goblin garden, and was caught in it. The place grimaced at me.

With the flowers it was similar, though far more difficult to detect in detail for description. I saw the smaller vegetable growth as impish, half-malicious. Even the terraces sloped ill, as though their ends had sagged since they had been so lavishly constructed; their varying angles gave a queerly bewildering aspect to their sequence that was unpleasant to the eye. One might wander among their deceptive lengths and get lost—lost among open terraces!—with the house quite close at hand. Unhomely seemed the entire garden, unable to give repose, restlessness in it everywhere, almost strife, and discord certainly.

Moreover, the garden grew into the house, the house into the garden, and in both was this idea of resistance to the natural—the spirit that says No to joy. All over it I was aware of the effort to achieve another end, the struggle to burst forth and escape into free, spontaneous expression that should be happy and natural, yet the effort forever frustrated by the weight of this dark shadow that rendered it abortive. Life crawled aside into a channel that was a cul-de-sac, then turned horribly upon itself. Instead of blossom and fruit, there were weeds. This approach of life I was conscious of—then dismal failure. There was no fulfillment. Nothing happened.

And so, through this singular mood, I came a little nearer to understand the unpure thing that had stammered out into expression through my sister's talent. For the unpure is merely negative; it has no existence; it is but the cramped expression of what is true, stammering its way brokenly over false boundaries that seek to limit and confine. Great, full expression of anything is pure, whereas here was only the incomplete, unfinished, and therefore ugly. There was a strife and pain and desire to escape. I found myself shrinking from house and grounds as one shrinks from the touch of the mentally arrested, those in whom life has turned awry. There was almost mutilation in it.

Past items, too, now flocked to confirm this feeling that I walked, liberty captured and half-maimed, in a monstrous garden. I remembered days of rain that refreshed the countryside, but left these grounds, cracked with the summer heat, unsatisfied and thirsty; and how the big winds, that cleaned the woods and fields elsewhere, crawled here with difficulty through the dense foliage that protected The Towers from the North and West and East. They were ineffective, sluggish currents. There was no real wind. Nothing happened. I began to realize—far more clearly than in my sister's fanciful explanation about "layers"—that here were many contrary influences at work, mutually destructive of one another. House and grounds were not haunted merely; they were the arena of past thinking and feeling, perhaps of terrible, impure beliefs, each striving to suppress the others, yet no one of them achieving supremacy because no one of them was strong enough, no one of them was true. Each, moreover, tried to win me over, though only one was able to reach my mind at all. For some obscure reason—possibly because my temperament had a natural bias towards the grotesque—it was the goblin layer. With me, it was the line of least resistance . . .

In my own thoughts this "goblin garden" revealed, of course, merely my personal interpretation. I felt now objectively what long ago my mind had felt subjectively. My work, essential sign of spontaneous life with me, had stopped dead; production had become impossible.

I stood now considerably closer to the cause of this sterility. The Cause, rather, turned bolder, had stepped insolently nearer. Nothing happened anywhere; house, garden, mind alike were barren, abortive, torn by the strife of frustrate impulse, ugly, hateful, sinful. Yet behind it all was still the desire of life—desire to escape—accomplish. Hope—an intolerable hope—I became startlingly aware—crowned torture.

And, realizing this, though in some part of me where Reason lost her hold, there rose upon me then another and a darker thing that caught me by the throat and made me shrink with a sense of revulsion that touched actual loathing. I knew instantly whence it came, this wave of abhorrence and disgust, for even while I saw red and felt revolt rise in me, it seemed that I grew partially aware of the layer next below the goblin. I perceived the existence of this deeper stratum. One opened the way for the other, as it were. There were so many, yet all inter-related; to admit one was to clear the way for all. If I lingered I should be caught—horribly. They struggled with such violence for supremacy among themselves, however, that this latest uprising was instantly smothered and crushed back, though not before a glimpse had been revealed to me, and the redness in my thoughts transferred itself to color my surroundings thickly and appallingly—with blood. This lurid aspect drenched the garden, smeared the terraces, lent to the very soil a tinge as of sacrificial rites, that choked the breath in me, while it seemed to fix me to the earth my feet so longed to leave. It was so revolting that at the same time I felt a dreadful curiosity as of fascination—I wished to stay. Between these contrary impulses I think I actually reeled a moment, transfixed by a fascination of the Awful. Through the lighter goblin veil I felt myself sinking down, down, down into this turgid layer that was so much more violent and so much more ancient. The upper layer, indeed, seemed fairy by comparison with this terror born of the lust for blood, thick with the anguish of human sacrificial victims.

Upper! Then I was already sinking; my feet were caught; I was actually in it! What atavistic strain, hidden deep within me, had been touched into vile response, giving this flash of intuitive comprehension, I cannot say. The coatings laid on by civilization are probably thin enough in all of us. I made a supreme effort. The sun and wind came back. I could almost swear I opened my eyes. Something very atrocious surged back into the depths, carrying with it a thought of tangled woods, of big stones standing in a circle, motionless, white figures, the one form bound with ropes, and the ghastly gleam of the knife. Like smoke upon a battlefield, it rolled away . . .

I was standing on the gravel path below the second terrace when the familiar goblin garden danced back again, doubly grotesque now, doubly mocking, yet, by way of contrast, almost welcome. My glimpse into the depths was momentary, it seems, and had passed utterly away.

The common world rushed back with a sense of glad relief, yet ominous now forever, I felt, for the knowledge of what its past had built upon. In street, in theater, in the festivities of friends, in music-room or playing field, even indeed in church—how could the memory of what I had seen and felt leave its hideous trace? The very structure of my Thought, it seemed to me, was stained.

What has been thought by others can never be obliterated until . . .

With a start my reverie broke and fled, scattered by a violent sound that I recognized for the first time in my life as wholly desirable. The returning motor meant that my hostess was back.

Yet, so urgent had been my temporary obsession, that my first presentation of her was—well, not as I knew her now. Floating along with a face of anguished torture I saw Mabel, a mere effigy captured by others' thinking, pass down into those depths of fire and blood that only just had closed beneath my feet. She dipped away. She vanished, her fading eyes turned to the last towards some savior who had failed her. And that strange intolerable hope was in her face.

The mystery of the place was pretty thick about me just then. It was the fall of dusk, and the ghost of slanting sunshine was as unreal as though badly painted. The garden stood at attention all about me. I cannot explain it, but I can tell it, I think, exactly as it happened, for it remains vivid in me forever—that, for the first time, something almost happened, myself apparently the combining link through which it pressed towards delivery:

I had already turned towards the house. In my mind were pictures—not actual thoughts—of the motor, tea on the verandah, my sister, Mabel—when there came behind me this tumultuous, awful rush—as I left the garden. The ugliness, the pain, the striving to escape, the whole negative and suppressed agony that was the Place, focused that second into a concentrated effort to produce a result. It was a blinding tempest of long-frustrate desire that heaved at me, surging appallingly behind me like an anguished mob. I was in the act of crossing the frontier into my normal self again, when it came, catching fearfully at my skirts. I might use an entire dictionary of descriptive adjectives yet come no nearer to it than this—the conception of a huge assemblage determined to escape with me, or to snatch me back among themselves. My legs trembled for an instant, and I caught my breath—then turned and ran as fast as possible up the ugly terraces.

At the same instant, as though the clanging of an iron gate cut short the unfinished phrase, I thought the beginning of an awful thing:

"The Damned . . ."

Like this it rushed after me from that goblin garden that had sought to keep me:

"The Damned!"

For there was sound in it. I know full well it was subjective, not actually heard at all; yet somehow sound was in it—a great volume, roaring and booming thunderously, far away, and below me. The sentence dipped back into the depths that gave it birth, unfinished. Its completion was prevented. As usual, nothing happened. But it drove behind me like a hurricane as I ran towards the house, and the sound of it I can only liken to those terrible undertones you may hear standing beside Niagara. They lie behind the mere crash of the falling flood, within it somehow, not audible to all—felt rather than definitely heard.

It seemed to echo back from the surface of those sagging terraces as I flew across their sloping ends, for it was somehow underneath them. It was in the rustle of the wind that stirred the skirts of the drooping wellingtonias. The beds of formal flowers passed it on to the creepers, red as blood, that crept over the unsightly building. Into the structure of the vulgar and forbidding house it sank away; The Towers took it home. The uncomely doors and windows seemed almost like mouths that had uttered the words themselves, and on the upper floors at that very moment I saw two maids in the act of closing them again.

And on the verandah, as I arrived breathless, and shaken in my soul, Frances and Mabel, standing by the tea table, looked up to greet me. In the faces of both were clearly legible the signs of shock. They watched me coming, yet so full of their own distress that they hardly noticed the state in which I came. In the face of my hostess, however, I read another and a bigger thing than in the face of Frances. Mabel knew. She had experienced what I had experienced. She had heard that awful sentence I had heard but heard it not for the first time; heard it, moreover, I verily believe, complete and to its dreadful end.

"Bill, did you hear that curious noise just now?" Frances asked it sharply before I could say a word. Her manner was confused; she looked straight at me; and there was a tremor in her voice she could not hide.

"There's wind about," I said, "wind in the trees and sweeping round the walls. It's risen rather suddenly." My voice faltered rather.

"No. It wasn't wind," she insisted, with a significance meant for me alone, but badly hidden. "It was more like distant thunder, we thought. How you ran too!" she added. "What a pace you came across the terraces!"

I knew instantly from the way she said it that they both had already heard the sound before and were anxious to know if I had heard it, and how. My interpretation was what they sought.

"It was a curiously deep sound, I admit. It may have been big guns at sea," I suggested, "forts or cruisers practicing. The coast isn't so very far, and with the wind in the right direction—"

The expression on Mabel's face stopped me dead.

"Like huge doors closing," she said softly in her colorless voice, "enormous metal doors shutting against a mass of people clamoring to get out." The gravity, the note of hopelessness in her tones, was shocking.

Frances had gone into the house the instant Mabel began to speak. "I'm cold," she had said; "I think I'll get a shawl." Mabel and I were alone. I believe it was the first time we had been really alone since I arrived. She looked up from the teacups, fixing her pallid eyes on mine. She had made a question of the sentence.

"You hear it like that?" I asked innocently. I purposely used the present tense.

She changed her stare from one eye to the other; it was absolutely expressionless. My sister's step sounded on the floor of the room behind us.

"If only—" Mabel began, then stopped, and my own feelings leaping out instinctively completed the sentence I felt was in her mind:

"—something would happen."

She instantly corrected me. I had caught her thought, yet somehow phrased it wrongly.

"We could escape!" She lowered her tone a little, saying it hurriedly. The "we" amazed and horrified me; but something in her voice and manner struck me utterly dumb. There was ice and terror in it. It was a dying woman speaking—a lost and hopeless soul.

In that atrocious moment I hardly noticed what was said exactly, but I remember that my sister returned with a grey shawl about her shoulders, and that Mabel said, in her ordinary voice again, "It is chilly, yes; let's have tea inside," and that two maids, one of them the grenadier, speedily carried the loaded trays into the morning-room and put a match to the logs in the great open fireplace. It was, after all, foolish to risk the sharp evening air, for dusk was falling steadily, and even the sunshine of the day just fading could not turn autumn into summer. I was the last to come in. Just as I left the verandah a large black bird swooped down in front of me past the pillars; it dropped from overhead, swerved abruptly to one side as it caught sight of me, and flapped heavily towards the shrubberies on the left of the terraces, where it disappeared into the gloom. It flew very low, very close. And it startled me, I think because in some way it seemed like my Shadow materialized—as though the dark horror that was rising everywhere from house and garden, then settling back so thickly yet so imperceptibly upon us all, were incarnated in that whirring creature that passed between the daylight and the coming night.

I stood a moment, wondering if it would appear again, before I followed the others indoors, and as I was in the act of closing the windows after me, I caught a glimpse of a figure on the lawn. It was some distance away, on the other side of the shrubberies, in fact where the bird had vanished. But in spite of the twilight that half magnified, half obscured it, the identity was unmistakable. I knew the housekeeper's stiff walk too well to be deceived. "Mrs. Marsh taking the air," I said to myself. I felt the necessity of saying it, and I wondered why she was doing so at this particular hour. If I had other thoughts they were so vague, and so quickly and utterly suppressed, that I cannot recall them sufficiently to relate them here.

And, once indoors, it was to be expected that there would come explanation, discussion, conversation, at any rate, regarding the singular noise and its cause, some uttered evidence of the mood that had been strong enough to drive us all inside. Yet there was none. Each of us purposely, and with various skill, ignored it. We talked little, and when we did it was of anything in the world but that. Personally, I experienced a touch of that same bewilderment which had come over me during my first talk with Frances on the evening of my arrival, for I recall now the acute tension, and the hope, yet dread, that one or other of us must sooner or later introduce the subject. It did not happen, however; no reference was made to it even remotely. It was the presence of Mabel, I felt positive, that prohibited. As soon might we have discussed Death in the bedroom of a dying woman.

The only scrap of conversation I remember, where all was ordinary and commonplace, was when Mabel spoke casually to the grenadier asking why Mrs. Marsh had omitted to do something or other—what it was I forget—and that the maid replied respectfully that "Mrs. Marsh was very sorry, but her 'and still pained her." I enquired, though so casually that I scarcely know what prompted the words, whether she had injured herself severely, and the reply, "She upset a lamp and burnt herself," was said in a tone that made me feel my curiosity was indiscreet, "but she always has an excuse for not doing things she ought to do." The little bit of conversation remained with me, and I remember particularly the quick way Frances interrupted and turned the talk upon the delinquencies of servants in general, telling incidents of her own at our flat with a volubility that perhaps seemed forced, and that certainly did not encourage general talk as it may have been intended to do. We lapsed into silence immediately she finished.

But for all our care and all our calculated silence, each knew that something had, in these last moments, come very close; it had brushed us in passing; it had retired; and I am inclined to think now that the large dark thing I saw, riding the dusk, probably bird of prey, was in some sense a symbol of it in my mind—that actually there had been no bird at all, I mean, but that my mood of apprehension and dismay had formed the vivid picture in my thoughts. It had swept past us, it had retreated, but it was now, at this moment, in hiding very close. And it was watching us.

Perhaps, too, it was mere coincidence that I encountered Mrs. Marsh, his housekeeper, several times that evening in the short interval between tea and dinner, and that on each occasion the sight of this gaunt, half-saturnine woman fed my prejudice against her. Once, on my way to the telephone, I ran into her just where the passage is somewhat jammed by a square table carrying the Chinese gong, a grandfather's clock and a box of croquet mallets. We both gave way, then both advanced, then again gave way—simultaneously. It seemed, impossible to pass. We stepped with decision to the same side, finally colliding in the middle, while saying those futile little things, half apology, half excuse, that are inevitable at such times. In the end she stood upright against the wall for me to pass, taking her place against the very door I wished to open. It was ludicrous.

"Excuse me—I was just going in—to telephone," I explained. And she sidled off, murmuring apologies, but opening the door for me while she did so. Our hands met a moment on the handle.

There was a second's awkwardness—it was too stupid. I remembered her injury, and by way of something to say, I enquired after it. She thanked me; it was entirely healed now, but it might have been much worse; and there was something about the "mercy of the Lord" that I didn't quite catch. While telephoning, however—London call, and my attention focused on it—realized sharply that this was the first time I had spoken with her; also, that I had—touched her.

It happened to be a Sunday, and the lines were clear. I got my connection quickly, and the incident was forgotten while my thoughts went up to

London. On my way upstairs, then, the woman came back into my mind, so that I recalled other things about her—how she seemed all over the house, in unlikely places often; how I had caught her sitting in the hall alone that night; how she was forever coming and going with her lugubrious visage and that untidy hair at the back that had made me laugh three years ago with the idea that it looked singed or burnt; and how the impression on my first arrival at The Towers was that this woman somehow kept alive, though its evidence was outwardly suppressed, the influence of her late employer and of his somber teachings. Somewhere with her was associated the idea of punishment, vindictiveness, revenge. I remembered again suddenly my odd notion that she sought to keep her present mistress here, a prisoner in this bleak and comfortless house, and that really, in spite of her obsequious silence, she was intensely opposed to the change of thought that had reclaimed Mabel to a happier view of life.

All this in a passing second flashed in review before me, and I discovered, or at any rate reconstructed, the real Mrs. Marsh. She was decidedly in the Shadow. More, she stood in the forefront of it, stealthily leading an assault, as it were, against The Towers and its occupants, as though, consciously or unconsciously, she labored incessantly to this hateful end.

I can only judge that some state of nervousness in me permitted the series of insignificant thoughts to assume this dramatic shape, and that what had gone before prepared the way and led her up at the head of so formidable a procession. I relate it exactly as it came to me. My nerves were doubtless somewhat on edge by now. Otherwise I should hardly have been a prey to the exaggeration at all. I seemed open to so many strange impressions.

Nothing else, perhaps, can explain my ridiculous conversation with her, when, for the third time that evening, I came suddenly upon the woman half-way down the stairs, standing by an open window as if in the act of listening. She was dressed in black, a black shawl over her square shoulders and black gloves on her big, broad hands. Two black objects, prayer books apparently, she clasped, and on her head she wore a bonnet with shaking beads of jet. At first I did not know her, as I came running down upon her from the landing; it was only when she stood aside to let me pass that I saw her profile against the tapestry and recognized Mrs. Marsh. And to catch her on the front stairs, dressed like this, struck me as incongruous—impertinent. I paused in my dangerous descent. Through the opened window came the sound of bells—church bells—a sound more depressing to me than superstition, and as nauseating. Though the action was ill judged, I obeyed the sudden prompting—was it a secret desire to attack, perhaps?—and spoke to her.

"Been to church, I suppose, Mrs. Marsh?" I said. "Or just going, perhaps?"

Her face, as she looked up a second to reply, was like an iron doll that moved its lips and turned its eyes, but made no other imitation of life at all.

"Some of us still goes, sir," she said unctuously.

It was respectful enough, yet the implied judgment of the rest of the world made me almost angry. A deferential insolence lay behind the affected meekness.

"For those who believe no doubt it is helpful," I smiled. "True religion brings peace and happiness, I'm sure—joy, Mrs. Marsh, joy!" I found keen satisfaction in the emphasis.

She looked at me like a knife. I cannot describe the implacable thing that shone in her fixed, stern eyes, nor the shadow of felt darkness that stole across her face. She glittered. I felt hate in her. I knew—she knew too—who was in the thoughts of us both at that moment.

She replied softly, never forgetting her place for an instant:

"There is joy, sir—in 'eaven—over one sinner that repenteth, and in church there goes up prayer to Gawd for those 'oo—well, for the others, sir, 'oo—"

She cut short her sentence thus. The gloom about her as she said it was like the gloom about a hearse, a tomb, a darkness of great hopeless dungeons. My tongue ran on of itself with a kind of bitter satisfaction:

"We must believe there are no others, Mrs. Marsh. Salvation, you know, would be such a failure if there were. No merciful, all-foreseeing God could ever have devised such a fearful plan—"

Her voice, interrupting me, seemed to rise out of the bowels of the earth:

"They rejected the salvation when it was offered to them, sir, on earth."

"But you wouldn't have them tortured forever because of one mistake in ignorance," I said, fixing her with my eye. "Come now, would you, Mrs. Marsh? No God worth worshipping could permit such cruelty. Think a moment what it means."

She stared at me, a curious expression in her stupid eyes. It seemed to me as though the "woman" in her revolted, while yet she dared not suffer her grim belief to trip. That is, she would willingly have had it otherwise but for a terror that prevented.

"We may pray for them, sir, and we do—we may 'ope." She dropped her eyes to the carpet.

"Good, good!" I put in cheerfully, sorry now that I had spoken at all. "That's more hopeful, at any rate isn't it?"

She murmured something about Abraham's bosom, and the "time of salvation not being forever," as I tried to pass her. Then a half gesture that she made stopped me. There was something more she wished to say—to ask. She looked up furtively. In her eyes I saw the "woman" peering out through fear.

"Per'aps, sir." she faltered, as though lightning must strike her dead, "per'aps, would you think, a drop of cold water, given in His name, might moisten—?"

But I stopped her, for the foolish talk had lasted long enough. "Of course," I exclaimed, "of course. For God is love, remember, and love means charity, tolerance, sympathy, and sparing others pain," and I hurried past her, determined to end the outrageous conversation for which yet I knew myself entirely to blame. Behind me, she stood stock-still for several minutes, half bewildered, half alarmed, as I suspected. I caught the fragment of another sentence, one word of it, rather—"punishment"—but the rest escaped me. Her arrogance and condescending tolerance exasperated me, while I was at the same time secretly pleased that I might have touched some string of remorse or sympathy in her after all. Her belief was iron; she dared not let it go; yet somewhere underneath there lurked the germ of a wholesome revulsion. She would help "them"—if she dared. Her question proved it.

Half ashamed of myself, I turned and crossed the hall quickly lest I should be tempted to say more, and in me was a disagreeable sensation as though I had just left the Incurable Ward of some great hospital. A reaction caught me as of nausea. Ugh! I wanted such people cleansed by fire. They seemed to me as centers of contamination whose vicious thoughts flowed out to stain God's glorious world. I saw myself, Frances, Mabel too especially, on the rack, while that odious figure of cruelty and darkness stood over us and ordered the awful handles turned in order that we might be "saved"—forced, that is, to think and believe exactly as she thought and believed.

I found relief for my somewhat childish indignation by letting myself loose upon the organ then. The flood of Bach and Beethoven brought back the sense of proportion. It proved, however, at the same time that there had been this growth of distortion in me, and that it had been provided apparently by my closer contact—for the first time—with that funereal personality, the woman who, like her master, believed that all holding views of God that differed from her own, must be damned eternally. It gave me, moreover, some faint clue perhaps, though a clue I was unequal of following up, to the nature of the strife and terror and frustrate influence in the house. That housekeeper had to do with it. She kept it alive. Her thought was like a spell she waved above her mistress's head.

VII

That night I was wakened by a hurried tapping at my door, and before I could answer, Frances stood beside my bed. She had switched on the light as she came in. Her hair fell straggling over her dressing gown. Her face was deathly pale, its expression so distraught it was almost haggard.

The eyes were very wide. She looked almost like another woman.

She was whispering at a great pace: "Bill, Bill, wake up, quick!"

"I am awake. What is it?" I whispered too. I was startled.

"Listen!" was all she said. Her eyes stared into vacancy.

There was not a sound in the great house. The wind had dropped, and all was still. Only the tapping seemed to continue endlessly in my brain. The clock on the mantelpiece pointed to half-past two.

"I heard nothing, Frances. What is it?" I rubbed my eyes; I had been very deeply asleep.

"Listen!" she repeated very softly, holding up one finger and turning her eyes towards the door she had left ajar. Her usual calmness had deserted her. She was in the grip of some distressing terror.

For a full minute we held our breath and listened. Then her eyes rolled round again and met my own, and her skin went even whiter than before.

"It woke me," she said beneath her breath, and moving a step nearer to my bed. "It was the Noise." Even her whisper trembled.

"The Noise!" The word repeated itself dully of its own accord. I would rather it had been anything in the world but that—earthquake, foreign cannon, collapse of the house above our heads! "The Noise, Frances! Are you sure?" I was playing really for a little time.

"It was like thunder. At first I thought it was thunder. But a minute later it came again—from underground. It's appalling." She muttered the words, her voice not properly under control.

There was a pause of perhaps a minute, and then we both spoke at once. We said foolish, obvious things that neither of us believed in for a second. The roof had fallen in, there were burglars downstairs, the safes had been blown open. It was to comfort each other as children do that we said these things; also it was to gain further time.

"There's some one in the house, of course," I heard my voice say finally, as I sprang out of bed and hurried into dressing gown and slippers. "Don't be alarmed. I'll go down and see," and from the drawer I took a pistol it was my habit to carry everywhere with me. I loaded it carefully while Frances stood stock-still beside the bed and watched. I moved towards the open door.

"You stay here, Frances," I whispered, the beating of my heart making the words uneven, "while I go down and make a search. Lock yourself in, girl. Nothing can happen to you. It was downstairs, you said?"

"Underneath," she answered faintly, pointing through the floor.

She moved suddenly between me and the door.

"Listen! Hark!" she said, the eyes in her face quite fixed; "it's coming again," and she turned her head to catch the slightest sound. I stood there watching her, and while I watched her, shook.

But nothing stirred. From the halls below rose only the whirr and quiet ticking of the numerous clocks. The blind by the open window behind us flapped out a little into the room as the draught caught it.

"I'll come with you, Bill—to the next floor," she broke the silence. "Then I'll stay with Mabel—till you come up again." The blind sank down with a long sigh as she said it.

The question jumped to my lips before I could repress it:

"Mabel is awake. She heard it too?"

I hardly know why horror caught me at her answer. All was so vague and terrible as we stood there playing the great game of this sinister house where nothing ever happened.

"We met in the passage. She was on her way to me."

What shook in me, shook inwardly. Frances, I mean, did not see it. I had the feeling just that the Noise was upon us, that any second it would boom and roar about our ears. But the deep silence held. I only heard my sister's little whisper coming across the room in answer to my question:

"Then what is Mabel doing now?"

And her reply proved that she was yielding at last beneath the dreadful tension, for she spoke at once, unable longer to keep up the pretence. With a kind of relief, as it were, she said it out, looking helplessly at me like a child:

"She is weeping and gna—"

My expression must have stopped her. I believe I clapped both hands upon her mouth, though when I realized things clearly again, I found they were covering my own ears instead. It was a moment of unutterable horror. The revulsion I felt was actually physical. It would have given me pleasure to fire off all the five chambers of my pistol into the air above my head; the sound—a definite, wholesome sound that explained itself—would have been a positive relief. Other feelings, though, were in me too, all over me, rushing to and fro. It was vain to seek their disentanglement; it was impossible. I confess that I experienced, among them, a touch of paralyzing fear—though for a moment only; it passed as sharply as it came, leaving me with a violent flush of blood to the face such as bursts of anger bring, followed abruptly by an icy perspiration over the entire body. Yet I may honestly avow that it was not ordinary personal fear I felt, nor any common dread of physical injury. It was, rather, a vast, impersonal shrinking—a sympathetic shrinking—from the agony and terror that countless others, somewhere, somehow, felt for themselves. The first sensation of a prison overwhelmed me in that instant, of bitter strife and frenzied suffering, and the fiery torture of the yearning to escape that was yet hopelessly uttered . . . It was of incredible power. It was real. The vain, intolerable hope swept over me.

I mastered myself, though hardly knowing how, and took my sister's hand.

It was as cold as ice, as I led her firmly to the door and out into the passage. Apparently she noticed nothing of my so near collapse, for I caught her whisper as we went. "You are brave, Bill; splendidly brave."

The upper corridors of the great sleeping house were brightly lit; on her way to me she had turned on every electric switch her hand could reach; and as we passed the final flight of stairs to the floor below, I heard a door shut softly and knew that Mabel had been listening—waiting for us. I led my sister up to it. She knocked, and the door was opened cautiously an inch or so. The room was pitch black. I caught no glimpse of Mabel standing there. Frances turned to me with a hurried whisper, "Billy, you will be careful, won't you?" and went in. I just had time to answer that I would not be long, and Frances to reply, "You'll find us here" when the door closed and cut her sentence short before its end.

But it was not alone the closing door that took the final words. Frances—by the way she disappeared I knew it—had made a swift and violent movement into the darkness that was as though she sprang. She leaped upon that other woman who stood back among the shadows, for, simultaneously with the clipping of the sentence, another sound was also stopped—stifled, smothered, choked back lest I should also hear it. Yet not in time. I heard it—a hard and horrible sound that explained both the leap and the abrupt cessation of the whispered words.

I stood irresolute a moment. It was as though all the bones had been withdrawn from my body, so that I must sink and fall. That sound plucked them out, and plucked out my self-possession with them. I am not sure that it was a sound I had ever heard before, though children, I half remembered, made it sometimes in blind rages when they knew not what they did. In a grown-up person certainly I had never known it. I associated it with animals rather—horribly. In the history of the world, no doubt, it has been common enough, alas, but fortunately today there can be but few who know it, or would recognize it even when heard. The bones shot back into my body the same instant, but red-hot and burning; the brief instant of irresolution passed; I was torn between the desire to break down the door and enter, and to run—run for my life from a thing I dared not face.

Out of the horrid tumult, then, I adopted neither course. Without reflection, certainly without analysis of what was best to do for my sister, myself or Mabel, I took up my action where it had been interrupted. I turned from the awful door and moved slowly towards the head of the stairs.

But that dreadful little sound came with me. I believe my own teeth chattered. It seemed all over the house—in the empty halls that opened into the long passages towards the music-room, and even in the grounds outside the building. From the lawns and barren garden, from the ugly terraces themselves, it rose into the night, and behind it came a curious driving sound, incomplete, unfinished, as of wailing for deliverance, the wailing of desperate souls in anguish, the dull and dry beseeching of hopeless spirits in prison.

That I could have taken the little sound from the bedroom where I actually heard it, and spread it thus over the entire house and grounds, is evidence, perhaps, of the state my nerves were in.

The wailing assuredly was in my mind alone. But the longer I hesitated, the more difficult became my task, and, gathering up my dressing gown, lest I should trip in the darkness, I passed slowly down the staircase into the hall below. I carried neither candle nor matches; every switch in room and corridor was known to me. The covering of darkness was indeed rather comforting than otherwise, for if it prevented seeing, it also prevented being seen. The heavy pistol, knocking against my thigh as I moved, made me feel I was carrying a child's toy, foolishly. I experienced in every nerve that primitive vast dread which is the Thrill of darkness. Merely the child in me was comforted by that pistol.

The night was not entirely black; the iron bars across the glass front door were visible, and, equally, I discerned the big, stiff wooden chairs in the hall, the gaping fireplace, the upright pillars supporting the staircase, the round table in the center with its books and flower-vases, and the basket that held visitors' cards. There, too, was the stick and umbrella stand and the shelf with railway guides, directory, and telegraph forms. Clocks ticked everywhere with sounds like quiet footfalls. Light fell here and there in patches from the floor above. I stood a moment in the hall, letting my eyes grow more accustomed to the gloom, while deciding on a plan of search. I made out the ivy trailing outside over one of the big windows . . . and then the tall clock by the front door made a grating noise deep down inside its body—it was the Presentation clock, large and hideous, given by the congregation of his church—and, dreading the booming strike it seemed to threaten, I made a quick decision. If others beside myself were about in the night, the sound of that striking might cover their approach.

So I tiptoed to the right, where the passage led towards the dining room. In the other direction were the morning- and drawing rooms, both little used, and various other rooms beyond that had been his, generally now kept locked. I thought of my sister, waiting upstairs with that frightened woman for my return. I went quickly, yet stealthily.

And, to my surprise, the door of the dining room was open. It had been opened. I paused on the threshold, staring about me. I think I fully expected to see a figure blocked in the shadows against the heavy sideboard, or looming on the other side beneath his portrait. But the room was empty; I felt it empty. Through the wide bow-windows that gave on to the verandah came an uncertain glimmer that even shone reflected in the polished surface of the dinner-table, and again I perceived the stiff outline of chairs, waiting tenantless all round it, two larger ones with high carved backs at either end. The monkey trees on the upper terrace, too, were visible outside against the sky, and the solemn crests of the wellingtonias on the terraces below. The enormous clock on the mantelpiece ticked very slowly, as though its machinery were running down, and I made out the pale round patch that was its face. Resisting my first inclination to turn the lights up—my hand had gone so far as to finger the friendly knob—I crossed the room so carefully that no single board creaked, nor a single chair, as I rested a hand upon its back, moved on the parquet flooring. I turned neither to the right nor left, nor did I once look back.

I went towards the long corridor filled with priceless objets d'art, that led through various antechambers into the spacious music-room, and only at the mouth of this corridor did I next halt a moment in uncertainty. For this long corridor, lit faintly by high windows on the left from the verandah, was very narrow, owing to the mass of shelves and fancy tables it contained. It was not that I feared to knock over precious things as I went, but, that, because of its ungenerous width, there would be no room to pass another person—if I met one. And the certainty had suddenly come upon me that somewhere in this corridor another person at this actual moment stood. Here, somehow, amid all this dead atmosphere of furniture and impersonal emptiness, lay the hint of a living human presence; and with such conviction did it come upon me, that my hand instinctively gripped the pistol in my pocket before I could even think. Either some one had passed along this corridor just before me, or some one lay waiting at its farther end—withdrawn or flattened into one of the little recesses, to let me pass. It was the person who had opened the door. And the blood ran from my heart as I realized it.

It was not courage that sent me on, but rather a strong impulsion from behind that made it impossible to retreat: the feeling that a throng pressed at my back, drawing nearer and nearer; that I was already half surrounded, swept, dragged, coaxed into a vast prison-house where there was wailing and gnashing of teeth, where their worm dieth not and their fire is not quenched. I can neither explain nor justify the storm of irrational emotion that swept me as I stood in that moment, staring down the length of the silent corridor towards the music-room at the far end, I can only repeat that no personal bravery sent me down it, but that the negative emotion of fear was swamped in this vast sea of pity and commiseration for others that surged upon me.

My senses, at least, were no whit confused; if anything, my brain registered impressions with keener accuracy than usual. I noticed, for instance, that the two swinging doors of baize that cut the corridor into definite lengths, making little rooms of the spaces between them, were both wide-open—in the dim light no mean achievement. Also that the fronds of a palm plant, some ten feet in front of me, still stirred gently from the air of someone who had recently gone past them. The long green leaves waved to and fro like hands. Then I went stealthily forward down the narrow space, proud even that I had this command of myself, and so carefully that my feet made no sound upon the Japanese matting on the floor.

It was a journey that seemed timeless. I have no idea how fast or slow I went, but I remember that I deliberately examined articles on each side of me, peering with particular closeness into the recesses of wall and window. I passed the first baize doors, and the passage beyond them widened out to hold shelves of books; there were sofas and small reading-tables against the wall.

It narrowed again presently, as I entered the second stretch. The windows here were higher and smaller, and marble statuettes of classical subject lined the walls, watching me like figures of the dead. Their white and shining faces saw me, yet made no sign. I passed next between the second baize doors. They, too, had been fastened back with hooks against the wall. Thus all doors were open—had been recently opened.

And so, at length, I found myself in the final widening of the corridor which formed an antechamber to the music-room itself. It had been used formerly to hold the overflow of meetings. No door separated it from the great hall beyond, but heavy curtains hung usually to close it off, and these curtains were invariably drawn. They now stood wide. And here—I can merely state the impression that came upon me—I knew myself at last surrounded. The throng that pressed behind me, also surged in front: facing me in the big room, and waiting for my entry, stood a multitude; on either side of me, in the very air above my head, the vast assemblage paused upon my coming. The pause, however, was momentary, for instantly the deep, tumultuous movement was resumed that yet was silent as a cavern underground. I felt the agony that was in it, the passionate striving, the awful struggle to escape. The semi-darkness held beseeching faces that fought to press themselves upon my vision, yearning yet hopeless eyes, lips scorched and dry, mouths that opened to implore but found no craved delivery in actual words, and a fury of misery and hate that made the life in me stop dead, frozen by the horror of vain pity. That intolerable, vain Hope was everywhere.

And the multitude, it came to me, was not a single multitude, but many; for, as soon as one huge division pressed too close upon the edge of escape, it was dragged back by another and prevented. The wild host was divided against itself. Here dwelt the Shadow I had "imagined" weeks ago, and in it struggled armies of lost souls as in the depths of some bottomless pit whence there is no escape. The layers mingled, fighting against themselves in endless torture. It was in this great Shadow I had clairvoyantly seen Mabel, but about its fearful mouth, I now was certain, hovered another figure of darkness, a figure who sought to keep it in existence, since to her thought were due those lampless depths of woe without escape . . . Towards me the multitudes now surged.

It was a sound and a movement that brought me back into myself. The great dock at the farther end of the room just then struck the hour of three. That was the sound. And the movement—? I was aware that a figure was passing across the distant center of the floor. Instantly I dropped back into the arena of my little human terror. My hand again clutched stupidly at the pistol butt. I drew back into the folds of the heavy curtain. And the figure advanced.

I remember every detail. At first it seemed to me enormous—this advancing shadow—far beyond human scale; but as it came nearer, I measured it, though not consciously, by the organ pipes that gleamed in faint colors, just above its gradual soft approach. It passed them, already halfway across the great room. I saw then that its stature was that of ordinary men. The prolonged booming of the clock died away. I heard the footfall, shuffling upon the polished boards. I heard another sound—a voice, low and monotonous, droning as in prayer. The figure was speaking. It was a woman. And she carried in both hands before her a small object that faintly shimmered—a glass of water. And then I recognized her.

There was still an instant's time before she reached me, and I made use of it. I shrank back, flattening myself against the wall. Her voice ceased a moment, as she turned and carefully drew the curtains together behind her, closing them with one hand. Oblivious of my presence, though she actually touched my dressing gown with the hand that pulled the cords, she resumed her dreadful, solemn march, disappearing at length down the long vista of the corridor like a shadow.

But as she passed me, her voice began again, so that I heard each word distinctly as she uttered it, her head aloft, her figure upright, as though she moved at the head of a procession:

"A drop of cold water, given in His name, shall moisten their burning tongues."

It was repeated monotonously over and over again, droning down into the distance as she went, until at length both voice and figure faded into the shadows at the farther end.

For a time, I have no means of measuring precisely, I stood in that dark corner, pressing my back against the wall, and would have drawn the curtains down to hide me had I dared to stretch an arm out. The dread that presently the woman would return passed gradually away. I realized that the air had emptied, the crowd her presence had stirred into activity had retreated; I was alone in the gloomy under-space of the odious building . . . Then I remembered suddenly again the terrified women waiting for me on that upper landing; and realized that my skin was wet and freezing cold after a profuse perspiration. I prepared to retrace my steps. I remember the effort it cost me to leave the support of the wall and covering darkness of my corner, and step out into the grey light of the corridor. At first I sidled, then, finding this mode of walking impossible, turned my face boldly and walked quickly, regardless that my dressing gown set the precious objects shaking as I passed. A wind that sighed mournfully against the high, small windows seemed to have got inside the corridor as well; it felt so cold; and every moment I dreaded to see the outline of the woman's figure as she waited in recess or angle against the wall for me to pass.

Was there another thing I dreaded even more? I cannot say. I only know that the first baize doors had swung to behind me, and the second ones were close at hand, when the great dim thunder caught me, pouring up with prodigious volume so that it seemed to roll out from another world. It shook the very bowels of the building. I was closer to it than that other time, when it had followed me from the goblin garden. There was strength and hardness in it, as of metal reverberation. Some touch of numbness, almost of paralysis, must surely have been upon me that I felt no actual terror, for I remember even turning and standing still to hear it better. "That is the Noise," my thought ran stupidly, and I think I whispered it aloud; "the Doors are closing." The wind outside against the windows was audible, so it cannot have been really loud, yet to me it was the biggest, deepest sound I have ever heard, but so far away, with such awful remoteness in it, that I had to doubt my own ears at the same time. It seemed underground—the rumbling of earthquake gates that shut remorselessly within the rocky Earth—stupendous ultimate thunder. They were shut off from help again. The doors had closed.

I felt a storm of pity, an agony of bitter, futile hate sweep through me. My memory of the figure changed then. The Woman with the glass of cooling water had stepped down from Heaven; but the Man—or was it Men?—who smeared this terrible layer of belief and Thought upon the world! . . .

I crossed the dining room—it was fancy, of course, that held my eyes from glancing at the portrait for fear I should see it smiling approval—and so finally reached the hall, where the light from the floor above seemed now quite bright in comparison. All the doors I closed carefully behind me; but first I had to open them. The woman had closed every one. Up the stairs, then, I actually ran, two steps at a time. My sister was standing outside Mabel's door. By her face I knew that she had also heard. There was no need to ask. I quickly made my mind up.

"There's nothing," I said, and detailed briefly my tour of search. "All is quiet and undisturbed downstairs." May God forgive me!

She beckoned to me, closing the door softly behind her. My heart beat violently a moment, then stood still.

"Mabel," she said aloud.

It was like the sentence of a judge, that one short word.

I tried to push past her and go in, but she stopped me with her arm. She was wholly mistress of herself, I saw.

"Hush!" she said in a lower voice. "I've got her round again with brandy. She's sleeping quietly now. We won't disturb her."

She drew me farther out into the landing, and as she did so, the clock in the hall below struck half-past three. I had stood, then, thirty minutes in the corridor below. "You've been such a long time." she said simply. "I feared for you," and she took my hand in her own that was cold and clammy.

VIII

And then, while that dreadful house stood listening about us in the early hours of this chill morning upon the edge of winter, she told me, with laconic brevity, things about Mabel that I heard as from a distance. There was nothing so unusual or tremendous in the short recital, nothing indeed I might not have already guessed for myself. It was the time and scene, the inference, too, that made it so afflicting: the idea that Mabel believed herself so utterly and hopelessly lost—beyond recovery damned.

That she had loved him with so passionate a devotion that she had given her soul into his keeping, this certainly I had not divined—probably because I had never thought about it one way or the other. He had "converted" her, I knew, but that she had subscribed whole-heartedly to that most cruel and ugly of his dogmas—this was new to me, and came with a certain shock as I heard it. In love, of course, the weaker nature is receptive to all manner of suggestion. This man had "suggested" his pet brimstone lake so vividly that she had listened and believed. He had frightened her into heaven; and his heaven, a definite locality in the skies, had its foretaste here on earth in miniature—The Towers, house, and garden. Into his dolorous scheme of a handful saved and millions damned, his enclosure, as it were, of sheep and goats, he had swept her before she was aware of it. Her mind no longer was her own. And it was Mrs. Marsh who kept the thought-stream open, though tempered, as she deemed, with that touch of craven, superstitious mercy.

But what I found it difficult to understand, and still more difficult to accept, was that, during her year abroad, she had been so haunted with a secret dread of that hideous after-death that she had finally revolted and tried to recover that clearer state of mind she had enjoyed before the religious bully had stunned her—yet had tried in vain. She had returned to The Towers to find her soul again, only to realize that it was lost eternally. The cleaner state of mind lay then beyond recovery. In the reaction that followed the removal of his terrible "suggestion," she felt the crumbling of all that he had taught her, but searched in vain for the peace and beauty his teachings had destroyed. Nothing came to replace these. She was empty, desolate, hopeless; craving her former joy and carelessness, she found only hate and diabolical calculation. This man, whom she had loved to the point of losing her soul for him, had bequeathed to her one black and fiery thing—the terror of the damned. His thinking wrapped her in this iron garment that held her fast.

All this Frances told me, far more briefly than I have here repeated it. In her eyes and gestures and laconic sentences lay the conviction of great beating issues and of menacing drama my own description fails to recapture. It was all so incongruous and remote from the world I lived in that more than once a smile, though a smile of pity, fluttered to my lips; but a glimpse of my face in the mirror showed rather the leer of a grimace. There was no real laughter anywhere that night.

The entire adventure seemed so incredible, here, in this twentieth century—but yet delusion, that feeble word, did not occur once in the comments my mind suggested though did not utter. I remembered that forbidding Shadow too; my sister's watercolors; the vanished personality of our hostess; the inexplicable, thundering Noise, and the figure of Mrs. Marsh in her midnight ritual that was so childish yet so horrible. I shivered in spite of my own "emancipated" cast of mind.

"There is no Mabel," were the words with which my sister sent another shower of ice down my spine. "He has killed her in his lake of fire and brimstone."

I stared at her blankly, as in a nightmare where nothing true or possible ever happened.

"He killed her in his lake of fire and brimstone," she repeated more faintly.

A desperate effort was in me to say the strong, sensible thing which should destroy the oppressive horror that grew so stiflingly about us both, but again the mirror drew the attempted smile into the merest grin, betraying the distortion that was everywhere in the place.

"You mean," I stammered beneath my breath, "that her faith has gone, but that the terror has remained?" I asked it, dully groping. I moved out of the line of the reflection in the glass.

She bowed her head as though beneath a weight; her skin was the pallor of grey ashes.

"You mean," I said louder, "that she has lost her—mind?"

"She is terror incarnate," was the whispered answer. "Mabel has lost her soul. Her soul is—there!" She pointed horribly below. "She is seeking it . . . ?"

The word "soul" stung me into something of my normal self again.

"But her terror, poor thing, is not—cannot be—transferable to us!" I exclaimed more vehemently. "It certainly is not convertible into feelings, sights and—even sounds!"

She interrupted me quickly, almost impatiently, speaking with that conviction by which she conquered me so easily that night.

"It is her terror that revived 'the Others.' It has brought her into touch with them. They are loose and driving after her. Her efforts at resistance have given them also hope—that escape, after all, is possible. Day and night they strive.

"Escape! Others!" The anger fast rising in me dropped of its own accord at the moment of birth. It shrank into a shuddering beyond my control. In that moment, I think, I would have believed in the possibility of anything and everything she might tell me. To argue or contradict seemed equally futile.

"His strong belief, as also the beliefs of others who have preceded him," she replied, so sure of herself that I actually turned to look over my shoulder, "have left their shadow like a thick deposit over the house and grounds. To them, poor souls imprisoned by thought, it was hopeless as granite walls—until her resistance, her effort to dissipate it—let in light. Now, in their thousands, they are flocking to this little light, seeking escape. Her own escape, don't you see, may release them all!"

It took my breath away. Had his predecessors, former occupants of this house, also preached damnation of all the world but their own exclusive sect? Was this the explanation of her obscure talk of "layers," each striving against the other for domination? And if men are spirits, and these spirits survive, could strong Thought thus determine their condition even afterwards?

So many questions flooded into me that I selected no one of them, but stared in uncomfortable silence, bewildered, out of my depth, and acutely, painfully distressed. There was so odd a mixture of possible truth and incredible, unacceptable explanation in it all; so much confirmed, yet so much left darker than before. What she said did, indeed, offer a quasi-interpretation of my own series of abominable sensations—strife, agony, pity, hate, escape—but so far-fetched that only the deep conviction in her voice and attitude made it tolerable for a second even. I found myself in a curious state of mind. I could neither think clearly nor say a word to refute her amazing statements, whispered there beside me in the shivering hours of the early morning with only a wall between ourselves and—Mabel. Close behind her words I remember this singular thing, however—that an atmosphere as of the Inquisition seemed to rise and stir about the room, beating awful wings of black above my head.

Abruptly, then, a moment's common sense returned to me. I faced her.

"And the Noise?" I said aloud, more firmly, "the roar of the closing doors? We have all heard that! Is that subjective too?"

Frances looked sideways about her in a queer fashion that made my flesh creep again. I spoke brusquely, almost angrily. I repeated the question, and waited with anxiety for her reply.

"What noise?" she asked, with the frank expression of an innocent child. "What closing doors?"

But her face turned from grey to white, and I saw that drops of perspiration glistened on her forehead. She caught at the back of a chair to steady herself, then glanced about her again with that sidelong look that made my blood run cold. I understood suddenly then. She did not take in what I said. I knew now. She was listening—for something else.

And the discovery revived in me a far stronger emotion than any mere desire for immediate explanation. Not only did I not insist upon an answer, but I was actually terrified lest she would answer. More, I felt in me a terror lest I should be moved to describe my own experiences below-stairs, thus increasing their reality and so the reality of all. She might even explain them too!

Still listening intently, she raised her head and looked me in the eyes. Her lips opened to speak. The words came to me from a great distance, it seemed, and her voice had a sound like a stone that drops into a deep well, its fate though hidden, known.

"We are in it with her, too, Bill. We are in it with her. Our interpretations vary—because we are—in parts of it only. Mabel is in it—all."

The desire for violence came over me. If only she would say a definite thing in plain King's English! If only I could find it in me to give utterance to what shouted so loud within me! If only—the same old cry—something would happen! For all this elliptic talk that dazed my mind left obscurity everywhere. Her atrocious meaning, nonetheless, flashed through me, though vanishing before it wholly divulged itself.

It brought a certain reaction with it. I found my tongue. Whether I actually believed what I said is more than I can swear to; that it seemed to me wise at the moment is all I remember. My mind was in a state of obscure perception less than that of normal consciousness.

"Yes, Frances, I believe that what you say is the truth, and that we are in it with her"—I meant to say *I* with loud, hostile emphasis, but instead I whispered it lest she should hear the trembling of my voice—"and for that reason, my dear sister, we leave tomorrow, you and I—today, rather, since it is long past midnight—we leave this house of the damned. We go back to London."

Frances looked up, her face distraught almost beyond recognition. But it was not my words that caused the tumult in her heart. It was a sound—the sound she had been listening for—so faint I barely caught it myself, and had she not pointed I could never have known the direction whence it came. Small and terrible it rose again in the stillness of the night, the sound of gnashing teeth. And behind it came another—the tread of stealthy footsteps. Both were just outside the door.

The room swung round me for a second. My first instinct to prevent my sister going out—she had dashed past me frantically to the door—gave place to another when I saw the expression in her eyes. I followed her lead instead; it was surer than my own. The pistol in my pocket swung uselessly against my thigh. I was flustered beyond belief and ashamed that I was so.

"Keep close to me, Frances," I said huskily, as the door swung wide and a shaft of light fell upon a figure moving rapidly. Mabel was going down the corridor. Beyond her, in the shadows on the staircase, a second figure stood beckoning, scarcely visible.

"Before they get her! Quick!" was screamed into my ears, and our arms were about her in the same moment. It was a horrible scene. Not that Mabel struggled in the least, but that she collapsed as we caught her and fell with her dead weight, as of a corpse, limp, against us. And her teeth began again. They continued, even beneath the hand that Frances clapped upon her lips . . .

We carried her back into her own bedroom, where she lay down peacefully enough. It was so soon over . . . The rapidity of the whole thing robbed it of reality almost. It had the swiftness of something remembered rather than of something witnessed. She slept again so quickly that it was almost as if we had caught her sleepwalking. I cannot say. I asked no questions at the time; I have asked none since; and my help was needed as little as the protection of my pistol. Frances was strangely competent and collected . . . I lingered for some time uselessly by the door, till at length, looking up with a sigh, she made a sign for me to go.

"I shall wait in your room next door," I whispered, "till you come." But, though going out, I waited in the corridor instead, so as to hear the faintest call for help. In that dark corridor upstairs I waited, but not long. It may have been fifteen minutes when Frances reappeared, locking the door softly behind her. Leaning over the banisters, I saw her.

"I'll go in again about six o'clock," she whispered, "as soon as it gets light. She is sound asleep now. Please don't wait. If anything happens I'll call—you might leave your door ajar, perhaps."

And she came up, looking like a ghost.

But I saw her first safely into bed, and the rest of the night I spent in an armchair close to my opened door, listening for the slightest sound. Soon after five o'clock I heard Frances fumbling with the key, and, peering over the railing again, I waited till she reappeared and went back into her own room. She closed her door. Evidently she was satisfied that all was well.

Then, and then only, did I go to bed myself, but not to sleep. I could not get the scene out of my mind, especially that odious detail of it which I hoped and believed my sister had not seen—the still, dark figure of the housekeeper waiting on the stairs below—waiting, of course, for Mabel.

IX

It seems I became a mere spectator after that; my sister's lead was so assured for one thing, and, for another, the responsibility of leaving Mabel alone—Frances laid it bodily upon my shoulders—was a little more than I cared about. Moreover, when we all three met later in the day, things went on so exactly as before, so absolutely without friction or distress, that to present a sudden, obvious excuse for cutting our visit short seemed ill-judged. And on the lowest grounds it would have been desertion. At any rate, it was beyond my powers, and Frances was quite firm that she must stay. We therefore did stay. Things that happen in the night always seem exaggerated and distorted when the sun shines brightly next morning; no one can reconstruct the terror of a nightmare afterwards, nor comprehend why it seemed so overwhelming at the time.

I slept till ten o'clock, and when I rang for breakfast, a note from my sister lay upon the tray, its message of counsel couched in a calm and comforting strain. Mabel, she assured me, was herself again and remembered nothing of what had happened; there was no need of any violent measures; I was to treat her exactly as if I knew nothing. "And, if you don't mind, Bill, let us leave the matter unmentioned between ourselves as well. Discussion exaggerates; such things are best not talked about. I'm sorry I disturbed you so unnecessarily; I was stupidly excited. Please forget all the things I said at the moment." She had written "nonsense" first instead of "things," then scratched it out. She wished to convey that hysteria had been abroad in the night, and I readily gulped the explanation down, though it could not satisfy me in the smallest degree.

There was another week of our visit still, and we stayed it out to the end without disaster. My desire to leave at times became that frantic thing, desire to escape; but I controlled it, kept silent, watched and wondered. Nothing happened. As before, and everywhere, there was no sequence of development, no connection between cause and effect; and climax, none whatever. The thing swayed up and down, backwards and forwards like a great loose curtain in the wind, and I could only vaguely surmise what caused the draught or why there was a curtain at all. A novelist might mold the queer material into coherent sequence that would be interesting but could not be true.

It remains, therefore, not a story but a history. Nothing happened.

Perhaps my intense dislike of the fall of darkness was due wholly to my stirred imagination, and perhaps my anger when I learned that Frances now occupied a bed in our hostess's room was unreasonable. Nerves were unquestionably on edge. I was forever on the lookout for some event that should make escape imperative, but yet that never presented itself. I slept lightly, left my door ajar to catch the slightest sound, even made stealthy tours of the house below-stairs while everybody dreamed in their beds. But I discovered nothing; the doors were always locked; I neither saw the housekeeper again in unreasonable times and places, nor heard a footstep in the passages and halls. The Noise was never once repeated. That horrible, ultimate thunder, my intensest dread of all, lay withdrawn into the abyss whence it had twice arisen. And though in my thoughts it was sternly denied existence, the great black reason for the fact afflicted me unbelievably. Since Mabel's fruitless effort to escape, the Doors kept closed remorselessly. She had failed; they gave up hope. For this was the explanation that haunted the region of my mind where feelings stir and hint before they clothe themselves in actual language. Only I firmly kept it there; it never knew expression.

But, if my ears were open, my eyes were opened too, and it were idle to pretend that I did not notice a hundred details that were capable of sinister interpretation had I been weak enough to yield. Some protective barrier had fallen into ruins round me, so that Terror stalked behind the general collapse, feeling for me through all the gaping fissures. Much of this, I admit, must have been merely the elaboration of those sensations I had first vaguely felt, before subsequent events and my talks with Frances had dramatized them into living thoughts. I therefore leave them unmentioned in this history, just as my mind left them unmentioned in that interminable final week. Our life went on precisely as before—Mabel unreal and outwardly so still; Frances, secretive, anxious, tactful to the point of slyness, and keen to save to the point of self-forgetfulness.

There were the same stupid meals, the same wearisome long evenings, the stifling ugliness of house and grounds, the Shadow settling in so thickly that it seemed almost a visible, tangible thing. I came to feel the only friendly things in all this hostile, cruel place were the robins that hopped boldly over the monstrous terraces and even up to the windows of the unsightly house itself. The robins alone knew joy; they danced, believing no evil thing was possible in all God's radiant world. They believed in everybody; their god's plan of life had no room in it for hell, damnation, and lakes of brimstone. I came to love the little birds. Had Samuel Franklyn known them, he might have preached a different sermon, bequeathing love in place of terror!

Most of my time I spent writing; but it was a pretence at best, and rather a dangerous one besides. For it stirred the mind to production, with the result that other things came pouring in as well. With reading it was the same. In the end I found an aggressive, deliberate resistance to be the only way of feasible defense. To walk far afield was out of the question, for it meant leaving my sister too long alone, so that my exercise was confined to nearer home. My saunters in the grounds, however, never surprised the goblin garden again. It was close at hand, but I seemed unable to get wholly into it. Too many things assailed my mind for any one to hold exclusive possession, perhaps.

Indeed, all the interpretations, all the "layers," to use my sister's phrase, slipped in by turns and lodged there for a time. They came day and night, and though my reason denied them entrance they held their own as by a kind of squatter's right. They stirred moods already in me, that is, and did not introduce entirely new ones; for every mind conceals ancestral deposits that have been cultivated in turn along the whole line of its descent. Any day a chance shower may cause this one or that to blossom. Thus it came to me, at any rate. After darkness the Inquisition paced the empty corridors and set up ghastly apparatus in the dismal halls; and once, in the library, there swept over me that easy and delicious conviction that by confessing my wickedness I could resume it later, since Confession is expression, and expression brings relief and leaves one ready to accumulate again. And in such mood I felt bitter and unforgiving towards all others who thought differently. Another time it was a Pagan thing that assaulted me—so trivial yet oh, so significant at the time—when I dreamed that a herd of centaurs rolled up with a great stamping of hoofs round the house to destroy it, and then woke to hear the horses tramping across the field below the lawns; they neighed ominously and their noisy panting was audible as if it were just outside my windows.

But the tree episode, I think, was the most curious of all—except, perhaps, the incident with the children which I shall mention in a moment—for its closeness to reality was so unforgettable.

Outside the east window of my room stood a giant wellingtonia on the lawn, its head rising level with the upper sash. It grew some twenty feet away, planted on the highest terrace, and I often saw it when closing my curtains for the night, noticing how it drew its heavy skirts about it, and how the light from other windows threw glimmering streaks and patches that turned it into the semblance of a towering, solemn image. It stood there then so strikingly, somehow like a great old-world idol, that it claimed attention. Its appearance was curiously formidable. Its branches rustled without visibly moving and it had a certain portentous, forbidding air, so grand and dark and monstrous in the night that I was always glad when my curtains shut it out. Yet, once in bed, I had never thought about it one way or the other, and by day had certainly never sought it out.

One night, then, as I went to bed and closed this window against a cutting easterly wind, I saw—that there were two of these trees. A brother wellingtonia rose mysteriously beside it, equally huge, equally towering, equally monstrous. The menacing pair of them faced me there upon the lawn. But in this new arrival lay a strange suggestion that frightened me before I could argue it away. Exact counterpart of its giant companion, it revealed also that gross, odious quality that all my sister's paintings held. I got the odd impression that the rest of these trees, stretching away dimly in a troop over the farther lawns, were similar, and that, led by this enormous pair, they had all moved boldly closer to my windows. At the same moment a blind was drawn down over an upper room; the second tree disappeared into the surrounding darkness.

It was, of course, this chance light that had brought it into the field of vision, but when the black shutter dropped over it, hiding it from view, the manner of its vanishing produced the queer effect that it had slipped into its companion—almost that it had been an emanation of the one I so disliked, and not really a tree at all! In this way the garden turned vehicle for expressing what lay behind it all . . . !

The behavior of the doors, the little, ordinary doors, seems scarcely worth mention at all, their queer way of opening and shutting of their own accord; for this was accountable in a hundred natural ways, and to tell the truth, I never caught one in the act of moving. Indeed, only after frequent repetitions did the detail force itself upon me, when, having noticed one, I noticed all. It produced, however, the unpleasant impression of a continual coming and going in the house, as though, screened cleverly and purposely from actual sight, some one in the building held constant invisible intercourse with—others.

Upon detailed descriptions of these uncertain incidents I do not venture, individually so trivial, but taken all together so impressive and so insolent. But the episode of the children, mentioned above, was different. And I give it because it showed how vividly the intuitive child-mind received the impression—one impression, at any rate—of what was in the air. It may be told in a very few words. I believe they were the coachman's children, and that the man had been in Mr. Franklyn's service; but of neither point am I quite positive.

I heard screaming in the rose-garden that runs along the stable walls—it was one afternoon not far from the tea-hour—and on hurrying up I found a little girl of nine or ten fastened with ropes to a rustic seat, and two other children—boys, one about twelve and one much younger—gathering sticks beneath the climbing rose trees. The girl was white and frightened, but the others were laughing and talking among themselves so busily while they picked that they did not notice my abrupt arrival. Some game, I understood, was in progress, but a game that had become too serious for the happiness of the prisoner, for there was a fear in the girl's eyes that was a very genuine fear indeed. I unfastened her at once; the ropes were so loosely and clumsily knotted that they had not hurt her skin; it was not that which made her pale. She collapsed a moment upon the bench, then picked up her tiny skirts and dived away at full speed into the safety of the stable-yard.

There was no response to my brief comforting, but she ran as though for her life, and I divined that some horrid boys' cruelty had been afoot. It was probably mere thoughtlessness, as cruelty with children usually is, but something in me decided to discover exactly what it was.

And the boys, not one whit alarmed at my intervention, merely laughed shyly when I explained that their prisoner had escaped, and told me frankly what their "game" had been. There was no vestige of shame in them, nor any idea, of course, that they aped a monstrous reality.

That it was mere pretence was neither here nor there. To them, though make-believe, it was a make-believe of something that was right and natural and in no sense cruel. Grown-ups did it too. It was necessary for her good.

"We was going to burn her up, sir," the older one informed me, answering my "Why?" with the explanation, "Because she wouldn't believe what we wanted 'er to believe."

And, game though it was, the feeling of reality about the little episode was so arresting, so terrific in some way, that only with difficulty did I confine my admonitions on this occasion to mere words. The boys slunk off, frightened in their turn, yet not, I felt, convinced that they had erred in principle. It was their inheritance. They had breathed it in with the atmosphere of their bringing-up. They would renew the salutary torture when they could—till she "believed" as they did.

I went back into the house, afflicted with a passion of mingled pity and distress impossible to describe, yet on my short way across the garden was attacked by other moods in turn, each more real and bitter than its predecessor. I received the whole series, as it were, at once. I felt like a diver rising to the surface through layers of water at different temperatures, though here the natural order was reversed, and the cooler strata were uppermost, the heated ones below. Thus, I was caught by the goblin touch of the willows that fringed the field; by the sensuous curving of the twisted ash that formed a gateway to the little grove of sapling oaks where fauns and satyrs lurked to play in the moonlight before Pagan altars; and by the cloaking darkness, next, of the copse of stunted pines, close gathered each to each, where hooded figures stalked behind an awful cross. The episode with the children seemed to have opened me like a knife. The whole Place rushed at me.

I suspect this synthesis of many moods produced in me that climax of loathing and disgust which made me feel the limit of bearable emotion had been reached, so that I made straight to find Frances in order to convince her that at any rate I must leave. For, although this was our last day in the house, and we had arranged to go next day, the dread was in me that she would still find some persuasive reason for staying on. And an unexpected incident then made my dread unnecessary. The front door was open and a cab stood in the drive; a tall, elderly man was gravely talking in the hall with the parlor maid we called the Grenadier. He held a piece of paper in his hand. "I have called to see the house," I heard him say, as I ran up the stairs to Frances, who was peering like an inquisitive child over the banisters . . .

"Yes," she told me with a sigh, I know not whether of resignation or relief, "the house is to be let or sold. Mabel has decided. Some Society or other, I believe—"

I was overjoyed: this made our leaving right and possible. "You never told me, Frances!"

"Mabel only heard of it a few days ago. She told me herself this morning. It is a chance, she says. Alone she cannot get it 'straight.'"

"Defeat?" I asked, watching her closely.

"She thinks she has found a way out. It's not a family, you see, it's a Society, a sort of Community—they go in for thought—"

"A Community!" I gasped. "You mean religious?"

She shook her head. "Not exactly," she said smiling, "but some kind of association of men and women who want a headquarters in the country—a place where they can write and meditate—think—mature their plans and all the rest—I don't know exactly what."

"Utopian dreamers?" I asked, yet feeling an immense relief come over me as I heard. But I asked in ignorance, not cynically. Frances would know. She knew all this kind of thing.

"No, not that exactly," she smiled. "Their teachings are grand and simple—old as the world too, really—the basis of every religion before men's minds perverted them with their manufactured creeds—"

Footsteps on the stairs, and the sound of voices, interrupted our odd impromptu conversation, as the Grenadier came up, followed by the tall, grave gentleman who was being shown over the house. My sister drew me along the corridor towards her room, where she went in and closed the door behind me, yet not before I had stolen a good look at the caller—long enough, at least, for his face and general appearance to have made a definite impression on me. For something strong and peaceful emanated from his presence; he moved with such quiet dignity; the glance of his eyes was so steady and reassuring, that my mind labeled him instantly as a type of man one would turn to in an emergency and not be disappointed. I had seen him but for a passing moment, but I had seen him twice, and the way he walked down the passage, looking competently about him, conveyed the same impression as when I saw him standing at the door—fearless, tolerant, wise. "A sincere and kindly character," I judged instantly, "a man whom some big kind of love has trained in sweetness towards the world; no hate in him anywhere." A great deal, no doubt, to read in so brief a glance! Yet his voice confirmed my intuition, a deep and very gentle voice, great firmness in it too.

"Have I become suddenly sensitive to people's atmospheres in this extraordinary fashion?" I asked myself, smiling, as I stood in the room and heard the door close behind me. "Have I developed some clairvoyant faculty here?" At any other time I should have mocked.

And I sat down and faced my sister, feeling strangely comforted and at peace for the first time since I had stepped beneath The Towers' roof a month ago. Frances, I then saw, was smiling a little as she watched me.

"You know him?" I asked.

"You felt it too?" was her question in reply. "No," she added, "I don't know him—beyond the fact that he is a leader in the Movement and has devoted years and money to its objects. Mabel felt the same thing in him that you have felt—and jumped at it."

"But you've seen him before?" I urged, for the certainty was in me that he was no stranger to her.

She shook her head. "He called one day early this week, when you were out. Mabel saw him. I believe—" she hesitated a moment, as though expecting me to stop her with my usual impatience of such subjects—"I believe he has explained everything to her—the beliefs he embodies, she declares, are her salvation—might be, rather, if she could adopt them."

"Conversion again!" For I remembered her riches, and how gladly a Society would gobble them.

"The layers I told you about," she continued calmly, shrugging her shoulders slightly—"the deposits that are left behind by strong thinking and real belief—but especially by ugly, hateful belief, because, you see—unfortunately there's more vital passion in that sort—"

"Frances, I don't understand a bit," I said out loud, but said it a little humbly, for the impression the man had left was still strong upon me and I was grateful for the steady sense of peace and comfort he had somehow introduced. The horrors had been so dreadful. My nerves, doubtless, were more than a little overstrained. Absurd as it must sound, I classed him in my mind with the robins, the happy, confiding robins who believed in everybody and thought no evil! I laughed a moment at my ridiculous idea, and my sister, encouraged by this sign of patience in me, continued more fluently.

"Of course you don't understand, Bill? Why should you? You've never thought about such things. Needing no creed yourself, you think all creeds are rubbish."

"I'm open to conviction—I'm tolerant," I interrupted.

"You're as narrow as Sam Franklyn, and as crammed with prejudice," she answered, knowing that she had me at her mercy.

"Then, pray, what may be his, or his Society's beliefs?" I asked, feeling no desire to argue, "and how are they going to prove your Mabel's salvation? Can they bring beauty into all this aggressive hate and ugliness?"

"Certain hope and peace," she said, "that peace which is understanding, and that understanding which explains all creeds and therefore tolerates them."

"Toleration! The one word a religious man loathes above all others! His pet word is damnation—"

"Tolerates them," she repeated patiently, unperturbed by my explosion, "because it includes them all."

"Fine, if true," I admitted, "very fine. But how, pray, does it include them all?"

"Because the key-word, the motto, of their Society is, 'There is no religion higher than Truth,' and it has no single dogma of any kind. Above all," she went on, "because it claims that no individual can be 'lost.' It teaches universal salvation. To damn outsiders is uncivilized, childish, impure. Some take longer than others—it's according to the way they think and live—but all find peace, through development, in the end. What the creeds call a hopeless soul, it regards as a soul having further to go. There is no damnation—"

"Well, well," I exclaimed, feeling that she rode her hobby horse too wildly, too roughly over me, "but what is the bearing of all this upon this dreadful place, and upon Mabel? I'll admit that there is this atmosphere—this—er—inexplicable horror in the house and grounds, and that if not of damnation exactly, it is certainly damnable. I'm not too prejudiced to deny that, for I've felt it myself."

To my relief she was brief. She made her statement, leaving me to take it or reject it as I would.

"The thought and belief its former occupants—have left behind. For there has been coincidence here, a coincidence that must be rare. The site on which this modern house now stands was Roman, before that Early Britain, with burial mounds, before that again, Druid—the Druid stones still lie in that copse below the field, the Tumuli among the ilexes behind the drive.

The older building Sam Franklyn altered and practically pulled down was a monastery; he changed the chapel into a meeting hall, which is now the music room; but, before he came here, the house was occupied by Manetti, a violent Catholic without tolerance or vision; and in the interval between these two, Julius Weinbaum had it, Hebrew of most rigid orthodox type imaginable—so they all have left their—"

"Even so," I repeated, yet interested to hear the rest, "what of it?"

"Simply this," said Frances with conviction, "that each in turn has left his layer of concentrated thinking and belief behind him; because each believed intensely, absolutely, beyond the least weakening of any doubt—the kind of strong belief and thinking that is rare anywhere today, the kind that wills, impregnates objects, saturates the atmosphere, haunts, in a word. And each, believing he was utterly and finally right, damned with equally positive conviction the rest of the world. One and all preached that implicitly if not explicitly. It's the root of every creed. Last of the bigoted, grim series came Samuel Franklyn."

I listened in amazement that increased as she went on. Up to this point her explanation was so admirable. It was, indeed, a pretty study in psychology if it were true.

"Then why does nothing ever happen?" I enquired mildly. "A place so thickly haunted ought to produce a crop of no ordinary results!"

"There lies the proof," she went on in a lowered voice, "the proof of the horror and the ugly reality. The thought and belief of each occupant in turn kept all the others under. They gave no sign of life at the time. But the results of thinking never die. They crop out again the moment there's an opening. And, with the return of Mabel in her negative state, believing nothing positive herself the place for the first time found itself free to reproduce its buried stores.

"Damnation, hell-fire, and the rest—the most permanent and vital thought of all those creeds, since it was applied to the majority of the world—broke loose again, for there was no restraint to hold it back. Each sought to obtain its former supremacy. None conquered. There results a pandemonium of hate and fear, of striving to escape, of agonized, bitter warring to find safety, peace—salvation. The place is saturated by that appalling stream of thinking—the terror of the damned. It concentrated upon Mabel, whose negative attitude furnished the channel of deliverance. You and I, according to our sympathy with her, were similarly involved. Nothing happened, because no one layer could ever gain the supremacy."

I was so interested—I dare not say amused—that I stared in silence while she paused a moment, afraid that she would draw rein and end the fairy tale too soon.

"The beliefs of this man, of his Society rather, vigorously thought and therefore vigorously given out here, will put the whole place straight. It will act as a solvent. These vitriolic layers actively denied, will fuse and disappear in the stream of gentle, tolerant sympathy which is love. For each member, worthy of the name, loves the world, and all creeds go into the melting-pot; Mabel, too, if she joins them out of real conviction, will find salvation—"

"Thinking, I know, is of the first importance," I objected, "but don't you, perhaps, exaggerate the power of feeling and emotion which in religion are au fond always hysterical?"

"What is the world," she told me, "but thinking and feeling? An individual's world is entirely what that individual thinks and believes—interpretation. There is no other. And unless he really thinks and really believes, he has no permanent world at all. I grant that few people think, and still fewer believe, and that most take ready-made suits and make them do. Only the strong make their own things; the lesser fry, Mabel among them, are merely swept up into what has been manufactured for them. They get along somehow. You and I have made for ourselves, Mabel has not. She is a nonentity, and when her belief is taken from her, she goes with it."

It was not in me just then to criticize the evasion, or pick out the sophistry from the truth. I merely waited for her to continue.

"None of us have Truth, my dear Frances," I ventured presently, seeing that she kept silent.

"Precisely," she answered, "but most of us have beliefs. And what one believes and thinks affects the world at large. Consider the legacy of hatred and cruelty involved in the doctrines men have built into their creeds where the sine qua non of salvation is absolute acceptance of one particular set of views or else perishing everlastingly—for only by repudiating history can they disavow it—"

"You're not quite accurate," I put in. "Not all the creeds teach damnation, do they? Franklyn did, of course, but the others are a bit modernized now surely?"

"Trying to get out of it," she admitted, "perhaps they are, but damnation of unbelievers—of most of the world, that is—is their rather favorite idea if you talk with them."

"I never have."

She smiled. "But I have," she said significantly, "so, if you consider what the various occupants of this house have so strongly held and thought and believed, you need not be surprised that the influence they have left behind them should be a dark and dreadful legacy. For thought, you know, does leave—"

The opening of the door, to my great relief, interrupted her, as the Grenadier led in the visitor to see the room. He bowed to both of us with a brief word of apology, looked round him, and withdrew, and with his departure the conversation between us came naturally to an end. I followed him out. Neither of us in any case, I think, cared to argue further.

And, so far as I am aware, the curious history of The Towers ends here too. There was no climax in the story sense. Nothing ever really happened. We left next morning for London. I only know that the Society in question took the house and have since occupied it to their entire satisfaction, and that Mabel, who became a member shortly afterwards, now stays there frequently when in need of repose from the arduous and unselfish labors she took upon herself under its aegis. She dined with us only the other night, here in our tiny Chelsea flat, and a jollier, saner, more interesting and happy guest I could hardly wish for. She was vital—in the best sense; the lay figure had come to life. I found it difficult to believe she was the same woman whose fearful effigy had floated down those dreary corridors and almost disappeared in the depths of that atrocious Shadow.

What her beliefs were now I was wise enough to leave unquestioned, and Frances, to my great relief, kept the conversation well away from such inappropriate topics. It was clear, however, that the woman had in herself some secret source of joy, that she was now an aggressive, positive force, sure of herself, and apparently afraid of nothing in heaven or hell. She radiated something very like hope and courage about her, and talked as though the world were a glorious place and everybody in it kind and beautiful. Her optimism was certainly infectious.

The Towers were mentioned only in passing. The name of Marsh came up—not the Marsh, it so happened, but a name in some book that was being discussed—and I was unable to restrain myself. Curiosity was too strong. I threw out a casual enquiry Mabel could leave unanswered if she wished. But there was no desire to avoid it. Her reply was frank and smiling.

"Would you believe it? She married," Mabel told me, though obviously surprised that I remembered the housekeeper at all; "and is happy as the day is long. She's found her right niche in life. A sergeant—"

"The army!" I ejaculated.

"Salvation Army," she explained merrily.

Frances exchanged a glance with me. I laughed too, for the information took me by surprise. I cannot say why exactly, but I expected at least to hear that the woman had met some dreadful end, not impossibly by burning.

"And The Towers, now called the Rest House," Mabel chattered on, "seems to me the most peaceful and delightful spot in England—"

"Really," I said politely.

"When I lived there in the old days—while you were there, perhaps, though I won't be sure."

Mabel went on, "the story got abroad that it was haunted. Wasn't it odd? A less likely place for a ghost I've never seen. Why, it had no atmosphere at all." She said this to Frances, glancing up at me with a smile that apparently had no hidden meaning. "Did you notice anything queer about it when you were there?"

This was plainly addressed to me.

"I found it—er—difficult to settle down to anything," I said, after an instant's hesitation. "I couldn't work there—"

"But I thought you wrote that wonderful book on the Deaf and Blind while you stayed with me," she asked innocently.

I stammered a little. "Oh no, not then. I only made a few notes—er—at The Towers. My mind, oddly enough, refused to produce at all down there. But—why do you ask? Did anything—was anything supposed to happen there?"

She looked searchingly into my eyes a moment before she answered:

"Not that I know of," she said simply.

THE JAPANNED BOX

Arthur Conan Doyle

It was a curious thing, said the private tutor; one of those grotesque and whimsical incidents which occur to one as one goes through life. I lost the best situation which I am ever likely to have through it. But I am glad that I went to Thorpe Place, for I gained—well, as I tell you the story you will learn what I gained.

I don't know whether you are familiar with that part of the Midlands which is drained by the Avon. It is the most English part of England. Shakespeare, the flower of the whole race, was born right in the middle of it. It is a land of rolling pastures, rising in higher folds to the westwards, until they swell into the Malvern Hills. There are no towns, but numerous villages, each with its grey Norman church. You have left the brick of the southern and eastern counties behind you, and everything is stone—stone for the walls, and lichened slabs of stone for the roofs. It is all grim and solid and massive, as befits the heart of a great nation.

It was in the middle of this country, not very far from Evesham, that Sir John Bollamore lived in the old ancestral home of Thorpe Place, and thither it was that I came to teach his two little sons. Sir John was a widower—his wife had died three years before—and he had been left with these two lads aged eight and ten, and one dear little girl of seven. Miss Witherton, who is now my wife, was governess to this little girl. I was tutor to the two boys. Could there be a more obvious prelude to an engagement? She governs me now, and I tutor two little boys of our own. But, there—I have already revealed what it was which I gained in Thorpe Place!

It was a very, very old house, incredibly old—pre-Norman, some of it—and the Bollamores claimed to have lived in that situation since long before the Conquest. It struck a chill to my heart when first I came there, those enormously thick grey walls, the rude crumbling stones, the smell as from a sick animal which exhaled from the rotting plaster of the aged building. But the modern wing was bright and the garden was well kept. No house could be dismal which had a pretty girl inside it and such a show of roses in front.

Apart from a very complete staff of servants there were only four of us in the household. These were Miss Witherton, who was at that time four-and-twenty and as pretty—well, as pretty as Mrs. Colmore is now—myself, Frank Colmore, aged thirty, Mrs. Stevens, the housekeeper, a dry, silent woman, and Mr. Richards, a tall military-looking man, who acted as steward to the Bollamore estates. We four always had our meals together, but Sir John had his usually alone in the library. Sometimes he joined us at dinner, but on the whole we were just as glad when he did not.

For he was a very formidable person. Imagine a man six feet three inches in height, majestically built, with a high-nosed, aristocratic face, brindled hair, shaggy eyebrows, a small, pointed Mephistophelian beard, and lines upon his brow and round his eyes as deep as if they had been carved with a penknife. He had grey eyes, weary, hopeless-looking eyes, proud and yet pathetic, eyes which claimed your pity and yet dared you to show it. His back was rounded with study, but otherwise he was as fine a looking man of his age—five-and-fifty perhaps—as any woman would wish to look upon.

But his presence was not a cheerful one. He was always courteous, always refined, but singularly silent and retiring. I have never lived so long with any man and known so little of him. If he were indoors he spent his time either in his own small study in the Eastern Tower, or in the library in the modern wing. So regular was his routine that one could always say at any hour exactly where he would be. Twice in the day he would visit his study, once after breakfast, and once about ten at night. You might set your watch by the slam of the heavy door. For the rest of the day he would be in his library—save that for an hour or two in the afternoon he would take a walk or a ride, which was solitary like the rest of his existence. He loved his children, and was keenly interested in the progress of their studies, but they were a little awed by the silent, shaggy-browed figure, and they avoided him as much as they could. Indeed, we all did that.

It was some time before I came to know anything about the circumstances of Sir John Bollamore's life, for Mrs. Stevens, the housekeeper, and Mr. Richards, the land-steward, were too loyal to talk easily of their employer's affairs. As to the governess, she knew no more than I did, and our common interest was one of the causes which drew us together. At last, however, an incident occurred which led to a closer acquaintance with Mr. Richards and a fuller knowledge of the life of the man whom I served.

The immediate cause of this was no less than the falling of Master Percy, the youngest of my pupils, into the mill-race, with imminent danger both to his life and to mine, since I had to risk myself in order to save him. Dripping and exhausted—for I was far more spent than the child—I was making for my room when Sir John, who had heard the hubbub, opened the door of his little study and asked me what was the matter. I told him of the accident, but assured him that his child was in no danger, while he listened with a rugged, immobile face, which expressed in its intense eyes and tightened lips all the emotion which he tried to conceal.

"One moment! Step in here! Let me have the details!" said he, turning back through the open door.

And so I found myself within that little sanctum, inside which, as I afterwards learned, no other foot had for three years been set save that of the old servant who cleaned it out. It was a round room, conforming to the shape of the tower in which it was situated, with a low ceiling, a single narrow, ivy-wreathed window, and the simplest of furniture. An old carpet, a single chair, a deal table, and a small shelf of books made up the whole contents. On the table stood a full-length photograph of a woman—I took no particular notice of the features, but I remember, that a certain gracious gentleness was the prevailing impression. Beside it were a large black japanned box and one or two bundles of letters or papers fastened together with elastic bands.

Our interview was a short one, for Sir John Bollamore perceived that I was soaked, and that I should change without delay. The incident led, however, to an instructive talk with Richards, the agent, who had never penetrated into the chamber which chance had opened to me. That very afternoon he came to me, all curiosity, and walked up and down the garden path with me, while my two charges played tennis upon the lawn beside us.

"You hardly realize the exception which has been made in your favour," said he. "That room has been kept such a mystery, and Sir John's visits to it have been so regular and consistent, that an almost superstitious feeling has arisen about it in the household. I assure you that if I were to repeat to you the tales which are flying about, tales of mysterious visitors there, and of voices overheard by the servants, you might suspect that Sir John had relapsed into his old ways."

"Why do you say relapsed?" I asked.

He looked at me in surprise.

"Is it possible," said he, "that Sir John Bollamore's previous history is unknown to you?"

"Absolutely."

"You astound me. I thought that every man in England knew something of his antecedents. I should not mention the matter if it were not that you are now one of ourselves, and that the facts might come to your ears in some harsher form if I were silent upon them. I always took it for granted that you knew that you were in the service of 'Devil' Bollamore."

"But why 'Devil'?" I asked.

"Ah, you are young and the world moves fast, but twenty years ago the name of 'Devil' Bollamore was one of the best known in London. He was the leader of the fastest set, bruiser, driver, gambler, drunkard—a survival of the old type, and as bad as the worst of them."

I stared at him in amazement.

"What!" I cried, "that quiet, studious, sad-faced man?"

"The greatest rip and debauchee in England! All between ourselves, Colmore. But you understand now what I mean when I say that a woman's voice in his room might even now give rise to suspicions."

"But what can have changed him so?"

"Little Beryl Clare, when she took the risk of becoming his wife. That was the turning point. He had got so far that his own fast set had thrown him over. There is a world of difference, you know, between a man who drinks and a drunkard. They all drink, but they taboo a drunkard. He had become a slave to it—hopeless and helpless. Then she stepped in, saw the possibilities of a fine man in the wreck, took her chance in marrying him though she might have had the pick of a dozen, and, by devoting her life to it, brought him back to manhood and decency. You have observed that no liquor is ever kept in the house. There never has been any since her foot crossed its threshold. A drop of it would be like blood to a tiger even now."

"Then her influence still holds him?"

"That is the wonder of it. When she died three years ago, we all expected and feared that he would fall back into his old ways. She feared it herself, and the thought gave a terror to death, for she was like a guardian angel to that man, and lived only for the one purpose. By the way, did you see a black japanned box in his room?"

"Yes."

"I fancy it contains her letters. If ever he has occasion to be away, if only for a single night, he invariably takes his black japanned box with him. Well, well, Colmore, perhaps I have told you rather more than I should, but I shall expect you to reciprocate if anything of interest should come to your knowledge."

I could see that the worthy man was consumed with curiosity and just a little piqued that I, the newcomer, should have been the first to penetrate into the untrodden chamber. But the fact raised me in his esteem, and from that time onwards I found myself upon more confidential terms with him.

And now the silent and majestic figure of my employer became an object of greater interest to me. I began to understand that strangely human look in his eyes, those deep lines upon his care-worn face. He was a man who was fighting a ceaseless battle, holding at arm's length, from morning till night, a horrible adversary who was forever trying to close with him—an adversary which would destroy him body and soul could it but fix its claws once more upon him. As I watched the grim, round-backed figure pacing the corridor or walking in the garden, this imminent danger seemed to take bodily shape, and I could almost fancy that I saw this most loathsome and dangerous of all the fiends crouching closely in his very shadow, like a half-cowed beast which slinks beside its keeper, ready at any unguarded moment to spring at his throat. And the dead woman, the woman who had spent her life in warding off this danger, took shape also to my imagination, and I saw her as a shadowy but beautiful presence which intervened for ever with arms uplifted to screen the man whom she loved.

In some subtle way he divined the sympathy which I had for him, and he showed in his own silent fashion that he appreciated it. He even invited me once to share his afternoon walk, and although no word passed between us on this occasion, it was a mark of confidence which he had never shown to anyone before. He asked me also to index his library (it was one of the best private libraries in England), and I spent many hours in the evening in his presence, if not in his society, he reading at his desk and I sitting in a recess by the window reducing to order the chaos which existed among his books. In spite of these close relations I was never again asked to enter the chamber in the turret.

And then came my revulsion of feeling. A single incident changed all my sympathy to loathing, and made me realize that my employer still remained all that he had ever been, with the additional vice of hypocrisy. What happened was as follows.

One evening Miss Witherton had gone down to Broadway, the neighbouring village, to sing at a concert for some charity, and I, according to my promise, had walked over to escort her back. The drive sweeps round under the eastern turret, and I observed as I passed that the light was lit in the circular room. It was a summer evening, and the window, which was a little higher than our heads, was open. We were, as it happened, engrossed in our own conversation at the moment and we had paused upon the lawn which skirts the old turret, when suddenly something broke in upon our talk and turned our thoughts away from our own affairs.

It was a voice—the voice undoubtedly of a woman. It was low—so low that it was only in that still night air that we could have heard it, but, hushed as it was, there was no mistaking its feminine timbre. It spoke hurriedly, gaspingly for a few sentences, and then was silent—a piteous, breathless, imploring sort of voice. Miss Witherton and I stood for an instant staring at each other. Then we walked quickly in the direction of the hall-door.

"It came through the window," I said.

"We must not play the part of eavesdroppers," she answered. "We must forget that we have ever heard it."

There was an absence of surprise in her manner which suggested a new idea to me.

"You have heard it before," I cried.

"I could not help it. My own room is higher up on the same turret. It has happened frequently."

"Who can the woman be?"

"I have no idea. I had rather not discuss it."

Her voice was enough to show me what she thought. But granting that our employer led a double and dubious life, who could she be, this mysterious woman who kept him company in the old tower? I knew from my own inspection how bleak and bare a room it was. She certainly did not live there. But in that case where did she come from? It could not be anyone of the household. They were all under the vigilant eyes of Mrs. Stevens. The visitor must come from without. But how?

And then suddenly I remembered how ancient this building was, and how probable that some mediaeval passage existed in it. There is hardly an old castle without one. The mysterious room was the basement of the turret, so that if there were anything of the sort it would open through the floor. There were numerous cottages in the immediate vicinity. The other end of the secret passage might lie among some tangle of bramble in the neighbouring copse. I said nothing to anyone, but I felt that the secret of my employer lay within my power.

And the more convinced I was of this the more I marvelled at the manner in which he concealed his true nature. Often as I watched his austere figure, I asked myself if it were indeed possible that such a man should be living this double life, and I tried to persuade myself that my suspicions might after all prove to be ill-founded. But there was the female voice, there was the secret nightly rendezvous in the turret-chamber—how could such facts admit of an innocent interpretation. I conceived a horror of the man. I was filled with loathing at his deep, consistent hypocrisy.

Only once during all those months did I ever see him without that sad but impassive mask which he usually presented towards his fellow-man. For an instant I caught a glimpse of those volcanic fires which he had damped down so long. The occasion was an unworthy one, for the object of his wrath was none other than the aged charwoman whom I have already mentioned as being the one person who was allowed within his mysterious chamber. I was passing the corridor which led to the turret—for my own room lay in that direction—when I heard a sudden, startled scream, and merged in it the husky, growling note of a man who is inarticulate with passion. It was the snarl of a furious wild beast. Then I heard his voice thrilling with anger. "You would dare!" he cried. "You would dare to disobey my directions!" An instant later the charwoman passed me, flying down the passage, white-faced and tremulous, while the terrible voice thundered behind her. "Go to Mrs. Stevens for your money! Never set foot in Thorpe Place again!" Consumed with curiosity, I could not help following the woman, and found her round the corner leaning against the wall and palpitating like a frightened rabbit.

"What is the matter, Mrs. Brown?" I asked.

"It's master!" she gasped. "Oh, 'ow 'e frightened me! If you had seen 'is eyes, Mr. Colmore, sir. I thought 'e would 'ave been the death of me."

"But what had you done?"

"Done, sir! Nothing. At least nothing to make so much of. Just laid my 'and on that black box of 'is—'adn't even opened it, when in 'e came and you 'eard the way 'e went on. I've lost my place, and glad I am of it, for I would never trust myself within reach of 'im again."

So it was the japanned box which was the cause of this outburst—the box from which he would never permit himself to be separated. What was the connection, or was there any connection between this and the secret visits of the lady whose voice I had overheard? Sir John Bollamore's wrath was enduring as well as fiery, for from that day Mrs. Brown, the charwoman, vanished from our ken, and Thorpe Place knew her no more.

And now I wish to tell you the singular chance which solved all these strange questions and put my employer's secret in my possession. The story may leave you with some lingering doubts as to whether my curiosity did not get the better of my honour, and whether I did not condescend to play the spy. If you choose to think so I cannot help it, but can only assure you that, improbable as it may appear, the matter came about exactly as I describe it.

The first stage in this denouement was that the small room in the turret became uninhabitable. This occurred through the fall of the worm-eaten oaken beam which supported the ceiling. Rotten with age, it snapped in the middle one morning, and brought down a quantity of plaster with it. Fortunately Sir John was not in the room at the time. His precious box was rescued from amongst the debris and brought into the library, where, henceforward, it was locked within his bureau. Sir John took no steps to repair the damage, and I never had an opportunity of searching for that secret passage, the existence of which I had surmised. As to the lady, I had thought that this would have brought her visits to an end, had I not one evening heard Mr. Richards asking Mrs. Stevens who the woman was whom he had overheard talking to Sir John in the library. I could not catch her reply, but I saw from her manner that it was not the first time that she had had to answer or avoid the same question.

"You've heard the voice, Colmore?" said the agent.

I confessed that I had.

"And what do you think of it?"

I shrugged my shoulders, and remarked that it was no business of mine.

"Come, come, you are just as curious as any of us. Is it a woman or not?"

"It is certainly a woman."

"Which room did you hear it from?"

"From the turret-room, before the ceiling fell."

"But I heard it from the library only last night. I passed the doors as I was going to bed, and I heard something wailing and praying just as plainly as I hear you. It may be a woman—"

"Why, what else *could* it be?"

He looked at me hard.

"There are more things in heaven and earth," said he. "If it is a woman, how does she get there?"

"I don't know."

"No, nor I. But if it is the other thing—but there, for a practical business man at the end of the nineteenth century this is rather a ridiculous line of conversation." He turned away, but I saw that he felt even more than he had said. To all the old ghost stories of Thorpe Place a new one was being added before our very eyes. It may by this time have taken its permanent place, for though an explanation came to me, it never reached the others.

And my explanation came in this way. I had suffered a sleepless night from neuralgia, and about midday I had taken a heavy dose of chlorodyne to alleviate the pain. At that time I was finishing the indexing of Sir John Bollamore's library, and it was my custom to work there from five till seven. On this particular day I struggled against the double effect of my bad night and the narcotic. I have already mentioned that there was a recess in the library, and in this it was my habit to work. I settled down steadily to my task, but my weariness overcame me and, falling back upon the settee, I dropped into a heavy sleep.

How long I slept I do not know, but it was quite dark when I awoke. Confused by the chlorodyne which I had taken, I lay motionless in a semi-conscious state. The great room with its high walls covered with books loomed darkly all round me. A dim radiance from the moonlight came through the farther window, and against this lighter background I saw that Sir John Bollamore was sitting at his study table. His well-set head and clearly cut profile were sharply outlined against the glimmering square behind him. He bent as I watched him, and I heard the sharp turning of a key and the rasping of metal upon metal. As if in a dream I was vaguely conscious that this was the japanned box which stood in front of him, and that he had drawn something out of it, something squat and uncouth, which now lay before him upon the table. I never realized—it never occurred to my bemuddled and torpid brain that I was intruding upon his privacy, that he imagined himself to be alone in the room. And then, just as it rushed upon my horrified perceptions, and I had half risen to announce my presence, I heard a strange, crisp, metallic clicking, and then the voice.

Yes, it was a woman's voice; there could not be a doubt of it. But a voice so charged with entreaty and with yearning love, that it will ring for ever in my ears. It came with a curious faraway tinkle, but every word was clear, though faint—very faint, for they were the last words of a dying woman.

"I am not really gone, John," said the thin, gasping voice. "I am here at your very elbow, and shall be until we meet once more. I die happy to think that morning and night you will hear my voice. Oh, John, be strong, be strong, until we meet again."

I say that I had risen in order to announce my presence, but I could not do so while the voice was sounding. I could only remain half lying, half sitting, paralysed, astounded, listening to those yearning distant musical words. And he—he was so absorbed that even if I had spoken he might not have heard me. But with the silence of the voice came my half articulated apologies and explanations. He sprang across the room, switched on the electric light, and in its white glare I saw him, his eyes gleaming with anger, his face twisted with passion, as the hapless charwoman may have seen him weeks before.

"Mr. Colmore!" he cried. "You here! What is the meaning of this, sir?"

With halting words I explained it all, my neuralgia, the narcotic, my luckless sleep and singular awakening. As he listened the glow of anger faded from his face, and the sad, impassive mask closed once more over his features.

"My secret is yours, Mr. Colmore," said he. "I have only myself to blame for relaxing my precautions. Half confidences are worse than no confidences, and so you may know all since you know so much. The story may go where you will when I have passed away, but until then I rely upon your sense of honour that no human soul shall hear it from your lips. I am proud still—God help me!—or, at least, I am proud enough to resent that pity which this story would draw upon me. I have smiled at envy, and disregarded hatred, but pity is more than I can tolerate.

"You have heard the source from which the voice comes—that voice which has, as I understand, excited so much curiosity in my household. I am aware of the rumours to which it has given rise. These speculations, whether scandalous or superstitious, are such as I can disregard and forgive. What I should never forgive would be a disloyal spying and eavesdropping in order to satisfy an illicit curiosity. But of that, Mr. Colmore, I acquit you.

"When I was a young man, sir, many years younger than you are now, I was launched upon town without a friend or adviser, and with a purse which brought only too many false friends and false advisers to my side. I drank deeply of the wine of life—if there is a man living who has drunk more deeply he is not a man whom I envy. My purse suffered, my character suffered, my constitution suffered, stimulants became a necessity to me, I was a creature from whom my memory recoils. And it was at that time, the time of my blackest degradation, that God sent into my life the gentlest, sweetest spirit that ever descended as a ministering angel from above. She loved me, broken as I was, loved me, and spent her life in making a man once more of that which had degraded itself to the level of the beasts.

"But a fell disease struck her, and she withered away before my eyes. In the hour of her agony it was never of herself, of her own sufferings and her own death that she thought. It was all of me. The one pang which her fate brought to her was the fear that when her influence was removed I should revert to that which I had been. It was in vain that I made oath to her that no drop of wine would ever cross my lips. She knew only too well the hold that the devil had upon me—she who had striven so to loosen it—and it haunted her night and day the thought that my soul might again be within his grip.

"It was from some friend's gossip of the sick room that she heard of this invention—this phonograph—and with the quick insight of a loving woman she saw how she might use it for her ends. She sent me to London to procure the best which money could buy. With her dying breath she gasped into it the words which have held me straight ever since. Lonely and broken, what else have I in all the world to uphold me? But it is enough. Please God, I shall face her without shame when He is pleased to reunite us! That is my secret, Mr. Colmore, and whilst I live I leave it in your keeping."

THE TOMB

H. P. Lovecraft

"Sedibus ut saltem placidis in morte quiescam."
—VIRGIL

In relating the circumstances which have led to my confinement within this refuge for the demented, I am aware that my present position will create a natural doubt of the authenticity of my narrative. It is an unfortunate fact that the bulk of humanity is too limited in its mental vision to weigh with patience and intelligence those isolated phenomena, seen and felt only by a psychologically sensitive few, which lie outside its common experience. Men of broader intellect know that there is no sharp distinction betwixt the real and the unreal; that all things appear as they do only by virtue of the delicate individual physical and mental media through which we are made conscious of them; but the prosaic materialism of the majority condemns as madness the flashes of super-sight which penetrate the common veil of obvious empiricism.

My name is Jervas Dudley, and from earliest childhood I have been a dreamer and a visionary. Wealthy beyond the necessity of a commercial life, and temperamentally unfitted for the formal studies and social recreations of my acquaintances, I have dwelt ever in realms apart from the visible world; spending my youth and adolescence in ancient and little-known books, and in roaming the fields and groves of the region near my ancestral home. I do not think that what I read in these books or saw in these fields and groves was exactly what other boys read and saw there; but of this I must say little, since detailed speech would but confirm those cruel slanders upon my intellect which I sometimes overhear from the whispers of the stealthy attendants around me. It is sufficient for me to relate events without analysing causes.

I have said that I dwelt apart from the visible world, but I have not said that I dwelt alone. This no human creature may do; for lacking the fellowship of the living, he inevitably draws upon the companionship of things that are not, or are no longer, living. Close by my home there lies a singular wooded hollow, in whose twilight deeps I spent most of my time; reading, thinking, and dreaming. Down its moss-covered slopes my first steps of infancy were taken, and around its grotesquely gnarled oak trees my first fancies of boyhood were woven. Well did I come to know the presiding dryads of those trees, and often have I watched their wild dances in the struggling beams of a waning moon—but of these things I must not now speak. I will tell only of the lone tomb in the darkest of the hillside thickets; the deserted tomb of the Hydes, an old and exalted family whose last direct descendant had been laid within its black recesses many decades before my birth.

The vault to which I refer is of ancient granite, weathered and discoloured by the mists and dampness of generations. Excavated back into the hillside, the structure is visible only at the entrance. The door, a ponderous and forbidding slab of stone, hangs upon rusted iron hinges, and is fastened *ajar* in a queerly sinister way by means of heavy iron chains and padlocks, according to a gruesome fashion of half a century ago. The abode of the race whose scions are here inurned had once crowned the declivity which holds the tomb, but had long since fallen victim to the flames which sprang up from a disastrous stroke of lightning. Of the midnight storm which destroyed this gloomy mansion, the older inhabitants of the region sometimes speak in hushed and uneasy voices; alluding to what they call "divine wrath" in a manner that in later years vaguely increased the always strong fascination which I felt for the forest-darkened sepulchre. One man only had perished in the fire. When the last of the Hydes was buried in this place of shade and stillness, the sad urnful of ashes had come from a distant land; to which the family had repaired when the mansion burned down. No one remains to lay flowers before the granite portal, and few care to brave the depressing shadows which seem to linger strangely about the water-worn stones.

I shall never forget the afternoon when first I stumbled upon the half-hidden house of death. It was in mid-summer, when the alchemy of Nature transmutes the sylvan landscape to one vivid and almost homogeneous mass of green; when the senses are well-nigh intoxicated with the surging seas of moist verdure and the subtly indefinable odours of the soil and the vegetation. In such surroundings the mind loses its perspective; time and space become trivial and unreal, and echoes of a forgotten prehistoric past beat insistently upon the enthralled consciousness. All day I had been wandering through the mystic groves of the hollow; thinking thoughts I need not discuss, and conversing with things I need not name. In years a child of ten, I had seen and heard many wonders unknown to the throng; and was oddly aged in certain respects. When, upon forcing my way between two savage clumps of briers, I suddenly encountered the entrance of the vault, I had no knowledge of what I had discovered. The dark blocks of granite, the door so curiously ajar, and the funereal carvings above the arch, aroused in me no associations of mournful or terrible character. Of graves and tombs I knew and imagined much, but had on account of my peculiar temperament been kept from all personal contact with churchyards and cemeteries. The strange stone house on the woodland slope was to me only a source of interest and speculation;

and its cold, damp interior, into which I vainly peered through the aperture so tantalisingly left, contained for me no hint of death or decay. But in that instant of curiosity was born the madly unreasoning desire which has brought me to this hell of confinement. Spurred on by a voice which must have come from the hideous soul of the forest, I resolved to enter the beckoning gloom in spite of the ponderous chains which barred my passage. In the waning light of day I alternately rattled the rusty impediments with a view to throwing wide the stone door, and essayed to squeeze my slight form through the space already provided; but neither plan met with success. At first curious, I was now frantic; and when in the thickening twilight I returned to my home, I had sworn to the hundred gods of the grove that at any cost I would some day force an entrance to the black, chilly depths that seemed calling out to me. The physician with the iron-grey beard who comes each day to my room once told a visitor that this decision marked the beginning of a pitiful monomania; but I will leave final judgment to my readers when they shall have learnt all.

The months following my discovery were spent in futile attempts to force the complicated padlock of the slightly open vault, and in carefully guarded inquiries regarding the nature and history of the structure. With the traditionally receptive ears of the small boy, I learned much; though an habitual secretiveness caused me to tell no one of my information or my resolve. It is perhaps worth mentioning that I was not at all surprised or terrified on learning of the nature of the vault. My rather original ideas regarding life and death had caused me to associate the cold clay with the breathing body in a vague fashion; and I felt that the great and sinister family of the burned-down mansion was in some way represented within the stone space I sought to explore. Mumbled tales of the weird rites and godless revels of bygone years in the ancient hall gave to me a new and potent interest in the tomb, before whose door I would sit for hours at a time each day. Once I thrust a candle within the nearly closed entrance, but could see nothing save a flight of damp stone steps leading downward. The odour of the place repelled yet bewitched me. I felt I had known it before, in a past remote beyond all recollection; beyond even my tenancy of the body I now possess.

The year after I first beheld the tomb, I stumbled upon a worm-eaten translation of Plutarch's *Lives* in the book-filled attic of my home. Reading the life of Theseus, I was much impressed by that passage telling of the great stone beneath which the boyish hero was to find his tokens of destiny whenever he should become old enough to lift its enormous weight. This legend had the effect of dispelling my keenest impatience to enter the vault, for it made me feel that the time was not yet ripe. Later, I told myself, I should grow to a strength and ingenuity which might enable me to unfasten the heavily chained door with ease; but until then I would do better by conforming to what seemed the will of Fate.

Accordingly my watches by the dank portal became less persistent, and much of my time was spent in other though equally strange pursuits. I would sometimes rise very quietly in the night, stealing out to walk in those churchyards and places of burial from which I had been kept by my parents. What I did there I may not say, for I am not now sure of the reality of certain things; but I know that on the day after such a nocturnal ramble I would often astonish those about me with my knowledge of topics almost forgotten for many generations. It was after a night like this that I shocked the community with a queer conceit about the burial of the rich and celebrated Squire Brewster, a maker of local history who was interred in 1711, and whose slate headstone, bearing a graven skull and crossbones, was slowly crumbling to powder. In a moment of childish imagination I vowed not only that the undertaker, Goodman Simpson, had stolen the silver-buckled shoes, silken hose, and satin small-clothes of the deceased before burial; but that the Squire himself, not fully inanimate, had turned twice in his mound-covered coffin on the day after interment.

But the idea of entering the tomb never left my thoughts; being indeed stimulated by the unexpected genealogical discovery that my own maternal ancestry possessed at least a slight link with the supposedly extinct family of the Hydes. Last of my paternal race, I was likewise the last of this older and more mysterious line. I began to feel that the tomb was mine, and to look forward with hot eagerness to the time when I might pass within that stone door and down those slimy stone steps in the dark. I now formed the habit of listening very intently at the slightly open portal, choosing my favourite hours of midnight stillness for the odd vigil. By the time I came of age, I had made a small clearing in the thicket before the mould-stained facade of the hillside, allowing the surrounding vegetation to encircle and overhang the space like the walls and roof of a sylvan bower. This bower was my temple, the fastened door my shrine, and here I would lie outstretched on the mossy ground, thinking strange thoughts and dreaming strange dreams.

The night of the first revelation was a sultry one. I must have fallen asleep from fatigue, for it was with a distinct sense of awakening that I heard the voices. Of those tones and accents I hesitate to speak; of their *quality* I will not speak; but I may say that they presented certain uncanny differences in vocabulary, pronunciation, and mode of utterance. Every shade of New England dialect, from the uncouth syllables of the Puritan colonists to the precise rhetoric of fifty years ago, seemed represented in that shadowy colloquy, though it was only later that I noticed the fact. At the time, indeed, my attention was distracted from this matter by another phenomenon; a phenomenon so fleeting that I could not take oath upon its reality. I barely fancied that as I awoke, a *light* had been hurriedly extinguished within the sunken sepulchre. I do not think I was either astounded or panic-stricken, but I know that I was greatly and permanently changed that night. Upon returning home I went with much directness to a rotting chest in the attic, wherein I found the key which next day unlocked with ease the barrier I had so long stormed in vain.

It was in the soft glow of late afternoon that I first entered the vault on the abandoned slope. A spell was upon me, and my heart leaped with an exultation I can but ill describe. As I closed the door behind me and descended the dripping steps by the light of my lone candle, I seemed to know the way; and though the candle sputtered with the stifling reek of the place, I felt singularly at home in the musty, charnel-house air. Looking about me, I beheld many marble slabs bearing coffins, or the remains of coffins. Some of these were sealed and intact, but others had nearly vanished, leaving the silver handles and plates isolated amidst certain curious heaps of whitish dust. Upon one plate I read the name of Sir Geoffrey Hyde, who had come from Sussex in 1640 and died here a few years later. In a conspicuous alcove was one fairly well-preserved and untenanted casket, adorned with a single name which brought to me both a smile and a shudder. An odd impulse caused me to climb upon the broad slab, extinguish my candle, and lie down within the vacant box.

In the grey light of dawn I staggered from the vault and locked the chain of the door behind me. I was no longer a young man, though but twenty-one winters had chilled my bodily frame. Early-rising villagers who observed my homeward progress looked at me strangely, and marvelled at the signs of ribald revelry which they saw in one whose life was known to be sober and solitary. I did not appear before my parents till after a long and refreshing sleep.

Henceforward I haunted the tomb each night; seeing, hearing, and doing things I must never reveal. My speech, always susceptible to environmental influences, was the first thing to succumb to the change; and my suddenly acquired archaism of diction was soon remarked upon. Later a queer boldness and recklessness came into my demeanour, till I unconsciously grew to possess the bearing of a man of the world despite my lifelong seclusion. My formerly silent tongue waxed voluble with the easy grace of a Chesterfield or the godless cynicism of a Rochester. I displayed a peculiar erudition utterly unlike the fantastic, monkish lore over which I had pored in youth; and covered the flyleaves of my books with facile impromptu epigrams which brought up suggestions of Gay, Prior, and the sprightliest of the Augustan wits and rimesters. One morning at breakfast I came close to disaster by declaiming in palpably liquorish accents an effusion of eighteenth-century Bacchanalian mirth; a bit of Georgian playfulness never recorded in a book, which ran something like this:

Come hither, my lads, with your tankards of ale,
And drink to the present before it shall fail;
Pile each on your platter a mountain of beef,
For 'tis eating and drinking that bring us relief:
  So fill up your glass,
  For life will soon pass;
When you're dead ye'll ne'er drink to your king or your lass!

Anacreon had a red nose, so they say;
But what's a red nose if ye're happy and gay?
Gad split me! I'd rather be red whilst I'm here,
Than white as a lily—and dead half a year!
  So Betty, my miss,
  Come give me a kiss;
In hell there's no innkeeper's daughter like this!

Young Harry, propp'd up just as straight as he's able,
Will soon lose his wig and slip under the table;
But fill up your goblets and pass 'em around—
Better under the table than under the ground!
  So revel and chaff
  As ye thirstily quaff:
Under six feet of dirt 'tis less easy to laugh!

The fiend strike me blue! I'm scarce able to walk,
And damn me if I can stand upright or talk!
Here, landlord, bid Betty to summon a chair;
I'll try home for a while, for my wife is not there!
  So lend me a hand;
  I'm not able to stand,
But I'm gay whilst I linger on top of the land!

About this time I conceived my present fear of fire and thunderstorms. Previously indifferent to such things, I had now an unspeakable horror of them; and would retire to the innermost recesses of the house whenever the heavens threatened an electrical display. A favourite haunt of mine during the day was the ruined cellar of the mansion that had burned down, and in fancy I would picture the structure as it had been in its prime. On one occasion I startled a villager by leading him confidently to a shallow sub-cellar, of whose existence I seemed to know in spite of the fact that it had been unseen and forgotten for many generations.

At last came that which I had long feared. My parents, alarmed at the altered manner and appearance of their only son, commenced to exert over my movements a kindly espionage which threatened to result in disaster. I had told no one of my visits to the tomb, having guarded my secret purpose with religious zeal since childhood; but now I was forced to exercise care in threading the mazes of the wooded hollow, that I might throw off a possible pursuer. My key to the vault I kept suspended from a cord about my neck, its presence known only to me. I never carried out of the sepulchre any of the things I came upon whilst within its walls.

One morning as I emerged from the damp tomb and fastened the chain of the portal with none too steady hand, I beheld in an adjacent thicket the dreaded face of a watcher. Surely the end was near; for my bower was discovered, and the objective of my nocturnal journeys revealed. The man did not accost me, so I hastened home in an effort to overhear what he might report to my careworn father. Were my sojourns beyond the chained door about to be proclaimed to the world? Imagine my delighted astonishment on hearing the spy inform my parent in a cautious whisper *that I had spent the night in the bower outside the tomb;* my sleep-filmed eyes fixed upon the crevice where the padlocked portal stood ajar! By what miracle had the watcher been thus deluded? I was now convinced that a supernatural agency protected me. Made bold by this heaven-sent circumstance, I began to resume perfect openness in going to the vault; confident that no one could witness my entrance. For a week I tasted to the full the joys of that charnel conviviality which I must not describe, when the thing happened, and I was borne away to this accursed abode of sorrow and monotony.

I should not have ventured out that night; for the taint of thunder was in the clouds, and a hellish phosphorescence rose from the rank swamp at the bottom of the hollow. The call of the dead, too, was different. Instead of the hillside tomb, it was the charred cellar on the crest of the slope whose presiding daemon beckoned to me with unseen fingers. As I emerged from an intervening grove upon the plain before the ruin, I beheld in the misty moonlight a thing I had always vaguely expected. The mansion, gone for a century, once more reared its stately height to the raptured vision; every window ablaze with the splendour of many candles. Up the long drive rolled the coaches of the Boston gentry, whilst on foot came a numerous assemblage of powdered exquisites from the neighbouring mansions. With this throng I mingled, though I knew I belonged with the hosts rather than with the guests. Inside the hall were music, laughter, and wine on every hand. Several faces I recognised; though I should have known them better had they been shrivelled or eaten away by death and decomposition. Amidst a wild and reckless throng I was the wildest and most abandoned. Gay blasphemy poured in torrents from my lips, and in my shocking sallies I heeded no law of God, Man, or Nature. Suddenly a peal of thunder, resonant even above the din of the swinish revelry, clave the very roof and laid a hush of fear upon the boisterous company. Red tongues of flame and searing gusts of heat engulfed the house; and the roysterers, struck with terror at the descent of a calamity which seemed to transcend the bounds of unguided Nature, fled shrieking into the night. I alone remained, riveted to my seat by a grovelling fear which I had never felt before. And then a second horror took possession of my soul. Burnt alive to ashes, my body dispersed by the four winds, *I might never lie in the tomb of the Hydes!* Was not my coffin prepared for me? Had I not a right to rest till eternity amongst the descendants of Sir Geoffrey Hyde? Aye! I would claim my heritage of death, even though my soul go seeking through the ages for another corporeal tenement to represent it on that vacant slab in the alcove of the vault. *Jervas Hyde* should never share the sad fate of Palinurus!

As the phantom of the burning house faded, I found myself screaming and struggling madly in the arms of two men, one of whom was the spy who had followed me to the tomb. Rain was pouring down in torrents, and upon the southern horizon were flashes of the lightning that had so lately passed over our heads. My father, his face lined with sorrow, stood by as I shouted my demands to be laid within the tomb; frequently admonishing my captors to treat me as gently as they could. A blackened circle on the floor of the ruined cellar told of a violent stroke from the heavens; and from this spot a group of curious villagers with lanterns were prying a small box of antique workmanship which the thunderbolt had brought to light. Ceasing my futile and now objectless writhing, I watched the spectators as they viewed the treasure-trove, and was permitted to share in their discoveries. The box, whose fastenings were broken by the stroke which had unearthed it, contained many papers and objects of value; but I had eyes for one thing alone. It was the porcelain miniature of a young man in a smartly curled bag-wig, and bore the initials "J. H." The face was such that as I gazed, I might well have been studying my mirror.

On the following day I was brought to this room with the barred windows, but I have been kept informed of certain things through an aged and simple-minded servitor, for whom I bore a fondness in infancy, and who like me loves the churchyard. What I have dared relate of my experiences within the vault has brought me only pitying smiles. My father, who visits me frequently, declares that at no time did I pass the chained portal, and swears that the rusted padlock had not been touched for fifty years when he examined it. He even says that all the village knew of my journeys to the tomb, and that I was often watched as I slept in the bower outside the grim facade, my half-open eyes fixed on the crevice that leads to the interior. Against these assertions I have no tangible proof to offer, since my key to the padlock was lost in the struggle on that night of horrors. The strange things of the past which I learnt during those nocturnal meetings with the dead he dismisses as the fruits of my lifelong and omnivorous browsing amongst the ancient volumes of the family library. Had it not been for my old servant Hiram, I should have by this time become quite convinced of my madness.

But Hiram, loyal to the last, has held faith in me, and has done that which impels me to make public at least a part of my story. A week ago he burst open the lock which chains the door of the tomb perpetually ajar, and descended with a lantern into the murky depths. On a slab in an alcove he found an old but empty coffin whose tarnished plate bears the single word "Jervas." In that coffin and in that vault they have promised me I shall be buried.

THE CASK OF AMONTILLADO

Edgar Allan Poe

The thousand injuries of Fortunato I had borne as I best could; but when he ventured upon insult, I vowed revenge. You, who so well know the nature of my soul, will not suppose, however, that I gave utterance to a threat. At length I would be avenged; this was a point definitively settled—but the very definitiveness with which it was resolved, precluded the idea of risk. I must not only punish, but punish with impunity. A wrong is unredressed when retribution overtakes its redresser. It is equally unredressed when the avenger fails to make himself felt as such to him who has done the wrong.

It must be understood, that neither by word nor deed had I given Fortunato cause to doubt my good will. I continued, as was my wont, to smile in his face, and he did not perceive that my smile now was at the thought of his immolation.

He had a weak point—this Fortunato—although in other regards he was a man to be respected and even feared. He prided himself on his connoisseurship in wine. Few Italians have the true virtuoso spirit. For the most part their enthusiasm is adopted to suit the time and opportunity—to practise imposture upon the British and Austrian millionaires. In painting and gemmary, Fortunato, like his countrymen, was a quack—but in the matter of old wines he was sincere. In this respect I did not differ from him materially: I was skilful in the Italian vintages myself, and bought largely whenever I could.

It was about dusk, one evening during the supreme madness of the carnival season, that I encountered my friend. He accosted me with excessive warmth, for he had been drinking much. The man wore motley. He had on a tight-fitting parti-striped dress, and his head was surmounted by the conical cap and bells. I was so pleased to see him, that I thought I should never have done wringing his hand.

I said to him—"My dear Fortunato, you are luckily met. How remarkably well you are looking today! But I have received a pipe of what passes for Amontillado, and I have my doubts."

"How?" said he. "Amontillado? A pipe? Impossible! And in the middle of the carnival!"

"I have my doubts," I replied; "and I was silly enough to pay the full Amontillado price without consulting you in the matter. You were not to be found, and I was fearful of losing a bargain."

"Amontillado!"

"I have my doubts."

"Amontillado!"

"And I must satisfy them."

"Amontillado!"

"As you are engaged, I am on my way to Luchesi. If any one has a critical turn, it is he. He will tell me—"

"Luchesi cannot tell Amontillado from Sherry."

"And yet some fools will have it that his taste is a match for your own."

"Come, let us go."

"Whither?"

"To your vaults."

"My friend, no; I will not impose upon your good nature. I perceive you have an engagement. Luchesi—"

"I have no engagement—come."

"My friend, no. It is not the engagement, but the severe cold with which I perceive you are afflicted. The vaults are insufferably damp. They are encrusted with nitre."

"Let us go, nevertheless. The cold is merely nothing. Amontillado! You have been imposed upon. And as for Luchesi, he cannot distinguish Sherry from Amontillado."

Thus speaking, Fortunato possessed himself of my arm. Putting on a mask of black silk, and drawing a *roquelaire* closely about my person, I suffered him to hurry me to my palazzo.

There were no attendants at home; they had absconded to make merry in honor of the time. I had told them that I should not return until the morning, and had given them explicit orders not to stir from the house. These orders were sufficient, I well knew, to insure their immediate disappearance, one and all, as soon as my back was turned.

I took from their sconces two flambeaux, and giving one to Fortunato, bowed him through several suites of rooms to the archway that led into the vaults. I passed down a long and winding staircase, requesting him to be cautious as he followed. We came at length to the foot of the descent, and stood together on the damp ground of the catacombs of the Montresors.

The gait of my friend was unsteady, and the bells upon his cap jingled as he strode.

"The pipe," said he.

"It is farther on," said I; "but observe the white web-work which gleams from these cavern walls."

He turned towards me, and looked into my eyes with two filmy orbs that distilled the rheum of intoxication.

"Nitre?" he asked, at length.

"Nitre," I replied. "How long have you had that cough?"

"Ugh! ugh! ugh!—ugh! ugh! ugh!—ugh! ugh! ugh!—ugh! ugh! ugh!—ugh! ugh! ugh!"

My poor friend found it impossible to reply for many minutes.

"It is nothing," he said, at last.

"Come," I said, with decision, "we will go back; your health is precious. You are rich, respected, admired, beloved; you are happy, as once I was. You are a man to be missed. For me it is no matter. We will go back; you will be ill, and I cannot be responsible. Besides, there is Luchesi—"

"Enough," he said; "the cough is a mere nothing; it will not kill me. I shall not die of a cough."

"True—true," I replied; "and, indeed, I had no intention of alarming you unnecessarily—but you should use all proper caution. A draught of this Medoc will defend us from the damps."

Here I knocked off the neck of a bottle which I drew from a long row of its fellows that lay upon the mould.

"Drink," I said, presenting him the wine.

He raised it to his lips with a leer. He paused and nodded to me familiarly, while his bells jingled.

"I drink," he said, "to the buried that repose around us."

"And I to your long life."

He again took my arm, and we proceeded.

"These vaults," he said, "are extensive."

"The Montresors," I replied, "were a great and numerous family."

"I forget your arms."

"A huge human foot d'or, in a field azure; the foot crushes a serpent rampant whose fangs are imbedded in the heel."

"And the motto?"

"*Nemo me impune lacessit.*"

"Good!" he said.

The wine sparkled in his eyes and the bells jingled. My own fancy grew warm with the Medoc. We had passed through walls of piled bones, with casks and puncheons intermingling, into the inmost recesses of the catacombs. I paused again, and this time I made bold to seize Fortunato by an arm above the elbow.

"The nitre!" I said: "see, it increases. It hangs like moss upon the vaults. We are below the river's bed. The drops of moisture trickle among the bones. Come, we will go back ere it is too late. Your cough—"

"It is nothing," he said; "let us go on. But first, another draught of the Medoc."

I broke and reached him a flagon of De Grave. He emptied it at a breath. His eyes flashed with a fierce light. He laughed and threw the bottle upwards with a gesticulation I did not understand.

I looked at him in surprise. He repeated the movement—a grotesque one.

"You do not comprehend?" he said.

"Not I," I replied.

"Then you are not of the brotherhood."

"How?"

"You are not of the masons."

"Yes, yes," I said, "yes, yes."

"You? Impossible! A mason?"

"A mason," I replied.

"A sign," he said.

"It is this," I answered, producing a trowel from beneath the folds of my *roquelaire*.

"You jest," he exclaimed, recoiling a few paces. "But let us proceed to the Amontillado."

"Be it so," I said, replacing the tool beneath the cloak, and again offering him my arm. He leaned upon it heavily. We continued our route in search of the Amontillado. We passed through a range of low arches, descended, passed on, and descending again, arrived at a deep crypt, in which the foulness of the air caused our flambeaux rather to glow than flame.

At the most remote end of the crypt there appeared another less spacious. Its walls had been lined with human remains, piled to the vault overhead, in the fashion of the great catacombs of Paris. Three sides of this interior crypt were still ornamented in this manner. From the fourth the bones had been thrown down, and lay promiscuously upon the earth, forming at one point a mound of some size. Within the wall thus exposed by the displacing of the bones, we perceived a still interior recess, in depth about four feet, in width three, in height six or seven. It seemed to have been constructed for no especial use in itself, but formed merely the interval between two of the colossal supports of the roof of the catacombs, and was backed by one of their circumscribing walls of solid granite.

It was in vain that Fortunato, uplifting his dull torch, endeavored to pry into the depths of the recess. Its termination the feeble light did not enable us to see.

"Proceed," I said; "herein is the Amontillado. As for Luchesi—"

"He is an ignoramus," interrupted my friend, as he stepped unsteadily forward, while I followed immediately at his heels. In an instant he had reached the extremity of the niche, and finding his progress arrested by the rock, stood stupidly bewildered. A moment more and I had fettered him to the granite. In its surface were two iron staples, distant from each other about two feet, horizontally. From one of these depended a short chain, from the other a padlock. Throwing the links about his waist, it was but the work of a few seconds to secure it. He was too much astounded to resist. Withdrawing the key I stepped back from the recess.

"Pass your hand," I said, "over the wall; you cannot help feeling the nitre. Indeed it is *very* damp. Once more let me *implore* you to return. No? Then I must positively leave you. But I must first render you all the little attentions in my power."

"The Amontillado!" ejaculated my friend, not yet recovered from his astonishment.

"True," I replied; "the Amontillado."

As I said these words I busied myself among the pile of bones of which I have before spoken. Throwing them aside, I soon uncovered a quantity of building stone and mortar. With these materials and with the aid of my trowel, I began vigorously to wall up the entrance of the niche.

I had scarcely laid the first tier of my masonry when I discovered that the intoxication of Fortunato had in a great measure worn off. The earliest indication I had of this was a low moaning cry from the depth of the recess. It was not the cry of a drunken man. There was then a long and obstinate silence. I laid the second tier, and the third, and the fourth; and then I heard the furious vibrations of the chain. The noise lasted for several minutes, during which, that I might hearken to it with the more satisfaction, I ceased my labors and sat down upon the bones. When at last the clanking subsided, I resumed the trowel, and finished without interruption the fifth, the sixth, and the seventh tier. The wall was now nearly upon a level with my breast. I again paused, and holding the flambeaux over the mason-work, threw a few feeble rays upon the figure within.

A succession of loud and shrill screams, bursting suddenly from the throat of the chained form, seemed to thrust me violently back. For a brief moment I hesitated—I trembled. Unsheathing my rapier, I began to grope with it about the recess: but the thought of an instant reassured me. I placed my hand upon the solid fabric of the catacombs, and felt satisfied. I reapproached the wall. I replied to the yells of him who clamored. I re-echoed—I aided—I surpassed them in volume and in strength. I did this, and the clamorer grew still.

It was now midnight, and my task was drawing to a close. I had completed the eighth, the ninth, and the tenth tier. I had finished a portion of the last and the eleventh; there remained but a single stone to be fitted and plastered in. I struggled with its weight; I placed it partially in its destined position.

But now there came from out the niche a low laugh that erected the hairs upon my head. It was succeeded by a sad voice, which I had difficulty in recognising as that of the noble Fortunato. The voice said—

"Ha! ha! ha!—he! he!—a very good joke indeed—an excellent jest. We will have many a rich laugh about it at the palazzo—he! he! he!—over our wine—he! he! he!"

"The Amontillado!" I said.

"He! he! he!—he! he! he!—yes, the Amontillado. But is it not getting late? Will not they be awaiting us at the palazzo, the Lady Fortunato and the rest? Let us be gone."

"Yes," I said, "let us be gone."

"*For the love of God, Montressor!*"

"Yes," I said, "for the love of God!"

But to these words I hearkened in vain for a reply. I grew impatient. I called aloud—

"Fortunato!"

No answer. I called again—

"Fortunato!"

No answer still. I thrust a torch through the remaining aperture and let it fall within. There came forth in return only a jingling of the bells. My heart grew sick—on account of the dampness of the catacombs. I hastened to make an end of my labor. I forced the last stone into its position; I plastered it up. Against the new masonry I re-erected the old rampart of bones. For the half of a century no mortal has disturbed them. *In pace requiescat!*